THE TCHAIKOVSKY HANDBOOK

Russian Music Studies

Malcolm Hamrick Brown, founding editor

THE TCHAIKOVSKY HANDBOOK

A Guide to the Man and His Music

Compiled by

ALEXANDER POZNANSKY

and

BRETT LANGSTON

Volume Two

Catalogue of Letters
Genealogy
Bibliography

INDIANA UNIVERSITY PRESS

Bloomington & Indianapolis

Published with the generous support of Allen W. Clowes.

This book is a publication of

Indiana University Press
601 North Morton Street
Bloomington, IN 47404-3797 USA

http://iupress.indiana.edu

Telephone orders 800-842-6796
Fax orders 812-855-7931
E-mail orders iuporder@indiana.edu

Library of Congress Cataloging-in-Publication Data

Poznansky, Alexander.
The Tchaikovsky handbook : a guide to the man and his music / compiled by Alexander
Poznansky and Brett Langston.
p.   cm. — (Russian music studies)
Includes bibliographical references (p.   ) and indexes.
Contents: vol. 1. Thematic catalogue of works ; Catalogue of photographs ; Autobiography—
vol. 2. Catalogue of letters ; Genealogy ; Bibliography.
ISBN 0-253-33921-9 (v. 1 : cloth : alk paper) — ISBN 0-253-33947-2 (v. 2 : cloth : alk. paper)
1. Tchaikovsky, Peter Ilich, 1840–1893—Bibliography.
2. Tchaikovsky, Peter Ilich, 1840–1893—Thematic catalogs.
I. Langston, Brett.
II. Title.
III. Russian music studies (Bloomington, Ind.)

ML134.C42 P69 2001
780'.92—dc21
[B]
2001039546

1 2 3 4 5 06 05 04 03 02

Contents

INTRODUCTION

Catalogue of Letters

Chaikovskii was an indefatigable writer of letters. Even though he may have not always enjoyed that particular endeavour, he possessed a strong sense of responsibility, and considered it a point of duty to answer each letter from his correspondents, who numbered over 350 individuals throughout his lifetime. His rigorous work schedule included a few hours dedicated specifically to letter writing, and he was capable of composing daily up to eighteen letters to various persons. This resulted in an epistolary corpus of over 5000 documents, most of them published, although it must be stressed that by no means all letters written by the composer are presently accounted for.

One cannot doubt that Chaikovskii's voluminous correspondence is the single most important source for factual biographical information. Its contents range from formal or cordial notes to colleagues and acquaintances, to deep thoughts on the nature of artistic creativity and the meaning of life, and intimate confessions about his private emotional experience. It must be remembered, however, that the composer was aware of the psychological ambivalence rooted in the very enterprise of letter writing, where the correspondents are often compelled both to reveal and conceal the truth about themselves [1]. This makes it imperative to place every letter into its proper biographical context, and one of our intentions in compiling this Catalogue of Chaikovskii's letters has been to facilitate such and similar investigative procedures.

The story of the composer's epistolary corpus, its collection and publication, involving twists and turns dependent on the vagaries of the Communist Party line and Soviet censorship, is told in the Introduction to the first volume of this Handbook. The present Catalogue, following the chronological principle, takes into account all publications of each letter both in original languages and in English translations. For the purpose of convenience, the numeration is made to agree with that found in the complete Russian edition of his letters (*PSSL*), published between 1959 and 1981 [2]. For documents which were not included in that edition, the suffixes "a", "b" and "c" have been employed, to avoid disruption to the chronological sequence.

For each of Chaikovskii's known letters, notes and telegrams, the following information is shown: the name of the recipient; the date and place of writing; the language in which it was written (if not in Russian); the present location of the original (or copies); references to its first publication, the volume and page numbers from *PSSL*, and any translations into English. An asterisk indicates that publication was incomplete or censored.

The Catalogue is supplemented with an Index of Correspondents, which contains basic biographical information about them, and a guide to the Locations of Chaikovskii's Autograph Letters, arranged geographically.

In a number of cases, Chaikovskii's correspondents were known by different forms of their names within and without Russia, and the most important variants are listed in the Index of Correspondents, with appropriate cross-references. As a general rule, the names of Russian citizens with European family names (e.g. Iurgenson/ Jurgenson), and of Russian emigres who adopted new names in their home countries (e.g.

---

(1)   See. vol. 1 of this Handbook, p. XXX .

(2)   P. I. Chaikovskii, *Polnoe sobranie sochinenii: Literaturnye proizvedeniia i perepiska*, vols. 5–17. Moscow: Gosudarstvennoe muzykal´noe izdatel´stvo, 1959–81 [see entry *156* in the bibliography].

Brodskii/Brodsky) are listed first in the Russian form, since this is normally how they were known to the composer. Similarly, foreigners who became Russian citizens are listed first under their Russified names, followed by the original (e.g. Al´brekht/Albrecht). However, Westerners who resided only temporarily in Russia appear under their original names, followed by the Russian transliteration (e.g. Harteveld/Gartevel´d), or have the patronymic elements of their names indicated by parentheses (e.g. 'Auer, Leopold (Semenovich)').

Genealogy of P. I. Chaikovskii

A number of studies concerning Chaikovskii's ancestry have been published in recent years, and in the concluding section of this handbook we present detailed charts showing the most up-to-date genealogical data for the composer and his relatives.

The composer's male line can be traced back to an eighteenth-century Ukrainian Cossack named Fëdor Chaika, who changed the family name to Chaikovskii. The composer's mother was descended from the d'Assier family, who left France in the wake of the revolution in 1789. The charts show a detailed history of these two families, so far as surviving records permit. We also include genealogies for the Miliukov family, into which the composer unhappily married in 1877, and also for the Davydov, Von Meck and Frolovskii families, whose intermarriage was contrived by the composer and his patroness, when Nadezhda von Meck's son Nikolai married Chaikovskii's niece Anna Davydova. As elsewhere in this handbook, all dates for pre-revolutionary events in Russia are shown in old style.

The lineage of the Chaikovskii family has been established back to the late seventeenth century, when they seem to have been considered as belonging to the Russian minor nobility, or gentry, as is apparent from the inclusion of the composer's grandfather Pëtr Fedorovich in a register of noble families published on the order of Catherine the Great in 1785. On the other hand, contemporary official sources on Russian heraldry do not contain any coats of arms for the Chaikovskiis, which justifies the composer's own humorous attitude towards the attempts of his relatives to demonstrate their aristocratic descent. (It is believed, for instance, that the coat of arms found on the seal preserved in the Klin House-Museum had been invented by the composer's uncle Pëtr Petrovich.) It was characteristic of the composer, according to his brother Modest, to insist on the common origins of his ancestors.

The Klin archives contain several documents pertaining to the history of Chaikovskii's family which must have been utilized by Modest in the course of his work on his brother's biography. These include an anonymous manuscript *The Clan Chaikovskii to 1894* [3], the memoirs of the composer's father Il´ia Petrovich, entitled *The Notes of a Mining School Cadet* [4], and the so-called *Certificate of A. M. Assier* [5], which deals with the origin and career of Chaikovskii's maternal grandfather. Taken with recently uncovered materials from archives in the Urals and St. Petersburg [6], these sources now enable us to describe the composer's ancestry with greater accuracy than has hitherto been possible [7].

---

(3)   'Rod Chaikovskikh k 1894 godu' [see *1879*].

(4)   'Zapiski kadeta Gornogo kadetskogo korpusa I. P. Chaikovskogo' [see *1895*].

(5)   'Attestat A. M. Assiera' [see *1874*].

(6)   V. I. Proleeva, *K rodoslovnoi P. I. Chaikovskogo: Zhizn´ i deiatel´nost´ P. F. Chaikovskogo.* Izhevsk: Udmurtiia, 1990 [see *1907*].

(7)   We are indebted to the research of our Russian colleagues Tamara Skvirskaia and Valerii Sokolov, who generously shared their findings with us.

The composer's grandfather was Fëdor Afanasievich Chaika ("Chaika" literally translates as "Seagull"). For some time he was believed to have been a member of the minor Polish nobility ("shliakhta"), but it has now been established that he was a Ukrainian Cossack who, most likely, served in the Omel´nitskii Division of the Mirgorodskii Cossack Regiment. It was reputed that he took part in the Battle of Poltava (1709), where Peter the Great secured a major victory over the Swedes. Chaika's son, Pëtr Fedorovich (the composer's grandfather) was the first to adopt the name Chaikovskii (thus according with the standard rules of Russian, rather than Ukrainian, nomenclature). He was an army physician and medical officer, formally ennobled by Catherine the Great, and eventually appointed to several governorship in the Ural region. One of his eleven children was the mining engineer Il´ia Petrovich who married (as his second wife) in 1833 to Aleksandra Andreevna Assier. Pëtr Il´ich Chaikovskii was their third child.

The composer's maternal great-grandfather Michel Assier was descended from a distinguish noble French family, and left his native France in the wake of the French Revolution, and settled in Dresden, Saxony. His son, and Chaikovskii's grandfather, André Assier, came to Russia in 1795 to become a teacher of German and French in the St. Petersburg Military School. He was granted Russian citizenship in 1800, and a later he successfully served as an official in the Customs Department and Ministry of Finances. The composer's mother Aleksandra was his fifth child.

The genealogy provides all available information about Chaikovskii's numerous relatives, both on his paternal and maternal lines, as well as about the families of his brother-in-law Lev Davydov, the composer's benefactress Nadezhda von Meck, and his wife Antonina Miliukova, all of which played important roles in his life.

In order to present as much detail as possible, the genealogical data is presented in 'narrative' format, generation by generation within each family, containing full details of the individuals' life events so far as they have been established. The genealogy is completed by a comprehensive name index, listing all the composer's known relatives.

Bibliography

The first bibliography related to Chaikovskii appeared in 1894, shortly after his death; it was compiled by Anatolii Molchanov and listed the publications of the composer's own critical writings [8]. The next steps were the surveys of literature about him published during the years of the revolution and the civil wars, as well as in the first two decades of the Soviet regime, respectively made by G. Nikol´skaia [9] and Nikolai Shemanin [10]. One should also mention the collection of bibliographical materials on Chaikovskii in Russian by Aleksandr Brianskii [11], and in particular the sections on Chaikovskii in the bibliographical volumes entitled *Literatura o muzyke* ("Literature on music") and *Sovetskaia literatura o muzyke*, which were published with some regularity in the Soviet Union between the years 1955 and 1974 [12]. Aside from the numerous lists of literature appended to monographs or articles on him and his music, the main source of

---

(8)   A. E. Molchanov, 'Bibliograficheskii ukazatel´ kriticheskikh statei P. I. Chaikovskogo', *Ezhegodnik imperatorskikh teatrov: Sezon 1892/93* (1894): 555–559 [see *14*].

(9)   G. Nikol´skaia, 'Chaikovskii v muzykal´noi literaturye revoliutsionnykh let', *Muzyka i revoliutsiia* (1928), 11: 51 [see *16*].

(10)   N. V. Shemanin, 'Literatura o P. I. Chaikovskom za 17 let (1917–1934)'. In: *Muzykal´noe nasledstvo: Sbornik materialov po istorii muzykal´noi kul´tury v Rossii*. Vyp. 1. Pod red. M. V. Ivanova-Boretskogo. Moskva: Ogiz, 1935: 76–93. [see *18*].

(11)   A. M Brianskii, 'Materialy k russkoi literature o P. I. Chaikovskom'. In: *P. I. Chaikovskii na stsene teatra opery i baleta im. S. M. Kirova* (1941): 421–449 [see *20*].

(12)   See entries *24–26, 30–31, 33, 35, 37*.

bibliographical information on Chaikovskii in English remains the relevant section in David Moldon's bibliography of Russian composers [13], which appeared in 1976 and is now considerably outdated.

It is clear, however, that none of the items referred to above meets all the necessary bibliographical requirements or provides an exemplary account of the subject, not to mention the fact that pertinent information is dispersed throughout a variety of editions, some of them not easily available, especially outside Russia.

The present bibliography, embracing over 6000 entries published prior to April 2000, attempts a comprehensive, if not necessarily exhaustive, coverage of literature on Chaikovskii, in languages ranging from Russian and English to Japanese. We focussed largely on works of scholarly rather than popular interest (although the latter are by no means left without representation), and we have felt free to supply an occasional annotation in places where we thought it might be expected. As far as the literature in Russian and English is concerned, our listings are close to complete. Most of the printed material (though not all of it) has been examined *de visu*.

The material is organized thematically and chronologically, and is divided into six main parts. The headings and sub-headings are self-explanatory, and the movement is from the general to the specific. Under the heading of 'Miscellanea' (Part 6) we offer a selection of references to fiction, plays, and poetry about Chaikovskii, as well as a listing of films, operas, musicals and ballets based on his life and music.

Cross-references have been introduced where an item falls under two or more headings. Within the divisions and subdivisions, entries are arranged according to the date of their first publication, with later editions noted immediately below. Lists of contents are shown for collections of essays or articles, while each individual piece of writing found therein is also itemized under the proper thematic heading. Review notices are included with the main entries. Throughout the bibliography, entry numbers are shown in italic type.

---

(13)   'Tchaikovsky, Piotr (1840–93)'. In: D. Moldon, *A bibliography of Russian composers*. London: White Lion [1976]: 295–326 [see *38*].

Abbreviations

General

A	Alto(s)
Akad.	Akademicheskii [academic]
arr.	arrangement, arranged by
Aufl.	Auflage [edition]
aut.	Autumn
B	Bass(es)
B.Cl.	bass clarinet
Bar	Baritone(s)
Bd.	Band [volume]
Bn	bassoon(s)
C.Ang.	cor anglais
ca.	circa
Calif.	California (USA)
Cel.	celesta
ch.	chast´ [part]
Cl.	clarinet(s)
coll.	collection
col(s).	column(s)
comp.	compiled (by)
Conn.	Connecticut (USA)
cond.	conductor
Contr.	contralto
Db.	double-bass(es)
dop.	dopolnenie [supplement(ed)]
ed.	editor(s), edition
f.	fond [collection]
facs.	facsimile(s)
Fl.	flute(s)
fol.	folio(s)
Gl.	glockenspiel
Gos.	Gosudarstvennoe [State]
hbk	hardback
Hn	horn(s)
Hp	harp(s)
hrsg.	herausgegeben [edited (by)]
illus.	illustrated
im.	imeni [named for]
ispr.	ispravlennoe [corrected]
izd.	izdanie [edition]
izdat.	izdatel´stvo [publishing house]
khudozh.	khudozhestvennyi [arts, artistic]
M. M.	Master of Music
Mass.	Massacheusetts (USA)
Mez.	mezzo-soprano
Middx.	Middlesex (England)
mm.	millimetres
movt(s).	movement(s)
MS(S)	manuscript(s)
muz.	muzykal´naia [musical]
no(s).	number(s)
N. Y.	New York
Ob.	oboe
otv.	otvetstvennyi [principal]
p, pp	page, pages
pbk	paperback
Penn.	Pennsylvania (USA)
pererab.	pererabotannoe [reworked]
Ph. D.	Doctor of Philosophy
pl.	plate (number)
podgot.	podgotovlen(nyi) [prepared (by)]
pod red.	pod redaktsiei [edited by]
pr.	printed
red.	redaktor [editor]
repr.	reprint, reprinted by
rev(s).	revised (by), revisions
RMS	Russian Musical Society
S	soprano(s)
sost.	sostavitel´, sostavlenie [compiler, compiled by]
spr.	spring
Str.	strings
sum.	summer
T	tenor(s)
Timp.	timpani
Tpt	trumpet(s)
tr.	translation, translator
Tbn.	trombone(s)
Univ.	University
var(s).	variation(s)
Vc.	cello(s)
Vla	viola(s)
Vln	violin(s)
vol(s).	volume(s)
vstup.	vstupitel´naia [introduction]
vyp.	vypusk [part]
win.	winter

Literary References

(shown in full in the bibliography section)

AIZ	*Aleksandr Il´ich Ziloti: Vospominaniia i pis´ma* (1963)
Al´shvang	A. A. Al´shvang, *P. Chaikovskii* (1959)
Baskin	V. S. Baskin, *P. I. Chaikovskii* (1895)
BBS	*Hans von Bülow: Briefe und Schriften.* Hrsg. von Marie von Bülow (Leipzig: Breitkopf & Härtel, 1895–1908) [8 vols.]
BC	*Perepiska M. A. Balakireva i P. I. Chaikovskogo* (1912)
BF	C. D. Bowen & B. von Meck, *Beloved friend* (1937)
Biulleten	*Biulleten´ Doma-Muzeia P. I. Chaikovskogo v Klinu*
Boccuni	*Il fanciullo di vetro: Petr Il´ic Cajkovskij a San Pietroburgo*, ed. M. Boccuni (1997)
BVP	*M. A. Balakirev: Vospominaniia i pis´ma* (1962)
Camner	J. Camner, *Great composers in historic photographs* (1981)
CH	*Chaikovskii, 1840–1893*, 2 vols (1990)
Chaikofosukii	*Chaikofosukii*, ed. Minoru Morita (1990)
CMS	*Chaikovskii na moskovskoi stsene* (1940)
ČS	*Čajkovskij-Studien*
CTP	P. I. Chaikovskii & S. I. Taneev, *Pis´ma* (1951)
DC	*Dnevniki P. I. Chaikovskogo* (1923)
DGC	*Dni i gody P. I. Chaikovskogo* (1940)
Diaries	*The diaries of Tchaikovsky*, ed. W. Lakond (1945)
Dombaev	G. S. Dombaev, *Tvorchestvo P. I. Chaikovskogo* (1958)
EIT	*Ezhegodnik Imperatorskikh Teatrov*
EFN	*E. F. Napravnik: Avtobiograficheskie, tvorcheskie materialy, dokumenty, pis´ma* (1959)
FC 2	*Famous composers and their work*, ed. J. K. Paine [et al], vol. 2 (1891)
Glebov	I. Glebov, *P. I. Chaikovskii: Ego zhizn´ i tvorchestvo* (1922)
Hervey	A. Hervey, 'Peter Ilitsch Tschaikowsky: A biographical sketch', *Strand*, 1 (1898)
IRM	*Istoriia russkoi muzyki v issledovaniiakh i materialakh* (1924)
JALS	*Journal of the American Liszt Society*
Kirov	*P. I. Chaikovskii na stsene Teatra opery i baleta S. M. Kirova (b. Mariinskii)* (1940)
KMV	I. A. Klimenko, *Moi vospominaniia o P. I. Chaikovskom* (1908)
KNB	*K novym beregam* [Moscow journal]
Knorr	I. Knorr, *Peter Jljtsch Tschaikowsky* (1900)
Kunin	I. Kunin, *Pëtr Il´ich Chaikovskii* (1958)
KVC	N. D. Kashkin, *Vospominaniia o P. I. Chaikovskom* (1896); 2nd ed. (1954)
Landon	R. Landon, *Tschaikowsky* (1912)
LF	P. I. Chaikovskii, *Letters to his family: An autobiography* (1981)
LNT	*L. N. Tolstoi: Polnoe sobranie sochinenii, iubeleinoe izd.* (1953)
Mason	D. G. Mason, 'Tschaikovsky and his music' (1902)
MF	*Muzykal´nye fel´etony i zametki Petra Il´icha Chaikovskogo* (1898)
MKS	P. I. Chaikovskii, *Muzykal´no kriticheskie stat´i*, 4-e izd. (1986)
MN	*Muzykal´naia nov´* [Moscow journal]
MNC	*Muzykal´noe nasledie Chaikovskogo* (1958)
Newmarch	R. Newmarch, *Tchaikovsky: His life and works* (1908)
Notes	Quarterly Journal of the Music Library Association
Očadlik	M. Očadlik, *Prazské dopisy P. I. Cajkovského* (1949)
ORK	*A. N. Ostrovskii i russkie kompozitory: Pis´ma* (1937)
OTC	V. V. Protopopov & N. V. Tumanina, *Opernoe tvorchestrvo Chaikovskovo* (1957)
PB	P. I. Chaikovskii, *Pis´ma k blizkim: izbrannoe* (1955)
PICH	*Pëtr Il´ich Chaikovskii* (1978)
PIU 1–2	P. I. Chaikovskii, *Perepiska s P. I. Iurgensonom*, vols. 1–2 (1938–52)
PM 1–3	P. I. Chaikovskii, *Perepiska s N. F. fon Mekk*, vols. 1–3 (1934–36)
PR	P. I. Chaikovskii, *Pis´ma k rodnym*, vol. 1 (1940)
Pribegina	*P. I. Chaikovskii*, ed. G. Pribegina (1984)
PRM	*Proshloe russkoi muzyki*, vol. 1 (1920)
PSSL 2–17	P. I. Chaikovskii, *Polnoe sobranie sochinenii: Literaturnye proizvedeniia i perepiska*, vols. 2–3, 5–17 (1959–81).
PSSM 1–63	P. I. Chaikovskii, *Polnoe sobranie sochinenii* [musical scores], vols. 1–63 (1940–90)
PT	*Pis´ma P. I. Chaikovskogo i S. I. Taneeva* (1916)
RdM	*Revue de musicologie* [journal]
RK 7	N. A. Rimskii-Korsakov, *Polnoe sobraniye sochinenii: Literaturnye proizvedeniia i perepiska*, vol. 7 (Moscow: Muzyka, 1970)

RM	*Russkaia mysl´* [journal]
SM	*Sovetskaia muzyka* [journal]
SN	*Sibirskii nabliudatel´* (Tomsk) [journal]
Šourek (1951)	O. Šourek, *Dvořák ve vzpominkách a dopisech*, 9th ed (Prague: Orbis, 1951)
Šourek (1954)	O. Šourek, *Dvořák im Erinnerungen und Briefe* (Prague: Orbis, 1954)
Štěpánek	V. Štěpánek, *Pražské návštěvy P. I. Čajkovského* (1952)
Streatfield	R. A. Streatfield, *Modern Music and Musicians* (1906)
TA	P. Vaidman, *Tvorcheskii arkhiv P. I. Chaikovskogo* (1988)
TGM	*Tschaikowsky-Gesellschaft Mitteilungen*
THC	*Tchaikovsky and his contemporaries* (1999)
TLD	A. Poznansky, *Tchaikovsky's last days* (1996)
TMBF	*To My Best Friend* (1993)
TQM	A. Poznansky, *Tchaikovsky: The quest for the inner man* (1991)
TS 2	*Schriften des Tschaikowsky-Studio*, vol. 2 (1968)
TT	A. Poznansky, *Tschaikowskys Tod* (1998)
TTOE	A. Poznansky, *Tchaikovsky through others' eyes* (1999)
TW	*Tchaikovsky and his world* (1998)
VC	*Vospominaniia o P. I. Chaikovskom* (1962); 2nd ed. (1973); 3rd ed. (1979); 4th ed. (1980)
VIS	Ia. Ravincher, *Vasilii Il´ch Safonov* (Moscow: Muzgiz, 1959)
VKG	*Vecherniaia krasnaia gazeta* [newspaper]
VM	*Vecherniaia Moskva* [newspaper]
VP	*Chaikovskii: Vospominaniia i pis´ma* (1924)
VPS	*Vystavka posviashchennaia 100-letiiu so dnia rozhdeniia P. I. Chaikovskogo* (1940)
Warrack	J. Warrack, *Tchaikovsky* (1973)
Werckmeister	K. Werckmeister, *Das neunzehnte Jahrhundert in Bildnissen*, vol. 5 (1901)
Yoffe	E. Yoffe, *Tchaikovsky in America* (1991)
ZC 1–3	M. I. Chaikovskii, *Zhizn´ Petra Il´icha Chaikovskogo*, vols. 1–3 (1900–02)
ZN	*P. I. Chaikovskii: Zabytoe i novoe* (1993)

Archives

ARM–YE	Yerevan, Armenia: Conservatory
CH–B	Basel, Switzerland: private coll.
CH–Bkoch	Basel, Switzerland: Louis Koch, private coll.
CH–Bps	Basel, Switzerland: Paul Sacher Stiftung. Bibliothek.
CZ–Pfoerster	Prague, Czech Republic: J. B. Foerster, private coll.
CZ–Pkadlic	Prague, Czech Republic: Emma Kadlic, private coll.
CZ–Pnm	Prague, Czech Republic: Národní Muzeum, Divadelí oddélení [National Museum, theatrical dept.]
CZ–Ps	Prague-Strahov, Czech Republic: Památník národního písemnictví, Literarní archív [Museum of National Literature, literary archive]
CZ–POm	Podebrady, Czech Republic: Podebrady Muzeum
CZ–ZL	Zlonice, Czech Republic: Památník Antonína Dvořáka [Dvořak museum].
D–AMlohss	Amühle, Germany: Eberhard Lohss, private coll.
D–Bds	Berlin, Germany: Deutsche Staatsbibliothek, Musikabteilung
D–Bmb	Berlin, Germany: Internationale Musikbibliothek, Verband Deutscher Komponisten und Musikwissenschaftler
D–Bmuck	Berlin, Germany: Peter Muck, private coll.
D–BShenn	Braunschweig, Germany: W. Henn, private coll.
D–EMmüller	Emden, Germany: Dr Gotthard Müller, private coll.
D–F	Frankfurt am Main, Germany: Stadt- und Universitätsbibliothek, Sammlung Manskopf
D–FF	Frankfurt, Germany: Frankfurter Stadtbibliothek, Musikbibliothek
D–H	Hamburg, Germany: Operntheater
D–Hoestrich	Hamburg, Germany: Dr. Oestrich, private coll.
D–LEmi	Leipzig, Germany: Leipziger Universität, Zweigbibliothek Musikwissenschaft und Musikpädagogik
D–Mtf	Munich, Germany: Tschaikowsky-Foundation
D–MZsch	Mainz, Germany: Archiv Schott Musik International
D–Tsiedentopf	Tübingen, Germany: Henning Siedentopf, private coll.
D–Tu	Tübingen, Germany: Tschaikowsky Gesellschaft, Eberhard-Karls-Universität, Universitätsbibliothek
D–WIaztmann	Wiesbaden, Germany: Horst Axtmann, private coll.

D–WÜ	Würzburg, Germany: private coll.
F–DI	Dieppe, France: Bibliothèque municipale
F–P	Paris, France: private coll.
F–Phofmann	Paris, France: Michael-Rostislav Hofman, private coll.
F–Pi	Paris, France: Bibliothèque de l'Institut de France
F–Plauwe	Paris, France: Eric van Lauwe, private coll.
F–Pn	Paris, France: Bibliothèque nationale de France, Département de la Musique
F–Po	Paris, France: Bibliothèque-Musée de l'Opéra
F–Psamarin	Paris, France: Charles Samarin, private coll.
GB–Cmaitland	Cambridge, England: Frederick Maitland, private coll.
GB–Cu	Cambridge:, England Cambridge University Library, Manuscripts and University Archives Department
GB–Gu	Glasgow, Scotland: University of Glasgow Library, special collections
GB–Lbl	London, England: British Library, Reference Division
GB–Lcm	London, England: Royal College of Music
GB–Lgetty	London, England: Hulton Getty, private archive
GB–Lpro	London, England: Public Record Office, Image Library (Kew)
GB–Lps	London, England: Royal Philharmonic Society
GB–Lrosenthal	London, England: Albi Rosenthal, private coll.
GB–Mcm	Manchester, England: Library of the Royal Northern College of Music
GE–Tir	Tbilissi, Georgia: Institut rukopisei imeni K. S. Kekelidze, Akademii Nauk Gruzii
H–Bkuna	Budapest, Hungary: Imre Kuna, private coll.
I–Nc	Naples, Italy: Conservatorio di Musica S Pietro a Majella Biblioteca
I–Rcolombo	Rome, Italy: Emilio Colombo, private coll.
I–Rsgambati	Rome, Italy: Giovanni Sgambati, private coll.
J–private	Japan: private coll.
KZ–AA	Alma-Ata, Kazakhstan: Gosudarstvennaia publichnaia biblioteka im. A. S. Pushkina [Pushkin State Public Library]
N–Bo	Bergen, Norway: Bergen offentlige bibliotek
NL–Ac	Amsterdam, The Netherlands: Concertgebouw Bibliotheek
NL–Amengelberg	Amsterdam, The Netherlands: Willem Mengelberg private coll.
NL–At	Amsterdam, The Netherlands: Toonkunst-Bibliotheek
RUS–KL	Klin, Russia: Gosudarstvennyi arkhiv doma-muzeia P. I. Chaikovskogo [P. I. Chaikovskii State House-Museum Archive]
RUS–Mbelza	Moscow, Russia: Igor Bel´za, private coll.
RUS–Mberggolts	Moscow, Russia: Genrietta, Berggolts, private coll.
RUS–Mcl	Moscow, Russia: Rossiiskii gosudarstvennyi arkhiv literatury i isskustva [Russian State Archive for Literature and the Arts]
RUS–Mcm	Moscow, Russia: Gosudarstvennyi tsentral´nyi muzei muzykal´noi kultury imeni M. I. Glinki [M. I. Glinka State Central Museum of Musical Culture]
RUS–Mf	Moscow, Russia: Gosudarstvennyi arkhiv Rossiiskoi Federatsii [State Archive of the Russian Federation]
RUS–Mfeldman	Moscow, Russia: K. I. Fel´dman, private coll.
RUS–Mgt	Moscow, Russia: Tret´iakov Gallery
RUS–Mia	Moscow, Russia: Tsentral´nyi istoricheskii arkhiv Moskvy [Moscow Central Historial Archive]
RUS–Mk	Moscow, Russia: Gosudarstvennaia Konservatoriia imeni P. I. Chaikovskogo, Nauchnaia muzykal´naia biblioteka im. S. I. Taneeva [Chaikovskii State Conservatory, Taneev music library]
RUS–Mkashkina	Moscow, Russia: Sof´ia Kashkina-Niuberg, private coll.
RUS–Mmt	Moscow, Russia: Tolstoi Museum
RUS–Mrg	Moscow, Russia: Rossiiskaia gosudarstvennaia biblioteka [Russian State Library]
RUS–Mt	Moscow, Russia: Gosudarstvennyi tsentral´nyi teatral´nyi muzei imeni A. Bakhrushina [Bakhrushin State Central Theatrical Museum]
RUS–Mteleshov	Moscow, Russia: N. D. Teleshov, private coll.
RUS–SPa	St. Petersburg, Russia: Tsentral´nyi gosudarstvennyi istoricheski arkhiv

	Sankt Peterburga [St. Petersburg Central State Historical Archive]
RUS–SPaa	St. Petersburg, Russia: Filial Arkhiva Rossiiskoi Akademii Nauk [Archive of the Russian Academy of Sciences]
RUS–SPf	St. Petersburg, Russia: Tsentral´nyi Gosudarstvennyi arkhiv kino-foto-fono-dokumentov [Central State Archive for cinemographic, photographic and phonographic documents]
RUS–SPia	St. Petersburg, Russia: Rossiiskii gosudarstvennyi istoricheskii arkhiv [Russian State Historical Archive]
RUS–SPil	St. Petersburg, Russia: Institut russkoi literatury (Pushkinskii Dom), Rossiiskoi Akademii nauk. Rukopisnyi otdel [Institute for Russian Literature (Pushkin House), Russian Academy of Sciences, manuscript department]
RUS–SPit	St. Petersburg, Russia: Rossiiskii institut istorii iskusstv, kabinet rukopisei [Russian Institute of Arts History, manuscript department]
RUS–SPk	St. Petersburg, Russia: Nauchnaia muzykal´naia biblioteka Sankt-Peterburgskoi gosudarstvennoi konservatorii imeni N. A. Rimskogo-Korsakova [Music library of the Rimskii-Korsakov State Conservatory in St. Petersburg]
RUS–SPsc	St. Petersburg, Russia: Rossiiskaia natsional´naia biblioteka, otdel rukopisei [Russian National Library, Manuscript Department]
RUS–SPsemenov	St. Petersburg, Russia: Ivan Semenov, private coll.
RUS–SPt	St. Petersburg, Russia: Sankt-Peterburgskaia gosudarstvennaia teatral´naia biblioteka [St. Petersburg State Theatrical Library]
RUS–SPtm	St. Petersburg, Russia: Sankt-Peterburgskii gosudarstvennyi muzei teatral´nogo i muzykal´nogo iskusstva, otdel rukopisei [St. Petersburg State Museum of Theatrical and Musical Arts, Manuscript Department]
RUS–SPtob	St. Petersburg, Russia: Tsentral´naia muzykal´naia biblioteka Gosudarstvennogo akademi-cheskogo Mariinskogo teatra [Central Musical library of the Mariinskii Theatre]
US–	Auburn (Alabama), USA: ANCrocker Malcolm J. Crocker, private coll.

US–Bgm	Boston (Mass.), USA: Isabella Stewart Gardner Museum Library.
US–Bpr	Boston (Mass.), USA: Boston Public Library, Dept. of Rare Books and Manuscripts
US–BHsachs	Beverley Hills (Calif.), USA: Charles W. Sachs, private coll.
US–BHsmith	Beverley Hills (Calif.), USA: Murray Johnson Smith, private coll.
US–Cn	Chicago (Illinois), USA: The Newberry Library
US–CA	Cambridge (Mass.), USA: Harvard University, Harvard College Library
US–CAM	Camarillo (Calif.), USA: St. John's Seminary, Laurence Doheny Memorial Library
US–CLbackford	Cleveland (Ohio), USA: G. P. Backford, private coll.
US–I	Ithaca (N. Y.), USA: Cornell University, Carl A. Kroch Library. Division of Rare and Manuscript Collections.
US–LJ	La Jolla (Calif.), USA: James S. Copley Library
US–NH	New Haven (Conn.), USA: Yale University, Irving S. Gilmore Music Library
US–NHub	New Haven (Conn.), USA: Yale University, Beinecke Rare Book and Manuscript Library
US–NYcorbis	New York (N. Y.), USA: Corbis Archive
US–NYcub	New York (N. Y.), USA: Columbia University, Butler Library (Rare Book & Manuscript Library)
US–NYdamrosch	New York (N. Y.), USA: Walter Damrosch, private coll.
US–NYmo	New York (N. Y.), USA: Library of the Metropolitan Opera Guild
US–NYpm	New York (N. Y), USA: Pierpont Morgan Library
US–NYtollefsen	New York (N. Y.), USA: Tollefsen private coll.
US–PHci	Philadelphia (Penn.), USA: Curtis Institute of Music Library
US–R	Rochester (N. Y.), USA: Sibley Music Library, Eastman School of Music, University of Rochester
US–STu	Stanford (Calif.), USA: Stanford University, Green Library (Dept. of Special Collections)
US–Wc	Washington (D. C.), USA: Library of Congress, Music Division

List of Illustrations

1. The Chaikovskii House-Museum at Klin, near Moscow, the main Russian archival repository for material related to the composer.

2. The first page of Chaikovskii's letter of Jul–Aug 1849 [no. 6] to his governess Fanny Dürbach.

3. The first and the last pages of Chaikovskii's letter of 10 Jul 1890 [No. 4169] to his brother Modest.

4. Chaikovskii's first letter to Nadezhda von Meck, 18–19 Dec 1876 [No. 524].

5. Nadezhda von Meck's first letter to Chaikovskii, 18 Dec 1876.

6. The first and last pages of Chaikovskii's letter of 30 Jan/11 Feb 1882 to Pëtr Iurgenson [No. 1952].

7. The cover of vol. 5 of Chaikovskii's collected letters (*PSSL*), where his correspondence was published from 1959.

8. The cover of *Proshloe Russkoi muzyki* ("Russian Music of the Past"), the first important collection of essays on Chaikovskii, which was published in 1920 (despite the imprint "1918" on its cover).

9. The cover of the first edition of *Vospominaniia o P. I. Chaikovskom* ("Recollections of P. I. Chaikovskii"), published in the Soviet Union in 1962.

10. Cover from vol. 2 of the Chaikovskii–von Meck correspondence, which was published in three volumes between 1934 and 1936 by the Soviet publishing house *Academia*.

11. The cover jacket from *Letters to His Family: An Autobiography*, the first collection of Chaikovskii's correspondence with his relatives published in England (1981), translated by Galina von Meck.

12. The title page from *Pis´ma k rodnym*, Chaikovskii's correspondence with his relatives, published in 1940, and less subject to censorship by the Soviet authorities than other editions.

13. The cover of the first edition of Chaikovskii's diaries (1923), edited by his brother Ippolit.

14. The cover of the first edition of Chaikovskii's diaries in an English translation by Wladimir Lakond (Walter Lake), published by W.W. Norton & Company, Inc (New York) in 1945.

15. The cover of Modest Chaikovskii's biography *Zhizn´ Petra Il´icha Chaikovskogo'* ["The Life of Pëtr Il´ich Chaikovskii"] published between 1900 and 1902 by Pëtr Iurgenson's publishing house.

16. The cover from the first edition of the libretto to the opera *The Oprichnik*, published by Bessel´ in St Petersburg (1874).

17. The cover from the first edition of libretto to the opera *The Enchantress*, published by Iurgenson in Moscow (1887).

18. The cover from Iwan Knorr's biography *Peter Tschaikowsky* published in Germany in 1900.

19. Boris Asaf´ev's study of Chaikovskii, published in 1921 by *Svetozar* in Petrograd.

20. The cover of the first guide to Chaikovskii works *Muzykal´noe nasledie Chaikovskogo* ("Chaikovskii's Musical Legacy"), published in 1958.

21. The cover of the periodical *Schriften des Tschaikowsky-Studio*, founded in 1965 by Louisa von Westernhagen in Hamburg, Germany.

22. The cover of Nina Berberova's recent Russian edition of her documentary novel *Chaikovskii*, originally published in 1936 in Berlin.

1. The Chaikovskii House-Museum at Klin,
near Moscow, the main Russian archival repository
for material related to the composer.

Chère Mlle Fanny)

Je ne puis vous dire comme j'étais content,
quand j'ai reçu votre lettre; je vous prie
chère Mlle Fanny ne vous fachez pas
contre moi; vous me dites, que vous avez
pleuré, de ce que je vous ai écrit, que c'est
ma paresse qui m'a empéché de vous écrire;
je tacherai une autrefois de ne jamais
etre paresseux, car je conviens que c'est
un mauvais sentiment, dont je me corigerai.
A présent, je veus vous va conter, comment
j'ai passé le temps le 20 de Juillet
le jour de fête de papa. Monsieur
Zélinzoff M. Tchaikovsky et Monsieur
Penn avec ses deux filles Suzanne et
Alice étaient arrivés chez nous. Le soir

*2. The first page of Chaikovskii's letter of Jul–Aug 1849 [no. 6]
to his governess Fanny Dürbach.*

*3. The first and the last pages of Chaikovskii's letter of
10 Jul 1890 [No. 4169] to his brother Modest.*

4. *Chaikovskii's first letter to Nadezhda von Meck,*
18–19 Dec 1876 [No. 524].

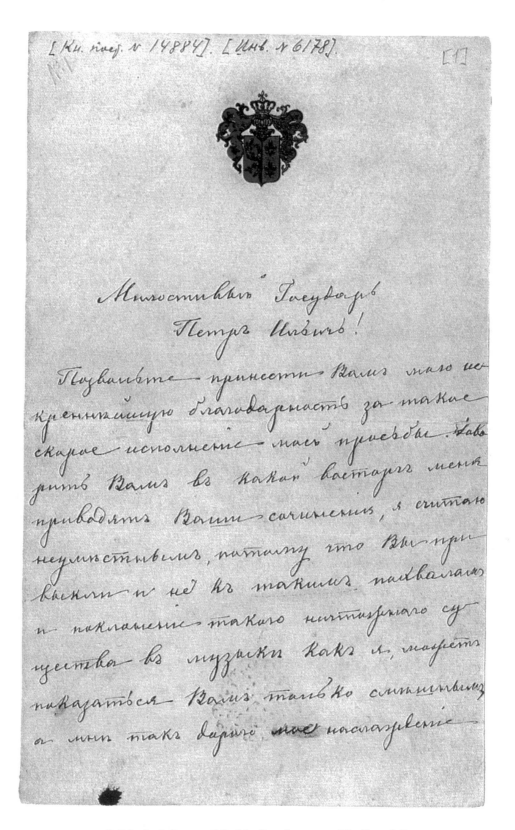

Милостивый Государь
Петръ Ильичъ!

Позвольте принести Вамъ мою ис-
креннѣйшую благодарность за такое
скорое исполненіе моей просьбы. Гово-
рить Вамъ въ какой востаргъ меня
приводятъ Ваши сочиненія, я считаю
неумѣстнымъ, потому что Вы при-
выкли и не къ такимъ похваламъ
и поклоненію такого ничтожнаго су-
щества въ музыкѣ какъ я, можетъ
показаться Вамъ только смѣшнымъ,
а мнѣ такъ дорого мое наслажденіе

5. *Nadezhda von Meck's first letter to Chaikovskii,*
18 Dec 1876.

*6. The first and last pages of Chaikovskii's letter
of 30 Jan/11 Feb 1882 to Pëtr Iurgenson [No. 1952].*

ЧАЙКОВСКИЙ

ПОЛНОЕ
СОБРАНИЕ СОЧИНЕНИЙ

V

МУЗГИЗ

7. *The cover of vol. 5 of Chaikovskii's collected letters (PSSL),
where his correspondence was published from 1959.*

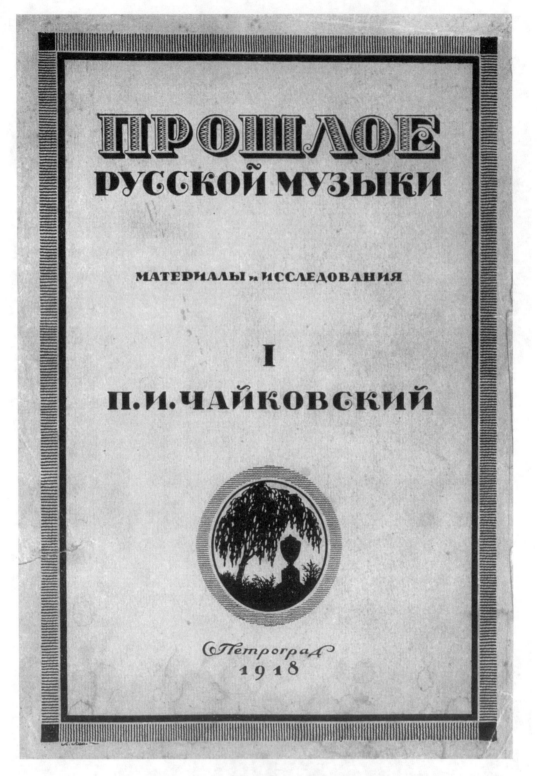

**ПРОШЛОЕ
РУССКОЙ МУЗЫКИ**

МАТЕРИАЛЫ и ИССЛЕДОВАНИЯ

I

П.И.ЧАЙКОВСКИЙ

Петроград
1918

8. The cover of Proshloe Russkoi muzyki
*("Russian Music of the Past"), the first important
collection of essays on Chaikovskii, which was published
in 1920 (despite the imprint "1918" on its cover).*

9. The cover of the first edition of
Vospominaniia o P. I. Chaikovskom
*("Recollections of P. I. Chaikovskii"), published
in the Soviet Union in 1962.*

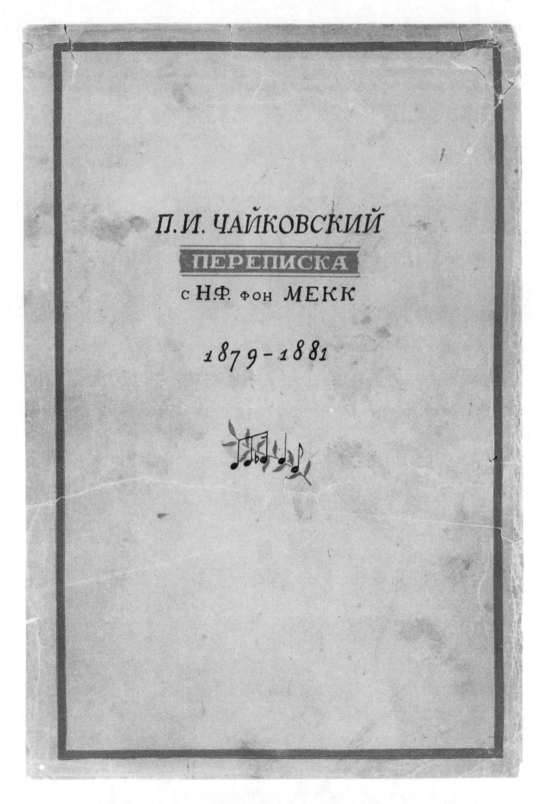

10. *Cover from vol. 2 of the Chaikovskii–von Meck correspondence,*
which was published in three volumes between 1934 and 1936
by the Soviet publishing house Academia.

An Autobiography by
Piotr Ilyich Tchaikovsky

Letters to His Family

11. The cover jacket from Letters to His Family:
An Autobiography, *the first collection of Chaikovskii's correspondence
with his relatives published in England (1981),
translated by Galina von Meck.*

П.И.ЧАЙКОВСКИЙ

Письма к родным

ТОМ
I

1850 – 1879

Редакция и Примечания
В. А. ЖДАНОВА

*Государственное
Музыкальное Издательство*
1940

12. *The title page from* Pis'ma k rodnym, *Chaikovskii's correspondence with his relatives, published in 1940, and less subject to censorship by the Soviet authorities than other editions.*

ДНЕВНИКИ
П.И.ЧАЙКОВСКОГО
1873-1891

ГОСУДАРСТВЕННОЕ

ИЗДАТЕЛЬСТВО

МУЗЫКАЛЬНЫЙ

СЕКТОР

*13. The cover of the first edition of Chaikovskii's diaries
(1923), edited by his brother Ippolit.*

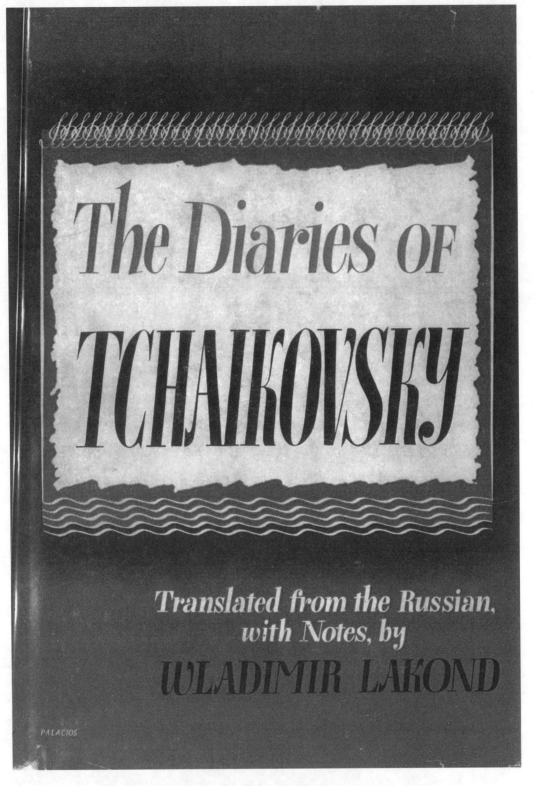

The Diaries of TCHAIKOVSKY

Translated from the Russian, with Notes, by

WLADIMIR LAKOND

PALACIOS

14. *The cover of the first edition of Chaikovskii's diaries in an English translation by Wladimir Lakond (Walter Lake), published by W.W. Norton & Company, Inc (New York) in 1945.*

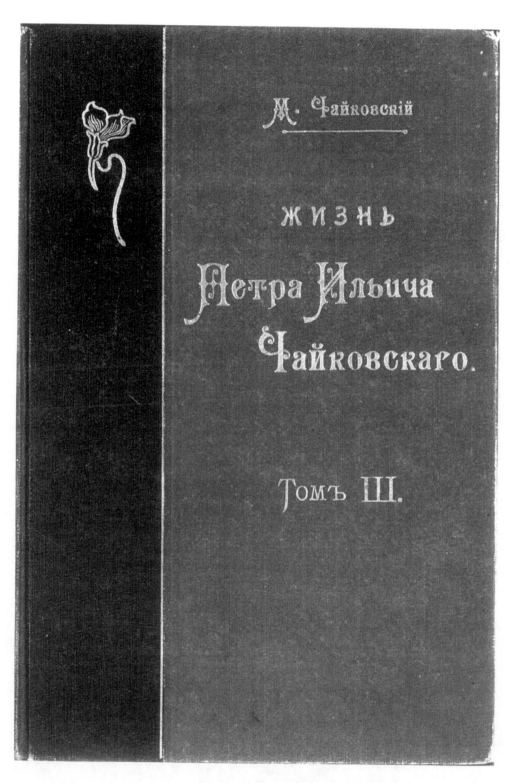

15. *The cover of Modest Chaikovskii's biography*
Zhizn' Petra Il'icha Chaikovskogo'
["The Life of Pëtr Il'ich Chaikovskii"] published between
1900 and 1902 by Pëtr Iurgenson's publishing house.

ОПРИЧНИКЪ

ОПЕРА ВЪ 4-ХЪ ДѢЙСТВІЯХЪ

(СЮЖЕТЪ ЗАИМСТВОВАНЪ ИЗЪ ДРАМЫ ЛАЖЕЧНИКОВА)

МУЗЫКА

П. ЧАЙКОВСКАГО.

Собственность издателей для всѣхъ странъ.

На основаніи договора заключеннаго издателями съ авторомъ, исполненіе этой оперы, какъ въ Россіи также и заграницею, зависитъ отъ обоюднаго ихъ согласія. Копіи съ партитуры должны быть снабжены печатью издателей, иначе будутъ считаться незаконными и преслѣдуемы какъ контрофакціи.

С.-ПЕТЕРБУРГЪ

у В. БЕССЕЛЯ и К°

Поступили въ продажу:
Полная опера для пѣнія съ фортепіано цѣна 15 руб.
„ „ „ одного фортепіано . . . . 8 „
Попурри изъ лучшихъ мотивовъ составленныя И. А. Помазанскимъ.
ЛИБРЕТТО ЦѢНА 50 КОП.

16. The cover from the first edition of the libretto to the opera
The Oprichnik, *published by Bessel' in St Petersburg (1874).*

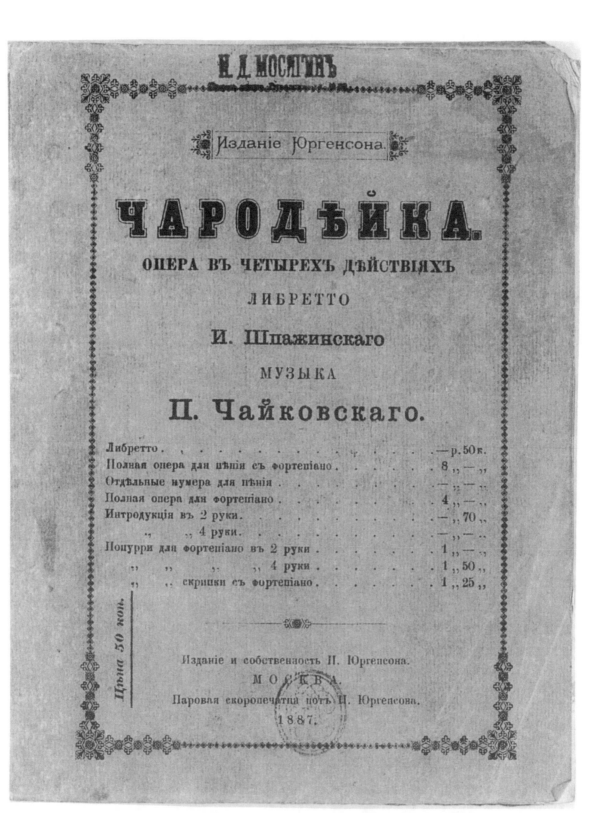

17. The cover from the first edition of the libretto to the opera
The Enchantress, *published by Iurgenson in Moscow (1887).*

18. The cover from Iwan Knorr's biography
Peter Tschaikowsky *published in Germany in 1900.*

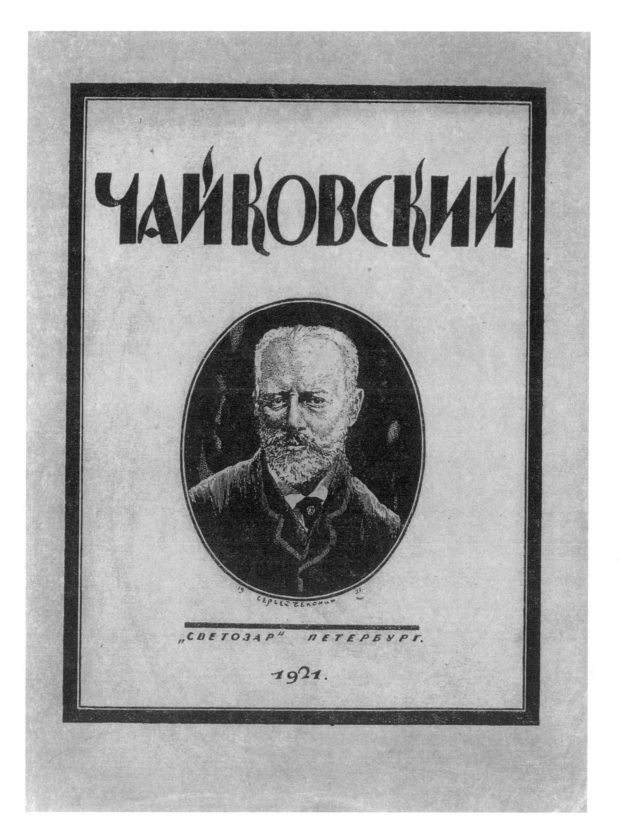

*19. Boris Asaf'ev's study of Chaikovskii,
published in 1921 by Svetozar in Petrograd.*

МУЗЫКАЛЬНОЕ
НАСЛЕДИЕ
ЧАЙКОВСКОГО

20. The cover of the first guide to Chaikovskii works
Muzykal'noe nasledie Chaikovskogo
("Chaikovskii's Musical Legacy"), published in 1958.

Schriften des

TSCHAIKOWSKY-STUDIO

I

21. The cover of the periodical
Schriften des Tschaikowsky-Studio,
founded in 1965 by Louisa von Westernhagen
in Hamburg, Germany.

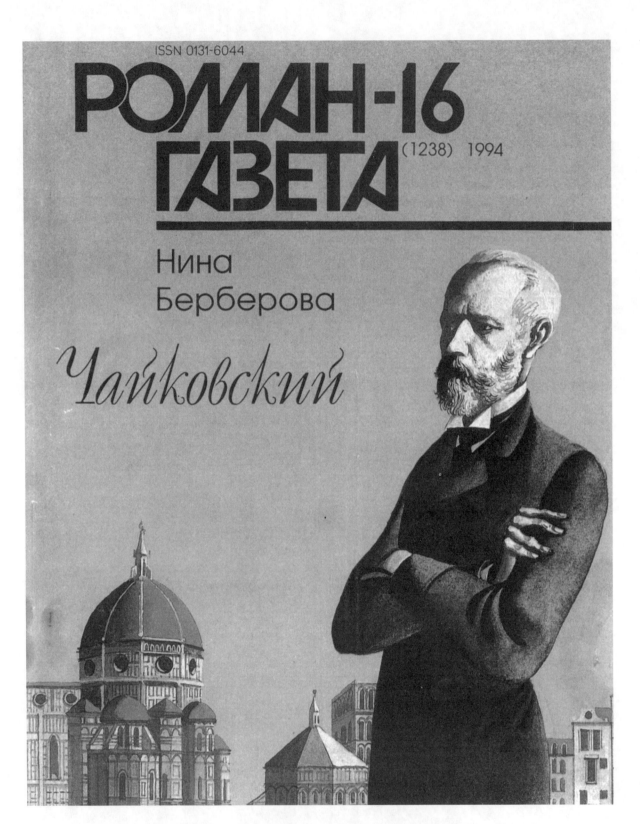

ISSN 0131-6044

РОМАН-16
ГАЗЕТА (1238) 1994

Нина
Берберова

Чайковский

22. *The cover of Nina Berberova's recent Russian edition of her documentary novel* Chaikovskii, *originally published in 1936 in Berlin.*

CATALOGUE OF LETTERS

CATALOGUE OF LETTERS

1848

1.   To Elizaveta & Vasilii Shobert
[summer 1848. Votkinsk] — in French.
RUS–SPsc (f. 834, No. 2, fol. 3–4).
PSSL 5: 3–4.

1a.   To Amalia Shobert
[summer 1848. Votkinsk] — in French.
RUS–SPsc (f. 834, No. 2, fol. 4).
PSSL 5: 40 ("Oct 1851", No. 38).

2.   To Frederika Dürbach
[1848. Votkinsk] — in French.
RUS–SPsc (f. 834, No. 2, fol. 1–2).
PSSL 5: 4.

3.   To Fanny Dürbach
[30 Oct 1848. Moscow] — in French.
Autograph lost; MS copy in RUS–KL.
ZC 1: 46–47 — *PSSL* 5: 5.

1849

4.   To Fanny Dürbach
[7 Jun 1849. Alapaevsk] — in French.
Autograph lost; MS copy in RUS–KL.
ZC 1: 51 — *PSSL* 5: 6.

5.   To Fanny Dürbach
[Jul–Aug 1849. Alapaevsk] — in French.
Autograph lost [facs. in Knorr: 16/17]; MS copy in
    RUS–KL.
ZC 1: 52–53 — *PSSL* 5: 7.

6.   To Fanny Dürbach
[Dec 1849. Alapaevsk] — in French.
Autograph lost; MS copy in RUS–KL.
PSSL 5: 9.

1850

7.   To Fanny Dürbach
[by 5 Mar 1850. Alapaevsk] — in French.
Autograph lost; MS copy in RUS–KL.
ZC 1: 56 — *PSSL* 5: 10.

8.   To Fanny Dürbach
2 May 1850. Alapaevsk — in French.
Autograph lost; MS copy in RUS–KL.
ZC 1: 56–57 — *PSSL* 5: 11.

9.   To Aleksandra & Il´ia Chaikovskii
[21 Oct 1850. St. Petersburg].
RUS–SPsc (f. 834, No. 33, fol. 3–4).
ZC 1: 65–66 — *PR*: 12–13 ("mid Nov") — *PSSL* 5:
    12–13.

10.   To Aleksandra & Il´ia Chaikovskii
8 Nov 1850 [St. Petersburg].
RUS–SPsc (f. 834, No. 33, fol. 1–2).
PR: 11–12 — *PSSL* 5: 14–15.

11.   To Aleksandra & Il´ia Chaikovskii
[23 Nov 1850. St. Petersburg].
RUS–SPsc (f. 834, No. 33, fol. 5–6).
PR: 13–14 — *PSSL* 5: 15–16.

12.   To Aleksandra & Il´ia Chaikovskii
[10 Dec 1850. St. Petersburg] — postscript to a
    letter from M. A. Vakar.
RUS–SPsc (f. 834, No. 33, fol. 7–8).
PR: 14 — *PSSL* 5: 16.

13.   To Aleksandra & Il´ia Chaikovskii
[17 Dec 1850. St. Petersburg].
RUS–SPsc (f. 834, No. 33, fol. 9–10) [facs. of p. 1 in
    PSSL 5: 16/17 — E. Garden, *Tchaikovsky* (1993):
    86/87 (No. 3)].
PR: 14–15 — *PSSL* 5: 17.

14.   To Aleksandra & Il´ia Chaikovskii
[24 Dec 1850. St. Petersburg] — in French and
    Russian.
RUS–SPsc (f. 834, No. 33, fol. 11–12).
PR: 15–16 — *PSSL* 5: 18.

1851

15.   To Aleksandra Chaikovskaia
1 Feb 1851. St. Petersburg — in French.
RUS–SPsc (f. 834, No. 33, fol. 13–14).
PR: 17–18 — *PSSL* 5: 20–21.

16.   To Aleksandra & Il´ia Chaikovskii
[18 Feb 1851. St. Petersburg].
RUS–SPsc (f. 834, No. 33, fol. 17–18).
PR: 20–21 — *PSSL* 5: 22 ("17 Feb").

17.   To Aleksandra & Il´ia Chaikovskii
[5 Mar 1851. St. Petersburg] — in French.
RUS–SPsc (f. 834, No. 33, fol. 15–16).
PR: 18–19 ("early Feb")— *PSSL* 5: 22–23.

18.   To Aleksandra & Il´ia Chaikovskii
[19 Mar 1851. St. Petersburg].
RUS–SPsc (f. 834, No. 33, fol. 19–20).
PR: 21 — *PSSL* 5: 24 ("18 Mar").

19.   To Aleksandra & Il´ia Chaikovskii
[7 Apr 1851. St. Petersburg] — postscript to a letter
    from Nikolai Chaikovskii.
RUS–SPsc (f. 834, No. 33, fol. 21–22).
PR: 21–22 — *PSSL* 5: 25.

20.   To Aleksandra & Il´ia Chaikovskii
[12 Apr 1851. St. Petersburg] — postscript to a letter
    from Nikolai Chaikovskii.
RUS–SPsc (f. 834, No. 33, fol. 23–24).
PR: 22 — *PSSL* 5: 25–26.

21.   To Aleksandra & Il´ia Chaikovskii
22 Apr 1851 [St. Petersburg].
RUS–SPsc (f. 834, No. 33, fol. 25–26).
PR: 23 — *PSSL* 5: 26.

22.   To Aleksandra & Il´ia Chaikovskii
[30 Apr 1851. St. Petersburg] — postscript to a letter
    from Nikolai Chaikovskii.
RUS–SPsc (f. 834, No. 33, fol. 27–28).
PR: 25 — *PSSL* 5: 27.

23.   To Aleksandra & Il´ia Chaikovskii
[? 13 May 1851. St. Petersburg] — in French.
RUS–SPsc (f. 834, No. 33, fol. 29–30).
PR: 23–24 ("mid Apr") — *PSSL* 5: 28.

24.   To Aleksandra & Il´ia Chaikovskii
[20 May 1851. St. Petersburg] — in French.
RUS–SPsc (f. 834, No. 33, fol. 33–34).
PR: 25–26 — *PSSL* 5: 29.

25.   To Aleksandra & Il´ia Chaikovskii
[26 or 27 May 1851. St. Petersburg] — in French.
RUS–SPsc (f. 834, No. 33, fol. 31–32).
PR: 26–27 — *PSSL* 5: 30–31.

26.   To Aleksandra & Il´ia Chaikovskii
[early Jun 1851. St. Petersburg] — in French.
RUS–SPsc (f. 834, No. 33, fol. 35–36).
PR: 28 — *PSSL* 5: 31–32.

27.   To Aleksandra & Il´ia Chaikovskii
[11 Jun 1851. St. Petersburg] — in French.
RUS–SPsc (f. 834, No. 33, fol. 37–38).
PR: 29 — *PSSL* 5: 32–33.

28.   To Aleksandra & Il´ia Chaikovskii
17 Jun [1851. St. Petersburg].
RUS–SPsc (f. 834, No. 33, fol. 41–42).
PR: 30 — *PSSL* 5: 34.

29.   To Aleksandra & Il´ia Chaikovskii
[25 Jun 1851. Nadino] — in French.
RUS–SPsc (f. 834, No. 33, fol. 39–40).
PR: 30–31 — *PSSL* 5: 34.

30.   To Il´ia Chaikovskii
17 Jul 1851 [St. Petersburg].
RUS–SPsc (f. 834, No. 33, fol. 43–44).
PR: 31 — *PSSL* 5: 35.

31. To Il´ia Chaikovskii

20 Jul 1851 [St. Petersburg].

RUS–SPsc (f. 834, No. 33, fol. 45–46).

PR: 32 — *PSSL* 5: 35–36.

32. To Aleksandra Chaikovskaia

7 Aug 1851 [St. Petersburg].

RUS–SPsc (f. 834, No. 33, fol. 47–48).

PR: 32–33 — *PSSL* 5: 36–37.

33. To Aleksandra Chaikovskaia

26 Aug 1851 [St. Petersburg].

RUS–SPsc (f. 834, No. 33, fol. 49–50).

PR: 33 — *PSSL* 5: 37.

34. To Aleksandra Chaikovskaia

[13 Sep 1851. St. Petersburg] — postscript to a letter from Il´ia Chaikovskii

RUS–KL (a^{17}, No. 16).

PSSL 5: 37.

35. To Aleksandra Chaikovskaia

[21 Sep 1851. St. Petersburg] — postscript to a letter from Il´ia Chaikovskii.

RUS–KL (a^{17}, No. 16).

PSSL 5: 38.

36. To Aleksandra & Il´ia Chaikovskii

[7 Oct 1851. St. Petersburg] — postscript to a letter from Nikolai Chaikovskii.

RUS–SPsc (f. 834, No. 33, fol. 51–52).

PR: 33–34 — *PSSL* 5: 38.

37. To Aleksandra & Il´ia Chaikovskii

28 Oct 1851 [St. Petersburg] — in French.

RUS–SPsc (f. 834, No. 33, fol. 53–54).

PR: 34 — *PSSL* 5: 39.

38. [see 1a]

39. To Aleksandra & Il´ia Chaikovskii

11 Nov 1851. St. Petersburg — in French.

RUS–SPsc (f. 834, No. 33, fol. 55–56).

PR: 35–36 — *PSSL* 5: 40–41.

40. To Aleksandra & Il´ia Chaikovskii

[18 Nov 1851. St. Petersburg] — in French.

RUS–SPsc (f. 834, No. 33, fol. 57–58).

PR: 36–37 — *PSSL* 5: 42.

41. To Aleksandra & Il´ia Chaikovskii

[23 Nov 1851. St. Petersburg] — postscript to a letter from Nikolai Chaikovskii.

RUS–SPsc (f. 834, No. 33, fol. 59–60).

PR: 37 — *PSSL* 5: 42–43.

42. To Aleksandra & Il´ia Chaikovskii

2 Dec 1851. St. Petersburg — in French.

RUS–SPsc (f. 834, No. 33, fol. 61–62).

PR: 37–38 — *PSSL* 5: 43.

43. To Aleksandra & Il´ia Chaikovskii

[10 Dec 1851. St. Petersburg] — in French.

RUS–SPsc (f. 834, No. 33, fol. 63–64).

PR: 39 — *PSSL* 5: 44–45.

44. To Aleksandra & Il´ia Chaikovskii

[25 Dec 1851. St. Petersburg] — postscript to a letter from Nikolai Chaikovskii.

RUS–SPsc (f. 834, No. 33, fol. 65–66).

PSSL 5: 45.

1852

45. To Aleksandra & Il´ia Chaikovskii

1 Jan 1852. St. Petersburg — in French.

RUS–SPsc (f. 834, No. 33, fol. 67–68).

PR: 40 — *PSSL* 5: 46.

46. To Aleksandra & Il´ia Chaikovskii

[early Jan 1852. St. Petersburg] — in French.

RUS–SPsc (f. 834, No. 33, fol. 69–70).

PR: 41–42 ("5–6 Jan") — *PSSL* 5: 47–48.

47. To Aleksandra & Il´ia Chaikovskii

[late Jan or Feb 1852. St. Petersburg] — in French.

RUS–SPsc (f. 834, No. 33, fol. 71–72).

PR: 42–43 ("Apr") — *PSSL* 5: 48–49.

48.   To Aleksandra & Il´ia Chaikovskii

[9 Mar 1852. St. Petersburg] — in French and
    Russian.

RUS–SPsc (f. 834, No. 33, fol. 73–74).

PR: 43–44 ("13 Mar") — *PSSL* 5: 50–51.

49.   To Aleksandra & Il´ia Chaikovskii

16 Mar 1852. St. Petersburg.

RUS–SPsc (f. 834, No. 33, fol. 75–76).

PR: 44–45 — *PSSL* 5: 51.

50.   To Aleksandra & Il´ia Chaikovskii

28 Mar 1852 [St. Petersburg].

RUS–SPsc (f. 834, No. 33, fol. 77–78).

PR: 45–46 — *PSSL* 5: 52.

1854

51.   To Viktor Ol´khovskii

[Jul 1854. Oranienbaum].

Autograph lost.

VKG (29 May 1933) — *PSSL* 5: 54.

52.   To Viktor Ol´khovskii

[autumn 1854. St. Petersburg].

Autograph lost.

VKG (29 May 1933) — *VM* (22 Aug 1936) — *PSSL*
    5: 54–55.

1856

53.   To Fanny Dürbach

22 Aug 1856. St. Petersburg — in French.

Autograph lost; MS copy in RUS–KL.

PSSL 5: 56–57.

1861

54.   To Aleksandra Davydova

10 Mar 1861. St. Petersburg.

RUS–SPsc (f. 834, No. 16, fol. 1–2).

ZC 1: 132–136 — *PR*: 47–49 — **PB*: 3–5 — *PSSL* 5:
    60–62 — *LF*: 3–4 [English tr.].

55.   To Aleksandra Davydova

9 Jun 1861. St. Petersburg.

RUS–SPsc (f. 834, No. 16, fol. 3–4).

**ZC* 1: 140 — *PR*: 49–50 — **PB*: 5 — *PSSL* 5: 63–
    64 — **LF*: 4–5 [English tr.].

56.   To Il´ia Chaikovskii

9/21 Jul 1861. Berlin.

RUS–SPsc (f. 834, No. 33, fol. 79–80).

**PR*: 50–52 — **PB*: 5–7 — **PSSL* 5: 64–66 — **ZN*:
    126 — **LF*: 5–6 [English tr.].

57.   To Il´ia Chaikovskii

17/29 Jul 1861. Antwerp.

RUS–SPsc (f. 834, No. 33, fol. 81–82).

PR: 52–53 — **PB*: 7–8 — *PSSL* 5: 66–67 — **LF*: 6–7
    [English tr.].

58.   To Il´ia Chaikovskii

29 Jul/10 Aug 1861. London.

RUS–SPsc (f. 834, No. 33, fol. 83–84).

PR: 53–54 — *PB*: 8–9 — *PSSL* 5: 67–68 — *LF*: 7–8
    [English tr.].

59.   To Il´ia Chaikovskii

12/24 Aug [1861]. Paris.

RUS–SPsc (f. 834, No. 33, fol. 85–86).

PR: 54–55 — *PB*: 9–10 — *PSSL* 5: 68–69 — *LF*: 8–9
    [English tr.].

60.   To Aleksandra Davydova

23 Oct 1861. St. Petersburg.

RUS–SPsc (f. 834, No. 16, fol. 5–6).

**ZC* 1: 144–145 — *PR*: 55–57 — *PB*: 10–11 — *PSSL*
    5: 69–71 — **LF*: 9–10 [English tr.].

61.   To Aleksandra Davydova

4 Dec 1861. St. Petersburg.

RUS–SPsc (f. 834, No. 16, fol. 7–8).

**ZC* 1: 147 — **PR*: 57–58 — **PB*: 11–12 — **PSSL*
    5: 71–72 — **LF*: 10–11 [English tr.].

1862

62.   To Aleksandra Davydova

[12 Apr 1862. St. Petersburg] — postscript to letter
    from Modest Chaikovskii.

RUS–SPsc (f. 834, No. 16, fol. 9–10).

PR: 59 — *PSSL* 5: 73.

63. To Aleksandra Davydova

10 Sep [1862]. St. Petersburg.

RUS–SPsc (f. 834, No. 16, fol. 11–12).

*ZC 1: 149–150 — *PR*: 59–61 — **PB*: 12–14 — *PSSL* 5: 73–75 — **LF*: 11–12 [English tr.].

1863

64. To Vasilii Kologrivov

[8 Jan 1863. St. Petersburg].

RUS–KL (a^{12}, No. 4a).

PSSL 5: 76.

65. To Vasilii Kologrivov

[Early 1863. St. Petersburg].

RUS–KL (a^{12}, No. 4b).

PSSL 5: 76.

66. To Aleksandra Davydova

15 Apr 1863 [St. Petersburg].

RUS–SPsc (f. 834, No. 16, fol. 13–15).

*ZC 1: 156–157 — *PR*: 62–63 — *PB*: 14–15 — *PSSL* 5: 77–78 — *LF*: 13–14 [English tr.].

1864

67. [To an unidentified correspondent]

[by 6 Jul 1864. St. Petersburg?].

US–Wc (ML95 T954).

*PSSL 5: 79–80.

68. To Aleksandra Davydova

28 Jul 1864 [Trostinets].

RUS–SPsc (f. 834, No. 16, fol. 16–17).

*ZC 1: 191 — *PR*: 64 — *PB*: 16 — *PSSL* 5: 80–81 — *LF*: 14–51 [English tr.].

69. To Vasilii Kologrivov

25 Aug 1864 [Trostinets].

RUS–KL (a^{12}, No. 4v).

PSSL 5: 81.

1865

70. To Aleksandra Davydova

24 Aug 1865. Kiev.

RUS–SPsc (f. 834, No. 16, fol. 18–19).

PR: 65–66 — *PB*: 16–17 — *PSSL* 5: 82–83 — *LF*: 15–16 [English tr.].

71. To Aleksandra Davydova

1 Sep 1865 [St. Petersburg].

RUS–SPsc (f. 834, No. 16, fol. 20–21).

PR: 66–67 — *PB*: 17–18 — *PSSL* 5: 83–84 — *LF*: 16–17 [English tr.].

72. To Aleksandra Davydova

8 Sep 1865 [St. Petersburg].

RUS–SPsc (f. 834, No. 16, fol. 22–23).

PR: 67–68 — **PB*: 18–19 — *PSSL* 5: 84–85 — **LF*: 17 [English tr.].

73. To Aleksandra Davydova

[early Oct 1865. St. Petersburg].

RUS–SPsc (f. 834, No. 16, fol. 24–25).

PR: 68–69 — **PB*: 19 — *PSSL* 5: 85–86 — *LF*: 17–18 [English tr.].

74. To Modest Chaikovskii

[mid Oct 1865. St. Petersburg].

RUS–KL (a^{3}, No. 1443).

PSSL 5: 86–87.

75. To Aleksandra Davydova

22 Oct [1865]. St. Petersburg.

RUS–SPsc (f. 834, No. 16, fol. 26–27).

PR: 69–70 — **PB*: 20 — *PSSL* 5: 87–88 — **LF*: 18–19 [English tr.].

76. To Elizaveta Chaikovskaia

29 Oct [1865]. [St. Petersburg].

RUS–SPsc (f. 834, No. 30, fol. 1–2).

PR: 70–71 — *PSSL* 5: 88–89.

1866

77. To Anatolii & Modest Chaikovskii

6 Jan [1866]. [Moscow].

Autograph lost; MS copy in RUS–KL.

ZC 1: 221 — *PR*: 72 — *PB*: 20–21— *PSSL* 5: 90 — *LF*: 19 [English tr.].

78.   To Anatolii & Modest Chaikovskii

10 Jan 1866 [Moscow].

Autograph lost; MS copy in RUS–KL.

ZC 1: 222–223 — *PR*: 72–73 — *PB*: 21–22 — *PSSL* 5: 91 — *LF*: 20 [English tr.].

79.   To Anatolii Chaikovskii

14 Jan 1866 [Moscow].

Autograph lost; MS copy in RUS–KL.

*ZC 1: 227–228 — *PR*: 73–74 — *PB*: 22–23 — *PSSL* 5: 92–93 — *LF*: 21 [English tr.].

80.   To Aleksandra & Lev Davydov

15 Jan 1866. Moscow.

RUS–SPsc (f. 834, No. 16, fol. 28–29).

*ZC 1: 228 — *PR*: 75–76 — *PB*: 23–24 — *PSSL* 5: 93–94 — *LF*: 22–23 [English tr.].

81.   To Elizaveta Chaikovskaia

15 Jan 1866. Moscow.

RUS–SPsc (f. 834, No. 30, fol. 3–4).

PR: 74–75 — *PB*: 23 — *PSSL* 5: 94–95 — *LF*: 21–22 [English tr.].

82.   To Modest Chaikovskii

16 Jan 1866. Moscow.

RUS–SPsc (f. 834, No. 36, fol. 1–2).

ZC 1: 229 — *PR*: 76–77 — **PB*: 24–25 — *PSSL* 5: 95–96 — **LF*: 23 [English tr.].

83.   To Anatolii & Modest Chaikovskii

23 Jan 1866 [Moscow].

Autograph lost; MS copy in RUS–KL.

*ZC 1: 230–231 — *PR*: 77–78 — *PB*: 25–26 — *PSSL* 5: 96–97 — *LF*: 23–24 [English tr.].

84.   To Anatolii & Modest Chaikovskii

30 Jan 1866 [Moscow].

Autograph lost; MS copy in RUS–KL.

*ZC 1: 231–233 — *PR*: 78–79 — *PB*: 26–27 — *PSSL* 5: 98–99 — *LF*: 24–25 [English tr.].

85.   To Anatolii Chaikovskii

6 Feb 1866 [Moscow].

Autograph lost; MS copy in RUS–KL.

*ZC 1: 233–234 — *PR*: 80–81 — *PB*: 27–28 — *PSSL* 5: 99–100 — *LF*: 26–27 [English tr.].

86.   To Aleksandra Davydova

7 Feb 1866 [Moscow].

RUS–SPsc (f. 834, No. 16, fol. 30–31).

*ZC 1: 234 — *PR*: 81–82 — **PB*: 29–30 — *PSSL* 5: 101–102 — **LF*: 27–28 [English tr.].

87.   To Modest Chaikovskii

[mid Feb 1866. Moscow].

RUS–SPsc (f. 834, No. 36, fol. 3–4).

PR: 82–83 — **PSSL* 5: 102–103.

88.   To Anatolii Chaikovskii

6 Mar 1866. Moscow.

Autograph lost; MS copy in RUS–KL.

*ZC 1: 236–237 — *PR*: 83–84 — **PB*: 30 — *PSSL* 5: 103–104 — **LF*: 28 [English tr.].

89.   To Anatolii & Modest Chaikovskii

7 Apr 1866 [Moscow].

Autograph lost; MS copy in RUS–KL.

*ZC 1: 237–239 — *PR*: 85 — *PB*: 30–31— *PSSL* 5: 104–105 — *LF*: 29 [English tr.].

90.   To Aleksandra & Lev Davydov

8 Apr 1866 [Moscow].

RUS–SPsc (f. 834, No. 16, fol. 32–33).

*ZC 1: 239 — *PR*: 86–87 — **PB*: 31–32 — *PSSL* 5: 106–107 — **LF*: 10–11 [English tr.].

91.   To Anatolii & Modest Chaikovskii

16 Apr [1866]. [Moscow].

Autograph lost; MS copy in RUS–KL.

*ZC 1: 239 — *PR*: 87–88 — *PSSL* 5: 107–108.

92.   To Anatolii Chaikovskii

25 Apr [1866]. [Moscow].

Autograph lost; MS copy in RUS–KL.

*ZC 1: 240–241 — *PR*: 88–89 — *PB*: 32–33 — *PSSL* 5: 108–109 — *LF*: 31–32 [English tr.].

93.   To Anatolii Chaikovskii

3 May 1866 [Moscow].

Autograph lost. MS copy in RUS–KL.

PR: 89 — *PSSL* 5: 109–110.

94.   To Aleksandra Davydova

14 May 1866 [Moscow].

RUS–SPsc (f. 834, No. 16, fol. 34–35).

ZC 1: 243–244 — *PR*: 90–91 — *PSSL* 5: 94–95.

95.   To Aleksandra Davydova

7 Jun [1866]. [Peterhof].

RUS–SPsc (f. 834, No. 16, fol. 36–39).

ZC 1: 245 — *PR*: 91–92 — *PSSL* 5: 111–113.

95a.   To Pëtr Iurgenson

11 Aug [1866]. [St. Petersburg].

RUS–KL (a³, No. 3310).

PSSL 17: 211.

96.   To Anatolii Chaikovskii

8 Nov [1866]. [Moscow].

Autograph lost; MS copy in RUS–KL.

ZC 1: 260–261 — *PR*: 93–94 — *PB*: 33–34 — *PSSL* 5: 113–114 — *LF*: 32 [English tr.].

97.   To Anatolii Chaikovskii

1 Dec 1866. Moscow.

Autograph lost; MS copy in RUS–KL.

ZC 1: 261 — *PR*: 94 — *PSSL* 5: 115–116.

97a.   To Pëtr Iurgenson

[1866–1869. Moscow] — note on visiting card.

RUS–Mcm

PSSL 17: 211.

1867

98.   To Anatolii Chaikovskii

2 May [1867]. [Moscow].

Autograph lost; MS copy in RUS–KL.

ZC 1: 268 — *PR*: 96 — *PB*: 34–35 — *PSSL* 5: 117 — *LF*: 32–33 [English tr.].

99.   To Aleksandr Ostrovskii

10 Jun 1867. Hapsal.

RUS–Mt (Ostrovskii coll.).

ORK: 157–158 — *PSSL* 5: 118–119.

100.   To Aleksandra Davydova

20 Jul [1867]. Hapsal.

RUS–SPsc (f. 834, No. 16, fol. 40–41).

ZC 1: 271 — *PR*: 96–97 — *PSSL* 5: 119–120.

101.   To Aleksandra Davydova

8 Aug 1867 [Hapsal].

RUS–SPsc (f. 834, No. 16, fol. 42–43).

ZC 1: 271–272 — *PR*: 97–98 — *PSSL* 5: 120–121.

102.   To Anatolii Chaikovskii

31 Aug [1867]. [Moscow].

Autograph lost; MS copy in RUS–KL.

ZC 1: 278 — *PR*: 98–99 — *PB*: 35 — *PSSL* 5: 121–122 — *LF*: 33 [English tr.].

103.   To Aleksandr Ostrovskii

[by 20 Sep 1867. Moscow].

RUS–Mt (Ostrovskii coll.).

ORK: 160 — *PSSL* 5: 122.

104.   To Anatolii Chaikovskii

28 Sep [1867]. [Moscow].

Autograph lost. MS copy in RUS–KL.

ZC 1: 278–279 — *PR*: 99–100 — *PB*: 35–36 — *PSSL* 5: 123 — *LF*: 34 [English tr.].

105.   To Ekaterina Alekseeva

4 Oct [1867]. Moscow.

RUS–SPsc (f. 834, No. 10).

PSSL 5: 105.

106.   To Aleksandra Davydova

11 Oct 1867. Moscow.

RUS–SPsc (f. 834, No. 16, fol. 44–45).

PR: 100–101 — *PSSL* 5: 125–126.

107.   To Modest Chaikovskii

[late Oct 1867. Moscow].

RUS–KL (a³, No. 1436).

PR: 96–96 — *PSSL* 5: 126–127.

108. To Anatolii Chaikovskii

[early Nov 1867; Moscow].

Autograph lost. MS copy in RUS–KL.

PR: 101–102 — **PB*: 36–37 — *PSSL* 5: 128–129 —
   *LF: 34–35 [English tr.].

109. To Modest Chaikovskii

25 Nov 1867 [Moscow].

RUS–SPsc (f. 834, No. 36, fol. 5–6).

*ZC 1: 280 — *PR*: 102–103 — *PB*: 37 — *PSSL* 5:
   128 — *LF*: 36 [English tr.].

110. To Anatolii Chaikovskii

12 Dec [1867]. [Moscow].

Autograph lost. MS copy in RUS–KL.

*ZC 1: 282 — *PR*: 103 — *PB*: 37–38 — *PSSL* 5:
   129 — *LF*: 36–37 [English tr.].

1868

111. To Milii Balakirev

21 Jan 1868. Moscow.

RUS–SPsc (f. 834, No. 11, fol. 1–2).

BC: 14 — *PSSL* 5: 131.

112. To Anatolii Chaikovskii

[27–28 Jan 1868. Moscow].

Autograph lost; MS copy in RUS–KL.

PR: 104–105 — **PB*: 38–39 — *PSSL* 5: 131–132 —
   *LF: 37 [English tr.].

113. To Anatolii Chaikovskii

[mid Feb 1868. Moscow].

Autograph lost. MS copy in RUS–KL.

PR: 105 ("early Feb") — *PB*: 39 ("early Feb") — *PSSL*
   5: 133 — *LF*: 37–38 ("early Feb") [English tr.].

114. To Milii Balakirev

25 Feb 1868. Moscow.

RUS–SPsc (f. 834, No. 11, fol. 3–4).

BC: 15 — *PSSL* 5: 134.

115. To Milii Balakirev

3 Mar [1868]. Moscow.

RUS–SPsc (f. 834, No. 11, fol. 5–6).

BC: 17 — *PSSL* 5: 134–135.

116. To Aleksandra Davydova

16 Apr 1868 [Moscow].

RUS–SPsc (f. 834, No. 16, fol. 46–49).

*ZC 1: 274 — *PR*: 106–107 — *PSSL* 5: 135–137.

117. To Aleksandra Davydova

20 Jul/1 Aug [1868]. Paris.

RUS–SPsc (f. 834, No. 16, fol. 50–52).

PR: 107–109 — **PB*: 40–41 — *PSSL* 5: 137–139 —
   *LF: 38–39 [English tr.].

118. To Anatolii Chaikovskii

10 Sep [1868]. [Moscow].

Autograph lost. MS copy in RUS–KL.

*ZC 1: 297–298 — *PR*: 109–110 — *PB*: 41–42 —
   PSSL 5: 139–140 — *LF*: 40 [English tr.].

119. To Modest Chaikovskii

13 [Sep 1868] (in MS: "13 Aug"). Moscow.

RUS–SPsc (f. 834, No. 36, fol. 7–8).

*ZC 1: 298–299 — *PR*: 110–111 — *PB*: 42–43 —
   PSSL 5: 140–141 — *LF*: 41 [English tr.].

120. To Aleksandra Davydova

24 Sep 1868. Moscow.

RUS–SPsc (f. 834, No. 16, fol. 53–54).

PR: 111–113 — *PSSL* 5: 141–143.

121. To Anatolii Chaikovskii

25 Sep [1868]. Moscow.

Autograph lost; MS copy in RUS–KL.

*ZC 1: 299–300 — *PR*: 113–114 — *PB*: 43–44 —
   PSSL 5: 143–144 — *LF*: 41–42 [English tr.].

122. To Anatolii Chaikovskii

21 Oct 1868 [Moscow].

Autograph lost; MS copy in RUS–KL.

ZC 1: 302–303 — *PR*: 114–115 — **PB*: 44–45 —
   PSSL 5: 144–145 — **LF*: 42–43 [English tr.].

123. To Modest Chaikovskii

[Nov 1868. Moscow].

RUS–SPsc (f. 834, No. 36, fol. 9–10).

*ZC 1: 303 — *PR*: 115–116 — **PB*: 45 — *PSSL* :
   146–147 — *LF*: 43–44 [English tr.].

124. To Modest Chaikovskii

[mid Dec 1868. Moscow].

RUS–SPsc (f. 834, No. 36, fol. 11–12).

*ZC 1: 303 — PR: 116–117 — PB: 46 — PSSL 5: 147–148 — LF: 44–45 [English tr.].

125. To Il´ia Chaikovskii

26 Dec 1868 [Moscow].

RUS–SPsc (f. 834, No. 33, fol. 87–89).

*ZC 1: 303–305 — PR: 117–119 — PB: 46–48 — PSSL 5: 148–150 — LF: 45–46 [English tr.].

126. To Milii Balakirev

[30 Dec 1868. Moscow].

RUS–SPsc (f. 834, No. 11, fol. 7–8).

BC: 21–22 — PSSL 5: 150–151.

127. To Modest Chaikovskii

[1868. Moscow].

RUS–KL (a³, No. 1439).

PSSL 5: 152.

128. To Pëtr Iurgenson

[1868. Moscow].

RUS–KL (a³, No. 2148).

PSSL 5: 152.

1869

129. To Anatolii Chaikovskii

[Jan 1869. Moscow].

Autograph lost. MS copy in RUS–KL.

*ZC 1: 308 — PR: 120–121 — *PB: 48–49 — PSSL 5: 153–154 — *LF: 47 [English tr.].

130. To Modest Chaikovskii

1 Feb 1869 [Moscow].

RUS–SPsc (f. 834, No. 36, fol. 13–14).

PR: 121–122 — PB: 49–50 — PSSL 5: 154–155 — LF: 48 [English tr.].

131. To Anatolii Chaikovskii

[15 Feb 1869. Moscow].

Autograph lost. MS copy in RUS–KL.

PR: 122–123 — *PB: 50 — PSSL 5: 156–157 — *LF: 49 [English tr.].

132. To Milii Balakirev

[mid Feb 1869. Moscow].

RUS–SPsc (f. 834, No. 11, fol. 11–12).

BC: 23 — PSSL 5: 157.

133. To Milii Balakirev

[13 Mar 1869. Moscow] — telegram.

RUS–SPsc

PSSL 5: 157.

134. To Milii Balakirev

13 Mar 1869 [Moscow].

RUS–SPsc (f. 834, No. 11, fol. 13–14).

BC: 24–26 — PSSL 5: 158–159.

135. To Modest Chaikovskii

[3 Apr 1869. Moscow].

RUS–KL (a³, No. 1438) [facs. of p. 1 in PSSL 5: 112/113].

PR: 123–124 — *PB: 51 — PSSL 5: 160 — *LF: 49–50 [English tr.].

136. To Anatolii Chaikovskii

[19 Apr 1869. Moscow].

Autograph lost; MS copy in RUS–KL.

PR: 124–125 — *PB: 51–52 — PSSL 5: 161 — *LF: 50 [English tr.].

137. To Anatolii Chaikovskii

[29 Apr–1 May 1869. Moscow].

Autograph lost; MS copy in RUS–KL.

PR: 125–126 ("late Apr") — PSSL 5: 162.

138. To Milii Balakirev

3 May 1869 [Moscow].

RUS–SPsc (f. 834, No. 11, fol. 15–16).

BC: 32–33 — PSSL 5: 162–163.

139. To Anatolii Chaikovskii

[3 or 4 May 1869. Moscow].

Autograph lost; MS copy in RUS–KL.

PR: 126 ("late Apr") — PSSL 5: 164.

140. To Anatolii Chaikovskii

[mid May 1869. Moscow].

Autograph lost; MS copy in RUS–KL.
PR: 126–127 — *PSSL* 5: 164.

141.   To Anatolii Chaikovskii
[by 20 May 1869. Moscow].
Autograph lost; MS copy in RUS–KL.
PR: 121 ("early Apr") — *PSSL* 5: 165.

142.   To Pëtr Iurgenson
[20 May 1869. Moscow].
RUS–KL (a³, No. 2180).
PSSL 5: 165.

143.   To Anatolii Chaikovskii
3 Aug [1869]. Moscow.
Autograph lost; MS copy in RUS–KL.
ZC 1: 327–328 — *PR*: 127–128 — *PB*: 52 — *PSSL*
    5: 165–166 — *LF*: 50–51 [English tr.].

144.   To Pavel Fëdorov
[6 Aug 1869. Moscow].
RUS–SPia (f. 497, op. 2, d. 22000).
Gatobovets (25 Mar 1935) — *PSSL* 5: 167.

145.   To Anatolii Chaikovskii
11 Aug [1869]. Moscow.
Autograph lost; MS copy in RUS–KL.
ZC 1: 328 — *PR*: 128–129 — *PB*: 52 — *PSSL* 5:
    168 — *LF*: 51–52 [English tr.].

146.   To Anatolii Chaikovskii
19 Aug [1869]. [Moscow].
Autograph lost; MS copy in RUS–KL.
ZC 1: 328–329 — *PR*: 129 — *PB*: 53–54 — *PSSL* 5:
    169 — *LF*: 52 [English tr.].

147.   To Modest Chaikovskii
[early Sep 1869. St. Petersburg].
RUS–KL (a³, No. 1441).
PSSL 5: 169.

148.   To Anatolii Chaikovskii
10 Sep 1869 [Moscow].
Autograph lost; MS copy in RUS–KL.
ZC 1: 329 — *PR*: 129–131 — *PSSL* 5: 170–171.

149.   To Aleksandra Davydova
[15–16 Sep 1869. Moscow].
RUS–SPsc (f. 834, No. 16, fol. 66–68).
PR: 131–132 — *PSSL* 5: 171–172.

150.   To Anatolii Chaikovskii
25 Sep 1869 [Moscow].
Autograph lost; MS copy in RUS–KL.
ZC 1: 329–330 — *PR*: 132–133 — *PB*: 54 — *PSSL*
    5: 172–173 — *LF*: 52 [English tr.].

151.   To Milii Balakirev
2 Oct [1869]. Moscow.
RUS–SPsc (f. 834, No. 11, fol. 17–18).
BC: 34–36 — *PSSL* 5: 174–175.

152.   To Milii Balakirev
[early Oct 1869. Moscow].
RUS–SPsc (f. 834, No. 11, fol. 19–20).
BC: 40 ("Oct") — *PSSL* 5: 175–176.

153.   To Anatolii Chaikovskii
7 Oct 1869 [Moscow].
Autograph lost; MS copy in RUS–KL.
ZC 1: 334 — *PR*: 133–134 — *PB*: 54–55 — *PSSL*
    5: 176–177 — *LF*: 53–54 [English tr.].

154.   To Stepan Gedeonov
12 Oct 1869 [Moscow].
RUS–SPsc (f. 834, No. 15).
SM (1939), 5: 56 — *PSSL* 5: 177–178.

155.   To Modest Chaikovskii
12 Oct [1869]. [Moscow].
RUS–SPsc (f. 834, No. 36, fol. 17–18).
ZC 1: 334 — *PR*: 134–135 — *PB*: 55–56 —
    PSSL 5: 179 — *LF*: 54 [English tr.].

156.   To Milii Balakirev
28 Oct 1869. Moscow
RUS–SPsc (f. 834, No. 11, fol. 21–23, 9–10).
BC: 40–42 — *PSSL* 5: 180–181.

157.   To Anatolii Chaikovskii
30 Oct 1869 [Moscow].

Autograph lost; MS copy in RUS–KL.

ZC 1: 334–335 — *PR*: 135–136 — *PB*: 56 — *PSSL*
5: 182–183 — *LF*: 54–55 [English tr.].

158. To Aleksandra Davydova

15 Nov [1869]. Moscow.

RUS–SPsc (f. 834, No. 16, fol. 55–56).

ZC 1: 335 — *PR*: 136–137 — *PB*: 57 — *PSSL* 5:
183–184 — *LF*: 55 [English tr.].

159. To Milii Balakirev

17 Nov 1869 [Moscow].

RUS–SPsc (f. 834, No. 11, fol. 24–28) [facs. of 2 p. in
PICH (1978): 60 — *CH* 1 (1990): 57].

BC: 44–48 — *PSSL* 5: 184–187.

160. To Anatolii Chaikovskii

18 [Nov 1869] (on MS: copy "18 Sep") [Moscow].

Autograph lost; MS copy in RUS–KL.

PR: 137–138 — *PB*: 57–58 — *PSSL* 5: 188–189 —
LF: 56 [English tr.].

161. To Modest Chaikovskii

18 [Nov 1869] (on MS copy: "18 Sep") [Moscow].

RUS–SPsc (f. 834, No. 36, fol. 15–16).

ZC 1: 335 — *PR*: 138–139 — *PB*: 58–59 — *PSSL* 5:
189–190 — *LF*: 57 [English tr.].

162. To Ivan Klimenko

[26 Nov 1869. Moscow].

Autograph lost; MS copy in RUS–KL.

KMV: 62–63 ("1871/1872") — *PSSL* 5: 190–191.

163. To Sergei Rachinskii

[Nov 1869. Moscow] — in French.

RUS–Mcl (f. 427).

Krasnyi arkhiv (1940), 3: 246 [Russian tr.] — *PSSL* 5:
191.

164. To Anatolii Chaikovskii

[by 4 Dec 1869. Moscow].

Autograph lost; MS copy in RUS–KL.

PR: 139–140 ("early Dec") — *PB*: 59 — *PSSL* 5:
192 — *LF*: 57–58 [English tr.].

165. To Anatolii Chaikovskii

7 Dec 1869 [Moscow].

Autograph lost; MS copy in RUS–KL.

PR: 140–141 — *PSSL* 5: 193.

166. To Modest Chaikovskii

[early Dec 1869. Moscow].

RUS–KL (a³, No. 1437).

PSSL 5: 193.

167. To Anatolii Chaikovskii

[mid Dec 1869. Moscow].

Autograph lost; MS copy in RUS–KL.

PR: 141 — *PSSL* 5: 194.

168. To Milii Balakirev

18 Dec [1869]. Moscow.

RUS–SPsc (f. 834, No. 11, fol. 29–30).

BC: 51–53 — *PSSL* 5: 194–195.

169. To Aleksandra Davydova

19 Dec [1869]. Moscow.

RUS–SPsc (f. 834, No. 16, fol. 57–58).

PR: 141–142 — *PB*: 60 — *PSSL* 5: 195–196 — *LF*:
58 [English tr.].

170. To Milii Balakirev

20 Dec 1869 [Moscow].

RUS–SPsc (f. 834, No. 11, fol. 31–32).

BC: 53 — *PSSL* 5: 197.

171. To Vasilii Bessel´

21 Dec 1869. Moscow.

RUS–Mcm (f. 42, No. 219).

KNB (1923), 1: 45 — *PSSL* 5: 197.

172. To Milii Balakirev

[late Dec 1869. Moscow].

RUS–SPsc (f. 834, No. 11, fol. 33–34).

BC: 54 — *PSSL* 5: 198.

173. To Milii Balakirev

[late Dec 1869. Moscow].

RUS–SPsc (f. 834, No. 11, fol. 35–36).

BC: 54 — *PSSL* 5: 198.

174. To Karl Al´brekht

[Dec 1869. Moscow].

RUS–Mcm (f. 37, No. 1).

PSSL 5: 199.

175. To Karl Al´brekht

[Dec 1869. Moscow].

RUS–Mcm (f. 37, No. 2).

PSSL 5: 199.

176. [To an unidentified correspondent]

[1869. Moscow].

RUS–Mcm (f. 37, No. 106).

PSSL 5: 199–200.

177. To Ivan Klimenko

[late 1860s. Moscow].

Autograph lost; MS copy in RUS–KL.

PSSL 5: 200.

1870

178. To Modest Chaikovskii

13 Jan 1870 [Moscow].

RUS–SPsc (f. 834, No. 36, fol. 19–20).

*ZC 1: 336 — *PR*: 143–144 — **PB*: 60–61 — **PSSL*
    5: 201–202 — **ZN*: 121 — **LF*: 59 [English tr.].

179. To Aleksandra Davydova

5 Feb [1870]. Moscow.

RUS–SPsc (f. 834, No. 16, fol. 59–60).

*ZC 1: 338 — *PR*: 144–145 — **PB*: 61–62 — **PSSL*
    5: 203–204 — **LF*: 59–60 [English tr.].

180. To Milii Balakirev

23 Feb 1870 [Moscow].

RUS–SPsc (f. 834, No. 11, fol. 37–38).

BC: 55–56 — *PSSL* 5: 204–205.

181. To Milii Balakirev

[25 Feb 1870. Moscow] — telegram.

RUS–SPsc

PSSL 5: 205.

182. To Anatolii Chaikovskii

[late Feb 1870. Moscow].

Autograph lost; MS copy in RUS–KL.

PR: 145–146 ("early Mar") — *PSSL* 5: 206.

183. To Modest Chaikovskii

[2–3 Mar 1870. Moscow].

RUS–SPsc (f. 834, No. 36, fol. 22–23).

*ZC 1: 339 — *PR*: 146–147 — *PB*: 62–63 — **PSSL*
    5: 206–207 — *LF*: 60–61 [English tr.].

184. To Anatolii Chaikovskii

7 Mar 1870. Moscow.

Autograph lost; MS copy in RUS–KL.

PR: 147–148 — **PB*: 63 — **PSSL* 5: 208 — **LF*: 61–
    62 [English tr.].

185. To Modest Chaikovskii

26 Mar 1870 [Moscow].

RUS–SPsc (f. 834, No. 36, fol. 24–25).

*ZC 1: 340–341 — *PR*: 148–149 — **PB*: 63–64 —
    *PSSL 5: 209–210 — **ZN*: 121 — **LF*: 62
    [English tr.].

186. To Karl Al´brekht

[Mar 1870. Moscow] — in German.

RUS–Mcm (f. 37, No. 110).

PSSL 5: 210.

187. To Ivan Klimenko

[1 Apr 1870. Moscow] — telegram.

Autograph lost; MS copy in RUS–KL.

KMV: 52–53 — *PSSL* 5: 21.

188. To Lev Davydov

[mid Apr 1870. Moscow].

RUS–SPsc (f. 834, No. 19, fol. 1–2).

PB: 64 — *PSSL* 5: 211–212 — *LF*: 62 [English tr.].

189. To Anatolii Chaikovskii

23 Apr 1870 [Moscow].

Autograph lost; MS copy in RUS–KL.

*ZC 1: 341 — *PR*: 150–151 — **PB*: 64–65 — *PSSL*
    5: 212–213 — **LF*: 63 [English tr.].

190. To Ivan Klimenko

1–4 May 1870. Moscow.

Autograph lost; MS copy in RUS–KL.

ZC 1: 341–343 — *KMV*: 55–56 — *PSSL* 5: 213–216.

191. To Milii Balakirev

[mid May 1870. Moscow].

RUS–SPsc (f. 834, No. 11, fol. 39–40).

BC: 58 — *PSSL* 5: 216–217.

192. To Milii Balakirev

[15 May 1870. Moscow] — telegram.

RUS–SPsc

BC: 58 — *PSSL* 5: 217.

193. To Nikolai Rubinshtein

18 May 1870. St. Petersburg.

RUS–Mcm (f. 37, No. 80).

ZC 1: 343–344 — *IRM* 1: 159–160 — *PSSL* 5: 217–218.

194. To Milii Balakirev

[1/13 Jun 1870]. Soden.

RUS–SPsc (f. 834, No. 11, fol. 41–42).

BC: 59 — *PSSL* 5: 218–219.

195. To Anatolii Chaikovskii

1/13 Jun 1870; Soden.

Autograph lost; MS copy in RUS–KL.

ZC 1: 345 — *PR*: 151–153 — *PB*: 65–66 — *PSSL* 5: 219–220 — *LF*: 63–64 [English tr.].

196. To Avdot´ia Bakhireva

2/14 Jun 1870 [Soden].

RUS–SPsc (f. 834, No. 13).

PSSL 5: 220–221.

197. To Il´ia Chaikovskii

2/14 Jun 1870. Soden.

RUS–SPsc (f. 834, No. 33, fol. 90–91).

PR: 153 — *PSSL* 5: 221–222.

198. To Modest Chaikovskii

7/19 Jun 1870. Soden.

RUS–SPsc (f. 834, No. 36, fol. 26–28).

ZC 1: 345–346 — *PR*: 154–155 — *PB*: 66–67 — *PSSL* 5: 222–223 — *LF*: 65 [English tr.].

199. To Aleksandra Davydova

24 Jun/6 Jul 1870. Soden.

RUS–SPsc (f. 834, No. 16, fol. 61–62).

ZC 1: 347 — *PR*: 156–158 — *PSSL* 5: 224–225.

200. To Anatolii Chaikovskii

24 Jun/6 Jul 1870. Soden.

Autograph lost; MS copy in RUS–KL.

ZC 1: 346–347 — *PR*: 155–156 — *PB*: 68–69 — *PSSL* 5: 225–226 — *LF*: 66 [English tr.].

201. To Il´ia Chaikovskii

12/24 Jul [1870]. Interlaken.

RUS–SPsc (f. 834, No. 33, fol. 29–30).

PR: 158–159 — *PSSL* 5: 227.

202. To Modest Chaikovskii

12/24 Jul 1870. Interlaken.

RUS–SPsc (f. 834, No. 36, fol. 29–30).

ZC 1: 348 — *PR*: 159–160 — *PB*: 69–70 — *PSSL* 5: 228–229 — *LF*: 67 [English tr.].

202a. To Modest Chaikovskii

[30 Aug 1870. St. Petersburg].

RUS–KL (b³, No. 6490).

PSSL 17: 212.

203. To Elizaveta Shobert

30 Aug [1870]. [St. Petersburg].

RUS–KL (a³, No. 462).

PSSL 5: 229.

204. To Anatolii Chaikovskii

4 Sep 1870 [Moscow].

Autograph lost; MS copy in RUS–KL.

PR: 160–161 — *PSSL* 5: 229–230.

205. To Milii Balakirev

6 Sep 1870. Moscow.

RUS–SPsc (f. 834, No. 11, fol. 43–44).

BC: 59–60 — *PSSL* 5: 230–231.

206. To Modest Chaikovskii

17 Sep 1870. Moscow.

RUS–SPsc (f. 834, No. 36, fol. 31–33).

PR: 161–162 — *PSSL* 5: 231–232.

207. To Milii Balakirev

25 Sep 1870. Moscow.

RUS–SPsc (f. 834, No. 11, fol. 45–46).

BC: 60 — *PSSL* 5: 232–233.

208. To Enrico Tamberlik

[by 1 Oct 1870. Moscow] — signed jointly by Chaikovskii, Nikolai Rubinshtein, Aleksandr Razmadze, Eduard Langer, Nikolai Kashkin, Wilhelm Fitzenhagen, Ferdinand Laub, Nikolai Hubert, Vladimir Kashperov, Giovanni Galvani.

Autograph lost

Moskovskie vedomosti (3 Oct 1870) — *PSSL* 5: 233.

209. To Modest Chaikovskii

5 Oct 1870 [Moscow].

RUS–SPsc (f. 834, No. 36, fol. 34–35).

ZC 1: 362–363 — *PR*: 162–163 — *PB*: 70 — *PSSL* 5: 234–235 — *LF*: 68 [English tr.].

210. To Anatolii Chaikovskii

[? 5 Oct 1870. Moscow].

Autograph lost. MS copy in RUS–KL.

PR: 163–164 — *PB*: 70–71 — *PSSL* 5: 235–236 — *LF*: 68 [English tr.].

211. To Modest Chaikovskii

[early–mid Oct 1870. Moscow].

RUS–SPsc (f. 834, No. 36, fol. 38–39).

PR: 164 — *PSSL* 5: 236.

212. To Milii Balakirev

[20–23 Oct 1870. Moscow].

RUS–SPsc (f. 834, No. 11, fol. 47–48).

BC: 61–62 ("late Oct/early Nov") — *PSSL* 5: 236–237.

213. To Ivan Klimenko

26 Oct 1870. Moscow.

Autograph lost; MS copy in RUS–KL.

ZC 1: 363 — *KMV:* 58–60 — *PSSL* 5: 237–238.

214. To Il´ia Chaikovskii

26 Oct 1870. Moscow.

RUS–SPsc (f. 834, No. 33, fol. 94–95).

PR: 164–165 — *PB*: 71 — *PSSL* 5: 239–240 — *LF*: 69 [English tr.].

215. To Modest Chaikovskii

1 Nov 1870. Moscow.

RUS–SPsc (f. 834, No. 36, fol. 36–37).

PR: 165–166 — *PSSL* 5: 240–241.

216. To Vasilii Bessel´

25 Nov 1870. Moscow.

RUS–Mcm (f. 42, No. 220).

KNB (1923), 2: 42–43 — *PSSL* 5: 241–242.

217. To Anatolii Chaikovskii

29 Nov 1870 [Moscow].

Autograph lost; MS copy in RUS–KL.

ZC 1: 364 — *PR*: 166–167 — *PSSL* 5: 242–243.

218. To Modest Chaikovskii

[7 Dec 1870. Moscow] — telegram.

RUS–KL (a³, No. 1444).

PSSL 5: 244.

219. To Aleksandra Davydova

20 Dec 1870. Moscow.

RUS–SPsc (f. 834, No. 16, fol. 64–64).

ZC 1: 364–365 — *PR*: 167–168 — *PB*: 71–72 — *PSSL* 5: 244–245 — *LF*: 69–70 [English tr.].

220. To Karl Al´brekht

[1870. Moscow].

RUS–Mcm (f. 37, No. 3).

PSSL 5: 245.

221. To Karl Al´brekht

[1870. Moscow].

RUS–Mcm (f. 37, No. 4).

PSSL 5: 246.

222. To Karl Al´brekht

[1870. Moscow].

RUS–Mcm (f. 37, No. 5).

PSSL 5: 246.

223. To Karl Al´brekht
[1867–1870. Moscow].
RUS–Mcm (f. 37, No. 6).
PSSL 5: 246.

224. [To German Larosh?]
[1867–1870. Moscow].
RUS–Mcm
PSSL 5: 246.

1871

225. To Vasilii Bessel´
9 Jan [1871]. [Moscow].
RUS–Mcm (f. 42, No. 221).
KNB (1923), 2: 43–44 — *PSSL* 5: 248.

226. To Milii Balakirev
10 [Jan] 1871. Moscow.
RUS–SPsc (f. 834, No. 11, fol. 49–50).
BC: 62–64 — *PSSL* 5: 249–250.

227. To Anatolii Chaikovskii
[Jan 1871. Moscow].
Autograph lost; MS copy in RUS–KL.
PR: 169 — *PSSL* 5: 250.

228. To Anatolii Chaikovskii
3 Feb 1871. Moscow
Autograph lost; MS copy in RUS–KL.
PR: 170 — *PSSL* 5: 251.

229. To Aleksandra Davydova
11 Feb 1871 [Moscow].
RUS–SPsc (f. 834, No. 16, fol. 65).
PR: 171 — *PSSL* 5: 252.

230. To Anatolii Chaikovskii
[mid Feb 1871. Moscow].
Autograph lost; MS copy in RUS–KL.
PR: 169 ("late Jan") — *PSSL* 5: 252–253.

231. To Il´ia Chaikovskii
14 Feb 1871 [Moscow].
RUS–SPsc (f. 834, No. 33, fol. 96–98).
*ZC 1: 365 — *PR:* 171–172 — *PSSL* 5: 253–254.

232. To Ivan Klimenko
[16 Mar 1871. Moscow].
Autograph lost; MS copy in RUS–KL.
PSSL 5: 254.

233. To Milii Balakirev
15 May 1871. Moscow.
RUS–SPsc (f. 834, No. 11, fol. 51–52).
BC: 65 — *PSSL* 5: 255.

234. To Anatolii Chaikovskii
17 May 1871 [Moscow].
Autograph lost; MS copy in RUS–KL.
PR: 173 — *PSSL* 5: 255–256.

235. To Milii Balakirev
29 May 1871. Moscow.
RUS–SPsc (f. 834, No. 11, fol. 53–55).
BC: 67 — *PSSL* 5: 235.

236. To Pëtr Iurgenson
15 Jul [1871]. Nizy.
RUS–KL (a³, No. 2852).
PSSL 5: 257.

237. To Anatolii Chaikovskii
3 Sep 1871 [Moscow].
Autograph lost; MS copy in RUS–KL.
PR: 173–174 — *PSSL* 5: 258.

238. To Mikhail Azanchevskii
11 Sep 1871. Moscow.
RUS–KL (a³, No. 2).
PSSL 5: 259–260.

239. To Ivan Klimenko
12 Sep 1871 [Moscow].
Autograph lost; MS copy in RUS–KL.
KMV: 60–62 — **PSSL* 5: 261–262.

240. To Nikolai Chaikovskii
28 Sep [1871]. Moscow.
RUS–SPsc (f. 834, No. 37, fol. 1–2).
*ZC 1: 372 — *PSSL* 5: 262–263.

241. To Milii Balakirev

8 Oct 1871. Moscow.

RUS–SPsc (f. 834, No. 11, fol. 56–57).

BC: 68–69 — *PSSL* 5: 263.

242. To Milii Balakirev

22 Oct 1871. Moscow.

RUS–SPsc (f. 834, No. 11, fol. 58–59).

BC: 70–71 — *PSSL* 5: 264.

243. To Anatolii Chaikovskii

2 Dec [1871]. Moscow.

RUS–KL (a³, No. 1083).

*ZC 1: 372–373 — *PR:* 174–175 — **PB:* 73 — **PSSL*
    5: 265–266 — *ZN:* 122 — **LF:* 71 [English tr.].

244. To Aleksandra Davydova

9 Dec 1871 [Moscow].

RUS–SPsc (f. 834. No. 16, fol. 69–70).

PR: 175–176 — **PB:* 73–74 — *PSSL* 5: 266–267 —
    LF: 71–72 [English tr.].

245. To Anna Merkling

16 Dec 1871. Moscow.

Autograph lost; MS copy in RUS–KL.

CTP 206–207 — *PSSL* 5: 267–269.

246. To Karl Al´brekht

[Nov–Dec 1871 . Moscow].

RUS–Mcm (f. 37, No. 7).

PSSL 5: 269.

246a. To Karl Al´brekht

Nov or Dec 1871 [Moscow].

RUS–KL (a³, No. 3311).

Not published.

247. To Karl Al´brekht

[1871. Moscow].

RUS–Mcm (f. 37, No. 8).

PSSL 5: 269.

248. To Karl Al´brekht

[1871. Moscow].

RUS–Mt (Al´brekht coll.).

PSSL 5: 270.

248a. To Karl Al´brekht

[1871–1877. Moscow].

RUS–Mcm (f. 37, No. 10).

PSSL 17: 212.

1872

249. To Anatolii Chaikovskii

1/13 Jan 1872. Nice.

RUS–KL (a³, No. 1078).

*ZC 1: 373–374 — *PR:* 177–178 — **PB:* 74–75 —
    PSSL 5: 271–272 — *LF:* 72–73 [English tr.].

250. To Pëtr Iurgenson

2/14 Jan 1872. Nice.

RUS–KL (a³, No. 2132a).

PSSL 5: 272.

251. To Il´ia Chaikovskii

31 Jan 1872. Moscow.

RUS–SPsc (f. 834, No. 33, fol. 99–100).

*ZC 1: 374 — *PR:* 179–180 — *PB:* 75–76 — *PSSL* 5:
    273 — *LF:* 73 [English tr.].

252. To Anatolii Chaikovskii

31 Jan [1872]. Moscow.

RUS–KL (a³, No. 1079).

*ZC 1: 374 — *PR:* 178–179 — *PSSL* 5: 273–275.

253. To Pëtr Iurgenson

[early Feb 1872. Moscow].

RUS–KL (a³, No. 2169).

PSSL 5: 275.

254. To Ivan Klimenko

[4 Feb 1872. Moscow].

Autograph lost; MS copy in RUS–KL.

KMV: 64 — *PSSL* 5: 275.

254a. To Stepan Gedeonov

[4 May 1872. Moscow].

RUS–SPia (f. 497, op. 2, d. 23068).

PSSL 17: 213.

255. To Eduard Nápravník

4 May 1872. Moscow.

RUS–SPtm (Gik 17195/2).
ZC 1: 377 — *VP* 105–106 — *PSSL* 5: 276.

256. To Pavel Fëdorov
4 May 1872. Moscow.
RUS–SPia (f. 497, op. 2, d. 23082) [facs. in *Kirov*: 24–
    25].
PSSL 5: 276–277.

257. To Il´ia Chaikovskii
8 May 1872. Moscow.
RUS–SPsc (f. 834, No. 33, fol. 101).
PR: 180 — *PSSL* 5: 277.

258. To Pëtr Iurgenson
[16 May 1872. Moscow].
RUS–KL (a³, No. 2134).
PSSL 5: 277.

258a. To Modest Chaikovskii
27 [May 1872]. Moscow.
RUS–KL (a³, No. 1442).
Not published.

259. To Ivan Klimenko
[by Jun 1872. Moscow].
Autograph lost; MS copy in RUS–KL.
PSSL 5: 278.

260. To Ivan Klimenko
[by Jun 1872. Moscow].
Autograph lost; MS copy in RUS–KL.
PSSL 5: 279.

261. To Ivan Klimenko
[by Jun 1872. Moscow].
Autograph lost; MS copy in RUS–KL.
KMV: 65 — *PSSL* 5: 278–279.

262. To Ivan Klimenko
[by Jun 1872. Moscow].
Autograph lost; MS copy in RUS–KL.
PSSL 5: 279.

263. To Pëtr Iurgenson
[by Jun 1872. Moscow].
RUS–KL (a³, No. 2149).
PSSL 5: 279.

264. To Karl Davydov
2 Jun [1872]. Kiev.
RUS–KL (a³, No. 157).
PSSL 5: 279–280.

265. To Iakov Polonskii
2 Jun [1872]. Kiev.
RUS–SPil (f. 241).
PSSL 5: 280.

266. To Modest Chaikovskii
[early Jun 1872. Kamenka].
RUS–SPsc (f. 834, No. 36, fol. 40–41).
PR: 180–181 — *PSSL* 5: 281.

267. Pëtr Iurgenson
30 Jun [1872]. Kamenka.
RUS–KL (a³, No. 2135).
*ZC 1: 379 — *PSSL* 5: 281–282.

268. To Anatolii Chaikovskii
5 Jul [1872]. Kiev.
RUS–KL (a³, No. 1080).
*ZC 1: 378 — *PR*: 181 — *PSSL* 5: 282–283.

269. To Pëtr Iurgenson
16 Jul [1872]. Nizy.
RUS–KL (a³, No. 2136).
PSSL 5: 283.

270. To Modest Chaikovskii
17–18 Jul [1872]. Vorozhba.
RUS–SPsc (f. 834, No. 36, fol. 42–43).
PR: 182 — *PSSL* 5: 283–284.

271. To Pëtr Iurgenson
8 Aug [1872]. [Usovo].
RUS–KL (a³, No. 2137).
PSSL 5: 284–285.

272. To Karl Al´brekht
[Aug–Sep 1872. Moscow].
RUS–Mcm (f. 37, No. 108).
PSSL 5: 285.

273. To Anatolii Chaikovskii
2 Sep [1872]. [Moscow].
RUS–KL (a³, No. 1081).
PR: 182–183 — *PSSL* 5: 285–286.

274. To Anatolii Chaikovskii
4 Sep [1872]. Moscow.
RUS–KL (a³, No. 1082).
**PR*: 183 — **PSSL* 5: 286–287.

275. To Modest Chaikovskii
2 Nov 1872 [Moscow].
RUS–SPsc (f. 834, No. 36, fol. 44–45).
**ZC* 1: 393–394 — *PR*: 184–185 — **PB*: 76 — *PSSL*
    5: 287–288 — **LF*: 74 [English tr.].

276. To Ivan Klimenko
15 Nov 1872. Moscow.
Autograph lost; MS copy in RUS–KL.
**ZC* 1: 394–395 — *KMV*: 65–67 — *PSSL* 5: 288–289.

277. To Il´ia Chaikovskii
22 Nov [1872]. Moscow.
RUS–SPsc (f. 834, fol. 33, No. 102–103).
**ZC* 1: 395–396 — *PR*: 185–186 — **PB*: 76–77 —
    PSSL 5: 290–291 — **LF*: 74–75 [English tr.].

278. To Ivan Klimenko
7 Dec 1872 [Moscow].
Autograph lost; MS copy in RUS–KL.
KMV: 68 — *PSSL* 5: 291.

279. To Il´ia Chaikovskii
9 Dec 1872 [Moscow].
RUS–SPsc (f. 834, No. 33, fol. 105–106).
**ZC* 1: 396 — *PR*: 186–187 — **PB*: 77–78 — *PSSL* 5:
    292 — **LF*: 75–76 [English tr.].

280. To Modest Chaikovskii
10 Dec [1872]. Moscow.
RUS–SPsc (f. 834, No. 36, fol. 46–47).

**ZC* 1: 396–397 — *PR*: 187–188 — **PB*: 78–79 —
    **PSSL* 5: 293–294 — **LF*: 76 [English tr.].

**281. To Nikolai Rubinshtein & Karl
       Al´brekht**
[1872. Moscow].
RUS–Mcm (f. 37, No. 81).
PSSL 5: 294.

282. To Pëtr Iurgenson
[1872. Moscow].
RUS–KL (a³, No. 2151).
PSSL 5: 294.

283. To Pëtr Iurgenson
[1872. Moscow].
RUS–KL (a³, No. 2150).
PSSL 5: 295.

1873

284. To Vasilii Bessel´
2 Jan 1873. Moscow.
RUS–Mcm (f. 42, No. 223).
KNB (1923), 2: 45–46 — *PSSL* 5: 296.

285. To Aleksandra Davydova
9 Jan [1873]. [Moscow].
RUS–SPsc (f. 834, No. 16, fol. 71–72).
PR: 189–190 — **PB*: 79 — *PSSL* 5: 297–298 — **LF*:
    76–77 [English tr.].

286. To Vladimir Stasov
15 Jan 1873. Moscow.
RUS–SPsc (f. 738, No. 343, fol. 1–3).
RM (1909), 3: 102–103 — *PSSL* 5: 298–299.

287. To Vladimir Stasov
27 Jan 1873. Moscow.
RUS–SPsc (f. 738, No. 343, fol. 4–6).
**ZC* 1: 400–401 — *RM* (1909), 3: 105–106 — *PSSL*
    5: 299–300.

288. To Il´ia Chaikovskii
5 Feb 1873. Moscow.
RUS–SPsc (f. 834, No. 33, fol. 107–108).

*ZC 1: 402 — PR: 190–191 — *PB: 79–80 — PSSL 5: 301–302 — *LF: 77–78 [English tr.].

289. To Modest Chaikovskii

13 Feb 1873. Moscow.

RUS–SPsc (f. 834, No. 36, fol. 48–49).

*ZC 1: 402–403 — PR: 191–193 — *PB: 80–81 — PSSL 5: 302–303 — *LF: 78–79 [English tr.].

290. To Vasilii Bessel´

21 Feb 1873. Moscow.

RUS–Mcm (f. 42, No. 224).

KNB (1923), 2: 46–47 — PSSL 5: 303–304.

291. To the editor of Golos

2 Mar 1873. Moscow.

Autograph lost

Golos (6 Mar 1873): 2 [col. 5] — Sankt Peterburge vedomosti (20 Mar 1873) — MF 119–121 — PSSL 2: 374 — PSSL 5: 304–305.

292. To Vasilii Bessel´

4 Mar 1873 [Moscow].

RUS–Mcm (f. 42, No. 225).

Novoe vremia (7 Oct 1896) — MN (1923), 1: 51 — PSSL 5: 306.

293. To Vasilii Bessel´

7 Mar 1873 [Moscow].

RUS–Mcm (f. 42, No. 226).

Novoe vremia (7 Oct 1896) — EIT (1896–97), 1: 25 — MN (1923), 1: 51–52 — PSSL 5: 307.

294. To Dmitrii Obolenskii

7 Mar 1873. Moscow.

RUS–SPa (f. 408, No. 165, fol. 14–15).

ZC 1: 437–438 — PSSL 5: 308–309.

295. To Vasilii Bessel´

[? 20 Mar 1873. Moscow].

RUS–Mcm (f. 42, No. 227).

MN (1923), 1: 52 — PSSL 5: 310.

296. To Vasilii Bessel´

25 Mar [1873]. [Moscow].

RUS–Mcm (f. 42, No. 228).

MN (1923), 1: 52 — PSSL 5: 310–311.

297. To Aleksandr Ostrovskii

[6 Apr 1873; Moscow];

RUS–Mt (Ostrovskii coll.).

ORK: 164–165 — PSSL 5: 311–312.

298. To Il´ia Chaikovskii

7 Apr 1873 [Moscow].

RUS–SPsc (f. 834, No. 33, fol. 109–110).

*ZC 1: 403–404 — PR: 193 — PB: 81–82 — PSSL 5: 312–313 — LF: 80 [English tr.].

299. To Vasilii Bessel´

21 Apr 1873 [Moscow].

RUS–Mcm (f. 42, No. 229).

*EIT (1896–97), 1: 25 — MN (1923), 1: 52–53 — *PSSL 5: 313–314.

300. To Nikolai Rimskii-Korsakov

21 Apr [1873]. [Moscow].

RUS–SPsc (f. 640, op. 1, No. 1015, fol. 35).

SM (1945), 3: 124 — PSSL 5: 314.

301. To Aleksandra Davydova & Modest Chaikovskii

27 Apr 1873. Moscow — partially in English.

RUS–SPsc (f. 834, No. 16, fol. 73–74).

PR: 193–195 — PSSL 5: 314–316.

302. To Pëtr Iurgenson

[Apr–May 1873. Moscow].

RUS–KL (a³, No. 2140).

*PSSL 5: 316.

303. To Vasilii Bessel´

[1 May 1873. Moscow].

RUS–Mcm (f. 42, No. 230).

MN (1923), 1: 53 — PSSL 5: 317.

304. To Vasilii Bessel´

1 May [1873]. Moscow.

RUS–Mcm (f. 42, No. 231).

EIT (1896–97), 1: 26 — MN (1923), 1: 53 — PSSL 5: 317–318.

305. To Vasilii Bessel´

[by 11 May 1873. St. Petersburg].

RUS–Mcm (f. 42, No. 232).

MN (1923), 1: 54 — *PSSL* 5: 318.

306.   To Aleksandr Ostrovskii

[12 May 1873. Moscow] — telegram.

RUS–Mt (Ostrovskii coll.).

PSSL 5: 318.

307.   To Karl Al´brekht

[16 May 1873. Moscow].

RUS–Mcm (f. 37, No. 11).

PSSL 5: 319.

308.   To Vasilii Bessel´

16 May [1873]. [Moscow].

RUS–Mcm (f. 42, No. 223).

MN (1923), 1: 54 — *PSSL* 5: 319.

309.   To Anatolii Chaikovskii

16 May 1873 [Moscow].

RUS–KL (a³, No. 1084).

PR: 195 — *PSSL* 5: 320.

310.   To Pëtr Iurgenson

[by 21 May 1873. Moscow].

RUS–KL (a³, No. 2138).

PSSL 5: 320.

311.   To Vasilii Bessel´

24 May [1873]. Moscow.

RUS–Mcm (f. 42, No. 234).

MN (1923), 1: 54 — *PSSL* 5: 321–322.

312.   To Il´ia Chaikovskii

24 May [1873]. [Moscow].

RUS–SPsc (f. 834, No. 33, fol. 111).

PR: 195–196 — *PB*: 82 — *PSSL* 5: 323 — *LF*: 80
[English tr.].

313.   To Pëtr Iurgenson

[by 25 May 1873. Moscow].

RUS–KL (a³, No. 2139).

PSSL 5: 323.

314.   To Pëtr Iurgenson

2 Jun [1873]. Nizy.

RUS–KL (a³, No. 2201).

PSSL 5: 324.

315.   To Vladimir Shilovskii

18 Jun [1873]. Kamenka.

RUS–Mt (Shilovskii coll.).

SM (1940), 5–6: 141 — *PSSL* 5: 324–325.

316.   To Il´ia Chaikovskii

23 Jul/4 August 1873. Paris.

RUS–SPsc (f. 834, No. 33, fol. 112–113).

PR: 196–197 — *PB*: 83 — *PSSL* 5: 325–326 — *LF*:
81 [English tr.].

317.   To Vasilii Bessel´

3 Sep [1873]. Moscow.

RUS–Mcm (f. 42, No. 235).

Novoe vremia (7 Oct 1896) — **EIT* (1896–97), 1:
26 — **ZC* 1: 416–417 — *MN* (1923), 1: 54–
55 — *PSSL* 5: 327.

318.   To Nikolai Rubinshtein

[early Oct 1873. Moscow].

RUS–Mcm (f. 37, No. 82).

IRM 1: 160 — *PSSL* 5: 328.

319.   To Pëtr Iurgenson

[early Oct 1873. Moscow].

RUS–KL (a³, No. 2177).

PSSL 5: 328.

320.   To Il´ia Chaikovskii

9 Oct 1873 [Moscow].

RUS–SPsc (f. 834, No. 33, fol. 114–115).

*ZC 1: 417–418 — *PR*: 197–198 — **PB*: 83–84 —
PSSL 5: 329 — *LF*: 81–82 [English tr.].

321.   To Vasilii Bessel´

10 Oct 1873 [Moscow].

RUS–Mcm (f. 42, No. 236).

Novoe vremia (7 Oct 1896) — **EIT* (1896–97), 1:
27 — **ZC* 1: 418 — *MN* (1923), 1: 55 — *PSSL*
5: 330.

322. To Vasilii Bessel´

18 Oct 1873. Moscow.

RUS–Mcm (f. 42, No. 237).

Novoe vremia (7 Oct 1896) — **EIT* (1896–97), 1: 28 — **ZC* 1: 418–419 — *MN* (1923), 1: 55, 3: 43 — *PSSL* 5: 330–331.

323. To Vasilii Bessel´

30 Oct [1873]. Moscow.

RUS–Mcm (f. 42, No. 238).

Novoe vremia (7 Oct 1896) — **EIT* (1896–97), 1: 29 — **ZC* 1: 419–420 — *MN* (1923), 3: 43 — *PSSL* 5: 332.

324. To Vasilii Bessel´

5 Nov [1873]. [Moscow].

RUS–Mcm (f. 42, No. 239).

Novoe vremia (7 Oct 1896) — **EIT* (1896–97), 1: 30 — *MN* (1923), 3: 43–44 — *PSSL* 5: 333.

325. To Anatolii Chaikovskii

[mid Nov 1873. Moscow].

RUS–KL (a³, No. 1286).

PSSL 5: 333–334.

326. To Vasilii Bessel´

28 Nov [1873]. Moscow.

RUS–Mcm (f. 42, No. 240).

Novoe vremia (7 Oct 1896) — **ZC* 1: 420 — *MN* (1923), 3: 44 — *PSSL* 5: 334.

327. To Modest Chaikovskii

28 Nov [1873]. Moscow.

RUS–SPsc (f. 834, No. 36, fol. 50–51).

*ZC 1: 420–421 — *PR*: 198–199 — **PB*: 84–88 — *PSSL* 5: 335–336 — **LF*: 82–83 [English tr.].

328. To Pëtr Iurgenson

[Oct–Nov 1873. Moscow].

RUS–KL (a³, No. 2174).

PSSL 5: 336.

329. To Pëtr Iurgenson

[Oct–Nov 1873. Moscow].

RUS–KL (a³, No. 2175).

PSSL 5: 336.

330. To Pëtr Iurgenson

[Oct–Nov 1873. Moscow].

RUS–KL (a³, No. 2176).

PSSL 5: 337.

331. To Karl Al´brekht

[by 6 Dec 1873. Moscow].

RUS–Mcm (f. 37, No. 12).

PSSL 5: 337.

332. To Vasilii Bessel´

6 Dec 1873 [Moscow].

RUS–Mcm (f. 37, No. 241).

*EIT (1896–97), 1: 31 — *MN* (1923), 3: 44 — *PSSL* 5: 338.

333. To Pëtr Iurgenson

[early Dec 1873. Moscow].

RUS–KL (a³, No. 2171).

PSSL 5: 338–339.

334. To Eduard Nápravník

[18 Dec 1873. Moscow].

RUS–SPtm (Gik 17195/3).

*ZC 1: 422–423 — *VP* 108–109 — *PSSL* 5: 339.

1874

335. To Vasilii Bessel´

[early Jan 1874. Moscow].

RUS–Mcm (f. 42, No. 242).

SM (1938), 6: 38 — *PSSL* 5: 340.

336. To Anatolii Chaikovskii

[24] Jan [1874] (in MS: "26 Jan") [Moscow].

RUS–KL (a³, No. 1085).

*ZC 1: 423 — *PR*: 200–201 — **PB*: 85–86 ("26 Jan") — **PSSL* 5: 341–342 — **LF*: 84 ("26 Jan") [English tr.]

337. To Vasilii Bessel´

[Jan 1874. Moscow].

RUS–Mcm (f. 42, No. 243).

SM (1938), 6: 38–39 — *PSSL* 5: 342.

338. To Vasilii Bessel´
[by 10 Feb 1874. Moscow].
RUS–Mcm (f. 42, No. 244).
PSSL 5: 342.

339. To Vasilii Bessel´
18 Feb [1874]. Moscow.
RUS–Mcm (f. 42, No. 245).
SM (1938), 6: 39 — *PSSL* 5: 343.

340. To Eduard Nápravník
19 Feb 1874 [Moscow].
RUS–SPtm (Gik 17195/4).
ZC 1: 424 — *VP* 109–110 — *PSSL* 5: 344.

341. To Vasilii Bessel´
[mid Mar 1874. Moscow].
RUS–Mcm (f. 42, No. 246).
PSSL 5: 344.

342. To Karl Al´brekht
[24 Mar 1874. St. Petersburg] — telegram.
RUS–Mcm (f. 37, No. 13).
PSSL 5: 345.

343. To Karl Al´brekht
25 Mar [1874]. St. Petersburg.
RUS–Mcm (f. 37, No. 14).
PSSL 5: 345.

344. To Karl Al´brekht
[25 Mar 1874. St. Petersburg] — telegram.
RUS–Mcm (f. 37, No. 15).
PSSL 5: 346.

345. To Sergei Taneev
25 Mar 1874. St. Petersburg.
Autograph lost; MS copy in RUS–KL.
PT 1 — *CTP* 3 — *PSSL* 5: 346.

346. To Iakov Polonskii
[11–12 Apr 1874. St. Petersburg].
RUS–Mcl (f. 403).
PSSL 5: 346.

347. To Modest Chaikovskii
17/[29] Apr 1874 (in MS: "17/19"). Venice.
RUS–SPsc (f. 834, No. 36, fol. 52–53).
ZC 1: 431–433 — *PR*: 201–202 — *PB*: 86–87 —
    PSSL 5: 347–348 — *LF*: 84–85 [English tr.].

348. To Pëtr Shchurovskii
17/29 Apr 1874. Venice.
RUS–Mt
CMS: 456–457 — *PSSL* 5: 348–349.

349. To Anatolii Chaikovskii
[19] Apr/1 May 1874 (in MS: "20 Apr"). Rome.
RUS–KL (a³, No. 1086).
ZC 1: 433–434 — *PR*: 202–204 — *PB*: 87–88 —
    PSSL 5: 349–350 — *LF*: 85–86 [English tr.].

350. To Anna Merkling
25 Apr/7 May 1874. Naples.
RUS–SPsc (f. 124, No. 4650).
CTP 207–209 — *PSSL* 5: 351–353.

351. To Modest Chaikovskii
27 Apr/9 May 1874. Florence.
RUS–SPsc (f. 834, No. 36, fol. 54–55).
ZC 1: 434–435 — *PR*: 204–205 — *PB*: 88–89 —
    PSSL 5: 353–354 — *LF*: 86–87 [English tr.].

352. To Vasilii Bessel´
18 May 1874 [Moscow].
RUS–Mcm (f. 42, No. 247).
EIT (1896–97), 1: 37–38 — *SM* (1938), 6: 39–40 —
    PSSL 5: 355–356.

353. To Vasilii Bessel´
30 May 1874. Moscow.
RUS–Mcm (f. 42, No. 248).
EIT (1896–97), 1: 38 — *SM* (1938), 6: 40–41 —
    PSSL 5: 356–357.

354. To Modest Chaikovskii
18 Jun 1874. Nizy — in French.
RUS–SPsc (f. 834, No. 36, fol. 56–57).
ZC 1: 439–440 — *PR*: 205–206 — *PB*: 90 — *PSSL*
    5: 358–359 — *LF*: 88 [English tr.].

355. To Bogomir Korsov
17 Jul 1874. Nizy — in French.
Autograph lost; MS copy in RUS–KL.
PSSL 5: 359–361.

356. To Elizaveta Lavrovskaia
17 Jul 1874. Nizy.
RUS–KL (a³, No. 262).
PSSL 5: 362–363.

357. To Karl Al´brekht
[late Aug 1874]. Usovo.
RUS–Mcm (f. 37, No. 17).
PSSL 5: 361.

358. To Vasilii Bessel´
4 Sep [1874]. [Moscow].
RUS–Mcm (f. 42, No. 249).
SM (1938), 6: 41 — *PSSL* 5: 363.

359. To Pëtr Iurgenson
[Sep 1874. Moscow].
RUS–KL (a³, No. 2141).
PSSL 5: 364.

360. To Vasilii Bessel´
13 Sep 1874 [Moscow].
RUS–Mcm (f. 42, No. 250).
SM (1938), 6: 41 — *PSSL* 5: 364.

361. To Nikolai Rimskii-Korsakov
13 Sep [1874]. Moscow.
Autograph lost; typed copy in RUS–KL.
PSSL 5: 365.

362. To Pëtr Iurgenson
[26 Sep 1874. Moscow].
RUS–KL (a³, No. 2172).
PSSL 5: 366.

363. To Pëtr Iurgenson
[26 Sep 1874. Moscow].
RUS–KL (a³, No. 2178).
PSSL 5: 366.

364. To Il´ia Chaikovskii
27 Sep 1874 [Moscow].
RUS–SPsc (f. 834, No. 33, fol. 116–117).
PR: 206–207 — *PSSL* 5: 366–367.

365. To Vladimir Stasov
28 Sep [1874]. Moscow.
RUS–SPsc (f. 738, No. 343, fol. 7–9).
RM (1909), 3: 107–108 — *PSSL* 5: 367–368.

366. To Vasilii Bessel´
19 Oct [1874]. Moscow.
RUS–Mcm (f. 42, No. 251).
SM (1938), 6: 41–42 — *PSSL* 5: 369–370.

367. To Eduard Nápravník
19 Oct 1874. Moscow.
RUS–SPtm (Gik 17195/5).
ZC 1: 447–448 — *VP* 110–111 — *PSSL* 5: 370–
371.

368. To Modest Chaikovskii
29 Oct [1874]. Moscow.
RUS–SPsc (f. 834, No. 36, fol. 58–59).
ZC 1: 448–449 — *PR*: 207–208 — *PB*: 90–91 —
PSSL 5: 371–372 — *LF*: 89–90 [English tr.].

369. To Vasilii Bessel´
9 Nov 1874. Moscow.
RUS–Mcm (f. 42, No. 252).
SM (1938), 6: 42–45 — *PSSL* 5: 373–376.

370. To Vladimir Stasov
16 Nov [1874]. [Moscow].
RUS–SPsc (f. 738, No. 343, fol. 10–12).
RM (1909), 3: 109–110 — *PSSL* 5: 377.

371. To Iosif Setov
18 Nov 1874. Moscow.
RUS–Mcl (f. 946).
OTC 84 — *PSSL* 5: 378–379.

372. To Anatolii Chaikovskii
21 Nov 1874. Moscow.
RUS–KL (a³, No. 1087).

*ZC 1: 451 — PR: 208–209 — *PB: 91–92 — PSSL 5: 379–380 — *LF: 90 [English tr.].

373. To Modest Chaikovskii

26 Nov 1874. Moscow.

RUS–SPsc (f. 834, No. 36, fol. 60–61).

*ZC 1: 451–452 — PR: 210–211 — *PB: 92–93 — *PSSL 5: 380–381 — *LF: 91 [English tr.].

374. To Iosif Setov

16 Dec 1874. Moscow.

RUS–Mcl (f. 946).

PSSL 5: 382.

375. To Modest Chaikovskii

[16 Dec 1874. Moscow].

RUS–SPsc (f. 834, No. 36, fol. 62–63).

PR: 211 — PB: 93 — PSSL 5: 383 — *LF: 92 [English tr.].

376. To Vasilii Bessel´

[17 Dec 1874. Moscow].

RUS–Mcm (f. 42, No. 253).

*EIT (1896–97), 1: 38 — SM (1938), 6: 45 — PSSL 5: 383.

377. To Modest Chaikovskii

[? 17 Dec 1874. Moscow].

RUS–SPsc (f. 834, No. 36, fol. 66–67).

PR: 214 ("mid Jan 1875") — *PB: 95–96 ("mid Jan 1875") — PSSL 5: 384 — *LF: 94 [English tr.].

378. To Modest Chaikovskii

[? 20–23 Dec 1874. Moscow].

RUS–SPsc (f. 834, No. 36, fol. 64–65).

PR: 211 ("late Dec") — PSSL 5: 384.

379. To Eduard Nápravník

[by 27 Dec 1874. Moscow].

RUS–SPtm (Gik 17195/6).

VP 113–114 — PSSL 5: 385.

380. To Pëtr Iurgenson

[1874. Moscow].

RUS–KL (a³, No. 2173).

PSSL 5: 385.

381. To Pëtr Iurgenson

[1874. Moscow].

RUS–KL (a³, No. 2152).

PSSL 5: 385.

1875

382. To Eduard Nápravník

1 Jan 1875 . Moscow.

RUS–SPtm (Gik 17195/7).

VP 115–116 — PSSL 5: 386–387.

383. To Nikolai Rimskii-Korsakov

4 Jan 1875. Moscow.

RUS–SPsc (f. 640, op. 1, No. 1015, fol. 1–1a).

SM (1945), 3: 124–125 — PSSL 5: 387.

384. To Modest Chaikovskii

6 Jan 1875 [Moscow].

RUS–SPsc (f. 834, No. 36, fol. 68–69).

*ZC 1: 454 — PR: 212–213 — *PB: 94 — PSSL 5: 388–389 — *LF: 92–93 [English tr.].

385. To Anatolii Chaikovskii

9 Jan 1875 [Moscow].

RUS–KL (a³, No. 1088).

*ZC 1: 455 — *PR: 213–214 — *PB: 95 — *PSSL 5: 389–390 — *ZN: 122 — *LF: 93 [English tr.]— TW: 60–61 [English tr.].

386. To Dmitrii Razumovskii

[12 Jan 1875. Moscow].

RUS–Mrg

PSSL 5: 390–392.

387. To the editor of *Golos*

[late Jan 1875. Moscow].

RUS–KL (a³, No. 254).

PSSL 5: 392.

388. To Modest Chaikovskii

[late Jan 1875. Moscow].

RUS–SPsc (f. 834, No. 36, fol. 70–71).

PR: 215 — *PB: 96 — PSSL 5: 392–393 — *LF: 96 [English tr.].

389. To Modest Chaikovskii

3 Feb [1875]. Moscow.

RUS–SPsc (f. 834, No. 36, fol. 72–73).

PR: 215 — **PB*: 96 — *PSSL* 5: 393 — **LF*: 94–95 [English tr.].

390. To Sergei Taneev

[5 Feb 1875. Moscow].

RUS–Mcl (f. 880).

CTP 4 — *PSSL* 5: 394.

391. To Modest Chaikovskii

13 Feb 1875. Moscow.

RUS–SPsc (f. 834, No. 36, fol. 74–75).

PR: 215–216 — **PB*: 97 — *PSSL* 5: 394–395 — **LF*: 95 [English tr.].

392. To Modest Chaikovskii

[by 23 Feb 1875. Moscow].

RUS–KL (a³, No. 1440).

PSSL 5: 395.

393. To Aleksandr Kuznetsov

7 Mar 1875. Moscow.

RUS–Mcl (f. 905).

PSSL 5: 396.

394. To Anatolii Chaikovskii

9 Mar 1875. Moscow.

RUS–KL (a³, No. 1090).

*ZC 1: 459–460 — *PR*: 216–217 — **PB*: 97–98 — *PSSL* 5: 396–397 — **LF*: 96 [English tr.].

395. To Modest Chaikovskii

12 Mar 1875. Moscow.

RUS–SPsc (f. 834, No. 36, fol. 78–79).

*ZC 1: 460–461 — *PR*: 218–219 — *PSSL* 5: 398–399.

396. To Vasilii Bessel´

22 Mar [1875]. Moscow.

RUS–Mcm (f. 42, No. 254).

SM (1938), 6: 45–46 — *PSSL* 5: 399–400.

397. To Modest Chaikovskii

27 [Mar 1875]. Moscow.

RUS–KL (a³, No. 2040).

PSSL 5: 401.

398. To Modest Chaikovskii

[30 or 31] Mar [1875]. Moscow.

RUS–SPsc (f. 834, No. 36, fol. 76–77).

PR: 219 — *PSSL* 5: 402.

399. To Pëtr Iurgenson

3 May [1875]. Moscow.

RUS–KL (a³, No. 2133).

PSSL 5: 402.

400. To Anatolii Chaikovskii

12 May 1875. Moscow.

RUS–KL (a³, No. 1091).

*ZC 1: 464–465 — *PR*: 219–220 — **PB*: 98–99 — *PSSL* 5: 403 — **LF*: 97 [English tr.].

400a. To the editor of *Russkie vedomosti*

[by 15 May 1875. Moscow] — signed "Storonnik Moskovskoi konservatorii" ('Advocate of the Moscow Conservatory' — Chaikovskii?).

Autograph lost

Russkie vedomosti (15 May 1875) — *SM* (1965), 5: 35–37.

401. To Nikolai Rimskii-Korsakov

18 May 1875. Moscow.

RUS–SPtob (VII.2.4.154).

SM (1945), 3: 125 — *PSSL* 5: 404.

402. To Sergei Taneev

[by 24 May 1875. Moscow].

RUS–Mcl (f. 880).

CTP 5 — *PSSL* 5: 405.

403. To Modest Chaikovskii

[by 24 May 1875. Moscow].

RUS–KL (a³, No. 2040).

PSSL 5: 405.

404. To Aleksandra Davydova

2 Jun 1875 [Usovo].

RUS–SPsc (f. 834, No. 17, fol. 1–2).

PR: 220–221 — *PSSL* 5: 405–406.

405.   **To Aleksei & Mikhail Sofronov**
19 Jun 1875. Usovo.
RUS–KL (a³, No. 391).
PSSL 5: 406–407.

406.   **To Modest Chaikovskii**
29 Jun 1875 [Moscow].
RUS–SPsc (f. 834, No. 36, fol. 80–81).
PR: 221 — *PSSL* 5: 407.

406a.   **To Hans von Bülow**
1 Jul 1875. Nizy — in French.
D–Bds
Muzykal´naia zhizn´ (1966), 23: 22 — *PSSL* 17: 213–214.

407.   **To Vasilii Bessel´**
8 Jul 1875. Nizy.
RUS–Mcm (f. 42, No. 255).
SM (1938), 6: 46–47 — *PSSL* 5: 407–409.

408.   **To Pëtr Iurgenson**
8 Jul 1875. Nizy.
RUS–KL (a³, No. 2142).
PSSL 5: 409.

409.   **To Sergei Taneev**
14 Aug 1875. Verbovka.
RUS–Mcl (f. 880).
PT 2 — *CTP* 5–6 — *PSSL* 5: 409–410.

410.   **To Lev Davydov**
30 Aug 1875. Usovo.
RUS–SPsc (f. 834, No. 19, fol. 3–4).
PR: 221–222 — *PSSL* 5: 411.

411.   **To Sergei Taneev**
[9 Sep 1875. Moscow].
RUS–Mcl (f. 880).
CTP 6 — *PSSL* 5: 411.

412.   **To Nikolai Rimskii-Korsakov**
10 Sep 1875. Moscow.
RUS–SPsc (f. 640, op. 1, No. 1015, fol. 2–3).
*ZC 1: 467–468 — *SM* (1945), 3: 125–126 — *PSSL* 5: 412–413.

413.   **To Modest Chaikovskii**
14 Sep [1875]. Moscow.
RUS–SPsc (f. 834, No. 36, fol. 82–83).
*ZC 1: 469 — *PR*: 222–223 — *PB*: 99 — *PSSL* 5: 414–415 — *LF*: 97–98 [English tr.].

413a.   **To Hans von Bülow**
21 Sep 1875. Moscow — in French.
US–NH (misc. 372, S–Z).
SM (1960), 5: 72–73 [Russian tr.] — *PSSL* 17: 215–216.

414.   **To Sergei Taneev**
[Sep 1875. Moscow].
RUS–Mcl (f. 880).
CTP 4 ("Mar–May 1875") — *PSSL* 5: 415.

415.   **To Sergei Taneev**
[Sep 1875. Moscow].
RUS–Mcl (f. 880).
CTP 5 ("Mar–May 1875") — *PSSL* 5: 416.

416.   **To Mariia Golovina**
20 Oct 1875. Moscow.
RUS–Mcl (f. 1336).
PSSL 5: 416.

417.   **To Nikolai Rimskii-Korsakov**
12 Nov 1875. Moscow.
RUS–SPsc (f. 640, op. 1, No. 1015, fol. 4–5) [facs. of p. 1 in *PSSL* 5: 384/385].
*ZC 1: 471–472 — *SM* (1945), 3: 128 — *PSSL* 5: 417–418.

418.   **To Hans von Bülow**
19 Nov 1875. Moscow — in French.
Autograph lost; MS copy in RUS–KL.
*BBS 6: 297 — *PSSL* 5: 418–419.

419.   **To Nikolai Bernard**
24 Nov [1875]. Moscow.
RUS–SPtob (VII.2.4.154).
Glebov (1922): 161 — *PSSL* 5: 420.

420.   **To Lev Kupernik**
26 Nov [1875]. [Moscow].

RUS–SPil (f. 232, No. 3).
PSSL 5: 421.

421. To Modest Chaikovskii
[27–28 Nov 1875. Moscow].
RUS–KL (a³, No. 2041).
PSSL 5: 421.

422. To Modest Chaikovskii
[5 Dec 1875. Moscow] — telegram.
RUS–KL (a³, No. 2887).
PSSL 5: 422.

423. To Modest Chaikovskii
[6–7 Dec 1875. Moscow].
RUS–KL (a³, No. 2973).
PSSL 5: 422.

424. To Mikhail Azanchevskii
8 Dec 1875. Moscow.
RUS–SPia (f. 497, op. 2, d. 23766).
PSSL 5: 422–423.

425. To Anatolii Chaikovskii
11 Dec 1875. Moscow.
RUS–KL (a³, No. 1092).
*ZC 1: 476–477 — PR: 223–224 — *PB: 99–100 —
    PSSL 5: 423–424 — *LF: 98–99 [English tr.].

426. To Nikolai Bernard
13 [Dec] 1875. Moscow (in MS: "13 Jan").
RUS–SPtob (VII.2.4.154).
Glebov (1922): 161 — *PSSL* 5: 425.

427. To Sergei Rachinskii
[18 Dec 1875. Moscow].
RUS–Mcl (f. 427).
Krasnyi arkhiv (1940), 3: 246 — *PSSL* 5: 426.

428. To Ekaterina Peresleni
[19 Dec 1875. Moscow].
RUS–KL (a³, No. 296).
PSSL 5: 426.

429. To Anatolii Chaikovskii
31 Dec 1875/12 Jan 1876 [Geneva].
RUS–KL (a³, No. 1093).
PR: 224–225 — *PB: 100–101 — *PSSL* 5: 427–
    428 — *LF: 99–100 [English tr.].

430. To Karl Al´brekht
[1875. Moscow].
RUS–Mcm (f. 37, No. 77).
PSSL 5: 428.

431. To Karl Al´brekht
[1875. Moscow].
RUS–Mcm (f. 37, No. 16).
PSSL 5: 428.

432. To Konstantin Shilovskii
[1875. Moscow].
RUS–Mt (Shilovskii coll.).
CMS: 300 — *PSSL* 5: 428–429.

432a. To Karl Al´brekht
[1875. ?Moscow].
RUS–KL (a³, No. 3312).
Not published.

433. To Ekaterina Peresleni
[early 1870s. Moscow].
RUS–KL (a³, No. 295).
PSSL 5: 429.

434. To Pavel Chokhin
[early 1870s. Moscow].
RUS–Mt
PSSL 5: 429–430.

435. To Pavel Chokhin
[early 1870s. Moscow].
RUS–Mt
PSSL 5: 430.

436. To Pëtr Iurgenson
[early 1870s. Moscow].
RUS–KL (a³, No. 2153).
PSSL 5: 430.

1876

437.   To Modest Chaikovskii

11/23 Jan 1876. Berlin.

RUS–KL (a³, No. 1446).

*ZC 1: 479–481 — PR: 226–227 — *PB: 101–102 —
   PSSL 6: 15–16 — *LF: 100–101 [English tr.].

438.   To Modest Chaikovskii

[12/24 Jan 1876. Berlin] — telegram; in French.

RUS–KL (a³, No. 1447).

PSSL 6: 16.

439.   To Modest Chaikovskii

20 Jan 1876. St. Petersburg.

RUS–KL (a³, No. 1445).

*ZC 1: 481 — PR: 227–228 — *PB: 102–103 — PSSL
   6: 17–18 — *LF: 101–102 [English tr.].

440.   To Nikolai Bernard

23 Jan 1876. St. Petersburg.

RUS–SPtob (VII.2.4.154).

Glebov (1922): 162 — PSSL 6: 19.

441.   To Eduard Nápravník

27 Jan 1876. Moscow.

RUS–SPtm (Gik 17195/8).

VP 116 — EFN 100 — PSSL 6: 19.

441a.   To Camille Saint-Saëns

27 Jan 1876. Moscow — in French.

F–DI

RdM 54 (1968), 1: 82 — PSSL 17: 218.

442.   To Modest Chaikovskii

28 Jan 1876. Moscow.

RUS–KL (a³, No. 1448).

*ZC 1: 481 — PR: 227–228 — *PB: 104 — *PSSL 6:
   20–21 — *LF: 102–103 [English tr.].

443.   To Hans von Bülow

1 Feb 1876. Moscow — in French.

CH–Bkoch (No. 322).

BBS 6: 297–298 — PSSL 6: 21–22.

444a.   To Anton Door

10 Feb [1876] (in MS: "1875"). Moscow — in
French.

Autograph lost

*Moskovskie vedomosti (28 Mar 1901) [Russian tr.] —
   *PSSL 6: 23 [Russian tr.] — Festschrift Otto Erich
   Deutsch (1963): 280–290 — PSSL 17: 220–221.

445.   To Modest Chaikovskii

10[–11] Feb [1876]. Moscow.

RUS–KL (a³, No. 1449).

*ZC 1: 482–483 — PR: 230–231 — *PB: 104–105 —
   PSSL 6: 24–25 — *LF: 103–104 [English tr.].

446.   To Anatolii Chaikovskii

10[–11] Feb 1876. Moscow.

RUS–KL (a³, No. 1089).

PR: 231–232 — PSSL 6: 26.

447.   To Konstantin Zvantsev

[11 Feb 1876. Moscow].

RUS–Mcl (f. 763).

PSSL 6: 27.

448.   To Karl Al´brekht

[Feb 1876. Moscow].

RUS–Mcm (f. 37, No. 18).

PSSL 6: 27.

449.   To Anatolii Chaikovskii

[late Feb–early Mar 1876. Moscow].

RUS–KL (a³, No. 1094).

PR: 224 — PSSL 6: 27.

450.   To Modest Chaikovskii

3 Mar 1876. Moscow.

RUS–KL (a³, No. 1450).

*ZC 1: 484 — *PR: 232–233 — *PB: 105–106 —
   *PSSL 6: 28 —*ZN: 123 — *LF: 104 [English
   tr.].

451.   To Karl Davydov

6 Mar 1876. Moscow.

RUS–KL (a³, No. 158).

PSSL 6: 29.

452. To Lev Kupernik

9 Mar 1876. Moscow.

RUS–SPil (f. 232, No. 4).

PSSL 6: 30.

453. To Anatolii Chaikovskii

17 Mar [1876]. Moscow.

RUS–KL (a³, No. 1095).

*ZC 1: 484–485 — *PR*: 233–234 — *PB*: 106 — *PSSL* 6: 30–31 — **LF*: 104–105 [English tr.].

454. To Nikolai Bernard

[17–18] Mar [1876]. [Moscow].

RUS–SPtob (VII.2.4.154).

Glebov (1922): 162 — *PSSL* 6: 31.

455. To Edward Dannreuther

18 Mar 1876. Moscow — in French.

Autograph lost.

Musical Times, 48 (1 Nov 1907): 717 — *RMG* (11 Nov 1907): 1034 [Russian tr.] — *PSSL* 6: 32.

455a. To Sergei Taneev

[? 20 Mar 1876. Moscow].

RUS–Mcl (f. 880).

CTP 151 ("1886") — *PSSL* 17: 222–223.

456. To Pëtr Iurgenson

[22 Mar 1876. Moscow].

RUS–KL (a³, No. 2143).

PSSL 6: 32–33.

457. To Modest Chaikovskii

24 Mar [1876]. Moscow.

RUS–KL (a³, No. 1451).

*ZC 1: 485 — *PR*: 234–235 — **PB*: 107 — **PSSL* 6: 33–34 — **LF*: 105–106 [English tr.].

458. To Karl Al´brekht

[?28 Mar 1876. Moscow].

RUS–Mcm (f. 37, No. 10).

PSSL 6: 34.

459. To Eduard Nápravník

[late Mar–early Apr 1876. Moscow].

RUS–SPtm (Gik 17195/9).

*ZC 1: 502–503 — *VP* 117 — *EFN* 100–101 — *PSSL* 6: 35.

460. To Mariia Kiseleva

[early Apr 1876. Glebovo].

RUS–SPt

PSSL 6: 36.

461. To Eduard Nápravník

[26 Apr 1876. Moscow] — telegram.

Autograph lost; typed copy in RUS–KL.

VP 116 — *EFN* 100 — *PSSL* 6: 36.

462. To Modest Chaikovskii

29 Apr 1876 [Moscow].

RUS–KL (a³, No. 1452).

*ZC 1: 486 — *PR*: 235–236 — **PB*: 107–108 — *PSSL* 6: 37–38 — **LF*: 106 [English tr.].

463. To Iakov Polonskii

4 May 1876. Moscow.

RUS–SPil

PSSL 6: 38–39.

464. To Anatolii Chaikovskii

19 May 1876. Moscow.

RUS–KL (a³, No. 1096).

*ZC 1: 486–487 — *PR*: 236–237 — *PSSL* 6: 39–40.

465. To Modest Chaikovskii

19 May 1876. Moscow.

RUS–KL (a³, No. 1453).

PR: 237–238 — *PSSL* 6: 40–41.

466. To Karl Al´brekht

2 Jun 1876. Kiev — in German.

RUS–Mcm (f. 37, No. 19).

PSSL 6: 41–42.

467. To Anatolii Chaikovskii

2 Jun [1876]. Kiev.

RUS–KL (a³, No. 1097).

PR: 238 — *PSSL* 6: 42–43.

468. To Modest Chaikovskii

2 Jun 1876. Kiev.

RUS–KL (a³, No. 1454).

PR: 239 — *PSSL* 6: 43.

469. To Aleksei Sofronov

7 Jun [1876]. Kamenka.

RUS–SPsc (f. 834, No. 25, fol. 1–2).

*PSSL 6: 44 — **ZN*: 125.

470. To Mikhail Sofronov

7 Jun [1876]. Kamenka.

RUS–KL (a³, No. 392).

PSSL 6: 44.

471. To Anatolii Chaikovskii

7 Jun 1876 . Kamenka.

RUS–KL (a³, No. 1098).

PR: 239–240 — *PSSL* 6: 45.

472. To Sergei Taneev

14 Jun 1876. Kamenka.

RUS–Mcl (f. 880).

CTP 6–7 — *PSSL* 6: 46–47.

473. To Konstantin Shilovskii

14 Jun 1876. Kamenka.

RUS–Mt (Shilovskii coll.).

CMS: 301–302 — *PSSL* 6: 47–48.

474. To Karl Al´brekht

16 Jun [1876]. Kamenka.

RUS–Mcm (f. 37, No. 20).

CMS: 258–259 — *PSSL* 6: 48.

475. To Anatolii Chaikovskii

16 Jun 1876 [Kamenka].

RUS–KL (a³, No. 1099).

PR: 240–241 — *PSSL* 6: 49.

476. To Modest Chaikovskii

[23 Jun/5 Jul 1876]. Vienna.

RUS–KL (a³, No. 1455).

*PSSL 6: 49–50 — *ZN*: 127–128 — *TW*: 61–63
[English tr.].

477. To Karl Al´brekht

2/14 Jul [1876]. Vichy.

RUS–Mcm (f. 37, No. 31).

CMS: 259–260 — *PSSL* 6: 50–51.

478. To Modest Chaikovskii

[2/14 Jul 1876]. Vichy.

RUS–KL (a³, No. 1456).

PR: 241 — *PSSL* 6: 51–52.

479. To Aleksei Sofronov

3/15 Jul 1876. Vichy.

RUS–SPsc (f. 834, No. 25, fol. 3–4).

*PSSL 6: 52–53 — **ZN*: 125.

480. To Anatolii Chaikovskii

3/15 Jul 1876. Vichy.

RUS–KL (a³, No. 1100).

*ZC 1: 487 — *PR*: 243–244 — *PB*: 108–109 — *PSSL*
6: 53–54 — *LF*: 107 [English tr.].

481. To Modest Chaikovskii

[3/15 Jul 1876] .Vichy.

RUS–KL (a³, No. 1457).

PR: 242 — *PSSL* 6: 54–55.

482. To Modest Chaikovskii

4/16 Jul [1876]. Vichy.

RUS–KL (a³, No. 1458).

PR: 244 — *PSSL* 6: 55–56.

483. To Anatolii Chaikovskii

6/18 Jul 1876. Vichy.

RUS–KL (a³, No. 1101).

PR: 244–245 — *PB*: 109–110 — *PSSL* 6: 56–57 —
LF: 108 [English tr.].

484. To Modest Chaikovskii

6/18 Jul 1876. Vichy.

RUS–KL (a³, No. 1459).

PR: 246 — *PSSL* 6: 57–58.

485. To Nikolai Konradi

7/19 Jul 1876. Vichy.

Autograph lost; MS copy in RUS–KL.

CTP 258 — *PSSL* 6: 58.

486.   To Modest Chaikovskii

7/19 Jul 1876. Vichy.

RUS–KL (a³, No. 1460).

*ZC 1: 488 — *PR*: 247 — *PSSL* 6: 59.

487.   To Aleksandra Davydova

13/25 Jul [1876]. Lyons.

RUS–SPsc (f. 834, No. 17, fol. 3–4).

PR: 247–248 — *PSSL* 6: 60–61.

488.   To Modest Chaikovskii

[27 Jul]/8 Aug 1876. Paris.

RUS–KL (a³, No. 1462).

*ZC 1: 489–490 — *PR*: 248–249 — *PSSL* 6: 61–62.

489.   To Mikhail Sofronov

29 Jul/[10 Aug] 1876. Paris.

RUS–KL (a³, No. 393).

PSSL 6: 62–63.

490.   To Modest Chaikovskii

2/14 Aug 1876. Bayreuth.

RUS–KL (a³, No. 1461).

*ZC 1: 490–491 — *PR*: 250–251 — *PB*: 110–111 —
    PSSL 6: 63–64 — *LF: 109 [English tr.].

491.   To Modest Chaikovskii

8/20 Aug [1876]. Vienna.

RUS–KL (a³, No. 1463).

*ZC 1: 494–495 — *PR*: 251–252 — *PB*: 111–112 —
    PSSL 6: 64–65 — *LF: 109–110 [English tr.].

492.   To Modest Chaikovskii

[19/31 Aug 1876]. Verbovka.

RUS–KL (a³, No. 1464).

PR: 252–253 — *PSSL* 6: 66 — *ZN: 121.

493.   To Nikolai Rimskii-Korsakov

7 Sep [1876]. Moscow.

RUS–SPsc (f. 640, op. 1, No. 1015, fol. 6–7).

*ZC 1: 499–500 — *SM* (1945), 3: 130–131 — *PSSL*
    6: 67–68.

494.   To Modest Chaikovskii

10 Sep 1876. Moscow.

RUS–KL (a³, No. 1465).

*ZC 1: 498–499 — *PR*: 253–254 — *PSSL* 6: 69 —
    ZN: 128–129 — *TW*: 63–64 [English tr.].

495.   To Lev Davydov

12 Sep [1876]. Moscow.

RUS–SPsc (f. 834, No. 19, fol. 5–6).

*ZC 1: 499 — *PR*: 254–255 — *PSSL* 6: 70.

496.   To Pëtr Iurgenson

16 Sep [1876]. [Moscow].

RUS–KL (a³, No. 2145).

PSSL 6: 71.

497.   To Modest Chaikovskii & Nikolai Konradi

17 Sep 1876. Moscow.

RUS–KL (a³, No. 1466).

*ZC 1: 501 — *PR*: 255–256 — *PB*: 112 — *PSSL* 6:
    71–72 — *LF: 110 [English tr.].

497a.   To Andronik Klimchenko

18 Sep 1876 [Moscow].

RUS–SPa (f. 408, op. 1, No. 206, fol. 30).

Not published.

498.   To Anatolii Chaikovskii

20 Sep 1876. Moscow.

RUS–KL (a³, No. 1102).

*ZC 1: 502 — *PR*: 256–257 — *PB*: 113 — *PSSL
    6: 72–73 — *ZN*: 126 — *LF: 110–111 [English tr.].

499.   To Aleksandra Davydova

20 Sep [1876]. Moscow.

RUS–SPsc (f. 834, No. 17, fol. 5–6).

PR: 258–259 — *PSSL* 6: 74–75.

500.   To Sergei Taneev

21 Sep [1876]. [Moscow].

RUS–Mcl (f. 880).

CTP 7 — *PSSL* 6: 75.

501.   To Modest Chaikovskii

28 Sep 1876 [Moscow].

RUS–KL (a³, No. 1467).

PR: 259–260 — **PSSL* 6: 75–76 — **ZN*: 121 — *TW*: 65–66 [English tr.].

502.   To Nikolai Rimskii-Korsakov

29 Sep 1876. Moscow.

RUS–SPsc (f. 640, op. 1, No. 1015, fol. 8–9).

*ZC 1: 503–504 — *SM* (1945), 3: 132–133 — *PSSL* 6: 76–77.

503.   To Aleksandra Davydova

6 Oct 1876 [Moscow].

RUS–SPsc (f. 834, No. 17, fol. 7–8).

*ZC 1: 504 — *PR*: 260–261 — *PSSL* 6: 78–79.

503a.   To Andronik Klimichenko

8 Oct 1876 [Moscow] — telegram.

RUS–SPa (f. 408, op. 1, No. 206, f. 29).

Not published.

503b.   To Andronik Klimchenko

8 Oct 1876 [Moscow].

RUS–SPa (f. 408, op. 1, No. 206, f. 31).

Not published.

503c.   To Andronik Klimichenko

12 Oct 1876 [Moscow] — telegram.

RUS–SPa (f. 408, op. 1, No. 206, f. 26).

Not published.

504.   To Anatolii Chaikovskii

14 Oct [1876]. [Moscow].

RUS–KL (a³, No. 1103).

*ZC 1: 505 — *PR*: 261–262 — *PSSL* 6: 79–80.

505.   To Modest Chaikovskii

14 Oct [1876]. Moscow.

RUS–KL (a³, No. 1468).

*ZC 1: 504–505 — *PR*: 262–263 — **PB*: 113–114 — *PSSL* 6: 80–81 — **LF*: 111 [English tr.].

506.   To Pëtr Iurgenson

[mid Oct 1876. Moscow].

RUS–KL (a³, No. 2146).

PSSL 6: 81–82.

507.   To Eduard Nápravník

18 Oct [1876]. Moscow.

RUS–SPtm (Gik 17195/10).

ZC 1: 505–506 — *VP* 118 — *EFN* 101–102 — *PSSL* 6: 82.

508.   To Karl Davydov

18 Oct 1876 [Moscow].

RUS–KL (a³, No. 159).

PSSL 6: 83.

509.   To Anatolii Chaikovskii

26 Oct [1876]. [Moscow].

RUS–KL (a³, No. 1104).

PR: 263 — *PSSL* 6: 83.

510.   To Pëtr Iurgenson

[late Oct 1876. Moscow].

RUS–KL (a³, No. 2147).

PSSL 6: 84.

511.   To Vasilii Bessel´

[early Nov 1876. Moscow].

RUS–Mcm (f. 42, No. 256).

PSSL 6: 84.

512.   To Pëtr Iurgenson

[early Nov 1876. Moscow].

RUS–KL (a³, No. 2179).

PSSL 6: 85.

513.   To Aleksandra Davydova

8 Nov 1876. Moscow.

RUS–SPsc (f. 834, No. 17, fol. 9–10).

*ZC 1: 506–507 — *PR*: 263–265 — **PB*: 114–115 — *PSSL* 6: 85–86 — **LF*: 112–113 [English tr.].

514.   To Eduard Nápravník

[?12–14 Nov 1876. Moscow] — telegram.

Autograph lost; typed copy in RUS–KL.

VP 230 — *EFN* 102 — *PSSL* 6: 87.

515.   To Pëtr Iurgenson

[?1–5 Dec 1876. Moscow].

RUS–KL (a³, No. 2144).

PSSL 6: 87.

516. To Lidiia Genke

2 Dec 1876 [Moscow].

RUS–Mcl (f. 905).

PSSL 6: 87–88.

517. To Sergei Taneev

2 Dec 1876. Moscow.

RUS–Mcl (f. 880).

*ZC 1: 509–510, 512–513 — *PT* 6–7 — *CTP* 10–11 — *PSSL* 6: 88–89.

518. To Sergei Taneev

5 Dec 1876. Moscow,

RUS–Mcl (f. 880).

*ZC 1: 514–515 — *PT* 8–9 — *CTP* 12–13 — *PSSL* 6: 90–91.

519. To Vasilii Avenarius

[8 Dec 1876. Moscow].

RUS–SPil (f. 221, No. 177).

PSSL 6: 91–92.

520. To Vladimir Stasov

11 Dec 1876. Moscow.

RUS–SPsc (f. 738, No. 343, fol. 13–15).

RM (1909), 3: 112–113 — *PSSL* 6: 92–93.

521. To Eduard Nápravník

15 Dec [1876]. Moscow.

RUS–SPtm (Gik 17195/11).

VP 118–119 — *EFN* 102 — *PSSL* 6: 94.

522. To Anatolii Chaikovskii

15 Dec 1876. Moscow.

RUS–KL (a³, No. 1105).

PR: 265–266 — *PSSL* 6: 94–95.

523. To Aleksandra & Lev Davydov

18 Dec [1876]. Moscow.

RUS–SPsc (f. 834, No. 17, fol. 11–12).

PR: 266–267 — *PSSL* 6: 95–96.

524. To Nadezhda von Meck

[18–19 Dec 1876. Moscow].

RUS–KL (a³, No. 3059) [facs. in *CH* 1 (1990): 74].

*ZC 2: 10–11 — *PM* 1: 3 — *PSSL* 6: 96–97 — *TMBF:* 3 [English tr.].

525. To Vladimir Stasov

19 Dec 1876. Moscow.

RUS–SPsc (f. 738, No. 343, fol. 16–19).

RM (1900), 3: 118–119 — *PSSL* 6: 97–99.

526. To Aleksandra Davydova

23 Dec 1876 [Moscow].

RUS–SPsc (f. 834, No. 17, fol. 13–14).

*ZC 1: 518–519 — *PR*: 267–268 — *PB: 115–116 — *PSSL* 6: 99–100 — *LF: 113–114 [English tr.].

527. To Lev Tolstoi

24 Dec 1876. Moscow.

RUS–Mmt

*ZC 1: 521–522 — *IRM 1: 115–116 — *LNT* 62: 298–299 — *PSSL* 6: 100–101.

528. To Sergei Taneev

25 Dec 1876. Moscow.

RUS–Mcl (f. 880).

*ZC 1: 516–517 — *PT* 11–12 — *CTP* 14–15 — *PSSL* 6: 102.

529. To Lidiia Genke

31 Dec 1876 [Moscow].

RUS–Mcl (f. 905).

PSSL 6: 103.

530. To Karl Al´brekht

[1876. Moscow].

RUS–Mt (Al´brekht coll.).

PSSL 6: 103.

530a. To Karl Al´brekht

[1876. ?Moscow].

RUS–KL (a³, No. 3313).

Not published.

1877

531. To Aleksandra Davydova

1 Jan [1877]. [Moscow].

RUS–SPsc (f. 834, No. 17, fol. 15–16).

PR: 269–270 — *PSSL* 6: 104–105.

532.   To Aleksandra Davydova

2 Jan 1877 [Moscow].

RUS–SPsc (f. 834, No. 17, fol. 17–18).

PR: 270–271 — *PSSL* 6: 105–106.

533.   To Modest Chaikovskii

2–[3] Jan [1877] (in MS: "2 Jan 1876"). Moscow.

RUS–KL (a^3, No. 1469).

ZC 1: 526–527 — *PR*: 271–272 — *PB*: 116–117 —
     PSSL 6: 106–107 — *LF*: 114 [English tr.].

534.   To Aleksandra Davydova

4 Jan 1877. Moscow.

RUS–SPsc (f. 834, No. 17, fol. 19–20).

PR: 272–273 — *PSSL* 6: 107–108.

535.   To Sergei Taneev

12 Jan [1877]. Moscow.

RUS–Mcl (f. 880).

CTP 15 — *PSSL* 6: 108.

536.   To Anatolii Chaikovskii

12 Jan 1877 [Moscow].

RUS–KL (a^3, No. 1106).

*ZC 1: 517 — **PR*: 273–274 — **PB*: 117 — **PSSL* 6:
     109 — *ZN*: 122 — **LF*: 115 [English tr.].

537.   To Aleksandra Davydova

19 Jan 1877. Moscow.

RUS–SPsc (f. 834, No. 17, fol. 21–22).

PR: 274 — *PSSL* 6: 109–110.

538.   To Modest Chaikovskii

19 Jan 1877. Moscow.

RUS–KL (a^3, No. 1470).

*PSSL 6: 110–111 — *ZN*: 129–131 — *TW*: 66–69
     [English tr.].

539.   To Sergei Taneev

29 Jan 1877. Moscow.

RUS–Mcl (f. 880).

*ZC 1: 517 — *PT* 12 — *CTP* 15 — *PSSL* 6: 111.

540.   To Ekaterina Peresleni

[early 1877. Moscow].

RUS–KL (a^3, No. 298).

PSSL 6: 111.

541.   To Vladimir Stasov

9 Feb 1877 [Moscow].

RUS–SPsc (f. 738, No. 343, fol. 20–22).

RM (1909), 3: 121–122 — *PSSL* 6: 112.

542.   To Nadezhda von Meck

[15–16 Feb 1877]. Moscow.

RUS–KL (a^3, No. 3060).

ZC 2: 11–12 — *PM* 4–5 — *PSSL* 6: 113 — *TMBF*: 4
     [English tr.].

543.   To Aleksandra Davydova

22 Feb [1877]. Moscow.

RUS–SPsc (f. 834, No. 17, fol. 23–24).

*ZC 1: 529–530 — *PR*: 275–276 — **PB*: 118 —
     PSSL 6: 113–114 — **LF*: 115–116 [English tr.].

544.   To Ekaterina Peresleni

[late Feb–early Mar 1877. Moscow].

RUS–KL (a^3, No. 297).

PSSL 6: 115.

545.   To Nadezhda von Meck

16 Mar [1877]. Moscow.

RUS–KL (a^3, No. 3061).

ZC 2: 14–16 — *PM* 1: 8–9 — *PSSL* 6: 115–116 —
     TMBF: 8–9 [English tr.].

546.   To Nadezhda von Meck

[19 Mar 1877. Moscow].

RUS–KL (a^3, No. 3062).

PSSL 6: 117.

547.   To Lidiia Genke

[20 Mar 1877. Moscow].

RUS–Mcl (f. 905).

PSSL 6: 117–118.

547a.   To Karl Al´brekht

[Mar–Apr 1877. Moscow].

RUS–Mcm (f. 37, No. 26).
PSSL 17: 223.

548. To Vladimir Stasov
8 Apr 1877 [Moscow].
RUS–SPsc (f. 738, No. 343, fol. 13–17).
RM (1909), 3: 122–124 — *PSSL* 6: 118–119.

548a. To Frits Hartvigson
13 Apr 1877. Moscow — in French.
F–Plauwe [facs. of p. 1 in *ČS* 3 (1998): 224].
ČS 3 (1998): 224–227.

549. To Elizaveta Chaikovskaia
18 Apr 1877 [Moscow].
RUS–SPsc (f. 834 , No. 30, fol. 5–6).
PR: 276 — *PSSL* 6: 120.

550. To Pëtr Iurgenson
[25 Apr 1877. Moscow].
RUS–KL (a³, No. 2168).
PSSL 6: 120.

551. To Sergei Taneev
25[–26] Apr [1877]. Moscow.
RUS–Mcl (f. 880).
*ZC 1: 531–532 — *PT* 15 — *CTP* 16–17 — *PSSL* 6: 121–122.

552. To Vladimir Stasov
29 Apr 1877 [Moscow].
RUS–SPsc (f. 738, No. 343, fol. 28–30).
RM (1909), 3: 125–126 — *PSSL* 6: 122–123.

553. To Nadezhda von Meck
1 May 1877 [Moscow].
RUS–KL (a³, No. 3063).
PM 1: 13 — *PSSL* 6: 124 — *TMBF:* 13 [English tr.].

554. To Nadezhda von Meck
1 May 1877. Moscow.
RUS–KL (a³, No. 3064).
*ZC 2: 16–18 — *PM* 1: 14–16 — *PSSL* 6: 125–127 — *TMBF:* 13–15 [English tr.].

555. To Nadezhda von Meck
2 May [1877]. [Moscow].
RUS–KL (a³, No. 3065).
PM 1: 17 — *PSSL* 6: 127 — *TMBF:* 16 [English tr.].

556. To Nadezhda von Meck
3 May 1877 [Moscow].
RUS–KL (a³, No. 3066).
PM 1: 17 — *PSSL* 6: 127 — *TMBF:* 17 [English tr.].

557. To Nadezhda von Meck
3 May 1877 [Moscow].
RUS–KL (a³, No. 3067).
PM 1: 18–20 — *PSSL* 6: 128–129 — *TMBF:* 17–19 [English tr.].

558. To Anatolii Chaikovskii
4 May 1877 [Moscow].
Autograph lost; MS copy in RUS–KL.
PSSL 6: 129–130.

559. To Modest Chaikovskii
4 May [1877]. [Moscow].
RUS–KL (a³, No. 1471).
PSSL 6: 130–131 — *ZN: 123 — *TW:* 70–71 [English tr.].

560. To Ivan Klimenko
[6 May 1877. Moscow].
Autograph lost; MS copy in RUS–KL.
KMV: 70 — *PSSL* 6: 130–131.

561. To Ivan Klimenko
8[–9] May 1877 [Moscow].
Autograph lost; MS copy in RUS–KL.
*ZC 1: 532 — *KMV:* 70–71 — *PSSL* 6: 131–132.

562. To Dmitrii Razumovskii
[17 May 1877. Moscow].
RUS–Mrg
PSSL 6: 132–133.

563. To Ivan Klimenko
18 May 1877 [Moscow].
Autograph lost; MS copy in RUS–KL.
KMV: 72 — *PSSL* 6: 133.

564.   To Anatolii Chaikovskii

18 May [1877]. [Moscow].

RUS–KL (a³, No. 1107).

PR: 277 — *PB*: 119 — *PSSL* 6: 133–134 — *LF*: 116–117 [English tr.].

565.   To Modest Chaikovskii

18 May [1877]. [Moscow].

RUS–KL (a³, No. 1472) [facs. of 1 p. in *PICH* (1978): 84].

*ZC 1: 532–534 — *PR*: 278–279 — **PB*: 119–121 — *PSSL* 6: 134–136 — **LF*: 117–118 [English tr.].

566.   To Lev Davydov

19 May 1877 [Moscow].

RUS–SPsc (f. 834, No. 19, fol. 7–8).

*ZC 1: 534–535 — *PR*: 279–280 — *PB*: 121–122 — *PSSL* 6: 136–137 — *LF*: 118–119 [English tr.].

567.   To Anatolii Chaikovskii

[22–27 May 1877. Moscow].

RUS–KL (a³, No. 1136).

PR: 276–277 — *PSSL* 6: 137–138.

567a. To Adelina Gippius

23 May 1877. Moscow.

Autograph lost; MS copy in RUS–SPia

A. V. Polovtsev, *Chaikovskii kak pisatel´* (1903): 47 — *Moskovskie vedomosti* (12 Nov 1903) — *PSSL* 17: 224.

568.   To Modest Chaikovskii

23 May 1877 [Moscow].

RUS–KL (a³, No. 1473).

*ZC 1: 535 — **PR*: 280–281 — **PSSL* 6: 138–139 — **ZN*: 123 — *TW*: 71–73 [English tr.].

569.   To Nadezhda von Meck

27 May [1877]. [Moscow].

RUS–KL (a³, No. 3068).

PM 1: 21–22 — *PSSL* 6: 139–140 — *TMBF*: 20–21 [English tr.].

570.   To Modest Chaikovskii

9 Jun [1877]. Glebovo.

RUS–KL (a³, No. 1474).

*ZC 1: 535–536 — *PR*: 281–282 — *PB*: 122 — *PSSL* 6: 141 — **LF*: 119–120 [English tr.].

571.   To Anatolii Chaikovskii

15 Jun [1877]. [Glebovo].

RUS–KL (a³, No. 1108).

PR: 282–283 — *PB*: 123 — *PSSL* 6: 142 — *LF*: 120–121 [English tr.].

572.   To Il´ia Chaikovskii

23 Jun 1877. Glebovo.

RUS–SPsc (f. 834, No. 33, fol. 118).

ZC 2: 19–20 — *PR*: 283 — *PSSL* 6: 143.

573.   To Anatolii Chaikovskii

23 Jun [1877]. Glebovo.

RUS–KL (a³, No. 1109).

*ZC 2: 19 — *PR*: 284 — *PSSL* 6: 143–144 — *TW*: 73–74 [English tr.].

574.   To Nadezhda von Meck

3 Jul 1877. Moscow.

RUS–KL (a³, No. 3069).

*ZC 2: 20–22 — *PM* 1: 25–28 — *PSSL* 6: 144–147 — *TMBF*: 23–26 [English tr.].

575.   To Aleksandra & Lev Davydov

5 Jul 1877. Moscow.

RUS–SPsc (f. 834, No. 17, fol. 25–26).

PR: 285–286 — *PSSL* 6: 148.

576.   To Sergei Taneev

5 Jul 1877 [Moscow].

RUS–Mcl (f. 880).

CTP 19–20 — *PSSL* 6: 148–149.

577.   To Modest Chaikovskii

5 Jul [1877]. Moscow.

RUS–KL (a³, No. 1475).

PR: 285 — *PSSL* 6: 150.

578.   To Vladimir Shilovskii

6 Jul [1877]. Moscow.

RUS–Mt (Shilovskii coll.).

SM (1940), 5–6: 142 — *PSSL* 6: 150–151.

579.   To Anatolii Chaikovskii
8 Jul 1877. St. Petersburg.
RUS–KL (a³, No. 1110).
*PR: 286–288 — *PSSL 6: 151–152 — *ZN: 124 —
TW: 75–77 [English tr.].

580.   To Modest Chaikovskii
8 Jul [1877]. St. Petersburg.
RUS–KL (a³, No. 1476).
*PR: 288 — *PSSL 6: 153 — *ZN: 124 — TW: 77–78
[English tr.].

581.   To Anatolii Chaikovskii
9 Jul [1877]. St. Petersburg.
RUS–KL (a³, No. 1111).
*PR: 289 — *PSSL 6: 153–154 — *ZN: 124 — TW:
79–80 [English tr.].

581a.   To Anatolii Chaikovskii
11 Jul 1877 [St. Petersburg].
RUS–KL (a³, No. 1112).
*PR: 289–290 — ZN: 131 — TW: 80–82 [English tr.].

582.   To Anna Aleksandrova-Levenson
13 Jul 1877. St. Petersburg.
Autograph lost; MS copy in RUS–KL.
SN (1905), 10: 100 — PSSL 6: 154–155.

583.   To Anatolii Chaikovskii
13 Jul 1877. St. Petersburg.
Autograph lost; incomplete MS copy in RUS–KL.
*PSSL 6: 155 — *TW: 82–83 [English tr.].

584.   To Nadezhda von Meck
15 Jul 1877. Moscow.
RUS–KL (a³, No. 3070) [facs. of p. 1 in D.
Mountfield, Tchaikovsky (1990): 37].
*ZC 2: 24 — PM 1: 29–30 — PSSL 6: 156–157 —
TMBF: 27–28 [English tr.].

585.   To Pëtr Iurgenson
[?15 Jul 1877]. Moscow.
RUS–KL (a³, No. 2167).
PSSL 6: 157.

586.   To Pëtr Iurgenson

[18 Jul 1877. Moscow].
RUS–KL (a³, No. 2154).
PSSL 6: 157.

587.   To Aleksandra Davydova
20 Jul 1877. Moscow.
RUS–SPsc (f. 834, No. 17, fol. 27–28).
PR: 290–291 — PSSL 6: 158.

588.   To Mikhail Sofronov
20 Jul 1877 [Moscow].
RUS–KL (a³, No. 394).
PSSL 6: 159.

589.   To Konstantin Shilovskii
25 Jul [1877]. Moscow.
RUS–Mt (Shilovskii coll.).
CMS: 302–303 — PSSL 6: 159–160.

590.   To Nadezhda von Meck
26 Jul [1877]. [Moscow].
RUS–KL (a³, No. 3071).
PM 1: 31 — PSSL 6: 160 — TMBF: 29 [English tr.].

591.   To Pëtr Iurgenson
26 Jul 1877 [Moscow].
RUS–KL (a³, No. 2155).
PSSL 6: 161.

592.   To Nadezhda von Meck
28 Jul 1877. Kiev.
RUS–KL (a³, No. 3072).
PM 1: 32–35 — PSSL 6: 161–164 — TMBF: 30–32
[English tr.].

593.   To Nadezhda von Meck
2 Aug [1877]. Kamenka.
RUS–KL (a³, No. 3073).
*ZC 2: 24–25 — PM 1: 35–36 — PSSL 6: 164–
165 — TMBF: 33–34 [English tr.].

594.   To Nadezhda von Meck
11 Aug 1877. Kamenka.
RUS–KL (a³, No. 3074).
*ZC 2: 25 — PM 1: 38–39 — PSSL 6: 166 — TMBF:
35–36 [English tr.].

595. To Nadezhda von Meck
12 Aug 1877. Kamenka.
RUS–KL (a³, No. 3075).
*ZC 2: 25–26 — *PM* 1: 39–41 — *PSSL* 6: 166–168 —
TMBF: 37–38 [English tr.].

596. To Anatolii Chaikovskii
27 Aug 1877. Kamenka.
RUS–KL (a³, No. 1113).
*ZC 2: 26–27 — *PR:* 291–292 — *PB:* 123–124 —
PSSL 6: 168–169 — *LF:* 121–122 [English tr.].

597. To Nadezhda von Meck
30 Aug 1877. Kamenka.
RUS–KL (a³, No. 3076).
*ZC 2: 27–28 — *PM* 1: 44–45 — *PSSL* 6: 170–171 —
TMBF: 41–42 [English tr.].

598. To Anatolii Chaikovskii
2 Sep [1877]. Kamenka.
RUS–KL (a³, No. 1114).
PR: 292–293 — *PSSL* 6: 171–172.

599. To Modest Chaikovskii
9 Sep 1877. Kiev.
RUS–KL (a³, No. 1477).
*ZC 2: 28–29 — *PR:* 294–295 — *PB:* 124–125 —
PSSL 6: 173–174 — *LF:* 122–123 [English tr.]—
TW: 83–85 [English tr.].

600. To Karl Al´brekht
[mid Sep 1877. Moscow].
RUS–Mcm (f. 37, No. 21).
PSSL 6: 174.

601. To Nadezhda von Meck
12 Sep 1877 [Moscow].
RUS–KL (a³, No. 3077).
*ZC 2: 29 — *PM* 1: 45–46 — *PSSL* 6: 175–176 —
TMBF: 42–43 [English tr.].

602. To Anatolii Chaikovskii
12 Sep 1877. Moscow.
RUS–KL (a³, No. 1115).
*ZC 2: 29 — *PR:* 295–296 — *PSSL* 6: 176–177.

603. To Pëtr Iurgenson
[mid Sep 1877. Moscow].
RUS–Mcm (f. 88, No. 70).
PSSL 6: 177.

604. To Pëtr Iurgenson
20 Sep 1877. Moscow.
RUS–KL (a³, No. 2157).
PSSL 6: 178.

605. To Karl Al´brekht
[24 Sep 1877. Moscow].
RUS–Mcm (f. 37, No. 22).
PSSL 6: 178.

606. To Karl Al´brekht
[24 Sep 1877. Moscow].
RUS–Mcm
PSSL 6: 178–179.

607. To Pëtr Iurgenson
[24 Sep 1877. Moscow].
RUS–KL (a³, No. 2156).
PSSL 6: 179.

608. To Karl Al´brekht
[1 Oct 1877. St. Petersburg] — telegram.
RUS–Mcm (f. 37, No. 23).
PSSL 6: 179.

608a. To Aleksei Sofronov
1 Oct [1877]. St. Petersburg.
RUS–SPsc (f. 834, No. 25, fol. 5).
Not published.

609. To Modest Chaikovskii
1 Oct [1877]. [St. Petersburg].
RUS–KL (a³, No. 1478).
PR: 296–297 — *PSSL* 6: 179–180.

609a. To Aleksei Sofronov
5/17 Oct 1877. Berlin.
RUS–SPsc (f. 834, No. 25, fol. 8–9).
Not published.

610. To Modest Chaikovskii
5/17 Oct 1877. Berlin.
RUS–KL (a³, No. 1479).
PR: 297–298 — **PSSL* 6: 180–181.

611. To Pëtr Iurgenson
5/17 Oct [1877]. Berln.
RUS–KL (a³, No. 2158).
PIU 1: 17 — *PSSL* 6: 181.

612. To Aleksandra Davydova
9/21 Oct 1877. Geneva.
RUS–SPsc (f. 834, No. 17, fol. 29–30).
PR: 298 — *PSSL* 6: 181–182.

613. To Modest Chaikovskii
9/21 Oct 1877. Geneva.
RUS–KL (a³, No. 1480).
PR: 299 — **PSSL* 6: 182–183.

614. To Anton Door
[mid Oct 1877. Clarens].
Autograph lost
Moskovskie vedomosti (28 Mar 1901) — *PSSL* 6: 183.

615. To Aleksandra Davydova
11/23 Oct 1877. Clarens.
RUS–SPsc (f. 834, No. 17, fol. 31).
PR: 300 — *PSSL* 6: 184.

616. To Nadezhda von Meck
11/23 Oct 1877. Clarens.
RUS–KL (a³, No. 3078).
PM 1: 48–50 — **PSSL* 6: 184–186 — *TMBF*: 45–47
[English tr.].

617. To Nikolai Rubinshtein
11/23 Oct 1877. Clarens.
RUS–Mcm (f. 37, No. 84).
IRM 1: 162–163 — *PSSL* 6: 176–187.

618. To Aleksandra Davydova
12/24 Oct 1877. Clarens.
RUS–SPsc (f. 834, No. 18, fol. 32–33).
PR: 300 — *PSSL* 6: 187–188.

619. To Aleksei Sofronov
16/28 Oct 1877. Clarens.
RUS–SPsc (f. 834, No. 25, fol. 10–11).
*PSSL 6: 188–189.

620. To Pëtr Iurgenson
16/28 Oct [1877]. Clarens.
RUS–KL (a³, No. 2159).
PIU 1: 17–18 — *PSSL* 6: 189.

621. To Modest Chaikovskii
17/29 Oct 1877. Clarens.
RUS–KL (a³, No. 1481).
*PR: 301–302 — **PSSL* 6: 189–190.

622. To Nadezhda von Meck
20 Oct/1 Nov 1877. Clarens.
RUS–KL (a³, No. 3079).
*ZC 2: 35–36 — *PM* 1: 53–54 — *PSSL* 6: 191–
192 — *TMBF*: 49–50 [English tr.].

623. To Nikolai Rubinshtein
20 Oct/1 [Nov] 1877. Clarens.
RUS–Mcm (f. 37, No. 83).
*ZC 2: 32–33 — *IRM* 1: 163–164 — *PSSL* 6: 192–
193.

623a. To Lauro Rossi
[20 Oct]/1 Nov 1877. Clarens — in French.
I–Nc
PSSL 17: 225.

624. To Karl Al´brekht
25 Oct/6 Nov 1877. Clarens.
Autograph lost; MS copy in RUS–KL.
CMS: 261–262 — *PSSL* 6: 194–195.

625. To Nadezhda von Meck
25 Oct/6 Nov 1877. Clarens.
RUS–KL (a³, No. 3080).
*ZC 2: 36–37 — *PM* 1: 54–59 — *PSSL* 6: 196–
200 — *TMBF*: 50–54 [English tr.].

626. To Nadezhda von Meck
25 Oct/6 Nov 1877. Clarens.

RUS–KL (a³, No. 3081).

PM 1: 59–60 — *PSSL* 6: 200–201 — *TMBF:* 55 [English tr.].

627.   To Aleksandra Davydova

26 Oct/7 Nov 1877. Clarens.

RUS–SPsc (f. 834, No. 17, fol. 34–37).

PR: 302–304 — *PSSL* 6: 202–203.

628.   To Aleksandra Davydova

[26–27 Oct/7–8 Nov 1877. Clarens].

Autograph lost; fragment of MS copy in RUS–KL.

PSSL 6: 204–205.

629.   To Aleksei Sofronov

[late Oct/early Nov 1877. Clarens].

RUS–SPsc (f. 834, No. 25, fol. 6–7).

*PSSL 6: 205 — **ZN:* 125.

630.   To Nikolai Rubinshtein

27 Oct/8 Nov 1877. Clarens.

RUS–Mcm (f. 37, No. 85).

*ZC 2: 37–38 — *IRM* 1: 165–166 — *PSSL* 6: 206–207.

631.   To Modest Chaikovskii

[27 Oct/8 Nov] 1877 (in MS: "26 Oct/6 Nov"). Clarens.

RUS–KL (a³, No. 1482).

PR: 304–306 — **PSSL* 6: 207–209.

632.   To Pëtr Iurgenson

[28 Oct]/9 Nov 1877 (in MS: "29 Oct"). Clarens.

RUS–KL (a³, No. 2160).

PIU 1: 18–19 — *PSSL* 6: 209–211.

633.   To Nadezhda von Meck

[29 Oct]/10 Nov 1877 (in MS: "30 Oct"). Clarens.

RUS–KL (a³, No. 3153).

*ZC 2: 38–39 — *PM* 1: 61–63 ("30 Oct/10 Nov") — *PSSL* 6: 212–214 — *TMBF:* 56–58 [English tr.].

634.   To Aleksandra Davydova

[31 Oct/12 Nov 1877] (in MS: "1/13 Nov"). Clarens.

RUS–SPsc (f. 834, No. 17, fol. 38–39).

PR: 307–308 — *PSSL* 6: 214–215.

635.   To Nadezhda von Meck

[1/13 Nov 1877]. Paris.

RUS–KL (a³, No. 3082).

*ZC 2: 39 — *PM* 1: 64–65 — *PSSL* 6: 216–217.

636.   To Nadezhda von Meck

2/14 Nov [1877]. Paris.

RUS–KL (a³, No. 3083).

PM 1: 65–67 — *PSSL* 6: 218–219.

637.   To Modest Chaikovskii

2/14[–3/15] Nov 1877. Paris.

RUS–KL (a³, No. 1483).

PR: 308–309 — **PSSL* 6: 219–220.

638.   To Nadezhda von Meck

6/18 Nov 1877. Florence.

RUS–KL (a³, No. 3084).

*ZC 2: 39–41 — *PM* 1: 67–69 — *PSSL* 6: 220–222 — *TMBF:* 59–60 [English tr.].

639.   To Nadezhda von Meck

7/19 Nov 1877. Rome.

RUS–KL (a³, No. 3085).

*ZC 2: 41–42 — *PM* 1: 69–71 — *PSSL* 6: 222–225 — *TMBF:* 60–62 [English tr.].

640.   To Nadezhda von Meck

[8/20–]9/21 Nov 1877. Rome.

RUS–KL (a³, No. 3086).

PM 1: 71–73 — *PSSL* 6: 225–226 — *TMBF:* 63–64 [English tr.].

641.   To Aleksandra Davydova

[8/20–9/21 Nov] 1877 (in MS: "9/21 Dec"). Rome.

RUS–SPsc (f. 834, No. 17, fol. 40–41).

PR: 309–311 — *PSSL* 6: 227–228.

642.   To Nikolai Rubinshtein

[9/21] Nov 1877. Rome.

RUS–Mcm (f. 37, No. 86).

*ZC 2: 42–43 — *IRM* 1: 166–168 — *PSSL* 6: 228–230.

643.   To Modest Chaikovskii

[10/22] Nov [1877]. Rome.

RUS–KL (a³, No. 1484).

*ZC 2: 43–44 — PR: 311–313 — PB: 125–127 —
*PSSL 6: 125–127 — LF: 123–125 [English tr.].

644. To Nadezhda von Meck
11/23 Nov 1877. Venice.
RUS–KL (a³, No. 3087).
*ZC 2: 44–45 — PM 1: 73–75 — PSSL 6: 233–235 —
TMBF: 64–65 [English tr.].

645. To Aleksandra Davydova
12/24 Nov 1877. Venice.
RUS–SPsc (f. 834, No. 17, fol. 42–43).
PR: 313–314 — *PSSL 6: 235–237.

646. To Nikolai Konradi
12/24 Nov 1877. Venice.
Autograph lost; MS copy in RUS–KL.
CTP 258 — PSSL 6: 237.

647. To Pëtr Iurgenson
13/25 Nov 1877. Venice.
RUS–KL (a³, No. 2161).
PIU 1: 19–21 — PSSL 6: 237–239.

648. To Nadezhda von Meck
16/28 Nov 1877. Venice.
RUS–KL (a³, No. 3088).
*ZC 2: 45–46 — PM 1: 81–82 — PSSL 6: 239–240 —
TMBF: 71–72 [English tr.].

649. To Aleksandra Davydova
18/30 Nov 1877. Venice.
RUS–SPsc (f. 834, No. 17, fol. 44–45).
PR: 314–315 — PB: 127–128 — PSSL 6: 241–242 —
LF: 125–126 [English tr.].

650. To Nadezhda von Meck
18/30 Nov 1877. Venice.
RUS–KL (a³, No. 3089).
*ZC 2: 46–48 — PM 1: 84–87 — PSSL 6: 242–244 —
TMBF: 74–76 [English tr.].

651. To Nadezhda von Meck
19 Nov/1 Dec 1877. Vienna.
RUS–KL (a³, No. 3090).

PM 1: 87 — PSSL 6: 245 — TMBF: 77 [English tr.].

651a. To Modest Chaikovskii
[20] Nov/1 Dec 1877 (in typed copy: "21 Nov"). Vienna
Autograph lost; typed copy in RUS–KL.
PSSL 17: 226.

652. To Nikolai Rubinshtein
[21 Nov/3 Dec] 1877 (in MS: "20 Nov/2 Dec"). Vienna.
RUS–Mcm (f. 37, No. 87).
IRM 1: 169 — PSSL 6: 245–246.

653. To Karl Al´brekht
[21 Nov/3 Dec] 1877 (in MS: "20 Nov/2 Dec"). Vienna.
RUS–Mcm (f. 37, No. 9).
PSSL 6: 246.

654. To Aleksandra Davydova
[21 Nov/3 Dec] 1877 (in MS: "21 Nov/2 Dec"). Vienna.
RUS–SPsc (f. 834, No. 17, fol. 46–47).
PR: 316 — PSSL 6: 247.

655. To Nadezhda von Meck
21 Nov/[3] Dec 1877 (in MS: "2 Dec"). Vienna.
RUS–KL (a³, No. 3091).
*ZC 2: 48–50 — PM 1: 88–90 — PSSL 6: 247–
250 — TMBF: 77–80 [English tr.].

656. To Nadezhda von Meck
[21 Nov/3 Dec 1877]. Vienna.
RUS–KL (a³, No. 3093).
*PM 1: 97–98 ("23 Nov") — PSSL 6: 250.

657. To Pëtr Iurgenson
21 Nov/[3 Dec] 1877 (in MS: "2 Dec"). Vienna.
RUS–KL (a³, No. 2162).
PSSL 6: 250.

658. To Nikolai Rubinshtein
[22–23 Nov/4–5 Dec 1877]. Vienna.
RUS–Mcm (f. 37, No. 88).
IRM 1: 169–170 — PSSL 6: 251.

659. To Nadezhda von Meck

23 Nov/5 Dec 1877. Vienna.

RUS–KL (a³, No. 3092).

*ZC 2: 50–52 — PM 1: 91–97 — PSSL 6: 251–257 — TMBF: 80– 86 [English tr.].

660. To Nikolai Kashkin

26 Nov/8 Dec 1877. Vienna.

RUS–KL (a³, No. 212).

*KVC (1896): 113–114 — *ZC 2: 52–53 —*KVC (1954): 130–132 — *PSSL 6: 258–260.

661. To Nadezhda von Meck

26 Nov/8 Dec 1877. Vienna.

RUS–KL (a³, No. 3094).

*ZC 2: 53–55 — PM 1: 98–100 — PSSL 6: 261–263 — TMBF: 87–89 [English tr.].

662. To Modest Chaikovskii

27 Nov/9 Dec 1877. Vienna.

RUS–KL (a³, No. 1485).

*PR: 316 — *PB: 128 — *PSSL 6: 263–264 — *ZN: 123 — *LF: 126 [English tr.].

663. To Pëtr Iurgenson

27 Nov/9 Dec 1877. Vienna.

RUS–KL (a³, No. 2163).

PIU 1: 21 — PSSL 6: 264–265.

664. To Nadezhda von Meck

27 Nov/9 Dec 1877. Vienna.

RUS–KL (a³, No. 3095).

PM 1: 100 — PSSL 6: 265–266 — TMBF: 89–90 [English tr.].

665. To Nadezhda von Meck

[30 Nov]/12 Dec 1877 (in MS: "29/12 Dec"). Vienna.

RUS–KL (a³, No. 3096).

*ZC 2: 56–57 — PM 1: 101–102 ("29 Nov/11 Dec") — PSSL 6: 266–268 — TMBF: 90–91 ("29 Nov/11 Dec") [English tr.].

666. To Anatolii Chaikovskii

1/13 Dec 1877. Vienna.

RUS–KL (a³, No. 1116).

PR: 317–318 — *PSSL 6: 268–269.

667. To Aleksandra & Lev Davydov

2/14 Dec [1877]. Venice.

RUS–SPsc (f. 834, No. 17, fol. 48–49).

PR: 320–321 — PSSL 6: 269–271.

668. To Nadezhda von Meck

2/14 Dec 1877. Venice.

RUS–KL (a³, No. 3097).

PM 1: 108–109 — PSSL 6: 271–272.

669. To Anatolii Chaikovskii

2/14 Dec 1877. Venice.

RUS–KL (a³, No. 1117).

PR: 318–320 — *PSSL 6: 272–273.

670. To Anatolii Chaikovskii

2/14[–3/15] Dec 1877. Venice.

RUS–KL (a³, No. 1118).

PR: 321–322 — *PSSL 6: 274.

671. To Karl Al´brekht

3/15 Dec 1877. Venice.

RUS–Mcm (f. 37, No. 24).

*ZC 2: 57–59 — *CMS: 263–266 — PSSL 6: 275–277.

672. To Anatolii Chaikovskii

3/15 Dec 1877. Venice.

RUS–KL (a³, No. 1119).

PR: 322–323 — *PB: 129 — PSSL 6: 278 — *LF: 127 [English tr.].

673. To Nadezhda von Meck

4/16 Dec 1877. Venice.

RUS–KL (a³, No. 3098).

PM 1: 109–110 — PSSL 6: 279–280 — TMBF: 96–97 [English tr.].

674. To Anatolii Chaikovskii

4/16 Dec [1877]. Venice.

RUS–KL (a³, No. 1120).

PR: 323–324 — PSSL 6: 280–281.

675. To Nikolai Rubinshtein

4/16 Dec [1877]. Venice.

RUS–Mcm (f. 37, No. 89).
IRM 1: 170 — *PSSL* 6: 281–282.

676.   To Modest Chaikovskii
4/16 Dec 1877. Venice.
RUS–KL (a³, No. 1487).
*ZC 2: 59 — PR: 324–325 — PSSL 6: 282–283.

677.   To Pëtr Iurgenson
5/17 Dec 1877. Venice.
RUS–KL (a³, No. 2164).
PIU 1: 22 — *PSSL* 6: 283–284.

678.   To Anatolii Chaikovskii
5/17–7/19 Dec [1877]. Venice.
RUS–KL (a³, No. 1121).
PR: 326–329 — *PSSL* 6: 285–287.

679.   To Nadezhda von Meck
[6/18] Dec 1877. Venice.
RUS–KL (a³, No. 3099).
PM 1: 110–115 ("5/17 Dec") — *PSSL* 6: 287–292 —
TMBF: 97–102 ("5/17 Dec") [English tr.].

680.   To Modest Chaikovskii
[6/18 Dec 1877. Venice].
RUS–KL (a³, No. 1488).
PR: 326 — *PB*: 129 — *PSSL* 6: 293 — *LF*: 100–127
[English tr.].

681.   To Sergei Taneev
7/19 Dec 1877. Venice.
RUS–Mcl (f. 880).
PT 16–17 — *CTP* 20–21 — *PSSL* 6: 293–295.

682.   To Aleksandra Davydova
8/20 Dec 1877. Venice.
RUS–SPsc (f. 834, No. 17, fol. 50–51).
PR: 329–330 — *PSSL* 6: 295–297.

683.   To Anatolii Chaikovskii
8/20–10/22 Dec 1877. Venice.
RUS–KL (a³, nos. 1122–1123).
*PR: 330–332 — *PB: 120–130 — *PSSL 6: 297–
298 — *ZN: 126–127.

684.   To Nadezhda von Meck
9/21 Dec 1877. Venice.
RUS–KL (a³, No. 3100).
*ZC 2: 62 — PM 1: 115–116 — PSSL 6: 298–299 —
TMBF: 102–103 [English tr.].

685.   To Modest Chaikovskii
[10/22 Dec 1877. Venice] — telegram; in French.
RUS–KL (a³, No. 1486).
PSSL 6: 299.

686.   To Anatolii Chaikovskii
11/23–14/26 Dec 1877 [Venice].
RUS–KL (a³, nos. 1124–1126).
*ZC 2: 64 — *PR: 332–334 — *PB: 130–131 —
*PSSL 6: 300–302 — *ZN: 124 — *LF: 127–129
[English tr.].

687.   To Karl Al´brekht
12/24 Dec 1877. Venice.
RUS–Mcm (f. 37, No. 25).
PSSL 6: 302.

688.   To Aleksandra Davydova
12/24 Dec 1877. Venice.
RUS–SPsc (f. 834, No. 17, fol. 53–54).
PR: 332–333 — *PSSL* 6: 303.

689.   To Nadezhda von Meck
12/24 Dec 1877. Venice.
RUS–KL (a³, No. 3101).
*ZC 2: 63–64 — PM 1: 117–118 — PSSL 6: 303–
304 — *TMBF*: 103–104 [English tr.].

690.   To Pëtr Iurgenson
15/27 Dec 1877. Venice.
RUS–KL (a³, No. 2165).
PIU 1: 23 — *PSSL* 6: 305–306.

691.   To Anatolii Chaikovskii
15/27–17/29 Dec 1877. Venice–Milan.
RUS–KL (a³, No. 1127).
PR: 335–336 — *PB*: 132–133 — *PSSL* 6: 306–307 —
LF: 129–130 [English tr.].

692.   To Nadezhda von Meck

16/28 Dec [1877]. Milan.

RUS–KL (a³, No. 3102).

*ZC 2: 64–66 — PM 1: 122–125 — PSSL 6: 307–312 — TMBF: 108–112 [English tr.].

693.   To Anatolii Chaikovskii

19/31 Dec 1877. San Remo.

RUS–KL (a³, No. 1128).

PR: 336–337 — PB: 133–134 — PSSL 6: 312–313 — LF: 131 [English tr.].

694.   To Karl Al´brekht

[20 Dec 1877/1 Jan 1878]. San Remo.

RUS–Mcm (f. 37, No. 25a).

PSSL 6: 313.

695.   To Anatolii Chaikovskii

20 Dec 1877/1 Jan 1878. San Remo.

RUS–KL (a³, No. 1129).

PR: 337–338 — PB: 134–135 — PSSL 6: 314 — LF: 132 [English tr.].

696.   To Nadezhda von Meck

20 Dec 1877/1 Jan 1878. San Remo.

RUS–KL (a³, No. 3103).

*ZC 2: 66–68 — PM 1: 128–131 — PSSL 6: 315–317 — *TMBF: 114–115 [English tr.].

697.   To Pëtr Iurgenson

20 Dec 1877/1 Jan 1878 [San Remo].

RUS–KL (a³, No. 2166).

PSSL 6: 318.

698.   To Nadezhda von Meck

21 Dec 1877/2 Jan 1878. San Remo.

RUS–KL (a³, No. 3104).

*ZC 2: 68–69 — PM 1: 131–133 — PSSL 6: 318–319 — TMBF: 116–118 [English tr.].

699.   To Nikolai Rubinshtein

21 Dec 1877/2 Jan 1878. San Remo.

RUS–Mcm (f. 37, No. 90).

*ZC 2: 69–70 — IRM 1: 170–171 — PSSL 6: 320.

700.   To Anatolii Chaikovskii

21 Dec 1877/2 Jan 1878. San Remo.

RUS–KL (a³, No. 1130).

PR: 338–339 — *PB: 135–136 — PSSL 6: 320–322 — *LF: 132–133 [English tr.].

701.   To Nadezhda von Meck

23 Dec 1877/4 Jan 1878. San Remo.

RUS–KL (a³, No. 3105).

PM 1: 133–134 — PSSL 6: 322–324 — TMBF: 118–119 [English tr.].

702.   To Nikolai Rubinshtein

23 Dec 1877/4 Jan 1878. San Remo.

RUS–Mcm (f. 37, No. 91).

*ZC 2: 71–72 — IRM 1: 171–172 — PSSL 6: 702.

703.   To Anatolii Chaikovskii

23 Dec 1877/4 Jan 1878. San Remo.

RUS–KL (a³, No. 1131).

*ZC 2: 70–71 — PR: 339–340 — PSSL 6: 325–326.

704.   To Aleksandra Davydova

24 Dec 1877/5 Jan 1878. San Remo.

RUS–SPsc (f. 834, No. 17, fol. 54–55).

PR: 341 — PB: 136–137 — PSSL 6: 327 — LF: 133–134 [English tr.].

705.   To Nadezhda von Meck

24 Dec 1877/5 Jan 1878. San Remo.

RUS–KL (a³, No. 3106).

*ZC 2: 72–73 — PM 1: 134–139 — PSSL 6: 328–332 — TMBF: 119–123 [English tr.].

706.   To Anatolii Chaikovskii

24 Dec 1877/5 Jan 1878 [San Remo].

RUS–KL (a³, No. 1132).

PR: 342 — PB: 137 — PSSL 6: 333 — LF: 134–135 [English tr.].

707.   To Nadezhda von Meck

24 Dec [1877]/5 Jan [1878]. San Remo.

RUS–KL (a³, No. 3107).

PM 1: 139–141 — *PSSL 6: 334–335 — TMBF: 124–125 [English tr.].

708.   To Anatolii Chaikovskii

24–25 Dec 1877/5–6 Jan 1878. San Remo.

RUS–KL (a³, No. 1133).

PR: 342–343 — *PSSL 6: 336–337.

709. To Anatolii Chaikovskii

[26 Dec 1877] /7 Jan [1878]. San Remo.

RUS–KL (a³, No. 1134).

ZC 2: 75 — *PR*: 343–344 — *PB*: 137–138 — *PSSL* 6: 337.

710. To Anatolii Chaikovskii

[28 Dec 1877/9 Jan 1878]. Milan.

RUS–KL (a³, No. 1135).

ZC 2: 75–76 — *PR*: 344 — *PB*: 138 — *PSSL* 6: 338 — *LF*: 135 [English tr.].

711. To Nadezhda von Meck

30 Dec 1877/[11] Jan 1878 (in MS: "10 Jan 1878"). Genoa

RUS–KL (a³, No. 3108).

PM 1: 141–142 — *PSSL* 6: 339–340 — *TMBF*: 125–126 [English tr.].

1878

712. To Nadezhda von Meck

1/13 Jan [1878]. San Remo.

RUS–KL (a³, No. 3109).

ZC 2: 76–77 — *PM* 1: 143–144 — *PSSL* 7: 13–14 — *TMBF*: 126–127 [English tr.].

713 . To Nikolai Rubinshtein

1/13 Jan 1878. San Remo.

RUS–Mcm (f. 37, No. 92).

ZC 2: 77–78 — *IRM* 1: 172–174 — *PSSL* 7: 14–16.

713a. To Robert von Tal´

1/13 Jan 1878. San Remo —in French.

Autograph lost (formerly F–P).

PSSL 17: 227.

714. To Pëtr Iurgenson

1/13 Jan [1878]. [San Remo].

RUS–KL (a³, No. 2181).

PIU 1: 27–28 — *PSSL* 7: 17.

715. To Anatolii Chaikovskii

1/13–4/16 Jan [1878]. San Remo.

RUS–KL (a³, No. 1137).

PR: 345–348 — *PB*: 138–139 — *PSSL* 7: 18–20 — *LF*: 135–136 [English tr.].

716. To Sergei Taneev

2/14 Jan 1878. San Remo.

RUS–Mcl (f. 880).

ZC 2: 78–82 — *PT* 17–20 — *CTP* 23–25 — *PSSL* 7: 20–23.

717. To Aleksandra Davydova

5/17 Jan 1878. San Remo.

RUS–SPsc (f. 834, No. 17, fol. 56–57).

PR: 348 — *PB*: 139–140 — *PSSL* 7: 24–25 — *LF*: 137 [English tr.].

718. To Anatolii Chaikovskii

5/17–7/19 Jan 1878 [San Remo].

RUS–KL (a³, No. 1138).

PR: 349–350 — *PB*: 140–141 — *PSSL* 7: 25–26 — *LF*: 137 [English tr.].

719. To Nadezhda von Meck

6/18 Jan 1878. San Remo.

RUS–KL (a³, No. 3110).

ZC 2: 82 — *PM* 1: 148–149 — *PSSL* 7: 26–27 — *TMBF*: 131–132 [English tr.].

720. To Karl Al´brekht

8/20 Jan 1878. San Remo.

RUS–Mbelza

ZC 2: 83–87 — *CMS*: 270–274 — *PSSL* 7: 28–31.

721. To Anatolii Chaikovskii

8/20–11/23 Jan 1878 [San Remo].

RUS–KL (a³, No. 1139).

PR: 350–353 — *PSSL* 7: 31–32.

722. To Nadezhda von Meck

9/21 Jan 1878. San Remo.

RUS–KL (a³, No. 3111).

PM 1: 149–153 — *PSSL* 7: 33–36 — *TMBF*: 132–136 [English tr.].

723. To Nadezhda von Meck

10/22 Jan 1878 [San Remo].

RUS–KL (a³, No. 3112).

PM 1: 153–156 — *PSSL* 7: 36–39 — *TMBF*: 136–137 [English tr.].

724. To Nadezhda von Meck

11/23 Jan 1878. San Remo.

RUS–KL (a³, No. 3113).

PM 1: 156–157 — *PSSL* 7: 39–41 — *TMBF*: 137–138 [English tr.].

725.   To Pëtr Iurgenson

12/24 Jan 1878 [San Remo].

RUS–KL (a³, No. 2182).

ZC 2: 87–88 — *PIU* 1: 28–29 — *PSSL* 7: 41–42.

726.   To Anatolii Chaikovskii

12/24–14/26 Jan 1878 [San Remo].

RUS–KL (a³, No. 1141).

PR: 353–354 — **PB*: 141–142 — **PSSL* 7: 43–44 — **LF*: 138–139 [English tr.].

727.   To Nikolai Rubinshtein

14/26 Jan 1878. San Remo.

RUS–Mcm (f. 37, No. 93).

*ZC 2: 91–92 — *IRM* 1: 174–177 — **PM* 1: 581–582 — *PSSL* 7: 44–46.

728.   To Nadezhda von Meck

14/26 Jan 1878. San Remo.

RUS–KL (a³, No. 3114).

*ZC 2: 88–91 — *PM* 1: 163–165 — *PSSL* 7: 47–49 — *TMBF*: 143–146 [English tr.].

729.   To Nadezhda von Meck

15/27 Jan 1878. San Remo.

RUS–KL (a³, No. 3115).

*ZC 2: 93–94 — *PM* 1: 165–166 — *PSSL* 7: 49–50.

730.   To Anatolii Chaikovskii

15/27–18/30 Jan 1878 [San Remo].

RUS–KL (a³, nos. 1142–1144).

PR: 354–358 — **PB*: 142–144 — **PSSL* 7: 51–54 — **LF*: 139–141 [English tr.].

731.   To Karl Al´brekht

[17/29 Jan 1878. San Remo] — telegram; in French.

RUS–Mcm (f. 37, No. 28).

PSSL 7: 55.

732.   To Nadezhda von Meck

17/29 Jan 1876. San Remo.

RUS–KL (a³, No. 3116).

PM 1: 167–168 — *PSSL* 7: 55–56 — **TMBF*: 146–147 [English tr.].

733.   To Pëtr Iurgenson

17/29 Jan 1878. San Remo.

RUS–KL (a³, No. 2183).

*PIU 1: 29–30 — **PSSL* 7: 57–58 — **ZN*: 126.

734.   To Anatolii Chaikovskii

19–21 Jan/31 Jan–2 Feb [1878]. [San Remo].

RUS–KL (a³, No. 1145).

PR: 358–359 — *PSSL* 7: 58–59.

735.   To Nadezhda von Meck

20–21 Jan/1–2 Feb 1878. San Remo.

RUS–KL (a³, No. 3117).

PM 1: 168–172 — *PSSL* 7: 59–63 — *TMBF*: 147–150 [English tr.].

736.   To Nadezhda von Meck

21–22 Jan/2–3 Feb 1878. San Remo–Nice.

RUS–KL (a³, No. 3118).

PM 1: 172–175 — *PSSL* 7: 64–67 — *TMBF*: 150–154 [English tr.].

737.   To Anatolii Chaikovskii

22–25 Jan/3–6 Feb 1878. Nice [–San Remo].

RUS–KL (a³, No. 1146).

PR: 359–361 — **PB*: 145–146 — *PSSL* 7: 67–68 — **LF*: 141–142 [English tr.].

738.   To Sergei Taneev

24 Jan/5 Feb [1878]. San Remo.

RUS–Mcl (f. 880).

*ZC 2: 94–95 — *PT* 23–25 — *CTP* 28–29 — *PSSL* 7: 68–70.

739.   To Pëtr Iurgenson

24 Jan/5 Feb 1878. San Remo.

RUS–KL (a³, nos. 2184, 2185).

*ZC 2: 95–96 —*PIU* 1: 30–31 — *PSSL* 7: 71–72.

740.   To Nadezhda von Meck

25 Jan/6 Feb 1878. San Remo.

RUS–KL (a³, No. 3119).

PM 1: 181–185 — *PSSL* 7: 72–75 — **TMBF*: 158–160 [English tr.].

741. To Pëtr Iurgenson

26 Jan/7 Feb 1878 [San Remo].

RUS–KL (a³, No. 2186).

PIU 1: 31 — *PSSL* 7: 76.

742. To Anatolii Chaikovskii

[26–28 Jan/7–9 Feb 1878] (in MS: "27/8–28/10") [San Remo].

RUS–KL (a³, No. 1147).

PR: 361–362 —*PB*: 146–147 — *PSSL* 7: 77–78 — *LF*: 143 [English tr.].

743. To Nadezhda von Meck

28 Jan/9 Feb 1878. San Remo.

RUS–KL (a³, No. 3120).

ZC 2: 97–99 — *PM* 1: 185–187 — *PSSL* 7: 78–80 — *TMBF*: 160–162 [English tr.].

744. To Anatolii Chaikovskii

29 Jan/10 Feb–1/13 Feb 1878 [San Remo].

RUS–KL (a³, No. 1148).

PR: 362–363 —*PB*: 147 — *PSSL* 7: 81–82 — *LF*: 143–144 [English tr.].

745. To Nikolai Rubinshtein

30 Jan/11 Feb 1878. San Remo.

RUS–Mcm (f. 37, No. 94).

ZC 2: 99–100 — *IRM* 1: 177–178 — *PSSL* 7: 83–84.

746. To Nadezhda von Meck

31 Jan/12 Feb [–1/13 Feb] 1878. San Remo.

RUS–KL (a³, No. 3121–3122).

ZC 2: 100–103 — *PM* 1: 190–195 — *PSSL* 7: 84–89 — *TMBF*: 163–168 [English tr.].

747. To Anatolii Chaikovskii

2/14 [–3/15] Feb 1878. San Remo.

RUS–KL (a³, No. 1149).

ZC 2: 103–105 — *PR*: 363–366 —*PSSL* 7: 90–92.

748. To Karl Al´brekht

3/15 Feb 1878. San Remo.

RUS–Mcm (f. 37, No. 29).

CMS: 275–276 — *PSSL* 7: 92–93.

749. To Nadezhda von Meck

3/15 Feb [1878]. San Remo.

RUS–KL (a³, No. 3123).

PM 1: 196–198 — *PSSL* 7: 94–96 — *TMBF*: 168–170 [English tr.].

750. To Pëtr Iurgenson

4/16 Feb [1878]. San Remo.

RUS–KL (a³, No. 2187).

PIU 1: 32 — *PSSL* 7: 96–97.

751. To Anatolii Chaikovskii

4/16–8/[20] Feb 1878 (in MS: "8/19") [San Remo].

RUS–KL (a³, No. 1150).

PR: 366–368 — *PSSL* 7: 98–99.

752. To Pëtr Iurgenson

5/17 Feb 1878. San Remo.

RUS–KL (a³, No. 2188).

PSSL 7: 99.

753. To Nadezhda von Meck

6/18 Feb 1878. San Remo.

RUS–KL (a³, No. 3124).

PM 1: 198–200 — *PSSL* 7: 100–101 — *TMBF*: 170–171 [English tr.].

754. To Nadezhda von Meck

8/20 Feb 1878. Nice.

RUS–KL (a³, No. 3125).

ZC 2: 106–107 — *PM* 1: 200–201 — *PSSL* 7: 101–102 — *TMBF*: 172–173 [English tr.].

755. To Nadezhda von Meck

9/21 Feb [1878]. Florence.

RUS–KL (a³, No. 3126).

ZC 2: 107–111 — *PM* 1: 201–205 — *PSSL* 7: 103–106 — *TMBF*: 173–177 [English tr.].

756. To Anatolii Chaikovskii

12/24 Feb 1878. Florence.

RUS–KL (a³, No. 1151).

PR: 368–370 — *PB*: 147–149 — *PSSL* 7: 107–108 — *LF*: 144–145 [English tr.].

757. To Lev Davydov

12/24 Feb [1878]. Florence.

RUS–KL (a³, No. 169).

PR: 370–371 — *PSSL* 7: 109–110.

758.   To Nadezhda von Meck

12/24 Feb 1878. Florence.

RUS–KL (a³, No. 3127).

*ZC 2: 111–114 — PM 1: 205–208 — PSSL 7: 111–113 — *TMBF: 177–179 [English tr.].

759.   To Anatolii Chaikovskii

13/25 [–14/26] Feb 1878. Florence .

RUS–KL (a³, No. 1152).

PR: 372–377 — *PB: 149–150 — *PSSL 7: 113–118 — *LF: 146 [English tr.].

760.   To Karl Al´brekht

14/26 Feb 1878. Florence.

Autograph lost; MS copy in RUS–KL.

*PSSL 7: 118–119.

761.   To Pëtr Iurgenson

14/26 Feb [1878]. Florence.

RUS–KL (a³, No. 2189).

*ZC 2: 114–115 — PIU 1: 33 — PSSL 7: 120–121.

762.   To Nadezhda von Meck

16/28 Feb 1878. Florence.

RUS–KL (a³, No. 3128).

*ZC 2: 115–116 — PM 1: 214–216 — PSSL 7: 121–123 — *TMBF: 182–183 [English tr.].

763.   To Nadezhda von Meck

17 Feb/1 Mar 1878. Florence .

RUS–KL (a³, No. 3129).

*ZC 2: 117–120 — PM 1: 216–220 — PSSL 7: 124–128 — TMBF: 183–188 [English tr.].

764.   To Anatolii Chaikovskii

[18 Feb/2 Mar] 1878. Florence.

RUS–KL (a³, No. 1153).

*PR: 377–378 — *PB: 150–151 — *PSSL 7: 128–129 — *LF: 147 [English tr.].

765.   To Nadezhda von Meck

20 Feb/4 Mar 1878. Florence.

RUS–KL (a³, No. 3130).

*ZC 2: 121–123 — PM 1: 220–223 — PSSL 7: 130–133 — TMBF: 188–191 [English tr.].

766.   To Anatolii Chaikovskii

[22 Feb/6 Mar] 1878. Florence.

RUS–KL (a³, No. 1154).

PR: 378–380 — *PB: 151–152 — *PSSL 7: 133–135 — *LF: 148–149 [English tr.].

767.   To Pëtr Iurgenson

22 Feb/[6] Mar 1878 (in MS: "4 Mar"). Florence.

RUS–KL (a³, No. 2191).

PSSL 7: 135.

768.   To Nadezhda von Meck

23 Feb/7 Mar 1878. Florence.

RUS–KL (a³, No. 3131).

PM 1: 223–224 — PSSL 7: 136–137.

769.   To Anatolii Chaikovskii

25 Feb/9 Mar 1878. Clarens.

RUS–KL (a³, No. 1154a).

*ZC 2: 123–124 — PR: 380–381 — PB: 152–153 — PSSL 7: 137–138 — *LF: 149 [English tr.].

770.   To Nadezhda von Meck

26 Feb/10 Mar 1878. Clarens.

RUS–KL (a³, No. 3132).

PM 1: 224–227 — PSSL 7: 139–142 — TMBF: 191–194 [English tr.].

771.   To Anatolii Chaikovskii

26 Feb/10 Mar 1878. Clarens.

RUS–KL (a³, No. 1155).

PR: 381–383 — *PSSL 7: 142–143.

772.   To Pëtr Iurgenson

27 Feb/11 Mar [1878]. Clarens.

RUS–KL (a³, No. 2190).

PIU 1: 34 — PSSL 7: 143–144.

773.   To Anatolii Chaikovskii

27 Feb/11 Mar–1/13 Mar [1878]. Clarens.

RUS–KL (a³, No. 1156).

PR: 384–385 — PSSL 7: 144–145.

774.   To Aleksandra Davydova

28 Feb/12 Mar 1878. Clarens.

RUS–SPsc (f. 834, No. 17, fol. 58–59).

PR: 383–384 — PSSL 7: 146–147.

775. To Nadezhda von Meck

28 Feb/12 Mar 1878. Clarens.

RUS–KL (a³, No. 3133).

*ZC 2: 124–125 — PM 1: 231–233 — PSSL 7: 148–149 — *TMBF: 196–197 [English tr.].

776. To Anatolii Chaikovskii

2/14–4/16 Mar 1878. Clarens.

RUS–KL (a³, No. 1158).

*PR: 386–387 — *PB: 153–154 — *PSSL 7: 150–151 — *LF: 150–151 [English tr.].

777. To Nadezhda von Meck

3/15 Mar 1878. Clarens.

RUS–KL (a³, No. 3134).

*ZC 2: 125–126 — PM 1: 233–235 — PSSL 7: 152–153 — TMBF: 198–199 [English tr.].

778. To Nadezhda von Meck

5/17 Mar 1878. Clarens.

RUS–KL (a³, No. 3135).

*ZC 2: 126–128 — PM 1: 235–238 — PSSL 7: 154–156 — *TMBF: 199–201 [English tr.].

779. To Anatolii Chaikovskii

5/17–8/20 Mar 1878 [Clarens].

RUS–KL (a³, No. 1159).

PR: 387–389 — PB: 154–155 — PSSL 7: 157–158 — *LF: 151–152 [English tr.].

780. To Nadezhda von Meck

7/19 Mar 1878. Clarens.

RUS–KL (a³, No. 3136).

*ZC 2: 128–131 — PM 1: 243–246 — PSSL 7: 159–162 — *TMBF: 205–208 [English tr.].

781. To Karl Al´brekht

9/21 Mar 1878 [Clarens].

RUS–Mcm (f. 37, No. 30).

CMS: 277–278 — PSSL 7: 163–164.

782. To Nadezhda von Meck

10/22 Mar 1878. Clarens.

RUS–KL (a³, No. 3137).

PM 1: 246–248 — PSSL 7: 164–165 — TMBF: 208–210 [English tr.].

783. To Anatolii Chaikovskii

9/21–11/23 Mar 1878 [Clarens].

RUS–KL (a³, No. 1160).

*PR: 389–390 — *PB: 155–156 — *PSSL 7: 166–167 — *LF: 152–153 [English tr.].

784. To Nadezhda von Meck

12/24 Mar 1878. Clarens.

RUS–KL (a³, No. 3138).

*ZC 2: 131–132 — PM 1: 251–252 — PSSL 7: 167–169 — *TMBF: 213–214 [English tr.].

785. To Nadezhda von Meck

13/25 Mar 1878. Clarens.

RUS–KL (a³, No. 3139).

PM 1: 253–255 — PSSL 7: 169–171 — TMBF: 214–215 [English tr.].

786. To Aleksandra Davydova

14/26 Mar 1878. Clarens.

RUS–SPsc (f. 834, No. 17, fol. 60–61).

PR: 390–391 — PSSL 7: 171–172.

787. To Nadezhda von Meck

14/26 Mar 1878. Clarens.

RUS–KL (a³, No. 3140).

*ZC 2: 132–134 — PM 1: 258–261 — PSSL 7: 173–175 — *TMBF: 217–219 [English tr.].

788. To Anatolii Chaikovskii

15/27 Mar 1878. Clarens.

RUS–KL (a³, No. 1161).

PR: 391–393 — *PB: 156–157 — *PSSL 7: 176–177 — *LF: 153–154 [English tr.].

789. To Pëtr Iurgenson

15/27 Mar 1878. Clarens.

RUS–KL (a³, No. 2192).

PIU 1: 36 — PSSL 7: 177–178.

790. To Nadezhda von Meck

16/28 Mar 1878. Clarens.

RUS–KL (a³, No. 3141).

*ZC 2: 134–138 — PM 1: 261–265 — PSSL 7: 179–182 — TMBF: 219–222 [English tr.].

791.   To Anatolii Chaikovskii

16/28–18/30 Mar 1878. Clarens.

RUS–KL (a^3, No. 1162).

PR: 393 — **PB*: 157 — *PSSL* 7: 183–184 — **LF*: 154–155 [English tr.].

792.   To Varvara Taneeva

17/29 Mar 1878. Clarens.

RUS–Mcl (f. 880).

CTP: 30 — *PSSL* 7: 184.

793.   To Nadezhda von Meck

18/30 Mar 1878. Clarens.

RUS–KL (a^3, No. 3142).

*ZC 2: 138–140 — *PM* 1: 265–266 — *PSSL* 7: 185–186 — **TMBF*: 222–223 [English tr.].

794.   To Nadezhda von Meck

19/31 Mar 1878. Clarens.

RUS–KL (a^3, No. 3143).

*ZC 2: 140–143 — *PM* 1: 266–270 — *PSSL* 7: 186–190 — **TMBF*: 223–226 [English tr.].

795.   To Anatolii Chaikovskii

19/31 Mar–22 Mar/3 Apr 1878 [Clarens].

RUS–KL (a^3, No. 1163).

PR: 394–396 — **PB*: 158–159 — *PSSL* 7: 190–192 — **LF*: 155–156 [English tr.].

796.   To Nadezhda von Meck

22 Mar/3 Apr 1878. Clarens.

RUS–KL (a^3, No. 3144).

PM 1: 274–275 — *PSSL* 7: 192–193 — **TMBF*: 228–229 [English tr.].

797.   To Anatolii Chaikovskii

23–25 Mar/4–6 Apr [1878]. Clarens.

RUS–KL (a^3, No. 1164).

*PR: 396–397 — **PB*: 159–160 — **PSSL* 7: 194–195 — **LF*: 156–157 [English tr.].

798.   To Nadezhda von Meck

24 Mar/5 Apr [1878]. Clarens.

RUS–KL (a^3, No. 3145).

*ZC 2: 144 — *PM* 1: 275–279 — *PSSL* 7: 195–199 — *TMBF*: 229–233 [English tr.].

799.   To Sergei Taneev

27 Mar/8 Apr [1878]. Clarens.

RUS–Mcl (f. 880) [facs. of 1 p. in *PICH* (1978): 92].

PT: 28–30 — *CTP*: 33–35 — *PSSL* 7: 200–202.

800.   To Pëtr Iurgenson

27 Mar/8 [Apr 1878]. Clarens.

RUS–KL (a^3, No. 2193).

*ZC 2: 149–151 — *PIU* 1: 37–38 — *PSSL* 7: 202–204.

801.   To Nadezhda von Meck

28 Mar/9 Apr 1878. Clarens.

RUS–KL (a^3, No. 3146).

PM 1: 284–285 — *PSSL* 7: 204–206 — **TMBF*: 235–236 [English tr.].

802.   To Anatolii Chaikovskii

29 Mar/10 Apr 1878. Clarens.

RUS–KL (a^3, No. 1165).

PR: 397–399 — **PB*: 160–161 — **PSSL* 7: 206–207 — **LF*: 157–158 [English tr.].

803.   To Nadezhda von Meck

30 Mar/11 Apr 1878 [Clarens].

RUS–KL (a^3, No. 3147).

PM 1: 285–287 — *PSSL* 7: 208–209.

804.   To Anatolii Chaikovskii

30 Mar/11 Apr–1/13 Apr 1878 [Clarens].

RUS–KL (a^3, No. 1166).

PR: 388–400 — *PB*: 161–162 — *PSSL* 7: 210–211 — **LF*: 158–159 [English tr.].

805.   To Nadezhda von Meck

1/13 Apr [1878]. [Clarens].

RUS–KL (a^3, No. 2921).

*ZC 2: 151–153 — *PM* 1: 287–289 — *PSSL* 7: 211–213 — **TMBF*: 237–239 [English tr.].

806.   To Nadezhda von Meck

4/16 Apr 1878. Clarens.

RUS–KL (a^3, No. 3148).

PM 1: 294–295 — *PSSL* 7: 214–215.

807.   To Sergei Taneev

4/16 Apr 1878. Clarens.

RUS–Mcl (f. 880).

PT: 31–33 — *CTP*: 35–38 — *PSSL* 7: 216–219.

808.   To Nadezhda von Meck

8/20 Apr 1878. Vienna.

RUS–KL (a³, No. 3149).

*ZC 2: 295–296 — *PM* 1: 295–296 — *PSSL* 7: 219–220 — *TMBF*: 241–241 [English tr.].

809.   To Nadezhda von Meck

12–13 Apr 1878. Kamenka.

RUS–KL (a³, No. 2922).

*ZC 2: 158–161 — *PM* 1: 297–301 — *PSSL* 7: 221–225 — **TMBF*: 242–245 [English tr.].

810.   To Pëtr Iurgenson

[14 Apr 1878. Kamenka] — telegram.

RUS–KL (a³, No. 2194).

PSSL 7: 225.

811.   To Nadezhda von Meck

15 Apr 1878. Kamenka.

RUS–KL (a³, No. 2923).

PM 1: 301–302 — *PSSL* 7: 226–227 — *TMBF*: 245–246 [English tr.].

812.   To Pëtr Iurgenson

15 Apr [1878]. Kamenka.

RUS–KL (a³, No. 2195) [fragment].

*PIU 1: 38–39 — *PSSL* 7: 227–228.

813.   To Nadezhda von Meck

17 Apr 1878. Kamenka.

RUS–KL (a³, No. 2924).

PM 1: 302–303 — *PSSL* 7: 228–229 — **TMBF*: 246–247 [English tr.].

814.   To Nikolai Rubinshtein

18 Apr 1878. Kamenka.

RUS–Mcm (f. 37, No. 95).

IRM 1: 178–179 — *PSSL* 7: 230–231.

815.   To Nadezhda von Meck

22 Apr 1878. Kamenka.

RUS–KL (a³, No. 2925).

PM 1: 307–309 — *PSSL* 7: 231–233 — **TMBF*: 249–250 [English tr.].

816.   To Pëtr Iurgenson

[22 Apr 1878. Kamenka].

RUS–KL (a³, No. 2196).

PSSL 7: 234.

817.   To Nadezhda von Meck

23 Apr [1878]. Kamenka.

RUS–KL (a³, No. 2926).

*ZC 2: 161–162 — *PM* 1: 310–311 — *PSSL* 7: 234–235 — *TMBF*: 251–252 [English tr.].

818.   To Pëtr Iurgenson

24 Apr [1878]. Kamenka.

RUS–KL (a³, No. 2197).

PIU 1: 39 — *PSSL* 7: 236.

819.   To Anatolii Chaikovskii

27 Apr [1878]. Kamenka.

RUS–KL (a³, No. 1167).

*ZC 2: 162 — *PR*: 400–401 — **PB*: 162–163 — **PSSL* 7: 236–237 — **LF*: 159–160 [English tr.].

820.   To Nadezhda von Meck

30 Apr 1878. Kamenka.

RUS–KL (a³, No. 2927).

*ZC 2: 163–164 — *PM* 1: 314–315 — *PSSL* 7: 238–239 — *TMBF*: 254–256 [English tr.].

821.   To Nadezhda von Meck

1 May [1878]. Kamenka.

RUS–KL (a³, No. 2928).

PM 1: 315–316 — *PSSL* 7: 240–241 — *TMBF*: 256–257 [English tr.].

822.   To Anatolii Chaikovskii

1 May 1878 [Kamenka].

RUS–KL (a³, nos. 1168, 1157).

PR 402–403, 713–714 — **PB*: 163–164 — **PSSL* 7: 241–244 — **LF*: 160–161 [English tr.].

823.   To Nadezhda von Meck

4 May 1878. Kamenka.

RUS–KL (a³, No. 2929).

PM 1: 317–319 — *PSSL* 7: 245–247 — *TMBF*: 257–259 [English tr.].

824.   To Pëtr Iurgenson

5 May [1878]. Kamenka.

RUS–KL (a³, No. 2198).

PSSL 7: 247–248.

825.   To Nadezhda von Meck

9 May 1878 [Kamenka].

RUS–KL (a³, No. 2930) [partly in MS copy].

PM 1: 322–324 — *PSSL* 7: 249–250 — *TMBF*: 261–263 [English tr.].

826.   To Anatolii Chaikovskii

10 May [1878]. Kamenka.

RUS–KL (a³, No. 1169).

PR: 403–404 — *PSSL* 7: 251.

827.   To Nadezhda von Meck

14 May [1878]. Kiev.

RUS–KL (a³, No. 2931).

ZC 2: 164 — *PM* 1: 325 — *PSSL* 7: 252.

828.   To Pëtr Iurgenson

15 May [1878]. Kiev.

RUS–KL (a³, No. 2334).

PIU 1: 39–40 — *PSSL* 7: 252–253.

829.   To Nadezhda von Meck

17 May 1878. Brailov.

RUS–KL (a³, No. 2932).

PM 1: 325–329 — *PSSL* 7: 253–256 — *TMBF*: 263–266 [English tr.].

830.   To Modest Chaikovskii

17 May [1878]. Brailov.

RUS–KL (a³, No. 1489).

*ZC 2: 164–166 — *PR*: 404–406 — *PB*: 164–165 — *PSSL* 7: 257–258 — **LF*: 161–162 [English tr.]

831.   To Aleksandra Davydova

18 May [1878]. Brailov.

RUS–SPsc (f. 834, No. 17, fol. 62–63).

PR: 406–407 — *PSSL* 7: 259–260.

832.   To Nadezhda von Meck

18–19 May [1878]. Brailov.

RUS–KL (a³, No. 2933).

*ZC 2: 166–167 — *PM* 1: 331–333 — *PSSL* 7: 260–262 — **TMBF*: 268–270 [English tr.].

833.   To Modest Chaikovskii

18–20 May 1878. Brailov.

RUS–KL (a³, No. 1490).

*ZC 2: 167–168 — **PR*: 407–412 — **PB*: 166–167 — **PSSL* 7: 262–267 — **ZN*: 122 — **LF*: 162–164 [English tr.]

834.   To Nadezhda von Meck

21 May 1878. Brailov.

RUS–KL (a³, No. 2934).

*ZC 2: 168–171 — *PM* 1: 333–338 — *PSSL* 7: 267–271 — **TMBF*: 270–273 [English tr.].

835.   To Pëtr Iurgenson

21 May [1878]. [Brailov].

RUS–KL (a³, No. 2200).

PIU 1: 40 — *PSSL* 7: 271–272.

836.   To Nikolai Konradi

22 May [1878]. Brailov.

Autograph lost; MS copy in RUS–KL.

CTP: 259 — *PSSL* 7: 272.

837.   To Anatolii Chaikovskii

22 May [1878]. Brailov.

RUS–KL (a³, No. 1170).

PR: 414–415 — *PSSL* 7: 273.

838.   To Modest Chaikovskii

22 May 1878 [Brailov].

RUS–KL (a³, No. 1491).

*PIU 1: 320 — *PR*: 413–414 — *PSSL* 7: 273–274.

839.   To Aleksandra Davydova

23 May [1878]. Brailov.

RUS–SPsc (f. 834, No. 19, fol. 9–10).

PSSL 7: 275–276.

840.   To Nadezhda von Meck

23 May 1878. Brailov.

RUS–KL (a³, No. 2935).

*ZC 2: 171–173 — *PM* 1: 340–342 — *PSSL* 7: 276–278 — **TMBF*: 274 [English tr.].

841.   To Nadezhda von Meck

25 May 1878. Brailov.

RUS–KL (a³, No. 2936).

PM 1: 345–346 — *PSSL* 7: 278–280 — *TMBF*: 277–278 [English tr.].

842.   To Modest Chaikovskii

25 May 1878. Brailov.

RUS–KL (a³, No. 1492).

*ZC 2: 173–175 — *PR*: 415–417 — *PB*: 167–169 — *PSSL* 7: 280–282 — **LF*: 164–166 [English tr.]

843.   To Nadezhda von Meck

27 May [1878]. Brailov.

RUS–KL (a³, No. 2937).

*ZC 2: 175–176 — *PM* 1: 346–349 — *PSSL* 7: 282–284 — **TMBF*: 279–280 [English tr.].

844.   To Modest Chaikovskii

27 May 1878. Brailov.

RUS–KL (a³, No. 1493).

PR: 417–418 — **PB*: 169–170 — *PSSL* 7: 285–286 — **LF*: 166–167 [English tr.].

845.   To Aleksandra Davydova

28 May [1878]. Brailov.

RUS–SPsc (f. 834, No. 17, fol. 64–65).

PR: 418–419 — *PSSL* 7: 286–287.

846.   To Nadezhda von Meck

29–30 May 1878. Brailov.

RUS–KL (a³, No. 2938).

*ZC 2: 177–178 — *PM* 1: 349–352 — *PSSL* 7: 287–291 — **TMBF*: 280–282 [English tr.].

847.   To Modest Chaikovskii

30 May [1878]. [Brailov].

RUS–KL (a³, No. 1494).

PR: 420 — *PSSL* 7: 291–292.

848.   To Nadezhda von Meck

2 Jun [1878]. Moscow.

RUS–KL (a³, No. 2939).

PM 1: 353–354 — *PSSL* 7: 292–293.

849.   To Nadezhda von Meck

[2 Jun 1878. Moscow].

RUS–KL (a³, No. 2940).

PM 1: 354 — *PSSL* 7: 293.

850.   To Nadezhda von Meck

6 Jun 1878. Nizy.

RUS–KL (a³, No. 2941).

*ZC 2: 355–357 — *PM* 1: 355–357 — *PSSL* 7: 293–296 — *TMBF*: 283–286 [English tr.].

851.   To Modest Chaikovskii

6 Jun [1878]. Nizy.

RUS–KL (a³, No. 1495).

PR: 420–421 — *PB*: 170 — *PSSL* 7: 296–297 — **LF*: 168 [English tr.].

852.   To Modest Chaikovskii

9 Jun [1878]. Nizy.

RUS–KL (a³, No. 1496).

PR: 421–422 — **PSSL* 7: 297–298.

853.   To Nadezhda von Meck

10 Jun 1878. Nizy.

RUS–KL (a³, No. 2942).

PM 1: 358–359 — *PSSL* 7: 298–300 — *TMBF*: 286–287 [English tr.].

854.   To Nadezhda von Meck

12 Jun 1878. Kiev .

RUS–KL (a³, No. 2943).

ZC 2: 180–181 — *PM* 1: 359–360 — *PSSL* 7: 300–301.

855.   To Modest Chaikovskii

12 Jun [1878]. Kiev.

RUS–KL (a³, No. 1497).

PR: 422–423 — *PSSL* 7: 301–302.

856.   To Modest Chaikovskii

15 Jun [1878]. Kamenka.

RUS–KL (a³, No. 1498).

PR: 423–424 — **PB*: 171 — *PSSL* 7: 302–303 — **LF*: 168–169 [English tr.].

857.   To Nadezhda von Meck

16 Jun 1878. Kamenka.

RUS–KL (a³, No. 2944).

PM 1: 363–366 — *PSSL* 7: 303–306 — *TMBF:* 289–
292 [English tr.].

858.   To Pëtr Iurgenson

16 Jun [1878]. Kamenka.

RUS–KL (a³, No. 2202).

PIU 1: 41 — *PSSL* 7: 306–307.

859.   To Nadezhda von Meck

17 Jun 1878. Kamenka.

RUS–KL (a³, No. 2945).

PM 1: 366–369 — *PSSL* 7: 308–311.

860.   To Modest Chaikovskii

18 Jun [1878]. Kamenka.

RUS–KL (a³, No. 1499).

PR: 424–426 — **PSSL* 7: 311–312.

861.   To Pëtr Iurgenson

[22 Jun 1878. Kamenka].

RUS–KL (a³, No. 2203).

PIU 1: 42 — *PSSL* 7: 313.

862.   To Nadezhda von Meck

24 Jun 1878. Kamenka.

RUS–KL (a³, No. 2946).

*ZC 2: 181–187 — *PM* 1: 371–377 — *PSSL* 7: 314–
319 — **TMBF:* 293–298 [English tr.].

863.   To Nadezhda von Meck

25 Jun 1878. Kamenka.

RUS–KL (a³, No. 2947).

*ZC 2: 187–188 — *PM* 1: 377–379 — *PSSL* 7: 320–
321 — **TMBF:* 298–299 [English tr.].

864.   To Nadezhda von Meck

29 Jun 1878. Verbovka.

RUS–KL (a³, No. 2948).

*ZC 2: 188 — *PM* 1 : 379–380 — *PSSL* 7: 322–
323 — *TMBF:* 300–301 [English tr.].

865.   To Pëtr Iurgenson

1 Jul 1878. Verbovka.

RUS–KL (a³, No. 2204).

PIU 1: 42–43 — *PSSL* 7: 323–325.

866.   To Nadezhda von Meck

4 Jul [1878]. Verbovka.

RUS–KL (a³, No. 2949).

*ZC 2: 188–189 — *PM* 1: 383–385 — *PSSL* 7: 325–
327 — *TMBF:* 303–304 [English tr.].

867.   To Modest Chaikovskii

[4] Jul [1878] (in MS: "7 Jul"). Verbovka.

RUS–KL (a³, No. 1500).

PR: 426–427 — *PSSL* 7: 327–328.

868.   To Nadezhda von Meck

6 Jul [1878]. Verbovka.

RUS–KL (a³, No. 2950).

PM 1: 385–389 — *PSSL* 7: 328–332 — *TMBF:* 304–
306 [English tr.].

869.   To Modest Chaikovskii

7 Jul 1878. Verbovka.

RUS–KL (a³, No. 1501).

PR: 427–428 — *PSSL* 7: 333–334.

869a. To Sergei Taneev

12 Jul 1878. Kamenka.

Autograph lost.

PT: 33–34 — *CTP:* 38–39 — *PSSL* 17: 229.

870.   To Pëtr Iurgenson

12 Jul [1878]. Verbovka.

RUS–KL (a³, No. 2205).

PIU 1: 44–45 — *PSSL* 7: 334–335.

871.   To Nadezhda von Meck

13 Jul 1878 [Verbovka].

RUS–KL (a³, No. 2951).

*ZC 2: 189–190 — *PM* 1: 390–391 — *PSSL* 7: 335–
337 — *TMBF:* 306–307 [English tr.].

872.   To Pëtr Iurgenson

[18 Jul 1878. Verbovka].

RUS–KL (a³, No. 2206).

*ZC 2: 190 — *PIU* 1: 45–46 — *PSSL* 7: 337–338.

873.   To Nikolai Konradi

19 Jul [1878]. Verbovka.

Autorgaph lost; MS copy in RUS–KL.

CTP: 259 — *PSSL* 7: 339.

874. To Nadezhda von Meck
19 Jul [1878]. Verbovka.
RUS–KL (a³, No. 2952).
PM 1: 395 — *PSSL* 7: 339–340.

875. To Anatolii Chaikovskii
19 Jul [1878]. Verbovka.
RUS–KL (a³, No. 1171).
PR: 428–429 — *PSSL* 7: 340–341.

876. To Nadezhda von Meck
21 Jul 1878. Verbovka.
RUS–KL (a³, No. 2953).
PM 1: 396–397 — *PSSL* 7: 341–342 — *TMBF*: 310–311 [English tr.].

877. To Karl Al´brekht
[22 Jul 1878]. Verbovka.
RUS–Mt
ZC 2: 192–193 — *CMS*: 279 — *PSSL* 7: 343.

878. To Anatolii Chaikovskii
[23 Jul 1878]. Verbovka.
RUS–KL (a³, No. 1172).
PR: 429–430 — *PSSL* 7: 344–345.

879. To Nadezhda von Meck
25 Jul 1878. Verbovka.
RUS–KL (a³, No. 2954).
PM 1: 397–399 — *PSSL* 7: 345–347 — *TMBF*: 312–313 [English tr.].

880. To Anatolii Chaikovskii
25 Jul [1878]. Verbovka.
RUS–KL (a³, No. 1173).
PR: 430–431 — *PSSL* 7: 347–348.

881. To Anatolii Chaikovskii
28 Jul [1878]. Verbovka.
RUS–KL (a³, No. 1174).
PR: 431–432 — *PSSL* 7: 348–349.

882. To Nadezhda von Meck
29 Jul 1878. Verbovka.
RUS–KL (a³, No. 2955).
PM 1: 399–400 — *PSSL* 7: 349–350.

883. To Pëtr Iurgenson
29 Jul [1878]. Verbovka.
RUS–KL (a³, No. 2207).
ZC 2: 191–192 — *PIU* 1: 46–47 — *PSSL* 7: 350–351.

884. To Anatolii Chaikovskii
31 Jul [1878]. Verbovka.
RUS–KL (a³, No. 1175).
PR: 432–434 — *PSSL* 7: 351–353.

885. To Pëtr Iurgenson
[? 2 Aug 1878]. Verbovka.
RUS–KL (a³, No. 2208).
PIU 1: 47–48 — *PSSL* 7: 353–354.

886. To Nadezhda von Meck
2–5 Aug [1878]. Verbovka.
RUS–KL (a³, No. 2956).
PM 1: 403–405 — *PSSL* 7: 354–356 — *TMBF*: 316–318 [English tr.].

887. To Anatolii Chaikovskii
3 Aug [1878]. Verbovka.
RUS–KL (a³, No. 1176).
PR: 434–435 — *PB*: 171–172 — *PSSL* 7: 357–358 — *LF*: 169–170 [English tr.].

888. To Pëtr Iurgenson
3 Aug [1878]. Verbovka.
RUS–KL (a³, No. 2209).
PSSL 7: 358.

889. To Nadezhda von Meck
[8 Aug 1878]. Vorozhba.
RUS–KL (a³, No. 2957).
PM 1: 406 — *PSSL* 359.

890. To Anatolii Chaikovskii
[8 Aug 1878]. Vorozhba.
RUS–KL (a³, No. 1206).
PR: 435–436 — *PSSL* 7: 359–360.

891. To Pëtr Iurgenson
[8 Aug 1878]. Vorozhba.
RUS–KL (a³, No. 2210).
PIU 1: 48 — *PSSL* 7: 360–361.

892.   To Nadezhda von Meck

12 Aug [1878]. Brailov.

RUS–KL (a³, No. 2958).

*ZC 2: 194–196 — PM 1: 407–409 — PSSL 7: 361–
363 — *TMBF: 318–319 [English tr.].

893.   To Anatolii Chaikovskii

12 Aug [1878]. Brailov.

RUS–KL (a³, No. 1177).

PR: 436–437 — *PSSL 7: 363–364.

894.   To Modest Chaikovskii

12 Aug [1878]. Brailov.

RUS–KL (a³, No. 1502).

PSSL 7: 364–365.

895.   To Nadezhda von Meck

13 Aug [1878]. Brailov.

RUS–KL (a³, No. 2959).

*ZC 2: 196–197 — PM 1: 409–411 — PSSL 7: 365–
366 — *TMBF: 319–320 [English tr.].

896.   To Anatolii Chaikovskii

[14 Aug 1878. Brailov] (in MS: "Verbovka").

RUS–KL (a³, No. 1178).

PR: 437 — PSSL 7: 367.

897.   To Nadezhda von Meck

14–17 Aug [1878]. Brailov.

RUS–KL (a³, No. 2960).

*ZC 2: 197–199 — PM 1: 411–412 — PSSL 7: 368–
371 — *TMBF: 320–321 [English tr.].

898.   To Modest Chaikovskii

16 Aug [1878]. Brailov.

RUS–KL (a³, No. 1503).

*ZC 2: 199 — PR: 438–439 — PB: 172–173 — *PSSL
7: 372–373 — *LF: 167 [English tr.] ("end of
May").

899.   To Anatolii Chaikovskii

17 Aug [1878]. Brailov.

RUS–KL (a³, No. 1179).

PR: 439 — PSSL 7: 373.

900.   To Modest Chaikovskii

21 Aug [1878]. Verbovka.

RUS–KL (a³, No. 1504).

PR: 439–440 — *PB: 173 — PSSL 7: 373–374 —
*LF: 170 [English tr.].

901.   To Nadezhda von Meck

25 Aug 1878. Verbovka.

RUS–KL (a³, No. 2961).

*ZC 2: 200 — PM 1: 420–422 — PSSL 7: 375–
376 — TMBF: 325–326 [English tr.].

902.   To Nadezhda von Meck

28 Aug [1878]. Verbovka.

RUS–KL (a³, No. 2962).

PM 1: 422–424 — PSSL 7: 376–378 — TMBF: 327–
328 [English tr.].

903.   To Modest Chaikovskii

28 Aug [1878]. Verbovka.

RUS–KL (a³, No. 1505).

PR: 440–441 — *PB: 173–174 — PSSL 7: 379 —
*LF: 170–171 [English tr.].

904.   To Modest Chaikovskii

29 Aug [1878]. Kiev.

RUS–KL (a³, No. 1506).

*ZC 2: 201–203 — *PR: 441–442 — *PSSL 7: 380–
381 — *ZN: 121.

905.   To Karl Al´brekht

[31 Aug 1878. Moscow].

RUS–Mcm (f. 37, No. 32).

PSSL 7: 382.

906.   To Nadezhda von Meck

4–10 Sep [1878]. St. Petersburg–Moscow.

RUS–KL (a³, No. 2963).

PM 1: 426–433 — PSSL 7: 382–389 — TMBF: 331–
338 [English tr.].

907.   To Modest Chaikovskii

[5 Sep 1878]. St. Petersburg.

RUS–KL (a³, No. 1507).

PR: 444–445 — PSSL 7: 389–390.

907a. To Hans von Bülow

5 Sep 1878. Moscow — in French.

D–Bds

PSSL 17: 229–230.

908. To Aleksandra & Lev Davydov

[8 Sep 1878. St. Petersburg].

RUS–SPsc (f. 834, No. 17, fol. 66–67) [postscript to a letter from Il´ia Chaikovskii].

PR: 445–446 — *PSSL* 7: 391–392.

909. To Nadezhda von Meck

10 Sep [1878]. Moscow.

RUS–KL (a³, No. 2964).

PM 1: 434 — *PSSL* 7: 392–393 — *TMBF*: 338–339 [English tr.].

910. To Anatolii Chaikovskii

11 Sep [1878]. Moscow.

RUS–KL (a³, No. 1180).

PR: 446 — *PSSL* 7: 393–394.

911. To Modest Chaikovskii

11 Sep [1878]. Moscow.

RUS–KL (a³, No. 1508).

PSSL 7: 394–395.

912. To Nadezhda von Meck

12–13 Sep [1878]. Moscow.

RUS–KL (a³, No. 2965).

PM 1: 436–438 — *PSSL* 7: 393–398 — *TMBF*: 339–342 [English tr.].

913. To Pëtr Iurgenson

[? 13–14 Sep 1878. Moscow].

RUS–KL (a³, No. 2211).

PSSL 7: 398.

914. To Avgust Bernard

15 Sep [1878]. Moscow.

RUS–SPsc (f. 124, No. 4649).

PSSL 7: 399.

915. To Anatolii Chaikovskii

16 Sep [1878]. Moscow.

RUS–KL (a³, No. 1181).

PR: 447–448 — **PB*: 174–175 — **PSSL* 7: 399–400 — **LF*: 166–167 [English tr.] ("18 Sep").

916. To Modest Chaikovskii

16 Sep [1878]. Moscow.

RUS–KL (a³, No. 1509).

*PSSL 7: 401 — *ZN*: 132 — *TW*: 85–86 [English tr.].

917. To Nadezhda von Meck

19 Sep [1878]. Moscow.

RUS–KL (a³, No. 2966).

PM 1: 438–439 — *PSSL* 7: 402–403.

918. To Pëtr Iurgenson

[20 Sep 1878. Moscow].

RUS–KL (a³, No. 2225).

PSSL 7: 403–404.

919. To Bogomir Korsov

[22 Sep 1878. Moscow] — in French.

RUS–KL (a³, No. 237).

SM (1959), 1: 75–76 [Russian tr.] — *PSSL* 7: 404–405.

920. To Modest Chaikovskii

23 Sep [1878]. Moscow.

RUS–KL (a³, No. 1510).

PSSL 7: 405–406.

921. To Anatolii Chaikovskii

23 Sep [1878]. Moscow.

RUS–KL (a³, No. 1182).

PR: 448 — *PB*: 175–176 — *PSSL* 7: 406–407 — *LF*: 172 [English tr.].

922. To Nadezhda von Meck

24 Sep [1878]. Moscow.

RUS–KL (a³, No. 2967).

*ZC 2: 213–215 — *PM* 1: 444–446 — *PSSL* 7: 407–409 — *TMBF*: 345–347 [English tr.].

923. To Eduard Nápravník

27 Sep 1878. Moscow.

RUS–SPtm (Gik 17195/12).

VP: 119 — *EFN*: 102–103 — *PSSL* 7: 409–410.

924. To Sergei Taneev

[28 Sep 1878. Moscow].

RUS–Mcl (f. 880).

PT: 34 — *CTP*: 39 — *PSSL* 7: 410–411.

925.   To Nadezhda von Meck

29 Sep 1878. Moscow.

RUS–KL (a³, No. 2968).

PM 1: 447 — *PSSL* 7: 411–412 — *TMBF*: 347–348 [English tr.].

926.   To Anatolii Chaikovskii

29 Sep [1878]. Moscow.

RUS–KL (a³, No. 1183).

*PR: 449–450 — *PB: 176 — *PSSL 7: 412–413 — *ZN: 125 — *LF: 174 [English tr.] ("29 Oct").

927.   To Nadezhda von Meck

30 Sep 1878. Moscow.

RUS–KL (a³, No. 2969).

PM 1: 447–449 — *PSSL* 7: 413–415 — *TMBF*: 348–349 [English tr.].

928.   To Bogomir Korsov

[late Sep 1878. Moscow] — in French.

RUS–KL (a³, No. 238).

PSSL 7: 416.

929.   To Pëtr Iurgenson

[Sep 1878. Moscow].

RUS–KL (a³, No. 2170).

PSSL 7: 416.

930.   To Nadezhda von Meck

2 Oct [1878]. Moscow.

RUS–KL (a³, No. 2970).

PM 1: 450 — *PSSL* 7: 416–417 — *TMBF*: 349–350 [English tr.].

931.   To Anatolii Chaikovskii

2 Oct [1878]. Moscow.

RUS–KL (a³, No. 1184).

PR: 450 — *PB*: 177 — *PSSL* 7: 418 — *LF*: 172–173 [English tr.].

932.   To Lev Davydov

7 Oct 1878 [Moscow].

RUS–SPsc (f. 834, No. 19, fol. 11–12).

PR: 451 — *PB: 177 — *PSSL* 7: 418–419 — *LF: 173 [English tr.].

932a.   To Karl Klindworth

7 Oct 1878. Moscow — in French.

D–MZsch

TGM 7 (2000): 16–17.

933.   To Bogomir Korsov

[7 Oct 1878. Moscow] — in French.

RUS–KL (a³, No. 241).

PSSL 7: 419.

934.   To Nadezhda von Meck

7 Oct 1878. Moscow.

RUS–Mcm (f. 171, No. 103).

PM 1: 452–453 — *PSSL* 7: 420–421 — *TMBF*: 351–352 [English tr.].

935.   To Sergei Taneev

[7 Oct 1878. Moscow].

RUS–Mcl (f. 880).

CTP: 39 — *PSSL* 7: 421.

936.   To Aleksei Sofronov

9 Oct [1878]. [St. Petersburg].

RUS–SPsc (f. 834, No. 25, fol. 14–15).

PSSL 7: 422.

937.   To Tat´iana Davydova

10 Oct [1878]. St. Petersburg.

RUS–SPsc (f. 834, No. 18, fol. 1–2).

PSSL 7: 422–423.

938.   To Nadezhda von Meck

10 Oct 1878. St. Petersburg.

RUS–Mcm (f. 171, No. 104).

*ZC 2: 215–216 — *PM* 1: 454 — *PSSL* 7: 423–424 — *TMBF*: 353 [English tr.].

939.   To Aleksei Sofronov

12 Oct [1878]. St. Petersburg.

RUS–SPsc (f. 834, No. 25, fol. 16–17).

PSSL 7: 425.

940.   To Nadezhda von Meck

14 Oct 1878. St. Petersburg.

RUS–Mcm (f. 171, No. 105).

PM 1: 456–457 — *PSSL* 7: 425–426 — *TMBF*: 355–356 [English tr.].

941. To Aleksei Sofronov

16 [Oct] 1878 (in MS: "16 Dec"). St. Petersburg.

RUS–SPsc (f. 834, No. 25, fol. 20–21).

PSSL 7: 427.

942. To Pëtr Iurgenson

[?16 Oct 1878. St. Petersburg].

RUS–KL (a³, No. 2224).

PIU 1: 49 — *PSSL* 7: 427–428.

943. To Nadezhda von Meck

18 Oct 1878. St. Petersburg.

RUS–Mcm (f. 171, No. 106).

PM 1: 458–459 — *PSSL* 7: 428–429 — *TMBF:* 356–357 [English tr.].

944. To Aleksei Sofronov

[? 18–19 Oct 1878. St. Petersburg].

RUS–SPsc (f. 834, No. 25, fol. 12–13).

PSSL 7: 429.

945. To Nadezhda von Meck

20 Oct 1878. St. Petersburg.

RUS–Mcm (f. 171, No. 107).

PM 1: 459–461 — *PSSL* 7: 430–431 — *TMBF:* 357–359 [English tr.].

946. To Pëtr Iurgenson

20 Oct [1878]. St. Petersburg.

RUS–KL (a³, No. 2212).

PIU 1: 50–51 — *PSSL* 7: 432–433.

947. To Nadezhda von Meck

21 Oct 1878. St. Petersburg.

RUS–Mcm (f. 171, No. 108).

PM 1: 461–462 — *PSSL* 7: 433–434 — *TMBF:* 359–360 [English tr.].

948. To Nadezhda von Meck

24 Oct 1878. St. Petersburg.

RUS–Mcm (f. 171, No. 109).

PM 1: 464–465 — *PSSL* 7: 434–435.

949. To Pëtr Iurgenson

24 Oct [1878]. St. Petersburg.

RUS–KL (a³, No. 2213).

PSSL 7: 436.

950. To Karl Davydov

25 Oct [1878]. [St. Petersburg].

RUS–KL (a³, No. 160).

PSSL 7: 436–437.

951. To Nikolai Rubinshtein

26 Oct [1878]. St. Petersburg.

RUS–Mcm (f. 37, No. 96).

IRM 1: 180 — *PSSL* 7: 437.

952. To Aleksei Sofronov

26 Oct [1878]. St. Petersburg.

RUS–SPsc (f. 834, No. 25, fol. 18–19).

PSSL 7: 437–438.

953. To Pëtr Iurgenson

26 Oct [1878]. St. Petersburg.

RUS–KL (a³, No. 2214).

PSSL 7: 438.

954. To Aleksandra Davydova

27 Oct [1878]. St. Petersburg.

RUS–SPsc (f. 834, No. 17, fol. 68–69).

PR: 451 — *PSSL* 7: 438.

955. To Nadezhda von Meck

27 Oct 1878. St. Petersburg.

RUS–Mcm (f. 171, No. 110).

PM 1: 466 — *PSSL* 7: 439 — *TMBF:* 362–363 [English tr.].

956. To Nadezhda von Meck

30 Oct [1878]. St. Petersburg.

RUS–KL (a³, No. 2888).

PM 1: 467–468 — *PSSL* 7: 440–441 — *TMBF:* 363–364 [English tr.].

957. To Anatolii Chaikovskii

[2 Nov 1878]. Moscow.

RUS–KL (a³, No. 1185).

PR: 451–452 — **PB:* 177–178 — **PSSL* 7: 441–442 — **LF:* 174–175 [English tr.].

958. To Anatolii Chaikovskii

[4 Nov 1878]. Kamenka.

RUS–KL (a³, No. 1186).

PR: 452–453 — **PB*: 178 — *PSSL* 7: 442–443 —
*LF: 175 [English tr.].

959.   To Nadezhda von Meck

6 Nov [1878]. Kamenka.

RUS–KL (a³, No. 2889).

PM 1: 473–478 — *PSSL* 7: 443–448 — **TMBF*: 368–
371 [English tr.].

960.   To Modest Chaikovskii

6 Nov [1878]. Kamenka.

RUS–KL (a³, No. 1511).

PR: 453–454 — **PSSL* 7: 448–449.

961.   To Anatolii Chaikovskii

6 Nov [1878]. Kamenka.

RUS–KL (a³, No. 1187).

PR: 454–456 — *PSSL* 7: 449–450.

962.   To Eduard Nápravník

7 Nov [1878]. Kamenka.

RUS–SPtm (Gik 17195/13).

VP: 120–122 — *EFN*: 103–105 — *PSSL* 7: 451–453.

963.   To Anatolii Chaikovskii

9 Nov [1878]. Kamenka.

RUS–KL (a³, No. 1188).

PR: 456–457 — **PB*: 178–179 — *PSSL* 7: 453–454 —
*LF: 176 [English tr.].

964.   To Pëtr Iurgenson

11 Nov 1878. Kamenka.

RUS–KL (a³, No. 2215).

PIU 1: 52–53 — *PSSL* 7: 455–456.

965.   To Nadezhda von Meck

13 Nov [1878]. Kamenka.

RUS–KL (a³, No. 2890).

PM 1: 478–479 — *PSSL* 7: 455–456.

966.   To Modest Chaikovskii

13 Nov [1878]. Kamenka.

RUS–KL (a³, No. 1512).

PR: 457–458 — **PB*: 179–180 — *PSSL* 457–458 —
*LF: 176–177 [English tr.].

967.   To Anatolii Chaikovskii

14 Nov [1878]. Kamenka.

RUS–KL (a³, No. 1189).

PR: 458–459 — *PSSL* 7: 458–459.

968.   To Pëtr Iurgenson

15 Nov [1878]. Kamenka.

RUS–KL (a³, No. 2216).

PIU 1: 53–54 — *PSSL* 7: 459–460.

969.   To Modest Chaikovskii

18/30 Nov 1878. Vienna.

RUS–KL (a³, No. 1513).

*ZC 2: 218 — **PR*: 459–460 — **PB*: 180–181 —
PSSL 7: 460–461 — **LF*: 177–178 [English tr.].

970.   To Nadezhda von Meck

21 Nov/[3] Dec 1878 (in MS: "2 Dec"). Florence.

RUS–KL (a³, No. 2891).

PM 1: 481–482 — *PSSL* 7: 462–463 — *TMBF*: 373–
374 [English tr.].

971.   To Anatolii Chaikovskii

21 Nov/[3] Dec 1878 (in MS: "2 Dec"). Florence.

RUS–KL (a³, No. 1190).

*ZC 2: 216–219 — *PR*: 461–462 — **PB*: 181–182 —
PSSL 7: 463–464 — **LF*: 178–179 [English tr.].

972.   To Modest Chaikovskii

21 Nov/[3] Dec 1878 (in MS: "2 Dec"). Florence.

RUS–KL (a³, No. 1514).

PR: 462 — **PSSL* 7: 465–466.

973.   To Nadezhda von Meck

21 Nov/[3] Dec 1878 (in MS: "2 Dec"). Florence.

RUS–KL (a³, No. 2892).

*ZC 2: 219–221 — *PM* 1: 483–485 — *PSSL* 7: 466–
468 — **TMBF*: 375–376 [English tr.].

974.   To Nadezhda von Meck

22 Nov/[4] Dec 1878 (in MS: "3 Dec"). Florence.

RUS–KL (a³, No. 2893).

*ZC 2: 221–223 — *PM* 1: 485–487 — *PSSL* 7: 468–
470 — *TMBF*: 3 76–378 [English tr.].

975. To Nadezhda von Meck

[23 Nov/5 Dec 1878. Florence].

RUS–KL (a³, No. 2894).

PM 1: 490–491 — *PSSL* 7: 470–471.

976. To Nadezhda von Meck

[23–24 Nov/5–6 Dec 1878. Florence].

RUS–KL (a³, No. 2895).

PM 1: 491–492 — *PSSL* 7: 471–472.

977. To Nadezhda von Meck

[24 Nov/6 Dec 1878. Florence].

RUS–KL (a³, No. 2896).

PM 1: 495–496 — *PSSL* 7: 473–474 — **TMBF*: 381–382 [English tr.].

978. To Pëtr Iurgenson

24 Nov/6 Dec 1878. Florence.

RUS–KL (a³, No. 2217).

*ZC 2: 223–224 — *PIU* 1: 55–56 — *PSSL* 7: 475–476.

979. To Aleksandra Davydova

25 Nov/7 Dec 1878 [Florence].

RUS–SPsc (f. 834, No. 17, fol. 70–71).

PR: 464–465 — *PSSL* 7: 476–477.

980. To Nadezhda von Meck

[25 Nov/7 Dec 1878]. Florence.

RUS–KL (a³, No. 2897).

PM 1: 495–497 — *PSSL* 7: 477–478 — **TMBF*: 382 [English tr.].

981. To Anatolii Chaikovskii

25 Nov/5 Dec 1878 (in MS: "23 Nov/5 Dec"). Florence.

RUS–KL (a³, No. 1191).

PR: 463–464 — **PB*: 182 — *PSSL* 7: 478–479 — **LF*: 179 [English tr.].

982. To Nadezhda von Meck

26 Nov/[8] Dec 1878 (in MS: "7 Dec") [Florence].

RUS–KL (a³, No. 2898).

PM 1: 500–501 — *PSSL* 7: 480–481.

983. To Nadezhda von Meck

[26 Nov/8 Dec 1878. Florence].

RUS–KL (a³, No. 2899).

PM 1: 499 — *PSSL* 7: 481 — *TMBF*: 384 [English tr.].

984. To Nadezhda von Meck

[26 Nov/8 Dec 1878. Florence].

RUS–KL (a³, No. 2900).

PM 1: 498 — *PSSL* 7: 482 — *TMBF*: 384 [English tr.].

985. To Nadezhda von Meck

[26 Nov/8 Dec 1878. Florence].

RUS–KL (a³, No. 2901).

PM 1: 499–500 — *PSSL* 7: 482–483 — *TMBF*: 384–385 [English tr.].

986. To Modest Chaikovskii

27 Nov/9 Dec 1878. Florence.

RUS–KL (a³, No. 1515).

PR: 465–466 — **PB*: 183 — **PSSL* 7: 484–485 — **LF*: 180 [English tr.].

987. To Nadezhda von Meck

[27–28 Nov/9–10 Dec 1878. Florence].

RUS–KL (a³, No. 2902).

*ZC 2: 227–230 — *PM* 1: 501–504 — *PSSL* 7: 485–488 — *TMBF*: 386–389 [English tr.].

988. To Nadezhda von Meck

28 Nov/10 Dec 1878 [Florence].

RUS–KL (a³, No. 2903).

PM 1: 508–509 — *PSSL* 7: 489–490 — **TMBF*: 390–391 [English tr.].

989. To Nadezhda von Meck

[29 Nov/11 Dec 1878. Florence].

RUS–KL (a³, No. 2904).

PM 1: 510 — *PSSL* 7: 490–491 — *TMBF*: 392–393 [English tr.].

990. To Karl Al´brekht

29 Nov/[10] Dec 1878. Florence.

RUS–Mt (Al´brekht coll.).

CMS: 280–281 — *PSSL* 7: 491–492.

991. To Anatolii Chaikovskii

29 Nov/11 Dec 1878. Florence.

RUS–KL (a[3], No. 1192).

PR: 467 — *PB*: 183–184 — *PSSL* 7: 492–493 — **LF*: 181 [English tr.].

992.   To Nadezhda von Meck

29 Nov/11 Dec 1878 [Florence].

RUS–KL (a[3], No. 2905).

*ZC 2: 231 — *PM* 1: 511–512 — *PSSL* 7: 493–495 — **TMBF*: 393 [English tr.].

993.   To Modest Chaikovskii

30 Nov/12 Dec 1878 [Florence].

RUS–KL (a[3], No. 1516).

PR: 468–469 — **PB*: 601 — *PSSL* 7: 495–496 — *TMBF*: 395 [English tr.].

994.   To Nadezhda von Meck

30 Nov/12 Dec [–1/12 Dec] 1878 [Florence].

RUS–KL (a[3], No. 2906).

PM 1: 515–517 — *PSSL* 7: 497–499 — **TMBF*: 395–396 [English tr.].

995.   To Nadezhda von Meck

1/13[–2/14] Dec 1878 [Florence].

RUS–KL (a[3], No. 2907).

PM 1: 519 — *PSSL* 7: 499–500 — **TMBF*: 397–398 [English tr.].

996.   To Nadezhda von Meck

[2/14 Dec 1878. Florence].

RUS–KL (a[3], No. 2913).

PM 1: 523 — *PSSL* 7: 500.

997.   To Nadezhda von Meck

2/14 Dec 1878 [Florence].

RUS–KL (a[3], No. 2908).

*ZC 2: 234–235 — *PM* 1: 520–523 — *PSSL* 7: 500–502 — **TMBF*: 398–399 [English tr.].

998.   To Anatolii Chaikovskii

[2/14 Dec 1878]. Florence.

RUS–KL (a[3], No. 1194).

PR: 469 — *PB*: 184–185 — *PSSL* 7: 503–504 — *LF*: 181–182 [English tr.].

999.   To Karl Al´brekht

3/15 [Dec 1878]. Florence.

RUS–Mcm (f. 37, No. 33).

PSSL 7: 504–505.

1000.   To Nadezhda von Meck

3/15 Dec [1878]. [Florence].

RUS–KL (a[3], No. 2909).

PM 1: 524–525 — *PSSL* 7: 505–506 — **TMBF*: 400–401 [English tr.].

1001.   To Anatolii Chaikovskii

3/15 Dec [1878]. Florence.

RUS–KL (a[3], No. 1193).

PR: 469–470 — *PSSL* 7: 507.

1002.   To Pëtr Iurgenson

3/15 [Dec 1878]. Florence.

RUS–KL (a[3], No. 2218).

PIU 1: 59 — *PSSL* 7: 508–509.

1003.   To Nadezhda von Meck

[4/16 Dec 1878]. Florence

RUS–KL (a[3], No. 2910).

*ZC 2: 235–236 — *PM* 1: 525–527 — *PSSL* 7: 509–510 — **TMBF*: 401–4029 [English tr.].

1004.   To Modest Chaikovskii

4/16 Dec [1878]. Florence.

RUS–KL (a[3], No. 1517).

*PR: 470–471 — **PB*: 185–186 — **PSSL* 7: 511–512 — **LF*: 182 [English tr.].

1005.   To Nadezhda von Meck

5/17 Dec 1878 [Florence].

RUS–KL (a[3], No. 2911).

*ZC 2: 236–238 — *PM* 1: 530–532 — *PSSL* 7: 512–514 — **TMBF*: 403–405 [English tr.].

1006.   To Anatolii Chaikovskii

[5/17 Dec 1878]. Florence.

RUS–KL (a[3], No. 1195).

PR: 471–473 — *PB*: 186–187 — *PSSL* 7: 515–516 — *LF*: 183–184 [English tr.].

1007.   To Nadezhda von Meck

6/18 Dec [1878]. [Florence].

RUS–KL (a[3], No. 2912).

PM 1: 533–535 — *PSSL* 7: 517–518 — **TMBF*: 405–406 [English tr.].

1008. To Modest Chaikovskii

6/18 Dec [1878]. Florence.

RUS–KL (a³, No. 1518).

PR: 473–474 — *PSSL* 7: 519–520.

1009. To Nadezhda von Meck

[7/19–8/20 Dec 1878. Florence].

RUS–KL (a³, No. 2914).

PM 1: 537 — *PSSL* 7: 520.

1010. To Nadezhda von Meck

8/20 Dec 1878 [Florence].

RUS–KL (a³, No. 2915).

*ZC 2: 238–239 — *PM* 1: 537–538 — *PSSL* 7: 520–521 — **TMBF:* 408–409 [English tr.].

1011. To Anatolii Chaikovskii

8/20 Dec 1878. Florence.

RUS–KL (a³, No. 1196).

PR: 474 — *PSSL* 7: 522–523.

1012. To Nadezhda von Meck

[10/22 Dec 1878. Florence].

RUS–KL (a³, No. 2916).

PM 1: 539–540 — *PSSL* 7: 523–524 — **TMBF:* 410–411 [English tr.].

1013. To Modest Chaikovskii

10/22 Dec 1878. Florence.

RUS–KL (a³, No. 1519).

*ZC 2: 239–240 — *PR*: 476–477 — **PB*: 187–188 — *PSSL* 7: 525–526 — **LF*: 184–185 [English tr.].

1014. To Pëtr Iurgenson

10/22 Dec 1878. Florence,

RUS–KL (a³, No. 2219).

PIU 1: 59–61 — *PSSL* 7: 526–528.

1015. To Nadezhda von Meck

11/23 Dec 1878 [Florence].

RUS–KL (a³, No. 2917).

PM 1: 541 — *PSSL* 7: 528–529.

1016. To Anatolii Chaikovskii

11/23 Dec 1878. Florence.

RUS–KL (a³, No. 1197).

PR: 477–478 — *PB*: 188–189 — **PSSL* 7: 529–530 — *LF*: 185–186 [English tr.].

1017. To Lev Davydov

12/24 Dec 1878. Florence.

RUS–SPsc (f. 834, No. 19, fol. 13–15).

PR: 478–479 — **PB*: 189–190 — *PSSL* 7: 531–532 — **LF*: 186–187 [English tr.].

1018. To Nadezhda von Meck

12/24 Dec 1878. Florence.

RUS–KL (a³, No. 2919).

PM 1: 542–543 — *PSSL* 7: 533–534 — **TMBF:* 411–412 [English tr.].

1019. To Modest Chaikovskii

12/24 Dec 1878. Florence.

RUS–KL (a³, No. 1520).

PR: 480 — *PSSL* 7: 534–535.

1020. To Nadezhda von Meck

13/25 Dec 1878 [Florence].

RUS–KL (a³, No. 2920).

*ZC 2: 240–241 — *PM* 1: 545–547 — *PSSL* 7: 535–538 — **TMBF:* 413–414 [English tr.].

1021. To Nadezhda von Meck

14/26 Dec 1878 [Florence].

RUS–KL (a³, No. 2860).

PM 1: 547–548 — *PSSL* 7: 538–539 — **TMBF:* 414–415 [English tr.].

1022. To Anatolii Chaikovskii

14/26 Dec 1878. Florence.

RUS–KL (a³, No. 1198).

PR: 481–482 —*PSSL* 7: 539–540.

1023. To Modest Chaikovskii

15/27 Dec 1878 [Florence].

RUS–KL (a³, No. 1521 & a², No. 29).

*ZC 2: 241–246 — *PR*: 482–485 — *PB*: 190–193 — *PSSL* 7: 541–543 — *LF*: 187–189 [English tr.].

1024. To Nadezhda von Meck

15/27–16/28 Dec 1878 [Florence].

RUS–KL (a³, No. 2861).

PM 1: 549–550 — *PSSL* 7: 543–545 — **TMBF:* 416– 417 [English tr.].

1025.   To Anatolii Chaikovskii
16/28 Dec 1878. Florence.
RUS–KL (a³, No. 1199).
PR: 485–486 — *PSSL* 7: 545–546.

1026.   To Nadezhda von Meck
18/30 Dec 1878. Paris.
RUS–KL (a³, No. 2862).
PM 1: 550–552 — *PSSL* 7: 546–547.

1027.   To Modest Chaikovskii
18/30 Dec 1878. Paris.
RUS–KL (a³, No. 1522).
PR: 486–487 — *PB*: 193–194 — *PSSL* 7: 548–549 —
   LF: 189–190 [English tr.].

1028.   To Pëtr Iurgenson
18/30 Dec 1878. Paris.
RUS–KL (a³, No. 2220).
PIU 1: 63–64 — *PSSL* 7: 549–550.

1029.   To Anatolii Chaikovskii
19/31 Dec 1878. Paris.
RUS–KL (a³, No. 1200).
PR: 487–488 — *PSSL* 7: 550–551.

1030.   To Karl Al´brekht
20 Dec 1878/1 Jan 1879. Paris.
RUS–Mcm (f. 37, No. 34).
CMS: 282 — *PSSL* 7: 551–552.

1031.   To Pëtr Iurgenson
20 Dec 1878/1 Jan 1879. Paris.
RUS–KL (a³, No. 2221).
PIU 1: 64–65 — *PSSL* 7: 552–554.

1032.   To Anatolii Chaikovskii
21 Dec 1878/2 Jan 1879. Paris.
RUS–KL (a³, No. 1201).
PR: 488–490 — *PSSL* 7: 554–556.

1033.   To Nadezhda von Meck
21 Dec 1878/2 Jan 1879. Paris.
RUS–KL (a³, No. 2863).
PM 1: 552–553 — *PSSL* 7: 556–557 — *TMBF*: 417–
   418 [English tr.].

1034.   To Nadezhda von Meck
22 Dec 1878/3 Jan 1879. Paris.
RUS–KL (a³, No. 2864).
PM 1: 553–554 — *PSSL* 7: 557–558 — *TMBF*:
   416–419 [English tr.].

1035.   To Modest Chaikovskii
22 Dec 1878/3 Jan 1879. Paris.
RUS–KL (a³, No. 1523).
PR: 490–492 — *PB*: 194 — *PSSL* 7: 559–561 —
   LF: 190–191 [English tr.].

1036.   To Anatolii Chaikovskii
23 Dec 1878/4 Jan 1879. Paris.
RUS–KL (a³, No. 1202).
PR: 493–494 — *PSSL* 7: 562–563.

1037.   To Nadezhda von Meck
24 Dec 1878/5 Jan 1879. Paris.
RUS–KL (a³, No. 2865).
ZC 1: 246–247 — *PM* 1: 558–559 — *PSSL* 7: 564–
   565 — *TMBF*: 420–421 [English tr.].

1038.   To Nadezhda von Meck
26 Dec 1878/7 Jan 1879. Paris.
RUS–KL (a³, No. 2866).
PM 1: 559–560 — *PSSL* 7: 565–566 — *TMBF*: 421
   [English tr.].

1039.   To Anatolii Chaikovskii
26 Dec 1878/7 Jan 1879. Paris.
RUS–KL (a³, No. 1203).
PR: 496 — *PSSL* 7: 567.

1040.   To Modest Chaikovskii
26 Dec 1878/7 Jan 1879. Paris
RUS–KL (a³, No. 1524).
PR: 495–496 — *PB*: 195 — *PSSL* 7: 567–568 —
   LF: 191 [English tr.].

1041.   To Nadezhda von Meck
[28 Dec 1878/9 Jan 1879] (in MS: "29 Dec/10 Jan").
Dijon.
RUS–KL (a³, No. 2867).
ZC 2: 561–562 — *PM* 1: 561–562 — *PSSL* 7:
   569 — *TMBF*: 421–422 [English tr.].

1042. To Anatolii Chaikovskii

[28 Dec 1878/9 Jan 1879]. Dijon.

RUS–KL (a³, No. 1204).

PR: 496–497 — *PB*: 195–196 — *PSSL* 7: 570–571 — **LF*: 191–192 [English tr.].

1043. To Modest Chaikovskii

29 Dec 1878/10 Jan 1879. Dijon.

RUS–KL (a³, No. 1525).

*ZC 2: 248–249 — *PR*: 498 — **PB*: 197 — *PSSL* 7: 571–572 — **LF*: 193 [English tr.].

1044. To Pëtr Iurgenson

29 Dec 1878/10 Jan 1879. Dijon.

RUS–KL (a³, No. 2222).

PIU 1: 67–68 — *PSSL* 7: 572–573.

1045. To Nadezhda von Meck

30 Dec 1878/11 Jan 1879. Clarens.

RUS–KL (a³, No. 2868).

PM 1: 562–563 — *PSSL* 7: 573–574 — **TMBF*: 422–423 [English tr.].

1046. To Anatolii Chaikovskii

30 Dec 1878/11 Jan 1879. Clarens.

RUS–KL (a³, No. 1205).

PR: 499 — *PSSL* 7: 575.

1047. To Modest Chaikovskii

30 Dec 1878/11 Jan 1879. Clarens.

RUS–KL (a³, No. 1526).

PR: 499–500 — *PB*: 197–198 — *PSSL* 7: 576 — *LF*: 194 [English tr.].

1048. To Pëtr Iurgenson

30 Dec 1878/11 Jan 1879. Clarens.

RUS–KL (a³, No. 2223).

PIU 1: 68 — *PSSL* 7: 577.

1049. To Nadezhda von Meck

31 Dec 1878/12 Jan 1879 . Clarens.

RUS–KL (a³, No. 2869).

*ZC 2: 250 — *PM* 1: 563–564 — *PSSL* 7: 578–579 — *TMBF*: 423–424 [English tr.].

1879

1050. To Anatolii Chaikovskii

1/13 Jan 1879. Clarens.

RUS–KL (a³, No. 1207).

*ZC 2: 250–251 — *PR*: 501–502 — **PB*: 195 — *PSSL* 8: 15–16 — **LF*: 194–195 [English tr.].

1051. To Modest Chaikovskii

2/14 Jan 1879. Clarens.

RUS–KL (a³, No. 1527).

*PR: 502–503 — **PB*: 199 — **PSSL* 8: 12 — **LF*: 195–196 [English tr.].

1052. To Nikolai Konradi

2/14 Jan 1879. Clarens.

Autograph lost; MS copy in RUS–KL.

CTP: 259–260 — *PSSL* 8: 18.

1053. To Pëtr Iurgenson

2/14 Jan 1879. Clarens.

RUS–KL (a³, No. 2226).

PSSL 8: 19.

1054. To Nadezhda von Meck

3/15 Jan 1879. Clarens.

RUS–KL (a³, No. 498).

PM 2: 14–15 — *PSSL* 8: 19–20.

1055. To Pëtr Iurgenson

3/15 Jan 1879. Clarens.

RUS–KL (a³, No. 2227).

PIU 1: 71–72 — *PSSL* 8: 21–22.

1056. To Sergei Taneev

4/16 Jan 1879. Clarens.

RUS–Mcl (f. 880).

PT: 34–35 — *CTP* 40–41 — *PSSL* 8: 22–23.

1057. To Anatolii Chaikovskii

4/16 Jan 1879. Clarens.

RUS–KL (a³, No. 1208).

*PR: 503–504 — **PB*: 200–201 — **PSSL* 8: 24–25 — **LF*: 196–197 [English tr.].

1058.   To Nadezhda von Meck

5/17 Jan 1879. Clarens.

RUS–KL (a³, No. 499).

*ZC 2: 251 — PM 2: 15–17 — PSSL 8: 25–27.

1059.   To Modest Chaikovskii

6/18 Jan 1879. Clarens.

RUS–KL (a³, No. 1528).

*PR: 504–506 — *PB: 201–202 — *PSSL 8: 27–28 —
    *LF: 197–198 [English tr.].

1060.   To Natal´ia Pleskaia

6/18 Jan 1879. Clarens.

RUS–Mcl (f. 905).

CTP: 362 — PSSL 8: 28–29.

1061.   To Pëtr Iurgenson

7/19 Jan 1879. Clarens.

RUS–KL (a³, No. 2228).

*PIU 1: 72–73 — *PSSL 8: 29–30.

1062.   To Anatolii Chaikovskii

7/19–8/20 Jan 1879. Clarens.

RUS–KL (a³, No. 1209).

PR: 506–507 — *PB: 203–204 — PSSL 8: 31–32 —
    *LF: 198–199 [English tr.].

1063.   To Nadezhda von Meck

8/20 Jan 1879. Clarens.

RUS–KL (a³, No. 500).

*ZC 2: 251–252 — PM 2: 19–20 — PSSL 8: 32–33.

1064.   To Anatolii Chaikovskii

9/21 Jan 1879. Clarens.

RUS–KL (a³, No. 1210).

*PR: 507–509 — *PB: 204–205 — *PSSL 8: 34–35 —
    *ZN: 122 — *LF: 199–200 [English tr.] — TW:
    87–88 [English tr.].

1065.   To Nadezhda von Meck

10/22 Jan 1879. Clarens.

RUS–KL (a³, No. 501).

PM 2: 20–24 — PSSL 8: 35–38.

1066.   To Modest Chaikovskii

10/22–11/23 Jan 1879. Clarens.

RUS–KL (a³, No. 1529).

*ZC 2: 252 — *PR: 509–510 — *PB: 205–206 —
    PSSL 8: 39–40 — *LF: 200–201 [English tr.].

1067.   To Nadezhda von Meck

13/25 Jan 1879. Clarens.

RUS–KL (a³, No. 502).

PM 2: 23–26 — PSSL 8: 40–42.

1068.   To Anatolii Chaikovskii

14/26 Jan 1879. Clarens.

RUS–KL (a³, No. 1211).

ZC 2: 252–253 — PR: 510–512 — PB: 206–207 —
    PSSL 8: 42–43 — *LF: 201–202 [English tr.].

1069.   To Pëtr Iurgenson

14/26 Jan 1879. Clarens.

RUS–KL (a³, No. 2229).

ZC 2: 253–254 — PIU 1: 74–75 — PSSL 8: 44–45.

1070.   To Nadezhda von Meck

15/27 Jan 1879. Clarens.

RUS–KL (a³, No. 503).

*ZC 2: 234–235 — PM 2: 28–30 — PSSL 8: 45–47.

1071.   To Modest Chaikovskii

[17/29] Jan 1879 (in MS: "16/28"). Clarens.

RUS–KL (a³, No. 1533).

*PR: 512 — *PB: 207–208 — *PSSL 8: 47–48 —
    *LF: 203 [English tr.].

1072.   To Vladimir Stasov

18/30 Jan 1879. Clarens.

RUS–SPsc (f. 738, No. 343, fol. 31–35).

RM (1909), 3: 129–132 — PSSL 8: 48–51.

1073.   To Nadezhda von Meck

18/30 Jan 1879. Clarens.

RUS–KL (a³, No. 504).

*ZC 2: 255–256 — PM 2: 30–32 — PSSL 8: 51–53.

1074.   To Anatolii Chaikovskii.

19/31 Jan 1879. Clarens

RUS–KL (a³, No. 1212).

*PR: 513–514 — *PB: 208–209 — *PSSL 8: 53–
    55 — *LF: 203–204 [English tr.].

1075. To Pëtr Iurgenson

19/31 Jan 1879. Clarens.

RUS–KL (a³, No. 2230).

*PIU 1: 76–77 — *PSSL 8: 55–56.

1076. To Nadezhda von Meck

20 Jan/1 Feb 1879. Clarens.

RUS–KL (a³, No. 505).

*ZC 2: 257 — PM 2: 32–34 — PSSL 8: 56–59.

1077. To Modest Chaikovskii

20 Jan/1 Feb 1879. Clarens.

RUS–KL (a³, No. 1530).

*ZC 2: 311–314 — PR: 514–518 — *PB: 209–212 —
    *PSSL 8: 59–62 — *LF: 204–207 [English tr.].

1078. To Aleksandra Davydova

21 Jan/2 Feb 1879. Clarens.

RUS–SPsc (f. 834, No. 17, fol. 72–73).

PR: 518–519 — PSSL 8: 63–64.

1079. To Anatolii Chaikovskii

22 Jan/3 Feb 1879. Clarens.

RUS–KL (a³, No. 1213).

*PR: 519–520 — *PSSL 8: 64–65.

1080. To Nadezhda von Meck

23 Jan/4 Feb 1879. Clarens.

RUS–KL (a³, No. 506).

*ZC 2: 257–259 — PM 2: 35–37 — PSSL 8: 65–67.

1081. To Modest Chaikovskii

24 Jan/5 Feb 1879. Clarens.

RUS–KL (a³, No. 1531).

*ZC 2: 259–260 — PR: 520–521 — PB: 212–213 —
    PSSL 8: 68–69 — LF: 207–208 [English tr.].

1082. To Nadezhda von Meck

25 Jan/6 Feb 1879. Clarens.

RUS–KL (a³, No. 507).

*ZC 2: 260 — PM 2: 37–39 — PSSL 8: 69–70.

1083. To Nadezhda von Meck

26 Jan/7 Feb 1879. Clarens.

RUS–KL (a³, No. 508).

PM 2: 39–40 — PSSL 8: 71–72.

1084. To Anatolii Chaikovskii

26 Jan/7 Feb 1879. Clarens.

RUS–KL (a³, No. 1214).

*PR: 522 — *PB: 213–214 — *PSSL 8: 72–73 —
    *LF: 208 [English tr.].

1085. To Modest Chaikovskii

27 Jan/8 Feb 1879. Clarens.

RUS–KL (a³, No. 1532).

*ZC 2: 260–261 — PR: 523–524 — *PB: 214–215 —
    *PSSL 8: 73–75 — *LF: 209 [English tr.].

1086. To Pëtr Iurgenson

27 Jan/8 Feb 1879. Clarens.

RUS–KL (a³, No. 2231).

*ZC 2: 262–261 ("2 Jan ") — PIU 1: 77–78 — PSSL
    8: 75–76.

1087. To Vladimir Stasov

29 Jan/10 Feb 1879. Clarens.

RUS–SPsc (f. 738, No. 343, fol. 36–39).

RM (1909), 3: 134–137 — PSSL 8: 77–79.

1088. To Anatolii Chaikovskii

29 Jan/10 Feb 1879. Clarens.

RUS–KL (a³, No. 1215).

PR: 524–526 — *PB: 216 — PSSL 8: 80–81 — *LF:
    210 [English tr.].

1089. To Nadezhda von Meck

30 Jan/11 Feb 1879. Clarens.

RUS–KL (a³, No. 509).

PM 2: 40–41 — PSSL 8: 82–83.

1090. To Modest Chaikovskii

31 Jan/12 Feb 1879. Clarens.

RUS–KL (a³, No. 1534).

*PR: 526–527 — *PSSL 8: 83–84.

1091. To Pëtr Iurgenson

1/13 Feb 1879. Clarens.

RUS–KL (a³, No. 2232).

PIU 1: 79–80 — PSSL 8: 84–85.

1092. To Nadezhda von Meck

[3]/15 Feb 1879 (in MS: "2/15 Feb"). Clarens.

RUS–KL (a³, No. 510).

*ZC 2: 262 — *PM* 2: 42–43 ("2/15 Feb") — *PSSL* 8: 85–87.

1093. To Anatolii Chaikovskii
[3/15] Feb 1879 (in MS: "2/15 Feb"). Clarens.
RUS–KL (a³, No. 1216).
PR: 527–528 — *PSSL* 8: 87–88.

1094. To Nadezhda von Meck
4/16 Feb 1879. Clarens.
RUS–KL (a³, No. 511).
PM 2: 43–44 — *PSSL* 8: 88–89.

1095. To Modest Chaikovskii
4/16 Feb 1879. Clarens
RUS–KL (a³, No. 1535).
PR: 528–529 — **PSSL* 8: 89–90.

1096. To Nadezhda von Meck
[6/18 Feb 1879]. Paris.
RUS–KL (a³, No. 512).
PM 2: 44–45 — *PSSL* 8: 90–91.

1097. To Anatolii Chaikovskii
6/18 Feb 1879. Paris.
RUS–KL (a³, No. 1217).
PR: 529–530 — *PSSL* 8: 91–92.

1098. To Pëtr Iurgenson
6/18 Feb 1879. Paris.
RUS–KL (a³, No. 2233).
*ZC 2: 263 — *PIU* 1: 80–81 — *PSSL* 8: 93–94.

1099. To Nadezhda von Meck
7/19 Feb 1879. Paris.
RUS–KL (a³, No. 513).
PM 2: 46–48 — *PSSL* 8: 94–96.

1100. To Modest Chaikovskii
7/19 Feb 1879. Paris.
RUS–KL (a³, No. 1536).
PR: 530–532 — **PB*: 217 — *PSSL* 8: 96–98 — **LF*: 210–211 [English tr.].

1101. To Nadezhda von Meck
8/20 Feb 1879. Paris.

RUS–KL (a³, No. 514).
PM 2: 49 — *PSSL* 8: 98.

1102. To Anatolii Chaikovskii
8/20 Feb 1879. Paris.
RUS–KL (a³, No. 1218).
PR: 532–533 — **PB*: 217–218 — *PSSL* 8: 98–99 — **LF*: 211–212 [English tr.].

1103. To Nadezhda von Meck
10/22 Feb [1879]. Paris.
RUS–KL (a³, No. 515).
*ZC 2: 264 — *PM* 2: 49–51 — *PSSL* 8: 100–101.

1104. To Modest Chaikovskii
10/22 Feb 1879. Paris.
RUS–KL (a³, No. 1538).
*ZC 2: 263–264 — *PR*: 534–535 — *PB*: 218–219 — *PSSL* 8: 102–103 — **LF*: 212–213 [English tr.].

1105. To Anatolii Chaikovskii
12/24 Feb 1879. Paris.
RUS–KL (a³, No. 1219).
PR: 535–536 — **PB*: 219–220 — *PSSL* 8: 103–104 — **LF*: 213–214 [English tr.].

1106. To Nadezhda von Meck
12/24–13/25 Feb [1879]. Paris.
RUS–KL (a³, nos. 516–517).
*ZC 2: 266 — *PM* 2: 52–53 — *PSSL* 8: 105–107.

1107. To Modest Chaikovskii
13/25 Feb 1879. Paris.
RUS–KL (a³, No. 1537).
**PR*: 536–537 — **PB*: 220–221 — **PSSL* 8: 108–109 — **LF*: 214–215 [English tr.].

1108. To Pëtr Iurgenson
13/25 Feb 1879. Paris.
RUS–KL (a³, No. 2234).
*ZC 2: 264–265 — *PIU* 1: 83–84 — *PSSL* 8: 109–110.

1109. To Aleksandra Davydova
15/27 Feb 1879. Paris.
RUS–SPsc (f. 834, No. 17, fol. 74–75).

PR: 537–539 — **PB*: 221–222 — *PSSL* 8: 111–112 —
*LF: 215 [English tr.].

1110.   To Anatolii Chaikovskii

15/27 Feb 1879. Paris.

RUS–KL (a³, No. 1220).

*PR: 539–541 — **PB*: 222–223 — **PSSL* 8: 112–
114 — **LF*: 216–217 [English tr.].

1111.   To Nadezhda von Meck

16/28–17/29 Feb 1879. Paris.

RUS–KL (a³, No. 521).

PM 2: 56–60 — *PSSL* 8: 114–118.

1112.   To Modest Chaikovskii

17 Feb/1 Mar 1879. Paris.

RUS–KL (a³, No. 1539).

*ZC 2: 266 — **PR*: 541 — **PB*: 223–224 — **PSSL* 8:
118–119 — **LF*: 217 [English tr.].

1113.   To Pëtr Iurgenson

[18 Feb/2 Mar 1879]. Paris.

RUS–KL (a³, No. 2235).

PSSL 8: 119.

1114.   To Pëtr Iurgenson

18 Feb/2 Mar 1879. Paris.

RUS–KL (a³, No. 2236).

PIU 1: 84–85 — *PSSL* 8: 119–120.

1115.   To Nadezhda von Meck

19–20 Feb/3–4 Mar 1879. Paris.

RUS–KL (a³, No. 522).

*ZC 2: 266–269 — *PM* 2: 62–66 — *PSSL* 8: 121–125.

1116.   To Anatolii Chaikovskii

[20] Feb/4 Mar 1879 (in MS: "21 Feb"). Paris.

RUS–KL (a³, No. 1221).

PR: 541–542 — **PB*: 224–225 — **PSSL* 8: 126 —
*LF: 217–218 [English tr.].

1117.   To Lev Davydov

22 Feb/6 Mar [1879]. Paris.

RUS–SPsc (f. 834, No. 19, fol. 16–18).

PR: 543–545 — *PSSL* 8: 127–128.

1118.   To Modest Chaikovskii

22 Feb/6 Mar [1879]. Paris.

RUS–KL (a³, No. 1540).

*ZC 2: 269–270 — **PR*: 542–543 — **PB*: 225–
226 — **PSSL* 8: 129–130 — **LF*: 219–220
[English tr.].

1119.   To Nadezhda von Meck

24 Feb/8 Mar 1879. Paris.

RUS–KL (a³, No. 518).

*ZC 2: 270–271 — *PM* 2: 66–68 — *PSSL* 8: 130–
132.

1120.   To Anatolii Chaikovskii

24 Feb/8 Mar 1879. Paris.

RUS–KL (a³, No. 1222).

PR: 545–547 — **PB*: 226–227 — *PSSL* 8: 132–
134 — **LF*: 219–220 [English tr.].

1121.   To Nadezhda von Meck

25 Feb/9 Mar 1879. Paris.

RUS–KL (a³, No. 523).

PM 2: 70–71 — *PSSL* 8: 134–135.

1122.   To the editor of *La Gazette Musicale*

[25 Feb/9 Mar 1879. Paris] — in French.

Autograph lost

La Gazette Musicale (16 Mar 1879) — *ZC* 2: 272 —
PSSL 8: 136.

1123.   To Pëtr Iurgenson

25 Feb/9 Mar 1879. Paris.

RUS–KL (a³, No. 2237).

PIU 1: 86–87 — *PSSL* 8: 137.

1124.   To Modest Chaikovskii

26 Feb/10 Mar 1879. Paris.

RUS–KL (a³, No. 1541).

*ZC 2: 271–272 — **PR*: 547–549 — **PB*: 227–
228 — **PSSL* 8: 138–139 — *ZN*: 132–134 —
*LF: 221–222 [English tr.]— *TW*: 88–91 [English
tr.].

1125.   To Pëtr Iurgenson

26 Feb/10 Mar 1879. Paris.

RUS–KL (a³, No. 2238).

*ZC 2: 275 — *PIU* 1: 87–88 — *PSSL* 8: 149–150.

1126.   To Nadezhda von Meck
[26 Feb/10 Mar 1879. Paris].
RUS–KL (a³, No. 596).
PM 2: 71 — *PSSL* 8: 141.

1127.   To Nadezhda von Meck
27 Feb/11 Mar 1879. Paris.
RUS–KL (a³, No. 519).
*ZC 2: 275–276 — *PM* 2: 71–73 — *PSSL* 8: 141–143.

1128.   To Pëtr Iurgenson
27 Feb/11 Mar 1879. Paris.
RUS–KL (a³, No. 2239).
ZC 2: 276 — *PIU* 1: 88 — *PSSL* 8: 143.

1129.   To Nadezhda von Meck
[28 Feb/12 Mar 1879. Paris].
RUS–KL (a³, No. 520).
PM 2: 74–75 — *PSSL* 8: 144.

1130.   To Anatolii Chaikovskii
28 Feb/12 Mar 1879. Paris.
RUS–KL (a³, No. 1223).
*PR: 549–550 — **PB*: 229 — **PSSL* 8: 144–145 —
      *LF: 222–223 [English tr.].

1131.   To Nadezhda von Meck
4/16 Mar 1879. Berlin.
RUS–KL (a³, No. 524).
PM 2: 73–78 — *PSSL* 8: 145–148.

1132.   To Nadezhda von Meck
6/18 Mar 1879. Berlin.
RUS–KL (a³, No. 525).
PM 2: 78–79 — *PSSL* 8: 148–149.

1133.   To Nadezhda von Meck
7/19 Mar 1879. Berlin.
RUS–KL (a³, No. 526).
PM 2: 80–81 — *PSSL* 8: 150–151.

1134.   To Pëtr Iurgenson
10 Mar [1879]. St. Petersburg.
RUS–KL (a³, No. 2287).
PIU 1: 141–142 ("10 Mar 1880") — *PSSL* 8: 151–
      152.

1135.   To Lev Davydov
12 M[ar 1879]. St. Petersburg.
RUS–SPsc (f. 834, No. 19, fol. 19–20).
PR: 550–551 — *PSSL* 8: 152–153.

1136.   To Nadezhda von Meck
13–22 Mar 1879. St. Petersburg.
RUS–KL (a³, nos. 527, 530).
*ZC 2: 278–280 — *PM* 2: 81–86 — *PSSL* 8: 153–
      157.

1137.   To Lidiia Kol´s
[?16–17 Mar 1879. Moscow].
RUS–KL (a³, No. 227).
PSSL 8: 157–158.

1138.   To Ekaterina Peresleni
20 Mar 1879. St. Petersburg.
RUS–KL (a³, No. 294).
PSSL 8: 158–159.

1139.   To Nadezhda von Meck
[24 Mar 1879. St. Petersburg].
RUS–KL (a³, No. 528).
PM 2: 85 ("20–21(?) Mar") — *PSSL* 8: 159.

1140.   To Nadezhda von Meck
[24 Mar 1879. St. Petersburg].
RUS–KL (a³, No. 531).
PM 2: 86–87 — *PSSL* 8: 159–161.

1141.   To Pëtr Iurgenson
[25 Mar 1879]. St. Petersburg.
RUS–KL (a³, No. 2240).
PSSL 8: 161.

1142.   To Nadezhda von Meck
[25–26 Mar 1879. St. Petersburg].
RUS–KL (a³, No. 529).
PM 2: 85 ("20–21(?) Mar") — *PSSL* 8: 161.

1143.   To Eduard Nápravník
29 Mar [1879]. [St. Petersburg].
RUS–SPtm (Gik 17195/15).
VP: 123 — *EFN*: 106 ("20 Mar") — *PSSL* 8: 162.

1144. To Pëtr Iurgenson

29 Mar [1879]. [St. Petersburg].

RUS–KL (a³, No. 2241).

PSSL 8: 162–163.

1145. To Nadezhda von Meck

31 Mar [1879]. [St. Petersburg].

RUS–KL (a³, No. 532).

PM 2: 88–89 — *PSSL* 8: 163–164.

1146. To Nadezhda von Meck

3 Apr 1879 [Moscow].

RUS–KL (a³, No. 533).

PM 2: 89–90 — *PSSL* 8: 164–165.

1147. To Anatolii Chaikovskii

4 Apr [1879]. [Moscow].

RUS–KL (a³, No. 1224).

PR: 551 — *PSSL* 8: 165.

1148. To Nadezhda von Meck

6 Apr [1879]. Moscow.

RUS–KL (a³, No. 534).

PM 2: 90 — *PSSL* 8: 165–166.

1149. To Aleksei Sofronov

[6 Apr 1879. Moscow] — written on the back of a
   letter dated 4 Apr 1879 from Nikolai Hubert.

RUS–KL (a⁴, No. 672).

PSSL 8: 166.

1150. To Nadezhda von Meck

9 Apr [1879]. Kamenka.

RUS–KL (a³, No. 535).

PM 2: 90–92 — *PSSL* 8: 166–167.

1151. To Anatolii Chaikovskii

9 Apr [1879]. Kamenka.

RUS–KL (a³, No. 1225).

PR: 551–553 — *PSSL* 8: 168–169.

1152. To Nadezhda von Meck

12 Apr 1879. Kamenka.

RUS–KL (a³, No. 536).

ZC 2: 283–284 — *PM* 2: 93–94 — *PSSL* 8: 169–170.

1153. To Anatolii Chaikovskii

12 Apr [1879]. Kamenka.

RUS–KL (a³, No. 1226).

PR: 553–554 — *PB*: 229–230 — *PSSL* 8: 170–
   171 — *LF*: 223 [English tr.].

1154. To Nadezhda von Meck

14 Apr 1879. Kamenka.

RUS–KL (a³, No. 537).

ZC 2: 284–285 — *PM* 2: 94–96 — *PSSL* 8: 172–
   174.

1155. To Pëtr Iurgenson

14 Apr 1879. Kamenka.

RUS–KL (a³, No. 2242).

PIU 1: 90–91 — *PSSL* 8: 175.

1156. To Anatolii Chaikovskii

16 Apr 1879. Kamenka.

RUS–KL (a³, No. 1227).

PR: 554–555 — *PSSL* 8: 176–177.

1157. To Pëtr Iurgenson

19 Apr 1879. Kamenka.

RUS–KL (a³, No. 2243).

PIU 1: 92–93 — *PSSL* 8: 177–178.

1158. To Karl Al´brekht

19 Apr [1879]. [Kamenka].

RUS–Mcm (f. 37, No. 35).

PSSL 8: 178–179.

1159. To Nadezhda von Meck

21 Apr 1879. Kamenka.

RUS–KL (a³, No. 538).

PM 1: 98–101 — *PSSL* 8: 179–181.

1160. To Anatolii Chaikovskii

21 Apr [1879]. Kamenka.

RUS–KL (a³, No. 1228).

PR: 555–556 — *PSSL* 8: 182–183.

1161. To Pëtr Iurgenson

22 Apr [1879]. Kamenka.

RUS–KL (a³, No. 2244).

ZC 2: 285–286 — *PIU* 1: 93 — *PSSL* 8: 183–184.

1162.   To Nadezhda von Meck
23 Apr 1879. Kamenka.
RUS–KL (a³, No. 539).
PM 2: 101–102 — *PSSL* 8: 184–185.

1163.   To Anatolii Chaikovskii
23 Apr [1879]. Kamenka.
RUS–KL (a³, No. 1229).
PR: 556–557 — *PSSL* 8: 185–186.

1164.   To Nadezhda von Meck
26 Apr [1879]. Kamenka.
RUS–KL (a³, No. 540).
PM 2: 102–103 — *PSSL* 8: 187–188.

1165.   To Anatolii Chaikovskii
28 Apr 1879. Kamenka.
RUS–KL (a³, No. 1230).
PR: 557–558 — *PSSL* 8: 188–189.

1166.   To Anatolii Chaikovskii
[28 Apr 1879. Kamenka].
RUS–KL (a³, No. 1232).
PSSL 8: 189.

1167.   To Nadezhda von Meck
29–30 Apr 1879. Kamenka.
RUS–KL (a³, No. 541).
PM 2: 104–106 — *PSSL* 8: 189–191.

1168.   To Anatolii Chaikovskii
[30 Apr 1879]. Kamenka.
RUS–KL (a³, No. 1231).
PR: 559, 723 — *PSSL* 8: 192–193.

1169.   To Nadezhda von Meck
4 May 1879. Brailov.
RUS–KL (a³, No. 542).
PM 2: 107–108 — *PSSL* 8: 193–195.

1170.   To Anatolii Chaikovskii
4 May 1879. Brailov.
RUS–KL (a³, No. 1233).
*ZC 2: 286 — *PR*: 559–561 — *PSSL* 8: 195–197.

1171.   To Nadezhda von Meck
5 May 1879. Brailov.
RUS–KL (a³, No. 543).
*ZC 2: 287 — *PM* 2: 110–112 — *PSSL* 8: 197–199.

1172.   To Modest Chaikovskii
5 May [1879]. Brailov.
RUS–KL (a³, No. 1542).
*ZC 2: 286–287 — *PR*: 561–562 — *PSSL* 8: 199–201.

1173.   To Pëtr Iurgenson
6 May 1879 [Brailov].
RUS–KL (a³, No. 2245).
PIU 1: 94 — *PSSL* 8: 201–202.

1174.   To Nadezhda von Meck
6–13 May [1879]. Brailov.
RUS–KL (a³, No. 544).
*ZC 2: 288–289 — *PM* 2: 112–119 — *PSSL* 8: 202–208.

1175.   To Anatolii Chaikovskii
8 May 1879. Brailov.
RUS–KL (a³, No. 1234).
*ZC 2: 289 — *PR*: 562–563 — *PSSL* 8: 209–210.

1176.   To Modest Chaikovskii
9 May [1879]. Brailov.
RUS–KL (a³, No. 1543).
PR: 564–565 — *PSSL* 8: 210–211.

1177.   To Vladimir Shilovskii
10 May 1879 [Brailov].
RUS–Mt (Shilovskii coll.).
*SM (1940), 5–6: 142–145 — *PSSL* 8: 211–214.

1178.   To Anatolii Chaikovskii
13 May [1879]. Fastov.
RUS–KL (a³, No. 1235).
*ZC 2: 290 — *PR*: 563–566 — *PSSL* 8: 214–215.

1179.   To Modest Chaikovskii
14 May [1879]. Kamenka.
RUS–KL (a³, No. 1544).
PR: 566–567 — *PSSL* 8: 215–216.

1180. To Anatolii Chaikovskii
15 May [1879]. [Kamenka].
RUS–KL (a³, No. 1236).
PR: 567–568 — *PSSL* 8: 216–217.

1181. To Konstantin Shilovskii
15 May 1879. Kamenka.
RUS–Mt (Shilovskii coll.).
CMS: 307–308 — *PSSL* 8: 217–218.

1182. To Pëtr Iurgenson
15 May [1879]. Kamenka.
RUS–KL (a³, No. 2246).
PIU 1: 95–96 — *PSSL* 8: 218–219.

1183. To Nadezhda von Meck
16 May 1879. Kamenka.
RUS–KL (a³, No. 545).
PM 2: 120–122 — *PSSL* 8: 220–221.

1184. To Nadezhda von Meck
17–18 May [1879]. Kamenka.
RUS–KL (a³, No. 546).
PM 2: 122–123 — *PSSL* 8: 221–222.

1185. To Anatolii Chaikovskii
[17]–18 May [1879] (in MS: "18 May"). Kamenka.
RUS–KL (a³, No. 1237).
PR: 568–569 ("18 May") — *PSSL* 8: 223–224.

1186. To Modest Chaikovskii
20 [May 1879] (in MS: "Jun"). Kamenka.
RUS–KL (a³, No. 1550).
PR: 570–571 — *PSSL* 8: 224–226.

1187. To Anatolii Chaikovskii
22 May 1879. Kamenka.
RUS–KL (a³, No. 1238).
PR: 572–573 — *PSSL* 8: 225–226.

1188. To Nadezhda von Meck
22–23 May [1879]. Kamenka.
RUS–KL (a³, No. 547).
ZC 2: 290–291 ("28 May") — *PM* 2: 124–127 — *PSSL* 8: 228–230.

1189. To Pëtr Iurgenson
24 May 1879. Kamenka.
RUS–KL (a³, No. 2247).
PIU 1: 97–98 — *PSSL* 8: 230–231.

1190. To Anatolii Chaikovskii
25 May 1879. Kamenka.
RUS–KL (a³, No. 1239).
PR: 573–574 — *PSSL* 8: 232–233.

1190a. To Pëtr Iurgenson
[25 Mar 1879]. St. Petersburg.
RUS–KL (a³, No. 2240).
Not published.

1191. To Modest Chaikovskii
26 May [1879]. Kamenka.
RUS–KL (a³, No. 1545).
PR: 574–575 — *PSSL* 8: 233–234.

1192. To Anatolii Chaikovskii
28 May [1879]. Kamenka.
RUS–KL (a³, No. 1240).
PR: 575–576 — *PSSL* 8: 234–235.

1193. To Nadezhda von Meck
29–30 May 1879. Kamenka.
RUS–KL (a³, No. 548).
ZC 2: 291 — *PM* 2: 128–130 — *PSSL* 8: 235–237.

1194. To Pëtr Iurgenson
31 May [1879]. Kamenka.
RUS–KL (a³, No. 2248).
PIU 1: 99 — *PSSL* 8: 238.

1195. To Anatolii Chaikovskii
1 Jun [1879]. Kamenka.
RUS–KL (a³, No. 1242).
PR: 576–577 — *PSSL* 8: 239.

1196. To Modest Chaikovskii
2 Jun [1879]. Kamenka.
RUS–KL (a³, No. 1546).
PR: 577–578 — *PSSL* 8: 240–241.

1197.   To Nadezhda von Meck
2–6 Jun [1879]. [Kamenka].
RUS–KL (a³, No. 552).
PM 2: 133–137 — *PSSL* 8: 241–244.

1198.   To Anatolii Chaikovskii
5 Jun [1879]. Kamenka.
RUS–KL (a³, No. 1243).
PR: 579–580 — *PSSL* 8: 244–245.

1199.   To Anatolii Chaikovskii
8 Jun [1879]. Kamenka.
RUS–KL (a³, No. 1244).
PR: 583–585 — **PSSL* 8: 246–247.

1200.   To Pëtr Iurgenson
8 Jun 1879 [Kamenka].
RUS–KL (a³, No. 2249).
PIU 1: 100–101 — *PSSL* 8: 247–248.

1201.   To Modest Chaikovskii
9 Jun [1879]. Kamenka.
RUS–KL (a³, No. 1547).
*ZC 2: 291–292 — *PR*: 580–583 ("8 Jun") — *PSSL* 8: 250–251.

1202.   To Pëtr Iurgenson
9 Jun 1879 [Kamenka].
RUS–KL (a³, No. 2250).
PIU 1: 101–102 — *PSSL* 8: 251–252.

1203.   To Anatolii Chaikovskii
12 Jun 1879 [Kamenka].
RUS–KL (a³, No. 1245).
PR: 583–586 — *PSSL* 8: 252–253.

1204.   To Nadezhda von Meck
12–13 Jun [1879]. [Kamenka].
RUS–KL (a³, No. 551).
*ZC 2: 292–293 — *PM* 2: 139–141 — *PSSL* 8: 253–255.

1205.   To Pëtr Iurgenson
14 Jun [1879]. [Kamenka].
RUS–KL (a³, No. 2251).
PIU 1: 102–103 — *PSSL* 8: 256–257.

1206.   To Anatolii Chaikovskii
15 Jun [1879]. Kamenka.
RUS–KL (a³, No. 1246).
PR: 588–589 — **PSSL* 8: 257–258.

1207.   To Modest Chaikovskii
15 Jun [1879]. Kamenka.
RUS–KL (a³, No. 1548).
PR: 586–588 — **PSSL* 8: 258–260.

1208.   To Sof´ia Iurgenson
16 Jun [1879]. Kamenka.
RUS–KL (a³, No. 486).
PIU 1: 330–331 — **CMS:* 81–82 — *PSSL* 8: 260–261.

1209.   To Modest Chaikovskii
17 [Jun 1879]. Kamenka.
RUS–KL (a³, No. 1549).
PR: 589–590 — *PSSL* 8: 261–262.

1210.   To Anatolii Chaikovskii
17 Jun [1879]. [Kamenka].
RUS–KL (a³, No. 1247).
PR: 590 — *PSSL* 8: 262.

1210a. To Edouard Colonne
18 Jun 1879. Kamenka — in French.
CH–B
TGM 7 (2000): 28–31.

1211.   To Anatolii Chaikovskii
[19 Jun 1879. Kamenka].
RUS–KL (a³, No. 1248).
PR: 590–591 — *PSSL* 8: 263.

1212.   To Nadezhda von Meck
20 Jun 1879 [Kamenka].
RUS–KL (a³, No. 550).
PM 2: 142–144 — *PSSL* 8: 263–265.

1213.   To Pëtr Iurgenson
20 Jun [1879]. Kamenka.
RUS–KL (a³, No. 2252).
PIU 1: 103–104 — *PSSL* 8: 266–267.

1214. To Aleksandra Davydova
21 Jun [1879]. Kiev.
RUS–SPsc (f. 834, No. 17, fol. 76–77).
PR: 591–592 — *PSSL* 8: 267–268.

1215. To Aleksandra Davydova
23 Jun [1879]. Nizy.
RUS–SPsc (f. 834, No. 17, fol. 78–79).
PR: 592–593 — *PSSL* 8: 268–269.

1216. To Modest Chaikovskii
24 Jun [1879]. Nizy.
RUS–KL (a³, No. 1551).
PR: 593–594 — *PSSL* 8: 269–270.

1217. To Nadezhda von Meck
27 Jun 1879. Nizy.
RUS–KL (a³, No. 549).
PM 2: 146–147 — *PSSL* 8: 270–271.

1218. To Pëtr Iurgenson
27 [Jun 1879]. Nizy.
RUS–KL (a³, No. 2253).
PSSL 8: 272.

1219. To Aleksei Sofronov
28 Jun 1879. Nizy.
RUS–SPsc (f. 834, No. 25, fol. 24–25).
PSSL 8: 272–273.

1220. To Aleksandra Davydova
29 Jun [1879]. Nizy.
RUS–SPsc (f. 834, No. 17, fol. 80–83).
PR: 594–597 — *PSSL* 8: 273–275.

1221. To Nadezhda von Meck
30 Jun 1879. Nizy.
RUS–KL (a³, No. 553).
PM 2: 147–148 — *PSSL* 8: 276–277.

1222. To Aleksandra Davydova
3 Jul [1879]. Nizy.
RUS–SPsc (f. 834, No. 17, fol. 84–85).
PR: 597–598 — *PSSL* 8: 277–278.

1223. To Nadezhda von Meck
3 Jul [1879]. Nizy.
RUS–KL (a³, No. 554).
PM 2: 149–151 — *PSSL* 8: 278–280.

1224. To Pëtr Iurgenson
4 Jul [1879]. Nizy.
RUS–KL (a³, No. 2254).
PSSL 8: 280.

1225. To Modest Chaikovskii
5 Jul [1879]. Nizy.
RUS–KL (a³, No. 1552).
PR: 598–600 — *PSSL* 8: 281–282.

1226. To Alina Konradi
5 Jul [1879]. Nizy.
RUS–SPsc (f. 834, No. 20).
PSSL 8: 282–283.

1227. To Nadezhda von Meck
8 Jul [1879]. Nizy.
RUS–KL (a³, No. 555).
PM 2: 151–152 — *PSSL* 8: 283–284.

1228. To Modest Chaikovskii
9 Jul [1879]. Kamenka.
RUS–KL (a³, No. 1553).
PR: 600–601 — *PSSL* 8: 284–285.

1229. To Nadezhda von Meck
10–11 Jul [1879]. [Kamenka].
RUS–KL (a³, No. 556).
PM 2: 157–158 — *PSSL* 8: 285–287.

1230. To Pëtr Iurgenson
14 Jul [1879]. Kamenka.
RUS–KL (a³, No. 2255).
PIU 1: 105–106 — *PSSL* 8: 287–288.

1231. To Modest Chaikovskii
15 Jul 1879. Kamenka.
RUS–KL (a³, No. 1554).
ZC 2: 296 — *PR*: 601–603 — *PSSL* 8: 288–289.

1232.   To Nadezhda von Meck
17 Jul 1879 [Kamenka].
RUS–KL (a³, No. 557).
*ZC 2: 296–297 — PM 2: 155–156 — PSSL 8: 290–291.

1233.   To Nadezhda von Meck
19 Jul 1879 [Kamenka].
RUS–KL (a³, No. 558).
PM 2: 157–158 — PSSL 8: 291–292.

1234.   To Nadezhda von Meck
20 Jul 1879 [Kamenka].
RUS–KL (a³, No. 559).
PM 2: 158–160 — PSSL 8: 292–294.

1235.   To Modest Chaikovskii
21 Jul 1879 [Kamenka].
RUS–KL (a³, No. 1555).
PR: 603–604 — PSSL 8: 294–295.

1236.   To Pëtr Iurgenson
24 Jul [1879]. Kamenka.
RUS–KL (a³, No. 2256).
PIU 1: 106, 108 — PSSL 8: 296.

1237.   To Nadezhda von Meck
24–25 Jul [1879]. Kamenka.
RUS–KL (a³, No. 561).
PM 2: 161–162 — PSSL 8: 297-298.

1238.   To Modest Chaikovskii
28 Jul [1879]. Kamenka.
RUS–KL (a³, No. 1556).
*PR: 604–605 — *PSSL 8: 298–299.

1239.   To Nadezhda von Meck
30–31 Jul [1879]. Kamenka.
RUS–KL (a³, No. 562).
*ZC 2: 297 — PM 2: 162–163 — PSSL 8: 299–302.

1240.   To Anatolii Chaikovskii
6 Aug [1879]. Kamenka.
RUS–KL (a³, No. 1249).
PR: 606–607 — PSSL 8: 302–303.

1241.   To Modest Chaikovskii
7 Aug [1879]. Kamenka.
RUS–KL (a³, No. 1557).
PR: 607–608 — PSSL 8: 303–304.

1242.   To Pëtr Iurgenson
7 Aug [1879]. Kamenka.
RUS–KL (a³, No. 2257).
PIU 1: 107–108 [as postscript to letter 1236] — PSSL 8: 304–305.

1243.   To Anatolii Chaikovskii
8 Aug 1879. Kamenka.
RUS–KL (a³, No. 1250).
PR: 608–609 — PSSL 8: 305–306.

1244.   To Nadezhda von Meck
8–9 Aug 1879. Simaki.
RUS–KL (a³, No. 563).
*ZC 2: 298 — PM 2: 166–167 — PSSL 8: 306–308.

1245.   To Anatolii Chaikovskii
9 Aug 1879. Simaki.
RUS–KL (a³, No. 1251).
PR: 609 — PB: 230 — PSSL 8: 308–309 — LF: 223–224 [English tr.].

1246.   To Modest Chaikovskii
9 Aug 1879. Simaki.
RUS–KL (a³, No. 1558).
*ZC 2: 298–299 — PSSL 8: 309–310.

1247.   To Pëtr Iurgenson
9 Aug [1879]. [Simaki].
RUS–KL (a³, No. 2258).
PIU 1: 108 — PSSL 8: 310.

1248.   To Nadezhda von Meck
9–11 Aug 1879 [Simaki].
RUS–KL (a³, No. 564).
*ZC 2: 299–300 — PM 2: 167–169 — PSSL 8: 310–312.

1249.   To Nadezhda von Meck
12 Aug 1879 [Simaki].

RUS–KL (a³, No. 565).

PM 2: 171 — *PSSL* 8: 312–313.

1250.   To Nadezhda von Meck

12 Aug [1879]. Simaki.

RUS–KL (a³, No. 566).

PM 2: 172–173 — *PSSL* 8: 313–314.

1251.   To Anatolii Chaikovskii

12 Aug [1879]. [Simaki].

RUS–KL (a³, No. 1252).

PR: 610 — *PB*: 231 — *PSSL* 8: 315 — *LF*: 224 [English tr.].

1252.   To Pëtr Iurgenson

12 Aug [1879]. [Simaki].

RUS–KL (a³, No. 2259) [facs. of p. 1 in *PSSL* 8: 320/321].

ZC 2: 301 — *PIU* 1: 109 — *PSSL* 8: 315–316.

1253.   To Anatolii Chaikovskii

13 Aug 1879. Simaki.

RUS–KL (a³, No. 1253).

PR: 610–611 — *PB*: 231–232 — *PSSL* 8: 316–317 — *LF*: 225 [English tr.].

1254.   To Nadezhda von Meck

13–15 Aug [1879]. Simaki.

RUS–KL (a³, No. 567).

PM 2: 173–175 — *PSSL* 8: 318–319.

1255.   To Anatolii Chaikovskii

15 Aug [1879]. Simaki.

RUS–KL (a³, No. 1254).

ZC 2: 301 — *PR*: 613–614 — *PSSL* 8: 320–321.

1256.   To Modest Chaikovskii

15 Aug [1879]. Simaki.

RUS–KL (a³, No. 1559).

ZC 2: 301–302 — *PR*: 611–613 — *PSSL* 8: 321–322.

1257.   To Nadezhda von Meck

16 Aug 1879 [Simaki].

RUS–KL (a³, No. 568).

PM 2: 176 — *PSSL* 8: 322.

1258.   To Nadezhda von Meck

16–19 Aug [1879]. [Simaki].

RUS–KL (a³, nos. 569, 3155).

ZC 2: 302–303 — *PM* 2: 177–180 — *PSSL* 8: 322–325.

1259.   To Modest Chaikovskii

21 Aug [1879]. [Simaki].

RUS–KL (a³, No. 1560).

PR: 614–615 — *PB*: 232 — *PSSL* 8: 325–326 — *LF*: 225–226 [English tr.].

1260.   To Nadezhda von Meck

21–23 Aug [1879]. [Simaki].

RUS–KL (a³, No. 570).

PM 2: 181–183 — *PSSL* 8: 326–328.

1261.   To Anatolii Chaikovskii

22 Aug [1879]. Simaki.

RUS–KL (a³, No. 1255).

PR: 615 — *PSSL* 8: 328–329.

1262.   To Modest Chaikovskii

22 Aug [1879]. [Simaki].

RUS–KL (a³, No. 1561).

PR: 613–616 — *PSSL* 8: 329–330.

1263.   To Nadezhda von Meck

24 Aug [1879]. Simaki.

RUS–KL (a³, No. 571).

PM 2: 186–188 — *PSSL* 8: 330–332.

1264.   To Pëtr Iurgenson

24 Aug [1879]. Simaki.

RUS–KL (a³, No. 2260).

ZC 2: 303–305 — *PIU* 1: 109–110 — *PSSL* 8: 332–334.

1265.   To Nadezhda von Meck

[24 Aug 1879. Simaki].

RUS–KL (a³, No. 572).

PM 2: 189 — *PSSL* 8: 334.

1266.   To Pëtr Iurgenson

[25 Aug 1879]. Simaki.

RUS–KL (a³, No. 2261).

ZC 2: 305 — *PIU* 1: 111 — *PSSL* 8: 335.

1267.   To Nadezhda von Meck

25–27 Aug [1879]. Simaki.

RUS–KL (a³, No. 573).

*ZC 2: 306 — *PM* 2: 191–194 — *PSSL* 8: 336–339.

1268.   To Nadezhda von Meck

[26 Aug 1879. Simaki].

RUS–KL (a³, No. 574).

PM 2: 189–190 — *PSSL* 8: 339.

1269.   To Anatolii Chaikovskii

26 Aug [1879]. [Simaki].

RUS–KL (a³, No. 1256).

*ZC 2: 505–506 — *PR*: 616–617 — *PSSL* 8: 340.

1270.   To Modest Chaikovskii

26 Aug [1879]. [Simaki].

RUS–KL (a³, No. 1562).

PR: 616 — *PSSL* 8: 341.

1271.   To Nadezhda von Meck

27 Aug [1879]. [Simaki].

RUS–KL (a³, No. 575).

PM 2: 191 — *PSSL* 8: 341.

1272.   To Pëtr Iurgenson

27 Aug [1879]. [Simaki].

RUS–KL (a³, No. 2262).

*ZC 2: 307–308 — *PIU* 1: 111–112 — *PSSL* 8: 342–343.

1273.   To Nadezhda von Meck

27–28 Aug [1879]. [Simaki].

RUS–KL (a³, No. 576).

*ZC 2: 306–307 — *PM* 2: 196–198 — *PSSL* 8: 343–345.

1274.   To Pëtr Iurgenson

[late Aug 1879. Simaki].

RUS–KL (a³, No. 2273).

*ZC 2: 308 — *PIU* 1: 112 — *PSSL* 8: 345.

1275.   To Anatolii Chaikovskii

28 Aug [1879]. [Simaki].

RUS–KL (a³, No. 1257).

PR: 617–618 — *PSSL* 8: 346.

1276.   To Nadezhda von Meck

29–31 Aug 1879. Simaki.

RUS–KL (a³, No. 577).

*ZC 2: 308–309 — *PM* 2: 200–203 — *PSSL* 8: 347–349.

1277.   To Nadezhda von Meck

30 Aug [1879]. [Simaki].

RUS–KL (a³, No. 578).

PM 2: 199–200 — *PSSL* 8: 350.

1278.   To Nadezhda von Meck

31 Aug [1879]. [Simaki].

RUS–KL (a³, No. 581).

PM 2: 205 — *PSSL* 8: 351.

1279.   To Lev Davydov

31 Aug [1879]. [Simaki].

RUS–SPsc (f. 834, No. 19, fol. 21–22).

PSSL 8: 351.

1280.   To Nadezhda von Meck

31 Aug [1879]. [Simaki].

RUS–KL (a³, No. 579).

PM 2: 203–205 — *PSSL* 8: 351–352.

1281.   To Modest Chaikovskii

31 Aug [1879]. [Simaki].

RUS–KL (a³, No. 1563).

*ZC 2: 309 — *PR*: 618–619 — *PSSL* 8: 353–354.

1282.   To Nadezhda von Meck

[31 Aug 1879. Simaki].

RUS–KL (a³, No. 580).

PM 2: 205 — *PSSL* 8: 354.

1283.   To Nadezhda von Meck

4 Sep [1879]. St. Petersburg.

RUS–KL (a³, No. 582).

PM 2: 206–207 — *PSSL* 8: 354–355.

1284.   To Modest Chaikovskii

4 Sep [1879]. [St. Petersburg].

RUS–KL (a³, No. 1564).

PR: 619–620 — *PSSL* 8: 356.

1285.   To Pëtr Iurgenson

[4 Sep 1879]. St. Petersburg.

RUS–KL (a³, No. 2263).

*ZC 2: 316–317 — PIU 1: 113 — PSSL 8: 357.

1286.   To Aleksei Sofronov

[6 Sep 1879. St. Petersburg].

RUS–SPsc (f. 834, No. 25, fol. 22–23).

PSSL 8: 358.

1287.   To Modest Chaikovskii

[6 Sep 1879]. St. Petersburg.

RUS–KL (a³, No. 1566).

PR: 620–621 ("10 Sep") — *PSSL 8: 358–359.

1288.   To Aleksandra Davydova

[8 Sep 1879]. St. Petersburg.

RUS–SPsc (f. 834, No. 17, fol. 86–87).

PR: 621–622 ("10 Sep") — PSSL 8: 359–360.

1289.   To Nadezhda von Meck

8 Sep [1879]. St. Petersburg.

RUS–KL (a³, No. 583).

*ZC 2: 217 — PM 2: 208–210 — PSSL 8: 360–362.

1290.   To Modest Chaikovskii

11 Sep [1879]. [St. Petersburg].

RUS–KL (a³, No. 1565).

PR: 622 — PSSL 8: 362.

1291.   To Pëtr Iurgenson

11 Sep [1879]. [St. Petersburg].

RUS–KL (a³, No. 2264).

PIU 1: 113–114 — PSSL 8: 362–363.

1292.   To Aleksei Sofronov

11 Sep [1879]. [St. Petersburg].

RUS–SPsc (f. 834, No. 25, fol. 26–27).

PSSL 8: 363.

1293.   To Nadezhda von Meck

13 Sep [1879]. St. Petersburg.

RUS–KL (a³, No. 584).

*ZC 2: 317–318 — PM 2: 210–211 — PSSL 8: 364–365.

1294.   To Nadezhda von Meck

15 Sep [1879]. St. Petersburg/

RUS–KL (a³, No. 585).

*ZC 2: 318–319 — PM 2: 213–214 — PSSL 8: 365–366.

1295.   To Pëtr Iurgenson

15 Sep [1879]. St. Petersburg.

RUS–KL (a³, No. 2265).

PIU 1: 114–115 — PSSL 8: 367.

1296.   To Eduard Nápravník

17 Sep [1879]. St. Petersburg.

Autograph lost; typed copy in RUS–KL.

VP: 123–124 — EFN: 106–107 — PSSL 8: 367–368.

1297.   To Nadezhda von Meck

17–25 Sep [1879]. St. Petersburg–Moscow–Grankino.

RUS–KL (a³, No. 586).

*ZC 2: 320–323 — PM 2: 217–221 — PSSL 8: 368–372.

1298.   To Anatolii Chaikovskii

20 Sep [1879]. Moscow.

RUS–KL (a³, No. 1258).

ZC 2: 319–320 — PR: 622–623 — PSSL 8: 372.

1299.   To Anatolii Chaikovskii

22 Sep [1879]. [Moscow].

RUS–KL (a³, No. 1259).

*ZC 2: 320 — PR: 623–624 — PSSL 8: 373.

1300.   To Pëtr Iurgenson

[? 22 Sep 1879. Moscow].

RUS–KL (a³, No. 3056).

PIU 1: 119 [as postscript to leter 1325] — PSSL 8: 373–374.

1301.   To Anatolii Chaikovskii

24 Sep [1879]. Grankino.

RUS–KL (a³, No. 1260).

*ZC 2: 321 — PR: 624–625 — PSSL 8: 374–375.

1302.   To Nadezhda von Meck

30 Sep 1879. Kamenka.

RUS–KL (a³, No. 587).

PM 2: 221–223 — PSSL 8: 376–378.

1303.   To Anatolii Chaikovskii

30 Sep [1879]. Kamenka.

RUS–KL (a³, No. 1261).

*ZC 2: 323 — *PR: 625–626 — *PSSL 8: 378–379.

1304.   To Pëtr Iurgenson

3 Oct [1879]. Kamenka.

RUS–KL (a³, No. 2266).

PIU 1: 116–117 — PSSL 8: 379–381.

1305.   To Anatolii Chaikovskii

4 Oct [1879]. Kamenka.

RUS–KL (a³, No. 1262).

PR: 626–627 — PSSL 8: 381–382.

1306.   To Modest Chaikovskii

4 Oct [1879]. Kamenka.

RUS–KL (a³, No. 1567).

PR: 627 — PSSL 8: 382–383.

1307.   To Nadezhda von Meck

5–7 Oct 1879. Kamenka.

RUS–KL (a³, No. 588).

*ZC 2: 323–324 — PM 2: 224–226 — PSSL 8: 383–385.

1308.   To Anatolii Chaikovskii

7 Oct [1879]. Kamenka.

RUS–KL (a³, No. 1263).

*ZC 2: 324 — *PR: 628–629 — PSSL 8: 385–387.

1309.   To Nadezhda von Meck

9 Oct 1879. Kamenka.

RUS–KL (a³, No. 589).

*ZC 2: 324–325 — PM 2: 226–227.

1310.   To Modest Chaikovskii

10 Oct [1879]. Kamenka.

RUS–KL (a³, No. 1568).

PR: 629–630 — *PB: 232–233 — PSSL 8: 388–389 — *LF: 226 [English tr.].

1311.   To Nadezhda von Meck

12 Oct [1879]. Kamenka.

RUS–KL (a³, No. 590).

*ZC 2: 325–326 — PM 2: 230–232 — PSSL 8: 389–391.

1312.   To Anatolii Chaikovskii

12 Oct [1879]. Kamenka.

RUS–KL (a³, No. 1264).

PR: 630–631 — *PB: 233 — PSSL 8: 391–392 — *LF: 227 [English tr.].

1313.   To Nadezhda von Meck

15–16 Oct 1879. Kamenka.

RUS–KL (a³, No. 591).

*ZC 2: 326–327 — PM 2: 233–234 — PSSL 8: 393–394.

1314.   To Anatolii Chaikovskii

17 Oct [1879]. Kamenka.

RUS–KL (a³, No. 1265).

PR: 631–632 — *PB: 234 — PSSL 8: 394–395 — *LF: 227–228 [English tr.].

1315.   To Nadezhda von Meck

18 Oct 1879. Kamenka.

RUS–KL (a³, No. 592).

PM 2: 235–236 — PSSL 8: 395–397.

1316.   To Anatolii Chaikovskii

18 Oct 1879. Kamenka.

RUS–KL (a³, No. 1266).

PR: 632 — PSSL 8: 397.

1317.   To Modest Chaikovskii

20 [Oct 1879]. [Kamenka].

RUS–KL (a³, No. 1569).

PR: 633 — PSSL 8: 398.

1318.   To Pëtr Iurgenson

20 Oct [1879]. Kamenka.

RUS–KL (a³, No. 2267).

*ZC 2: 327–328 — PIU 1: 117–118 — PSSL 8: 398–399.

1319.   To Pëtr Iurgenson

21 Oct [1879]. [Kamenka].

RUS–KL (a³, No. 2268).

PIU 1: 118–119 — PSSL 8: 399.

1320. To Nadezhda von Meck
21–22 Oct [1879]. Kamenka.
RUS–KL (a³, No. 593).
PM 2: 237–238 — *PSSL* 8: 400–401.

1321. To Nadezhda von Meck
24 Oct [1879]. Kamenka.
RUS–KL (a³, No. 594).
*ZC 2: 328 — *PM* 2: 238–239 — *PSSL* 8: 402.

1322. To Nadezhda von Meck
29[–30] Oct [1879]. St. Petersburg.
RUS–KL (a³, No. 595).
PM 2: 239–240 — *PSSL* 8: 402–403.

1323. To Eduard Nápravník
[31 Oct 1879. St. Petersburg].
RUS–SPtm (Gik 17195/18).
VP: 124 — *EFN*: 107 — *PSSL* 8: 403–404.

1324. To Nadezhda von Meck
1 Nov 1879. St. Petersburg.
RUS–KL (a³, No. 597).
PM 2: 240–241 — *PSSL* 8: 404–405.

1325. To Pëtr Iurgenson
1 Nov 1879. St. Petersburg.
RUS–KL (a³, No. 2269).
PIU 1: 118–119 — *PSSL* 8: 405.

1326. To Nadezhda von Meck
3 Nov [1879]. St. Petersburg.
RUS–KL (a³, No. 598).
PM 2: 241–242 — *PSSL* 8: 406.

1327. To Nadezhda von Meck
4 Nov 1879. St. Petersburg.
RUS–KL (a³, No. 599).
PM 2: 243–244 — *PSSL* 8: 406–408.

1328. To Pëtr Iurgenson
4 Nov [1879]. St. Petersburg.
RUS–KL (a³, No. 2270).
PIU 1: 119–120 — *PSSL* 8: 408–409.

1329. To Nikolai Rubinshtein
8 Nov [1879]. St. Petersburg.
RUS–Mcm (f. 37, No. 97).
*ZC 2: 329 — *IRM* 1: 180 — *PSSL* 8: 409.

1330. To Pëtr Iurgenson
8 Nov [1879]. [St. Petersburg].
RUS–KL (a³, No. 2271).
PSSL 8: 410.

1331. To Pëtr Iurgenson
[8 Nov 1879]. St. Petersburg.
RUS–KL (a³, No. 2272).
PIU 1: 120 — *PSSL* 8: 410–411.

1332. To Anatolii Chaikovskii
11/23 Nov 1879. Berlin.
RUS–KL (a³, No. 1267).
*ZC 2: 329–330 — *PR*: 633–634 — *PSSL* 8: 411–
412.

1332a. To Mme Fernow
[12]/24 Nov 1879. Berlin.
J–private
*ČS 3 (1998): 188–189.

1333. To Anatolii Chaikovskii
12/[24] Nov 1879. Berlin.
RUS–KL (a³, No. 1268).
*ZC 2: 330 — *PR*: 634–635 — **PB*: 234 — *PSSL* 8:
412–413 — **LF*: 228 [English tr.].

1334. To Nadezhda von Meck
[13/25–14/26 Nov 1879]. Paris.
RUS–KL (a³, No. 600).
PM 2: 246–248 — *PSSL* 8: 413–415.

1335. To Anatolii Chaikovskii
14/26 Nov 1879. Paris.
RUS–KL (a³, No. 1269).
PR: 635 — *PSSL* 8: 415–416.

1336. To Modest Chaikovskii
14/[26] Nov [1879]. Paris.
RUS–KL (a³, No. 1570).
PSSL 8: 416.

1337.   To Nadezhda von Meck
14/26–15/27 Nov [1879]. Paris.
RUS–KL (a³, No. 601).
*ZC 2: 330 — PM 2: 249–251 — PSSL 8: 417–419.

1338.   To Nadezhda von Meck
[16/28 Nov 1879. Paris].
RUS–KL (a³, No. 602).
PM 2: 252 — PSSL 8: 419.

1339.   To Anatolii Chaikovskii
16/28 Nov 1879. Paris.
RUS–KL (a³, No. 1270).
PR: 636 — *PSSL 8: 420.

1340.   To Modest Chaikovskii
16/28 Nov 1879. Paris.
RUS–KL (a³, No. 1571).
*PSSL 8: 421.

1341.   To Nadezhda von Meck
18/[30] Nov 1879. Paris.
RUS–KL (a³, No. 603).
*ZC 2: 331 — PM 2: 253–254 — PSSL 8: 421–422.

1342.   To Modest Chaikovskii
18/[30] Nov [1879]. Paris.
RUS–KL (a³, No. 1572).
PR: 636–637 — PSSL 8: 423.

1343.   To Nadezhda von Meck
[19 Nov/1 Dec 1879. Paris].
RUS–KL (a³, No. 604).
PM 2: 254 — PSSL 8: 424.

1344.   To Anatolii Chaikovskii
19 Nov/1 Dec 1879. Paris.
RUS–KL (a³, No. 1271).
PR: 637–638 — PSSL 8: 424–425.

1345.   To Pëtr Iurgenson
19 Nov/1 Dec 1879. Paris.
RUS–KL (a³, No. 2274).
*ZC 2: 332 — PIU 1: 121–122 — PSSL 8: 425.

1346.   To Nadezhda von Meck
19–20 Nov/1–2 Dec 1879. Paris.
RUS–KL (a³, No. 605).
*ZC 2: 332–333 — PM 2: 255–257 — PSSL 8: 426–428.

1347.   To Nadezhda von Meck
21 Nov/3 Dec 1879. Paris.
RUS–KL (a³, No. 606).
*ZC 2: 333–334 — PM 2: 258–259 — PSSL 8: 429.

1348.   To Modest Chaikovskii
21 Nov/3 Dec 1879. Paris.
RUS–KL (a³, No. 1573).
PR: 638 — PSSL 8: 430.

1349.   To Anatolii Chaikovskii
22 Nov/[4 Dec 1879]. Paris.
RUS–KL (a³, No. 1272).
*ZC 2: 334–335 — PR: 639 — PSSL 8: 430–431.

1350.   To Il´ia Chaikovskii
22 Nov/[4 Dec] 1879. Paris.
RUS–SPsc (f. 834, No. 33, fol. 104, 119–120).
PR: 640 — PSSL 8: 432.

1351.   To Nadezhda von Meck
22–23 Nov/[4–5 Dec 1879]. Paris.
RUS–KL (a³, No. 607).
*ZC 2: 335 — PM 2: 259–261 — PSSL 8: 432–433.

1352.   To Nadezhda von Meck
24–25 Nov/[6–7 Dec 1879]. Paris.
RUS–KL (a³, No. 608).
*ZC 1: 120–121 — *ZC 2: 335–337 — PM 2: 262–264 — PSSL 8: 434–435.

1353.   To Anatolii Chaikovskii
25 Nov/7 Dec [1879]. Paris
RUS–KL (a³, No. 1273).
PR: 640–641 — *PB: 234–235 — *PSSL 8: 436–437 — *LF: 228 [English tr.].

1354.   To Adolf Fürstner
[26 Nov]/8 Dec 1879. Paris — in French.
Original lost; autograph copy in RUS–KL.
*ZC 2: 339–340 — PSSL 8: 437–438.

1355. To Pëtr Iurgenson
26 Nov/8 Dec 1879. Paris.
RUS–KL (a³, No. 2275).
ZC 2: 338–339 — *PIU* 1: 124 — *PSSL* 8: 438–439.

1356. To Nadezhda von Meck
26–27 Nov/8–9 Dec 1879. Paris.
RUS–KL (a³, No. 609).
ZC 2: 337–338 — *PM* 2: 265–266 — *PSSL* 8: 439–441.

1357. To Anatolii Chaikovskii
27 Nov/9 Dec 1879. Paris.
RUS–KL (a³, No. 1274).
ZC 2: 342–343 — *PR*: 641–644 — *PSSL* 8: 441–444.

1358. To Nadezhda von Meck
27–28 Nov/9–10 Dec 1879. Paris.
RUS–KL (a³, No. 610).
ZC 2: 340–344 — *PM* 2: 267–271 — *PSSL* 8: 444–448.

1359. To Modest Chaikovskii
28 Nov/10 Dec 1879. Paris.
RUS–KL (a³, No. 1574).
PR: 644–645 — *PSSL* 8: 448–449.

1360. To Nadezhda von Meck
30 Nov/12 Dec 1879. Paris.
RUS–KL (a³, No. 611).
PM 2: 272 — *PSSL* 8: 449–450.

1361. To Anatolii Chaikovskii
30 Nov/12 Dec 1879. Paris.
RUS–KL (a³, No. 1275).
PR: 645–646 — *PSSL* 8: 450–451.

1362. To Modest Chaikovskii
30 Nov/12 Dec 1879. Paris.
RUS–KL (a³, No. 1575).
PR: 646–647 — *PSSL* 8: 451–452.

1363. To Pëtr Iurgenson
30 Nov/12 Dec 1879. Paris.
RUS–KL (a³, No. 2276).
ZC 2: 344 — *PIU* 1: 124–125 — *PSSL* 8: 452–453.

1364. To Nadezhda von Meck
2/14 Dec 1879. Paris.
RUS–KL (a³, No. 612).
ZC 2: 344–345 — *PM* 2: 273–275 — *PSSL* 8: 453–455.

1365. To Anatolii Chaikovskii
3/15 Dec 1879. Paris.
RUS–KL (a³, No. 1276).
PR: 647 — *PB*: 233 — *PSSL* 8: 455–456 — *LF*: 229 [English tr.].

1366. To Nadezhda von Meck
3/15–4/16 Dec 1879. Paris.
RUS–KL (a³, No. 613).
ZC 2: 345 — *PM* 2: 275–276 — *PSSL* 8: 456–457.

1367. To Anatolii Chaikovskii
5/17 Dec 1879. Paris.
RUS–KL (a³, No. 1277).
PR: 648 — *PSSL* 8: 458.

1368. To Pëtr Iurgenson
5/17 Dec 1879. Paris.
RUS–KL (a³, No. 2277).
PSSL 8: 458.

1369. To Anatolii Chaikovskii
7/19 Dec 1879. Turin.
RUS–KL (a³, No. 1278).
ZC 2: 346 — *PR*: 648–649 — *PB*: 235–236 — *PSSL* 8: 458–459 — *LF*: 229 [English tr.].

1370. To Modest Chaikovskii
[7/19 Dec 1879. Turin] — telegram; in French.
RUS–KL (a³, No. 3159).
PSSL 8: 459.

1371. To Nadezhda von Meck
9/21 Dec 1879. Rome.
RUS–KL (a³, No. 614).
PM 2: 277–278 — *PSSL* 8: 459–460.

1372. To Anatolii Chaikovskii
9/21 Dec 1879. Rome.
RUS–KL (a³, No. 1279).

*ZC 2: 346–347 — PR: 649 — PB: 236 — PSSL 8:
461 — *LF: 229 [English tr.].

1373.   To Pëtr Iurgenson

9/21 Dec 1879. Rome.

RUS–KL (a³, No. 2278).

PSSL 8: 462.

1374.   To Nadezhda von Meck

12/24 [Dec] 1879. Rome.

RUS–KL (a³, No. 615).

*ZC 2: 347–348 — PM 2: 278–279 — PSSL 8: 462–
463.

1375.   To Anatolii Chaikovskii

12/24 Dec 1879. Rome.

RUS–KL (a³, No. 1280).

PR: 649–650 — *PSSL* 8: 463–464.

1376.   To Natal´ia Pleskaia

13/25 Dec 1879. Rome.

RUS–Mcl (f. 905).

CTP: 362–363 — *PSSL* 8: 464–465.

1377.   To Nadezhda von Meck

13/25–15/27 Dec 1879. Rome.

RUS–KL (a³, No. 616).

*ZC 2: 348–349 — PM 2: 280–281 — PSSL 8: 465–
466.

1378.   To Lev Davydov

14/26 Dec 1879. Rome.

RUS–KL (a³, No. 170).

PSSL 8: 467.

1379.   To Anatolii Chaikovskii

16/28 Dec 1879. Rome.

RUS–KL (a³, No. 1281).

PR: 650–651 — *PSSL* 8: 468–469.

1380.   To Pëtr Iurgenson

16/28 Dec [1879]. Rome.

RUS–KL (a³, No. 2279).

*ZC 2: 349–350 — PIU 1: 127 — PSSL 8: 469–470.

1381.   To Nadezhda von Meck

16/28–18/30 Dec 1879. Rome.

RUS–KL (a³, No. 617).

*ZC 2: 350–352 — PM 2: 281–282 — PSSL 8: 470–
471.

1382.   To Anatolii Chaikovskii

18/30–19/31 Dec 1879. Rome.

RUS–KL (a³, No. 1282).

*ZC 2: 350–351 — PR: 651–652 — PB: 237 — PSSL
8: 472–473 — *LF: 230–231 [English tr.].

1383.   To Sergei Taneev

[19/31 Dec 1879]. Rome.

RUS–Mcl (f. 880).

*ZC 2: 357 — PT: 35–36 — CTP 41 — PSSL 8: 473.

1384.   To Pëtr Iurgenson

19/31 Dec 1879. Rome.

RUS–KL (a³, No. 2280).

*ZC 2: 352 — PIU 1: 128 — PSSL 8: 473–474.

1385.   To Nadezhda von Meck

20–21 Dec 1879/1–2 Jan 1880. Rome.

RUS–KL (a³, No. 618).

*PM 2: 283–284 — PSSL 8: 474–476.

1386.   To Vasilii Bessel´

21 Dec 1879/2 Jan 1880. Rome.

RUS–Mcm (f. 42, No. 257).

SM (1938), 6: 47–49 — *PSSL* 8: 476–478.

1387.   To Nadezhda von Meck

22–24 Dec 1879/3–5 Jan 1880. Rome.

RUS–KL (a³, No. 619).

*ZC 2: 353 — PM 2: 285–287 — PSSL 8: 479–481.

1388.   To Natal´ia Pleskaia

23 Dec 1879/4 Jan 1880. Rome.

RUS–Mcl (f. 905).

CTP: 363–364 — *PSSL* 8: 481–482.

1389.   To Anatolii Chaikovskii

23 Dec 1879/4 Jan 1880. Rome.

RUS–KL (a³, No. 1283).

*ZC 2: 353–354 — PR: 652–653 — PB: 237–238 —
LF: 231–232 [English tr.].

1390.   To the *Hôtel Constanzy*

[? 23 Dec 1879/4 Jan 1880. Rome] — in French.

RUS–KL (a³, No. 255).

PSSL 8: 484.

1391.   To Anatolii Chaikovskii

26 Dec 1879/7 Jan 1880 [Rome].

RUS–KL (a³, No. 1284).

*PR: 654 — **PSSL* 8: 484–485.

1392.   To Nadezhda von Meck

27–29 Dec 1879/8–10 Jan 1880 [Rome].

RUS–KL (a³, No. 620).

*ZC 2: 354–357 — *PM* 2: 287–290 — *PSSL* 8: 485–
488

1393.   To Anatolii Chaikovskii

31 Dec 1879/12 Jan 1880. Rome.

RUS–KL (a³, No. 1285).

PR: 655–656 — **PB*: 239 — *PSSL* 8: 488–489 —
*LF: 232–233 [English tr.].

1394.   To Nadezhda von Meck

31 Dec 1879/12 Jan 1880–3/15 Jan 1880. Rome.

RUS–KL (a³, No. 621).

PM 2: 290–292 — *PSSL* 8: 490–492.

1880

1395.   To Lev Davydov

4/16 Jan [1880]. Rome.

RUS–SPsc (f. 834, No. 19, fol. 23–24).

PSSL 9: 13.

1396.   To Sergei Taneev

4/16 Jan [1880]. Rome.

RUS–Mcl (f. 880).

*ZC 2: 360–362 — **PT*: 41–43 — *CTP*: 46–48 —
PSSL 9: 14–16.

1397.   To Pëtr Iurgenson

4/16 Jan 1880. Rome.

RUS–KL (a³, No. 2282).

*ZC 2: 363–364 — *PIU* 1: 134–135 — *PSSL* 9: 17–
18.

1398.   To Karl Al´brekht

6/18 Jan 1880. Rome.

RUS–Mcm (f. 37, No. 36).

*ZC 2: 364 — *CMS*: 283 — *PSSL* 9: 18–19.

1399.   To Anatolii Chaikovskii

6/18 Jan 1880. Rome.

RUS–KL (a³, No. 1287).

PSSL 9: 19–20.

1400.   To Nadezhda von Meck

7/19–8/20 Jan 1880. Rome.

RUS–KL (a³, No. 622).

PM 2: 294–295 — *PSSL* 9: 20–21.

1401.   To Anatolii Chaikovskii

8/20 Jan [1880]. Rome.

RUS–KL (a³, No. 1288).

PSSL 9: 21–22.

1402.   To Anatolii Chaikovskii

10/22 [Jan 1880]. Rome.

RUS–KL (a³, No. 1289).

PSSL 9: 22–23.

1403.   To Nadezhda von Meck

11/23 Jan 1880. Rome.

RUS–KL (a³, No. 623).

PM 2: 295–296 — *PSSL* 9: 23–24.

1404.   To Pëtr Iurgenson

11/23 Jan 1880. Rome.

RUS–KL (a³, No. 2283).

*ZC 2: 364 — *PIU* 1: 135 — *PSSL* 9: 24.

1405.   To Anatolii Chaikovskii

12/24 Jan 1880. Rome.

RUS–KL (a³, No. 1290).

PSSL 9: 25.

1406.   To Nadezhda von Meck

12/24–13/25 Jan 1880. Rome.

RUS–KL (a³, No. 624).

*ZC 2: 365–366 — *PM* 2: 296–298 — *PSSL* 9: 26–
27.

1407. To Anatolii Chaikovskii
15/27 Jan 1880. Rome.
RUS–KL (a³, No. 1291).
PSSL 9: 27–28.

1408. To Nadezhda von Meck
16/28–17/29 Jan 1880. Rome.
RUS–KL (a³, No. 625).
*ZC 2: 366–368 — PM 2: 299–302 — PSSL 9: 29–31.

1409. To Anatolii Chaikovskii
19/31 Jan 1880 [Rome].
RUS–KL (a³, No. 1292).
*ZC 2: 370 — PSSL 9: 31–32.

1410. To Nadezhda von Meck
19/31 Jan–21 Jan/2 Feb 1880. Rome.
RUS–KL (a³, No. 626).
PM 2: 302–303 — *PSSL* 9: 32–33.

1411. To Anatolii Chaikovskii
22 Jan/3 Feb 1880. Rome.
RUS–KL (a³, No. 1293).
*PB: 240 — PSSL 9: 34 — *LF: 233 [English tr.].

1412. To Nadezhda von Meck
[24] Jan/5 Feb 1880 (in MS: "23 Jan"). Rome.
RUS–KL (a³, No. 627).
*ZC 2: 370–371 — PM 2: 305–306 — PSSL 9: 34–36.

1413. To Vasilii Bessel´
[25] Jan/6 Feb 1880 (in MS: "24 Jan"). Rome.
RUS–Mcm (f. 42, No. 258).
SM (1938), 6: 49–50 — *PSSL* 9: 36–37.

1414. To Karl Davydov
[25] Jan/6 Feb 1880 (in MS: "24 Jan"). Rome.
RUS–KL (a³, No. 161).
PSSL 9: 37–38.

1415. To Pëtr Iurgenson
[25] Jan/6 Feb 1880 (in MS: "24 Jan"). Rome.
RUS–KL (a³, No. 2284).
*ZC 2: 371–372 — PIU 1: 136–137 — PSSL 9: 38–39.

1416. To Nadezhda von Meck
27 Jan/8 Feb 1880. Rome.
RUS–KL (a³, No. 628).
*ZC 2: 373 — PM 2: 306–307 — PSSL 9: 39–40.

1417. To Anatolii Chaikovskii
28 Jan/9 Feb 1880. Rome.
RUS–KL (a³, No. 1294).
PB: 240–241 — *PSSL* 9: 40–41 — *LF*: 234 [English tr.].

1418. To Anatolii Chaikovskii
31 Jan/12 Feb 1880. Rome.
RUS–KL (a³, No. 1295).
*PB: 241 — PSSL 9: 41–42 — *LF: 234–235 [English tr.].

1419. To Nadezhda von Meck
31 Jan/12 Feb–2/14 Feb 1880. Rome.
RUS–KL (a³, No. 629).
PM 2: 307–308 — *PSSL* 9: 42–44.

1420. To Nadezhda von Meck
4/16–6/18 Feb 1880. Rome.
RUS–KL (a³, No. 630).
*ZC 2: 373–375 — PM 2: 310–312 — PSSL 9: 44–46.

1421. To Anatolii Chaikovskii
5/17 Feb 1880. Rome.
RUS–KL (a³, No. 1296).
PSSL 9: 47–48.

1422. To Pëtr Iurgenson
5/17 Feb [1880]. Rome.
RUS–KL (a³, No. 2285).
*ZC 2: 375 — PIU 1: 137–138 — PSSL 9: 48–49.

1423. To Nadezhda von Meck
8/20–10/22 Feb 1880. Rome.
RUS–KL (a³, No. 631).
*ZC 2: 376–377 — PM 2: 312–313 — PSSL 9: 49:50.

1424. To Anatolii Chaikovskii
10/22 Feb 1880. Rome.
RUS–KL (a³, No. 1297).
PSSL 9: 51–52.

1425.   To Nadezhda von Meck

12/24–14/26 Feb 1880. Rome.

RUS–KL (a³, No. 632).

PM 2: 314–315 — *PSSL* 9: 52–53.

1426.   To Anatolii Chaikovskii

14/26 Feb 1880. Rome.

RUS–KL (a³, No. 1298).

PSSL 9: 53–54.

1427.   To Nadezhda von Meck

16/28 Feb–28 Feb/1 Mar 1880. Rome.

RUS–KL (a³, No. 633).

*ZC 2: 377–378 — *PM* 2: 316–318 — *PSSL* 9: 54–57.

1428.   To Anatolii Chaikovskii

18 Feb/1 Mar 1880. Rome.

RUS–KL (a³, No. 1299).

PSSL 9: 57–58.

1429.   To Anatolii Chaikovskii

20 Feb/[3 Mar 1880]. Rome.

RUS–KL (a³, No. 1300).

PSSL 9: 58–59.

1430.   To Pëtr Iurgenson

20 Feb/[3 Mar 1880]. Rome.

RUS–KL (a³, No. 2286).

*ZC 2: 379 — *PIU* 1: 139–140 — *PSSL* 9: 59–60.

1431.   To Nadezhda von Meck

25 Feb/8 Mar 1880. Rome.

RUS–KL (a³, No. 634).

PM 2: 319–320 — *PSSL* 9: 60–61.

1432.   To Anatolii Chaikovskii

25 Feb/8 Mar 1880. Rome.

RUS–KL (a³, No. 1301).

PSSL 9: 61–62.

1433.   To Modest Chaikovskii

26 [Feb]/9[Mar 1880]. Rome.

RUS–KL (a³, No. 1576) [incomplete].

*ZC 2: 379–380 — *PB*: 241–242 — *PSSL* 9: 62–63 —
LF: 235 [English tr.].

1434.   To Anatolii Chaikovskii

28 Feb/11 Mar 1880. Paris.

Autograph lost; MS copy in RUS–KL.

PSSL 9: 63–64.

1435.   To Modest Chaikovskii

28 Feb/11 Mar 1880. Paris.

RUS–KL (a³, No. 1577).

PSSL 9: 64–65.

1436.   To Nadezhda von Meck

29 Feb/12 Mar 1880. Paris.

RUS–KL (a³, No. 635).

PM 2: 320 — *PSSL* 9: 65–66.

1437.   To Modest Chaikovskii

1/13 Mar 1880. Paris.

RUS–KL (a³, No. 1578).

*PB: 242–243 — **PSSL* 9: 66–67 — **LF*: 235–236
[English tr.].

1438.   To Modest Chaikovskii

2/14 Mar 1880. Paris.

RUS–KL (a³, No. 1579).

*PSSL 9: 67–68.

1439.   To Nadezhda von Meck

4/16 Mar 1880. Berlin.

RUS–KL (a³, No. 636).

PM 2: 323 — *PSSL* 9: 68–69.

1440.   To Modest Chaikovskii

4/16 Mar 1880. Berlin.

RUS–KL (a³, No. 1580).

*ZC 2: 380–381 — **PB*: 243–244 — **PSSL* 9: 69–
71 — **LF*: 236–237 [English tr.].

1441.   To Modest Chaikovskii

5/17 Mar 1880. Berlin.

RUS–KL (a³, No. 1581).

*ZC 2: 381–382 — **PB*: 244–245 — **PSSL* 9: 71–
72 — **LF*: 238–239 [English tr.].

1442.   To Nadezhda von Meck

8 Mar [1880]. St. Petersburg.

RUS–KL (a³, No. 637).

PM 2: 324–325 — *PSSL* 9: 72–73.

1443.   To Modest Chaikovskii
8 Mar [1880]. St. Petersburg.
RUS–KL (a³, No. 1582).
PSSL 9: 74–75.

1444.   To Nadezhda von Meck
10 Mar [1880]. St. Petersburg.
RUS–KL (a³, No. 638).
*ZC 2: 382 — PM 2: 325–326 — PSSL 9: 76.

1445.   To Modest Chaikovskii
[11] Mar 1880. St. Petersburg.
RUS–KL (a³, No. 1583).
PSSL 9: 77–79.

1446.   To Vasilii Bessel´
[13 Mar 1880. St. Petersburg].
RUS–Mcm (f. 42, No. 259).
SM (1938), 6: 50 — *PSSL* 9: 79.

1447.   To Eduard Nápravník
13 Mar [1880]. [St. Petersburg].
RUS–SPtm (Gik 17195/14).
VP: 122 ("1879") — *EFN*106 ("1879") — *PSSL* 9:
80.

1448.   To Nikolai Konradi
14 Mar [1880]. St. Petersburg.
Autograph lost; MS copy in RUS–KL.
CTP: 260–261 — *PSSL* 9: 80.

1449.   To Eduard Nápravník
[14 Mar 1880. St. Petersburg].
RUS–SPtm (Gik 17195/16).
VP: 124 ("1879") — *EFN*: 106 ("1879") — *PSSL* 9:
81.

1450.   To Modest Chaikovskii
14 Mar [1880]. [St. Petersburg].
RUS–KL (a³, No. 1584).
*ZC 2: 383–385 — PB: 245–247 — *PSSL 9: 81–
83 — LF: 238–240 [English tr.].

1451.   To Nadezhda von Meck
16 Mar [1880]. St. Petersburg.
RUS–KL (a³, No. 639).
*ZC 2: 385 — PM 2: 327–328 — PSSL 9: 83–84.

1452.   To Modest Chaikovskii
16 Mar [1880]. [St. Petersburg].
RUS–KL (a³, No. 1585).
PSSL 9: 85.

1453.   To Evgenii Al´brekht
[mid Mar 1880. St. Petersburg].
RUS–SPtob (VII.2.4.154).
Kirov: 412 — *PSSL* 9: 85.

1454.   To Modest Chaikovskii
19 Mar [1880]. St. Petersburg.
RUS–KL (a³, No. 1586).
*PB: 247 — PSSL 9: 86–87 — *LF: 240 [English tr.].

1455.   To Pëtr Iurgenson
19 Mar [1880]. St. Petersburg.
RUS–KL (a³, No. 2288).
PIU 1: 143–144 — *PSSL* 9: 87–88.

1456.   To Nadezhda von Meck
20–24 Mar [1880]. St. Petersburg.
RUS–KL (a³, No. 640).
*ZC 2: 385–386 — PM 2: 329–331 — PSSL 9: 88–
90.

1457.   To Modest Chaikovskii
22 Mar [1880]. St. Petersburg.
RUS–KL (a³, No. 1587).
*ZC 2: 386 — *PB: 248 — PSSL 9: 90–91 — *LF:
241 [English tr.].

1458.   To Modest Chaikovskii
27 M[ar] 1880 [St. Petersburg].
RUS–KL (a³, No. 1588).
*PB: 248 — PSSL 9: 91–92 — *LF: 241 [English tr.].

1459.   To Pëtr Iurgenson
27 M[ar 1880]. St. Petersburg.
RUS–KL (a³, No. 2289).
PIU 1: 144–145 — *PSSL* 9: 92–93.

1460.   To Nadezhda von Meck
27–28 Mar [1880]. St. Petersburg.
RUS–KL (a³, No. 641).
PM 2: 332–333 — *PSSL* 9: 93–94.

1461. To Evgenii Al´brekht

28 Mar 1880 [St. Petersburg].

RUS–SPtob (VII.2.4.154).

Kirov: 412–413 — *PSSL* 9: 94.

1462. To Pëtr Iurgenson

29 Mar [1880]. [St. Petersburg].

RUS–KL (a³, No. 2290).

ZC 2: 388 — *PIU* 1: 145 — *PSSL* 9: 95.

1463. To Vasilii Bessel´

[1 Apr 1880. St. Petersburg].

RUS–Mcm (f. 42, No. 260).

PSSL 9: 96.

1464. To Karl Davydov

[1 Apr 1880. St. Petersburg].

RUS–KL (a³, No. 167) [facs. in *K. Iu. Davydov* (1950): 24–25].

PSSL 9: 96–97.

1464a. To Eduard Langer

1 Apr 1880 [St. Petersburg].

RUS–KL (a³, No. 3329).

Not published.

1465. To Nadezhda von Meck

2 Apr [1880]. Moscow.

RUS–KL (a³, No. 642).

ZC 2: 388 — *PM* 2: 333 — *PSSL* 9: 97.

1466. To Anatolii Chaikovskii

2 Apr [1880]. Moscow.

RUS–KL (a³, No. 1302).

PSSL 9: 98.

1467. To Nadezhda von Meck

3 Apr 1880. Moscow.

RUS–KL (a³, No. 643).

ZC 2: 389–390 — *PM* 2: 335–336 — *PSSL* 9: 98–100.

1468. To Modest Chaikovskii

3 Apr [1880]. Moscow.

RUS–KL (a³, No. 1589).

PSSL 9: 100–101.

1469. To Sergei Taneev

[early April 1880]. Moscow.

RUS–Mcl (f. 880).

PSSL 9: 101.

1470. To Vasilii Bessel´

7 Apr [1880]. Moscow.

RUS–Mcm (f. 42, No. 261).

SM (1938), 6: 50–51 — *PSSL* 9: 101–102.

1471. To Anatolii Chaikovskii

7 Apr [1880]. [Moscow].

RUS–Mcl (f. 905).

PSSL 9: 102–103.

1472. To Modest Chaikovskii

7 Apr [1880]. Moscow.

RUS–KL (a³, No. 1590).

PB: 249 — *PSSL* 9: 103 — *LF*: 242 [English tr.].

1473. To Nadezhda von Meck

9 Apr [1880]. Moscow.

RUS–KL (a³, No. 644).

PM 2: 338–339 — *PSSL* 9: 104.

1474. To Nadezhda von Meck

10 Apr [1880]. Moscow.

RUS–KL (a³, No. 645).

PM 2: 339–340 — *PSSL* 9: 104–105.

1475. To Eduard Nápravník

10 Apr [1880]. Moscow.

RUS–SPtm (Gik 17195/17).

VP: 125–126 — *EFN*: 107–108 — *PSSL* 9: 106.

1476. To Pëtr Iurgenson

13 Apr [1880]. [Kamenka].

RUS–KL (a³, No. 2291).

PSSL 9: 107.

1477. To Modest Chaikovskii

[16 Apr 1880. Kamenka] — telegram; in French.

RUS–KL (a³, No. 1593).

PSSL 9: 107.

1478.   To Nadezhda von Meck
15 Apr [1880]. Kamenka.
RUS–KL (a³, No. 646).
PM 2: 341–342 — *PSSL* 9: 107–108.

1479.   To Nadezhda von Meck
18 Apr 1880. Kamenka.
RUS–KL (a³, No. 647).
*ZC 2: 390–391 — *PM* 2: 342–343 — *PSSL* 9: 109–
110.

1480.   To Pëtr Iurgenson
18 Apr [1880]. Kamenka.
RUS–KL (a³, No. 2292).
PIU 1: 146 — *PSSL* 9: 110–111.

1481.   To Pëtr Iurgenson
19 Apr [1880]. Kamenka.
RUS–KL (a³, No. 2293).
*ZC 2: 391 — *PIU* 1: 146–147 — *PSSL* 9: 111.

1482.   To Modest Chaikovskii
[? 22 Apr 1880. Kamenka].
RUS–KL (a³, No. 1591).
PSSL 9: 112.

1483.   To Nadezhda von Meck
24 Apr 1880 [Kamenka].
RUS–KL (a³, No. 648).
PM 2: 344–345 — *PSSL* 9: 112–113.

1484.   To Alina Konradi
25 Apr 1880. Kamenka.
RUS–KL (a³, No. 230).
PSSL 9: 114–115.

1485.   To Nadezhda von Meck
[28]–30 Apr 1880 (in MS: "27 Apr") [Kamenka].
RUS–KL (a³, nos. 649–650).
*ZC 2: 392 — *PM* 2: 345–347 — *PSSL* 9: 115–117.

1486.   To Pëtr Iurgenson
30 Apr 1880. Kamenka.
RUS–KL (a³, No. 2294).
PIU 1: 148 — *PSSL* 9: 117–118.

1487.   To Anatolii Chaikovskii
3 May [1880]. Kamenka.
RUS–KL (a³, No. 1303).
PSSL 9: 118–119.

1488.   To Pëtr Iurgenson
3 May [1880]. Kamenka.
RUS–KL (a³, No. 2295).
*PIU 1: 148–149 — **PSSL* 9: 110.

1489.   To Nadezhda von Meck
3–7 May [1880]. Kamenka.
RUS–KL (a³, No. 651).
PM 2: 348–350 — *PSSL* 9: 120–122.

1490.   To Anatolii Chaikovskii
5 May [1880]. Kamenka.
RUS–KL (a³, No. 1304).
PSSL 9: 123.

1491.   To Anatolii Chaikovskii
8–9 May [1880]. Kamenka.
RUS–KL (a³, No. 1305).
PSSL 9: 123–124.

1492.   To Pëtr Iurgenson
10 May [1880]. Kamenka.
RUS–KL (a³, No. 2296).
PIU 1: 149 — *PSSL* 9: 125.

1493.   To Nadezhda von Meck
12–14 May [1880]. Kamenka.
RUS–KL (a³, No. 652).
*ZC 2: 392 — *PM* 2: 351–352 — *PSSL* 9: 125–127.

1494.   To Nikolai Lents
13 May 1880 [Kamenka].
Autograph lost
Den´ (25 Oct 1913) ["1886"] — *PSSL* 9: 127.

1495.   To Nikolai Rubinshtein
13 May [1880]. Kamenka.
RUS–KL (a³, No. 339).
IRM 1: 180–181 — *PSSL* 9: 128.

1495a. To Pëtr Iurgenson
13 May 1880. Kamenka.
US–Wc (Moldenhauer coll., box 55).
Not published.

1496. To Ivan Zeifert
15 May 1880. Kamenka.
RUS–SPtob (VII.2.4.154).
Kirov: 419 — *PSSL* 9: 129.

1497. To Anatolii Chaikovskii
15 May [1880]. Kamenka.
RUS–KL (a³, No. 1306).
*PB: 249 — *PSSL* 9: 130 — *LF: 242–243 [English tr.].

1498. To Pëtr Iurgenson
16 May 1880 [Kamenka].
RUS–KL (a³, No. 2297).
*PIU 1: 150 — *PSSL 9: 131.

1499. To Anatolii Chaikovskii
18 May [1880]. Kamenka.
RUS–KL (a³, No. 1307).
PSSL 9: 132.

1500. To Nadezhda von Meck
19–21 May 1880. Kamenka.
RUS–KL (a³, No. 653).
PM 2: 352–354 — *PSSL* 9: 133–134.

1501. To Pëtr Iurgenson
20 May [1880]. Kamenka.
RUS–KL (a³, No. 2298).
PIU 1: 150 — *PSSL* 9: 134–135.

1502. To Pëtr Iurgenson
22 May 1880. Kamenka.
RUS–KL (a³, No. 2299).
PIU 1: 151–152 — *PSSL* 9: 136.

1503. To Sergei Taneev
22 May [1880]. Kamenka.
RUS–Mcl (f. 880).
PT: 43–44 — *CTP*: 48–49 — *PSSL* 9: 136–137.

1504. To Nadezhda von Meck
24–28 May [1880]. [Kamenka].
RUS–KL (a³, No. 654).
PM 2: 354–358 — *PSSL* 9: 137–141.

1505. To Anatolii Chaikovskii
25 May [1880]. Kamenka.
RUS–KL (a³, No. 1308).
PSSL 9: 141–142.

1506. To Anatolii Chaikovskii
30 May [1880]. Kamenka.
RUS–KL (a³, No. 1241).
PSSL 9: 142–143.

1507. To Aleksandr Zhedrinskii
2 Jun 1880. Kamenka.
RUS–KL (a³, No. 2983).
PSSL 9: 143–144.

1508. To Nadezhda von Meck
2 Jun [1880]. [Kamenka].
RUS–KL (a³, No. 655).
PM 2: 358–359 — *PSSL* 9: 144–145.

1509. To Nadezhda von Meck
5 Jun [1880]. Kamenka.
RUS–KL (a³, No. 656).
*ZC 2: 392–393 — *PM* 2: 359–360 — *PSSL* 9: 145–146.

1510. To Anatolii Chaikovskii
5 Jun [1880]. Kamenka.
RUS–KL (a³, No. 1309).
PSSL 9: 147.

1511. To Anatolii Chaikovskii
12 Jun 1880. Kamenka.
RUS–KL (a³, No. 1310).
PSSL 9: 148–149.

1512. To Nadezhda von Meck
14–28 Jun 1880. Kamenka.
RUS–KL (a³, No. 657).
*ZC 2: 393–394 — *PM* 2: 362–363 — *PSSL* 9: 149–152.

1513. To Anatolii Chaikovskii
17 Jun [1880]. Kamenka.
RUS–KL (a³, No. 1311).
PSSL 9: 153–154.

1514.   To Pëtr Iurgenson
17 Jun [1880]. Kamenka.
RUS–KL (a³, No. 2300).
*ZC 2: 394 — PIU 1: 153 — PSSL 9: 154–155.

1515.   To Modest Chaikovskii
22 Jun 1880. Kamenka.
RUS–KL (a³, No. 1592).
PSSL 9: 155–156.

1516.   To Anatolii Chaikovskii
23 Jun [1880]. Kamenka.
RUS–KL (a³, No. 1312).
PSSL 9: 156–157.

1517.   To Pëtr Iurgenson
23 Jun 1880. Kamenka.
RUS–KL (a³, No. 2301).
*ZC 2: 394–395 — PIU 1: 154–155 — PSSL 9: 157–

1518.   To Karl Al´brekht
24 Jun 1880. Kamenka.
RUS–Mcm (f. 37, No. 37).
CMS: 287–290 — PSSL 9: 158–161.

1519.   To Anatolii Chaikovskii
28 Jun [1880]. Kamenka.
RUS–KL (a³, No. 1313).
PSSL 9: 161–163.

1520.   To Modest Chaikovskii
28 Jun 1880. Kamenka.
RUS–KL (a³, No. 1594).
PSSL 9: 163–166.

1521.   To Nadezhda von Meck
2 Jul [1880]. Brailov.
RUS–KL (a³, No. 658).
PM 2: 366–367 — PSSL 9: 166–167.

1522.   To Lev Davydov
3 Jul [1880]. Brailov.
RUS–SPsc (f. 834, No. 19, fol. 25–26).
PSSL 9: 167–168.

1523.   To Nadezhda von Meck
3 Jul [1880]. Brailov.
RUS–KL (a³, No. 659).
PM 2: 367–368 — PSSL 9: 168–169.

1524.   To Anatolii Chaikovskii
3 Jul [1880]. Brailov.
RUS–KL (a³, No. 1314).
PSSL 9: 170.

1525.   To Pëtr Iurgenson
3 Jul [1880]. Brailov.
RUS–KL (a³, No. 2302).
*ZC 2: 397–400 — PIU 1: 156–158 — PSSL 9: 170–
173.

1526.   To Modest Chaikovskii
4 Jul [1880]. Brailov.
RUS–KL (a³, No. 1595).
*ZC 2: 396–397 — *PB: 250 — PSSL 9: 173–175 —
*LF: 243 [English tr.].

1527.   To Nadezhda von Meck
4–7 Jul [1880]. Brailov.
RUS–KL (a³, No. 660).
*ZC 2: 400–402 — PM 2: 369–372 — PSSL 9: 175–
178.

1528.   To Modest Chaikovskii
7 Jul [1880]. Brailov.
RUS–KL (a³, No. 1596).
*PB: 251 — PSSL 9: 178–179 — *LF: 244 [English
tr.].

1529.   To Nadezhda von Meck
[8 Jul 1880. Brailov/Simaki].
RUS–KL (a³, No. 661).
*ZC 2: 402–403 — PM 2: 372–373 — PSSL 9: 180–
181.

1530.   To Lev Davydov
8 Jul [1880]. Simaki.
RUS–SPsc (f. 834, No. 19, fol. 27–28).
PSSL 9: 181–182.

1531. To Anatolii Chaikovskii

8–9 Jul 1880. Simaki.

RUS–KL (a³, No. 1315).

PSSL 9: 182–183.

1532. To Modest Chaikovskii

8–10 Jul 1880. Simaki.

RUS–KL (a³, No. 1597).

*ZC 2: 403 — **PB*: 251–252 — *PSSL* 9: 183–185 —
*LF: 245 [English tr.].

1533. To Nadezhda von Meck

9–11 Jul 1880. Simaki.

RUS–KL (a³, No. 662).

*ZC 2: 404 — *PM* 2: 375–376 — *PSSL* 9: 185–186.

1534. To Nadezhda von Meck

12–15 Jul 1880. Simaki.

RUS–KL (a³, No. 663).

*ZC 2: 404–405 — PM 2: 376–380 — *PSSL* 9: 187–190.

1535. To Anatolii Chaikovskii

13 Jul [1880]. Simaki.

RUS–KL (a³, No. 1316).

PSSL 9: 191.

1536. To Modest Chaikovskii

13 Jul [1880]. [Simaki].

RUS–KL (a³, No. 1598).

PSSL 9: 191–193.

1537. To Nikolai Konradi

15 Jul [1880]. Simaki.

Autograph lost; MS copy in RUS–KL.

CTP: 260 ("15 Aug") — *PSSL* 9: 193.

1538. To Anatolii Chaikovskii

15 Jul [1880]. [Simaki].

RUS–KL (a³, No. 1317).

PSSL 9: 194.

1539. To Nadezhda von Meck

16–19 Jul 1880 [Simaki].

RUS–KL (a³, No. 664).

*ZC 2: 405–406 — *PM* 2: 380–383 — *PSSL* 9: 195–198.

1540. To Pëtr Iurgenson

18 Jul 1880. Simaki.

RUS–KL (a³, No. 2303).

PIU 1: 159–160 — *PSSL* 9: 198–199.

1541. To Modest Chaikovskii

18–19 Jul [1880]. [Simaki].

RUS–KL (a³, No. 1599).

*ZC 2: 405–406 — PB: 252–254 — *PSSL* 9: 199–202 — *LF: 246–247 [English tr.].

1542. To Aleksandr Zhedrinskii

20 Jul [1880]. [Simaki].

RUS–KL (a³, No. 2984).

PSSL 9: 202–203.

1543. To Pëtr Iurgenson

20 Jul [1880]. Simaki.

RUS–KL (a³, No. 2304).

PIU 1: 160–161 — *PSSL* 9: 203–204.

1544. To Sergei Taneev

21 Jul [1880]. [Simaki].

RUS–Mcl (f. 880).

*ZC 2: 408–410 — *PT*: 45–48 — *CTP*: 50–53 — *PSSL* 9: 204–208.

1545. To Pëtr Iurgenson

21 Jul [1880]. [Simaki].

RUS–KL (a³, No. 2305).

PIU 1: 161 — *PSSL* 9: 208–209.

1546. To Nadezhda von Meck

21–24 Jul [1880]. Simaki.

RUS–KL (a³, nos. 665, 560).

*ZC 2: 410 — *PM* 2: 383–386 — *PSSL* 9: 209–211.

1547. To Lev Davydov

22 Jul [1880]. Simaki.

RUS–KL (a³, No. 171).

*PB: 254–255 — *PSSL* 9: 211–213 — *LF: 247–248 [English tr.].

1548.   **To Modest Chaikovskii**

22–24 Jul [1880]. [Simaki].

RUS–KL (a³, No. 1600).

PSSL 9: 213–214.

1549.   **To Pëtr Iurgenson**

23 Jul [1880]. [Simaki].

RUS–KL (a³, No. 2306).

PSSL 9: 214–215.

1550.   **To Nadezhda von Meck**

25–29 Jul [1880]. Simaki.

RUS–KL (a³, No. 666).

PM 2: 386–388 — *PSSL* 9: 215–218.

1551.   **To Modest Chaikovskii**

26 Jul [1880]. Simaki.

RUS–KL (a³, No. 1601).

PB: 255–256 — *PSSL* 9: 218–219 — **LF*: 248–249 [English tr.].

1552.   **To Nadezhda von Meck**

31 Jul–2 Aug [1880]. Kamenka.

RUS–KL (a³, No. 667).

PM 2: 390–391 — *PSSL* 9: 219–220.

1553.   **To Modest Chaikovskii**

31 Jul–2 Aug [1880]. Kamenka.

RUS–KL (a³, No. 1602).

*ZC 2: 410–411 ("31 Jun") — *PSSL* 9: 220–221.

1554.   **To Sergei Taneev**

1 Aug 1880. Kamenka.

RUS–Mcl (f. 880).

Belyi kamen´, 1 (1907): 60–61 — *PT*: 52–54 — *CTP*: 56–58 — *PSSL* 9: 222–224.

1555.   **To Pëtr Iurgenson**

[1–2 Aug 1880]. Kamenka.

RUS–KL (a³, No. 2307).

PIU 1: 162–163 — *PSSL* 9: 225–226.

1556.   **To Pëtr Iurgenson**

3 Aug [1880]. [Kamenka].

RUS–KL (a³, No. 2308).

ZC 2: 411–412 — *PIU* 1: 163 — *PSSL* 9: 226–227.

1557.   **To Nadezhda von Meck**

7 Aug [1880]. [Kamenka].

RUS–KL (a³, No. 668).

*ZC 2: 412–413 — *PM* 2: 391–393 — *PSSL* 9: 227–228.

1558.   **To Modest Chaikovskii**

7 Aug 1880 [Kamenka].

RUS–KL (a³, No. 1603).

*PSSL 9: 229–230.

1559.   **To Pëtr Iurgenson**

8 Aug [1880]. Kamenka.

RUS–KL (a³, No. 2309).

PIU 1: 163–164 — *PSSL* 9: 230–231.

1560.   **To Modest Chaikovskii**

9 Aug [1880]. [Kamenka].

RUS–KL (a³, No. 1604).

*PSSL 9: 231.

1561.   **To Nadezhda von Meck**

9–18 Aug [1880]. Kamenka.

RUS–KL (a³, No. 669) [facs. of 2 sections in *Internationales Tschaikowsky-Fest. Tübingen 23.–27. Oktober 1993: Programm* (1993): 100].

*ZC 2: 415–416 — *PM* 2: 396–399 — *PSSL* 9: 232–235.

1562.   **To Pëtr Iurgenson**

12 Aug 1880 [Kamenka].

RUS–KL (a³, No. 2310).

*ZC 2: 413–414 — *PIU* 1: 164–165 — *PSSL* 9: 235–236.

1563.   **To Pëtr Iurgenson**

13 Aug [1880]. [Kamenka].

RUS–KL (a³, No. 2311).

PIU 1: 165–166 — *PSSL* 9: 237.

1564.   **To Modest Chaikovskii**

15 Aug [1880]. Kamenka.

RUS–KL (a³, No. 1605).

PSSL 9: 238.

1565.   **To Sergei Taneev**

15–24 Aug 1880. Kamenka.

RUS–Mcl (f. 880).

Belyi kamen´, 1 (1907): 65–67 — **PT:* 59–61 — *CTP:* 61–63 — *PSSL* 9: 238–241.

1566. To Pëtr Iurgenson
[mid Aug 1880. Kamenka].
RUS–KL (a³, No. 2326).
PIU 1: 166–167 — *PSSL* 9: 242–243.

1567. To Modest Chaikovskii
19 Aug 1880 [Kamenka].
RUS–KL (a³, No. 1606).
PSSL 9: 243–244.

1568. To Nikolai Kashkin
21 Aug [1880]. [Kamenka].
RUS–KL (a³, No. 213).
PSSL 9: 244–245.

1569. To Karl Al´brekht
24 Aug [1880]. Kamenka.
RUS–Mcm (f. 37, No. 38).
PSSL 9: 245.

1570. To Nadezhda von Meck
24 Aug [1880]. Kamenka.
RUS–KL (a³, No. 670).
PM 2: 399–401 — *PSSL* 9: 245–246.

1571. To Nadezhda von Meck
26–31 Aug [1880]. Kamenka.
RUS–KL (a³, No. 671).
PM 2: 402–403 — *PSSL* 9: 247–248.

1572. To Pëtr Iurgenson
29 Aug [1880]. [Kamenka].
RUS–KL (a³, No. 2312).
PSSL 9: 249.

1573. To Pëtr Iurgenson
29 Aug [1880]. Kamenka.
RUS–KL (a³, No. 2313).
PIU 1: 167–168 — *PSSL* 9: 249–250.

1574. To Sergei Taneev
1 Sep [1880]. Kamenka.
RUS–Mcl (f. 880).
PT: 62–63 — *CTP:* 63–64 — *PSSL* 9: 250–251.

1575. To Eduard Langer
1 Sep 1880 [Kamenka].
RUS–Mfeldman
PSSL 9: 251–252.

1576. To Anatolii Chaikovskii
1 [Sep 1880]. [Kamenka].
RUS–KL (a³, No. 1319).
PSSL 9: 252–253.

1577. To Pëtr Iurgenson
1 Sep 1880 [Kamenka].
RUS–KL (a³, No. 2314).
*ZC 2: 419–420 — *PIU* 1: 168 — *PSSL* 9: 253.

1578. To Nadezhda von Meck
1–6 Sep 1880. Kamenka.
RUS–KL (a³, No. 672).
*ZC 2: 420–421 — *PM* 2: 404–407 — *PSSL* 9: 254–256.

1579. To Eduard Nápravník
5 Sep 1880. Kamenka.
Autograph lost; typed copy in RUS–KL.
VP: 127–128 — *EFN:* 109 — *PSSL* 9: 257.

1580. To Anatolii Chaikovskii
5 Sep 1880. Kamenka.
RUS–KL (a³, No. 1320).
PSSL 9: 258.

1581. To Pëtr Iurgenson
6 Sep 1880 [Kamenka].
RUS–KL (a³, No. 2315).
PIU 1: 169 — *PSSL* 9: 259.

1582. To Pëtr Iurgenson
[6 Sep 1880. Kamenka].
RUS–KL (a³, No. 2316).
PIU 1: 169 — *PSSL* 9: 260.

1583. To Anatolii Chaikovskii
7 Sep [1880]. Kamenka.
RUS–KL (a³, No. 1321).
PB: 256–257 — *PSSL* 9: 260–261 — *LF:* 249 [English tr.].

1584.   To Pëtr Iurgenson
[7 Sep 1880]. Kamenka.
RUS–KL (a³, No. 2317).
PIU 1: 169–170 — *PSSL* 9: 261–262.

1584a. To Elizaveta Chaikovskaia
9 Sep 1880. Kamenka.
RUS–SPsc (f. 834, No. 30, fol. 7–9).
PSSL 9: 281 ("19 Sep", No. 1598).

1585.   To Nadezhda von Meck
9–12 Sep [1880]. Kamenka.
RUS–KL (a³, No. 673).
*ZC 2: 421–423 — *PM* 2: 408–411 — *PSSL* 9: 262–264.

1586.   To Eduard Nápravník
12 Sep [1880]. Kamenka.
Autograph lost; typed copy in RUS–KL.
VP: 128–129 — *EFN*: 109–110 — *PSSL* 9: 265.

1587.   To Anatolii Chaikovskii
12 Sep [1880]. Kamenka.
RUS–KL (a³, No. 1322).
PSSL 9: 266.

1588.   To Pëtr Iurgenson
12 Sep [1880]. [Kamenka].
RUS–KL (a³, No. 2318).
PIU 1: 172 — *PSSL* 9: 267.

1589.   To Nadezhda von Meck
13 Sep [1880]. Kamenka.
RUS–KL (a³, No. 674).
PM 2: 411 — *PSSL* 9: 267–268.

1590.   To Anatolii Chaikovskii
[13] Sep [1880]. Kamenka.
RUS–KL (a³, No. 1323).
PSSL 9: 267–268.

1591.   To Pëtr Iurgenson
13 Sep [1880]. Kamenka.
RUS–KL (a³, No. 2319).
PIU 1: 173–175 — *PSSL* 9: 269–272.

1592.   To Nadezhda von Meck
15 Sep [1880]. Kamenka.
RUS–KL (a³, No. 675).
PM 2: 413–416 — *PSSL* 9: 272–275.

1593.   To Pëtr Iurgenson
15 Sep [1880]. Kamenka.
RUS–KL (a³, No. 2320).
PIU 1: 175–176 — *PSSL* 9: 275.

1594.   To Anatolii Chaikovskii
16 Sep [1880]. Kamenka.
RUS–KL (a³, No. 1324).
PSSL 9: 277.

1595.   To Vasilii Bessel´
18 Sep [1880]. Kamenka.
RUS–Mcm (f. 42, No. 262).
SM (1938), 6: 51 — *PSSL* 9: 278.

1596.   To Pëtr Iurgenson
18 Sep 1880 [Kamenka].
RUS–KL (a³, No. 2321).
PIU 1: 176 — *PSSL* 9: 278–279.

1597.   To Nadezhda von Meck
19 Sep [1880]. Kamenka.
RUS–KL (a³, No. 676).
PM 2: 416 — *PSSL* 9: 279280.

1598.   [see 1584a]

1599.   To Anatolii Chaikovskii
21 Sep [1880]. Kamenka.
RUS–KL (a³, No. 1325).
*PB: 257 — *PSSL* 9: 282 — *LF: 250 [English tr.].

1600.   To Pëtr Iurgenson
21 Sep 1880 [Kamenka].
RUS–KL (a³, No. 2322).
PIU 1: 176 — *PSSL* 9: 282–283.

1601.   To Nadezhda von Meck
21–25 Sep 1880. Kamenka.
RUS–KL (a³, No. 4677).
PM 2: 419–420 — *PSSL* 9: 283–284.

1602. To Anna Merkling

27 Sep 1880. Kamenka.

Autograph lost; MS copy in RUS–KL.

CTP: 209–210 — *PSSL* 9: 284–285.

1603. To Nadezhda von Meck

27–30 Sep 1880. Kamenka.

RUS–KL (a³, No. 678).

ZC 2: 424 — *PM* 2: 422–424 — *PSSL* 9: 285–287.

1604. To Anatolii Chaikovskii

29 Sep [1880]. Kamenka.

RUS–KL (a³, No. 1327).

PSSL 9: 288–289.

1605. To Anatolii Chaikovskii

1 Oct [1880]. Kamenka.

RUS–KL (a³, No. 1328).

PB: 257–258 — *PSSL* 9: 289 — *LF*: 250–251 [English tr.].

1606. To Nadezhda von Meck

3 Oct [1880]. Kamenka.

RUS–KL (a³, No. 679).

PM 2: 424 — *PSSL* 9: 290.

1607. To Nadezhda von Meck

5 Oct 1880. Kamenka.

RUS–KL (a³, No. 680).

PM 2: 425–426 — *PSSL* 9: 290–292.

1608. To Anatolii Chaikovskii

6 Oct [1880]. Kamenka.

RUS–KL (a³, No. 1330).

PSSL 9: 292–293.

1609. To Nadezhda von Meck

8–10 Oct [1880]. Kamenka.

RUS–KL (a³, No. 681).

ZC 2: 425–426 — *PM* 2: 427–429 — *PSSL* 9: 293–295.

1610. To Pëtr Iurgenson

9 Oct [1880]. Kamenka.

RUS–KL (a³, No. 2323).

PIU 1: 177 — *PSSL* 9: 295–296.

1611. To Anatolii Chaikovskii

11 Oct [1880]. Kamenka.

RUS–KL (a³, No. 1331).

PSSL 9: 296–297.

1612. To Pëtr Iurgenson

11 Oct [1880]. Kamenka.

RUS–KL (a³, No. 2324).

PIU 1: 177 — *PSSL* 9: 297–298.

1613. To Nadezhda von Meck

14–16 Oct 1880. Kamenka.

RUS–KL (a³, No. 682).

ZC 2: 426–427 — *PM* 2: 431–433 — *PSSL* 9: 298–300.

1614. To Anatolii Chaikovskii

17 Oct [1880]. Kamenka.

RUS–KL (a³, No. 1332) [facs. of 2 pages in *MNC* (1958): 47].

PB: 258 — *PSSL* 9: 301–302 — *LF*: 251 [English tr.].

1615. To Nadezhda von Meck

22 Oct [1880]. Kamenka.

RUS–KL (a³, No. 683).

PM 2: 435–436 — *PSSL* 9: 302–304.

1616. To Anatolii Chaikovskii

24 Oct [1880]. Kamenka.

RUS–KL (a³, No. 1333).

PSSL 9: 304–305.

1617. To Nadezhda von Meck

24–27 Oct 1880. Kamenka.

RUS–KL (a³, No. 684).

ZC 2: 427–429 — *PM* 2: 438–440 — *PSSL* 9: 305–307.

1618. To Aleksei Sofronov

27 Oct [1880]. Kamenka.

RUS–SPsc (f. 834, No. 25, fol. 28–29).

PSSL 9: 307–308.

1619. To Pëtr Iurgenson

27 Oct [1880]. Kamenka.

RUS–KL (a³, No. 2325).

ZC 2: 429 — *PIU* 1: 179 — *PSSL* 9: 308–30

1620.   To Vasilii Bessel´

[29 Oct 1880. Kamenka] — note on visiting card.

RUS–Mcm (f. 42, No. 263).

SM (1938), 6: 51 — *PSSL* 9: 309.

1621.   To Nadezhda von Meck

31 Oct [1880]. Kamenka.

RUS–KL (a³, No. 685).

PM 2: 442–443 — *PSSL* 9: 309–311.

1622.   To Anatolii Chaikovskii

31 Oct [1880]. Kamenka.

RUS–KL (a³, No. 1324).

PSSL 9: 311.

1623.   To Anatolii Chaikovskii

5 Nov [1880]. Kamenka.

RUS–KL (a³, No. 1335).

PSSL 9: 312.

1624.   To Nadezhda von Meck

7 Nov 1880. Kamenka.

RUS–KL (a³, No. 686).

ZC 2: 430 — *PM* 2: 445–446 — *PSSL* 9: 312–313.

1625.   To Grand Duke Konstantin Konstantinovich

[7 Nov 1880. Kamenka].

RUS–SPil (f. 137, No. 78/1).

PSSL 9: 313–314.

1626.   To Pëtr Iurgenson

[mid Nov 1880. Moscow].

RUS–KL (a³, No. 2281).

PSSL 9: 314.

1627.   To Nadezhda von Meck

12 Nov 1880. Moscow.

RUS–KL (a³, No. 687).

PM 2: 447 — *PSSL* 9: 315.

1628.   To Nadezhda von Meck

17 Nov [1880]. Moscow.

RUS–KL (a³, No. 688).

PM 2: 448 — *PSSL* 9: 316.

1629.   To Modest Chaikovskii

17–18 Nov [1880]. Moscow.

RUS–KL (a³, No. 1607).

PB: 259 — *PSSL* 9: 317 — *LF*: 252 [English tr.].

1630.   To Karl Al´brekht

[mid Nov 1880. Moscow].

RUS–Mcm (f. 37, No. 39).

PSSL 9: 317.

1631.   To Nadezhda von Meck

[20–]21 Nov [1880]. Moscow.

RUS–KL (a³, No. 689).

PM 2: 448–449 — *PSSL* 9: 318.

1632.   To Nadezhda von Meck

27 Nov 1880. St. Petersburg.

RUS–KL (a³, No. 690).

ZC 2: 431–432 — *PM* 2: 450–452 — *PSSL* 9: 319–320.

1633.   To Karl Al´brekht

[27 Nov–2 Dec 1880. St. Petersburg].

RUS–Mcm

PSSL 9: 321.

1634.   To Karl Davydov

[1 Dec 1880. St. Petersburg].

RUS–KL (a³, No. 168).

PSSL 9: 321.

1635.   To Vasilii Bessel´

[1–7 Dec 1880. St. Petersburg] — note on visiting card.

RUS–Mcm (f. 42, No. 264).

PSSL 9: 321–322.

1636.   To Nadezhda von Meck

[2–5 Dec 1880]. St. Petersburg.

RUS–KL (a³, No. 696a).

ZC 2: 432–433 — *PM* 2: 452–454 — *PSSL* 9: 322–323.

1637.   To Modest Chaikovskii

8 Dec [1880]. Moscow.

RUS–KL (a³, No. 1608).

PB: 259 — *PSSL* 9: 323–324 — *LF*: 252 [English tr.].

1638. To Pëtr Iurgenson

[8 Dec 1880. Moscow].

RUS–KL (a³, No. 2445).

PSSL 9: 324.

1639. To Karl Al´brekht

[mid Dec 1880. Moscow].

RUS–Mcm (f. 37, No. 41).

PSSL 9: 324.

1640. To Anna Aleksandrova-Levenson

9 Dec 1880 [Moscow].

Autograph lost; MS copy in RUS–KL.

SN (1905), 10: 101 — *PSSL* 9: 325.

1641. To Nadezhda von Meck

9 Dec 1880. Moscow.

RUS–KL (a³, No. 691).

PM 2: 454–456 — *PSSL* 9: 325–326.

1642. To Pëtr Iurgenson

[9 Dec 1880. Moscow].

RUS–KL (a³, No. 2444).

PSSL 9: 327.

1643. To Eduard Nápravník

11 Dec 1880 [Moscow].

Autograph lost; typed copy in RUS–KL.

VP: 130–132 — *EFN*: 111–112 — *PSSL* 9: 327–329.

1644. To Modest Chaikovskii

12 Dec 1880. Moscow.

RUS–KL (a³, No. 1609).

PB: 259–260 — *PSSL* 9: 329–330 — *LF*: 253 [English tr.].

1645. To Anna Maslova

13 Dec 1880 [Moscow].

RUS–KL (a³, No. 271).

PSSL 9: 330.

1646. To Sergei Taneev

13 Dec [1880]. [Moscow].

RUS–Mcl (f. 880).

CTP: 65–66 — *PSSL* 9: 331.

1647. To Modest Chaikovskii

14 Dec 1880. Moscow.

RUS–KL (a³, No. 1610).

PB: 260–261 — *PSSL* 9: 331–332 — *LF*: 253–254 [English tr.].

1648. To Nadezhda von Meck

14–17 Dec [1880]. Moscow.

RUS–KL (a³, No. 692).

ZC 2: 433–434 — *PM* 2: 456–458 — *PSSL* 9: 332–333.

1649. To Leontii Tkachenko

16 Dec [1880]. Moscow.

RUS–SPsc (f. 834, No. 29, fol. 1–2).

ZC 2: 435–436 — *PSSL* 9: 335.

1650. To Karl Al´brekht

[18 Dec 1880. Moscow].

RUS–Mcm (f. 37, No. 40).

PSSL 9: 336.

1651. To Modest Chaikovskii

18–[19] Dec 1880. Moscow.

RUS–KL (a³, No. 1611).

ZC 2: 436 — *PB*: 261–262 — *PSSL* 9: 336–338 — *LF*: 254–255 [English tr.].

1652. To Modest Chaikovskii

[21 Dec 1880. Moscow].

RUS–KL (a³, No. 1612).

ZC 2: 436–437 — *PB*: 262 — *PSSL* 9: 340–341 — *LF*: 255–256 [English tr.].

1653. To Anatolii Chaikovskii

22–[23 Dec 1880]. Kiev.

RUS–KL (a³, No. 1336).

PB: 263 — *PSSL* 9: 340–341 — *LF*: 256 [English tr.].

1654. To Nadezhda von Meck

23 Dec [1880]. Kiev.

RUS–KL (a³, No. 693).

PM 2: 458–459 — *PSSL* 9: 341–342.

1655. To Anatolii Chaikovskii

25 Dec [1880]. Kamenka.

RUS–KL (a³, No. 1337).
PSSL 9: 342–343.

1656.   To Aleksei Sofronov
26 Dec [1880]. Kamenka.
RUS–SPsc (f. 834, No. 25, fol. 30–31).
PSSL 9: 343.

1657.   To Modest Chaikovskii
26 Dec [1880]. Kamenka.
RUS–KL (a³, No. 1613).
PSSL 9: 343–344.

1658.   To Nadezhda von Meck
28 Dec [1880]. Kamenka.
RUS–KL (a³, No. 694).
PM 2: 461–462 — *PSSL* 9: 344–346.

1659.   To Aleksei Sofronov
29 Dec 1880. Kamenka.
RUS–SPsc (f. 834, fol. 25, No. 32–33).
PSSL 9: 346.

1660.   To Nadezhda von Meck
30 Dec 1880–5 Jan 1881. Kamenka.
RUS–KL (a³, No. 695).
PM 2: 462–465 — *PSSL* 9: 346–349.

1881

1661.   To Modest Chaikovskii
2 Jan 1881. Kamenka.
RUS–KL (a³, No. 1614).
PB: 263–264 — *PSSL* 10: 13–15 — *LF*: 256–257
   [English tr.].

1662.   To Aleksandr Tarnavich
[2–3 Jan 1881. Kamenka].
RUS–KL (a³, No. 407).
PSSL 10: 13.

1663.   To Karl Al´brekht
[3 Jan 1881. Kamenka] — telegram.
RUS–Mcm (f. 37, No. 43).
PSSL 10: 15–16.

1664.   To Leontii Tkachenko
[10 Jan 1881. Moscow].
RUS–SPsc (f. 834, No. 29, fol. 3).
PSSL 10: 16.

1665.   To Nadezhda von Meck
12 Jan 1881. Moscow.
RUS–KL (a³, No. 696).
*ZC 2: 445–446 — *PM* 2: 466–467 — *PSSL* 10: 16–
   17.

1665a.   To Leontii Tkachenko
[mid Jan or late Sep 1881. Moscow].
RUS–SPsc (f. 834, No. 29, fol. 36–37).
Not published.

1666.   To Ekaterina Sinel´nikova
17 Jan 1881. Moscow.
RUS–Mcl (f. 905).
PSSL 10: 18.

1667.   To Nadezhda von Meck
19–21 Jan 1881. Moscow.
RUS–KL (a³, No. 697).
*ZC 2: 446–447 — *PM* 2: 467–469 — *PSSL* 10: 18–
   20.

1668.   To Nadezhda von Meck
22 Jan [1881] (in MS: "1880"). Moscow.
RUS–KL (a³, No. 698).
PM 2: 469–470 — *PSSL* 10: 20–21.

1669.   To Aleksandr Tarnavich
[mid Jan 1881. Moscow].
RUS–KL (a³, No. 409).
PSSL 10: 21.

1670.   To Nadezhda von Meck
26 Jan 1881. St. Petersburg.
RUS–KL (a³, No. 699).
*ZC 2: 447–448 — *PM* 2: 470–471 — *PSSL* 10: 22–
   23.

1671.   To Nadezhda von Meck
27 Jan–1 Feb 1881. St. Petersburg.
RUS–KL (a³, No. 700).
*ZC 2: 448–450 — *PM* 2: 471–473 — *PSSL* 10: 23–
   25.

1672. To Aleksei Sofronov

29 Jan [1881]. St. Petersburg.

RUS–SPsc (f. 834, No. 25, fol. 36–37).

PSSL 10: 26.

1673. To Anatolii Chaikovskii

1 Feb [1881]. St. Petersburg.

RUS–KL (a³, No. 1338).

PB: 264 — *PSSL* 10: 26–27 — *LF*: 257–258 [English tr.].

1674. To Aleksei Sofronov

2 Feb 1881. St. Petersburg.

RUS–SPsc (f. 834, No. 25, fol. 38–39).

PSSL 10: 27.

1675. To Karl Al´brekht

[7 Feb 1881. St. Petersburg] — telegram.

RUS–Mcm (f. 37, No. 42).

PSSL 10: 28.

1676. To Nadezhda von Meck

7 Feb 1881. St. Petersburg.

RUS–KL (a³, No. 701).

*ZC 2: 450–451 — *PM* 2: 475–476 — *PSSL* 10: 28–29.

1677. To Aleksei Sofronov

10 Feb 1881 [St. Petersburg].

RUS–SPsc (f. 834, No. 25, fol. 40–41).

PSSL 10: 29–30.

1678. To Nadezhda von Meck

11 Feb 1881. St. Petersburg.

RUS–KL (a³, No. 702).

*ZC 2: 451 — *PM* 2: 476–477 — *PSSL* 10: 30–31.

1679. To Eduard Nápravník

14 Feb 1881. St. Petersburg.

Autograph lost; typed copy in RUS–KL.

EFN: 112–113 — *PSSL* 10: 31.

1680. To Nadezhda von Meck

[15 Feb 1881. Vil´na] — telegram.

RUS–KL (a³, No. 703).

PM 2: 477 — *PSSL* 10: 32.

1681. To Nadezhda von Meck

16/28 Feb 1881. Vienna.

RUS–KL (a³, No. 704).

*ZC 2: 453–454 — *PM* 2: 478–479 — *PSSL* 10: 32–33.

1682. To Anatolii Chaikovskii

16/28 Feb 1881. Vienna.

RUS–KL (a³, No. 1339).

*PB: 264–265 — *PSSL* 10: 33–34 — **LF*: 258 [English tr.].

1683. To Modest Chaikovskii

16/28 Feb 1881. Vienna.

RUS–KL (a³, No. 1615).

*PB: 265–266 — *PSSL* 10: 34–35 — **LF*: 258–259 [English tr.].

1684. To Nadezhda von Meck

19 Feb/3 Mar 1881. Florence.

RUS–KL (a³, No. 705).

*ZC 2: 456–457 — *PM* 2: 479–480 — *PSSL* 10: 35–36.

1685. To Anatolii Chaikovskii

19 Feb/3 Mar 1881. Florence.

RUS–KL (a³, No. 1340).

PSSL 10: 36–37.

1686. To Modest Chaikovskii

19 Feb/3 Mar 1881 [Florence].

RUS–KL (a³, No. 1616).

PB: 266 — *PSSL* 10: 37–38 — *LF*: 259–260 [English tr.].

1687. To Aleksei Sofronov

19 Feb/3 Mar [1881]. Florence.

RUS–SPsc (f. 834, No. 25, fol. 42–43).

PSSL 10: 38.

1688. To Nadezhda von Meck

19 Feb/3 Mar [1881]. Florence.

RUS–KL (a³, No. 706).

*ZC 2: 457 — *PM* 2: 480 — *PSSL* 10: 39.

1689. To Modest Chaikovskii

20 Feb/4 Mar 1881. Rome.

RUS–KL (a³, No. 1617).
*ZC 2: 457 — PSSL 10: 39–41.

1690. To Anatolii Chaikovskii
21 Feb/5 Mar 1881. Rome.
RUS–KL (a³, No. 1341).
PSSL 10: 41–42.

1691. To Pëtr Iurgenson
21 Feb/5 Mar 1881. Rome.
RUS–KL (a³, No. 2327).
PIU 1: 183 — PSSL 10: 42–43.

1692. To Nadezhda von Meck
21–23 Feb/5–7 Mar 1881. Rome.
RUS–KL (a³, No. 707).
*ZC 2: 457–458 — PM 2: 480–484 — PSSL 10: 43–46.

1693. To Modest Chaikovskii
22 Feb/6 Mar 1881. Rome.
RUS–KL (a³, No. 1618).
PSSL 10: 46–47.

1693a. To Enrico Bevignani
[23 Feb]/7 Mar 1881 [Rome].
Autograph auctioned at Christie's, London in 1994 [see ČS 3 (1998): 185].
Not published.

1694. To Anatolii Chaikovskii
23 Feb/7 Mar 1881. Rome.
RUS–KL (a³, No. 1342).
PSSL 10: 47–48.

1695. To Modest Chaikovskii
25 Feb/9 Mar 1881. Rome.
RUS–KL (a³, No. 1619).
*ZC 2: 458–459 — *PB: 267 — PSSL 10: 49–50 — *LF: 260 [English tr.].

1696. To Aleksei Sofronov
26 Feb/10 Mar 1881. Rome.
RUS–SPsc (f. 834, No. 25, fol. 44–45).
PSSL 10: 50–51.

1697. To Modest Chaikovskii
26–27 Feb/10–11 Mar 1881. Rome.
RUS–KL (a³, No. 1620).
*ZC 2: 459 — PSSL 10: 51–52.

1698. To Anatolii Chaikovskii
1/13 Mar 1881. Naples.
RUS–KL (a³, No. 1343).
PSSL 10: 52–53.

1699. To Pëtr Iurgenson
1/13 Mar 1881. Naples.
RUS–KL (a³, No. 2328).
PIU 1: 185–186 — PSSL 10: 53–54.

1700. To Nadezhda von Meck
3/15 Mar 1881. Naples.
RUS–KL (a³, No. 708).
*ZC 2: 460–461 — PM 2: 484 — PSSL 10: 54–55.

1701. To Modest Chaikovskii
3/15 Mar 1881. Naples.
RUS–KL (a³, No. 1621).
*ZC 2: 460 — *PSSL 10: 55–58.

1702. To Tat´iana Davydova
4/16 Mar 1881. Naples.
RUS–SPsc (f. 834, No. 18, fol. 3–4).
PSSL 10: 58–59.

1703. To Anatolii Chaikovskii
6/18 Mar 1881. Naples.
RUS–KL (a³, No. 1344).
PSSL 10: 59–60.

1704. To Nadezhda von Meck
10/22 Mar 1881. Nice.
RUS–KL (a³, No. 709).
*ZC 2: 461–462 — PM 2: 487–488 — PSSL 10: 60–61.

1705. To Aleksei Sofronov
10/22 Mar 1881. Nice.
RUS–SPsc (f. 834, No. 25, fol. 46–47).
PSSL 10: 61–62.

1706. To Sergei Taneev
10/22 Mar 1881. Nice.
RUS–Mcl (f. 880).
PT: 66 — *CTP*: 67–68 — *PSSL* 10: 62.

1707. To Modest Chaikovskii
10/[22] Mar [1881]. Nice.
RUS–KL (a³, No. 1622).
ZC 2: 461 — *PSSL* 10: 63.

1708. To Anatolii Chaikovskii
11/23 Mar [1881]. Nice.
RUS–KL (a³, No. 1345).
PB: 267 — *PSSL* 10: 63–64 — *LF*: 261 [English tr.].

1709. To Modest Chaikovskii
13/25 Mar 1881 [Paris].
RUS–KL (a³, No. 1623).
ZC 2: 462 — *PB*: 268 — *PSSL* 10: 64–65 — *LF*: 261–262 [English tr.].

1710. To the editor of *Moskovskie vedomosti*
[14]/26 Mar 1881 [Paris] — letter article *The Last Days of N. G. Rubinshtein's Life* (315).
RUS–Mcl [incomplete].
Moskovskie vedomosti (23 Mar 1881) — *Russkie vedomosti* (24 Mar 1881) — *ZC* 2: 463–465 — *PSSL* 10: 65–67.

1711. To Nadezhda von Meck
15/27 Mar 1881. Paris.
RUS–KL (a³, No. 710).
PM 2: 489–490 — *PSSL* 10: 67–68.

1712. To Nadezhda von Meck
16/28 Mar 1881. Paris.
RUS–KL (a³, No. 711).
ZC 2: 466–468 — *PM* 2: 491–493 — *PSSL* 10: 69–71.

1713. To Sergei Flerov
16/[28] Mar 1881 (in MS: "24 Mar"). Paris.
RUS–Mcl (f. 905).
PSSL 10: 71–72.

1714. To Lev Davydov
17/29 Mar 1881. Paris.
RUS–SPsc (f. 834, No. 19, fol. 29–30).
PSSL 10: 72.

1715. To Anatolii Chaikovskii
17/29 Mar 1881. Paris.
RUS–KL (a³, No. 1346).
ZC 2: 633–634 — *PB*: 268–269 — *PSSL* 10: 73 — *LF*: 262 [English tr.].

1716. To Modest Chaikovskii
17/29 Mar 1881. Paris.
RUS–KL (a³, No. 1624).
ZC 2: 467 — *PB*: 269–270 — *PSSL* 10: 73–74 — *LF*: 263 [English tr.].

1717. To Lev Davydov
19/31 Mar 1881. Paris.
RUS–SPsc (f. 834, No. 19, fol. 1717).
PSSL 10: 74–75.

1718. To Nadezhda von Meck
20 Mar/1 Apr 1881. Paris.
RUS–KL (a³, No. 713).
PM 2: 493–494 — *PSSL* 10: 75–76.

1719. To Anatolii Chaikovskii
26 Mar [1881]. St. Petersburg.
RUS–KL (a³, No. 1347).
PSSL 10: 76.

1720. To Aleksei Sofronov
28 Mar [1881]. St. Petersburg.
RUS–SPsc (f. 834, No. 25, fol. 48–49).
PSSL 10: 77.

1721. To Nadezhda von Meck
30 Mar 1881. St. Petersburg.
RUS–KL (a³, No. 712).
PM 2: 497–498 — *PSSL* 10: 77–78.

1722. To Anatolii Chaikovskii
30 Mar 1881 [St. Petersburg].
RUS–KL (a³, No. 1348).
PSSL 10: 78.

1723.   To Nadezhda von Meck
31 Mar 1881. St. Petersburg.
RUS–KL (a³, No. 714).
PM 2: 498 — *PSSL* 10: 79.

1724.   To Aleksandr Zhedrinskii
2 Apr [1881]. St. Petersburg].
RUS–KL (a³, No. 274).
PSSL 10: 79.

1725.   To Nadezhda von Meck
2 Apr 1881. St. Petersburg.
RUS–KL (a³, No. 715).
PM 2: 498–499 — *PSSL* 10: 80–81.

1726.   To Nadezhda von Meck
8 Apr [1881]. St. Petersburg.
RUS–KL (a³, No. 716).
PM 2: 500–501 — *PSSL* 10: 81–82.

1727.   To Pëtr Iurgenson
9 Apr [1881]. St. Petersburg.
RUS–KL (a³, No. 2329).
PIU 1: 187–188 — *PSSL* 10: 82.

1728.   To Anna Aleksandrova-Levenson
15 Apr 1881. St. Petersburg.
GB–Lbl (Add. 50483, ff. 141–147).
SN (1905), 10: 102–103 — *PSSL* 10: 83.

1729.   To Nadezhda von Meck
18 Apr 1881. St. Petersburg
RUS–KL (a³, No. 717).
PM 2: 502–503 — *PSSL* 10: 83–85.

1730.   To Aleksei Sofronov
20 Apr [1881]. St. Petersburg.
RUS–SPsc (f. 834, No. 26, fol. 1–2).
PSSL 10: 85.

1731.   To Aleksei Sofronov
[25 Apr 1881. Moscow].
RUS–SPsc (f. 834, No. 25, fol. 34–35).
PSSL 10: 86.

1732.   To Nadezhda von Meck
29 Apr 1881. Kamenka.
RUS–KL (a³, No. 718).
ZC 2: 468 — *PM* 2: 504–505 — *PSSL* 10: 86–87.

1733.   To Anatolii Chaikovskii
30 Apr 1881. Kamenka.
RUS–KL (a³, No. 1349).
PSSL 10: 87–88.

1734.   To Modest Chaikovskii
30 Apr [1881]. Kamenka.
RUS–KL (a³, No. 1625).
PSSL 10: 88–89.

1735.   To Nadezhda von Meck
30 Apr 1881. Kamenka.
RUS–KL (a³, No. 719).
PM 2: 505–507 — *PSSL* 10: 89–91.

1736.   To German Konradi
1 May 1881. Kamenka.
RUS–SPsc (f. 834, No. 21) [rough draft dated 30 Apr
    in RUS–KL (a³, No. 229)].
PSSL 10: 91–93.

1737.   To Pëtr Iurgenson
1 May [1881]. Kamenka.
RUS–KL (a³, No. 2330).
PSSL 10: 94.

1738.   To Aleksei Sofronov
2 May [1881]. Kamenka.
RUS–SPsc (f. 834, No. 26, fol. 3–4).
PSSL 10: 94–95.

1739.   To Pëtr Iurgenson
2 May [1881]. Kamenka.
RUS–KL (a³, No. 2331).
PIU 1: 188 — *PSSL* 10: 95.

1740.   To Karl Davydov
5 May 1881. Kamenka.
RUS–Mcl
Muzykal´noe obrazovanie (1926), 5–6: 44–45 — *PSSL*
    10: 95–96.

1741. To Anatolii Chaikovskii
6 May [1881]. Kamenka.
RUS–KL (a³, No. 1350).
*PSSL 10: 97–98 — *ZN: 125.

1742. To Modest Chaikovskii
7 May 1881. Kamenka.
RUS–KL (a³, No. 1626).
*PSSL 10: 98–99 — *ZN: 126.

1743. To Pëtr Iurgenson
7 May 1881. Kamenka.
RUS–KL (a³, No. 2332).
*ZC 2: 469 — PIU 1: 189 — PSSL 10: 100.

1744. To Nadezhda von Meck
8 May 1881. Kamenka.
RUS–KL (a³, No. 720).
*ZC 2: 469 — PM 2: 509 — PSSL 10: 101–102.

1745. To Pëtr Iurgenson
8 May 1881. Kamenka.
RUS–KL (a³, No. 2333).
*ZC 2: 469–470 ("6 May") — PIU 1: 190 — PSSL
10: 102.

1746. To Aleksei Sofronov
10 May [1881]. Kamenka.
RUS–KL (a³, No. 373).
PM 2: 634–635 — PSSL 10: 102–103.

1747. To Nadezhda von Meck
10–13 May [1881]. Kamenka.
RUS–KL (a³, No. 721).
PM 2: 511–512 — PSSL 10: 103–104.

1748. To Modest Chaikovskii
11 May [1881]. Kamenka.
RUS–KL (a³, No. 1627).
PSSL 10: 105.

1749. To Pëtr Iurgenson
11 May [1881]. Kamenka.
RUS–KL (a³, No. 2688).
PIU 1: 191–192 — PSSL 10: 105–106.

1750. To Sergei Rachinskii
13 May 1881. Kamenka.
RUS–SPsc (f. 631, fol. 107–108).
*ZC 2: 470–471 — PSSL 10: 106–107.

1751. To Anatolii Chaikovskii
13 May [1881]. Kamenka.
RUS–KL (a³, No. 1351).
PSSL 10: 107–108.

1752. To Nadezhda von Meck
15 May 1881 [Kamenka].
RUS–KL (a³, No. 722).
PM 2: 512 — PSSL 10: 108–109.

1753. To Modest Chaikovskii
16 May 1881 [Kamenka].
RUS–KL (a³, No. 1628).
PSSL 10: 109–110.

1754. To Nadezhda von Meck
17 May 1881. Kamenka.
RUS–KL (a³, No. 723).
*ZC 2: 471 — PM 2: 512–514 — PSSL 10: 110–111.

1755. To Sergei Flerov
17 May [1881]. Kamenka
RUS–Mcl
CMS: 461 — PSSL 10: 111.

1756. To Aleksei Sofronov
18 May [1881]. Kamenka.
RUS–KL (a³, No. 372).
PSSL 10: 112.

1757. To Pëtr Iurgenson
18 May 1881 [Kamenka].
RUS–KL (a³, No. 3306).
PSSL 10: 112.

1758. To Pëtr Iurgenson
18 May [1881]. [Kamenka].
RUS–KL (a³, No. 2335).
PSSL 10: 113.

1759.   To Konstantin Pobedonostsev

19 May 1881. Kamenka.

RUS–KL (a^3, No. 303).

K. P. Pobedonostsev i ego korrespondenty (1923): 403–
404 — *PSSL* 10: 113–115.

1760.   To Anatolii Chaikovskii

19 May [1881]. Kamenka.

RUS–KL (a^3, No. 1352).

PSSL 10: 115.

1761.   To Pëtr Iurgenson

19 May [1881]. [Kamenka].

RUS–KL (a^3, No. 2199).

PSSL 10: 116.

1762.   To Nadezhda von Meck

21 May 1881. Kamenka.

RUS–KL (a^3, No. 724).

PM 2: 514–516 — *PSSL* 10: 116–117.

1763.   To Anatolii Chaikovskii

21 May 1881. Kamenka.

RUS–KL (a^3, No. 1353).

PSSL 10: 117–118.

1764.   To Modest Chaikovskii

22 May [1881]. Kamenka.

RUS–KL (a^3, No. 1629).

PSSL 10: 119.

1765.   To Modest Chaikovskii

24 May 1881. Kamenka.

RUS–KL (a^3, No. 1630).

*PB: 270–271 — *PSSL* 10: 119–121 — **LF*: 263–264
[English tr.].

1766.   To Nadezhda von Meck

24–27 May 1881. Kamenka.

RUS–KL (a^3, No. 725).

PM 2: 516–517 — *PSSL* 10: 122–123.

1767.   To Pëtr Iurgenson

25 May 1881. Kamenka.

RUS–KL (a^3, No. 2336).

PIU 1: 192 — *PSSL* 10: 123.

1768.   To Anatolii Chaikovskii

28 May 1881. Kamenka.

RUS–KL (a^3, No. 1354).

PSSL 10: 124–125.

1769.   To Modest Chaikovskii

31 May 1881. Kamenka.

RUS–KL (a^3, No. 1631).

PSSL 10: 125–127.

1770.   To Konstantin Pobedonostsev

1 Jun 1881. Kamenka.

RUS–Mrg

K. P. Pobedonostsev i ego korrespondenty (1923): 235 —
PSSL 10: 127.

1771.   To Nadezhda von Meck

2 Jun 1881. Kamenka.

RUS–KL (a^3, No. 726).

*ZC 2: 471–472 — *PM* 2: 517–518 — *PSSL* 10: 127–
128.

1772.   To Konstantin Pobedonostsev

4 Jun 1881. Kamenka

RUS–Mrg

K. P. Pobedonostsev i ego korrespondenty (1923): 235 —
PSSL 10: 236.

1773.   To Aleksei Sofronov

4 Jun [1881]. Kamenka.

RUS–SPsc (f. 834, No. 26, fol. 7–8).

PSSL 10: 129–130.

1774.   To Sergei Flerov

4 Jun [1881]. Kamenka.

RUS–Mcl (f. 905).

*Russkoe obozrenie (Nov 1893): 453 — *PSSL* 10: 130–
131.

1775.   To Anatolii Chaikovskii

4 Jun [1881]. [Kamenka].

Autograph lost; MS copy in RUS–KL.

PSSL 10: 131–132.

1776.   To Pëtr Iurgenson

4 Jun [1881]. Kamenka.

RUS–KL (a³, No. 2337).
*ZC 2: 472 — *PIU* 1: 193–194 — *PSSL* 10: 1776.

1777.   To Pëtr Iurgenson
5 Jun [1881]. Kamenka.
RUS–KL (a³, No. 2338).
PIU 1: 194 — *PSSL* 10: 133.

1778.   To Modest Chaikovskii
5–7 Jun [1881]. Kamenka.
RUS–KL (a³, No. 1632).
PSSL 10: 133–135.

1779.   To Pëtr Iurgenson
6 Jun [1881]. [Kamenka],
RUS–KL (a³, No. 2339).
PIU 1: 195 — *PSSL* 10: 135.

1780.   To Nadezhda von Meck
6–11 Jun 1881. Kamenka.
RUS–KL (a³, No. 727).
PM 2: 519–520 — *PSSL* 10: 136–137.

1781.   To Konstantin Pobedonostsev
7 Jun 1881. Kamenka.
RUS–KL (a³, No. 304).
K. P. Pobedonostsev i ego korrespondenty (1923): 404–405 — *PSSL* 10: 138.

1782.   To Anatolii Chaikovskii
11 Jun [1881]. Kamenka.
RUS–KL (a³, No. 1355).
PSSL 10: 138–139.

1783.   To Anna Aleksandrova-Levenson
13 Jun 1881. Kamenka.
Autograph lost; MS copy in RUS–KL.
SN (1905), 10: 103 — *PSSL* 10: 139.

1784.   To Nadezhda von Meck
14 Jun 1881. Kamenka.
RUS–KL (a³, No. 728).
PM 2: 521–522 — *PSSL* 10: 140.

1785.   To Modest Chaikovskii
14 Jun [1881]. Kamenka.

RUS–KL (a³, No. 1633).
PSSL 10: 140–142.

1786.   To Eduard Nápravník
17 Jun 1881. Kamenka.
Autograph lost; typed copy in RUS–KL.
*ZC 2: 472–473 — *VP:* 132–134 — *EFN:* 113–114 — *PSSL* 10: 142–143.

1787.   To Josef Sklenář
17 [Jun] 1881 (in MS: "May"). Kamenka.
CZ–Pnm
Stěpánek (1952): 125 — *PSSL* 10: 144.

1788.   To Anatolii Chaikovskii
18 Jun 1881 [Kamenka].
RUS–KL (a³, No. 1356).
PSSL 10: 145–146.

1789.   To Nadezhda von Meck
20 Jun 1881 [Kamenka].
RUS–KL (a³, No. 729).
PM 2: 523–524 — *PSSL* 10: 147–148.

1790.   To Modest Chaikovskii
21 Jun [1881]. [Kamenka].
RUS–KL (a³, No. 1634).
*ZC 2: 473 ("24 Jun") — *PB: 271 — *PSSL* 10: 148–149 — *LF: 264–265 [English tr.] ("24 Jun").

1791.   To Pëtr Iurgenson
21 Jun [1881]. Kamenka.
RUS–KL (a³, No. 2340).
*ZC 2: 474–475 — *PIU* 1: 196–197 — *PSSL* 10: 149–150.

1792.   To Modest Chaikovskii
22 Jun [1881]. Kamenka.
RUS–KL (a³, No. 1635).
*ZC 2: 475 — *PSSL* 10: 150–152.

1793.   To Nadezhda von Meck
23–26 Jun 1881. Kamenka.
RUS–KL (a³, No. 730).
PM 2: 525–526 — *PSSL* 10: 152–153.

1794.   **To Anatolii Chaikovskii**
24 Jun [1881]. Kamenka.
RUS–KL (a³, No. 1357).
PSSL 10: 153–154.

1794a.   **To Aleksei Sofronov**
24 Jun 1881. Kamenka
RUS–KL (a³, No. 3314).
Not published.

1795.   **To Sergei Taneev**
27 Jun [1881]. Kamenka.
RUS–Mcl (f. 880).
ZC 2: 475–476 (”2 Jun”) — *PT:* 66–67 (”2 Jun”) —
     CTP: 69–70 — *PSSL* 10: 154–155.

1796.   **To Anatolii Chaikovskii**
28 Jun [1881]. Kamenka.
RUS–KL (a³, No. 1358).
PSSL 10: 155–156.

1797.   **To Modest Chaikovskii**
28 Jun [1881]. Kamenka.
RUS–KL (a³, No. 1636).
PSSL 10: 156–157.

1798.   **To Aleksandr Tarnavich**
29 Jun 1881. Kamenka.
RUS–KL (a³, No. 401).
PSSL 10: 157.

1799.   **To Nadezhda von Meck**
30 Jun [1881]. Kamenka.
RUS–KL (a³, No. 731).
PM 2: 527–528 — *PSSL* 10: 158–159.

1800.   **To Aleksei Sofronov**
1 Jul 1881 [Kamenka].
RUS–KL (a³, No. 374).
PSSL 10: 159.

1801.   **To Eduard Nápravník**
3 Jul 1881. Kamenka.
Autograph lost; typed copy in RUS–KL.
ZC 2: 477–478 — *VP:* 136–137 — *EFN:* 115–116 —
     PSSL 10: 160.

1802.   **To Anatolii Chaikovskii**
3 Jul [1881]. Kamenka.
RUS–KL (a³, No. 1359).
PSSL 10: 161.

1803 .   **To Pëtr Iurgenson**
3 Jul 1881. Kamenka.
RUS–KL (a³, No. 2341).
PIU 1: 197–198 — *PSSL* 10: 161–162.

1804.   **To Nadezhda von Meck**
3–4 Jul [1881]. Kamenka.
RUS–KL (a³, No. 732).
ZC 2: 476–477 — *PM* 2: 529–530 — *PSSL* 10: 162–
     163.

1805.   **To Modest Chaikovskii**
5 Jul [1881]. Kamenka.
RUS–KL (a³, No. 1637).
PSSL 10: 164–165.

1806.   **To Nadezhda von Meck**
7–11 Jul [1881]. Kamenka.
RUS–KL (a³, No. 733).
PM 2: 531–534 — *PSSL* 10: 165–168.

1807.   **To Anatolii Chaikovskii**
9 Jul [1881]. Kamenka.
RUS–KL (a³, No. 1360).
PSSL 10: 168.

1808.   **To Anatolii Chaikovskii**
11 Jul [1881]. [Kamenka].
RUS–KL (a³, No. 1361).
PSSL 10: 169.

1809.   **To Modest Chaikovskii**
11 Jul [1881]. [Kamenka].
RUS–KL (a³, No. 1638).
PSSL 10: 169–170.

1810.   **To Pëtr Iurgenson**
11 Jul [1881]. [Kamenka].
RUS–KL (a³, No. 2342).
PIU 1: 199 — *PSSL* 10: 170.

1811. To Aleksei Sofronov
16 Jul [1881]. Kamenka.
RUS–KL (a³, No. 375).
PSSL 10: 171.

1812. To Anatolii Chaikovskii
16 Jul [1881]. [Kamenka].
RUS–KL (a³, No. 1362).
PSSL 10: 171–172.

1813. To Nadezhda von Meck
17 Jul [1881]. Kamenka.
RUS–KL (a³, No. 734).
PM 2: 534 — *PSSL* 10: 172.

1814. To Anatolii Chaikovskii
18 Jul [1881]. [Kamenka].
RUS–KL (a³, No. 1363).
PSSL 10: 173.

1815. To Modest Chaikovskii
19 Jul [1881]. [Kamenka].
RUS–KL (a³, No. 1639).
*PSSL 10: 173–175.

1816. To Nadezhda von Meck
22 Jul [1881]. Kiev.
RUS–KL (a³, No. 735).
PM 2: 535 — *PSSL* 10: 175.

1817. To Anatolii Chaikovskii
22 Jul [1881]. Kiev.
RUS–KL (a³, No. 1364).
PSSL 10: 176.

1818. To Modest Chaikovskii
22 Jul [1881]. Kiev.
RUS–KL (a³, No. 1640).
PSSL 10: 176–177.

1819. To Modest Chaikovskii
26 Jul [1881]. Kamenka.
RUS–KL (a³, No. 1641).
*PSSL 10: 177–178.

1820. To Nadezhda von Meck
30 Jul [1881]. Kamenka.
RUS–KL (a³, No. 736).
PM 2: 536–538 — *PSSL* 10: 178–179.

1821. To Pëtr Iurgenson
31 Jul [1881]. Kamenka.
RUS–KL (a³, No. 2343).
*ZC 2: 478 — *PIU* 1: 199–200 — *PSSL* 10: 180–181.

1822. To Aleksei Sofronov
2 Aug [1881]. Kamenka.
RUS–KL (a³, No. 376).
PSSL 10: 181.

1823. To Modest Chaikovskii
2 Aug [1881]. [Kamenka] (in MS: "Kiev").
RUS–KL (a³, No. 1642).
PSSL 10: 182.

1824. To Modest Chaikovskii
3 Aug [1881]. [Kamenka].
RUS–KL (a³, No. 1643).
PSSL 10: 182–183.

1825. To Nadezhda von Meck
4 Aug [1881]. Kamenka.
RUS–KL (a³, No. 737).
PM 2: 538–539 — *PSSL* 10: 183–185.

1826. To Sergei Taneev
5 Aug 1881 [Kamenka].
RUS–Mcl (f. 880).
*Maski (1913/14), 2: 1–3 — *PT*: 71–73 — *CTP*: 71–73 — *PSSL* 10: 185–188.

1827. To Anna Aleksandrova-Levenson
6 Aug 1881. Kamenka.
Autograph lost; MS copy in RUS–KL.
PSSL 10: 188–189.

1828. To Modest Chaikovskii
9 Aug [1881]. Kamenka.
RUS–KL (a³, No. 1644).
*ZC 2: 479 — *PSSL* 10: 189–190.

1829.   To Leontii Tkachenko
[? 9–10 Aug 1881]. Kamenka.
RUS–SPsc (f. 834, No. 29, fol. 4–5).
PSSL 10: 190.

1830.   To Nikolai Konradi
10 Aug [1881]. Kamenka.
Autograph lost; MS copy in RUS–KL.
CTP: 261 — *PSSL* 10: 190–191.

1831.   To Nadezhda von Meck
10 Aug [1881]. Kamenka.
RUS–KL (a³, No. 738).
PM 2: 540–541 — *PSSL* 10: 191–192.

1832.   To Pëtr Iurgenson
10 Aug 1881 [Kamenka].
RUS–KL (a³, No. 2344).
PIU 1: 200–201 — *PSSL* 10: 192–194.

1833.   To Elizaveta Chaikovskaia
14 Aug 1881. Kamenka.
RUS–SPsc (f. 834, No. 30, fol. 10–12).
PSSL 10: 193–194.

1834.   To Modest Chaikovskii
14 Aug [1881]. [Kamenka].
RUS–KL (a³, No. 1645).
ZC 2: 479 — *DGC* 245 — *PSSL* 10: 195–197.

1835.   To Pëtr Iurgenson
16 Aug [1881]. Kamenka.
RUS–KL (a³, No. 2345).
PIU 1: 203–204 — *PSSL* 10: 198–199.

1836.   To Nadezhda von Meck
19 Aug [1881]. Kamenka.
RUS–KL (a³, No. 739).
PM 2: 542–543 — *PSSL* 10: 199–200.

1837.   To Pëtr Iurgenson
19 Aug [1881]. Kamenka.
RUS–KL (a³, No. 2346).
PIU 1: 205–206 — *PSSL* 10: 200–201.

1838.   To Modest Chaikovskii
23 Aug [1881]. Kamenka.
RUS–KL (a³, No. 1646).
PB: 272 — *PSSL* 10: 201–202 — *LF*: 265 [English tr.].

1839.   To Sergei Taneev
23–25 Aug 1881. Kamenka.
RUS–Mcl (f. 880).
Maski (1913/14), 2: 6–7 — *ZC* 2: 480–482 — *PT*: 77–79 — *CTP*: 76–78 — *PSSL* 10: 203–205.

1840.   To Nadezhda von Meck
24 Aug [1881]. Kamenka.
RUS–KL (a³, No. 740).
ZC 2: 479–480 — *PM* 2: 545–547 — *PSSL* 10: 205–207.

1841.   To Leontii Tkachenko
26 Aug 1881. Kamenka.
RUS–SPsc (f. 834, No. 29, fol. 6–7).
PSSL 10: 208.

1842.   To Nadezhda von Meck
29 Aug [1881]. Kamenka.
RUS–KL (a³, No. 741).
PM 2: 547–548 — *PSSL* 10: 208–209.

1843.   To Modest Chaikovskii
29–30 Aug [1881]. Kamenka.
RUS–KL (a³, No. 1647).
PSSL 10: 209–211.

1844.   To Aleksandr Tarnavich
31 Aug [1881]. Kamenka.
RUS–KL (a³, No. 403).
PSSL 10: 212.

1845.   To Anatolii Chaikovskii
31 Aug [1881]. Kamenka.
RUS–KL (a³, No. 1318).
PSSL 10: 212–213.

1846.   To Pëtr Iurgenson
31 Aug [1881]. Kamenka.
RUS–KL (a³, No. 2347).
PIU 1: 206 — *PSSL* 10: 213–214.

1847.   To Leontii Tkachenko

31 Aug–6 Sep 1881. Kamenka.

RUS–KL (a³, No. 410).

PSSL 10: 214–217.

1848.   To Milii Balakirev

1 Sep 1881. Kamenka.

RUS–SPsc (f. 834, No. 12, fol. 1–3).

BC: 72 — *BVP* 163 —*PSSL* 10: 217–218.

1849.   To Pëtr Iurgenson

1 Sep 1881 [Kamenka].

RUS–KL (a³, No. 2348).

PIU 1: 207 — *PSSL* 10: 218.

1850.   To Nadezhda von Meck

2–3 Sep [1881]. Kamenka.

RUS–KL (a³, No. 742).

*ZC 2: 482–484 — *PM* 2: 549–52 — *PSSL* 10: 219–
221.

1851.   To Anna Alexandrova–Levenson

3 Sep [1881]. Kamenka.

RUS–KL (a³, No. 2977).

PSSL 10: 221–222.

1852.   To Modest Chaikovskii

4 Sep 1881 [Kamenka].

RUS–KL (a³, No. 1648).

PSSL 10: 222–224.

1853.   To Lev Davydov

9 Sep 1881. Kiev.

RUS–SPsc (f. 834, No. 19, fol. 33–34).

PSSL 10: 225.

1854.   To Nadezhda von Meck

11 Sep [1881]. Moscow.

RUS–KL (a³, No. 743).

PM 2: 552 — *PSSL* 10: 226.

1854a.   To Leontii Tkachenko

[? 11–29 Sep 1881. Moscow].

RUS–SPsc (f. 834, No. 29, fol. 34–35).

Not published.

1855.   To Nadezhda von Meck

13 Sep 1881. Moscow.

RUS–KL (a³, No. 744).

PM 2: 553–554 — *PSSL* 10: 226–227.

1855a.   To Leontii Tkachenko

[? 14 Sep 1881. Moscow].

RUS–SPsc (f. 834, No. 29, fol. 30–31).

Not published.

1856.   To Nadezhda von Meck

15 Sep [1881]. [Moscow].

RUS–KL (a³, No. 745).

PM 2: 555 — *PSSL* 10: 227–228.

1857.   To Nadezhda von Meck

17 Sep 1881 [Moscow].

RUS–KL (a³, No. 746).

PM 2: 555 — *PSSL* 10: 228.

**1857a.   To the Editor of *Signale für die
musikalische Welt***

17 Sep 1881. Moscow — in German.

Autograph lost

Signale für die musikalische Welt, 57 (Oct 1881): 898 —
ČS 3 (1998): 536.

1858.   To Modest Chaikovskii

18 Sep [1881]. Moscow.

RUS–KL (a³, No. 1649).

PSSL 10: 228.

1859.   To Nadezhda von Meck

19 Sep 1881. Moscow.

RUS–KL (a³, No. 747).

PM 2: 556–557 — *PSSL* 10: 229–210.

1860.   To Anatolii Chaikovskii

2–3 Oct 1881 [Kiev].

RUS–KL (a³, No. 1365).

*ZC 2: 487–488 — **PB*: 272–273 — *PSSL* 10: 230–
231 — **LF*: 266 [English tr.].

1861.   To Anatolii Chaikovskii

5 Oct [1881]. Kamenka.

RUS–KL (a³, No. 1366).

PSSL 10: 232–233.

1862.   To Nadezhda von Meck
5 Oct 1881. Kamenka.
RUS–KL (a³, No. 748).
PM 2: 559–561 — *PSSL* 10: 233–235.

1863.   To Pëtr Iurgenson
8 Oct [1881]. Kamenka.
RUS–KL (a³, No. 2349).
ZC 2: 488 — *PIU* 1: 208–209 — *PSSL* 10: 235–236.

1864.   To Nadezhda von Meck
9 Oct [1881]. Kamenka.
RUS–KL (a³, No. 749).
PM 2: 561–562 — *PSSL* 10: 236–237.

1865.   To Anatolii Chaikovskii
10 Oct [1881]. Kamenka.
RUS–KL (a³, No. 1367).
PSSL 10: 237–238.

1866.   To Pëtr Iurgenson
10 Oct 1881 [Kamenka].
RUS–KL (a³, No. 2350).
PSSL 10: 238.

1867.   To Pëtr Iurgenson
11 Oct [1881]. Kamenka.
RUS–KL (a³, No. 2351).
ZC 2: 488–489 — *PIU* 1: 209 — *PSSL* 10: 239.

1868.   To Nikolai Kashkin
12 Oct 1881. Kamenka.
RUS–KL (a³, No. 214).
PSSL 10: 240.

1869.   To Modest Chaikovskii
12 Oct 1881. Kamenka.
RUS–KL (a³, No. 1650).
ZC 2: 489–490 — *PB*: 273 — *PSSL* 10: 241 — *LF*: 267 [English tr.].

1870.   To Nadezhda von Meck
14 Oct 1881. Kamenka.
RUS–KL (a³, No. 750).
PM 2: 563–564 — *PSSL* 10: 242.

1871.   To Anatolii Chaikovskii
16 Oct [1881]. Kamenka.
RUS–KL (a³, No. 1368).
PSSL 10: 243.

1872.   To Modest Chaikovskii
17 Oct [1881]. Kamenka.
RUS–KL (a³, No. 1651).
PSSL 10: 244–245.

1873.   To Anatolii Chaikovskii
18 Oct [1881]. Kamenka.
RUS–KL (a³, No. 1369).
PSSL 10: 245.

1874.   To Pëtr Iurgenson
19 Oct [1881]. Kamenka.
RUS–KL (a³, No. 2352).
PIU 1: 209–210 — *PSSL* 10: 246.

1875.   To Pëtr Iurgenson
20 Oct 1881. Kamenka.
RUS–KL (a³, No. 2353).
PIU 1: 210–211 — *PSSL* 10: 247–248.

1876.   To Nadezhda von Meck
20 Oct 1881. Kamenka.
RUS–KL (a³, No. 751).
PM 2: 564–567 — *PSSL* 10: 248–250.

1877.   To Nadezhda von Meck
22–24 Oct 1881. Kamenka.
RUS–KL (a³, No. 752).
PM 2: 567–569 — *PSSL* 10: 250–252.

1878.   To Anatolii Chaikovskii
25 Oct [1881]. Kamenka.
RUS–KL (a³, No. 1370).
PB: 252–253 — *PSSL* 10: 273–274 — *LF*: 267 [English tr.].

1879.   To Modest Chaikovskii
25 Oct [1881]. Kamenka.
RUS–KL (a³, No. 1652).
PSSL 10: 253–255.

1880. To Pëtr Iurgenson
27 Oct [1881]. Kamenka.
RUS–KL (a³, No. 2354).
*ZC 2: 490 — PIU 1: 211–213— PSSL 10: 255–257.

1881. To Modest Chaikovskii
28 Oct [1881]. Kamenka.
RUS–KL (a³, No. 1653).
PSSL 10: 257–258.

1882. To Pëtr Iurgenson
31 Oct [1881]. Kiev.
RUS–KL (a³, No. 2355).
*ZC 2: 490–491 — PIU 1: 213 — PSSL 10: 258–259.

1883. To Aleksei Sofronov
1 Nov [1881]. Kiev.
RUS–KL (a³, No. 377).
PSSL 10: 259–260.

1884. To Nadezhda von Meck
3 Nov 1881. Kiev.
RUS–KL (a³, No. 753).
PM 2: 569–570 — PSSL 10: 260–261.

1884a. [To an unidentified corresponent]
3 Nov 1881. Kiev.
US–Bpr
Not published.

1885. To Pëtr Iurgenson
5 Nov [1881]. Kiev.
RUS–KL (a³, No. 2356).
PIU 1: 213–214 — PSSL 10: 261–262.

1886. To Modest Chaikovskii
6 Nov [1881]. Kiev.
RUS–KL (a³, No. 1654).
PSSL 10: 262.

1887. To Aleksei Sofronov
7 Nov [1881]. Kiev.
RUS–KL (a³, No. 2971).
PSSL 10: 262–263.

1888. To Pëtr Iurgenson
7 Nov [1881]. Kiev.
RUS–KL (a³, No. 2357).
PIU 1: 214–215 — PSSL 10: 263–264.

1889. To Nadezhda von Meck
8–9 Nov 1881. Kiev.
RUS–KL (a³, No. 754).
*ZC 2: 491–492 — PM 2: 570–571 — PSSL 10: 264–265.

1890. To Pëtr Iurgenson
9 Nov [1881]. Kiev.
RUS–KL (a³, No. 2358).
PIU 1: 215 — PSSL 10: 266.

1891. To Aleksei Sofronov
14/26 Nov [1881]. Vienna.
RUS–SPsc (f. 834, No. 26, fol. 9–10).
PSSL 10: 266–267.

1892. To Anatolii Chaikovskii
14/26 Nov [1881]. Vienna.
RUS–KL (a³, No. 1371).
PSSL 10: 267–268.

1893. To Nadezhda von Meck
16/28 Nov 1881. Venice.
RUS–KL (a³, No. 755).
PM 2: 571–572 — PSSL 10: 268–269.

1894. To Pëtr Iurgenson
16/28 Nov [1881]. Venice.
RUS–KL (a³, No. 2359).
*ZC 2: 493–494 — PIU 1: 215–216 — PSSL 10: 269–270.

1895. To Anatolii Chaikovskii
16/28 Nov [1881]. Venice.
RUS–KL (a³, No. 1372).
*ZC 2: 492–493 — PB: 274 — PSSL 10: 270–271 — *LF: 268 [English tr.].

1896. To Nadezhda von Meck
[18/30 Nov 1881. Florence].
RUS–KL (a³, No. 759).
PM 2: 573 — PSSL 10: 271.

1897.   To Nadezhda von Meck
19 Nov/1 Dec 1881. Florence.
RUS–KL (a³, No. 756).
PM 2: 574–576 — *PSSL* 10: 271–273.

1898.   To Leontii Tkachenko
21 Nov/3 Dec 1881. Rome.
RUS–SPsc (f. 834, No. 29, fol. 8–9).
PSSL 10: 273–274.

1899.   To Anatolii Chaikovskii
21 Nov/3 Dec [1881]. Rome.
RUS–KL (a³, No. 1373).
PSSL 10: 274–275.

1900.   To Nadezhda von Meck
23 Nov/5 Dec 1881. Rome.
RUS–KL (a³, No. 757).
ZC 2: 494 — *PM* 2: 576–577 — *PSSL* 10: 275–276.

1901.   To Aleksei Sofronov
23 Nov/5 Dec 1881. Rome.
RUS–KL (a³, No. 378).
PSSL 10: 276–277.

1902.   To Nadezhda von Meck
26 Nov/8 Dec–27 Nov/9 Dec 1881. Rome.
RUS–KL (a³, No. 758).
ZC 2: 494–495 — *PM* 2: 578–580 — *PSSL* 10: 277–279.

1903.   To Anatolii Chaikovskii
27 Nov/9 Dec 1881. Rome.
RUS–KL (a³, No. 1374).
PSSL 10: 279–280.

1904 .   To Lev Kupernik
1/13 Dec [1881]. Rome.
RUS–SPil (f. 232, No. 5).
Sovetskaia kul´tura (11 Aug 1962) — *PSSL* 10: 280.

1905.   To Anatolii Chaikovskii
1/13–3/15 Dec 1881. Rome.
RUS–KL (a³, No. 1375).
PB: 275 — *PSSL* 10: 281–282 — *LF*: 268–269 [English tr.].

1906.   To Nadezhda von Meck
1/13–4/16 Dec 1881. Rome.
RUS–KL (a³, No. 760).
ZC 2: 495–497 — *PM* 2: 580–581 — *PSSL* 10: 282–284.

1907.   To Aleksei Sofronov
6/18 Dec 1881. Rome.
RUS–KL (a³, No. 379).
PSSL 10: 284–285.

1908.   To Nadezhda von Meck
6/18–9/21 Dec 1881. Rome.
RUS–KL (a³, No. 761).
ZC 2: 497–498 — *PM* 2: 582–583 — *PSSL* 10: 285–287.

1909.   To Eduard Nápravník
7/19 Dec 1881. Rome
Autograph lost; typed copy in RUS–KL.
EFN: 116–117 — *PSSL* 10: 287–288.

1910.   To Anatolii Chaikovskii
12/24 Dec 1881. Rome
RUS–KL (a³, No. 1376).
PB: 275–276 — *PSSL* 10: 288–289 — *LF*: 269–270 [English tr.].

1911.   To Pëtr Iurgenson
12/24 Dec 1881. Rome.
RUS–KL (a³, No. 2360).
PIU 1: 218–219 — *PSSL* 10: 290.

1912.   To Nadezhda von Meck
14/26–15/27 Dec [1881] (in MS: "1882"). Rome.
RUS–KL (a³, No. 762).
ZC 2: 499–500, 505–506 — *PM* 2: 585–587 — *PSSL* 10: 291–292.

1913.   To Aleksei Sofronov
15/27 Dec [1881] (in MS: "1882"). Rome.
RUS–KL (a³, No. 381).
PSSL 10: 293–294.

1914.   To Pëtr Iurgenson
15/27 Dec 1881. Rome.
RUS–KL (a³, No. 2361).

ZC 2: 504–505 — *PIU* 1: 219–220 — *PSSL* 10: 294–295.

1915. To Anatolii Chaikovskii

18/30–19/[31] Dec 1881 [Rome] (in MS: "Kiev").

RUS–KL (a³, No. 1377).

ZC 2: 505 — *PB*: 276–277 — *PSSL* 10: 295–296 — *LF*: 271–272 [English tr.].

1916. To Nadezhda von Meck

22–23 Dec 1881/3–4 Jan 1882. Rome.

RUS–KL (a³, No. 763).

ZC 2: 506–507 — *PM* 2: 588–590 — *PSSL* 10: 297–299.

1917. To Aleksei Sofronov

24 Dec 1881/5 Jan 1882. Rome.

RUS–KL (a³, No. 380).

PSSL 10: 299–300.

1918. To Eduard Nápravník

26 Dec 1881/[7 Jan 1882]. Rome.

Autograph lost; typed copy in RUS–KL.

EFN: 119–120 — *PSSL* 10: 300–301.

1919. To Anatolii Chaikovskii

26 Dec 1881/[7 Jan 1882]. Rome.

RUS–KL (a³, No. 1378).

PB: 277 — *PSSL* 10: 301–302 — *LF*: 271 [English tr.].

1920. To Anna Merkling

27 Dec 1881/8 Jan 1882. Rome.

Autograph lost; MS copy in RUS–KL.

ZC 2: 507–508 — *CTP*: 210–211 — *PSSL* 10: 302–305.

1921. To Andronik Klimchenko

29 Dec 1881/10 Jan 1882. Rome.

RUS–KL (a³, No. 226).

SM (1939), 8: 60 — *PSSL* 10: 305.

1922. To Aleksei Sofronov

29 Dec 1881/10 Jan 1882. Rome.

RUS–KL (a³, No. 382).

PSSL 10: 306.

1923. To Pëtr Iurgenson

29 Dec 1881/10 Jan 1882. Rome.

RUS–KL (a³, No. 2362).

ZC 2: 498–499 — *PIU* 1: 221–222 — *PSSL* 10: 306–307.

1882

1924. To Adol´f Brodskii

1/13 Jan 1882. Rome,

GB–Mcm

The Listener (19 Apr 1962) [English tr.] — *Sovetskaia kul´tura* (11 Aug 1962) — *PSSL* 11: 15–16.

1925. To Anatolii Chaikovskii

2/14 Jan 1882. Rome.

Autograph lost; partial MS copy in RUS–KL.

PSSL 11: 16–17.

1926. To Pëtr Iurgenson

4/16 Jan 1882. Rome.

RUS–KL (a³, No. 2363).

ZC 2: 509 — *PIU* 1: 226 — *PSSL* 11: 17–18.

1927. To Nadezhda von Meck

5/17–6/18 Jan 1882. Rome.

RUS–KL (a³, No. 764).

PM 3: 13–14 — *PSSL* 11: 19.

1928. To Anatolii Chaikovskii

9/21 Jan 1882. Rome.

Autograph lost; MS copy in RUS–KL.

ZC 2: 509–510 — *PB*: 278 — *PSSL* 11: 20–21 — *LF*: 271–272 [English tr.].

1929. To Anatolii Chaikovskii

10/22 Jan 1882. Rome.

RUS–KL [MS copy — incomplete].

PSSL 11: 21.

1930. To Pëtr Iurgenson

10/22 Jan 1882. Rome.

RUS–KL (a³, No. 2364).

ZC 2: 510 — *PIU* 1: 228–229 — *PSSL* 11: 22.

1931.   **To Anatolii Chaikovskii**

12/[24] Jan 1882. Rome

Autograph lost; MS copy in RUS–KL.

PSSL 11: 23–24.

1932.   **To Nadezhda von Meck**

13/[25] Jan 1882. Rome.

RUS–KL (a³, No. 765).

*ZC 2: 511 — *PM* 3: 16 — *PSSL* 11: 24.

1933.   **To Nikolai Bernard**

14/26 Jan 1882. Rome.

RUS–SPtob (VII.2.4.154).

Glebov (1922): 163 — *PSSL* 11: 25.

1934.   **To Pëtr Iurgenson**

14/26 Jan 1882. Rome.

RUS–KL (a³, No. 2365).

ZC 2: 511 — *PIU* 1: 229 — *PSSL* 11: 26.

1935.   **To Anna Merkling**

15/27 Jan 1882 [Rome].

Autograph lost; MS copy in RUS–KL.

CTP: 212 — *PSSL* 11: 26–27.

1936.   **To Nadezhda von Meck**

16/28 Jan–20 Jan/1 Feb 1882 [Rome].

RUS–KL (a³, No. 766).

*ZC 2: 511–512 — *PM* 2: 17–18 — *PSSL* 11: 27–28.

1937.   **To Anatolii Chaikovskii**

[16]/28 Jan [1882] ("17 Jan"). Rome.

Autograph lost; MS copy in RUS–KL.

*ZC 2: 512–513 — **PB*: 278 — *PSSL* 11: 29 — **LF*: 272 [English tr.].

1938.   **To Aleksei Sofronov**

18/[30] Jan [1882]. Rome.

RUS–KL (a³, No. 383).

PSSL 11: 30.

1939.   **To Pëtr Iurgenson**

18/[30] Jan 1882. Rome.

RUS–KL (a³, No. 2366).

PIU 1: 231–233 — *PSSL* 11: 31–33.

1940.   **To Leontii Tkachenko**

19/31 Jan 1882. Rome.

RUS–SPsc (f. 834, No. 29, fol. 10–12).

*ZC 2: 513–514 — *PSSL* 11: 33–34.

1941.   **To Natal´ia Pleskaia**

22 Jan/[3 Feb] 1882. Rome.

RUS–Mcl (f. 905).

CTP: 364 — *PSSL* 11: 35.

1942.   **To Aleksei Sofronov**

22 Jan/3 Feb 1882. Rome.

RUS–KL (a³, No. 384).

PSSL 11: 35–36.

1943.   **To Sergei Flerov**

22 Jan/3 Feb 1882. Rome.

RUS–Mcm (f. 37, No. 98).

**Iu. Slonimskii, *Chaikovskii i baletnyi teatr ego vremenii* (1956): 240–241 ["to Sergei Bakhrushin"] — *PSSL* 11: 36–37.

1944.   **To Anatolii Chaikovskii**

22 Jan/3 Feb 1882. Rome

Autograph lost; MS copy in RUS–KL.

*ZC 2: 514–515 — **PB*: 278–279 — *PSSL* 11: 37–38 — **LF*: 272–273 [English tr.].

1945.   **To Pëtr Iurgenson**

22 Jan/[3 Feb] 1882. Rome.

RUS–KL (a³, No. 2367).

*ZC 2: 515 — *PSSL* 11: 38–39.

1946.   **To Anatolii Chaikovskii**

25 Jan/6 Feb 1882. Rome.

Autograph lost; MS copy in RUS–KL.

PSSL 11: 39–40.

1947.   **To Nadezhda von Meck**

25–26 Jan/6–[7] Feb 1882. Rome.

RUS–KL (a³, No. 767).

PM 3: 19–21 — *PSSL* 11: 40–42.

1948.   **To Anna Aleksandrova-Levenson**

28 Jan/9 Feb 1882. Rome.

RUS–KL (a³, No. 3).

SN (1905), 10: 104 — *PSSL* 11: 42–43.

1949.   To Nadezhda von Meck
30 Jan/[11 Feb 1882] (in MS: "1881"). Rome.
RUS–KL (a³, No. 768).
*ZC 2: 516–517 — PM 3: 22–23 — PSSL 11: 43–44.

1950.   To Aleksei Sofronov
30 Jan/11 Feb 1882. Rome.
RUS–KL (a³, No. 2872).
PSSL 11: 44–45.

1951.   To Anatolii Chaikovskii
30 Jan/11 Feb 1882. Rome.
Autograph lost; MS copy in RUS–KL.
PSSL 11: 45–46.

1952.   To Pëtr Iurgenson
30 Jan/11 Feb 1882. Rome.
RUS–KL (a³, No. 2368) [facs. in PIU 1: 232/233].
*ZC 2: 515–516 — PIU 1: 233 — PSSL 11: 47.

1953.   To Nadezhda von Meck
1/13–3/[15] Feb 1882 [Rome].
RUS–KL (a³, No. 769).
PM 3: 23–25 — PSSL 11: 48–49.

1954.   To Pëtr Iurgenson
1/13 Feb 1882. Rome.
RUS–KL (a³, No. 2369).
*ZC 2: 517–518 — PIU 1: 233–235 — PSSL 11: 50–
    51.

1955.   To Pëtr Iurgenson
5/17 Feb 1882. Rome.
RUS–KL (a³, No. 2370).
*ZC 2: 517–518 — PIU 1: 235–236 — PSSL 11: 51–
    52.

1956.   To Sergei Flerov
[6]/18 Feb [1882]. Rome.
RUS–Mt
CMS: 464 — PSSL 11: 53.

1957.   To Anatolii Chaikovskii
6/18 Feb 1882. Rome.
Autograph lost; MS copy in RUS–KL.
PSSL 11: 53.

1958.   To Nadezhda von Meck
7/19–8/20 Feb 1882. Rome.
RUS–KL (a³, No. 770).
PM 3: 26–27 — PSSL 11: 54–55.

1959.   To Anatolii Chaikovskii
[8/20] Feb 1882 (in MS copy: "7/19 Feb"). Rome.
Autograph lost; MS copy in RUS–KL.
*ZC 2 : 519 —*PB: 279 — PSSL 11: 55–56 — *LF:
    273 [English tr.].

1960.   To Modest Chaikovskii
10/22 Feb [1882]. Naples.
RUS–KL (a³, No. 1655).
*ZC 2: 520 — PSSL 11: 56–59.

1961.   To Nadezhda von Meck
11/23 Feb 1882 [Naples].
RUS–KL (a³, No. 771).
PM 3: 28–29 — PSSL 11: 59.

1962.   To Aleksei Sofronov
11/23 Feb 1882. Naples.
RUS–KL (a³, No. 385).
PSSL 11: 60.

1963.   To Anatolii Chaikovskii
11/23 Feb 1882. Naples.
Autograph lost; MS copy in RUS–KL.
PSSL 11: 60–61.

1964.   To Modest Chaikovskii
[11]/23 Feb [1882]. [Naples].
RUS–KL (a³, No. 1656).
PSSL 11: 61.

1965.   To Pëtr Iurgenson
11/23 Feb 1882. Naples.
RUS–KL (a³, No. 2373).
PIU 1: 236 — PSSL 11: 62.

1966.   To Pëtr Iurgenson
[12/24 Feb 1882. Naples] — telegram; in French.
RUS–KL (a³, No. 2399).
PSSL 11: 62.

1967.   To Nadezhda von Meck
13/25–[14/26] Feb 1882. Naples.
RUS–KL (a³, No. 772).
*ZC 2: 521–522 — *PM* 3: 29–32 — *PSSL* 11: 63–65.

1968.   To Anna Aleksandrova-Levenson
14/26 Feb 1882. Naples.
RUS–KL (a³, No. 4).
SN (1905), 10: 104–105 — *PSSL* 11: 66.

1969.   To Aleksei Sofronov
16/28 Feb 1882. Naples.
RUS–KL (a³, No. 386).
PSSL 11: 67.

1970.   To Anatolii Chaikovskii
16/28 Feb [1882]. Naples.
Autograph lost; MS copy in RUS–KL.
PSSL 11: 67–68.

1971.   To Pëtr Iurgenson
18 Feb/2 Mar [1882]. Naples.
RUS–KL (a³, No. 2374).
PIU 1: 236–237 — *PSSL* 11: 68–69.

1972.   To Nadezhda von Meck
21 Feb/5 Mar [1882]. Naples.
RUS–KL (a³, No. 773).
PM 3: 33–34 — *PSSL* 11: 70.

1973.   To Anatolii Chaikovskii
21 Feb/[5] Mar 1882 (in MS: "1 Mar"). Naples.
Autograph lost; MS copy in RUS–KL.
PSSL 11: 71.

1974.   To Nadezhda von Meck
22 Feb/6 Mar 1882. Naples.
RUS–KL (a³, No. 774).
PM 3: 34–35 — *PSSL* 11: 71–73.

1975.   To "Monsieur Vincenzo"
[22 Feb]/6 Mar 1882. Naples — in French.
RUS–KL (a⁵, No. 7).
PSSL 11: 73.

1976.   To Pëtr Iurgenson
[22 Feb/6 Mar 1882. Naples] — telegram; in French.
RUS–KL (a³, No. 2400).
PSSL 11: 73.

1977.   To Pëtr Iurgenson
[23] Feb/[7 Mar 1882] (in MS: "21 Feb"). Naples.
RUS–KL (a³, No. 2371).
*ZC 2: 522 — *PIU* 1: 237–238 — *PSSL* 11: 73.

1978.   To Pëtr Iurgenson
[23] Feb/7 Mar–[24 Feb/8 Mar] 1882 (in MS: "22
      Feb/7 Mar"). Naples,
RUS–KL (a³, No. 2372).
PIU 1: 240–241 — *PSSL* 11: 74–76.

1979.   To Aleksei Sofronov
24 Feb/8 Mar 1882. Naples.
RUS–KL (a³, No. 387).
PSSL 11: 76–77.

1980.   To Anatolii Chaikovskii
24 Feb/8 Mar 1882. Naples.
Autograph lost; MS copy in RUS–KL.
PSSL 11: 77–78.

1981.   To Nadezhda von Meck
27 Feb/11 Mar–28 Feb/[12] Mar 1882. Naples.
RUS–KL (a³, No. 775).
*ZC 2: 523–524 — *PM* 3: 37–39 — *PSSL* 11: 78–80.

1982.   To Anatolii Chaikovskii
1/[13]–2/[14] Mar 1882. Naples.
Autograph lost; MS copy in RUS–KL.
PSSL 11: 80–81.

1983.   To Pëtr Iurgenson
2/[14] Mar 1882. Naples.
RUS–KL (a³, No. 2375).
PIU 1: 243–244 — *PSSL* 11: 82–83.

1984.   To Pëtr Iurgenson
4/[16] Mar [1882]. Naples.
RUS–KL (a³, No. 2376).
PIU 1: 244 — *PSSL* 11: 83–84.

1985. To Pëtr Iurgenson
[4/16 Mar 1882. Naples] — telegram; in French.
RUS–KL (a³, No. 2401).
PSSL 11: 84.

1986. To Natal´ia Pleskaia
6/18 Mar [1882]. Naples.
RUS–Mcl (f. 905).
CTP: 364–365 — *PSSL* 11: 84–85.

1987. To Nadezhda von Meck
7/19 Mar 1882. Naples.
RUS–KL (a³, No. 776).
*ZC 2: 524–526 — *PM* 3: 39–41 — *PSSL* 11: 85–87.

1988. To Nadezhda von Meck
9/21 Mar [1882]. Naples.
RUS–KL (a³, No. 777).
PM 3: 42 — *PSSL* 11: 88–89.

1989. To Anatolii Chaikovskii
10/[22] Mar 1882. Naples.
Autograph lost; MS copy in RUS–KL.
PSSL 11: 89.

1990. To Nadezhda von Meck
17/29 Mar [1882]. Florence.
RUS–KL (a³, No. 778).
*ZC 2: 527 — *PM* 3: 43 — *PSSL* 11: 90.

1991. To Nadezhda von Meck
[18/30 Mar 1882. Florence].
RUS–KL (a³, No. 779).
PM 3: 44 — *PSSL* 11: 91.

1992. To Nadezhda von Meck
20 Mar/[1 Apr 1882]. Florence.
RUS–KL (a³, No. 780).
PM 3: 45 — *PSSL* 11: 91.

1993. To Nadezhda von Meck
22 Mar/[3 Apr] 1882. Vienna.
RUS–KL (a³, No. 781).
PM 3: 45–46 — *PSSL* 11: 91–92.

1994. To Modest Chaikovskii
22 Mar/[3 Apr 1882]. [Vienna].
RUS–KL (a³, No. 1657).
PSSL 11: 92–93.

1995. To Modest Chaikovskii
24 Mar [1882]. Warsaw.
RUS–KL (a³, No. 1658).
*ZC 2: 527–528 — *PB*: 279–280 — *PSSL* 11: 94 —
  LF: 274 [English tr.].

1996. To Modest Chaikovskii
28 Mar [1882]. Moscow.
RUS–KL (a³, No. 1659).
PSSL 11: 95.

1997. To Modest Chaikovskii
[29 Mar 1882. Moscow].
RUS–KL (a³, No. 1660).
PSSL 11: 95–96.

1998. To Nadezhda von Meck
31 Mar [1882]. Moscow.
RUS–KL (a³, No. 782).
PM 3: 46 — *PSSL* 11: 96–97.

1999. To Mikhail Lentovskii
1 Apr [1882]. [Moscow].
RUS–Mt
CMS: 468 — *PSSL* 11: 97.

2000. To Modest Chaikovskii
1 Apr [1882]. Moscow.
RUS–KL (a³, No. 1661).
PB: 280 — *PSSL* 11: 97–98 — *LF*: 274–275
  [English tr.].

2001. To Nadezhda von Meck
3–5 Apr [1882]. Moscow.
RUS–KL (a³, No. 783).
PM 3: 47–48 — *PSSL* 11: 98–99.

2002. To Modest Chaikovskii
4 Apr [1882]. [Moscow].
RUS–KL (a³, No. 1662).
PSSL 11: 100.

2003.   To Karl Al´brekht
[early Apr 1882. Moscow].
RUS–Mcm (f. 37, No. 44).
PSSL 11: 100.

2004.   To Anna Avramova
[early–mid Apr 1882. Moscow].
RUS–KL (a³, No. 1).
PSSL 11: 101.

2005.   To Elizaveta Kashkina
[6–7 Apr 1882. Moscow].
RUS–Mkashkina
PSSL 11: 101.

2006.   To Modest Chaikovskii
[8–9 Apr 1882. Moscow].
RUS–KL (a³, No. 1663).
*PB: 281 — *PSSL* 11: 101–102 — **LF*: 275 [English
   tr.].

2007.   To Anatolii Chaikovskii
10 Apr [1882]. Moscow.
Autograph lost; MS copy in RUS–KL.
PSSL 11: 103.

2008.   To Adol´f Brodskii
15 Apr [1882]. Moscow.
GB–Mcm
*ZC 2: 528–529 — *PSSL* 11: 104.

2009.   To Nadezhda von Meck
16–26 Apr [1882]. Moscow–Kamenka.
RUS–KL (a³, No. 784).
*ZC 2: 529–530 — *PM* 3: 51–54 — *PSSL* 11: 105–
   107.

2010.   To Pëtr Iurgenson
24 Apr [1882]. Kiev.
RUS–KL (a³, No. 2377).
*ZC 2: 530–531 — *PIU* 1: 245 — *PSSL* 11: 108–109.

2011.   To Anatolii Chaikovskii
24 Apr–7 May 1882. Kiev–Kamenka.
Autograph lost; partial MS copy in RUS–KL.
PSSL 11: 109–111.

2012.   To Aleksei Sofronov
2 May [1882]. Kamenka.
RUS–SPsc
*PSSL 11: 111–112.

2013.   To Adol´f Brodskii
4 May [1882]. Kamenka.
GB–Mcm
*ZC 2: 531–532 — *PSSL* 11: 112–113.

2014.   To Natal´ia Pleskaia
4 May [1882]. Kamenka.
RUS–Mcl (f. 880).
CTP: 365 — *PSSL* 11: 113–114.

2015.   To Nadezhda von Meck
5 May 1882. Kamenka.
RUS–KL (a³, No. 785).
PM 3: 55–56 — *PSSL* 11: 114–115.

2016.   To Leontii Tkachenko
6 May [1882]. Kamenka.
RUS–SPsc (f. 834, No. 29, fol. 13–14).
PSSL 11: 115–116.

2017.   To Anna Davydova
10 May [1882]. Kamenka.
RUS–Mrg
PSSL 11: 116.

2018.   To Modest Chaikovskii
10 May [1882]. Kamenka.
RUS–KL (a³, No. 1664).
PSSL 11: 117–118.

2019.   To Pëtr Iurgenson
11 May [1882]. Kamenka.
RUS–KL (a³, No. 2835).
PSSL 11: 119.

2020.   To Anatolii Chaikovskii
13 May [1882]. Kamenka.
Autograph lost; MS copy in RUS–KL.
PSSL 11: 119–120.

2021.   To Modest Chaikovskii
15 May [1882]. Kamenka.
RUS–KL (a³, No. 1665).
PSSL 11: 120–121.

2022.   To Aleksei Sofronov
16 May [1882]. Kamenka.
RUS–SPsc (f. 834, No. 26, fol. 13–14).
PSSL 11: 121–122.

2023.   To Anna Merkling
17 May 1882. Kamenka.
Autograph lost; MS copy in RUS–KL.
CTP: 212–213 — *PSSL* 11: 122–123.

2024.   To Pëtr Iurgenson
17 May [1882]. Kamenka.
RUS–KL (a³, No. 2378).
PIU 1: 246–247 — *PSSL* 11: 123–124.

2025.   To Nadezhda von Meck
17–[18] May 1882. Kamenka.
RUS–KL (a³, No. 786).
PM 3: 57–58 — *PSSL* 11: 124–125.

2026.   To Modest Chaikovskii
19–21 May [1882]. Kamenka.
RUS–KL (a³, No. 1666).
ZC 2: 532–534 — *PB*: 281–282 — *PSSL* 11: 125–127 — *LF*: 276 [English tr.].

2027.   To Nadezhda von Meck
23–27 May [1882]. Kamenka.
RUS–KL (a³, No. 787).
PM 3: 60–61 — *PSSL* 11: 128–129.

2028.   To Pëtr Iurgenson
24 May [1882]. Kamenka.
RUS–KL (a³, No. 2379).
PIU 1: 247 — *PSSL* 11: 129–130.

2029.   To Aleksandr Shidlovskii
26 May 1882. Kamenka.
Autograph lost; typed copy in RUS–KL.
ZC 2: 534–535 — *PSSL* 11: 130–131.

2030.   To Sergei Morozov
27 May [1882]. Kamenka.
RUS–SPil (f. 53, No. 77, fol. 1–2).
PSSL 11: 132.

2031.   To Modest Chaikovskii
27 May 1882 [Kamenka].
RUS–KL (a³, No. 1667).
ZC 2: 535 — *PSSL* 11: 132–134.

2032.   To Pëtr Iurgenson
27 May [1882]. Kamenka.
RUS–KL (a³, No. 2606).
PSSL 11: 134.

2033.   To Modest Chaikovskii
29 May [1882]. Kamenka.
RUS–KL (a³, No. 1668).
PSSL 11: 134–135.

2034.   To Nadezhda von Meck
29 May–3 Jun [1882]. [Kamenka].
RUS–KL (a³, No. 788).
ZC 2: 535–536 — *PM* 3: 61–63 — *PSSL* 11: 135–137.

2035.   To Aleksandr Zhedrinskii
30 May [1882]. Kamenka.
RUS–KL (a³, No. 2982) [incomplete].
PSSL 11: 138.

2036.   To Adol´f Brodskii
3 Jun [1882]. Kamenka.
RUS–Mcm (f. 385, No. 634) [facs. in *SM* (1959), 1: 81].
SM (1959), 1: 81–82 — *PSSL* 11: 138–139.

2037.   To Aleksei Sofronov
3 Jun [1882]. Kamenka.
RUS–SPsc (f. 834, No. 26, fol. 17–18).
PSSL 11: 139.

2038.   To Pëtr Iurgenson
3 Jun [1882]. [Kamenka].
RUS–KL (a³, No. 2380).
PIU 1: 250 — *PSSL* 11: 140.

2039.   To Nadezhda von Meck
4 Jun [1882]. Kamenka.
RUS–KL (a³, No. 789).
PM 3: 63–64 — *PSSL* 11: 140.

2040.   To Leontii Tkachenko
4 Jun [1882]. Kamenka.
RUS–SPsc (f. 834, No. 29, fol. 15–16).
*ZC 2: 537 — *PSSL* 11: 141–142.

2041.   To Nadezhda von Meck
7–9 Jun 1882. Grankino.
RUS–KL (a³, No. 790).
*ZC 2: 538 — *PM* 3: 64–66 — *PSSL* 11: 142–144.

2042.   To Aleksei Sofronov
12 Jun [1882]. Grankino.
RUS–SPsc (f. 834, No. 26, fol. 15–16).
PSSL 11: 144–145.

2043.   To Pëtr Iurgenson
12 Jun [1882]. Grankino.
RUS–KL (a³, No. 2381).
*ZC 2: 538–540 — *PIU* 1: 250–251 — *PSSL* 11: 145–146.

2044.   To Nadezhda von Meck
16 Jun 1882. Grankino.
RUS–KL (a³, No. 791).
PM 3: 66–67 — *PSSL* 11: 147–148.

2045.   To Anna Aleksandrova-Levenson
18 Jun [1882]. Grankino.
RUS–KL (a³, No. 3347).
SN (1905), 10: 105 — *PSSL* 11: 148–150.

2046.   To Anna Merkling
18 Jun 1882. Grankino
Autograph lost; MS copy in RUS–KL.
*ZC 2: 340 — *CTP*: 213–214 — *PSSL* 11: 150–151.

2047.   To Leontii Tkachenko
19 Jun [1882]. Grankino.
RUS–SPsc (f. 834, No. 29, fol. 17–18).
*ZC 2: 540–541 — *PSSL* 11: 151–152.

2048.   To Pëtr Iurgenson
19 Jun [1882]. Grankino.
RUS–KL (a³, No. 2382).
PSSL 11: 152–153.

2049.   To Aleksei Sofronov
22 Jun 1882 [Grankino].
RUS–SPsc (f. 834, No. 26, fol. 19–20).
PSSL 11: 153–154.

2050.   To Anatolii Chaikovskii
22 Jun [1882]. Grankino.
Autograph lost; MS copy in RUS–KL.
PSSL 11: 154–155.

2051.   To Nadezhda von Meck
24 Jun [1882]. Grankino.
RUS–KL (a³, No. 792).
PM 3: 68–69 — *PSSL* 11: 155–156.

2052.   To Lev Davydov
26 Jun [1882]. Grankino.
RUS–SPsc (f. 834, No. 19, fol. 35–36).
PSSL 11: 156–157.

2053.   To Nadezhda von Meck
26 Jun [1882]. Grankino.
RUS–KL (a³, No. 793).
PM 3: 69–70 — *PSSL* 11: 157.

2054.   To Pëtr Iurgenson
26 Jun [1882]. Grankino.
RUS–KL (a³, No. 2383).
PSSL 11: 158.

2055.   To Nadezhda von Meck
30 Jun [1882]. Grankino.
RUS–KL (a³, No. 794).
*ZC 2: 541–542 — *PM* 3: 70–71 — *PSSL* 11: 158–159.

2056.   To Aleksei Sofronov
30 Jun 1882. Grankino.
RUS–SPsc (f. 834, No. 26, fol. 21–22).
PSSL 11: 159.

2057. To Nadezhda von Meck

5 Jul 1882. Grankino.

RUS–KL (a³, No. 795).

*ZC 2: 542 — *PM* 3: 72–73 — *PSSL* 11: 160–161.

2058. To Lev Davydov

11 Jul [1882]. Grankino.

RUS–SPsc (f. 834, No. 19, fol. 37–38).

PSSL 11: 161.

2059. To Sergei Taneev

11 Jul [1882]. Grankino.

RUS–Mcl (f. 880).

PT: 82 — *CTP*: 80–81 — *PSSL* 11: 162.

2060. To Pëtr Iurgenson

11 Jul [1882]. Grankino.

RUS–KL (a³, No. 2384).

PIU 1: 253–254 — *PSSL* 11: 163.

2061. To Nadezhda von Meck

12–13 Jul 1882. Grankino.

RUS–KL (a³, No. 796).

PM 3: 73–74 — *PSSL* 11: 164–165.

2062. To Aleksei Sofronov

14 [Jul 1882] (in MS: "14 Apr") [Grankino].

RUS–SPsc (f. 834, No. 26, fol. 23–24).

PSSL 11: 165–166.

2063. To Pëtr Iurgenson

14 Jul 1882 [Grankino].

RUS–KL (a³, No. 2385).

PIU 1: 254 — *PSSL* 11: 166.

2064. To Pëtr Iurgenson

16–17 Jul 1882 [Grankino].

RUS–KL (a³, nos. 2386–2387).

PIU 1: 254–255 — *PSSL* 11: 167–168.

2065. To Lev Davydov

17 Jul [1882]. Grankino.

RUS–KL (a³, No. 174).

PSSL 11: 168–169.

2066. To Anatolii Chaikovskii

17 Jul 1882 [Grankino].

Autograph lost; MS copy in RUS–KL.

PSSL 11: 169.

2067. To Nadezhda von Meck

20 Jul [1882]. Grankino.

RUS–KL (a³, No. 797).

PM 3: 75–77 — *PSSL* 11: 170–171.

2068. To Leontii Tkachenko

26 Jul [1882]. Kamenka.

RUS–SPsc (f. 834, No. 29, fol. 19–21).

*ZC 2: 542 — *PSSL* 11: 172–173.

2069. To Pëtr Iurgenson

26 Jul [1882]. Kamenka.

RUS–KL (a³, No. 2388).

*ZC 2: 542–543 — *PIU* 1: 255–256 — *PSSL* 11: 173–174.

2070. To Nadezhda von Meck

27 Jul 1882. Kamenka.

RUS–KL (a³, No. 798).

PM 3: 78–80 — *PSSL* 11: 174–175.

2071. To Sergei Taneev

28 Jul [1882]. Kamenka.

RUS–Mcl (f. 880).

PT: 82–84 ("26 Jul") — *CTP*: 81–82 — *PSSL* 11: 176–177.

2072. To Anna Aleksandrova-Levenson

29 Jul [1882]. Kamenka.

Autograph lost

SN (1905), 10: 101 ("1879") — *PSSL* 11: 178.

2073. To Nadezhda von Meck

3 Aug 1882. Kamenka.

RUS–KL (a³, No. 799).

PM 3: 81–83 —*PSSL* 11: 178–180.

2074. To the Maslov family

[10 Aug 1882. Moscow] — postscript to a letter from Sergei Taneev.

RUS–Mcl

PSSL 11: 181.

2075.   To Nadezhda von Meck

10 Aug [1882]. Moscow.

RUS–KL (a³, No. 800).

PM 3: 85 — *PSSL* 11: 181.

2076.   To Nadezhda von Meck

11 Aug [1882]. [Moscow].

RUS–KL (a³, No. 801).

PM 3: 85–86 — *PSSL* 11: 182–183.

2077.   To Modest Chaikovskii

15–16 Aug [1882]. Moscow.

RUS–KL (a³, No. 1669).

*ZC 2: 544–545 — **PB*: 282–283 — **PSSL* 11: 183–185 — **LF*: 276–277 [English tr.].

2078.   To Nadezhda von Meck

17–[18] Aug [1882]. Moscow.

RUS–KL (a³, No. 802).

PM 3: 88 — *PSSL* 11: 185–186.

2079.   To Nadezhda von Meck

20 Aug [1882]. Kiev.

RUS–KL (a³, No. 803).

PM 3: 89–90 — *PSSL* 11: 186–187.

2080.   To Leontii Tkachenko

20 Aug [1882]. Kiev.

RUS–SPsc (f. 834, No. 29, fol. 22–23).

PSSL 11: 187–188.

2081.   To Modest Chaikovskii

20 Aug [1882]. Kiev.

RUS–KL (a³, No. 1670).

PSSL 11: 188.

2082.   To Pëtr Iurgenson

20 Aug [1882]. Kiev.

RUS–KL (a³, No. 2389).

PIU 1: 256 — *PSSL* 11: 189.

2083.   To Anatolii Chaikovskii

22 Aug 1882. Kamenka.

Autograph lost; MS copy in RUS–KL.

*ZC 2: 546 — *PSSL* 11: 189–190.

2084.   To Nadezhda von Meck

22–25 Aug 1882. Kamenka.

RUS–KL (a³, No. 804).

*ZC 2: 546–547 ("23 Aug") — *PM* 3: 92–94 — *PSSL* 11: 190–191.

2085.   To Modest Chaikovskii

23 Aug [1882]. Kamenka.

RUS–KL (a³, No. 1671).

*PB: 281–283 — *PSSL* 11: 192–193 — **LF*: 277–278 [English tr.].

2086.   [see 2146a].

2087.   To Aleksandr Shidlovskii

26 Aug 1882. Kamenka.

Autograph lost; MS copy in RUS–KL.

PSSL 11: 194–196.

2088.   To Nadezhda von Meck

28 Aug 1882. Kamenka.

RUS–KL (a³, No. 805).

PM 3: 95–96 — *PSSL* 11: 196–197.

2089.   To Anatolii Chaikovskii

29 Aug [1882]. Kamenka.

Autograph lost; MS copy in RUS–KL.

PSSL 11: 198.

2090.   To Modest Chaikovskii

30 Aug 1882 [Kamenka].

RUS–KL (a³, No. 1672).

*ZC 2: 547 — *PB*: 284 — *PSSL* 11: 198–199 — **LF*: 278–279 [English tr.].

2091.   To Nadezhda von Meck

31 Aug–2 Sep 1882. Kamenka.

RUS–KL (a³, No. 806).

PM 3: 96–97 — *PSSL* 11: 200–201.

2092.   To Anna Aleksandrova-Levenson

1 Sep 1882. Kamenka.

RUS–Mrg

PSSL 11: 202.

2093. To Nikolai Hubert

1 Sep [1882]. Kamenka.

RUS–KL (a³, No. 105).

PSSL 11: 202–203.

2094. To Karl Al´brekht

1 Sep [1882]. Kamenka.

RUS–Mcm (f. 37, No. 45).

PSSL 11: 203.

2095. To Aleksandr Shidlovskii

[1 Sep 1882. Kamenka].

Autograph lost; MS copy in RUS–KL.

PSSL 11: 204.

2095a. To Pëtr Iurgenson

2 Sep 1882. Kamenka.

RUS–KL (a³, No. 3307).

Not published.

2096. To Aleksei Sofronov

2 Sep [1882]. Kamenka.

RUS–SPsc (f. 834, No. 26, fol. 25–26).

PSSL 11: 204–205.

2097. To Pëtr Iurgenson

2 Sep [1882]. Kamenka.

RUS–SPsc (f. 834, No. 26, fol. 26) [post–script to
    letter 2096].

PSSL 11: 205.

2098. To Anatolii Chaikovskii

5 Sep 1882. Kamenka.

Autograph lost; MS copy in RUS–KL.

PSSL 11: 206.

2099. To Nikolai Konradi

6 Sep 1882. Kamenka.

Autograph lost; MS copy in RUS–KL.

CTP: 261–262 — *PSSL* 11: 207–208.

2100. To Aleksandra Hubert

7 Sep 1882. Kamenka.

RUS–KL (a³, No. 41).

PRM 19 — *PSSL* 11: 208–209.

2101. To Nadezhda von Meck

9 Sep 1882. Kamenka.

RUS–KL (a³, No. 807).

PM 3: 100–101 — *PSSL* 11: 209–210.

2102. To Pëtr Iurgenson

10 Sep [1882]. Kamenka.

RUS–KL (a³, No. 2390).

PIU 1: 256–257 — *PSSL* 11: 210–211.

2103. To Modest Chaikovskii

10–13 Sep 1882. Kamenka.

RUS–KL (a³, No. 1673).

*ZC 2: 550 — **PB*: 285 — *PSSL* 11: 211–213 —
    *LF: 279 [English tr.].

2104. To Aleksei Sofronov

11 Sep 1882. Kamenka.

RUS–SPsc (f. 834, No. 26, fol. 27–28).

PSSL 11: 213–214.

2105. To Anatolii Chaikovskii

12 Sep 1882. Kamenka.

Autograph lost; MS copy in RUS–KL.

PSSL 11: 213–215.

2106. To Aleksandr Tarnavich

[12–14 Sep 1882]. Kamenka.

RUS–KL (a³, No. 408).

PSSL 11: 215.

2107. To Nadezhda von Meck

14 Sep [1882]. Kamenka.

RUS–KL (a³, No. 808).

PM 3: 101–102 — *PSSL* 11: 216–217.

2108. To Pëtr Iurgenson

15 Sep [1882]. Kamenka.

RUS–KL (a³, No. 2391).

*PIU 1: 259 — **PSSL* 11: 217–218.

2109. To Modest Chaikovskii

17 Sep [1882. Kamenka].

RUS–KL (a³, No. 1674).

PSSL 11: 218–219.

2110.   To Aleksei Sofronov
18 Sep [1882]. Kamenka.
RUS–SPsc (f. 834, No. 26, fol. 29–30).
PSSL 11: 219–220.

2111.   To Anatolii Chaikovskii
18 Sep [1882]. Kamenka.
Autograph lost; MS copy in RUS–KL.
*ZC 2: 551 — *PB: 285–286 — *PSSL* 11: 220–221 —
    *LF: 279–280 [English tr.].

2112.   To Modest Chaikovskii
20 Sep 1882 [Kamenka].
RUS–KL (a³, No. 1675).
*ZC 2: 551 — *PB: 286 — *PSSL* 11: 221–223 — *LF:
    280–281 [English tr.].

2113.   To Pëtr Iurgenson
20 Sep [1882]. Kamenka.
RUS–KL (a³, No. 2392).
PIU 1: 260 — *PSSL* 11: 223–224.

2114.   To Eduard Nápravník
21 Sep [1882]. Kamenka.
Autograph lost; typed copy in RUS–KL.
*ZC 2: 552–553 — *VP*: 141–143 — *EFN*: 120–121 —
    PSSL 11: 224–225.

2115.   To Pëtr Iurgenson
[22 Sep 1882. Kamenka] — telegram.
RUS–KL (a³, No. 2403).
PSSL 11: 225.

2116.   To Nadezhda von Meck
22–24 Sep 1882. Kamenka.
RUS–KL (a³, No. 809).
PM 3: 104–106 — *PSSL* 11: 226–227.

2117.   To Anatolii Chaikovskii
26 [Sep 1882]. Kiev
RUS–KL (a³, No. 1326).
PSSL 11: 228.

2118.   To Modest Chaikovskii
28 Sep [1882]. Kamenka.
RUS–KL (a³, No. 1676).
PSSL 11: 229.

2119.   To Nadezhda von Meck
28 Sep–8 Oct 1882. Kamenka.
RUS–KL (a³, No. 810).
PM 3: 107–109 — *PSSL* 11: 230–232.

2120.   To Iosif Kotek
[29 Sep 1882. Kamenka] — telegram.
RUS–KL (a³, No. 251).
PSSL 11: 232.

2121.   To Matvei Luznii
29 Sep 1882 [Kamenka].
Autograph lost
Krasnyi arkhiv (1940), 3: 246–248 — *PSSL* 11: 232–
    235.

2121a.   To Leontii Tkachenko
[30 Sep 1882. Kamenka].
RUS–SPsc (f. 834, No. 29, fol. 32–33).
Not published.

2122.   To Leontii Tkachenko
1 Oct [1882]. Kamenka.
RUS–SPsc (f. 834, No. 29, fol. 24–25).
PSSL 11: 235–236.

2123.   To Modest Chaikovskii
1–4 Oct [1882]. Kamenka.
RUS–KL (a³, No. 1677).
*ZC 2: 553–554 — *PB: 287–288 — *PSSL* 11: 236–
    238 — *LF: 281–282 [English tr.].

2124.   To Anatolii Chaikovskii
3 Oct [1882]. Kamenka.
RUS–KL (a³, No. 1329).
*ZC 2: 424–425 ("2 Oct") — *PB: 287 — *PSSL* 11:
    238–239 — *LF: 281 [English tr.].

2125.   To Pëtr Iurgenson
3 Oct [1882]. Kamenka.
RUS–KL (a³, No. 2393).
PIU 1: 262 — *PSSL* 11: 239.

2126.   To Eduard Nápravník
7 Oct 1882. Kamenka.
Autograph lost; typed copy in RUS–KL.
VP: 144–146 — *EFN*: 122–123 — *PSSL* 11: 240–241.

2127.   To Milii Balakirev

8 Oct 1882. Kamenka.

RUS–SPsc (f. 834, No. 12, fol. 4–6).

BC: 73–74 — *BVP* 164–165 — *PSSL* 11: 241–242.

2128.   To Nikolai Hubert

8 Oct 1882 [Kamenka].

RUS–KL (a³, No. 106).

PSSL 11: 243.

2129.   To Aleksei Sofronov

8 Oct 1882. Kamenka.

RUS–SPsc (f. 834, No. 26, fol. 31–32).

PSSL 11: 244.

2130.   To Sergei Taneev

8 Oct [1882]. Kamenka.

RUS–Mcl (f. 880).

PT: 88 — *CTP*: 87 — *PSSL* 11: 244–245.

2131.   To Anatolii Chaikovskii

9 Oct 1882. Kamenka.

Autograph lost; MS copy in RUS–KL.

PSSL 11: 245–247.

2132.   To Modest Chaikovskii

11 Oct [1882]. Kamenka.

RUS–KL (a³, No. 1678).

PSSL 11: 247–248.

2133.   To Pëtr Iurgenson

12 [Oct 1882]. Kamenka.

RUS–KL (a³, No. 2394).

PIU 1: 263 — *PSSL* 11: 248–249.

2134.   To Aleksandr Tarnavich

13 Oct [1882. Kamenka].

RUS–KL (a³, No. 404).

PSSL 11: 249.

2135.   To Nadezhda von Meck

14 Oct [1882]. Kamenka.

RUS–KL (a³, No. 811).

PM 3: 111–112 — *PSSL* 11: 250–251.

2136.   To Anatolii Chaikovskii

17 Oct [1882]. Kamenka.

Autograph lost; MS copy in RUS–KL.

PSSL 11: 251–252.

2137.   To Modest Chaikovskii

18 Oct 1882. Kamenka.

RUS–KL (a³, No. 1679).

ZC 2: 554–555 — *PSSL* 11: 252–253.

2138.   To Nadezhda von Meck

19–26 Oct [1882]. Kamenka.

RUS–KL (a³, No. 812).

PM 3: 113–115 — *PSSL* 11: 253–256.

2139.   To Nadezhda von Meck

20 Oct [1882]. Kamenka.

RUS–KL (a³, No. 813).

PM 3: 112–113 — *PSSL* 11: 256–257.

2140.   To Aleksei Sofronov

20 Oct 1882 [Kamenka].

RUS–SPsc (f. 834, No. 26, fol. 33–34).

PSSL 11: 257–258.

2141.   To Pëtr Iurgenson

20 Oct 1882. Kamenka.

RUS–KL (a³, No. 2395).

ZC 2: 555 — *PIU* 1: 263–264 — *PSSL* 11: 258–259.

2142.   To Pëtr Iurgenson

[21 Oct 1882. Kamenka] — telegram.

RUS–KL (a³, No. 2402).

PSSL 11: 259.

2143.   To Pëtr Iurgenson

23 Oct [1882]. Kamenka.

RUS–KL (a³, No. 2396).

PIU 1: 264–265 — *PSSL* 11: 260.

2144.   To Anatolii Chaikovskii

24 Oct [1882]. Kamenka.

Autograph lost; MS copy in RUS–KL.

PSSL 11: 260–261.

2145.   To Modest Chaikovskii

25 Oct [1882]. Kamenka.

RUS–KL (a³, No. 1680).

*ZC 2: 557–558 — *PB: 288 — *PSSL 11: 262–
263 — *LF: 282 [English tr.].

2146.   To Nikolai von Meck

[late Oct 1882. Kamenka].

Autograph lost; MS copy in RUS–KL.

PSSL 11: 263–265.

2146a. To Modest Chaikovskii

[? 27–29 Oct 1882 . Kamenka] — postscript to a
letter from German Larosh.

RUS–KL (b¹⁰, No. 3665).

PSSL 11: 193 ("25–26 Aug", as No. 2086) — PSSL
17: 232.

2147.   To Aleksandr Ostrovskii

28 Oct 1882. Kamenka.

RUS–Mt (Ostrovskii coll.).

ORK: 166–167 — PSSL 11: 265–266.

2148.   To Sergei Taneev

29 Oct 1882. Kamenka.

RUS–Mcl (f. 880).

*ZC 2: 558–559 — PT: 90–91 — CTP: 89 — PSSL
11: 266–267.

2149.   To Nadezhda von Meck

30 Oct–3 Nov [1882]. Kamenka.

RUS–KL (a³, No. 814).

PM 3: 115–117 — PSSL 11: 268–270.

2150.   To Aleksandr Tarnavich

31 Oct [1882]. [Kamenka].

RUS–KL (a³, No. 405).

PSSL 11: 270.

2151.   To Anatolii Chaikovskii

31 Oct [1882]. [Kamenka].

Autograph lost; MS copy in RUS–KL.

PSSL 11: 271.

2152.   To Modest Chaikovskii

1 Nov [1882]. Kamenka.

RUS–KL (a³, No. 1681).

PSSL 11: 272–273.

2153.   To Anna Merkling

2 Nov [1882]. Kamenka.

Autograph lost; MS copy in RUS–KL.

CTP: 214 — PSSL 11: 273–274.

2154.   To Anatolii Chaikovskii

7 Nov [1882]. Kamenka.

Autograph lost; MS copy in RUS–KL.

PSSL 11: 274–275.

2155.   To Leontii Tkachenko

8 Nov [1882]. Kamenka.

RUS–SPsc (f. 834, No. 29, fol. 26–27).

*ZC 2: 559–560 — PSSL 11: 275–276.

2156.   To Modest Chaikovskii

8 Nov [1882]. Kamenka.

RUS–KL (a³, No. 1682).

*PB: 288–289 — PSSL 11: 277–278 — *LF: 283
[English tr.].

2157.   To Nadezhda von Meck

9–10 Nov [1882]. Kamenka.

RUS–KL (a³, No. 815).

*ZC 2: 560–561 — PM 3: 119–120 — PSSL 11: 278–
280.

2158.   To Milii Balakirev

12 Nov 1882. Kamenka.

RUS–SPsc (f. 834, No. 12, fol. 7–11).

BC: 77–80 — BVP 167–169 — PSSL 11: 281–282.

2159.   To Anna Aleksandrova-Levenson

13 Nov 1882. Kamenka.

Autograph lost; typed copy in RUS–KL (a⁷, No.
1113).

SN (1905), 10: 106 — PSSL 11: 282–283.

2160.   To Aleksandr Tarnavich

15 Nov [1882]. [Kamenka].

RUS–KL (a³, No. 406).

PSSL 11: 283.

2161.   To Nadezhda von Meck

17 Nov 1882. Kiev.

RUS–KL (a³, No. 816).

*ZC 2: 561 — PM 3: 121 — PSSL 11: 283–284.

2162.   To Pëtr Iurgenson

[17 Nov 1882. Kiev] — telegram.

RUS–KL (a³, No. 2398).

PSSL 11: 284.

2163.   To Modest Chaikovskii

18 Nov [1882]. Kiev.

RUS–KL (a³, No. 1683).

PSSL 11: 284–285.

2164.   To Modest Chaikovskii

21 Nov [1882]. Moscow.

RUS–KL (a³, No. 1684).

*ZC 2: 561–562 — *PB: 289 — PSSL 11: 285–286 —
   *LF: 283 [English tr.].

2165.   To Nadezhda von Meck

22–26 Nov [1882]. Moscow.

RUS–KL (a³, No. 817).

*ZC 2: 562–563 ("23 Nov") — PM 3: 122–124 —
   PSSL 11: 286–288.

2166.   To Vladmir Shilovskii

28 Nov [1882]. [Moscow].

RUS–SPsc (f. 834, No. 14, fol. 5–7).

PSSL 11: 288–289.

2167.   To Sergei Taneev

[30 Nov 1882. Moscow].

RUS–Mcl (f. 880).

PSSL 11: 289.

2168.   To Modest Chaikovskii

2 Dec [1882]. Moscow.

RUS–KL (a³, No. 1685).

PSSL 11: 289–290.

2169.   To Aleksei Sofronov

[5 Dec 1882. Moscow].

RUS–SPsc (f. 834, No. 26, fol. 11–12).

PSSL 11: 290.

2170.   To Nadezhda von Meck

5 Dec [1882]. Moscow.

RUS–KL (a³, No. 818).

*ZC 2: 563 — PM 3: 125–126 — PSSL 11: 290–291.

2171.   To Modest Chaikovskii

8 Dec [1882]. Moscow.

RUS–KL (a³, No. 1686).

*PB: 289 — *PSSL 11: 291–292 — *LF: 284 [English
   tr.].

2172.   To Sergei Morozov

10 Dec 1882. Moscow.

RUS–SPil (f. 53, No. 77, fol. 3–4).

PSSL 11: 292.

2173.   To Nadezhda von Meck

12–13 Dec [1882]. Moscow.

RUS–KL (a³, No. 819).

*ZC 2: 564 — PM 3: 127–128 — PSSL 11: 293–294.

2174.   To Anatolii Chaikovskii

[15 Dec 1882. St. Petersburg].

Autograph lost; MS copy in RUS–KL.

PSSL 11: 294–295.

2175.   To Aleksei Sofronov

21 Dec 1882. St. Petersburg.

RUS–SPsc (f. 834, No. 26, fol. 35–36).

PSSL 11: 295.

2176.   To Anatolii Chaikovskii

21 Dec [1882]. St. Petersburg.

Autograph lost; MS copy in RUS–KL.

PSSL 11: 295–296.

2177.   To Lev Davydov

25 Dec [1882]. St. Petersburg.

RUS–SPsc (f. 834, No. 19, fol. 39–40).

*PB: 290 — PSSL 11: 296–297 — *LF: 284 [English
   tr.].

2178.   To Nadezhda von Meck

25 Dec [1882]. St. Petersburg.

RUS–KL (a³, No. 820).

PM 3: 128–130 — PSSL 11: 297–299.

2179.   To Anatolii Chaikovskii
25 Dec [1882]. St. Petersburg.
Autograph lost; MS copy in RUS–KL.
PSSL 11: 299–300.

2180.   To Pëtr Iurgenson
25 Dec [1882]. St. Petersburg.
RUS–KL (a³, No. 2397).
PIU 1: 265–266 — *PSSL* 11: 300.

2181.   To Pavel Tret´iakov
26 Dec 1882. St. Petersburg.
RUS–Mgt
*A. P. Botkina, *Pavel Mikhailovich Tret´iakov v zhizni i iskusstve* (1951): 198 — *PSSL* 11: 301.

2182.   To Eduard Nápravník
[28 Dec 1882. St. Petersburg].
Autograph lost; typed copy in RUS–KL.
VP: 147 — *EFN*: 124 — *PSSL* 11: 302.

2183.   To Modest Chaikovskii
30 Dec 1882/[11 Jan 1883]. Berlin.
RUS–KL (a³, No. 1687).
ZC 2: 565 — *PB*: 290–291 — *PSSL* 11: 302–303 — *LF*: 285 [English tr.].

2184.   To Nadezhda von Meck
31 Dec [1882]/[12 Jan 1883]. Berlin.
RUS–KL (a³, No. 821).
ZC 2: 565–566 — *PM* 3: 130–132 — *PSSL* 11: 303–305.

1883

2185.   To Nikolai Konradi
3/15 Jan 1883. Paris
Autograph lost; MS copy in RUS–KL.
CTP: 262–263 — *PSSL* 12: 13.

2186.   To Anatolii Chaikovskii
3/15 Jan 1883. Paris
Autograph lost; MS copy in RUS–KL.
PSSL 12: 14.

2187.   To Modest Chaikovskii
3/15 Jan [1883] (in MS: "1882"). Paris.
RUS–KL (a³, No. 1688).
PSSL 12: 15.

2188.   To Pëtr Iurgenson
3/15 Jan 1883. Paris
RUS–KL (a³, No. 2404).
PIU 1: 271–272 — *PSSL* 12: 15–16.

2189.   To Nadezhda von Meck
3/15–5/17 Jan 1883. Paris
RUS–KL (a³, No. 822).
PM 3: 134–136 — *PSSL* 12: 17–19.

2190.   To Pëtr Iurgenson
5/[17] Jan 1883. Paris
RUS–KL (a³, No. 2405).
ZC 2: 566–567 — *PIU* 1: 272–273 — *PSSL* 12: 19–21.

2191.   To Aleksei Sofronov
8/20 Jan [1883]. Paris.
RUS–SPsc (f. 834, No. 26, fol. 37–38).
PSSL 12: 22–23.

2192.   To Modest Chaikovskii
8/20 Jan [1883]. Paris.
RUS–KL (a³, No. 1689).
PSSL 12: 23.

2193.   To Pëtr Iurgenson
9/[21] Jan [1883]. Paris.
RUS–SPsc (f. 834, No. 38).
PSSL 12: 24.

2194.   To Anna Merkling
10/22 Jan 1883. Paris.
Autograph lost; MS copy in RUS–KL.
ZC 2: 567–568 — *CTP*: 215 — *PSSL* 12: 24–25.

2195.   To Nadezhda von Meck
11/23 Jan 1883. Paris.
RUS–KL (a³, No. 823).
ZC 2: 568–569 — *PM* 3: 138–139 — *PSSL* 12: 26–27.

2196. To Vladimir Shilovskii

13/25 Jan 1883. Paris.

RUS–SPsc (f. 834, No. 14, fol. 8–9).

PSSL 12: 28–29.

2197. To Eduard Nápravník

14/26 Jan 1883. Paris.

RUS–KL (a³, No. 3357).

ZC 2: 569–570 — VP: 150–151 *— EFN:* 126–127 —
     PSSL 12: 29–30.

2198. To Aleksei Sofronov

14/26 Jan 1883. Paris.

RUS–SPsc (f. 834, No. 26, fol. 39–40).

PSSL 12: 31.

2199. To Leontii Tkachenko

14/26 Jan 1883. Paris.

RUS–SPsc (f. 834, No. 29, fol. 28–29).

PSSL 12: 31.

2200. To Anatolii Chaikovskii

14/26 Jan [1883]. Paris.

Autograph lost; MS copy in RUS–KL.

PSSL 12: 32.

2201. To Nadezhda von Meck

15/27 Jan 1883. Paris.

RUS–KL (a³, No. 824).

PM 3: 139–140 — *PSSL* 12: 33–34.

2202. To Pëtr Iurgenson

[16]/28 Jan 1883 (in MS: "14/28"). Paris.

RUS–KL (a³, No. 2406).

PIU 1: 274–275 — *PSSL* 12: 34.

2203. To Praskov´ia Chaikovskaia

[19]/31 Jan 1883 (in MS: "12/31"). Paris.

Autograph lost; MS copy in RUS–KL.

PSSL 12: 35–36.

2204. To Nadezhda von Meck

19/31 Jan–24 Jan/5 Feb 1883. Paris.

RUS–KL (a³, No. 825).

PM 3: 142–144 — *PSSL* 12: 36–38.

2205. To Anatolii Chaikovskii

21 Jan/2 Feb [1883]. Paris.

Autograph lost; MS copy in RUS–KL.

PSSL 12: 39.

2206. To Pëtr Iurgenson

21 Jan/2 Feb 1883 [Paris].

RUS–KL (a³, No. 2407).

PIU 1: 275–276 — *PSSL* 12: 39–40.

2207. To Anna Merkling

24 Jan/5 Feb 1883. Paris.

Autograph lost; MS copy in RUS–KL.

CTP: 215–216 — *PSSL* 12: 41.

2208. To Aleksei Sofronov

24 Jan/5 Feb 1883. Paris.

RUS–SPsc (f. 834, No. 26, fol. 41–42).

PSSL 12: 41–42.

2209. To Nadezhda von Meck

26 Jan/7 Feb 1883. Paris.

RUS–KL (a³, No. 826).

PM 3: 144–145 — *PSSL* 12: 42–43.

2210. To Noël Pascal

[late Jan/early Feb 1883. Paris] — in French.

Autograph lost; rough draft in RUS–KL (a⁴, No.
     6179).

PSSL 12: 44.

2211. To Anatolii Chaikovskii

28 Jan/9 Feb 1883. Paris.

Autograph lost; MS copy in RUS–KL.

PSSL 12: 44–45.

2212. To Anna Merkling

29 Jan/[10 Feb] 1883. Paris.

Autograph lost; MS copy in RUS–KL.

CTP: 216 — *PSSL* 12: 45–46.

2213. To Pëtr Iurgenson

29 Jan/[10 Feb]–2/14 Feb 1883. Paris.

RUS–KL (a³, No. 2408).

ZC 2: 571 — PIU 1: 277–278 — *PSSL* 12: 46–48.

2214.   To Lev Davydov

31 Jan/12 Feb 1883. Paris.

RUS–SPsc (f. 834, No. 19, fol. 41–42).

PSSL 12: 48–49.

2215.   To Nadezhda von Meck

31 Jan/12 Feb–9/21 Feb 1883. Paris.

RUS–KL (a³, No. 827).

*ZC 2: 573 ("5 Feb") — *PM* 3: 148–152 — *PSSL* 12: 49–53.

2216.   To Sergei Taneev

2/[14] Feb [1883]. Paris.

RUS–Mcl (f. 880).

*ZC 2: 571–572 — **PT*: 93–94 — *CTP*: 91–92 — *PSSL* 12: 54.

2217.   To Anatolii Chaikovskii

4/[16] Feb [1883]. Paris.

Autograph lost; MS copy in RUS–KL.

PSSL 12: 55–56.

2218.   To Pëtr Iurgenson

4/16 Feb 1883. Paris.

RUS–KL (a³, No. 2409).

*ZC 2: 572 — *PIU* 1: 279–280 — *PSSL* 12: 56–57.

2219.   To Pëtr Iurgenson

6/[18] Feb 1883 [Paris].

RUS–KL (a³, No. 2410).

*ZC 2: 573–574 — **PIU* 1: 280–281 — *PSSL* 12: 58–59.

2220.   To Aleksei Sofronov

7/[19] Feb 1883. Paris.

RUS–SPsc (f. 834, No. 26, fol. 43–44).

PSSL 12: 59–60.

2221.   To Pëtr Iurgenson

9/[21] Feb [1883]. Paris.

RUS–KL (a³, No. 2411).

*ZC 2: 574–575 — *PIU* 1: 281–282 — *PSSL* 12: 60–61.

2222.   To Anatolii Chaikovskii

11/23 Feb 1883 [Paris].

Autograph lost; MS copy in RUS–KL.

PSSL 12: 61–62.

2223.   To Aleksei Sofronov

12/[24] Feb 1883. Paris.

RUS–SPsc (f. 834, No. 26, fol. 45–46).

PSSL 12: 62–63.

2224.   To Nadezhda von Meck

14/26–16/28 Feb 1883. Paris.

RUS–KL (a³, No. 828).

*ZC 2: 575 ("16 Feb") — *PM* 3: 153–155 — *PSSL* 12: 63–65.

2225.   To Pëtr Iurgenson

16/[28] Feb [1883]. Paris.

RUS–KL (a³, No. 2412).

PSSL 12: 65.

2226.   To Anatolii Chaikovskii

18 Feb/2 Mar 1883. Paris.

Autograph lost; MS copy in RUS–KL.

PSSL 12: 66.

2227.   To Nadezhda von Meck

21–24 Feb/5–8 Mar [1883]. Paris.

RUS–KL (a³, No. 829).

*ZC 2: 575–576 — *PM* 3: 156–157 — *PSSL* 12: 67–69.

2228.   To Anatolii Chaikovskii

25 Feb/[9 Mar 1883]. Paris.

Autograph lost; MS copy in RUS–KL.

*ZC 2: 576 — **PB*: 291 — *PSSL* 12: 70–71 — **LF*: 285–286 [English tr.].

2229.   To Aleksei Sofronov

26 Feb/[10 Mar 1883]. Paris.

RUS–SPsc (f. 834, No. 26, fol. 47–48).

PSSL 12: 71–72.

2230.   To Pëtr Iurgenson

26 Feb/10 Mar– 1/13 Mar 1883. Paris.

RUS–KL (a³, No. 2413).

PIU 1: 284–285 — *PSSL* 12: 72–73.

2231.   To Anna Aleksandrova-Levenson

1/13 Mar 1883. Paris.

Autograph lost

SN (1905), 10: 106–107 — *PSSL* 12: 74.

2232.   To Anna Merkling

1/13 Mar 1883. Paris.

Autograph lost; MS copy in RUS–KL.

CTP: 216–217 — *PSSL* 12: 75.

2233.   To Anatolii Chaikovskii

3/[15] Mar [1883]. Paris.

Autograph lost; MS copy in RUS–KL.

PSSL 12: 76.

2234.   To Nadezhda von Meck

3/15–4/16 Mar 1883. Paris.

RUS–KL (a³, No. 830).

PM 3: 157–158 — *PSSL* 12: 77–78.

2235.   To Pëtr Iurgenson

[7]/19 Mar 1883. Paris.

RUS–KL (a³, No. 2417).

ZC 2: 577–578 — *PIU* 1: 291–292 — *PSSL* 12: 78–79.

2236.   To Nadezhda von Meck

9/21 Mar [1883]. Paris.

RUS–KL (a³, No. 831).

ZC 2: 576–577 — *PM* 3: 158–160 — *PSSL* 12: 80–81.

2237.   To Aleksei Sofronov

11/23 Mar 1883. Paris.

RUS–SPsc (f. 834, No. 26, fol. 49–50).

PSSL 12: 82.

2238.   To Anatolii Chaikovskii

12/24 Mar [1883]. Paris.

Autograph lost; MS copy in RUS–KL.

PSSL 12: 83.

2239.   To Pëtr Iurgenson

12/24 Mar [1883]. Paris.

RUS–KL (a³, No. 2419).

ZC 2: 577 — *PIU* 1: 289–290 — *PSSL* 12: 83–84.

2240.   To Nadezhda von Meck

14/26–16/28 Mar 1883. Paris.

RUS–KL (a³, No. 832).

PM 3: 161–164 — *PSSL* 12: 84–87.

2241.   To Anatolii Chaikovskii

17/[29]–18/[30] Mar [1883]. Paris.

Autograph lost; MS copy in RUS–KL.

PSSL 12: 87–88.

2242.   To Pëtr Iurgenson

[20] Mar/1 Apr 1883 (in MS: "19 Mar").Paris.

RUS–KL (a³, No. 2416).

ZC 2: 578–579 ("19 Mar") — *PIU* 1: 292–293 — *PSSL* 12: 88–89.

2243.   To Sof´ia Malozemova

[21] Mar/1 Apr 1883 (in MS: "20 Mar"). Paris.

RUS–KL (a³, No. 12).

PSSL 12: 90–91.

2244.   To Nadezhda von Meck

[21] Mar/2 Apr 1883 (in MS: "20 Mar"). Paris.

RUS–KL (a³, No. 833).

PM 3: 165–166 — *PSSL* 12: 91–92.

2245.   To Pëtr Iurgenson

23 Mar/[4 Apr 1883]. Paris.

RUS–KL (a³, No. 2418).

PIU 1: 293–294 — *PSSL* 12: 93–94.

2246.   To Pëtr Iurgenson

24 Mar/[5 Apr 1883]. [Paris].

RUS–KL (a³, No. 2420).

PSSL 12: 94–95.

2247.   To Anatolii Chaikovskii

25 Mar/[6 Apr] 1883. Paris.

Autograph lost; MS copy in RUS–KL.

PSSL 12: 95–96.

2248.   To Pëtr Iurgenson

25 Mar/[6 Apr 1883]. [Paris].

RUS–KL (a³, No. 2421).

PIU 1: 294–295 — *PSSL* 12: 96–97.

2249.   To Nadezhda von Meck
26 Mar/[7 Apr] 1883. Paris.
RUS–KL (a³, No. 834).
PM 3: 166–167 — *PSSL* 12: 97–98.

2250.   To Pëtr Iurgenson
26 Mar/[7 Apr 1883]. [Paris].
RUS–KL (a³, No. 2426).
PIU 1: 295 — *PSSL* 12: 99.

2251.   To Aleksei Sofronov
30 Mar/[11 Apr 1883]. Paris.
RUS–SPsc (f. 834, No. 26, fol. 51–52).
PSSL 12: 100.

2252.   To Anatolii Chaikovskii
1/13 Apr 1883. Paris.
Autograph lost; MS copy in RUS–KL.
PSSL 12: 100–101.

2253.   To Sergei Taneev
1/[13]–3/[15] Apr [1883]. Paris.
RUS–Mcl (f. 880).
ZC 2: 579–580 — *PT*: 100–101 — *CTP*: 96–97 —
   PSSL 12: 101–103.

2254.   To Pëtr Iurgenson
6/[18] Apr [1883]. Paris.
RUS–KL (a³, No. 2422).
ZC 2: 580–583 — *PIU* 1: 298–300 — *PSSL* 12:
   104–106.

2255.   To Nadezhda von Meck
6/[18] Apr [1883]. Paris.
RUS–KL (a³, No. 835).
PM 3: 169–170 — *PSSL* 12: 106–107.

2256.   To Modest Chaikovskii
7/[19] Apr [1883]. Paris.
RUS–KL (a³, No. 1690).
PB: 292 — *PSSL* 12: 108–109 — *LF*: 286–287
   [English tr.].

2257.   To Anatolii Chaikovskii
8/[20] Apr 1883 [Paris].

Autograph lost; MS copy in RUS–KL.
PSSL 12: 109–110.

2258.   To Modest Chaikovskii
9/[21] Apr [1883]. Paris.
RUS–KL (a³, No. 1691).
PB: 292–293 — *PSSL* 12: 110–111 — *LF*: 287–288
   [English tr.].

2259.   To Wladyslaw Pachulski
10/22 Apr 1883. Paris.
US–Wc
SM (1959), 12: 66–69 — *PSSL* 12: 111–116.

2260.   To Modest Chaikovskii
11/23 Apr 1883. Paris.
RUS–KL (a³, No. 1692).
PSSL 12: 116–117.

2261.   To Modest Chaikovskii
13/25 Apr [1883]. Paris.
RUS–KL (a³, No. 1693).
ZC 2: 583 — *PSSL* 12: 117–118.

2262.   To Modest Chaikovskii
14/26 Apr 1883 [Paris].
RUS–KL (a³, No. 1694).
ZC 2: 584 — *PB*: 293–294 — *PSSL* 12: 119–
   120 — *LF*: 288 [English tr.].

2263.   To Pëtr Iurgenson
14/26 Apr 1883. Paris.
RUS–KL (a³, No. 2423).
ZC 2: 583–584 — *PIU* 1: 300–301 — *PSSL* 12:
   120–121.

2264.   To Anatolii Chaikovskii
15/[27] Apr [1883]. Paris.
Autograph lost; MS copy in RUS–KL.
PSSL 12: 122.

2265.   To Nadezhda von Meck
16/[28] Apr 1883. Paris.
RUS–KL (a³, No. 836).
ZC 2: 584 — *PM* 3: 172–173 — *PSSL* 12: 123–124.

2266. To Modest Chaikovskii
16/[28] Apr [1883]. Paris.
RUS–KL (a³, No. 1695).
*PSSL 12: 124–125.

2267. To Pëtr Iurgenson
17/[29] Apr [1883]. Paris.
RUS–KL (a³, No. 2424).
PIU 1: 301–302 — PSSL 12: 126–127.

2268. To Modest Chaikovskii
18/30 Apr [1883]. [Paris].
RUS–KL (a³, No. 1696).
*PB: 294–295 — *PSSL 12: 127–129 — *LF: 289–290 [English tr.].

2269. To Natal´ia Pleskaia
20 Apr/[2 May 1883]. Paris.
RUS–Mcl (f. 905).
CTP: 365–36 — PSSL 12: 130.

2270. To Modest Chaikovskii
20 Apr/[2 May] 1883. Paris.
RUS–KL (a³, No. 1697).
*PB: 295–296 — PSSL 12: 131–132 — *LF: 290 [English tr.].

2271. To Anatolii Chaikovskii
21 Apr/[3 May 1883]. Paris.
Autograph lost; MS copy in RUS–KL.
PSSL 12: 132–133.

2272. To Modest Chaikovskii
22 Apr/[4 May] 1883. Paris.
RUS–KL (a³, No. 1698).
*PSSL 12: 133–134.

2273. To Nadezhda von Meck
23 Apr/[5 May] 1883. Paris.
RUS–KL (a³, No. 837).
PM 3: 174–175 — PSSL 12: 134–135.

2274. To Nikolai Konradi
24 Apr/6 May 1883. Paris.
Autograph lost; MS copy in RUS–KL.
CTP: 263 — PSSL 12: 136.

2275. To Modest Chaikovskii
25–26 Apr/7–[8] May 1883 [Paris].
RUS–KL (a³, No. 1699).
*ZC 2: 622–623 — PSSL 12: 137–140.

2276. To Anna Merkling
27 Apr/[9 May] 1883. Paris.
Autograph lost; MS copy in RUS–KL.
CTP: 217 — PSSL 12: 140–141.

2277. To Modest Chaikovskii
27 Apr/[9 May] 1883. Paris.
RUS–KL (a³, No. 1700).
PSSL 12: 142–144.

2278. To Lev Davydov
28 Apr/[10 May] 1883. Paris.
RUS–SPsc (f. 834, No. 19, fol. 43–44).
PSSL 12: 144–145.

2279. To Aleksei Sofronov
28 Apr/[10 May] 1883. Paris.
RUS–SPsc (f. 834, No. 26, fol. 53–54).
PSSL 12: 145–146.

2280. To Pëtr Iurgenson
28 Apr/[10 May] 1883. Paris.
RUS–KL (a³, No. 2425).
*ZC 2: 584–585 — PIU 1: 302–303 — PSSL 12: 146–147.

2281. To Nadezhda von Meck
29 Apr/11 May [1883]. Paris.
RUS–KL (a³, No. 838).
*ZC 2: 585 — PM 3: 176–178 — PSSL 12: 147–149.

2282. To Anatolii Chaikovskii
29 Apr/11 May 1883. Paris.
Autograph lost; MS copy in RUS–KL.
PSSL 12: 149–150.

2283. To Modest Chaikovskii
1/[13] May [1883]. [Paris].
RUS–KL (a³, No. 1701).
PSSL 12: 150–151.

2284.   To Modest Chaikovskii
2/[14]–3/[15] May [1883]. [Paris].
RUS–KL (a³, No. 1702).
*PSSL 12: 151–153.

2285.   To Nadezhda von Meck
3/[15] May 1883. Paris.
RUS–KL (a³, No. 839).
*ZC 2: 585–586 — PM 3: 179–181 — PSSL 12: 153–155.

2286.   To Modest Chaikovskii
5/[17] May [1883]. [Paris].
RUS–KL (a³, No. 1703).
PSSL 12: 156–157.

2287.   To Anatolii Chaikovskii
7/19 May [1883]. Paris.
Autograph lost; MS copy in RUS–KL.
PSSL 12: 158.

2288.   To Modest Chaikovskii
7/19 May 1883. Paris.
RUS–KL (a³, No. 1704).
PSSL 12: 158–160.

2289.   To Nadezhda von Meck
8/[20] May 1883. Paris.
RUS–KL (a³, No. 840).
PM 3: 181–183 — PSSL 12: 160–161.

2290.   To Nadezhda von Meck
9/[21] May [1883]. Paris.
RUS–KL (a³, No. 841).
PM 3: 183–184 — PSSL 12: 162.

2291.   To the editor of *Le Gaulois*
[10]/22 May 1883. Paris — in French.
Autograph lost
Le Gaulois (23 May 1883) — PSSL 12: 163.

2292.   To Nadezhda von Meck
12/24 May 1883. Berlin
RUS–KL (a³, No. 842).
*ZC 2: 586–587 — PM 3: 184–185 — PSSL 12: 164–165.

2293.   To Anatolii Chaikovskii
16 May [1883]. St. Petersburg.
Autograph lost; MS copy in RUS–KL.
PSSL 12: 165.

2294.   To Nadezhda von Meck
19 May [1883]. St. Petersburg.
RUS–KL (a³, No. 843).
*ZC 2: 589 — PM 3: 185–186 — PSSL 12: 165–166.

2295.   To Nadezhda von Meck
24 May [1883]. St. Petersburg.
RUS–KL (a³, No. 844).
*ZC 2: 589 — PM 3: 188–189 — PSSL 12: 167–168.

2296.   To Anna Aleksandrova-Levenson
31 May 1883. Podushkino.
Autograph lost
SN (1905), 10: 107 — PSSL 12: 168.

2297.   To Karl Davydov
31 May [1883]. Podushkino.
RUS–KL (a³, No. 162).
PSSL 12: 169.

2298.   To Nadezhda von Meck
1–8 Jun 1883. Podushkino.
RUS–KL (a³, No. 845).
PM 3: 189–191 — PSSL 12: 170–171.

2299.   To Modest Chaikovskii
8–9 Jun [1883]. Podushkino.
RUS–KL (a³, No. 1705).
*PSSL 12: 172–173.

2300.   To Nikolai Hubert
15 Jun 1883. Podushkino.
RUS–KL (a³, No. 107).
PRM 20–23 — PSSL 12: 173–175.

2301.   To Lev Davydov
15 Jun 1883 [Podushkino].
RUS–SPsc (f. 834, No. 19, fol. 45–46).
PSSL 12: 175–176.

2302. To Nadezhda von Meck

15 Jun 1883. Podushkino.

RUS–KL (a³, No. 846).

*ZC 2: 590 — PM 3: 191–192 — PSSL 12: 177–178.

2303. To Modest Chaikovskii

20 Jun [1883]. Podushkino.

RUS–KL (a³, No. 1706).

*ZC 2: 622 — *PSSL 12: 178–179.

2304. To Nikolai Konradi

22 Jun [1883]. Podushkino.

Autograph lost; MS copy in RUS–KL.

CTP: 264 — PSSL 12: 180.

2305. To Nadezhda von Meck

27 Jun [1883]. Podushkino.

RUS–KL (a³, No. 847).

*ZC 2: 590–591 — PM 3: 193–194 — PSSL 12: 181–182.

2306. To Lev Davydov

28 Jun 1883. Podushkino.

RUS–SPsc (f. 834, No. 19, fol. 47–48).

PSSL 12: 182–183.

2307. To Nikolai Hubert

2 Jul 1883. Podushkino.

RUS–KL (a³, No. 108).

PRM 24–26 — PSSL 12: 183–185.

2308. To Modest Chaikovskii

3–4 Jul [1883]. Podushkino.

RUS–KL (a³, No. 1707).

*ZC 2: 591 — *PB: 296 — PSSL 12: 185–186 — *LF: 291 [English tr.].

2309. To Nadezhda von Meck

8 Jul 1883. Podushkino.

RUS–KL (a³, No. 848).

*ZC 2: 591–592 — PM 3: 195–197 — PSSL 12: 187–188.

2310. To Modest Chaikovskii

14 Jul [1883]. Podushkino.

RUS–KL (a³, No. 1708).

*ZC 2: 592–593 — PB: 297 — PSSL 12: 189–190 — LF: 292 [English tr.].

2311. To Nadezhda von Meck

17 Jul 1883. Podushkino.

RUS–KL (a³, No. 849).

PM 3: 198–199 — PSSL 12: 190–191.

2312. To Pëtr Iurgenson

18 Jul [1883]. [Podushkino].

RUS–KL (a³, No. 2427).

PIU 1: 303 — PSSL 12: 191–192.

2313. To Nadezhda von Meck

18 Jul 1883. Podushkino.

RUS–KL (a³, No. 850).

PM 3: 199–202 — PSSL 12: 192–195.

2314. To Modest Chaikovskii

18 Jul 1883. Podushkino.

RUS–KL (a³, No. 1709).

PSSL 12: 195–196.

2315. To Adolph Strauss

25 Jul 1883 [Moscow].

RUS–KL (a³, No. 465).

PSSL 12: 196.

2316. To Modest Chaikovskii

26 Jul [1883]. Moscow.

RUS–KL (a³, No. 1710).

*PB: 297–298 — PSSL 12: 197–198 — *LF: 293 [English tr.].

2317. To Nadezhda von Meck

27 Jul [1883]. Podushkino.

RUS–KL (a³, No. 851).

PM 3: 202–203 — PSSL 12: 198–199.

2318. To Pëtr Iurgenson

28 Jul 1883. Podushkino.

RUS–KL (a³, No. 2428).

*ZC 2: 593–594 — PIU 1: 304–305 — PSSL 12: 200–201.

2319.   To Anna Aleksandrova-Levenson

1 Aug 1883. Podushkino.

Autograph lost

SN (1903), 10: 107–108 — *PSSL* 12: 202.

2320.   To Nadezhda von Meck

1 Aug 1883. Podushkino.

RUS–KL (a³, No. 852).

*ZC 2: 594–595 — *PM* 3: 205–206 — *PSSL* 12: 203–204.

2321.   To Modest Chaikovskii

1 Aug 1883. Podushkino.

RUS–KL (a³, No. 1711).

PSSL 12: 204–205.

2322.   To Nikolai Konradi

1 Aug [1883]. Podushkino.

Autograph lost; MS copy in RUS–KL.

CTP: 264–265 — *PSSL* 12: 205–206.

2323.   To Nadezhda von Meck

4 Aug [1883]. Podushkino.

RUS–KL (a³, No. 853).

PM 3: 207 — *PSSL* 12: 206.

2324.   To Anna Merkling

8 Aug 1883. Podushkino.

Autograph lost; MS copy in RUS–KL.

CTP: 218 — *PSSL* 12: 207.

2325.   To Nadezhda von Meck

10 Aug 1883 [Podushkino].

RUS–KL (a³, No. 854).

*ZC 2: 595–596 — *PM* 3: 208–209 — *PSSL* 12: 208–209.

2326.   To Modest Chaikovskii

10 Aug [1883]. Podushkino.

RUS–KL (a³, No. 1712).

PB: 299 — *PSSL* 12: 209–210 — *LF*: 294 [English tr.].

2327.   To Karl Al´brekht

[11 Aug 1883. Podushkino].

RUS–Mcm (f. 37, No. 46).

PSSL 12: 211.

2328.   To Modest Chaikovskii

12 Aug [1883]. [Podushkino].

RUS–KL (a³, No. 1713).

PB: 299–300 — *PSSL* 12: 211–212 — *LF*: 294–295 [English tr.].

2329.   To Anna Merkling

16 Aug 1883 [Podushkino].

Autograph lost; MS copy in RUS–KL.

CTP: 218 — *PSSL* 12: 212.

2330.   To Natal´ia Pleskaia

16 Aug [1883]. [Podushkino].

RUS–Mcl (f. 905).

CTP: 366 — *PSSL* 12: 212–213.

2331.   To Nadezhda von Meck

19 Aug [1883]. Podushkino.

RUS–KL (a³, No. 855).

*ZC 2: 596 — *PM* 3: 209–211 — *PSSL* 12: 213–214.

2332.   To Eduard Nápravník

19 Aug 1883. Podushkino.

Autograph lost; typed copy in RUS–KL.

VP: 151–152 (“29 Aug”) — *Kirov*: 60 (“29 Aug”) — *EFN*: 127 (“Aug”) — *PSSL* 12: 215.

2333.   To Natal´ia Pleskaia

22 Aug [1883]. [Podushkino].

RUS–Mcl (f. 905).

CTP: 366–367 — *PSSL* 12: 216.

2334.   To Nadezhda von Meck

23 Aug [1883]. [Podushkino].

RUS–KL (a³, No. 856).

PM 3: 212–213 — *PSSL* 12: 216–217.

2334a.   To Pëtr Iurgenson

[? Aug 1883. Podushkino].

RUS–KL (a³, No. 2429).

Not published.

2334b. To Pëtr Iurgenson

[Aug 1883?. Podushkino].

RUS–KL (a³, No. 2430).

Not published.

2335. To Eduard Nápravník

31 Aug 1883. Podushkino.

Autograph lost; typed copy in RUS–KL.

VP: 152–154 — *EFN*: 127–128 — *PSSL* 12: 217–218.

2336. To Nadezhda von Meck

1 Sep [1883]. Moscow.

RUS–KL (a³, No. 857).

PM 3: 215 — *PSSL* 12: 219.

2337. To Anatolii Chaikovskii

4 Sep [1883]. Kiev

Autograph lost; MS copy in RUS–KL.

PSSL 12: 220.

2338. To Modest Chaikovskii

4 Sep [1883]. Kiev.

RUS–KL (a³, No. 1714).

PSSL 12: 220–221.

2339. To Nadezhda von Meck

6 Sep 1883. Verbovka.

RUS–KL (a³, No. 858).

PM 3: 217–218 — *PSSL* 12: 221–222.

2340. To Anatolii Chaikovskii

6 Sep [1883]. Verbovka.

Autograph lost; MS copy in RUS–KL.

PSSL 12: 222–223.

2341. To Modest Chaikovskii

6 Sep [1883]. Verbovka.

RUS–KL (a³, No. 1715).

*ZC 2: 602 — *PSSL* 12: 223–225.

2342. To Nadezhda von Meck

8–10 Sep [1883]. Verbovka.

RUS–KL (a³, No. 859).

*ZC 2: 602 — *PM* 3: 218–221 — *PSSL* 12: 225–227.

2343 . To Eduard Nápravník

10 Sep 1883 [Verbovka].

Autograph lost; typed copy in RUS–KL.

VP: 156–157 — *EFN*: 130 — *PSSL* 12: 228.

2344. To Modest Chaikovskii

10–12 Sep [1883]. Verbovka.

RUS–KL (a³, No. 1716).

*ZC 2: 602–603 — **PB*: 300 — *PSSL* 12: 229–231 — **LF*: 295 [English tr.].

2345. To Praskov´ia Chaikovskaia

11 Sep [1883]. Verbovka.

Autograph lost; MS copy in RUS–KL.

PSSL 12: 231–232.

2346. To Pëtr Iurgenson

12 Sep [1883]. Verbovka.

RUS–KL (a³, No. 2431).

PIU 1: 306 — *PSSL* 12: 233.

2347. To Nadezhda von Meck

16 Sep 1883. Verbovka.

RUS–KL (a³, No. 861).

PM 3: 221–222 — *PSSL* 12: 234–235.

2348. To Modest Chaikovskii

19 Sep 1883. Verbovka.

RUS–KL (a³, No. 1717).

*ZC 2: 603–605 — *PB*: 301 — *PSSL* 12: 235–237 — **LF*: 296 [English tr.].

2349. To Nadezhda von Meck

21–22 Sep [1883]. Verbovka.

RUS–KL (a³, No. 860).

PM 3: 222–223 — *PSSL* 12: 238–239.

2350. To Aleksandr Sokolov

22 Sep 1883. Kamenka.

RUS–KL (a³, No. 14).

PSSL 12: 239.

2351. To Anatolii Chaikovskii

24–25 Sep [1883]. Verbovka.

RUS–KL (a³, No. 1379).

PSSL 12: 239–240.

2352.   To Pëtr Iurgenson
25 Sep [1883]. Verbovka.
RUS–KL (a³, No. 2432).
*ZC 2: 604 — PIU 1: 307–308 — PSSL 12: 241.

2353.   To Praskov´ia Chaikovskaia
26 Sep [1883]. [Verbovka].
RUS–KL (a³, No. 421).
PSSL 12: 242.

2354.   To Modest Chaikovskii
26 Sep [1883]. Verbovka.
RUS–KL (a³, No. 1718).
*ZC 2: 605 — PSSL 12: 243–244.

2355.   To Nadezhda von Meck
27 Sep [1883]. Verbovka.
RUS–KL (a³, No. 862).
PM 3: 225 — PSSL 12: 244–245.

2356.   To Nadezhda von Meck
28–30 Sep [1883]. Verbovka.
RUS–KL (a³, No. 863).
*ZC 2: 605–607 — PM 3: 226–228 — PSSL 12: 245–
    247.

2357.   To Modest Chaikovskii
3 Oct [1883]. Verbovka.
RUS–KL (a³, No. 1719).
*ZC 2: 607 — PSSL 12: 248.

2358.   To Nadezhda von Meck
5 Oct [1883]. Kamenka.
RUS–KL (a³, No. 864).
PM 3: 229–230 — PSSL 12: 249.

2359.   To Pëtr Iurgenson
5 Oct [1883]. Kamenka.
RUS–KL (a³, No. 2433).
PIU 1: 309 — PSSL 12: 250.

2360.   To Anna Merkling
6 Oct 1883 [Kamenka].
Autograph lost; MS copy in RUS–KL.
CTP: 218–219 — PSSL 12: 251.

2361.   To Modest Chaikovskii
8 Oct 1883 [Verbovka].
RUS–KL (a³, No. 1720).
PSSL 12: 252.

2362.   To Anatolii Chaikovskii
9 Oct 1883. Kamenka.
RUS–KL (a³, No. 1380).
PSSL 12: 252–253.

2363.   To Modest Chaikovskii
10 Oct 1883 [Kamenka].
RUS–KL (a³, No. 1721).
*ZC 2: 607 — PSSL 12: 253–254.

2364.   To Nadezhda von Meck
11–19 Oct [1883]. Kamenka.
RUS–KL (a³, No. 865).
*ZC 2: 607–608 — PM 3: 230–231 — PSSL 12: 255–
    256.

2365.   To Pëtr Iurgenson
13 Oct [1883]. [Kamenka].
RUS–KL (a³, No. 2434).
PSSL 12: 256–257.

2366.   To Aleksandra Hubert
13 Oct [1883]. [Kamenka].
RUS–KL (a³, No. 42).
PRM 26 — PSSL 12: 257.

2367.   To Pëtr Iurgenson
14 Oct [1883]. [Kamenka].
RUS–KL (a³, No. 2435) [facs. in PSSL 12: 256/257].
PSSL 12: 257–258.

2368.   To Karl Al´brekht
17 Oct [1883]. Kiev.
RUS–Mcm (f. 37, No. 47).
CMS: 290 — PSSL 12: 258.

2369.   To Praskov´ia Chaikovskaia
17 Oct [1883]. Kiev.
Autograph lost; MS copy in RUS–KL.
PSSL 12: 259.

2370. To Modest Chaikovskii
17 Oct [1883]. Kiev.
RUS–KL (a³, No. 1722).
PSSL 12: 260–261.

2371. To Anna Aleksandrova-Levenson
19 Oct 1883. Kamenka.
Autograph lost.
*ZC 2: 608 — *SN* (1905), 10: 108 — *PSSL* 12: 261.

2372. To Pëtr Iurgenson
19 Oct [1883]. [Kamenka].
RUS–KL (a³, No. 2436).
PSSL 12: 262.

2373. To Pëtr Iurgenson
20 Oct [1883]. [Kamenka].
RUS–KL (a³, No. 2437).
PSSL 12: 262.

2374. To Modest Chaikovskii
20–24 Oct 1883. Kamenka.
RUS–KL (a³, No. 1723).
*PB: 599 — *PSSL* 12: 263–265.

2375. To Nikolai Konradi
22 Oct 1883. Kamenka.
Autograph lost; MS copy in RUS–KL.
CTP: 265 — *PSSL* 12: 265–266.

2376. To Anatolii Chaikovskii
23 Oct [1883]. Kamenka.
Autograph lost; MS copy in RUS–KL.
PSSL 12: 266–267.

2377. To Nadezhda von Meck
25 Oct [1883]. Kamenka.
RUS–KL (a³, No. 866).
*ZC 2: 608–609 — *PM* 3: 231–232 — *PSSL* 12: 267–268.

2378. To Praskov´ia Chaikovskaia
30 Oct [1883]. Kamenka.
Autograph lost; MS copy in RUS–KL.
PSSL 12: 269.

2379. To Modest Chaikovskii
31 Oct 1883 [Kamenka].
RUS–KL (a³, No. 1724).
PSSL 12: 269–270.

2380. To Nadezhda von Meck
1 Nov [1883]. Kamenka.
RUS–KL (a³, No. 867).
*ZC 2: 609 — *PM* 3: 234–235 — *PSSL* 12: 271–272.

2381. To Pëtr Iurgenson
1 Nov 1883. Kamenka.
RUS–KL (a³, No. 2438).
*ZC 2: 610 — *PIU* 1: 310 — *PSSL* 12: 272–273.

2382. To Pëtr Iurgenson
3 Nov 1883 [Kamenka].
RUS–KL (a³, No. 2439).
PIU 1: 310 — *PSSL* 12: 273.

2383. To Anatolii Chaikovskii
6 Nov [1883]. Kamenka.
Autograph lost; MS copy in RUS–KL.
PSSL 12: 274.

2384. To Nikolai Konradi
7 Nov [1883]. Kamenka.
Autograph lost; MS copy in RUS–KL.
CTP: 266 — *PSSL* 12: 274–275.

2385. To Karl Tavaststjerna
8 Nov [1883]. Kamenka.
RUS–Mcl (f. 905).
PSSL 12: 275.

2386. To Modest Chaikovskii
8 Nov 1883 [Kamenka].
RUS–KL (a³, No. 1725).
PSSL 12: 276.

2387. To Pëtr Iurgenson
8 Nov [1883]. [Kamenka].
RUS–KL (a³, No. 2440).
PIU 1: 311 — *PSSL* 12: 276–277.

2388.   To Pëtr Iurgenson
9 Nov [1883]. [Kamenka].
RUS–KL (a³, No. 2441).
PIU 1: 311 — *PSSL* 12: 277.

2389.   To Pëtr Iurgenson
11 Nov [1883]. [Kamenka].
RUS–KL (a³, No. 2442).
PSSL 12: 278.

2390.   To Pëtr Iurgenson
13 Nov [1883]. [Kamenka].
RUS–KL (a³, No. 2443).
*ZC 2: 610 — *PSSL* 12: 278.

2391.   To Modest Chaikovskii
14 Nov 1883. Kamenka.
RUS–KL (a³, No. 1726).
PSSL 12: 279.

2392.   To Nadezhda von Meck
15 Nov [1883]. Kamenka.
RUS–KL (a³, No. 868).
*ZC 2: 610 — *PM* 3: 235–236 — *PSSL* 12: 279–280.

2393.   To Ivan Vsevolozhskii
20 Nov 1883. Moscow — in French.
RUS–SPia (f. 652, op. 1, d. 608, fol. 1–2).
PSSL 12: 280–281.

2394.   To Nadezhda von Meck
23 Nov [1883]. Moscow.
RUS–KL (a³, No. 869).
*ZC 2: 611 — *PM* 3: 236 — *PSSL* 12: 282–283.

2395.   To Nadezhda von Meck
2 Dec [1883]. St. Petersburg.
RUS–KL (a³, No. 870).
*ZC 2: 611–612 — *PM* 3: 237 — *PSSL* 12: 283–284.

2396.   To Pëtr Iurgenson
2 Dec [1883]. [St. Petersburg].
RUS–KL (a³, No. 2477).
PSSL 12: 284.

2397.   To Nadezhda von Meck
11 Dec [1883]. Moscow.
RUS–KL (a³, No. 871).
*ZC 2: 612–613 — *PM* 3: 239–240 — *PSSL* 12: 284–285.

2398.   To Bogomir Korsov
12 Dec [1883]. [Moscow] — in French.
RUS–KL (a³, No. 250).
PSSL 12: 286.

2399.   To Bogomir Korsov
[13 Dec 1883. Moscow] — in French.
RUS–KL (a³, No. 252).
PSSL 12: 286.

2400.   To Milii Balakirev
14 Dec 1883. Moscow.
RUS–SPsc (f. 834, No. 12, fol. 12–13).
BC: 80 — *BVP* 169 — *PSSL* 12: 286–287.

2400a.   To Nikolai Kristoforov [?]
15 Dec 1883.[Moscow].
Autograph auctioned at Sotherby's, London in 1995
     [see *ČS* 3 (1998): 165].
Not published.

2401.   To Vera Tret´iakova
20 Dec 1883. Moscow.
RUS–Mgt
PSSL 12: 287–288.

2402.   To Nadezhda von Meck
21 Dec [1883]. Moscow.
RUS–KL (a³, No. 872).
*ZC 2: 613–614 — *PM* 3: 241–243 — *PSSL* 12: 288–290.

2403.   To Nadezhda von Meck
31 Dec 1883. Moscow.
RUS–KL (a³, No. 873).
PM 3: 245–246 — *PSSL* 12: 290–291.

2404.   To Pëtr Iurgenson
[1883. Moscow].
RUS–KL (a³, No. 2414).
PSSL 12: 291.

2405. To Pëtr Iurgenson

[1883. Moscow].

RUS–KL (a³, No. 2415).

PSSL 12: 291.

1884

2406. To Karl Al´brekht

3 Jan [1884]. [Moscow].

RUS–Mcm (f. 37, No. 48).

PSSL 12: 292.

2407. To Nadezhda von Meck

6 Jan [1884]. Moscow.

RUS–KL (a³, No. 874).

PM 3: 247 — *PSSL* 12: 292–293.

2408. To Il´ia Slatin

6 Jan 1884. Moscow.

RUS–KL (a³, No. 357).

PSSL 12: 294.

2409. To Pëtr Iurgenson

[9 Jan 1884. Moscow].

RUS–KL (a³, No. 2446).

PIU 2: 3 — *PSSL* 12: 294.

2410. To Ivan Vsevolozhskii

14 Jan 1884. Moscow.

RUS–SPia (f. 652, op. 1, d. 608, fol. 3–4).

PSSL 12: 294–296.

2411. To Nadezhda von Meck

14 Jan 1884. Moscow.

RUS–KL (a³, No. 875).

ZC 2: 614–615 — *PM* 3: 248–250 — *PSSL* 12: 296–298.

2412. To Modest Chaikovskii

16 Jan [1884]. Moscow.

RUS–KL (a³, No. 1727).

ZC 2: 615 — *PB*: 301–302 — *PSSL* 12: 299 — *LF*: 297 [English tr.].

2413. To Nadezhda von Meck

20 Jan 1884. Moscow.

RUS–KL (a³, No. 876).

ZC 2: 615–616 — *PM* 3: 250–251 — *PSSL* 12: 300–301.

2414. To Modest Chaikovskii

20 Jan [1884]. [Moscow].

RUS–KL (a³, No. 1728).

PB: 302 — *PSSL* 12: 301 — *LF*: 297–298 [English tr.].

2415. To Eduard Nápravník

22 Jan 1884. Moscow.

Autograph lost; typed copy in RUS–KL.

ZC 2: 616–617 — *VP*: 157–158 — *EFN*: 130–131 — *PSSL* 12: 302.

2416. To Modest Chaikovskii

24 Jan [1884]. [Moscow].

RUS–KL (a³, No. 1729).

PB: 302–303 — *PSSL* 12: 303 — *LF*: 298 [English tr.].

2417. To Vladimir Shilovskii

24 Jan [1884]. [Moscow].

RUS–SPsc (f. 834, No. 14, fol. 1).

PSSL 12: 303.

2418. To Nadezhda von Meck

27 Jan 1884 [Moscow].

RUS–KL (a³, No. 877).

ZC 2: 617 — *PM* 3: 253 — *PSSL* 12: 304–305.

2418a. To Iakov Gartung

[? 2–3 Feb 1884. Moscow].

RUS–KL (a³, No. 3058).

PSSL 17: 232.

2419. To Nadezhda von Meck

3 Feb 1884. Moscow.

RUS–KL (a³, No. 878).

ZC 2: 617–618 — *PM* 3: 254–255 — *PSSL* 12: 305–306.

2420. To Ippolit Al´tani

4 Feb 1884 [Moscow].

RUS–Mcm (f. 88, No. 178).

PSSL 12: 306.

2421.   To Pavel Borisov
4 Feb 1884 [Moscow].
RUS–Mcl (f. 905).
PSSL 12: 301.

2422.   To Bogomir Korsov
4 Feb [1884]. [Moscow] — in French.
RUS–KL (a³, No. 240).
SM (1959), 1: 76 [Russian tr.] — *PSSL* 12: 307.

2423.   To Eduard Nápravník
[4 Feb 1884. Moscow] — telegram.
Autograph lost; typed copy in RUS–KL.
VP: 158 ("6 Feb") — *EFN: 131* — *PSSL* 12: 308.

2424.   To Emiliia Pavlovskaia
4 Feb 1884 [Moscow].
RUS–Mt (Pavlovskaia coll.).
*ZC 2: 621 — SM (1934), 8: 64 — CMS: 316 —
     PSSL* 12: 308.

2425.   To Pëtr Iurgenson
[5 Feb 1884. Smolensk] — telegram.
RUS–KL (a³, No. 2481).
PSSL 12: 308.

2426.   To Nadezhda von Meck
7/19 Feb 1884. Berlin.
RUS–KL (a³, No. 879).
ZC 2: 620, 624 — PM 3: 255–256 — PSSL 12: 309.

2427.   To Anatolii Chaikovskii
7/[19] Feb [1884]. Berlin.
Autograph lost; MS copy in RUS–KL.
PSSL 12: 310.

2428.   To Modest Chaikovskii
7/[19] Feb 1884. Berlin.
RUS–KL (a³, No. 1730).
PB: 303 — *PSSL* 12: 310–311 — *LF*: 298–299
     [English tr.].

2429.   To Pëtr Iurgenson
7/[19] Feb 1884. Berlin.
RUS–KL (a³, No. 2447).
PIU 2: 3 — PSSL 12: 311.

2430.   To Aleksandr Tarnavich
7/[19] Feb 1884. Berlin.
RUS–KL (a³, No. 402).
PSSL 12: 312.

2431.   To Aleksei Sofronov
8/[20] Feb [1884]. Berlin.
RUS–SPsc (f. 834, No. 27, fol. 9–10).
PSSL 12: 312.

2432.   To Pëtr Iurgenson
8/[20] Feb [1884]. Berlin.
RUS–KL (a³, No. 2448).
PIU 2: 4 — PSSL 12: 313.

2433.   To Praskov´ia Chaikovskaia
10/22 Feb 1884 [Paris].
RUS–KL (a³, No. 422).
ZC 2: 625 — PSSL 12: 313–314.

2434.   To Modest Chaikovskii
10/22 Feb 1884. Paris.
RUS–KL (a³, No. 1731).
PSSL 12: 314–315.

2435.   To Nadezhda von Meck
13/[25] Feb 1884. Paris.
RUS–KL (a³, No. 880).
PM 3: 257–258 — PSSL 12: 315–316.

2436.   To Modest Chaikovskii
13/25 Feb 1884. Paris.
RUS–KL (a³, No. 1732).
*ZC 2: 625 — *PB*: 303–304 — *PSSL* 12: 316–
     319 — *LF*: 299–300 [English tr.].

2437.   To Anatolii Chaikovskii
16/28 Feb 1884. Paris.
RUS–KL (a³, No. 1381).
PSSL 12: 319–320.

2438.   To Aleksei Sofronov
18 Feb/[1 Mar 1884]. [Paris.].
RUS–SPsc (f. 834, No. 27, fol. 1–2).
PSSL 12: 320.

2439.   To Pëtr Iurgenson

18 Feb/[1 Mar] 1884 [Paris].

RUS–KL (a³, No. 2449).

*ZC 2: 626–627 — PIU 2: 5–6 — PSSL 12: 321.

2440.   To Modest Chaikovskii

18–19 Feb/[1–2 Mar 1884]. Paris.

RUS–KL (a³, No. 1733).

*ZC 2: 626 — *PB: 304–305 — *PSSL 12: 321–324 — *LF: 300 [English tr.].

2441.   To Nadezhda von Meck

19 Feb/[2 Mar 1884]. Paris.

RUS–KL (a³, No. 881).

PM 3: 259–260 — PSSL 12: 324–325.

2442.   To Aleksei Sofronov

22 Feb/[5 Mar] 1884 [Paris].

RUS–SPsc (f. 834, No. 27, fol. 3–4).

PSSL 12: 325.

2443.   To Praskov´ia Chaikovskaia

23 Feb/[6 Mar] 1884. Paris.

RUS–KL (a³, No. 423).

PSSL 12: 326.

2444.   To Modest Chaikovskii

23 Feb/[6 Mar 1884]. Paris.

RUS–KL (a³, No. 1734).

*ZC 2: 627 — PB: 305 — PSSL 12: 327–328 — *LF: 300–301 [English tr.].

2445.   To Pëtr Iurgenson

[24 Feb/7 Mar 1884. Paris] — telegram; in French.

RUS–KL (a³, No. 2482).

PSSL 12: 328.

2446.   To Aleksei Sofronov

26 Feb/9 Mar 1884. Paris.

RUS–SPsc (f. 834, No. 27, fol. 5–6).

PSSL 12: 329.

2447.   To Pëtr Iurgenson

26 Feb/9 Mar 1884 [Paris].

RUS–KL (a³, No. 2450).

*ZC 2: 627 ("22 Feb") — PIU 2: 6 — PSSL 12: 329–330.

2448.   To Nadezhda von Meck

27 Feb/[10 Mar] 1884. Paris.

RUS–KL (a³, No. 882).

*ZC 2: 627–628 — PM 3: 261–262 — PSSL 12: 330–332.

2449.   To Nadezhda von Meck

29 Feb/12 Mar 1884 [Paris].

RUS–KL (a³, No. 883).

*ZC 2: 628–629 — PM 3: 263 — PSSL 12: 332–333.

2450.   To Anatolii Chaikovskii

29 Feb/12 Mar 1884 [Paris].

RUS–KL (a³, No. 1382).

PSSL 12: 333.

2451.   To Pëtr Iurgenson

[29 Feb/12 Mar 1884. Paris] — telegram; in French.

RUS–KL (a³, No. 2483).

PSSL 12: 333.

2451a.   To Eduard Nápravník

4 Mar 1884. St. Petersburg

RUS–KL (a³, No. 3332).

Not published.

2452.   To Nadezhda von Meck

8 Mar [1884]. St. Petersburg.

RUS–KL (a³, No. 884).

PM 3: 263–264 — PSSL 12: 334.

2453.   To Anatolii Chaikovskii

10 Mar [1884]. St. Petersburg.

RUS–KL (a³, No. 1384).

*ZC 2: 629–630 — PSSL 12: 334–335.

2453a.   To Alfred Bruneau

11/23 Mar 1884. St. Petersburg — in French.

D–Tu [facs. of p. 1 in TGM 5 (1998): 15 — ČS 3 (1998): 201].

TGM 5 (1998): 14 — ČS 3 (1998): 200–202.

2454.   To Nadezhda von Meck

13 Mar [1884]. St. Petersburg.

RUS–KL (a³, No. 885).

*ZC 2: 630–631 — PM 3: 265–266 — PSSL 12: 335–336.

2455.   To Pëtr Iurgenson

[16 Mar 1884. St. Petersburg].

RUS–KL (a³, No. 2451).

PIU 2: 7 — PSSL 12: 337.

2455a. To Anton Arenskii

[? late Mar/early Apr 1884. Moscow].

RUS–SPil (f. 504, No. 69, fol. 1).

PSSL 17: 232.

2456.   To Nadezhda von Meck

23 Mar 1884 [Moscow].

RUS–KL (a³, No. 886).

PM 3: 266–267 — PSSL 12: 337–338.

2457.   To Modest Chaikovskii

24–25 Mar [1884]. Moscow.

RUS–KL (a³, No. 1735).

*ZC 2: 631 — *PB: 306 — PSSL 12: 338–339 — *LF: 301–302 [English tr.].

2458.   To Eduard Nápravník

26 Mar [1884]. Moscow.

Autograph lost; typed copy in RUS–KL.

*ZC 2: 631–632 — VP: 159–160 — EFN: 131–132 — PSSL 12: 340.

2459.   To Sergei Taneev

1 Apr 1884 [Moscow].

RUS–Mcl (f. 880).

*ZC 2: 632–633 — PT: 105–106 — CTP: 101–102 — PSSL 12: 341.

2460.   To Modest Chaikovskii

1 Apr 1884. Moscow.

RUS–KL (a³, No. 1736).

PB: 306–307 — PSSL 12: 342 — *LF: 302 [English tr.].

2461.   To Nadezhda von Meck

1–12 Apr 1884. Moscow–[Kamenka].

RUS–KL (a³, No. 887).

PM 3: 269–271 — PSSL 12: 343–345.

2462.   To Modest Chaikovskii

7 Apr [1884]. [Moscow].

RUS–KL (a³, No. 1737).

PSSL 12: 345–346.

2463.   To Anatolii Chaikovskii

12 Apr [1884]. Kamenka.

RUS–KL (a³, No. 1383).

PSSL 12: 346–347.

2464.   To Modest Chaikovskii

12 Apr 1884. Kamenka.

RUS–KL (a³, No. 1738).

*ZC 2: 633–634 — *PB: 307–308 — PSSL 12: 347–348 — *LF: 303 [English tr.].

2465.   To Sergei Taneev

14 Apr [1884]. Kamenka.

RUS–Mcl (f. 880).

*ZC 2: 636–637 — PT: 108–110 — CTP: 104–105 — PSSL 12: 348–350.

2466.   To Nikolai Chaikovskii

14 Apr 1884. Kamenka.

RUS–SPsc (f. 834, No. 37, fol. 3–4).

PSSL 12: 351.

2467.   To Nadezhda von Meck

16–19 [Apr 1884] (in MS: "16 Jul"). Kamenka.

RUS–KL (a³, No. 888).

*ZC 2: 637–639 — PM 3: 271–273 — PSSL 12: 352–354.

2468.   To Modest Chaikovskii

18 Apr 1884. Kamenka.

RUS–KL (a³, No. 1739).

*ZC 2: 638–639 — *PB: 308 — PSSL 12: 354–355 — *LF: 304 [English tr.].

2469.   To Praskov´ia Chaikovskaia

20 Apr [1884]. Kamenka.

RUS–KL (a³, No. 424).

*ZC 2: 639–640 — *PB: 309 — PSSL 12: 355–356 — *LF: 305 [English tr.].

2470. To Anna Aleksandrova-Levenson

21 Apr 1884. Kamenka.

RUS–SPsc (f. 834, No. 9).

PSSL 12: 356–357.

2471. To Modest Chaikovskii

22 Apr [1884]. Kamenka.

RUS–KL (a³, No. 1740).

PB: 309–310 — *PSSL* 12: 357 — *LF*: 305–306 [English tr.].

2472. To Karl Davydov

24 Apr [1884]. Kamenka.

RUS–KL (a³, No. 163).

PSSL 12: 358.

2473. To Pëtr Iurgenson

24 Apr [1884]. Kamenka.

RUS–KL (a³, No. 2452).

A. A. Nikolaev, *Fortepiannoe tvorchestvo Chaikovskogo* (1949): 77 — *PIU* 2: 8–9 — *PSSL* 12: 358–359.

2474. To Nadezhda von Meck

24–27 Apr [1884]. Kamenka.

RUS–KL (a³, No. 889).

PM 3: 274–275 — *PSSL* 12: 359–360.

2475. To Modest Chaikovskii

25 Apr [1884]. [Kamenka].

RUS–KL (a³, No. 1741).

PSSL 12: 360–361.

2476. To Karl Al´brekht

[26 Apr 1884. Kamenka] — telegram.

RUS–Mcm (f. 37, No. 49).

PSSL 12: 362.

2477. To Anna Merkling

27 Apr 1884. Kamenka.

Autograph lost; MS copy in RUS–KL.

ZC 2: 640–641 — *CTP*: 219–220 — *PSSL* 12: 362–363.

2478. To Praskov´ia Chaikovskaia

27 Apr 1884. Kamenka.

RUS–KL (a³, No. 425).

PSSL 12: 363–364.

2479. To Ippolit Al´tani

28 Apr 1884. Kamenka.

RUS–Mcm (f. 7, No. 54).

PSSL 12: 364.

2480. To Pëtr Iurgenson

28 Apr [1884]. [Kamenka].

RUS–KL (a³, No. 2453).

PIU 2: 9 — *PSSL* 12: 365.

2481. To Modest Chaikovskii

2 May 1884. Kamenka.

RUS–KL (a³, No. 1742).

PB: 310–311 — *PSSL* 12: 365–366 — *LF*: 306–307 [English tr.].

2482. To Nadezhda von Meck

3 May 1884. Kamenka.

RUS–KL (a³, No. 890).

PM 3: 276–277 — *PSSL* 12: 366–367.

2483. To Nadezhda von Meck

4 May 1884. Kamenka.

RUS–KL (a³, No. 891).

PM 3: 277–278 — *PSSL* 12: 367–368.

2484. To Anatolii Chaikovskii

4 May 1884. Kamenka.

Autograph lost; MS copy in RUS–KL.

PSSL 12: 368.

2485. To Pëtr Iurgenson

8 May [1884]. Kamenka.

RUS–KL (a³, No. 2454).

PIU 2: 10 — *PSSL* 12: 369.

2486. To Sof´ia Iurgenson

8 May [1884]. Kamenka.

RUS–KL (a³, No. 487).

PSSL 12: 370.

2487. To Nikolai Konradi

9 May 1884. Kamenka.

Autograph lost; MS copy in RUS–KL.

CTP: 266–267 — *PSSL* 12: 370–371.

2488.   To Nadezhda von Meck
9 May 1884. Kamenka.
RUS–KL (a^3, No. 892).
*ZC 2: 643–644 — PM 3: 279–280 — PSSL 12: 371–
   373.

2489.   To Pëtr Iurgenson
11 May [1884]. [Kamenka].
RUS–KL (a^3, No. 2455).
PSSL 12: 373.

2490.   To Praskov´ia Chaikovskaia
13 May [1884]. Kamenka.
RUS–KL (a^3, No. 426).
PSSL 12: 373–374.

2491.   To Modest Chaikovskii
17 May [1884]. Kamenka.
RUS–KL (a^3, No. 1743).
PSSL 12: 374–375.

2491a.   To German Larosh
19 May 1884. Kamenka — partly in English.
CH–B
TGM 7 (2000): 31–35.

2492.   To Anatolii Chaikovskii
19 May [1884]. Kamenka.
RUS–KL (a^3, No. 1385).
PSSL 12: 375–376.

2493.   To Pëtr Iurgenson
21 May [1884]. Kamenka.
RUS–KL (a^3, No. 2456).
*ZC 2: 645 — PIU 2: 10–11 — PSSL 12: 376–377.

2494.   To Nadezhda von Meck
21–26 May [1884]. Kamenka.
RUS–KL (a^3, No. 893).
PM 3: 280–282 — PSSL 12: 378–380.

2495.   To Nikolai Hubert
26 May 1884. Kamenka.
RUS–KL (a^3, No. 109).
PRM 27–28 — PSSL 12: 380–381.

2496.   To Praskov´ia Chaikovskaia
26 May 1884. Kamenka.
RUS–KL (a^3, No. 427).
PSSL 12: 381–382.

2497.   To Modest Chaikovskii
28 May 1884 [Kamenka].
RUS–KL (a^3, No. 1744).
PSSL 12: 382.

2498.   To Pëtr Iurgenson
31 May [1884]. Kamenka.
RUS–KL (a^3, No. 2457).
*ZC 2: 645–647 — PIU 2: 11–12 — PSSL 12: 382–
   384.

2499.   To Anatolii Chaikovskii
2 Jun 1884. Kamenka.
RUS–KL (a^3, No. 1387).
PSSL 12: 385–386.

2500.   To Modest Chaikovskii
2 Jun 1884. Kamenka.
RUS–KL (a^3, No. 1745).
PSSL 12: 386.

2501.   To Aleksandr Zhedrinskii
7 Jun 1884. Kamenka.
RUS–Mcl (f. 905).
PSSL 12: 387.

2502.   To Nadezhda von Meck
7 Jun 1884. Kamenka.
RUS–KL (a^3, No. 894).
PM 3: 283 — PSSL 12: 387–388.

2503.   To Praskov´ia Chaikovskaia
12 Jun [1884]. Grankino.
RUS–KL (a^3, No. 428).
*ZC 2: 647 — PSSL 12: 388–389.

2504.   To Pëtr Iurgenson
12–[13] Jun 1884. Grankino.
RUS–KL (a^3, No. 2458).
PIU 2: 13–14 — PSSL 12: 389.

2505. To Nadezhda von Meck
16 Jun [1884]. Grankino.
RUS–KL (a³, No. 895).
PM 3: 285 — *PSSL* 12: 390–391.

2506. To Anatolii Chaikovskii
20 Jun [1884]. Grankino.
RUS–KL (a³, No. 1386).
PSSL 12: 391–392.

2507. To Pëtr Iurgenson
20 Jun [1884]. Grankino.
RUS–KL (a³, No. 2459).
ZC 2: 647–648 — *PIU* 2: 14 — *PSSL* 12: 393.

2508. To Lev Davydov
23 Jun 1884. Grankino.
RUS–SPsc (f. 834, No. 19, fol. 49–50).
PSSL 12: 393–394.

2509. To Nadezhda von Meck
26 Jun [1884]. Grankino.
RUS–KL (a³, No. 896).
ZC 2: 648 — *PM* 3: 285–286 — *PSSL* 12: 394–395.

2510. To Praskov´ia Chaikovskaia
27 Jun 1884. Grankino.
RUS–KL (a³, No. 429).
PSSL 12: 395–396.

2511. To Pëtr Iurgenson
27 Jun 1884. Grankino.
RUS–KL (a³, No. 2460).
PIU 2: 15–16 — *PSSL* 12: 396.

2512. To Sergei Taneev
30 Jun 1884. Grankino.
RUS–Mcl (f. 880).
ZC 2: 648–649 — *PT*: 114–115 — *CTP*: 107–108 —
PSSL 12: 397–398.

2513. To Anatolii Chaikovskii
4 Jul [1884]. [Grankino].
RUS–KL (a³, No. 1388).
PSSL 12: 398.

2514. To Nadezhda von Meck
5 Jul 1884. Grankino.
RUS–KL (a³, No. 897).
PM 3: 287–288 — *PSSL* 12: 399.

2515. To Pëtr Iurgenson
7 Jul [1884]. [Grankino].
RUS–KL (a³, No. 2461).
PSSL 12: 400.

2516. To Lev Davydov
11 Jul [1884]. Grankino.
RUS–SPsc (f. 834, No. 19, fol. 51–52).
PSSL 12: 400–401.

2517. To Anatolii Chaikovskii
11 Jul [1884]. Grankino.
RUS–KL (a³, No. 1389).
PSSL 12: 401.

2518. To Nadezhda von Meck
14–17 Jul 1884. Grankino.
RUS–KL (a³, No. 898).
ZC 2: 649–650 — *PM* 3: 288–290 — *PSSL* 12: 402–
403.

2519. To Nadezhda von Meck
23 Jul 1884. Skabeevo.
RUS–KL (a³, No. 899).
ZC 2: 652–653 ("25 Jul") — *PM* 3: 291–292 —
PSSL 12: 403–405.

2520. To Sergei Taneev
23 Jul 1884. Skabeevo.
RUS–Mcl (f. 880).
ZC 2: 653–656 — *PT*: 115–118 — *CTP* 110–112 —
PSSL 12: 405–408.

2521. To Modest Chaikovskii
23 Jul [1884]. Skabeevo.
RUS–KL (a³, No. 1746).
ZC 2: 650–651 ("27 Jul") — *PB*: 311–312 —
PSSL 12: 408–410 — *LF*: 307–308 [English
tr.].

2522.   To Pëtr Iurgenson
24 Jul [1884]. [Skabeevo].
RUS–KL (a³, No. 2462).
PSSL 12: 410–411.

2523.   To Modest Chaikovskii
26 Jul 1884. Skabeevo.
RUS–KL (a³, No. 1747).
ZC 2: 651–652 ("28 Jul") — *PB*: 312–313 — *PSSL*
    12: 411–412 — *LF*: 308–309 [English tr.].

2524.   To Nadezhda von Meck
28 Jul [1884]. Skabeevo.
RUS–KL (a³, No. 900).
PM 3: 292 — *PSSL* 12: 412–413.

2525.   To Nadezhda von Meck
1 Aug [1884]. Klimovka.
RUS–KL (a³, No. 901).
ZC 2: 656 — *PM* 3: 293 — *PSSL* 12: 413–414.

2526.   To Modest Chaikovskii
1 Aug [1884]. Skabeevo.
RUS–KL (a³, No. 1748).
PSSL 12: 414–415.

2527.   To Modest Chaikovskii
6 Aug [1884]. Skabeevo.
RUS–KL (a³, No. 1749).
ZC 2: 656–658 — *PB*: 313–315 — *PSSL* 12: 415–
    417 — *LF*: 309–310 [English tr.].

2528.   To Nadezhda von Meck
8 Aug 1884. Skabeevo.
RUS–KL (a³, No. 902).
PM 3: 294–295 — *PSSL* 12: 417–418.

2529.   To Nadezhda von Meck
11–15 Aug 1884. Skabeevo.
RUS–KL (a³, No. 903).
PM 3: 297–299 — *PSSL* 12: 418–420.

2530.   To Pëtr Iurgenson
14 Aug [1884]. [Skabeevo].
RUS–KL (a³, No. 2463).
PSSL 12: 420.

2531.   To Pëtr Iurgenson
19 Aug [1884]. [Skabeevo].
RUS–KL (a³, No. 2464).
PSSL 12: 420–421.

2532.   To Sergei Taneev
20 Aug [1884]. [Skabeevo].
RUS–Mcl (f. 880).
PT: 118–119 — *CTP*: 113 — *PSSL* 12: 421.

2533.   To Nadezhda von Meck
21 Aug 1884. Skabeevo.
RUS–KL (a³, No. 904).
PM 3: 299 — *PSSL* 12: 421–422.

2534.   To Nadezhda von Meck
23 Aug [1884]. [Skabeevo].
RUS–KL (a³, No. 905).
PM 3: 301–304 — *PSSL* 12: 422–425.

2535.   To Nadezhda von Meck
27 Aug 1884. Moscow.
RUS–KL (a³, No. 906).
PM 3: 305–306 — *PSSL* 12: 425.

2536.   To Natal´ia Pleskaia
28 Aug [1884]. Skabeevo.
RUS–Mcl (f. 905).
CTP: 367 — *PSSL* 12: 426.

2537.   To Nadezhda von Meck
30 Aug [1884]. [Skabeevo].
RUS–KL (a³, No. 907).
PM 3: 307 — *PSSL* 12: 427.

2538.   To Modest Chaikovskii
1 Sep [1884]. Skabeevo.
RUS–KL (a³, No. 1750).
PB: 315 — *PSSL* 12: 427–428 — *LF*: 310–311
    [English tr.].

2539.   To Anatolii Chaikovskii
2 Sep [1884]. Moscow.
RUS–KL (a³, No. 1390).
PSSL 12: 428–429.

2540.   To Nadezhda von Meck

3 Sep [1884]. Pleshcheevo.

RUS–KL (a³, No. 908).

PM 3: 308–309 — *PSSL* 12: 429.

2541.   To Praskov´ia Chaikovskaia

4 Sep [1884]. Pleshcheevo.

RUS–KL (a³, No. 430).

PSSL 12: 430.

2542.   To Modest Chaikovskii

4 Sep [1884]. Pleshcheevo.

RUS–KL (a³, No. 1751).

ZC 2: 658–659 — *PB*: 315–316 — *PSSL* 12: 430–431 — *LF*: 311 [English tr.].

2543.   To Nadezhda von Meck

4–6 Sep [1884]. Pleshcheevo.

RUS–KL (a³, No. 909).

PM 3: 309–310 — *PSSL* 12: 431–432.

2544.   To Modest Chaikovskii

7–11 Sep [1884]. Pleshcheevo.

RUS–KL (a³, nos. 1752, 659).

ZC 2: 659–660 — *PB*: 316–317 — *PSSL* 12: 433–434 — *LF*: 312 [English tr.].

2545.   To Nadezhda von Meck

8–10 Sep [1884]. Pleshcheevo.

RUS–KL (a³, No. 910).

ZC 2: 660–661 — *PM* 3: 310–312 — *PSSL* 12: 435–437.

2546.   To Praskov´ia Chaikovskaia

9 Sep [1884]. Pleshcheevo.

RUS–KL (a³, No. 431).

PSSL 12: 438.

2547.   To Praskov´ia Chaikovskaia

11 Sep 1884 [Pleshcheevo].

RUS–KL (a³, No. 432).

PSSL 12: 439.

2548.   To Pëtr Iurgenson

[11 Sep 1884. Podol´ok] — telegram.

RUS–KL (a³, No. 2484).

PSSL 12: 439.

2549.   To Nadezhda von Meck

13–18 Sep [1884]. Pleshcheevo.

RUS–KL (a³, No. 911).

ZC 2: 661 ("20 Sep") — *PM* 3: 313–314 — *PSSL* 12: 439–441.

2550.   To Eduard Nápravník

14 Sep 1884. Pleshcheevo.

Autograph lost; typed copy in RUS–KL.

VP: 160 — *EFN*: 132 — *PSSL* 12: 441.

2551.   To Anatolii Chaikovskii

19 Sep [1884]. Pleshcheevo.

RUS–KL (a³, No. 1391).

PSSL 12: 442.

2552.   To Aleksandra Hubert

20 Sep [1884]. Pleshcheevo.

RUS–KL (a³, No. 43).

PRM 28 — *PSSL* 12: 443.

2553.   To Sergei Taneev

20 Sep [1884]. Pleshcheevo.

RUS–Mcl (f. 880).

CTP: 114 — *PSSL* 12: 443.

2554.   To Modest Chaikovskii

20 Sep [1884]. Pleshcheevo.

RUS–KL (a³, No. 1754).

PB: 317–318 — *PSSL* 12: 443–444 — *LF*: 312–313 [English tr.].

2555.   To Pëtr Iurgenson

20 Sep [1884]. Pleshcheevo.

RUS–KL (a³, No. 2465).

PSSL 12: 445.

2556.   To Nadezhda von Meck

24 Sep 1884. Pleshcheevo.

RUS–KL (a³, No. 912).

PM 3: 315–316 — *PSSL* 12: 445–446.

2557.   To Sergei Taneev

25 Sep 1884. Pleshcheevo.

RUS–Mcl (f. 880).

PT: 119 — *CTP*: 114 — *PSSL* 12: 447.

2558.   To Modest Chaikovskii

25 Sep [1884]. Pleshcheevo.

RUS–KL (a³, No. 1755).

PB: 318 — *PSSL* 12: 447–448 — *LF*: 313–314 [English tr.].

2559.   To Pëtr Iurgenson

25 Sep [1884]. [Pleshcheevo].

RUS–KL (a³, No. 2466).

PSSL 12: 449.

2560.   To Sergei Taneev

28 Sep [1884]. Pleshcheevo.

RUS–Mcl (f. 880).

ZC 2: 661–665 — *PT*: 120–122 — *CTP*: 115–118 — *PSSL* 12: 449–453.

2561.   To Pëtr Iurgenson

30 Sep [1884]. [Pleshcheevo].

RUS–KL (a³, No. 2457).

PSSL 12: 453.

2562.   To Nadezhda von Meck

1–3 Oct 1884. Pleshcheevo.

RUS–KL (a³, No. 913).

ZC 2: 665–666 — *PM* 3: 316–317 — *PSSL* 12: 453–454.

2563.   To Pëtr Iurgenson

3 Oct 1884. Pleshcheevo.

RUS–KL (a³, No. 2472).

ZC 2: 666 — *PIU* 2: 16 — *PSSL* 12: 455–456.

2564.   To Bogomir Korsov

8 Oct 1884. St. Petersburg — in French.

RUS–KL (a³, No. 239) [facs. of 2 p. in *MNC* (1958): 69].

PSSL 12: 456–457.

2565.   To Pëtr Iurgenson

9 Oct [1884]. [St. Petersburg].

RUS–KL (a³, No. 2463).

PIU 2: 17 — *PSSL* 12: 459.

2566.   To Nadezhda von Meck

12 Oct [1884]. St. Petersburg.

RUS–KL (a³, No. 914).

ZC 2: 666 — *PM* 3: 318 — *PSSL* 12: 460.

2567.   To Loius de Fourcaud

12 Oct [1884]. St. Petersburg — in French.

Autograph auctioned by J. A. Stargardt, Marburg, in 1944.

PSSL 12: 461.

2568.   To Pëtr Iurgenson

12 Oct [1884]. [St. Petersburg].

RUS–KL (a³, No. 2469).

PIU 2: 17–18 — *PSSL* 12: 462.

2569.   To Pëtr Iurgenson

[15 Oct 1884. St. Petersburg] — telegram.

RUS–KL (a³, No. 2485).

PSSL 12: 462.

2570.   To Aleksandr Ostrovskii

18 Oct 1884 [St. Petersburg].

RUS–Mt (Ostrovskii coll.).

ORK: 167 — *PSSL* 12: 463.

2571.   To Glikeria Fedotova

20 Oct 1884. St. Petersburg.

RUS–KL (a³, No. 415).

PSSL 12: 464.

2572.   To Milii Balakirev

[? 21 Oct 1884]. St. Petersburg — note on visiting card.

RUS–SPsc (f. 834, No. 12, fol. 43).

BVP 169 — *PSSL* 12: 464.

2573.   To Vasilii Bessel´

22 Oct 1884. St. Petersburg.

RUS–Mcm (f. 42, No. 265).

SM (1938), 6: 51–52 — *PSSL* 12: 465.

2574.   To Nadezhda von Meck

22 Oct 1884. St. Petersburg.

RUS–KL (a³, No. 915).

ZC 2: 672 — *PM* 3: 319–320 — *PSSL* 12: 465–466.

2575. To Eduard Nápravník

25 Oct [1884]. [St. Petersburg].

Autograph lost; typed copy in RUS–KL.

VP: 162 — *EFN*: 134 — *PSSL* 12: 466.

2576. To Anatolii Chaikovskii

25 Oct [1884]. St. Petersburg.

RUS–KL (a³, No. 1392).

*PB: 319 — *PSSL* 12: 467 — **LF*: 314–315 [English tr.].

2577. To Pëtr Iurgenson

26 Oct [1884]. [St. Petersburg].

RUS–KL (a³, No. 2470).

*ZC 2: 672 — *PIU* 2: 18 — *PSSL* 12: 467–468.

2578. To Nadezhda von Meck

28 Oct [1884]. St. Petersburg.

RUS–KL (a³, No. 916).

PM 3: 320–321 — *PSSL* 12: 468–469.

2579. To Pëtr Iurgenson

28 Oct [1884]. [St. Petersburg].

RUS–KL (a³, No. 2471).

PSSL 12: 469.

2580. To Milii Balakirev

31 Oct [1884]. [St. Petersburg].

RUS–SPsc (f. 834, No. 12, fol. 14–16).

BC: 83–84 — *BVP* 171–172 — *PSSL* 12: 470–471.

2581. To Eduard Nápravník

1 Nov [1884]. [St. Petersburg].

Autograph lost; typed copy in RUS–KL.

VP: 162–163 — *EFN*: 134–135 — *PSSL* 12: 472.

2582. To Nadezhda von Meck

3/15 Nov 1884. Berlin.

RUS–KL (a³, No. 917).

PM 3: 321–322 — *PSSL* 12: 473–474.

2583. To Praskov´ia Chaikovskaia

3/15 Nov 1884. Berlin.

RUS–KL (a³, No. 433).

*ZC 2: 673 — *PB*: 319–320 — *PSSL* 12: 475 — *LF*: 315 [English tr.].

2584. To Modest Chaikovskii

3/15 Nov 1884. Berlin.

RUS–KL (a³, No. 1757).

*ZC 2: 673–674 — *PSSL* 12: 476.

2585. To Anatolii Chaikovskii

7/[19] Nov [1884]. Munich.

RUS–KL (a³, No. 1393).

PSSL 12: 476–477.

2586. To Modest Chaikovskii

7/[19] Nov 1884. Munich.

RUS–KL (a³, No. 1756).

*ZC 2: 674–675 — *PB*: 320–321 — *PSSL* 12: 478–479 — *LF*: 3 [English tr.].

2587. To Pëtr Iurgenson

7/[19] Nov 1884. Munich.

RUS–KL (a³, No. 2473).

PIU 2: 20 — *PSSL* 12: 480.

2588. To Lev Davydov

9/[21] Nov [1884]. Munich.

RUS–KL (a³, No. 172).

PSSL 12: 481.

2589. To Nadezhda von Meck

12/24 Nov [1884]. Davos.

RUS–KL (a³, No. 918).

PM 3: 323–324 — *PSSL* 12: 481–482.

2590. To Anna Merkling

12/24 Nov 1884. Davos.

Autograph lost; MS copy in RUS–KL.

CTP: 220–221 — *PSSL* 12: 482–483.

2591. To Praskov´ia Chaikovskaia

12/24 Nov [1884]. Davos.

RUS–KL (a³, No. 434).

PSSL 12: 483–484.

2592. To Modest Chaikovskii

12/24 Nov [1884]. Davos.

RUS–KL (a³, No. 1758).

*ZC 2: 675–677 — **PB*: 321–322 — *PSSL* 12: 485–486 — **LF*: 317–318 [English tr.].

2593.   To Nikolai Konradi
14/[26] Nov 1884. Davos.
Autograph lost; MS copy in RUS–KL.
CTP: 267 — *PSSL* 12: 486–487.

2594.   To Milii Balakirev
17/[29] Nov [1884]. Davos.
RUS–SPsc (f. 834, No. 12, fol. 17–18).
BC: 85–86 — *BVP* 173–174 — *PSSL* 12: 487–488.

2595.   To Vladimir Stasov
[17/29] Nov 1884 (in MS: "18 Nov"). Davos.
RUS–SPsc (f. 738, No. 343, fol. 41–43).
RM (1909), 3: 138–139 ("18 Nov") — *PSSL* 12: 489.

2596.   To Pëtr Iurgenson
17/29 Nov 1884. Davos.
RUS–KL (a³, No. 2474).
ZC 2: 677 — *PIU* 2: 21–22 — *PSSL* 12: 490.

2597.   To Nadezhda von Meck
18/30 Nov [1884]. Zurich.
RUS–KL (a³, No. 919).
ZC 2: 678 — *PM* 3: 324–325 — *PSSL* 12: 491–492.

2598.   To Anatolii Chaikovskii
18/30 Nov 1884. Zurich.
RUS–KL (a³, No. 1394).
PSSL 12: 492–493.

2599.   To Modest Chaikovskii
18/30 Nov [1884]. Zurich.
RUS–KL (a³, No. 1759).
ZC 2: 677–678 — *PB*: 322–323 — *PSSL* 12: 493–
494 — *LF*: 318 [English tr.].

2600.   To Pëtr Iurgenson
18/30 Nov [1884]. Zurich.
RUS–KL (a³, No. 2475).
ZC 2: 678–679 — *PIU* 2: 22 — *PSSL* 12: 494–495.

2601.   To Modest Chaikovskii
21 Nov/[3 Dec] 1884. Paris.
RUS–KL (a³, No. 1760).
PB: 323–324 — *PSSL* 12: 496 — *LF*: 319 [English tr.].

2602.   To Pëtr Iurgenson
[22 Nov/4 Dec 1884. Paris] — telegram; in French.
RUS–KL (a³, No. 2486).
PSSL 12: 497.

2603.   To Vladimir Stasov
23 Nov/[5 Dec] 1884. Paris.
RUS–SPsc (f. 738, No. 343, fol. 44–46).
RM (1909), 3: 140–141 — *PSSL* 12: 497–498.

2604.   To Vladimir Stasov
[23 Nov/5 Dec 1884. Paris] — telegram; in French.
RUS–SPsc
PSSL 12: 498.

2605.   To Nadezhda von Meck
24 Nov/6 Dec 1884. Paris.
RUS–KL (a³, No. 920).
ZC 2: 679 — *PM* 3: 325–326 — *PSSL* 12: 498–499.

2606.   To Modest Chaikovskii
24 Nov/[6 Dec] 1884. Paris.
RUS–KL (a³, No. 1761).
PB: 601 — *PSSL* 12: 499–500.

2607.   To Sergei Taneev
26 Nov/8 Dec 1884. Paris.
Autograph lost; typed copy in RUS–KL.
PT: 124 — *CTP*: 119 — *PSSL* 12: 500–501.

2608.   To Praskov´ia Chaikovskaia
26 Nov/[8 Dec] 1884. Paris.
RUS–KL (a³, No. 435).
PSSL 12: 501.

2609.   To Vladimir Stasov
30 Nov/12 Dec 1884. Paris.
RUS–SPsc (f. 738, No. 343, fol. 47–49).
RM (1909), 3: 142–143 — *PSSL* 12: 502.

2610.   To Modest Chaikovskii
30 Nov/12 Dec 1884. Paris.
RUS–KL (a³, No. 1762).
ZC 2: 679–680 — *PB*: 324 — *PSSL* 12: 502–
503 — *LF*: 319–320 [English tr.].

2611.   To Milii Balakirev

1/13 Dec 1884. Paris.

RUS–SPsc (f. 834, No. 12, fol. 19–20).

BC: 86–87 — *BVP* 174 — *PSSL* 12: 503–504.

2612.   To Eduard Nápravník

1/13 Dec 1884. Paris.

Autograph lost; typed copy in RUS–KL.

VP: 163–164 — *EFN*: 135 — *PSSL* 12: 505.

2613.   To Emiliia Pavlovskaia

1/13 Dec 1884. Paris.

RUS–Mt (Pavlovskaia coll.).

*SM (1934), 8: 63 — *CMS*: 316–317 — *PSSL* 12: 506.

2614.   To Aleksei Sofronov

1/13 Dec 1884. Paris.

RUS–SPsc (f. 834, No. 27, fol. 7–8).

PSSL 12: 506.

2615.   To Pëtr Iurgenson

1/13 Dec [1884]. Paris.

RUS–KL (a³, No. 2476).

PIU 2: 22 — *PSSL* 12: 507.

2616.   To Vladimir Stasov

3/15 Dec 1884. Paris.

RUS–SPsc (f. 738, No. 343, fol. 50–52).

RM (1909), 3: 143–144 — *PSSL* 12: 507–508.

2617.   To Modest Chaikovskii

3/15 Dec 1884. Paris.

RUS–KL (a³, No. 1763).

*ZC 2: 680–681 — *PB*: 324–325 — *PSSL* 12: 508–509 — *LF*: 320 [English tr.].

2617a.   To Ivan Vsevolozhskii

[9 Dec 1884. St. Petersburg].

RUS–SPia (f. 652, op. 1, d. 608, fol. 39–40).

Not published.

2618.   To Nadezhda von Meck

9 Dec 1884. St. Petersburg.

RUS–KL (a³, No. 921).

PM 3: 327–328 — *PSSL* 12: 509–510.

2619.   To Sergei Taneev

9 Dec 1884. St. Petersburg.

RUS–Mcl (f. 880).

PT: 127 — *CTP*: 122 — *PSSL* 12: 510.

2620.   To Nadezhda von Meck

18 Dec [1884]. Moscow.

RUS–KL (a³, No. 922).

PM 3: 328–329 — *PSSL* 12: 511–512.

2621.   To Pavel Pchel´nikov

18 Dec [1884]. Moscow.

RUS–KL (a³, No. 332).

PSSL 12: 512.

2622.   To Aleksei Suvorin

18 Dec 1884. Moscow.

RUS–Mcl (f. 459).

Krasnyi arkhiv (1940), 3: 248–249 — *PSSL* 12: 513.

2623.   To Modest Chaikovskii

18 Dec [1884]. Moscow.

RUS–KL (a³, No. 1764).

PB: 325–326 — *PSSL* 12: 514 — *LF*: 321 [English tr.].

2624.   To Lidiia Genke

[mid Dec 1884. Moscow].

RUS–Mcl (f. 905).

PSSL 12: 515.

2625.   To Pëtr Iurgenson

23 Dec [1884]. [Moscow].

RUS–KL (a³, No. 2478).

PSSL 12: 515.

2626.   To Vasilii Kandaurov

25 Dec [1884]. [Moscow].

RUS–KL (a³, No. 235).

Biulleten´ (1949), 2: 17 — *PSSL* 12: 515.

2627.   To Lidiia Genke

[26 Dec 1884. Moscow].

RUS–Mcl (f. 905).

PSSL 12: 516.

2628.   To Vasilii Kandaurov
26 Dec [1884]. [Moscow].
RUS–KL (a³, No. 234).
Biulleten´ (1949), 2: 18 — *PSSL* 12: 516.

2629.   To Andrei Arends
[27–29 Dec 1884. Moscow].
RUS–Mt
PSSL 12: 517.

2630.   To Emiliia Pavlovskaia
29 Dec [1884]. [Moscow].
RUS–Mt (Pavlovskaia coll.).
CMS: 318–319 — *PSSL* 12: 517–518.

2631.   To Vasilii Kandaurov
[31 Dec 1884. Moscow].
RUS–KL (a³, No. 233).
Biulleten´ (1949), 2: 20 — *PSSL* 12: 518.

2632.   To Pëtr Iurgenson
31 Dec [1884]. [Moscow].
RUS–KL (a³, No. 2479).
PSSL 12: 518.

2633.   To Aleksandra Iurgenson
[late Dec 1884. Moscow].
RUS–KL (a³, No. 474).
SM (1939), 8: 61 — *PSSL* 12: 519.

2634.   To Karl Al´brekht
[1884. Moscow] — note on visiting card.
RUS–Mcm (f. 37, No. 50).
PSSL 12: 519.

2634a. To Hugo Bock
[23 Dec 1884. Moscow] — telegram; in German.
RUS–KL (a³, No. 2979).
PSSL 17: 233.

2634b. To Bogomir Korsov
[?1884–1887. Moscow].
RUS–KL (a³, No. 246).
PSSL 17: 233.

2635.   To Nadezhda von Meck
1 Jan 1885. Moscow.
RUS–KL (a³, No. 923).
*ZC 3: 16–17 — PM 3: 331–332 — PSSL 13: 13–14.

2636.   To Modest Chaikovskii
1 Jan 1885 [Moscow].
RUS–KL (a³, No. 1765).
PB: 326 — *PSSL* 13: 15 — *LF:* 321 [English tr.].

2637.   To Modest Chaikovskii
2 Jan [1885]. [Moscow].
RUS–KL (a³, No. 1766).
PSSL 13: 16.

2638.   To Nadezhda von Meck
5 Jan [1885]. Moscow.
RUS–KL (a³, No. 924).
*ZC 3: 17 — PM 3: 332–334 — PSSL 13: 17–18.

2639.   To Eduard Nápravník
5 Jan 1885. Moscow.
Autograph lost; typed copy in RUS–KL.
*ZC 3: 17–18 — VP: 164–168 — EFN: 136–138 —
   PSSL 13: 19–21.

2640.   To Andrei Arends
[7 Jan 1885. Moscow].
RUS–Mt
PSSL 13: 22.

2641.   To Evgeniia Zhukovskaia
8 Jan 1885. Moscow.
RUS–KL (a³, No. 3299).
PSSL 13: 22–23.

2642.   To Vasilii Kandaurov
[8–9 Jan 1885. Moscow].
RUS–Mrg
PSSL 13: 23.

2643.   To Emiliia Meyer
8 Jan 1885. Moscow.
RUS–Mcl (f. 905).
PSSL 13: 24.

2643a. To Iuliia Chistiakova-Mikhalevskaia

9 Jan 1885. Moscow.

RUS–KL (a³, No. 3300).

Not published.

2644. To Modest Chaikovskii

[10–12 Jan 1885. Moscow].

RUS–KL (a³, No. 2042).

PSSL 13: 24.

2645. To Pëtr Iurgenson

[16 Jan 1885. St. Petersburg] — telegram.

RUS–KL (a³, No. 2486a).

PSSL 13: 24.

2646. To Nadezhda von Meck

18 Jan 1885. Moscow.

RUS–KL (a³, No. 925).

*ZC 3: 20–21 — *PM* 3: 337–338 — *PSSL* 13: 25–26.

2647. To Pavel Pchel´nikov

18 Jan 1885 [Moscow].

RUS–KL (a³, No. 309).

PSSL 13: 27.

2648. To Pavel Pchel´nikov

19 Jan 1885 [Moscow].

RUS–KL (a³, No. 310).

PSSL 13: 27–28.

2648a. To Vasilii Kandaurov

[21 Jan 1885. Moscow].

RUS–SPtm (Gik. 17121/27).

SM (1990), 6: 102.

2648b. To Anatolii Liadov

26 Jan [1885]. Moscow.

RUS–SPsc (f. 449, No. 65, fol. 34–35).

PSSL 17: 234 [No. 2648a].

2649. To Emiliia Pavlovskaia

26 Jan 1885. Moscow.

RUS–Mt (Pavlovskaia coll.).

*SM (1934), 8: 63 — *CMS*: 321–322 — *PSSL* 13: 28–29.

2650. To Nadezhda von Meck

28 Jan 1885. Moscow.

RUS–KL (a³, No. 926).

PM 3: 340–341 — *PSSL* 13: 29–30.

2651. To Modest Chaikovskii

29 Jan [1885]. Moscow.

RUS–KL (a³, No. 1767).

PB: 326–327 — *PSSL* 13: 30 — *LF*: 322 [English tr.].

2652. To Nadezhda von Meck

3 Feb 1885 [Moscow].

RUS–KL (a³, No. 927).

*ZC 3: 23–24 — *PM* 3: 341–342 — *PSSL* 13: 31–32.

2653. To Nadezhda von Meck

10 Feb 1885. St. Petersburg.

RUS–KL (a³, No. 928).

PM 3: 343 — *PSSL* 13: 32.

2654. To Pëtr Iurgenson

[12 Feb 1885. St. Petersburg] — telegram.

RUS–KL (a³, No. 2487).

PSSL 13: 33.

2655. To Modest Chaikovskii

14 Feb [1885]. Maidanovo.

RUS–KL (a³, No. 1768).

*ZC 3: 25–26 — *PB*: 327 — *PSSL* 13: 33–34 — **LF*: 322–323 [English tr.].

2656. To Praskov´ia & Anatolii Chaikovskii

14 Feb [1885]. Maidanovo.

RUS–KL (a³, No. 1395).

PSSL 13: 34.

2657. To Nadezhda von Meck

16 Feb 1885. Maidanovo.

RUS–KL (a³, No. 929).

PM 3: 343–344 — *PSSL* 13: 35.

2658. To Modest Chaikovskii

17–19 Feb 1885. Maidanovo.

RUS–KL (a³, No. 1769).

*ZC 3: 26 — *PB*: 327–328 — *PSSL* 13: 36 — *LF*: 323–324 [English tr.].

2659. To Pëtr Iurgenson
18 Feb [1885]. Maidanovo.
RUS–KL (a³, No. 2488).
*ZC 3: 26 ("19 Feb") — PIU 2: 26 — PSSL 13: 37.

2660. To Pëtr Iurgenson
19 Feb [1885]. [Maidanovo].
RUS–KL (a³, No. 2857).
PSSL 13: 38.

2661. To Emiliia Pavlovskaia
20 Feb 1885. Maidanovo.
RUS–Mt (Pavlovskaia coll.).
*ZC 3: 26–27 — SM (1934), 8: 63–64 — CMS: 322–
323 — PSSL 13: 38–39.

2662. To Modest Chaikovskii
25 Feb [1885]. Maidanovo.
RUS–KL (a³, No. 1770).
*ZC 3: 28 — *PB: 328 — PSSL 13: 39–40 — *LF:
324 [English tr.].

2663. To Praskov´ia & Anatolii Chaikovskii
26 Feb [1885]. [Maidanovo].
RUS–KL (a³, No. 1396).
PSSL 13: 41.

2664. To Aleksandra & Nikolai Hubert
26 Feb [1885]. Maidanovo.
RUS–KL (a³, No. 88).
PSSL 13: 41.

2664a. To Iuliia Chistiakova-Mikhalevskaia
26 Feb 1885. Moscow.
RUS–KL (a³, No. 3301).
Not published.

2665. To Anna Merkling
28 Feb 1885. Maidanovo.
Autograph lost; MS copy in RUS–KL.
*CTP: 221 — PSSL 13: 41–42.

2666. To Modest Chaikovskii
4 Mar 1885. Maidanovo.
RUS–KL (a³, No. 1771).

*ZC 3: 28 — *PB: 329 — PSSL 13: 43 — *LF: 324–
325 [English tr.].

2667. To Nadezhda von Meck
5 Mar 1885. Maidanovo.
RUS–KL (a³, No. 930).
*ZC 3: 28–30 — PM 3: 346–347 — PSSL 13: 44–45.

2668. To Pëtr Iurgenson
[6–7 Mar 1885. Maidanovo].
RUS–KL (a³, No. 2502).
PSSL 13: 46.

2669. To Pëtr Iurgenson
8 Mar [1885]. [Maidanovo].
RUS–KL (a³, No. 2489).
ZC 3: 31 — PIU 2: 26–27 — PSSL 13: 46.

2670. To the Slavonic Charitable Society
8 Mar 1885. Maidanovo.
RUS–SPa (f. 343, op. 2, No. 21).
PSSL 13: 47.

2671. To Modest Chaikovskii
13 Mar [1885]. Moscow.
RUS–KL (a³, No. 1772).
PB: 329–330 — PSSL 13: 47–48 — LF: 325 [English
tr.].

2672. To Emiliia Pavlovskaia
14 Mar 1885. Maidanovo.
RUS–Mt (Pavlovskaia coll.).
*ZC 3: 31–32 — SM (1934), 8: 64 — CMS: 326–
327 — PSSL 13: 48–49.

2673. To Modest Chaikovskii
15 Mar [1885]. [Maidanovo].
RUS–KL (a³, No. 1773).
*ZC 3: 32 — PB: 330 — PSSL 13: 50 — LF: 325–326
[English tr.].

2674. To Aleksandra Hubert
16 Mar 1885. Maidanovo.
RUS–KL (a³, No. 44).
*PRM 28–29 — PSSL 13: 51–52.

2675.   To Pëtr Iurgenson

[25 Mar 1885. Moscow].

RUS–KL (a³, No. 2501).

PIU 2: 27 — *PSSL* 13: 52–53.

2676.   To Karl Al´brekht

[27 Mar 1885. Moscow].

RUS–Mcm

PSSL 13: 53.

2676a.   To Nikolai Hubert

[29 Mar 1885. Moscow].

RUS–KL (a³, No. 114).

PRM 63 — *PSSL* 17: 234.

2677.   To Emiliia Pavlovskaia

1 Apr 1885 [St. Petersburg].

RUS–Mt (Pavlovskaia coll.).

CMS: 329 — *PSSL* 13: 53–54.

2678.   To Nadezhda von Meck

3–9 Apr 1885. Maidanovo.

RUS–KL (a³, No. 931).

ZC 3: 32–34 — *PM* 3: 349–351 — *PSSL* 13: 54–56.

2679.   To Nikolai Rimskii-Korsakov

6 Apr 1885. Maidanovo.

RUS–SPsc (f. 640, op. 1, No. 1015, fol. 10–14).

ZC 3: 34–36 — *SM* (1945), 3: 133–134 — *RK* 7 (1970): 45–47 — *PSSL* 13: 57–58.

2680.   To Modest Chaikovskii

8 Apr 1885. Moscow.

RUS–KL (a³, No. 1774).

PB: 330–331 — *PSSL* 13: 59–60 — *LF*: 326 [English tr.].

2681.   To Anatolii Galli

11 Apr 1885 [Maidanovo].

RUS–KL (a³, No. 3308).

PSSL 13: 60.

2682.   To Nikolai Konradi

11 Apr 1885. Maidanovo.

Autograph lost; MS copy in RUS–KL.

CTP: 267–268 — *PSSL* 13: 61.

2683.   To Anatolii Chaikovskii

11 Apr 1885 [Maidanovo].

RUS–KL (a³, No. 1397).

PSSL 13: 62.

2684.   To Pëtr Iurgenson

[?11 Apr 1885. Maidanovo].

RUS–KL (a³, No. 2480).

PSSL 13: 62.

2685.   To Emiliia Pavlovskaia

12 Apr 1885. Maidanovo.

RUS–Mt (Pavlovskaia coll.).

ZC 3: 38–41 — *CMS*: 332–335 — *PSSL* 13: 63–65.

2686.   To Nadezhda von Meck

15 Apr 1885. Maidanovo.

RUS–KL (a³, No. 932).

PM 3: 351–352 — *PSSL* 13: 65–66.

2687.   To Natal´ia Pleskaia

15 Apr 1885. Maidanovo.

RUS–Mcl (f. 905).

CTP: 367–368 — *PSSL* 13: 67.

2688.   To Modest Chaikovskii

15 Apr [1885]. Maidanovo.

RUS–KL (a³, No. 1775).

ZC 3: 41–42 — *PB*: 331 — *PSSL* 13: 67–68 — *LF*: 327 [English tr.].

2689.   To Nadezhda von Meck

20 Apr 1885. Maidanovo.

RUS–KL (a³, No. 933).

ZC 3: 42 — *PM* 3: 354–355 — *PSSL* 13: 68–70.

2690.   To Pavel Pereletskii

21 Apr 1885. Maidanovo.

RUS–KL (a³, No. 301) [facs. in *RV* (1903), 11: 441–444].

RV (1903), 11: 440 — *SM* (1939), 8: 56 — *PSSL* 13: 71.

2691.   To Pavel Pchel´nikov

[mid–late Apr 1885. Moscow].

RUS–KL (a³, No. 334).

PSSL 13: 72.

2692. To Aleksandra Hubert
[? 23 Apr 1885. Moscow].
RUS–KL (a³, No. 46).
PRM 30 — *PSSL* 13: 72.

2693. To Lev Davydov
26 Apr 1885. Maidanovo.
RUS–KL (a³, No. 173).
PSSL 13: 72–73.

2694. To Modest Chaikovskii
26 Apr 1885. Maidanovo.
RUS–KL (a³, No. 1776).
*ZC 3: 42–43 — **PB*: 74 — *PSSL* 13: 74 — **LF*:
327–328 [English tr.].

2695. To Pëtr Iurgenson
26 Apr 1885. Maidanovo.
RUS–KL (a³, No. 2980).
*ZC 3: 43 — *PIU* 2: 27 — *PSSL* 13: 74–75.

2696. To Pëtr Iurgenson
26 Apr 1885. Maidanovo.
RUS–KL (a³, No. 2490).
PSSL 13: 75.

2697. To Nadezhda von Meck
28 Apr 1885. Maidanovo.
RUS–KL (a³, No. 934).
PM 3: 356–357 — *PSSL* 13: 76–77.

2698. To Emiliia Pavlovskaia
28 Apr 1885. Maidanovo.
RUS–Mt (Pavlovskaia coll.).
CMS: 340–341 — *PSSL* 13: 77.

2699. To Modest Chaikovskii
28 Apr [1885]. Maidanovo.
RUS–KL (a³, No. 1777).
PSSL 13: 77–78.

2700. To Anatolii Chaikovskii
29 Apr [1885]. [Maidanovo].
RUS–KL (a³, No. 1398).
PSSL 13: 78–79.

2701. To Nadezhda von Meck
30 Apr 1885. Maidanovo.
RUS–KL (a³, No. 935).
PM 3: 357–358 — *PSSL* 13: 79.

2702. To Anatolii Chaikovskii
2 May [1885]. [Maidanovo].
RUS–KL (a³, No. 1399).
PSSL 13: 80.

2703. To Pëtr Iurgenson
2 May 1885. Maidanovo.
RUS–KL (a³, No. 2491).
*PIU 2: 27–28 — *PSSL* 13: 80–81.

2704. To Ippolit Al´tani
[2] May 1885 (in MS: "3 May"). Maidanovo..
RUS–Mcm (f. 7, No. 55).
PSSL 13: 82.

2705. To Emiliia Pavlovskaia
7 May 1885. Maidanovo.
RUS–Mt (Pavlovskaia coll.).
CMS: 342–343 — *PSSL* 13: 82–83.

2706. To Karl Al´brekht
9 May 1885. Maidanovo [in MS: "Klin"].
RUS–Mcm (f. 37, No. 51).
PSSL 13: 83.

2707. To Nadezhda von Meck
9 May 1885 [Maidanovo].
RUS–KL (a³, No. 936).
*ZC 3: 43–44 — *PM* 3: 358–359 — *PSSL* 13: 83–84.

2708. To Emiliia Pavlovskaia
9 May 1885 [Maidanovo].
RUS–Mt (Pavlovskaia coll.).
CMS: 343–344 — *PSSL* 13: 84–85.

2709. To Nadezhda von Meck
18 May 1885. Moscow.
RUS–KL (a³, No. 937).
*ZC 3: 44–45 — *PM* 3: 359–360 — *PSSL* 13: 85–86.

2710. To Emiliia Pavlovskaia
18 May [1885]. Moscow.
RUS–Mt (Pavlovskaia coll.).
ZC 3: 45 — *CMS*: 345–346 — *PSSL* 13: 87.

2711. To Pëtr Iurgenson & Sergei Taneev
[20 May 1885. Smolensk].
RUS–Mcl (f. 931).
CTP: 122 — *PSSL* 13: 88.

2712. To Nadezhda von Meck
26 May [1885]. Moscow.
RUS–KL (a³, No. 938).
ZC 3: 45–46 — *PM* 3: 360–361 — *PSSL* 13: 88–89.

2713. To Sof´ia Iurgenson
26 May [1885]. [Moscow].
RUS–KL (a³, No. 490).
PSSL 13: 90.

2713a. To Karl Al´brekht
[29 May 1885. Moscow].
RUS–Mcm (f. 37, No. 52).
PSSL 17: 234.

2714. To Nadezhda von Meck
31 May 1885. Moscow.
RUS–KL (a³, No. 939).
ZC 3: 46–47 — *PM* 3: 362–363 — *PSSL* 13: 90–91.

2714a. To Aleksandra Hubert
[? May 1885. Moscow].
RUS–KL (a³, No. 82).
PRM 64 — *PSSL* 17: 235.

2715. To Nadezhda von Meck
2 Jun [1885]. Maidanovo.
RUS–KL (a³, No. 940).
ZC 3 :47–49 — *PM* 3: 363–365 — *PSSL* 13: 92–93.

2716. To Karl Al´brekht
3 Jun 1885. Maidanovo.
RUS–Mcm (f. 37, No. 53).
PSSL 13: 94.

2717. To Iuliia Shpazhinskaia
3 Jun 1885. Maidanovo.
RUS–KL (a³, No. 2051).
CTP: 289 — *PSSL* 13: 94–95.

2718. To Anna Merkling
4 Jun 1885. Maidanovo.
Autograph lost; MS copy in RUS–KL.
CTP: 222 — *PSSL* 13: 95–96.

2719. To Nikolai Solov´ev
5 Jun 1885. Maidanovo.
RUS–Mcl (f. 949).
SM (1956), 4: 118–119 — *PSSL* 13: 96–97.

2720. To Aleksandra Hubert
11 Jun [1885]. Maidanovo.
RUS–KL (a³, No. 85).
PSSL 13: 97–98.

2721a. To Sof´ia Iurgenson
[by 13 Jun 1885. Maidanovo].
RUS–KL (a³, No. 489).
Not published.

2721. To Nadezhda von Meck
13 Jun 1885. Maidanovo.
RUS–KL (a³, No. 941).
ZC 3: 53 — *PM* 3: 366–367 — *PSSL* 13: 98–99.

2722. To Sergei Taneev
13 Jun 1885. Maidanovo.
RUS–Mcl (f. 880).
ZC 3: 49–50 — *PT*: 128–129 — *CTP*: 124 — *PSSL*
13: 100–101.

2723. To Sof´ia Iurgenson
13 Jun 1885 [Maidanovo].
RUS–Mcm (f. 37, No. 103).
PSSL 13: 101.

2724. To Sof´ia Iurgenson
[14–15 Jun 1885. Maidanovo].
RUS–KL (a³, No. 495).
PSSL 13: 101–102.

2725.   To Sof´ia Iurgenson
[20 Jun 1885. Maidanovo].
RUS–KL (a³, No. 492).
PSSL 13: 102.

2726.   To Pëtr Iurgenson
26 Jun 1885. Maidanovo.
RUS–KL (a³, No. 2492).
PIU 2: 28–29 — *PSSL* 13: 103.

2727.   To Nadezhda von Meck
28 Jun [1885]. Maidanovo.
RUS–KL (a³, No. 942).
PM 3: 368 — *PSSL* 13: 104.

2728.   To Sergei Taneev
28 Jun 1885. Maidanovo.
RUS–Mcl (f. 880).
*ZC 3: 53–55 — *PT*: 134–136 — *CTP*: 128–129 —
    PSSL 13: 105–106.

2729.   To Nikolai Konradi
1 Jul 1885. Maidanovo.
Autograph lost; MS copy in RUS–KL.
*ZC 3: 56 — *CTP*: 268–269 — *PSSL* 13: 107.

2730.   To Sof´ia Iurgenson
[3 Jul 1885. Maidanovo].
RUS–KL (a³, No. 494).
PSSL 13: 108.

2730a.   To German Larosh
3 Jul 1885. Maidanovo.
US–NHub
Not published.

2731.   To Nadezhda von Meck
6 Jul [1885]. Maidanovo.
RUS–KL (a³, No. 943).
PM 3: 370 — *PSSL* 13: 108–109.

2732.   To Anna Merkling
6 Jul 1885. Maidanovo.
Autograph lost; MS copy in RUS–KL.
CTP: 222–223 — *PSSL* 13: 109–110.

2733.   To Sergei Taneev
8 Jul [1885]. Maidanovo.
RUS–Mcl (f. 880).
PT: 139–140 — *CTP*: 132 — *PSSL* 13: 110–111.

2734.   To Sof´ia Iurgenson
[8–9 Jul 1885. Maidanovo].
RUS–KL (a³, No. 493).
PSSL 13: 112.

2735.   To Vasilii Safonov
10 Jul 1885. Maidanovo.
RUS–KL (a³, No. 340).
PSSL 13: 113.

2736.   To Sergei Taneev
10 Jul [1885]. [Maidanovo].
RUS–Mcl (f. 880).
PT: 140 — *CTP*: 133 — *PSSL* 13: 113.

2737.   To Ol´ga & Nikolai Chaikovskii
10 Jul 1885. Maidanovo.
RUS–SPsc (f. 834, No. 37, fol. 5–6).
PSSL 13: 114.

2738.   To Nikolai Konradi
14 Jul [1885]. [Maidanovo].
Autograph lost; MS copy in RUS–KL.
CTP: 269 — *PSSL* 13: 115.

2739.   To Sof´ia Iurgenson
[?14 Jul 1885. Maidanovo].
RUS–Mcm (f. 37, No. 104).
PSSL 13: 115.

2740.   To Nadezhda von Meck
19 Jul [1885]. Maidanovo.
RUS–KL (a³, No. 944).
PM 3: 372–373 — *PSSL* 13: 116–117.

2741.   To Emiliia Pavlovskaia
20 Jul 1885. Maidanovo.
RUS–Mt (Pavlovskaia coll.).
*ZC 3: 56 — *CMS*: 350–353 — *PSSL* 13: 117–119.

2742. To Vasilii Safonov
26 Jul 1885. Maidanovo.
RUS–KL (a³, No. 341).
PSSL 13: 120.

2743. To Sof´ia Iurgenson
[late Jul 1885. Maidanovo].
RUS–KL (a³, No. 491).
PSSL 13: 120–121.

2744. To Natal´ia Pleskaia
31 Jul 1885. Maidanovo.
RUS–Mcl (f. 905).
CTP: 368 — *PSSL* 13: 121–122.

2745. To Nadezhda von Meck
3–10 Aug 1885. Maidanovo.
RUS–KL (a³, No. 945).
ZC 3: 57 — *PM* 3: 373–375 — *PSSL* 13: 122–124.

2746. To Pëtr Iurgenson
[? early Aug 1885. Maidanovo].
RUS–Mcl
PSSL 13: 124.

2747. To Emiliia Pavlovskaia
10 Aug 1885. Maidanovo.
RUS–Mt (Pavlovskaia coll.).
CMS: 356–357 — *PSSL* 13: 125–126.

2748. To Vasilii Safonov
15 Aug 1885. Maidanovo.
RUS–KL (a³, No. 342).
PSSL 13: 124.

2749. To Wladyslaw Pachulski
16 Aug [1885]. Maidanovo.
US–Wc
SM (1959), 12: 69–71 — *PSSL* 13: 127–128.

2750. To Nikolai Chaikovskii
19 Aug 1885. Maidanovo.
RUS–SPsc (f. 834, No. 37, fol. 7–8).
PSSL 13: 128–129.

2751. To Pëtr Iurgenson
21 Aug [1885]. [Maidanovo].
RUS–KL (a³, No. 2493).
ZC 3: 57–58 — *PIU* 2: 29 — *PSSL* 13: 129–130.

2752. To Ivan Vsevolozhskii
22 Aug 1885. Maidanovo.
RUS–KL (a³, No. 3156).
PSSL 13: 130–131.

2753. To Pëtr Iurgenson
[23 Aug 1885. Maidanovo].
RUS–Mcl
PSSL 13: 131.

2754. To Aleksandra & Nikolai Hubert
23 Aug [1885]. [Maidanovo].
RUS–KL (a³, No. 89).
PSSL 13: 131–132.

2755. To Sergei Taneev
[26 Aug 1885. Maidanovo] — telegram.
RUS–Mcm (f. 37, No. 101).
CTP: 134 — *PSSL* 13: 132.

2756. To Vasilii Safonov
30 Aug 1885. Maidanovo.
RUS–KL (a³, No. 343).
PSSL 13: 132–133.

2757. To Sergei Taneev
30 Aug [1885]. [Maidanovo].
RUS–Mcl (f. 880).
CTP: 135 — *PSSL* 13: 134.

2758. To Félix Mackar
31 Aug 1885. Maidanovo — in French.
F–Pn
RdM 54 (1968), 1: 42 — *PSSL* 13: 134–135.

2759. To Nadezhda von Meck
31 Aug 1885. Maidanovo.
RUS–KL (a³, No. 946).
ZC 3: 58 — *PM* 3: 376–377 — *PSSL* 13: 136.

2760.   To Wladyslaw Pachulski
31 Aug 1885. Maidanovo.
US–Wc
SM (1959), 12: 71–72 — *PSSL* 13: 137–138.

2761.   To Modest Chaikovskii
3 Sep [1885]. Maidanovo.
RUS–KL (a³, No. 1778).
PSSL 13: 139.

2762.   To Félix Mackar
8 Sep 1885 [Maidanovo] — in French.
F–Pn
RdM 54 (1968), 1: 42–44 — *PSSL* 13: 139–141.

2762a.   To Emiliia Pavlovskaia
9 [Sep] 1885 (in MS: "9 Oct"). Maidanovo..
RUS–Mt (Pavlovskaia coll.).
ZC 3: 70 ("9 Sep") — *CMS*: 357–358 ("9 Sep") —
   PSSL 13: 166–167 [as No. 2787].

2763.   To Vasilii Bessel´
[early–mid Sep 1885]. Maidanovo.
RUS–Mcm (f. 42, No. 266).
SM (1938), 6: 52 — *PSSL* 13: 143–144.

2764.   To Nadezhda von Meck
11 Sep 1885. Maidanovo.
RUS–KL (a³, No. 947).
ZC 3: 70–71 — *PM* 3: 377–378 — *PSSL* 13: 144–
   145.

2765.   To Milii Balakirev
13 Sep 1885. Maidanovo.
RUS–SPsc (f. 834, No. 12, fol. 21–23).
BC: 88–90 — *BVP* 170–171 — *PSSL* 13: 145–146.

2766.   To Anna Merkling
13 Sep 1885. Maidanovo.
Autograph lost; MS copy in RUS–KL.
ZC 3: 71–72 — *CTP*: 223–224 — *PSSL* 13: 146–
   147.

2767.   To Modest Chaikovskii
13 Sep [1885]. Maidanovo.
RUS–KL (a³, No. 1779).
PSSL 13: 148.

2767a.   To Pëtr Iurgenson
[13 Sep 1885. Maidanovo] — telegram.
RUS–KL (a³, No. 2553).
PSSL 17: 235.

2768.   To Milii Balakirev
[? 20–22 Sep 1885]. Maidanovo.
RUS–SPsc (f. 834, No. 12, fol. 24–27).
BC: 90–92 — *BVP* 177–178 ("22 Sep") — *PSSL* 13:
   149–150 ("20 Sep").

2769.   To Anna Merkling
20 Sep 1885 [Maidanovo].
Autograph lost; MS copy in RUS–KL.
CTP: 224–225 — *PSSL* 13: 150–151.

2770.   To Praskov´ia Chaikovskaia
20 Sep [1885]. Maidanovo.
RUS–KL (a³, No. 436).
PSSL 13: 151–152.

2771.   To Modest Chaikovskii
20 Sep 1885. Maidanovo.
RUS–KL (a³, No. 1780).
ZC 3: 72–73 — *PB*: 332–333 — *PSSL* 13: 152–
   153 — *LF*: 328 [English tr.].

2772.   To Nadezhda von Meck
22 Sep 1885. Maidanovo.
RUS–KL (a³, No. 948).
PM 3: 379–380 — *PSSL* 13: 153–154.

2773.   To Aleksandra Hubert
24 Sep [1885]. Maidanovo.
RUS–KL (a³, No. 47).
PRM 30–31 — *PSSL* 13: 154.

2774.   To Pëtr Iurgenson
[?24 Sep 1885. Maidanovo].
RUS–KL (a³, No. 2503).
PSSL 13: 155.

2775.   To Anton Arenskii
25 Sep 1885. Maidanovo.
RUS–SPil (f. 504, No. 74, fol. 1–4).
ZC 3: 73–74 — *PSSL* 13: 155–156.

2776.   To Praskov´ia Chaikovskaia
25 Sep 1885. Maidanovo.
RUS–KL (a³, No. 437).
PSSL 13: 157–158.

2777.   To Pëtr Iurgenson
25 Sep [1885]. [Maidanovo].
RUS–KL (a³, No. 2494).
PIU 2: 29–30 — *PSSL* 13: 158–159.

2778.   To Nadezhda von Meck
27 Sep 1885. Maidanovo.
RUS–KL (a³, No. 949).
*ZC 3: 74–75 — *PM* 3: 380–381 — *PSSL* 13: 159–
160.

2779.   To Modest Chaikovskii
27 Sep 1885. Maidanovo.
RUS–KL (a³, No. 1781).
PB: 333 — *PSSL* 13: 160–161 — **LF*: 329 [English
tr.].

2780.   To Karl Al´brekht
30 Sep 1885 [Maidanovo].
RUS–Mcm (f. 37, No. 54).
PSSL 13: 161.

2781.   To Pëtr Iurgenson
30 Sep [1885]. [Maidanovo].
RUS–KL (a³, No. 2495).
PSSL 13: 162.

2782.   To Anna Aleksandrova-Levenson
6 Oct 1885 [Maidanovo].
Autograph lost; typed copy in RUS–KL.
PSSL 13: 162.

2783.   To Praskov´ia Chaikovskaia
6 Oct [1885]. Maidanovo.
RUS–KL (a³, No. 438).
PSSL 13: 163.

2784.   To Modest Chaikovskii
6 Oct 1885. Maidanovo.
RUS–KL (a³, No. 1782).

*ZC 3: 75 ("1 Oct") — **PB*: 334 — **PSSL* 13:
164 — **LF*: 329–330 [English tr.].

2785.   To Nikolai Chaikovskii
6 Oct [1885]. Maidanovo.
RUS–SPsc (f. 834, No. 37, fol. 9–10).
PSSL 13: 165.

2786.   To Vasilii Bessel´
7 Oct [1885]. [Maidanovo].
RUS–KL (a³, No. 13).
PSSL 13: 166.

2787.   [see 2762a]

2788.   To Modest Chaikovskii
9 Oct 1885. Maidanovo.
RUS–KL (a³, No. 1783).
*ZC 3: 75 — *PB*: 334–335 — *PSSL* 13: 167–168 —
*LF: 330 [English tr.].

2789.   To Pëtr Iurgenson
9 Oct 1885 [Maidanovo].
RUS–KL (a³, No. 2496).
*ZC 3: 75–76 — *PIU* 2: 30–31 — *PSSL* 13: 168–169.

2790.   To Anna Merkling
[by 10 Oct] 1885. Maidanovo.
Autograph lost; MS copy in RUS–KL.
CTP: 224 ("mid Sep 1885") — *PSSL* 13: 169–170.

2791.   To Nadezhda von Meck
11 Oct 1885. Maidanovo.
RUS–KL (a³, No. 950).
*ZC 3: 76–77 — *PM* 3: 383–385 — *PSSL* 13: 170–
172.

2792.   To Anna Merkling
11 Oct 1885 [Maidanovo].
Autograph lost; MS copy in RUS–KL.
CTP: 225 — *PSSL* 13: 172.

2793.   To Nadezhda von Meck
13 Oct 1885 [Maidanovo].
RUS–KL (a³, No. 951).
PM 3: 385–386 — *PSSL* 13: 173.

2794.   To Praskov´ia Chaikovskaia
13 Oct 1885. Maidanovo.
RUS–KL (a³, No. 439).
PSSL 13: 174–175.

2795.   To Nikolai Konradi
15 Oct [1885]. Maidanovo.
Autograph lost; MS copy in RUS–KL.
CTP: 269–270 — *PSSL* 13: 176.

2796.   To Nikolai Chaikovskii
16 Oct [1885]. Maidanovo.
RUS–SPsc (f. 834, No. 37, fol. 11–12).
PSSL 13: 177.

2797.   To Modest Chaikovskii
17 Oct 1885. Maidanovo.
RUS–KL (a³, No. 1784).
*ZC 3: 78 — *PB*: 335–336 — *PSSL* 13: 178–179 —
    **LF*: 331 [English tr.].

2798.   To Modest Chaikovskii
24 Oct [1885]. Moscow.
RUS–KL (a³, No. 1785).
PB: 336 — *PSSL* 13: 179–180 — *LF*: 332 [English
    tr.].

2799.   To Vladimir Shilovskii
24 Oct [1885]. [Moscow].
RUS–SPsc (f. 834, No. 14, fol. 2–4).
PSSL 13: 180.

2800.   To Nadezhda von Meck
27 Oct 1885. Khar´kov.
RUS–KL (a³, No. 952).
PM 3: 386–387 — *PSSL* 13: 181–182.

2801.   To Praskov´ia Chaikovskaia
27 Oct 1885. Khar´kov.
RUS–KL (a³, No. 440).
PB: 336–337 — *PSSL* 13: 182–183 — *LF*: 332–333
    [English tr.].

2802.   To Aleksandr Ostrovskii
30 Oct 1885. Kamenka.
RUS–Mt (Ostrovskii coll.).
ORK: 168–169 — *PSSL* 13: 183–184.

2803.   To Modest Chaikovskii
30 Oct 1885. Kamenka.
.RUS–KL (a³, No. 1786).
PSSL 13: 184–185.

2804.   To Nikolai Chaikovskii
30 Oct 1885 [Kamenka].
RUS–SPsc (f. 834, No. 37, fol. 13–14).
PSSL 13: 155–156.

2805.   To Praskov´ia Chaikovskaia
4 Nov [1885]. Kamenka.
RUS–KL (a³, No. 441).
PB: 337–338 — *PSSL* 13: 187 — *LF*: 333–334
    [English tr.].

2806.   To Nadezhda von Meck
5 Nov 1885. Kamenka.
RUS–KL (a³, No. 953).
PM 3: 387–388 — *PSSL* 13: 188–189.

2807.   To Praskov´ia Chaikovskaia
9 Nov 1885. Kamenka.
RUS–KL (a³, No. 442).
PSSL 13: 189–190.

2808.   To Vladimir Shilovskii
15 Nov 1885 [Moscow].
RUS–Mt (Shilovskii coll.).
PSSL 13: 190.

2808a. To Mariia Klimentova–Muromtseva
[? 16 Nov 1885. Moscow].
RUS–KL (a³, No. 224).
PSSL 17: 236.

2809.   To Modest Chaikovskii
[17 Nov 1885. Moscow].
RUS–KL (a³, No. 1787).
PB: 338–339 — *PSSL* 13: 191 — *LF*: 334–335
    [English tr.].

2810.   To Praskov´ia Chaikovskaia
18 Nov 1885. Maidanovo.
RUS–KL (a³, No. 443).
PSSL 13: 192.

2811. To Anna Aleksandrova-Levenson

19 Nov [1885]. Maidanovo.

RUS–KL (a³, No. 6).

PSSL 13: 193.

2812. To Nadezhda von Meck

19 Nov 1885. Maidanovo.

RUS–KL (a³, No. 954).

ZC 3: 78–79 — *PM* 3: 391–392 — *PSSL* 13: 194.

2813. To Modest Chaikovskii

19 Nov 1885. Maidanovo.

RUS–KL (a³, No. 1788).

**PB*: 339 — **PSSL* 13: 195 — **LF*: 335 [English tr.].

2814. To Nikolai Chaikovskii

19 Nov [1885]. Maidanovo.

RUS–SPsc (f. 834, No. 37, fol. 15–16).

PSSL 13: 196.

2815. To Mariia Ermolova

[20–21 Nov 1885. Maidanovo].

Autograph lost; typed copy in RUS–KL.

ZC 3: 79–81 — *PSSL* 13: 196–197.

2816. To Milii Balakirev

21 Nov 1885. Maidanovo.

RUS–SPsc (f. 834, No. 12, fol. 28–30).

BC: 92 — *BVP* 179 — *PSSL* 13: 198.

2817. To Pëtr Iurgenson

21 Nov [1885]. [Maidanovo].

RUS–KL (a³, No. 2497).

PIU 2: 31 — *PSSL* 13: 198.

2818. To Modest Chaikovskii

21 Nov [1885]. [Maidanovo].

RUS–KL (a³, No. 1789).

**ZC* 3: 79 — *PB*: 339–340 — *PSSL* 13: 199 — *LF*: 336 [English tr.].

2819. To Félix Mackar

22 Nov 1885. Maidanovo — in French.

F–Pn

RdM 54 (1968), 1: 45–47 — *SM* (1970), 9: 61–63 [Russian tr.] — *PSSL* 13: 200–202.

2820. To Iuliia Shpazhinskaia

22 Nov [1885]. Maidanovo.

RUS–KL (a³, No. 2052).

CTP: 289 — *PSSL* 13: 204–205.

2821. To Praskov´ia Chaikovskaia

25 Nov 1885. Maidanovo.

RUS–KL (a³, No. 444).

PSSL 13: 205–206.

2822. To Vladimir Stasov

27 Nov 1885. Maidanovo.

RUS–SPsc (f. 738, No. 343, fol. 53–55).

RM (1900), 3: 144–145 — *PSSL* 13: 206–207.

2823. To Modest Chaikovskii

27 Nov 1885. Maidanovo.

RUS–KL (a³, No. 1790).

PSSL 13: 207–208.

2824. To Milii Balakirev

4 Dec 1885. Maidanovo.

RUS–SPsc (f. 834, No. 12, fol. 31–33).

BC: 93 — *BVP* 180 — *PSSL* 13: 208.

2825. To Vadim Peresleni

4 Dec [1885]. Maidanovo.

RUS–KL (a³, No. 293).

PSSL 13: 209.

2826. To Praskov´ia Chaikovskaia

4 Dec 1885. Maidanovo.

RUS–KL (a³, No. 445).

**PB*: 340 — *PSSL* 13: 209–210 — **LF*: 336–337 [English tr.].

2827. To Vladimir Stasov

[? 5 Dec 1885]. Maidanovo.

RUS–SPsc (f. 738, No. 343, fol. 56b–57).

PSSL 13: 210.

2828. To Mikhail Ippolitov-Ivanov

6 Dec 1885. Maidanovo.

RUS–KL (a³, No. 177–178).

**ZC* 3: 81 — *Biulleten´* (1947), 1: 10–11.

2829.   To Pavel Pchel´nikov

8 Dec [1885]. Maidanovo.

RUS–KL (a³, No. 311).

PSSL 13: 212–213.

2829a.   To Karl Klindworth

9 Dec 1885. Maidanovo — in French.

D–MZsch

TGM 7 (2000): 19–20.

2830.   To Félix Mackar

9 Dec 1885. Maidanovo — in French.

F–Pn

RdM 54 (1968), 1: 47–49 ("9/12 Dec") — *PSSL* 13: 213–215.

2831.   To Anna Merkling

9 Dec 1885. Maidanovo.

Autograph lost; MS copy in RUS–KL.

CTP: 225 — *PSSL* 13: 216–217.

2832.   To Modest Chaikovskii

9 Dec 1885 [Maidanovo].

RUS–KL (a³, No. 1791).

ZC 3: 81–82 — *PB*: 341 — *PSSL* 13: 217–218 — *LF*: 337 [English tr.].

2833.   To Nadezhda von Meck

11 Dec 1885. Maidanovo.

RUS–KL (a³, No. 955).

ZC 3: 82–83 — *PM* 3: 392–393 — *PSSL* 13: 218–220.

2834.   To Sergei Taneev

11 Dec 1885. Maidanovo.

RUS–Mcl (f. 880).

ZC 3: 83 — *PT*: 142 — *CTP*: 136–137 — *PSSL* 13: 220–221.

2835.   To Praskov´ia Chaikovskaia

11 Dec 1885. Maidanovo.

RUS–KL (a³, No. 446).

PB: 341–342 — *PSSL* 13: 221–222 — *LF*: 338 [English tr.].

2836.   To Modest Chaikovskii

20 Dec [1885]. [Moscow].

RUS–KL (a³, No. 1792).

PSSL 13: 222.

2836a.   To Hans von Bülow

22 Dec 1885 [Maidanovo] (in MS: "Klin").

Autograph auctioned by W. Heyer of Berlin, 1926.

Musiker-Autographen aus der Sammlung Wilhelm Heyer in Köln. Auktionkatalog 6–7 Dec 1926, Beschreibendes Verzeichnis von Georg Kinsky. Berlin, 1926: 105.

2837.   To Vera Genke

22 Dec [1885]. [Maidanovo].

RUS–Mcl (f. 905).

PSSL 13: 222–223.

2838.   To Mikhail Ippolitov–Ivanov

22 Dec [1885]. Maidanovo.

RUS–KL (a³, No. 179).

ZC 3: 83–84 ("23 Dec") — *Biulleten´* (1947), 1: 13–14 — *PSSL* 13: 223–224.

2839.   To Félix Mackar

22 Dec 1885. Maidanovo — in French.

F–Pn

RdM 54 (1968), 1: 49–50 — *PSSL* 13: 224–225.

2840.   To Praskov´ia Chaikovskaia

22 Dec 1885. Maidanovo.

RUS–KL (a³, No. 447).

PB: 342–343 — *PSSL* 13: 226–228 — *LF*: 338–339 [English tr.].

2841.   To Pëtr Iurgenson

22 Dec [1885]. [Maidanovo].

RUS–KL (a³, No. 2498).

PSSL 13: 229.

2842.   To Pëtr Iurgenson

22 Dec [1885]. [Maidanovo].

RUS–KL (a³, No. 2499).

ZC 3: 84–85 — *PIU* 2: 31–32 — *PSSL* 13: 229–230.

2843.   To Nadezhda von Meck

23 Dec 1885 [Maidanovo].

RUS–KL (a³, No. 956).

PM 3: 396 — *PSSL* 13: 230–231.

2844.   To Karl Al´brekht

[28 Dec 1885]. [Maidanovo].

RUS–KL (a³, No. 11).

PSSL 13: 231–232.

2845.   To Vasilii Orlov

28 Dec 1885 [Maidanovo].

Autograph lost; MS copy in RUS–KL.

PSSL 13: 232.

2846.   To Pëtr Iurgenson

[28 Dec 1885. Maidanovo].

RUS–KL (a³, No. 2500).

PSSL 13: 233.

2847.   To Iuliia Shpazhinskaia

31 Dec 1885. St. Petersburg.

RUS–KL (a³, No. 2053).

CTP: 290 — *PSSL* 13: 233–234.

2847a.   To Aleksandra Hubert

[? 1885].

RUS–KL (a³, No. 45).

PRM 30.

1886

2848.   To Pëtr Iurgenson

[6 Jan 1886. St. Petersburg] — telegram.

RUS–KL (a³, No. 2536).

PSSL 13: 235.

2849.   To Pëtr Iurgenson

7 Jan 1886 [St. Petersburg].

RUS–KL (a³, No. 2504).

ZC 3: 85–86 — *V. Beliaev, *Aleksandr Konstantinovich
  Glazunov* (1922): 99 — *SM* (1938), 10/11: 150 —
  PIU 2: 35 — *PSSL* 13: 235–236.

2850.   To Karl Davydov

12 Jan 1886 [St. Petersburg].

RUS–KL (a³, No. 164).

PSSL 13: 236.

2851.   To Georgii Katuar

13 Jan 1886. Maidanovo.

RUS–KL (a³, No. 205).

SM (1945), 3: 48–49 — *PSSL* 13: 237–238.

2852.   To Nadezhda von Meck

13 Jan 1886. Maidanovo.

RUS–KL (a², No. 957).

ZC 3: 86–87 — *PM* 3: 398–399 — *PSSL* 13: 238–
  239.

2853.   To Anatolii Chaikovskii

13 Jan 1886. Maidanovo.

RUS–KL (a³, No. 3160).

PB: 343–344 — *PSSL* 13: 239–240 — *LF*: 339–340
  [English tr.].

2854.   To Félix Mackar

14 Jan 1886. Maidanovo — in French.

F–Pn

RdM 54 (1968), 1: 51–53 — *SM* (1970), 9: 63–64
  [Russian tr.] — *PSSL* 13: 241–244.

2855.   To Nadezhda von Meck

14 Jan 1886. Maidanovo.

RUS–KL (a³, No. 958).

ZC 3: 87–88 — *PM* 3: 400–401 — *PSSL* 13: 246–
  248.

2856.   To Anna Aleksandrova-Levenson

15 Jan 1886 [Maidanovo].

Autograph lost; typed copy in RUS–KL.

PSSL 13: 249.

2857.   To Anna Aleksandrova-Levenson

[16 Jan 1886. Maidanovo].

Autograph lost; MS copy in RUS–KL.

PSSL 13: 249.

2858.   To Pëtr Iurgenson

[mid Jan 1886. Maidanovo].

RUS–KL (a³, No. 2533).

PSSL 13: 250.

2859.   To Karl Al´brekht

[17–18 Jan 1886. Maidanovo].

RUS–Mcm (f. 37, No. 55).

ZC 3: 88–89 — *PSSL* 13: 250.

2860.   To Modest Chaikovskii

19 [Jan 1886] (in MS: "19 Nov"). Maidanovo.

RUS–KL (a³, No. 1793).

*ZC 3: 89 — PSSL 13: 251.

2861.   To Ippolit Shpazhinskii

19 Jan [1886]. Maidanovo.

RUS–KL (a⁸, No. 463).

Kul´tura teatra (1921), 6: 39–40 — CMS: 432–433 —
    PSSL 13: 252.

2862.   To Pëtr Iurgenson

19 Jan 1886 [Maidanovo].

RUS–KL (a³, No. 2505).

PIU 2: 36 — PSSL 13: 252–253.

2863.   To Nadezhda von Meck

23 Jan 1886. Maidanovo.

RUS–KL (a³, No. 959).

*ZC 3: 90–91 — PM 3: 402–403 — PSSL 13: 253–
254.

2864.   To Praskov´ia Chaikovskaia

23 Jan 1886. Maidanovo.

RUS–KL (a³, No. 3248).

PB: 344 — PSSL 13: 255–256 — *LF: 340–341
    [English tr.].

2865.   To Iuliia Shpazhinskaia

23 Jan 1886 [Maidanovo].

RUS–KL (a³, No. 2054).

CTP: 290–291 — PSSL 13: 256.

2866.   To Pëtr Iurgenson

[23 Jan 1886. Klin] — telegram.

RUS–KL (a³, No. 2537).

PSSL 13: 257.

2867.   To Pëtr Iurgenson

[23 Jan 1886. Klin] — telegram.

RUS–KL (a³, No. 2538).

PSSL 13: 257.

2868.   To Aleksandr Ostrovskii

24 Jan [1886]. [Maidanovo].

RUS–Mt (Ostrovskii coll.).

ORK: 169–170 — PSSL 13: 257.

2869.   To Sergei Taneev

24 Jan 1886 [Maidanovo].

RUS–Mcm (f. 88, No. 181).

PSSL 13: 258.

2870.   To Sergei Taneev

27 Jan [1886]. [Maidanovo].

RUS–Mcl (f. 880).

PSSL 13: 258.

2871.   To Modest Chaikovskii

28 Jan 1886. Moscow.

RUS–KL (a³, No. 1794).

*ZC 3: 91 — PB: 344–345 — PSSL 13: 259 — *LF:
    341 [English tr.].

2872.   To Vasilii Orlov

30 Jan 1886. Maidanovo.

Autograph lost; typed copy in RUS–KL.

PSSL 13: 259–260.

2873.   To Nikolai Rimskii-Korsakov

30 Jan 1886. Maidanovo.

RUS–SPsc (f. 640, op. 1, No. 1015, fol. 15–17).

*ZC 3: 91–93 — SM (1945), 3: 136–137 — RK 7
    (1970): 48–50 — PSSL 13: 261–262.

2874.   To Modest Chaikovskii

30 Jan [1886]. Maidanovo.

RUS–KL (a³, No. 1795).

*ZC 3: 91 — *PB: 345 — PSSL 13: 262–263 — *LF:
    341 [English tr.].

2875.   To Ippolit Shpazhinskii

30 Jan 1886. Maidanovo.

RUS–Mt (Shpazhinskii coll.).

Kul´tura teatra (1921), 6: 38 — CMS: 433–435 —
    PSSL 13: 263–265.

2876.   To Praskov´ia Chaikovskaia

31 Jan 1886. Moscow.

RUS–KL (a³. No. 3249).

PB: 346 — PSSL 13: 265–266 — *LF: 342 [English
    tr.].

2877.   To Nadezhda von Meck

4 Feb 1886. Moscow.

RUS–KL (a³, No. 960).

ZC 3: 93 — *PM* 3: 403–404 — *PSSL* 13: 267.

2878. To Aleksandra Iurgenson

[4 Feb 1886. Moscow].

RUS–KL (a³, No. 469).

SM (1939), 8: 61 — *PSSL* 13: 268.

2879. To Nadezhda von Meck

6 Feb 1886. Moscow.

RUS–KL (a³. No. 961).

*ZC 3: 93–94 — *PM* 3: 404–405 — *PSSL* 13: 268–269.

2880. To Vasilii Filatov

6 Feb [1886]. Maidanovo.

RUS–KL (a³, No. 3317).

PSSL 13: 270.

2881. To Praskov´ia Chaikovskaia

6 Feb [1886]. Maidanovo.

RUS–KL (a³, No. 3250).

PSSL 13: 270–271.

2882. To Modest Chaikovskii

6 Feb 1886. Maidanovo.

RUS–KL (a³, No. 1796).

PB: 346–347 — *PSSL* 13: 272–273 — **LF*: 343–344 [English tr.].

2883. To Karl Al´brekht

13 Feb [1886]. [Moscow].

RUS–Mcm (f. 37, No. 56).

PSSL 13: 273.

2884. To Georgii Katuar

13 Feb 1886. Maidanovo.

RUS–KL (a³, No. 206).

SM (1945), 3: 50–51 — *PSSL* 13: 274–275.

2885. To Modest Chaikovskii

13 Feb 1886. Maidanovo.

RUS–KL (a³, No. 1797).

*PB: 347–348 — *PSSL* 13: 275–276 — **LF*: 344 [English tr.].

2886. To Iuliia Shpazhinskaia

13 Feb [1886]. [Moscow].

RUS–KL (a³, No. 2055).

CTP: 291 — *PSSL* 13: 276.

2887. To Pëtr Iurgenson

13 Feb [1886]. [Maidanovo].

RUS–KL (a³, No. 2506).

PIU 2: 36–37 — *PSSL* 13: 277.

2888. To Nadezhda von Meck

14 Feb 1886. Maidanovo.

RUS–KL (a³, No. 962).

*ZC 3: 94 — *PM* 3 :405–406 — *PSSL* 13: 277–278.

2889. To Anna Merkling

14 Feb 1886. Maidanovo.

Autograph lost; MS copy in RUS–KL.

CTP: 226 — *PSSL* 13: 278–279.

2890. To Anatolii Chaikovskii

14 Feb [1886]. Maidanovo.

RUS–KL (a³, No. 3161).

PSSL 13: 279–280.

2891. To Iuliia Shpazhinskaia

[17 Feb 1886. Moscow].

RUS–KL (a³, No. 2056).

CTP: 291 — *PSSL* 13: 281.

2892. To Aleksandra Hubert

19 Feb [1886]. Maidanovo.

RUS–KL (a³, No. 49).

PRM 31–32 — *PSSL* 13: 281–282.

2893. To Vasilii Safonov

19 Feb 1886. Maidanovo.

RUS–KL (a³, No. 344).

VIS: 198–199 — *PSSL* 13: 282–283.

2894. To Modest Chaikovskii

19 Feb [1886]. Maidanovo.

RUS–KL (a³, No. 1798).

PSSL 13: 283–284.

2895. To Anna Merkling
20 Feb 1886. Maidanovo.
Autograph lost; MS copy in RUS–KL.
CTP: 226 — *PSSL* 13: 284.

2896. To Nadezhda von Meck
21–25 Feb 1886. Maidanovo.
RUS–KL (a³, No. 963).
PM 3: 408–409 — *PSSL* 13: 285–286.

2897. To Praskov´ia Chaikovskaia
25 Feb 1886 [Maidanovo].
RUS–KL (a³, No. 3251).
PSSL 13: 286–287.

2898. To Modest Chaikovskii
25 Feb [1886]. Maidanovo.
RUS–KL (a³, No. 1799).
PSSL 13: 287–288.

2899. To Konstantin Pobedonostsev
[26 Feb 1886]. Maidanovo.
RUS–KL (a³, No. 306).
* V. Metallov, *Sinodal´noe uchilshche tserkovnogo peniia* (1911): 43 — *K. P. Pobedonostsev i ego korrespondenty,* 1 (1923) — *PSSL* 13: 288–289.

2900. To Anatolii Chaikovskii
27 Feb 1886 [Maidanovo].
RUS–KL (a³, No. 3162).
PSSL 13: 289–290.

2900a. To Modest Chaikovskii
27 Feb [1886]. [Maidanovo].
US–NYtollefsen
PSSL 17: 236.

2901. To Andrei Shishkov
27 Feb 1886 [Maidanovo].
RUS–Mcm (f. 88, No. 200); rough draft in RUS–KL (a³, No. 461).
Moskovskie vedomosti (19 Feb 1902) — *V. Metallov, *Sinodal´noe uchilshche tserkovnogo peniia* (1911): 43–44 — *PSSL* 13: 290–292.

2902. To Karl Davydov
28 Feb 1886 [Maidanovo].
RUS–KL (a³, No. 165).
PSSL 13: 292.

2903. To Modest Chaikovskii
28 Feb [1886]. [Maidanovo].
RUS–KL (a³, No. 1300).
PSSL 13: 292–293.

2904. To Iuliia Shpazhinskaia
28 Feb [1886]. [Maidanovo].
RUS–KL (a³, No. 2057).
CTP: 292 — *PSSL* 13: 293–294.

2905. To Aleksandra & Nikolai Hubert
[6 Mar 1886. Moscow].
RUS–KL (a³, No. 90).
PRM 32–33 ("1886") — *PSSL* 13: 294.

2906. To Aleksandra Iurgenson
[6 Mar 1886. Moscow].
RUS–KL (a³, No. 473).
SM (1939), 8: 61 — *PSSL* 13: 295.

2907. To Aleksandra Iurgenson
[6 Mar 1886. Moscow].
RUS–KL (a³, No. 472).
SM (1939), 8: 61 — *PSSL* 13: 295.

2908. To Aleksandra & Nikolai Hubert
[8 Mar 1886. Moscow].
RUS–KL (a³, No. 91).
PRM 32 ("early Mar 1886") — *PSSL* 13: 296.

2909. To Aleksandr Ostrovskii
8 Mar 1886 [Moscow].
RUS–Mt (Ostrovskii coll.).
ORK: 170 — *PSSL* 13: 296.

2910. To Iuliia Shpazhinskaia
8 Mar 1886. Moscow.
RUS–KL (a³, No. 2058).
CTP: 292 — *PSSL* 13: 297.

2911.   To Iuliia Shpazhinskaia
11 Mar [1886]. [Moscow].
RUS–KL (a³, No. 2059).
CTP: 293 — *PSSL* 13: 298.

2912.   To Milii Balakirev
13 Mar 1886. Maidanovo.
RUS–SPsc (f. 834, No. 12, fol. 34–36).
BC: 95–96 — *BVP* 181–182 — *PSSL* 13: 298–299.

2913.   To Nadezhda von Meck
13 Mar [1886]. Maidanovo.
RUS–KL (a³, No. 964).
*ZC 3: 96097 — *PM* 3: 410–411 — *PSSL* 13: 300.

2914.   To Praskov´ia Chaikovskaia
13 Mar [1886]. Maidanovo.
RUS–KL (a³, No. 3252).
PB: 348 — *PSSL* 13: 301 — **LF*: 345 [English tr.].

2914a.   To Ol´ga Chaikovskaia
[17 Mar 1886. St. Petersburg].
RUS–SPsc (f. 834, No. 31, fol. 17).
PSSL 17: 237.

2915.   To Eduard Nápravník
20 Mar 1886 [Maidanovo].
Autograph lost; typed copy in RUS–KL.
VP: 168 — *EFN*: 138–139 — *PSSL* 13: 302.

2916.   To Praskov´ia Chaikovskaia
20 Mar 1886. Maidanovo.
RUS–KL (a³, No. 3253).
PSSL 13: 302–303.

2917.   To Pëtr Iurgenson
[22 Mar 1886. Moscow].
RUS–KL (a³, No. 2858).
PSSL 13: 303.

2918.   To Nadezhda von Meck
29 Mar [1886]. Vladikavkaz.
RUS–KL (a³, No. 965).
PM 3: 411 — *PSSL* 13: 304.

2919.   To Modest Chaikovskii
29 Mar 1886. Vladikavkaz.
RUS–KL (a³, No. 1801).
PB: 348–349 — *PSSL* 13: 304–305 — *LF*: 345–346
    [English tr.].

2920.   To Pëtr Iurgenson
29 Mar [1886]. Vladikavkaz.
RUS–KL (a³, No. 2507).
PIU 2: 37–38 — *PSSL* 13: 305–306.

2921.   To Modest Chaikovskii
1 Apr [1886]. Tiflis.
RUS–KL (a³, No. 1802).
*ZC 3: 98–99 — **PB*: 349–351 — *PSSL* 13: 306–
    308 — **LF*: 346–347 [English tr.].

2922.   To Nadezhda von Meck
1–12 Apr 1886. Tiflis.
RUS–KL (a³, No. 966).
*ZC 3: 100 — *PM* 3: 411–412 — *PSSL* 13: 308–310.

2922a.   To Iuliia Shpazhinskaia
[? early Apr 1886. Tiflis].
RUS–KL (a³, No. 2076).
Not published.

2923.   To Aleksandra Hubert
3 Apr [1886]. Tiflis
RUS–KL (a³, No. 50).
PRM 33–34 — *PSSL* 13: 310–311.

2924.   To Félix Mackar
3 Apr 1886. Tiflis — in French.
F–Pn
RdM 54 (1968), 1: 54 — *PSSL* 13: 311–312.

2925.   To Al´bert Repman
3 Apr [1886]. Tiflis.
RUS–Mcm (f. 37, No. 99).
PSSL 13: 312.

2926.   To Pëtr Iurgenson
3 Apr [1886]. Tiflis.
RUS–KL (a³, No. 2508).
PIU 2: 38 — *PSSL* 13: 313.

2927.   To Pëtr Iurgenson

4 Apr 1886 [Tiflis].

RUS–KL (a³, No. 2509).

PIU 2: 38–39 — *PSSL* 13: 314.

2928.   To Ippolit Shpazhinskii

6 Apr [1886] (in MS: "1885"). Tiflis.

RUS–Mt (Shpazhinskii coll.).

Kul´tura teatra (1921), 6: 38 ("1885") — *CMS:* 436–
437 — *PSSL* 13: 314–315.

2929.   To Modest Chaikovskii

9 Apr 1886. Tiflis.

RUS–KL (a³, No. 1803).

PB: 351 — *PSSL* 13: 315–316 — *LF:* 347–348
[English tr.].

2930.   To Iuliia Shpazhinskaia

9 Apr [1886]. Tiflis.

RUS–KL (a³, No. 2060).

*Sovetskoe iskusstvo (6 Jul 1937) — *CTP:* 293–294 —
PSSL 13: 317–318.

2931.   To Pëtr Iurgenson

15 Apr [1886]. Tiflis

RUS–KL (a³, No. 2510).

*ZC 3: 101–102 — *PIU* 2: 39–40 — *PSSL* 13: 319–
320.

2932.   To Emiliia Pavlovskaia

17 Apr 1886. Tiflis

RUS–Mt (Pavlovskaia coll.).

CMS: 359–360 — *PSSL* 13: 321–322.

2933.   To Modest Chaikovskii

17 Apr 1886. Tiflis

RUS–KL (a³, No. 1804).

*ZC 3: 102–103 — **PB:* 351–352 — *PSSL* 13: 322–
323 — **LF:* 348–349 [English tr.].

2934.   To Ippolit Al´tani

18 Apr 1886. Tiflis

RUS–Mcm (f. 7, No. 56).

PSSL 13: 323.

2935.   To Pëtr Iurgenson

[20 Apr 1886. Tiflis] — telegram.

RUS–KL (a³, No. 2535).

PSSL 13: 324.

2936.   To Boris Iurgenson

21 Apr 1886. Tiflis.

RUS–KL (a³, No. 475).

PSSL 13: 324–325.

2937.   To Nadezhda von Meck

23 Apr [1886]. Tiflis.

RUS–KL (a³, No. 967).

PM 3: 413–414 — *PSSL* 13: 325–326.

2938.   To Modest Chaikovskii

23 Apr 1886. Tiflis.

RUS–KL (a³, No. 1805).

*ZC 3: 103 — *PB:* 352–353 — *PSSL* 13: 326–327 —
*LF: 349–350 [English tr.].

2939.   To Karl Davydov

28 Apr 1886. Tiflis.

RUS–KL (a³, No. 166).

PSSL 13: 328.

2940.   To Modest Chaikovskii

28 Apr [1886]. Tiflis.

RUS–KL (a³, No. 1806).

PSSL 13: 328–329.

2941.   To Pëtr Iurgenson

28 Apr 1886. Tiflis.

RUS–KL (a³, No. 2511).

PIU 2: 40 — *PSSL* 13: 329.

2942.   To Praskov´ia Chaikovskaia

1–3 May 1886 [Black Sea].

RUS–KL (a³, No. 3163).

*ZC 3: 107–108 ["to Anatolii Chaikovskii"] —
*Sovetskaia kul´tura (18 Jun 1957) ["to Anatolii
Chaikovskii"] — *PSSL* 13: 329–331.

2943.   To Modest Chaikovskii

1–3 May 1886 [Black Sea].

RUS–KL (a³, No. 1807).

*PB: 353–355 — *PSSL* 13: 331–333 — **LF:* 350–351
[English tr.].

2944.   To Iuliia Shpazhinskaia

2–3 May [1886]. [Black Sea].

RUS–KL (a³, No. 2061).

CTP: 294–205 — *PSSL* 13: 333–334.

2945.   To Nadezhda von Meck

3 May 1886. At sea, near Constantinople.

RUS–KL (a³, No. 968).

PM 3: 415–416 — *PSSL* 13: 335–336.

2946.   To Anna Merkling

3 May 1886 [Black Sea].

Autograph lost; MS copy in RUS–KL.

CTP: 227 — *PSSL* 13: 336–337.

2947.   To Anatolii Chaikovskii

6–11/[23] May 1886. Adriatic Sea–[Marseille].

RUS–KL (a³, No. 3164).

*ZC 3: 108–109 — **Sovetskaia kul´tura* (18 Jun 1957) — *PSSL* 13: 337–339.

2948.   To Modest Chaikovskii

6–11/[23] May 1886 [Adriatic Sea–Marseille].

RUS–KL (a³, nos. 1808–1809).

*ZC 3: 109 — *PB*: 355–357 — *PSSL* 13: 340–342 — *LF*: 351–352 [English tr.].

2949.   To Camille Saint–Saëns

[12]/24 May 1886. Marseilles — in French.

F–DI

RdM 54 (1968), 1: 82 — *PSSL* 13: 342.

2950.   To Modest Chaikovskii

[12/24 May 1886. Marseilles] — telegram; in French.

RUS–KL (a³, No. 1810).

PSSL 13: 343.

2951.   To Nadezhda von Meck

13/[25] May 1886. Marseilles.

RUS–KL (a³, No. 969).

PM 3: 417–418 — *PSSL* 13: 343–344.

2952.   To Praskov´ia Chaikovskaia

16/[28]–18/[30] May 1886 (in MS: "16/29 May"). Paris.

RUS–KL (a³, No. 3254).

PSSL 13: 344–345.

2953.   To Modest Chaikovskii

16/[28]–18/[30] May 1886. Paris.

RUS–KL (a³, No. 1811).

*PB: 357 — *PSSL* 13: 345–347 — **LF*: 353–334 [English tr.].

2954.   To Pëtr Iurgenson

17/[29] May 1886. Paris.

RUS–KL (a³, No. 2512).

*ZC 2: 41 — *PSSL* 13: 347–348.

2955.   To Nadezhda von Meck

19/[31] May 1886. Paris.

RUS–KL (a³, No. 970).

*ZC 3: 110–111 — *PM* 3: 418–419 — *PSSL* 13: 348–349.

2956.   To Praskov´ia Chaikovskaia

25 May/[6 Jun] 1886. Paris.

RUS–KL (a³, No. 3255).

*ZC 3: 111–112 — *PSSL* 13: 349–350.

2957.   To Modest Chaikovskii

25 May/[6 Jun] 1886. Paris.

RUS–KL (a³, No. 1812).

*PB: 357–358 — *PSSL* 13: 351–352 — **LF*: 354–355 [English tr.].

2958.   To Georgii Katuar

27 May/[8 Jun] 1886. Paris.

RUS–KL (a³, No. 207).

SM (1945), 3: 53–54 — *PSSL* 13: 352–353.

2959.   To Modest Chaikovskii

27 May/[8 Jun] 1886. Paris.

RUS–KL (a³, No. 1813).

*ZC 3: 112–113 — **PB*: 338–339 — *PSSL* 13: 353–355 — **LF*: 355 [English tr.].

2960.   To Iuliia Shpazhinskaia

28 May/[9 Jun]–1/[13] Jun 1886. Paris.

RUS–KL (a³, No. 2062).

CTP: 295–296 — *PSSL* 13: 355–356.

2961.   To Praskov´ia Chaikovskaia

1/13 Jun 1886. Paris.

RUS–KL (a³, No. 3165).

*ZC 3: 113 — *PB: 359 — PSSL 13: 356–357 — *LF: 356 [English tr.].

2962.   To Modest Chaikovskii

1/13 Jun 1886 [Paris].

RUS–KL (a³, No. 1814).

*PB: 360 — PSSL 13: 357–358 — *LF: 356–357 [English tr.].

2963.   To Pëtr Iurgenson

1/13 Jun 1886. Paris.

RUS–KL (a³, No. 2513).

PIU 2: 42–43 — PSSL 13: 358–359.

2964.   To Nadezhda von Meck

3/15 Jun 1886. Paris.

RUS–KL (a³, No. 971).

PM 3: 421–422 — PSSL 13: 359–360.

2965.   To Edouard Colonne

[5]/17 Jun 1886. Paris — in French.

F–Po

RdM 54 (1968), 1: 84–85 — PSSL 13: 360–361.

2966.   To Nadezhda von Meck

5/[17] Jun 1886. Paris.

RUS–KL (a³, No. 972).

PM 3: 422–423 — PSSL 13: 362–363.

2967.   To Anatolii Brandukov

[6/18 Jun 1886. Paris].

RUS–KL (a³, No. 16).

PSSL 13: 353.

2968.   To Praskov´ia Chaikovskaia

[7]/19 Jun [1886]. [Paris].

RUS–KL (a³, No. 3257).

PSSL 13: 363–364.

2968a.   To Pauline Viardot-García

[9/21 Jun 1886. Paris] — in French.

F–Pn

PSSL 17: 237–238.

2969.   To Camille Saint–Saëns

[9]/21 Jun 1886. Paris — in French.

F–DI

RdM 54 (1968), 1: 83 — PSSL 13: 364.

2970.   To Félix Mackar

[11/23 Jun 1886]. Paris — in French.

F–Pn

RdM 54 (1968), 1: 54 — PSSL 13: 365.

2971.   To Modest Chaikovskii

11/23 Jun [1886]. Paris.

RUS–KL (a³, No. 1815).

*ZC 3: 313–314 — *PB: 360–361 — PSSL 13: 365–366 — *LF: 357 [English tr.].

2972.   To Anatolii Brandukov

[12 Jun 1886. Paris].

RUS–KL (a³, No. 15).

PSSL 13: 367.

2973.   To Modest Chaikovskii

16 Jun [1886]. St. Petersburg.

RUS–KL (a³, No. 1816).

PSSL 13: 367–368.

2974.   To Praskov´ia Chaikovskaia

17 Jun [1886]. St. Petersburg.

RUS–KL (a³, No. 3256).

PSSL 13: 368–369.

2975.   To Nadezhda von Meck

17–18 Jun 1886. St. Petersburg–Maidanovo.

RUS–KL (a³, No. 973).

*ZC 3: 115–116 — PM 3: 423–424 — PSSL 13: 369–370.

2976.   To Anna Aleksandrova-Levenson

18 Jun 1886 [Maidanovo].

Autograph lost

SN (1905), 10: 105 — PSSL 13: 371.

2977.   To Iuliia Shpazhinskaia

18 Jun [1886]. [Maidanovo].

RUS–KL (a³, No. 2063).

CTP: 296–297 — PSSL 13: 371.

2978. To Pëtr Iurgenson
18 Jun 1886. Maidanovo.
RUS–KL (a³, No. 2514).
PIU 2: 43 — *PSSL* 13: 372.

2979. To Modest Chaikovskii
19 Jun 1886. Maidanovo.
RUS–KL (a³, No. 1817).
PSSL 13: 372–373.

2980. To Félix Mackar
22 Jun 1886. Moscow — in French.
F–Pn
RdM 54 (1968), 1: 55 — *PSSL* 13: 373–374.

2981. To Pëtr Iurgenson
22 Jun [1886]. [Moscow].
RUS–KL (a³, No. 2515).
PIU 2: 43–44 — *PSSL* 13: 376.

2982. To Pëtr Iurgenson
23 Jun [1886]. [Maidanovo].
RUS–KL (a³, No. 2516).
PIU 2: 44 — *PSSL* 13: 377.

2983. To Aleksandra & Nikolai Hubert
24 Jun 1886. Maidanovo.
RUS–KL (a³, No. 92).
PSSL 13: 377–379.

2984. To Anatolii Chaikovskii
24 Jun 1886. Maidanovo.
RUS–KL (a³, No. 3166).
PSSL 13: 379–380.

2984a. To Max Erdmannsdörfer
25 Jun 1886 [Maidanovo] (in MS: "Klin").
Autograph lost; MS copy in RUS–KL
Not published.

2985. To Modest Chaikovskii
25–26 Jun 1886. Maidanovo.
RUS–KL (a³, No. 1818).
*ZC 3: 116 — *PB: 361 — *PSSL* 13: 380–381 — *LF:
357–358 [English tr.].

2986. To Pëtr Iurgenson
26 Jun [1886]. [Maidanovo].
RUS–KL (a³, No. 2517).
PSSL 13: 382.

2987. To Pëtr Iurgenson
[27–28 Jun 1886. Klin] — telegram.
RUS–KL (a³, No. 2540).
PSSL 13: 382.

2987a. To Édouard Lalo
28 Jun 1886. Maidanovo — in French.
Autograph auctioned by J. A. Stargardt, Berlin in
1997.
*ČS 3 (1998): 188.

2988. To Nadezhda von Meck
28 Jun 1886. Maidanovo.
RUS–KL (a³, No. 974).
*ZC 3: 117 — *PM* 3: 425–426 — *PSSL* 13: 383–384.

2989. To Nikolai Konradi
1 Jul 1886. Maidanovo.
Autograph lost; MS copy in RUS–KL.
*CTP: 270 — *PSSL* 13: 384–385.

2990. To Iuliia Shpazhinskaia
1 Jul 1886 [Maidanovo].
RUS–KL (a³, No. 2064).
*CTP: 297 — *PSSL* 13: 385.

2991. To Aleksandra Iurgenson
1 Jul [1886]. [Maidanovo].
RUS–KL (a³, No. 470).
PSSL 13: 386.

2992. To Pëtr Iurgenson
1 Jul [1886]. [Maidanovo].
RUS–KL (a³, No. 2518).
PIU 2: 44 — *PSSL* 13: 386–387.

2993. To Modest Chaikovskii
4 Jul [1886]. Maidanovo.
RUS–KL (a³, No. 1819).
PSSL 13: 388–389.

2994.   To Pëtr Iurgenson

5 Jul [1886]. Moscow.

RUS–KL (a³, No. 2519).

PIU 2: 45 — *PSSL* 13: 389–390.

2995.   To Mikhail Ippolitov–Ivanov

7 Jul 1886. Maidanovo.

RUS–KL (a³, No. 180).

*ZC 3: 117–118 — **Iskusstvo*, 3 (1927), 4: 144–145 —
    Biulleten´ (1947), 1: 18–20 — *PSSL* 13: 390–392.

2996.   To Ippolit Shpazhinskii

7 Jul 1886. Maidanovo.

Autograph lost.

Kul´tura teatra (1921), 6: 40 — *CMS:* 441–442 —
    PSSL 13: 393.

2997.   To Anatolii Brandukov

8 Jul 1886. Maidanovo.

RUS–KL (a³, No. 17).

PSSL 13: 394.

2998.   To Nadezhda von Meck

8 Jul 1886. Maidanovo.

RUS–KL (a³, No. 975).

PM 3: 427–428 — *PSSL* 13: 394–395.

2999.   To Praskov´ia Chaikovskaia

8 Jul 1886. Maidanovo.

RUS–KL (a³, No. 3258).

PSSL 13: 396–397.

3000.   To Karl Al´brekht

11 Jul [1886]. [Maidanovo].

RUS–Mcm (f. 37, No. 57).

PSSL 13: 397.

3001.   To Sergei Taneev

11 Jul 1886. Maidanovo.

RUS–Mcl (f. 880).

*ZC 3: 118–119 — *CTP:* 139–140 — *PSSL* 13: 397–
    399.

3002.   To Iuliia Shpazhinskaia

11 Jul 1886. Maidanovo.

RUS–KL (a³, No. 2065).

CTP: 297–298 — *PSSL* 13: 399–401.

3003.   To Pëtr Iurgenson

11 Jul 1886. Maidanovo.

RUS–KL (a³, No. 2520).

*PIU 2: 45 — *PSSL* 13: 401–402.

3004.   To Aleksandra & Nikolai Hubert

13 Jul 1886. Maidanovo.

RUS–KL (a³, No. 93).

PSSL 13: 402–403.

3005.   To Praskov´ia Chaikovskaia

18 Jul 1886. Maidanovo.

RUS–KL (a³, No. 3259).

PSSL 13: 403–404.

3006.   To Modest Chaikovskii

18 Jul 1886. Maidanovo.

RUS–KL (a³, No. 1820).

PSSL 13: 404–406.

3007.   To Pëtr Iurgenson

18 Jul [1886]. Maidanovo.

RUS–KL (a³, No. 2521).

PSSL 13: 406–407.

3008.   To Pëtr Iurgenson

19 Jul 1886. Maidanovo.

RUS–KL (a³, No. 2522).

*ZC 3: 120–121 — *PIU* 2: 46–47 — *PSSL* 13: 407–
    408.

3009.   To Anatolii Brandukov

20 Jul 1886 [Maidanovo].

RUS–KL (a³, No. 18).

PSSL 13: 408–409.

3010.   To Marie Tayau

20 Jul 1886. Maidanovo — in French.

US–NYpm (Morgan coll.).

PSSL 13: 410.

3011.   To Mikhail Ippolitov-Ivanov

23 Jul 1886. Maidanovo.

RUS–KL (a³, No. 181).

*ZC 3: 121–122 — *Biulleten´* (1947), 1: 24–25 —
    PSSL 13: 411–412.

3012. To Nikolai Konradi
25 Jul 1886. Maidanovo.
Autograph lost; MS copy in RUS–KL.
CTP: 271 — *PSSL* 13: 412–414.

3013. To Emiliia Pavlovskaia
25 Jul 1886. Maidanovo.
RUS–Mt (Pavlovskaia coll.).
*ZC 3: 122–123 — *CMS*: 367–369 — *PSSL* 13: 414–416.

3014. To Vadim Peresleni
25 Jul [1886]. [Maidanovo].
RUS–KL (a³, No. 287).
PSSL 13: 417.

3014a. To Pauline Erdmannsdörfer-Richter
25 Jul 1886. Maidanovo — in French.
D–Tu [facs. of p. 1 in *ČS* 3 (1998): 214].
PSSL 17: 239 — *ČS* 3 (1998): 214–216.

3015. To Nadezhda von Meck
29 Jul 1886. Moscow.
RUS–KL (a³, No. 976).
PM 3: 429–430 — *PSSL* 13: 417–418.

3016. To Sergei Taneev
29 Jul [1886]. Moscow.
RUS–Mcl (f. 880).
*ZC 3: 123–124 — *PT*: 143–144 — *CTP*: 141 — *PSSL* 13: 419.

3017. To Anatolii Chaikovskii
29 Jul [1886]. Moscow.
RUS–KL (a³, No. 3260).
PSSL 13: 420–421.

3018. To Anatolii Chaikovskii
30 Jul [1886]. Maidanovo.
RUS–KL (a³, No. 3167).
PSSL 13: 421.

3019. To Iuliia Shpazhinskaia
30 Jul 1886. Maidanovo.
RUS–KL (a³, No. 2066).
CTP: 299–300 — *PSSL* 13: 422–424.

3020. To Modest Chaikovskii
31 Jul 1886. Maidanovo.
RUS–KL (a³, No. 1821).
PSSL 13: 424–425.

3020a. To Fëdor Ivanov [?]
[July 1886. Moscow] — note on visiting card.
RUS–Mt
PSSL 17: 240.

3021. To Karl Al´brekht
2 Aug [1886]. [Maidanovo].
RUS–Mcm (f. 37, No. 58).
PSSL 13: 425–426.

3022. To Praskov´ia Chaikovskaia
2 Aug 1886. Maidanovo.
RUS–KL (a³, No. 3261).
PSSL 13: 426–427.

3022a. To Aleksandra L´vova
4 Aug 1886. Maidanovo.
RUS–Mia (f. 1341, op. 1/1121).
Not published.

3023. To Nadezhda von Meck
4 Aug 1886. Maidanovo.
RUS–KL (a³, No. 977).
*ZC 3: 125–126 — *PM* 3: 430–431 — *PSSL* 13: 427–428.

3024. To Modest Chaikovskii
6 Aug [1886]. Maidanovo.
RUS–KL (a³, No. 1822).
*ZC 3: 126 — **PB*: 361–362 — *PSSL* 13: 429–430 — **LF*: 358 [English tr.].

3025. To Pëtr Iurgenson
8 Aug [1886]. [Maidanovo].
RUS–KL (a³, No. 2523).
PSSL 13: 430.

3026. To Iuliia Shpazhinskaia
13 Aug 1886. Maidanovo.
RUS–KL (a³, No. 2067).
CTP: 300–301 — *PSSL* 13: 430–432.

3027. To Pëtr Iurgenson
13 Aug [1886]. [Maidanovo].
RUS–KL (a³, No. 2524).
*PIU 2: 47 — *PSSL* 13: 432.

3028.   To Pëtr Iurgenson
16 Aug [1886]. Maidanovo.
RUS–KL (a³, No. 2525).
PIU 2: 47–48 — *PSSL* 13: 433.

3029.   To Anatolii Brandukov
16 Aug [1886]. Maidanovo.
RUS–KL (a³, No. 19).
PSSL 13: 433–434.

3030.   To Aleksandra & Nikolai Hubert
18 Aug 1886 [Maidanovo].
RUS–KL (a³, No. 94).
PSSL 13: 434.

3031.   To Félix Mackar
18 Aug 1886. Maidanovo — in French.
F–Pn
RdM 54 (1968), 1: 56 — *SM* (1970), 9: 64 [Russian
    tr.] — *PSSL* 13: 435.

3032.   To Anatolii Brandukov
20 Aug [1886]. [Maidanovo].
RUS–KL (a³, No. 20).
PSSL 13: 436.

3033.   To Pëtr Iurgenson
20 Aug 1886 [Maidanovo].
RUS–KL (a³, No. 2526).
PIU 2: 48 — *PSSL* 13: 436–437.

3034.   To Ippolit Al´tani
[?28 Aug 1886. Moscow].
RUS–KL (a³, No. 2886).
PSSL 13: 437.

3035.   To Georgii Katuar
30 Aug [?1886]. [Maidanovo].
RUS–KL (a³, No. 211).
PSSL 13: 438.

3036.   To Anatolii Chaikovskii
30 Aug [1886]. [Maidanovo].
RUS–KL (a³, No. 3168).
PB: 362–363 — *PSSL* 13: 438–439 — *LF*: 359
    [English tr.].

3036a.   To Anna Aleksandrova-Levenson
3 Sep 1886. Maidanovo.
RUS–KL (a³, No. 3324).
PSSL 17: 240.

3037.   To Nadezhda von Meck
3 Sep 1886. Maidanovo.
RUS–KL (a³, No. 978).
PM 3: 432–434 — *PSSL* 13: 439–440.

3038.   To Ivan Popov
3 Sep 1886. Maidanovo.
RUS–KL (a³, No. 299).
PSSL 13: 441.

3039.   To Sergei Taneev
3 Sep 1886.[Maidanovo].
RUS–Mcl (f. 880).
PT: 145 — *CTP*: 142 — *PSSL* 13: 442.

3040.   To Praskov´ia Chaikovskaia
3 Sep 1886. Maidanovo.
RUS–KL (a³, No. 3262).
PSSL 13: 442–443.

3041.   To Modest Chaikovskii
3 Sep [1886]. [Maidanovo].
RUS–KL (a³, No. 1823).
ZC 3: 127–128 — *PB*: 363 — *PSSL* 13: 443–
    444 — *LF*: 360 [English tr.].

3042.   To Nadezhda von Meck
9 Sep 1886. Maidanovo.
RUS–KL (a³, No. 979).
PM 3: 435–436 — *PSSL* 13: 445–446.

**3043.   To   Grand   Duke   Konstantin
Konstantinovich**
9 Sep 1886. Maidanovo.
RUS–SPil (f. 137, No. 78/2).
ZC 3: 129–130 — *PSSL* 13: 447.

3044.   To Modest Chaikovskii
9 Sep 1886 [Maidanovo].
RUS–KL (a³, No. 1824).
ZC 3: 130–131 — *PB*: 364 — *PSSL* 13: 448–
    449 — *LF*: 361 [English tr.].

3045.   To Pëtr Iurgenson

9 Sep [1886]. [Maidanovo].

RUS–KL (a³, No. 2527).

PIU 2: 48 — *PSSL* 13: 450.

3046.   To Anna Merkling

12 Sep 1886. Maidanovo.

Autograph lost; MS copy in RUS–KL.

CTP: 227–228 — *PSSL* 13: 450–451.

3047.   To Nikolai Rimskii-Korsakov

17 Sep [1886]. [Moscow].

RUS–SPsc (f. 640, op. 1, No. 1015, fol. 18–19).

*ZC 3: 269–270 ("1888") — *SM* (1945), 3: 137 —
    RK 7 (1970): 50 — *PSSL* 13: 451–452.

**3048.   To   Grand   Duke   Konstantin
            Konstantinovich**

[18 Sep 1886. Maidanovo].

RUS–SPil (f. 137, No. 78/3).

PSSL 13: 452–453.

3049.   To Praskov´ia Chaikovskaia

18 Sep 1886. Maidanovo.

RUS–KL (a³, No. 3263).

PB: 365–366 — *PSSL* 13: 453–454 — *LF*: 361–362
    [English tr.].

3050.   To Modest Chaikovskii

18 Sep 1886. Maidanovo.

RUS–KL (a³, No. 1825).

*ZC 3: 131 — **PB*: 364–365 — *PSSL* 13: 454–455 —
    *LF: 362–363 [English tr.].

3051.   To Pëtr Iurgenson

18 Sep [1886]. [Maidanovo].

RUS–KL (a³, No. 2528).

PSSL 13: 456.

3052.   To Vasilii Bessel´

19 Sep 1886. Maidanovo.

RUS–Mcm (f. 42, No. 268).

SM (1938), 6: 52 — *PSSL* 13: 456–457.

3053.   To Karl Al´brekht

20 Sep [1886]. [Maidanovo].

RUS–Mcm (f. 37, No. 59).

PSSL 13: 457.

3054.   To Nikolai Konradi

20 Sep 1886. Maidanovo.

Autograph lost; MS copy in RUS–KL.

CTP: 272 — *PSSL* 13: 458–459.

3055.   To Aleksandr Ziloti

22 Sep 1886 [Moscow].

RUS–KL (a³, No. 2995).

AIZ: 80 — *PSSL* 13: 459.

3056.   To Nadezhda von Meck

23 Sep 1886. Maidanovo.

RUS–KL (a³, No. 980).

*ZC 3: 133–134 — *PM* 3: 439–440 — *PSSL* 13: 460–
    461.

3057.   To Eduard Nápravník

23 Sep [1886]. [Maidanovo].

Autograph lost; typed copy in RUS–KL.

EFN: 139 — *PSSL* 13: 461.

3058.   To Anatolii Chaikovskii

23 Sep 1886. Maidanovo.

RUS–KL (a³, No. 3169).

PSSL 13: 462–463.

3059.   To Iuliia Shpazhinskaia

23 Sep 1886. Maidanovo.

RUS–KL (a³, No. 2068).

CTP: 301–302 — *PSSL* 13: 463–464.

3060.   To Nadezhda von Meck

26 Sep 1886. Maidanovo.

RUS–KL (a³, No. 981).

*ZC 3: 134 — *PM* 3: 440–441 — *PSSL* 13: 464–465.

3061.   To Pëtr Iurgenson

[26 Sep 1886. Klin] — telegram.

RUS–KL (a³, No. 2539).

PSSL 13: 466.

3062.   To Modest Chaikovskii

29 Sep [1886]. Moscow.

RUS–KL (a³, No. 1826).

*PB: 366 — *PSSL* 13: 466–467 — **LF*: 363 [English
    tr.].

3063.   To Nikolai Lents

[30 Sep 1886]. Maidanovo.

Autograph lost; typed copy in RUS–KL.

Den´ (25 Oct 1913) — *PSSL* 13: 467–468.

3064.   To Iuliia Shpazhinskaia

[30] Sep 1886 (in MS: "29 Sep"). Maidanovo.

RUS–KL (a³, No. 2069).

CTP: 302 ("29 Sep") — *PSSL* 13: 468–469.

3065.   To Evgenii Al´brekht

5 Oct 1886 [Moscow].

RUS–SPtob (VII.2.4.154).

Muzykal´noe obozrenie (30 Oct 1886) — Glebov (1922): 170–171 — *PSSL* 13: 470–471.

3066.   To Evgenii Al´brekht

5 Oct 1886. Moscow.

RUS–SPtob (VII.2.4.154).

Glebov (1922): 170 — *PSSL* 13: 471–472.

3067.   To Nadezhda von Meck

5 Oct [1886]. Maidanovo.

RUS–KL (a³, No. 982).

*ZC 3: 135–136 — *PM* 3: 443 — *PSSL* 13: 472–473.

3068.   To Iuliia Shpazhinskaia

5 Oct 1886. Maidanovo.

RUS–KL (a³, No. 2070).

CTP: 303–304 — *PSSL* 13: 473–474.

3069.   To Modest Chaikovskii

7 Oct [1886]. Maidanovo.

RUS–KL (a³, No. 1827).

PB: 366–367 — *PSSL* 13: 475 — *LF*: 364 [English tr.].

3070.   To Eduard Nápravník

7 Oct [1886]. [Maidanovo].

US–ANcrocker

EFN: 140 — *PSSL* 13: 476.

3071.   To Vadim Peresleni

8 Oct [1886]. [Maidanovo].

RUS–KL (a³, No. 290).

PSSL 13: 476.

3072.   To Pëtr Iurgenson

[8 Oct 1886]. [Maidanovo].

RUS–KL (a³, No. 2981).

PSSL 13: 477.

3073.   To Modest Chaikovskii

10 Oct [1886]. [Maidanovo].

RUS–KL (a³, No. 1828).

*ZC 3: 137 — *PB*: 367 — *PSSL* 13: 477 — *LF*: 364–365 [English tr.].

3074.   To Nikolai Rimskii-Korsakov

11 Oct 1886. Maidanovo.

RUS–SPsc (f. 640, op. 1, No. 1015, fol. 20–21).

*ZC 3: 279 ("1888") — *SM* (1945), 3: 137–138 — *RK* 7 (1970): 51 — *PSSL* 13: 478.

3075.   To Praskov´ia Chaikovskaia

11 Oct 1886 [Maidanovo].

RUS–KL (a³, No. 3170).

PSSL 13: 479.

3076.   To Aleksandra Hubert

17 Oct [1886]. [Maidanovo].

RUS–KL (a³, No. 51).

PRM 35 — *PSSL* 13: 480.

3077.   To Pëtr Iurgenson

17 Oct [1886]. [Maidanovo].

RUS–KL (a³, No. 2529).

PSSL 13: 480.

3078.   To Pëtr Iurgenson

21 Oct [1886]. [St. Petersburg].

RUS–KL (a³, No. 2625).

PIU 2: 48–49 — *PSSL* 13: 481.

3079.   To Vladimir Sabler

22 Oct 1886 [St. Petersburg].

RUS–SPil (No. 24514).

PSSL 13: 482.

3080.   To Nadezhda von Meck

26 Oct 1886. St. Petersburg.

RUS–KL (a³, No. 983).

PM 3: 445–446 — *PSSL* 13: 482–483.

3081.   To Pëtr Iurgenson
26 Oct 1886. St. Petersburg.
RUS–KL (a³, No. 2530).
PIU 2: 49 — *PSSL* 13: 483–484.

3082.   To Félix Mackar
27 Oct 1886 [St. Petersburg] — in French.
F–Pn
RdM 54 (1968), 1: 57 — *PSSL* 13: 484–486.

3082a.   To Aleksandr Adlerberg
[? Oct–Nov 1886. St. Petersburg].
RUS–SPsc (f. 834, No. 39).
PSSL 17: 241.

3083.   To Evgenii Al´brekht
4 Nov [1886]. [St. Petersburg].
RUS–SPtob (VII.2.4.154).
Kirov: 413 — *PSSL* 13: 487.

3084.   To Vasilii Bessel´
4 Nov [1886]. [St. Petersburg].
RUS–Mcm (f. 42, No. 267).
PSSL 13: 488.

3085.   To Nadezhda von Meck
4 Nov 1886. St. Petersburg.
RUS–KL (a³, No. 984).
*ZC 3: 139 — *PM* 3: 447 — *PSSL* 13: 488–489.

3086.   To Ol´ga Nápravník
[4 Nov 1886. St. Petersburg].
RUS–KL (a³, No. 2993).
PSSL 13: 489.

3087.   To Praskov´ia Chaikovskaia
4 Nov 1886. St. Petersburg.
RUS–KL (a³, No. 3171).
*PB: 368 — *PSSL* 13: 489–490 — **LF:* 365 [English tr.].

3088.   To Iuliia Shpazhinskaia
4 Nov 1886. St. Petersburg.
RUS–KL (a³, No. 2072).
CTP: 304–305 — *PSSL* 13: 490–491.

3089.   To Eduard Nápravník
[8 Nov 1886. St. Petersburg] — note on visiting card.
RUS–KL (a³, No. 3333).
EFN: 140 ("9 Nov 1886") — *PSSL* 13: 491.

3090.   To Nikolai Konradi
[10] Nov 1886 (in MS copy: "12 Nov"). Maidanovo.
Autograph lost; MS copy in RUS–KL.
CTP: 272–273 ("12 Nov") — *PSSL* 13: 491–492.

3091.   To Nadezhda von Meck
10 Nov 1886. Maidanovo.
RUS–KL (a³, No. 985).
PM 3: 447–449 — *PSSL* 13: 492–494.

3092.   To Praskov´ia Chaikovskaia
10 Nov 1886. Maidanovo.
RUS–KL (a³, No. 3264).
*ZC 3: 139–140 — **PB:* 368 — *PSSL* 13: 494–495 — **LF:* 365–366 [English tr.].

3093.   To Iuliia Shpazhinskaia
10 Nov 1886. Maidanovo.
RUS–KL (a³, No. 2073).
CTP: 305–307 — *PSSL* 13: 495–498.

3094.   To Pëtr Iurgenson
10 Nov 1886 [Maidanovo].
RUS–KL (a³, No. 2531).
PIU 2: 49–51 — *PSSL* 13: 498–500.

3095.   To Eduard Nápravník
[13 Nov 1886. Klin] — telegram.
Autograph lost; typed copy in RUS–KL.
EFN: 140 — *PSSL* 13: 501.

3096.   To Emiliia Pavlovskaia
[13 Nov 1886. Klin] — telegram.
RUS–KL (a³, No. 277).
CMS: 370 — *PSSL* 13: 501.

3097   To   Aleksandra   Aleksandrova-Kochetova
14 Nov 1886. Maidanovo.
RUS–Mcm (f. 88, No. 8).
PSSL 13: 501.

3098.   To Aleksandra Hubert
14 Nov [1886]. [Maidanovo].
RUS–KL (a³, No. 52).
PRM 35–36 — *PSSL* 13: 502.

3099.   To Aleksandr Ziloti
14 Nov [1886]. Maidanovo.
RUS–KL (a³, No. 2996).
AIZ: 81 — *PSSL* 13: 502–503.

3100.   To Gennadi Kondrat´ev
14 Nov 1886. Maidanovo.
RUS–SPil (No. 25438).
PSSL 13: 503.

3101.   To Vladimir Nápravník
14 Nov [1886]. Maidanovo.
Autograph lost; typed copy in RUS–KL.
PSSL 13: 504.

3102.   To Fëdor Oom
[14 Nov 1886. Maidanovo].
Autograph lost; rough draft in RUS–KL (a⁴, No. 3144).
PSSL 13: 504 [draft].

3103.   To Modest Chaikovskii
14 Nov 1886 [Maidanovo].
RUS–KL (a³, No. 1829).
ZC 3: 140–141 — *PB*: 369 — *PSSL* 13: 505–506 — *LF*: 366–367 [English tr.].

3104.   To Pëtr Iurgenson
14 Nov [1886]. Maidanovo.
RUS–KL (a³, No. 2982).
ZC 3: 141 — *PIU* 2: 51–52 — *PSSL* 13: 506–507.

3105.   To Nadezhda von Meck
14–24 Nov 1886. Maidanovo.
RUS–KL (a³, No. 986).
PM 3: 450–451 — *PSSL* 13: 507–508.

3106.   To Iuliia Shpazhinskaia
14–24 Nov 1886. Maidanovo.
RUS–KL (a³, No. 2074).
CTP: 307–308 — *PSSL* 13: 509–510.

3107.   To Vladimir Nápravník
16 Nov [1886]. [Maidanovo].
Autograph lost; typed copy in RUS–KL.
PSSL 13: 510.

3108.   To Modest Chaikovskii
19 [Nov 1886] (in MS: "19 Dec") [Moscow].
RUS–KL (a³, No. 1833).
ZC 3: 141–142 — *PB*: 369–370 — *PSSL* 13: 511 — *LF*: 367 [English tr.].

3109.   To Sof´ia Iurgenson
[19 Nov 1886. Moscow].
RUS–KL (a³, No. 497).
PSSL 13: 512.

3110.   To Anton Arenskii
24 Nov 1886 [Moscow].
RUS–SPil (f. 504, No. 74, fol. 5–6).
ZC 3: 143–144 — *PSSL* 13: 512–513.

3111.   To Adol´f Brodskii
26 Nov 1886. Moscow.
GB–Mcm
PSSL 13: 513–514.

3112.   To Praskov´ia Chaikovskaia
26 Nov 1886. Moscow.
RUS–KL (a³, No. 3265).
PSSL 13: 515.

3113.   To Modest Chaikovskii
26 Nov [1886]. [Moscow].
RUS–KL (a³, No. 1830).
ZC 3: 142 — *PB*: 370 — *PSSL* 13: 516 — *LF*: 367–368 [English tr.].

3113a.   To Mariia Klimentova–Muromtseva
27 Nov [1886]. [Moscow].
RUS–Mcl (f. 774).
PSSL 17: 241.

3114.   To Vladimir Stasov
2 Dec 1886. Moscow.
RUS–SPsc (f. 738, No. 343, fol. 58–60).
RM (1909), 3: 146 — *PSSL* 13: 517.

3115. To Modest Chaikovskii

4 Dec 1886 [Moscow].

RUS–KL (a³, No. 1831).

*ZC 3: 149–150 — PB: 371 — PSSL 13: 517–518 — LF: 368–369 [English tr.].

3116. To Iuliia Shpazhinskaia

4 Dec 1886 [Moscow].

RUS–KL (a³, No. 2075).

CTP: 308–309 — PSSL 13: 519–520.

3117. To Aleksandra & Nikolai Hubert

[5 Dec 1886. Moscow].

RUS–KL (a³, No. 104).

PRM 63 — PSSL 13: 521.

3118. To Nadezhda von Meck

9 Dec 1886. Moscow.

RUS–KL (a³, No. 987).

PM 3: 452–453 — PSSL 13: 520–521.

3119. To Iakov Gartung

11 Dec [1886]. [Moscow].

RUS–KL (a³, No. 3057).

PSSL 13: 522.

3120. To Pavel Tret´iakov

15 Dec 1886 [Moscow].

RUS–Mgt

PSSL 13: 523.

3121. To Praskov´ia Chaikovskaia

15 Dec 1886. Moscow.

RUS–KL (a³, No. 3266).

*PB: 371–372 — PSSL 13: 523–524 — *LF: 369 [English tr.].

3122. To Modest Chaikovskii

15 Dec [1886]. [Moscow].

RUS–KL (a³, No. 1832).

PSSL 13: 524.

3123. To Vasilii Bessel´

18 Dec [1886]. [Moscow].

RUS–Mcm (f. 42, No. 269).

SM (1938), 6: 53 ("12 Dec") — PSSL 13: 525.

3123a. To the editor of Muzykal´noe obozrenie

18 Dec 1886. Moscow.

RUS–Mcm (f. 42, No. 270).

*Muzykal´noe obozrenie (24 Dec 1886): 111 — *ZC 3: 148 — *SM (1938), 6: 53 — PSSL 13: 545–546.

3124. To Vasilii Bessel´

18 Dec [1886]. [Moscow].

RUS–Mcm (f. 42, No. 271).

SM (1938), 6: 53–54 — PSSL 13: 525.

3125. To Sergei Taneev & Karl Al´brekht

20 Dec [1886]. [Moscow] — note on visiting card.

RUS–Mcm (f. 37, No. 60).

PSSL 13: 526.

3126. To Vera Tret´iakova

20 Dec [1886]. [Moscow].

RUS–Mgt

A. P. Botkina, Pavel Mikhailovich Tret´iakov v zhizni i iskusstve (1951): 198 — PSSL 13: 526.

3127. To Vasilii Bessel´

[21 Dec 1886. Moscow] — telegram.

RUS–Mcm (f. 42, No. 272).

SM (1938), 6: 54 — PSSL 13: 527.

3128. To Lidiia Genke

22 Dec [1886]. [Moscow].

RUS–Mcl (f. 905).

PSSL 13: 528.

3129. To Aleksandra Hubert

24 Dec [1886]. [Moscow].

RUS–KL (a³, No. 48).

PSSL 13: 528.

3130. To Ivan Vsevolozhskii

25 Dec 1886. Moscow — in French.

RUS–SPia (f. 652, op. 1, d. 608, fol. 5–9).

PSSL 13: 528–530.

3131. To Nadezhda von Meck

26 Dec 1886. Maidanovo.

RUS–KL (a³, No. 988).

*ZC 3: 150–151 — PM 3: 454–455 — PSSL 13: 531–532.

3132.   To Anna Merkling
26 Dec 1886 [Maidanovo].
Autograph lost; MS copy in RUS–KL.
CTP: 228–229 — *PSSL* 13: 533.

3133.   To Eduard Nápravník
26 [Dec] 1886 (in MS: "26 Oct") [Maidanovo].
RUS–KL (a³, No. 3358).
VP: 170–172 — *EFN*: 141–142 — *PSSL* 13: 533–545.

3134.   To Anatolii Chaikovskii
26 Dec 1886 [Maidanovo].
RUS–KL (a³, No. 3172).
*PB: 372 — *PSSL* 13: 535–537 — *LF: 369–370
   [English tr.].

3135.   To Nikolai Chaikovskii
26 Dec 1886 [Maidanovo].
RUS–SPsc (f. 834, No. 37, fol. 17).
PSSL 13: 537.

3136.   To Iuliia Shpazhinskaia
26 [Dec] 1886 (in MS: "26 Oct"). Maidanovo.
RUS–KL (a³, No. 2071).
CTP: 310 — *PSSL* 13: 538.

3137.   To Ivan Popov
[28–29 Dec 1886. Maidanovo].
RUS–KL (a³, No. 2870).
PSSL 13: 539.

3138.   To Vasilii Bessel´
[29 Dec 1886. Maidanovo].
RUS–Mcm (f. 42, No. 273).
SM (1938), 6: 54 — *PSSL* 13: 539–540.

3139.   To Eduard Nápravník
31 Dec [1886]. Maidanovo.
Autograph lost; typed copy in RUS–KL.
VP: 174–175 — *PSSL* 13: 540–541.

3139a.   To Max Erdmannsdörfer
[1886–1888. Moscow] — note on visiting card; in
   German.
RUS–KL (a³, No. 3315).
PSSL 17: 242.

3139b.   To Modest Chaikovskii
[1886].
RUS–KL (a³, No. 3303).
Not published.

1887

3140.   To Eduard Nápravník
1 Jan [1887]. [Maidanovo].
Autograph lost; typed copy in RUS–KL.
VP: 175 — *EFN*: 144 — *PSSL* 14: 13.

3141.   To Emiliia Pavlovskaia
2 Jan 1887 [Maidanovo].
RUS–Mt (Pavlovskaia coll.).
CMS: 370–371 — *PSSL* 14: 13–14.

3142.   To Iuliia Shpazhinskaia
4 Jan 1887. Maidanovo.
RUS–KL (a³, No. 2077).
CTP: 310–311 — *PSSL* 14: 14–15.

3143.   To Nadezhda von Meck
5 Jan 1887. Maidanovo.
RUS–KL (a³, No. 989).
*ZC 3: 151 — *PM* 3: 456–457 — *PSSL* 14: 16–17.

3144.   To Emiliia Pavlovskaia
[13 Jan 1887. Moscow] — telegram.
RUS–KL (a³, No. 278).
CMS: 374 — *PSSL* 14: 17.

3145.   To Karl Al´brekht
[14 Jan 1887. Moscow].
RUS–Mt (Al´brekht coll.).
PSSL 14: 17.

3146.   To Nadezhda von Meck
14 Jan [1887] (in MS: "1886"). Moscow.
RUS–KL (a³, No. 990).
*ZC 3: 151–152 — *PM* 3: 458–459 — *PSSL* 14: 18.

3147.   To Eduard Nápravník
14 Jan [1887]. Moscow.
Autograph lost; typed copy in RUS–KL.
VP: 176 — *EFN*: 145 — *PSSL* 14: 19.

3148. To Aleksandra Hubert

16 Jan [1887]. [Moscow].

RUS–KL (a³, No. 53).

PRM 36–37 — *PSSL* 14: 19.

3149. To Emiliia Pavlovskaia

[20 Jan 1887. Moscow] — telegram.

RUS–KL (a³, No. 279).

CMS: 378 — *PSSL* 14: 20.

3150. To Emiliia Pavlovskaia

20 Jan 1887. Moscow.

RUS–Mt (Pavlovskaia coll.).

*ZC 3: 154–155 — *CMS:* 378–380 — *PSSL* 14: 20–22.

3151. To Vladimir Shilovskii

20 Jan [1887]. [Moscow].

RUS–SPsc (f. 834, No. 14, fol. 10–12).

PSSL 14: 22.

3152. To Emiliia Pavlovskaia

21 Jan 1887 [Moscow].

RUS–Mt (Pavlovskaia coll.).

CMS: 381–382 — *PSSL* 14: 22–23.

3153. To Nadezhda von Meck

22 Jan 1887. Moscow.

RUS–KL (a³, No. 991).

PM 3: 460–461 — **CMS:* 158 — *PSSL* 14: 23–24.

3154. To Eduard Nápravník

[22 Jan 1887. Moscow] — telegram.

Autograph lost; typed copy in RUS–KL.

VP: 177 — *EFN:* 146 — *PSSL* 14: 25.

3155. To Praskov´ia Chaikovskaia

22 Jan 1887 [Moscow].

RUS–KL (a³, No. 3267).

*PB: 372–373 — *PSSL* 14: 25–26 — **LF:* 370–371 [English tr.].

3156. To Modest Chaikovskii

22 Jan [1887]. [Moscow].

RUS–KL (a³, No. 1834).

*PB: 373 — *PSSL* 14: 26–27 — **LF:* 371 [English tr.].

3157. To Vladimir Shilovskii

22 Jan [1887]. [Moscow].

RUS–SPsc (f. 834, No. 14, fol. 13–15).

PSSL 14: 27.

3158. To Pavel Pchel´nikov

23 Jan [1887]. [Moscow].

RUS–KL (a³, No. 330).

PSSL 14: 27–28.

3159. To Iuliia Shpazhinskaia

24 Jan [1887]. [Moscow].

RUS–KL (a³, No. 2078).

CTP: 311–312 — *PSSL* 14: 28–29.

3160. To Vladimir Shilovskii

25 Jan [1887]. [Moscow].

RUS–SPsc (f. 834, No. 14, fol. 16–17).

PSSL 14: 29.

3161. To Mariia Klimentova-Muromtseva

[26 Jan 1887. Moscow] — note on visiting card.

RUS–Mcl (f. 774).

PSSL 14: 30.

3162. To Modest Chaikovskii

26 Jan 1887 [Moscow].

RUS–KL (a³, No. 1835).

*ZC 3: 157–158 — **PB:* 374 — *PSSL* 14: 30–31 — **LF:* 371–372 [English tr.].

3163. To the St. Petersburg. Philharmonic Society

27 Jan 1887. Moscow.

Autograph lost

100-letnii iubilei Peterburgskogo Filarmonicheskogo obshchestva (1902): 80 — *PSSL* 14: 31.

3164. To Emiliia Pavlovskaia

[27 Jan 1887. Moscow] — telegram.

RUS–KL (a³, No. 280).

CMS: 384 — *PSSL* 14: 32.

3165. To Bogomir Korsov

28 Jan [1887]. [Moscow] — in French.

RUS–KL (a³, No. 251).

PSSL 14: 32.

3166.   To Grand Duke Konstantin Konstantinovich

29 Jan 1887. Maidanovo.

RUS–SPil (f. 137, No. 78/4).

PSSL 14: 33.

3167.   To Praskov´ia Chaikovskaia

29 Jan 1887. Maidanovo.

RUS–KL (a³, No. 3268).

PSSL 14: 34.

3168.   To Modest Chaikovskii

29 Jan 1887. Maidanovo.

RUS–KL (a³, No. 1836).

ZC 3: 158 — *PB*: 374–375 — *PSSL* 14: 34–35 —
   LF: 372 [English tr.].

3168a. To K. E. Weber

30 Jan [1887]. [Maidanovo] (in MS: "Klin").

Autograph lost; photocopy in RUS–KL

Not published.

3169.   To Adol´f Brodskii

[31 Jan 1887. Klin] — telegram.

GB–Mcm

PSSL 14: 35.

3170.   To Félix Mackar

[early Feb 1887]. Maidanovo — in French.

F–Pn

RdM 54 (1968), 1: 58–59 — *SM* (1970), 9: 64–65 —
   PSSL 14: 36–37.

3171.   To Nadezhda von Meck

2 Feb 1887. Maidanovo.

RUS–KL (a³, No. 992).

ZC 3: 158–159 — *PM* 3: 462–463 — *PSSL* 14: 37–
   38.

3172.   To Modest Chaikovskii

4 Feb [1887]. [Maidanovo].

RUS–KL (a³, No. 1837).

PSSL 14: 39.

3173.   To Sof´ia Iurgenson

7 Feb 1887. Maidanovo.

RUS–KL (a³, No. 2557).

PSSL 14: 39.

3174.   To Iuliia Shpazhinskaia

7 Feb 1887. Maidanovo.

RUS–KL (a³, No. 2079).

CTP: 312–313 — *PSSL* 14: 40–41.

3175.   To Nadezhda von Meck

9 Feb 1887. Maidanovo.

RUS–KL (a³, No. 993).

ZC 3: 159–160 — *PM* 3: 463–464 — *PSSL* 14: 42–
   43.

3176.   To Félix Mackar

10 Feb 1887. Maidanovo — in French.

F–Pn

RdM 54 (1968), 1: 59 — *SM* (1970), 9: 65 [Russian
   tr.] — *PSSL* 14: 43–44.

3177.   To Vladimir Pogozhev

10 Feb 1887. Maidanovo.

RUS–KL (a³, No. 2872).

VP: 27–28 — *PSSL* 14: 45.

3178.   To Sof´ia Iurgenson

11 Feb 1887. Maidanovo.

RUS–KL (a³, No. 488).

PSSL 14: 46.

3179.   To Aleksandra Hubert

11 Feb [1887]. Maidanovo.

RUS–KL (a³, No. 54).

PRM 37 — *PSSL* 14: 46–47.

3180.   To Anna Merkling

12 Feb 1887 [Maidanovo].

Autograph lost; MS copy in RUS–KL.

CTP: 229 — *PSSL* 14: 47.

3181.   To Modest Chaikovskii

12 Feb [1887]. [Maidanovo].

RUS–KL (a³, No. 1838).

PB: 375 — *PSSL* 14: 47–48 — *LF*: 372–373
   [English tr.].

3182. To Pëtr Iurgenson

12 Feb 1887. Maidanovo.

RUS–KL (a³, No. 2558).

PIU 2: 55 — *PSSL* 14: 48.

3183. To Sergei Taneev

14 Feb [1887]. [Maidanovo].

RUS–KL (a³, No. 397).

SM (1937), 6: 77 — *CTP:* : 143–144 — *PSSL* 14: 49–50.

3184. To Eduard Nápravník

15 Feb 1887 [Maidanovo].

Autograph lost; typed copy in RUS–KL.

VP: 178 — *EFN:* 146 — *PSSL* 14: 51.

3185. To Pëtr Iurgenson

17 Feb [1887]. [Maidanovo].

RUS–KL (a³, No. 2831).

PIU 2: 56 — *PSSL* 14: 51.

3186. To Anatolii Brandukov

[18 Feb 1887]. Maidanovo.

RUS–KL (a³, No. 21).

PSSL 14: 52.

3187. To Félix Mackar

18 Feb 1887 [Maidanovo] — in French.

F–Pn

RdM 54 (1968), 1: 60 — *SM* (1970), 9: 55 [Russian tr.] — *PSSL* 14: 52–53.

3188. To Ivan Popov

19 Feb [1887]. [Moscow].

RUS–KL (a³, No. 300).

PSSL 14: 54.

3189. To Nadezhda von Meck

20 Feb 1887. Moscow.

RUS–KL (a³, No. 994).

ZC 3: 160 — PM 3: 465–466 — PSSL 14: 54–55.

3190. To Praskov´ia Chaikovskaia

27 Feb 1887. St. Petersburg.

RUS–KL (a³, No. 3269).

PB: 375–376 — *PSSL* 14: 55–56 — *LF:* 373 [English tr.].

3191. To Bogomir Korsov

1 Mar [1887]. [St. Petersburg] — in French.

RUS–KL (a³, No. 248).

PSSL 14: 56.

3192. To Emiliia Pavlovskaia

[2 Mar 1887. St. Petersburg] — telegram.

RUS–KL (a³, No. 281).

CMS: 385 — *PSSL* 14: 57.

3193. To Vladimir Stasov

[8 Mar 1887. St. Petersburg].

RUS–SPsc (f. 738, No. 343, fol. 61).

RM (1909), 3: 146 — *PSSL* 14: 57.

3194. To Nadezhda von Meck

10 Mar 1887. St. Petersburg.

RUS–KL (a³, No. 995).

*ZC 3: 161–162 — PM 3: 467–469 — *CMS:* 159 — PSSL* 14: 58–59.

3195. To Vasilii Sidorov

[10 Mar 1887. St. Petersburg].

Autograph lost; rough draft in RUS–KL (a⁴, No. 3977).

PSSL 14: 60 [draft].

3196. To Iuliia Shpazhinskaia

10 Mar [1887]. St. Petersburg.

RUS–KL (a³, No. 2080).

CTP: 314 — *PSSL* 14: 60.

3197. To Milii Balakirev

11 Mar [1887]. [St. Petersburg].

RUS–SPsc (f. 834, No. 12, fol. 37, 44).

BC: 97 — *BVP* 183 — *PSSL* 14: 61.

3198. To Nadezhda von Meck

12 Mar 1887. Maidanovo.

RUS–KL (a³, No. 996).

ZC 3: 162 — PM 3: 469–470 — PSSL 14: 61–62.

3199. To Praskov´ia Chaikovskaia

12 Mar 1887. Maidanovo.

RUS–KL (a³, No. 3270).

PB: 376 — *PSSL* 14: 62–63 — *LF:* 374 [English tr.].

3200.   To Ippolit Al´tani

14 Mar [1887]. [Maidanovo].

RUS–Mcm (f. 7, No. 58).

PSSL 14: 63–64.

3201.   To Modest Chaikovskii

15 Mar [1887]. [Maidanovo].

RUS–KL (a³, No. 1839).

*ZC 3: 163–164 — **PB*: 377 — *PSSL* 14: 64–65 —
   *LF: 375 [English tr.].

3202.   To Iuliia Shpazhinskaia

15 Mar 1887. Maidanovo.

RUS–KL (a³, No. 2051).

CTP: 314–315 — *PSSL* 14: 65–66.

3203.   To Semen Kruglikov

21 Mar [1887]. Moscow.

RUS–KL (a³, No. 256).

PSSL 14: 67.

3204.   To Félix Mackar

23 Mar 1887. Maidanovo — in French.

F–Pn

RdM 54 (1968), 1: 60–61 — *SM* (1970), 9: 65–66
   [Russian tr.] — *PSSL* 14: 67–68.

3205.   To Nadezhda von Meck

23 Mar 1887. Maidanovo.

RUS–KL (a³, No. 997).

PM 3: 472 — *PSSL* 14: 69–70.

3206.   To Praskov´ia Chaikovskaia

23 Mar [1887]. [Maidanovo].

RUS–KL (a³, No. 3279).

PSSL 14: 70–71.

3207.   To Modest Chaikovskii

23 Mar [1887]. Maidanovo.

RUS–KL (a³, No. 1840).

*PB: 377–378 — *PSSL* 14: 71–72 — **LF*: 375–376
   [English tr.].

3208.   To Anna Merkling

25 Mar 1887 [Maidanovo].

Autograph lost; MS copy in RUS–KL.

CTP: 229–230 — *PSSL* 14: 72–73.

3209.   To Pëtr Iurgenson

25 Mar [1887]. [Maidanovo].

RUS–KL (a³, No. 2559).

PIU 2: 56 — *PSSL* 14: 73.

3210.   To Iuliia Shpazhinskaia

26 Mar 1887 [Maidanovo].

RUS–KL (a³, No. 2082).

*Proletarskaia pravda (9 Sep 1938) [Ukrainian tr.] —
   *Sovetskoe iskusstvo (10 Sep 1938) — *CTP*: 316–
   317 — *PSSL* 14: 74–76.

3211.   To Sergei Taneev

28 Mar [1887]. [Maidanovo].

RUS–Mcl (f. 880).

CTP: 144–145 — *PSSL* 14: 76.

3212.   To Sof´ia Chaikovskaia

28 Mar 1887. Maidanovo.

RUS–SPsc (f. 834, No. 32).

PSSL 14: 77.

3213.   To Anton Rubinshtein

30 Mar 1887. Maidanovo.

RUS–SPsc (f. 124, No. 4652).

PIU 2: 286–287 — *PSSL* 14: 77–78.

3214.   To Karl Al´brekht

[1 Apr 1887. Maidanovo] — telegram.

RUS–Mcm (f. 37, No. 61).

PSSL 14: 78.

3215.   To Anton Arenskii

2 Apr 1887. Maidanovo.

RUS–SPil (f. 54, No. 74, fol. 7–12).

*ZC 3: 144–147 — *PSSL* 14: 78–81.

3216.   To Félix Mackar

4 Apr 1887. Maidanovo — in French.

F–Pn

RdM 54 (1968), 1: 61–62 — *PSSL* 14: 82–83.

3217.   To Praskov´ia Chaikovskaia

4 Apr [1887]. Maidanovo.

RUS–KL (a³, No. 3271).

PSSL 14: 83–84.

3218. To Modest Chaikovskii
4 Apr [1887]. Maidanovo.
RUS–KL (a³, No. 1841).
PSSL 14: 84–85.

3219. To Pëtr Iurgenson
4 Apr 1887. Maidanovo.
RUS–KL (a³, No. 2560).
PIU 2: 57 — *PSSL* 14: 85–86.

3219a. To Jacques Dusautoy
4 Apr 1887. Maidanovo — in French.
D–Tu [facs. in *Bisher unbekannte Briefe und musikalische Arbeiten Čajkovskijs* (1994): 5–8 — *Internationales Čajkovskij-Symposium Tübingen 1993: Bericht* (1995): 23–26].
Bisher unbekannte Briefe und musikalische Arbeiten Čajkovskijs (1994): 4 — *Internationales Čajkovskij-Symposium Tübingen 1993: Bericht* (1995): 21–35.

3220. To Aleksandra Hubert
7 Apr 1887. Maidanovo.
RUS–KL (a³, No. 55).
PRM 37–38 — *PSSL* 14: 86–87.

3221. To Pëtr Iurgenson
7 Apr 1887. Maidanovo.
RUS–KL (a³, No. 2561).
PIU 2: 58 — *PSSL* 14: 87.

3222. To Modest Chaikovskii
10 Apr [1887]. Maidanovo.
RUS–KL (a³, No. 1842).
PSSL 14: 88.

3223. To Iuliia Shpazhinskaia
10 Apr 1887. Maidanovo.
RUS–KL (a³, No. 2083).
CTP: 318 — *PSSL* 14: 89–90.

3224. To Pëtr Iurgenson
10 Apr 1887. Maidanovo.
RUS–KL (a³, No. 2562).
PIU 2: 59 — *PSSL* 14: 90–91.

3225. To Pëtr Iurgenson
[12 Apr 1887. Maidanovo].
RUS–KL (a³, No. 2592).
PSSL 14: 91.

3226. To Praskov´ia & Anatolii Chaikovskii
15 Apr [1887]. Maidanovo.
RUS–KL (a³, No. 3272).
PSSL 14: 92.

3227. To Camille Saint-Saëns
18 Apr 1887 [Maidanovo] — in French.
F–DI
RdM 54 (1968), 1: 83 — *PSSL* 14: 92.

3228. To Pëtr Iurgenson
[18 Apr 1887. Klin] — telegram.
RUS–KL (a³, No. 2541).
PSSL 14: 93.

3229. To Vladimir Nápravník
19 Apr [1887]. Maidanovo.
Autograph lost; typed copy in RUS–KL.
EFN: 189–190 — *PSSL* 14: 93.

3230. To Pëtr Iurgenson
19 Apr [1887]. Maidanovo.
RUS–KL (a³, No. 2563).
PIU 2: 59–60 — *PSSL* 14: 94.

3231. To Aleksandra Sviatlovskaia
19 Apr [1887]. [Maidanovo].
RUS–KL (a³, No. 8).
PSSL 14: 94.

3232. To Modest Chaikovskii
20 Apr [1887]. [Maidanovo].
RUS–KL (a³, No. 1843).
PB: 378 — *PSSL* 14: 94–95 — *LF*: 376 [English tr.].

3233. To Pëtr Iurgenson
20 Apr [1887]. [Maidanovo].
RUS–KL (a³, No. 2564).
PSSL 14: 95.

3234.   To Pëtr Iurgenson
23 Apr [1887]. [Maidanovo].
RUS–KL (a³, No. 2566).
PIU 2: 60 — *PSSL* 14: 95–96.

3235.   To Pëtr Iurgenson
[23 Apr 1887. Klin] — telegram.
RUS–KL (a³, No. 2542).
PIU 2: 60 — *PSSL* 14: 96.

3236.   To Emiliia Pavlovskaia
23 Apr 1887 [Maidanovo].
RUS–Mt (Pavlovskaia coll.).
CMS: 386 — *PSSL* 14: 96.

3237.   To Pëtr Iurgenson
23 Apr [1887]. [Maidanovo].
RUS–KL (a³, No. 2565).
PSSL 14: 97.

3238.   To Karl Al´brekht
24 Apr [1887]. [Maidanovo] — in German.
RUS–Mcm (f. 37, No. 62).
PSSL 14: 97.

3239.   To Nadezhda von Meck
24 Apr 1887. Maidanovo.
RUS–KL (a³, No. 998).
*ZC 3: 165–166 — *PM* 3: 473–474 — *PSSL* 14: 98–99.

3240.   To Aleksandra Hubert
26 Apr [1887]. [Maidanovo].
RUS–KL (a³, No. 56).
PRM 38–39 — *PSSL* 14: 99–100.

3241.   To Praskov´ia & Anatolii Chaikovskii
26 Apr 1887. Maidanovo.
RUS–KL (a³, No. 3273).
PSSL 14: 100.

3242.   To Modest Chaikovskii
26 Apr 1887 [Maidanovo].
RUS–KL (a³, No. 1844).
PSSL 14: 100–101.

3243.   To Georgii Katuar
27 Apr 1887. Maidanovo.
RUS–KL (a³, No. 208).
PSSL 14: 101.

3244.   To Illarion Vorontsov-Dashkov
28 Apr 1887 [Maidanovo].
RUS–Mcl (f. 829).
PSSL 14: 102.

3245.   To Bogomir Korsov
28 Apr [1887]. [Maidanovo] — in French.
RUS–Mcm (f. 88, No. 184).
SM (1959), 1: 76 ("26 Apr") [Russian tr.] — *PSSL* 14: 102–103.

3246.   To Vladimir Stasov
29 Apr 1887. Maidanovo.
RUS–SPsc (f. 738, No. 343, fol. 62–64).
RM (1909), 3: 147–148 — *PSSL* 14: 103–104.

3247.   To Modest Chaikovskii
29 Apr [1887]. [Maidanovo].
RUS–KL (a³, No. 1845).
PSSL 14: 104–105.

3248.   To Modest Chaikovskii
1 May [1887]. [Maidanovo].
RUS–KL (a³, No. 1846).
PSSL 14: 105–106.

3249.   To Nadezhda von Meck
5 May 1887. Maidanovo.
RUS–KL (a³, No. 999).
*ZC 3: 166–167 ("13 May") — *PM* 3: 475 — *PSSL* 14: 106–107.

3250.   To Praskov´ia Chaikovskaia
7 May [1887]. Maidanovo.
RUS–KL (a³, No. 3274).
PSSL 14: 107–108.

3251.   To Iuliia Shpazhinskaia
7 May [1887]. Maidanovo.
RUS–KL (a³, No. 2084).
CTP: 319 — *PSSL* 14: 108.

3252. To Aleksandra Hubert
9 May [1887]. [Maidanovo].
RUS–KL (a³, No. 57).
PRM 39 — *PSSL* 14: 109.

3253. To Pëtr Iurgenson
9 May [1887]. [Maidanovo].
RUS–KL (a³, No. 2567).
PIU 2: 61 — *PSSL* 14: 109–110.

3254. To Aleksei Sofronov
11 May [1887]. [St. Petersburg].
RUS–SPsc (f. 834, No. 27, fol. 11–12).
PSSL 14: 110.

3255. To Ivan Vsevolozhskii
13 May 1887 [St. Petersburg].
RUS–SPia (f. 652, op. 1, d. 608, fol. 10–11).
PSSL 14: 110–111.

3256. To Bogomir Korsov
13 May [1887]. [St. Petersburg] — in French.
RUS–KL (a³, No. 247).
SM (1959), 1: 77 [Russian tr.] — *PSSL* 14: 111.

3257. To Nadezhda von Meck
14 May 1887. St. Petersburg.
RUS–KL (a³, No. 1000).
PM 3: 476 — *PSSL* 14: 112.

3258. To Praskov´ia Chaikovskaia
14 May 1887 [St. Petersburg].
RUS–KL (a³, No. 3275).
PSSL 14: 113.

3259. To Nadezhda von Meck
20 May 1887. Moscow.
RUS–KL (a³, No. 1001).
PM 3: 476–477 — *PSSL* 14: 113–114.

3260. To Praskov´ia Chaikovskaia
20 May [1887]. [Moscow].
RUS–KL (a³, No. 3276).
PSSL 14: 114.

3261. To Modest Chaikovskii
20 May [1887]. [Moscow].
RUS–KL (a³, No. 1847).
PSSL 14: 114–115.

3262. To Iuliia Shpazhinskaia
20 May 1887 [Moscow].
RUS–KL (a³, No. 2085).
CTP: 319 — *PSSL* 14: 115.

3263. To Aleksandra Hubert
26 May [1887]. Caspian Sea.
RUS–KL (a³, No. 86).
PSSL 14: 116.

3264. To Nadezhda von Meck
28 May 1887. Caspian Sea.
RUS–KL (a³, No. 1002).
*ZC 3: 167–168 — *PM* 3: 477–478 — *PSSL* 14: 116–117.

3265. To Nadezhda von Meck
30 May 1887. Tiflis.
RUS–KL (a³, No. 1003).
*ZC 3: 168–169 — *PM* 3: 478–479 — *PSSL* 14: 117–118.

3266. To Iuliia Shpazhinskaia
4 Jun 1887 [Tiflis].
RUS–KL (a³, No. 2086).
*Zara Vostoka (6 May 1940) — *CTP*: 320–321 — *PSSL* 14: 118–121.

3267. To Pëtr Iurgenson
4 Jun 1887. Tiflis.
RUS–KL (a³, No. 2568).
PIU 2: 61–62 — *PSSL* 14: 121–122.

3268. To Nadezhda von Meck
13 Jun 1887. Borzhom.
RUS–KL (a³, No. 1004).
PM 3: 482–483 — *PSSL* 14: 122–123.

3269. To Tsar Aleksandr III
18 Jun 1887. Borzhom.
RUS–SPia (f. 1412, op. 55, d. 9).
PSSL 14: 124–125.

3270. To Aleksandra & Nikolai Hubert
20 Jun 1887. Borzhom.
RUS–KL (a³, No. 96).
PSSL 14: 125–126.

3271. To Mikhail Ippolitov-Ivanov
20 Jun [1887]. Borzhom.
RUS–KL (a³, No. 182).
*ZC 3: 169–170 — Iskusstvo, 3 (1927), 4: 147 —
Biulleten´ (1947), 1: 31–33 — PSSL 14: 127–128.

3272. To Ol´ga Chaikovskaia
21 Jun 1887. Borzhom.
RUS–SPsc (f. 834, No. 31, fol. 1–2).
PSSL 14: 129–130.

3273. To Nadezhda von Meck
22 Jun [1887]. Borzhom.
RUS–KL (a³, No. 1005).
PM 3: 484–486 — *PSSL* 14: 130–132.

3274. To Pavel Iurasov
[23 Jun 1887. Borzhom] — telegram.
RUS–KL (a³, No. 468).
PSSL 14: 132.

3275. To Pëtr Iurgenson
24 Jun [1887]. Borzhom.
RUS–KL (a³, No. 2569).
*ZC 3: 170–171 — PIU 2: 63–64 — PSSL 14: 132–
133.

3276. To Nadezhda von Meck
26 Jun 1887. Borzhom.
RUS–KL (a³, No. 1006).
*ZC 3: 171–172 — PM 3: 486–487 — PSSL 14: 134–
135.

3277. To Anna Merkling
26 Jun 1887. Borzhom.
Autograph lost; MS copy in RUS–KL.
CTP: 230–231 — *PSSL* 14: 135–137.

3278. To Nadezhda von Meck
27 Jun 1887. Borzhom.
RUS–KL (a³, No. 1007).
PM 3: 487–488 — *PSSL* 14: 137–138.

3279. To Iuliia Shpazhinskaia
27 Jun 1887. Borzhom.
RUS–KL (a³, No. 2087).
Zara Vostoka (6 May 1940) — *CTP*: 322 — *PSSL* 14:
138–139.

3280. To Nadezhda von Meck
1 Jul 1887. Borzhom.
RUS–KL (a³, No. 1008).
PM 3: 489 — *PSSL* 14: 140.

3281. To Pëtr Iurgenson
1 Jul 1887. Borzhom.
RUS–KL (a³, No. 2570).
*ZC 3: 172 — PIU 2: 64 — PSSL 14: 141.

3282. To Aleksandra & Nikolai Hubert
4 Jul 1887. Borzhom.
RUS–KL (a³, No. 97).
PSSL 14: 142.

3283. To Nadezhda von Meck
5 Jul [1887]. Borzhom.
RUS–KL (a³, No. 1009).
PM 3: 490 — *PSSL* 14: 143.

3283a. To Anna Aleksandrova-Levenson
[early Jun 1887]. Borzhom.
RUS–KL (a³, No. 3327).
Not published.

3284. To Praskov´ia Chaikovskaia
6 Jul 1887. Batum.
RUS–KL (a³, No. 458).
*ZC 3: 172–173 — *PB: 378–379 — PSSL 14: 143–
144 — *LF: 377 [English tr.].

3285. To Modest Chaikovskii
8–9 Jul 1887 [Black Sea].
RUS–KL (a³, No. 1848).
*ZC 3: 173 — PB: 379–380 — PSSL 14: 144–145 —
LF: 377–378 [English tr.].

3286. To Nikolai Konradi
10 Jul 1887. Odessa.
Autograph lost; MS copy in RUS–KL.
CTP: 273–274 — *PSSL* 14: 146.

3287. To Modest Chaikovskii

16/[28] Jul 1887. Aachen.

RUS–KL (a³, No. 1849).

*ZC 3: 174–176 — *PSSL* 14: 147–150.

3288. To Aleksei Sofronov

18/[30] Jul 1887. Aachen.

RUS–SPsc (f. 834, No. 27, fol. 13–14).

PSSL 14: 150–151.

3289. To Praskov´ia Chaikovskaia

19/[31] Jul 1887. Aachen.

RUS–KL (a³, No. 3277).

*ZC 3: 176 — *PSSL* 14: 151–152.

3290. To Nikolai Hubert

20 Jul/[1 Aug] 1887. Aachen.

RUS–KL (a³, No. 110).

PSSL 14: 153–154.

3291. To Nadezhda von Meck

20 Jul/[1 Aug] 1887. Aachen.

RUS–KL (a³, No. 1010).

PM 3: 492–493 — *PSSL* 14: 154–155.

3292. To Boris Iurgenson

20 Jul/[1 Aug] 1887. Aachen.

RUS–KL (a³, No. 476).

PSSL 14: 155–156.

3293. To Mikhail Ippolitov-Ivanov

22 Jul/[3 Aug] 1887. Aachen.

RUS–KL (a³, No. 183).

Iskusstvo, 3 (1927), 4: 148 — *Biulleten´* (1947), 1: 36 — *PSSL* 14: 156–157.

3294. To Sergei Taneev

22 Jul/[3 Aug] 1887. Aachen.

RUS–Mcl (f. 880).

PT: 147 — *CTP*: 145–146 — *PSSL* 14: 157–158.

3295. To Iuliia Shpazhinskaia

22 Jul/[3 Aug] 1887. Aachen.

RUS–KL (a³, No. 2058).

CTP: 323 — *PSSL* 14: 158–159.

3296. To Nikolai Konradi

23 Jul/[4 Aug] 1887. Aachen.

Autograph lost; MS copy in RUS–KL.

*ZC 3: 177–178 — *CTP*: 274–275 — *PSSL* 14: 160–161.

3297. To Emiliia Pavlovskaia

23 Jul/[4 Aug] 1887. Aachen.

RUS–Mt (Pavlovskaia coll.).

CMS: 390–391 — *PSSL* 14: 161–162.

3298. To Modest Chaikovskii

25 Jul/[6 Aug] 1887. Aachen.

RUS–KL (a³, No. 1850).

PSSL 14: 163–164.

3299. To Anna Aleksandrova-Levenson

26 Jul/[7 Aug] 1887. Aachen.

Autograph lost; MS copy in RUS–KL.

PSSL 14: 164–165.

3300. To Anna Merkling

26 Jul/[7 Aug] 1887. Aachen.

Autograph lost; MS copy in RUS–KL.

CTP: 231–232 — *PSSL* 14: 165–166.

3301. To Modest Chaikovskii

27 Jul/[8 Aug] 1887 [Aachen.].

RUS–KL (a³, No. 1851).

PSSL 14: 166–168.

3302. To Nikolai Konradi

28 Jul/[9 Aug] 1887. Aachen.

Autograph lost; MS copy in RUS–KL.

CTP: 275 — *PSSL* 14: 169–170.

3303. To Nadezhda von Meck

29 Jul/[10 Aug] 1887 [Aachen].

RUS–KL (a³, No. 1011).

PM 3: 493–494 — *PSSL* 14: 170–171.

3304. To Modest Chaikovskii

29 Jul/[10 Aug] 1887. Aachen.

RUS–KL (a³, No. 1852).

PSSL 14: 171–172.

3305.   To Pëtr Iurgenson
29 Jul/[10 Aug 1887]. Aachen.
RUS–KL (a³, No. 2571).
*ZC 3: 178 — *PIU 2: 66–67 — PSSL 14: 172–173.

3306.   To Emiliia Pavlovskaia
30 Jul/[11 Aug] 1887. Aachen.
RUS–Mt (Pavlovskaia coll.).
*ZC 3: 178–179 — CMS: 395–396 — PSSL 14: 173–175.

3307.   To Modest Chaikovskii
30 Jul/[11 Aug] 1887. Aachen.
RUS–KL (a³, No. 1853).
PSSL 14: 175–177.

3308.   To Praskov´ia Chaikovskaia
31 Jul/[12 Aug] 1887. Aachen.
RUS–KL (a³. No. 3278).
PSSL 14: 178.

3309.   To Modest Chaikovskii
1/[13] Aug 1887 [Aachen].
RUS–KL (a³, No. 1854).
PSSL 14: 179–180.

3310.   To Anatolii Brandukov
[4/16 Aug 1887. Paris] — note on visiting card.
RUS–KL (L.R., No. 2).
PSSL 14: 180.

3311.   To Praskov´ia Chaikovskaia
5/[17] Aug 1887 [Aachen].
RUS–KL (a³, No. 3328).
PSSL 14: 180–181.

3312.   To Iuliia Shpazhinskaia
6/[18] Aug 1887. Aachen.
RUS–KL (a³, No. 2059).
CTP: 324–325 — PSSL 14: 181–183.

3313.   To Aleksei Sofronov
7/[19] Aug 1887. Aachen.
RUS–SPsc (f. 834, No. 27, fol. 15–16).
PSSL 14: 183–184.

3314.   To Mariia Slavina
8/20 Aug 1887. Aachen.
RUS–KL (a³, No. 3152).
PSSL 14: 184–190.

3315.   To Praskov´ia Chaikovskaia
8/[20] Aug 1887. Aachen.
RUS–KL (a³, No. 3280).
PSSL 14: 191.

3316.   To Praskov´ia, Anatolii & Modest Chaikovskii
9/[21] Aug 1887. Aachen.
RUS–KL (a³, No. 3281).
PSSL 14: 191–192.

3317.   To Anatolii Brandukov
13/25 Aug 1887. Aachen.
RUS–KL (a³, No. 22).
PSSL 14: 192.

3318.   To Vasilii Filatov
13/25 Aug 1887. Aachen.
RUS–KL (a³, No. 3318).
PSSL 14: 193.

3319.   To Modest Chaikovskii
14/[26] Aug 1887 [Aachen].
RUS–KL (a³, No. 1855).
PSSL 14: 193.

3320.   To Aleksei Sofronov
15/[27] Aug 1887. Aachen.
RUS–SPsc (f. 834, No. 27, fol. 17–18).
PSSL 14: 194.

3321.   To Modest Chaikovskii
16/[28] Aug 1887 [Aachen].
RUS–KL (a³, No. 1856).
PSSL 14: 194–195.

3322.   To Modest Chaikovskii
16/[28] Aug 1887 [Aachen.].
RUS–KL (a³, No. 1857).
PSSL 14: 195.

3323. To Modest Chaikovskii
17/[29] Aug [1887]. [Aachen].
RUS–KL (a³, No. 1858).
PSSL 14: 195–196.

3324. To Sergei Taneev
18/[30 Aug 1887] (in MS: "18 Jun") [Aachen].
RUS–Mcl (f. 880).
PT: 149 — *CTP*: 147 — *PSSL* 14: 196.

3325. To Modest Chaikovskii
19/[31] Aug [1887]. [Aachen].
RUS–KL (a³, No. 1859).
PSSL 14: 197.

3326. To Modest Chaikovskii
20 Aug/[1 Sep] 1887 [Aachen.].
RUS–KL (a³, No. 1860).
PSSL 14: 197–198.

3327. To Anatolii Chaikovskii
23 Aug/[4 Sep 1887]. Aachen.
RUS–KL (a³, No. 3173).
PSSL 14: 198–199.

3328. To Modest Chaikovskii
23 Aug/[4 Sep] 1887. Aachen.
RUS–KL (a³, No. 1861).
PSSL 14: 199.

3329. To Anatolii Brandukov
26 Aug [7 Sep] 1887. Berlin
RUS–KL (a³, No. 23).
PSSL 14: 199–200.

3330. To Modest Chaikovskii
[29 Aug 1887. St. Petersburg].
RUS–KL (a³, No. 1862).
PSSL 14: 200.

3331. To Modest Chaikovskii
30 Aug 1887 [Maidanovo].
RUS–KL (a³, No. 1863).
PSSL 14: 201.

3332. To Pëtr Iurgenson
30 Aug [1887]. Maidanovo.
RUS–KL (a³, No. 2574).
PIU 2: 67 — *PSSL* 14: 201.

3333. To Pëtr Iurgenson
30 Aug [1887]. [Maidanovo].
RUS–KL (a³, No. 2575).
PIU 2: 68 — *PSSL* 14: 201–202.

3334. To Pëtr Iurgenson
[30 Aug 1887. Maidanovo].
RUS–KL (a³, No. 2573).
PSSL 14: 202.

3335. To Nadezhda von Meck
31 Aug–9 Sep 1887. Maidanovo.
RUS–KL (a³, No. 1012).
PM 3: 494–496 — *PSSL* 14: 202–204.

3336. To Sergei Taneev
2 Sep [1887]. [Maidanovo].
RUS–Mcl (f. 880).
PT: 149 — *CTP*: 148 — *PSSL* 14: 205.

3337. To Emiliia Pavlovskaia
3 Sep 1887 [Maidanovo].
RUS–Mt (Pavlovskaia coll.).
CMS: 401 — *PSSL* 14: 205–206.

3338. To Emiliia Pavlovskaia
[3 Sep 1887. Klin] — telegram.
RUS–KL (a³, No. 282).
CMS: 400 — *PSSL* 14: 206.

3339. To Anatolii Chaikovskii
3 Sep 1887. Maidanovo.
RUS–KL (a³, No. 1402).
ZC 3: 180–181 — *PSSL* 14: 206–207.

3340. To Modest Chaikovskii
3 Sep 1887 [Maidanovo].
RUS–KL (a³, No. 1864).
ZC 3: 181 — *PSSL* 14: 207–208.

3341.   To Pëtr Iurgenson
[3 Sep 1887. Klin] — telegram.
RUS–KL (a³, No. 2556).
PSSL 14: 208.

3342.   To Avgust Gerke
[8 Sep 1887. St. Petersburg].
RUS–SPia
PSSL 14: 208.

3343.   To Aleksandra & Nikolai Hubert
9 Sep 1887. Maidanovo.
RUS–KL (a³, No. 98).
PRM 40 — *PSSL* 14: 209.

3344.   To Paul Pabst
9 Sep 1887. Maidanovo — in French.
RUS–KL (a³, No. 3350).
PSSL 14: 209–210.

3345.   To Pëtr Iurgenson
9 Sep [1887]. [Maidanovo].
RUS–KL (a³, No. 2575).
PSSL 14: 210.

3346.   To Emiliia Pavlovskaia
10 Sep 1887. Maidanovo.
RUS–Mt (Pavlovskaia coll.).
CMS: 402 — *PSSL* 14: 211.

3347.   To Emiliia Pavlovskaia
11 Sep [1887]. [Maidanovo].
RUS–Mt (Pavlovskaia coll.).
CMS: 402–403 — *PSSL* 14: 211–212.

3348.   To Iuliia Shpazhinskaia
11 Sep 1887. Maidanovo.
RUS–KL (a³, No. 2090).
CTP: 325–326 — *PSSL* 14: 212–214.

3349.   To Ivan Klimenko
[?13 Sep 1887. Moscow].
Autograph lost; MS copy in RUS–KL.
KMV: 73 — *PSSL* 14: 214.

3350.   To Aleksandr Uspenskii
13 Sep 1887. Moscow.
RUS–KL (a³, No. 414).
PSSL 14: 215.

3351.   To Anatolii Chaikovskii
14 Sep 1887. Maidanovo.
RUS–KL (a³, No. 3174).
PSSL 14: 215–216.

3352.   To Modest Chaikovskii
14 Sep 1887. Maidanovo.
RUS–KL (a³, No. 1865).
PSSL 14: 216–217.

3353.   To Pëtr Iurgenson
14 Sep 1887 [Maidanovo].
RUS–KL (a³, No. 2576).
PSSL 14: 217.

3354.   To Anatolii Chaikovskii
17 Sep [1887]. [Maidanovo].
RUS–KL (a³, No. 3175).
PSSL 14: 217–218.

3355.   To Pëtr Iurgenson
18 Sep 1887. Maidanovo.
RUS–KL (a³, No. 2577).
PSSL 14: 218.

3356.   To Pëtr Iurgenson
[18 Sep 1887. Klin] — telegram.
RUS–KL (a³, No. 2557).
PSSL 14: 218.

3357.   To Eduard Nápravník
19 Sep 1887 [Maidanovo].
RUS–SPtm (Gik 15849) [facs. in *SM* (1990), 6: 100–101].
*VP: 178–179 — *EFN: 147 — *PSSL 14: 219 — *SM* (1990), 6: 99.

3358.   To Emiliia Pavlovskaia
19 Sep 1887 [Maidanovo].
RUS–Mt (Pavlovskaia coll.).
CMS: 406–407 — *PSSL* 14: 220.

3359.   To Pëtr Iurgenson
[19 Sep 1887. Klin] — telegram.
RUS–KL (a³, No. 2555).
PSSL 14: 220.

3360.   To Nadezhda von Meck
21–25 Sep 1887. Maidanovo.
RUS–KL (a³, No. 1013).
PM 3: 497–500 — *PSSL* 14: 220–223.

3361.   To Emiliia Pavlovskaia
21 Sep 1887. Maidanovo.
RUS–Mt (Pavlovskaia coll.).
*ZC 3: 182 — *CMS*: 408–409 — *PSSL* 14: 223–224.

3362.   To Karl Al´brekht
22 Sep 1887. Moscow.
RUS–Mcm
PSSL 14: 225.

3363.   To Emiliia Pavlovskaia
22 Sep [1887]. [Maidanovo].
RUS–Mt (Pavlovskaia coll.).
CMS: 409–410 — *PSSL* 14: 226.

3364.   To Eduard Nápravník
[23 Sep 1887. Moscow] — telegram.
Autograph lost; typed copy in RUS–KL.
VP: 180 — *EFN*: 148 — *PSSL* 14: 226.

3365.   To Pëtr Iurgenson
[24 Sep 1887. Klin] — telegram.
RUS–KL (a³, No. 2544).
PSSL 14: 227.

3366.   To Eduard Nápravník
25 Sep [1887]. Maidanovo.
Autograph lost; typed copy in RUS–KL.
VP: 180–181 — *EFN*: 149 — *PSSL* 14: 227.

3367.   To Ippolit Shpazhinskii
25 Sep [1887]. Maidanovo.
RUS–Mt (Shpazhinskii coll.).
Kul´tura teatra (1921), 6: 40–42 — *Allgemeine
   Musikzeitung* (1934), 13: 158–160 [German tr.] —
   CMS: 449–451 — *PSSL* 14: 227–230.

3368.   To Pëtr Iurgenson
[25 Sep 1887. Klin] — telegram.
RUS–KL (a³, No. 2554).
PSSL 14: 230.

3369.   To Pëtr Iurgenson
25 Sep 1887 [Maidanovo].
RUS–KL (a³, No. 2578).
*ZC 3: 183 — *PIU* 2: 68 — *PSSL* 14: 230–231.

3370.   To Emiliia Pavlovskaia
26 Sep [1887]. [Maidanovo].
RUS–Mt (Pavlovskaia coll.).
CMS: 412–413 — *PSSL* 14: 231.

3371.   To Pëtr Iurgenson
[26 Sep 1887. Klin] — telegram.
RUS–KL (a³, No. 2548).
PSSL 14: 232.

3372.   To Pëtr Iurgenson
28 Sep 1887 [Maidanovo].
RUS–KL (a³, No. 2579).
PIU 2: 69 — *PSSL* 14: 232–233.

3373.   To Mikhail Ippolitov-Ivanov
1 Oct 1887. St. Petersburg.
RUS–KL (a³, No. 184).
Biulleten´ (1947), 1: 39–40 — *PSSL* 14: 233–234.

3374.   To Nadezhda von Meck
1 Oct [1887]. St. Petersburg.
RUS–KL (a³, No. 1014).
*ZC 3: 183–184 — *PM* 3: 501 — *PSSL* 14: 234–235.

3374a.   To Nikolai Chaikovskii
[1 Oct 1887. St. Petersburg] — in French and
   Russian.
RUS–SPsc (f. 834, No. 37, fol. 33).
PSSL 17: 242.

3375.   To Pëtr Iurgenson
[5 Oct 1887. St. Petersburg] — telegram.
RUS–KL (a³, No. 2545).
PSSL 14: 235.

3376.   To Pëtr Iurgenson
5 Oct 1887. St. Petersburg.
RUS–KL (a³, No. 2580).
PIU 2: 70–71 — *PSSL* 14: 236.

3377.   To Velabín Urbánek
8 Oct 1887. St. Petersburg — in French.
US–CA.
PSSL 14: 237–238.

3378.   To Aleksandra Hubert
9 Oct [1887]. St. Petersburg.
RUS–KL (a³, No. 58).
PRM 40 — *PSSL* 14: 238.

3379.   To Aleksei Sofronov
9 Oct [1887. St. Petersburg].
RUS–SPsc (f. 834, No. 27, fol. 32).
PSSL 14: 238.

3380.   To Pëtr Iurgenson
9 Oct [1887]. St. Petersburg.
RUS–KL (a³, No. 2581).
PIU 2: 71 — *PSSL* 14: 239.

3381.   To Modest Chaikovskii
10 Oct 1887 [St. Petersburg].
RUS–KL (a³, No. 1866).
PSSL 14: 240.

3382.   To Pëtr Iurgenson
10 Oct [1887]. [St. Petersburg].
RUS–KL (a³, No. 2582).
PIU 2: 72 — *PSSL* 14: 240.

3383.   To Pëtr Iurgenson
[13 Oct 1887. St. Petersburg] — telegram.
RUS–KL (a³, No. 2546).
PSSL 14: 241.

3384.   To Otto Schneider
15 Oct 1887. St. Petersburg — in German.
US–Wc.
PSSL 14: 241.

3385.   To Pëtr Iurgenson
[15 Oct 1887. St. Petersburg] — telegram.
RUS–KL (a³, No. 2552).
PSSL 14: 242.

3386.   To Pëtr Iurgenson
15 Oct 1887 [St. Petersburg].
RUS–KL (a³, No. 2583).
PIU 2: 72 — *PSSL* 14: 242–243.

3387.   To Sergei Taneev
[16 Oct 1887. St. Petersburg] — telegram.
RUS–Mcm (f. 37, No. 102).
CTP: 148 — *PSSL* 14: 243.

3388.   To Nadezhda von Meck
[19] Oct [1887] (in MS: "18 Oct"). St. Petersburg.
RUS–KL (a³, No. 1015).
ZC 3: 184 — *PM* 3: 502–503 — *PSSL* 14: 244–245.

3389.   To Aleksandra Iurgenson
26 Oct 1887 [St. Petersburg].
RUS–KL (a³, No. 471).
SM (1939), 8: 61 — *PSSL* 14: 245.

3390.   To Otto Schneider
27 Oct 1887. St. Petersburg — in German.
D–Bmuck.
PSSL 14: 246.

3391.   To Félix Mackar
28 Oct 1887. St. Petersburg — in French.
F–Pn
RdM 54 (1968), 1: 62–63 — *SM* (1970), 9: 66–67
    [Russian tr.] — *PSSL* 14: 248–249.

3392.   To Iuliia Shpazhinskaia
28 Oct [1887]. St. Petersburg.
RUS–KL (a³, No. 2091).
CTP: 327 — *PSSL* 14: 249–251.

3393.   To Nikolai Rimskii-Korsakov
30 Oct [1887]. [St. Petersburg].
RUS–SPsc (f. 640, op. 1, No. 1015, fol. 22–23).
ZC 3: 138–139 — *SM* (1945), 3: 138–139 — *RK* 7
    (1970): 53–54 — *PSSL* 14: 251–252.

3394.   To Boris Fitingof–Shel´

31 Oct 1887 [St. Petersburg].

RUS–SPsc (f. 817, No. 1, f. 182–184).

PSSL 14: 252.

3395.   To Aleksandr Ziloti

4 Nov [1887]. [St. Petersburg].

RUS–KL (a³, No. 2997).

RMG (1908), 43: 931 — *AIZ:* 82 — *PSSL* 14: 253.

3395a.   To Velabín Urbánek

6 Nov 1887. St. Petersburg — in French.

CH–B.

TGM 7 (2000): 36–38.

3396.   To Pëtr Iurgenson

[6 Nov 1887. St. Petersburg] — telegram.

RUS–KL (a³, No. 2547).

PSSL 14: 253.

3397.   To Semen Kruglikov

11 Nov [1887]. [Moscow].

RUS–KL (a³, nos. 257, 260).

PSSL 14: 254.

3398.   To Pëtr Iurgenson

[12 Nov 1887. Moscow].

RUS–KL (a³, No. 2584).

PSSL 14: 254.

3399.   To Nadezhda von Meck

13 Nov [1887]. Moscow.

RUS–KL (a³, No. 1016).

ZC 3: 186–187 — *PM* 3: 503–504 — *PSSL* 14: 255.

3400.   To Modest Chaikovskii

15 Nov 1887 [Moscow].

RUS–KL (a³, No. 1868).

ZC 3: 187–188 — *PB:* 380 — *PSSL* 14: 256 — *LF:* 379 [English tr.].

3401.   To Pavel Tret´iakov

15 Nov 1887 [Moscow].

RUS–Mgt.

A. P. Botkina, *Pavel Mikhailovich Tret´iakov v zhizni i iskusstve* (1951): 199 — *PSSL* 14: 257.

3402.   To Vladimir Shilovskii [?]

15 Nov 1887 [Moscow].

RUS–Mcm (f. 88, No. 183).

PSSL 14: 257.

3403.   To Eduard Nápravník

16 Nov 1887. Moscow.

Autograph lost; typed copy in RUS–KL.

ZC 3: 188 — *VP:* 182–183 — *EFN:* 150–151 — *PSSL* 14: 258.

3403a.   To Karl Al´brekht

17 Nov [1887]. [Moscow] — in German.

RUS–Mcm (f. 37, No. 63).

Not published.

3404.   To Leopold Auer

17 Nov 1887. Maidanovo — in French.

RUS–Mcl (f. 701).

Voprosy muzykal´no–ispolnitel´slkogo iskusstva, 2 (1958): 257–258 [Russian tr.] — L. Raaben, *L. Auer* (1962): 100–101 [Russian tr.] — *PSSL* 14: 258–259.

3405.   To Pavel Pchel´nikov

17 Nov 1887. Maidanovo.

RUS–KL (a³, No. 312).

PSSL 14: 260–261.

3406.   To Vera Timanova

17 Nov 1887. Maidanovo.

RUS–SPsc (f. 770, No. 3).

PSSL 14: 261.

3407.   To Iuliia Shpazhinskaia

17 Nov 1887. Maidanovo.

RUS–KL (a³, No. 2092).

CTP: 328–329 — *PSSL* 14: 262–263.

3408.   To Pëtr Iurgenson

17 Nov 1887. Maidanovo.

RUS–KL (a³, No. 2585).

PIU 2: 73 — *PSSL* 14: 263–264.

3409.   To Georgii Katuar

18 Nov 1887. Maidanovo.

RUS–KL (a³, No. 209).

PSSL 14: 264.

3410.   To Sergei Taneev

18 Nov [1887]. [Maidanovo].

RUS–Mcl (f. 880).

CTP: 150 — *PSSL* 14: 264–265.

3411.   To Mikhail Ippolitov-Ivanov

19 Nov 1887. Maidanovo.

RUS–KL (a³, No. 185).

Biulleten´ (1947), 1: 41–42 — *PSSL* 14: 265–266.

3412.   To Pelagea Pushechnikova

19 Nov [1887]. Maidanovo.

RUS–KL (a³, No. 3325).

PSSL 14: 266.

3413.   To Modest Chaikovskii

19 Nov [1887]. Maidanovo.

RUS–KL (a³, No. 1869).

*ZC 3: 188–189 — **PB:* 380–381 — *PSSL* 14: 267 —
   *LF: 379–380 [English tr.].

3414.   To Feodos´ia Velinskaia

20 Nov 1887 [Maidanovo].

RUS–KL (a³, No. 2994).

PSSL 14: 268.

3414a. To Mariia Klimentova–Muromtseva

[21 Nov 1887. Moscow].

RUS–KL (a³, No. 225).

PSSL 17: 243.

3415.   To Emiliia Pavlovskaia

24 Nov 1887 [Maidanovo].

RUS–Mt (Pavlovskaia coll.).

CMS: 413 — *PSSL* 14: 268.

3416.   To Pëtr Iurgenson

24 Nov [1887]. [Maidanovo].

RUS–KL (a³, No. 2586).

*ZC 3: 189 — *PIU* 2: 73 — *PSSL* 14: 269.

3417.   To Leopold Auer

[24 Nov 1887]. Maidanovo — in French.

RUS–Mcl (f. 701).

Voprosy muzykal´no–ispolnitel´skogo iskusstva, 2 (1958):
   258 [Russian tr.] — L. Raaben, *L. Auer* (1962):
   101–102 [Russian tr.] — *PSSL* 14: 269–270.

3418.   To Ivan Vsevolozhskii

25 Nov 1887. Maidanovo.

RUS–Mcl (f. 726) [facs. in I. Andronnikov, *Rasskaziy
   portrety, ocherki, stat´i*, 3-e izd. (1971): 200–201].

PSSL 14: 271–272.

3419.   To Nadezhda von Meck

25 Nov 1887. Maidanovo.

RUS–KL (a³, No. 1017).

*ZC 3: 190–191 — *PM* 3: 505–507 — *PSSL* 14: 273–
   274.

3420.   To Iuliia Shpazhinskaia

25 Nov 1887. Maidanovo.

RUS–KL (a³, No. 2093).

CTP: 329–330 — *PSSL* 14: 275–276.

3421.   To Iuliia Shpazhinskaia

27 Nov 1887. Maidanovo.

RUS–KL (a³, No. 2094).

CTP: 330–331 — *PSSL* 14: 277.

3422.   To Ivan Vsevolozhskii

28 Nov 1887. Maidanovo — in French.

RUS–SPia (f. 652, op. 1, d. 608, fol. 41).

PSSL 14: 278 [Russian tr. only].

3423.   To Leopold Auer

30 Nov 1887. Moscow — in French.

RUS–Mcl (f. 701).

Voprosy muzykal´no–ispolnitel´skogo iskusstva, 2 (1958):
   259 [Russian tr.] — L. Raaben, *L. Auer* (1962):
   102–103 [Russian tr.] — *PSSL* 14: 278.

3423a. To Aleksandra & Nikolai Hubert

30 Nov [1887]. [Moscow].

RUS–KL (a³, No. 95).

PRM 36 — *PSSL* 17: 243.

3424.   To Nadezhda von Meck

30 Nov 1887. Moscow.

RUS–KL (a³, No. 1018).

PM 3: 507–508 — *PSSL* 14: 279–280.

3425. To Georgii Katuar
[late Nov 1887. Moscow].
RUS–KL (a³, No. 210).
PSSL 14: 280.

3426. To Modest Chaikovskii
1 Dec 1887 [Maidanovo].
RUS–Mcl (f. 908).
PSSL 14: 280–281.

3427. To Pëtr Iurgenson
1 Dec 1887 [Maidanovo].
RUS–KL (a³, No. 2587).
PIU 2: 74–75 — *PSSL* 14: 281–282.

3428. To Karl Al´brekht
2 Dec [1887]. [Maidanovo].
RUS–Mcm (f. 37, No. 64).
PSSL 14: 282–283.

3429. To Iuliia Shpazhinskaia
4 Dec 1887. Maidanovo.
RUS–KL (a³, No. 2095).
CTP: 331 — *PSSL* 14: 283–284.

3430. To Félix Mackar
6 Dec 1887. Maidanovo — in French.
F–Pn
RdM 54 (1968), 1: 63–65 — *PSSL* 14: 284–286.

3431. To Karl Al´brekht
[7 Dec 1887]. Maidanovo.
RUS–Mcm (f. 37, No. 65).
CMS: 292 — *PSSL* 14: 288.

3432. To Pëtr Iurgenson
[10 Dec 1887. St. Petersburg] — telegram.
RUS–KL (a³, No. 2549).
PSSL 14: 289.

3433. To Pëtr Iurgenson
[11 Dec 1887. St. Petersburg] — telegram.
RUS–KL (a³, No. 2550).
PSSL 14: 289.

3434. To Aleksandr Glazunov
13 Dec 1887 [St. Petersburg].
Autograph lost; typed copy in RUS–KL.
SM (1945), 3: 57 — *PSSL* 14: 289–290.

3435. To Grand Duke Konstantin Konstantinovich
15 Dec 1887 [St. Petersburg].
RUS–SPil (f. 137, No. 78/5).
ZC 3: 191–192 — *PSSL* 14: 290–291.

3435a. To Pëtr Iurgenson
15/27 Dec [1887]. Berlin.
RUS–KL (a³, No. 2590).
Not published.

3436. To Anatolii Chaikovskii
17/29 Dec 1887. Berlin.
RUS–KL (a³, No. 3176).
PB: 381 — *PSSL* 14: 291–292 — *LF*: 380 [English tr.].

3437. To Pëtr Iurgenson
17/29 Dec 1887. Berlin.
RUS–KL (a³, No. 2588).
PIU 2: 75–76 — *PSSL* 14: 292–293.

3438. To Modest Chaikovskii
18/30 Dec 1887. Berlin.
RUS–KL (a³, No. 1870).
ZC 3: 199–201 ("10/18 Dec") — *PB*: 382 — *PSSL* 14: 293–294 — *LF*: 380–381 [English tr.].

3439. To Praskov´ia & Anatolii Chaikovskii
21 Dec 1887/2 Jan [1888]. Leipzig.
RUS–KL (a³, No. 3178).
PB: 384 — *PSSL* 14: 294–295 — *LF*: 382–383 [English tr.].

3440. To Modest Chaikovskii
21 Dec 1887/2 Jan [1888]. Leipzig.
RUS–KL (a³, No. 1871).
ZC 3: 201–203 — *PB*: 383–384 — *PSSL* 14: 296–297 — *LF*: 381–382 [English tr.].

3441.   To Otto Schneider

[21 Dec 1887]/2 Jan 1888. Leipzig — in German.

D–BShenn

PSSL 14: 297.

3442.   To Pëtr Iurgenson

24–25 Dec 1887/5–6 Jan 1888. Leipzig.

RUS–KL (a³, No. 2589).

*ZC 3: 203–204 — *PIU* 2: 76–78 — *PSSL* 14: 298–
299.

3443.   To Aleksandr Ziloti

[27 Dec 1887]/8 Jan [1888] (in MS: "8 Jan 1888").
Berlin.

RUS–KL (a³, No. 2998).

*RMG (1908), 43: 931–942 — *AIZ:* 82–84 — *PSSL*
14: 300–301.

3444.   To Adol´f Brodskii

[28 Dec 1887]/9 Jan [1888]. [Berlin].

GB–Mcm

PSSL 14: 302.

3445.   To Nadezhda von Meck

[28] Dec 1887/9 Jan 1888 (in MS: "29 Dec"). Berlin.

RUS–KL (a³, No. 1019).

PM 3: 509–510 — *PSSL* 14: 302–303.

**3446.   To   Grand   Duke   Konstantin
Konstantinovich**

[28] Dec 1887/9 Jan 1888 (in MS: "29 Dec"). Berlin.

RUS–SPil (f. 137, No. 78/6).

PSSL 14: 304–305.

3447.   To Anatolii Chaikovskii

[28] Dec 1887/9 Jan [1888] (in MS: "29 Dec")
[Berlin].

RUS–KL (a³, No. 1400).

PB: 384–385 — *PSSL* 14: 305–306 — *LF*: 383–384
[English tr.].

3448.   To Pëtr Iurgenson

[28 Dec 1887]/9 Jan 1888. Berlin.

RUS–KL (a³, No. 2591).

*ZC 3: 204 ("23 Dec 1887") — *PIU* 2: 78 — *PSSL*
14: 307–308.

3449.   To Aleksandra & Nikolai Hubert

30 Dec 1887/11 Jan 1888. Lubeck.

RUS–KL (a³, No. 99).

PRM 40–42 — *PSSL* 14: 308–309.

3450.   To Nadezhda von Meck

30 Dec 1887/11 [Jan] 1888. Lubeck.

RUS–KL (a³, No. 1020).

PM 3: 510–511 — *PSSL* 14: 309–310.

3451.   To Aleksei Sofronov

30 Dec 1887/11 Jan 1888. Lubeck.

RUS–SPsc (f. 834, No. 27, fol. 19–20).

PSSL 14: 311.

**3452.   To Praskov´ia & Anatolii
Chaikovskii**

30 Dec 1887/11 Jan 1888–10/22 Jan 1888. Lubeck–
Hamburg.

RUS–KL (a³, No. 3177).

*PB: 387–388 — *PSSL* 14: 312–314 — **LF*: 386–387
[English tr.].

3453.   To Modest Chaikovskii

30 Dec 1887/11 Jan 1888–6/18 Jan 1888. Lubeck–
Hamburg.

RUS–KL (a³, No. 1872).

*ZC 3: 205–207 — *PB*: 385–387 — *PSSL* 14: 314–
316 — **LF*: 384–385 [English tr.].

3454.   To Iuliia Shpazhinskaia

31 Dec 1887/12 Jan 1888. Lubeck.

RUS–KL (a³, No. 2095).

CTP: 331–332 — *PSSL* 14: 317–318.

3455.   To Sergei Taneev

[1887. Moscow].

RUS–Mcl (f. 880).

CTP: 151 — *PSSL* 14: 318.

1888

3456.   To Nikolai Kashkin

1/13–9/21 Jan 1888. Lubeck–Hamburg.

RUS–KL (a³, No. 216).

*Teatr (25 Oct 1908) — *PSSL* 14: 319–320.

3457. To Vera Tret´iakova

1/13 Jan 1888. Lubeck.

RUS–Mgt

AIZ: 410–411 — *PSSL* 14: 321–322.

3458. To Ivan Vsevolozhskii

[2/14 Jan 1888. Lubeck] — telegram; in French.

RUS–SPia

PSSL 14: 322.

3459. To Ivan Vsevolozhskii

2/14 Jan 1888. Lubeck.

RUS–SPia (f. 652, op. 1, d. 608, fol. 42–43).

PSSL 14: 323.

3460. To Nadezhda von Meck

2/14–10/22 Jan 1888. Lubeck–Hamburg.

RUS–KL (a³, No. 1021).

PM 3: 512–513 — *PSSL* 14: 324–325.

3461. To Vladimir Pogozhev

2/14 Jan 1888. Lubeck.

RUS–KL (a³, No. 2873).

VP: 39–41 — *PSSL* 14: 325–326.

3462. To Félix Mackar

[6]/18 Jan 1888. Hamburg — in French.

F–Pn

RdM 54 (1968), 1: 66 — *PSSL* 14: 327–328.

3463. To Aleksandr Ziloti

9/21 Jan 1888. Hamburg.

RUS–KL (a³, No. 2999).

RMG (1908), 43: 932 ("21 Jan/4 Feb") — *AIZ*: 85 —
   PSSL 14: 329.

3464. To Modest Chaikovskii

[9/21 Jan 1888. Hamburg] — telegram; in French.

RUS–KL (a³, No. 2045).

PSSL 14: 330.

3465. To Aleksandr Ziloti

[10/22 Jan 1888. Hamburg].

RUS–KL (a³, No. 3000).

AIZ: 85 — *PSSL* 14: 330.

3465a. To Josef Sittard

[10]/22 Jan 1888. Hamburg — in German.

D–Tsiedentopf

H. Siedentopf, *Musiker der Spätromantik* (1979): 77 —
   PSSL 17: 244.

3466. To Nikolai Kashkin

[10]/22 Jan [1888]. Hamburg.

RUS–KL (a³, No. 217).

Teatr (25 Oct 1908) — *PSSL* 14: 330.

3467. To Edouard Colonne

[10]/22 Jan 1888 [Hamburg] — in French.

US–CAM

PSSL 14: 331.

3468. To Modest Chaikovskii

10/22 [Jan 1888]. Hamburg.

RUS–KL (a³, No. 1873).

ZC 3: 207–208 — PB: 388 — PSSL 14: 331–332 —
   LF: 387 [English tr.].

3469. To Marie von Bülow

[12]/24 Jan 1888 [Magdeburg] — in French.

GB–Lbl (Eg. 3246, ff. 1–2b) [facs. in R. F. Sharp,
   Makers of Music (1913): 238/239].

PSSL 14: 332–333.

3470. To Aleksandra & Nikolai Hubert

12/24 Jan 1888. Magdeburg.

RUS–KL (a³, No. 100).

PRM 42–43 — *PSSL* 14: 334.

3471. To Vladimir Nápravník

12/24 Jan 1888. Magdeburg.

Autograph lost; typed copy in RUS–KL.

ZC 3: 211–212 — EFN: 190–191 — PSSL 14: 335–
   336.

3472. To Modest Chaikovskii

12/24–15/27 Jan [1888]. Magdeburg–Leipzig.

RUS–KL (a³, No. 1874).

ZC 3: 210–211 — PB: 389–390 — PSSL 14: 336–
   337 — *LF*: 388 [English tr.].

3473. To Pëtr Iurgenson

13/25 Jan [1888]. Magdeburg.

RUS–KL (a³, No. 2593).

*ZC 3: 212 — *PIU 2: 81 — PSSL* 14: 338–339.

3474. To Félix Mackar

[14]/26 Jan [1888]. Leipzig — in French.

F–Pn

RdM 54 (1968), 1: 67 — *SM* (1970), 9: 67 [Russian tr.] — *PSSL* 14: 339–340.

3475. To Edouard Colonne

[14]/26 Jan [1888]. Leipzig — in French.

Autograph lost; photocopy in RUS–KL.

PSSL 14: 341–342.

3476. To Aleksei Sofronov

15/27 Jan 1888. Leipzig.

RUS–SPsc (f. 834, No. 27, fol. 21–22).

PSSL 14: 342–343.

3477. To Anatolii Chaikovskii

20 Jan/1 Feb 1888. Leipzig.

RUS–KL (a³, No. 3179).

PSSL 14: 343–344.

3478. To Modest Chaikovskii

20 Jan/1 Feb 1888. Leipzig.

RUS–KL (a³, No. 1875).

ZC 3: 212–213 — PB: 390 — PSSL 14: 345 — *LF: 389 [English tr.].

3479. To Iuliia Shpazhinskaia

20 Jan/1 Feb 1888. Leipzig.

RUS–KL (a³, No. 2097).

CTP: 332–334 — *PSSL* 14: 346–348.

3480. To Pëtr Iurgenson

20 Jan/1 Feb–[24] Jan/5 Feb 1888. Leipzig-Berlin.

RUS–KL (a³, No. 2594).

ZC 3: 213–214 — PIU 2: 83–85 — PSSL 14: 348–350.

3481. To Nikolai Hubert

[23 Jan]/4 Feb 1888. Berlin.

RUS–KL (a³, No. 111).

PRM 43–44 — *PSSL* 14: 350–351.

3482. To Nadezhda von Meck

23 Jan/4 Feb 1888 [Berlin].

RUS–KL (a³, No. 1022).

PM 3: 515–516 — *PSSL* 14: 351–352.

3483. To Aleksei Sofronov

23 Jan/5 Feb 1888. Berlin

RUS–SPsc (f. 834, No. 27, fol. 23–24).

PSSL 14: 353.

3484. To Modest Chaikovskii

[23 Jan]/4 Feb 1888. Berlin.

RUS–KL (a³, No. 1876).

ZC 3: 214 — PB: 391 — PSSL 14: 353–354 — *LF: 390 [English tr.].

3485. To Francesco Berger

[25 Jan]/6 Feb 1888. Berlin — in French.

GB–Lps

PSSL 14: 354–355.

3486. To Aleksandra & Nikolai Hubert

[28 Jan]/9 Feb 1888 [Berlin].

RUS–KL (a³, No. 101).

PRM 44–45 — *PSSL* 14: 356.

3487. To Nadezhda von Meck

[30 Jan]/11 Feb [1888]. Leipzig.

RUS–KL (a³, No. 1024).

ZC 3: 215–216 — PM 3: 516–517 — PSSL 14: 357.

3488. To Praskov´ia Chaikovskaia

[30 Jan]/11 Feb 1888. Leipzig.

RUS–KL (a³, No. 3282).

ZC 3: 217 — PB: 391–392 — PSSL 14: 358 — *LF: 390–391 [English tr.].

3489. To Pëtr Iurgenson

[30 Jan/11 Feb 1887. Leipzig] — telegram; in German.

RUS–KL (a³, No. 2635).

PSSL 14: 359.

3490. To Modest Chaikovskii

2/14 Feb [1888]. Prague.

RUS–KL (a³, No. 1877).

PB: 392–393 — *PSSL* 14: 359–360 — *LF*: 392 [English tr.].

3491. To Aleksei Sofronov

4/16 Feb 1888. Prague.

RUS–SPsc (f. 834, No. 27, fol. 25–26).

PSSL 14: 361.

3492. To Pëtr Iurgenson

[4/16 Feb 1888. Prague].

RUS–KL (a³, No. 2595).

PIU 2: 85 — *PSSL* 14: 361–362.

3493. To Francesco Berger

[8]/20 Feb 1888. Prague — in German.

GB–Lps

PSSL 14: 362.

3494. To Nadezhda von Meck

10/22 Feb [1888]. Prague.

RUS–KL (a³, No. 1023).

PM 3: 517–518 — *PSSL* 14: 363–364.

3495. To Praskov´ia & Anatolii Chaikovskii

[10]/22 Feb 1888. Prague.

RUS–KL (a³, No. 3180).

ZC 3: 224 — *PB*: 394 — *PSSL* 14: 364–365 — *LF*: 393 [English tr.].

3496. To Modest Chaikovskii

10/22 Feb [1888]. Prague.

RUS–KL (a³, No. 1878).

PB: 393–394 — *PSSL* 14: 365–366 — *LF*: 393–394 [English tr.].

3497. To Iuliia Shpazhinskaia

14/26 Feb 1888. Paris.

RUS–KL (a³, No. 2098).

CTP: 334 — *PSSL* 14: 366–367.

3498. To Nadezhda von Meck

15/27 Feb 1888. Paris.

RUS–KL (a³, No. 1025).

PM 3: 519–520 — *PSSL* 14: 367–368.

3499. To Edvard Grieg

[19 Feb]/2 Mar 1888. Paris — in German.

N–Bo

SM (1940), 5–6: 145–147 [Russian tr.] — O. Levasheva, *Edvard Grig* (1962): 746–747 [Russian tr.] — *PSSL* 14: 368–369.

3500. To Nikolai Konradi

19 Feb/2 Mar [1888]. [Paris].

Autograph lost; MS copy in RUS–KL.

CTP: 276 — *PSSL* 14: 370.

3501. To Anatolii Chaikovskii

[19 Feb]/2 Mar 1888. Paris.

RUS–KL (a³, No. 3181).

PB: 394–395 — *PSSL* 14: 371 — *LF*: 394–395 [English tr.].

3502. To Modest Chaikovskii

[22 Feb/5 Mar 1888. Paris] — telegram; in French.

RUS–KL (a³, No. 2046).

PSSL 14: 372.

3503. To Pëtr Iurgenson

[22 Feb/5 Mar 1888. Paris] — telegram; in French.

RUS–KL (a³, No. 2633).

PSSL 14: 372.

3504. To Louis Diémer

[23 Feb]/6 Mar [1888]. [Paris] — in French.

D–LEmi

PSSL 14: 372.

3505. To Vladimir Nápravník

[23 Feb]/6 Mar 1888. Paris.

Autograph lost; MS copy in RUS–KL.

EFN: 191 — *PSSL* 14: 373.

3506. To Francesco Berger

[24 Feb]/7 Mar 1888. Paris — in German.

Autograph lost [facs. in E. Evans, *Tschaikovsky* (1906): 120 — E. Garden, *Tchaikovsky* (1993): 86/87 [No. 8]].

Muscial Times (1 Jan 1927): 39 — *PSSL* 14: 374.

3507. To Modest Chaikovskii

[25 Feb]/8 Mar 1888. Paris.

RUS–KL (a³, No. 1879).

PB: 395–396 — *PSSL* 14: 374–376 — *LF*: 395–396 [English tr.].

3508. To Marie Benardaky

[1]/13 Mar 1888. Paris.

US–STu

PSSL 14: 376.

3509.   To Varvara Zarudnaia

1/13 Mar 1888 [Paris].

RUS–Mcm (f. 2, No. 5113).

Iskusstvo, 3 (1927), 4: 150 — *PSSL* 14: 377.

3510.   To Aleksei Sofronov

1/13 Mar 1888 [Paris].

RUS–SPsc (f. 834, No. 27, fol. 27–28).

PSSL 14: 378.

3511.   To Modest Chaikovskii

1/13 Mar [1888]. [Paris].

RUS–KL (a³, No. 1880).

PB: 396–397 — *PSSL* 14: 378 — *LF*: 396 [English tr.].

3512.   To Pëtr Iurgenson

1/13 Mar 1888 [Paris].

RUS–KL (a³, No. 2596).

ZC 3: 233 — *PIU* 2: 85–86 — *PSSL* 14: 379.

3513.   To Pëtr Iurgenson

[5/17 Mar 1888. Paris] — telegram; in French.

RUS–KL (a³, No. 2634).

PSSL 14: 380.

3514.   To Émil Blavet

[6]/18 Mar 1888 [Paris] — in French.

F–Pn.

RdM 54 (1968), 1: 88 — *PSSL* 14: 380.

3515.   To Nikolai Rimskii-Korsakov

8/20 Mar 1888. London.

RUS–SPsc (f. 640, op. 1, No. 1015, fol. 24–27).

ZC 3: 234–236 — *SM* (1945), 3: 139–140 — *RK* 7 (1970): 55–56 — *PSSL* 14: 381–383.

3516.   To Anatolii Chaikovskii

8/20 Mar [1888]. London.

RUS–KL (a³, No. 3183).

PSSL 14: 383.

3517.   To Modest Chaikovskii

8/20 Mar [1888]. London.

RUS–KL (a³, No. 1881).

PB: 397–398 — *PSSL* 14: 384 — *LF*: 396–397 [English tr.].

3518.   To Pëtr Iurgenson

8/20 Mar [1888]. London.

RUS–KL (a³, No. 2597).

PIU 2: 86 — *PSSL* 14: 384–385.

3519.   To Nadezhda von Meck

11/23 Mar 1888. London.

RUS–KL (a³, No. 1026).

ZC 3: 233–234 — *PM* 3: 521–522 — *PSSL* 14: 385–386.

3520.   To Modest Chaikovskii

[11/23 Mar 1888. London] — telegram; in French.

RUS–KL (a³, No. 2047).

PSSL 14: 386.

3521.   To Aleksei Sofronov

[12]/24 Mar [1888]. [London].

RUS–SPsc (f. 834, No. 27, fol. 37).

PSSL 14: 387.

3522.   To Anatolii Chaikovskii

12/24 Mar [1888]. London.

RUS–KL (a³, No. 3184).

PSSL 14: 387.

3523.   To Modest Chaikovskii

12/24 Mar [1888]. [London].

RUS–KL (a³, No. 1883).

PB: 398 — *PSSL* 14: 388 — *LF*: 397 [English tr.].

3524.   To Iuliia Shpazhinskaia

[12]/24 Mar [1888]. London.

RUS–KL (a³, No. 2099).

CTP: 334–335 — *PSSL* 14: 388.

3525.   To Pëtr Iurgenson

12/24 Mar 1888. London.

RUS–KL (a³, No. 2598).

PIU 2: 86–87 — *PSSL* 14: 389.

3526.   To Adol´f Brodskii

[15]/27 Mar 1888. Vienna.

GB–Mcm.

PSSL 14: 389.

3527. To Edvard Válečka

[15]/27 Mar 1888. Vienna.

CZ–Ps [facs. in M. Očadlik, *Pražské dopisy P. I. Čajkovského* (1949)].

Stěpánek (1952): 128 [Czech tr.] — *Puti razvitiia i vzaimosviazi russkogo i chekhoslovatskogo iskusstva* (1970): 180 — *PSSL* 14: 390.

3528. To Aleksandra Hubert

[15]/27 Mar 1888. Vienna.

RUS–KL (a³, No. 59).

PRM 45 — *PSSL* 14: 391.

3529. To Antonin Dvořák

[15]/27 Mar 1888. Vienna — in German.

CZ–ZL.

Šourek (1951): 102 [Czech tr.] — Stěpánek (1952): 127 [Czech tr.] — Šourek (1954) [German and English trs]. — *SM* (1964), 4: 73 — *Dvorzhak v pis´makh i vospominaniiakh* (1964): 83–84 [Russian tr.] — *PSSL* 14: 391–392.

3529a. To Konstantin Koninskii

[15/27 Mar 1888]. Vienna.

Autograph lost.

RMG (9 Jan 1899), 2: 51.

3530. To Adolf Patera

[15]/27 Mar 1888. Vienna.

CZ–Ps.

Stěpánek (1952): 125–126 [Czech tr.] — *PSSL* 14: 393.

3531. To Modest Chaikovskii

15/27 Mar [1888]. Vienna.

RUS–KL (a³, No. 1881).

PB: 398–399 — *PSSL* 14: 394 — *LF*: 397–398 [English tr.].

3532. To Pëtr Iurgenson

15/27 Mar [1888]. [Vienna].

RUS–KL (a³, No. 2599).

PSSL 14: 394.

3533. To Nadezhda von Meck

22 Mar 1888. Taganrog.

RUS–KL (a³, No. 1027).

ZC 3: 237 — PM 3: 523–524 — PSSL 14: 395.

3534. To Modest Chaikovskii

22 Mar 1888. Taganrog.

RUS–KL (a³, No. 1882).

ZC 3: 237–238 — PB: 399–400 — PSSL 14: 396 — *LF*: 398–399 [English tr.].

3535. To Pëtr Iurgenson

27 Mar 1888 [Tiflis].

RUS–KL (a³, No. 2600).

PSSL 14: 396.

3536. To Emiliia Pavlovskaia

28 Mar 1888. Tiflis.

RUS–Mt (Pavlovskaia coll.).

CMS: 416 — *PSSL* 14: 397.

3537. To Vladimir Pogozhev

28 Mar 1888. Tiflis.

RUS–KL (a³, No. 2874).

VP: 41–43 — *PSSL* 14: 397–398.

3538. To Aleksei Sofronov

28 Mar 1888 [Tiflis].

RUS–SPsc (f. 834, No. 27, fol. 29–30).

PSSL 14: 399.

3539. To Modest Chaikovskii

28 Mar 1888. Tiflis.

RUS–KL (a³, No. 1885).

*ZC 3: 238–239 — PB: 399–400 — *LF*: 399–400 [English tr.].

3540. To Pëtr Iurgenson

28 Mar 1888. Tiflis.

RUS–KL (a³, No. 2601).

ZC 3: 239 — PIU 2: 87–88 — PSSL 14: 401–402.

3541. To Nadezhda von Meck

29 Mar 1888. Tiflis.

RUS–KL (a³, No. 1028).

PM 3: 524–525 — PSSL 14: 402–404.

3542. To Iuliia Shpazhinskaia

29 Mar 1888. Tiflis.

RUS–KL (a³, No. 2100).

CTP: 335–336 — *PSSL* 14: 404–405.

3543.   To Mikhail Ippolitov-Ivanov

4 Apr [1888]. [Tiflis].

RUS–Mcm (f. 2, No. 5119).

Iskusstvo, 3 (1927), 4: 151 — *Biulleten´* (1947), 1: 42–43 — *PSSL* 14: 405.

3544.   To Modest Chaikovskii

7 Apr 1888 [Tiflis].

RUS–KL (a³, No. 1886).

PSSL 14: 406.

3545.   To Pëtr Iurgenson

7 Apr 1888 [Tiflis].

RUS–KL (a³, No. 2602).

PIU 2: 90 — *PSSL* 14: 406–407.

3546.   To Anatolii Brandukov

13 Apr 1888 [Tiflis].

RUS–KL (a³, No. 24).

PSSL 14: 407.

3547.   To Nadezhda von Meck

13 Apr 1888. Tiflis.

RUS–KL (a³, No. 1029).

PM 3: 526–527 — *PSSL* 14: 407–409.

3548.   To Anatolii Chaikovskii

[16 Apr 1888. Vladikavkaz] — telegram.

RUS–KL (a³, No. 3185).

PSSL 14: 409.

3549.   To Praskov´ia & Anatolii Chaikovskii

21 Apr [1888]. Moscow.

RUS–KL (a³, No. 3186).

PSSL 14: 409–410.

3550.   To Ippolit Shpazhinskii

[mid Apr 1888. Moscow].

RUS–KL (a³, No. 464) [fragment].

*CMS: 453–454 — *PSSL* 14: 410–411.

3551.   To Iuliia Shpazhinskaia

[23] Apr 1888 (in MS: "24 Apr"). Frolovskoe.

RUS–KL (a³, No. 2101).

CTP: 336 ("24 Apr") — *PSSL* 14: 411–412.

3552.   To Edvard Grieg

24 Apr/6 May 1888. Frolovskoe — in German.

N–Bo

SM (1940), 5–6: 147 — O. Levasheva, *Edvard Grig* (1962): 749 [Russian tr.] — *PSSL* 14: 413–414.

3553.   To Nadezhda von Meck

24 Apr 1888. Frolovskoe.

RUS–KL (a³, No. 1030).

*ZC 3: 240 — *PM* 3: 528–529 — *PSSL* 14: 415–416.

3554.   To Vladimir Pogozhev

25 Apr 1888. Frolovskoe.

RUS–KL (a³, No. 2875).

PSSL 14: 417.

3555.   To Anatolii Chaikovskii

25 Apr 1888. Frolovskoe.

RUS–KL (a³, No. 3187).

*PB: 401 — *PSSL* 14: 417–418 — *LF: 401 [English tr.].

3556.   To Pëtr Iurgenson

25 Apr 1888. Frolovskoe.

RUS–KL (a³, No. 2603).

PIU 2: 90–91 — *PSSL* 14: 419.

3557.   To Félix Mackar

27 Apr 1888. Frolovskoe — in French.

F–Pn

RdM 54 (1968), 1: 58–69 — *SM* (1970), 9: 67–68 [Russian tr.] — *PSSL* 14: 420–421.

3558.   To Akhilles Alferaki

28 Apr 1888. Frolovskoe.

Autograph lost; MS copy in RUS–KL.

PSSL 14: 422.

3559.   To Aleksandra Hubert

28 Apr 1888 [Frolovskoe].

RUS–KL (a³, No. 60).

PRM 46 — *PSSL* 14: 422–423.

3560.   To Vladimir Pogozhev

28 Apr 1888. Frolovskoe.

RUS–KL (a³, No. 2876).

PSSL 14: 423.

3561. To Nadezhda von Meck

9 May 1888. Frolovskoe.

RUS–KL (a³, No. 1031).

PM 3: 530–531 — *PSSL* 14: 423–424.

3562. To Praskov´ia Chaikovskaia

9 May 1888. Frolovskoe.

RUS–KL (a³, No. 3188).

PSSL 14: 425.

3563. To Iuliia Shpazhinskaia

9 May 1888. Frolovskoe.

RUS–KL (a³, No. 2102).

CTP: 337 — *PSSL* 14: 426–427.

3563a. To Marie Benardaky

10 May 1888 [Frolovskoe].

US–Wc (ML31.H43i.C5).

PSSL 17: 245–246.

3563b. To Léonce Détroyat

10 May 1888. Frolovskoe — in French.

Autograph auctioned in Paris, 1992.

*A. Lischké, *Piotr Ilyitch Tchaikovsky* (1993): 542.

3564. To Grand Duke Konstantin Konstantinovich

10 May 1888. Frolovskoe.

RUS–SPil (f. 137, No. 78/7).

PSSL 14: 428.

3565. To Pëtr Iurgenson

10 May [1888]. Frolovskoe.

RUS–KL (a³, No. 2604).

PIU 2: 91 — *PSSL* 14: 428–429.

3566. To Ivan Vsevolozhskii

11 May 1888 [Frolovskoe].

RUS–KL (a³, No. 31).

PSSL 14: 429–430.

3567. To Sergei Taneev

[11 May 1888. Klin] — telegram.

RUS–KL (a³, No. 396).

CTP: 151 — *PSSL* 14: 430 ·

3568. To Modest Chaikovskii

15 May 1888 [Frolovskoe].

RUS–KL (a³, No. 1887).

ZC 3: 241 — *PB*: 401–402 — *PSSL* 14: 430–431 — *LF*: 401–402 [English tr.].

3569. To Desirée Artôt–Padilla

16 May 1888 [Frolovskoe] (in MS: "Klin") — in French.

RUS–Mcl (f. 905).

CTP: 372–373 — *PSSL* 14: 431–432.

3570. To Pëtr Iurgenson

16 May [1888]. Frolovskoe.

RUS–KL (a³, No. 2605).

PIU 2: 91 — *PSSL* 14: 433.

3571. To Varvara Zarudnaia

18 May 1888 [Frolovskoe].

RUS–Mcm (f. 2, No. 5114).

ZC 3: 241–242 — *PSSL* 14: 434–435.

3572. To Nadezhda von Meck

18 May 1888. Frolovskoe.

RUS–KL (a³, No. 1032).

PM 3: 532 — *PSSL* 14: 435–436.

3573. To Modest Chaikovskii

19 May 1888 [Frolovskoe].

RUS–KL (a³, No. 1888).

PSSL 14: 436.

3574. To Grand Duke Konstantin Konstantinovich

20 May 1888. Frolovskoe.

RUS–SPil (f. 137, No. 78/8).

ZC 3: 242–243 — *PSSL* 14: 437–438.

3575. To Ol´ga Chaikovskaia

20 May 1888 [Frolovskoe].

RUS–SPsc (f. 834, No. 31, fol. 3).

PSSL 14: 438.

3575a. To Pëtr Iurgenson

[late May 1888. Moscow].

RUS–KL (a³, No. 2534).

PSSL 17: 246.

3576.   To Nadezhda von Meck
24 May [1888]. Moscow.
RUS–KL (a³, No. 1033).
PM 3: 533–534 — *PSSL* 14: 438–439.

3577.   To Sergei Taneev
[late May 1888. Moscow].
RUS–Mcl (f. 880).
CTP: 162 ("May 1889") — *PSSL* 14: 440.

3578.   To   Grand   Duke   Konstantin Konstantinovich
30 May 1888. Frolovskoe.
RUS–SPil (f. 137, No. 78/9).
ZC 3: 244–246 — *PSSL* 14: 440–442.

3579.   To Praskov´ia Chaikovskaia
30 May 1888. Frolovskoe.
RUS–KL (a³, No. 3283).
PSSL 14: 443.

3580.   To Iuliia Shpazhinskaia
30 May 1888. Frolovskoe.
RUS–KL (a³, No. 2103).
CTP: 338 — *PSSL* 14: 443–444.

3581.   To Pëtr Iurgenson
30 [May 1888] (in MS: "30 Jun") [Frolovskoe].
RUS–KL (a³, No. 2609).
PIU 2: 91–92 — *PSSL* 14: 445.

3582.   To Nadezhda von Meck
1 Jun [1888]. Frolovskoe.
RUS–KL (a³, No. 1034).
ZC 3: 247 — *PM* 3: 534–535 — *PSSL* 14: 445–446.

3583.   To Pëtr Iurgenson
1 Jun 1888 [Frolovskoe].
RUS–KL (a³, No. 2607).
PIU 2: 92 — *PSSL* 14: 446–447.

3584.   To Nadezhda von Meck
4 Jun 1888. Frolovskoe.
RUS–KL (a³, No. 1035).
PM 3: 536–537 — *PSSL* 14: 448.

3585.   To Modest Chaikovskii
6 Jun 1888. Frolovskoe.
RUS–Mcl (f. 908).
PSSL 14: 449–450.

3586.   To Praskov´ia Chaikovskaia
6 Jun 1888. Frolovskoe.
RUS–KL (a³, No. 3284).
PSSL 14: 450–451.

3587.   To Vladimir Nápravník
7 Jun 1888. Frolovskoe.
Autograph lost; MS copy in RUS–KL.
EFN: 192 — *PSSL* 14: 451–452.

3587a.   To Julius Laube
10 Jun 1888 [Frolovskoe] (in MS: "Klin") — in German.
D–WIaxtmann [facs. of p. 1 in *ČS* 3 (1998): 218].
ČS 3 (1998): 218–222.

3588.   To Nadezhda von Meck
10 Jun 1888. Frolovskoe.
RUS–KL (a³, No. 1036).
ZC 3: 247–248 — *PM* 3: 538 — *PSSL* 14: 452.

3589.   To   Grand   Duke   Konstantin Konstantinovich
11 Jun 1888. Frolovskoe.
RUS–SPil (f. 137, No. 78/10).
ZC 3: 248–250 — *PSSL* 14: 453–454.

3590.   To Iuliia Shpazhinskaia
13 Jun [1888]. Frolovskoe.
RUS–KL (a³, No. 2104).
CTP: 338–339 — *PSSL* 14: 455–456.

3591.   To Edouard Colonne
14 Jun 1888 [Frolovskoe] — in French.
F–P; photocopy in RUS–KL.
PSSL 14: 456–458.

3592.   To Anna Merkling
14 Jun 1888. Frolovskoe.
Autograph lost; MS copy in RUS–KL.
CTP: 232 — *PSSL* 14: 459–460.

3593. To Anatolii Chaikovskii

14 Jun 1888 [Frolovskoe].

RUS–KL (a³, No. 3192).

PSSL 14: 460.

3953a. To Anatolii Chaikovskii

14 Jun [1888]. Frolovskoe.

RUS–KL (a³, No. 3190).

Not published.

3594. To Ol´ga Chaikovskaia

14 Jun 1888. Frolovskoe.

RUS–SPsc (f. 834, No. 31, fol. 4–5).

PSSL 14: 461.

3595. To Varvara Zarudnaia & Mikhail Ippolitov-Ivanov

17 Jun 1888. Frolovskoe.

RUS–Mcm (f. 2, No. 5115).

ZC 3: 250 — *Iskusstvo*, 3 (1927), 4: 152 — *Biulleten´* (1947), 1: 45–46 — *PSSL* 14: 462–463.

3596. To Vadim Peresleni

17 Jun [1888]. Frolovskoe.

RUS–KL (a³, No. 289).

PSSL 14: 463.

3597. To Modest Chaikovskii

17 Jun [1888]. Frolovskoe.

RUS–KL (a³, No. 1889).

*PB: 402–403 — *PSSL* 14: 463–464 — *LF*: 402–403 [English tr.].

3598. To Pëtr Iurgenson

18 Jun [1888]. [Frolovskoe] — note on visiting card.

RUS–KL (a³, No. 2608).

PSSL 14: 465.

3598a. To Léonce Détroyat

20 Jun 1888 [Frolovskoe] (in MS: "Klin") — in French.

F–Plauwe [facs. of last page in *ČS* 3 (1998): 243].

ČS 3 (1998): 239–248.

3599. To Georgii Kartsov

22 Jun 1888. Frolovskoe.

RUS–Mcl (f. 980).

PSSL 14: 465–466.

3600. To Nadezhda von Meck

22 Jun 1888. Frolovskoe.

RUS–KL (a³, No. 1037).

ZC 3: 250–251 — *PM* 3: 538–539 — *PSSL* 14: 466–467.

3601. To Anna Merkling

22 Jun 1888. Frolovskoe.

Autograph lost; MS copy in RUS–KL.

CTP: 232 — *PSSL* 14: 468.

3602. To Modest Chaikovskii

26 Jun [1888]. Moscow.

RUS–KL (a³, No. 1890).

PB: 403–404 — *PSSL* 14: 468–469 — *LF*: 403–404 [English tr.].

3603. To Ludvik Kuba

27 Jun 1888. Frolovskoe.

CZ–POm [facs. in *Hudebni rozhledy* (1953), 16: 761].

Hudebni rozhledy (1953), 16: 760 [Czech tr.] — *Slaviane* (1956), 10: 50 — I. Belza, *Iz istorii russko-cheshskikh sviazei* (1956): 12–13 — *PSSL* 14: 469–470.

3604. To Vladimir Nápravník

27 Jun 1888. Frolovskoe.

Autograph lost; MS copy in RUS–KL.

EFN: 192–194 — *PSSL* 14: 471–472.

3605. To Nadezhda von Meck

1 Jul 1888. Frolovskoe.

RUS–KL (a³, No. 1038).

ZC 3: 254–256 ("17 Jul") — *PM* 3: 541–542 — *PSSL* 14: 472–474.

3606. To Anna Merkling

1 Jul 1888. Frolovskoe.

Autograph lost; MS copy in RUS–KL.

CTP: 233 — *PSSL* 14: 474–475.

3607. To Anatolii Chaikovskii

1 Jul 1888. Frolovskoe.

RUS–KL (a³, No. 3191).

PB: 404 — *PSSL* 14: 475–476 — *LF*: 404 [English tr.].

3608.   To Pëtr Iurgenson
1 Jul [1888]. [Frolovskoe].
RUS–KL (a³, No. 2610).
PIU 2: 93 — *PSSL* 14: 476.

3609.   To Iuliia Shpazhinskaia
6 Jul 1888. Moscow.
RUS–KL (a³, No. 2105).
CTP: 339–340 — *PSSL* 14: 477.

3610.   To Modest Chaikovskii
7 Jul 1888. St. Petersburg.
RUS–KL (a³, No. 1891).
PSSL 14: 478.

3610a.   [To an unidentified correspondent]
[11 Jul 1888. St. Petersburg].
RUS–KL (a³, No. 2989).
PSSL 17: 247.

3611.   To Aleksandra & Nikolai Hubert
12 Jul 1888. Frolovskoe.
RUS–KL (a³, No. 102).
PRM 46–48 — *PSSL* 14: 479–480.

3612.   To Varvara Zarudnaia & Mikhail Ippolitov-Ivanov
12 Jul 1888. Frolovskoe.
RUS–KL (a³, No. 186).
Biulleten´ (1947), 1: 48–49 — *PSSL* 14: 480–481.

3613.   To Nadezhda von Meck
12 Jul 1888. Frolovskoe.
RUS–KL (a³, No. 1039).
PM 3: 543–544 — *PSSL* 14: 482.

3614.   To Vladimir Nápravník
12 Jul 1888 [Frolovskoe].
Autograph lost; typed copy in RUS–KL.
EFN: 194 — *PSSL* 14: 483.

3615.   To Anatolii Chaikovskii
12 Jul 1888 [Frolovskoe].
RUS–KL (a³, No. 3192).
PB: 404–405 — *PSSL* 14: 484 — *LF*: 404–405
    [English tr.].

3616.   To Modest Chaikovskii
12 Jul 1888. Frolovskoe.
RUS–KL (a³, No. 1892).
ZC 3: 256 — *PSSL* 14: 484.

3617.   To Iuliia Shpazhinskaia
12 Jul 1888. Frolovskoe.
RUS–KL (a³, No. 2106).
CTP: 340 — *PSSL* 14: 485.

3618.   To Pëtr Iurgenson
12 Jul [1888]. Frolovskoe.
RUS–KL (a³, No. 2611).
PIU 2: 93 — *PSSL* 14: 486.

3619.   To Pëtr Iurgenson
[13 Jul 1888. Klin] — telegram.
RUS–KL (a³, No. 2636).
PSSL 14: 486.

3620.   To Pëtr Iurgenson
13 Jul [1888]. [Frolovskoe].
RUS–KL (a³, No. 2612).
PIU 2: 93–94 — *PSSL* 14: 486–487.

3621.   To Nikolai Konradi
17 Jul 1888 [Frolovskoe].
Autograph lost; MS copy in RUS–KL.
CTP: 276 — *PSSL* 14: 487.

3622.   To Modest Chaikovskii
18 Jul [1888]. Frolovskoe.
RUS–KL (a³, No. 1893).
PSSL 14: 487.

3623.   To Akhilles Alferaki
20 Jul 1888. Frolovskoe.
Autograph lost; typed copy in RUS–KL.
ZC 3: 257–261 — *SM* (1938), 10/11: 146–148 —
    PSSL 14: 488–491.

3624.   To Nadezhda von Meck
25 Jul 1888. Frolovskoe.
RUS–KL (a³, No. 1040).
ZC 3: 261 — *PM* 3: 545–546 — *PSSL* 14: 491–492.

3625. To Anatolii Chaikovskii

25 Jul 1888 [Frolovskoe].

RUS–KL (a³, No. 3193).

PB: 405 — *PSSL* 14: 492–493 — *LF*: 405 [English tr.].

3626. To Iuliia Shpazhinskaia

25 Jul 1888 [Frolovskoe].

RUS–KL (a³, No. 2107).

CTP: 340–341 — *PSSL* 14: 493.

3627. To Modest Chaikovskii

[29 Jul 1888. Klin] — telegram.

RUS–KL (a³, No. 2048).

PSSL 14: 493.

3628. To Anna Aleksandrova-Levenson

30 Jul [1888]. Frolovskoe.

RUS–KL (a³, No. 3321).

SM (1938), 8: 143 — *PSSL* 14: 494.

3629. To Lidiia Genke

[late Jul 1888]. Frolovskoe.

RUS–Mcl (f. 905).

PSSL 14: 494–495.

3630. To Praskov´ia Chaikovskaia

1 Aug [1888]. Frolovskoe.

RUS–KL (a³, No. 3285).

PB: 405–406 — *PSSL* 14: 495–496 — *LF*: 405–406 [English tr.].

3631. To Vladimir Shilovskii

1 Aug [1888]. Frolovskoe.

RUS–SPsc (f. 834, No. 14, fol. 18–20).

PSSL 14: 496.

3632. To Pëtr Iurgenson

[1 Aug 1888. Klin] — telegram.

RUS–KL (a³, No. 2672).

PSSL 14: 497.

3633. To Pëtr Iurgenson

1 Aug [1888]. [Frolovskoe].

RUS–KL (a³, No. 2613).

PSSL 14: 497.

3634. To Nikolai Konradi

[?1 Aug 1888. Frolovskoe].

Autograph lost; MS copy in RUS–KL.

PSSL 14: 497.

3635. To Mikhail Ippolitov-Ivanov

4 Aug [1888]. Frolovskoe.

RUS–KL (a³, No. 187).

*ZC 3: 262 — *SM* (1938), 10/11: 151–152 — *Biulleten´* (1947), 1: 52–53.

3636. To Ivan Vsevolozhskii

7 Aug 1888. Frolovskoe.

RUS–Mcl (f. 726) [facs. in I. V. Remezov, *V. I. Suk* (1933): 6/7.

I. Remezov, *V. I. Suk* (1933): 6–7 — **I. Remezov, Viacheslav Suk* (1951): 14 — *PSSL* 14: 499.

3637. To Nadezhda von Meck

7 Aug 1888. Frolovskoe.

RUS–KL (a³, No. 1041).

PM 3: 546–547 — *PSSL* 14: 500–501.

3638. To Anatolii Chaikovskii

7 Aug [1888]. [Frolovskoe].

RUS–KL (a³, No. 3194).

PSSL 14: 501.

3639. To Pëtr Iurgenson

9 Aug 1888 [Frolovskoe].

RUS–KL (a³, No. 2615).

*ZC 3: 262–263 — *PIU* 2: 95 — *PSSL* 14: 501–502.

3640. To Vladimir Argutinskii-Dolgorukov

11 Aug [1888]. [Frolovskoe].

RUS–Mcl (f. 1900).

PSSL 14: 502.

3640a. To Natal´ia Pleskaia

11 Aug [1888]. [Frolovskoe].

RUS–Mcl (f. 905).

PSSL 17: 247.

3641. To Pëtr Iurgenson

11 Aug [1888]. [Frolovskoe].

RUS–KL (a³, No. 2616).

*ZC 3: 263–264 — *PIU* 2: 95–96 — *PSSL* 14: 503.

3642.   To Nikolai Hubert

12 Aug [1888]. [Frolovskoe].

RUS–KL (a³, No. 112).

PRM 48 — *PSSL* 14: 504.

3643.   To Ivan Vsevolozhskii

13 Aug 1888. Frolovskoe.

RUS–KL (a³, No. 32).

*Iu. Slonimskii, *P. I. Chaikovskii i baletnyi teatr ego vremenii* (1956): 170 — *PSSL* 14: 504–505.

3644.   To Nadezhda von Meck

14 Aug 1888. Frolovskoe.

RUS–KL (a³, No. 1042).

ZC 3: 264–265 — *PM* 3: 548–549 — *PSSL* 14: 505–506.

3645.   To Iuliia Shpazhinskaia

14 Aug [1888]. Frolovskoe.

RUS–KL (a³, No. 2108).

CTP: 341 — *PSSL* 14: 507.

3646.   To Pëtr Iurgenson

14 Aug 1888. Frolovskoe.

RUS–KL (a³, No. 2617).

ZC 3: 264 — *PIU* 2: 96 — *PSSL* 14: 508.

3647.   To Ivan Vsevolozhskii

22 Aug 1888. Moscow — in French.

Autograph lost; MS copy in RUS–KL.

*Iu. Slonimskii, *P. I. Chaikovskii i baletnyi teatr ego vremeni* (1956): 170–171 — *PSSL* 14: 509–510.

3648.   To Nadezhda von Meck

22 [Aug] 1888 (in MS: "22 Sep"). Moscow.

RUS–KL (a³, No. 1045).

PM 3: 549–550 — *PSSL* 14: 510–511.

3649.   To Anatolii Chaikovskii

22 Aug 1888. Moscow.

RUS–KL (a³, No. 3195).

PSSL 14: 511–512.

3650.   To Modest Chaikovskii

22 Aug [1888]. Moscow.

RUS–KL (a³, No. 1894).

PB: 406 — *PSSL* 14: 512 — *LF*: 406 [English tr.].

3651.   To   Grand   Duke   Konstantin Konstantinovich

26 Aug 1888. Kamenka.

RUS–SPil (f. 137, No. 78/11).

ZC 3: 266–267 — *PSSL* 14: 513–515.

3652.   To Emil von Sauer

27 Aug 1888. Kamenka — in French.

D–EMmüller.

SM (1965), 9: 48 [Russian tr.] — *PSSL* 14: 515–516.

3653.   To Nadezhda von Meck

3 Sep 1888. Moscow.

RUS–KL (a³, No. 1043).

PM 3: 550–551 — *PSSL* 14: 517–518.

3654.   To Modest Chaikovskii

4 Sep 1888. Moscow.

RUS–KL (a³, No. 1895).

PSSL 14: 518.

3655.   To Edvard Grieg

5 Sep 1888 [Frolovskoe] (in MS: "Klin") — in German.

N–Bo.

SM (1940), 5–6: 147–148 [Russian tr.] — O. Levasheva, *Edvard Grig* (1962): 750 [Russian tr.] — *PSSL* 14: 519.

3656.   To Václav Suk

5 Sep [1888]. [Frolovskoe].

RUS–Mcl (f. 877) [facs. in I. Remezov, *V. I. Suk* (1933): 10 — I. Remezov, *Viacheslav Suk* (1951): 12/13].

I. Remezov, *V. I. Suk* (1933): 7 — *I. Remezov, *Viacheslav Suk* (1951): 15 — *PSSL* 14: 520.

3657.   To Anatolii Chaikovskii

5 Sep [1888]. [Frolovskoe].

RUS–KL (a³, No. 3196).

PSSL 14: 521.

3658.   To Iuliia Shpazhinskaia

5 Sep 1888. Frolovskoe.

RUS–KL (a³, No. 2109).

CTP: 341 — *PSSL* 14: 522.

3659. To Willy Burmester

7 Sep 1888 [Frolovskoe] (in MS: "Klin") — in German.

D–AMlohss [facs. in W. Burmester, *Fünfzig Jahre Künstlerleben* (1926): 64/65 — *ČS* 3: 276].

W. Burmester, *Fünfzig Jahre Künstlerleben* (1926): 67 — *Muzykal'noe nasledstvo*, 1 (1962): 367–368 — *PSSL* 14: 522–523 — *ČS* 3: 277.

3660. To Aleksandr Ziloti

7 Sep [1888]. [Frolovskoe].

RUS–KL (a³, No. 3001).

AIZ: 67 — *PSSL* 14: 524.

3661. To Modest Chaikovskii

7 Sep 1888. Frolovskoe.

RUS–KL (a³, No. 1896).

*PB: 406–407 — *PSSL* 14: 524–525 — **LF*: 407 [English tr.].

3662. To Pëtr Iurgenson

7 Sep [1888]. [Frolovskoe].

RUS–KL (a³, No. 2619).

PIU 2: 97–98 — *PSSL* 14: 525–526.

3663. To German Larosh

10 Sep [1888]. [Frolovskoe].

Autograph lost; photocopy in RUS–KL.

PSSL 14: 526–527.

3664. To Vladimir Pogozhev

10 Sep 1888. Frolovskoe.

RUS–KL (a³, No. 2877).

VP: 44–46 — **CTP*: 342–343 — *PSSL* 14: 527–528.

3665. To Iuliia Shpazhinskaia

10 Sep 1888. Frolovskoe.

RUS–KL (a³, No. 2110).

CTP: 342 — *PSSL* 14: 529–530.

3666. To Pëtr Iurgenson

10 Sep [1888]. Frolovskoe.

RUS–KL (a³, No. 2620).

PIU 2: 98 — *PSSL* 14: 530.

3667. To Pëtr Iurgenson

10 Sep 1888 [Frolovskoe].

RUS–KL (a³, No. 2621).

PIU 2: 98–99 — *PSSL* 14: 531–532.

3668. To Marie Červinková-Riegrová

12 Sep 1888. Frolovskoe.

CZ–Ps.

Lidovy noviny (25 Jan 1937) [Czech tr.] — Štěpánek (1952): 130–132 [Czech tr.] — *Muzykal'naia zhizn'* (Apr 1965), 8: 6 — *PSSL* 14: 532–533.

3669. To Nadezhda von Meck

14 Sep 1888. Frolovskoe.

RUS–KL (a³, No. 1044).

*ZC 3: 268–269 — *PM* 3: 551–552 — *PSSL* 14: 534–535.

3670. To Anatolii Chaikovskii

14 Sep 1888. Frolovskoe.

RUS–KL (a³, No. 3197).

PSSL 14: 535–536.

3671. To Pëtr Iurgenson

14 Sep [1888]. [Frolovskoe].

RUS–KL (a³, No. 2622).

PIU 2: 99 — *PSSL* 14: 536.

3672. To Modest Chaikovskii

19 Sep [1888]. Moscow.

RUS–KL (a³, No. 1897).

PB: 407 — *PSSL* 14: 537 — *LF*: 407–408 [English tr.].

3673. To Aleksandr Ziloti

20 Sep [1888]. [Moscow].

RUS–KL (a³, No. 3022).

AIZ: 88 — *PSSL* 14: 537.

3673a. To Viacheslav Kotek

21 Sep 1888. Frolovskoe.

RUS–KL (a³, No. 3320).

Not published.

3674. To Eduard Nápravník

21 Sep 1888. Frolovskoe.

F–Plauwe [facs. of p. 1 in *ČS* 3: 230].

VP: 185–186 — *EFN*: 152–153 — *PSSL* 14: 538–539 — *ČS* 3: 229, 231 [German tr.].

3675.   To Grand Duke Konstantin Konstantinovich

21 Sep 1888. Frolovskoe.

RUS–SPil (f. 137, No. 78/12).

*ZC 3: 270–275 — PSSL 14: 539–543.

3675a.   To Sergei Taneev

21 Sep [1888]. [Moscow].

RUS–Mcl (f. 880).

CTP: 177 ("1891") — PSSL 17: 248.

3676.   To Adolf Čech

21 [Sep] 1888 (in MS: "21 Nov") [Frolovskoe] (in MS: "Klin") — in German.

CZ–Pkadlic [facs. in M. Očadlik, Pražské dopisy P. I. Čajkovského (1949)].

Stěpánek (1952): 133 — SM (1952), 7: 68 [Russian tr.] — PSSL 14: 543–544.

3677.   To Pëtr Iurgenson

22 Sep [1888]. [Frolovskoe].

RUS–KL (a³, No. 2658).

PSSL 14: 545.

3677a.   To Eduard Nápravník

23 Sep 1888 [Frolovskoe] (in MS: "Klin").

Autograph lost; photocopy in RUS–KL.

Not published.

3678.   To Nadezhda von Meck

24 Sep [1888].

RUS–KL (a³, No. 1046).

PM 3: 553–554 — PSSL 14: 545–546.

3679.   To Modest Chaikovskii

27 Sep [1888]. [Frolovskoe].

RUS–KL (a³, No. 1898).

PB: 407–408 — PSSL 14: 546 — LF: 408 [English tr.].

3680.   To Pëtr Iurgenson

[27 Sep 1888. Klin] — telegram.

RUS–KL (a³, No. 2637).

PSSL 14: 547.

3681.   To Aleksandra Hubert

29 Sep [1888]. [Moscow].

RUS–KL (a³, No. 61).

PRM 48 — PSSL 14: 547.

3682.   To Vladimir Pogozhev

1 Oct 1888. Frolovskoe.

RUS–KL (a³, No. 2878).

VP: 47–48 — PSSL 14: 547–549.

3683.   To Anatolii Chaikovskii

1 Oct 1888 [Frolovskoe].

RUS–KL (a³, No. 3198).

*PB: 408 — PSSL 14: 549–550 — *LF: 408–409 [English tr.].

3684.   To Iuliia Shpazhinskaia

1 Oct 1888. Frolovskoe.

RUS–KL (a³, No. 2111).

CTP: 343–344 — PSSL 14: 550–551.

3685.   To Grand Duke Konstantin Konstantinovich

2 Oct 1888. Frolovskoe.

RUS–SPil (f. 137, No. 78/13).

*ZC 3: 275–278 — PSSL 14: 551–554.

3686.   To Modest Chaikovskii

4 Oct [1888]. Frolovskoe.

RUS–KL (a³, No. 1899).

PSSL 14: 555.

3687.   To Aleksandr Ziloti

5 Oct [1888]. [Frolovskoe].

Autograph lost

RMG (1908), 43: 932 ("1891") — AIZ: 88 — PSSL 14: 555–556.

3688.   To Anna Brodskaia

8 Oct 1888. Frolovskoe.

GB–Mcm

PSSL 14: 556–557.

3689.   To Willy Burmester

[8] Oct 1888 (in printed copy: "2 Oct"). Frolovskoe — in German.

Autograph lost

W. Burmester, Fünfzig Jahre Künstlerleben (1926): 66–67 — Muzykal´noe nasledstvo, 1 (1962): 369 — PSSL 14: 557–558.

3690.   To Félix Mackar

8 Oct 1888 [Frolovskoe] (in MS: "Klin") — in French.
F–Pn

RdM 54 (1968), 1: 64–71 — *SM* (1970), 9: 68–70
  [Russian tr.] — *PSSL* 14: 558–560.

3691.   To Anna Merkling

8 Oct 1888. Frolovskoe.
Autograph lost; MS copy in RUS–KL.
*ZC 3: 278–279 — *CTP*: 233–234 — *PSSL* 14: 562–
  563.

3692.   To Pëtr Iurgenson

8 Oct [1888]. [Frolovskoe].
RUS–KL (a³, No. 2623).
PSSL 14: 563.

3693.   To German Larosh

9 Oct [1888]. [Frolovskoe].
Autograph lost
PSSL 14: 564.

3694.   To František Šubert

10 Oct 1888 [Frolovskoe] — in French.
CZ–Ps [facs. in M. Očadlik, *Pražské dopisy P. I.
  Čajkovského* (1949)].
Štěpánek (1952): 132–133 [Czech tr.] — *PSSL* 14:
  564–565.

3695.   To Modest Chaikovskii

14 Oct [1888]. [Frolovskoe].
RUS–KL (a³, No. 1867).
PSSL 14: 566.

3696.   To František Šubert

16 Oct 1888 [Frolovskoe] — in French.
CZ–Ps [facs. in M. Očadlik, *Pražské dopisy P. I.
  Čajkovského* (1949)].
Štěpánek (1952): 135–136 [Czech tr.] — *PSSL* 14:
  566–567.

3697.   To Praskov´ia Chaikovskaia

16 Oct [1888]. Frolovskoe.
RUS–KL (a³, No. 3286).
PB: 409 — *PSSL* 14: 567–568 — *LF*: 409 [English
  tr.].

3698.   To Modest Chaikovskii

16 Oct [1888]. [Frolovskoe].
RUS–KL (a³, No. 2009).
PB: 408–409 — *PSSL* 14: 568–569 — *LF*: 409–410
  [English tr.].

3699.   To Pëtr Iurgenson

16 Oct [1888]. [Frolovskoe].
RUS–KL (a³, No. 2624).
PIU 2: 101 — *PSSL* 14: 569.

3700.   To Desirée Artôt-Padilla

17 Oct 1888 [Frolovskoe] (in MS: "Klin") — in
French.
RUS–Mcl (f. 905).
CTP: 373–374 — *PSSL* 14: 569–570.

3701.   To Anatolii Chaikovskii

17 Oct 1888. Frolovskoe.
RUS–KL (a³, No. 3199).
*PB: 410 — *PSSL* 14: 571–572 — **LF*: 410–411
  [English tr.].

3702.   To Adolf Čech

17 Oct 1888 [Frolovskoe] — in German.
CZ–Pkadlic [facs. in M. Očadlik, *Pražské dopisy P. I.
  Čajkovského* (1949)].
Štěpánek (1952): 136 — *SM* (1952), 7: 68 [Russian
  tr.] — *PSSL* 14: 572–573.

3703.   To Pëtr Iurgenson

[17 Oct 1888. Frolovskoe].
RUS–KL (a³, No. 2625).
PSSL 14: 573.

3704.   To Ekaterina Larosh

19 Oct 1888 [Frolovskoe].
Autograph lost; photocopy in RUS–KL.
PSSL 14: 574.

3705.   To Iuliia Shpazhinskaia

19 Oct 1888. Frolovskoe.
RUS–KL (a³, No. 2112).
CTP: 344–345 — *PSSL* 14: 574–575.

3706.   To Aleksandra Hubert

[22 Oct 1888. Moscow].

RUS–KL (a³, No. 62).

PRM 49 — *PSSL* 14: 576.

3707.   To Emiliia Pavlovskaia

22 Oct [1888]. [Moscow].

RUS–Mt (Pavlovskaia coll.).

CMS: 417 — *PSSL* 14: 576–577.

3708.   To Emiliia Pavlovskaia

25 Oct [1888]. [Moscow].

RUS–Mt (Pavlovskaia coll.).

CMS: 417–418 — *PSSL* 14: 577–578.

3709.   To Pëtr Iurgenson

26 Oct [1888]. [Frolovskoe].

RUS–KL (a³, No. 2627).

PSSL 14: 578.

3710.   To Mikhail Ippolitov-Ivanov

27 Oct 1888. Frolovskoe.

RUS–KL (a³, No. 188).

ZC 3: 279–280 — *Biulleten´* (1947), 1: 56–57 —
    PSSL 14: 578–579.

3711.   To Nadezhda von Meck

27 Oct 1888. Frolovskoe.

RUS–KL (a³, No. 1047).

ZC 3: 280–821 — *PM* 3: 554–555 — *PSSL* 14: 579–
    580.

3712.   To Anatolii Chaikovskii

27 Oct [1888]. Frolovskoe.

RUS–KL (a³, No. 3200).

PB: 410–411 — *PSSL* 14: 581 — *LF*: 411 [English
    tr.].

3712a.   To Léonce Détroyat

28 Oct 1888. Frolovskoe — in French.

Autograph auctioned in Paris, 1992.

*A. Lischké, *Piotr Ilyitch Tchaikovsky* (1993): 543.

3713.   To František Šubert

28 Oct 1888 [Frolovskoe] — in French.

CZ–Ps [facs. in M. Očadlik, *Pražské dopisy P. I.
    Čajkovského* (1949)].

Stěpánek (1952): 137–138 [Czech tr.] — *PSSL* 14:
    581–582.

3714.   To Emil von Sauer

28 Oct 1888 [Frolovskoe] — in French.

D–EMmüller

SM (1965), 9: 48 [Russian tr.] — *PSSL* 14: 583.

3715.   To Pavel Tret´iakov

30 Oct 1888. Frolovskoe.

RUS–Mgt

PSSL 14: 584–585.

3716.   To Aleksandr Ziloti

30 Oct 1888 [Frolovskoe].

RUS–KL (a³, No. 3002).

AIZ: 89 — *PSSL* 14: 585.

3717.   To Pëtr Iurgenson

30 Oct [1888]. [Frolovskoe].

RUS–KL (a³, No. 2628).

PIU 2: 101–102 — *PSSL* 14: 585–586.

3718.   To Boris Iurgenson

[Oct 1888. Frolovskoe].

RUS–KL (a³, No. 483).

PSSL 14: 586.

3719.   To Sergei Taneev

[?Oct 1888. Moscow].

RUS–Mcl (f. 880).

CTP: 155 — *PSSL* 14: 587.

3720.   To Ivan Vsevolozhskii

3 Nov 1888 [St. Petersburg].

RUS–SPia (f. 652, op. 1, d. 608, fol. 40).

PSSL 14: 587.

3721.   To Sergei Taneev

[3 Nov 1888. St. Petersburg] — telegram.

Autograph lost; typed copy in RUS–KL.

CTP: 156 — *PSSL* 14: 587–588.

3722. To Milii Balakirev

8 Nov [1888]. [St. Petersburg].

RUS–SPsc (f. 834, No. 12, fol. 38–39).

BC: 97–98 — *BVP* 184 — *PSSL* 14: 588.

3723. To Eduard Nápravník

[8 Nov 1888. St. Petersburg].

Autograph lost; typed copy in RUS–KL.

VP: 186–287 — *EFN:* 153 — *PSSL* 14: 589.

3724. To Ol´ga Nápravník

10 Nov 1888 [St. Petersburg].

RUS–KL (a³, No. 2991).

PSSL 14: 589.

3724a. To Nikolai Lents

12 Nov 1888 [St. Petersburg] — noted on the MS score of Lents' two-piano arrangement of *Francesca da Rimini*

RUS–Mcm (f. 88, No. 28).

PSSL 17: 248.

3725. To Nadezhda von Meck

13 Nov 1888 [St. Petersburg].

RUS–KL (a³, No. 1048).

*ZC 3: 285 — *PM* 3: 556 — *PSSL* 14: 590.

3726. To Anatolii Chaikovskii

[13] Nov 1888 (in MS: "12 Nov") [St. Petersburg].

RUS–KL (a³, No. 3201).

PB: 411 — *PSSL* 14: 591 — *LF:* 411 [English tr.].

3727. To Iuliia Shpazhinskaia

[13] Nov 1888 (in MS: "12 Nov") [St. Petersburg].

RUS–KL (a³, No. 2113).

CTP: 345 ("12 Nov") — *PSSL* 14: 591–592.

3728. To Pëtr Iurgenson

[23 Nov/5 Dec 1888. Prague] — telegram; in German.

RUS–KL (a³, No. 2653).

PSSL 14: 592.

3729. To Pëtr Iurgenson

[24 Nov/6 Dec 1888. Prague] — telegram; in German.

RUS–KL (a³, No. 2654).

PSSL 14: 592.

3730. To Ludvik Kuba

26 Nov/8 Dec 1888. Vienna.

CZ–POm [facs. in I. Belza, *Iz istorii russko-cheshskikh sviazei* (1956): 8/9].

Hudebni rozhledy (1953), 16: 761 [Czech tr.] — **Slaviane* (1956), 10: 50 — I. Belza, *Iz istorii russko-cheshskikh sviazei* (1956): 13–14 — *PSSL* 14: 593.

3731. To Nadezhda von Meck

26 Nov/8 Dec 1888. Vienna.

RUS–KL (a³, No. 1049).

*ZC 3: 285–286 — *PM* 3: 557–558 — *PSSL* 14: 593–594.

3732. To Adolf Patera

26 Nov/8 Dec 1888 [Vienna].

CZ–Ps

Stěpánek (1952): 139–140 [Czech tr.] — *PSSL* 14: 595.

3733. To Praskov´ia Chaikovskaia

26 Nov/8 Dec [1888]. Vienna.

RUS–KL (a³, No. 3287).

PB: 411–412 — *PSSL* 14: 595–596 — *LF:* 412 [English tr.].

3734. To Iuliia Shpazhinskaia

26 Nov/8 Dec 1888. Vienna.

RUS–KL (a³, No. 2114).

CTP: 345–346 — *PSSL* 14: 596–597.

3735. To Pëtr Iurgenson

30 Nov [1888]. St. Petersburg.

RUS–KL (a³, No. 2629).

PSSL 14: 597.

3736. To Grand Duke Konstantin Konstantinovich

1 Dec 1888. Frolovskoe.

RUS–SPil (f. 137, No. 78/14).

*ZC 3: 286–287 — *PSSL* 14: 598–599.

3737. To Praskov´ia Chaikovskaia

1 Dec [1888]. Frolovskoe.

RUS–KL (a³, No. 3288).

PSSL 14: 599.

3738. To Nadezhda von Meck

2 Dec 1888. Frolovskoe.

RUS–KL (a³, No. 1050).

*ZC 3: 289 — PM 3: 558–559 — PSSL 14: 600–601.

3739. To Edvard Válečka

15 Dec 1888. St. Petersburg.

CZ–Ps [facs. in M. Očadlik, Pražké dopisy P. I. Čajkovského (1949)].

Stěpánek (1952): 142 [Czech tr.] — PSSL 14: 601–602.

3740. To Paul Taffanel

15 Dec 1888. St. Petersburg — in French.

F–Psamarin.

RdM 54 (1968), 1: 87 — PSSL 14: 602.

3741. To Ol´ga Chaikovskaia

17 Dec [1888]. [St. Petersburg].

RUS–SPsc (f. 834, No. 31, fol. 15–16).

PSSL 14: 603.

3742. To Nikolai Abramychev

[mid Dec 1888. St. Petersburg].

RUS–SPsc (f. 230, No. 21, fol. 1).

*PSSL 14: 604.

3743. To Anatolii Chaikovskii

19 Dec [1888]. [St. Petersburg].

RUS–KL (a³, No. 3202).

*PB: 412 — PSSL 14: 604–605 — *LF: 412–413 [English tr.].

3744. To Pëtr Iurgenson

19 Dec 1888. St. Petersburg.

RUS–KL (a³, No. 2630).

PIU 2: 102–103 — PSSL 14: 605.

3745. To Adolf Čech

23 Dec 1888. St. Petersburg — in German.

CZ–Pkadlic [facs. in M. Očadlik, Pražké dopisy P. I. Čajkovského (1949)].

Stěpánek (1952): 143 — SM (1952), 7: 68–69 [Russian tr.] — PSSL 14: 606.

3746. To Pëtr Iurgenson

23 Dec 1888 [St. Petersburg].

RUS–KL (a³, No. 2631).

PIU 2: 103–104 — PSSL 14: 607.

3747. To Félix Mackar

26 Dec 1888 [Frolovskoe] — in French.

F–Pn.

RdM 54 (1968), 1: 72 — PSSL 14: 608.

3748. To Nadezhda von Meck

26 Dec 1888. Frolovskoe.

RUS–KL (a³, No. 1051).

PM 3: 559–561 — PSSL 14: 609–611.

3749. To Adolf Patera

26 Dec 1888. Frolovskoe.

CZ–Ps.

Stěpánek (1952): 144 [Czech tr.] — PSSL 14: 611–612.

3750. To Iuliia Shpazhinskaia

26 Dec [1888]. Frolovskoe.

RUS–KL (a³, No. 2115).

CTP: 346 — PSSL 14: 612–613.

3751. To Aleksandr Ziloti

27 Dec 1888. Frolovskoe.

RUS–KL (a³, No. 3003).

AIZ: 89–91 — PSSL 14: 613–615.

1889

3752. To Nikolai Bernard

3 Jan 1889 [Frolovskoe].

RUS–SPtob (VII.2.4.154) [facs. in Avtografy muzykal´-nykh deiatelei 1839–1889 (supp. to Nuvellist) (1889): 34].

Glebov (1924): 163–164 ("4 Jan") — PSSL 15A: 13.

3753. To Aleksandr Ziloti

4 Jan 1889 [Frolovskoe].

RUS–KL (a³, No. 3004).

AIZ: 92 — PSSL 15A: 13.

3754. To Pëtr Iurgenson

4 Jan 1889 [Frolovskoe].

RUS–KL (a³, No. 2638).

*ZC 3: 290 — *PIU 2: 107–108 — PSSL 15A: 14.

3754a. To Hermann Wolff

5 Jan [1889] (in MS: "1888") [Frolovskoe] (in MS: "Klin") — in French.

Autograph auctioned at Sotheby's, London, 1995 [see *ČS* 3 (1998): 165].

Not published.

3755. To Aleksandr Ziloti

5 Jan [1889]. [Frolovskoe].

RUS–KL (a³, No. 3005).

AIZ: 93 — *PSSL* 15A: 15.

3756. To Anatolii Chaikovskii

5 Jan 1889 [Frolovskoe].

RUS–KL (a³, No. 3204).

*PB: 16 — *PSSL* 15A: 16 — **LF*: 413 [English tr.].

3757. To Pëtr Iurgenson

5 Jan [1889]. [Frolovskoe].

RUS–KL (a³, No. 2639).

PIU 2: 108 — *PSSL* 15A: 17.

3758. To Ivan Vsevolozhskii

6 Jan 1889. Frolovskoe.

RUS–SPia (f. 652, op. 1, d. 608, fol. 17–18).

PSSL 15A: 17.

3759. To Nadezhda von Meck

8 Jan 1889. Frolovskoe.

RUS–KL (a³, No. 1052).

PM 3: 564–565 — *PSSL* 15A: 18–19.

3760. To Fëdor Bekker

9 Jan 1889 [Frolovskoe].

RUS–SPtob (VII.2.4.154).

PSSL 15A: 20.

3761. To Ivan Vsevolozhskii

9 Jan 1889. Frolovskoe.

RUS–SPia (f. 652, op. 1, d. 608, fol. 14–16).

PSSL 15A: 20–21.

3762. To Anna Merkling

9 Jan 1889. Frolovskoe.

Autograph lost; MS copy in RUS–KL.

CTP: 234 — *PSSL* 15A: 21–22.

3763. To Adolf Patera

9 Jan 1889 [Frolovskoe] (in MS: "Klin").

CZ–Ps

Stěpánek (1952): 145–148 [Czech tr.] — *Antonin Dvorzhak* (1967): 212–215 — *PSSL* 15A: 22–24.

3763a. To Vasilii Safonov

9 [Jan 1889] (in MS: "9 Nov 1888") [Frolovskoe].

RUS–KL (a³, No. 345).

VIS: 199–200 — *PSSL* 17: 248–249.

3764. To Modest Chaikovskii

9 Jan 1889. Frolovskoe.

RUS–KL (a³, No. 1900).

PB: 413 — *PSSL* 15A: 24–25 — *LF*: 413 [English tr.].

3765. To Modest Chaikovskii

9 Jan 1889 [Frolovskoe].

RUS–Mcl (f. 908).

PSSL 15A: 25.

3766. To Iuliia Shpazhinskaia

9 Jan 1889. Frolovskoe.

RUS–KL (a³, No. 2116).

CTP: 346–347 — *PSSL* 15A: 26–27.

3767. To Pëtr Iurgenson

9 Jan [1889]. [Frolovskoe].

RUS–KL (a³, No. 2640).

PSSL 15A: 28.

3768. To Félix Mackar

13 [Jan] 1889 (in MS: "Feb") [Frolovskoe] — in French.

F–Pn

RdM 54 (1968), 1: 72–73 — *PSSL* 15A: 28–29.

3769. To František Šubert

13 Jan 1889 [Frolovskoe] — in French.

RUS–Mcl (f. 774).

PSSL 15A: 29–30.

3770. To Mariia Klimentova–Muromtseva

13 Jan 1889 [Frolovskoe].

RUS–KL (a³, No. 218).

PSSL 15A: 31.

3771. To Pëtr Iurgenson

18 Jan [1889]. [Frolovskoe].

RUS–KL (a³, No. 2641).

PIU 2: 109 — *PSSL* 15A: 31.

3772. To Antonin Dvořák

18 Jan 1889. Frolovskoe.

CZ–ZL

Šourek (1951): 103–104 [Czech tr.] — Šourek (1954) [German tr.] — *SM* (1954), 5: 48 — *Dvorzhak v pis´makh i vospominaniiakh* (1964): 85 — *PSSL* 15A: 32.

3772a. To Paulina Erdmannsdörfer-Richter

18 Jan 1889. Frolovskoe — in French.

Autograph lost

PSSL 17: 250.

3773. To Pëtr Iurgenson

18 Jan 1889. Frolovskoe.

RUS–KL (a³, No. 2642).

PIU 2: 109–110 — *PSSL* 15A: 33–34.

3774. To Elizaveta Lavrovskaia

20 Jan 1889. St. Petersburg.

RUS–KL (a³, No. 263).

V. Shkov, ´Etu rol´ ia pisal dlia Vas´, *Kalininskaia pravda* (13 Oct 1970) — *PSSL* 15A: 34.

3774a. To Edouard Colonne

22 Jan 1889. St. Petersburg — in French.

US–CAM (Estelle Doheny coll.).

Not published.

3775. To Aleksei Sofronov

[24 Jan 1889. St. Petersburg].

RUS–SPsc (f. 834, No. 27, fol. 31).

PSSL 15A: 35.

3776. To Aleksandr Ziloti

28 Jan/9 Feb 1889. Berlin.

RUS–KL (a³, No. 3006).

AIZ: 94 — *PSSL* 15A: 35–36.

3777. To Pëtr Iurgenson

28 Jan/9 Feb 1889. Berlin.

RUS–KL (a³, No. 2643).

PIU 2: 112 — *PSSL* 15A: 36–37.

3778. To Modest Chaikovskii

30 Jan/11 Feb 1889. Cologne.

RUS–KL (a³, No. 1901).

ZC 3: 291 — *PB*: 413 — *PSSL* 15A: 37–38 — *LF*: 414 [English tr.].

3779. To Freidrich Sieger

[1/13 Feb 1889. Frankfurt] — in German.

NL–Ac

PSSL 15A: 38.

3780. To Aleksei Sofronov

2/14 Feb 1889. Frankfurt.

RUS–SPsc (f. 834, No. 27, fol. 33–34).

PSSL 15A: 39.

3781. To Anatolii Chaikovskii

2/14 Feb 1889. Frankfurt.

RUS–KL (a³, No. 3203).

PB: 414 — *PSSL* 15A: 39 — *LF*: 414 [English tr.].

3782. To Modest Chaikovskii

2/14 Feb [1889]. [Frankfurt].

RUS–KL (a³, No. 1902).

PB: 414 — *PSSL* 15A: 40 — *LF*: 414–415 [English tr.].

3783. To Pëtr Iurgenson

2/14 Feb 1889. Frankfurt.

RUS–KL (a³, No. 2644).

PIU 2: 114 — *PSSL* 15A: 40.

3784. To Willy Burmester

[5]/17 Feb 1889. Dresden — in German.

Priv. coll. of Dr Oestrich, Hamburg

W. Burmester, *Fünfzig Jahre Künstlerleben* (1926): 68 — *Muzykal´noe nasledstvo*, 1 (1962): 370 [Russian tr.] — *PSSL* 15A: 40–41.

3785. To Hermann Wolff

[5]/17 Feb [1889]. [Dresden] — in French.

GB–Lrosenthal

RdM 54 (1968), 1: 88 — *PSSL* 15A: 41.

3786. To Pëtr Iurgenson
5/17 Feb [1889]. Dresden.
RUS–KL (a³, No. 2645).
PIU 2: 114 — *PSSL* 15A: 42.

3787. To Pëtr Iurgenson
[5]/17 Feb [1889]. Dresden.
RUS–KL (a³, No. 2646).
ZC 3: 295 — *PIU* 2: 114–115 — *PSSL* 15A: 43.

3788. To Grand Duke Konstantin Konstantinovich
7/19 Feb 1889. Dresden.
RUS–SPil (f. 137, No. 78/15).
PSSL 15A: 43–44.

3789. To Aleksandr Ziloti
7/19 Feb 1889. Dresden.
RUS–KL (a³, No. 3007) [facs. of 2 pages in *PSSL* 15A: 160/161].
*RMG (1908), 43: 933 — *AIZ:* 95 — *PSSL* 15A: 44–45.

3790. To Modest Chaikovskii
8/20–9/21 Feb [1889]. Dresden.
RUS–KL (a³, No. 1903).
*ZC 3: 295 — *PB*: 414–415 — *PSSL* 15A: 45 — **LF*: 415 [English tr.].

3790a. To Desirée Artôt-Padilla
10/22 Feb 1889. Berlin.
Autograph lostl; photocopy in RUS–KL.
Not published.

3791. To Julius von Bernuth
[10/22 Feb 1889. Berlin] — in German.
Autograph lost; rough draft in RUS–KL (a⁴, No. 264).
PSSL 15A: 46 [draft].

3792. To Nadezhda von Meck
11/23 Feb 1889. Berlin.
RUS–KL (a³, No. 1054).
*ZC 3: 295–296 — *PM* 3: 565–566 — *PSSL* 15A: 46–47.

3793. To Anna Brodskaia
13/25 Feb 1889. Berlin.
GB–Mcm.
PSSL 15A: 47–48.

3793a. To Félix Mackar
13/25 Feb 1889. Berlin — in French.
US–Wc (Moldenhauer coll., box 55).
Not published.

3794. To Aleksandr Glazunov
15/27 Feb 1889 [Berlin].
Autograph lost; MS copy in RUS–KL.
*ZC 3: 297 — *SM* (1945), 3: 58–60 — *PSSL* 15A: 48–50.

3795. To Modest Chaikovskii
15/27 Feb 1889. Berlin.
RUS–KL (a³, No. 1904).
*ZC 3: 296 ("5 Feb") — *PB*: 415 — *PSSL* 15A: 51 — *LF*: 415–416 [English tr.].

3796. To Edouard Colonne
[16]/28 Feb [1889]. Berlin — in French.
RUS–KL (a³, No. 228).
PSSL 15A: 52.

3797. To Félix Mackar
[16]/28 Feb 1889 [Berlin] — in French.
RUS–KL (a³, No. 268).
PSSL 15A: 52.

3798. To František Šubert
[16]/28 Feb 1889 [Berlin] — in German.
RUS–KL (a³, No. 465).
PSSL 15A: 53.

3799. To Adolf Patera
17 Feb/1 Mar 1889. Leipzig.
CZ–Ps.
Stěpánek (1952): 150–151 [Czech tr.] — *Antonin Dvorzhak* (1967): 215–216 — *PSSL* 15A: 53–54.

3800. To Antonín Dvořák
17 Feb/1 Mar 1889. Leipzig.
CZ–ZL [facs. in *Antonin Dvorzhak* (1967): 208–211 — facs. of p. 1 in *Musical Quarterly*, 51 (Jul 1965), 3: 494].
Šourek (1951): 104–105 [Czech tr.] — *SM* (1951), 11: 79 — *Hudebni rozhledy* (1952), 17: 23–24 [Czech tr.] — Šourek (1954) [German tr.] — *Dvorzhak v pis´makh i vospominaniiakh* (1964): 85–86 — **Musical Quarterly* 51 (Jul 1965), 3: 494 [English tr.] — *PSSL* 15A: 32.

3801.   To Nikolai Konradi

17 Feb/1 Mar 1889. Leipzig.

Autograph lost; MS copy in RUS–KL.

CTP: 276–277 — *PSSL* 15A: 56.

3802.   To   Grand   Duke   Konstantin Konstantinovich

17 Feb/1 Mar 1889 [Leipzig].

RUS–SPil (f. 137, No. 78/16).

PSSL 15A: 57–58.

3803.   To Aleksei Sofronov

17 Feb/1 Mar 1889. Leipzig.

RUS–KL (a³, No. 388).

PSSL 15A: 58–59.

3804.   To Pëtr Iurgenson

17 Feb/1 Mar 1889. Leipzig.

RUS–KL (a³, No. 2647).

ZC 3: 298–299 — *PIU* 2: 115 — *PSSL* 15A: 59–60.

3805.   To Vladimir Davydov

20 Feb/4 Mar 1889. Geneva.

RUS–KL (a³, No. 115).

PSSL 15A: 60–61.

3806.   To Praskov´ia & Anatolii Chaikovskii

20 Feb/4 Mar 1889. Geneva.

RUS–KL (a³, No. 3205).

PB: 413–416 — *PSSL* 15A: 62 — *LF*: 416–417 [English tr.].

3807.   To Nadezhda von Meck

21 Feb/5 Mar 1889. Geneva.

RUS–KL (a³, No. 1053).

ZC 3: 299–300 — *PM* 3: 566–567 — *PSSL* 15A: 62–63.

3808.   To Félix Mackar

[21 Feb/5 Mar] 1889 (in MS: "9 Mar"). Geneva — in French.

F–Pn

RdM 54 (1968), 1: 73–74 — *PSSL* 15A: 64–65.

3809.   To Vladimir Davydov

28 Feb/12 Mar [1889]. Hamburg.

RUS–KL (a³, No. 116).

PSSL 15A: 65.

3810.   To Anna Merkling

[28 Feb]/12 Mar 1889 (in MS copy: "12/22"). Hamburg.

Autograph lost; MS copy in RUS–KL.

CTP: 234–235 — *PSSL* 15A: 66.

3811.   To Adolf Patera

28 Feb/12 Mar 1889. Hamburg.

CZ–Ps

Stěpánek (1952): 152–153 [Czech tr.] — *Antonin Dvorzhak* (1967): 216–217 — *PSSL* 15A: 67.

3812.   To Modest Chaikovskii

28 Feb/12 Mar [1889]. Hamburg.

RUS–KL (a³, No. 1905).

PB: 416–417 — *PSSL* 15A: 68 — *LF*: 417–418 [English tr.].

3813.   To Pëtr Iurgenson

4/16 Mar 1889. Hamburg.

RUS–KL (a³, No. 2648).

PIU 2: 116–117 — *PSSL* 15A: 69.

3814.   To Vladimir Davydov

5/17 Mar 1889. Hannover.

RUS–KL (a³, No. 117).

ZC 3: 301–302 — *PB*: 418 — *PSSL* 15A: 70–71 — *LF*: 418 [English tr.].

3815.   To Nadezhda von Meck

5/17 Mar 1889. Hannover.

RUS–KL (a³, No. 1055).

PM 3: 568–569 — *PSSL* 15A: 71–72.

3816.   To Daniel Rahter

5/17 Mar [1889]. Hannover — in Germam.

US–CA (Kilgour coll.) [facs. in *Notes*, 17 (1960), 4: 557].

Notes, 17 (1960), 4: 557 — *PSSL* 15A: 72–73.

3817.   To Anatolii Chaikovskii

5/17 Mar [1889]. Hannover.

RUS–KL (a³, No. 3182).

PSSL 15A: 73–74.

3818. To Modest Chaikovskii

5/17 Mar [1889]. Hannover.

RUS–KL (a³, No. 1906).

*ZC 3: 302–303 — PB: 417–418 — PSSL 15A: 74–75 — *LF: 419 [English tr.].

3819. To Iuliia Shpazhinskaia

5/17 Mar 1889 [Hannover] (in MS: "Hamburg").

RUS–KL (a³, No. 2117).

CTP: 348–349 — PSSL 15A: 75–76.

3819a. [To an unknown 'Madame']

[5]/17 Mar 1889. Hannover — in French

Autograph lost [facs. of p. 1 in Knorr: 64/65].

Not published.

3820. To Aleksandr Ziloti

9/21 Mar [1889]. Paris.

RUS–KL (a³, No. 3008).

*RMG (1908), 43: 933–934 — AIZ: 96–97 — PSSL 15A: 76–77.

3820a. To Josef Sittard

[9]/21 Mar 1889. Paris — in German.

D–Tsiedentopf

H. Siedentopf, *Musiker der Spätromantik* (1979): 77 — PSSL 17: 250–251.

3821. To Pëtr Iurgenson

9/21 Mar 1889. Paris.

RUS–KL (a³, No. 2649).

*ZC 3: 647 — *PIU 2: 118 — PSSL 15A: 78.

3822. To Aleksei Sofronov

10/22 Mar 1889. Paris.

RUS–SPsc (f. 834, No. 27, fol. 35–36).

PSSL 15A: 79.

3823. To Modest Chaikovskii

10/22 Mar 1889. Paris.

RUS–KL (a³, No. 1907).

PSSL 15A: 79–80.

3824. To Nadezhda von Meck

13/25 Mar [1889]. Paris.

RUS–KL (a³, No. 1056).

PM 3: 570 — PSSL 15A: 80–81.

3825. To Modest Chaikovskii

21 Mar/2 Apr 1889. Paris.

RUS–KL (a³, No. 1908).

*ZC 3: 305 ("22 Mar/2 Apr") — *PB: 419 — PSSL 15A: 81–82 — *LF: 419–420 [English tr.].

3826. To Pëtr Iurgenson

21 Mar/2 Apr 1889. Paris.

RUS–KL (a³, No. 2650).

*ZC 3: 304–305 — *PIU 2: 119–120 — PSSL 15A: 82–83.

3827. To Pëtr Iurgenson

21 Mar/2 Apr 1889. Paris.

RUS–KL (a³, No. 2651).

*ZC 3: 304–305 — *PIU 2: 120 — PSSL 15A: 84–85.

3828. To Modest Chaikovskii

[24 Mar/5 Apr 1889. Paris] — telegram; in French.

RUS–KL (a³, No. 2049).

PSSL 15A: 85.

3829. To Modest Chaikovskii

25 Mar/[6] Apr 1889 (in MS: "6 Apr"). Paris.

RUS–KL (a³, No. 1909).

*ZC 3: 305 ("25 Mar/7 Apr") — PB: 419–420 ("26 Mar/7 Apr") — PSSL 15A: 86 — *LF: 420 [English tr.].

3830. To Vladimir Davydov

[29 Mar]/10 Apr 1889 (in MS: "30 Mar"). London.

RUS–KL (a³, No. 118).

*ZC 3: 307–308 — PB: 420–422 — PSSL 15A: 87–88 — *LF: 421–422 [English tr.].

3831. To Nadezhda von Meck

[29] Mar/[10 Apr] 1889 (in MS: "30 Mar"). London.

RUS–KL (a³, No. 1057).

PM 3: 571 — PSSL 15A: 89–90.

3832. To Pëtr Iurgenson

[29] Mar/10 Apr 1889. London.

RUS–KL (a³, No. 2652).

PIU 2: 121–122 — PSSL 15A: 90–91.

3833.   To Aleksei Sofronov
31 Mar/12 Apr 1889. London.
RUS–SPsc (f. 834, No. 27, fol. 38–39).
PSSL 15A: 92.

3834.   To Félix Mackar
[8/20 Apr 1889]. Constantinople — in French.
F–Pn
RdM 54 (1968), 1: 74 — *PSSL* 15A: 92.

3835.   To Modest Chaikovskii
8/[20] Apr 1889. Constantinople.
RUS–KL (a³, No. 1910).
ZC 3: 308–309 — *PB*: 422 — *PSSL* 15A: 93 — *LF*:
   422–423 [English tr.].

3836.   To Aleksandra Hubert
13 Apr 1889. Tiflis.
RUS–KL (a³, No. 63).
PRM 49–50 — *PSSL* 15A: 93–94.

3837.   To Pëtr Iurgenson
13 Apr 1889. Tiflis.
RUS–KL (a³, No. 2653).
PIU 2: 123 — *PSSL* 15A: 94–95.

3838.   To Aleksei Suvorin
15 Apr 1889. Tiflis.
RUS–Mcl (f. 459).
Krasnii arkhiv (1940), 3: 249–250 — *Sovetskoe iskusstvo*
   (29 Mar 1940): 4 — *PSSL* 15A: 95–97.

3839.   To Modest Chaikovskii
15 Apr [1889]. Tiflis.
RUS–KL (a³, No. 1911).
PSSL 15A: 97–98.

3839a. To Vasilii Sapel´nikov
17 Apr 1889. Tiflis.
Autograph lost; photocopy in RUS–KL.
Not published.

3840.   To Aleksei Sofronov
17 Apr [1889]. Tiflis.
RUS–SPsc (f. 834, No. 27, fol. 40–41).
PSSL 15A: 98.

3841.   To Pëtr Iurgenson
19 Apr [1889]. Tiflis.
RUS–KL (a³, No. 2654).
PSSL 15A: 99.

3842.   To Nadezhda von Meck
20 Apr 1889. Tiflis.
RUS–KL (a³, No. 1058).
ZC 3: 309–310 — *PM* 3: 572 — *PSSL* 15A: 99–100.

3843.   To Marius Petipa
26 Apr 1889. Tiflis — in French.
Autograph lost
Memuary Mariusa Petipa (1906): 70–71 — *PSSL* 15A:
   100–101 [Russian trs].

3844.   To Vladimir Pogozhev
26 Apr 1889. Tiflis.
RUS–KL (a³, No. 2879).
VP: 50 — *PSSL* 15A: 101.

3845.   To Modest Chaikovskii
26 Apr 1889 [Tiflis].
RUS–KL (a³, No. 1912).
PSSL 15A: 102.

3846.   To Pëtr Iurgenson
26 Apr 1889 [Tiflis].
RUS–KL (a³, No. 2655).
PIU 2: 124–125 — *PSSL* 15A: 103.

**3847.   To   Grand   Duke   Konstantin
   Konstantinovich**
1 May 1889. Tiflis.
RUS–SPil (f. 137, No. 78/17).
PSSL 15A: 104–105.

3848.   To Iuliia Shpazhinskaia
1 May 1889. Tiflis.
RUS–KL (a³, No. 2118).
CTP: 349 — *PSSL* 15A: 106–107.

3849.   To Anatolii Chaikovskii
4 May [1889]. Vladikavkaz.
RUS–KL (a³, No. 3206).
PSSL 15A: 106–107.

3850.   To Aleksandra Hubert

9 May 1889 [Moscow].

RUS–KL (a³, No. 64).

PRM 50 — *PSSL* 15A: 107.

3851.   To Anatolii Brandukov

10 May 1889. Moscow.

RUS–KL (a³, No. 25).

PSSL 15A: 107–108.

3852.   To Aleksei Suvorin

10 May 1889. Moscow.

RUS–Mcl (f. 459).

Krasnyi arkhiv (1940), 3: 250 — *PSSL* 15A: 108–109.

3852a. To Karl Al´brekht

[? 11 May 1889. Moscow].

RUS–Mcm.

PSSL 17: 251.

3853.   To Karl Al´brekht

12 May 1889. Moscow.

RUS–Mcm (f. 37, No. 66). Unfinished draft in RUS–Mcl (f. 37, No. 67).

PSSL 15A: 109–110; draft in *PSSL* 15A: 228.

3854.   To Berta Foerstrová-Lautererová

12 May 1889. Moscow — in German.

CZ–Pfoerster.

Stěpánek (1952): 153–154 [Czech tr.] — *SM* (1952), 7: 70 [Russian tr.] — *PSSL* 15A: 110.

3855.   To Anatolii Chaikovskii

12 May 1889. Moscow.

RUS–KL (a³, No. 3207).

*ZC 3: 310 — *PB*: 422–423 — *PSSL* 15A: 111–112 — *LF*: 423 [English tr.].

3856.   To Pëtr Iurgenson

[12 May 1889. Moscow].

RUS–KL (a³, No. 2659).

PSSL 15A: 112.

3857.   To Aleksandr Ziloti

[13 May 1889. Moscow].

RUS–KL (a³, No. 3055).

PSSL 15A: 113.

3858.   To Mikhail Ippolitov-Ivanov

19 May 1889. Frolovskoe.

RUS–KL (a³, No. 189).

Iskusstvo, 3 (1927), 4: 155 — *Biulleten´* (1947), 1: 58–59 — *PSSL* 15A: 113.

3859.   To Nadezhda von Meck

19 May 1889. Frolovskoe.

RUS–KL (a³, No. 1059).

*ZC 3: 310–311 — *PM* 3: 573–574 — *PSSL* 15A: 113–114.

3860.   To Sergei Taneev

19 May [1889]. Frolovskoe.

RUS–Mcl (f. 880).

CTP: 160 — *PSSL* 15A: 115.

3861.   To Anatolii Chaikovskii

19 May [1889]. Frolovskoe.

RUS–KL (a³, No. 3189).

PSSL 15A: 115–116.

3861a. To Ethel Smyth

19/31 May 1889 [Frolovskoe] (in MS: "Klin") — in French.

Autograph lost; photocopy in RUS–KL.

ČS 3 (1998): 187.

3862.   To Elizaveta Lavrovskaia

22 May 1889. Frolovskoe.

RUS–KL (a³, No. 261).

Kalininskaia pravda (13 Oct 1970) — *PSSL* 15A: 117.

3863.   To Sergei Taneev

22 May [1889]. [Frolovskoe].

RUS–Mcl (f. 880).

CTP: 161 — *PSSL* 15A: 117.

3864.   To Anatolii Chaikovskii

22 May 1889. Frolovskoe.

RUS–KL (a³, No. 3208).

PSSL 15A: 118.

3865.   To Iuliia Shpazhinskaia

22 May 1889. Frolovskoe.

RUS–KL (a³, No. 2119).

CTP: 350 — *PSSL* 15A: 119–120.

3866.   To Aleksandra Hubert

[24 May 1889. Klin] — telegram.

RUS–KL (a³, No. 103).

PSSL 15A: 120.

3867.   To Berta Foerstrová-Lautererová

26 May 1889 [Frolovskoe] (in MS: "Klin") — in German.

CZ–Pfoerster.

Stěpánek (1952): 154–155 [Czech tr.] — *SM* (1952), 7: 70 [Russian tr.] — *PSSL* 15A: 120–121.

3867a. To Nikolai Sitovskii

[by June 1889. Moscow].

RUS–Mcm (f. 37, No. 100).

PSSL 17: 252.

3868.   To Adol´f Brodskii

2 Jun [1889]. [Frolovskoe] (in MS: "Klin").

GB–Mcm.

PSSL 15A: 122.

3869.   To Modest Chaikovskii

2 Jun [1889. Frolovskoe].

RUS–KL (a³, No. 1913).

PSSL 15A: 123.

3870.   To Iuliia Shpazhinskaia

2 Jun 1889 [Frolovskoe].

RUS–KL (a³, No. 2120).

CTP: 350–351 — *PSSL* 15A: 123–124.

3871.   To Praskov´ia Chaikovskaia

6 Jun [1889]. [Frolovskoe].

RUS–KL (a³, No. 3289).

PSSL 15A: 124–125.

3872.   To Grand Duke Konstantin Konstantinovich

7 Jun 1889. Frolovskoe.

RUS–SPil (f. 137, No. 78/18).

PSSL 15A: 125–126.

3873.   To Pëtr Iurgenson

7 Jun [1889]. Frolovskoe.

RUS–KL (a³, No. 2655).

ZC 3: 312 — *PRM* 51 — *PIU* 2: 126 — *PSSL* 15A: 127.

3874.   To Aleksandr Ziloti

12 Jun [1889]. [Frolovskoe].

RUS–KL (a³, No. 3009).

RMG (1908), 47: 1045–1046 — *AIZ*: 98–99 — *PSSL* 15A: 128.

3875.   To Mikhail Ippolitov-Ivanov

12 Jun 1889. Frolovskoe.

RUS–KL (a³, No. 190).

ZC 3: 312–313 — *Biulleten´* (1947), 1: 1–62 — *PSSL* 15A: 129–130.

3876.   To Mariia Klimentova–Muromtseva

13 Jun 1889. Frolovskoe.

RUS–KL (a³, No. 219).

PSSL 15A: 130–131.

3877.   To Adol´f Brodskii

16 Jun 1889 [Frolovskoe] (in MS: "Klin").

GB–Mcm.

PSSL 15A: 131.

3878.   To Aleksandr Ziloti

16 Jun [1889]. [Frolovskoe].

RUS–KL (a³, No. 3010).

RMG (1908), 47: 1046 ("16 Jul") — *AIZ*: 99 — *PSSL* 15A: 132.

3879.   To Ippolit Al´tani

18 Jun 1889 [Frolovskoe] (in MS: "Klin").

RUS–Mcm (f. 7, No. 57).

PSSL 15A: 133.

3880.   To Aleksandra Hubert

18 Jun [1889]. Frolovskoe.

RUS–KL (a³, No. 65).

PRM 51 — *PSSL* 15A: 134.

3881. To Aleksandr Ziloti

18 Jun [1889]. [Frolovskoe].

RUS–KL (a³, No. 3011).

RMG (1908), 47: 1046 ("18 Jul") — *AIZ:* 100 —
PSSL 15A: 134.

3882. To Nikolai Khristoforov

18 Jun [1889]. [Frolovskoe].

RUS–SPtob (VII.2.4.154).

Kirov: 417 — *PSSL* 15A: 134–135.

3883. To Mariia Klimentova–Muromtseva

19 Jun 1889. Frolovskoe.

RUS–KL (a³, No. 220).

PSSL 15A: 135–136.

3884. To Anatolii Chaikovskii

19 Jun 1889. Frolovskoe.

RUS–KL (a³, No. 3209).

PSSL 15A: 136–137.

3885. To Anna Aleksandrova-Levenson

26 Jun [1889]. [Frolovskoe].

ARM–YE.

PSSL 15A: 137.

3886. To Nadezhda von Meck

26 Jun 1889. Frolovskoe.

RUS–KL (a³, No. 1060).

ZC 3: 313 — PM 3: 575–576 — PSSL 15A: 138–
139.

3887. To Adelina Bolska

26 Jun 1889 [Frolovskoe] (in MS: "Moscow").

RUS–Mcm (f. 314, No. 6).

PSSL 15A: 139–140.

3888. To Ippolit Chaikovskii

26 Jun 1889 [Frolovskoe] (in MS: "Klin").

RUS–SPsc (f. 834, No. 35, fol. 1–2).

PSSL 15A: 140–141.

3889. To Anna Merkling

27 Jun 1889. Frolovskoe.

Autograph lost; MS copy in RUS–KL.

CTP: 235 — *PSSL* 15A: 141.

3889a. To Vasilii Sapel´nikov

[27 Jun 1889. Frolovskoe] (in MS: "Moscow").

Autograph lost; photocopy in RUS–KL.

Not published.

3890. To Anna Merkling

30 Jun 1889 [Frolovskoe].

Autograph lost; MS copy in RUS–KL.

CTP: 235–236 — *PSSL* 15A: 142.

3891. To Vasilii Safonov

30 Jun 1889 [Frolovskoe].

RUS–KL (a³, No. 347).

VIS: 200–201 — *PSSL* 15A: 143–144.

3892. To Ekaterina Larosh

30 Jun [1889]. [Frolovskoe].

Autograph lost; photocopy in RUS–KL.

PSSL 15A: 144–145.

3893. To Aleksandr Iurgenson

1 Jul [1889]. [Frolovskoe].

RUS–Mcl (f. 905).

AIZ: 100 ("to Aleksandr Ziloti") — *PSSL* 15A: 145.

3894. To Grand Duke Konstantin Konstantinovich

2 Jul [1889]. [Frolovskoe].

RUS–SPil (f. 137, No. 78/19).

PSSL 15A: 146–147.

3895. To Anatolii Chaikovskii

3 Jul [1889]. [Frolovskoe].

RUS–KL (a³, No. 3210).

PSSL 15A: 147.

3896. To Aleksandra Hubert

6 Jul [1889]. [Frolovskoe].

RUS–KL (a³, No. 66).

PRM 51 — *PSSL* 15A: 148.

3897. To Boris Iurgenson

8 Jul 1889 [Frolovskoe].

RUS–KL (a³, No. 477).

PSSL 15A: 148.

3898.   To Adol´f Brodskii

9 Jul 1889 [Frolovskoe].

GB–Mcm [facs. in *Sovetskaia kul´tura* (11 Aug 1962)].

PSSL 15A: 149.

3899.   To Eduard Nápravník

9 Jul 1889 [Frolovskoe].

RUS–KL (a³, No. 3334).

*ZC 3: 313–314 — *VP*: 187–189 — *EFN*: 153–155 — *PSSL* 15A: 150–151.

3900.   To Iuliia Shpazhinskaia

9 Jul 1889 [Frolovskoe].

RUS–KL (a³, No. 2121).

CTP: 351 — *PSSL* 15A: 152–153.

3901.   To Osip Iurgenson

9 Jul 1889. Moscow.

RUS–KL (a³, No. 484).

PIU 2: 299 — *PSSL* 15A: 153–154.

3902.   To Aleksandra Hubert

10 Jul [1889]. [Moscow].

RUS–KL (a³, No. 67).

PRM 52–55 — *PSSL* 15A: 154.

3903.   To Nadezhda von Meck

12 Jul 1889. Frolovskoe.

RUS–KL (a³, No. 1061).

*ZC 3: 314–315 — *PM* 3: 578–579 — *PSSL* 15A: 155–156.

3904.   To Anatolii Chaikovskii

12 Jul 1889 [Frolovskoe].

RUS–KL (a³, No. 3211).

*PB: 423 — *PSSL* 15A: 156–157 — **LF*: 424 [English tr.].

3905.   To Aleksandra Hubert

17 Jul [1889]. [Frolovskoe].

RUS–KL (a³, No. 68).

PRM 53 — *PSSL* 15A: 157.

3905a.   To Léonce Détroyat

17 Jul 1889. Frolovskoe — in French.

Autograph auctioned in Paris, 1992.

**A. Lischké, *Piotr Ilyitch Tchaikovsky* (1993): 543.

3906.   To Semen Kruglikov

22 Jul 1889 [Frolovskoe] (in MS: "Klin").

RUS–KL (a³, No. 258).

PSSL 15A: 158.

3907.   To Aleksandr Ziloti

23 Jul 1889. Frolovskoe.

KKL (a³, No. 3012).

RMG (1908), 47: 1046–1047 — *AIZ*: 101 — *PSSL* 15A: 158–159.

3908.   To Iuliia Shpazhinskaia

23 Jul 1889 [Frolovskoe].

RUS–KL (a³, No. 2122).

CTP: 351–352 — *PSSL* 15A: 159–160.

3909.   To Nadezhda von Meck

25 Jul 1889. Frolovskoe.

RUS–KL (a³, No. 1062).

*ZC 3: 315–316 — *PM* 3: 580–581 — *PSSL* 15A: 160–161.

3910.   To Desirée Artôt-Padilla

27 Jul 1889 [Frolovskoe] — in French.

D–Mtf

PSSL 15A: 161.

3911.   To Aleksandr Ziloti

28 Jul [1889]. [Frolovskoe].

RUS–KL (a³, No. 3013).

*RMG (1908), 47: 1047 ("28 Jun") — **AIZ*: 101–102 — *PSSL* 15A: 162.

3912.   To Vladimir Nápravník

31 Jul [1889]. [Frolovskoe].

Autograph lost; typed copy in RUS–KL.

EFN: 194–195 — *PSSL* 15A: 163.

3913.   To Eduard Nápravník

31 Jul 1889 [Frolovskoe].

RUS–KL (a³, No. 3335).

*ZC 3: 316 — *VP*: 193 — *EFN*: 157–158 — *PSSL* 15A: 164.

3914.   To Anatolii Chaikovskii

31 Jul 1889 [Frolovskoe].

RUS–KL (a³, No. 3212).

*PB: 424 — *PSSL* 15A: 165 — **LF*: 424 [English tr.].

3915. To Aleksandr Ziloti
5 Aug [1889]. [Frolovskoe].
RUS–KL (a³, No. 3014).
AIZ: 102 — *PSSL* 15A: 165–166.

3916. To Boris & Aleksandr Iurgenson
5 Aug [1889]. [Frolovskoe].
RUS–KL (a³, No. 482).
PSSL 15A: 166.

3917. To Nadezhda von Meck
7 Aug 1889 [Moscow].
RUS–KL (a³, No. 1063).
PM 3: 581 — *PSSL* 15A: 167.

3917a. To Karl Al´brekht
[8 Aug 1889. Moscow].
RUS–Mcm (f. 37, No. 76).
PSSL 17: 252.

3918. To Konstantin Rukavishnikov
8 Aug 1889 [Moscow].
RUS–SPil (No. 21439).
PSSL 15A: 167.

3919. To Mikhail Ippolitov-Ivanov
9 Aug 1889 [Frolovskoe].
RUS–KL (a³, No. 191).
*ZC 3: 316–317 — Biulleten´ (1947), 1: 64–65 —
PSSL 15A: 168.

3919a. To Wladyslaw Pachulski
9 Aug 1889. Frolovskoe.
CH–Bps.
**Muzykal´noe obozrenie* (20 Nov 1992): 8.

3920. To Nadezhda von Meck
13 Aug 1889 [Frolovskoe].
RUS–KL (a³, No. 1064).
PM 3: 582–583 — *PSSL* 15A: 169–170.

3921. To Pëtr Iurgenson
13 Aug [1889]. [Frolovskoe].
RUS–KL (a³, No. 2657).
PIU 2: 127 — *PSSL* 15A: 170.

3922. To Semen Kruglikov
16 Aug [1889]. [Frolovskoe].
RUS–KL (a³, No. 259).
PSSL 15A: 171.

3923. To Aleksandr Ziloti
17 Aug 1889 [Frolovskoe].
Autograph lost.
**RMG* (1908), 47: 1047 — **AIZ*: 102 — **PSSL* 15A:
171.

3924. To Anna Merkling
21 Aug 1889 [Frolovskoe].
Autograph lost; MS copy in RUS–KL.
CTP: 236 — *PSSL* 15A: 172.

3925. To Anatolii Chaikovskii
21 Aug [1889]. Frolovskoe.
RUS–KL (a³, No. 3213).
PB: 424 — *PSSL* 15A: 172 — *LF*: 424–425 [English
tr.].

3926. To Anatolii Chaikovskii
31 Aug 1889. Kamenka
RUS–KL (a³, No. 3214).
**PB*: 424–425 — *PSSL* 15A: 173 — **LF*: 425–426
[English tr.].

3927. To Modest Chaikovskii
31 Aug 1889. Kamenka
RUS–KL (a³, No. 1914).
PSSL 15A: 174.

3928. To Iuliia Shpazhinskaia
2 Sep 1889. Kamenka
RUS–KL (a³, No. 2123).
CTP: 352–353 — *PSSL* 15A: 175.

3929. To Varvara Zarudnaia
8 Sep [1889]. [Frolovskoe].
RUS–Mcm (f. 2, No. 5116).
**ZC 3: 317–318 — *PSSL* 15A: 176–177.

3930. To Georgii Meklenburg-Strelitskii
8 Sep 1889. Frolovskoe.
RUS–Mf.
Krasnyi arkhiv (1940), 3: 251 — *PSSL* 15A: 177–178.

3931. To Anatolii Chaikovskii

8 Sep 1889. Frolovskoe.

RUS–KL (a³, No. 3215).

PSSL 15A: 178–179.

3931a. To the Committee of the New Symphonic Society (Vienna)

8 Sep 1889 [Frolovskoe] — in French.

Autograph auctioned in Vienna, 1994.

*ČS 3 (1998): 186.

3932. [To an unidentified correspondent]

[? 11 Sep 1889. Moscow] — rough draft on an undated letter from Aleksandra Hubert; in French.

RUS–KL.

PSSL 15A: 179.

3933. To Anatolii Brandukov

12 Sep [?1889]. [Moscow].

RUS–KL (a³, No. 30).

PSSL 15A: 179.

3934. To Aleksei Sofronov

12 Sep 1889 [Moscow].

RUS–SPsc (f. 834, No. 27, fol. 42–43).

PSSL 15A: 180.

3935. To Willy Burmester

13 Sep [1889]. [Moscow] — in German.

Autograph lost

W. Burmester, *Fünfzig Jahre Künstlerleben* (1926): 66 ("1888") — *Muzykal´noe nasledstvo*, 1 (1962): 369 ("1888") [inc. Russian tr.] — *PSSL* 15A: 180.

3936. To Félix Mackar

13 Sep 1889 [Moscow] — in French.

F–Pn

RdM 54 (1968), 1: 74 — *PSSL* 15A: 181.

3937. To Modest Chaikovskii

13 Sep [1889]. Moscow.

RUS–KL (a³, No. 1915).

PB: 425–426 — *PSSL* 15A: 181–182 — *LF*: 426 [English tr.].

3938. To Adol´f Brodskii

15 Sep 1889. Moscow.

GB–Mcm

PSSL 15A: 182–183.

3939. To Aleksandr Khimichenko

15 Sep 1889. Moscow.

RUS–KL (a³, No. 3345) [facs. in *P. I. Chaikovskii na Ukraini* (1940): 112/113].

Radian´ska muzyka (1940), 2 — *PSSL* 15A: 183.

3940. To Aleksandra Hubert

[18–19 Sep 1889. Moscow].

RUS–KL (a³, No. 69).

PRM 53 — *PSSL* 15A: 184.

3941. To Anna Leshetitskaia-Frideburg

19 Sep 1889 [Moscow].

RUS–KL (a³, No. 3304).

PSSL 15A: 184.

3942. To Aleksandr Glazunov

25 Sep 1889 [St. Petersburg].

Autograph lost; MS copy in RUS–KL.

PSSL 15A: 185.

3943. To Freidrich Sieger

[1 Oct] 1889 (in MS: "30 Sep") [Moscow] — in French.

US–NYmo

PSSL 15A: 185–186.

3944. To Nikolai Rimskii-Korsakov

1 Oct [1889]. [Moscow].

RUS–SPsc (f. 640, op. 1, No. 1015, fol. 28–29).

SM (1945), 3: 141 — *RK* 7 (1970): 58 — *PSSL* 15A: 187.

3945. To Anatolii Chaikovskii

1 Oct 1889. Moscow.

RUS–KL (a³, No. 3216).

PB: 426 — *PSSL* 15A: 187 — *LF: 427 [English tr.].

3946. To Modest Chaikovskii

1 Oct [1889]. [Moscow].

RUS–KL (a³, No. 1916).

PSSL 15A: 189.

3947. To Nadezhda von Meck

2 Oct 1889. Moscow.

RUS–KL (a³, No. 1065).

*ZC 3: 322 — PM 3: 583–584 — PSSL 15A: 189–191.

3948. To Pëtr Iurgenson

[3 Oct 1889. Moscow].

RUS–KL (a³, No. 2855).

PSSL 15A: 191.

3949. To Adol´f Brodskii

4 Oct 1889. Moscow.

GB–Mcm [facs. in Sovetskaia kul´tura (11 Aug 1962)].

PSSL 15A: 192.

3950. To Iakov Polonskii

4 Oct 1889. Moscow.

RUS–SPil

PSSL 15A: 192–193.

3951. To Nikolai Rimskii-Korsakov

5 Oct 1889 [Moscow].

RUS–SPsc (f. 640, op. 1, No. 1015, fol. 30–31).

SM (1945), 3: 141 — RK 7 (1970): 59 — PSSL 15A: 193–194.

3952. To Anna Aleksandrova-Levenson

6 Oct [1889]. [Moscow].

RUS–KL (a³, No. 5).

PSSL 15A: 195.

3953. To Pëtr Iurgenson

[6 Oct 1889. Moscow].

RUS–KL (a³, No. 2665).

PSSL 15A: 195.

3954. To Aleksandra Hubert

[8 Oct 1889. Moscow].

RUS–KL (a³, No. 84).

PSSL 15A: 195.

3955. To Sergei Taneev

[?7–9 Oct 1889. Moscow].

RUS–Mcl (f. 880).

CTP: 200 (undated) — PSSL 15A: 196.

3956. To Anna Voitkevich

9 Oct 1889. Moscow.

RUS–KL (a³, No. 283).

PSSL 15A: 196.

3956a. To the editor of Moskovskie vedomosti

9 Oct 1889. Moscow.

unknown

Moskovskie vedomosti (11 Oct 1889) — Muzykal´naia zhizn´ (1992), 17/18: 24.

3957. To Nadezhda von Meck

12 Oct 1889. Moscow.

RUS–KL (a³, No. 1066).

*ZC 3: 322 — PM 3: 585–586 — PSSL 15A: 196–197.

3958. To Anton Chekhov

14 Oct 1889 [Moscow].

RUS–Mrg [facs. in E. Balabanovich, Chekhov i Chaikovskii (1962): 12/13; 2-e izd. (1970): 64/65].

I. R. Eiges, Muzyka v zhizni i tvorchestve A. P. Chekhova (1953): 27–28 — PSSL 15A: 198.

3958a. To Vasilii Sapel´nikov

14 Oct 1889. Moscow — partly in French.

US–NHub

Not published.

3959. To Grand Duke Konstantin Konstantinovich

15 Oct 1889. Moscow.

RUS–SPil (f. 137, No. 78/20).

*ZC 3: 323–325 — PSSL 15A: 198–200.

3960. To Anatolii Brandukov

16 Oct 1889 [Moscow].

RUS–KL (a³, No. 27).

PSSL 15A: 200.

3961. To Modest Chaikovskii

16 Oct [1889]. [Moscow].

RUS–KL (a³, No. 1917).

ZC 3: 325–326 — PB: 426–427 — PSSL 15A: 201 — *LF: 427–428 [English tr.].

3962.   To Anton Chekhov

20 Oct 1889 [Moscow].

RUS–Mrg

*E. Balabanovich, *Chekhov i Chaikovskii* (1962): 24; 2–e izd. (1970): 105 — *PSSL* 15A: 202.

3963.   To Vasilii Safonov

[late Oct 1889. Moscow].

RUS–KL (a³, No. 346).

PSSL 15A: 202.

3964.   To Anna Aleksandrova-Levenson

27 Oct 1889 [Moscow].

RUS–KL (a³, No. 3326).

PSSL 15A: 203.

3965.   To Lidiia Genke

27 Oct 1889 [Moscow].

RUS–Mcl (f. 905).

PSSL 15A: 203–204.

3966.   To Grand Duke Konstantin Konstantinovich

29 Oct 1889. Moscow.

RUS–SPil (f. 137, No. 78/21).

ZC 3: 328–330 — *PSSL* 15A: 204–205.

3967.   To Aleksandr Glazunov

2 Nov 1889 [St. Petersburg].

RUS–KL (a³, No. 38).

PSSL 15A: 206.

3968.   To Elizaveta Lavrovskaia

2 Nov 1889 [St. Petersburg].

RUS–Mcl (f. 787).

PSSL 15A: 207.

3969.   To Ekaterina & German Larosh

4 Nov 1889 [St. Petersburg] — partly in French.

Autograph lost; photocopy in RUS–KL.

PSSL 15A: 208.

3970.   To Aleksandr Glazunov

8 Nov 1889. St. Petersburg.

Autograph lost; MS copy in RUS–KL.

SM (1945), 3: 60 — *PSSL* 15A: 208–209.

3971.   To Ol´ga Chaikovskaia

8 Nov [1889]. [St. Petersburg].

RUS–SPsc (f. 834, No. 31, fol. 11–12).

PSSL 15A: 209.

3972.   To Avgust Gerke

9 Nov 1889. St. Petersburg.

RUS–SPsc (f. 654, op. 1, No. 118, fol. 1–2).

PSSL 15A: 209–210.

3973.   To Iuliia Shpazhinskaia

11 Nov 1889 [Moscow].

RUS–KL (a³, No. 2124).

CTP: 353 — *PSSL* 15A: 210–211.

3974.   To Avgust Gerke

14 Nov 1889 [St. Petersburg].

RUS–SPsc (f. 654, No. 118).

PSSL 15A: 211.

3975.   To Nadezhda von Meck

22 Nov 1889. Moscow.

RUS–KL (a³, No. 1067).

PM 3: 587–588 — *PSSL* 15A: 212–213.

3976.   To Grand Duke Konstantin Konstantinovich

22 Nov 1889. Moscow.

RUS–SPil (f. 137, No. 78/22).

PSSL 15A: 213.

3976a. To Karl Klindworth

27 Nov 1889. Moscow — in German.

D–MZsch

TGM 7 (2000): 22–23.

3977.   To Vladimir Frolov

28 Nov 1889 [Moscow].

RUS–KL (a³, No. 3305).

PSSL 15A: 214.

3978.   To Sergei Ziloti

1 Dec 1889 [St. Petersburg].

RUS–KL (a³, No. 3316).

PSSL 15A: 214.

3979.   To Ol´ga & Varvara Nápravník
4 Dec [?1889]. [St. Petersburg].
RUS–KL (a³, No. 2990).
PSSL 15A: 215.

3980.   To Elizaveta Chaikovskaia
8 Dec 1889 [St. Petersburg].
RUS–SPsc (f. 834, No. 30 fol. 13–15).
PSSL 15A: 215.

3981.   To Félix Mackar
10 Dec 1889. St. Petersburg — in French.
F–Pn
RdM 54 (1968), 1: 75 — *PSSL* 15A: 215–216.

3982.   To Vasilii Safonov
10 Dec 1889. St. Petersburg.
RUS–KL (a³, No. 348).
VIS: 200–201 — *PSSL* 15A: 217.

3983.   To Pëtr Iurgenson
[11] Dec 1889 (in MS: "12 Dec"). St. Petersburg.
RUS–KL (a³, No. 2660).
PIU 2: 128 ("12 Dec") — *PSSL* 15A: 217.

3984.   To Pëtr Iurgenson
[late Dec 1889. St. Petersburg].
RUS–KL (a³, No. 2661).
PSSL 15A: 218.

3985.   To Nadezhda von Meck
17–26 Dec 1889. St. Petersburg–Moscow.
RUS–KL (a³, No. 1068).
*ZC 3: 337 — *PSSL* 15A: 218–220.

3986.   To Pëtr Iurgenson
[?18 Dec 1889. Moscow].
RUS–KL (a³, No. 2662).
PSSL 15A: 221.

3987.   To Pëtr Iurgenson
18 Dec 1889 [St. Petersburg].
RUS–KL (a³, No. 2664).
PSSL 15A: 221.

3988.   To Pavel Pchel´nikov
21 Dec 1889 [St. Petersburg].
RUS–KL (a³, No. 313).
PSSL 15A: 222.

3989.   To Anna Aleksandrova-Levenson
[22 Dec 1889. Moscow].
RUS–Mberggolts
PSSL 15A: 222.

3990.   To Aleksandr Glazunov
23 Dec 1889. Moscow.
Autograph lost; MS copy in RUS–KL.
SM (1945), 3: 61 — *PSSL* 15A: 223.

3991.   To Pëtr Iurgenson
[28 Dec 1889. Moscow].
RUS–KL (a³, No. 2711).
PSSL 15A: 223.

3992.   To Anatolii Liadov
[29 Dec 1889. St. Petersburg].
RUS–SPsc (f. 449, No. 65, fol. 5–6).
PSSL 15A: 224.

3992a. To Zinaida Larosh
[1889].
RUS–KL (a³, No. 3346).
Not published.

1890

3993.   To Aleksandr Glazunov
2 Jan 1890 [St. Petersburg].
Autograph lost; MS copy in RUS–KL.
PSSL 15B: 13.

3994.   To Anatolii Liadov
2 Jan [1890] (in MS: "1889") [St. Petersburg].
RUS–SPsc (f. 449, No. 65, fol. 1–2).
PSSL 15B: 13–14.

3995.   To Osip Iurgenson
[2 Jan 1890. St. Petersburg].
RUS–SPsc
PSSL 15B: 14.

3996.   **To Pavel Tret´iakov**
3 Jan [1890]. [St. Petersburg].
RUS–KL (a³, No. 413).
PSSL 15B: 14.

3997.   **To Aleksei Suvorin**
3–[4] Jan 1890. St. Petersburg.
RUS–Mcl (f. 459).
Krasnyi arkhiv (1940), 3: 244 — *PSSL* 15B: 15.

3998.   **To Edouard Colonne**
7 Jan 1890 [Moscow] — in French.
F–Po
RdM 54 (1968), 1: 85 — *PSSL* 15B: 15.

3999.   **To Pëtr Iurgenson**
[8 Jan 1890. Moscow].
RUS–KL (a³, No. 2663).
*PSSL 15B: 16.

4000.   **To Pëtr Iurgenson**
[8 Jan 1890. Moscow].
RUS–KL (a³, No. 2729).
PSSL 15B: 16.

4001.   **To Aleksandr Ziloti**
[mid Jan 1890. St. Petersburg].
RUS–KL (a³, No. 3054).
AIZ: 103 — *PSSL* 15B: 17.

4002.   **To Pëtr Iurgenson**
12 Jan 1890 [St. Petersburg].
RUS–KL (a³, No. 2666).
PSSL 15B: 17.

4003.   **To Aleksandr Glazunov**
[14 Jan 1890. St. Petersburg].
RUS–KL (a³, No. 39).
PSSL 15B: 17.

4004.   **To Pëtr Iurgenson**
14 Jan [1890]. [St. Petersburg].
RUS–KL (a³, No. 2667).
PSSL 15B: 18.

4005.   **To Anatolii Chaikovskii**
16/28 Jan 1890. Berlin.
Autograph lost; MS copy in RUS–KL.
PSSL 15B: 18–19.

4006.   **To Modest Chaikovskii**
16/28 Jan 1890. Berlin.
RUS–KL (a³, No. 1918).
*ZC 3: 341 — *PB*: 427 — *PSSL* 15B: 19 — **LF*: 429
[English tr.].

4007.   **To Pëtr Iurgenson**
[16/28 Jan 1890. Berlin] — telegram; in German.
RUS–KL (a³, No. 2730).
PSSL 15B: 19.

4008.   **To Ekaterina & German Larosh**
18/30 Jan 1890. Florence.
Autograph lost; photocopy in RUS–KL.
PSSL 15B: 20.

4009.   **To Modest Chaikovskii**
18/30 Jan 1890. Florence.
RUS–KL (a³, No. 1919).
*ZC 3: 341–342 — *PB*: 427–428 — *PSSL* 15B: 20–
21 — *LF*: 429–430 [English tr.].

4010.   **To Pëtr Iurgenson**
[18/30 Jan 1890. Florence] — telegram; in French.
RUS–KL (a³, No. 2731).
PSSL 15B: 21.

4011.   **To Anatolii Chaikovskii**
23 Jan/4 Feb 1890. Florence.
RUS–KL (a³, No. 1403).
PSSL 15B: 21–22.

4012.   **To Modest Chaikovskii**
23 Jan/4 Feb 1890 [Florence].
RUS–KL (a³, No. 1921).
*ZC 3: 343 — *PB*: 429–429 — *PSSL* 15B: 22–24 —
*LF: 430–431 [English tr.].

4012a.   **To Pëtr Iurgenson**
[24–25 Jan/5–6 Feb 1890. Florence].
RUS–KL (a³, No. 2856) [ending only].
Not published.

4013. To Modest Chaikovskii

25 Jan/[6 Feb] 1890. Florence.

RUS–KL (a³, No. 1920).

*ZC 3: 344–345 — PB: 429–430 — PSSL 15B: 24–25 — LF: 431–432 [English tr.].

4014. To Iuliia Shpazhinskaia

26 Jan/7 Feb 1890. Florence.

RUS–KL (a³, No. 2125).

CTP: 354–355 — PSSL 15B: 26–27.

4015. To Pëtr Iurgenson

26 Jan/7 Feb 1890. Florence.

RUS–KL (a³, No. 2669).

PIU 2: 134 — PSSL 15B: 27–28.

4016. To Ekaterina & German Larosh

28 Jan/9 Feb 1890. Florence.

Autograph lost; photocopy in RUS–KL.

PSSL 15B: 28–29.

4017. To Pëtr Iurgenson

28 Jan/9 Feb 1890 [Florence].

RUS–KL (a³, No. 2668).

*ZC 3: 342–343 ("22 Jan") — PIU 2: 134–135 — PSSL 15B: 29–30.

4018. To Aleksandr Glazunov

30 Jan/11 Feb 1890. Florence.

Autograph lost; MS copy in RUS–KL.

*ZC 3: 345–346 — SM (1945), 3: 60–61 — *A. K. Glazunov: Pis´ma, stat´i, vospominaniia (1958): 144–145 — PSSL 15B: 30–32.

4019. To Antonina Chaikovskaia

30 Jan/11 Feb 1890 [Florence].

RUS–KL.

PSSL 15B: 32–34.

4020. To Pëtr Iurgenson

30 Jan/[11] Feb 1890 (in MS: "10 Feb"). Florence.

RUS–KL (a³, No. 2670).

*ZC 3: 347 — *PIU 2: 135 — PSSL 15B: 34–35.

4021. To Aleksandr Ziloti

1/13 Feb 1890. Florence.

RUS–KL (a³, No. 175).

*RMG (1908), 43: 934–935, 47: 1041 — AIZ: 105–106 — PSSL 15B: 36–37.

4022. To Modest Chaikovskii

2/14 Feb 1890. Florence.

RUS–KL (a³, No. 1922).

*ZC 3: 347 — *PB: 430–431 — PSSL 15B: 38–39 — *LF: 432–433 [English tr.].

4023. To Osip Iurgenson

2/14 Feb 1890. Florence.

RUS–Mcl (f. 931).

PSSL 15B: 39.

4024. To Pëtr Iurgenson

2/14 Feb 1890. Florence.

RUS–KL (a³, No. 2671).

*PIU 2: 135–136 — PSSL 15B: 39–40.

4025. To Anna Merkling

6/18 Feb 1890. Florence.

Autograph lost; MS copy in RUS–KL.

CTP: 236–237 — PSSL 15B: 40–41.

4026. To Anatolii Chaikovskii

6/18 Feb 1890. Florence.

RUS–KL (a³, No. 1404).

PSSL 15B: 41–42.

4027. To Modest Chaikovskii

6/18 Feb 1890. Florence.

RUS–KL (a³, No. 1923).

*ZC 3: 348–349 — *Sovetskoe iskusstvo (30 Aug 1938) — PB: 431–433 — PSSL 15B: 42–43 — *LF: 433–434 [English tr.].

4028. To Anna Merkling

7/19 Feb 1890. Florence.

Autograph lost; MS copy in RUS–KL.

*ZC 3: 349 — CTP: 237 — PSSL 15B: 44–45.

4029. To Mariia Klimentova–Muromtseva

10/22 Feb 1890. Florence.

RUS–KL (a³, No. 221).

PSSL 15B: 45.

4030. To Ambroise Thomas

[10]/22 Feb 1890. Florence — in French.

RUS–KL (a³, No. 411).

PSSL 15B: 46.

4031. To Nikolai Konradi

10/22 Feb 1890. Florence.

Autograph lost; MS copy in RUS–KL.

CTP: 277 — *PSSL* 15B: 46–47.

4032. To Aleksei Maslov-Bezhetskii

13/25 Feb [1890]. Florence.

RUS–SPsc (f. 834, No. 40).

PSSL 15B: 47.

4033. To Anna Merkling

13/25 Feb 1890. Florence.

Autograph lost; MS copy in RUS–KL.

CTP: 237–238 — *PSSL* 15B: 48.

4034. To Modest Chaikovskii

13/25 Feb 1890 [Florence].

RUS–KL (a³, No. 1924).

ZC 3: 349–350 ("12/25 Feb") — *PB*: 433–434 —
   PSSL 15B: 48–49 — *LF*: 435–436 [English tr.].

4035. To Pëtr Iurgenson

[14/26 Feb 1890. Florence] — telegram; in German.

RUS–KL (a³, No. 2732).

PSSL 15B: 50.

4036. To Pëtr Iurgenson

14/26 Feb 1890. Florence.

RUS–KL (a³, No. 2673).

PIU 2: 139 — *PSSL* 15B: 50.

4037. To German Larosh

15/27 Feb 1890. Florence.

Autograph lost; photocopy in RUS–KL.

PSSL 15B: 51–52.

4038. To Ekaterina Larosh

15/27 Feb [1890]. Florence.

Autograph lost; photocopy in RUS–KL.

PSSL 15B: 52–53.

4038a. To Karl Klindworth

16/28 Feb 1890. Florence — in French.

D–MZsch

TGM 7 (2000): 25–27.

4039. To the Moscow Branch of the Russsian Musical Society

17 Feb/1 Mar 1890. Florence.

RUS–KL (a³, No. 338).

Muzyka i revoliutsiia (1928), 11: 27–29 — *PSSL* 15B:
   53–56.

4040. To Pëtr Iurgenson

17 Feb/1 Mar [1890]. Florence.

RUS–KL (a³, No. 2674).

ZC 3: 351 — *Muzyka i revoliutsiia* (1928), 11: 29 —
   PIU 2: 139–140 — *PSSL* 15B: 57.

4041. To Mariia Klimentova–Muromtseva

19 Feb/3 Mar 1890 [Florence].

RUS–KL (a³, No. 222).

PSSL 15B: 58–59.

4042. To Anna Merkling

19 Feb/3 Mar 1890. Florence.

Autograph lost; MS copy in RUS–KL.

ZC 3: 351–352 ("18 Feb") — *CTP*: 238 ("18 Feb/2
   Mar") — *PSSL* 15B: 59–60.

4043. To Pëtr Iurgenson

19 Feb/3 Mar 1890. Florence.

RUS–KL (a³, No. 2675).

ZC 3: 352–353 — *Muzyka i revoliutsiia* (1928), 11:
   29–30 — *PIU* 2: 140–141 — *PSSL* 15B: 60–61.

4044. To Modest Chaikovskii

20 Feb/4 Mar 1890 [Florence].

RUS–KL (a³, No. 1925) [facs. in *Kirov*: 119].

ZC 3: 354–355 — *PB*: 434–437 — *PSSL* 15B: 62–
   64 — *LF*: 436–438 [English tr.].

4045. To Modest Chaikovskii

21 Feb/5 Mar [1890]. [Florence].

RUS–KL (a³, No. 1926).

ZC 3: 355 — *PB*: 437 — *PSSL* 15B: 64–65 — *LF*:
   438–439 [English tr.].

4046. To Nikolai Chaikovskii

22 Feb/6 Mar [1890]. Florence.

RUS–SPsc (f. 834, No. 37, fol. 18–19).

PB: 437–438 — *PSSL* 15B: 65–66 — *LF*: 439–440
[English tr.].

4047. To Anatolii Chaikovskii

[23] Feb/7 Mar 1890 (in MS: "24 Feb"). Florence.

RUS–KL (a³, No. 1405).

PSSL 15B: 66–67.

4048. To Pëtr Iurgenson

23 Feb/7 Mar 1890 [Florence].

RUS–KL (a³, No. 2676).

PIU 2: 141.

4049. To Modest Chaikovskii

[24] Feb/8 Mar 1890 (in MS: "25 Feb"). Florence.

RUS–KL (a³, No. 1927).

Sovetskoe iskusstvo (30 Aug 1938) — *PB*: 438–444 —
PSSL 15B: 68–73 — *LF*: 440–444 [English tr.].

4050. To Desirée Artôt–Padilla

25 Feb/9 Mar 1890. Florence — in French.

RUS–Mcl (f. 905).

CTP: 374–375 — *PSSL* 15B: 73–75.

4051. To Modest Chaikovskii

[25] Feb/9 Mar 1890 (in MS: "26 Feb") [Florence].

RUS–KL (a³, No. 1928).

ZC 3: 356 ("26 Feb") — *PB*: 444 — *PSSL* 15B: 77 —
LF: 444–445 [English tr.].

4052. To Wladyslaw Pachulski

27 Feb/11 Mar 1890. Florence.

US–Wc

SM (1959), 12: 72–74 — *PSSL* 15B: 78–80.

4053. To Modest Chaikovskii

27 Feb/11 Mar 1890 [Florence].

RUS–KL (a³, No. 1929).

ZC 3: 356–357 — *PB*: 445 — *PSSL* 15B: 81 — *LF*:
445 [English tr.].

4054. To Pëtr Iurgenson

28 Feb/12 Mar 1890 [Florence].

RUS–KL (a³, No. 2677).

PIU 2: 143 — *PSSL* 15B: 81–82.

4055. To Modest Chaikovskii

2/14 Mar 1890. Florence.

RUS–KL (a³, No. 1930).

PB: 445–446 — *PSSL* 15B: 83 — *LF*: 446
[English tr.].

4056. To Modest Chaikovskii

[3/15 Mar 1890. Florence] — telegram; in French.

RUS–KL (a³, No. 2050).

PSSL 15B: 84.

4057. To Pëtr Iurgenson

3/15 Mar [1890]. Florence.

RUS–KL (a³, No. 2678).

PIU 2: 143–144 — *PSSL* 15B: 84–85.

4058. To Modest Chaikovskii

3/15 Mar 1890 [Florence].

RUS–KL (a³, No. 1931).

ZC 3: 357–358 — *PB*: 446–448 — *PSSL* 15B: 85–
88 — *LF*: 447–449 [English tr.].

4059. To Anna Merkling

5/17 Mar 1890 [Florence].

Autograph lost; MS copy in RUS–KL.

ZC 3: 358–359 — *CTP*: 239 — *PSSL* 15B: 89–90.

4060. To Modest Chaikovskii

5/17 Mar 1890 [Florence].

RUS–KL (a³, No. 1932).

ZC 3: 358 — *PB*: 448–449 — *PSSL* 15B: 90 — *LF*:
449–450 [English tr.].

4061. To Pëtr Iurgenson

5/17 Mar 1890 [Florence].

RUS–KL (a³, No. 2679).

PIU 2: 144–146 — *PSSL* 15B: 91–93.

4062. To Nikolai Konradi

6/18 Mar 1890. Florence

Autograph lost; MS copy in RUS–KL.

CTP: 278 — *PSSL* 15B: 92–93.

4063.   To Pëtr Iurgenson

[6/18 Mar 1890. Florence] — telegram; in German.

RUS–KL (a³, No. 2733).

PSSL 15B: 94.

4064.   To Nikolai Khristoforov

7/19 Mar [1890]. Florence.

RUS–SPtob (VII.2.4.154).

Kirov: 418 — *PSSL* 15B: 95.

4065.   To Anatolii Chaikovskii

7/19 Mar 1890. Florence.

RUS–KL (a³, No. 1406).

PSSL 15B: 95–96.

4066.   To Pëtr Iurgenson

8/20 Mar [1890]. Florence.

RUS–KL (a³, No. 2680).

PIU 2: 247 — *PSSL* 15B: 96–97.

4067.   To Modest Chaikovskii

9/21 Mar 1890 [Florence].

RUS–KL (a³, No. 1933).

PB: 449 — *PSSL* 15B: 97–98 — **LF*: 450 [English tr.].

4068.   To Félix Mackar

[14]/26 Mar 1890. Florence — in French.

F–Pn

RdM 54 (1968), 1: 75–76 — *PSSL* 15B: 98–99.

4069.   To Wladyslaw Pachulski

14/26 Mar 1890. Florence.

US–Wc

SM (1959), 12: 74–75 — *PSSL* 15B: 100–102.

4070.   To Modest Chaikovskii

14/26 Mar 1890 [Florence].

RUS–KL (a³, No. 1934).

ZC 3: 359 — *PB*: 450 — *PSSL* 15B: 102 — **LF*: 450–451 [English tr.].

4071.   To Modest Chaikovskii

18/30 Mar 1890 [Florence].

RUS–KL (a³, No. 1935).

*ZC 3: 359 — *PB*: 450 — *PSSL* 15B: 103 — *LF*: 491 [English tr.].

4072.   To Modest Chaikovskii

19/31 Mar 1890 [Florence].

RUS–KL (a³, No. 1936).

*ZC 3: 360–361 — *PB*: 450–451 — *PSSL* 15B: 103–104 — *LF*: 451–452 [English tr.].

4073.   To Pëtr Iurgenson

19/31 Mar [1890]. Florence.

RUS–KL (a³, No. 2681).

*ZC 3: 359–360 — *PIU* 2: 148–149 — *PSSL* 15B: 104–105.

4074.   To Nikolai Konradi

20 Mar/1 Apr 1890. Florence.

Autograph lost; MS copy in RUS–KL.

CTP: 278–279 — *PSSL* 15B: 105–106.

4075.   To Iuliia Shpazhinskaia

20 Mar/1 Apr 1890. Florence.

RUS–KL (a³, No. 2126).

CTP: 355–356 — *PSSL* 15B: 106–107.

4076.   To Aleksandr Ziloti

[22 Mar/3 Apr 1890]. Florence.

RUS–KL (a³, No. 3016).

AIZ: 105–106 — *PSSL* 15B: 107–108.

4077.   To Modest Chaikovskii

23 Mar/4 Apr [1890]. [Florence].

RUS–KL (a³, No. 1937).

PB: 452 — *PSSL* 15B: 108 — *LF*: 452–453 [English tr.].

4078.   To Ivan Vsevolozhskii

26 Mar/7 Apr 1890. Florence.

RUS–KL (a³, No. 33) [facs. in *Kirov:* 114/115].

Orfei (1922), 1: 180–181— *PSSL* 15B: 108–111.

4079.   To Modest Chaikovskii

26 Mar/7 Apr [1890]. [Florence].

RUS–KL (a³, No. 1938).

*ZC 3: 361–362 — *PB*: 452–454 — *PSSL* 15B: 111–113 — *LF*: 453–454 [English tr.].

4080.   To Vladimir Davydov

27 Mar/8 Apr 1890. Rome.

RUS–Mcl (f. 905).

PSSL 15B: 114.

4081.   To Nadezhda von Meck

27 Mar/8 Apr 1890. Rome.

RUS–KL (a³, No. 1069).

PM 3: 591–592 — *PSSL* 15B: 115–116.

4082.   To Anna Merkling

27 Mar/8 Apr 1890. Rome.

Autograph lost; MS copy in RUS–KL.

CTP: 240 — *PSSL* 15B: 116–117.

4083.   To Modest Chaikovskii

27 Mar/8 Apr 1890 [Rome].

RUS–KL (a³, No. 1939).

*ZC 3: 362–363 — *PB*: 454–455 — *PSSL* 15B: 117–118 — *LF*: 455–456 [English tr.].

4084.   To Pëtr Iurgenson

[27 Mar/8 Apr 1890. Rome] — telegram; in German.

RUS–KL (a³, No. 2734).

PSSL 15B: 119.

4085.   To Pëtr Iurgenson

28 Mar/9 Apr 1890. Rome.

RUS–KL (a³, No. 2682).

*ZC 3: 363–364 — *PIU* 2: 150–152 — *PSSL* 15B: 119–121.

4086.   To Anatolii Chaikovskii

29 Mar/10 Apr 1890. Rome.

RUS–KL (a³, No. 1407).

PB: 455–456 — *PSSL* 15B: 121–122 — *LF*: 456 [English tr.].

4087.   To German Larosh

2/[14] Apr [1890]. Rome.

Autograph lost; photocopy in RUS–KL.

PSSL 15B: 122.

4088.   To Félix Mackar

3/15 Apr 1890. Rome — in French.

F–Pn

RdM 54 (1968), 1: 76–77 — *SM* (1970), 9: 71 [Russian tr.] — *PSSL* 15B: 123–124.

4089.   To Modest Chaikovskii

3/15 Apr 1890. Rome.

RUS–KL (a³, No. 264).

*ZC 3: 364 — **PB*: 456 — *PSSL* 15B: 124–125 — **LF*: 456–457 [English tr.].

4090.   To Pëtr Iurgenson

3/15 Apr [1890]. Rome.

RUS–KL (a³, No. 2683).

PIU 2: 153–154 — *PSSL* 15B: 125–126.

4091.   To Giovanni Sgambati

[6]/18 Apr [1890]. Rome — in French.

I–Rsgambati

PSSL 15B: 127.

4092.   To Nadezhda von Meck

7/19 Apr 1890. Rome.

RUS–KL (a³, No. 1070).

*ZC 3: 364–365 — *PM* 3: 594–595 — *PSSL* 15B: 127–129.

4093.   To Anna Merkling

7/19 Apr 1890. Rome.

Autograph lost; MS copy in RUS–KL.

CTP: 240 — *PSSL* 15B: 129.

4094.   To Grand Duke Konstantin Konstantinovich

7/19 Apr [1890]. Rome.

RUS–SPil (f. 137, No. 78/23).

PSSL 15B: 129–130.

4095.   To Modest Chaikovskii

7/19 Apr 1890. Rome.

RUS–KL (a³, No. 1941).

*ZC 3: 365 — *PB*: 457 — *PSSL* 15B: 132 — *LF*: 457–458 [English tr.].

4096.   To Pëtr Iurgenson

9/[21] Apr [1890]. [Rome].

RUS–KL (a³, No. 2684).

PIU 2: 154 — *PSSL* 15B: 133.

4097.   To Pëtr Iurgenson

11/23 [Apr] 1890 (in MS: "Feb"). Rome.

RUS–KL (a³, No. 2672).

PIU 2: 155–156 — *PSSL* 15B: 133.

4098.   To Sergei Taneev

13/[25] Apr 1890. Rome.

RUS–Mcl (f. 880).

CTP: 165 — *PSSL* 15B: 134–135.

4099.   To Praskov´ia & Anatolii Chaikovskii

17/29 Apr 1890. Rome.

RUS–KL (a³, No. 1408).

PB: 457–458 — *PSSL* 15B: 135–136 — *LF*: 458
[English tr.].

4100.   To Pëtr Iurgenson

26 Apr [1890]. St. Petersburg.

RUS–KL (a³, No. 2685).

PIU 2: 156 — *PSSL* 15B: 136.

4101.   To Ivan Vsevolozhskii

1 May 1890. St. Petersburg.

RUS–KL (a³, No. 185).

Orfei (1922), 1: 185 — *PSSL* 15B: 137.

4102.   To Pëtr Iurgenson

[1 May 1890. St. Petersburg] — telegram.

RUS–KL (a³, No. 2735).

PSSL 15B: 137.

4103.   To Anna Rebezova

3 May 1890. Frolovskoe.

RUS–SPsc (654, op. 1, No. 111).

PSSL 15B: 138.

4104.   To Pëtr Iurgenson

3 May [1890]. Frolovskoe.

RUS–KL (a³, No. 2686).

PIU 2: 156–157 — *PSSL* 15B: 138–139.

4105.   To Aleksandra Hubert

5 May [1890]. [Frolovskoe].

RUS–KL (a³, No. 71).

PRM 53 — *PSSL* 15B: 139–140.

4106.   To Aleksandr Ziloti

5 May [1890]. [Frolovskoe].

RUS–KL (a³, No. 3017).

AIZ: 109 — *PSSL* 15B: 140.

4107.   To Mikhail Ippolitov-Ivanov

5 May 1890. Frolovskoe.

RUS–KL (a³, No. 192).

*ZC 3: 366–367— *Biulleten´* (1947), 2: 1–3 — *PSSL*
15B: 140–142.

4108.   To Pavel Pchel´nikov

[5 May 1890. Frolovskoe] (in MS: "Klin").

RUS–KL (a³, No. 314).

PSSL 15B: 142–143.

4109.   To Anatolii Chaikovskii

5 May 1890 [Frolovskoe].

RUS–KL (a³, No. 1409).

PB: 459 — *PSSL* 15B: 143–144 — **LF*: 459–460
[English tr.].

4110.   To Modest Chaikovskii

5 May [1890]. Frolovskoe.

RUS–KL (a³, No. 1492).

*ZC 3: 366 — *PB*: 459 — *PSSL* 15B: 144–145 —
*LF: 458–459 [English tr.].

4111.   To Pëtr Iurgenson

8 May [1890]. [Frolovskoe].

RUS–KL (a³, No. 2687).

PSSL 15B: 145–146.

4112.   To Modest Chaikovskii

14 May [1890]. [Frolovskoe].

RUS–KL (a³, No. 1493).

*ZC 3: 368 — *PB*: 460 — *PSSL* 15B: 146–147 —
*LF: 460 [English tr.].

4113.   To Pëtr Iurgenson

14 May 1890 [Frolovskoe].

RUS–KL (a³, No. 2689).

PSSL 15B: 147–148.

4114.   To   Grand   Duke   Konstantin   Konstantinovich
18 May 1890. Frolovskoe.
RUS–SPil (f. 137, No. 78/24).
ZC 3: 368–370 — *PSSL* 15B: 148–150.

4115.   To Pëtr Iurgenson
18 May [1890]. [Frolovskoe].
RUS–KL (a³, No. 2690).
PIU 2: 158 — *PSSL* 15B: 150–151.

4116.   To German Larosh
22 May [1890]. Frolovskoe.
US–BHsachs
PSSL 15B: 151–152.

4117.   To Modest Chaikovskii
22 May [1890]. Frolovskoe.
RUS–KL (a³, No. 1944).
PSSL 15B: 152.

4118.   To Pëtr Iurgenson
22 May [1890]. [Frolovskoe].
RUS–KL (a³, No. 2691).
PIU 2: 158–159 — *PSSL* 15B: 153.

4119.   To Vladimir Pogozhev
24 May 1890 [Frolovskoe].
RUS–KL (a³, No. 2880).
VP: 59–60 — *PSSL* 15B: 154–155.

4120.   To Pëtr Iurgenson
24 May 1890 [Frolovskoe].
RUS–KL (a³, No. 2692).
*ZC 3: 371 — *PIU* 2: 159 — *PSSL* 15B: 155.

4121.   To Nikolai Khristoforov
24 May 1890 [Frolovskoe].
RUS–SPtob (VII.2.4.154).
PSSL 15B: 156.

4122.   To Anatolii Chaikovskii
24 May 1890. Frolovskoe.
RUS–KL (a³, No. 1410).
PSSL 15B: 156–157.

4123.   To Pëtr Iurgenson
25 May [1890]. [Frolovskoe].
RUS–KL (a³, No. 2693).
PIU 2: 159–160 — *PSSL* 15B: 157–158.

4124.   To Nikolai Konradi
26 May [1890]. [Frolovskoe].
Autograph lost; MS copy in RUS–KL.
*CTP: 279 — *PSSL* 15B: 158.

4125.   To Pëtr Iurgenson
26 May [1890]. [Frolovskoe].
RUS–KL (a³, No. 2694).
PIU 2: 160 — *PSSL* 15B: 158–159.

4126.   To Pëtr Iurgenson
28 May [1890]. [Frolovskoe].
RUS–KL (a³, No. 2695).
PIU 2: 161 — *PSSL* 15B: 159–160.

4127.   To Pëtr Iurgenson
29 May [1890]. [Frolovskoe].
RUS–KL (a³, No. 2696).
PIU 2: 161–163 — *PSSL* 15B: 160–162.

4128.   To Pëtr Iurgenson
29 May [1890]. [Frolovskoe].
RUS–KL (a³, No. 2697).
PIU 2: 163–164 — *PSSL* 15B: 162–163.

4129.   To Pëtr Iurgenson
31 May [1890]. [Frolovskoe].
RUS–KL (a³, No. 2699).
PIU 2: 164–165 — *PSSL* 15B: 163–164.

4130.   To Vladimir Pogozhev
31 May [1890]. Frolovskoe.
RUS–KL (a³, No. 2881).
VP: 61 — *PSSL* 15B: 164.

4131.   To Pëtr Iurgenson
31 May [1890]. [Frolovskoe].
RUS–KL (a³, No. 2693).
PIU 2: 164 — *PSSL* 15B: 165.

4132.   To Pavel Pchel´nikov

31 May [1890]. [Frolovskoe] (in MS: "Klin").

RUS–KL (a³, No. 315).

PSSL 15B: 165–166.

4133.   To Nadezhda von Meck

2 Jun 1890. Frolovskoe.

RUS–KL (a³, No. 1074).

*ZC 3: 371–372 — *PM* 3: 596–597 — *PSSL* 15B: 166–167.

4134.   To Anna Aleksandrova-Levenson

4 Jun 1890 [Frolovskoe].

RUS–KL (a³, No. 3348).

PSSL 15B: 168.

4135.   To Mikhail Ippolitov-Ivanov

4 Jun 1890. Frolovskoe.

RUS–KL (a³, No. 193).

*ZC 3: 373 — *Biulleten´* (1947), 2: 8–9 — *PSSL* 15B: 168–169.

4136.   To Nikolai Khristoforov

4 Jun [1890]. [Frolovskoe].

RUS–SPtob (VII.2.4.154).

Kirov: 418 — *PSSL* 15B: 170.

4136a. To Ambroise Thomas

4 June 1890 [Frolovskoe] (in MS: "Klin").

Autograph auctioned by Sotherby's, London, 1998.

*TGM 6 (1999): 7–9.

4137.   To Pëtr Iurgenson

4 Jun 1890 [Frolovskoe].

RUS–KL (a³, No. 2700).

PIU 2: 166–168 — *PSSL* 15B: 170–171.

4138.   To Pëtr Iurgenson

4 Jun 1890 [Frolovskoe].

RUS–KL (a³, No. 2701).

*ZC 3: 372 — *PIU* 2: 165–166 — *PSSL* 15B: 172.

4139.   To Vladimir Davydov

5 Jun 1890 [Frolovskoe].

RUS–KL (a³, No. 119).

*ZC 3: 373–374 — *PSSL* 15B: 173–174.

4140.   To German Larosh

5 Jun [1890]. [Frolovskoe].

Autograph lost; photocopy in RUS–KL.

PSSL 15B: 174.

4141.   To Karl Al´brekht

12 Jun [1890]. [Frolovskoe] (in MS: "Klin").

RUS–Mt (Al´brekht coll.).

CMS: 294–295 — *PSSL* 15B: 175.

4142.   To Aleksandr Ziloti

12 Jun 1890 [Frolovskoe] (in MS: "Klin").

RUS–KL (a³, No. 3018).

AIZ: 110 — *PSSL* 15B: 176.

4143.   To Anna Merkling

[12 Jun] 1890 [Frolovskoe] (in MS: "Klin").

Autograph lost; MS copy in RUS–KL.

CTP: 241 — *PSSL* 15B: 177.

4144.   To Anatolii Chaikovskii

12 Jun 1890. Frolovskoe.

RUS–KL (a³, No. 1411).

*ZC 3: 374–375 — **PB:* 461–462 — *PSSL* 15B: 178–179 — **LF:* 461 [English tr.].

4145.   To Modest Chaikovskii

12 Jun [1890]. Frolovskoe.

RUS–KL (a³, No. 1945).

*PB: 460–461 — *PSSL* 15B: 188–189 — **LF:* 461–462 [English tr.].

4146.   To Pëtr Iurgenson

12 Jun 1890 [Frolovskoe].

RUS–KL (a³, No. 2702).

PIU 2: 169 — *PSSL* 15B: 181.

4147.   To Anatolii Chaikovskii

14 Jun [1890]. [Frolovskoe].

RUS–KL (a³, No. 1412).

PSSL 15B: 181–182.

4148.   To Aleksandr Ziloti

15 Jun 1890 [Frolovskoe].

RUS–KL (a³, No. 3019).

AIZ: 110–111 — *PSSL* 15B: 182–183.

4149. To Modest Chaikovskii

15 Jun 1890 [Frolovskoe].

RUS–KL (a³, No. 1946).

ZC 3: 375–376 — *PB*: 461–462 — *PSSL* 15B: 183–184 — *LF*: 462–463 [English tr.].

4150. To Edouard Colonne

19 Jun 1890 [Frolovskoe] (in MS: "Klin") — in French.

F–P; photocopy in RUS–KL.

PSSL 15B: 185–186.

4151. To Anatolii Chaikovskii

19 Jun 1890. Frolovskoe.

RUS–KL (a³, No. 1413).

PB: 463 — *PSSL* 15B: 187 — *LF*: 463 [English tr.].

4152. To Pëtr Iurgenson

19 Jun [1890]. [Frolovskoe].

RUS–KL (a³, No. 2703).

PIU 2: 169–170 — *PSSL* 15B: 187–188.

4153. To Anton Arenskii

[?20–21 Jun 1890. Frolovskoe] (in MS: "Klin").

RUS–KL (LR, No. 3).

ZC 3: 423 (undated) — *PSSL* 15B: 188–189.

4154. To Anatolii Chaikovskii

21 Jun 1890. Frolovskoe.

RUS–KL (a³, No. 1414).

ZC 3: 376 — *PB*: 464 — *PSSL* 15B: 189–190 — *LF*: 463–464 [English tr.].

4155. To Modest Chaikovskii

21 Jun 1890 [Frolovskoe].

RUS–KL (a³, No. 1947).

ZC 3: 376–377 — *PB*: 463–464 — *PSSL* 15B: 190–191 — *LF*: 464 [English tr.].

4156. To Pëtr Iurgenson

25 Jun [1890]. [Frolovskoe].

RUS–KL (a³, No. 2704).

PIU 2: 170 — *PSSL* 15B: 191–192.

4157. To Pëtr Iurgenson

28 Jun [1890]. [Frolovskoe].

RUS–KL (a³, No. 2705).

PSSL 15B: 192.

4158. To Nadezhda von Meck

30 Jun 1890. Frolovskoe.

RUS–KL (a³, No. 1072).

ZC 3: 377 — *PM* 3: 597–598 — *PSSL* 15B: 192–193.

4159. To Modest Chaikovskii

30 Jun [1890]. [Frolovskoe].

RUS–KL (a³, No. 1948).

ZC 3: 377–378 — *PB*: 465 — *PSSL* 15B: 193–194 — *LF*: 465 [English tr.].

4160. To Nadezhda von Meck

1 Jul 1890. Frolovskoe.

RUS–KL (a³, No. 1073).

PM 3: 598 — *PSSL* 15B: 195.

4161. To Nadezhda von Meck

2 Jul 1890. Frolovskoe.

RUS–KL (a³, No. 1074).

ZC 3: 378 — *PM* 3: 599 — *PSSL* 15B: 195–196.

4162. To Anna Merkling

2 Jul 1890 [Frolovskoe].

Autograph lost; MS copy in RUS–KL.

CTP: 241–242 — *PSSL* 15B: 196.

4163. To Pëtr Iurgenson

2 Jul [1890]. [Frolovskoe].

RUS–KL (a³, No. 2706).

ZC 3: 378 — *PIU* 2: 171 — *PSSL* 15B: 197.

4164. To Wladyslaw Pachulski

3 Jul 1890. Frolovskoe.

US–NYpm (Heineman MS 211).

SM (1959), 12: 75–78 — *PSSL* 15B: 198–202.

4165. To Anatolii Chaikovskii

4 Jul 1890. Frolovskoe.

RUS–KL (a³, No. 1415).

PSSL 15B: 202–203.

4166.   To Modest Chaikovskii

4 Jul 1890. Frolovskoe.

RUS–KL (a³, No. 1949).

*ZC 3: 379 — PB: 465–466 — PSSL 15B: 203–204 —
LF: 465–466 [English tr.].

4167.   To Nikolai Konradi

6 Jul [1890]. Moscow.

Autograph lost; MS copy in RUS–KL.

CTP: 279 — PSSL 15B: 205.

4168.   To Herr Baske

9 Jul 1890. Frolovskoe.

D–Bmb

Österreichische Musikzeitschrift (1961), 2 — PSSL 15B:
205–206.

4169.   To Modest Chaikovskii

10 Jul [1890]. Frolovskoe.

RUS–KL (a³, No. 1950) [facs. in Pikovaia dama (1935):
54/55].

*ZC 3: 381 — *PB: 466–477 — PSSL 15B: 206–
207 — *LF: 466–467 [English tr.].

4170.   To Pëtr Iurgenson

10 Jul 1890. Frolovskoe.

RUS–KL (a³, No. 2707).

*ZC 3: 380 — PIU 2: 172 — PSSL 15B: 207–208.

4171.   To Mikhail Ippolitov-Ivanov

13 Jul 1890. Frolovskoe.

RUS–KL (a³, No. 194).

Iskusstvo, 3 (1927), 4: 159–160 — Biulleten´ (1947), 2:
13–15 — PSSL 15B: 209–210.

4172.   To Anatolii Chaikovskii

13 Jul 1890. Frolovskoe.

RUS–KL (a³, No. 1416).

*ZC 3: 381–382 — PSSL 15B: 210–212.

4173.   To Evgenii Al´brekht

14 Jul 1890 [Frolovskoe] (in MS: "Klin").

RUS–SPtob (VII.2.4.154).

Kirov: 413–414 — PSSL 15B: 212–213.

4174.   To Nikolai Khristoforov

14 Jul 1890 [Frolovskoe].

RUS–SPtob (VII.2.4.154).

Kirov: 418 — PSSL 15B: 213.

4175.   To Pëtr Iurgenson

15 Jul [1890]. [Frolovskoe].

RUS–KL (a³, No. 2708).

PIU 2: 173 — PSSL 15B: 213–214.

4175a. To Pëtr Iurgenson

[15 Jul 1890. Frolovskoe].

RUS–KL (a³, No. 2712).

Not published.

4176.   To Aleksandr Ziloti

17 [Jul] 1890 (in MS: "Feb") [Frolovskoe].

RUS–KL (a³, No. 3020).

AIZ: 112 — PSSL 15B: 214.

4177.   To Iuliia Shpazhinskaia

17 Jul 1890. Frolovskoe.

RUS–KL (a³, No. 2127).

CTP: 356–357 — PSSL 15B: 215–216.

4178.   To Pëtr Iurgenson

17 Jul [1890]. Frolovskoe.

RUS–KL (a³, No. 2709).

PIU 2: 173 — PSSL 15B: 216–217.

4179.   To Varvara Zarudnaia

20 Jul 1890. Frolovskoe.

RUS–Mcm (f. 2, No. 5117).

Iskusstvo, 3 (1927), 4: 160–162 — PSSL 15B: 217–
219.

4180.   To Nikolai Konradi

20 Jul 1890 [Frolovskoe].

Autograph lost; MS copy in RUS–KL.

CTP: 280 — PSSL 15B: 219–220.

4181.   To German Larosh

21 Jul [1890]. Frolovskoe.

US–Wc (Moldenhauer coll., box 55).

PSSL 15B: 220–221.

4182. To Pëtr Iurgenson

[21 Jul 1890. Klin] — telegram.

RUS–KL (a³, No. 2736).

PSSL 15B: 221.

4183. To Pëtr Iurgenson

21 Jul [1890]. [Frolovskoe].

RUS–KL (a³, No. 2710).

PIU 2: 174 — *PSSL* 15B: 221.

4184. To Ivan Vsevolozhskii

22 Jul 1890. Frolovskoe.

RUS–KL (a³, No. 35).

PSSL 15B: 222.

4185. To Nadezhda von Meck

[31] Jul 1890 (in MS: "30 Jul"). St. Petersburg.

RUS–KL (a³, No. 1075).

PM 3: 600–601 ("30 Jul") — *PSSL* 15B: 222–224.

4186. To Ivan Vsevolozhskii

1 Aug 1890. St. Petersburg.

RUS–KL (a³, No. 36).

Pikovaia dama (1935): 66–68 — *PSSL* 15B: 225–226.

4187. To Evgenii Al´brekht

2 Aug [1890]. Frolovskoe.

RUS–SPtob (VII.2.4.154).

Kirov: 414–416 — *PSSL* 15B: 227–229.

4188. To Anatolii Chaikovskii

2 Aug [1890]. [Frolovskoe].

RUS–KL (a³, No. 1417).

*PB: 467 — *PSSL* 15B: 229 — **LF*: 467 [English tr.].

4189. To Modest Chaikovskii

2 Aug [1890]. [Frolovskoe].

RUS–KL (a³, No. 2978).

PSSL 15B: 230.

4190. To Pëtr Iurgenson

2 Aug [1890]. Frolovskoe.

RUS–KL (a³, No. 2713).

PIU 2: 174–175 — *PSSL* 15B: 230–231.

4191. To Nikolai Khristoforov

4 Aug 1890. Frolovskoe.

RUS–SPtob (VII.2.4.154).

PSSL 15B: 232–233.

4192. To Pëtr Iurgenson

[4] Aug [1890] (in MS: "8 Aug") [Frolovskoe].

RUS–KL (a³, No. 2614).

PSSL 15B: 233.

4193. To Aleksandr Ziloti

5 Aug [1890]. [Frolovskoe].

RUS–KL (a³, No. 3021).

*RMG (1908), 47: 1047–1048 — *AIZ*: 113 — *PSSL* 15B: 234.

4194. To Eduard Nápravník

5 Aug [1890]. Frolovskoe.

RUS–KL (a³, No. 3336).

ZC 3: 385–386 — *VP*: 193–196 — *EFN*: 158–159 — *PSSL* 15B: 235–236.

4195. To Grand Duke Konstantin Konstantinovich

5 Aug [1890]. Frolovskoe.

RUS–SPil (f. 137, No. 78/25).

ZC 3: 382–385 ("3 Aug") — *PSSL* 15B: 236–239.

4196. To Pavel Tret´iakov

6 Aug 1890 [Moscow].

RUS–Mgt

A. P. Botkina, *Pavel Mikhailovich Tret´iakov v zhizni i isuksstve* (1951): 200 — *PSSL* 15B: 240–241.

4197. To Nikolai Figner

6–7 Aug 1890. Moscow.

Autograph lost

Novosti i birzhevaia gazeta (25 Oct 1894) — **N. N. Figner, Vospominaniia, pis´ma, materialy* (1968): 180 — *PSSL* 15B: 241–242.

4197a. To Monsieur de Fernow

14 Aug 1890 [Grankino] — in French.

Autograph auctioned by Sotheby's, London, 1996.

*ČS 3 (1998): 184.

4198.   To Ivan Vsevolozhskii
18 Aug 1890. Kamenka — in French.
RUS–SPia (f. 652, op. 1, d. 608, fol. 46–47).
PSSL 15B: 242–243 [Russian tr. only].

4199.   To Pëtr Iurgenson
[19 Aug 1890. Kamenka] — telegram.
RUS–KL (a³, No. 2737).
PSSL 15B: 243.

4200.   To Pëtr Iurgenson
19 Aug 1890. Kamenka.
RUS–KL (a³, No. 2714).
ZC 3: 386–387 — *PIU* 2: 175–176 — *PSSL* 15B: 243–244.

4201.   To Anatolii Chaikovskii
22 Aug 1890 [Kamenka].
RUS–KL (a³, No. 1418).
PSSL 15B: 245.

4202.   To Pëtr Iurgenson
22 Aug [1890]. Kamenka.
RUS–KL (a³, No. 2618).
PIU 2: 176–177 — *PSSL* 15B: 246–247.

4203.   To Pavel Tret´iakov
[23 Aug 1890]. Kamenka.
RUS–Mgt
PSSL 15B: 247.

4204.   To Iuliia Shpazhinskaia
23 Aug 1890. Kamenka.
RUS–KL (a³, No. 2128).
CTP: 357–358 — *PSSL* 15B: 247–248.

4205.   To Pavel Tret´iakov
24 Aug 1890. Kamenka.
RUS–Mgt
A. P. Botkina, *Pavel MikhailovichTret´iakov v zhizni i iskusstve* (1951): 200–201.

4206.   To Eduard Nápravník
25 Aug 1890. Kamenka.
Autograph lost; typed copy in RUS–KL.
ZC 3: 387 — *VP*: 198–200 — *EFN*: 162 — *PSSL* 15B: 250.

4207.   To Pëtr Iurgenson
25 Aug [1890]. Kamenka.
RUS–KL (a³, No. 2715).
PSSL 15B: 251.

4208.   To Ekaterina Larosh
26 Aug 1890. Kamenka.
Autograph lost; photocopy in RUS–KL.
PSSL 15B: 251–252.

4209.   To Pëtr Iurgenson
2 Sep 1890. Kiev.
RUS–KL (a³, No. 2716).
ZC 3: 400 — *PIU* 2: 178 — *PSSL* 15B: 252.

4210.   To Vladimir Pogozhev
3 Sep 1890. Kiev.
RUS–KL (a³, No. 2882).
PSSL 15B: 253.

4211.   To Pavel Pchel´nikov
3 Sep 1890. Kiev.
RUS–KL (a³, No. 316).
PSSL 15B: 253.

4212.   To Nadezhda von Meck
4 Sep 1890 [Khar´kov].
RUS–KL (a³, No. 1076).
PM 3: 602–603 — *PSSL* 15B: 254–255.

4213.   To Modest Chaikovskii
4 Sep 1890. Khar´kov.
RUS–KL (a³, No. 1951).
PSSL 15B: 255–256.

4214.   To Ivan Vsevolozhskii
9 Sep 1890. Tiflis.
RUS–SPia (f. 652, op. 1, d. 608, fol. 44–45).
PSSL 15B: 256–257.

4215.   To Pëtr Iurgenson
[9 Sep 1890. Tiflis] — telegram.
RUS–KL (a³, No. 2738).
PSSL 15B: 257.

4216. To Pëtr Iurgenson

14 Sep 1890 [Tiflis].

RUS–KL (a³, No. 2717).

*ZC 3: 400–401 — PIU 2: 179–180 — PSSL 15B: 257–258.

4217. To Ekaterina Larosh

15 Sep 1890. Tiflis.

Autograph lost; photocopy in RUS–KL.

PSSL 15B: 259.

4218. To Modest Chaikovskii

15 Sep 1890. Tiflis.

RUS–KL (a³, No. 1952).

*ZC 3: 401 — PB: 467 — PSSL 15B: 260 — *LF: 467 [English tr.].

4219. To Eduard Nápravník

19 Sep [1890]. Tiflis.

RUS–KL (a³, No. 3337).

*VP: 201 — EFN: 163–165 — PSSL 15B: 261–262.

4220. To Vladimir Nápravník

20 Sep [1890]. Tiflis.

Autograph lost; typed copy in RUS–KL.

EFN: 195 — PSSL 15B: 263.

4220a. To Ol´ga Nápravník

[21 Sep 1890. Tiflis] — telegram.

RUS–SPit (f. 21, 3, 220).

Not published

4221. To Nadezhda von Meck

22 Sep 1890. Tiflis.

RUS–KL (a³, No. 1077).

*ZC 3: 394–396 — PM 3: 605–606 — PSSL 15B: 263–265.

4222. To Isaak Khalatov

22 Sep [1890]. Tiflis.

Autograph lost

V. D. Korganov, *Chaikovskii na Kavkaze* (1940): xiii — PSSL 15B: 265–266.

4223. To Anna Merkling

28 Sep 1890. Tiflis.

Autograph lost; MS copy in RUS–KL.

*ZC 3: 403 — CTP: 242 — PSSL 15B: 266.

4224. To Pëtr Iurgenson

28 Sep [1890]. Tiflis.

RUS–KL (a³, No. 2718).

*ZC 3: 402–403 — PIU 2: 180–182 — PSSL 15B: 267–269.

4225. To Eduard Nápravník

3 Oct 1890. Tiflis.

RUS–KL (a³, No. 3338).

*VP 203 — EFN: 167–168 — PSSL 15B: 269–270.

4226. To Pëtr Iurgenson

3 Oct [1890]. Tiflis.

RUS–KL (a³, No. 2719).

*ZC 3: 403–404 — PIU 2: 183 — PSSL 15B: 270–271.

4227. To Pëtr Iurgenson

[4 Oct 1890. Tiflis] — telegram.

RUS–KL (a³, No. 2739).

PSSL 15B: 271.

4228. To Vladimir Davydov

[5] Oct 1890 (in MS: "4 Oct"). Tiflis.

RUS–KL (a³, No. 120).

PSSL 15B: 271–272.

4229. To Eduard Nápravník

[5] Oct 1890 (in MS: "4 Oct"). Tiflis.

RUS–KL (a³, No. 3339).

*VP: 203 ("4 Oct") — EFN: 166–169 ("4 Oct") — PSSL 15B: 272–273.

4230. To Aleksandr Ziloti

[? 5–6 Oct 1890. Tiflis].

Autograph lost; MS copy in RUS–KL.

PSSL 15B: 274.

4231. To Modest Chaikovskii

10 Oct 1890 [Tiflis].

RUS–KL (a³, No. 468).

PB: 466 — PSSL 15B: 274–275 — LF: 468 [English tr.].

4232.   To Pëtr Iurgenson

14 Oct 1890. Tiflis.

RUS–KL (a³, No. 2720).

*ZC 3: 404–405 — PIU 2: 185–186 — PSSL 15B: 275–276.

4233.   To Praskov´ia Chaikovskaia

[?15 Oct 1890. Tiflis].

RUS–KL (a³, No. 457).

PSSL 15B: 277.

4234.   To Pëtr Iurgenson

15 Oct 1890. Tiflis.

RUS–KL (a³, No. 2721).

*ZC 3: 405 — PIU 2: 186 — PSSL 15B: 277–278.

4235.   To Anna Merkling

16 Oct 1890. Tiflis.

Autograph lost; MS copy in RUS–KL.

*ZC 3: 406–407 — CTP: 242–243 — PSSL 15B: 278–279.

4236.   To Modest Chaikovskii

16 Oct [1890]. Tiflis.

RUS–KL (a³, No. 1954).

PB: 468–469 — PSSL 15B: 279–280 — LF: 469 [English tr.].

4237.   To Pëtr Iurgenson

16 Oct [1890]. Tiflis.

RUS–KL (a³, No. 2722).

*ZC 3: 405–406 — PIU 2: 186–187 — PSSL 15B: 280–281.

4238.   To Eduard Nápravník

19 Oct 1890. Tiflis.

RUS–KL (a³, No. 3340).

*ZC 3: 407 — *VP: 204 — EFN: 170 — PSSL 15B: 282.

4239.   To Bagrat Mirimanian

22 Oct 1890. Tiflis

US–STu

V. D. Korganov, Chaikovskii na Kavkaze (1940): 87 — PSSL 15B: 283.

4240.   To Pëtr Iurgenson

[22 Oct 1890. Tiflis] — telegram.

RUS–KL (a³, No. 2773).

PSSL 15B: 283.

4241.   To Pavel Tret´iakov

[?23 Oct 1890. Mtskhet] — telegram.

RUS–Mgt

PSSL 15B: 283.

4242.   To Vladimir Argutinskii-Dolgorukov

[27 Oct 1890. Taganrog].

RUS–Mcl (f. 1900).

PSSL 15B: 283–284.

4243.   To Praskov´ia Chaikovskaia

27 Oct 1890. Taganrog.

RUS–KL (a³, No. 448).

PB: 469 — PSSL 15B: 284–285 — *LF: 469–470 [English tr.].

4244.   To Pëtr Iurgenson

[28 Oct 1890. Taganrog] — telegram.

RUS–KL (a³, No. 2740).

PSSL 15B: 285.

4244a.   To Sergei Taneev

[? 31 Oct 1890. Moscow].

RUS–Mcl (f. 880).

CTP: 199 — PSSL 17: 253.

4245.   To Aleksei Suvorin

2 Nov 1890. Frolovskoe.

RUS–Mcl (f. 459).

Krasnyi arkhiv (1940), 3: 252 — PSSL 15B: 285.

4246.   To the editor of Novoe vremia

2 Nov 1890. Frolovskoe.

Autograph lost

Novoe vremia (4 Nov 1890) — Novosti dnia (6 Nov 1890) — PSSL 15B:286.

4247.   To Praskov´ia Chaikovskaia

2 Nov 1890. Frolovskoe.

RUS–KL (a³, No. 449).

PSSL 15B: 286–287.

4248.   To Modest Chaikovskii

2 Nov 1890. Frolovskoe.

RUS–KL (a³, No. 1956).

PB: 470 — *PSSL* 15B: 287–288 — *LF*: 470–471
    [English tr.].

4249.   To Pëtr Iurgenson

3 Nov [1890]. Frolovskoe.

RUS–KL (a³, No. 2723).

ZC 3: 409 — *PIU* 2: 187–188 — *PSSL* 15B: 290.

4250.   To Ippolit Prianishnikov

5 Nov [1890]. Frolovskoe.

Autograph lost.

Odesskii listok (26 Jun 1896) — *RMG* (1896), 8: 951–
    952 — *PSSL* 15B: 290–291.

4251.   To Pëtr Iurgenson

5 Nov 1890.[Frolovskoe].

RUS–KL (a³, No. 2724).

ZC 3: 410 — *PIU* 2: 188–189 — *PSSL* 15B: 291–
    292.

4252.   To Pëtr Iurgenson

12 Nov [1890]. [St. Petersburg].

RUS–KL (a³, No. 2725).

ZC 3: 410 — *PIU* 2: 190 — *PSSL* 15B: 292–293.

4253.   To Modest Chaikovskii

[14 Nov 1890. St. Petersburg].

RUS–KL.

PSSL 15B: 293.

4254.   To Ol´ga Nápravník

14 Nov [1890]. [St. Petersburg].

RUS–KL (a³, No. 2992).

PSSL 15B: 294.

4255.   To Leopold Auer

15 Nov 1890 [St. Petersburg] — in French.

RUS–Mcl (f. 701).

PSSL 15B: 294.

4256.   To Pëtr Iurgenson

15 Nov 1890 [St. Petersburg].

RUS–KL (a³, No. 2726).

PIU 2: 191 — *PSSL* 15B: 295.

4257.   To Nikolai Khristoforov

17 Nov 1890. St. Petersburg.

RUS–SPtob (VII.2.4.154).

Kirov: 418 — *PSSL* 15B: 296.

4258.   To Osip Iurgenson

[19 Nov 1890. St. Petersburg].

RUS–Mcl (f. 931).

PSSL 15B: 296.

4259.   To German Larosh

[21 Nov 1890. St. Petersburg].

Autograph lost; photocopy in RUS–KL.

PSSL 15B: 296.

4260.   To Praskov´ia Chaikovskaia

21 Nov 1890 [St. Petersburg].

RUS–KL (a³, No. 450).

PB: 470–471 — *PSSL* 15B: 297 — *LF*: 471 [English
    tr.].

4261.   To Pëtr Iurgenson

23 Nov 1890 [St. Petersburg].

RUS–KL (a³, No. 2727).

PIU 2: 192 — *PSSL* 15B: 298.

4262.   To Boris Fitingof–Shel´

[28 Nov 1890. St. Petersburg] — postcard.

RUS–SPsc (f. 817, No. 1, fol. 181).

PSSL 15B: 298.

4262a. To Pëtr Iurgenson

28 Nov [1890]. [St. Petersburg].

RUS–KL (a³, No. 2828).

PIU 2: 257–258 ("1892") — *PSSL* 17: 253.

4263.   To Henryk Pachulski

30 Nov 1890 [St. Petersburg].

Autograph lost; typed copy in RUS–KL.

PSSL 15B: 299.

4264.   To Modest Chaikovskii

[3 Dec 1890. St. Petersburg].

RUS–KL (a³, No. 1955).

PSSL 15B: 299.

4264a. To Osip Iurgenson

3 Dec 1890 [St. Petersburg].

RUS–KL (a³, No. 3354).

Not published.

4265. To Ekaterina Larosh

[early Dec 1890. St. Petersburg], note on visiting card.

Autograph lost; photocopy in RUS–KL.

PSSL 15B: 300.

4266. To Elizaveta Chaikovskaia

4 Dec [1890]. [St. Petersburg].

RUS–SPsc (f. 834, No. 30, fol. 16, 18, 20).

PSSL 15B: 300.

4267. To Ol´ga Chaikovskaia

[4] Dec [1890] (in MS: "5 Dec") [St. Petersburg].

RUS–SPsc (f. 834, No. 31, fol. 13–14).

PSSL 15B: 301.

4267a. To Ekaterina Larosh

[6 Dec 1890. St. Petersburg].

Autograph auctioned by Sotheby's, New York, 1997.

Fine books and Americana (25 Nov 1997): 8 [auction catalogue]

4268. To Wilhelm Harteveld

[8 Dec 1890. St. Petersburg] — telegram.

RUS–KL (a³, No. 168).

PSSL 15B: 301.

4269. To Mikhail Petukhov

9 Dec 1890 [St. Petersburg].

RUS–Mcl (f. 905).

PSSL 15B: 301.

4270. To Pavel Pchel´nikov

9 Dec 1890 [St. Petersburg].

RUS–KL (a³, No. 317).

PSSL 15B: 302.

4271. To Ekaterina Larosh

[?9 Dec 1890. St. Petersburg].

Autograph lost; photocopy in RUS–KL.

PSSL 15B: 302.

4272. To Pëtr Iurgenson

[12 Dec 1890. Kiev] — telegram.

RUS–KL (a³, No. 2741).

PSSL 15B: 302.

4273. To Modest Chaikovskii

[14] Dec [1890] (in MS: "13 Dec"). Kiev.

RUS–KL (a³, No. 1957).

ZC 3: 414 — *PB*: 471 — *PSSL* 15B: 303 — *LF*: 471–472 [English tr.].

4273a. To Anton Arenskii

[21 Dec 1890. Kiev] — telegram.

RUS–SPil (f. 504, No. 72).

Not published.

4274. To Aleksandra Hubert

21 Dec 1890. Kiev.

RUS–KL (a³, No. 72).

PRM 55 — *PSSL* 15B: 304.

4275. To Modest Chaikovskii

21 Dec 1890 [Kiev].

RUS–KL (a³, No. 1958).

ZC 3: 415–416 — *PB*: 471–472 — *PSSL* 15B: 304–305 — *LF*: 472 [English tr.].

4276. To Grand Duke Konstantin Konstantinovich

23 Dec 1890. Kamenka.

RUS–SPil (f. 137, No. 78/26).

PSSL 15B: 305–306.

4276a. To Grand Duke Konstantin Konstantinovich

23 Dec 1890. Kamenka -- telegramm

RUS-SPil (f. 137, No. 78)

Not published

4277. To Pëtr Iurgenson

[23 Dec 1890. Kamenka] — telegram.

RUS–KL (a³, No. 2742).

PSSL 15B: 306.

4278. To Pëtr Iurgenson

23 Dec 1890. Kamenka.

RUS–KL (a³, No. 2728).

ZC 3: 416 — *PIU* 2: 193 — *PSSL* 15B: 307.

4279. To Mikhail Ippolitov-Ivanov

24 Dec 1890. Kamenka.

RUS–KL (a³, No. 195).

ZC 3: 416–418 — *Biulleten´* (1947), 2: 20–22.

4280.   To Vladimir Pogozhev
24 Dec 1890. Kamenka.
RUS–KL (a³, No. 2883).
VP: 70–75 — *PSSL* 15B: 309–312.

4281.   To Praskov´ia Chaikovskaia
24 Dec 1890. Kamenka.
RUS–KL (a³, No. 451).
PSSL 15B: 313.

4282.   To Iakov Kalishevskii
31 Dec 1890. Kamenka.
Autograph lost
Muzyka i penie (1903), 5: 2 — *PSSL* 15B: 314.

4282a.   To Mar´ia Kondrat´eva
[? 1890–1892. St. Petersburg].
RUS–Mcl (f. 905).
PSSL 17: 254.

4282b.   To Bogomir Korsov
[1890s. Moscow] — in French.
RUS–KL (a³, No. 253).
PSSL 17: 254.

1891

4283.   To Modest Chaikovskii
1 Jan 1891. Kamenka.
RUS–KL (a³, No. 1959).
*ZC 3: 418 — *PB: 472–473 — *PSSL* 16A: 13–14 —
    *LF: 473 [English tr.].

4284.   To Aleksandra Hubert
4 Jan 1891. Moscow.
RUS–KL (a³, No. 73).
PRM 55–56 — *PSSL* 16A: 14–15.

4285.   To Sergei Taneev
[5] Jan [1891] (in MS: "4 Jan 1890") [Moscow].
RUS–Mcl (f. 880).
CTP: 167 — *PSSL* 16A: 15.

4286.   To Nikolai Kashkin
[5] Jan [1891] (in MS: "4 Jan") [Moscow].
RUS–KL (a³, No. 215).
PSSL 16A: 16.

4287.   To Aleksandra Hubert
[5] Jan [1891] (in MS: "4 Jan") [Moscow].
RUS–KL (a³, No. 70).
PRM 56 — *PSSL* 16A: 16.

4288.   To Pavel Vargunin
6 Jan 1891 [Frolovskoe] (in MS: "Klin").
RUS–Mt
PSSL 16A: 17.

4288a.   To Louis Gallet
6 Jan 1891 [Frolovskoe] (in MS: Klin) — in French.
F–Plauwe
ČS 3 (1998): 249–255.

4289.   To Vladimir Pogozhev
6 Jan 1891. Frolovskoe.
RUS–KL (a³, No. 2884).
VP: 78–79 — *PSSL* 16A: 17–18.

4290.   To Anatolii Chaikovskii
6 Jan 1891 [Frolovskoe].
Autograph lost; MS copy in RUS–KL.
PSSL 16A: 18.

4291.   To Modest Chaikovskii
6 Jan 1891 [Frolovskoe].
RUS–KL (a³, No. 1960).
*PB: 473 — *PSSL* 16A: 19–20 — *LF: 473–474
    [English tr.].

4292.   To Pëtr Iurgenson
6 Jan 1891 [Frolovskoe].
RUS–KL (a³, No. 2744).
PSSL 16A: 20.

4293.   To Anna Merkling
6 Jan 1891 [Frolovskoe] (in MS: "Klin").
Autograph lost; MS copy in RUS–KL.
PSSL 16A: 21.

4293a.   To Anna Rebezova
6 Jan 1891 [Frolovskoe] (in MS: "Klin").
RUS–Mcm (f. 88, No. 341).
PSSL 17: 254–255.

4293b.   To Friedrich Sieger

6 Jan 1891 [Frolovskoe] (in MS: "Klin") — in French.

D–FF [facs. in *TGM* 5 (1998): 12/13].

TGM 5 (1998): 11.

4294.   To Aleksandr Ziloti

[? 6–7 Jan 1891. Frolovskoe].

RUS–KL (a³, No. 3022).

AIZ: 115 ("6 Jan") — *PSSL* 16A: 22.

4295.   To Evgenii Al´brekht

7 Jan 1891 [Frolovskoe].

RUS–SPtob (VII.2.4.154).

Kirov: 416 — *PSSL* 16A: 22.

4296.   To Ivan Vsevolozhskii

11 Jan 1891 [Frolovskoe] (in MS: "Klin").

RUS–SPia (f. 652, op. 1, d. 608, fol. 19–20).

PSSL 16A: 23.

4297.   To Aleksandr Ziloti

11 Jan [1891]. [Frolovskoe].

RUS–KL (a³, No. 3023).

AIZ: 115 — *PSSL* 16A: 24.

4298.   To Félix Mackar

11 Jan 1891 [Frolovskoe] (in MS: "Klin") — in French.

F–Pn

RdM 54 (1968), 1: 77–78 — *SM* (1970), 9: 72 [Russian tr.] — *PSSL* 16A: 24–25.

4299.   To Georgii Meklenburg-Strelitskii

11 Jan 1891 [Frolovskoe] (in MS: "Klin").

RUS–Mf

Krasnii arkhiv (1940), 3: 252 — *PSSL* 16A: 26.

4300.   To Modest Chaikovskii

[11 Jan 1891]. Frolovskoe.

RUS–KL (a³, No. 1985).

*ZC 3: 424–425 — *PB:* 473–474 — *PSSL* 16A: 27 — **LF:* 474–475 [English tr.].

4301.   To Pëtr Iurgenson

11 Jan [1891]. [Frolovskoe].

RUS–KL (a³, No. 2743).

PSSL 16A: 28.

4302.   To Sergei Taneev

14 Jan 1891 [Frolovskoe].

RUS–Mcl (f. 880).

*ZC 3: 421–423 — *PT:* 162–163 — *CTP:* 169–170 — *PSSL* 16A: 28–30.

4303.   To Nikolai Rimskii-Korsakov

15 Jan 1891 [Frolovskoe] (in MS: "Klin").

RUS–SPsc (f. f. 640, op. 1, No. 1015, fol. 32–32a).

*ZC 3: 424 — *SM* (1945), 3: 143 — *RK* 7 (1970): 62 — *PSSL* 16A: 30.

4304.   To Vladimir Shervud

15 Jan 1891. Frolovskoe.

RUS–KL (a³, No. 3323).

PSSL 16A: 31–32.

4305.   To Pëtr Iurgenson

15 Jan [1891]. [Frolovskoe].

RUS–KL (a³, No. 2745).

*ZC 3: 425 — *PIU* 2: 197–198 — *PSSL* 16A: 33 — Yoffe: 13 [English tr.].

4306.   To Aleksandr Ziloti

17 Jan [1891]. [Frolovskoe].

Autograph lost; photocopy in RUS–KL.

PSSL 16A: 33–34.

4307.   To Nikolai Rimskii-Korsakov

17 Jan 1891 [Frolovskoe] (in MS: "Klin").

RUS–SPsc (f. 640, op. 1, No. 1015, fol. 33–34).

*ZC 3: 424 — *SM* (1945), 3: 143 — *RK* 7 (1970): 63 — *PSSL* 16A: 34.

4308.   To František Šubert

17 Jan 1891 [Frolovskoe] (in MS: "Klin") — in French.

CZ–Ps [facs. in: F. A. Šubert, *Moje vzpominky* (1902): 110–111 — M. Očadlik, *Pražské dopisy P. I. Čajkovského* (1949) — J. Wenig, *Sie waren in Prag* (1971): 186].

Štěpánek (1952): 156 [Czech tr.] — *PSSL* 16A: 35.

4309.   To Pëtr Iurgenson

17 Jan [1891]. [Frolovskoe].

RUS–KL (a³, No. 2746).

*ZC 3: 425 — *PIU* 2: 198–199 — *PSSL* 16A: 36 — Yoffe: 14–15 [English tr.].

4310. To Pëtr Iurgenson

[17 Jan 1891. Frolovskoe].

RUS–KL (a³, No. 2762).

PSSL 16A: 37.

4311. To Pëtr Iurgenson

17 Jan [1891]. [Frolovskoe].

RUS–KL (a³, No. 2787).

PIU 2: 199 — *PSSL* 16A: 37–38.

4312. To Anatolii Chaikovskii

22 Jan 1891 [Frolovskoe] (in MS: "Klin").

RUS–KL (a³, No. 1419).

ZC 3: 425–426 — *PB*: 474 — *PSSL* 16A: 38–39 —
LF: 475 [English tr.] — Yoffe: 15–16 [English
tr.].

4313. To Karl Al´brekht

[23 Jan 1891. Klin] — telegram.

RUS–Mcm (f. 37, No. 68).

PSSL 16A: 39.

4314. To Aleksandra Hubert

23 Jan 1891 [Frolovskoe].

RUS–KL (a³, No. 74).

PRM 56–57 — *PSSL* 16A: 39–40.

4315. To Félix Mackar

23 Jan 1891 [Frolovskoe] (in MS: "Klin") — in
French.

F–Pn

RdM 54 (1968), 1: 79 — *PSSL* 16A: 40–41 — Yoffe:
17–18 [English tr.].

4316. To Pëtr Iurgenson

23 Jan 1891 [Frolovskoe].

RUS–KL (a³, No. 2747).

PIU 2: 199–200 — *PSSL* 16A: 42.

4317. To Pëtr Iurgenson

[27 Jan 1891. Moscow].

RUS–KL (a³, No. 2783).

PSSL 16A: 43.

4318. To Praskov´ia Chaikovskaia

[30] Jan 1891 (in MS: "29 Jan"). St. Petersburg.

RUS–KL (a³, No. 452).

PB: 475 — *PSSL* 16A: 43–44 — *LF*: 475–476
[English tr.].

4318a. To Félix Mackar

31 Jan/12 Feb 1891. St. Petersburg — in French.

D–WÜ

TGM 6 (1999): 9–15.

4319. To Pëtr Iurgenson

31 Jan [1891]. St. Petersburg.

RUS–KL (a³, No. 2748).

PIU 2: 201–202 — *PSSL* 16A: 44–45 — Yoffe: 16–17
[English tr.].

4320. To Ekaterina Larosh

1 Feb [1891]. [St. Petersburg].

Autograph lost; photocopy in RUS–KL.

PSSL 16A: 45.

4321. To Aleksandr Ziloti

5 Feb [1891]. St. Petersburg.

RUS–KL (a³, No. 3024).

AIZ: 116 — *PSSL* 16A: 46.

4322. To Pëtr Iurgenson

6 Feb [1891]. St. Petersburg.

RUS–KL (a³, No. 2749).

PIU 2: 202–203 — *PSSL* 16A: 46–47.

4323. To Pëtr Iurgenson

[10 Feb 1891. St. Petersburg].

RUS–KL (a³, No. 2763).

PSSL 16A: 48.

4324. To Ivan Vsevolozhskii

12 Feb 1891. Frolovskoe.

RUS–SPia (f. 652, op. 1, d. 608, fol. 21–27); rough
draft in RUS–KL (a¹³, No. 2).

PSSL 16A: 48–51 [draft: *PIU* 2: 304–305 — *PSSL*
16A: 305–310].

4325. To Aleksandr Glazunov

12 Feb 1891. Frolovskoe.

Autograph lost; typed copy in RUS–KL.

SM (1945), 3: 64 — *PSSL* 16A: 52.

4326.   To Mikhail Ippolitov-Ivanov

12 Feb 1891. Frolovskoe.

RUS–KL (a³, No. 196).

Biulleten´ (1947), 2: 25–26 — *PSSL* 16A: 52–53.

4327.   To Aleksandra L´vova

12 Feb 1891. Frolovskoe.

RUS–Mrg

PSSL 16A: 53–54.

4328.   To Mikhail Petukhov

12 Feb 1891. Frolovskoe.

RUS–SPil (f. 123, op. 3, No. 137).

PSSL 16A: 54.

4329.   To Anatolii Chaikovskii

12 Feb 1891. Frolovskoe.

RUS–KL (a³, No. 1420).

PB: 475–476 — *PSSL* 16A: 54–55 — *LF*: 476
[English tr.] — Yoffe: 17–18 [English tr.].

4330.   To Pëtr Iurgenson

12 Feb 1891. Frolovskoe.

RUS–KL (a³, No. 2750).

ZC 3: 427–428 — *PIU* 2: 203–204 — *PSSL* 16A: 56.

4331.   To Aleksandr Ziloti

14 Feb 1891 [Frolovskoe].

RUS–KL (a³, No. 3025).

AIZ: 117 — *PSSL* 16A: 57.

4332.   To Pëtr Iurgenson

[16 Feb 1891]. Frolovskoe.

RUS–KL (a³, No. 2764).

ZC 3: 426–427 — *PIU* 2: 204–205 — *PSSL* 16A: 58.

4333.   To Anna Merkling

16 Feb 1891 [St. Petersburg].

Autograph lost; MS copy in RUS–KL.

CTP: 243 — *PSSL* 16A: 59.

4334.   To Pëtr Iurgenson

19 Feb [1891]. St. Petersburg.

RUS–KL (a³, No. 2751).

PIU 2: 206 — *PSSL* 16A: 59–60.

4335 .   To Félix Mackar

20 Feb 1891. St. Petersburg — in French.

F–Pn

RdM 54 (1968), 1: 79–80 — *PSSL* 16A: 60.

4336.   To Aleksandr Ziloti

22 Feb 1891 [Frolovskoe].

RUS–KL (a³, No. 3026).

AIZ: 117–118 — *PSSL* 16A: 61.

4337.   To Nikolai Konradi

[24 Feb 1891. Frolovskoe].

Autograph lost; MS copy in RUS–KL.

PSSL 16A: 62.

4338.   To Praskov´ia Chaikovskaia

25 Feb 1891. Frolovskoe.

RUS–KL (a³, No. 453).

PB: 476–477 — *PSSL* 16A: 62–63 — *LF*: 477–478
[English tr.].

4339.   To Modest Chaikovskii

25 Feb [1891]. Frolovskoe.

RUS–KL (a³, No. 1961).

ZC 3: 430 — *PB*: 476 — *PSSL* 16A: 63–64 — *LF*:
477 [English tr.].

4340.   To Ivan Armsgeimer

28 Feb 1891. Frolovskoe.

RUS–KL (a³, No. 2986) [facs. in *Biulleten´* (1951), 1:
33–34 — *Avtografy P. I. Chaikovskogo v arkhive
Doma–muzeia v Klinu*, vyp. 2 (1952): 10/11].

PSSL 16A: 64–65.

4341.   To Pëtr Iurgenson

2 Mar [1891]. [Moscow].

RUS–KL (a³, No. 2752).

PSSL 16A: 65.

4342.   To Vladimir Davydov

8/20 Mar [1891]. Berlin.

RUS–KL (a³, No. 121).

ZC 3: 430–431 — *PSSL* 16A: 66 — Yoffe: 25–26
[English tr.].

4343. To Anatolii Chaikovskii

8/20 Mar 1891. Berlin.

RUS–KL (a³, No. 1421).

PB: 477–478 — *PSSL* 16A: 67 — *LF*: 478–479
[English tr.] — Yoffe: 26–27 [English tr.].

4344. To Pëtr Iurgenson

8/20 Mar 1891. Berlin.

RUS–KL (a³, No. 2753).

*PIU 2: 207 — **PSSL* 16A: 68 — Yoffe: 27–28
[English tr.].

4345. To Pëtr Iurgenson

12/24 Mar 1891. Paris.

RUS–KL (a³, No. 2754).

*ZC 3 — *PIU* 2: 207–208 — *PSSL* 16A: 69.

4346. To Ivan Vsevolozhskii

13/25 Mar [1891]. Paris.

RUS–SPia (f. 652, op. 1, d. 608, fol. 34–35) [facs. in
Neva (1974), 7: 220].

PSSL 16A: 70.

4347. To Wladyslaw Pachulski

[14]/26 Mar 1891 (in MS: "13/26"). Paris.

US–Wc

SM (1959), 12: 78 — *PSSL* 16A: 71 — Yoffe: 28–29
[English tr.].

4348. To Vladimir Davydov

[15]/27 Mar 1891 (in MS: "14/27"). Paris.

RUS–KL (a³, No. 122).

*PB: 478 — *PSSL* 16A: 72 — **LF*: 479 [English tr.].

4349. To Iulii Konius

[15]/27 [Mar] 1891 (in MS: "27 May") [Paris] — in
French.

Autograph lost; MS copy in RUS–KL.

PSSL 16A: 73.

4350. To Ekaterina Larosh

[15]/27 Mar [1891]. Paris.

Autograph lost; photocopy in RUS–KL.

PSSL 16A: 73.

4351. To Eduard Nápravník

[15/27 Mar 1891. Paris].

RUS–KL (a³, No. 3341).

VP: 205 ("Mar 1891") — *EFN*: 171 ("21 Mar") —
PSSL 16A: 74.

4352. To Grand Duke Konstantin Konstantinovich

15/27 Mar 1891. Paris.

RUS–SPil (f. 137, No. 78/27).

PSSL 16A: 74–75 — Yoffe: 29–30 [English tr.].

4353. To Grand Duke Konstantin Konstantinovich

[15]/27 Mar 1891. Paris — in French.

RUS–SPil (f. 137, No. 78/28).

PSSL 16A: 75.

4354. To Pëtr Iurgenson

17/29 Mar [1891]. [Paris].

RUS–KL (a³, No. 2755).

*ZC 3: 433 — **PIU* 2: 208 — *PSSL* 16A: 76 —
Yoffe: 30–31 [English tr.].

4355. To Nikolai Konradi

20 Mar/1 Apr 1891. Paris.

Autograph lost; MS copy in RUS–KL.

CTP: 280 — *PSSL* 16A: 76–77.

4356. To Ekaterina Larosh

24 Mar/5 Apr 1891 [Paris].

Autograph lost; photocopy in RUS–KL.

PSSL 16A: 77.

4357. To Jacques Dusotoir

[25 Mar]/6 Apr 1891 [Paris].

RUS–KL (a³, No. 3297).

PSSL 16A: 78.

4358. To Eduard Nápravník

[25 Mar]/6 Apr [1891]. Paris.

Autograph lost; typed copy in RUS–KL.

EFN: 178 ("6 Apr") — *PSSL* 16A: 79.

4359. To Anna Merkling

30 Mar/11 Apr 1891. Rouen.

Autograph lost; MS copy in RUS–KL.

CTP: 243–244 — *PSSL* 16A: 79–80.

4360.   To Praskov´ia Chaikovskaia

30 Mar/11 [Apr] 1891. Rouen.

RUS–KL (a³, No. 454).

*PB: 478–479 — PSSL 16A: 80–81 — *LF: 480 [English tr.].

4361.   To Pëtr Iurgenson

30 Mar/11 Apr [1891]. Rouen.

RUS–KL (a³, No. 2756).

PIU 2: 209–210 — PSSL 16A: 81–82 — Yoffe: 31–32 [English tr.].

4362.   To Vladimir Davydov

30 Mar/11 Apr 1891. Rouen.

RUS–KL (a³, No. 123).

PSSL 16A: 83.

4362a.   To Clotilde Kleeberg

[30 Mar]/11 Apr 1891 [Rouen] — in French.

D–F

Bisher unbekannte Briefe und musikalische Arbeiten Čajkovskijs (1994): 12–14 — Internationales Čajkovskij-Symposium Tübingen 1993: Bericht (1995): 36–38.

4363.   To Ivan Vsevolozhskii

3/15 Apr 1891. Rouen.

RUS–SPia (f. 652, op. 1, d. 608, fol. 28–33).

PSSL 16A: 83–86 — Yoffe: 32–35 [English tr.].

4364.   To Modest Chaikovskii

3/15 Apr 1891 [Rouen].

RUS–KL (a³, No. 1962).

*ZC 3: 435–436 — PB: 479–480 — PSSL 16A: 86–87 — LF: 480–481 [English tr.] — Yoffe: 36–37 [English tr.].

4365.   To Modest Chaikovskii

[4/16] Apr 1891 (in MS: "5/17") [Paris].

RUS–KL (a³, No. 1963).

*ZC 3: 435 — PB: 481 — PSSL 16A: 88 — LF: 481–482 [English tr.] — Yoffe: 37–38 [English tr.].

4365a.   To Ivan Vsevolozhskii

[5/17 Apr 1891. Rouen].

RUS–KL (a³, No. 3321).

Not published.

4366.   To Aleksei Sofronov

5/17 Apr [1891]. Rouen.

RUS–SPsc (f. 834, No. 28, fol. 1–2).

PSSL 16A: 89 — Yoffe: 38–39 [English tr.].

4367.   To Modest Chaikovskii

6/18–15/27 Apr 1891. Atlantic Ocean–New York.

RUS–KL (a³, No. 1964).

*ZC 3: 437–446 ("9–15 Apr") — *PB: 481–486 — PSSL 16A: 89–98 — *LF: 482–488 [English tr.] — Yoffe: 39–49 [English tr.].

4367a.   To Anna Merkling

[15/27 Apr 1891. New York].

Autograph lost; MS copy in RUS–KL.

PSSL 17: 255.

4368.   To Praskov´ia & Anatolii Chaikovskii

15/27 Apr 1891. New York

RUS–KL (a³, No. 1422).

PSSL 16A: 98 — Yoffe: 55–56 [English tr.].

4369.   To Vladimir Davydov

18/30 Apr 1891. New York.

RUS–KL (a³, No. 124).

*ZC 3: 451–452 — PB: 488–489 — PSSL 16A: 99–100 — LF: 489–490 [English tr.] — Yoffe: 62–64 [English tr.].

4370.   To Eduard Nápravník

20 Apr/2 May 1891. New York.

RUS–KL (a³, No. 3342).

VP: 209–211 — EFN: 174–175 — PSSL 16A: 101–102 — Yoffe: 68–71 [English tr.].

4371.   To Anatolii Chaikovskii

21 Apr/3 May 1891. New York.

RUS–KL (a³, No. 1423).

*PB: 490 — PSSL 16A: 103–104 — *LF: 490 [English tr.] — Yoffe: 72–73 [English tr.].

4372.   To Nikolai Konradi

22 Apr/4 May 1891. New York.

Autograph lost; MS copy in RUS–KL.

CTP: 281 — PSSL 16A: 104–105 — Yoffe: 76–77 [English tr.].

4373.   To Anna Merkling

22 Apr/4 May 1891. New York.

Autograph lost; MS copy in RUS–KL.

*CTP:*244–245 — *PSSL* 16A: 105–106 — Yoffe: 77–78 [English tr.].

4374.   To Iulii Konius

[23 Apr]/5 May 1891. New York.

Autograph lost; MS copy in RUS–KL.

*ZC 3: 460 — *PSSL* 16A: 106–107 — Yoffe: 80–81 [English tr.].

4375.   To Aleksei Sofronov

23 Apr/5 May 1891. New York.

RUS–SPsc (f. 834, No. 28, fol. 3–4).

PSSL 16A: 107–108 — Yoffe: 81 [English tr.].

4375a.   [To an unidentified correspondent]

[26 Apr]/8 May 1891. New York.

US–NH (John Carter Glenn coll., MSS 9/1/1).

TGM 7 (2000): 42.

4376.   To Modest Chaikovskii

27 Apr/9 May 1891 [New York].

RUS–KL (a³, No. 1965).

PB: 490–491 — *PSSL* 16A: 108–109 — *LF*: 490–491 [English tr.] — Yoffe: 103–104 [English tr.].

4377.   To Nikolai Chaikovskii

27 Apr/9 May 1891 [New York].

RUS–SPsc (f. 834, No. 37, fol. 20–21).

PSSL 16A: 109–110 — Yoffe: 104–106 [English tr.].

4378.   To Modest Chaikovskii

[29 Apr/11 May] 1891 (in MS: "28 Apr/10 May"). New York.

RUS–KL (a³, No. 1966).

PB: 491 — *PSSL* 16A: 111 — *LF*: 491–492 [English tr.] — Yoffe: 113 [English tr.].

4379.   To Modest Chaikovskii

[29 Apr]/11 May 1891 (in MS: "22 Apr"). Utica, on the way to Niagara Falls.

RUS–KL (a³, No. 1967).

*ZC 3: 469 — *PB*: 491–492 — *PSSL* 16A: 111–112 — *LF*: 492 [English tr.] — Yoffe: 114–115 [English tr.].

4380.   To Vladimir Davydov

2/[14] May [1891]. New York.

RUS–KL (a³, No. 125).

PB: 492–493 — *PSSL* 16A: 112–113 — **LF*: 492–493 [English tr.] — Yoffe: 128 [English tr.].

4381.   To Georgii Konius

2/14 May 1891. New York.

RUS–Mcm (f. 88, No. 328).

*ZC 3: 473–474 — *PSSL* 16A: 113–114.

4382.   To Anatolii Chaikovskii

14/26 May 1891. Atlantic Ocean.

RUS–KL (a³, No. 1424).

*PB: 493 — *PSSL* 16A: 114–115 — **LF*: 493 [English tr.].

4382a. To Aleksandr Glazunov

24 May 1891. St Petersburg

Autograph lost; MS copy in RUS-SPit (f. 21, No. 886, fol 8).

Not published.

4383.   To Giulio Riccordi

28 May 1891. St. Petersburg — in French.

Autograph lost; photocopy in RUS–KL.

PSSL 16A: 115–116.

4384.   To Vladimir Nápravník

29 May 1891 [Maidanovo] (in MS: "Klin").

Autograph lost; typed copy in RUS–KL.

EFN: 196 — *PSSL* 16A: 116–117 — Yoffe: 160–161 [English tr.].

4385.   To William von Sachs

29 [May] 1891 (in MS: "29 Jun") [Maidanovo] (in MS: "Klin").

RUS–Mt

PSSL 16A: 117–118 — Yoffe: 161–162 [English tr.].

4386.   To Ippolit Chaikovskii

29 May 1891 [Maidanovo] (in MS: "Klin").

RUS–SPsc (f. 834, No. 33, fol. 3–5).

*PB: 493–494 — *PSSL* 16A: 119 — **LF*: 494 [English tr.] — Yoffe: 158–159 [English tr.].

4387.   To Nikolai Chaikovskii

29 May 1891 [Maidanovo] (in MS: "Klin").

RUS–SPsc (f. 834, No. 37, fol. 22–23).

PSSL 16A: 120 — Yoffe: 159–160 [English tr.].

4388.   To Iuliia Shpazhinskaia

29 May 1891 [Maidanovo] (in MS: "Klin").

RUS–KL (a³, No. 2129).

CTP: 358 — *PSSL* 16A: 120–121.

4389.   To Vasilii Bessel´ & Co.

2 Jun 1891. Maidanovo.

RUS–Mcm (f. 42, No. 274).

SM (1938), 6: 54–55 — *PSSL* 16A: 121–122.

4390.   To Anna Merkling

2 Jun 1891 [Maidanovo].

Autograph lost; MS copy in RUS–KL.

CTP: 245 — *PSSL* 16A: 122–123.

4391.   To N. Nikolaev

2 Jun [1891]. [Maidanovo] (in MS: "Klin").

RUS–KL (a³, No. 3152).

Radian´ska muzyka (1940), No. 2 — *PSSL* 16A: 123–124.

4392.   To Anton Rubinshtein

2 Jun 1891 [Maidanovo].

RUS–SPsc (f. 654, op. 1, No. 81).

PSSL 16A: 124.

4393.   To Praskov´ia Chaikovskaia

2 Jun 1891 [Maidanovo] (in MS: "Klin").

RUS–KL (a³, No. 455) — incomplete

PSSL 16A: 124–125.

4394.   To Mikhail Ippolitov-Ivanov

3 Jun 1891 [Maidanovo] (in MS: "Klin").

RUS–KL (a³, No. 197).

*ZC 3: 487–488 — **Iskusstvo*, 3 (1927), 4: 165–166 — *Biulleten´* (1947), 2: 30–33 — *PSSL* 16A: 125–127.

4395.   To Anna Merkling

3 Jun 1891 [Maidanovo].

Autograph lost; MS copy in RUS–KL.

CTP: 245 — *PSSL* 16A: 127 — Yoffe: 162 [English tr.].

4396.   To Osip Paleček

3 Jun 1891 [Maidanovo] (in MS: "Klin").

RUS–KL (a³, No. 283).

SM (1965), 9: 46 — *PSSL* 16A: 128.

4397.   To Pëtr Iurgenson

3 Jun 1891. Maidanovo.

RUS–KL (a³, No. 2757).

*ZC 3: 488 — *PIU* 2: 211–213 — *PSSL* 16A: 129–130 — Yoffe: 162–165 [English tr.].

4397a.   To Anna Aleksandrova-Levenson

[early June 1891. Moscow] — note on visiting card.

Autograph lost; typed copy in RUS–KL.

PSSL 17: 255.

4398.   To Wladyslaw Pachulski

6 Jun 1891. Moscow.

RUS–SPsc (f. 834, No. 22).

*ZC 3: 398–399 — *PM* 3: 611–612 — *PSSL* 16A: 131–132 — Yoffe: 167–168 [English tr.].

4399.   To Vladimir Davydov

11 Jun [1891]. Maidanovo.

RUS–KL (a³, No. 126).

PSSL 16A: 133.

4400.   To Aleksandr Ziloti

11 Jun 1891. Maidanovo.

RUS–KL (a³, No. 176).

RMG (1908), 43: 1043–1044 — *AIZ*: 118–120 — *PSSL* 16A: 134–136 — Yoffe: 169–171 [English tr.].

4401.   To Anna Merkling

11 Jun 1891. Maidanovo.

Autograph lost; MS copy in RUS–KL.

CTP: 245–246 — *PSSL* 16A: 136–137.

4402.   To Vasilii Filatov

11 Jun [1891]. Maidanovo.

RUS–KL (a³, No. 3319(

PSSL 16A: 137.

4403.   To Modest Chaikovskii

11 Jun [1891]. [Maidanovo].

RUS–KL (a³, No. 1968).

PSSL 16A: 137–138.

4404. To Iuliia Shpazhinskaia

11 Jun [1891]. [Maidanovo] (in MS: "Klin").

RUS–KL (a³, No. 2130).

CTP: 358–359 — *PSSL* 16A: 138–139.

4405. To Aleksandr Ziloti

14 Jun 1891. Maidanovo.

RUS–KL (a³, No. 3027).

*RMG (1908), 47: 1043–1044 — *AIZ*: 120–123 — *PSSL* 16A: 139–142.

4406. To Nikolai Konradi

14 Jun 1891. Maidanovo.

Autograph lost; MS copy in RUS–KL.

CTP: 281–282 — *PSSL* 16A: 142.

4407. To Osip Paleček

14 Jun 1891 [Maidanovo] (in MS: "Klin").

RUS–KL (a³, No. 284).

SM (1965), 9: 47 — *PSSL* 16A: 143.

4408. To Pëtr Iurgenson

14 Jun [1891]. Maidanovo.

RUS–KL (a³, No. 2758).

PIU 2: 213–214 — *PSSL* 16A: 144.

4409. To Boris Iurgenson

14 Jun 1891. Maidanovo.

RUS–KL (a³, No. 478).

PSSL 16A: 145–146.

4410. To Iulii Konius

15 Jun 1891 [Maidanovo] (in MS: "Klin").

Autograph lost; MS copy in RUS–KL.

*ZC 3: 489 — *PSSL* 16A: 146–147.

4411. To Karl Al´brekht

16 [Jun] 1891 (in MS: "16 May"). Maidanovo.

RUS–Mcm (f. 37, No. 69).

PSSL 16A: 148.

4412. To Varvara Zarudnaia

17 Jun 1891 [Maidanovo] (in MS: "Klin").

RUS–Mcm (f. 2, No. 5118).

Iskusstvo, 3 (1927), 4: 167 — *PSSL* 16A: 148–149.

4413. To Modest Chaikovskii

17 Jun [1891]. [Maidanovo].

RUS–KL (a³, No. 1969).

PB: 494 — *PSSL* 16A: 149–150 — *LF*: 494 [English tr.].

4414. To Aleksandra Hubert

18 Jun 1891. Maidanovo.

RUS–KL (a³, No. 75).

PRM 57 — *PSSL* 16A: 150.

4415. To Karl Val´tz

[? 18–19 Jun 1891. Maidanovo] (in MS: "Klin").

RUS–Mt (Val´tz coll.).

SM (1933), 6: 100 — *CMS*: 475 — *PSSL* 16A: 150–151.

4416. To Boris Iurgenson

19 Jun [1891]. Maidanovo.

RUS–KL (a³, No. 480).

PSSL 16A: 152.

4417. To Iakov Kalishevskii

20 Jun 1891 [Maidanovo] (in MS: "Klin").

Autograph lost

Muzyka i penie (1903), 5: 2–3 — **Chaikovskii na Ukraine* (1940): 33–34 [Ukrainian tr.] — *PSSL* 16A: 152–153 — Yoffe: 173–174 [English tr.].

4418. To Anatolii Chaikovskii

22 Jun 1891. Maidanovo.

RUS–KL (a³, No. 1425).

PSSL 16A: 154–155.

4419. To Aleksandra Hubert

25 Jun 1891 [Maidanovo].

RUS–KL (a³, No. 76).

PRM 58 — *PSSL* 16A: 155.

4420. To Vladimir Davydov

25 Jun 1891 [Maidanovo] (in MS: "Klin").

RUS–KL (a³, No. 127).

*ZC 3: 489–490 — *PB: 494–495 — *PSSL* 16A: 155–156 — *LF: 495 [English tr.].

**4421.　To Mikhail Ippolitov-Ivanov &
Varvara Zarudnaia**

25 Jun 1891 [Maidanovo] (in MS: "Klin").

RUS–KL (a³, No. 198).

*ZC 3: 489 — *Iskusstvo, 3 (1927), 4: 168 — Biulleten´
(1947), 2: 37–38 — PSSL 16A: 157–158.

4422.　To Iakov Kalishevskii

25 Jun 1891 [Maidanovo] (in MS: "Klin").

Autograph lost

Muzyka i penie (1903), 5: 3 — PSSL 16A: 158–159.

4423.　To Iulii Konius

25 Jun 1891 [Maidanovo].

Autograph lost; MS copy in RUS–KL.

PSSL 16A: 159.

4424.　To Bogomir Korsov

25 Jun 1891 [Maidanovo] (in MS: "Klin") — in
French.

RUS–KL (a³, nos. 242, 236).

Sovetskoe iskusstvo (6 May 1940) [Russian tr.] — SM
(1959), 1: 77 [Russian tr.] — *V. Protopopov,
´Ivan Susanin´ Glinki (1961): 279–280 [Russian
tr.] — PSSL 16A: 160–161.

4425.　To Modest Chaikovskii

25 Jun 1891 [Maidanovo].

RUS–KL (a³, No. 1970).

PSSL 16A: 161.

4426.　To Nikolai Konradi

26 Jun 1891. Maidanovo.

Autograph lost; incomplete MS copy in RUS–KL.

*ZC 3: 490–491 — CTP: 282 — PSSL 16A: 162–163.

4427.　To Modest Chaikovskii

26 Jun [1891]. [Maidanovo].

RUS–KL (a³, No. 1971).

PSSL 16A: 163.

4428.　To Boris Iurgenson

26 Jun [1891]. [Maidanovo].

RUS–KL (a³, No. 481).

PSSL 16A: 163–164.

4429.　To Sergei Taneev

27 [Jun] 1891 (in MS: "27 Jul") [Maidanovo] (in
MS: "Klin").

RUS–Mcl (f. 880).

*ZC 3: 497–499 ("27 Jul") — PT: 168–170 — CTP:
173–175 — PSSL 16A: 164–166.

**4430.　To Ol´ga, Nikolai & Georgii
Chaikovskii**

27 Jun 1891 [Maidanovo].

RUS–SPsc (f. 834, No. 31, fol. 6).

PSSL 16A: 167.

4431.　To Anton Arenskii

7 Jul 1891 [Maidanovo].

RUS–SPil (f. 504, No. 74, fol. 13–16).

*ZC 3: 491–492 — *G. Tsypin, A. S. Arenskii (1966):
24 — PSSL 16A: 167–168.

4432.　To Walter Damrosch

7 Jul 1891 [Maidanovo] (in MS: "Klin") — in French
and German.

US–Wc (ML31.B4. box 6, folder 52).

PSSL 16A: 169–170 — Yoffe: 175–176 [English tr.].

4433.　To Aleksandr Ziloti

7 Jul [1891]. [Maidanovo] (in MS: "Klin").

RUS–KL (a³, No. 3028).

AIZ: 124–125 — PSSL 16A: 171.

4434.　To Iakov Kalishevskii

7 Jul 1891 [Maidanovo] (in MS: "Klin").

Autograph lost

Muzyka i penie (1903), 5: 3 — PSSL 16A: 172–173.

4435.　To Iulii Konius

7 Jul 1891 [Maidanovo].

Autograph lost; MS copy in RUS–KL.

PSSL 16A: 173.

4436.　To Vladimir Davydov

8 Jul [1891]. [Maidanovo].

RUS–KL (a³, No. 128).

PSSL 16A: 173–174.

4437.   To Ekaterina Larosh

8 Jul 1891 [Maidanovo] (in MS: "Klin").

Autograph lost; photocopy in RUS–KL.

PSSL 16A: 174–175.

4438.   To Anna Merkling

8 Jul 1891 [Maidanovo].

Autograph lost; MS copy in RUS–KL.

*ZC 3: 493–494 — *CTP*: 246 — *PSSL* 16A: 175–176.

4439.   To Anatolii Chaikovskii

8 Jul 1891 [Maidanovo].

RUS–KL (a³, No. 1426).

*ZC 3: 492–493 — *PB*: 495–496 — *PSSL* 16A: 176–
177 — *LF*: 495–496 [English tr.].

4439a. To Modest Chaikovskii

[8 Jul 1891. Maidanovo].

RUS–KL (a³, No. 2043).

PSSL 17: 256.

4440.   To Vladimir Davydov

11 Jul 1891 [Maidanovo].

RUS–KL (a³, No. 129).

*ZC 3: 494 — **PB*: 496 — *PSSL* 16A: 177–178 —
*LF: 496 [English tr.] ("to Lev Davydov").

4441.   To Aleksandra Hubert

18 Jul 1891. Maidanovo.

RUS–KL (a³, No. 77).

PRM 58 — *PSSL* 16A: 179.

4442.   To Vladimir Davydov

22 Jul 1891 [Maidanovo] (in MS: "Klin").

RUS–KL (a³, No. 130).

*ZC 3: 494 — **PB*: 496–497 — *PSSL* 16A: 179–
180 — **LF*: 497 [English tr.].

4443.   To Aleksandr Ziloti

22 Jul [1891]. [Maidanovo].

RUS–KL (a³, No. 3029).

AIZ: 126 — *PSSL* 16A: 181.

4444.   To Aleksandr Litke

22 Jul 1891 [Maidanovo].

RUS–KL (a³, No. 267).

PSSL 16A: 182.

4445.   To Nikolai Konradi

25 Jul 1891 [Maidanovo].

Autograph lost; MS copy in RUS–KL.

CTP: 283 — *PSSL* 16A: 183.

4446.   To Vladimir Nápravník

25 Jul 1891. Maidanovo.

Autograph lost; typed copy in RUS–KL.

EFN: 196–197 — *PSSL* 16A: 184 — Yoffe: 176–177
[English tr.].

4447.   To Anatolii Chaikovskii

25 Jul 1891 [Maidanovo].

RUS–KL (a³, No. 1427).

*ZC 3: 495 — *PSSL* 16A: 185.

4448.   To Modest Chaikovskii

25 Jul 1891 [Maidanovo].

RUS–KL (a³. No. 1972).

*ZC 3: 496–497 — *PB*: 497–498 — *PSSL* 16A:
186 — *LF*: 497–498 [English tr.].

4449.   To Akhilles Alferaki

1 Aug 1891 [Maidanovo].

Autograph lost; typed copy in RUS–KL.

*ZC 3: 500–501 — *PSSL* 16A: 187.

4450.   To Vladimir Davydov

1 Aug 1891 [Maidanovo] — partly in French.

RUS–KL (a³, No. 131).

*ZC 3: 499–500 — *PB*: 498–499 — *PSSL* 16A: 188–
189 — *LF*: 498–499 [English tr.].

4451.   To Aleksandr Ziloti

7 Aug 1891. Maidanovo.

RUS–KL (a³, No. 3030).

AIZ: 127 — *PSSL* 16A: 189.

4452.   To Modest Chaikovskii

7 Aug 1891. Maidanovo.

RUS–KL (a³, No. 1973).

*ZC 3: 501–502 — *PB*: 499–500 — *PSSL* 16A: 190–
191 — *LF*: 499–500 [English tr.].

4453.   To Iulii Konius

8 Aug 1891 [Maidanovo].

Autograph lost; MS copy in RUS–KL.

PSSL 16A: 191.

4454.   To Pëtr Iurgenson

8 Aug [1891]. [Maidanovo].

RUS–KL (a³, No. 2759).

PIU 2: 214 — *PSSL* 16A: 191–192.

4455.   To Ippolit Chaikovskii

9 Aug [1891]. [Maidanovo] (in MS: "Klin").

RUS–SPsc (f. 834, No. 35, fol. 6–7).

PSSL 16A: 192–193.

4456.   To Anatolii Chaikovskii

10 Aug 1891. Maidanovo.

RUS–KL (a³, No. 1428).

PSSL 16A: 193–194.

4457.   To Aleksei Sofronov

15 Aug [1891]. [Ukolovo].

RUS–SPsc (f. 834, No. 28, fol. 18–19).

PSSL 16A: 195.

4458.   To Pavel Peterssen

22 Aug 1891. Kamenka.

RUS–SPsc (f. 124, No. 4651, fol. 1–3).

PSSL 16A: 195.

4459.   To Pëtr Iurgenson

22 Aug [1891]. Kamenka.

RUS–KL (a³, No. 2760).

PIU 2: 215 — *PSSL* 16A: 196.

4460.   To Karl Al´brekht

[1 Sep 1891. Moscow].

RUS–Mcm (f. 37, No. 111).

PSSL 16A: 196.

4461.   To Evgenii Al´brekht

2 Sep [1891]. [Maidanovo] (in MS: "Klin").

RUS–SPtob (VII.2.4.154).

PSSL 16A: 197.

4462.   To Evgenii Al´brekht

2 Sep 1891. Maidanovo.

RUS–SPtob (VII.2.4.154).

PSSL 16A: 197–198.

4463.   To Anna Merkling

2 Sep 1891 [Maidanovo].

Autograph lost; MS copy in RUS–KL.

CTP: 246–247 — *PSSL* 16A: 198.

4464.   To Pavel Peterssen

2 Sep 1891 [Maidanovo] (in MS: "Klin").

RUS–SPsc (f. 124, No. 4651, fol. 4–6).

PSSL 16A: 199.

4465.   To Anatolii Chaikovskii

2 Sep [1891]. [Maidanovo].

RUS–KL (a³, No. 1429).

PB: 500–501 — *PSSL* 16A: 199–200 — *LF*: 500–501
    [English tr.].

4466.   To Praskov´ia Chaikovskaia

2 Sep 1891. Maidanovo.

RUS–KL (a³, No. 456).

PSSL 16A: 201.

4467.   To Ippolit Chaikovskii

2 Sep 1891. Maidanovo.

RUS–SPsc (f. 834, No. 35, fol. 8–9).

PSSL 16A: 201–202.

4468.   To Iuliia Shpazhinskaia

2 Sep 1891 [Maidanovo] (in MS: "Klin").

RUS–KL (a³, No. 2131).

CTP: 359–360 — *PSSL* 16A: 202–203.

4468a. To Georgii Chaikovskii

5 Sep [1891]. [Maidanovo].

RUS–SPsc (f. 834, No. 34).

PSSL 17: 256.

4469.   To Modest Chaikovskii

5 Sep [1891]. [Maidanovo].

RUS–KL (a³, No. 1974).

*ZC 3: 504–505 — *PSSL* 16A: 203–205.

4470.   To Pëtr Iurgenson

7 Sep 1891 [Maidanovo].

RUS–KL (a³, No. 2761).

PIU 2: 215–216 — *PSSL* 16A: 205–206 — Yoffe: 178–179 [English tr.].

4471.   To Anton Arenskii

8 Sep 1891 [Maidanovo].

RUS–SPil (f. 504, No. 74, fol. 15).

PSSL 16A: 206.

4472.   To Aleksandr Ziloti

8 Sep 1891. Maidanovo.

RUS–KL (a³, No. 3031).

AIZ: 127–128 — *PSSL* 16A: 207.

4473.   To Pëtr Iurgenson

8 Sep 1891 [Maidanovo].

RUS–KL (a³, No. 2765).

PIU 2: 216 — *PSSL* 16A: 207–208.

4474.   To Bogomir Korsov

12 Sep 1891 [Maidanovo] — in French.

RUS–KL (a³, No. 243).

PSSL 16A: 208.

4475.   To Anna Merkling

12 Sep 1891 [Maidanovo].

Autograph lost; MS copy in RUS–KL.

PSSL 16A: 209.

4476.   To Bogomir Korsov

15 Sep 1891. Maidanovo — in French.

RUS–KL (a³, No. 244).

PSSL 16A: 209.

4477.   To Sophie Menter

22 Sep 1891 [Maidanovo] (in MS: "Klin").

US–NYpm (Morgan coll.).

PSSL 16A: 210–211.

4478.   To Anna Merkling

22 Sep 1891 [Maidanovo].

Autograph lost; MS copy in RUS–KL.

PSSL 16A: 212.

4479.   To Pavel Peterssen

22 Sep 1891 [Maidanovo] (in MS: "Klin").

RUS–SPsc

PSSL 16A: 213.

4480.   To Anatolii Chaikovskii

22 Sep 1891 [Maidanovo].

RUS–KL (a³, No. 1430).

*PB: 301 — *PSSL* 16A: 214 — **LF:* 501 [English tr.].

4481.   To Pëtr Iurgenson

22 Sep [1891]. [Maidanovo].

RUS–KL (a³, No. 2766).

PIU 2: 216–217 — *PSSL* 16A: 214–215 — Yoffe: 187 [English tr.].

4482.   To Pëtr Iurgenson

[23 Sep 1891. Maidanovo].

RUS–KL (a³, No. 2784).

PIU 2: 217 — *PSSL* 16A: 215.

4483.   To Aleksandr Ziloti

25 Sep [1891]. [Maidanovo].

RUS–KL (a³, No. 3033).

AIZ: 128 — *PSSL* 16A: 215.

4484.   To Sergei Taneev

25 Sep 1891 [Maidanovo].

RUS–Mcl (f. 880).

CTP: 178 — *PSSL* 16A: 216.

4485.   To Karl Al´brekht

[27 Sep 1891. Maidanovo].

RUS–Mcm (f. 37, No. 70).

CMS: 297 — *PSSL* 16A: 216.

4486.   To Bogomir Korsov

[28 Sep 1891. Maidanovo] — in French.

RUS–KL (a³, No. 249).

PSSL 16A: 216.

4487.   To Pëtr Iurgenson

29 Sep [1891]. [Moscow].

RUS–KL (a³, No. 2767).

PIU 2: 217 — *PSSL* 16A: 217.

4488.   To Anna & Adol´f Brodskii

30 Sep 1891 [Moscow].

GB–Mcm

PSSL 16A: 217 — Yoffe: 188 [English tr.].

4489.   To Adolf Čech

[? 30 Sep–1 Oct 1891. Maidanovo] — in German.

Autograph lost. Rough draft (including German tr. by
    German Larosh) in RUS–KL (a⁴, No. 6635).

Chaikovkskii i zarubezhnye muzykanty (1970): 190–191—
    PSSL 16A: 218 [German tr. — *PSSL* 16A: 309].

4490.   To Iakov Kalishevskii

1 Oct [1891]. [Maidanovo] (in MS: "Klin").

Autograph lost

Muzyka i penie (1903), 5: 3 — *PSSL* 16A: 218–219.

4491.   To Milii Balakirev

1 Oct 1891 [Maidanovo] (in MS: "Klin").

RUS–SPsc (f. 834, No. 12, fol. 40–41).

BC: 98–99 — *BVP* 184–185 — *PSSL* 16A: 219–220.

4492.   To Anatolii Chaikovskii

1 Oct 1891 [Maidanovo].

RUS–KL (a³, No. 1431).

PB: 501–502 — *PSSL* 16A: 220–221 — *LF*: 502
    [English tr.].

4493.   To Iuliia Shpazhinskaia

1 Oct [1891]. [Maidanovo] (in MS: "Klin").

RUS–KL (a³, No. 2132).

CTP: 360 — *PSSL* 16A: 221–222.

4494.   To Vladimir Nápravník

2 Oct 1891 [Maidanovo].

Autograph lost; typed copy in RUS–KL.

ZC 3: 508 — *EFN*: 197–198 — *PSSL* 16A: 222–223.

4495.   To Pëtr Iurgenson

3 Oct 1891 [Maidanovo].

RUS–KL (a³, No. 2768).

PIU 2: 218 — *PSSL* 16A: 224.

4496.   To Francesco Berger

[? 3–5 Oct 1891. Maidanovo] — note on visiting card.

US–NYcub (Schang coll.).

F. C. Schang, *Visiting Cards of Celebrities* (1971) —
    PSSL 16A: 225.

4497.   To Pëtr Iurgenson

5 Oct 1891 [Maidanovo].

RUS–KL (a³, No. 2769).

PIU 2: 218–219 — *PSSL* 16A: 225–226.

4498.   To Aleksandr Ziloti

6 Oct [1891]. [Maidanovo].

RUS–KL (a³, No. 3034).

RMG (1908), 4: 1048 ("5 Oct") — *AIZ:* 129 —
    PSSL 16A: 226.

4499.   To Anna Merkling

7 Oct 1891 [Maidanovo].

Autograph lost; MS copy in RUS–KL.

CTP: 248 — *PSSL* 16A: 227.

4500.   To Eduard Nápravník

7 Oct 1891 [Maidanovo].

RUS–KL (a³, No. 3343).

VP: 212–213 — *EFN:* 176–177 — *PSSL* 16A: 227–
    228.

4501.   To Vadim Peresleni

7 Oct [1891]. [Maidanovo] (in MS: "Klin").

RUS–KL (a³, No. 292).

PSSL 16A: 229.

4502.   To Modest Chaikovskii

7 Oct [1891]. [Maidanovo].

RUS–KL (a³, No. 1975).

PB: 502 — *PSSL* 16A: 229 — *LF*: 502 [English tr.].

4503.   To Iakov Kalishevskii

8 Oct 1891 [Maidanovo].

Autograph lost

Muzyka i penie (1903), 5: 3 — *PSSL* 16A: 230.

4504.   To Ekaterina Larosh

8 Oct 1891. Maidanovo.

Autograph lost; photocopy in RUS–KL.

PSSL 16A: 230–231.

4505.   To Pëtr Iurgenson

8 Oct [1891]. [Maidanovo].

RUS–KL (a³, No. 2981).

PSSL 16A: 231 — Yoffe: 180 [English tr.].

4506. To Pëtr Iurgenson
8 Oct [1891]. [Maidanovo].
RUS–KL (a³, No. 2770).
PIU 2: 219 — *PSSL* 16A: 232.

4507. To Modest Chaikovskii
11 Oct [1891]. [Maidanovo].
RUS–KL (a³, No. 1976).
PSSL 16A: 232–233.

4508. To Vladimir Davydov
12 Oct 1891 [Maidanovo].
RUS–KL (a³, No. 132).
PSSL 16A: 233 — Yoffe: 181 [English tr.].

4509. To Vladimir Davydov
13 Oct 1891 [Maidanovo].
RUS–KL (a³, No. 133).
PSSL 16A: 234.

4510. To Eduard Nápravník
13 Oct 1891 [Maidanovo].
RUS–KL (a³, No. 3344).
VP: 215 — *EFN*: 178 — *PSSL* 16A: 234–235.

4511. To Pëtr Iurgenson
13 Oct 1891 [Maidanovo].
RUS–KL (a³, No. 2771).
PSSL 16A: 235 — Yoffe: 180 [English tr.].

4512. To Vladimir Pogozhev
16 Oct 1891 [Maidanovo].
RUS–Mcl
PSSL 16A: 235–236.

4513. To Adolf Čech
[16 Oct 1891. Maidanovo] (in MS: "Klin") — in German.
CZ–Pkadlic [facs. in Očadlik, *Pražské dopisy P. I. Čajkovského* (1949)].
Stěpánek (1952): 158–159 [Czech tr.] —*SM* (1952), 7: 69 [Russian tr.] — *PSSL* 16A: 236–237.

4514. To Mikhail Ippolitov-Ivanov
17 Oct 1891 [Maidanovo].
RUS–KL (a³, No. 199).
Biulleten´ (1947), 2: 41–43 — *PSSL* 16A: 238–239.

4515. To Ado´lf Brodskii
19 Oct 1891. Maidanovo.
GB–Mcm
The Listener (19 Apr 1962) [English tr.] — *PSSL* 16A: 239–241 — Yoffe: 190–192 [English tr.].

4516. To Aleksandra Hubert
19 Oct 1891 [Maidanovo].
RUS–KL (a³, No. 78).
PRM 58–59 — *PSSL* 16A: 241–242.

4517. To Modest Chaikovskii
20 Oct 1891. Maidanovo.
RUS–KL (a³, No. 1977).
*PB: 502–503 — *PSSL* 16A: 242–243 — **LF*: 503 [English tr.].

4518. To Pëtr Iurgenson
21 Oct [1891]. [Moscow].
RUS–KL (a³, No. 2772).
PSSL 16A: 243.

4519. To Modest Chaikovskii
22 Oct [1891]. Moscow.
Autograph lost; rough draft in RUS–KL (a³, No. 1978).
PSSL 16A: 244–248 [draft].

4520. To Leopoldine Lafitte
23 Oct [1891]. [Moscow] — in French.
RUS–KL (a³, No. 265).
PSSL 16A: 248.

4521. To Aleksei Sofronov
[23 Oct 1891. Moscow].
RUS–KL (a³, No. 389).
PSSL 16A: 249.

4522. To Anton Chekhov
23 Oct [1891. Moscow].
RUS–Mrg
ZC 3: 326–328 ("24 Oct 1889") — *Slovo*, 2 (1914): 218–221 — **I. R. Eiges, Muzyka v zhizni i tvorchestve A. P. Chekhova* (1953): 38–39 — *PSSL* 16A: 249–250.

4523.   To Pavel Peterssen

24 Oct [1891]. Moscow.

RUS–KL (a³, No. 302).

PSSL 16A: 250–251.

4523a. To Vasilii Safonov

24 Oct [1891]. [Moscow].

Autograph lost [facs. in *Radians´ka muzyka* (1940), 2: 41].

PSSL 17: 257.

4524.   To Aleksei Kartavov

25 Oct 1891. Moscow.

RUS–SPsc (f. 341, No. 299, fol. 1–2).

PSSL 16A: 251.

4525.   To Sergei Taneev

25 Oct 1891 [Moscow].

RUS–Mcl (f. 880).

ZC 3: 509 — *PT*: 172–173 — *CTP*: 178 — *PSSL* 16A: 252.

4526.   To Mikhail Lentovskii

27 Oct [1891]. [Moscow].

RUS–Mt

PSSL 16A: 252–253.

4527.   To Anatolii Chaikovskii

27 Oct [1891]. Moscow.

RUS–KL (a³, No. 1432).

ZC 3: 509–510 ("31 Oct") — *PB*: 503 — *PSSL* 16A: 253 — *LF*: 503 [English tr.].

4528.   To Modest Chaikovskii

27 Oct 1891 [Moscow].

RUS–KL (a³, No. 1979).

PSSL 16A: 254–255.

4529.   To Osip Paleček

28 Oct 1891. Moscow.

RUS–KL (a³, No. 285).

SM (1965), 9: 47 — *PSSL* 16A: 255.

4530.   To Modest Chaikovskii

29 Oct 1891. Moscow.

RUS–KL (a³, No. 1980).

PSSL 16A: 256.

4531.   To   Grand   Duke   Konstantin Konstantinovich

31 Oct 1891. Moscow.

RUS–SPil (f. 137, No. 78/29).

ZC 3: 510–511 — *PSSL* 16A: 257–258 — Yoffe: 182–184 [English tr.].

4531a. To Aleksei Sofronov

[31 Oct 1891. Moscow] — postcard.

RUS–Mcm (f. 88, No. 223).

PSSL 17: 257.

4532.   To Aleksei Kartavov

2 Nov [1891]. Moscow.

RUS–SPsc (f. 341, No. 299, fol. 3).

PSSL 16A: 259.

4533.   To Pëtr Iurgenson

[2 Nov 1891. Moscow].

RUS–KL (a³, No. 2785).

PSSL 16A: 259.

4533a. To Sergei Taneev

[? 2–3 Nov 1881. Moscow].

RUS–Mcl (f. 880).

CTP: 191 ("1889–1893") — *PSSL* 17: 258.

4534.   To Aleksandra Hubert

3 Nov 1891 [Moscow].

RUS–KL (a³, No. 113).

PRM 59 — *PSSL* 16A: 260.

4535.   To Pavel Pchel´nikov

3 Nov [1891]. [Moscow].

RUS–KL (a³, No. 331).

PSSL 16A: 260.

4536.   To Lidiia Genke

[5 Nov 1891. Moscow].

RUS–Mcl (f. 905).

PSSL 16A: 261.

4537.   To Mariia Klimentova–Muromtseva

8 Nov [1891]. [Moscow].

RUS–Mcl (f. 774).

PSSL 16A: 261.

4538. To Elena Samoilova

8 Nov 1891 [Moscow].

US–CLbackford.

PSSL 16A: 261.

4539. To Anatolii Chaikovskii

8 Nov [1891]. Moscow.

RUS–KL (a³, No. 1433).

PB: 503–504 — *PSSL* 16A: 262 — *LF*: 504 [English tr.].

4540. To Aleksei Kartavov

10 Nov 1891. Moscow.

RUS–SPsc (f. 341, No. 299, fol. 4–5).

PSSL 16A: 263.

4541. To Václav Suk

[10 Nov 1891. Moscow] — note on visiting card.

RUS–KL (a³, No. 2976).

PSSL 16A: 264.

4542. To Pavel Pchel´nikov

10 Nov 1891. Moscow.

RUS–KL (a³, No. 318).

PSSL 16A: 264.

4543. To Vladimir Alpers

11 Nov 1891 [Maidanovo].

RUS–KL (a³, No. 3157).

PSSL 16A: 265.

4544. To Aleksandra Hubert

11 Nov 1891 [Maidanovo].

RUS–KL (a³, No. 79).

PRM 60 — *PSSL* 16A: 265.

4545. To Vladimir Nápravník

11 Nov 1891 [Maidanovo].

Autograph lost; typed copy in RUS–KL.

EFN: 198–100 — *PSSL* 16A: 266.

4546. To Pëtr Iurgenson

11 Nov [1891]. [Maidanovo].

RUS–KL (a³, No. 2774).

PIU 2: 219 — *PSSL* 16A: 267.

4547. To Vera Genke

12 Nov [1891]. Maidanovo.

RUS–Md (f. 905).

PSSL 16A: 267.

4548. To Vladimir Davydov

14 Nov [1891]. [Maidanovo].

RUS–KL (a³, No. 134).

PSSL 16A: 268.

4549. To Nikolai Konradi

14 Nov 1891 [Maidanovo].

Autograph lost; MS copy in RUS–KL.

CTP: 283 — *PSSL* 16A: 268.

4550. To Bogomir Korsov

14 Nov 1891. Maidanovo — in French.

Autograph lost; typed copy in RUS–KL.

SM (1959), 1: 78–79 [Russian tr.] — *PSSL* 16A: 268–270.

4551. To Ekaterina Larosh

14 Nov 1891. Maidanovo.

Autograph lost; photocopy in RUS–KL.

PSSL 16A: 272–273.

4552. To Pavel Peterssen

14 Nov [1891]. [Maidanovo] (in MS: "Klin").

RUS–SPsc (f. 124, No. 4651, fol. 14–15).

PSSL 16A: 273.

4553. To Modest Chaikovskii

14 Nov [1891]. [Maidanovo].

RUS–KL (a³, No. 1981).

PSSL 16A: 274.

4554. To František Šubert

14 Nov 1891 [Maidanovo] (in MS: "Klin") — in French.

CZ–Ps [facs. in M. Očadlik, *Pražké dopisy P. I. Čajkovského* (1949)].

Stěpánek (1952): 156 [Czech tr.] — *PSSL* 16A: 275.

4555. To Pëtr Iurgenson

14 Nov [1891]. [Maidanovo].

RUS–KL (a³, No. 2775).

PIU 2: 220 — *PSSL* 16A: 275.

4556.　To Aleksandr Ziloti

15 Nov [1891]. [Maidanovo].

RUS–KL (a³, No. 3035).

RMG (1908), 47: 1049 — *AIZ*: 129 — *PSSL* 16A: 276.

4557.　To Pëtr Iurgenson

15 Nov 1891 [Maidanovo].

RUS–KL (a³, No. 2776).

PIU 2: 220–221 — *PSSL* 16A: 276–277.

4558.　To Bogomir Korsov

18 Nov 1891. Maidanovo — partly in French.

RUS–Mcm

SM (1959), 1: 80 [Russian tr.] — *PSSL* 16A: 277–278.

4559.　To Mariia Klimentova–Muromtseva

19 Nov [1891]. [Maidanovo].

RUS–Mcl (f. 774).

PSSL 16A: 279–280.

4560.　To Varvara, Sof´ia & Anna Maslova

19 Nov [1891]. [Maidanovo].

RUS–KL (a³, No. 270).

PSSL 16A: 280.

4561.　To Bogomir Korsov

20 Nov 1891 [Maidanovo] — in French.

RUS–KL (a³, No. 245).

PSSL 16A: 281.

4562.　To Pëtr Iurgenson

20 Nov [1891]. [Maidanovo].

RUS–KL (a³, No. 2777).

PIU 2: 221 — *PSSL* 16A: 282.

4563.　To Modest Chaikovskii

22 Nov [1891]. [Maidanovo].

RUS–KL (a³, No. 1982).

PSSL 16A: 282–283.

4564.　To Iulii Konius

23 Nov 1891 [Maidanovo].

Autograph lost; MS copy in RUS–KL.

PSSL 16A: 283–284 — Yoffe: 189–190 [English tr.].

4565.　To Pëtr Iurgenson

24 Nov [1891]. [Maidanovo].

RUS–KL (a³, No. 2827).

PSSL 16A: 284–285.

4566.　To Milii Balakirev

[29 Nov 1891. St. Petersburg].

RUS–SPsc (f. 834, No. 12, fol. 42).

BC: 100 — *BVP* 186 — *PSSL* 16A: 285.

4567.　To Pëtr Iurgenson

29 Nov [1891]. [St. Petersburg].

RUS–KL (a³, No. 2778).

PIU 2: 222 — *PSSL* 16A: 285–286.

4568.　To Pëtr Iurgenson

4 Dec 1891 [St. Petersburg].

RUS–KL (a³, No. 2779).

PIU 2: 222 — *PSSL* 16A: 286.

4569.　To Aleksandr Zverzhanskii

9 Dec 1891 [Maidanovo] (in MS: "Klin").

RUS–KL (a³, No. 2298).

PSSL 16A: 287.

4570.　To Eduard Nápravník

9 Dec [1891]. [Maidanovo] (in MS: "Klin").

Autograph lost; typed copy in RUS–KL.

EFN: 178 — *PSSL* 16A: 287.

4571.　To Sergei Taneev

9 Dec 1891 [Maidanovo].

RUS–Mcl (f. 880).

PT: 174 — *CTP*: 179–180 — *PSSL* 16A: 287–288.

4572.　To Pëtr Iurgenson

9 Dec 1891. Maidanovo.

RUS–KL (a³, No. 2780).

PIU 2: 223 — *PSSL* 16A: 288.

4573.　To Praskov´ia & Anatolii Chaikovskii

14 Dec 1891. Maidanovo.

RUS–KL (a³, No. 1434).

ZC 3: 516–517 — *PSSL* 16A: 289–290.

4574. To Modest Chaikovskii

14 Dec [1891]. Maidanovo.

RUS–KL (a³, No. 1983).

*PB: 504–505 — *PSSL* 16A: 290–292 — *LF: 505 [English tr.].

4575. To František Šubert

14 Dec 1891 [Maidanovo] — in French.

CZ–Pnm.

Stěpánek (1952): 157–158 [Czech tr.] — *PSSL* 16A: 275.

4576. To Osip Iurgenson

14 Dec 1891. Maidanovo.

RUS–KL.

PSSL 16A: 294.

4577. To Aleksei Sofronov

15 Dec [1891]. Moscow.

RUS–SPsc (f. 834, No. 28, fol. 5).

PSSL 16A: 294.

4578. To Modest Chaikovskii

16 Dec [1891]. [Moscow].

RUS–KL (a³, No. 1984).

PB: 505 — *PSSL* 16A: 294–295 — *LF*: 506 [English tr.].

4579. To Il´ia Slatin

[18 Dec 1891. Kiev] — telegram.

RUS–KL (a³, No. 368).

PSSL 16A: 295.

4580. To Carl Reinecke

21 Dec 1891. Kiev.

US–NHub.

SM (1965), 9: 48–49 — *PSSL* 16A: 295–296.

4581. To František Šubert

21 Dec 1891. Kiev — in German.

CZ–Pnm [facs. in M. Očadlik, *Pražké dopisy P. I. Čajkovského* (1949)].

Stěpánek (1952): 159 [Czech tr.] — *PSSL* 16A: 296.

4582. To Nikolai Konradi

23 Dec 1891. Kiev.

Autograph lost; MS copy in RUS–KL.

*ZC 3: 518 — *CTP*: 283–284 — *PSSL* 16A: 297.

4583. To Vladimir Davydov

25 Dec 1891. Kamenka,

RUS–KL (a³, No. 135).

PSSL 16A: 298–299.

4584. To Vladimir Davydov

29 Dec 1891. Warsaw.

RUS–KL (a³, No. 136).

*ZC 3: 519 — *PSSL* 16A: 299–300.

4585. To Anatolii Chaikovskii

29 Dec 1891. Warsaw.

RUS–KL (a³, No. 1435).

PSSL 16A: 301.

4586. To Pëtr Iurgenson

29 Dec 1891. Warsaw.

RUS–KL (a³, No. 2781).

*ZC 3: 519 — *PIU* 2: 224–225 — *PSSL* 16A: 302.

4587. To Aleksei Sofronov

30 Dec 1891. Warsaw.

RUS–SPsc (f. 834, No. 28, fol. 6–7).

PSSL 16A: 303.

4588. To Nikolai Konradi

31 Dec 1891. Warsaw.

Autograph lost; MS copy in RUS–KL.

*ZC 3: 519–520 — *CTP*: 284 — *PSSL* 16A: 303–304.

4589. To Pëtr Iurgenson

31 Dec 1891 [Warsaw].

RUS–KL (a³, No. 2782).

PIU 2: 225 — *PSSL* 16A: 304.

4589a. To Eduard Nápravník

[? Dec 1891. Warsaw].

Autograph auctioned in Tutzing, 1994 [see *ČS* 3 (1998): 186].

Not published.

4589b. To Modest Chaikovskii

[1891 or 1892].

RUS–KL (a³, No. 3309).

Not published.

1892

4590.   To Modest Chaikovskii

3 Jan [1892]. Warsaw.

RUS–KL (a³, No. 1986).

*ZC 3: 520 — PB: 506 — PSSL 16B: 13 — LF: 506 [English tr.].

4591.   To Anna Merkling

4/16 Jan 1892. Berlin.

Autograph lost; MS copy in RUS–KL.

*ZC 3: 521 — CTP: 249 — PSSL 16B: 14.

4592.   To Pavel Pchel´nikov

[4/16] Jan 1892 (in MS: "3/15"). Berlin.

RUS–KL (a³, No. 319).

PSSL 16B: 15.

4593.   To Vladimir Davydov

7/19 Jan 1892. Hamburg.

RUS–KL (a³, No. 137).

*ZC 3: 521–522 — *PB: 506–507 — PSSL 16B: 15–16 — *LF: 507 [English tr.].

4594.   To Nikolai Konradi

8/20 Jan [1892]. Hamburg.

Autograph lost; MS copy in RUS–KL.

*ZC 3: 524–525 — CTP: 284–285 — PSSL 16B: 17.

4595.   To Praskov´ia & Anatolii Chaikovskii

8/20 Jan 1892. Hamburg.

RUS–KL (a³, No. 3290).

*PB: 507 — PSSL 16B: 18 — *LF: 507–508 [English tr.].

4596.   To Iulii Konius

10/22 Jan 1892 [Paris].

Autograph lost; MS copy in RUS–KL.

PSSL 16B: 18–19.

4597.   To Modest Chaikovskii

10/22 Jan 1892 [Paris].

RUS–KL (a³, No. 1987).

*ZC 3: 525 — PB: 508 — PSSL 16B: 20 — LF: 508 [English tr.].

4597a.   To Osip Iurgenson

10/22 Jan 1892 [Paris].

RUS–KL (a³, No. 3352).

SM (1990), 6: 96.

4598.   To Pëtr Iurgenson

10/22 Jan 1892 [Paris].

RUS–KL (a³, No. 2786).

*ZC 3: 525 — PIU 2: 229–230 — PSSL 16B: 21–22.

4599.   To Vladimir Davydov

12/24 Jan 1892. Paris.

RUS–KL (a³, No. 138).

*ZC 3: 525–526 — PB: 508–509 — PSSL 16B: 22–23 — LF: 508–509 [English tr.].

4600.   To Aleksei Sofronov

12/24 Jan 1892. Paris.

RUS–SPsc (f. 834, No. 28, fol. 8–9).

PSSL 16B: 23–24.

4601.   To Aleksei Sofronov

13/25 Jan 1892 [Paris].

RUS–SPsc (f. 834, No. 28, fol. 10–11).

PSSL 16B: 24–25.

4602.   To Edouard Colonne

16/[28] Jan 1892 [Paris] — in French.

F–Pn

RdM 54 (1968), 1: 85 — PSSL 16B: 25.

4603.   To William von Sachs

[17]/29 Jan 1892. Paris — in French.

US–NYpm

PSSL 16B: 25–26 — Yoffe: 185–186 [English tr.].

4604.   To Pëtr Iurgenson

25 Jan 1892. St. Petersburg.

RUS–KL (a³, No. 2788).

PIU 2: 230–231 — PSSL 16B: 27.

4605.   To Aleksandr Ziloti

26 Jan 1892. St. Petersburg.

RUS–KL (a³, No. 3036).

AIZ: 130 — PSSL 16B: 27–28.

4606. To Pëtr Iurgenson

28 Jan 1892 [Maidanovo].

RUS–KL (a³, No. 2789).

PIU 2: 231 — *PSSL* 16B: 28–29.

4607. To Henrik Hennings

29 Jan/10 Feb 1892 [Maidanovo] (in MS: "Klin") —
in French.

D–H.

PSSL 16B: 29–30.

4608. To Pëtr Iurgenson

29 Jan 1892 [Maidanovo].

RUS–KL (a³, No. 2790).

*ZC 3: 527 — *PIU* 2: 232 — *PSSL* 16B: 31.

4609. To Pëtr Iurgenson

30 Jan [1892]. [Maidanovo].

RUS–KL (a³, No. 2791).

*ZC 3: 527 — *PIU* 2: 232 — *PSSL* 16B: 31–32.

4610. To Modest Chaikovskii

31 [Jan] 1892 (in MS: "Dec") [Maidanovo].

RUS–KL (a³, No. 1988).

PSSL 16B: 32–33.

4611. To Pëtr Iurgenson

31 Jan 1892. Maidanovo.

RUS–KL (a³, No. 2792).

PIU 2: 233 — *PSSL* 16B: 33.

4612. To Daniël de Lange

1/13 Feb 1892 [Maidanovo] (in MS: "Klin") — in
French.

NL–At.

RdM 54 (1968), 1: 89 — *PSSL* 16B: 34.

4612a. To Osip Iurgenson

2 Feb [1892]. [Maidanovo] (in MS: "Klin").

Autograph lost; photocopy in RUS–KL.

Not published.

4613. To Ivan Vsevolozhskii

3 Feb 1892 [Maidanovo] (in MS: "Klin").

RUS–SPia (f. 652, op. 1, d. 608, fol. 48).

PSSL 16B: 34–35.

4614. To Karl Al´brekht

4 Feb [1892]. [Maidanovo].

RUS–Mcm (f. 37, No. 71).

PSSL 16B: 35.

4615. To Aleksandra Hubert

4 Feb [1892]. [Maidanovo].

RUS–KL (a³, No. 80).

PRM 60 — *PSSL* 16B: 36.

4616. To Anatolii Chaikovskii

9 Feb 1892. Maidanovo.

RUS–KL (a³, No. 3217).

*ZC 3: 527–528 — *PB*: 509–510 — *PSSL* 16B: 37–
38 — *LF*: 510 [English tr.].

4617. To Ivan Vsevolozhskii

13 Feb 1892. Moscow.

RUS–SPia (f. 652, op. 1, d. 608, fol. 37–38).

PSSL 16B: 38–39.

4618. To Ekaterina Larosh

13 Feb 1892. Moscow.

Autograph lost; photocopy in RUS–KL.

PSSL 16B: 39.

4619. To Eduard Nápravník

16 Feb–5 Mar 1892. Moscow–St. Petersburg.

RUS–KL (a³, No. 3359).

VP: 218 — *EFN*: 178–179 — *PSSL* 16B: 40.

4620. To Bernhardt Pollini

16 Feb 1892. Moscow — in French.

RUS–KL (a³, No. 307).

PSSL 16B: 40.

4621. To František Šubert

16 Feb 1892. Moscow — in French.

RUS–KL (a³, No. 467).

PSSL 16B: 41.

4622. To Eduard Nápravník

19 Feb 1892. Maidanovo.

RUS–KL (a³, No. 3360).

VP: 217–218 — *EFN*: 180 — *PSSL* 16B: 41–42.

4623.   To Modest Chaikovskii
19 Feb [1892]. [Moscow].
RUS–KL (a³, No. 1989).
PSSL 16B: 43.

4624.   To Evgenii Al´brekht
20 Feb [1892]. [Moscow].
RUS–SPtob (VII.2.4.154).
Kirov: 416 — *PSSL* 16B: 43.

4625.   To Modest Chaikovskii
20 Feb [1892]. [Maidanovo].
RUS–KL (a³, No. 1990).
PSSL 16B: 43–44.

4626.   To Aleksandr Fedotov
21 Feb 1892 [Maidanovo] (in MS: "Klin").
RUS–Mt (Fedotov coll.).
SM (1933), 6: 101 — *CMS:* 480–481 — *PSSL* 16B:
    44–45.

4627.   To Anatolii Chaikovskii
22 Feb [1892]. Maidanovo.
RUS–KL (a³, No. 3218).
*ZC 3: 528 — *PB:* 510 — *PSSL* 16B: 46 — *LF:* 511
    [English tr.].

4628.   To Vadim Peresleni
[25 Feb 1892. Maidanovo].
RUS–KL (a³, No. 291).
PSSL 16B: 47.

4629.   To Vadim Peresleni
27 Feb [1892]. [Maidanovo].
RUS–KL (a³, No. 288).
PSSL 16B: 47.

4630.   To Vladimir Bibikov
28 Feb 1892 [St. Petersburg].
RUS–KL (a³, No. 2987).
PSSL 16B: 47.

4631.   To Ivan Zeifert
1 Mar [1892]. [St. Petersburg].
RUS–SPtob
PSSL 16B: 48.

4632.   To Arsenii Koreshchenko
1 Mar [1892]. [St. Petersburg].
RUS–KL (a³, No. 231).
Biulleten´ (1951), 1: 36–37 — *SM* (1972), 11: 92–
    93 — *PSSL* 16B: 48–49.

4633.   To Aleksandr Khimichenko
3 Mar [1892]. St. Petersburg.
Autograph lost [facs. in *Radian´skaia muzyka* (1940),
    2: 45].
Radians´kaia muzyka (1940), 2: 44–46 — *PSSL* 16B:
    49–50.

4634.   To Pëtr Iurgenson
6 Mar [1892]. St. Petersburg.
RUS–KL (a³, No. 2793).
PIU 2: 234 — *PSSL* 16B: 50–51.

4635.   [To an unidentified correspondent]
8/20 Mar 1892. St. Petersburg — in French.
US–R
PSSL 16B: 51–52.

4636.   To Karl Al´brekht
9 Mar [1892]. Maidanovo.
RUS–Mcl
PSSL 16B: 52.

4637.   To Aleksandr Glazunov
9 Mar 1892 [Maidanovo].
Autograph lost; typed copy in RUS–KL.
SM (1945), 3: 64 — *PSSL* 16B: 53.

4638.   To Iulii Konius
9 Mar 1892 [Maidanovo].
Autograph lost; MS copy in RUS–KL.
*ZC 3: 531 — *PSSL* 16B: 53–54.

4639.   To František Šubert
9 Mar 1892 [Maidanovo] (in MS: "Klin") — in
    French.
CZ–Pnm
Štěpánek (1952): 161 [Czech tr.] — *PSSL* 16B: 55.

4640.   To Boris Iurgenson
9 Mar [1892]. [Maidanovo].
RUS–KL (a³, No. 479).
PSSL 16B: 55–56.

4641. To Pëtr Iurgenson

9 Mar 1892. Maidanovo.

RUS–KL (a³, No. 2794).

*ZC 3: 530 — PIU 2: 234–235 — PSSL 16B: 56–57.

4642. To Aleksandr Ziloti

13 Mar 1892. Maidanovo.

RUS–KL (a³, No. 3037).

AIZ: 132–133 — PSSL 16B: 57–58.

4643. To Pëtr Iurgenson

14 Mar [1892]. Maidanovo.

RUS–KL (a³, No. 2795).

PIU 2: 236 — PSSL 16B: 58–59.

4644. To Modest Chaikovskii

17 Mar 1892 [Maidanovo].

RUS–KL (a³, No. 1991).

PSSL 16B: 59–60.

4645. To Pëtr Iurgenson

18 Mar [1892]. [Maidanovo].

RUS–KL (a³, No. 2796).

*ZC 3: 531–532 — PIU 2: 237–238 — PSSL 16B: 61–62.

4646. To Pëtr Iurgenson

20 Mar [1892]. [Maidanovo].

RUS–KL (a³, No. 2797).

PIU 2: 239 — PSSL 16B: 63.

4647. To Pëtr Iurgenson

21 Mar [1892]. [Maidanovo].

RUS–KL (a³, No. 2798).

PIU 2: 239–240 — PSSL 16B: 63–64.

4648. To Anatolii Chaikovskii

23 Mar [1892]. Maidanovo.

RUS–KL (a³, No. 3219).

ZC 3: 532–533 — *PB: 511 — PSSL 16B: 64–65 — *LF: 511–512 [English tr.].

4649. To Pëtr Iurgenson

25 Mar [1892]. [Maidanovo].

RUS–KL (a³, No. 2799).

*ZC 3: 533 — PIU 2: 241 — PSSL 16B: 65.

4650. To Leopoldine Lafitte

[27 Mar 1892. Maidanovo] — in French.

RUS–KL (a³, No. 266).

PSSL 16B: 66.

4651. To Ippolit Prianishnikov

27 Mar 1892. Maidanovo.

Autograph lost

Odesskii listok (26 Jun 1896) — PSSL 16B: 66–67.

4652. To Praskov´ia Chaikovskaia

27 Mar [1892]. [Maidanovo].

RUS–KL (a³, No. 3291).

PSSL 16B: 67.

4653. To Pëtr Iurgenson

27 Mar [1892]. [Maidanovo].

RUS–KL (a³, No. 2800).

*ZC 3: 533 — PIU 2: 241 — PSSL 16B: 68.

4654. To Albert Gutmann

28 Mar/10 [Apr] 1892 (in MS: "28/10 Mar"). St. Petersburg — in German.

US–Wc

PSSL 16B: 69.

4655. To Pëtr Iurgenson

29 Mar [1892]. [St. Petersburg].

RUS–KL (a³, No. 2801).

PIU 2: 242 — PSSL 16B: 70.

4656. To Aleksandr Ziloti

6 Apr 1892. Moscow.

RUS–KL (a³, No. 3038).

AIZ: 134 — PSSL 16B: 70–71.

4657. To Mikhail Ippolitov-Ivanov

6 Apr 1892 [Moscow].

RUS–KL (a³, No. 201).

*ZC 3: 533 — *Iskusstvo, 3 (1927), 4: 170 — Biulleten´ (1947), 2: 46–47 — PSSL 16B: 71–72 — Yoffe: 194–195 [English tr.].

4658. To Modest Chaikovskii

6 Apr [1892]. Moscow.

RUS–KL (a³, No. 1992).

*PB: 511–512 — PSSL 16B: 73 — *LF: 512 [English tr.].

4659. To Praskov´ia Chaikovskaia
[early–mid Apr 1892. Moscow].
RUS–KL (a³, No. 3293).
PSSL 16B: 73.

4660. To Sergei Taneev
[10 Apr 1892. Moscow].
RUS–Md (f. 880).
CTP: 182 — *PSSL* 16B: 74.

4661. To Pëtr Iurgenson
10 Apr [1892]. [Moscow].
RUS–KL (a³, No. 2802).
PIU 2: 242 — *PSSL* 16B: 74.

4662. To Adelina Bolska
11 Apr 1892 [Moscow].
RUS–Mcm (f. 314, No. 7).
PSSL 16B: 74.

4663. To Eduard Nápravník
13 Apr 1892 [Moscow].
RUS–KL (a³, no;. 3361).
*ZC 3: 533–534 — *VP*: 220–221 — *EFN*: 182–183 —
   PSSL 16B: 76.

4664. To Modest Chaikovskii
14 Apr 1892. Moscow.
RUS–KL (a³, No. 1993).
*ZC 3: 534 — *PB*: 512 — *PSSL* 16B: 77 — *LF*: 513
   [English tr.].

4665. To Karl Al´brekht
[17 Apr 1892. Moscow].
RUS–Mcm (f. 37, No. 72).
PSSL 16B: 77.

4666. To Eduard Nápravník
[17 Apr 1892. Moscow] — telegram.
Autograph lost; typed copy in RUS–KL.
VP: 222 — *EFN*: 183 — *PSSL* 16B: 78.

4666a. To Anatolii Chaikovskii
19 Apr 1892 [Moscow].
RUS–KL (a³, No. 3220).
Not published.

4667. To Praskov´ia Chaikovskaia
19 Apr 1892 [Moscow].
RUS–KL (a³, No. 3294).
PSSL 16B: 78.

4668. To Modest Chaikovskii
20 Apr 1892. Moscow.
RUS–KL (a³, No. 1994).
*ZC 3: 534 — *PB*: 512 — *PSSL* 16B: 78–79 — *LF*:
   513 [English tr.].

4669. To Karl Al´brekht
22 Apr [1892]. [Moscow].
RUS–Mcm (f. 37, No. 73).
PSSL 16B: 79.

4670. To Praskov´ia Chaikovskaia
22 Apr [1892]. [Moscow].
RUS–KL (a³, No. 459).
PSSL 16B: 80.

4671. To Anatolii Chaikovskii
23 Apr 1892. Moscow.
RUS–KL (a³, No. 3221).
*ZC 3: 534–535 — *PB*: 512–513 — *PSSL* 16B: 80–
   81 — *LF*: 513–514 [English tr.].

4672. To Praskov´ia Chaikovskaia
[23–25 Apr 1892. Moscow].
RUS–KL (a³, No. 3295).
PSSL 16B: 81–82.

4673. To Evgenii Al´brekht
[25 Apr 1892. Moscow].
RUS–SPtob (VII.2.4.154).
PSSL 16B: 82.

4674. To Pavel Pchel´nikov
28 Apr 1892 [Moscow].
RUS–KL (a³, No. 320).
PSSL 16B: 82–83.

4675. To Pëtr Iurgenson
28 Apr 1892 [Moscow].
RUS–KL (a³, No. 2808).
PSSL 16B: 83.

4676.   To Pëtr Iurgenson

28 Apr [1892]. [Moscow].

RUS–KL (a³, No. 2803).

PIU 2: 243 — *PSSL* 16B: 83.

4677.   To Ludvik Kuba

2 May [1892]. St. Petersburg.

CZ–POm

Hudebni rozhledy (1953), 16: 761 — I. Belza, *Iz istorii russko-cheshskikh muzykal'nykh sviazei*, 2 (1956): 14 — *PSSL* 16B: 84.

4678.   To Modest Chaikovskii

2 May [1892]. St. Petersburg.

RUS–KL (a³, No. 1995).

*PB: 513 — *PSSL* 16B: 85 — **LF*: 514 [English tr.].

4679.   To Pëtr Iurgenson

2 May [1892]. [St. Petersburg].

RUS–KL (a³, No. 2804).

PIU 2: 243 — *PSSL* 16B: 86.

4680.   To Sergei Borisoglebskii

5 May 1892 [Klin].

RUS–KL (a³, No. 2974).

PSSL 16B: 87.

4681.   To Aleksandra Hubert

5 May [1892]. [Klin].

RUS–KL (a³, No. 87).

PSSL 16B: 87.

4681a.   To Frederic Lamond

[5]/17 May 1892 [Klin] — in French.

GB–Gu (Lamond coll. No. 4631).

Net Volksdageblad (2 May 1940) [Dutch tr.] — *VC* (1973): 298–299 [Russian tr.] — *PSSL* 17: 202–203 [Russian tr, as No. 5059 ("Oct 1893")] — *TGM* 7 (2000): 42–43.

4682.   To Theodore Thomas

5 May 1892. Klin.

US–Cn

PSSL 16B: 88 — Yoffe: 195–196 [English tr.].

4683.   To Pëtr Iurgenson

5 May 1892. Klin.

RUS–KL (a³, No. 2805).

*PIU 2: 244 — **PSSL* 16B: 88–89 — Yoffe: 196–197 [English tr.].

4684.   To Arsenii Koreshchenko

7 May 1892. Klin.

RUS–KL (a³, No. 232).

Biulleten' (1951), 1: 37–38 — *SM* (1972), 11: 92–93 — *PSSL* 16B: 89–90.

4685.   To Iakov Grot

10 May 1892. Klin.

RUS–SPaa (f. 137, op. 3, No. 1007, fol. 1–2).

Vestnik Akademii Nauk SSSR (1933), 12: 37–38 — *PSSL* 16B: 90–91.

4686.   To Pëtr Iurgenson

10 May 1892. Klin.

RUS–KL (a³, No. 2806).

*ZC 3: 537 — *PIU* 2: 244 — *PSSL* 16B: 91–92.

4687.   To Pëtr Iurgenson

12 May [1892]. [Klin].

RUS–KL (a³, No. 2807).

PIU 2: 245 — *PSSL* 16B: 92–93.

4688.   To Sergei Borisoglebskii

13 May [1892]. [Klin].

RUS–KL (a³, No. 2975).

PSSL 16B: 93.

4689.   To Pëtr Iurgenson (?)

13 May 1892. Klin.

RUS–KL (a³, No. 2975a).

PSSL 16B: 94.

4690.   To Praskov'ia Chaikovskaia

14 May 1892. Klin.

RUS–KL (a³, No. 3292).

PSSL 16B: 94–95.

4691.   To Pavel Pchel'nikov

16 May 1892 [Moscow].

RUS–KL (a³, No. 321).

PSSL 16B: 95.

4692.   To Nikolai Konradi

20 May 1892 [Klin].

Autograph lost; MS copy in RUS–KL.

*ZC 3: 538 — *CTP*: 285 — *PSSL* 16B: 95–96.

4693.   To Anna Merkling

20 May 1892. Klin.

Autograph lost; MS copy in RUS–KL.

CTP: 249–250 — *PSSL* 16B: 96–97.

4694.   To Vladimir Nápravník

20 May 1892 [Klin].

Autograph lost; typed copy in RUS–KL.

EFN: 199–200 — *PSSL* 16B: 98.

4695.   To Modest Chaikovskii

20 May 1892. Klin.

RUS–KL (a³, No. 1996).

*ZC 3: 538 — *PSSL* 16B: 99–100.

4696.   To Eugen Zabel

24 May 1892. Klin — in French and German.

Autograph lost

E. Zabel, *Anton Rubinstein: Ein Künstlerleben* (1892): 271–276 — *Teatral´nyi mirok* (10 Jan 1893): 11–12 [Russian tr.] — *Nuvellist* (Feb 1893), 2: 3–4 [Russian tr.] — *Nationalzeitung* (1895): 162 — *ZC* 3: 538–542 [Russian tr.] — *PSSL* 16B: 100–105.

4697.   To Vasilii Ostrovskii

25 May 1892. Klin.

RUS–KL (a³, No. 276).

PSSL 16B: 106.

4698.   To Iosif Setov

25 May 1892 [Klin].

RUS–KL (a³, No. 356).

PSSL 16B: 106–107.

4699.   To Iulii Konius

26 May 1892. Klin.

Autograph lost; MS copy in RUS–KL.

PSSL 16B: 107.

4700.   To Aleksei Sofronov

31 May 1892 [St. Petersburg].

RUS–SPsc (f. 834, No. 28, fol. 12–13).

PSSL 16B: 107–108.

4701.   To Modest Chaikovskii

31 May 1892 [St. Petersburg].

RUS–KL (a³, No. 1997).

PSSL 16B: 108–109.

4702.   To Gustav Besson

[May 1892. St. Petersburg] — telegram.

RUS–SPil

Nuvellist (Sep 1893), 5: 6–7 — *PSSL* 16B: 109.

4703.   To Aleksei Sofronov

2 Jun 1892 [St. Petersburg].

RUS–SPsc (f. 834, No. 28, fol. 14–15).

PSSL 16B: 109.

4704.   To Pavel Pchel´nikov

7/[19] Jun 1892 [Paris].

RUS–KL (a³, No. 322).

PSSL 16B: 110.

4705.   To Aleksandr Ziloti

[early Jun 1892. Paris].

RUS–KL (a³, No. 3053).

AIZ: 134–135 — *PSSL* 16B: 110.

4706.   To Modest Chaikovskii

11/23 Jun [1892]. Paris.

RUS–KL (a³, No. 1998).

*ZC 3: 544 — *PSSL* 16B: 110–111.

4707.   To Aleksei Sofronov

17/[29] Jun [1892]. Vichy.

RUS–SPsc (f. 834, No. 28, fol. 16–17).

PSSL 16B: 111–112.

4708.   To Pavel Dunaevskii

18/30 Jun 1892. Vichy.

RUS–Mcm (f. 88, No. 199).

PSSL 16B: 112.

4709.   To Eduard Nápravník

18/30 Jun 1892. Vichy.

RUS–KL (a³, No. 3362).

*ZC 3: 545 — VP: 222–223 — EFN: 185 — PSSL 16B: 113.

4710.   To Modest Chaikovskii

19 Jun/1 Jul 1892 [Vichy].

RUS–KL (a³, No. 1999).

*ZC 3: 545 — PSSL 16B: 114–115.

4711.   To Pëtr Iurgenson

20 Jun/2 Jul 1892 [Vichy].

RUS–KL (a³, No. 2809).

*ZC 3: 546 — PIU 2: 246 — PSSL 16B: 116 — Yoffe: 197 [English tr.].

4712.   To Aleksandr Ziloti

22 Jun/4 Jul [1892]. Vichy.

RUS–KL (a³, No. 3039).

AIZ: 135–136 — PSSL 16B: 116–117.

4713.   To Mojmír Urbánek

[22 Jun]/4 Jul 1892 [Vichy] — in French.

CZ–Pnm.

PSSL 16B: 118.

4714.   To Pëtr Iurgenson

22 Jun/4 Jul [1892]. Vichy.

RUS–KL (a³, No. 2810).

PIU 2: 247 — PSSL 16B: 119 — Yoffe: 197 [English tr.].

4715.   To Aleksandr Ziloti

28 Jun/10 Jul [1892]. [Vichy].

RUS–KL (a³, No. 3040).

AIZ: 137–138 — PSSL 16B: 120.

4716.   To Anna Merkling

[28 Jun/10 Jul] 1892 (in MS: "22 Jun/10 Jul"). Vichy.

Autograph lost; MS copy in RUS–KL.

CTP: 250–251 — PSSL 16B: 121–122.

4717.   To Modest Chaikovskii

29 Jun/[11] Jul 1892 (in MS: "12 Jul"). Vichy.

RUS–KL (a³, No. 2000).

*ZC 3: 546 — PSSL 16B: 122–123.

4718.   To Nikolai, Ol´ga & Georgii Chaikovskii

30 Jun 1892. Vichy.

RUS–SPsc (f. 834, No. 37, fol. 24–25).

PSSL 16B: 123–124.

4719.   To Emilio Colombo

[1]/13 Jul 1892 [Vichy] — in French.

I–Rcolombo.

Novyi zhurnal, 85 (1966): 272–273 — PSSL 16B: 124–125.

4720.   To Pëtr Iurgenson

1/[13] Jul 1892. Vichy.

RUS–KL (a³, No. 2811).

*ZC 3: 546–547 — PIU 2: 247–248 — PSSL 16B: 125–126.

4721.   To Vasilii Bertenson

9 Jul 1892 [St. Petersburg].

RUS–Mcl (f. 39).

*Istoricheskii vestnik (Jun 1912): 810 — PSSL 16B: 126.

4722.   To Nikolai Konradi

9 Jul [1892]. St. Petersburg.

Autograph lost; MS copy in RUS–KL.

*ZC 3: 547 — CTP: 286 — PSSL 16B: 127.

4723.   To Pëtr Iurgenson

11 Jul 1892 [Klin].

RUS–KL (a³, No. 2812).

PIU 2: 248 — PSSL 16B: 128.

4723a. To Pavel Peterssen

13 Jul 1892. Klin.

RUS–SPa (f. 408, op. 1, No. 338, fol. 16–17).

Not published.

4724.   To Sergei Taneev

13 Jul 1892. Klin.

RUS–Mcl (f. 880).

*ZC 3: 549–550 — PT: 177 — CTP: 184.

4725.   To Pëtr Iurgenson

13 Jul [1892]. Klin.

RUS–KL (a³, No. 2813).

PIU 2: 248 — *PSSL* 16B: 129–130.

4726.   To Pëtr Iurgenson

[14 Jul 1892. Klin].

RUS–KL (a³, No. 2830).

PIU 2: 249 — *PSSL* 16B: 130.

4727.   To Pëtr Iurgenson

15 Jul [1892]. [Klin].

RUS–KL (a³, No. 2814).

PIU 2: 249 — *PSSL* 16B: 131.

4728.   To Pëtr Iurgenson

15 Jul [1892]. [Klin].

RUS–KL (a³, No. 2815).

PIU 2: 249–250 — *PSSL* 16B: 131–132.

4729.   To Mikhail Ippolitov-Ivanov

16 Jul 1892. Klin.

RUS–KL (a³, No. 201).

*ZC 3: 550–551 — **Iskusstvo*, 3 (1927), 4: 171–172 — *Biulleten´* (1947), 2: 49–51 — *PSSL* 16B: 132–133.

4730.   To Anatolii Chaikovskii

16 Jul 1892. Klin.

RUS–KL (a³, No. 3222).

PSSL 16B: 133–134.

4731.   To Pëtr Iurgenson

16 Jul [1892]. [Klin].

RUS–KL (a³, No. 2816).

PIU 2: 250–251 — *PSSL* 16B: 134.

4732.   To Vladimir Davydov

17 Jul 1892. Klin.

RUS–KL (a³, No. 139).

*ZC 3: 551 — *PSSL* 16B: 135.

4733.   To Anna Merkling

17 Jul 1892. Klin.

Autograph lost; MS copy in RUS–KL.

*ZC 3: 551–552 — *CTP*: 251–252 — *PSSL* 16B: 136.

4734.   To Modest Chaikovskii

17 Jul 1892. Klin.

RUS–KL (a³, No. 2001).

*ZC 3: 552 — *PB*: 514 — *PSSL* 16B: 137–138 — *LF*: 515 [English tr.].

4735.   To Pëtr Iurgenson

17 Jul [1892]. [Klin].

RUS–KL (a³, No. 2817).

PIU 2: 251 — *PSSL* 16B: 138.

4736.   To Pëtr Iurgenson

19 Jul 1892 [Klin].

RUS–KL (a³, No. 2818).

PIU 2: 251–252 — *PSSL* 16B: 139.

4737.   To Pëtr Iurgenson

20 Jul 1892. Klin.

RUS–KL (a³, No. 2819).

PIU 2: 252 — *PSSL* 16B: 139–140.

4738.   To Anatolii Chaikovskii

21 Jul 1892. Klin.

RUS–KL (a³, No. 3223).

PSSL 16B: 140–141.

4739.   To Ekaterina Larosh

22 Jul 1892. Klin.

Autograph lost; photocopy in RUS–KL.

PSSL 16B: 141–142.

4740.   To Pëtr Iurgenson

25 Jul [1892]. [Klin].

RUS–KL (a³, No. 2820).

PIU 2: 253 — *PSSL* 16B: 142–143.

4741.   To Pëtr Iurgenson

27 Jul [1892]. [Klin].

RUS–KL (a³, No. 2821).

*ZC 3: 552–553 — *PIU* 2: 253–254 — *PSSL* 16B: 143–144.

4742.   To Modest Chaikovskii

30 Jul [1892]. Moscow.

RUS–KL (a³, No. 2002).

*ZC 3: 553 — *PB*: 514–515 — *PSSL* 16B: 144–145 — *LF*: 516 [English tr.].

4743.   To Vladimir Davydov
1 Aug [1892]. Klin.
RUS–KL (a³, No. 140).
PSSL 16B: 145.

4743a. To Pavel Peterssen
2 Aug 1892. Klin.
RUS–KL (a³, No. 3158).
Not published.

4744.   To Modest Chaikovskii
2 Aug [1892]. Klin.
RUS–KL (a³, No. 2003).
**PB*: 515 — *PSSL* 16B: 146 — **LF*: 516 [English tr.].

4745.   To Pëtr Iurgenson
2 Aug [1892]. [Klin].
RUS–KL (a³, No. 2823).
PIU 2: 254 — *PSSL* 16B: 147.

4746.   To Sergei Taneev
3 Aug [1892]. [Klin].
RUS–Mcl (f. 880).
**ZC* 3: 553 — *PT*: 179 — *CTP*: 186 — *PSSL* 16B:
148.

4747.   To Pëtr Iurgenson
5–6 Aug [1892]. [Klin].
RUS–KL (a³, No. 2823).
**PIU* 2: 255 — **PSSL* 16B: 148–149.

4748.   [To an undientfied "Mademoiselle"]
9 Aug 1892 [? Klin].
Autograph lost; photocopy in RUS–KL.
PSSL 16B: 149.

4749.   To Pavel Peterssen
9 Aug [1892]. Klin.
RUS–SPsc (f. 124, No. 4651, fol. 12–13).
PSSL 16B: 150.

4750.   To Sergei Taneev
11 Aug 1892. Moscow.
RUS–Mcl (f. 880).
PT: 180 — *CTP*: 18 — *PSSL* 16B: 151.

4751.   To Anna Merkling
12 Aug 1892. Klin.
Autograph lost; MS copy in RUS–KL.
CTP: 252 — *PSSL* 16B: 152.

4752.   To Vladimir Davydov
12 Aug [1892]. Klin.
RUS–KL (a³, No. 141).
**ZC* 3: 553–554 — *PB*: 515–516 — *PSSL* 16B: 153–
154 — *LF*: 517 [English tr.].

4753.   To Vladimir Davydov
14 Aug [1892]. Moscow.
RUS–KL (a³, No. 142).
**ZC* 3: 554 — *PB*: 516 — **LF*: 517–518 [English tr.].

4754.   To Anatolii Chaikovskii
14 Aug [1892]. Moscow.
RUS–KL (a³, No. 3224).
**ZC* 3: 554 — *PSSL* 16B: 155.

4755.   To Modest Chaikovskii
14 Aug [1892]. Moscow.
RUS–KL (a³, No. 2004).
PSSL 16B: 156.

4755a. To Andrei Arends
16 Aug 1892 [Klin].
RUS–Mteleshov
PSSL 17: 258.

4756.   To Pëtr Iurgenson
20 Aug [1892]. [Klin].
RUS–KL (a³, No. 2824).
PIU 2: 256 — *PSSL* 16B: 156–157.

4757.   To Pëtr Iurgenson
25 Aug [1892]. [Klin].
RUS–KL (a³, No. 2825).
PIU 2: 256–257 — *PSSL* 16B: 157–158.

4758.   To Karl Al´brekht
27 Aug [1892]. [Klin].
RUS–Mcm (f. 37, No. 74).
PSSL 16B: 158.

4759.   To Mikhail Ippolitov-Ivanov

27 Aug [1892]. Klin.

RUS–KL (a³, No. 202).

Biulleten´ (1947), 2: 53–55 — *PSSL* 16B: 158–159.

4760.   To Anatolii Chaikovskii

27 Aug [1892]. [Klin].

RUS–KL (a³, No. 3225).

PSSL 16B: 160.

4761.   To Vladimir Davydov

28 Aug [1892]. Klin.

RUS–KL (a³, No. 143).

ZC 3: 555 — *PB*: 517 — *PSSL* 16B: 160–161 — *LF*: 518–519 [English tr.].

4762.   To Daniil Ratgauz

30 Aug 1892. Moscow.

Autograph lost

Novosti dnia (5 Oct 1894) — *ZC* 3: 555–556 — *PSSL* 16B: 161–162.

4763.   To Stepan Smolenskii

1 Sep [1892]. Moscow.

RUS–KL (a³, No. 371).

PSSL 16B: 162.

4764.   To Vasilii Orlov

1 Sep [1892]. [Moscow].

Autograph lost; MS copy in RUS–KL.

PSSL 16B: 163.

4765.   To Henryk Pachulski

[3 Sep 1892. St. Petersburg] — telegram.

RUS–KL (a³, No. 236).

PSSL 16B: 163.

4766.   To Pëtr Iurgenson

4 Sep [1892]. St. Petersburg.

RUS–KL (a³, No. 2826).

PIU 2: 257 — *PSSL* 16B: 164.

4767.   To Modest Chaikovskii

7/19–10/[22] Sep 1892. Vienna.

RUS–KL (a³, No. 2005).

ZC 3: 566–56 — *PB*: 517–518 — *PSSL* 16B: 164–165 — *LF*: 519 [English tr.].

4768.   To Lev Kupernik

10/22 Sep [1892]. Itter.

RUS–SPil (f. 232, No. 6).

PSSL 16B: 165–166.

4769.   To Pavel Peterssen

10/22 Sep 1892 [Itter].

RUS–SPsc (f. 834, No. 23).

PSSL 16B: 166–167.

4770.   To Anatolii Chaikovskii

10/22 Sep 1892. Itter

RUS–KL (a³, No. 3226).

PSSL 16B: 167.

4771.   To Anton Door

[12/24 Sep 1892. Itter].

Autograph lost

Neue Freie Presse ([18]/30 Mar 1901) [German tr.] — *Moskovskie vedomosti* (28 Mar 1901) ("10/22 Sep 1892") — *ZC* 3: 569 — *PSSL* 16B: 168.

4772.   To Modest Chaikovskii

15/27 Sep [1892]. Itter.

RUS–KL (a³, No. 2006).

ZC 3: 570 — *PB*: 518–519 — *PSSL* 16B: 168–169 — *LF*: 520 [English tr.].

4773.   To František Šubert

[17/29 Sep 1892. Itter] — telegram; in German.

CZ–Pnm

Štěpánek (1952): 162 [Czech tr.] — *PSSL* 16B: 169.

4774.   To Pavel Pchel´nikov

22 Sep/4 Oct 1892. Itter

RUS–KL (a³, No. 323).

PSSL 16B: 169–170.

4775.   To Modest Chaikovskii

[22 Sep]/4 Oct 1892. Itter

RUS–KL (a³, No. 2007).

ZC 3: 571 — *PB*: 519 — *PSSL* 16B: 170–171 — *LF*: 520 [English tr.].

4776.   To František Šubert

[22 Sep/4 Oct 1892. Itter] — telegram; in German.

CZ–Pnm

Štěpánek (1952): 163 [Czech tr.] — *PSSL* 16B: 171.

4777. To František Šubert

[25 Sep/7 Oct 1892. Salzburg] — telegram; in German.

CZ–Pnm.

Stěpánek (1952): 163 [Czech tr.] — *PSSL* 16B: 171.

4777a. To Berta Foerstrová-Lautererová

[26–27 Sep/8–9 Oct 1892. Prague] — in German.

H–Bkuna.

PSSL 17: 259.

4778. To Georgii Konius

7 [Oct] 1892 (in MS: "Nov"). Klin.

Autograph lost; MS copy in RUS–KL.

PSSL 16B: 172.

4779. To Lev Kupernik

7 Oct 1892. Klin.

RUS–SPil (f. 232, No. 7).

PSSL 16B: 172–173.

4780. To Il´ia Slatin

7 [Oct] 1892 (in MS: "Nov"). Klin.

RUS–KL (a³, No. 358).

ZC 3: 573–574 — PSSL 16B: 173–174.

4781. To Anatolii Chaikovskii

7 [Oct] 1892 (in MS: "Nov"). Klin.

Autograph lost; MS copy in RUS–KL.

PB: 519–520 — *PSSL* 16B: 174–175 — **LF:* 521 [English tr.].

4782. To Aleksandr Vinogradskii

9 Oct 1892. Klin.

RUS–Mcm (f. 96, No. 3977).

Iz arkhivov russkikh muzykantov. Moscow, 1962: 161–162 — *PSSL* 16B: 175–176.

4782a. To Sergei Taneev

9 Oct [1892]. [Klin].

RUS–Mcl (f. 880).

CTP: 187 — *PSSL* 17: 259.

4783. To Vladimir Pogozhev

[11 Oct 1892. Klin].

RUS–KL (a³, No. 2885).

PSSL 3A: xxiv — *PSSL* 16B: 176.

4784. To Modest Chaikovskii

12 Oct 1892 [Klin].

RUS–KL (a³, No. 2008).

**ZC* 3: 574 — **PB:* 520 — *PSSL* 16B: 177 — **LF:* 521 [English tr.].

4785. To Sergei Taneev

14 Oct 1892 [Moscow].

RUS–KL (a³, No. 399).

**ZC* 3: 574 — *PT:* 180–181 — *CTP:* 188 — *PSSL* 16B: 178.

4786. To Eduard Nápravník

18 Oct 1892. Klin.

RUS–KL (a³, No. 3363).

**ZC* 3: 574–575 — *VP:* 225–226 — *EFN:* 185–186 — *PSSL* 16B: 178–179.

4787. To Pavel Pchel´nikov

18 Oct 1892. Klin.

RUS–KL (a³, No. 324).

PSSL 16B: 179–180.

4788. To Anatolii Chaikovskii

18 Oct 1892. Klin.

RUS–KL (a³, No. 3227).

PSSL 16B: 180.

4789. To Aleksandr Ziloti

23 Oct 1892. Klin.

RUS–KL (a³, No. 3041).

AIZ: 138–139 — *PSSL* 16B: 181–182.

4790. To Josef Bohuslav Foerster

23 Oct 1892. Klin — in French.

CZ–Pfoerster.

SM (1952), 7: 70–71 — *PSSL* 16B: 183.

4790a. To Mojmír Urbánek

26 Oct/7 Nov 1892. Klin — in German.

CZ–Pnm.

PSSL 17: 259.

4791. To František Šubert

26 Oct 1892. Klin — in French.

CZ–Ps.

Stěpánek (1952): 164 [Czech tr.] — *PSSL* 16B: 184.

4792.   To Aleksei Sofronov

28 Oct 1892 [St. Petersburg].

RUS–SPsc (f. 834, No. 28, fol. 20–21).

PSSL 16B: 184.

4793.   To Iakov Grot

29 Oct 1892 [St. Petersburg].

RUS–SPil (f. 13, No. 17).

PSSL 16B: 185.

4794.   To Sergei Taneev

3 Nov [1892]. [St. Petersburg].

RUS–Mcl (f. 880).

*ZC 3: 577–578 ("3 Dec") — *PT* 181–182 ("3 Dec") — *CTP*: 188–189 — *PSSL* 16B: 185–186.

4795.   To Evgenii Al´brekht

4 Nov 1892 [St. Petersburg].

RUS–SPtob (VII.2.4.154).

PSSL 16B: 186.

4796.   To Ružena Vykoukalová-Bradačeva

4 Nov 1892 [St. Petersburg] — in French.

Autograph auctioned by J. A. Stargardt, Marburg, 1971.

Chaikovskii i zarubezhnye muzykanty (1970): 178 — *PSSL* 16B: 187.

4797.   To Lev Kupernik

4 Nov [1892]. St. Petersburg.

RUS–SPil (f. 232, No. 8).

PSSL 16B: 187.

4798.   To Lev Kupernik

5 Nov [1892]. St. Petersburg.

RUS–SPil (f. 232, No. 9).

PSSL 16B: 188.

4798a. To Anatolii Chaikovskii

7 Nov 1892. St. Petersburg.

RUS–KL (a³, No. 3228).

Not published.

4799.   To Nikolai Chaikovskii

7 Nov [1892]. St. Petersburg — in French.

RUS–SPsc (f. 834, No. 31, fol. 19–20).

PSSL 16B: 188.

4800.   To Pavel Pchel´nikov

8 Nov 1892 [St. Petersburg].

RUS–KL (a³, No. 325).

PSSL 16B: 189.

4801.   To Sergei Taneev

8 Nov 1892 [St. Petersburg].

RUS–Mcl (f. 880).

CTP: 189 — *PSSL* 16B: 189–190.

4802.   To Ol´ga Chaikovskaia

9 Nov 1892 [St. Petersburg].

RUS–SPsc (f. 834, No. 31, fol. 7–8).

PSSL 16B: 190.

4803.   To Pavel Pchel´nikov

10 Nov 1892 [St. Petersburg].

RUS–KL (a³, No. 326).

PSSL 16B: 191.

4804.   To Anatolii Chaikovskii

11 Nov 1892 [St. Petersburg].

RUS–KL (a³, No. 3229).

*ZC 3: 576 — **PB*: 520–521 — *PSSL* 16B: 191–192 — **LF*: 522 [English tr.].

4805.   To Bernhardt Pollini

14 Nov 1892. St. Petersburg — in French.

US–NYpm (Morgan coll. MA 2717).

PSSL 16B: 192–193.

4806.   To Sergei Taneev

14 Nov [1892]. [St. Petersburg].

RUS–Mcl (f. 880).

CTP: 189–190 — *PSSL* 16B: 193–194.

4807.   To William von Sachs

15 Nov 1892. St. Petersburg — in French.

US–NYpm (Morgan coll.).

PSSL 16B: 194–195.

4808.   To Ol´ga Chaikovskaia

21 Nov 1892. St. Petersburg.

RUS–SPsc (f. 834, No. 31, fol. 9–10).

PSSL 16B: 195–196.

4809. To Henri Delabordé

23 Nov 1892. St. Petersburg — in French.

F–Pi.

RdM 54 (1968), 1: 88 — *PSSL* 16B: 196.

4810. To Paul Collin

24 Nov 1892. St. Petersburg — in French.

F–Phofmann.

*M. R. Hofmann, *Tchaïkovsky* (1959) — *SM* (1960), 5: 74 [Russian tr.] — *PSSL* 16B: 197.

4811. To Aleksei Sofronov

24 Nov [1892]. [St. Petersburg].

RUS–SPsc (f. 834, No. 28, fol. 22–23).

PSSL 16B: 198.

4812. To Anatolii Chaikovskii

24 Nov 1892. St. Petersburg.

RUS–KL (a³, No. 3230).

*ZC 3: 576–577 — *PB: 521 — *PSSL* 16B: 198–199 — *LF: 522 [English tr.].

4812a. To Viacheslav Tenishev

3 Dec 1892 [St. Petersburg].

RUS–KL (a³, No. 3330).

PSSL 17: 260.

4812b. To John Peile

[4]/16 Dec 1892 [St. Petersburg] — in French.

GB–Cu (Add.MS 4251/1409).

G. Norris, *Stanford, the Cambridge Jubilee and Tchaikovsky* (1980): 267 [English tr.] — *TGM* 7 (2000): 44.

4813. To Il´ia Gintsburg

5 Dec [1892]. [St. Petersburg].

RUS–KL (a³, No. 37).

PSSL 16B: 199.

4814. To Sergei Taneev

[5 Dec 1892. St. Petersburg] — telegram.

RUS–Mcl (f. 880).

CTP: 190 — *PSSL* 16B: 199.

4815. To Sergei Taneev

6 Dec [1892]. [St. Petersburg].

RUS–Mcl (f. 880).

CTP: 190 — *PSSL* 16B: 200.

4816. To Elena Glazunova

7 Dec 1892 [St. Petersburg].

RUS–SPsemenov.

PSSL 16B: 200.

4817. To Ernest Keller

7 Dec 1892 [St. Petersburg] — in French; note on visiting card.

RUS–SPsc (f. 346, No. 5, fol. 126–127).

PSSL 16B: 200.

4818. To Sergei Taneev

7 Dec 1892 [St. Petersburg].

RUS–Mcl (f. 880).

CTP: 190 — *PSSL* 16B: 201.

4819. To Anatolii Chaikovskii

7 Dec [1892]. [St. Petersburg].

RUS–KL (a³, No. 3231).

*ZC 3: 581 — *PB: 521 — *PSSL* 16B: 201 — *LF: 523 [English tr.] ("9 Dec").

4819a. To Elizaveta Chaikovskaia

[?early Dec 1892 or mid Oct 1893. St. Petersburg].

RUS–SPsc (f. 834, No. 30, fol. 17, 19, 21).

PSSL 17: 260.

4820. To Anatolii Chaikovskii

10 Dec [1892]. [St. Petersburg].

RUS–KL (a³, No. 3232).

*ZC 3: 581–582 — *PB: 522 — *PSSL* 16B: 202 — *LF: 523–524 [English tr.].

4821. To Karl Al´brekht

11 Dec [1892]. [St. Petersburg].

RUS–Mcm (f. 37, No. 75).

PSSL 16B: 203.

4822. To Aleksandr Glazunov

11 Dec 1892 [St. Petersburg].

RUS–KL (a³, No. 40).

SM (1945), 3: 64 — *PSSL* 16B: 203.

4823.   To Porfirii Molchanov

[11 Dec] 1892. St. Petersburg.

RUS–KL (a³, No. 3154).

Bol´shevistskoe znamia [Odessa] (5 Jul 1946) — *PSSL* 16B: 204.

4824.   To William von Sachs

11 Dec 1892. St. Petersburg — in French.

US–NYpm (Morgan coll.).

PSSL 16B: 204.

4825.   To Vasilii Safonov

11 Dec 1892 [St. Petersburg].

RUS–KL (a³, No. 349).

VIS: 208–209 — *PSSL* 16B: 205.

4826.   To Modest Chaikovskii

11 Dec [1892]. [St. Petersburg].

RUS–KL (a³, No. 2010).

PSSL 16B: 206.

4827.   To Vladimir Davydov

14/26 Dec 1892 [Berlin].

RUS–KL (a³, No. 144).

*ZC 3: 582–583 — *PB*: 522–523 — *PSSL* 16B: 206–207 — *LF*: 524 [English tr.].

4828.   To Modest Chaikovskii

14/26 Dec [1892]. Berlin.

RUS–KL (a³, No. 2011).

PSSL 16B: 207.

4829.   To Vladimir Davydov

16/28 Dec 1892 [Berlin].

RUS–KL (a³, No. 145).

*ZC 3: 538–584 — *PB*: 523–524 — *PSSL* 16B: 208 — **LF*: 525 [English tr.].

4830.   To Nikolai Konradi

18/30 Dec 1892 [Berlin].

Autograph lost; MS copy in RUS–KL.

*ZC 3: 584 — *CTP*: 286–287 — *PSSL* 16B: 209.

4831.   To Praskov´ia Chaikovskaia

18/30 Dec 1892. Basel.

RUS–KL (a³, No. 3293).

PB: 524–525 — *PSSL* 16B: 209–210 — *LF*: 525–526 [English tr.].

4832.   To František Šubert

[18]/30 Dec 1892. Basel — in French.

CZ–Ps [facs. in M. Očadlik, *Pražské dopisy P. I. Čajkovského* (1949)].

Štěpánek (1952): 165 [Czech tr.] — *PSSL* 16B: 210–211.

4833.   To Modest Chaikovskii

19/31 Dec 1892. Basel.

RUS–KL (a³, No. 2012).

*ZC 3: 585 — *PB*: 525 — *PSSL* 16B: 211–212 — *LF*: 526 [English tr.].

4834.   To Pëtr Iurgenson

20 Dec 1892/[1 Jan 1893]. [Montpelier].

RUS–KL (a³, No. 2829).

PIU 2: 258 — *PSSL* 16B: 212.

4835.   To Nikolai Chaikovskii

22 Dec 1892/3 Jan 1893. Paris.

RUS–SPsc (f. 834, No. 37, fol. 26–29).

*ZC 3: 585–587 — *PB*: 525–527 — *PSSL* 16B: 212–214 — *LF*: 527–528 [English tr.].

4836.   To Modest Chaikovskii

24 Dec 1892/5 Jan 1893. Paris.

RUS–KL (a³, No. 2013).

*ZC 3: 587–588 — *PB*: 527–528 — *PSSL* 16B: 214–215 — **LF*: 528–529 [English tr.].

4837.   To the Editor of *Paris*.

[29 Dec 1892/10 Jan 1893]. Brussels — in French.

Autograph lost; typed copy in RUS–KL.

*Paris. (1/13 Jan 1893) — **ZC* 3: 592–593 [Russian tr.] — *PSSL* 16B: 216–217.

4838.   To Anna Merkling

31 Dec 1892/12 Jan [1893]. Brussels.

Autograph lost; MS copy in RUS–KL.

CTP: 253 — *PSSL* 16B: 219.

4839.   To Aleksei Sofronov

31 Dec 1892/12 Jan 1893. Brussels.

RUS–SPsc (f. 834, No. 28, fol. 24–25).

PSSL 16B: 219–220.

1893

4840.   To Vladimir Davydov

4/16 Jan 1893. Paris.

RUS–KL (a³, No. 146).

PSSL 17: 13–14.

4841.   To Karl von Ledebur

[4]/16 Jan 1893. Paris — in French.

Autograph lost

K. von Ledebur, *Aus meinem* Tagebuche (1897): 175–
   176 — PSSL 17: 14–15.

4842.   To Vladmir Nápravník

4/16 Jan 1893. Paris.

Autograph lost; typed copy in RUS–KL.

EFN: 200–201 — *PSSL* 17: 16.

4843.   To Anatolii Chaikovskii

4/16 Jan 1893. Paris.

RUS–KL (a³, No. 3233).

ZC 3: 588–589 — *PSSL* 17: 17–18.

4844.   To Modest Chaikovskii

4/16 Jan 1893. Paris.

RUS–KL (a³, No. 2014).

ZC 3: 589 — *PB*: 528–529 — *PSSL* 17: 18–19 —
   LF: 530 [English tr.].

4844a. To Marie de Lynen

[5]/17 Jan 1893. Paris.

US–NHub

Not published.

4845.   To Ekaterina Larosh

7/19 Jan 1893. Paris.

Autograph lost; photocopy in RUS–KL.

PSSL 17: 19–20.

4846.   To Vladmir Nápravník

15 Jan [1893]. Odessa.

Autograph lost; typed copy in RUS–KL.

EFN: 201 — *PSSL* 17: 20–21.

4847.   To Vasilii Safonov

15 Jan 1893. Odessa.

RUS–KL (a³, No. 350).

VIS: 210–211 — *PSSL* 17: 22.

4848.   To Lev Kupernik

[mid Jan 1893. Odessa].

RUS–SPil (f. 232, No. 10).

PSSL 17: 23.

4849.   [To an unidentified correspondent]

23 Jan 1893. Odessa.

RUS–KL.

PSSL 17: 23–24.

4850.   To Anna Merkling

[24] Jan 1893. Odessa.

Autograph lost; MS copy in RUS–KL.

ZC 3: 598–599 — *CTP*: 253–254 — *PSSL* 17: 24–
   25.

4851.   To Vladimir Makovskii

27 Jan 1893. Kamenka.

RUS–KL (a³, No. 269).

SM (1939), 8: 57 — *PSSL* 17: 26.

4852.   To Modest Chaikovskii

28 Jan 1893. Kamenka.

RUS–KL (a³, No. 2015).

ZC 3: 599 — *PB*: 529–530 — *PSSL* 17: 27 — *LF*:
   530–531 [English tr.].

4853.   To Anatolii Chaikovskii

29 Jan 1893. Kamenka.

Autograph lost; MS copy in RUS–KL.

PB: 530 — *PSSL* 17: 28–29 — *LF*: 531–532 [English
   tr.].

4854.   To Il´ia Slatin

2 Feb 1893 [Khar´kov].

RUS–KL (a³, No. 359).

PSSL 17: 29.

4855.   To Charles Villiers Stanford

[3–4 Feb 1893]. Klin — in French.

GB–Lcm (MS 4253, No. 158).

SM (1965), 9: 49–50 — *PSSL* 17: 29–30.

4856.   To Iulii Konius

5 Feb [1893]. Klin.

Autograph lost; MS copy in RUS–KL.

PSSL 17: 31–32 — Yoffe: 198–200 [English tr.].

4856a.   To Francis Jameson

5/17 Feb 1893. Klin — in French.

US–LJ (No. 2521).

SM (1990), 6: 92–93.

4857.   To Il´ia Slatin

5 Feb 1893 [Klin].

RUS–KL (a³, No. 360).

PSSL 17: 34.

4858.   To Modest Chaikovskii

5 Feb 1893. Klin.

RUS–KL (a³, No. 2016).

ZC 3: 600–601 — *PB*: 530–531 — *PSSL* 17: 34–
35 — *LF*: 532–533 [English tr.].

4858a.   [To an unidentified correspondent]

5 Feb 1893. Klin.

US–PHci.

Not published.

4859.   To Natal´ia Pleskaia

6 Feb 1893. Klin.

RUS–Mcl (f. 905).

CTP: 368–369 — *PSSL* 17: 36–37.

4860.   To Aleksandr Shidlovskii

7 Feb 1893. Klin.

Autograph lost; MS copy in RUS–KL.

PSSL 17: 37.

4861.   To Vasilii Safonov

[8 Feb 1893. Klin] — telegram.

RUS–Mcm (f. 80, No. 1047).

PSSL 17: 37.

4862.   To Josef Bohuslav Foerster

8 Feb 1893. Klin — in French.

CZ–Pfoerster [facs. in *SM* (1952), 7: 71–72].

PSSL 17: 38–39.

4863.   To Vasilii Safonov

[10 Feb 1893. Klin] — telegram.

RUS–Mcm (f. 80, No. 1048).

PSSL 17: 41.

4864.   To Anatolii Chaikovskii

10 Feb [1893]. Klin.

RUS–KL (a³, No. 3234).

ZC 3: 602 — *PB*: 531–532 — *PSSL* 17: 42 — *LF*:
533 [English tr.].

4865.   To Vladimir Davydov

11 Feb 1893. Klin.

RUS–KL (a³, No. 147) [facs. of 2 p. in *PICH* (1978):
145].

ZC 3: 602–603 — *PB*: 532–533 — *PSSL* 17: 42–
43 — *LF*: 534 [English tr.].

4866.   To Ružena Vykoukalová-Bradačeva

[16] Feb 1893 (in MS: "28 Feb") [Moscow] (in MS:
"Klin") — in French.

Autograph lost [facs. in *Divadelní listy* (20 Oct 1902)].

PSSL 17: 44.

4867.   To Aleksandr Ziloti

16 Feb [1893]. Moscow.

RUS–KL (a³, No. 3042).

AIZ: 141–142 — *PSSL* 17: 44–45.

4868.   To Aleksei Kartavov

16 Feb 1893. Moscow.

RUS–KL (a³, No. 204).

PSSL 17: 45–46.

4869.   To Vladimir Stasov

16 Feb 1893. Moscow.

RUS–SPsc (f. 738, No. 343, fol. 65b–66).

RM (1909), 3: 149 — *PSSL* 17: 46.

4870.   To Charles Villiers Stanford

[20 Feb 1893. Klin] — in French.

GB–Lcm (MS 4253, No. 159).

SM (1965), 9: 49–50 — *PSSL* 17: 46–47.

4871.   To Nikolai Kuznetsov

20 Feb [1893]. Moscow.

RUS–KL (a³, No. 2871).

PSSL 17: 47.

4872.   To the Editor of *Russkie vedomosti*

26 Feb [1893]. Moscow.

RUS–SPsc (f. 834, No. 24) [rough draft, not sent].

ZC 3: 603–604 — *SM* (1938), 10/11: 152–153 — *PSSL* 17: 48–49.

4873.   To Pavel Pchel´nikov

27 Feb [1893]. Moscow.

RUS–KL (a³, No. 335).

PSSL 17: 49.

4874.   To Aleksandr Ziloti

28 Feb 1893. Klin.

RUS–KL (a³, No. 3043).

AIZ: 143–144 — *PSSL* 17: 50.

4875.   To Robert Kajanus

28 Feb 1893. Klin — in German.

Autograph lost; photocopy in RUS–Mcm

PSSL 17: 51.

4876.   To Konstantin Mikhailov-Stoian

[28 Feb 1893. Klin].

Autograph lost

K. I. Mikhailov-Stoian, *Ispovel´ tenor*, tom 2 (1896): 93 (undated) — *PSSL* 17: 52.

4877.   To Iosif Suprunenko

28 Feb 1893. Klin.

RUS–KL (a³, No. 395).

Neva (1959), 5: 223–224 — *PSSL* 17: 52.

4878.   To Modest Chaikovskii

28 Feb [1893]. Klin.

RUS–KL (a³, No. 2017).

ZC 3: 604–605 — *PB*: 533 — *PSSL* 17: 53 — *LF*: 535 [English tr.].

4879.   To Pavel Pchel´nikov

1 Mar 1893. Klin.

RUS–KL (a³, No. 327).

PSSL 17: 54.

4880.   To Vladimir Shilovskii

2 Mar [1893]. Klin.

RUS–SPsc (f. 834, No. 14, fol. 21–22).

ZC 3: 605–606 —*PSSL* 17: 54–55.

4881.   To Iakov Grot

4 Mar 1893 [Klin].

RUS–SPaa (f. 137, op. 3, No. 1007, fol. 3–4).

Vestnik Akademii nauk SSSR (1933), 12: 40 — *PSSL* 17: 56.

4882.   To Alfred Hipkins

4 Mar 1893. Klin — in French.

US–NYpm (MFC T249.X).

PSSL 17: 56–57.

4883.   To Anatolii Chaikovskii

4 Mar 1893. Klin.

RUS–KL (a³, No. 3235).

ZC 3: 606 — *PB*: 533–534 — *PSSL* 17: 57–58 — *LF*: 535–536 [English tr.].

4884.   To Andrei Chaikovskii

4 Mar 1893. Klin.

RUS–KL (a³, No. 413).

PSSL 17: 58.

4885.   To Mariia Klimentova-Muromtseva

7 Mar [1893]. [Moscow].

RUS–KL (a³, No. 223).

PSSL 17: 59.

4886.   To Lev Kupernik

7 Mar [1893]. Moscow.

RUS–SPil (f. 232, No. 11).

PSSL 17: 59.

4887.   To Stepan Smolenskii

8 Mar 1893 [Moscow].

RUS–KL (a³, No. 369).

SM (1959), 12: 83 — *PSSL* 17: 60.

4888.   To Modest Chaikovskii

8 Mar [1893]. Moscow.

RUS–KL (a³, No. 2018).

ZC 3: 607 — *PB*: 534 — *PSSL* 17: 60–61 — *LF*: 536 [English tr.].

4889.   To Vladimir Shilovskii

9 Mar [1893]. Moscow.

RUS–SPsc (f. 834, No. 14, fol. 23–24).

ZC 3: 606 — *PSSL* 17: 61–62.

4890.   To Pavel Pchel´nikov

10 Mar 1893 [Moscow].

RUS–KL (a³, No. 328).

PSSL 17: 62.

4891.   To Ivan Klimenko

[11 Mar 1893. Khar´kov] — telegram.

Autograph lost

KMV: 74 — *PSSL* 17: 62.

4892.   To Anatolii Brandukov

18 Mar [1893]. [Moscow].

RUS–KL (a³, No. 29).

PSSL 17: 63.

4893.   To Il´ia Slatin

18 Mar [1893]. [Klin].

RUS–KL (a³, No. 361).

PSSL 17: 63.

4894.   To Anna Aleksandrova-Levenson

19 Mar 1893 [Moscow].

RUS–KL (a³, No. 3323).

PSSL 17: 64.

4894a. To Alma Aronson

19 Mar [1893]. Klin — in French.

US–I (Noyes coll. E173 N95, pt. 13).

TGM 7 (2000): 45–46.

4895.   To Lev Kupernik

19 Mar 1893. Klin.

RUS–SPil (f. 232, No. 12).

PSSL 17: 64–65.

4896.   To Anna Merkling

19 Mar 1893. Klin.

Autograph lost; MS copy in RUS–KL.

CTP: 254 — *PSSL* 17: 66.

4897.   To Modest Chaikovskii

19 Mar 1893. Klin.

RUS–KL (a³, No. 2019).

*ZC 3: 608–609 — *PB: 535 — *PSSL* 17: 67 — *LF:
537 [English tr.].

4898.   To Vladimir Shilovskii

19 Mar [1893]. Klin.

RUS–SPsc (f. 834, No. 14, fol. 25).

PSSL 17: 67–68.

4899.   To Modest Chaikovskii

21 Mar [1893]. [Klin].

RUS–KL (a³, No. 2020).

PSSL 17: 68.

4900.   To Josef Bohuslav Foerster

24 Mar 1893. Klin — in French.

CZ–Pfoerster [facs. in *SM* (1950), 12: 87–88].

J. B. Foerster (1949): 61 — *SM* (1950), 12: 87–88
[Russian tr.] — I. F. Belza, *Ocherki razvitiia
cheshskoi muzykal´noi klassiki* (1951): 376 — *PSSL*
17: 68–69.

4901.   To Mikhail Ippolitov-Ivanov

[25] Mar 1893 (in MS: "24 Mar"). Klin.

US–NH (misc. 372, S–Z).

*ZC 3: 609 — *Biulleten´* (1947), 2: 58–59 — *PSSL*
17: 70.

4902.   To Anatolii Chaikovskii

[25] Mar 1893 (in MS: "24 Mar"). Klin.

RUS–KL (a³, No. 3236).

*ZC 3: 609–610 — *PSSL* 17: 71.

4903.   To Andrei Chaikovskii

[25] Mar 1893 (in MS: "24 Mar") [Klin].

RUS–KL (a³, No. 419).

PSSL 17: 72.

4904.   To Boris Iurgenson

28 Mar 1893 [St. Petersburg] — noted on the MS of
Sergei Taneev's orchestration of Chaikovskii's
quartet *Night*

RUS–Mcm (f. 88, No. 128).

PSSL 17: 72.

4905.   To Georgii Konius

5 Apr 1893 [Klin].

Autograph lost; MS copy in RUS–KL.

*ZC 3: 610 — *PSSL* 17: 73.

4906. To Lev Kupernik

5 Apr 1893. Klin.

RUS–SPil (f. 232, No. 13).

PSSL 17: 74–75.

4907. To Natal´ia Pleskaia

5 Apr 1893. Klin.

RUS–Mcl (f. 905).

CTP: 369 — *PSSL* 17: 75.

4908. To Vasilii Salin

[5 Apr 1893]. [Klin].

KZ–AA

Sovetskaia Moldavia (27 Mar 1941): 4 — *PSSL* 17: 76.

4909. To Eduard Nápravník

5 Apr 1893. Klin.

Autograph lost; typed copy in RUS–KL.

VP: 226–227 — *EFN*: 186 — *PSSL* 17: 76.

4910. To Il´ia Slatin

5 Apr 1893. Klin.

RUS–KL (a³, No. 362).

PSSL 17: 77.

4911. To Stepan Smolenskii

5 Apr 1893. Klin.

RUS–KL (a³, No. 370).

SM (1959), 12: 83 — *PSSL* 17: 77–78.

4912. To Aleksandr Shidlovskii

5 Apr 1893. Klin.

Autograph lost; MS copy in RUS–KL.

PSSL 17: 78.

4913. To Vladimir Davydov

11 Apr 1893 [Klin].

RUS–KL (a³, No. 148).

*ZC 3: 611 — **PB*: 535 — *PSSL* 17: 79 — **LF*: 537
[English tr.].

4913a. To Stepan Smolenskii

11 Apr 1893. Klin.

RUS–SPsc (f. 631, fol. 159–[159a]).

Not published.

4914. To Aleksandra Sviatlovskaia

13 Apr 1893. Klin.

RUS–KL (a³, No. 7).

PSSL 17: 80.

4915. To Anatolii Chaikovskii

13 Apr 1893. Klin.

RUS–KL (a³, No. 3237).

PSSL 17: 80–81.

4916. To Vladimir Davydov

15 Apr 1893 [Klin].

RUS–KL (a³, No. 149).

*ZC 3: 611 — *PB*: 535–536 — *PSSL* 17: 81–82 —
LF: 537–538 [English tr.].

4917. To Ekaterina Larosh

15 Apr 1893 [Klin].

Autograph lost; photocopy in RUS–KL.

PSSL 17: 82–83.

4918. To Il´ia Slatin

15 Apr 1893. Klin.

RUS–KL (a³, No. 363).

PSSL 17: 83–84.

4919. To Modest Chaikovskii

17 Apr [1893]. Klin.

RUS–KL (a³, No. 2021).

*ZC 3: 611–613 — *PB*: 536–537 — *PSSL* 17: 84–
85 — **LF*: 538–539 [English tr.].

4920. To Il´ia Slatin

20 Apr 1893 [Klin].

RUS–KL (a³, No. 364).

PSSL 17: 86.

4921. To Modest Chaikovskii

22–23 Apr 1893. Moscow.

RUS–KL (a³, No. 2022).

*ZC 3: 613 — *PB*: 537–538 — *PSSL* 17: 86–87 —
*LF: 539–540 [English tr.].

4922. To Aleksei Sofronov

27 Apr [1893]. [Klin].

RUS–SPsc (f. 834, No. 28, fol. 26–27).

PSSL 17: 87–88.

4923.　To Pavel Pchel´nikov

2 May 1893 [Moscow].

RUS–KL (a³, No. 329).

PSSL 17: 88.

4924.　To Pëtr Iurgenson

2 May [1893]. [Moscow].

RUS–KL (a³, No. 2832).

*ZC 3: 613–614 — *PIU* 2: 261 — *PSSL* 17: 89.

4925.　To Aleksandr Ziloti

3 May [1893]. Klin.

RUS–KL (a³, No. 3044).

AIZ: 145–146 — *PSSL* 17: 89–90.

4926.　To Il´ia Slatin

3 May [1893]. Klin.

RUS–KL (a³, No. 365).

PSSL 17: 90–91.

4927.　To Daniil Ratgauz

5 May 1893. Klin.

Autograph lost; photocopy in RUS–KL.

*Novosti dnia (5 Oct 1894) — **Golos Moskvy* (25 Oct 1911) — **PSSL* 17: 91.

4928.　To Andrei Chaikovskii

5 May [1893]. Klin.

RUS–KL (a³, No. 420).

PSSL 17: 92.

4929.　To Pëtr Iurgenson

5 May 1893 [Klin].

RUS–KL (a³, No. 2833).

ZC 3: 614 — *PIU* 2: 261–262.

4930.　To Pëtr Iurgenson

6 May 1893. St. Petersburg.

RUS–KL (a³, No. 2834).

*ZC 3: 614–615 — *PIU* 2: 262 — *PSSL* 17: 93.

4930a.　To Osip Iurgenson

12 May 1893 [St. Petersburg].

RUS–KL (a³, No. 485).

Not published.

4931.　To Vladimir Davydov

15/27 May [1893]. Berlin.

RUS–KL (a³, No. 150).

*ZC 3: 615–616 — *PSSL* 17: 94.

4932.　To Aleksandr Ziloti

15/27 May 1893. Berlin.

RUS–KL (a³, No. 3045).

AIZ: 146 — *PSSL* 17: 94–95.

4933.　To Aleksei Sofronov

15/27 May [1893]. Berlin.

RUS–SPsc (f. 834, No. 28, fol. 28–29).

PSSL 17: 95.

4934.　To Modest Chaikovskii

15/27 May [1893]. Berlin.

RUS–KL (a³, No. 2023).

*ZC 3: 616–617 — **PB*: 538 — *PSSL* 17: 96 — **LF*: 540 [English tr.].

4935.　To Vladimir Davydov

17/29 May [1893]. London.

RUS–KL (a³, No. 151).

*ZC 3: 617–618 — **PB*: 539–540 — *PSSL* 17: 97–98 — **LF*: 541 [English tr.].

4936.　To Lev Kupernik

17/29 May 1893. London.

RUS–SPil (f. 232, No. 14).

PSSL 17: 98–99.

4937.　To Anatolii Chaikovskii

17/29 May [1893]. London.

RUS–KL (a³, No. 3238).

*ZC 3: 617 — *PB*: 538–539 — *PSSL* 17: 99–100 — **LF*: 541–542 [English tr.].

4938.　To Frits Hartvigson

[22 May]/3 Jun 1893. London — in German.

Autograph auctioned by J. Stargardt, Marburg, 1979.

*PSSL 17: 100–101.

4939.　To Aleksandr Ziloti

[22 May]/3 Jun [1893]. London.

RUS–KL (a³, No. 3046).

AIZ: 148 — *PSSL* 17: 101–102.

4940. To Modest Chaikovskii

[22 May]/3 Jun [1893]. London.

RUS–KL (a³, No. 2024).

*ZC 3: 619 — PB: 540–541 — PSSL 17: 102–103 —
*LF: 542–543 [English tr.].

4941. To Frederick Maitland

[24 May]/5 [Jun] 1893 (in MS: "5 May"). London —
in French.

GB–Cmaitland.

SM (1965), 9: 49 — PSSL 17: 103–104.

4942. To Pëtr Iurgenson

[24 May]/5 Jun 1893. London.

RUS–KL (a³, No. 2837).

PIU 2: 265 — PSSL 17: 104–105.

4943. To Frits Hartvigson

[26 May]/7 Jun [1893]. [London] — in German.

Autograph lost (formerly in the possession of J.
MacNutt, London).

PSSL 17: 105.

4943a. To Frits Hartvigson

[26 May]/8 [Jun 1893]. [London] — noted on the
back of Hartvigson's visiting card; in German.

Autograph auctioned by Sotheby's, London, 1998.

TGM 6 (1999): 6.

4944. To Aleksandra Sviatlovskaia

27 [May]/[8 Jun] 1893 (in MS: "27 Apr") [London].

RUS–KL (a³, No. 9).

PSSL 17: 105–106.

4945. To Modest Chaikovskii

[29 May]/10 Jun [1893]. London.

RUS–KL (a³, No. 2025).

*ZC 3: 619–620 — PB: 541 — PSSL 17: 106 — LF:
543 [English tr.].

4946. To Adelina Bolska

[29 May/10 Jun–30 May/11 Jun 1893]. [London] —
in French.

RUS–Mcm (f. 314, No. 8).

PSSL 17: 107.

4947. To Aleksei Sofronov

1/[13] Jun [1893]. Cambridge.

RUS–SPsc (f. 834, No. 28, fol. 30–31).

PSSL 17: 107–108.

4948. To Nikolai Konradi

3/15 Jun 1893. Paris.

Autograph lost; MS copy in RUS–KL.

ZC 3: 625 — CTP: 287 — PSSL 17: 108–109.

4949. To Vladimir Nápravník

3/15 Jun 1893. Paris.

Autograph lost; typed copy in RUS–KL.

EFN: 202–203 — PSSL 17: 110.

4950. To Daniil Ratgauz

3/15 Jun 1893. Paris.

Autograph lost.

Novosti dnia (5 Oct 1894) — Golos Moskvy (25 Oct
1911) — PSSL 17: 111.

4951. To Emil Hatzfeld

[3]/15 Jun 1893 [Paris] — in French.

Autograph lost.

R. Landon, Tschaikowsky [n.d.]: 28 — PSSL 17: 111–
112.

4952. To Anatolii Chaikovskii

3/15 Jun [1893]. Paris.

RUS–KL (a³, No. 3239).

PB: 541–542 — PSSL 17: 112–113 — LF: 544–545
[English tr.].

4953. To Aleksandr Shidlovskii

3/15 Jun [1893]. Paris.

Autograph lost; MS copy in RUS–KL.

PSSL 17: 114.

4954. To Pëtr Iurgenson

3/15 Jun [1893]. Paris.

RUS–KL (a³, No. 2836).

*ZC 3: 624–625 — PIU 2: 263–264 — PSSL 17:
114–115.

4955.   To Anatolii Chaikovskii

[6]/18 Jun [1893] (in MS: "5/18"). Paris.

RUS–KL (a³, No. 3240).

PSSL 17: 115.

4956.   To Modest Chaikovskii

[6]/18 Jun [1893] (in MS: "5/18"). Paris.

RUS–KL (a³, No. 2026).

PB: 543 — *PSSL* 17: 116 — *LF*: 545–546 [English tr.].

4957.   To Konstantin Koninskii

19 Jun 1893 [Grankino].

RUS–Mt [facs. of harmonisation in *RMG* (1899), 1: 16].

*RMG (1899), 1: 15–16 — *PSSL* 17: 117.

4958.   To Natal´ia Pleskaia

19 Jun 1893. Grankino

RUS–Mcl (f. 905).

CTP: 370 — *PSSL* 17: 118–119.

4959.   To Anatolii Chaikovskii

19 Jun 1893. Grankino.

RUS–KL (a³, No. 3241).

*ZC 3: 626–627 — *PB*: 543–544 — *PSSL* 17: 119 — *LF*: 546 [English tr.].

4959a.   To Pavel Peterssen

23 Jun 1893. Grankino.

RUS–Mcl (f. 1919).

PSSL 17: 261–262.

4960.   To Vasilii Safonov

23 Jun 1893. Grankino.

RUS–KL (a³, No. 353).

SM (1939), 8: 57 — *VIS*: 212–213 ("23 Jul") — *PSSL* 17: 120.

4961.   To Modest Chaikovskii

23 Jun [1893]. Grankino.

RUS–KL (a³, No. 2027).

*PB: 544 — *PSSL* 17: 121–122 — *LF: 546–547 [English tr.].

4962.   To Pëtr Iurgenson

23 Jun 1893. Grankino.

RUS–KL (a³, No. 2838).

PIU 2: 264–265 — *PSSL* 17: 122–123.

4963.   To Iulian Poplavskii

26 Jun [1893]. Grankino.

Autograph lost; photocopy in RUS–Mcl (f. 905).

PSSL 17: 124.

4964.   To Pëtr Iurgenson

26 Jun [1893]. Grankino.

RUS–KL (a³, No. 2839).

PIU 2: 265.

4965.   To Aleksei Sofronov

1 Jul [1893]. Grankino.

RUS–SPsc (f. 834, No. 28, fol. 32–33).

PSSL 17: 125.

4966.   To Vasilii Safonov

3 Jul [1893]. [Grankino].

RUS–KL (a³, No. 351).

SM (1939), 8: 55 — *VIS*: 211–212 — *PSSL* 17: 125–126.

4967.   To Pëtr Iurgenson

[3] Jul 1893 (in MS: "2 Jul"). Grankino.

RUS–KL (a³, No. 2840).

PIU 2: 265 — *PSSL* 17: 126–127.

4968.   To Anatolii Chaikovskii

6 Jul [1893]. Ukolovo.

RUS–KL (a³, No. 3242).

*ZC 3: 627 — *PB: 544–545 — *PSSL* 17: 127–128 — *LF: 547 [English tr.].

4969.   To Sergei Taneev

[18] Jul [1893] (in MS: "19 Jul") [Moscow].

RUS–KL (a³, No. 400).

CTP: 193 — *PSSL* 17: 128.

4970.   To Pëtr Iurgenson

[18] Jul 1893 (in MS: "19 Jul") [Klin].

RUS–KL (a³, No. 2841).

PSSL 17: 129.

4971.   To Francesco Berger
19 Jul 1893. Klin — in German.
GB–Lps
PSSL 17: 129.

4972.   To Vladimir Davydov
19 Jul [1893]. Klin.
RUS–KL (a³, No. 152).
**ZC* 3: 627 — *PSSL* 17: 130–131.

4973.   To Aleksandr Ziloti
19 Jul 1893. Klin.
RUS–KL (a³, No. 3047).
AIZ: 151 — *PSSL* 17: 131–132.

4974.   To Mikhail Ippolitov-Ivanov
19 Jul 1893. Klin.
RUS–KL (a³, No. 203).
**ZC* 3: 609 — **Iskusstvo*, 3 (1927), 4: 175 — *Biulleten´*
    (1947), 2: 62–63 — *PSSL* 17: 132–133.

4975.   To Anna Merkling
19 Jul 1893. Klin.
Autograph lost; MS copy in RUS–KL.
PSSL 17: 133–134.

4976.   To Pavel Peterssen
19 Jul 1893. Klin.
RUS–Mcl (f. 1919).
PSSL 17: 134.

4977.   To Daniil Ratgauz
19 Jul 1893. Klin.
RUS–KL (a³, No. 336).
Sovetskoe Iskusstvo (9 Jul 1940) — *PSSL* 17: 135.

4978.   To Aleksandra Sviatlovskaia
19 Jul 1893 [Klin].
RUS–KL (a³, No. 3351).
PSSL 17: 136.

4979.   To Anatolii Chaikovskii
19 Jul 1893 [Klin].
RUS–KL (a³, No. 3243).
PB: 545 — *PSSL* 17: 136–137 — *LF:* 548 [English
    tr.].

4980.   To Praskov´ia Chaikovskaia
[20–21 Jul] 1893. Klin.
RUS–KL (a³, No. 3297).
PSSL 17: 137.

4981.   To Pëtr Iurgenson
21 Jul 1893 [Klin].
RUS–KL (a³, No. 2842).
PSSL 17: 138–139.

4982.   To Eduard Nápravník
22 Jul [1893]. Klin.
RUS–KL (a³, No. 3364).
VP: : 229–230 — *EFN:* 188 — *PSSL* 17: 140.

4983.   To Sergei Taneev
22 Jul 1893 [Klin].
RUS–Mcl (f. 880).
PT: 1916 — *CTP:* 195 — *PSSL* 17: 141.

4984.   To Modest Chaikovskii
22 Jul [1893]. [Klin].
RUS–KL (a³, No. 2028).
**ZC* 3: 627–628 — **PB:* 546 — *PSSL* 17: 142–
    143 — **LF:* 548–549 [English tr.].

4985.   To Aleksandr Ziloti
23 Jul 1893. Klin.
RUS–KL (a³, No. 3048).
AIZ: 151–152 — *PSSL* 17: 143–144.

4986.   To Georgii Konius
23 Jul 1893 [Klin].
Autograph lost; MS copy in RUS–KL.
**ZC* 3: 628–629 — *PSSL* 17: 144–145.

4987.   To Ol´ga & Nikolai Chaikovskii
23 Jul 1893. Klin.
RUS–SPsc (f. 834, No. 37, fol. 30–32).
PSSL 17: 145–146.

4988.   To Pëtr Iurgenson
24 Jul [1893]. [Klin].
RUS–KL (a³, No. 2843).
PSSL 17: 146.

4989.   To Aleksandr Ziloti

26 Jul [1893]. Klin.

RUS–KL (a³, No. 3049).

AIZ: 153–154 — *PSSL* 17: 147–148.

4990.   To Vasilii Safonov

26 Jul [1893]. [Klin].

RUS–KL (a³, No. 352).

Iu. D. Engel, *Glazami sovremenika* (1971): 494 — *PSSL* 17: 148.

4991.   To Modest Chaikovskii

26 Jul 1893 [Klin].

RUS–KL (a³, No. 2029).

PSSL 17: 148–149.

4992.   To Pëtr Iurgenson

[27–28] Jul 1893 (in MS: "26 Jul") [Klin].

RUS–KL (a³, No. 2841).

PIU 2: 268 — *PSSL* 17: 149.

4993.   To Anna Merkling

28 Jul 1893 [Klin].

Autograph lost; MS copy in RUS–KL.

CTP: 255 — *PSSL* 17: 150.

4994.   To Aleksandr Ziloti

1 Aug [1893]. Klin.

RUS–KL (a³, No. 3050).

AIZ: 154–155 — *PSSL* 17: 151.

4995.   To Ekaterina Larosh

1 Aug 1893. Klin.

US–BHsmith

PSSL 17: 152–153.

4996.   To Daniil Ratgauz

1 Aug 1893. Klin.

RUS–KL (a³, No. 337).

ZC 3: 629 — *Golos Moskvy* (25 Oct 1911) — **RMG* (1912), 23/24: 531 — *Sovetskoe iskusstvo* (9 Jul 1940) — *PSSL* 17: 153–154.

4997.   To Sergei Taneev

1 Aug [1893]. Klin.

RUS–Mcl (f. 880).

PT: 187 — *CTP*: 196 — *PSSL* 17: 154.

4998.   To Vladimir Davydov

[2] Aug 1893 (in MS: "3 Aug"). Klin.

RUS–KL (a³, No. 153) [facs. of 2 p. in *MNC* (1958): 252–253].

*ZC 3: 629–630 — **PB*: 546–547 — *PSSL* 17: 155 — **LF*: 549–550 [English tr.].

4999.   To Pavel Peterssen

2 Aug 1893 [Klin].

RUS–SPil (f. 221, No. 23) [facs. in *SM* (1953), 10: 47–48].

SM (1953), 10: 47–48 — *PSSL* 17: 156.

5000.   To Modest Chaikovskii

3 Aug [1893]. Klin.

RUS–KL (a³, No. 2030).

PSSL 17: 157.

5001.   To Pëtr Iurgenson

3 Aug [1893]. [Klin].

RUS–KL (a³, No. 2845).

PSSL 17: 157–158.

5002.   To Vladimir Davydov

4 Aug [1893]. [Klin].

RUS–KL (a³, No. 154).

*ZC 3: 630 — *PSSL* 17: 158–159.

5003.   To Pavel Peterssen

7 Aug 1893 [Klin].

RUS–Mrg

SM (1953), 10: 48 — *PSSL* 17: 159–160.

5004.   To Aleksandr Ziloti

8 Aug [1893]. [Klin].

RUS–KL (a³, No. 3051).

AIZ: 156–157 — *PSSL* 17: 160–161.

5005.   To Pavel Peterssen

11 Aug [1893]. [Klin].

RUS–KL (a³, No. 2988) [facs. in *Avtografy P. I. Chaikovskogo v arkhive Doma–muzeia na Klinu*, vyp 2 (1952): 132–133].

SM (1953), 10: 48 — *PSSL* 17: 161–162.

5006.   To Modest Chaikovskii

11 Aug 1893. Klin.

RUS–KL (a³, No. 2031).

PSSL 17: 162.

5007.   To Vasilii Safonov

12 Aug [1893]. Klin.

RUS–KL (a³, No. 354).

SM (1939), 8: 58 — *PSSL* 17: 163.

5008.   To Sergei Taneev

12 Aug [1893]. Klin.

RUS–Mcl (f. 880).

PT: 1916 — *CTP*: 197–198 — *PSSL* 17: 163–164.

5009.   To Anatolii Chaikovskii

12 Aug [1893]. [Klin].

RUS–KL (a³, No. 3244).

*PB: 547 — *PSSL* 17: 164–165 — **LF*: 550 [English tr.].

5010.   To Pëtr Iurgenson

12 Aug [1893]. Klin.

RUS–KL (a³, No. 2846).

PIU 2: 269–270 — *PSSL* 17: 165–166.

5011.   To Modest Chaikovskii

13 Aug [1893]. [Klin].

RUS–KL (a³, No. 2032).

PSSL 17: 166.

5012.   To Modest Chaikovskii

[14 Aug 1893. Klin] — telegram.

RUS–KL (a³, No. 2033).

PSSL 17: 167.

5013.   To Iulii Konius

[16 Aug 1893. Klin].

Autograph lost; MS copy in RUS–KL.

PSSL 17: 167.

5014.   To Aleksandra Hubert

20 Aug [1893]. [Klin].

RUS–KL (a³, No. 81).

PRM 61 — *PSSL* 17: 167–168.

5015.   To Vladimir Davydov

20 Aug [1893]. [Klin].

RUS–KL (a³, No. 155).

*PB: 548–549 — *PSSL* 17: 168–169 — **LF*: 551 [English tr.].

5016.   To Iulii Konius

20 Aug 1893 [Klin].

Autograph lost; MS copy in RUS–KL.

*PSSL 17: 169–170.

5017.   To Anatolii Chaikovskii

20 Aug 1893 [Klin].

RUS–KL (a³, No. 3245).

PB: 547–548 — *PSSL* 17: 171 — *LF*: 550–551 [English tr.].

5018.   To Modest Chaikovskii

20 Aug [1893]. [Klin].

RUS–KL (a³, No. 2034).

PSSL 17: 172.

5019.   To Pëtr Iurgenson

20 Aug [1893]. [Klin].

RUS–KL (a³, No. 2847).

ZC 3: 631–632 — *PIU* 2: 270–271 — *PSSL* 17: 172–174.

5019a.   To Aleksandr Ziloti

20 Aug 1893 [Klin].

D–F [facs. in *Bisher unbekannte Briefe und musikalische Arbeiten Čajkovskijs* (1994): 14] — *Internationales Čajkovskij-Symposium Tübingen 1993: Bericht* (1995): 39].

Bisher unbekannte Briefe und musikalische Arbeiten Čajkovskijs (1994): 15 — *Internationales Čajkovskij-Symposium Tübingen 1993: Bericht* (1995): 38, 40.

5020.   To Michat Hertz

23 Aug 1893 [St. Petersburg] (in MS: "Moscow") — in German.

RUS–Mt

CMS: 484–485 — *Chaikovskii i zarubezhnye muzykanty* (1970): 86 — *PSSL* 17: 174–175.

5021.   To Hugo Bock

[28 Aug]/9 Sep [1893]. [Hamburg] — in French.

Autograph lost

Berliner Börsen-Courier (5 Feb 1927) — *PSSL* 17: 176.

5022.   To Vasilii Safonov

31 Aug [1893]. [St. Petersburg].

RUS–Mcm (f. 88, No. 180).

PSSL 17: 176–177.

5023.   To Mikhail Ippolitov-Ivanov

[3 Sep 1893. St. Petersburg].

Autograph lost; typed copy in RUS–KL.

PSSL 17: 177.

5024.   To Aleksei Sofronov

3 Sep [1893]. [St. Petersburg].

RUS–KL (a³, No. 390).

PSSL 17: 177–178.

5025.   To Pëtr Iurgenson

3 Sep [1893]. [St. Petersburg].

RUS–KL (a³, No. 2848).

*PIU 2: 272 — **PSSL* 17: 178.

5026.   To Mikhail Mikeshin

[? 3 Sep 1893. St. Petersburg].

RUS–Mt

Peterburgskaia zhizn' (1893), 53: 498 — *PSSL* 17: 178–
179.

5027.   To Pëtr Iurgenson

[4 Sep 1893. St. Petersburg].

RUS–KL (a³, No. 2849).

PIU 2: 272 — *PSSL* 17: 179.

5028.   To Modest Chaikovskii

9 Sep [1893]. [Moscow].

RUS–KL (a³, No. 2035).

PB: 549 — *PSSL* 17: 180 — *LF*: 552 [English tr.].

5029.   To Modest Chaikovskii

12 Sep [1893]. Mikhailovskoe.

RUS–KL (a³, No. 2036).

*ZC 3: 634 — *PSSL* 17: 180.

5030.   To Sigismund Stojowski

15 Sep 1893. Mikhailovskoe (in MS: "Spasskoe") —
in French.

US–NH (misc. 372, S–Z) [facs. in *SM* (1960), 5: 78].

SM (1960), 5: 78 [Russian tr.] — *PSSL* 17: 181.

5031.   To Modest Chaikovskii

17 Sep [1893]. [Moscow].

RUS–KL (a³, No. 2037).

PSSL 17: 182.

5032.   To Aleksandra Hubert

[? 17 Sep 1893. Moscow].

RUS–KL (a³, No. 83).

PRM 64 — *PSSL* 17: 183.

5033.   To Pavel Pchel´nikov

[mid Sep 1893. Moscow].

RUS–KL (a³, No. 333).

PSSL 17: 183.

5034.   To Sergei Taneev

[18 Sep 1893. Moscow].

RUS–Mcl (f. 880).

PT: 188 — *CTP*: 198 — *PSSL* 17: 183.

5035.   To Anatolii Chaikovskii

20 Sep 1893 [Moscow].

RUS–KL (a³, No. 3246).

*PB: 549 — *PSSL* 17: 184 — **LF*: 552 [English tr.].

5035a.   [To an unidentified French musician]

20 Sep 1893. Moscow — in French.

RUS–KL (a³, No. 272).

Not published.

5036.   To Sergei Taneev

[mid–late Sep 1893. Moscow].

RUS–Mcl (f. 880).

CTP: 185 ("1889–1893") — *PSSL* 17: 185.

5037.   To Pavel Peterssen

21 Sep 1893. Moscow.

RUS–Mcl (f. 1919).

PSSL 17: 185.

**5038.   To   Grand   Duke   Konstantin
Konstantinovich**

21 Sep 1893. Moscow.

RUS–SPil (f. 137, No. 78/30).

ZC 3: 634–636.

5039. To Sof´ia Iurgenson
22 Sep [1893]. [Moscow].
RUS–KL (a³, No. 496).
PSSL 17: 187.

5040. To Il´ia Slatin
23 Sep 1893. Moscow.
RUS–KL (a³, No. 366).
PSSL 17: 188.

5041. To German Larosh
24 Sep 1893 [Moscow].
Autograph lost; photocopy in RUS–KL.
PSSL 17: 188–189.

5042. To Modest Chaikovskii
24 Sep [1893]. [Moscow].
RUS–KL (a³, No. 2038).
*ZC 3: 635 — *PB*: 550 — *PSSL* 17: 189 — **LF*: 552–553 [English tr.].

5043. To Aleksandr Ziloti
25 Sep 1893. Klin.
RUS–KL (a³, No. 3052).
AIZ: 168 — *PSSL* 17: 190.

5044. To William von Sachs
25 Sep 1893. Klin — in French.
US–NYpm (Morgan coll.).
PSSL 17: 192.

5045. To Modest Chaikovskii
25 Sep [1893]. Klin.
RUS–KL (a³, No. 2039).
*ZC 3: 636 — *PSSL* 17: 192–193.

5046. To Grand Duke Konstantin Konstantinovich
26 Sep 1893. Klin.
RUS–SPil (f. 137, No. 78/31).
ZC 3: 636–638 — *PSSL* 17: 193–194.

5047. To Vladimir Davydov
27 Sep 1893. Klin.
RUS–KL (a³, No. 156).
PSSL 17: 194–195.

5048. To Il´ia Slatin
27 Sep 1893 [Klin].
RUS–KL (a³, No. 367).
PSSL 17: 195.

5049. To Anatolii Chaikovskii
27 Sep 1893. Klin.
RUS–KL (a³, No. 3247).
PSSL 17: 196.

5050. To Anatolii Brandukov
27 Sep [1893]. Klin.
RUS–KL (a³, No. 26).
PSSL 17: 196–197.

5051. To Anna Merkling
29 Sep 1893 [Klin].
Autograph lost; MS copy in RUS–KL.
CTP: 255–256 — *PSSL* 17: 197–198.

5052. To Pëtr Iurgenson
30 Sep 1893 [Klin].
RUS–KL (a³, No. 2850).
PIU 2: 273 — *PSSL* 17: 198.

5053. To Iulian Poplavskii
2 Oct [1893]. [Klin].
RUS–Mcl (f. 905).
PSSL 17: 198.

5054. To Sergei Remezov
2 Oct [1893]. Klin.
RUS–Mcm (f. 88, No. 179).
SM (1946), 1: 84 — *PSSL* 17: 199.

5055. To Vasilii Safonov
2 Oct [1893]. Klin.
RUS–KL (a³, No. 355).
SM (1939), 8: 58 — *PSSL* 17: 200.

5056. To Anatolii Brandukov
[5 Oct 1893. Klin] — telegram.
RUS–KL (a³, No. 28).
PSSL 17: 200.

5057.   To Sigismund Stojowski

[7 Oct 1893]. Klin — in French.

US–NH (misc. 372, S–Z).

SM (1960), 5: 78–79 [Russian tr.] — *PSSL* 17: 200–201 ("6 Oct").

5058.   To Sergei Taneev

[8 Oct 1893]. Moscow.

RUS–Mcl (f. 880).

CTP: 199 — *PSSL* 17: 202.

5059.   [see 4681a]

5060.   To Iulii Konius

18 Oct [1893]. [St. Petersburg].

Autograph lost; MS copy in RUS–KL.

ZC 3: 646 — *PSSL* 17: 203.

5061.   To Iosif Pribik

18 Oct 1893 [St. Petersburg].

Autograph lost

Odesskoe obozrenie teatrov (1913) — *PSSL* 17: 204.

5062.   To Pëtr Iurgenson

18 Oct [1893]. [St. Petersburg].

RUS–KL (a³, No. 2851) [facs. in *Chaikofosukii* (1990): 115].

ZC 3: 645–646 — *PIU* 2: 273 — *PSSL* 17: 205.

5063.   To Willem Kes

19 Oct 1893 [St. Petersburg] — in French.

Estate of W. Mengel´berg, Amsterdam.

RdM 54 (1968), 1: 89–90 — *PSSL* 17: 206.

5064 .   To Ol´ga Nápravník

[21 Oct 1893. St. Petersburg].

Autograph lost

ZC 3: 648 — *PSSL* 17: 206.

5065.   To Ivan Grekov

[21 Oct 1893. St. Petersburg].

Autograph lost

Odesskii listok (27 Oct 1893) — *Novosti dnia* (31 Oct 1893) — *Novosti i birzhevaia gazeta* (1 Nov 1893) — *PSSL* 17: 207.

Undated

5065a.   To Modest Chaikovskii

[date & place unknown].

RUS–KL (a³, No. 2044) — fragment only

Not published.

5065b.   [To an unknown "Madame"]

[date & place unknown] — in French.

RUS–KL (a³, No. 275).

Not published.

INDEX OF CORRESPONDENTS

ABRAMYCHEV, Nikolai Ivanovich (1854–1931). Pianist.

1 letter (1888) — 3742.

RUS–SPsc.

ADLERBERG, Aleksandr Vladimirovich (1818–88). Former minister at the Imperial Court.

1 letter (1886) — 3082a.

RUS–SPsc.

ALBRECHT — see AL´BREKHT.

AL´BREKHT, Evgenii Karlovich [ALBRECHT, Eugen Maria] (1842–94). Violinist, Director of the St. Petersburg Chamber Music Society, Manager of the Central Musical Library.

13 letters (1880, 1886, 1890–92) — 1453, 1461, 3065, 3066, 3083, 4173, 4187, 4295, 4461, 4462, 4624, 4673, 4795.

RUS–SPtob.

AL´BREKHT, Karl Karlovich [ALBRECHT, Konstantin] (1836–93). Cellist and inspector at the Moscow Conservatory.

100 letters (1869–87, 1889–92) — 174, 175, 186, 220, 221, 222, 223, 246, 246a, 247, 248, 248a, 272, 281, 307, 331, 342, 343, 344, 357, 430, 431, 432a, 448, 458, 466, 474, 477, 530, 530a, 547a, 600, 605, 606, 608, 624, 653, 671, 687, 694, 720, 731, 748, 760, 781, 877, 905, 990, 999, 1030, 1158, 1398, 1518, 1569, 1630, 1633, 1639, 1650, 1663, 1675, 2003, 2094, 2327, 2368, 2406, 2476, 2634, 2676, 2706, 2713a, 2716, 2780, 2844, 2859, 2883, 3000, 3021, 3053, 3125, 3145, 3213, 3238, 3362, 3403a, 3428, 3431, 3852a, 3853, 3917, 4141, 4313, 4411, 4460, 4485, 4614, 4636, 4665, 4669, 4758, 4821.

RUS–KL (5), RUS–Mbelza (1), RUS–Mcl (1), RUS–Mcm (87), RUS–Mt (5), unknown (1).

[246a, 432a, 530a, 3403a not published].

ALEKSANDROVA-KOCHETOVA, Aleksandra Dorimedontovna (b. SOKOLOVA; 1833–1902). Soprano at the Bol´shoi Theatre in Moscow, and professor at the Moscow Conservatory.

1 letter (1886) — 3097.

RUS–Mcm.

ALEKSANDROVA-LEVENSON, Anna Iakovlevna (1856–1930). Pianist and Chaikovskii's student at the Moscow Conservatory.

33 letters (1877, 1880–91, 1893) — 582, 1640, 1728, 1783, 1827, 1851, 1948, 1968, 2045, 2072, 2092, 2159, 2231, 2296, 2319, 2371, 2470, 2782, 2811, 2856, 2857, 2976, 3036a, 3283a, 3299, 3628, 3885, 3952, 3964, 3989, 4134, 4397a, 4894.

ARM–YE (1), GB–Lbm (1), RUS–KL (12), RUS–Mberggoltz, RUS–Mrg (1), RUS–SPsc (1), unknown (17).

[3283a not published].

ALEKSEEVA, Ekaterina Andreevna (b. ASSIER; 1805–82). Older sister of the composer's mother. Amateur singer (contralto).

1 letter (1867) — 105.

RUS–SPsc.

ALEXANDER III (*Tsar*; 1845–94). Emperor of Russia from 1881.

1 letter (1887) — 3269.

RUS–SPia.

ALFERAKI, Akhilles Nikolaevich [ALFERAKI, Achilles] (1846–1919). Pianist, composer and artist.

3 letters (1888, 1891) — 3558, 3623, 4449.

Locations unknown.

ALPERS, Vladimir Mikhailovich (1863–1921). Composer and journalist.

1 letter (1891) — 4543.

RUS–KL.

AL´TANI, Ippolit Karlovich [ALTANI, Ippolit] (1846–1919). Principal conductor at the Bol´shoi Theatre in Moscow.

7 letters (1884–87, 1889) — 2420, 2479, 2704, 2934, 3034, 3200, 3879.

RUS–KL (1), RUS–Mcm (6).

ARENDS, Andrei Fedorovich [ARENDS, Heinrich] (1855– 1924). Conductor, violinist and composer, and former student of Chaikovskii's at the Moscow Conservatory.

3 letters (1884–85, 1892) — 2629, 2640, 4755a.
RUS–Mt (2), RUS–Mteleshov (1).

ARENSKII, Anton (Antonii) Stepanovich (1861–1905). Composer, pianist, conductor and professor at the Moscow Conservatory.

8 letters (1884–87, 1889–91, n.d.) — 2455a, 2775, 3110, 3215, 4153, 4273a, 4431, 4471.

RUS–KL (1), RUS–SPil (7).

[4273a not published].

ARGUTINSKII-DOLGORUKOV, Vladimir Nikolaevich (1874–1941). Artist, collector and employee of the Russian Foreign Ministry.

2 letters (1888, 1890) — 3640, 4242.

RUS–Md.

ARMSGEIMER, Ivan Ivanovich [ARMSHEIMER, Johann Jozef] (1860–1933). German-born ballet composer, conductor, and trumpet and cornet player at the Mariinskii Theatre in St. Petersburg.

1 letter (1891) — 4340.

RUS–KL.

ARMSHEIMER — see ARMSGEIMER.

ARONSON, Alma. Unknown correspondent

1 letter (1893) — 4894a.

US–I.

ARTÔT–PADILLA, Desirée (b. ARTÔT, Marguerite-Joséphine Desirée Montagney; 1835–1907). Belgian opera singer, and former fiancée of the composer.

5 letters (1888–90) — 3569, 3700, 3790a, 3910, 4050.

D–Mtf (1), RUS–Md (3), unknown (1).

[3790a not published].

AUER, Leopold (Semenovich) (1845–1930). Hungarian-born violinist and conductor, and professor at the St. Petersburg Conservatory.

4 letters (1888, 1890) — 3404, 3417, 3423, 4255

RUS–Md (4).

AVENARIUS, Vasilii Petrovich (1839–1919). Dramatist, writer of children's literature and translator.

1 letter (1876) — 519.

RUS–SPil.

AVRAMOVA, Anna Konstantinovna (1848–1918). Pianist and tutor at the Moscow Conservatory.

1 letter (1882) — 2004.

RUS–KL.

AZANCHEVSKII, Mikhail Pavlovich (1837–81). Director of the St. Petersburg Conservatory.

2 letters (1871, 1875) — 238, 424.

RUS–KL (1), RUS–SPia (1).

BAKHIREVA, Avdot´ia Iakovlevna (d. 1880). Governess to Anatolii and Modest Chaikovskii during the 1850s.

1 letter (1870) — 196.

RUS–SPsc.

BALAKIREV, Milii Alekseevich (1837–1910). Composer, pianist, conductor, and founder of the Free Music School in St. Petersburg.

46 letters (1868–71, 1881–88, 1891) — 111, 114, 115, 126, 132, 133, 134, 138, 151, 152, 156, 159, 168, 170, 172, 173, 180, 181, 191, 192, 194, 205, 207, 212, 226, 233, 235, 241, 242, 1848, 2127, 2158, 2400, 2572, 2580, 2594, 2611, 2765, 2768, 2816, 2824, 2912, 3197, 3722, 4491, 4566

RUS–SPsc (46).

BASKE, Herr. German amateur musician.

1 letter (1890) — 4168.

D–Bmb.

BECKER — see BEKKER.

BEKKER, Fëdor Fedorovich [BECKER, Fëdor] (1851–1901). Singer (baritone) and choirmaster.

1 letter (1889) — 3760.

RUS–SPtob.

BENARDAKY, Marie (b. LEIBROCK, Mariia Pavlovna; d. 1913). Singer, former student at the St. Petersburg Conservatory.

2 letters (1888) — 3508, 3563a.

US–STu (1), US–Wc (1).

BERGER, Francesco (1834–1933). English pianist, composer, and secretary of the London Philharmonic Society.

5 letters (1888, 1891, 1893) — 3485, 3493, 3506, 4496, 4971.

GB–Lps (3); US–NYcub (1); unknown (1).

BERNARD, Avgust Rudol´fovich [BERNARD, August] (1852–1908). Student, later teacher at the St. Petersburg Conservatory.

1 letter (1878) — 399.

RU–SPsc.

BERNARD, Nikolai Matveevich (1844–1905). Musical publisher, and son of the founder of the St. Petersburg publishing firm M. I. Bernard.

6 letters (1875–76, 1882, 1889) — 419, 426, 440, 454, 1933, 3752.

RU–SPtob (6).

BERNUTH, Julius von (1830–1902). German conductor and impressario.

1 letter (1889) — 3791.

Location unknown (rough draft in RUS–KL).

BERTENSON, Vasilii Bernardovich (1853–1933). Physician.

1 letter (1892) — 4721.

RUS–Mcl.

BESSEL´, Vasilii Vasil´evich (1843–1907). Music publisher, violist, contemporary of Chaikovskii's at the St. Petersburg Conservatory, later editor of the journal *Muzykal´noe obozrenie*.

55 letters (1869–71, 1873–76, 1879–80, 1884–86, 1891) — 171, 216, 225, 284, 290, 292, 293, 295, 296, 299, 303, 304, 305, 308, 311, 317, 321, 322, 323, 324, 326, 332, 335, 337, 338, 339, 341, 352, 353, 358, 360, 366, 369, 376, 396, 407, 511, 1386, 1413, 1446, 1463, 1470, 1595, 1620, 1635, 2573, 2763, 2786, 3052, 3084, 3123, 3124, 3127, 3138, 4389.

RUS–KL (1), RUS–Mcm (54).

BESSON, Gustav August (1820–75). Musical instrument manufacturer.

1 letter (1892) — 4702.

Location unknown.

BEVIGNANI, Enrico Modesto (1841–1903). Conductor at the Bol´shoi Theatre in Moscow.

1 letter (1881) — 1693a.

Location unknown.

Not published.

BIBIKOV, Vladimir Illarionovich. Civil servant.

1 letter (1892) — 4630.

RUS–KL.

BLAVET, Émil. Journalist on the French newspaper *Figaro*.

1 letter (1888) — 3514.

F–Pn.

BOCK, Hugo (1848–1932). Son of Gustav Bock, co-founder of the Berlin music–publishing firm Bote & Bock.

2 letters (1884, 1893) — 2634a, 5021.

RUS–KL (1), unknown (1).

BOLSKA, Adelina Iulianovna (b. SKOMPSKA; *later* SCZAWINSKA-BROCHOCKI, *Countess*; 1863–1930). Soprano at the Bol´shoi Theatre in Moscow.

3 letters (1889, 1892–93) — 3887, 4662, 4946.

RUS–Mcm.

BORISOGLEBSKII, Sergei Alekseevich (1863–1926). Opera singer (baritone) with the Imperial Theatres.

2 letters (1892) — 4680, 4688.

RUS–KL.

BORISOV, Pavel Borisovich (1850–1904). Singer (baritone).

1 letter (1884) — 2421.

RUS–KL.

BRANDUKOV, Anatolii Andreevich (1856–1930). Cellist, teacher, conductor, and former student of Chaikovskii's at the Moscow Conservatory.

17 letters (1886–89, 1893, n.d.) — 2967, 2972, 2997, 3009, 3029, 3032, 3186, 3310, 3317, 3329, 3546, 3851, 3933, 3960, 4892, 5050, 5056.

RUS–KL.

BRODSKAIA, Anna L´vovna [BRODSKY, Anna] (b. SKADOVSKAIA; 1855–?). Wife of Adol´f Brodskii.

3 letters (1888–91) — 3688, 3793, 4488.

GB–Mcm.

BRODSKII, Adol´f Davidovich [BRODSKY, Adolph] (1851–1929). Violinist and concertmaster.

15 letters (1882, 1886–89, 1891) — 1924, 2008, 2013, 2036, 3111, 3169, 3444, 3526, 3868, 3877, 3898, 3938, 3949, 4488, 4515

GB–Mcm (14), RUS–Mcm (1).

BRODSKY — *see* BRODSKAIA, BRODSKII.

BRUNEAU, Alfred (1857–1934). French composer and critic, and President of the International Composer's Union in Paris.

1 letter (1884) — 2453a.

D–Tu.

BÜLOW, Hans (Guido) von (1830–94). German pianist, conductor, composer and music critic.

6 letters (1875–76, 1878, 1885) — 406a, 413a, 418, 443, 907a, 2836a.

CH–Bkoch (1), D–Bds (2), US–NH (1), US–Wc (1), unknown (1).

BÜLOW, Marie von (b. SCHLANZER; 1857–1941). Second wife of Hans von Bülow.

1 letter (1888) — 3469.

GB–Lbl.

BURMESTER, Willy (1869–1933). German violinst.

4 letters (1888–89) — 3659, 3689, 3784, 3935.

D–AMlohss (1), D–EMoestrich (1), unknown (2).

CATOIRE — *see* KATUAR.

ČECH, Adolf (1841–1903). Principal conductor at the National Theatre in Prague.

5 letters (1888, 1891) — 3676, 3702, 3745, 4489, 4513.

CZ–Pkadlic (4), unknown (1).

ČERVINKOVÁ-RIEGROVÁ, Marie (1854–95). Czech writer, translator and librettist.

1 letter (1888) — 3668.

CZ–Ps.

CHAIKOVSKAIA, Aleksandra Andreevna (b. ASSIER; 1813–54). Mother of the composer.

39 letters (1850–52) — 9, 10, 11, 12, 13, 14, 15, 16, 17, 18, 19, 20, 21, 22, 23, 24, 25, 26, 27, 28, 29, 32, 33, 34, 35, 36, 37, 39, 40, 41, 42, 43, 44, 45, 46, 47, 48, 49, 50.

RUS–KL (2), RUS–SPsc (4).

CHAIKOVSKAIA, Antonina Ivanova (b. MILIUKOVA; 1849–1917). Wife of the composer.

1 letter (1890) — 4019.

RUS–KL.

CHAIKOVSKAIA, Elizaveta Mikhailovna (b. LIPPORT). The composer's stepmother, third wife of Il'ia Petrovich Chaikovskii.

8 letters (1865–66, 1877, 1880–81, 1889–90, n.d.) — 76, 81, 549, 1584a, 1833, 3980, 4266, 4819a.

RUS–SPsc.

CHAIKOVSKAIA, Ol'ga Sergeevna (b. DENIS'EVA). Wife of the composer's brother Nikolai.

14 letters (1885–93) — 2737, 2914a, 3272, 3575, 3594, 3741, 3971, 4267, 4430, 4718, 4802, 4808, 4987.

RUS–SPsc.

CHAIKOVSKAIA, Praskov'ia Vladimirovna (b. KONSHINA; 1864–1956). Wife of the composer's brother Anatolii.

108 letters (1883–93) — 2203, 2345, 2353, 2369, 2378, 2433, 2443, 2469, 2478, 2490, 2496, 2503, 2510, 2541, 2546, 2547, 2583, 2591, 2608, 2656, 2663, 2770, 2776, 2783, 2794, 2801, 2805, 2807, 2810, 2821, 2826, 2835, 2840, 2864, 2876, 2881, 2897, 2914, 2916, 2942, 2952, 2956, 2961, 2968, 2974, 2999, 3005, 3022, 3040, 3049, 3075, 3087, 3092, 3112, 3121, 3155, 3167, 3190, 3199, 3206, 3217, 3226, 3241, 3250, 3258, 3260, 3284, 3289, 3308, 3311, 3315, 3316, 3439, 3452, 3488, 3495, 3549, 3562, 3579, 3586, 3630, 3697, 3733, 3737, 3806, 3871, 4099, 4233, 4243, 4247, 4260, 4281, 4318, 4338, 4360, 4368, 4393, 4466, 4573, 4595, 4652, 4659, 4667, 4670, 4672, 4690, 4831, 4980.

RUS–KL (104), unknown (4).

CHAIKOVSKAIA, Sof'ia Petrovna (b. NIKONOVA; 1843–1920). Wife of the composer's brother Ippolit.

1 letter (1887) — 3212.

RUS–SPsc.

CHAIKOVSKII, Anatolii Il'ich (1850–1915). Younger brother of the composer.

562 letters (1866–93) — 77, 78, 79, 83, 84, 85, 88, 89, 91, 92, 93, 96, 97, 98, 102, 104, 108, 110, 112, 113, 118, 121, 122, 129, 131, 136, 137, 139, 140, 141, 143, 145, 146, 148, 150, 153, 157, 160, 164, 165, 167, 182, 184, 189, 195, 200, 204, 210, 217, 227, 228, 230, 234, 237, 243, 249, 252, 268, 273, 274, 309, 325, 336, 349, 372, 385, 394, 400, 425, 429, 446, 449, 453, 464, 467, 471, 475, 480, 483, 498, 504, 509, 522, 536, 558, 564, 567, 571, 573, 579, 581, 581a, 583, 596, 598, 602, 666, 669, 670, 672, 674, 678, 683, 686, 691, 693, 695, 700, 703, 706, 708, 709, 710, 715, 718, 721, 726, 730, 734, 737, 742, 744, 747, 751, 756, 759,

CHAIKOVSKII, Andrei Petrovich (1841–1920).
Cousin of the composer, and commander of the
98th Yurevskii Regiment.

CHAIKOVSKII, Georgii Nikolaevich [DAVYDOV,
Georges-Léon] (1883–1940). Son of the
composer's niece, Tat'iana Davydova; later
adopted by NIkolai & Ol'ga Chaikovskii.

CHAIKOVSKII, Il'ia Petrovich (1795–80). Father
of the composer.

CHAIKOVSKII, Ippolit Il'ich (1843–1927).
Younger brother of the composer.

CHAIKOVSKII, Modest Il'ich (1850–1916).
Writer, dramatist and younger brother of the
composer.

1567, 1629, 1637, 1644, 1647, 1651, 1652, 1657,
1661, 1683, 1686, 1689, 1693, 1695, 1697, 1701,
1707, 1709, 1716, 1734, 1742, 1748, 1753, 1764,
1765, 1769, 1778, 1785, 1790, 1792, 1797, 1805,
1809, 1815, 1818, 1819, 1823, 1824, 1828, 1834,
1838, 1843, 1852, 1858, 1869, 1872, 1879, 1881,
1886, 1960, 1964, 1994, 1995, 1996, 1997, 2000,
2002, 2006, 2018, 2021, 2026, 2031, 2033,
2077, 2081, 2085, 2090, 2103, 2109, 2112, 2118,
2123, 2132, 2137, 2145, 2146a, 2152, 2156,
2163, 2164, 2168, 2171, 2183, 2187, 2192, 2256,
2258, 2260, 2261, 2262, 2266, 2268, 2270, 2272,
2275, 2277, 2283, 2284, 2286, 2288, 2299, 2303,
2308, 2310, 2314, 2316, 2321, 2326, 2328, 2338,
2341, 2344, 2348, 2354, 2357, 2361, 2363, 2370,
2374, 2379, 2386, 2391, 2412, 2414, 2416, 2428,
2434, 2436, 2440, 2444, 2457, 2460, 2462, 2464,
2468, 2471, 2475, 2481, 2491, 2497, 2500, 2521,
2523, 2526, 2527, 2538, 2542, 2544, 2554, 2558,
2584, 2586, 2592, 2599, 2601, 2606, 2610, 2617,
2623, 2636, 2637, 2644, 2651, 2655, 2658, 2662,
2666, 2671, 2673, 2680, 2688, 2694, 2699, 2761,
2767, 2771, 2779, 2784, 2788, 2797, 2798, 2803,
2809, 2813, 2818, 2823, 2832, 2836, 2860, 2871,
2874, 2882, 2885, 2894, 2898, 2900a, 2903,
2919, 2921, 2929, 2933, 2938, 2940, 2943, 2948,
2950, 2953, 2957, 2959, 2962, 2971, 2973, 2979,
2985, 2993, 3006, 3020, 3024, 3041, 3044, 3050,
3062, 3069, 3073, 3103, 3108, 3113, 3115, 3122,
3139b, 3156, 3162, 3168, 3172, 3181, 3201,
3207, 3218, 3222, 3232, 3242, 3247, 3248, 3261,
3285, 3287, 3298, 3301, 3304, 3307, 3309, 3316,
3319, 3321, 3322, 3323, 3325, 3326, 3328, 3330,
3331, 3340, 3352, 3381, 3400, 3413, 3426, 3438,
3440, 3453, 3464, 3468, 3472, 3478, 3484, 3490,
3496, 3502, 3507, 3511, 3517, 3520, 3523, 3531,
3534, 3539, 3544, 3568, 3573, 3585, 3597, 3602,
3610, 3616, 3622, 3627, 3650, 3654, 3661, 3672,
3679, 3686, 3695, 3698, 3764, 3765, 3778, 3782,
3790, 3795, 3812, 3818, 3823, 3825, 3828, 3829,
3835, 3839, 3845, 3869, 3927, 3937, 3946, 3961,
4006, 4009, 4012, 4013, 4022, 4027, 4034, 4044,
4045, 4049, 4051, 4053, 4055, 4056, 4058, 4060,
4067, 4070, 4071, 4072, 4077, 4079, 4083, 4089,
4095, 4110, 4112, 4117, 4145, 4149, 4155, 4159,
4166, 4169, 4189, 4213, 4218, 4231, 4236, 4248,
4253, 4264, 4273, 4275, 4283, 4291, 4300, 4339,
4364, 4365, 4367, 4376, 4378, 4379, 4403, 4413,
4425, 4427, 4439a, 4448, 4452, 4469, 4502,
4507, 4517, 4519, 4528, 4530, 4553, 4589b,
4563, 4574, 4578, 4590, 4597, 4610, 4623, 4625,
4644, 4658, 4664, 4666a, 4668, 4678, 4695,
4701, 4706, 4710, 4717, 4734, 4742, 4744, 4755,
4767, 4772, 4775, 4784, 4826, 4828, 4833, 4836,
4844, 4852, 4858, 4878, 4888, 4897, 4899, 4919,
4921, 4934, 4940, 4945, 4956, 4961, 4984, 4991,
5000, 5006, 5011, 5012, 5018, 5028, 5029, 5031,
5042, 5045, 5065a

RUS–KL (628), RUS–Md (3), RUS–SPsc (41), US–
NYtollefsen (1), unknown (7).

[3139b, 4589b, 4666a, 5065a not published].

CHAIKOVSKII, Nikolai Il´ich (1838–1911). Older
brother of the composer.

16 letters (1871, 1884–87, 1890–93) — 240, 2466,
2737, 2750, 2785, 2796, 2804, 2814, 3135,
3374a, 4046, 4377, 4387, 4430, 4718, 4799,
4835, 4987.

RUS–SPsc.

CHEKHOV, Anton Pavlovich (1860–1904). Writer
and dramatist.

3 letters (1889, 1891) — 3958, 3962, 4522.

RUS–Mrg.

**CHISTIAKOVA-MIKHALEVSKAIA,   Iuliia
Iosifovna** (b. KOTEK). Sister of Iosif Kotek.

2 letters (1885) — 2643a, 2664a.

RUS–KL.

Not published.

CHOKIN, Pavel Aleksandrovich. Friend of Vladimir
Shilovskii.

2 letters (n.d.) — 434, 435.

RUS–Mt.

COLES — see KOL´S.

COLLIN, Paul (1843–1915). French poet and
translator.

1 letter (1892) — 4810.

F–Phofmann.

COLOMBO, Emilio (1875–1937). Italian musician.

1 letter (1892) — 4719.

I–Rcolombo.

COLONNE, Edouard (b. COLONNE, Judas; 1838–
1910). French conductor, violinist and composer,
editor of *La Gazette Musicale*.

10 letters (1879, 1886, 1888–90, 1892) — 1122,
1210a, 2965, 3467, 3475, 3591, 3774a, 3796,
3998, 4150, 4602.

CH–B (1), F–P (2), F–Pn (1), F–Po (2), RUS–KL (1)
US–CAM (2), unknown (1).

[3774a not published].

CONRADI — *see* KONRADI.

CONUS — *see* KONIUS.

DAMROSCH, Walter (1862–1930). American
conductor, pianist and composer.

1 letter (1891) — 4432.

US–Wc.

DANNREUTHER, Edward (1844–1905). English pianist.

1 letter (1876) — 455.

Location unknown.

DAVYDOV, Georges Léon — *see* CHAIKOVSKII, Georgii Nikolaevich.

DAVYDOV, Karl Iul´evich (1838–89). Cellist, composer and conductor. Professor and director of the St. Petersburg Conservatory.

13 letters (1872, 1875, 1878, 1880, 1883–84, 1886) — 264, 451, 508, 950, 1414, 1464, 1634, 1740, 2297, 2472, 2850, 2902, 2939.

RUS–KL (12), RUS–Mcl (1).

DAVYDOV, Lev Vasil´evich (1837–96). Husband of the composer´s sister Aleksandra.

37 letters (1866, 1870, 1875–85) — 80, 90, 188, 410, 495, 523, 566, 575, 667, 757, 908, 932, 1017, 1117, 1135, 1279, 1378, 1395, 1522, 1530, 1547, 1714, 1717, 1853, 2052, 2058, 2065, 2177, 2214, 2278, 2301, 2306, 2508, 2516, 2588, 2693.

RUS–KL (6), RUS–SPsc (31).

DAVYDOV, Vladimir L´vovich (1871–1906). Son of the composer´s sister Aleksandra.

43 letters (1889–93) — 3805, 3809, 3814, 3830, 4080, 4139, 4228, 4342, 4348, 4362, 4369, 4380, 4399, 4420, 4436, 4440, 4442, 4450, 4508, 4509, 4548, 4583, 4584, 4593, 4599, 4732, 4743, 4752, 4753, 4761, 4827, 4829, 4840, 4865, 4913, 4916, 4931, 4935, 4972, 4998, 5002, 5015, 5047.

RUS–KL (42), RUS–Mcl (1).

DAVYDOVA, Aleksandra Il´inichna (b. CHAIKOVSKAIA; 1842–91). Younger sister of the composer.

79 letters (1861–71, 1873, 1875–79) — 54, 55, 60, 61, 62, 63, 66, 68, 70, 71, 72, 73, 75, 80, 86, 90, 94, 95, 100, 101, 106, 116, 117, 120, 149, 158, 169, 179, 199, 219, 229, 244, 285, 301, 404, 487, 499, 503, 513, 523, 526, 531, 532, 534, 537, 543, 575, 587, 612, 615, 618, 627, 628, 634, 641, 645, 649, 654, 667, 682, 688, 704, 717, 774, 786, 831, 839, 845, 908, 954, 979, 1078, 1109, 1214, 1215, 1220, 1222, 1288.

RUS–SPsc (78), unknown (1).

DAVYDOVA, Anna L´vovna (1863–1942). Daughter of the composer's sister Aleksandra. Later married to Nikolai von Meck.

1 letter (1882) — 2017.

RUS–Mrg.

DAVYDOVA, Tat´iana L´vovna (1861–87). Eldest daughter of the composer's sister Aleksandra.

2 letters (1878, 1881) — 937, 1702.

RUS–SPsc.

DELABORDE, Henri (*Count*, 1811–99). French critic, Secretary of the Académie Française.

1 letter (1892) — 4809.

F–Pi.

DÉTROYAT, (Pierre) Léonce (1829–98). French journalist and librettist.

4 letters (1888, 1889) — 3563b, 3598a, 3712a, 3905a.

F–Plauwe (1), unknown (3).

DIÉMER, Louis (1843–1919). French pianist, professor at the Paris Conservatory.

1 letter (1888) — 3504.

D–LEmi.

DOOR, Anton (Andreevich) (1833–1919). Pianist and professor at the Moscow and Vienna Conservatories

3 letters (1876, 1877, 1892) — 444a, 614, 4771.

Locations unknown.

DUNAEVSKII, Pavel Fëdorovich (1862–1911). Operatic baritone and director.

1 letter (1892) — 4708.

RUS–Mcm.

DÜRBACH, Fanny (1822–1901). Chaikovskii's governess from 1844 to 1848

6 letters (1848–50, 1856) — 3, 4, 5, 6, 7, 8, 53.

Locations unknown.

DÜRBACH, Frederika. Younger sister of Fanny Dürbach.

1 letter (1848) — 2.

RUS–SPsc.

DUSAUTOY, Jacques. French composer and pianist.

2 letters (1887, 1891) — 3219a, 4357.

D–Tu (1), RUS–KL (1).

DVOŘÁK, Antonín (1841–1904). Czech composer, conductor, and professor at the Prague Conservatory.

3 letters (1888–89) — 3529, 3772, 3800.

CZ–ZL.

ERDMANNSDÖRFER, Max (1848–1905). German conductor, composer and teacher, principal conductor of the Moscow branch of the RMS from 1882

2 letters (1886, n.d.) — 2984a, 3139a.

RUS–KL (1), unknown (1).

[2984a not published].

ERDMANNSDÖRFER-RICHTER, Paulina (1847–1916). German pianist, and wife of Max Erdmannsdörfer.

2 letters (1886, 1889) — 3014a, 3772a.

D–Tu (1), unknown (1)

ERMOLOVA, Mariia Nikolaevna (1853–1928). Actress at the Malyi Theatre in Moscow.

1 letter (1886) — 2815.

Location unknown.

FËDOROV, Pavel Stepanovich (1809–79). Author and translator.

2 letters (1869, 1872) — 144, 256.

RUS–SPia.

FEDOTOV, Aleksandr Filippovich (1841–95). Actor, director, teacher and dramatist.

1 letter (1892) — 4626.

RUS–Mt.

FEDOTOVA, Glikeriia Nikolaevna (1846–1925). Actress at the Malyi Theatre in Moscow.

1 letter (1884) — 2571.

RUS–KL.

FERNOW, *Madame*. German artist.

1 letter (1879) — 1332a.

J–private.

Not published.

FERNOW, *Monsieur* de. American agent.

1 letter (1890) — 4197a.

Location unknown.

FIGNER, Nikolai Nikolaevich (1857–1918). Principal tenor with the Imperial Opera in St. Petersburg.

1 letter (1890) — 4197.

Location unknown.

FILATOV, Vasilii Nikolaevich. Servant to Anatolii Chaikovskii in Tiflis.

3 letters (1886–87, 1891) — 2880, 3318, 4402.

RUS–KL.

FITINGHOFF-SCHELL — *see* FITINGOF-SHEL´.

FITINGOF-SHEL´, Boris Aleksandrovich [FITINGHOFF-SCHELL, *Baron*] (1829–1901). Composer.

2 letters (1887, 1890) — 3394, 4262.

RUS–SPsc.

FLEROV, Sergei Vasil´evich (1841–1901). Teacher, journalist and musical critic.

5 letters (1881–82, 1884) — 1713, 1755, 1774, 1943, 1956.

RUS–Mcl (2), RUS–Mcm (1), Mt (2).

FOERSTER, Josef Bohuslav (1859–1951). Czech composer and music critic.

3 letters (1892–93) — 4790, 4862, 4900.

CZ–Pfoerster.

FOERSTROVÁ-LAUTEREROVÁ, Berta (1869–1936). Czech soprano, and wife of Josef Bohuslav Foerster.

3 letters (1889, 1892) — 3854, 3867, 4777a.

CZ–Pfoerster (2), H–Bkuna (1).

FON-MEKK — *see* MECK.

FOUCARD, Louis de. French writer and music critic.

1 letter (1884) — 2567.

Location unknown.

FROLOV, Vladmir Iakovlevich (d. 1895). Clarinettist with the Bol´shoi Theatre Orchestra in Moscow.

1 letter (1889) — 3977.

RUS–KL.

FÜRSTNER, Adolf (1833–1908). German music publisher.

1 letter (1879) — 1354.

Location unknown.

GALLET, Louis (1835–98). French writer and librettist.

1 letter (1891) — 4288a.

F–Plauwe.

GALLI, Anatolii Ivanovich (1845–1915). Pianist and professor at the Moscow Conservatory.
1 letter (1885) — 2681.
RUS–KL.

GARTEVEL´D — *see* HARTEVELD.

GARTUNG, Iakov Fëdorvich [HARTUNG, Iakov] (1842–1900). Chemical engineer, and brother-in-law of Pavel Tret´iakov.
2 letters (1884, 1886) — 2418a, 3119.
RUS–KL.

(LE) GAULOIS. Letter to the editor [Maurice Ordonneau] of the Parisian newspaper.
1 letter (1884) — 2291.
Location unknown.

(LA) GAZETTE MUSICALE. Letter to the editor [Edouard Colonne] of the French journal.
1 letter (1879) — 1122.
Location unknown.

GEDEONOV, Stepan Aleksandrovich (1816–78). Historian and director of the Imperial Theatres in St. Petersburg.
2 letters (1869, n. d.) — 154, 254a.
RUS–SPia (1), RUS–SPsc (1).

GENKE, Lidiia Petrovna (1838–1901). Elder sister of Il´ia Chaikovskii, and aunt of the composer.
9 letters (1876–77, 1884, 1886, 1888–89, 1891) — 516, 529, 547, 2624, 2627, 3128, 3629, 3965, 4536.
RUS–Mcl.

GENKE, Vera Emil´evna (later OLËNINA; 1868–1960). Daughter of Lidiia Genke.
2 letters (1885, 1891) — 2837, 4547.
RUS–Mcl.

GERKE, Avgust Antonovich (1841–1902). Lawyer, and contemporary of Chaikovskii's at the Imperial School of Jurisprudence.
3 letters (1887, 1889) — 3342, 3972, 3974.
RUS–SPia (1), RUS–SPsc (2).

GINTSBURG, Il´ia Iakovlevich [GINZBURG, Il´ia] (1859–1939). Sculptor.
1 letter (1892) — 4813.
RUS–KL.

GINZBURG — *see* GINTSBURG.

GIPPIUS, Adelina Eduardovna. Pianist and music teacher.
1 letters (1876) — 567a.
Location unknown.

GLAZUNOV, Aleksandr Konstantinovich (1865–1936). Composer, conductor and professor at the St. Petersburg Conservatory.
13 letters (1887, 1889–92) — 3434, 3794, 3942, 3967, 3970, 3990, 3993, 4003, 4018, 4325, 4382a, 4637, 4822.
RUS–KL (3), unknown (10).

GLAZUNOVA, Elena Pavlovna (b. TURYGINA; d. 1925). Mother of Aleksandr Glazunov.
1 letter (1892) — 4816.
RUS–SPsemenov.

GOLOS. Letters to the editor [Andrei Kraevskii] of the Moscow Journal.
2 letters (1873, 1875) — 291, 387.
RUS–KL (1), unknown (1).

GOLOVINA, Mariia Alekseevna (d. 1878). Pianist and student of Chaikovskii's at the Moscow Conservatory.
1 letter (1875) — 416.
RUS–Mcl.

GÖRING, Gottfried — *see* KORSOV, Bogomir Bogomirovich.

GREKOV, Ivan Nikolaevich (1849–1919). Actor at the Malyi Theatre, Moscow, and manager of the Odessa Opera House.
1 letter (1893) — 5065.
Location unknown.

GRIEG, Edvard (Hagerup) (1843–1907). Norwegian composer, pianist and conductor.
3 letters (1888) — 3499, 3552, 3655.
N–Bo.

GROT, Iakov Karlovich (1812–93). Vice-President of the Academy of Sciences, and editor of the *Dictionary of the Russian Language*.
3 letters (1892–93) — 4685, 4793, 4881.
RUS–SPaa (2), RUS–SPil (1).

GUBERT — *see* HUBERT.

GUTMANN, Albert. Organiser of the 1892 International Musical Exhibition in Vienna.

1 letter (1892) — 4654.

US–Wc.

HARTEVELD, Wilhelm Julius Napoleon [GARTEVEL´D, Wil´gel´m Napolenovich] (1859–1927). Swedish-born composer, conductor and pianist, resident in Russia from 1882 to 1918.

1 letter (1890) — 4268

RUS–KL.

HARTUNG — *see* GARTUNG.

HARTVIGSON, Frits (1841–1919). Danish pianist.

4 letters (1877, 1893) — 548a, 4938, 4943, 4943a.

F–Plauwe (1), unknown (3).

HATZFELD, Emil (1857–?). English music publisher and amateur composer.

1 letter (1893) — 4951.

Location unknown.

HENNINGS, Henrik. Danish musician and teacher.

1 letter (1892) — 4607.

D–H.

HERTZ, Michał (1844–?). Polish conductor, composer and music teacher.

1 letter (1893) — 5020.

RUS–Mt.

HIPKINS, Alfred (James) (1826–1903). English pianist and musicologist.

1 letter (1893) — 4882.

US–NYpm.

HOTEL CONSTANZY. Guest–house in Rome, where Chaikovskii stayed during 1879 and 1880.

1 letter to the *Hotel Constanzy* (n. d.) — 1390.

RUS–KL.

HUBERT, Aleksandra [GUBERT, Aleksandra Ivanovna] (b. BATALINA, 1950–1937). Pianist, and wife of Nikolai Hubert. Later a director of the Moscow Conservatory.

65 letters (1882–93) — 2100, 2366, 2552, 2674, 2684, 2692, 2714a, 2720, 2754, 2773, 2847a, 2892, 2905, 2908, 2923, 2983, 3004, 3030, 3076, 3098, 3117, 3129, 3148, 3179, 3220, 3240, 3252, 3263, 3270, 3282, 3343, 3378, 3423a, 3449, 3470, 3486, 3528, 3559, 3611, 3681, 3706, 3836, 3850, 3866, 3880, 3896, 3902, 3905, 3940, 3954, 4105, 4274, 4284, 4287, 4314, 4414, 4419, 4441, 4516, 4534, 4544, 4615, 4681, 5014, 5032.

RUS–KL.

[2847a not published].

HUBERT, Nikolai [GUBERT, Nikolai Al´bertovich] (1840–88). Chaikovskii's contemporary at the St. Petersburg conservatory, later a professor and director of the Moscow Conservatory.

25 letters (1882–88) — 2093, 2128, 2300, 2307, 2495, 2676a, 2684, 2754, 2905, 2908, 2983, 3004, 3030, 3117, 3270, 3282, 3290, 3343, 3423a, 3449, 3470, 3481, 3496, 3611, 3642.

RUS–KL.

IMPERATORSKOE RUSSKOE MUZYKAL´NOE OBSHCHESTVO — *see* RUSSIAN MUSICAL SOCIETY.

IPPOLITOV-IVANOV, Mikhail Mikhailovich (1859–1935). Composer, conductor and professor at the Moscow Conservatory.

30 letters (1885–93) — 2828, 2838, 2995, 3011, 3271, 3293, 3373, 3411, 3543, 3595, 3612, 3635, 3710, 3858, 3875, 3919, 4107, 4135, 4171, 4279, 4326, 4394, 4421, 4514, 4657, 4729, 4759, 4901, 4974, 5023.

RUS–KL (26), RUS–Mcl (1), RUS–Mcm (1), USA–NH (1), unknown (1).

IURASOV, Pavel Ivanovich. Accountant for Pëtr Iurgenson's publishing firm.

1 letter (1887) — 3274.

RUS–KL.

IURGENSON, Aleksandr Osipovich [JURGENSON, Alexander] (d. 1890). Son of Osip Iurgenson.

2 letters (1889) — 3893, 3916.

RUS–KL (1), RUS–Mcl (1).

IURGENSON, Aleksandra Petrovna (*later* SNEGIREVA; 1869–1946). Daughter of Pëtr Iurgenson.

6 letters (1884, 1886–87, n.d.) — 2633, 2878, 2906, 2907, 2991, 3389.

RUS–KL.

IURGENSON, Boris Petrovich [IURGENSON, Boris] (1868–1935). Son of Pëtr Iurgenson.

10 letters (1886–89, 1891–93) — 2936, 3292, 3718, 3897, 3916, 4409, 4416, 4428, 4640, 4904.

RUS–KL (9), RUS–Mcm (1).

IURGENSON, Osip (Iosif) Ivanovich [JURGENSON, Josef] (1829–1910). Older brother of Pëtr Iurgenson.

9 letters (1889–91, n. d.) — 3901, 3995, 4023, 4258, 4612a, 4624a, 4576, 4597a, 4930a.

RUS–KL (5), RUS–Mcl (2), RUS–SPsc (1), unknown (1).

[4264a, 4612a, 4930a not published].

IURGENSON, Pëtr Ivanovich [JURGENSON, Peter] (1836–1903). Chaikovskii's principal publisher.

741 letters (1866, 1868–69, 1871–93, n.d.) — 95a, 97a, 128, 142, 236, 250, 253, 258, 263, 267, 269, 271, 282, 283, 302, 310, 313, 314, 319, 328, 329, 330, 333, 359, 362, 363, 380, 381, 399, 408, 436, 456, 496, 506, 510, 512, 515, 550, 585, 586, 591, 603, 604, 607, 611, 620, 632, 647, 657, 663, 677, 690, 697, 714, 725, 733, 739, 741, 750, 752, 761, 767, 772, 789, 800, 810, 812, 816, 818, 824, 828, 835, 858, 861, 865, 870, 872, 883, 885, 888, 891, 913, 918, 929, 942, 946, 949, 953, 964, 968, 978, 1002, 1014, 1028, 1031, 1044, 1048, 1053, 1055, 1061, 1069, 1075, 1086, 1091, 1098, 1108, 1113, 1114, 1123, 1125, 1128, 1134, 1141, 1144, 1155, 1157, 1161, 1173, 1182, 1189, 1190a, 1194, 1200, 1202, 1205, 1213, 1218, 1224, 1230, 1236, 1242, 1247, 1252, 1264, 1266, 1272, 1274, 1285, 1291, 1295, 1300, 1304, 1318, 1319, 1325, 1328, 1330, 1331, 1345, 1355, 1363, 1368, 1373, 1380, 1384, 1397, 1404, 1415, 1422, 1430, 1455, 1459, 1462, 1476, 1480, 1481, 1486, 1488, 1492, 1495a, 1498, 1501, 1502, 1514, 1517, 1525, 1540, 1543, 1545, 1549, 1555, 1556, 1559, 1562, 1563, 1566, 1572, 1573, 1577, 1581, 1582, 1584, 1588, 1591, 1593, 1596, 1600, 1610, 1612, 1619, 1626, 1638, 1642, 1691, 1699, 1727, 1737, 1739, 1743, 1745, 1749, 1757, 1758, 1761, 1767, 1776, 1777, 1779, 1791, 1803, 1810, 1821, 1832, 1835, 1837, 1846, 1849, 1863, 1866, 1867, 1874, 1875, 1880, 1882, 1885, 1888, 1890, 1894, 1911, 1914, 1923, 1926, 1930, 1934, 1939, 1945, 1952, 1954, 1955, 1965, 1966, 1971, 1976, 1977, 1978, 1983, 1984, 1985, 2010, 2019, 2024, 2028, 2032, 2038, 2043, 2048, 2054, 2060, 2063, 2064, 2069, 2082, 2095a, 2097, 2102, 2108, 2113, 2115, 2125, 2133, 2141, 2142, 2143, 2162, 2180, 2188, 2190, 2193, 2202, 2206, 2213, 2218, 2219, 2221, 2225, 2230, 2235, 2239, 2242, 2245, 2246, 2248, 2250, 2254, 2263, 2267, 2280, 2312, 2318, 2334a, 2334b, 2346, 2352, 2359, 2365, 2367, 2372, 2373, 2381, 2382, 2387, 2388, 2389, 2390, 2396, 2404, 2405, 2409, 2425, 2429, 2432, 2439, 2445, 2447, 2451, 2455, 2473, 2480, 2485, 2489, 2493, 2498, 2504, 2507, 2511, 2515, 2522, 2530, 2531, 2548, 2555, 2559, 2561, 2563, 2565, 2568, 2569, 2577, 2579, 2587, 2596, 2600, 2602, 2615, 2625, 2632, 2645, 2654, 2659, 2660, 2668, 2669, 2675, 2684, 2695, 2696, 2703, 2711, 2726, 2746, 2751, 2753, 2767a, 2774, 2777, 2781, 2789, 2817, 2841, 2842, 2846, 2848, 2849, 2858, 2862, 2866, 2867, 2887, 2917, 2920, 2926, 2927, 2931, 2935, 2941, 2954, 2963, 2978, 2981, 2982, 2986, 2987, 2992, 2994, 3003, 3007, 3008, 3025, 3027, 3028, 3033, 3045, 3051, 3061, 3072, 3077, 3078, 3081, 3094, 3104, 3182, 3185, 3209, 3219, 3221, 3224, 3225, 3228, 3230, 3233, 3234, 3235, 3237, 3253, 3267, 3275, 3281, 3305, 3332, 3333, 3334, 3341, 3345, 3353, 3355, 3356, 3359, 3365, 3368, 3369, 3371, 3372, 3375, 3376, 3380, 3382, 3383, 3385, 3386, 3396, 3398, 3416, 3427, 3432, 3433, 3435a, 3437, 3442, 3448, 3473, 3480, 3489, 3492, 3503, 3512, 3513, 3518, 3525, 3532, 3535, 3540, 3545, 3556, 3565, 3570, 3575a, 3581, 3583, 3598, 3608, 3618, 3619, 3620, 3632, 3633, 3639, 3641, 3646, 3662, 3666, 3667, 3671, 3677, 3680, 3692, 3699, 3703, 3709, 3717, 3728, 3729, 3735, 3744, 3746, 3754, 3757, 3767, 3771, 3773, 3777, 3783, 3786, 3787, 3804, 3813, 3821, 3826, 3827, 3832, 3837, 3841, 3846, 3856, 3873, 3921, 3948, 3953, 3983, 3984, 3986, 3987, 3991, 3999, 4000, 4002, 4004, 4007, 4010, 4012a, 4015, 4017, 4020, 4024, 4035, 4036, 4040, 4043, 4048, 4054, 4057, 4061, 4063, 4066, 4073, 4084, 4085, 4090, 4096, 4097, 4100, 4102, 4104, 4111, 4113, 4115, 4118, 4120, 4123, 4125, 4126, 4127, 4128, 4129, 4131, 4137, 4138, 4146, 4152, 4156, 4157, 4163, 4170, 4175, 4175a, 4178, 4182, 4183, 4190, 4192, 4199, 4200, 4202, 4207, 4209, 4215, 4216, 4224, 4226, 4227, 4232, 4234, 4237, 4240, 4244, 4249, 4251, 4252, 4256, 4261, 4262a, 4272, 4277, 4278, 4262a, 4292, 4301, 4305, 4309, 4310, 4311, 4316, 4317, 4319, 4322, 4323, 4330, 4332, 4334, 4341, 4344, 4345, 4354, 4361, 4397, 4408, 4454, 4459, 4470, 4473, 4481, 4482, 4487, 4495, 4497, 4505, 4506, 4511, 4518, 4533, 4546, 4555, 4557, 4562, 4565, 4567, 4568, 4572, 4586, 4589, 4598, 4604, 4606, 4608, 4609, 4611, 4634, 4641, 4643, 4645, 4646, 4647, 4649, 4653, 4655, 4661, 4675, 4676, 4679, 4683, 4686, 4687, 4689, 4711, 4714, 4720, 4723, 4725, 4726, 4727, 4728, 4731, 4735, 4736, 4737, 4740, 4741, 4745, 4747, 4756, 4757, 4766, 4834, 4924, 4929, 4930, 4942, 4954, 4962, 4964, 4967, 4970, 4981, 4988, 4992, 5001, 5010, 5019, 5025, 5027, 5052, 5062

RUS–KL (733), RUS–Mcl (3), RUS–Mcm (2), RUS–SPsc (2), US–Wc (1).

[1190a, 1495a, 2095a, 2334a, 2334b, 3435a, 4012a, 4175a not published].

IURGENSON, Sof´ia Ivanovna [IURGENSON, Sofia] (1840–1911). Wife of Pëtr Iurgenson

15 letters (1879, 1884–87, 1893) — 1208, 2486, 2713, 2721a, 2723, 2724, 2725, 2730, 2734, 2739, 2743, 3109, 3173, 3178, 5039.

RUS–KL (13), RUS–Mcm (2).

[2721a not published].

IVANOV, Fëdor Alekseevich (1853–1919). Choral conductor and composer.

1 letter (n. d.) — 3020a.

RUS–Mt.

IVANOVA, Varvara — see ZARUDNAIA, Varvara Mikhailovna.

JAMESON, Francis Arthur. Englishman.

1 letter (1893) — 4856a

US–LJ.

JURGENSON — see IURGENSON.

KAJANUS, Robert (1856–1933). Finnish conductor and composer, and founder of the Finland Symphony Orchestra.

1 letter (1893) — 4875.

Location unknown.

KALISHEVSKII, Iakov Stepanovich (1856–1923). Baritone, and choirmaster of the Sofinskii Cathedral in Kiev.

6 letters (1890–91) — 4282, 4417, 4422, 4434, 4490, 4503.

Locations unknown.

KANDAUROV, Vasilii Alekseevich (1830–88). Civil servant and librettist.

5 letters (1884–85) — 2626, 2628, 2631, 2642, 2648a.

RUS–KL (3), RUS–Mrg (1), RUS–SPtm (1).

KARTAVOV, Aleksei Fëdorovich. Impressario at the Khar´kov Opera Theatre.

4 letters (1891, 1893) — 4524, 4532, 4540, 4868.

RUS–KL (1), RUS–SPsc (3).

KARTSOV, Georgii Pavlovich (1862–1930). Cousin of the composer.

1 letter (1888) — 3599.

RUS–Mcl.

KASHKIN, Nikolai Dmitrievich (1839–1920) Pianist, music critic and professor at the Moscow Conservatory.

6 letters (1877, 1880–81, 1888, 1891) — 660, 1568, 1868, 3456, 3466, 4286.

RUS–KL.

KASHKINA, Elizaveta Konstantinovna (1846–1910). Wife of Nikolai Kashkin.

1 letter (1882) — 2005.

RUS–Mkashkina.

KATUAR, Georgii L´vovich [CATOIRE, Georges] (1861–1926). Composer, musicologist and teacher.

7 letters (1886–87) — 2851, 2884, 2958, 3035, 3243, 3409, 3425.

RUS–KL.

KELLER, Ernest (Iosifovich) (1849–?). Flutist with the orchestra of the Imperial Theates in St. Petersburg.

1 letter (1892) — 4817.

RUS–SPsc.

KES, Willem (1856–1934). Dutch violinist, composer and conductor.

1 letter (1893) — 5063.

NL–Amengelberg.

KHALATOV, Isaak Bogdanovich. Head of the Tiflis Artistic Society.

1 letter (1890) — 4222.

Location unknown.

KHIMICHENKO, Aleksandr Vasil´evich (1856–1947). Flutist and teacher.

2 letters (1889, 1892) — 3939, 4633.

RUS–KL (2).

KHRISTOFOROV, Nikolai Osipovich (1836–92). Director of the Central Music Library of the Imperial Theatres.

8 letters (1883, 1889–90) — 2400a, 3882, 4064, 4121, 4136, 4174, 4191, 4257.

RUS–SPtob.

[2400a not published].

KISELEVA, Mariia Vladimirovna (d. 1921). Mother of Konstantin and Vladimir Shilovskii.

1 letter (1877) — 460.

RUS–SPt.

KLEEBERG, Clotilde (1866–1909). French pianist.

1 letter (1891) — 4362a.

D–F.

KLIMCHENKO, Andronik Mikhailovich (1831–1909). Director of the St. Petersburg Conservatory, and Chairman of the Artists' Mutual Benefit Society.

5 letters (1876, 1881) — 497a, 503a, 503b, 503c, 1921.

RUS–KL (1), RUS–SPa (4).

[497a, 503a, 503b, 503c not published].

KLIMENKO, Ivan Aleksandrovich (1841–1914). Architect, and friend of the composer.

19 letters (1869–72, 1877, 1887, 1893, n.d.) — 162, 177, 187, 190, 213, 232, 239, 254, 259, 260, 261, 262, 276, 278, 560, 561, 563, 3349, 4891.

Locations unknown.

KLIMENTOVA-MUROMTSEVA, Mariia Nikolaevna (1856–1946). Soprano at the Bol'shoi Theatre in Moscow.

12 letters (1884–87, 1889–91, 1893) — 2808a, 3113a, 3161, 3414a, 3770, 3876, 3883, 4029, 4041, 4537, 4559, 4885.

RUS–KL (8), RUS–Mcl (4).

KLINDWORTH, Karl (1830–1916). German pianist, conductor, and professor at the Moscow Conservatory.

4 letters (1878, 1885, 1889, 1890) — 932a, 2829a, 3976a, 4038a.

D–MZsch.

KOLOGRIVOV, Vasilii Alekseevich (1827–75). Director of the RMS and inspector at the St. Petersburg Conservatory.

3 letters (1864) — 64, 65, 69.

RUS–KL.

KOL'S, Lidiia Vasil'evna [COLES, Lidia]. Moscow pianist.

1 letter (n. d.) — 1138.

RUS–KL.

KONDRAT'EV, Gennadi Petrovich (1834–1905). Baritone and director with the St. Petersburg Imperial Theatres.

1 letter (1886) — 3100.

RUS–SPil.

KONDRAT'EVA, Mariia Sergeevna. Wife of the composer's friend Nikolai Kondrat'ev.

1 letter (n. d.) — 4282a.

RUS–Mcl.

KONINSKII, Konstantin Martynovich. Choirmaster and conductor.

2 letters (1881, 1893) — 3529a, 4857.

RUS–Mt (1), unknown (1).

KONIUS, Georgii Eduardovich [CONUS, Georges] (1862–1933). Composer, musicologist and lecturer at the Moscow Conservatory.

5 letters (1891–93) — 4381, 4778, 4905, 4986, 5060.

RUS–Mcl (1), unknown (4).

KONIUS, Iulii Eduardovich [CONUS, Jules] (1869–1942). Violinist, teacher, and composer; younger brother of Georgii Konius.

13 letters (1891–93) — 4349, 4374, 4410, 4423, 4435, 4453, 4564, 4596, 4638, 4699, 4856, 5013, 5016.

Locations unknown.

KONRADI, Alina Ivanovna [CONRADI, Alina] (b. MEYER, later BRIULLOVA; 1849–1932). Mother of Nikolai Konradi.

2 letters (1879–80) — 1226, 1484.

RUS–KL (1), RUS–SPsc (1).

KONRADI, German Karlovich [CONRADI, Hermann] (1833–82). Father of Nikolai Konradi.

1 letter (1881) — 1736.

RUS–SPsc.

KONRADI, Nikolai Germanovich [CONRADI, Nikolai] (1868–1922). Pupil of the composer's brother Modest.

53 letters (1876–93) — 485, 497, 646, 836, 873, 1052, 1448, 1537, 1830, 2099, 2185, 2274, 2304, 2322, 2375, 2384, 2487, 2593, 2682, 2729, 2738, 2795, 2989, 3012, 3054, 3090, 3286, 3296, 3302, 3500, 3621, 3634, 3801, 4031, 4062, 4074, 4124, 4167, 4180, 4337, 4355, 4372, 4406, 4426, 4445, 4549, 4582, 4588, 4594, 4692, 4722, 4830, 4948.

RUS–KL (1), unknown (52).

KONSTANTIN KONSTANTINOVICH
[ROMANOV] (*Grand Duke*; 1858–1914), Vice-President of the RMS from 1892; poet, amateur pianist and composer.
32 letters (1880, 1886–91, 1893) — 1625, 3043, 3048, 3166, 3435, 3446, 3564, 3574, 3578, 3589, 3651, 3675, 3685, 3736, 3788, 3802, 3847, 3872, 3894, 3959, 3966, 3976, 4094, 4114, 4195, 4276, 4276a, 4352, 4353, 4531, 5038, 5046.
RUS–SPil.

KORESHCHENKO, Arsenii Nikolaevich (1870–1921). Composer, pianist, conductor, teacher and music critic.
2 letters (1892) — 4632, 4684.
RUS–KL.

KORSOV, Bogomir Bogomirovich (b. GÖRING, Gottfried; 1845–1920). Baritone at the St. Petersburg opera, later at the Bol´shoi Theatre in Moscow.
21 letters (1874, 1878, 1883–84, 1887, 1891, n.d.) — 355, 919, 928, 933, 2398, 2399, 2422, 2564, 2634b, 3165, 3191, 3245, 3256, 4424, 4474, 4476, 4486, 4550, 4558, 4561, 4828b.
RUS–KL (17), RUS–Mcm (2), unknown (2).

KOTEK, Iosif Iosifovich (1855–85). Violinist and student of Chaikovskii's at the Moscow Conservatory.
1 letter (1882) — 2120.
RUS–KL.

KOTEK, Viacheslav Iosifovich (b. 1870). Younger brother of Iosif Kotek.
1 letter (1888) — 3673a.
RUS–KL.
Not published.

KRUGLIKOV, Semën Nikolaevch (1851–1910). Music critic, and editor of the journal *Artist*.
4 letters (1887, 1889) — 3203, 3397, 3906, 3922.
RUS–KL.

KUBA, Ludvik (1863–1956). Czech writer and artist.
3 letters (1888, 1892) — 3603, 3730, 4677.
CZ–POm.

KUPERNIK, Lev Abramovich (1845–1904). Lawyer, writer and theatre critic.
12 letters (1875–76, 1881, 1892–93) — 420, 452, 1904, 4768, 4779, 4797, 4798, 4848, 4886, 4895, 4906, 4936.
RUS–SPil.

KUZNETSOV, Aleksandr Vasil´evich (1847–1910). Cellist, teacher, and contemporary of Chaikovskii's at the St. Petersburg Conservatory.
1 letter (1875) — 393.
RUS–Mcl.

KUZNETSOV, Nikolai Dmitrievich (1850–1930). Artist.
1 letter (1893) — 4871.
RUS–KL.

LAFITTE, Leopoldine (d. 1930). Tutor to the Litke family, and later to Tat´iana Chaikovskii (daughter of Anatolii & Praskov´ia Chaikovskii).
2 letters (1891–92) — 4520, 4650.
RUS–KL.

LALO, Édouard (-Victoire-Antoine) (1823–92). French composer.
1 letter (1886) — 2987a.
Location unknown.
Not published in full.

LAMOND, Frederic (Frederick Archibald) (1868–1948). Scottish pianist, teacher and composer.
1 letter (1892) — 4681a.
GB–Gu.

LANGE, Danïel de (1841–1918). Dutch composer, cellist, pianist and teacher.
1 letter (1892) — 4612.
NL–At.

LANGER, Eduard Leont´evich [LANGER, Eduard Leopold] (1835–1905). Pianist and professor at the Moscow Conservatory.
2 letters (1880) — 1464a, 1575.
RUS–KL (1), RUS–Mfeldman (1).
[1464a not published].

LAROCHE — *see* LAROSH.

LAROSH, Ekaterina Ivanovna [LAROCHE, Ekaterina] (b. SINEL´NIKOVA). Third wife of German Larosh.
23 letters (1881, 1888–93) — 1666, 3704, 3892, 3969, 4008, 4016, 4038, 4208, 4217, 4265, 4267a, 4271, 4320, 4350, 4356, 4437, 4504, 4551, 4618, 4739, 4845, 4917, 4995.
RUS–Mcl (1), US–BHsmith (1), unknown (21).

LAROSH, German Avgustovich [LAROCHE, Hermann] (1845–1904). Music and literary critic, professor of music history at the Moscow and St. Petersburg Conservatories, fellow student of Chaikovskii's at the St. Petersburg Conservatory.

15 letters (1884–85, 1888–90, 1893, n.d.) — 224, 2491a, 2730a, 3663, 3693, 3969, 4008, 4016, 4037, 4087, 4116, 4140, 4181, 4259, 5041.

CH–B (1), RUS–Mcm (1), US–BHsachs (1), US–NHub (1), US–Wc (1), unknown (10).

[2730a not published].

LAROSH, Zinaida Germanovna [LAROCHE, Zinaida] (1869–1959). Translator, daughter of German Larosh.

1 letter (1889) — 3992a.

RUS–KL.

Not published.

LAUBE, Julius. Conductor of the Pavlovsk orchestra.

1 letter (1888) — 3587a.

D–WIaxtmann.

LAVROVSKAIA, Elizaveta Andreevna (later. *Countess* TSERTELEVA, 1845–1919). Contralto, and professor at the Moscow Conservatory.

4 letters (1874, 1889) — 356, 3774, 3862, 3968.

RUS–KL (3), RUS–Mcl (1).

LEDEBUR, Karl von (1840–1913). Director of the Schwerin Hoftheater, Germany.

1 letter (1893) — 4841.

Location unknown.

LENTOVSKII, Mikhail Valentinovich (1843–1906). Operatic impresario and writer.

2 letters (1882, 1891) — 1999, 4526.

RUS–Mt.

LENTS, Nikolai Konstantinovich [LENZ, Nikolai] (1858–?). Lawyer and composer.

3 letters (1880, 1886, 1893) — 1494, 3063, 3724a.

RUS–Mcm (1), unknown (2).

LENZ — *see* LENTS.

LESHETITSKAIA — *see* LESZETYCKI.

LESZETYCKI, Anna [LESHETITSKAIA, Anna Karlovna] (b. FRIDEBURG; 1829–1903). Singer (contralto) and vocal teacher; first wife of pianist Teodor Leszetycki.

1 letter (1889) — 3941.

RUS–KL.

LEVENSON — see ALEKSANDROVA-LEVENSON.

LIADOV, Anatolii Konstantinovich (1855–1914). Composer and professor at the St. Petersburg Conservatory.

3 letters (1885, 1889–90) — 2648b, 3992, 3994.

RUS–SPsc.

LITKE, Aleksandr Nikolaevich (1868–1918). Cousin of the composer.

1 letter (1891) — 4444.

RUS–KL.

LITKE, Amaliia — *see* SHOBERT, Amaliia Vasil´evna.

LUZIN, Matvei Ivanovich [*later* Bishop Mikhail] (1830–87). Bishop of Uman´sk.

1 letter (1882) — 2121.

Location unknown.

L´VOVA, Aleksandra Aleksandrovna (1831–1916). Maid of honour, benefactress.

1 letter (1886) — 3022a.

RUS–Mia

Not published.

L´VOVA, Aleksandra Dmitrievna (b. SHIDLOV-SKAIA; 1849–1932). Poet.

1 letter (1891) — 4327.

RUS–Mrg.

LYNEN, Marie de. Unknown correspondent.

1 letter (1893) — 4844a.

US–NHub.

Not published.

MACKAR, Félix (1837–1903). French music publisher.

36 letters (1885–91) — 2758, 2762, 2819, 2830, 2839, 2854, 2924, 2970, 2980, 3031, 3082, 3170, 3176, 3187, 3204, 3215, 3391, 3430, 3462, 3474, 3557, 3690, 3747, 3768, 3793a, 3797, 3808, 3834, 3936, 3981, 4068, 4088, 4298, 4315, 4318a, 4335.

D–WÜ (1), F–Pn (33), RUS–KL (1), US–Wc (1).

MAITLAND, Frederick William (1850–1906). Professor of Law at Christ College at Cambridge University, England.

1 letter (1893) — 4941.

GB–Cmaitland.

MAKOVSKII, Vladimir Egorovich (1846–1920). Painter, and professor at the Academy of Arts in St. Petersburg.

1 letter (1893) — 4851.

RUS–KL.

MALOZEMOVA, Sofiia Aleksandrovna (1846–1908). Pianist, teacher and professor at the Moscow Conservatory.

1 letter (1884) — 2243.

RUS–KL.

MASLOV, Fëdor Ivanovich (1840–1915). Contemporary of Chaikovskii's at the Imperial School of Jurisprudence, and colleague at the Ministry of Justice.

1 letter (1882) — 2074.

RUS–KL.

MASLOVA, Anna Ivanovna. Sister of Fëdor Maslov

3 letters (1880, 1882, 1891) — 1645, 2074, 4560.

RUS–KL.

MASLOVA, Sof´ia Ivanovna (d. 1902). Sister of Fëdor Maslov.

2 letters (1882, 1891) — 2074, 4560.

RUS–KL.

MASLOVA, Varvara Ivanovna (d. 1905). Sister of Fëdor Maslov

2 letters (1882, 1891) — 2074, 4560.

RUS–KL.

MASLOV-BEZHETSKII, Aleksei Nikolaevich (1853–?). Writer and dramatist.

1 letter (1890) — 4032.

RUS–SPsc.

MECK, Anna von — *see* DAVYDOVA, Anna L´vovna.

MECK, Nadezhda von [MEKK, Nadezhda Filaretovna] (b. FROLOVSKAIA; 1831–94). Correspondent and benefactress of the composer.

768 letters (1876–90) — 524, 542, 545, 546, 553, 554, 555, 556, 557, 569, 574, 584, 590, 592, 593, 594, 595, 597, 601, 616, 622, 625, 626, 633, 635, 636, 638, 639, 640, 644, 648, 650, 651, 655, 656, 659, 661, 664, 665, 668, 673, 679, 684, 689, 692, 696, 698, 701, 705, 707, 711, 712, 719, 722, 723, 724, 728, 729, 732, 735, 736, 740, 743, 746, 749, 753, 754, 755, 758, 762, 763, 765, 768, 770, 775, 777, 778, 780, 782, 784, 785, 787, 790, 793, 794, 796, 798, 801, 803, 805, 806, 808, 809, 811, 813, 815, 817, 820, 821, 823, 825, 827, 829, 832, 834, 840, 841, 843, 846, 848, 849, 850, 853, 854, 857, 859, 862, 863, 864, 866, 868, 871, 874, 876, 879, 882, 886, 889, 892, 895, 897, 901, 902, 906, 909, 912, 917, 922, 925, 927, 930, 934, 938, 940, 943, 945, 947, 948, 955, 956, 959, 965, 970, 973, 974, 975, 976, 977, 980, 982, 983, 984, 985, 987, 988, 989, 992, 994, 995, 996, 997, 1000, 1003, 1005, 1007, 1009, 1010, 1012, 1015, 1018, 1020, 1021, 1024, 1026, 1033, 1034, 1037, 1038, 1041, 1045, 1049, 1054, 1058, 1063, 1065, 1067, 1070, 1073, 1076, 1080, 1082, 1083, 1089, 1092, 1094, 1096, 1099, 1101, 1103, 1106, 1111, 1115, 1119, 1121, 1126, 1127, 1129, 1131, 1132, 1133, 1136, 1139, 1140, 1142, 1145, 1146, 1148, 1150, 1152, 1154, 1159, 1162, 1164, 1167, 1169, 1171, 1174, 1183, 1184, 1188, 1193, 1197, 1204, 1212, 1217, 1221, 1223, 1227, 1229, 1232, 1233, 1234, 1237, 1239, 1244, 1248, 1249, 1250, 1254, 1257, 1258, 1260, 1263, 1265, 1267, 1268, 1271, 1273, 1276, 1277, 1278, 1280, 1282, 1283, 1289, 1293, 1294, 1297, 1302, 1307, 1309, 1311, 1313, 1315, 1320, 1321, 1322, 1324, 1326, 1327, 1334, 1337, 1338, 1341, 1343, 1346, 1347, 1351, 1352, 1356, 1358, 1360, 1364, 1366, 1371, 1374, 1377, 1381, 1385, 1387, 1392, 1394, 1400, 1403, 1406, 1408, 1410, 1412, 1416, 1419, 1420, 1423, 1425, 1427, 1431, 1436, 1439, 1442, 1444, 1451, 1456, 1460, 1465, 1467, 1473, 1474, 1478, 1479, 1483, 1485, 1489, 1493, 1500, 1504, 1508, 1509, 1512, 1521, 1523, 1527, 1529, 1533, 1534, 1539, 1546, 1550, 1552, 1557, 1561, 1570, 1571, 1578, 1585, 1589, 1592, 1597, 1601, 1603, 1606, 1607, 1609, 1613, 1615, 1617, 1621, 1624, 1627, 1628, 1631, 1632, 1636, 1641, 1648, 1654, 1658, 1660, 1665, 1667, 1668, 1670, 1671, 1676, 1678, 1680, 1681, 1684, 1688, 1692, 1700, 1704, 1711, 1712, 1718, 1721, 1723, 1725, 1726, 1729, 1732, 1735, 1744, 1747, 1752, 1754, 1762, 1766, 1771, 1780, 1784, 1789, 1793, 1799, 1804, 1806, 1813, 1816, 1820, 1825, 1831, 1836, 1840, 1842, 1850, 1854, 1855, 1856, 1857, 1859, 1862, 1864, 1870, 1876, 1877, 1884, 1889, 1893, 1896, 1897, 1900, 1902, 1906, 1908, 1912, 1916, 1927, 1932, 1936, 1947, 1949, 1953, 1958, 1961, 1967, 1972, 1974, 1981, 1987, 1988, 1990, 1991, 1992, 1993, 1998, 2001, 2009, 2015, 2025, 2027, 2034, 2039, 2041, 2044, 2051, 2053, 2055, 2057, 2061, 2067, 2070, 2073, 2075, 2076, 2078, 2079, 2084, 2088, 2091, 2101, 2107, 2116, 2119, 2135, 2138, 2139, 2149, 2157, 2161, 2165, 2170, 2173, 2178, 2184, 2189, 2195, 2201, 2204, 2209, 2215, 2224, 2227, 2234, 2236, 2240, 2244, 2249, 2255, 2265, 2273, 2281, 2285, 2289, 2290, 2292, 2294, 2295, 2298, 2302, 2305, 2309, 2311,

MECK, Nikolai von [MEKK, Nikolai Karlovich] (1863–1929). Lawyer, son of Nadezhda von Meck, later married to the composer's niece Anna Davydova.

1 letter (1882) — 2146.

Location unknown.

MECKLENBURG-STRELITZ — *see* MEKLENBURG-STRELITSKII.

MEKLENBURG-STRELITSKII, Georgii Georgievich [MECKLENBURG-STRELITZ, Georg-Alexander] (*Count*; 1859–1920). Founder of the Meklenburg Quartet.

2 letters (1889, 1891) — 3930, 4299.

RUS–Mf.

MENTER, Sophie (1846–1918). German pianist, composer and professor at the St. Petersburg Conservatory.

1 letter (1891) — 4477.

US–NYpm.

MERKLING, Anna Petrovna (b. CHAIKOVSKAIA; 1830–1911). Daughter of Pëtr Petrovich Chaikovskii (the composer's paternal uncle).

MEYER, Emiliia (Karlovna). Paternal aunt of Nikolai Konradi.

1 letter (1885) — 2643.

RUS–Md.

MIKESHIN, Mikhail Osipovich (1836–1936). Artist, sculptor and writer.

1 letter (1893) — 5026.

RUS–Mt.

MIKHAILOV-STOIAN, Konstantin Ivanovich [*alias* MIKHAILOV; *alias* SVETLOV-STOIAN] (b. STOIAN; 1850–1914). Baritone at the Bol'shoi Theatre, Moscow.

1 letter (1893) — 4876.

Location unknown.

MIRIMANIAN, Bagrat Moiseevich. Music store proprietor in Tiflis.

1 letter — 4239.

US–STu.

MOLCHANOV, Porfirii Iustinovich (1863–1945). Composer, professor at the Odessa Conservatory.

1 letter (1892) — 4823.

RUS–KL.

MOROZOV, Sergei Iakovlevich (1850–?). Cellist and music teacher.

2 letters (1882) — 2030, 2172.

RUS–SPil.

MOSKOVSKIE VEDOMOSTI. Letters to the editor of the Moscow journal.

2 letters (1881, 1889) — 1710, 3956a.

RUS–Md (1), unknown (1).

MUROMTSEVA — *see* KLIMENTOVA-MUROMTSEVA.

MUZYKAL´NOE OBOZRENIE. Letter to the editor
   [Vasilii Bessel´] of the St. Petersburg journal.
1 letter (1886) — 3123a.
RUS–Mcm.

NÁPRAVNÍK, Eduard (Frantsevich) (1839–1916).
   Czech composer and conductor at the Imperial
   Opera in St. Petersburg.
85 letters (1872–76, 1878–93) — 255, 334, 340, 367,
   379, 382, 441, 459, 461, 507, 514, 521, 923, 962,
   1143, 1296, 1323, 1447, 1449, 1475, 1579, 1586,
   1643, 1679, 1786, 1801, 1909, 1918, 2114, 2126,
   2182, 2197, 2332, 2335, 2343, 2415, 2423,
   2451a, 2458, 2550, 2575, 2581, 2612, 2639,
   2915, 3057, 3070, 3089, 3095, 3133, 3139, 3140,
   3147, 3154, 3184, 3357, 3364, 3366, 3403, 3674,
   3677a, 3723, 3899, 3913, 4194, 4206, 4219,
   4225, 4229, 4238, 4351, 4358, 4370, 4500, 4510,
   4570, 4589a, 4619, 4622, 4663, 4666, 4709,
   4786, 4909, 4982.
F–Plauwe (1), RUS–KL (21), RUS–SPtm (18), US–
   ANcrocker (1), unknown (44).
[2451a, 3677a, 4589a not published].

NÁPRAVNÍK, Ol´ga Eduardovna (b. SCHRÖDER;
   1839–1916). Singer (contralto) with the Imperial
   Theatres in St. Petersburg, and wife of Eduard
   Nápravník.
4 letters (1886, 1888, 1890, 1893) — 3086, 3724,
   4254, 5064.
RUS–KL (3), unknown (1).

NÁPRAVNÍK, Ol´ga Eduardovna (1870–1920).
   Daughter of Eduard & Ol´ga Nápravník.
2 letters (1889, 1890) — 3979, 4220a.
RUS–KL (1), RUS–SPit (1).
[4220a not published].

NÁPRAVNÍK, Varvara Eduardovna (1873–1942).
   Daughter of Eduard & Ol´ga Nápravník.
1 letter (1889) — 3979.
RUS–KL.

NÁPRAVNÍK, Vladimir Eduardovich (1869–1948).
   Son of Eduard & Ol´ga Nápravník.
18 letters (1886–93) — 3101, 3107, 3229, 3471,
   3505, 3587, 3604, 3614, 3912, 4220, 4384, 4446,
   4494, 4545, 4694, 4842, 4846, 4949.
Locations unknown.

NEUEN SYMPHONISCHEN GESELLSCHAFT
   Letter to the Committee of the New Symphonic
   Society in Vienna.
1 letter (1889) — 3931a.

Location unknown.
Not published in full.

NEW SYMPHONIC SOCIETY — *see* NEUEN
SYMPHONISCHEN GESELLSCHAFT.

NIKOLAEV, N. Unknown correspondent in St.
   Petersburg.
1 letter (1891) — 4391.
RUS–KL.

NOVOE VREMIA. Letter to the editor of the St.
   Petersburg newspaper.
1 letter (1890) — 4246.
Location unknown.

OBOLENSKII, Dmitrii Aleksandrovich (1822–
   1881). Prince, Vice–President of the RMS.
1 letter (1873) — 294.
RUS–SPa.

OL´KHOVSKII, Viktor Ivanovich. Poet and writer,
   distant relative of Chaikovskii.
2 letters (1854) — 51, 52.
Location unknown.

OOM, Fëdor Adol´fovich (1826–98). Secretary to
   the Empress Mariia Fëdorovna.
1 letter (1886) — 3102.
Location unknown.

ORLOV, Vasilii Sergeevich (1856–1907). Church
   choirmaster in Moscow.
3 letters (1885–86, 1892) — 2845, 2872, 4764.
Locations unknown.

OSTROVSKII, Aleksandr Nikolaevich (1823–86).
   Dramatist, translator and librettist.
9 letters (1867, 1873, 1882–84, 1886) — 99, 103,
   297, 306, 2147, 2570, 2802, 2868, 2909.
RUS–Mt.

OSTROVSKII, Vasilii Aleksandrovich (1866–
   1942). Singer (baritone).
1 letter (1892) — 4697.
RUS–KL.

PABST, (Christian Georg) Paul [PABST, Pavel
   Avgustovich] (1854–97). German pianist,
   composer and professor at the Moscow
   Conservatory.
1 letter (1887) — 3344.
RUS–KL.

PACHULSKI, Henryk [PAKHUL´SKII, Genrikh Al´bertovich] (1859–1921). Polish composer and pianist, brother of Wladyslaw.

2 letters (1890, 1892) — 4263, 4765.

RUS–KL (1), unknown (1).

PACHULSKI, Wladyslaw [PAKHUL´SKII, Vladislav Al´bertovich] (d. 1919). Violinist, amateur composer, and son-in-law to Nadezhda von Meck.

9 letters (1883, 1885, 1889–91) — 2259, 2749, 2760, 3919a, 4052, 4069, 4164, 4347, 4398.

CH–Bps (1), RUS–SPsc (1), US–NYpm (1), US–Wc (6).

PAKHUL´SKII — see PACHULSKI.

PALEČEK, Osip Osipovich (Iosif Iosifovich) [PALECHEK, Josef] (1842–1916). Czech singer (bass), music teacher, and founder of the St. Petersburg Conservatory´s opera class.

3 letters (1891) — 4396, 4407, 4529.

RUS–KL.

PARIS. Letter to the editor of the Parisian newspaper (received by its reporter Michel Delines).

1 letter (1892) — 4837.

Location unknown.

PASCAL, Noël. Parisian doctor.

1 letter (1883) — 2210.

RUS–KL.

PATERA, Adolf (1836–1912). Librarian of the Czech Museum, and head of the Society of Artists in Prague.

6 letters (1888–89) — 3530, 3732, 3749, 3763, 3799, 3811.

CZ–Ps.

PAVLOVSKAIA, Emiliia Karlovna (b. BERMAN; 1853–1935). Opera artist at the Mariinskii Theatre in St. Petersburg.

40 letters (1884–88) — 2424, 2613, 2630, 2649, 2661, 2672, 2677, 2685, 2698, 2705, 2708, 2710, 2741, 2747, 2787, 2932, 3013, 3096, 3141, 3144, 3149, 3150, 3152, 3164, 3192, 3236, 3297, 3306, 3337, 3338, 3346, 3347, 3358, 3361, 3363, 3370, 3415, 3536, 3707, 3708.

RUS–KL (6), RUS–Mt (34).

PCHEL´NIKOV, Pavel Mikhailovich (1851–1913). Director of the Moscow Imperial Theatres.

27 letters (1884–85, 1887, 1889–93, n.d.) — 2621, 2647, 2648, 2691, 2829, 3158, 3405, 3988, 4108, 4132, 4211, 4270, 4535, 4542, 4592, 4674, 4691, 4704, 4774, 4787, 4800, 4803, 4873, 4879, 4890, 4923, 5033.

RUS–KL.

PEILE, John (1837–1910). Professor and Vice-Chancellor of Christ College at Cambridge University.

1 letter (1892) — 4812b.

GB–Cu.

PERELETSKII, Pavel Alekseevich. Teacher from Rybinsk.

1 letter (1885) — 2690.

RUS–KL.

PERESLENI, Ekaterina Vasil´evna (1822–98). Older sister of Lev Davydov.

5 letters (1875, 1877, 1879, n.d.) — 428, 433, 540, 544, 1138.

RUS–KL.

PERESLENI, Vadim Vladimirovich. Nephew of Lev Davydov, and son of Ekaterina Peresleni.

7 letters (1885–86, 1888, 1891, 1892) — 2825, 3014, 3071, 3596, 4501, 4628, 4629.

RUS–KL.

PETERSSEN, Pavel Leont´evich (1831–95). Pianist and director of the RMS in St. Petersburg.

15 letters (1891–93) — 4458, 4464, 4479, 4523, 4552, 4723a, 4743a, 4749, 4769, 4959a, 4976, 4999, 5003, 5005, 5037.

RUS–KL (3), RUS–Mcl (3), RUS–Mrg (1), RUS–SPa (1), RUS–SPil (1), RUS–SPsc (6).

[4723a, 4743a not published].

PETIPA, Marius (Ivanovich) (1822–1910). French balletmaster with the Imperial Theatres in St. Petersburg.

1 letter (1889) — 3843.

Location unknown.

PETUKHOV, Mikhail Onisiforovich (1843–94). Journalist and music critic.

2 letters (1890–91) — 4269, 4328.

RUS–Mcl (1), RUS–SPil (1).

PLESKAIA, Natal´ia Andreevna (1837–?). Niece of Lev Davydov.

16 letters (1879, 1882–85, 1888, 1893) — 1060, 1376, 1388, 1941, 1986, 2014, 2269, 2330, 2333, 2536, 2687, 2744, 3640a, 4859, 4907, 4958.

RUS–Mcl.

POBEDONOSTSEV, Konstantin Petrovich (1827–1906). Russian statesman.
5 letters (1881, 1886) — 1759, 1770, 1772, 1781, 2899.
RUS–KL (3), RUS–Mrg (2).

POGOZHEV, Vladimir Petrovich (1851–1935). Official at the Imperial Theatres in St. Petersburg.
15 letters (1887–92) — 3177, 3461, 3537, 3554, 3560, 3664, 3682, 3844, 4119, 4130, 4210, 4280, 4289, 4512, 4783.
RUS–KL (14), RUS–Mcl (1).

POHL, Baruch — *see* POLLINI, Bernard.

POLLINI, Bernard (b. POHL, Baruch; 1838–97). Director of the Hamburg Opera Theatre.
2 letters (1892) — 4620, 4805.
RUS–KL (1), US–NYpm (1).

POLONSKII, Iakov Petrovich (1819–98). Poet and librettist.
4 letters (1872, 1874, 1876, 1889) — 265, 346, 463, 3950.
RUS–Mcl (1), RUS–SPil (3).

POPLAVSKII, Iul´ian Ignat´evich (1871–1958). Cellist and writer.
2 letters (1893) — 4963, 5053.
RUS–Mcl (1), unknown (1).

POPOV, Ivan Petrovich. Member of the Russian Choral Society in Moscow.
3 letters (1886–87) — 3038, 3137, 3188.
RUS–KL.

PRIANISHNIKOV, Ippolit Petrovich (1847–1921). Singer (baritone) at the Kiev Opera Theatre, music teacher and opera impressario.
3 letters (1890, 1892) — 4250, 4651.
Locations unknown.

PRIBIK, Iosif Viacheslavovich [PRIBIQUE, Josef] (1855– 1937). Composer, conductor and music teacher.
1 letter (1893) — 5061.
Location unknown.

PRIBIQUE — *see* PRIBIK.

PUSHECHNIKOVA, Pelagea Sofirovna (b. BALABANOVA; 1862–1935). Teacher at the Music School in Khar´kov.
1 letter (1887) — 3412.
RUS–KL.

RACHINSKII, Sergei Aleksandrovich (1836–1902). Artist, writer and professor of botany at Moscow University.
3 letters (1869, 1875, 1881) — 163, 427, 1750.
RUS–Mcl (2), RUS–SPsc (1).

RAHTER, Daniel (1828–91). German music publisher, with offices in Hamburg and St. Petersburg.
1 letter (1889) — 3816.
US–CA.

RATGAUZ, Daniil Maksimovich [RATHAUS, Daniel] (1868–1937). Poet.
5 letters (1892–93) — 4762, 4927, 4950, 4977, 4996.
RUS–KL (2), unknown (3).

RATHAUS — *see* RATGAUZ.

RAZUMOVSKII, Dmitrii Vasil´evich (1818–89). Priest and professor of church music history at the Moscow Conservatory.
2 letters (1875, 1877) — 386, 562.
RUS–Mrg.

REBEZOVA, Anna Antonovna (b. RUBINSHTEIN, later TILLING; 1869–1915). Daughter of Anton Rubinshtein.
2 letters (1890–91) — 4103, 4293a.
RUS–Mcm (1), RUS–SPsc (1).

REINECKE, Carl (Heinrich Karsten) (1824–1910). German pianist, conductor, composer, and director of the Leipzig Conservatory.
1 letter (1891) — 4580.
US–NHub.

REMEZOV, Sergei Mikhailovich (1854–?). Pianist and music teacher.
1 letter (1893) — 5054.
RUS–Mcm.

REPMAN, Al´bert Khristianovich (1834–?). State Secretary to the Empress Mariia Fedorovna.
1 letter (1885) — 2925.
RUS–KL.

RICCORDI, Giulio (1840–1912). Italian music publisher.
1 letter (1891) — 4383.
Location unknown.

RIMSKII-KORSAKOV, Nikolai Andreevich (1844–1908). Composer, conductor and professor at the St. Petersburg Conservatory.

18 letters (1873–76, 1885–89, 1891) — 300, 361, 383, 401, 412, 417, 493, 502, 2679, 2873, 3047, 3074, 3393, 3515, 3944, 3951, 4303, 4307.

RUS–SPsc (16), RUS–SPtob (1), unknown (1).

ROMANOV, Aleksandr Aleksandrovich — *see* ALEXANDER III, *Tsar.*

ROMANOV, Konstantin Konstantinovich — *see* KONSTANTIN KONSTANTINOVICH, *Grand Duke.*

ROSSI, Lauro (1810–85). Italian composer, conductor and music teacher, director of the Collegia di Musica in Naples.

1 letter (1877) — 623a.

I–Nc.

RUBINSHTEIN, Anna — *see* REBEZOVA, Anna.

RUBINSHTEIN, Anton Grigor´evich [RUBINSTEIN, Anton] (1829–94). Composer, pianist, conductor and founder of the St. Petersburg Conservatory; older brother of Nikolai Rubinshtein.

2 letters (1887, 1891) — 3213, 4392.

RUS–SPsc.

RUBINSHTEIN, Nikolai Grigor´evich [RUBINSTEIN, Nikolai] (1835–81). Pianist, conductor and founder of the Moscow Conservatory; younger brother of Anton Rubinshtein.

19 letters (1870, 1872–73, 1877–80) — 193, 281, 318, 617, 623, 630, 642, 652, 658, 675, 699, 702, 713, 727, 745, 814, 951, 1329, 1495.

RUS–KL (2), RUS–Mcl (17).

RUBINSTEIN — *see* RUBINSHTEIN.

RUKAVISHNIKOV, Konstantin Vasil´evich (1843–1915). Principal director of the Moscow branch of the RMS.

1 letter (1889) — 3918.

RUS–SPil.

RUSSIAN MUSICAL SOCIETY [Imperatorskoe Russkoe muzykal´noe obshchestvo]. Letter to the Moscow branch of the RMS.

1 letter (1890) — 4039.

RUS–KL.

RUSSKIE VEDOMOSTI. Letters to the editor of the Moscow newspaper.

2 letters (1875, 1893) — 400a, 4872.

RUS–SPsc [1 draft], unknown (1).

SABLER, Vladimir Karlovich (1847–1919). Lawyer.

1 letter (1886) — 3079.

RUS–SPil.

SACHS, William (Wilhelm) von. Austrian music critic and journalist, living in New York.

5 letters (1891–93) — 4385, 4603, 4807, 4824, 5044.

RUS–Mt (1), US–NYpm (4).

SAFONOV, Vasilii Il´ich (1852–1918). Pianist, conductor, professor and director of the Moscow Conservatory.

20 letters (1885–86, 1889, 1891–93) — 2735, 2742, 2748, 2756, 2893, 3763a, 3891, 3963, 3982, 4523a, 4825, 4847, 4861, 4863, 4960, 4966, 4990, 5007, 5022, 5055.

RUS–KL (16), RUS–Mcm (3), unknown (1).

ST. PETERSBURG PHILHARMONIC SOCIETY [Sankt Peterburgskoe filarmonicheskoe obshchestvo].

1 letter (1887) — 3163.

Location unknown.

SAINT–SAËNS, (Charles) Camille (1833–1921). French composer, pianist, organist and conductor

4 letters (1876, 1886–87) — 441a, 2949, 2969, 3227.

F–DI.

SALIN, Vasilii Zakharovich (1843–1907). Violinist and contemporary of Chaikovskii's at the St. Petersburg Conservatory.

1 letter (1893) — 4908.

KZ–AA.

SAMOILOVA, Elena Al´bertovna (b. ZABEL). Singer (soprano), student of Desirée Artôt.

1 letter (1891) — 4538.

US–CLbackford.

SANKT PETERBURGSKOE FILARMON- ICHESKOE OBSHCHESTVO — *see* ST. PETERSBURG PHILHARMONIC SOCIETY.

SAPEL´NIKOV, Vasilii L´vovich (1868–1941). Pianist.

3 letters (1889) — 3839a, 3889a, 3958a.

US–NHub (1), unknown (2).

Not published.

SAUER, Emil (Georg Konrad) von (1862–1942). German pianist, composer and music teacher.
2 letters (1888) — 3652, 3714.
D–EMmüller.

SCHNEIDER, Otto (1851–90). Director of the Berlin Philharmonic Orchestra.
3 letters (1887) — 3384, 3390, 3441.
D–Bmuck (1), D–BShenn (1), US–Wc (1).

SCHOBERT — *see* SHOBERT.

SEIFERT — *see* ZEIFERT.

SETOV, Iosif Iakovlevich (b. SETGOFER, 1835–94). Opera singer (tenor) and manager of the Kiev Opera Theatre.
3 letters (1874, 1892) — 371, 374, 4698.
RUS–KL (1), RUS–Mcl (2).

SGAMBATI, Giovanni (1843–1914). Italian pianist, composer and conductor.
1 letter (1890) — 4091.
I–Rsgambati.

SHCHUROVSKII, Pëtr Andreevich (1850–1908). Conductor, composer, and music critic for the journal *Moskovskie vedomosti*.
1 letter (1874) — 348.
RUS–Mt.

SHERVUD, Vladimir Osipovich [SHERWOOD, Vladimir] (1833–97). Moscow architect.
1 letter (1891) — 4304.
RUS–KL.

SHERWOOD — *see* SHERVUD.

SHIDLOVSKII, Aleksandr Ivanovich (1852–?). History teacher, and coachman to the Davydov family at Kamenka.
6 letters (1882, 1893) — 2029, 2087, 2095, 4860, 4912, 4953.
Locations unknown.

SHILOVSKII, Konstantin Stepanovich (1849–1893). Artist, poet and musician.
4 letters (1875–77, 1879) — 432, 473, 589, 1181.
RUS–Mt.

SHILOVSKII, Vladimir Stepanovich (*Count* VASIL′EV-SHILOVSKII) (1852–93). Student of music theory with Chaikovskii in the 1870s.

16 letters (1873, 1877, 1879, 1882–85, 1887–88, 1893) — 315, 578, 1177, 2166, 2196, 2417, 2799, 2808, 3151, 3157, 3160, 3402, 3631, 4880, 4889, 4898.
RUS–Mcm (1), RUS–Mt (4), RUS–SPsc (11).

SHISHKOV, Andrei Nikolaevich (d. 1909). Manager of the Synod Publishing House.
1 letter (1886) — 2901.
RUS–Mcm.

SHOBERT, Amaliia Vasil′evna [SCHOBERT, Amaliia] (later *Countess* LITKE; 1841–1912). Cousin of the composer, daughter of Elizaveta Shobert.
1 letter (1848) — 1a.
RUS–SPsc.

SHOBERT, Elizaveta Andreevna [SCHOBERT, Elizaveta] (b. ASSIER; 1823–?). Younger sister of the composer′s mother, Aleksandra Chaikovskaia.
2 letters (1848, 1870) — 1, 203.
RUS–KL (1), RUS–SPsc (1).

SHOBERT, Vasilii Vasil′evich (d. 1849). Uncle of the composer, husband of Elizaveta Shobert
1 letter (1848) — 1.
RUS–SPsc.

SHPAZHINSKAIA, Iuliia Petrovna (b. POROKHITSEVA; d. 1919). Pianist, and wife of Ippolit Shpazhinskii.
83 letters (1885–91) — 2407, 2717, 2820, 2847, 2865, 2886, 2891, 2904, 2910, 2911, 2922a, 2930, 2944, 2960, 2977, 2990, 3002, 3019, 3026, 3059, 3064, 3068, 3088, 3093, 3106, 3116, 3136, 3142, 3159, 3174, 3196, 3202, 3210, 3223, 3251, 3262, 3266, 3279, 3295, 3312, 3348, 3392, 3407, 3420, 3421, 3429, 3454, 3479, 3497, 3524, 3542, 3551, 3563, 3580, 3590, 3609, 3617, 3626, 3645, 3658, 3665, 3684, 3705, 3727, 3734, 3750, 3766, 3819, 3848, 3865, 3870, 3900, 3908, 3928, 3973, 4014, 4075, 4177, 4204, 4388, 4404, 4468, 4493.
RUS–KL.
[2922a not published].

SHPAZHINSKII, Ippolit Vasil′evich (1848–1917). Dramatist and librettist.
6 letters (1886–88) — 2861, 2875, 2928, 2996, 3367, 3550.
RUS–KL (1), RUS–Mt (4), unknown (1).

SIDOROV, Vasilii Mikhailovich. Poet and collector of autographs.
1 letter (1887) — 3195.
Location unknown.

SIEGER, Friedrich. Musical writer, critic, director of the Frankfurt–am–Main Museum–Gesellschaft.
3 letters (1889, 1891) — 3779, 3943, 4293b.
D–FF (1), NL–Ac (1), US–NYmo (1).

SIGNALE FÜR DIE MUSIKALISCHE WELT. Letter to the editor of the German music journal.
1 letter (1881) — 1857a.
Location unknown.

SILOTI — *see* ZILOTI.

SINEL'NIKOVA, Ekaterina — *see* LAROSH, Ekaterina.

SITOVSKII, Nikolai Prokof'evich (d. 1890). Secretary of the Arts Committee at the Moscow Conservatory, and director of the RMS.
1 letter (n. d.) — 3867a.
RUS–Mcm.

SITTARD, Josef (1846–1903). German musicologist, organist, teacher and music critic.
2 letters (1888–89) — 3465a, 3820a.
D–Tsiedentopf.

SKLENÁŘ, Josef (d. 1890). Secretary of the Prague National Theatre.
1 letter (1881) — 1787.
CZ–Pnm.

SKOMPSKA, Adelina — *see* BOL'SKA, Adelina.

SLATIN, Il'ia Il'ich (1845–1931). Pianist, conductor, and director of the Khar'kov branch of the RMS.
12 letters (1884, 1891–93) — 2408, 4579, 4780, 4854, 4857, 4893, 4910, 4918, 4920, 4926, 5040, 5048.
RUS–KL.

SLAVIANSKOE BLAGOTVORITEL'NOE OBSHCHESTVO — *see* SLAVONIC CHARITABLE SOCIETY

SLAVINA, Mariia Aleksandrovna (1858–1951). Mezzo-soprano with the Imperial Theatres in St. Petersburg.
1 letter (1887) — 3314.
RUS–KL.

SLAVONIC CHARITABLE SOCIETY [Slavianskoe blagotvoritel'noe obshchestvo]. Founded in St. Petersburg in 1877.
1 letter (1885) — 2670.
RUS–SPa.

SMOLENSKII, Stepan Vasil'evich (1848–1909). Choirmaster, and Russian church music historian.
4 letters (1892–93) — 4763, 4887, 4911, 4913a.
RUS–KL (3), RUS–SPsc (1).
[4913a not published].

SMYTH, Ethel (Mary) (1858–1943). English composer and conductor.
1 letter (1889) — 3861a.
Location unknown.

SOFRONOV, Aleksei Ivanovich (1859–1925). Chaikovskii's manservant from 1871.
118 letters (1875–84, 1887–93, n.d.) — 405, 469, 479, 608a, 609a, 619, 629, 936, 939, 941, 944, 952, 1149, 1219, 1286, 1292, 1618, 1656, 1659, 1672, 1674, 1677, 1687, 1696, 1705, 1720, 1730, 1731, 1738, 1746, 1756, 1773, 1794a, 1800, 1811, 1822, 1883, 1887, 1891, 1901, 1907, 1913, 1917, 1922, 1938, 1942, 1950, 1962, 1969, 1979, 2012, 2022, 2037, 2042, 2049, 2056, 2062, 2096, 2104, 2110, 2129, 2140, 2169, 2175, 2191, 2198, 2208, 2220, 2223, 2229, 2237, 2251, 2279, 2431, 2438, 2442, 2446, 2614, 3254, 3288, 3313, 3320, 3379, 3451, 3476, 3483, 3491, 3510, 3521, 3538, 3775, 3780, 3803, 3822, 3833, 3840, 3934, 4366, 4375, 4457, 4521, 4531a, 4577, 4587, 4600, 4601, 4700, 4703, 4707, 4792, 4811, 4839, 4922, 4933, 4947, 4965, 5024.
RUS–KL (24), RUS–Mcm (1), RUS–SPsc (93).
[608a, 609a, 1794a not published].

SOFRONOV, Mikhail Ivanovich (1848–1932). The composer's manservant from 1871 to 1876, and older brother of Aleksei Sofronov.
4 letters (1875–77) — 405, 470, 489, 588.
RUS–KL.

SOKOLOV, Aleksandr Petrovich. Opera singer at the Bol'shoi Theatre in Moscow.
1 letter (1883) — 2350.
RUS–KL.

SOLOV'EV, Nikolai Feopemptovich (1846–1916). Composer, music critic, and professor at the St. Petersburg Conservatory.
1 letter (1885) — 2719.
RUS–Mcl.

STANFORD, Charles Villiers (1852–1924). Irish composer, director and teacher. Professor of music at Cambridge University.
2 letters (1893) — 4855, 4870.
GB–Lcm.

STASOV, Vladimir Vasil´evich (1824–1906). Art historian, critic, and director of the arts section of the St. Petersburg Public Library.
22 letters (1873–74, 1876–77, 1879, 1884–87, 1893) — 286, 287, 365, 370, 520, 525, 541, 548, 552, 1072, 1087, 2595, 2603, 2604, 2609, 2616, 2822, 2827, 3114, 3193, 3246, 4869.
RUS–SPsc.

STOIAN, Konstantin — see MIKHAILOV-STOIAN, Konstantin Ivanovich.

STOJOWSKI, Sigismund (1870–1946). Polish pianist and composer.
2 letters (1893) — 5030, 5057.
US–NH.

STRAUSS, Adolph (1864–1939). Pianist and teacher.
1 letter (1883) — 2315.
RUS–KL.

ŠUBERT, František Adolf (1849–1915). Czech journalist and writer, and director of the National Theatre in Prague.
16 letters (1888–89, 1891–92) — 3694, 3696, 3713, 3769, 3798, 4308, 4554, 4575, 4581, 4621, 4639, 4773, 4776, 4777, 4791, 4832.
CZ–Pnm (7), CZ–Ps (6), RUS–KL (2), RUS–Mcl (1).

SUK, Václav [SUK, Viacheslav Ivanovich] (1861–1933). Czech violinist, conductor and composer.
2 letters (1888, 1891) — 3656, 4541.
RUS–KL (1), RUS–Mcl (1).

SUPRUNENKO, Iosif Grigor´evich (1861–1936). Music teacher and singer with the Odessa opera company.
1 letter (1893) — 4877.
RUS–KL.

SUVORIN, Aleksei Sergeevich (1834–1912). Journalist, writer, dramatist and publisher.
5 letters (1884, 1889–90) — 2622, 3838, 3852, 3997, 4245.
RUS–Mcl.

SVETLOV, Konstantin — see MIKHAILOV-STOIAN, Konstantin Ivanovich.

SVETLOV-STOIAN, Konstantin — see MIKHAILOV-STOIAN, Konstantin Ivanovich.

SVIATLOVSKAIA, Aleksandra Vladimirovna (later MÜLLER; 1856–1923). Opera singer (soprano) at the Bol´shoi Theatre in Moscow.
4 letters (1887, 1893) — 3231, 4914, 4944, 4978.
RUS–KL (4).

TAFFANEL, (Claude) Paul (1844–1908). French flute virtuoso, composer, conductor and teacher.
1 letter (1888) — 3740.
F–Psamarin.

TAL´, Robert Khristianovich von. Russian consul in Paris.
1 letter (1878) — 713a.
Location unknown

TAMBERLIK, Enrico (1820–89). Italian singer (tenor).
1 letter (1870) — 208.
Location unknown.

TANEEV, Sergei Ivanovich (1856–1915). Composer, pianist, conductor, musicologist and professor/director of the Moscow Conservatory.
114 letters (1874–93) — 345, 390, 402, 409, 411, 414, 415, 455a, 472, 500, 517, 518, 528, 535, 539, 551, 576, 681, 716, 738, 799, 807, 869a, 924, 935, 1056, 1383, 1396, 1469, 1503, 1544, 1554, 1565, 1574, 1646, 1706, 1795, 1826, 1839, 2059, 2071, 2130, 2148, 2167, 2216, 2253, 2459, 2465, 2512, 2520, 2532, 2553, 2557, 2560, 2607, 2619, 2711, 2722, 2728, 2733, 2736, 2755, 2757, 2834, 2869, 2870, 3001, 3016, 3039, 3183, 3211, 3294, 3324, 3336, 3387, 3410, 3455, 3567, 3577, 3675a, 3719, 3721, 3675a, 3860, 3863, 3955, 4098, 4244a, 4285, 4302, 4429, 4484, 4525, 4533a, 4571, 4660, 4724, 4746, 4750, 4782a, 4785, 4794, 4801, 4806, 4814, 4815, 4818, 4969, 4983, 4997, 5008, 5034, 5036, 5058.
RUS–KL (4), RUS–Mcl (103), RUS–Mcm (3), unknown (4).

TANEEVA, Varvara Pavlovna (1822–89). Mother of Sergei Taneev.
1 letter (1878) — 792.
RUS—Mcl.

TARNAVICH, Aleksandr Danilovich (1834–?). Priest at Kamenka.
9 letters (1881–82, 1884) — 1662, 1669, 1798, 1844, 2106, 2134, 2150, 2160, 2430.
RUS–KL.

TAVASTSJERNA, Karl August (1860–98). German writer, sculptor and architect.
1 letter (1883) — 2385.
RUS–Mcl.

TAYAU, Marie (Augustine Anne) (1855–92). Parisian violinist.
1 letter (1886) — 3010.
US–NYpm.

VOITKEVICH, Anna Mikhailovna. Friend of Varvara Zarudnaia in Tiflis.
1 letter (1889) — 3956.
RUS–KL.

VON MECK — *see* MECK.

VORONTSOV-DASHKOV, Illarion Ivanovich (*Count*; 1837–1916). Minister to the Imperial Court.
1 letter (1887) — 3244.
RUS–Md.

VSEVOLOZHSKII, Ivan Aleksandrovich (1835–1909). Director of the Imperial Theatres.
30 letters (1883–92) — 2393, 2410, 2617a, 2752, 3130, 3255, 3418, 3422, 3458, 3459, 3566, 3636, 3643, 3647, 3720, 3758, 3761, 4078, 4101, 4184, 4186, 4198, 4214, 4296, 4324, 4346, 4363, 4365a, 4613, 4617.
RUS–KL (8), RUS–Md (2), RUS–SPia (19), unknown (1).
[2617a, 4365a not published].

VYKOUKALOVÁ-BRADAČEVA, Ružena. Czech opera singer (mezzo–soprano) at the National Theatre in Prague.
2 letters (1892–93) — 4796, 4866.
Locations unknown.

WALTZ — *see* VAL´TS.

WEBER, K. E. Unknown correspondent.
1 letter (1887) — 3168a.
Location unknown.
Not published.

WOLFF, Hermann (1845–1902). German musician.
2 letters (1889) — 3754a, 3785.
GB–Lrosenthal (1), unknown (1).

ZABEL, Eugen. German music critic and journalist.
1 letter (1892) — 4696.
Location unknown.

ZARUDNAIA, Varvara Mikhailovna (*later* IVANOVA; 1857–1939). Singer (soprano) with the Kiev and Tiflis operas theatres, professor at the Moscow Conservatory, and wife of Mikhail Ippolitov-Ivanov.
5 letters (1888–91) — 3509, 3571, 3595, 3612, 3929, 4179, 4412, 4421.
RUS–KL (2), RUS–Mcm (6).

ZEIFERT, Ivan Ivanovich [SEIFERT, Jan] (1833–aft.1910). Cellist, teacher, professor at the St. Petersburg Conservatory and director of the St. Petersburg Philharmonic Society.
2 letters (1880, 1892) — 1496, 4631.
RUS–Md (1), RUS–SPtob (1).

ZHEDRINSKII, Aleksandr Aleksandrovich (1859–1919). Lawyer and senator in St. Petersburg.
5 letters (1880–82, 1884) — 1507, 1542, 1724, 2035, 2501.
RUS–KL (4), RUS–Md (1).

ZHUKOVSKAIA, Evgeniia Iosifovna (b. KOTEK). Older sister of Iosif Kotek.
1 letter (1885) — 2641.
RUS–KL.

ZILOTI, Aleksandr Il´ich [SILOTI, Alexander] (1863–1945). Pianist, conductor and professor at the Moscow Conservatory.
67 letters (1886–93, n.d.) — 3055, 3099, 3395, 3443, 3463, 3465, 3660, 3673, 3687, 3716, 3751, 3753, 3755, 3776, 3789, 3820, 3857, 3874, 3878, 3881, 3907, 3911, 3915, 3923, 4001, 4021, 4076, 4106, 4142, 4148, 4176, 4193, 4230, 4294, 4297, 4306, 4321, 4331, 4336, 4400, 4405, 4433, 4443, 4451, 4472, 4483, 4498, 4556, 4605, 4642, 4656, 4705, 4712, 4715, 4789, 4867, 4874, 4925, 4932, 4939, 4973, 4985, 4989, 4994, 5004, 5019a, 5043.
D–F (1), RUS–KL (62), US–NYpm (1), unknown (3).

ZILOTI, Sergei Il´ich [SILOTI, Sergei] (1862–1914). Older brother of Aleksandr Ziloti.
1 letter (1889) — 3978.
RUS–KL.

ZVANTSEV, Konstantin Ivanovich (1825–90). Author, librettist and translator.
1 letter (1876) — 447.
RUS–Md.

ZVERZHANSKII, Aleksandr Georgievich (b. 1874). Pianist and musicologist.
1 letter (1891) — 4569.
RUS–KL.

To unidentified correspondents
12 letters (1864, 1869, 1888–89, 1892, 1893) — 67, 176, 1884a, 3610a, 3932, 4375a, 4635, 4748, 4858a, 5035a, 5065b.
RUS–KL (5), RUS–Mcm (1), RUS–Mkiselev (1), US–Bpr (1), US–NH (1), US–PHci (1), US–R (1), US–Wc (1), unknown (1).
[1884a, 3861a, 4858a, 5035a, 5065b not published].

LOCATIONS OF CHAIKOVSKII'S AUTOGRAPH LETTERS

Armenia *(1)*
ARM–YE *(1)* — 3885

Czech Republic *(40)*
CZ–Pfoerster *(5)* — 3854, 3867, 4790, 4862, 4900
CZ–Pkadlic *(4)* — 3676, 3702, 3745, 4513
CZ–Pnm *(9)* — 1787, 4575, 4581, 4639, 4713, 4773, 4776, 4777, 4790a
CZ–POm *(3)* — 3603, 3730, 4677
CZ–Ps *(16)* — 3527, 3530, 3668, 3694, 3696, 3713, 3732, 3739, 3749, 3763, 3799, 3811, 4308, 4554, 4791, 4832
CZ–ZL *(3)* — 3529, 3772, 3800

France *(49)*
F–DI *(4)* — 441a, 2949, 2969, 3227
F–Phofman *(1)* — 4810
F–Pi *(1)* — 4809
F–Plauwe *(4)* — 548a, 3598a, 3674, 4822a
F–Pn *(36)* — 2758, 2762, 2819, 2830, 2839, 2854, 2924, 2968a, 2970, 2980, 3031, 3082, 3170, 3176, 3187, 3204, 3216, 3391, 3430, 3462, 3474, 3514, 3557, 3690, 3747, 3768, 3808, 3834, 3936, 3981, 4068, 4088, 4298, 4315, 4335, 4602
F–Po *(2)* — 2965, 3998
F–Psamarin *(1)* — 3740

Germany *(26)*
D–AMlohss *(1)* — 3659
D–Bds *(2)* — 406a, 907a
D–Bmb *(1)* — 4168
D–Bmuck *(1)* — 3390
D–BShenn *(1)* — 3441
D–EMmüller *(2)* — 3652, 3714
D–F *(2)* —4362a, 5019a
D–FF *(1)* — 4293b
D–MZsch *(4)* — 932a, 2829a, 3976a, 4038a
D–H *(1)* — 4607
D–Hoestrich *(1)* — 3784
D–LEmi *(1)* — 3504
D–Mtf *(1)* — 3910
D–Tsiedentopf *(2)* — 3465a, 3820a
D–Tu *(3)* — 2453a, 3014a, 3219a

D–WIaxtmann *(1)* — 3587a
D–WÜ *(1)* — 4318a

Great Britain *(27)*
GB–Cmaitland *(1)* — 4941
GB–Cu *(1)* — 4812b
GB–Gu *(1)* — 4681a
GB–Lbl *(2)* — 1728, 3469
GB–Lcm *(2)* — 4855, 4870
GB–Lps *(3)* — 3485, 3493, 4971
GB–Lrosenthal *(1)* — 3785
GB–Mcm *(16)* — 1924, 2008, 2013, 3111, 3169, 3444, 3526, 3688, 3793, 3868, 3877, 3898, 3938, 3949, 4488, 4515

Hungary *(1)*
H–Bkuna *(1)* — 4777a

Italy *(3)*
I–Nc *(1)* — 623a
I–Rcolombo *(1)* — 4719
I–Rsgambati *(1)* — 4091

Japan *(1)*
J–private — 1332a

Kazakhstan *(1)*
KZK–AA *(1)* — 4908

The Netherlands *(3)*
NL–Ac *(1)* — 3779
NL–At *(1)* — 4612
NL–Amengelberg *(1)* — 5063

Norway *(3)*
N–Bo *(3)* — 3499, 3552, 3655

Russia *(4502)*
RUS–KL *(3355)* — 34, 35, 64, 65, 69, 74, 95a, 107, 127, 128, 135, 142, 147, 166, 202a, 203, 218, 236, 238, 243, 246a, 249, 250, 252, 253, 258, 258a, 263, 264, 267, 268, 269, 271, 273, 274, 282, 283, 302, 309, 310, 313, 314, 319, 325

RUS–KL [continued] — 328, 329, 330, 333, 336, 349, 356, 359, 362, 363, 372, 380, 381, 385, 387, 392, 394, 397, 399, 400, 403, 405, 408, 421, 422, 423, 425, 428, 429, 432a, 433, 436, 437, 438, 439, 442, 445, 446, 449, 450, 451, 453, 456, 457, 462, 464, 465, 467, 468, 470, 471, 475, 476, 478, 480, 481, 482, 483, 484, 486, 488, 489, 490, 491, 492, 494, 496, 497, 498, 501, 504, 505, 506, 508, 509, 510, 512, 515, 522, 524, 530a, 533, 536, 538, 540, 542, 544, 545, 546, 550, 553, 554, 555, 556, 557, 559, 564, 565, 567, 568, 569, 570, 571, 573, 574, 577, 579, 580, 581, 581a, 584, 585, 586, 588, 590, 591, 592, 593, 594, 595, 596, 597, 598, 599, 601, 602, 604, 607, 609, 610, 611, 613, 616, 620, 621, 622, 625, 626, 631, 632, 633, 635, 636, 637, 638, 639, 640, 643, 644, 647, 648, 650, 651, 655, 656, 657, 659, 660, 661, 662, 663, 664, 665, 666, 668, 669, 670, 672, 673, 674, 676, 677, 678, 679, 680, 683, 684, 685, 686, 689, 690, 691, 692, 693, 695, 696, 697, 698, 700, 701, 703, 705, 706, 707, 708, 709, 710, 711, 712, 714, 715, 718, 719, 721, 722, 723, 724, 725, 726, 728, 729, 730, 732, 733, 734, 735, 736, 737, 739, 740, 741, 742, 743, 744, 746, 747, 749, 750, 751, 752, 753, 754, 755, 756, 757, 758, 759, 761, 762, 763, 764, 765, 766, 767, 768, 769, 770, 771, 772, 773, 775, 776, 777, 778, 779, 780, 782, 783, 784, 785, 787, 788, 789, 790, 791, 793, 794, 795, 796, 797, 798, 800, 801, 802, 803, 804, 805, 806, 808, 809, 810, 811, 812, 813, 815, 816, 817, 818, 819, 820, 821, 822, 823, 824, 825, 826, 827, 828, 829, 830, 832, 833, 834, 835, 837, 838, 840, 841, 842, 843, 844, 846, 847, 848, 849, 850, 851, 852, 853, 854, 855, 856, 857, 858, 859, 860, 861, 862, 863, 864, 865, 866, 867, 868, 869, 870, 871, 872, 874, 875, 876, 878, 879, 880, 881, 882, 883, 884, 885, 886, 887, 888, 889, 890, 891, 892, 893, 894, 895, 896, 897, 898, 899, 900, 901, 902, 903, 904, 906, 907, 909, 910, 911, 912, 913, 915, 916, 917, 918, 919, 920, 921, 922, 925, 926, 927, 928, 929, 930, 931, 933, 944, 946, 949, 950, 953, 956, 957, 958, 959, 960, 961, 963, 964, 965, 966, 967, 968, 969, 970, 971, 972, 973, 974, 975, 976, 977, 978, 980, 981, 982, 983, 984, 985, 986, 987, 988, 989, 991, 992, 993, 994, 995, 996, 997, 998, 1000, 1001, 1002, 1003, 1004, 1005, 1006, 1007, 1008, 1009, 1010, 1011, 1012, 1013, 1014, 1015, 1016, 1018, 1019, 1020, 1021, 1022, 1023, 1024, 1025, 1026, 1027, 1028, 1029, 1031, 1032, 1033, 1034, 1035, 1036, 1037, 1038, 1039, 1040, 1041, 1042, 1043, 1044, 1045, 1046, 1047, 1048, 1049, 1050, 1051, 1053, 1054, 1055, 1057, 1058, 1059, 1061, 1062, 1063, 1064, 1065, 1066, 1067, 1068, 1069, 1070, 1071, 1073, 1074, 1075, 1076, 1077, 1079, 1080, 1081, 1082, 1083, 1084, 1085, 1086, 1088, 1089, 1090, 1091, 1092, 1093, 1094, 1095, 1096, 1097, 1098, 1099, 1100, 1101, 1102, 1103, 1104, 1105, 1106, 1107, 1108, 1110, 1111, 1112, 1113, 1114, 1115, 1116, 1118, 1119, 1120, 1121, 1123, 1124, 1125, 1126, 1127, 1128, 1129, 1130, 1131, 1132, 1133, 1134, 1136, 1137, 1138, 1139, 1140, 1141, 1142, 1144, 1145, 1146, 1147, 1148, 1149, 1150, 1151, 1152, 1153, 1154, 1155, 1156, 1157, 1159, 1160, 1161, 1162, 1163, 1164, 1165, 1166, 1167, 1168, 1169, 1170, 1171, 1172, 1173, 1174, 1175, 1176, 1178, 1179, 1180, 1182, 1183, 1184, 1185, 1186, 1187, 1188, 1189, 1190, 1190a, 1191, 1192, 1193, 1194, 1195, 1196, 1197, 1198, 1199, 1200, 1201, 1202, 1203, 1204, 1205, 1206, 1207, 1208, 1209, 1210, 1211, 1212, 1213, 1216, 1217, 1218, 1221, 1223, 1224, 1225, 1227, 1228, 1229, 1230, 1231, 1232, 1233, 1234, 1235, 1236, 1237, 1238, 1239, 1240, 1241, 1242, 1243, 1244, 1245, 1246, 1247, 1248, 1249, 1250, 1251, 1252, 1253, 1254, 1255, 1256, 1257, 1258, 1259, 1260, 1261, 1262, 1263, 1264, 1265, 1266, 1267, 1268, 1269, 1270, 1271, 1272, 1273, 1274, 1275, 1276, 1277, 1278, 1280, 1281, 1282, 1283, 1284, 1285, 1287, 1289, 1290, 1291, 1293, 1294, 1295, 1297, 1298, 1299, 1300, 1301, 1302, 1303, 1304, 1305, 1306, 1307, 1308, 1309, 1310, 1311, 1312, 1313, 1314, 1315, 1316, 1317, 1318, 1319, 1320, 1321, 1322, 1324, 1325, 1326, 1327, 1328, 1330, 1331, 1332, 1333, 1334, 1335, 1336, 1337, 1338, 1339, 1340, 1341, 1342, 1343, 1344, 1345, 1346, 1347, 1348, 1349, 1351, 1352, 1353, 1354, 1355, 1356, 1357, 1358, 1359, 1360, 1361, 1362, 1363, 1364, 1365, 1366, 1367, 1368, 1369, 1370, 1371, 1372, 1373, 1374, 1375, 1377, 1378, 1379, 1380, 1381, 1382, 1384, 1385, 1387, 1389, 1390, 1391, 1392, 1393, 1394, 1397, 1399, 1400, 1401, 1402, 1403, 1404, 1405, 1406, 1407, 1408, 1409, 1410, 1411, 1412, 1414, 1415, 1416, 1417, 1418, 1419, 1420, 1421, 1422, 1423, 1424, 1425, 1426, 1427, 1428, 1429, 1430, 1431, 1432, 1433, 1435, 1436, 1437, 1438, 1439, 1440, 1441, 1442, 1443, 1444, 1445, 1450, 1451, 1452, 1454, 1455, 1456, 1457, 1458, 1459, 1460, 1462, 1464, 1464a, 1465, 1466, 1467, 1468, 1472, 1473, 1474, 1476, 1477, 1478, 1479, 1480, 1481, 1482, 1483, 1484, 1485, 1486, 1487, 1488, 1489, 1490, 1491, 1492, 1493, 1495, 1497, 1498, 1499, 1500, 1501, 1502, 1504, 1505, 1506, 1507, 1508, 1509, 1510, 1511, 1512, 1513, 1514, 1515, 1516, 1517, 1519, 1520, 1521, 1523, 1524, 1525, 1526, 1527, 1528, 1529, 1531, 1532, 1533, 1534, 1535, 1536, 1538, 1539, 1540, 1541, 1542, 1543, 1545, 1546, 1547, 1548, 1549, 1550, 1551, 1552, 1553, 1555, 1556, 1557, 1558, 1559, 1560, 1561, 1562, 1563, 1564, 1566, 1567, 1568, 1570, 1571, 1572, 1573, 1576, 1577, 1578, 1580, 1581, 1582, 1583, 1584, 1585, 1587, 1588, 1589, 1590, 1591, 1592, 1593, 1594, 1596, 1597, 1599, 1600, 1601, 1603, 1604,   1605,   1606,   1607,   1608,   1609,

RUS–KL [continued] — 2882, 2884, 2885, 2886, 2887, 2888, 2890, 2891, 2892, 2893, 2894, 2896, 2897, 2898, 2899, 2900, 2902, 2903, 2904, 2905, 2906, 2907, 2908, 2910, 2911, 2913, 2914, 2916, 2917, 2918, 2919, 2920, 2921, 2922, 2922a, 2923, 2926, 2927, 2929, 2930, 2931, 2933, 2935, 2936, 2937, 2938, 2939, 2940, 2941, 2942, 2943, 2944, 2945, 2947, 2948, 2950, 2951, 2952, 2953, 2954, 2955, 2956, 2957, 2958, 2959, 2960, 2961, 2962, 2963, 2964, 2966, 2967, 2968, 2971, 2972, 2973, 2974, 2975, 2977, 2978, 2979, 2981, 2982, 2983, 2984, 2985, 2986, 2987, 2988, 2990, 2991, 2992, 2993, 2994, 2995, 2997, 2998, 2999, 3002, 3003, 3004, 3005, 3006, 3007, 3008, 3009, 3011, 3014, 3015, 3017, 3018, 3019, 3020, 3022, 3023, 3024, 3025, 3026, 3027, 3028, 3029, 3030, 3032, 3033, 3034, 3035, 3036, 3036a, 3037, 3038, 3040, 3041, 3042, 3044, 3045, 3049, 3050, 3051, 3055, 3056, 3058, 3059, 3060, 3061, 3062, 3064, 3067, 3068, 3069, 3071, 3072, 3073, 3075, 3076, 3077, 3078, 3080, 3081, 3085, 3086, 3087, 3088, 3089, 3091, 3092, 3093, 3094, 3096, 3098, 3099, 3102, 3103, 3104, 3105, 3106, 3108, 3109, 3112, 3113, 3115, 3116, 3117, 3118, 3119, 3121, 3122, 3129, 3131, 3133, 3134, 3136, 3137, 3139a, 3139b, 3142, 3143, 3144, 3146, 3148, 3149, 3153, 3155, 3156, 3158, 3159, 3162, 3164, 3165, 3167, 3168, 3168a, 3171, 3172, 3173, 3174, 3175, 3177, 3178, 3179, 3181, 3182, 3183, 3185, 3186, 3188, 3189, 3190, 3191, 3192, 3194, 3195, 3196, 3198, 3199, 3201, 3202, 3203, 3205, 3206, 3207, 3209, 3210, 3217, 3218, 3219, 3220, 3221, 3222, 3223, 3224, 3225, 3226, 3228, 3230, 3231, 3232, 3233, 3234, 3235, 3237, 3239, 3240, 3241, 3242, 3243, 3247, 3248, 3249, 3250, 3251, 3252, 3253, 3256, 3257, 3258, 3259, 3260, 3261, 3262, 3263, 3264, 3265, 3266, 3267, 3268, 3270, 3271, 3273, 3274, 3275, 3276, 3278, 3279, 3280, 3281, 3282, 3283, 3283a, 3284, 3285, 3287, 3289, 3290, 3291, 3292, 3293, 3295, 3298, 3301, 3303, 3304, 3305, 3307, 3308, 3309, 3310, 3311, 3312, 3314, 3315, 3316, 3317, 3318, 3319, 3321, 3322, 3323, 3325, 3326, 3327, 3328, 3329, 3330, 3331, 3332, 3333, 3334, 3335, 3338, 3339, 3340, 3341, 3343, 3344, 3345, 3348, 3350, 3351, 3352, 3353, 3354, 3355, 3356, 3359, 3360, 3365, 3368, 3369, 3371, 3372, 3373, 3374, 3375, 3376, 3378, 3380, 3381, 3382, 3383, 3385, 3386, 3388, 3389, 3392, 3395, 3396, 3397, 3398, 3399, 3400, 3405, 3407, 3408, 3409, 3411, 3412, 3413, 3414, 3414a, 3416, 3419, 3420, 3421, 3423a, 3424, 3425, 3427, 3429, 3432, 3433, 3435a, 3436, 3437, 3438, 3439, 3440, 3442, 3443, 3445, 3447, 3448, 3449, 3450, 3452, 3453, 3454, 3456, 3460, 3461, 3463, 3464, 3465, 3466, 3468, 3470, 3472, 3473, 3477, 3478, 3479, 3480, 3481, 3482, 3484, 3486, 3487, 3488, 3489, 3490, 3492, 3494, 3495, 3496, 3497, 3498, 3501, 3502, 3503, 3507, 3511, 3512, 3513, 3516, 3517, 3518, 3519, 3520, 3522, 3523, 3524, 3525, 3528, 3531, 3532, 3533, 3534, 3535, 3537, 3539, 3540, 3541, 3542, 3544, 3545, 3546, 3547, 3548, 3549, 3550, 3551, 3553, 3554, 3555, 3556, 3559, 3560, 3561, 3562, 3563, 3565, 3566, 3567, 3568, 3570, 3572, 3573, 3575a, 3576, 3579, 3580, 3581, 3582, 3583, 3584, 3586, 3588, 3590, 3593, 3593a, 3596, 3597, 3598, 3600, 3602, 3605, 3607, 3608, 3609, 3610, 3610a, 3611, 3612, 3613, 3615, 3616, 3617, 3618, 3619, 3620, 3622, 3624, 3625, 3626, 3627, 3628, 3630, 3632, 3633, 3635, 3637, 3638, 3639, 3641, 3642, 3643, 3644, 3645, 3646, 3648, 3649, 3650, 3653, 3654, 3657, 3658, 3660, 3661, 3662, 3664, 3665, 3666, 3667, 3669, 3670, 3671, 3672, 3673, 3673a, 3677, 3678, 3679, 3680, 3681, 3682, 3683, 3684, 3686, 3692, 3695, 3697, 3698, 3699, 3701, 3703, 3705, 3706, 3709, 3710, 3711, 3712, 3716, 3717, 3718, 3724, 3725, 3726, 3727, 3728, 3729, 3731, 3733, 3734, 3735, 3737, 3738, 3743, 3744, 3746, 3748, 3750, 3751, 3753, 3754, 3755, 3756, 3757, 3759, 3763a, 3764, 3766, 3767, 3770, 3771, 3773, 3774, 3776, 3777, 3778, 3781, 3782, 3783, 3786, 3787, 3789, 3790, 3791, 3792, 3795, 3796, 3797, 3798, 3803, 3804, 3805, 3806, 3807, 3809, 3812, 3813, 3814, 3815, 3817, 3818, 3819, 3820, 3821, 3823, 3824, 3825, 3826, 3827, 3828, 3829, 3830, 3831, 3832, 3835, 3836, 3837, 3839, 3841, 3842, 3844, 3845, 3846, 3848, 3849, 3850, 3851, 3855, 3856, 3857, 3858, 3859, 3861, 3862, 3864, 3865, 3866, 3869, 3870, 3871, 3873, 3874, 3875, 3876, 3878, 3880, 3881, 3883, 3884, 3886, 3891, 3895, 3896, 3897, 3899, 3900, 3901, 3902, 3903, 3904, 3905, 3906, 3907, 3908, 3909, 3911, 3913, 3914, 3915, 3916, 3917, 3919, 3920, 3921, 3922, 3925, 3926, 3927, 3928, 3931, 3932, 3933, 3937, 3939, 3940, 3941, 3945, 3946, 3947, 3948, 3952, 3953, 3954, 3956, 3957, 3960, 3961, 3963, 3964, 3967, 3973, 3975, 3977, 3978, 3979, 3982, 3983, 3984, 3985, 3986, 3987, 3988, 3991, 3992a, 3996, 3999, 4000, 4001, 4002, 4003, 4004, 4006, 4007, 4009, 4010, 4011, 4012, 4012a, 4013, 4014, 4015, 4017, 4019, 4020, 4021, 4022, 4024, 4026, 4027, 4029, 4030, 4034, 4035, 4036, 4039, 4040, 4041, 4043, 4044, 4045, 4047, 4048, 4049, 4051, 4053, 4054, 4055, 4056, 4057, 4058, 4060, 4061, 4063, 4065, 4066, 4067, 4070, 4071, 4072, 4073, 4075, 4076, 4077, 4078, 4079, 4081, 4083, 4084, 4085, 4086, 4089, 4090, 4092, 4095, 4096, 4097, 4099, 4100, 4101, 4102, 4104, 4105, 4106, 4107, 4108, 4109, 4110, 4111, 4112, 4113, 4115, 4117, 4118, 4119, 4120, 4122, 4123, 4125, 4126, 4127, 4128, 4129, 4130, 4131, 4132, 4133, 4134, 4135, 4137, 4138, 4139, 4142, 4144, 4145, 4146, 4147, 4148, 4149, 4151, 4152, 4153, 4154, 4155, 4156, 4157,

RUS–SPtob *(30)* — 401, 419, 426, 440, 454, 1453, 1461, 1496, 1933, 3065, 3066, 3083, 3752, 3760, 3882, 4064, 4121, 4136, 4173, 4174, 4187, 4191, 4257, 4295, 4461, 4462, 4624, 4631, 4673, 4795

Switzerland *(5)*

CH–B *(3)* — 1210a, 2491a, 3395a

CH–Bkoch *(1)* — 443

CH–Bps *(1)* — 3919a

United States of America *(50)*

US–ANcrocker *(1)* — 3070

US–Bpr *(1)* — 1884a

US–BHsachs *(1)* — 4116

US–BHsmith *(1)* — 4995

US–Cn *(1)* — 4682

US–CA *(2)* — 3377, 3816

US–CAM *(2)* — 3467, 3774a

US–CLbackford *(1)* — 4538

US–I *(1)* — 4894a

US–LJ *(1)* — 4856a

US–NH *(5)* — 413a, 4375a, 4901, 5030, 5057

US–NHub *(4)* — 2730a, 3958a, 4580, 4844a

US–NYcub *(1)* — 4496

US–NYmo *(1)* — 3943

US–NYpm *(9)* — 3010, 4164, 4306, 4477, 4603, 4805, 4807, 4824, 5044, 4882

US–NYtollefsen *(1)* — 2900a

US–PHci *(1)* — 4858a

US–R] *(1)* — 4635

US–STu *(2)* — 3508, 4239

US–Wc *(14)* — 67, 1495a, 2259, 2749, 2760, 3384, 3563a, 3793a, 4052, 4069, 4181, 4347, 4432, 4654

Unknown *(534)* — 3, 4, 5, 6, 7, 8, 51, 52, 53, 77, 78, 79, 83, 84, 85, 88, 89, 91, 92, 93, 96, 97, 98, 102, 104, 108, 110, 112, 113, 118, 121, 122, 129, 131, 136, 137, 139, 140, 141, 143, 145, 146, 148, 150, 153, 157, 160, 162, 164, 165, 167, 177, 182, 184, 187, 189, 190, 195, 200, 204, 208, 210, 213, 217, 227, 228, 230, 232, 234, 237, 239, 245, 254, 259, 260, 261, 262, 276, 278, 291, 345, 355, 361, 400a, 418, 444a, 455, 461, 485, 514, 558, 560, 561, 563, 582, 583, 614, 624, 628, 646, 651a, 713a, 760, 836, 869a, 873, 934, 938, 940, 943, 945, 947, 948, 955, 1052, 1122, 1296, 1434, 1448, 1494, 1537, 1579, 1586, 1602, 1640, 1643, 1679, 1693a,

1775, 1783, 1786, 1801, 1827, 1830, 1857a,, 1909, 1918, 1920, 1925, 1928, 1929, 1931, 1935, 1937, 1944, 1946, 1951, 1957, 1959, 1963, 1970, 1973, 1980, 1982, 1989, 2007, 2011, 2020, 2023, 2029, 2046, 2050, 2066, 2072, 2083, 2087, 2089, 2095, 2098, 2099, 2105, 2111, 2114, 2121, 2126, 2131, 2136, 2144, 2146, 2151, 2153, 2154, 2159, 2174, 2176, 2179, 2182, 2185, 2186, 2194, 2200, 2203, 2205, 2207, 2211, 2212, 2217, 2222, 2226, 2228, 2231, 2232, 2233, 2238, 2241, 2247, 2252, 2257, 2264, 2271, 2274, 2276, 2282, 2287, 2291, 2293, 2296, 2304, 2319, 2322, 2324, 2329, 2332, 2335, 2337, 2340, 2343, 2345, 2360, 2369, 2371, 2375, 2376, 2378, 2383, 2384, 2400a, 2415, 2423, 2427, 2458, 2477, 2484, 2487, 2550, 2567, 2575, 2581, 2590, 2593, 2607, 2612, 2639, 2665, 2682, 2718, 2729, 2732, 2738, 2766, 2769, 2782, 2790, 2792, 2795, 2815, 2831, 2836a, 2845, 2856, 2857, 2872, 2889, 2895, 2915, 2946, 2976, 2984a, 2987a, 2989, 2996, 3012, 3046, 3054, 3057, 3063, 3090, 3095, 3101, 3107, 3132, 3139, 3140, 3147, 3154, 3163, 3180, 3184, 3208, 3229, 3277, 3286, 3296, 3299, 3300, 3302, 3349, 3364, 3366, 3403, 3434, 3471, 3475, 3500, 3505, 3506, 3529a, 3558, 3563b, 3587, 3591, 3592, 3601, 3604, 3606, 3614, 3621, 3623, 3634, 3647, 3663, 3677a, 3687, 3689, 3691, 3693, 3704, 3712a, 3721, 3723, 3754a, 3762, 3772a, 3772, 3790a, 3794, 3801, 3819a, 3839a, 3843, 3861a, 3889, 3889a, 3890, 3892, 3905a, 3912, 3923, 3924, 3931a, 3935, 3942, 3956a, 3969, 3970, 3990, 3993, 4005, 4008, 4016, 4018, 4025, 4028, 4031, 4033, 4037, 4038, 4042, 4059, 4062, 4074, 4082, 4087, 4093, 4124, 4136a, 4140, 4143, 4150, 4162, 4167, 4180, 4197, 4197a, 4206, 4208, 4217, 4220, 4222, 4223, 4230, 4235, 4246, 4250, 4259, 4263, 424267a, 65, 4271, 4282, 4290, 4293, 4320, 4325, 4333, 4337, 4349, 4350, 4355, 4356, 4358, 4359, 4367a, 4372, 4373, 4374, 4383, 4384, 4390, 4395, 4401, 4406, 4410, 4417, 4422, 4423, 4426, 4434, 4435, 4437, 4438, 4445, 4446, 4449, 4453, 4463, 4475, 4478, 4490, 4494, 4499, 4503, 4504, 4523a, 4545, 4549, 4550, 4551, 4564, 4570, 4582, 4588, 4589a, 4591, 4594, 4596, 4612a, 4618, 4633, 4637, 4638, 4651, 4666, 4692, 4693, 4694, 4696, 4699, 4716, 4722, 4733, 4739, 4748, 4751, 4762, 4764, 4771, 4778, 4781, 4796, 4830, 4837, 4838, 4841, 4842, 4845, 4846, 4850, 4853, 4856, 4860, 4866, 4875, 4876, 4891, 4896, 4905, 4909, 4912, 4917, 4927, 4938, 4943, 4943a, 4948, 4949, 4950, 4951, 4953, 4963, 4975, 4986, 4993, 5013, 5016, 5021, 5023, 5041, 5051, 5060, 5061, 5064, 5065

Total = 5248 letters

GENEALOGY OF

P. I. CHAIKOVSKII

CHAIKOVSKII

Pëtr Il´ich Chaikovskii

PËTR IL´ICH CHAIKOVSKII [the composer]. Born on 25 Apr 1840 in Votkinsk, Russia, the son of Il´ia Petrovich Chaikovskii (1795–1880) & Aleksandra Andreevna (b. ASSIER, 1812–54) [see below]. Studied in the Imperial School of Jurisprudence (1850–59) and the St. Petersburg Conservatory (1862–65); clerk at the Ministry of Justice in St. Petersburg from (1859–63); Professor of Music Theory at the Moscow Conservatory (1866–78). Awarded the Order of St. Vladimir (4th Class) on 23 Feb 1884 "as a sign of the particular benevolence" of Tsar Alexander III.

On 6 Jul 1877 he married Antonina Ivanovna Miliukova (1848–1917) at the Church of St. George, Malaia Nikitskaia Street, Moscow; they separated in Sep 1877 but never divorced.

Pëtr Il´ich died from complications arising from cholera at Malaia Morskaia 13 in St. Petersburg on 25 Oct 1893, and was buried on 28 Oct 1893 in Tikhvinskoe Cemetery at the Aleksandr Nevskii Monastery, St. Petersburg.

Il´ia Petrovich Chaikovskii

IL´IA PETROVICH CHAIKOVSKII [father of the composer]. Born 20 Jul 1795 in Glazov, Viatka Province, Russia, the fifth son of Pëtr Fedorovich Chaikovskii (1745–1818) and Anastasiia Stepanovna (b. POSOKHOVA; 1751–?) [see below]. Administrator of the Onezhskii salt board; Director of the Kamsko-Votkinsk iron works from 1837, later administrator at the Alapaevsk and Nizhne-Nev´ianskie works; Director of the St. Petersburg Technological Institute from 1858. He married first on 11 Sep 1827 to Mariia Karlovna KEIZER (d. 1831); second on 1 Oct 1833 to Aleksandra Andreevna ASSIER (1812–54); third in 1865 to Elizaveta Mikhailovna LIPPORT (1829–1910). Il´ia Petrovich died in St. Petersburg, Russia on 9 Jan 1880, and had eight children:

1. **Zinaida Il´inichna** [half-sister of the composer]. Born in 1829, the only child of Il´ia Petrovich and Mariia Karlovna. In Jan 1854 she married Evgenii Ivanovich OL´KHOVSKII (1824–76). Zinaida Il´inishna died on 13 Jan 1878, and had five children:
    (a) Mikhail Evgen´evich (1854–1929).
    (b) Evgeniia Evgen´evna. Married to KONOVALOV.
    (c) Mariia Evgen´evna. Married to TORSHILOV.
    (d) Aleksandr Evgen´evich.
    (e) Anatolii Evgen´evich.

2. **Ekaterina Il´inichna** [sister of the composer]. Born in 1836 or 1837, the eldest daughter of Il´ia Petrovich and Aleksandra Andreevna; she died in infancy.

3. **Nikolai Il´ich** [brother of the composer]. Born on 9 May 1838, the eldest son of Il´ia Petrovich and Aleksandra Andreevna. He worked as a mining engineer. In 1872 he married Ol´ga Sergeevna DENIS´EVA (who died c.1919). Nikolai Il´ich died on 21 Nov 1911 in Moscow, and was buried at Novodevich´e Cemetery, Moscow. He adopted one child in 1886:
    (a) Georgii Nikolaevich (Georges-Léon). Born on 26 Apr 1883 in Paris, France, the natural son of Tat´iana L´vovna DAVYDOVA [niece of Nikolai Il´ich] and Stanislaw Mikhailovich BLUMENFEL´D. Georgii Nikolaevich died in 1940.

4. **Pëtr Il´ich** [the composer]. Born on 25 Apr 1840 in Votkinsk, Russia [see above].

5. **Aleksandra Il´inichna** [sister of the composer]. Born on 28 Dec 1841 in Votkinsk, Russia the youngest daughter of Il´ia Petrovich and Aleksandra Andreevna. On 6 Nov 1860 she married Lev Vasil´evich DAVYDOV (1837–96). Aleksandra Il´inichna died in Kamenka (Kiev Region), Ukraine on 28

Mar 1891, and was buried next to her daughter Tat´iana L´vovna in the cemetery at the Aleksandr Nevskii Monastery, St. Petersburg (neither grave site has survived). She had seven children [see also under DAYVDOV]:

> (a) Tat´iana L´vovna (1861–87).
> (b) Vera L´vovna (1863–88).
> (c) Anna L´vovna (1864–1942).
> (d) Natal´ia L´vovna (1868–1956).
> (e) Dmitrii L´vovich (1870–1929).
> (f) Vladimir L´vovich (1871–1906).
> (g) Iurii (Georgii) L´vovich (1877–1965).

6   Ippolit Il´ich [brother of the composer]. Born on 10 Apr 1845 in Votkinsk, Russia, the fourth son of Il´ia Petrovich and Aleksandra Andreevna. Russian Naval officer; captain in the merchant marines; curator of the composer's house-museum at Klin from 1919. In Jun 1869 he married Sofiia Petrovna NIKONOVA (1843–1920). Ippolit Il´ich died in 1927, and was buried at the Dem´ianovo Cemetery, near Klin. He had one child:

> (a) Natal´ia Ippolitovna was born in 1876. She married Nikolai Ivanovich ALEKSEEV. Natal´ia Ippolitovna died in 1970, and had three children:
>> (i)   Mariana Nikolaevna.
>> (ii)   Irina Nikolaevna.
>> (iii) Kseniia (Oksana) Nikolaevna.

7   Anatolii Il´ich [brother of the composer]. Born on 1 May 1850 in Alapaevsk, Russia, the fifth son of Il´ia Petrovich and Aleksandra Andreevna, and a twin brother to Modest Il´ich, Civil servant, lawyer; State Prosecutor in Tiflis; State Senator. In Apr 1882 he married Praskov´ia Vladimirovna KONSHINA (1864–1956). Anatolii Il´ich died on 20 Jan 1915, and was buried in the Nikol´skoe Cemetery at t he Aleksandr Nevskii Monastery, St. Petersburg (the grave site does not survive). He had one child:

> (a) Tat´iana Anatolevna. Born in Mar 1883 in Tiflis, Georgia. She married first to VENEVITINOV; second to Baron UNGERN-STERNBERG; third to Warren CROSS. Tat´iana Anatolevna had five children:
>> (i)   Vladimir VENEVITINOV.
>> (ii)   Elena VENEVITINOV.
>> (iii) Apollinariia VENEVITINOV.
>> (iv)   Margarita UNGERN-STERNBERG.
>> (v)   Mariia UNGERN-STERNBERG.

8.   Modest Il´ich [brother of the composer]. Born on 1 May 1850 in Alapaevsk, Russia, the sixth son of Il´ia Petrovich and Aleksandra Andreevna, and twin brother to Anatolii Il´ich. Author, translator, playwright and librettist; founder and director of the composer's house-museum at Klin from 1895. Modest Il´ich died on 2 Jan 1916, and was buried at the Dem´ianovo Cemetery, near Klin.

Pëtr Fedorovich Chaikovskii

PËTR FEDOROVICH CHAIKOVSKII [grandfather of the composer]. Born in 1745 in Nikolaevka (Poltava Region), Ukraine, the second child of Fëdor Afanas´evich CHAIKA (c.1695–1767) & Anna (b. 1717) [see below], and the first to adopt the name CHAIKOVSKII. Army physician from 1777, later a medical officer in Kungur (Perm´ Region), before transferring to Viatka in 1782. He was granted nobility in the Viatka region in 1785, and became a member of Viatka City Council in 1789. Governor of Slobodskoi from 1795, later governor of Glazov. Recipient of the Order of St. Vladimir (4th class). In 1776 he married Anastasiia Stepanovna POSOKHOVA (born in 1751). Pëtr Fedorovich died in 1818, and had eleven children:

1.   Vasilii Petrovich [uncle of the composer]. Born in 1777. State Senator. Vasilii Petrovich had one child:

> (a) Pëtr Vasil´evich.

2.   Evdokiia Petrovna [aunt of the composer]. Born in 1780. Married to Vasilii Pavlovich POPOV (b. 1774), and had three children:

   (a)   Mariia Vasil´evna (b. 1803).
   (b)   Anastasiia Vasil´evna (1807–94).
   (c)   Aleksei Vasil´evich (b. 1810).

3.   Ekaterina Petrovna [aunt of the composer]. Born in 1783. Married to Vasilii Parfënovich SHIROKSHIN (born in 1776), and had two children:

   (a)   Nikolai Vasil´evich (b. 1808).
   (b)   Pëtr Vasil´evich (b. 1810).

4.   Ivan Petrovich [uncle of the composer]. Born in 1785. Army officer, awarded the Order of St. George (4th class) for bravery. Ivan Petrovich was killed in Paris in 1813, fighting in the Napoleonic Wars.

5   Aleksandra Petrovna [aunt of the composer]. Born in 1786. Married to Ivan Fedorovich EVREINOV, and had one child:

   (a)   Pëtr Ivanovich (1812–?1849), who had three children:
      (i)   Mariia Petrovna (1843–1920).
      (ii)   Elena Petrovna (1847–1915),
      (iii) Pëtr Petrovich (1850–66).

6   Pëtr Petrovich [uncle of the composer]. Born in 1789. Major-General. Recipient of the Order of St. George (4th class). Married to Evdokiia Petrovna BERENS [Elizaveta von BERENS] (b. 1780). Pëtr Petrovich died in Feb 1871, and had eight children:

   (a)   Anna Petrovna (1830–1911). Married first to EGOROV; second to Pëtr Ivanovich MERKLING, by whom she had one child:
      (i)   Lidiia Petrovna. Married to PETS.
   (b)   Sof´ia Petrovna (1833–88).
   (c)   Aleksandra Petrovna (1836–99). Married to Pavel Petrovich KARTSOV (1821–?82), and had eleven children:
      (i)   Pëtr Pavlovich (died in childhood).
      (ii)   Elizaveta Pavlovna (1858–1908).
      (iii)   Mikhail Pavlovich (1860–1909).
      (iv)   Georgii Pavlovich (1862–1931). Married to Aleksandra Valerianovna PANAEVA (1853–1942)
      (v)   Nikolai Pavlovich (1862–1918).
      (vi)   Mariia Pavlovna (1864–1927). Married to EVREMEEV.
      (vii)   Ekaterina Pavlovna (1866–1941). Married to OBUKHOV.
      (viii) Praskov´ia Pavlovna (b. 1870). Married to KORBE.
      (ix)   Lidiia Pavlovna (1872–1945).
      (x)   Pëtr Pavlovich (1874–?1930).
      (xi)   Aleksandra Pavlovna. Married first to FONVIZIN; second to HARTVIG.
   (d)   Il´ia Petrovich (1837–91). Engineer.
   (e)   Lidiia Petrovna (1838–1901). Married to Emil Iakovlevich GENKE (1828–88), and had six children:
      (i)   Pëtr Emil´evich (1862–1908).
      (ii)   Sergei Emil´evich (1866–1905).
      (iii)   Vera Emil´evna (1871–1960). Married to OLENIN.
      (iv)   Vladimir Emil´evich (1875–1916).
      (v)   Anna Emil´evna (1879–1965).
      (vi)   Ivan Emil´evich (1880–1961).
   (f)   Mitrofan Petrovich (1840–1903). General. Married to Tat´iana Petrovna BESTUZHEVA, and had one child:
      (i)   Natal´ia Mitrofanovna. Married to RACHINSKII.
   (g)   Andrei Petrovich (1841–1920). Commander of the 98th Iurevskii Infantry Regiment. Married Mariia Mikhailovna VEBER (1851–1930), and had six children:
      (i)   Natal´ia Andreevna (1876–1966). Married to Pavel Vladimirovich BURMEISTER.
      (ii)   Elizaveta Andreevna (1877–1967).
      (iii)   Ekaterina Andreevna (1879-1968). Married to Mikhail SHOROKHOV.
      (iv)   Pëtr Andreevich (1880–1950?).
      (v)   Ol´ga Andreevna (1881–1902).
      (vi)   Andrei Andreevich (1882–1970).

(h) Nadezhda Petrovna (b. 1841). Married to Sergei POROKHOVSHCHIKOV, and had four children:

    (i)   Aleksandr Sergeevich (1864–1945).

    (ii)   Pëtr Sergeevich (1867–1952).

    (iii) Sergei Sergeevich (1870–1903).

    (iv) Iurii Sergeevich (1873–1937).

    (v)   Georgii Sergeevich.

7. **Anna Petrovna** [aunt of the composer]. Born in 1790; died in early childhood.

8. **Mariia Petrovna** [aunt of the composer]. Born in 1792; died in early childhood.

9. **Vladimir Petrovich** [uncle of the composer]. Born in 1793. Army officer; Governor of Okhansk (Perm´ region). Married to Mariia Petrovna KAMENSKAIA (d. 1842). Vladimir Petrovich died in 1850, and had four children:

    (a) Nikolai Vladimirovich (b. 1828).

    (b) Boris Vladimirovich (?1831–93), who had two children:

        (i)   Georgii Borisovich (1884–1951).

        (ii)   Anna Boris´evna (1893–1980).

    (c) Pëtr Vladimirovich (b. 1833).

    (d) Lidiia Vladimirovna (1836–92). Married to Nikolai Ivanovich OL´KHOVSKII (1819–92), and had five children:

        (i)   Ekaterina Nikolaevna (1859–1930). Married in 1892 to Lev Vasil´evich DAVYDOV (1837–96) [widower of the composer's sister Aleksandra Il´inshina].

        (ii)   Vladimir Nikolaevich.

        (iii) Mariia Nikolaevna. Married to BULATSEL´.

        (iv) Nikolai Nikolaevich.

        (v)   Ignatii Nikolaevich.

10. **Il´ia Petrovich** [father of the composer]. Born in 1795 [see above].

11. **Olimpiada Petrovna** [aunt of the composer]. Born in 1801. Married to Ivan Ivanovich ANTIPOV. Olimpiada Petrovna died in 1874, and had seven children:

    (a) Pëtr Ivanovich (b. 1819).

    (b) Ekaterina Ivanovna (b. 1822).

    (c) Aleksandr Ivanovich (1824–87), who had two children:

        (i)   Anna Aleksandrovna. Married to TERSKII.

        (ii)   Natal´ia Aleksandrovna (1863–1909). Married to BIRIUKOV.

    (d) Mikhail Ivanovich (1824–97), who had one child:

        (i)   Zinaida Mikhailovna (1861–1957). Married to GAGIN.

    (e) Aleksei Ivanovich (d. 1913).

    (f) Elizaveta Ivanovna. Married to NOVOV.

    (g) Appolinariia Ivanovna. Married to TIMASHEV.

Fëdor Afanas´evich Chaika

FËDOR AFANAS´EVICH CHAIKA [great-grandfather of the composer]. Born *c.*1695 at Nikolaevka (Poltava Region), Ukraine. A Cossack in the Omel´nitskii Division of the Mirgorodskii Regiment, who reputedly fought under Peter the Great at the Battle of Poltava. He married Anna (b. 1717), also known as "Chaichikha". Fëdor Afanas´evich died in 1767, and had five children:

1. **Danilo Fedorovich.** Born in 1738.

2. **Pëtr Fedorovich.** Born in 1745 [see above].

3. **Mikhailo Fedorovich.** Born in 1748.

4. **Matvei Fedorovich.** Born in 1750.

5. **Aleksei Fedorovich.** Born in 1760.

ASSIER

Andrei Mikhailovich Assier

ANDREI (ANDRÉ) MIKHAILOVICH ASSIER [maternal grandfather of the composer]. Born in 1779 in Dresden, Saxony, son of Michel d'Assier. Brought to Russia as a teacher of German and French for the St. Petersburg Military School by the Russian general Petr Melissino in 1795, and received Russian citizenship in 1800. Later a Customs and Ministry of Finances official. Awarded the Order of St. Vladimir (4th Class) and the Order of St. Anne (2nd Class). He married first in 1800 to Ekaterina Mikhailovna POPOVA (1778–1816); second to Amalia Grigor´evna GOGEL´. Andrei Mikhailovich died c.1836, and had seven children:

1. **Mikhail Andreevich** [uncle of the composer]. Born on 25 Sep 1802, to Andrei Mikhailovich & Ekaterina Mikhailovna. Army officer.

2. **Ekaterina Andreevna** [aunt of the composer]. Born on 14 Feb 1805, to Andrei Mikhailovich & Ekaterina Mikhailovna. Singer. She married Aleksandr Stepanovich ALEKSEEV. Ekaterina Andreevna died on 17 Jan 1882, and was buried at Smolenskoe Cemetery in St. Petersburg. She had one child:
    (a) Ivan Aleksandrovich, who had three children:
        (i)   Sof´ia Ivanovna. Married to PALECHEK.
        (ii) Nikolai Ivanovich.
        (iii) Ekaterina Ivanovna.

3. **Nikolai Andreevich** [uncle of the composer]. Born on 25 Jul 1809, to Andrei Mikhailovich & Ekaterina Mikhailovna

4. **Andrei Andreevich** [uncle of the composer]. Born on 4 Apr 1811, to Andrei Mikhailovich & Ekaterina Mikhailovna. Colonel. Andrei Andrevich died in the 1880s, and had three children:
    (a) Mikhail Andreevich.
    (b) Agnes Andreevna.
    (c) Nikolai Andreevich.

5. **Aleksandra Andreevna** [mother of the composer]. Born on 30 July 1812 in St. Petersburg to Andrei Mikhailovich & Ekaterina Mikhailovna. Married on 1 Oct 1833 to Il´ia Petrovich CHAIKOVSKII (1795–1880). Aleksandr Andreevna died of cholera on 13 Jun 1854, and was buried at Smolenskoe Cemetery in St. Petersburg. She had seven children [see under CHAIKOVSKII].

6. **Elizaveta Andreevna** [aunt of the composer]. Born in 1823, to Andrei Mikhailovich & Amalia Grigor´evna. Married to Vasilii SHOBERT, and had three children:
    (a) Amaliia Vasil´evna (1841–1912). Married to Count Nikolai Fedorovich LITKE (1839–87), and had five children:
        (i)   Nikolai Nikolaevich.
        (ii) Fëdor Nikolaevich.
        (iii) Aleksandr Nikolaevich (b. 9 Dec 1868; d. 1918).
        (iv) Konstantin Nikolaevich (d. 1916). Colonel in the Guards Regiment.
        (v)   Pëtr Nikolaevich.
    (b) Wilhelmina Vasil´evna. Married to VON GAN, and had one child:
        (i)   Evgeniia.
    (c) Ekaterina Vasil´evna (d. 1866).

7. **Pavel Andreevich** [uncle of the composer]. Born in 1824, to Andrei Mikhailovich & Amalia Grigor´evna.

POPOV

Mikhail Ivanovich Popov

MIKHAIL IVANOVICH POPOV [great-grandfather of the composer]. Born *c.*1752 in Moscow, the eldest son of Ivan Ivanovich & Tat´iana Petrovna [see below]. Studied at the Kiev Academy (1763–69) and the Aleksandr Nevskii Seminary in St. Petersburg (1770–74). Appointed Deacon at the Nikolaveskii Cathedral in St. Petersburg in 1774, and at the Church of St. Sergiev from 1790. He married Anna Dmitrievna RYKOVSKAIA (b. *c.*1752) at the Church of St. Sergiev in St. Petersburg on 1 Jun 1774. Mikahil Ivanovich died from a fever on 16 Mar 1792 in St. Petersburg, and was buried at the Otkhenskii Cemetery. He had five children:

1. **Varvara Mikhailovna** [great-aunt of the composer]. Born *c.*1776.

2. **Ekaterina Mikhailovna** [grandmother of the composer]. Born on 8 Oct 1778 in St. Petersburg. Married in 1800 to Andrei Mikhailovich ASSIER (1779–?1836). Ekaterina Mikhailovna died on 5 Sep 1816, and was buried at Smolenskoe Cemetery in St. Petersburg. She had 5 children [see under ASSIER].

3. **Nikolai Mikhailovich** [great-uncle of the composer]. Born on 18 Aug 1779 in St. Petersburg. Senior official at the Ministry of Finance. Awarded the Order of St. Vladimir (3rd and 4th Class) and Order of St. Anne (2nd Class). In 1823 he married Anna Vilminovna MERTENS, daughter of Vilmina Fedorovich MERTENS, a Privy Councillor. Nikolai Mikhailovich died on 27 Sep 1869, and was buried at the Smolenskoe Cemetery in St. Petersburg. He had six children:
    - (a) Aleksandr Nikolaevich (b. 15 May 1824).
    - (b) Vladimir Nikolaevich (b. 3 Jul 1826).
    - (c) Nadezhda Nikolaevna (b. 10 Mar 1831).
    - (d) Nikolai Nikolaevich (b. 24 Jan 1834).
    - (e) Kirill Nikolaevich (b. 25 Nov 1835).
    - (f) Ekaterina Nikolaevna (b. 13 Mar 1837).

4. **Mariia Mikhailovna** [great-aunt of the composer]. Born *c.*1783.

5. **Sergei Mikhailovich** [great-uncle of the composer]. Born 23 May 1785 in St. Petersburg. Civil servant, rising to the rank of Titular Councillor (9th Grade). Sergei Mikhaikovich died on 24 Mar 1851, and was buried at Smolenskoe Cemetery in St. Petersburg.

Ivan Ivanovich Popov

IVAN IVANOVICH (IOANN IOANNOVICH) POPOV [great-great-grandfather of the composer]. Born *c.*1732. Deacon at the Church of St. Nikita in Moscow; later an army chaplain in Kiev (1763–69), and Priest at the Church of St. Sergiev in St. Petersburg (1770–83). He married Tat´iana Petrovna (b. ?1736). Ivan Ivanovich died from consumption on 8 Jan 1783, and was buried at Okhtenskii Cemetery in St. Petersburg. He had three children:

1. **Mikhail Ivanovich** [great-grandfather of the composer]. Born *c.*1752 [see above].

2. **Argippina Ivanovna**. Born in 1756. Married in 1772 to Ivan STEPANOVICH[?] (Ioann STEFANOV) (1743–98). Argippina Ivanovna died from consumption on 1 Jun 1798, and was buried at Okhtenskii Cemetery in St. Petersburg. She had four children:
    - (a) Semën Ivanovich (b. 1774).
    - (b) Tat´iana Ivanovna (b. 1777).
    - (c) Ivan Ivanovich (b. 1778).
    - (d) Elizaveta Ivanovna (b. after 1778; d. 1783).

3. **Marfa Ivanovna**. Born *c.*1763.

RYKOVSKII

Dmitrii Iakovlevich Rykovskii

DMITRII IAKOVLEVICH RYKOVSKII [great-great-grandfather of the composer]. Born *c.*1722. Graduated from the Aleksandr Nevskii Seminary in St. Petersburg, where he served as Deacon from 1744, Priest from 1747, and later Steward. Dmitrii Iakovlevich died in Mar 1757 in St. Petersburg. He had two children:

1. **Iakov Dmitrievich**. Born *c.*1747. Graduated from the Aleksandr Nevskii Seminary in 1769, where he then served as Deacon.

2. **Anna Dmitrievna**. Born *c.*1752 in St. Petersburg. Married 1 Jun 1774 to Mikhail Ivanovich POPOV (?1752–92). Anna Dmitrievna died after 1823, and had five children [see under POPOV].

DAVYDOV

Lev Vasil´evich Davydov

LEV VASILI´EVICH DAVYDOV [brother-in-law of the composer]. Born in 1837, the sixth son of Vasilii L´vovich Davydov (1792–1855) & Aleksandra Ivanovna (b. POTAPOVA; 1802–95) [see below]. Estate manager at Kamenka (Kiev Region), Ukraine. He married first on 6 Nov 1860 to Aleksandra Il´inichna CHAIKOVSKAIA (1841–91) [sister of the composer]; second to Ekaterina Nikolaevna OL´KHOVSKAIA (1859–1930) [cousin of the composer]. Lev Vasil´evich died in 1896, and had eight children:

1. **Tat´iana L´vovna** [niece of the composer]. Born on 6 Sep 1861 at Kamenka (Kiev Region), Ukraine, to Lev Vasil´evich and Aleksandra Il´inichna. Tat´iana L´vovna died on 19 Jan 1887 in St. Petersburg, and was buried in the cemetery at the Aleksandr Nevskii Monastery, St. Petersburg (the grave site has not survived). She had one illegitimate child by Stanislav Mikhailovich BLUMENFEL´D (1850–97):
    (a) Georgii Nikolaevich (Georges-Lèon). Born on 26 Apr 1883 in Paris, France. Adopted by Tat´iana L´vovna's uncle Nikolai Chaikovskii in 1886. Georgii Nikolaevich died in 1940.

2. **Vera L´vovna** [niece of the composer]. Born on 16 Mar 1863 at Kamenka (Kiev Region), Ukraine, to Lev Vasil´evich and Aleksandra Il´inichna. In Nov 1881 she married Nikolai Aleksandrovich RIMSKII-KORSAKOV (1852–1908). Vera L´vovna died on 19 Nov 1888 in Nice, France, and had two chldren:
    (a) Irina Nikolaevna.
    (b) Aleksandra Nikolaevna.

3. **Anna L´vovna** [niece of the composer]. Born on 9 Dec 1864 at Kamenka (Kiev Region), Ukraine, to Lev Vasil´evich and Aleksandra Il´inichna. On 11 Jan 1884 she married Nikolai Karlovich VON MECK (1863–1929), son of Otto Georg Karl VON MECK (1821–76) & Nadezhda Filaretovna (b. FROLOVSKAIA; 1831–94). Anna L´vovna died in 1942, and had six children [see also under VON MECK]:
    (a) Kira Nikolaevna (1885–1969).
    (b) Mark Nikolaevich (1890–1918).
    (c) Galina Nikolaevna (1891–1985).
    (d) Attal Nikolaevich (1894–1915).
    (f) Elena Nikolaevna (1897–1926). Adopted (born as Elena Aleksandrovna KHAKMAN).
    (e) Liutsella Nikolaevna (1899–1933).

4. **Natal´ia L´vovna** [niece of the composer]. Born on 19 May 1868 at Kamenka (Kiev Region), Ukraine, to Lev Vasil´evich and Aleksandra Il´inichna. After 1889, she married her widowed brother-in-law Nikolai Aleksandrovich RIMSKII-KORSAKOV (1852–1908). Natal´ia L´vovna died in 1956, and had two children:
    (a) Sergei Nikolaevich.
    (b) Vladimir Nikolaevich.

5. **Dmitrii L´vovich** [nephew of the composer]. Born on 8 Aug 1870 at Kamenka (Kiev Region), Ukraine, to Lev Vasil´evich and Aleksandra Il´inichna. He married Natal´ia Mikhailovna GUDIM-LEVKOVICH (1875–1933). Dmitrii L´vovich died in 1929, and had four children:
    (a) Denis Dmitrevich.
    (b) Liudmila Dmitrevna.
    (c) Vasilii Dmitrevich.
    (d) Kirill Dmitrievich.

6. **Vladimir L´vovich (Bob)** [nephew of the composer]. Born on 2 Dec 1871 at Kamenka (Kiev Region), Ukraine, to Lev Vasil´evich & Aleksandra Il´inichna. He studied at the Imperial School of Jurisprudence in St Petersburg (1883–93), then chose a military career, retiring as a lieutenant from the Imperial Preobrazhenskii Regiment in 1900; moved to the composer''s house at Klin, where on 14 Dec 1906 commited suicide. Vladimir L´vovich is buried at Dem´ianovo Cemetery, near Klin.

7. **Georgii L´vovich (Iurii)** [nephew of the composer]. Born on 24 Apr/6 May 1876 in Geneva, Switzerland, to Lev Vasil´evich and Aleksandra Il´inichna. He graduated from Bonn Agricultural Academy in 1898. From 1908 to1917 he was a director of the Kiev branch of the Russian Musical Society, and helped to found the Kiev Conservatory. In 1937 he joined the staff of the composer's house-museum at Klin, where he became curator in 1945. He married Margarita Nikolaevna LOPUKHINA (1864–1931). Iurii L´vovich died on 16 Apr 1965 at Klin, and was buried at the Dem´ianovo Cemetery, near Klin. He had four children:
    (a) Irina Georgievna [Iur'evna] (1900–89). Married to SOKOLINSKII.
    (b) Tat´iana Georgievna [Iur'evna] (1902–25).
    (c) Kseniia Iur´evna [Georgievna]. Born in 1905. Curator of the composer's house-museum at Klin until 1989. She married Efim Davydovich GERSHOVSKII (1906–69). Kseniia Iur´evna died on 12 Sep 1992, and was buried at the Dem´ianovo Cemetery, near Klin. She had two children:
        (i) Lev Efimovich. Born in 1946.
        (ii) Georgii Efimovich. Born in 1949. Married to Natal´ia Iur´evna VOLKOVA (b. 1950).
    (d) Georgii Iurevich.

8. **Lev L´vovich**. Born in 1892, to Lev Vasil´evich & Ekaterina Nikolaevna.

Vasilii L´vovich Davydov

VASILII L´VOVICH DAVYDOV. Born in 1792, the third son of Lev Denisovich Davydov (1743–1801). & Ekaterina Nikolaevna (b. SAMOILOVA; 1755–1825) [see below]. A participant in the Decembrist uprising. He married Aleksandra Ivanovna POTAPOVA (1802–95). Vasilii L´vovich died in 1855, and had thirteen children:

1. **Mariia Vasil´evna**. Born in 1819. Married to Robert Karlovich FELEIZEN. Mariia Vasil´evna died in 1845.

2. **Mikhail Vasil´evich**. Born in 1820. Married to Elena Pavlovna. Mikhail Vasil´evich died in 1880.

3. **Ekaterina Vasil´evna**. Born in 1822. Married to Vladimir Mikhailovich PERESLENI. Ekaterina Vasil´evna died in 1904, and had four children:
    (a) Aleksandra Vladimirovna (1862–1937)
    (b) Vadim Vladimirovich.
    (c) Nikolai Vladimirovich (d. 1914).
    (d) Sof´ia Vladimirovna. Married to DRASHUSOV.

4. **Elizaveta Vasil´evna**. Born in 1823. Died in 1906.

5. **Pëtr Vasil´evich**. Born in 1825. Married to Elizaveta Sergeevna TRUBETSKAIA (1834–1918). Pëtr Vasil´evich died in 1912, and had three children:
    (a) Vasilii Petrovich (1870–97). Married to O. A. LIVEN.
    (b) Zinaida Petrovna.
    (c) Ekaterina Petrovna.

6. **Nikolai Vasil´evich**. Born in 1826. Nikolai Vasil´evich died in 1916, and had three illegitimate children by Pelageia Osipovna:
    (a) Mariia Nikolaevna
    (b) Varvara Nikolaevna. Born in 1864. Married first to Aleksandr (Axel) SANDBERG; second to DIKOV. Varvara Nikolaevna died in 1912, and had three children:
        (i) Nikolai Aleksandrovich.
        (ii) Vera Aleksandrovna.
        (iii) Natal´ia Aleksandrovna.
    (c) Nina Nikolaevna, Married to PISAREV, and had two children:
        (i) Aleksandr (1897–1975).
        (ii) Ekaterina.

7. **Vasilii Vasil´evich**. Born in 1829. Married to Aleksandra Mikhailovna. Vasilii Vasil´evich died in 1873.

8. **Aleksandra Vasil´evna**. Born in 1831. Died in 1917.

9. **Ivan Vasil´evich**. Born in 1834. Died in 1850.

10. **Lev Vasil´evich**. Born in 1837 [see above].

11. **Sof´ia Vasil´evna**. Born in 1840. Married to Fedosii Kazimovich DE STAL´ (b. 1829). Sof´ia Vasil´evna died in 1918.

12. **Vera Vasil´evna**. Born in 1843. Married to Ivan Ivanovich BUTAKOV (1822–82). Vera Vasil´evna died in 1923.

13. **Aleksei Vasil´evich**. Born in 1847. He married Mariia Nikolaevna TRUBAZHEVA (1852–1936). Aleksei Vasil´evich died in 1903, and had five children:
    (a) Lev Alekseevich. Born in 1868. He married Margarita Nikolaevna LOPUKHINA (1864–1931); the marriage was later dissolved. Lev Alekseevich died in 1935.
    (b) Grigorii Alekseevich. Born in 1870. Died in 1919.
    (c) Vera Alekseevna. Born in 1871.
    (d) Natal´ia Alekseevna. Born in 1874. Died after 1918.
    (e) Mariia Alekseevna.

Lev Denisovich Davydov

LEV DENISOVICH DAVYDOV. Born in 1743, the second son of Denis Vasil´evich Davydov (b. 1722). & Anna Andreevna (b. KOPYCHEVA) [see below]. He married Ekaterina Nikolaevna SAMOILOVA (1755–1825), daughter of Nikolai Borisovich SAMOILOV (1727–91) & Mariia Aleksandrovna (b. POTEMKINA; d.1774). Lev Denisovich died in 1801, and had four children:

1. **Aleksandr L´vovich**. Born in 1773. He married Duchess Aglaia Aneglica Gabrielle DE GRAMONT (1787–1843). Aleksandr L´vovich died in 1833, and had one child:
    (a) Adele Aleksandrovna. Born in 1810. Died in 1882,

2. **Sof´ia L´vovna**. Born in 1774. Married to Andrei Mikhailovich BOROZDIN (b. 1785).

3. **Pëtr L´vovich**. Born in 1777. Married first to Natal´ia Vladimirovna ORLOVA (1789–1819); second to Varvara LIKHAREVA. Pëtr L´vovich died in 1843.

3. **Vasilii L´vovich**. Born in 1792 [see above].

Denis Vasil´evich Davydov

DENIS VASIL´EVICH DAVYDOV. Born in 1722, the son of Vasilii Vasil´evich Davydov (1699–1795). He married Anna Andreevna KOPYCHEVA, and had five children:

1. **Vasilii Denisovich**. Married to Elena Evdokimovna SHCHERBININA (d. 1813). Vasilii Denisovich died in 1802, and had four children:
   (a) Denis Vasil´evich. Born in 1784. Married to Sof´ia Nikolaevna CHIRKOVA (1795–1880). Denis Vasil´evich died in 1839.
   (b) Evdokim Vasil´evich. Born in 1786. Married to Ekaterina Nikolaevna ERMOLOVA. Evdokim Vasil´evich died in 1843.
   (c) Aleksandra Vasil´evna. Born in 1789. Married to BEGICHEV.
   (d) Lev Vasil´evich.

2. **Lev Denisovich**. Born in 1743 [see above].

3. **Dmitrii Denisovich**.

4. **Vladimir Denisovich**.

5. **Mariia Denisovna**. Married to Pëtr Alekseevich ERMOLOV. Mariia Denisovna died in 1813, and had one child:
   (a) Aleksei Petrovich. Born in 1777. Died in 1861.

VON MECK

Otto Georg Karl von MECK

OTTO GEORG KARL VON MECK. Born on 22 Jun 1821, the only son of Otto Adam von Meck (1790–1830) & Wilhelmina (b. HOFFERBERG) [see below]. He married on 14 Jan 1848 to Nadezhda Filaretovna FROLOVSKAIA (1831–94), daughter of Filaret Vasil´evich FROLOVSKII & Anastasiia Dmitrievna (b. POTEMKINA). Otto George Karl died on 26 Jan 1876, and had eleven children:

1. **Elizaveta Karlovna**. Born on 28 Nov 1848. Married to Aleksandr Aleksandrovich IOLSHIN [ËLSHIN] (d. 1929). Elizaveta Karlovna died on 30 Aug 1907, and had one child:
   (a) Lidiia Aleksandrovna IOLSHINA. Married to her cousin Vladimir Aleksandrovich FROLOVSKII (1870–1940)

2. **Aleksandra Karlovna**. Born in 1849. Married to Pavel Aleksandrovich BENNINGSEN [BENNIGSEN] (b. 1845). Aleksandra Karlovna died in 1920, and had four children:
   (a) Emmanuil Pavlovich (1875-1955).
   (b) Georgii Pavlovich (1879-1962).
   (c) Adam Pavlovich (1885-ca.1950).
   (d) Ekaterina Pavlovna.

3. **Vladimir Karlovich**. Born on 15 Jun 1852. Married to Elizaveta Mikhailovna POPOVA (1861–92). Vladimir Karlovich died on 2 Nov 1893, and had one child:
   (a) Vladimir Vladimirovich. Born on 14 Jul 1877. Married to Varvara KARPOVA (b. 1889). Vladimir Vladimirovich died in 1932.

4. **Iuliia Karlovna**. Born in 1853. Married to Wladyslaw PACHULSKI (Vladislav Al´bertovich PAKHUL´SKII) (d. 1919). Iuliia Karlovna died in 1915.

5. **Lidiia Karlovna**. Born on 1 Jun 1855. Married to Friedrich VON LÖWIS. Lidiia Karlovna died on 9 Oct 1903.

6. **Nikolai Karlovich**. Born on 16 Apr 1863. President of the Board of the Moscow–Kazan Railway; from 1919 worked in the Peoples Comissariat of Communications. On 11 Jan 1884 he married Anna L′vovna DAVYDOVA (1864–1942) [niece of the composer]. Nikolai Karlovich was arrested by the State Secret Police (OGPU) on 5 Sep 1928 on false charges of sabotage, in connection with the so-called called "Shakhty affair", and was executed on 23 May 1929. He had six children:

(a) Kira Nikolaevna. Born in 1885. Married to Aleksandr ZAPOL′SKII. Kira Nikolaevna died in 1969, and had five children:

    (i) Anna Aleksandrovna (d. 1995). Married to Tadeusz ZEMINSKI.

    (ii) Kira Aleksandrovna (d. 1945).

    (iii) Konstantin Aleksandrovich (1906–22).

    (iv) Irena Aleksandrovna.

    (v) Iadviga Aleksandrovna (b. 1928). Married to Cheslav Cheslavovich LUZYNA.

(b) Mark Nikolaevich. Born on 9 Mar 1890. Married to Ol′ga RODZIANKO. Mark Nikolaevich died in 1918.

(c) Galina Nikolaevna. Born on 12 Oct 1891 in Moscow. Married first in 1913 to Noël PERROTT; second to Dmitrii ORLOVSKII. Galina Nikolaevna died in Apr 1985, and had one child:

    (i) Anna PERROTT (1915–95). Married to Geoffrey COURTNEY.

(d) Attal Nikolaevich. Born on 11 Sep 1894. Died in 1915.

(e) Elena Nikolaevna. Born in 1897 as Elena Aleksandrovna KHAKMAN; adopted in 1903 by Nikolai Karlovich & Anna L′vovna von Meck. Married to Nikolai Sergeevich MOISEEV (d. 1933). Elena Nikolaevna died in 1926, and had two children:

    (i) Nikita Nikolaevich (b. 1918).

    (ii) Sergei Nikolaevich (1923–48).

(f) Liutsella Nikolaevna. Born on 8 Aug 1899. Married first to Aleksei Aleksandrovich KORNOUKHOV (1889–1967); second to Aleksei Vasil′evich RAT'KO (1900–75). Liutsella Nikolaevna died in 1933, and had two children:

    (i) Tat′iana Alekseevna KORNOUKHOVA (b. 1918). Married first to Evgenii Evgen′evich SEBENTSOV (1915–82); second to Lev Vladimirovich TOKAREV (1904–91).

    (ii) Vasilii Alekseevich RAT'KO (b. 1928). Married to Tamara Aleksandrovna BOZHIKOVA.

7. **Aleksandr Karlovich**. Born on 6 Jun 1864. Married to Anna Georgievna FRANK (d. 1914). Aleksandr Karlovich died on 15 Mar 1911, and had one son:

(a) Georgii Aleksandrovich. Born on 14 Oct 1888. Died in 1962.

8. **Sof′ia Karlovna**. Born in 1867. Married first to Aleksei Aleksandrovich RIMSKII-KORSAKOV (1860–1920); second to GOLITSYN. Sof′ia Karlovna died in 1935, and had two children:

(a) Natal′ia Alekseevna RIMSKAIA-KORSAKOVA. Married to Aleksei Alekseevich VERSHININ.

(b) Georgii Alekseevich RIMSKII-KORSAKOV. Married to Nadezhda Ivanovna.

9. **Maksimilian Karlovich**. Born on 17 Jan 1869. Married to Ol′ga Mikhailovna KIRIIAKOVA. Maksimilian Karlovich died on 15 May 1950.

10. **Mikhail Karlovich**. Born on 17 Jan 1870. Died on 12 Jun 1883.

11. **Liudmila Karlovna**. Born in 1872 [reputedly the daughter of Aleksandr Aleksandrovich IOLSHIN (ËLSHIN), brother-in-law to Otto Georg Karl]. Married to Andrei Aleksandrovich SHIRINSKII-SHIKHMATOV (1868–1927). Liudmila Karlovna died in 1946, and had two children:

(a) Mikhail Andreevich.

(b) Anikita Andreevich.

Otto Adam von Meck

OTTO ADAM VON MECK. Born on 9 May 1790, the only known son of George Johann von Meck (b. 1745) & Sophia Elisabeth (b. VON MARTINI; 1762–?) [see below]. He married Wilhelmina HOFFERBERG. Otto Adam died on 27 Apr 1830, and had one child:

1. **Otto Georg Karl**. Born on 22 Jun 1821 [see above].

Georg Johann von Meck

GEORG JOHANN VON MECK. Born on 15 Feb 1745, the son of Otto Johann von Meck (1714–87) & Anna Christina (b. VON KREIDENER). Married in 1776 to Sophia Elisabeth von MARTINI (b. 11 Feb 1762), and one known child:

1. **Otto Adam.** Born on 9 May 1790 [see above].

FROLOVSKII

Filaret Vasil´evich Frolovskii

FILARET VASIL´EVICH FROLOVSKII. Married to Anastasiia Dmitrievna POTEMKINA, daughter of Dmitrii Dem´ianovich POTEMKIN, and had three children:

1. **Nadezhda Filaretovna.** Born on 29 Jan 1831 in Znamenskoe (Smolensk Region). Married on 14 Jan 1848 to Otto Georg Karl VON MECK (1821–76), Nadezhda Filaretovna died on 14/26 Jan 1894 in Nice, France, and was buried in the Novo-Alekseevskii Cemetery, Moscow (the grave has not survived). She had eleven children [see also under VON MECK]:
    (a) Elizaveta Karlovna (1848–1903).
    (b) Aleksandra Karlovna (1849–1920).
    (c) Vladimir Karlovich (1852–92).
    (d) Iuliia Karlovna (1853–1915).
    (e) Lidiia Karlovna (1855–1910).
    (f) Nikolai Karlovich (1863–1929).
    (g) Aleksandr Karlovich (1864–1911).
    (h) Sof´ia Karlovna (1867–1935)
    (i) Maksimilian Karlovich (1869–1955).
    (j) Mikhail Karlovich (1871–83).
    (k) Liudmila Karlovna (1872–1946).

2. **Vladimir Filaretovich.** Died in 1890, and had one child:
    (a) Nikolai Vladimirovich, who had one child:
        (i)   Natal´ia Nikolaevna. Married to ANDREEV.

3. **Aleksandr Filaretovich.** Married to Varvara, and had four children:
    (a) Aleksandr Aleksandrovich. Born in 1831. Married to Mariia Mikhailovna ALPERS. Aleksandr Aleksandrovich died in 1894, and had three children:
        (i)   Aleksandr Aleksandrovich.
        (ii)   Boris Aleksandrovich.
        (iii)   Elena Aleksandrovna.
    (b) Aleksei Aleksandrovich.
    (c) Vladimir Aleksandrovich. Born in 1870. Married to his cousin Lidiia Aleksandrovna IOLSHINA (ËLSHINA), Vladimir Aleksandrovich died c. 1940.
    (d) Sergei Aleksandrovich.

MILIUKOV

Antonina Ivanovna Miliukova

ANTONINA IVANOVNA MILIUKOVA [wife of the composer]. Born on 23 Jun 1848, the second daughter of Ivan Andreevich Miliukov (1811–71) and Ol´ga Nikanorovna (b. IAMINSKAIA; 1821–81) [see below]. On 6 Jul 1877 at the Church of St. George in Moscow, she married Pëtr Il´ich CHAIKOVSKII (1840–93); they separated in Sep 1877, but never divorced. In 1896 she was admitted to a mental hospital in St. Petersburg, where she spent four years and was then released; in 1901 she was re-admitted there and was soon transferred to a mental asylum at Udel´naia near St. Petersburg, Antonina Ivanovna remained there until her death on 18 Feb 1917, and was buried in Severnoe Cemetery, St. Petersburg (the grave site has not survived). She had three illegitimate children:

1. **Mariia Aleksandrovna.** Born on 13 Feb 1881. Died in an orphanage on 2 Jan 1882.

2. **Pëtr Petrovich.** Born on 24 Aug 1882. Died in an orphanage on 9 Jun 1890.

3. **Antonina Petrovna.** Born on 24 Oct 1884. Died in an oprhanage on 8 Mar 1887.

Ivan Andreevich Miliukov

IVAN ANDREEVICH MILIUKOV [father-in-law of the composer]. Born on 24 Feb 1811, the son of Andrei Miliukov (1777–1831) and Aksin´ia Ivanovna (b. GOLOSOVA). On 25 Jan 1839 he married Ol´ga Nikanorovna IAMINSKAIA (b. 14 Aug 1821; d. Feb 1881), the daughter of Nikanor Vasil´evich IAMINSKII (1792–1855) & Elizaveta Aleksandrovna (1802–35). Ivan Andreevich died on 2 Apr 1871, and had ten children:

1. **Aleksandr Ivanovich** [brother-in-law of the composer]. Born on 16 Jul 1840. Married on 7 May 1872 to Anastasiia KHVOSTOVA (1842–1911). Died on 3 May 1885, and had three children:
    (a) Aleksandr Aleksandrovich. Born on 9 Sep 1874. Died in 1942, and had one child:
        (i)   Aleksandr Aleksandrovich (1901–70).
    (b) Nina Aleksandrovna. Born in 1880. Died in infancy.
    (c) Iurii Aleksandrovich. Born on 15 Dec 1882. Died after 1918.

2. **Elizaveta Ivanovna** [sister-in-law of the composer]. Born on 24 Jun 1842. Died in 1912.

3. **Nikolai Ivanovich** [brother-in-law of the composer]. Born in 1844. Died in 1846.

4. **Mikhail Ivanovich** [brother-in-law of the composer]. Born on 15 May 1845. Died on 24 Mar 1869.

5. **Antonina Ivanovna** [wife of the composer]. Born in 1848. Died in 1917 [see above].

6. **Ol´ga Ivanovna** [sister-in-law of the composer]. Born on 6 Sep 1851.

7. **Mariia Ivanovna** [sister-in-law of the composer]. Born in 1854. Died after 1930.

8. **Aglaida (Adel´) Ivanovna** [sister-in-law of the composer]. Born in 1855. Died after 1890.

9. **Ivan[?] Ivanovich** [brother-in-law of the composer]. Born in 1857.

10. **Anna Ivanovna** [sister-in-law of the composer]. Born in 1859.

354   Genealogy

Index of Names

(Page numbers in bold type relate to principal entries)

ALEKSEEV
Aleksandr Stepanovich 345
Ivan Aleksandrovich 345
Nikolai Ivanovich 342
Nikolai Ivanovich 345

ALEKSEEVA
Ekaterina Andreevna — *see* Assier
Ekaterina Ivanovna 345
Irina Nikolaevna 342
Kseniia Nikolaevna 342
Mariana Nikolaevna 342
Natal´ia Ippolitovna — *see* Chaikovskaia
Oksana Nikolaevna — *see* Kseniia Nikolaevna
Sof´ia Ivanovna 345

ALPERS
Mariia Mikhailovna 352

ANDREEVA
Natal´ia Nikolaevna — *see* Frolovskaia

ANTIPOV
Aleksandr Ivanovich (1824–87) 344
Aleksei Ivanovich (d. 1913) 344
Ivan Ivanovich 344
Mikhail Ivanovich (1824–97) 344
Pëtr Ivanovich (b. 1819) 344

ANTIPOVA
Anna Aleksandrovna 344
Appolinariia Ivanovna 344
Ekaterina Ivanovna (b. 1822) 344
Elizaveta Ivanovna 344
Natal´ia Aleksandrovna (1863–1909) 344
Olimpiada Petrovna — *see* Chaikovskaia
Zinaida Mikhailovna (1861–1957) 344

ASSIER
Agnes Andreevna 345
Aleksandra Andreevna (1812–54) 341, **345**
Amalia Grigor´evna — *see* Gogel´
Andrei Andreevich (1811–1880s) **345**
Andrei (André) Mikhailovich (1779–?1836) **345**, 346
Ekaterina Andreevna (1805–82) **345**
Ekaterina Mikhailovna — *see* Popova
Elizaveta Andreevna (b. 1823) **345**
Michel d' 345
Mikhail Andreevich (b. 1802) **345**
Mikhail Andreevich 345
Nikolai Andreevich (b. 1809) **345**
Nikolai Andreevich 345
Pavel Andreevich (b. 1824) **345**

BEGICHEVA
Aleksandra Vasil´evna — *see* Davydova

BENNINGSEN [BENNIGSEN]
Adam Pavlovich (1885-ca.1950) 350
Aleksandra Karlovna — *see* Von Meck
Ekaterina Pavlovna 350
Emmanuil Pavlovich (1875-1955) 350
Georgii Pavlovich (1879-1962) 350
Pavel Aleksandrovich (b. 1845) 350

BERENS
Elizaveta von — *see* Berens, Evdokiia Petrovna
Evdokiia Petrovna (b. 1780) 343

BESTUZHEVA
Tat´iana Petrovna 343

BIRIUKOVA
Natal´ia Aleksandrovna — *see* Antipova

BLUMENFEL´D
Stanislaw Mikhailovich (1850–97) 341, 347

BOROZDIN
Andrei Mikhailovich (b. 1785) 349

BOROZDINA
Sof´ia L´vovna — *see* Davydova

BOZHIKOVA
Tamara Aleksandrovna 351

BULATSEL´
Mariia Nikolaevna — *see* Ol´khovskaia

BURMEISTER
Natal´ia Petrovna — *see* Chaikovskaia

BUTAKOV
Ivan Ivanovich (1822–82) 349
Vera Vasil´evna — *see* Davydova

CHAIKA
Aleksei Fedorovich **344**
Anna ("Chaichikha") 342, 344
Danilo Fedorovich (b. 1738) **344**
Matvei Fedorovich (b. 1750) **344**
Mikhailo Fedorovich (b. 1748) **344**
Fëdor Afanas´evich (c.1695–1767) 342, **344**
Pëtr Fedorovich — *see* Chaikovskii

CHAIKOVSKAIA
Aleksandra Andreevna — *see* Assier
Aleksandra Il´inichna (1841–91) **341–342**, 344, 347, 348
Aleksandra Petrovna (b. 1786) **343**
Aleksandra Petrovna (1836–99) **343**
Anastasiia Stepanovna — *see* Posokhova
Anna Boris´evna (1893–1980) 344
Anna Petrovna (b. 1790) **344**
Anna Petrovna (1830–1911) **343**

IOLSHINA (ËLSHINA)
Elizaveta Karlovna — *see* Von Meck

IOLSHINA (ËLSHINA) — *continued*
Lidiia Aleksandrovna　350,, 351

KAMENSKAIA
Mariia Petrovna (d. 1842)　344

KARPOVA
Varvara (b. 1889)　350

KARTSOV
Georgii Pavlovich (1862–1931)　343
Mikhail Pavlovich (1860–1909)　343
Nikolai Pavlovich (1862–1918)　343
Pavel Petrovich (1821–?82)　343
Pëtr Pavlovich (d. inf.)　343
Pëtr Pavlovich (1874–?1930)　343

KARTSOVA
Aleksandra Pavlovna　343
Aleksandra Petrovna — *see* Chaikovskaia
Aleksandra Valerianovna — *see* Panaeva
Ekaterina Pavlovna (1866–1941)　343
Elizaveta Pavlovna (1858–1908)　343
Lidiia Pavlovna (1872–1945)　343
Mariia Pavlovna (1864–1927)　343
Praskov´ia Pavlovna (b. 1870)　343

KEIZER
Mariia Karlovna (d. 1831)　341

KHAKMAN
Elena Aleksandrovna — *see* Von Meck, Elena
Nikolaevna

KHVOSTOVA
Anastasiia (1842–1911)　353

KIRIIAKOVA
Ol´ga Mikhailovna　351

KONOVALOVA
Evgeniia Evgen´evna — *see* Ol´khovskaia

KONSHINA
Praskov´ia Vladimirovna (1864–1956)　342

KOPYCHEVA
Anna Andreevna　349, 350

KORBE
Praskov´ia Pavlovna — *see* Kartsova

KORNOUKHOV
Aleksei Aleksandrovich (1889–1967)　351

KORNOUKHOVA
Liutsella Nikolaevna — *see* Von Meck
Tat´iana Alekseevna (b. 1918)　351

LIKHAREVA
Varvara　349

LIPPORT
Elizaveta Mikhailovna (1829–1910)　341

LITKE
Aleksandr Nikolaevich (1868–1918)　345
Amaliia Vasil´evna — *see* Shobert
Fëdor Nikolaevich　345

LITKE — *continued*
Konstantin Nikolaevich (d. 1916)　345
Nikolai Fedorovich (1839–87)　345
Nikolai Nikolaevich　345
Pëtr Nikolaevich　345

LOPUKHINA
Margarita Nikolaevna (1864–1931)　348, 349

LUZYNA
Cheslav Cheslavovich　351
Iadviga Aleksandrovna — *see* Zapol´skaia

MECK — *see* VON MECK

MERKLING
Anna Petrovna (1830–1911)　343
Lidiia Petrovna　343
Pëtr Ivanovich　343

MERTENS
Anna Vilminova　346
Vilmina Fedorovich　346

MILIUKOV
Aleksandr Aleksandrovich (1874–1942)　353
Aleksandr Aleksandrovich (1901–70)　353
Aleksandr Ivanovich (1840–85)　**353**
Andrei (1777–1831)　353
Iurii Aleksandrovich (b. 1882)　353
Ivan Andreevich (1811–71)　**353**
Ivan Ivanovich (b. 1857)　**353**
Mikhail Ivanovich (1845–69)　**353**
Nikolai Ivanovich (1844–46)　**353**
Pëtr Petrovich (1882–90)　**353**

MILIUKOVA
Aglaida (Adel´) Ivanovna (b. 1855)　**353**
Aksin´ia Ivanovna — *see* Golosova
Anastasiia — *see* Khvostova
Anna Ivanovna (b. 1859)　**353**
Antonina Ivanovna (1848–1917)　341, **353**
Antonina Petrovna (1884–87)　**353**
Elizaveta Ivanovna (1842–1912)　**353**
Mariia Aleksandrovna (1881–82)　**353**
Mariia Ivanovna (b. 1854)　**353**
Nina Aleksandrovna (b. 1880)　**353**
Ol´ga Ivanovna (b. 1851)　**353**
Ol´ga Nikanorovna — *see* Iaminskaia

MOISEEV
Nikita Nikolaevich (b. 1918)　351
Nikolai Sergeevich (d. 1933)　351
Sergei Nikolaevich (1923–48)　351

MOISEEVA
Elena Nikolaevna — *see* Von Meck

NIKONOVA
Sofiia Petrovna (1843–1920)　342

NOVOVA
Elizaveta Ivanovna — *see* Antipova

OBUKHOVA
Ekaterina Pavlovna — *see* Kartsova

OLENINA
Vera Emil´evna — *see* Genke

BIBLIOGRAPHY

PART 1

CATALOGUES & BIBLIOGRAPHIES

1.1. CATALOGUES
1.1.1. Thematic Catalogues
1.1.2. General

1.2. BIBLIOGRAPHIES

1.3. DISCOGRAPHIES

1.4. FILMOGRAPHIES & VIDEOGRAPHIES

1.5. CHRONOLOGIES

1.6. ENCYCLOPEDIAS

1.1. CATALOGUES

1.1.1. Thematic Catalogues

[1]   **[IURGENSON, B. P.]** *Catalogue thématique des œuvres de P. Tschaïkowsky*. Rédigé par B. Jurgenson. Moscou: P. Jurgenson [1897]. 168 p, music.

Works are listed according to opus number, with incipits. Text in French, Russian and German.

Review: N. F. Findeizen, *Russkaia muzykal´naia gazeta* (Sep 1897), 9: 1242–1243.

— [repr.] New York: Am-Rus Music Corp. [1940]. 168 p, music.

— [repr.] London: H. Baron, 1965. 168 p, music.

1.1.2. General

[2]   **IURGENSON, P. I.** *Sochineniia P. Chaikovskogo*. Moskva: P. Iurgenson, 1888. 40 p.

— [new ed.] *P. Chaikovskii: Sochineniia*. Moskva: P. Iurgenson, 1894. 71 p.

— [new ed.] *Polnyi katalog sochinenii P. Chaikovskogo*. Moskva; Leiptsig: P. Iurgenson [1902]. 41 p.

The 1902 ed. was also issued bound with *Zhizn´ Petra Il´icha Chaikovskogo*, tom 3 (1902) [see *1453*].

[3]   **[MORDVINOV, V. R.]** 'Spisok muzykal´nykh sochinenii P. I. Chaikovskogo'. In: *Pamiatnaia knizhka pravoviedov XX vypuska 1859 goda*. Sankt Peterburg: [Imperatorskoe Uchilishche Pravovedeniia], 1894: 212–233.

— [repr.] In: *Pëtr Il´ich Chaikovskii: Biograficheskie o nem svedeniia i spisok muzykal´nykh sochinenii* (1894): 17–35 [see *1451*].

[4]   *Verzeichniss der Compositionen von P. Tschaikowsky im Verlage von D. Rahter, Leipzig*. Einzige autorisierte, vom Componisten revedirte Ausgabe. Leipzig: D. Rahter, 1900. 23 p. illus.

[5]   **NEWMARCH, R. H.** 'Chronological list of Tchaikovsky's compositions from 1866–1893'. In: M. I. Chaikovskii, *The life and letters of Peter Ilich Tchaikovsky* (1906): 726–749 [see *1453*].

[6]   *Peter Tschaikowsky: A complete list of his compositions*. Edition of the original publishers. Preface by Rosa Newmarch. London: Breitkopf & Härtel, 1912. 40 p, illus.

A publisher's sales catalogue, listing Chaikovskii's published works and numerous arrangements by others.

[7]   **SHEMANIN, N. V.** 'Notografiia i bibliografiia proizvedenii P. I. Chaikovskogo'. In: *Dni i gody P. I. Chaikovskogo: Letopis´ zhizni i tvorchestva* (1940): 653–739 [see *85*].

[8]   *Prospekt akademicheskogo izdaniia polnogo sobraniia sochinenii P. I. Chaikovskogo*. Moskva; Leningrad: Gos. muz. izdat., 1946. 16 p.

Prospectus for the complete edition of Chaikovskii's works [see *118*].

[9]   'List of Tchaikovsky's works for the stage'. In: *Russian symphony: Thoughts about Tchaikovsky* (1947): 213–263 [see *587*].

Also covering Chaikovskii's orchestral, chamber-instrumental and vocal works.

[10] **DOMBAEV. G. S.** *Muzykal´noe nasledie P. I. Chaikovskogo: Spravochnik*. Sost. G. Dombaev. Moskva: Sovetskii kompozitor, 1958. 77 p.

A series of tables showing the dates of composition, first performance, publication and other data for each of Chaikovskii's works. See also *11*.

[*11*]   *Systematisches Verzeichnis der Werke von Pjotr Iljitsch Tschaikowsky: Ein Handbuch für die Musikpraxis.*
Hrsg. vom Tschaikowsky-Studio, Institut International. Vorwort von Louisa von Westernhagen.
Hamburg: H. Sikorski [1973]. 112 p. ISBN: 3–920880–08–0.

Based on G. S. Dombaev, *Muzykal'noe nasledie P. I. Chaikovskogo* (1958) [see *10*].

Reviews: G. Eberle, *Neue Zeitschrift für Musik*, 134 (1973), 12: 828–829 — *Musikhandel*, 25 (1974), 2: 112 —
B. Schwarz, *Notes*, 31 (1974/75), 1: 61–62 — D. Gojowy, *Musik und Bildung*, 7 (1975): 389 — *Musik und
Gesellschaft*, 25 (Jul 1975): 433–434 — D. Gojowy, *Die Musikforschung*, 29 (1976), 4: 478–479.

[*12*]   *Petr Il´ic Cajkovskij (1840–1893): New Edition of the Complete Works. Invitation to subscribe / Neue
Ausgabe Samtlicher Werke. Enladung zur subscription.* Moskva: Muzyka; Mainz: Schott, 1993, 15 p.

Prospectus for the new edition of the complete works [see *120*], listing the contents of each volume.

[*13*]   **'Chronologisches Verzeichnis der musikalischen Werke Peter Tschaikowskys'**. In: G. A. Larosh,
Peter Tschaikowsky: Aufsätze und Erinnerungen (1993): 282–298 [see *2406*].

1.2. BIBLIOGRAPHIES

[*14*]   **MOLCHANOV, A. E. 'Bibliograficheskii ukazatel´ kriticheskikh statei P. I. Chaikovskogo'**,
Ezhegodnik imperatorskikh teatrov: Sezon 1892/93 (1894): 555–559.

A listing of Chaikovskii's newspaper review articles.

[*15*]   **[CHAIKOVSKII, M. I.] 'Bibliografiia P. I. Chaikovskogo, sobrannaia Modestom Il´ichom i
khraniashchaiasia v vitrine muzeia v Klinu'**. In: *Proshloe russkoi muzyki*, tom 1 (1920): 183–184 [see
584].

[*16*]   **NIKOL´SKAIA, G. 'Chaikovskii v muzykal´noi literaturye revoliutsionnykh let'**, *Muzyka i revoliutsiia*
(1928), 11: 51.

[*17*]   **'Chaikovskii, Pëtr Il´ich'**. In: G. Orlov, *Muzykal´naia literatura: Muzykal´nyi ukazatel´ knizhnoi i
zhurnal´noi literatury o muzyke na russkom iazyke.* Leningrad: Leningradskaia filarmoniia, 1935: 111–121.

[*18*]   **SHEMANIN, N. V. 'Literatura o P. I. Chaikovskom za 17 let (1917–1934)'**. In: *Muzykal´noe
nasledstvo: Sbornik materialov po istorii muzykal´noi kul´tury v Rossii.* Vyp. 1. Pod red. M. V. Ivanova-
Boretskogo. Moskva: Ogiz, 1935: 76–93.

[*19*]   **VOROB´EV, M. P. *P. I. Chaikovskii: Kratkii ukazatel´ literatury (K stoletiiu so dnia rozhdeniia, 7 maia
1840 g.–7 maia 1940 g.).*** Molotov, 1940. 12 p. (*Molotovskaia oblastnaia biblioteka im. A. M. Gor´kogo i
Molotovskii oblastnoi teatr opery i baleta*).

[*20*]   **BRIANSKII, A. M. 'Materialy k russkoi literature o P. I. Chaikovskom'**. In: *P. I. Chaikovskii na stsene
teatra opery i baleta im. S. M. Kirova* (1941): 421–449 [see *2542*].

[*21*]   **'K voprosu o bibliografii'**. In: *Avtografy P. I. Chaikovskogo v arkhive doma-muzeia v Klinu: Spravochnik* [vyp.
1] (1950): 93–94 [see *102*].

[*22*]   **FERNANDES, Kh. E. *Pëtr Il´ich Chaikovskii: Bibliograficheskaia pamiatka k 60-letiiu so dnia smerti*.**
Izhevsk: Respublikanskaia biblioteka Udmurtskoi ASSR im. A. S. Pushkina, 1953. 4 p.

[*23*]   *Pëtr Il´ich Chaikovskii: Kratkii rekomendatel´nyi ukazatel´.* Sost. I. F. Kunin. Pod obshchei red. V. V.
Iakovleva. Moskva: Gos. ordena Lenina biblioteka SSSR im. V. I. Lenina, 1953. 47 p, illus. (*Velikie deiateli
russkogo iskusstva*).

Contents: 'Predislovie': 3–4 — 'Vazhneishie muzykal´nye proizvedeniia P. I. Chaikovskogo': 5–6 [see *2345*] —
'P. I. Chaikovskii: Velikii russkii kompozitor': 7–11 [see *903*] — 'Iz vyskazyvanii P. I. Chaikovskogo': 12–17
[see *2062*] — 'Literaturnye proizvedeniia P. I. Chaikovskogo': 17 [see *5434*] — 'Osnovnye daty zhizni i
tvorchestva P. I. Chaikovskogo': 18–30 [see *86*] — 'Chto chitat´ o P. I. Chaikovskom': 31–45.

[24]   'P. I. Chaikovskii, 1840–1893'. In: S. L. Uspenskaia, *Literatura o muzyke 1948–1953: Bibliograficheskii ukazatel´*. Red. Iu. N. Masanov. Moskva: Izdat. Vsesoiuznoi knizhnoi palaty, 1955: 83–88.

[25]   'P. I. Chaikovskii, 1840–1893'. In: S. L. Uspenskaia, *Literatura o muzyke 1954–1956: Bibliograficheskii ukazatel´*. Red. N. A. Lavrova. Moskva: Izdat. Vsesoiuznoi knizhnoi palaty, 1958: 42–44.

[26]   'P. I. Chaikovskii, 1840–1893'. In: *Sovetskaia literatura o muzyke: Bibliograficheskii ukazatel´ za 1957 god.* Sost. S. Uspenskaia i B. Iagolim. Moskva: Sovetskii kompozitor, 1959: 32–33.

[27]   'Sovetskie publikacie o Čajkovskom', *Slovenská hudba*, 3 (Nov/Dec 1959): 546–547.

[28]   'Chaikovskii, P. I.'. In: *Muzykal´naia bibliografiia russkoi periodicheskoi pechati XIX veka.* Sost. T. N. Livanova i O. A. Vinogradova. Moskva: Sovetskii kompozitor, 1960–1975. Vyp. 5: *(1861–1870)*, chast 1: 331–332; Vyp. 6: *(1871–1880)*, chast 2: 351–358.

[29]   'P. I. Chaikovskii, 1840–1893: Knigi, zhurnaly i gazetnye stat´i'. In: *Informatsionnyi ukazatel´ bibliograficheskikh spiskov i kartotek sostavlennykh bibliotekami Sovetskogo Soiuza.* Vyp. 7. Moskva, 1962: 25.
        Lists 252 titles up to Feb 1962.

[30]   'P. I. Chaikovskii, 1840–1893'. In: *Sovetskaia literatura o muzyke: Bibliograficheskii ukazatel´ knig, zhurnal´nykh statei i retsenzii za 1958–1959 gg.* Sost. S. Uspenskaia i G. Koltypina. Moskva: Sovetskii kompozitor, 1963: 43–45.

[31]   'P. I. Chaikovskii, 1840–1893'. In: *Sovetskaia literatura o muzyke, 1918–1947: Bibliograficheskii ukazatel´ knig.* Sost. I. I. Startsev. Red. S. L. Uspenskaia. Moskva: Gos. muz. izdat, 1963: 81–95.

[32]   POGOSOVA, Z. *Pëtr Il´ich Chaikovskii: K 125-letiiu so dnia rozhdeniia.* Rekomendatel´nyi spisok literatury. Sost. Z. Pogosova. Essentuki, 1965. (*Essentukskaia kurortnaia biblioteka*).

[33]   'P. I. Chaikovskii, 1840–1893'. In: *Sovetskaia literatura o muzyke, 1960–1962.* Sost. S. Uspenskaia, A. Kolbanovskaia, I. Startsev, B. Iagolim. Moskva: Sovetskii kompozitor, 1967: 106–110.

[34]   BULAI, L. G. & IVANOVA, N. P. *P. I. Chaikovskii: Bibliograficheskii ukazatel´.* K 75-letiiu so dnia smerti. L´vov: Gos. nauchnaia biblioteka, 1968. 58 p.
        Text in Ukrainian.

[35]   'P. I. Chaikovskii, 1840–1893'. In: *Sovetskaia literatura o muzyke: Bibliograficheskii ukazatel´ knig, zhurnal´nykh statei i retsenzii za 1963–1965 gg.* Sost. A. Kolbanovskaia, G. Koltypina, B. Iagolim. Moskva: Sovetskii kompozitor, 1971: 94–97.

[36]   'Chaikovskii, Piotr Il´ich'. In: *New York Public Library: Dictionary Catalog of the Slavonic Collection.* 2nd ed., revised and enlarged. Vol. 6. Boston, G. K Hall & Co, 1974: 728–746.

[37]   'P. I. Chaikovskii, 1850–1893'. In: *Sovetskaia literatura o muzyke: Bibliograficheskii ukazatel´ knig, zhurnal´nykh statei i retsenzii 1966–1967 gg.* Sost. G. B. Koltypina, B. S. Iagolim. Moskva: Sovetskii kompozitor, 1974: 80–81.

[38]   MOLDON, D. 'Tchaikovsky, Piotr (1840–93)'. In: D. Moldon, *A bibliography of Russian composers.* London: White Lion [1976]: 295–326. ISBN 0-7284-0101-0.

[39]   'Tchaikovskii, Peter Ilich, 1840–1893'. In: *Historical sets, Collected editions, and monuments of music: A guide to their contents.* Comp. by Anna Harriet Heyer. Vol. 1. Chicago: American Library Association, 1980: 653–656.
        A guide to the contents of *P. I. Chaikovskii: Polnoe sobranie sochinenii* [see *118*].

[40]   'Chaikovskii, Pëtr Il´ich (1840–1893), kompozitor'. In: *Istoriia dorevoliutsionnoi Rossii v dnevnikakh i vospominaniiakh: Annotirovannyi ukazatel´ knig i publikatsii v zhurnalakh* [5 vols.]. Moskva: Kniga [1981–89]. Tom 3, chast 3: 334–344; Tom 5, chast 2: 348–350.

[*41*]   'Chaikovskii, Piotr Il´ich'. In: *New York Public Library: Dictionary catalog of the music collection*. Vol. 7. 2nd ed. Boston: G. K. Hall, 1982: 47–79. ISBN 0–8161–0374–7.

[*42*]   'P. I. Chaikovsky'. In: *The catalogue of printed music in the British Library to 1980*. Ed. Laureen Baillie. Vol. 11. London; New York: K. G. Saur, 1982: 101–159.

        Lists Chaikovskii's published scores held by the British Library.

[*43*]   POLIAKOVA, I. S. 'Bibliografiia'. In: *Sovetskaia muzykal´naia entsiklopediia*, tom 6. (1982): 185–189 [see *1660*].

[*44*]   ZABOROV, P. R. 'P. I. Chaikovskii i russkaia literatura', *Russkaia literatura* (May/Jun 1984), 3: 245–249.

[*45*]   'Čajkovskij, Petr I.'. In: *Bayerische Staatsbibliothek: Katalog der Musikdrucke, BSB-Musik*. Bd. 3. München; New York: K. G. Saur, 1988: 1036–1048. ISBN 3–5983–0560–5.

[*46*]   SHOKHMAN, G. 'Vzgliad s drugikh beregov', *Sovetskaia muzyka* (1990), 6: 134–141.

        A survey of Western publications on Chaikovskii, 1980–89.

[*47*]   'Chronologisches Verzeichnis von Tschaikowskys theoretischen Werken, Schriften und Übersetzungen'. In: G. A. Larosh, *Peter Tschaikowsky: Aufsätze und Erinnerungen* (1993): 299–305 [see *2406*].

[*48*]   RUBTSOVA, V. 'Piotr Czajkowski w rodzimej literaturze muzykologicznej' / 'Russian musical writings on Tchaikovsky', *Muzyka*, 39 (1994), 1: 109–112.

        Text in Polish, with a summary in English.

1.3. DISCOGRAPHIES

[*49*]   HOLT, R. 'Tchaikovsky and the gramophone', *Gramophone* (Aug 1928), 8: 94–96.

[*50*]   'Peter Ilich Tchaikovsky (1840–1893)'. In: T. H. Tyler & J. F. Brogan, *Encyclopedia of the world's best recorded music*. New York: The Gramophone Shop, 1930: 194–196.

        — 2nd ed. *The Gramophone Shop encyclopedia of recorded music*. Comp. by R. D. Darrel; with a foreword by Lawrence Gilman. New York: The Gramophone Shop, 1936: 472–478.

        — 3rd ed. New York: The Gramophone Shop, 1942: 468–474.

        — 4th ed. New Yok, The Gramophone Shop, 1948: 527–536.

        — [repr.] Westport, Ct.: Greenwood Press, 1970: 527–536.

[*51*]   HALLIDAY, J. *Tchaikovsky on records*. With foreword by Artur Rodzinski. New York: Four Corners [1942]. 89 p, illus.

[*52*]   BIANCOLLI, L. 'Complete list of recordings by the Philharmonic-Symphony Society of New York'. In: L. Biancolli, *Tschaikowsky and his orchestral music* (1944): 46–48 [see *4372*].

[*53*]   'Tchaikovsky, Peter Ilyich (1840–1893)'. In: D. Hall, *The record book: A guide to the world of the phonograph*. International ed. New York, O. Durrell, 1948: 1212–1233.

[*54*]   'Quelques beaux enregistrements de Tchaikowsky', *Disques*, 5 (Dec 1952): 652–653.

        Survey of recordings. See also *56, 57, 60*.

[*55*]   'Tchaikovsky, Peter Ilich (1840–1893)'. In: F. F. Clough & G. J. Cuming, *World's encyclopedia of recorded music*. London: Sidgwick & Jackson, 1952–1957 [4 vols. in 3]. Vol. 1: 613–628; Vol. 2: 845–847; Vol. 3: 222–230; Vol. 4: 460–475.

[56]   'Peter-Illitch Tchaikowsky', *Disques* (Sep/Oct 1953): 562–563.

[57]   'Peter Illitch Tchaikowsky', *Disques* (Jan/Feb 1954): 72–74.

[58]   INDCOX, J. F. 'Tchaikovsky recordings on microgroove', *High Fidelity*, 4 (Aug 1954): 55–58; (Oct 1954): 89–99; 5 (May 1955): 85–89.

[59]   'All Tchaikovsky', *Musical America*, 74 (Sep 1954): 17.

[60]   'Peter-Illitch Tchaikowsky', *Disques* (Apr 1955): 358–361, illus.

[61]   BRIGGS, J. *The collector's Tchaikovsky and the five*. Philadelphia: Lippincott [1959]: 10–149 (*Keystone Books on Music*; *KB–9*).

An annotated discography, with the first half of the book devoted to Chaikovskii. Includes a short biographical sketch: 11–98 — Discography: 99–149.

[62]   'Tchaikovsky, Peter (1840–93)'. In: *The stereo record guide*. Comp. by Edward Greenfield, Ivan March and Dennis Stevens; ed. by Ivan March. London: Long Playing Record Library, 1960–61 [2 vols.]. Vol. 1: 188–207; Vol. 2: 521–533.

— [rev. ed.] *The Penguin stereo record guide*. Harmondsworth, Middx.; New York: Penguin, 1977: 1018–1057.

— [rev. ed.] *The new Penguin stereo record and cassette guide*. Comp. by Edward Greenfied, Robert Layton, Ivan March. Ed. by Ivan March. Harmondsworth, Middx.; New York: Penguin Books, 1982: 766–802.

— [rev. ed.] *The Penguin guide to compact discs, cassettes, and LPs*. Comp. by Edward Greenfield, Robert Layton, and Ivan March. Harmondsworth, Middx.; New York: Penguin Books, 1986: 921–955.

— [rev. ed.] *The new Penguin guide to compact discs and cassettes*. Comp. by Edward Greenfield, Robert Layton, and Ivan March. Harmondsworth, Middx.; New York: Penguin Books, 1988: 1095–1137.

— New ed., rev. and updated. *The Penguin guide to compact discs and cassettes*. Comp. by Ivan March, Edward Greenfield and Robert Layton. Ed. by Ivan March. London; New York: Penguin Books, 1996: 1330–1371. (*Penguin handbooks*).

[63]   BLASL, F. 'Werke von P. I. Tschaikowsky auf Langspielplatten', *Musikerziehung*, 14 (Sep 1960): 36–40.

[64]   'Tschaikowsky, Peter Iljitsch'. In: *Opern auf Schallplatten, 1900–1962: Ein historischer Katalog vollstandiger oder nahezu vollstandiger Aufnahmen als Beitrag zur Geschichte der Auffuhrungspraxis*. Wien: Universal Edition, 1974: 151–154.

[65]   PETROV, I. 'Izdanie v gramzapisi', *Sovetskaia kul´tura* (7 Dec 1979): 8.

Concerning a complete set of recordings of Chaikovskii's music, issued on the Russian label 'Melodiya'.

[66]   'Piotr (Peter) Ilych Tchaikovsky'. In: A. Cohn, *Recorded classical music: A critical guide to compositions and performances*. New York: Schirmer Books; London: Collier Macmillan, 1981: 1877–1895. ISBN 0–0287–0640–4.

[67]   'Tchaikovsky, Peter Ilych (1840–1893)'. In: J. R. Bennett, *Melodiya: A Soviet Russian L. P. discography*. Comp. by John R. Bennett; foreword by Boris Semeonoff and Anatoli Zhelezny. Westport, Conn. : Greenwood Press, 1981: 606–649. (*Discographies*; 6).

[68]   *P. I. Chaikovskii, 1840–1990: Katalog videomaterialov*. Sost. A. V. Balukova, I. V. Kognovitskaia, L. Fëdorova. Moskva: Teleradiofond, 1988: 198 p. [2 vols.]

A catalogue of audio-visual materials on Chaikovskii held by Soviet State Television.

[69]   *P. I. Chaikovskii, 1840–1990: Katalog zvukozapisei*. Moskva: Teleradiofond, 1988.

A catalogue of sound recordings of Chaikovskii's music in the archives of Soviet State Radio.

Tom 2: Opery. 164 p.

Tom 3: Stsenicheskaia muzyka. 136 p.

Tom 5: Kamerno-instrumental´naia muzyka. 147 p.

Tom 6: Romansy (soch. do 1875 g.). 120 p.

Tom 7: Romansy (soch. 1878–84 gg.). 106 p.

Tom 8: Romansy (vokal´nye ansambli). 148 p.

[*70*]   **SWED, M. 'Piotr Ilyich Tchaikovsky'.** In: *The Metropolitan Opera guide to recorded opera.* Ed. by Paul Gruber. New York: Metropolitan Opera Guild; W. W. Norton, 1993: 551–561.

Comparison of recordings of *Evgenii Onegin* and *The Queen of Spades.*

[*71*]   **FREED, R. 'Basic Tchaikovsky: A critical discography of orchestral music on CD'**, *Stereo Review,* 58 (Nov 1993): 78–80, illus.

[*72*]   **'Tchaikovsky on disc'**, *Classic CD* (Nov 1993), 42: 26–27 [suppl.], illus.

[*73*]   **SVEJDA, J. 'Tchaikovsky, Piotr Ilyich'.** In: J. Svejda, *The record shelf guide to classical CDs and audiocassettes.* Rocklin (Calif.): Prima, 1995: 543–551.

[*74*]   **'Overview: Tchaikovsky'**, *American Record Guide,* 60 (1997), 4: 54–67.

[*75*]   **TEACHOUT, T. 'Tchaikovsky on CD: A select discography'.** In: T. Teachout, 'Tchaikovsky's passion' (1999): 58–59 [see *1695*].

See also *1512, 1554, 2587, 2606, 2689, 2969, 3000, 3052, 3076, 3088, 3103, 3178, 3321, 3420, 3660, 3677, 3824, 3974, 4071, 4072, 4093, 4102, 4219, 4240, 4241, 4272, 4292, 4372, 4423, 4428, 4433, 4479, 4497, 4530, 4599, 4644, 4649, 4706, 4720, 4728, 4856, 4890, 4961, 4962, 4965, 4986, 4988, 5075, 5111, 5114, 5137, 5142, 5256, 5309, 5405.*

1.4. FILMOGRAPHIES & VIDEOGRAPHIES

[*76*]   **'Tchaikovsky, Peter'.** In: D. L. Parker & E. Siegel, *Guide to dance in film: A catalog of U. S. productions including dance sequences with names of dancers, choreographers, directors, and other details.* Detroit: Gale Research [1978]: 208. (*Performing arts information guide series;* 3).

[*77*]   **'Tchaikovsky, Peter Ilich'.** In: C. R. Croissant, *Opera performances in video format: A checklist of commercially released recordings.* Canton (Mass.): Music Library Association, 1991: 60–62. (*MLA index & bibliography series;* 26).

[*78*]   **'Tchaikovsky, Peter Ilyich'.** In: *The Dance film and video guide.* Comp. by Deirdre Towers. Princeton (N. J.): Dance Horizons; Princeton Book Co. [1991]: 150.

[*79*]   **'Tchaikovsky'.** In: *Opera mediagraphy: Video recordings and motion pictures.* Comp. by Sharon G. Almquist. Westport (Conn.): Greenwood Press [1993]: 56–58, 136–137. (*Music reference collection;* 40).

[*80*]   **ROBINSON, H. 'Pyotr Ilyich Tchaikovsky'.** In: *The Metropolitan opera guide to opera on video.* Ed. by Paul Gruber. New York: Metropolitan Opera Guild; W. W. Norton, 1997: 332–343.

[*81*]   **'Tchaikovsky, Piotr Ilyich'.** In: *An opera videography.* Comp. by Charles H. Parsons. Lewiston (N. Y.): Edwin Mellen Press, 1997: 276–281. (*Mellen opera reference index;* 20).

[*82*]   **'Tchaikovsky, Peter Ilyich'.** In: *Dance on camera: A guide to dance films and videos.* Ed. by Louise Spain; foreword by Jacques D'Amboise. Lanham (Md.); London: Scarecrow Press; New York: Neal-Schuman, 1998: 162.

1.5. CHRONOLOGIES

[*83*]   GLEBOV, I. [ASAF´EV, B. V.] 'Khronograf zhizni P. I. Chaikovskogo i vazhneishikh aktov ego tvorchestva'. In: I. Glebov, *P. I. Chaikovskii: Ego zhizn´ i tvorchestvo* (1922): 153–174 [see *1470*].

[*84*]   'Letopis´ zhizni i tvorchestva P. I. Chaikovskogo', *Sovetskoe iskusstvo* (2 Aug 1938): 4.

The preparation of *Dni i gody P. I. Chaikovskogo* [see *85*].

[*85*]   ***Dni i gody P. I. Chaikovskogo: Letopis´ zhizni i tvorchestva***. Sost. E. Zaidenshnur, V. Kiselev, A. Orlova, N. Shemanin. Pod red. V. Iakovleva. Moskva; Leningrad: Muzgiz, 1940. 744 p, music, illus. (*Trudy Doma-muzeia P. I. Chaikovskogo v Klinu*).

A day-by-day listing of the most significant events in the composer's life, including quotations from letters, diaries and newspaper articles.

Contents: V. V. Iakovev, 'Ot redaktora': 3–10 — 'Letopis´ zhizni i tvorchestva P. I. Chaikovskogo': 11–652 — N. V. Shemanin, 'Notografiia i bibliografiia proizvedenii P. I. Chaikovskogo': 653–739 [see *7*].

[*86*]   'Osnovnye daty zhizni i tvorchestva P. I. Chaikovskogo'. In: *Pëtr Il´ich Chaikovskii: Kratkii rekomendatel´nyi ukazatel´* (1953): 18–30 [see *23*].

[*87*]   DOMBAEV, G. S. *Tvorchestvo Petra Il´icha Chaikovskogo v materialakh i dokumentakh*. Sost. G. Dombaev. Pod red. Gr. Bernandta. Moskva: Gos. muz. izdat., 1958. 635 p, music, illus.

Presents a chronological list of references for all the composer's musical and literary works, using extracts from correspondence, diaries, articles, reviews, etc. Includes bibliography and comprehensive indexes.

Review: A. A. Orlova, 'Kniga o Chaikovskom', *Sovetskaia muzyka* (1960), 1: 187–190.

[*88*]   DAVYDOV, Iu. L. 'Khronologiia poslednikh let zhizni i tvorchestva'. In: Iu. L. Davydov, *Klinskie gody tvorchestva Chaikovskogo* (1965): 117–126 [see *1243*].

[*89*]   ORLOVA, E. M. 'Daty zhizni i deiatel´nosti P. I. Chaikovskogo'. In: E. M. Orlova, *Pëtr Il´ich Chaikovskii* (1980): 243–255 [see *1537*].

[*90*]   POLIAKOVA, I. S. 'Osnovnye daty zhizni i deiatel´nosti'. In: *Sovetskaia muzykal´naia entsiklopediia*, tom 6 (1982): 183–185 [see *1660*].

[*91*]   ROZANOVA, Iu. A. 'Sozdavaia novuiu letopis´ zhizni i tvorchestva Chaikovskogo'. In: *Chaikovskii: K 150-letiiu so dnia rozhdeniia. Voprosy istorii, teorii i ispolnitel´stva* (1990): 4–17 [see *591*].

[*92*]   MORITA, M. 'Chaikofosukii Nendaijun denki'. In: M. Morita, *Shin Chaikofuskii kou* (1993): 305–363 [see *1550*].

1.6. ENCYCLOPEDIAS

[*93*]   'Entsiklopediia "Zhizn´ i tvorchestvo P. I. Chaikovskogo"', *Sovetskoe iskusstvo* (13 Mar 1948): 1.

A projected two-volume encyclopedia devoted to the life and works of Chaikovskii, edited by Boris Asaf´ev (which was not realized).

[*94*]   KORABEL´NIKOVA, L. Z. 'Entsiklopediia Chaikovskogo: Rossiiskii fond fundamental´nykh issledovanii', *Muzykal´naia akademiia* (1993), 4: 213–214.

Report on the compilation of an encyclopedia on the composer, as part of the projected New Complete Edition of his works [see *120*]. See also *95, 96*.

[95]   **KORABEL´NIKOVA, L. Z.** 'Wszystko o Czajkovskim' / 'Everything on Tchaikovsky', *Muzyka*, 39
        (1994), 1: 112–114.
        Work in Russia on the Chaikovskii encyclopedia. Text in Polish, with a summary in English.

[96]   **KORABEL´NIKOVA, L. Z.** 'Chaikovskii Entsiklopediia: Sud´ba proekta', *Muzykal´noe obozrenie*
        (1997), 9: 11.
        Progress on the projected Chaikovskii encyclopedia.

PART 2

SOURCES AND DOCUMENTS

2.1. MANUSCRIPTS
2.1.1. Archival Holdings
2.1.2. General

2.2. SCORES
2.2.1. Critical Editions
2.2.2. Facsimile Editions

2.3. LITERARY WORKS
2.3.1. Books
2.3.2. Articles and Interviews
2.3.3. Translations

2.4. CORRESPONDENCE
2.4.1. Collected Editions
2.4.2. Selections

2.5. DIARIES AND NOTEBOOKS
2.5.1. Critical Editions
2.5.2. Diary Extracts
2.5.3. Notebooks

2.6. MEMOIRS
2.6.1. Collections
2.6.2. Individual

2.7. PICTORIAL COLLECTIONS

2.8. SOUND RECORDINGS

2.1. MANUSCRIPTS

2.1.1. Archival Holdings

[*97*]   **ENGEL´, Iu. D. 'Rukopisi P. I. Chaikovskogo'**, *Khronika zhurnala "Muzykal´nyi Sovremennik"* (1916), 20: 3–5.

A short general description of Chaikovskii's manuscripts which were donated to the library of the Moscow Conservatory in 1905 by Modest Chaikovskii. See also *98*.

[*98*]   **'Bibliograficheskie i arkhivnye spravki o sochineniiakh P. I. Chaikovskogo i ego muzykal´nyi arkhiv'**. In: *Proshloe russkoi muzyki*, tom 1 (1920): 140–171 [see *584*].

A detailed list of the composer's manuscripts in the archives of the Moscow Conservatory, including those donated by Modest Chaikovskii in 1905 (see *97*).

[*99*]   **MAMUNA, N. V. 'Notnye avtografy i neizdannye pis´ma P. I. Chaikovskogo'**. In: *P. I. Chaikovskii na stsene teatra opery i baleta im. S. M. Kirova* (1941): 405–422 [see *2542*].

Includes descriptions of Chaikovskii's autographs in RUS–SPtob: 405–409 — Publication of letters from Chaikovskii to Evgenii Al´brekht: 410–416 — Nikolai Khristoforov: 416–418 — Iosif Zeifert: 419 — Letter from Modest Chaikovskii to Vladimir Pogozhev: 408.

[*100*] **ORLOVA, E. V. 'Perechen´ i kratkaia kharakteristika notnykh eskizov, chernovykh i chistovykh rukopisei romansov, khraniashchikhsia v arkhive P. I. Chaikovskogo v Dome-muzee v Klinu'**. In: E. V. Orlova, *Romansy Chaikovskogo* (1948): 139–142 [see *5248*].

Describing 29 manuscript scores and sketches of Chaikovskii's songs, preserved in the archives of the Chaikovskii Museum at Klin (RUS–KL).

[*101*] **NIKOLAEV, A. A. 'Perechen´ rukopisei fortepiannykh sochinenii P. I. Chaikovskogo, khraniashchikhsia v Gosudarstvennom tsentral´nom muzee muzykal´noi kul´tury im. M. I. Glinki'**. In: A. A. Nikolaev, *Fortepiannoe nasledie Chaikovskogo* (1949): 204–205 [see *5350*].

— [rev. repr.] In: A. A. Nikolaev, *Fortepiannoe nasledie Chaikovskogo*, 2-e izd. (1958): 275–277 [see *5350*].

[*102*] *Avtografy P. I. Chaikovskogo v arkhive doma-muzeia v Klinu: Spravochnik*. Pod obshchei red. Z. V. Korotkovoi-Leviton. (*Komitet po delam iskusstv pri Sovete Ministrov SSSR. Otdel nauchno-issledovatel´skikh uchrezhdenii. Gos. Dom-muzei P. I. Chaikovskogo*).

[*Vyp. 1*] Sost. nauchnye sotrudniki Doma-muzeia P. I. Chaikovskogo: K. Iu. Davydova, E. M. Orlova, G. R. Freindling. Moskva; Leningrad: Gos. muz. izdat., 1950. 96 p, music, illus.

Contents: 'Arkhiv P. I. Chaikovskogo v Dome-muzee': 3–6 [see *1217*] — 'Avtografy k muzykal´nym proizvedeniiam': 9–76 — 'Zapisnye knizhki i dnevniki': 79–92 [see *368*] — 'K voprosu o bibliografii': 93–94 [see *21*].

Vyp. 2. Sost. K. Davydova. Moskva; Leningrad: Gos. muz. izdat., 1952. 332 p, illus.

An annotated catalogue of Chaikovskii's letters to 119 correspondents (1866–93).

Review: V. V. Protopopov, 'Poleznye spravochniki', *Sovetskaia muzyka* (1951), 7: 99–101 [vyp. 2].

[*103*] *Chaikovskii, Pëtr Il´ich (1840–1893 gg.): Opis´ dokumental´nykh materialov lichnogo fonda No. 905*. Krainie daty dokumental´nykh materialov 1859–1922 gg. Sost. i podgot. k pechati G. D. Andreevoi. Pod red. V. A. Kiseleva. Moskva: Glavnoe arkhivnoe upravlenie Tsentral´nyi gos. arkhiv literatury i iskusstva SSSR, 1955. 20 p.

Catalogue of documents in the Central State Archive for Literature and the Arts, Moscow, with 105 items dating from 1859 to 1922.

[*104*]   ***Rukopisi P. I. Chaikovskogo v fondakh Gosudarstvennogo tsentral´nogo muzeia muzykal´noi kultury im.***
          M. I. Glinki: Katalog-spravochnik. Sost. B. V. Dobrokhotov i V. A. Kiselev. Pod obshchei red. V. A.
          Kiseleva. [Moskva], 1955. 98 p. (*Ministerstvo kul´tury SSSR*).

          Stencilled copy of typescript.

          — [2-e izd.] *Avtografy P. I. Chaikovskogo v fondakh Gosudarstvennogo tsentral´nogo muzeia muzykal´noi kultury imeni*
          M. I. Glinki: Katalog-spravochnik. Sost. B. V. Dobrokhotov i V. A. Kiselev. Pod obshchei red. V. A. Kiseleva.
          Moskva: Gos. tsentral´naia muzei muzykal´nyi kultury im. M. I. Glinki, 1956. 77 p. (*Ministerstvo kul´tury*
          SSSR).

          Lists 412 items (musical scores, literary manuscripts, letters, notes and miscellania).

[*105*]   'Tchaikovsky, Pyotr Il´ych, 1840–1893'. In: *Music letters in the Pierpont Morgan Library: A catalogue*. Ed.
          by J. Rigbie Turner. Vol. 2. [New York:] 1991:384–385.

[*106*]   **SKVIRSKAIA, T. Z. 'Avtografy P. I. Chaikovksogo v Otdele rukopisei Peterburgskoi**
          konservatorii'. In: *Peterburgskii muzykal´nyi arkhiv: Sbornik statei i materialov*. Vyp. 1. Sankt Peterburg:
          Kanon, 1997: 117–122.

2.1.2. General

[*107*]   **'Neizdannyi muzykal´nyi otryvok Chaikovskogo'**, *Russkaia muzykal´naia gazeta* (Jan 1899), 1: 15–16.

          Facs. of Chaikovskii's autograph arrangement of the folk-song 'Tis Not the Wind That Bends the Branches'.
          See also *108*.

          — [repr.] *Russkaia muzykal´naia gazeta* (20 Oct 1913), 42: 924.

[*108*]   **TITKOV, V. 'Pis´mo v redaktsiiu po povodu avtografa P. I. Chaikovskogo'**, *Russkaia muzykal´naia*
          gazeta (30 Sep 1900), 40: 924.

[*109*]   **POPOV, S. S. 'Novoe o zabytykh muzykal´nykh proizvedeniiakh P. I. Chaikovskogo'**, *Sovetskaia*
          muzyka (1933), 6: 102–104.

          The discovery of the manuscripts of Chaikovskii's melodrama for the Domovoi Scene in the play *The Voevoda*,
          and the *Overture in C minor*.

[*110*]   **'Naideny rukopisi P. I. Chaikovskogo'**, *Sovetskoe iskusstvo* (6 Sep 1946): 7.

          The Klin house-musuem's acquisition of Chaikovskii's autograph manuscripts of the suite from the ballet *The*
          Nutcracker, the symphony *Manfred*, and 15 letters from Chaikovskii to Vladimir Pogozhev.

[*111*]   **'Nasledie velikogo kompozitora: Rabota nad arkhivom P. I. Chaikovskogo'**, *Vechernii Leningrad* (20
          Apr 1947): 3.

          Work on reconstructing the scores of Chaikovskii's unfinished *Symphony* in E-flat major, the opera *The Voevoda*
          and the original version of the *Variations on a Rococo Theme*, from the surviving manuscripts.

[*112*]   **'Za rubezhom: FRG'**, *Muzykal´naia zhizn´* (1961), 8: 12.

          A short note regarding the auction of Chaikovskii's autobiography in Munich.

[*113*]   **KULAKOVSKAIA, T. 'Napisannye ego rukoi'**, *Teatral´naia zhizn´* (1965), 9: 30.

          An exhibition of Chaikovskii's manuscripts at the M. I. Glinka Museum of Musical Culture in Moscow.

[*114*]   **VAIDMAN, P. E. *Tvorcheskii arkhiv P. I. Chaikovskogo***. Moskva: Muzyka, 1988. 174 p, music, illus.
          ISBN: 5-7140-0200-8.

          Study of Chaikovskii's manuscripts and working methods. Includes: 'Kratkoe opisanie zapisnykh knizhek P. I.
          Chaikovskogo': 161–164 [see *370*].

          Adapted from dissertation (summary published Moskva: Institut iskusstvoznaniia, 1989, 23 p).

[*115*]   **VAIDMAN, P. E. 'Novye dokumenty P. I. Chaikovskogo: Obzor istochnikov'**. In: *P. I. Chaikovskii:*
          Zabytoe i novoe (1995): 135 [see *598*].

          Concerning recently-discovered letters and autograph manuscripts by Chaikovskii.

[116] 'Avtografy Chekhova, Chaikovskogo i Nikolaia budut predstavleny na auktsione "LG"', *Literaturnaia gazeta* (10 Apr 1996).

An auction of famous autographs in Russia, including a signed photograph of Chaikovskii.

[117] VAIDMAN, P. E. 'P. I. Chaikovskii: Novye stranitsy biografii po materialam rukopisei uchenicheskikh rabot kompozitora'. In: *Peterburgskii muzykal´nyi arkhiv: Sbornik statei i materialov*. Vyp. 2. Sankt Peterburg: Kanon, 1998: 134–143.

A study of Chaikovskii's manuscripts dating from his years at the St. Petersburg Conservatory, and Schumann's influence on Chaikovskii.

See also *290, 500, 1210, 3421, 3798, 5187, 5385, 5390.*

2.2. SCORES

2.2.1. Critical Editions

[118] CHAIKOVSKII, P. I. *Polnoe sobranie sochinenii*. Obshchaia red. B. V. Asaf´eva. Redaktsionnaia komissiia: A. N. Aleksandrov, B. V. Asaf´ev, S. S. Bogatyrev, A. B. Gol´denveizer, T. N. Khrennikov, B. L. Iavorskii, N. Ia. Miaskovskii, M. S. Pekelis, V. V. Protopopov, K. K. Sakva, Iu. A. Shaporin, V. Ia. Shebalin, I. P. Shishov, M. O. Shteinberg, L. S. Sidel´nikov. Moskva; Leningrad, 1940–90 [63 vols.].

Note: In some vocal works the original texts have been altered by the Soviet publishers, and musical quotations from the Imperial Russian Anthem have also been excised or re-written (although in such cases the original version is normally given in footnotes or appendices to the scores). See also *8, 39, 801, 981, 4972, 4973, 4974, 4975, 5119, 5158.*

Tom 1A: Opernoe tvorchestvo: "Voevoda", soch. 3. Partitura (deistvie pervoe). Tom podgot. P. Lammom. Moskva: Gos. muz. izdat., 1953. xiv, 323 p.

Tom 1B: Opernoe tvorchestvo: "Voevoda", soch. 3. Partitura (deistvie vtoroe). Tom podgot. P. Lammom. Moskva: Gos. muz. izdat., 1953. 185 p.

Tom 1V: Opernoe tvorchestvo: "Voevoda", soch. 3. Partitura (deistvie tret´e). Tom podgot. P. Lammom. Moskva: Gos. muz. izdat., 1953. 213 p.

Tom 1 (dop.): *Opernoe tvorchestvo: "Voevoda".* Perelozhenie dlia peniia s fortepiano. Tom podgot. P. Lammom. Moskva: Gos. muz. izdat., 1953. xiv, 431 p, illus.

Tom 2: Opernoe tvorchestvo: Otryvki iz oper "Undina" i "Mandragora". Partitury i perelozheniia dlia peniia s fortepiano. Tom podgot. R. Berberovym. Moskva; Leningrad: Gos. muz. izdat., 1950. xiii, 223 p, illus.

Contents: 'Otryvki iz opery "Undina": Pesnia Undiny': 2–43 — 'Final I akta': 44–90 — '"Khor tsvetov i nasekomykh" iz opery "Mandragora"': 93–158 — 'Perelozheniia dlia peniia s fortepiano: "Pesnia Undiny"': 161–168 — 'Final I akta': 169–189 — "Khor tsvetov i nasekomykh": 191–221.

Tom 3A: Opernoe tvorchestvo: "Oprichnik". Partitura (deistviia pervoe i vtoroe). Tom podgot. A. N. Dmitrievym. Moskva: Gos. muz. izdat., 1959. xix, 313 p, illus.

Tom 3B: Opernoe tvorchestvo: "Oprichnik". Partitura (deistviia tret´e i chetvertoe). Tom podgot. A. N. Dmitrievym. Moskva: Gos. muz. izdat., 1959. 383 p.

Tom 4: Opernoe tvorchestvo: "Evgenii Onegin", soch. 24. Partitura. Red. Ivana Shishova. Moskva: Gos. muz. izdat., 1948. xiv, 536 p, illus.

Tom 5A: Opernoe tvorchestvo: "Orleanskaia deva". Partitura (deistviia pervoe i vtoroe). Tom podgot. V. D. Vasil´evym. Moskva: Muzyka, 1964. xviii, 517 p.

Tom 5B: Opernoe tvorchestvo: "Orleanskaia deva". Partitura (deistviia tret´e i chetvertoe). Tom podgot. V. D. Vasil´evym. Moskva: Muzyka, 1964. 449 p.

Tom 6A: Opernoe tvorchestvo: "Mazepa". Partitura (deistvie pervoe). Tom podgot. V. D. Vasil´evym. Moskva: Muzyka, 1969. xvii, 336 p, illus.

Tom 6B: Opernoe tvorchestvo: "Mazepa". Partitura (deistviia vtoroe i tret´e). Tom podgot. V. D. Vasil´evym. Moskva: Muzyka, 1969. 483 p.

Tom 7A: Opernoe tvorchestvo: "Cherevichki". Partitura (deistviia pervoe i vtoroe). Tom podgot. V. D. Vasil´evym. Moskva: Gos. muz. izdat., 1951. xiv, 425 p.

Tom 7B: Opernoe tvorchestvo: "Cherevichki". Partitura (deistviia tret´e i chetvertoe). Tom podgot. V. D. Vasil´evym. Moskva: Gos. muz. izdat., 1951. 281 p.

Tom 8A: Opernoe tvorchestvo: "Charodeika". Partitura (deistviia pervoe i vtoroe). Red. Ivana Shishova. Moskva: Gos. muz. izdat., 1948. xiii, 523 p.

Tom 8B: Opernoe tvorchestvo: "Charodeika". Partitura (deistviia tret´e i chetvertoe). Red. Ivana Shishova. Moskva: Gos. muz. izdat., 1948. xiii, 503 p.

Tom 9A: Opernoe tvorchestvo: "Pikovaia dama", soch. 68. Partitura (deistvie pervoe). Red. Anatoliia Dmitrieva. Moskva: Gos. muz. izdat., 1950. xix, 293 p, illus.

Tom 9B: Opernoe tvorchestvo: "Pikovaia dama", soch. 68. Partitura (deistvie vtoroe). Red. Anatoliia Dmitrieva. Moskva: Gos. muz. izdat., 1950. 279 p.

Tom 9V: Opernoe tvorchestvo: "Pikovaia dama", soch. 68. Partitura (deistvie tret´e). Red. Anatoliia Dmitrieva. Moskva: Gos. muz. izdat., 1950. 277 p.

Tom 10: Opernoe tvorchestvo: "Iolanta", soch. 69. Partitura. Tom podgot. V. D. Vasil´evym. Moskva: Gos. muz. izdat., 1953. xiv, 360 p, illus.

Tom 11A: Baletnoe tvorchestvo: "Lebedinoe ozero", soch. 20. Partitura (deistviia pervoe i vtoroe). Tom podgot. I. Iordan i G. Kirkorom. Moskva: Gos. muz. izdat., 1957. xvi, 401 p, illus.

Tom 11B: Baletnoe tvorchestvo: "Lebedinoe ozero", soch. 20. Partitura (deistviia tret´e i chetvertoe). Tom podgot. I. Iordan i G. Kirkorom. Moskva: Gos. muz. izdat., 1957. 411 p.

Tom 12A: Baletnoe tvorchestvo: "Spiashchaia krasavitsa", soch. 66. Partitura (prolog). Tom podgot. A. Dmitrievym. Moskva: Gos. muz. izdat., 1957. xix, 244 p.

Tom 12B: Baletnoe tvorchestvo: "Spiashchaia krasavitsa", soch. 66. Partitura (deistvie pervoe). Tom podgot. A. Dmitrievym. Moskva: Gos. muz. izdat., 1957. 272 p.

Tom 12V: Baletnoe tvorchestvo: "Spiashchaia krasavitsa", soch. 66. Partitura (deistvie vtoroe). Tom podgot. A. Dmitrievym. Moskva: Gos. muz. izdat., 1957. 257 p.

Tom 12G: Baletnoe tvorchestvo: "Spiashchaia krasavitsa", soch. 66. Partitura (deistvie tret´e). Tom podgot. A. Dmitrievym. Moskva: Gos. muz. izdat., 1957. 375 p.

Tom 13A: Baletnoe tvorchestvo: "Shchelkunchik", soch. 71. Partitura (deistvie pervoe). Tom podgot. V. Vasil´evym. Moskva: Gos. muz. izdat., 1955. xvi, 310 p.

Tom 13B: Baletnoe tvorchestvo: "Shchelkunchik", soch. 71. Partitura (deistvie vtoroe). Tom podgot. V. Vasil´evym. Moskva: Gos. muz. izdat., 1955. 301 p.

Tom 14: Muzyka k dramaticheskim spektakliam. Tom podgot. I. N. Iordan. Moskva: Gos. muz. izdat., 1962. xix, 395 p, illus.

Contents: 'Muzyka k "Dmitriu Samozvantsu i Vasiliiu Shuiskomu"': 3–15 — 'Kuplety k "Sevil´skomu tsiriul´niku"': 19 — 'Muzyka k "Snegurochke", soch. 12': 23–274 — 'Muzyka dlia monologa Domovogo v p´ese "Voevoda"': 277–282 — 'Muzyka k tragedii "Gamlet"': 285–395.

Tom 15A: Sochineniia dlia orkestra: Pervaia simfoniia, "Zimnie grezy", soch. 13. Partitura. Red. S. S. Bogatyreva. Moskva: Gos. muz. izdat., 1957. xiii, 168 p.

Tom 15B: Sochineniia dlia orkestra: Vtoraia simfoniia, soch. 17. Partitura. Tom podgot. S. S. Bogatyrevym. Moskva: Gos. muz. izdat., 1954. ix, 303 p, illus.

Contents: 'Vtoraia redaktsiia (1879)': 3–165 — 'Pervaia redaktsiia (1872)': 169–298.

Tom 16A: Sochineniia dlia orkestra: Tret´ia simfoniia, soch. 29. Partitura. Red. Pavla Berlinskogo. Moskva: Gos. muz. izdat., 1949. 209 p, illus.

Tom 16B: Sochineniia dlia orkestra: Chetvertaia simfoniia, soch. 36. Partitura. Red. Pavla Berlinskogo. Moskva: Gos. muz. izdat., 1949. 220 p, illus.

Tom 17A: Sochineniia dlia orkestra: Piataia simfoniia, soch. 64. Partitura. Tom podgot. G. V. Kirkorom. Moskva: Gos. muz. izdat., 1963. xii, 227 p, illus.

Tom 17B: Sochineniia dlia orkestra: Shestaia simfoniia ("Pateticheskaia"), soch. 74. Partitura. Tom podgot. I. N. Iordan. Moskva: Gos. muz. izdat., 1963. xvi, 243 p, illus.

Tom 18: Sochineniia dlia orkestra: "Manfred", soch. 58. Partitura. Red. Evgeniia Makarova. Moskva: Gos. muz. izdat., 1949. xv, 319 p.

Tom 19A: Sochineniia dlia orkestra: Pervaia siuita, soch. 43. Partitura. Red. Borisa Karpova. Moskva: Gos. muz. izdat., 1948. xiii, 200 p.

Tom 19B: *Sochineniia dlia orkestra: Vtoraia siuita, soch. 53.* Partitura. Red. Borisa Karpova. Moskva: Gos. muz. izdat., 1948. xiii, 291 p.

Tom 20: *Sochineniia dlia orkestra: Partitury.* Red. Ivana Shishova. Moskva: Gos. muz. izdat., 1946. 366 p, illus.

Contents: 'Tret´ia siuita, soch. 55': 3–222 — '"Motsartiana" (chetvertaia siuita), soch. 61': 225–298 — '"Serenada dlia strunnogo orkestra", soch. 48': 301–366.

Tom 21: *Sochineniia dlia orkestra: Uvertiury.* Tom podgot. P. Lammom. Moskva: Gos. muz. izdat., 1952. 300 p.

Contents: 'Uvertiura "Groza" (op. post. 76)': 3–82 — 'Uvertiura F-dur (pervaia redaktsiia, 1865)': 85–117 — 'Uvertiura F-dur (vtoraia redaktsiia, 1866)': 121–210 — 'Uvertiura c-moll': 213–300.

Tom 22: *Sochineniia dlia orkestra: Partitury.* Tom podgot. I. N. Iordan. Moskva: Gos. muz. izdat., 1960. xiii, 184 p.

Contents: 'Torzhestvennaia uvertiura na datskii gimn, soch. 15': 3–79 — '"Fatum" (op. post. 77)': 81–174 — 'Prilozhenie' [op. 15]: 175–184.

Tom 23: *Sochineniia dlia orkestra: "Romeo i Dzhul´etta", uvertiura-fantaziia.* Partitura. Red. Anatoliia Drozdova i Igoria Belza. Moskva: Gos. muz. izdat., 1950. 223 p, illus.

Contents: 'Pervaia redaktsiia (1869)': 3–86 — 'Tret´e (okonchatel´naia) redaktsiia (1880)': 89–195 — 'Fragment vtoroi redaktsii (1870)': 199–223.

Tom 24: *Sochineniia dlia orkestra: Partitury.* Tom podgot. I. N. Iordan. Moskva: Gos. muz. izdat., 1961. xix, 336 p, illus.

Contents: "Serenada k imeninam N. G. Rubinshteina": 3–8 — '"Buria", soch. 18': 13–114 — '"Slavianskii marsh", soch. 31': 117–181 — '"Francheska da Rimini", soch. 32': 187–336.

Tom 25: *Sochineniia dlia orkestra: Partitury.* Tom podgot. A. A. Nikolaevym. Moskva: Gos. muz. izdat., 1961. xviii, 238 p, illus.

Contents: '"Ital´ianskoe kaprichchio", soch. 45': 3–96 — '"1812 god", soch. 49': 99–186 — "Torzhestvennyi marsh": 189–231 — 'Prilozheniia' [op. 49]: 235–238.

Tom 26: *Sochineniia dlia orkestra: Partitury.* Tom podgot. I. N. Iordan. Moskva: Gos. muz. izdat., 1961. xvii, 245 p, illus.

Contents: "Elegiia": 5–11 — "Pravovedskii marsh": 15–41 — '"Gamlet" (uvertiura-fantaziia), soch. 67': 47–149 — '"Voevoda" (op. post. 78)': 155–239 — 'Prilozheniia' [op. 67]: 242–245.

Tom 27: *Vokal´nye sochineniia s orkestrom: Partitury.* Tom podgot. I. N. Iordan. Moskva: Gos. muz. izdat., 1960. xv, 517 p, illus.

Contents: "K radosti": 3–185 — "Kantata v pamiat´ dvukhsotoi godovshchiny rozhdeniia Petra Velikogo": 189–337 — "Khor k iubileiu O. A. Petrova": 341–357 — "Moskva": 361–451 — "Na son griadushchii": 455–470 — '"Rassvet", soch. 46, no. 6': 473–485 — '"Ia li v pole da ne travushka byla", soch. 47, no. 7': 489–500 — '"Legenda", soch. 54, no. 5': 501–505 — 'Prilozheniia': 509–517.

Tom 28: *Sochineniia dlia fortepiano s orkestrom: Partitury.* Tom podgot. A. Gol´denveizerom. Moskva: Gos. muz. izdat., 1955. xvi, 347 p, illus.

Contents: 'Pervyi kontsert, soch. 23': 5–161 — 'Vtoroi kontsert, soch. 44': 167–347.

Tom 29: *Sochineniia dlia fortepiano s orkestrom: Partitury.* Tom podgot. A. Gol´denveizerom. Moskva: Gos. muz. izdat., 1954. xiv, 254 p, illus.

Contents: 'Kontsertnaia fantaziia, soch. 56': 5–155 — 'Tretii kontsert, soch. 75': 161–254.

Tom 30A: *Sochineniia dlia skripki s orkestrom: Partitury.* Red. Valentiny Ratskovskoi. Moskva: Gos. muz. izdat., 1949. xiii, 172 p, illus.

Contents: '"Sérénade mélancolique", soch. 26': 3–16 — '"Valse-scherzo", soch. 35': 19–46 — 'Kontsert, soch. 35': 49–170.

Tom 30B: *Sochineniia dlia violoncheli s orkestrom: Partitury.* Tom podgot. V. Kubatskim. Moskva: Gos. muz. izdat., 1956. xiii, 94 p.

Contents: '"Variatsii na temu rokoko", soch. 33': 5–46 — '"Pezzo capriccioso", soch. 62': 47–69 — '"Andante cantabile" iz Pervogo kvarteta': 71–79 — '"Noktiurn", soch. 19, no. 4': 83–89 — 'Prilozheniia' [op. 33]: 93–94.

Tom 31: Kamernye ansambli: Partitury. Tom podgot. An. Aleksandrovym. Moskva: Gos. muz. izdat., 1955. xiii, 161 p (+ 4 parts), illus.

Contents: 'Neokonchennyi kvartet (1865)': 3–20 — 'Pervyi kvartet, soch. 11': 25–60 — 'Vtoroi kvartet, soch. 22': 63–109 — 'Tretii kvartet, soch. 30': 115–161.

Tom 32A: Kamernye ansambli: Partitury. Tom podgot. A. Gol´denveizerom. Moskva: Gos. muz. izdat., 1951. xii, 150 p (+ 2 parts), illus.

Contents: 'Trio (dlia fortepiano, skripki i violoncheli), soch. 50': 5–151.

Tom 32B: Kamernye ansambli: Partitury. Tom podgot. A. Gol´denveizerom. Moskva: Gos. muz. izdat., 1952. 108 p (+ 6 parts), illus.

Contents: '"Souvenir de Florence" (sekstet), soch. 70': 5–86 — 'Prilozheniia': 89–108.

Tom 33: Vokal´nye sochineniia s orkestrom: Perelozhenie dlia peniia s fortepiano. Tom podgot. G. V. Kirkorom. Moskva: Muzyka, 1965. xviii, 314 p, illus.

Contents: "K radosti": 3–82 — "Kantata v pamiat´ dvukhsotoi godovshchiny rozhdeniia Petra Velikogo": 85–146 — "Khor k iubileiu O. A. Petrova": 149–158 — "Moskva": 159–207 — "Na son griadushchii": 211–214 — 'Muzyka k "Snegurochke", soch. 12': 217–314.

Tom 34: Opernoe tvorchestvo: "Oprichnik". Perelozhenie dlia peniia s fortepiano. Tom podgot. A. N. Dmitrievym. Moskva: Gos. muz. izdat., 1959. xix, 378 p, illus.

Tom 35: Opernoe tvorchestvo: "Kuznets Vakula", soch. 14. Perelozhenie dlia peniia s fortepiano. Tom podgot. V. D. Vasil´evym. Moskva: Gos. muz. izdat., 1956. xviii, 423 p, illus.

Tom 36: Opernoe tvorchestvo: "Evgenii Onegin", soch. 24. Perelozhenie dlia peniia s fortepiano, Red. Ivana Shishova. Moskva: Gos. muz. izdat., 1946. xiv, 298 p, illus.

Tom 37: Opernoe tvorchestvo: "Orleanskaia deva". Perelozhenie dlia peniia s fortepiano. Tom podgot. V. D. Vasil´evym. Moskva: Gos. muz. izdat., 1963. xviii, 512 p, illus.

Tom 38: Opernoe tvorchestvo: "Mazepa". Perelozhenie dlia peniia s fortepiano. Tom podgot. V. D. Vasil´evym. Moskva: Muzyka, 1968. xx, 397 p, illus.

Tom 39: Opernoe tvorchestvo: "Cherevichki". Perelozhenie dlia peniia s fortepiano. Tom podgot. V. D. Vasil´evym. Moskva: Gos. muz. izdat., 1951. xiv, 383 p, illus.

Tom 40A: Opernoe tvorchestvo: "Charodeika". Perelozhenie dlia peniia s fortepiano (deistviia pervoe i vtoroe). Red. Ivana Shishova. Moskva: Gos. muz. izdat., 1949. xii, 264 p, illus.

Tom 40B: Opernoe tvorchestvo: "Charodeika". Perelozhenie dlia peniia s fortepiano (deistviia tret´e i chetvertoe). Red. Ivana Shishova. Moskva: Gos. muz. izdat., 1949. xii, 219 p, illus.

Tom 41: Opernoe tvorchestvo: "Pikovaia dama", soch. 68. Perelozhenie dlia peniia s fortepiano. Red. Anatoliia Dmitrieva. Moskva: Gos. muz. izdat., 1950. xiii, 423 p, illus.

Tom 42: Opernoe tvorchestvo: "Iolanta", soch. 69. Perelozhenie dlia peniia s fortepiano S. I. Taneeva. Tom podgot. V. D. Vasil´evym. Moskva: Gos. muz. izdat., 1953. x, 232 p.

Tom 43: Khory i ansambli. Red. Ivana Shishova i N. Shemanina. Moskva; Leningrad: Gos. muz. izdat., 1941. 155 p.

Contents: "Na son griadushchii": 5–8 — "Vecher": 9–11 — "Nochevala tuchka zolotaia": 12–13 — "Blazhen, kto ulybaetsia": 14–17 — "Privet Antonu Grigor´evichu Rubinshteinu": 18–22 — "Solovushko": 23–25 — "Ne kukushechka vo syrom boru": 26–29 — "Chto smolknul veseliia glas": 30–33 — "Bez pory da bez vremeni": 34–42 — "Noch´": 43–55 — "Priroda i liubov´": 59–82 — 'Shest´ duetov, soch. 46': 85–150.

Tom 44: Romansy i pesni. Red. Ivana Shishova i N Shemanina. Moskva: Gos. muz. izdat., 1940. xvi, 300 p, illus.

Contents: "Moi genii, moi angel, moi drug": 3–4 — "Pesn´ Zemfiry": 5–7 — "Mezza notte": 8–11 — 'Shest´ romansov, soch. 6': 15–42 — "Zabyt´ tak skoro": 45–49 — 'Shest´ romansov, soch. 16': 53–86 — "Unosi moe serdtse": 89–94 — "Glazki vesny golubye": 95–99 — 'Shest´ romansov, soch. 25': 103–132 — "Khotel by v edinoe slovo": 135–138 — "Ne dolgo nam guliat´": 139–142 — 'Shest´ romansov, soch. 27': 145–177 — 'Shest´ romansov, soch. 28': 181–209 — 'Shest´ romansov, soch. 38': 213–245 — 'Sem´ romansov, soch. 47': 249–295.

Tom 45: Romansy i pesni. Red. I. Shishova i N Shemanina. Moskva: Gos. muz. izdat., 1940. 239 p, illus.

Contents: 'Shestnadtsat´ pesen dlia detei, soch. 54': 3–68 — 'Shest´ romansov, soch. 57': 71–97 — 'Dvenadtsat´ romansov, soch. 60': 101–158 — 'Shest´ romansov, soch. 63': 161–186 — 'Shest´ romansov, soch. 65': 189–211 — 'Shest´ romansov, soch. 73': 215–236.

Tom 46A: *Sochineniia dlia fortepiano s orkestrom: Perelozhenie dlia dvukh fortepiano.* Tom podgot. A. Gol′denveizerom. Moskva: Gos. muz. izdat., 1954. xvi, 244 p, illus.

Contents: 'Pervyi kontsert, soch. 23': 5–127 — 'Vtoroi kontsert, soch. 44': 131–244.

Tom 46B: *Sochineniia dlia fortepiano s orkestrom: Perelozhenie dlia dvukh fortepiano.* Tom podgot. A. Gol′denveizerom. Moskva: Gos. muz. izdat., 1954. x, 122 p, illus.

Contents: 'Kontsertnaia fantaziia, soch. 56': 5–70 — 'Tretii kontsert, soch. 75': 73–122.

Tom 47: *Sochineniia dlia orkestra: Perelozhenie dlia fortepiano v chetyre ruki avtora.* Tom podgot. S. Bogatyrevym. Moskva: Gos. muz. izdat., 1961. ix, 162 p, illus.

Contents: 'Vtoraia simfornia, soch. 17: Vtoraia redaktsiia (1879)': 5–89 – 'Pervaia redaktsiia (1872)': 93–162.

Tom 48: *Sochineniia dlia orkestra: Perelozhenie dlia fortepiano v chetyre ruki avtora.* Tom podgot. I. N. Iordan. Moskva: Muzyka, 1964. xv, 214 p, illus.

Contents: '"Manfred", soch. 58': 5–126 — 'Shestaia simfoniia ("Pateticheskaia"), soch. 74': 131–214.

Tom 49: *Sochineniia dlia orkestra: Perelozhenie dlia fortepiano v chetyre ruki avtora.* Tom podgot. B. Karpovym. Moskva: Gos. muz. izdat., 1952. xix, 295 p, illus.

Contents: 'Pervaia siuita, soch. 43': 5–79 — 'Vtoraia siuita, soch. 53': 85–169 — 'Tret′ia siuita, soch. 55': 175–265 — 'Prilozheniia' [op. 53, op. 55]: 269– 295.

Tom 50A: *Sochineniia dlia orkestra: Perelozhenie avtora dlia fortepiano v chetyre ruki.* Tom podgot. I. N. Iordan. Moskva: Muzyka, 1965. ix, 97 p, illus.

Contents: 'Torzhestvennaia uvertiura na datskii gimn, soch. 15': 1–40 — "Ital′ianskoe kaprichchio, soch. 45": 45–90 — 'Prilozhenie' [op. 15]: 93–97.

Tom 50B: *Sochineniia dlia orkestra: Perelozhenie avtora dlia fortepiano v chetyre ruki i dve ruki.* Tom podgot. I. N. Iordan. Moskva: Muzyka, 1965. ix, 101 p, illus.

Contents: 'Perelozhenie dlia chetyrekh ruk: "Serenada dlia strunnogo orkestra", soch. 48': 3–68 — 'Perelozhenie dlia dvukh ruk: "Slavianskii marsh", soch. 31': 71–86 — "Torzhestvennyi marsh": 81–96 — 'Prilozheniia': 99–101.

Tom 51A: *Sochineniia dlia fortepiano.* Red. Ivana Shishova. Moskva: Gos. muz. izdat., 1945. 120 p, illus.

Contents: "Tema s variatsiiami": 3–24 — 'Sonata': 27–77 — 'Dve p′esy, soch. 1': 81–102 — '"Vospominaniia o Gapsale", soch. 2': 105–120.

Tom 51B: *Sochineniia dlia fortepiano.* Red. Ivana Shishova. Moskva: Gos. muz. izdat., 1946. 215 p, illus.

Contents: '"Valse-Caprice", soch. 4': 3–20 — '"Romance", soch. 5': 23–28 — '"Valse-scherzo", soch. 7': 31–40 — '"Capriccio", soch. 8': 43–53 — 'Trois morceaux, soch. 9': 57–77 — 'Deux morceaux, soch. 10': 81–88 — 'Shest′ p′es, soch. 19': 91–135 — 'Shest′ p′es na odnu temu, soch. 21': 139–177 — 'Tri transkriptsii romansov dlia fortepiano (soch. 16)': 181–193 — 'Popurri iz opery "Voevoda"': 197–214.

Tom 52: *Sochineniia dlia fortepiano.* Red. Anatoliia Drozdova. Moskva: Gos. muz. izdat., 1948. 241 p.

Contents: '"Vremena goda", soch. 37-bis': 3–62 — "Marsh Dobrovol′nogo flota": 65–70 — 'Dvenadtsat′ p′es srednei trudnosti, soch. 40': 73–136 — '"Detskii al′bom", soch. 39': 139–170 — '"Grande sonate", soch. 37': 173–241.

Tom 53: *Sochineniia dlia fortepiano.* Red. Anatoliia Drozdova. Moskva: Gos. muz. izdat., 1949. 235 p, illus.

Contents: 'Shest′ p′es, soch. 51': 3–53 — "Ekspromt-kapris": 57–60 — '"Dumka", soch. 59': 63–74 — "Val′s-skertso": 77–82 — "Ekspromt": 85–88 — "Voennyi marsh": 91–94 — 'Vosemnadtsat p′es, soch. 72': 97–225 — "Strastnoe priznanie": 229–231 — 'Prilozhenie' [op. 40, no. 9]: 235.

Tom 54: *Baletnoe tvorchestvo: "Shchelkunchik", soch. 54: Oblegchennoe perelozhenie dlia fortepiano v dve ruki avtora.* Tom podgot. V. Vasil′evym. Moskva: Gos. muz. izdat., 1956. 166 p.

Tom 55A: *Sochineniia dlia skripki s fortepiano.* Red. Ivana Shishova i N. Shemanina. Moskva: Gos. muz. izdat., 1946. 153 p (+ 1 part, 61 p), illus.

Contents: '"Sérénade mélancolique", soch. 26': 3–14 — '"Valse-scherzo", soch. 34': 15–39 — 'Kontsert (dlia skripki s orkestrom), soch. 35': 39–104 — '"Vospominanie o dorogom meste", soch. 42': 105–134 — '"Iumoreska", soch. 10, no. 2': 137–142 — 'Andante iz tret′ego kvarteta': 143–153.

Tom 55B: *Sochineniia dlia violoncheli s orkestrom: Perelozhenie dlia violoncheli s fortepiano.* Tom podgot. V. Kubatskim. Moskva: Gos. muz. izdat., 1956. xiii, 63 p (+ 1 part).

Contents: '"Variatsii na temu rokoko", soch. 33': 5–42 — '"Pezzo capriccioso", soch. 62': 43–53 — 'Prilozhenie (Pervonachal′nyu variant 4-i variatsii)': 57–63.

Tom 56: Baletnoe tvorchestvo: "Lebedinoe ozero", soch. 20. Perelozhenie dlia fortepiano v dve ruki N. D. Kashkina. Tom podgot. I. Iordan i G. Kirkorom. Moskva: Gos. muz. izdat., 1958. xvi, 275 p, illus.

Tom 57: Baletnoe tvorchestvo: "Spiashchaia krasavitsa", soch. 66. Perelozhenie dlia fortepiano v dve ruki A. I. Ziloti. Tom podgot. A. Dmitrievym. Moskva: Gos. muz. izdat., 1954. x, 269 p, illus.

Tom 58: Ucheincheskie raboty. Tom podgot. I. N. Iordan. Moskva: Muzyka, 1967. xi, 210 p., illus.

Contents: 'Raboty po kompozitsii: Allegretto moderato D-dur': 3 — 'Allegretto E-dur': 4–5 — 'Allegro vivace B-dur': 6–8 — 'Andante molto G-dur': 9 — 'Adagio C-dur': 10 — 'Andante ma non troppo e-moll': 11–13 — 'Adagio molto Es-dur': 14–16 — 'Allegro c-moll': 17–25 — 'Adagio F-dur': 26–28 — 'Allegro ma non tanto G-dur': 29–32 — 'Largo i Allegro D-dur': 33–39 — 'Agitato e-moll': 40–59 — 'Andante ma non troppo i Allegro moderato A-dur': 60–89 — 'Allegro vivo c-moll': 90–118 — 'Instrumentovki raboty drugikh avtora: K. M. Veber, "Menuetto capriccioso"': 121–135 — 'R. Shuman, "Simfonicheskie etiudy"': 136–176 — 'L. Betkhoven, Ekspozitsiia 1-i chasti sonaty': 177–201 — 'Prilozhenie (Allegro f-moll dlia fortepiano)': 205–210.

Tom 59: Obrabotki proizvedenii drugikh avtorov: Partitura. Tom podgot. I. N. Iordan. Moskva: Muzyka, 1970. 327 p, illus.

Contents: 'I. Gungl´, "Vozvrashchenie val´sa"': 17–23 — 'A. Diubiuk, "Mariia-Dagmara"': 24–34 — '"Gott Erhalte" (Avstriiskii gymn)': 35–42 — 'R. Shuman, "Veshchii son"': 43–59 — 'G. Larosh, "Uvertiura-fantaziia"': 60–178 — 'S. Menter, "Vengerskaia rapsodiia"': 179–266 — 'A. Stradella, "O del mio dolce ardor"': 269–275 — 'D. Chimarosa, Trio iz opery "Tainyi brak"': 276–304 — 'F. List, "Ful´skii korol´"': 305–318 — 'A. Dargomyzhskii, "Nochevala tuchka zolotaia"': 319–327.

Tom 60: Obrabotki proizvedenii drugikh avtorov: Perelozheniia dlia fortepiano v dve i chetyre ruki, i dlia peniia a cappella i v soprovozhdenii fortepiano. Tom podgot. G. V. Kirkorom. Moskva: Muzyka, 1971. xv, 272 p, illus.

Contents: 'A. Dargomyzhskii, "Malorossiiskii kazachok"': 3–13 — 'K. Veber, "Perpetuum mobile"': 14–28 — 'E. Tarnovskaia, "Ia pomniu vse"': 31–38 — 'A. Rubinshtein, "Ivan Groznyi"': 39–92 — 'A. Rubinshtein, "Don-Kikhot"': 93–148 — 'D. Ober, "Chernoe domino" (khor i rechitativy k opere)': 151–187 — '"Gaudeamus igitur"': 188–190 — 'V. Motsart, "Svad´ba Figaro" (rechitativy k opere)': 191–272.

Tom 61: Obrabotki i redaktirovanie narodnykh pesen. Red. Sof´i Ziv. Moskva: Gos. muz. izdat., 1949. 232 p, illus.

Contents: '"50 russkikh narodnykh pesen" (dlia fortepiano v 4 ruki)': 3–58 — '"Russkie narodnye pesni dlia odnogo golosa s soprovozhdeniem fortepiano" (sobrannye V. Prokuninym, pod red. P. Chaikovskogo)': 61–220 — '"Detskie pesni na russkie i malorossiiskie napevy s akompanementom fortepiano" (sost. M. Mamontovoi, pod red. P. Chaikovskogo)': 223–232.

Tom 62: Sochineniia zakonchennye S. I. Taneevym. Red. Ivana Shishova. Moskva: Gos. muz. izdat., 1948. xiii, 298 p, illus.

Contents: 'Andante i final dlia fortepiano s orkestrom, soch. 79: Partitura': 3–133 — 'Perelozhenie dlia dvukh fortepiano': 135–208 — '"Romeo i Dzhul´etta" (duet dlia soprano i tenora s orkestrom): Partitura': 211–263 — 'Perelozhenie dlia peniia s fortepiano': 267–292 — '"Momento lirico"': 295–298.

Tom 63: Sochineniia dlia khora bez soprovozhdeniia. Tom podgot. L. Z. Korabel´nikovoi i M. P. Rakhmanovoi. Moskva: Muzyka, 1990. 279 p, illus.

Contents: '"Liturgiia sviatogo Ioanna Zlatousta", soch. 41': 19–66 — '"Vsenoshchnoe bdenie", soch. 52': 69–202 — 'Deviat´ dukhovno-muzykal´nykh sochinenii': 205–249 — '"Angel vopiiashe": 257–262 — '"Gimn v chest´ sviatykh Kirilla i Mefodiia": 263–264 — '"Pravovedcheskaia pesn´"': 265–266 — '"Legenda", soch. 54, no. 5': 267–269 — 'Prilozheniia': 270–272.

Reviews: 'Akademicheskoe izdanie proizvedenii P. I. Chaikovskogo', *Sovetskaia muzyka* (1936), 6: 93 [preview] — 'K stoletiiu so dnia rozhdeniia P. I. Chaikovskogo', *Sovetskoe iskusstvo* (19 May 1938): 1 [preview] — V. August, 'Pochemu ne izdaiut proizvedenii Chaikovskogo?', *Leningradskaia pravda* (18 Mar 1940): 3 — 'Sobranie sochinenii Chaikovskogo', *Izvestiia* (20 May 1940): 4 — 'Akademicheskoe izdanie sochinenii P. I. Chaikovskogo', *Leningradskaia pravda* (19 Apr 1941): 1 [vols. 43–45] — 'Akademicheskoe izdanie sochinenii P. I. Chaikovskogo', *Izvestiia* (16 May 1941): 4 [preparation of vol. 62] — '137 tomov: Novye izdaniia muzykal´noi klassiki', *Sovetskoe iskusstvo* (19 Apr 1945): 1 — R. M. 'Notografiia i bibliografiia', *Sovetskaia muzyka* (1949), 2: 111–112 [vol. 4] — A. Nikolaev, 'Znachitel´noe sobytie v muzykal´noi zhizni', *Sovetskaia muzyka* (1950), 3: 105–107 [vols. 51A, 51B, 52, 53] — 'Die werkgeschichtlichen Einführungen der alten Čajkovskij-Gesamtausgabe', *Tschaikowsky-Gesellschaft Mitteilungen* (2000) [see *3782*].

— [repr. (in 143 vols.)] Belwin Mills, N. Y.: E. Kalmus [1974].

The vols. from the original series were divided or combined for this reprint, and the Russian editorial prefaces were omitted.

[*119*]   **P. Tschaikowsky: Sinfonie Nr. 6 h-Moll, Op. 74, 'Pathétique'.** Einführung und Analyse von Thomas Kohlhase. München: Wilhelm Goldmann; Mainz: B. Schott, 1983. [388] p, illus. ISBN: 3–4423–3054–8.

Miniature score with analysis in German text.

[120]   **P. I. Čajkovskij: New edition of the complete works.** Published in association with the Čajkovskij Society, Klin-Tubingen; The Čajkovskij Museum, Klin; The Institute of the Russian Federation for the Study of the Arts. Editorial Board: Ljudmila Z. Korabel´nikova, Valentina V. Rubcova, Polina E. Vajdman and Thomas Kohlhase. Moskva: Muzyka; Mainz: Schott, 1993+. [76 vols. planned].

          Vol. 39b: *Symphony No. 6 in B minor, 'Pathétique', op. 74: Full score.* Ed. by Thomas Kohlhase, with the assistance of Polina Vajdman. Moskva: Muzyka; Mainz: Schott, 1993. xiii, 228 p.

          Text in English and Russian. No further vols. published to date. See also *12, 94, 95, 96, 1043, 4749, 5363.*

[121]   **P. Tchaikovsky: The complete sacred choral works.** Ed. Vladimir Morosan. Madison, Conn.: Musica Russia, 1996. cxix, 477 p, music, illus. (*Monuments of Russian sacred music*; 2 (1–3)). ISBN 0-9629460–4-4.

          Text in Russian and English.

          Contents: P. Meyendorff, 'Russian liturgical worship': xvii-xl — V. Morosan, 'The sacred choral works of Peter Tchaikowsky': xli-cxix [see *5160*] — '"Liturgy of St. John Chrysostom", op. 41': 3–98 — '"All-Night Vigil", op. 52': 99–314 — 'Nine Sacred Choruses': 315–390 — "The Angel Cried Out": 393–398. 'Appendices: "Hymn in Honor of Saints Cyril and Methodius" (1885) — "A Legend" (1889) — '"Our Father" (a variant)': 403–428.

2.2.2. Facsimile Editions

[122]   'Podlinnaia partitura P. I. Chaikovskogo "Stseny Domovogo" (melodrama) iz p´esy A. N. Ostrovskogo 'Voevoda' (1886 g.)'. In: *Chaikovskii na Moskovskoi stsene* (1940): 489–500 [see *2538*].

          Facs. of Chaikovskii's autograph score.

[123]   **CHAIKOVSKII, P. I.** *Shestaia simfoniia, "Pateticheskaia": Chernovaia rukopis´, 1893.* Predislovie Iu. Shaporina. [Moskva: Giprotis, 1962]. 36 p.

          Facs. of Chaikovskii's sketches for the *Symphony No. 6.*

[124]   **P. Tchaikovsky: Sixth Symphony, "Pathétique".** Preface, research and commentary by Galina Pribegina; tr. from the Russian by Xenia Danko. Moscow: State Music Publishers, 1970. xvii, 139 p, illus.

          Facs. of the autograph score. English and Russian text. See also *4658.*

          Review: M. Serebrovskii, 'Shestaia Chaikovskogo, god izdaniia 1971', *Sovetskaia kul´tura* (5 Aug 1971): 3.

[125]   **CHAIKOVSKII, P. I.** *"Vremena goda", dlia fortepiano: Faksimile.* Moskva: Muzyka, 1978. 44 p.

          Facs. of the autograph score of *The Seasons.* Notes in Russian by Elena Orlova, with English tr. by Kseniia Danko, and German tr. by Valerij Jerochin.

[126]   **CHAIKOVSKII, P. I.** *Detskii al´bom / Album pour enfants / Kinderalbum / Children's album.* Moskva: Muzyka [1992]. 39 p, music.

          Facsimile of the original edition (P. Iurgenson, Moscow, 1878).

          — [repr.] Mainz; New York: Schott [1994]. 39 p, music.

[127]   **CHAIKOVSKII, P. I.** *"Children's Album", for piano: Facsimile / "Kinderalbum", für Klavier: Faksimile / "Detskii al´bom", dlia fortepiano: Faksimile.* Commentary by Ol´ga Zakharova. Moscow; Vienna: Minex 1993. [22] p, music, illus.

          Facsimile of the autograph score. Includes commentary in Russian, English and German.

          — [repr.] Mainz; Moskva: Schott, 1997. [22] p, music, illus.

[*128*] **P. Tschaikowsky: Zwölf Stücke für Klavier, Opus 40**. Nach dem Autograph und den Ausgaben des Originalverlegers hrsg. von Ludmila Korabel′nikova und Polina Vajdman; Fingersatz von Klaus Schilde. München: Henle [1995]. xiii, 64 p. of music.

Facs. edition of the autograph score, with editorial and historical notes in German, English and French.

2.3. LITERARY WORKS

2.3.1. Books

GUIDE TO THE PRACTICAL STUDY OF HARMONY (1872)

[*129*] **CHAIKOVSKII, P. I. Rukovodstvo k prakticheskomu izucheniiu garmonii**. Uchebnik sost. professorom Moskovskoi konservatorii P. Chaikovskim. Moskva [printed Leipzig]: P. Iurgenson, 1871. vi, 155 p, music.

Review: P. A. Shchurovskii, 'Uchebnik garmonii P. I. Chaikovskogo', *Moskovskie vedomosti* (21 Aug 1872).

— 2-e izd. Moskva: P. Iurgenson, 1876. vi, 155 p.

Review: K. Galler, 'Muzykal′naia bibliografiia', *Muzykal′nyi svet* (6 Mar 1877): 117.

— [repr.] Moskva: P. Iurgenson, 1881, 1885, 1891, 1902, 1905, 1914.

— [repr.] In: P. I. Chaikovskii, *Polnoe sobranie sochinenii: Literaturnye proizvedeniia i perepiska*, tom III-a (1957): 1–162 [see *156*].

— [English tr.] *Guide to the practical study of harmony*. By P. Tschaikowsky. Tr. from the German version of P. Juon by Emil Krall and James Liebling. Leipzig [pr. Moscow]: P. Jurgenson, 1900. 137 p, music.

— [English tr. (repr.)] Canoga Park, Calif.: Summit Pub. Co. [1970]. 137 p, music. ISBN: 0–8778–6001–7.

Review: W. Piston, *Notes*, 27 (Jun 1971), 4: 707–708.

— [English tr. (repr.)] Bonn-Bad Godesberg: Forberg-Jurgenson, 1976. 137 p, music.

Review: *Musical Times*, 118 (Nov 1977): 9, 17.

— [English tr. (repr.)] Pro-Am Music Resources, 1983. ISBN 0–9124–8358–X.

Review: P. Standford, *Musical Times*, 125 (Sep 1984): 503.

— [German tr.] *Leitfaden zum praktischen Erlernen der Harmonie*. Verfasst von P. Tschaikowsky. Aus dem Russischen übersezt von Paul Juon. Leipzig, Moskau: P. Jurgenson [1899]. vi, 137 p, music, illus.

See also *5439–5444*.

A SHORT MANUAL OF HARMONY
Textbook (1875)

[*130*] **CHAIKOVSKII, P. I. Kratkii uchebnik garmonii: Prisposoblennyi k chteniiu dukhovno-muzykal′nykh sochinenii v Rossii**. Moskva [pr. Leipzig]: P. Iurgenson, 1875. 79 p, music.

Review: 'P. I. Chaikovskii o ego "Kratkom uchebnike garmonii"', *Tserkhovnyi vestnik* (1881), No. 32.

— [repr.] Moskva: P. Iurgenson, 1895. 79 p, music.

— [repr.] In: P. I. Chaikovskii, *Polnoe sobranie sochinenii: Literaturnye proizvedeniia i perepiska*, tom III-a (1957): 164–216 [see *156*].

2.3.2. Articles and Interviews

[*131*] *Muzykal′nye fel′etony i zametki Petra Il′icha Chaikovskogo (1868–1876)*. S prilozheniem portreta, avtobiograficheskogo opisaniia puteshestvia zagranitsu v 1888 godu i predisloviia G. A. Larosha. Moskva: S. P. Iakovlev, 1898. xxxii, 397 p, illus.

Contents: G. A. Larosh, 'Predislovie': i–xxxii [see *5425*] — 'I. Muzykal′nye fel′etony i zametki (1868–1876)': 1–353 — 'II. Avtobiograficheskoe opisanie puteshestviia zagranitsu v 1888 godu': 355–391 [see *13*]. See also *2047, 5426*.

Reviews: Eusebias, 'P. I. Chaikovskii, kak muzykal´nyi kritik', *Sankt Peterburgskie vedomosti* (1898), No. 332 — Debbl´iu, *Volzhskii vestnik* (6 Jan 1898) — I. Vasil´ev, 'P. I. Chaikovskii v svoikh kriticheskikh stat´iakh', *Moskovskie vedomosti* (24 Feb 1898) — V. Chechott, *Kievlianin* (28 Feb 1898) — M, *Russkaia muzykal´naia gazeta* (Apr 1898), 4: 428 — E. N. Borman, 'P. I. Chaikovskii: Retsenzent i muzykal´nyi fel´etonist', *Severnyi kur´er* (12 Nov 1899) — B. D. K. 'Chaikovskii: Retsenzent', *Kavkaz* (19 Jan 1900).

[132]   *Musikalische Einnerungen und Feuilletons von Peter Tschaikowsky*. In deutscher übesetzung, hrsg. von Heinrich Stümcke. Berlin: Harmonie [1899]. v, 127 p.

Contents: 'Einleitung': 1–16 — 'Erinnerungen an Leipzig, Berlin und Hamburg. I-XII': 17–72 — 'Kritiken und Feuilletons: Mozart, "Don Juan"': 75–76 — 'Beethovens "Eroica"': 77–78 — 'Beethovens "Fidelio"': 79 — 'Schumann als Symphoniker': 80–85 — 'Mendelssohn, Schumann und Brahms': 86-88 — 'Auber': 89–90 — 'Verdi': 91–93 — '"Afrikanerin" und "Troubadour"': 94–97 — 'Christine Nillsson und Adelina Patti': 98–102 — 'Rimski-Korssakow': 103–106 — 'Hans von Bülow': 107–110 — 'Bayreuth 1876, I–III': 111–125 — 'Personen-und Sach-Register': 126-127.

— 2. aufl. *Erinnerungen eines Musikers*. Von P. I. Tschaikowsky. In deutscher Übertragung und in auswahl mit einer Einleitung, hrsg. von Heinrich Stümcke. Neue durchges. und vermehren Auflage. Leipzig: P. Reclam jun. [1922]. 147 p. (*Reclams Universal-Bibliothek*; nr. 6285–6286).

[133]   **CHAIKOVSKII, P. I.** *Muzykal´no-kriticheskie stat´i*. Vstup. stat´ia i poiasneniia V. V. Iakovleva. Moskva: Gos. muz. izdat., 1953. iv, 436 p, illus.

Rev. repr. of P. I. Chaikovskii, *Polnoe sobranie sochinenii: Literaturnye proizvedeniia i perepiska*, tom II (1953) [see *156*].

Contents: V. V. Iakovlev, 'Chaikovskii—kritik': 1–22 [see *5433*] — 'Muzykal´no-kriticheskie stat´i (1868–1876)': 25–328 — "Vagner i ego muzyka": 329–332 [see *144*] — "Avtobiograficheskoe opisanie puteshestviia za granitsu v 1888 godu": 333–364 [see *138*] — "Beseda s Chaikovskim v noiabre 1892 g. v Peterburge": 367–373 [see *141*] — "Pis´mo v redaktsiiu *Golosa*": 374 — 'Primechaniia i poiasneniia': 375–438.

Review: M. Sokol´skii, 'Perechityvaia stat´i Chaikovskogo', *Sovetskaia muzyka* (1953), 11: 72–75.

— ["4-e izd."] Leningrad: Muzyka, 1986. 368 p, illus.

Contents: M. Ovchinnikov: 'Chaikovskii—kritik': 4–24 [see *5438*] — 'Muzykal´no-kriticheskie stat´i': 25–285 — "Avtobiograficheskoe opisanie puteshestviia za granitsu v 1888 godu": 286–316 [see *138*] — 'Prilozheniia: "Beseda s Chaikovskim v noiabre 1892 g. v Peterburge": 317–323 [see *141*] — 'Pis´mo v redaktsiiu *Golosa*': 323–324 — '"Ivan Susanin" na milanskoi stsene': 324–329 — 'Primechaniia': 330–365.

[134]   *P. I. Tschaikowsky: Erinnerungen und Musikkritiken*. Hrsg. von Richard Petzoldt. Mit einem Aufsatz "Tschaikowski als Kritiker", von Wassili Jakowlew. Leipzig: P. Reclam jun. [1961]. 261 p.

Based on P. I. Chaikovskii, *Muzykal´no-kriticheskie stat´i* (1953) [see *133*].

Review: *Musik in der Schule*, 13 (1962), 10: 478–479.

— [2., veründ. Aufl.] *Erinnerungen und Musikkritiken von Peter I. Tschaikowski*. Mit einem Aufsatz 'Tschaikowski als Kritiker', von Wassili Jakowlew. Hrsg. von Richard Petzoldt und Lothar Fahlbusch. Aus der Russische übersetzung von Lothar Fahlbusch. Hrsg. von Richard Petzoldt und Lothar Fahlbusch. Leipzig: P. Reclam, 1974. 262 p. (*Reclams Universal-Bibliothek*; 554).

— [repr.] Wiesbaden: VMA-Verlag [c.1981]. 262 p.

Reviews: H. Gerlach, *Musik und Gesellschaft*, 25 (1975): 433–434 — *Neue Zeitschrift für Musik*, 1 (1975), 1: 67.

[135]   **KUNIN, I. F.** 'Dva interv´iu u P. I. Chaikovskogo', *Sovetskaia muzyka* (1965), 5: 30–35, illus.

Includes: "U P. I. Chaikovskogo" (1892): 30-34 [see *145*] — "U avtora "Iolanty" (1892): 34–35 [see *147*]. With commentary by I. F. Kunin and V. V. Protopopov.

[136]   *P. I. Chaykovski: Muzikal´no-kritičeski stat´i*. Sastav. Andrej E. Koralov. Prev. ot rus. Sofiia: Muzika, 1977. 416 p.

Based on P. I. Chaikovskii, *Muzykal´no-kriticheskie stat´i* (1953) [see *133*]. Text in Bulgarian.

See also *14, 376, 2047, 2048, 2051, 2055, 2056, 2076, 2079, 5426*.

AUTOBIOGRAPHICAL ACCOUNT OF A TOUR ABROAD IN THE YEAR 1888

Diary-Article (1888)

[*137*]   **CHAIKOVSKII, P. I. 'Iz dnevnika'**, *Russkii vestnik*, 230 (1894), 2: 165–203.

Abridged version of Chaikovskii's account of his conducting tour of Western Europe in 1888. With an introduction by Modest Chaikovskii.

— [repr.] 'Avtobiograficheskoe opisanie puteshestviia zagranitsu v 1888 godu'. In: *Muzykal´nye fel´etony i zametki Petra Il´icha Chaikovskogo* (1898): 355–391 [see *131*].

— [English tr. (abridged)] 'Diary of my tour in 1888'. In: R. H. Newmarch, *Tchaikovsky: His life and works* (1900): 168–225 [see *1455*].

[*138*]   **CHAIKOVSKII. P. I. 'Avtobiograficheskoe opisanie puteshestviia za granitsu v 1888 godu'**. In: P. I. Chaikovskii, *Polnoe sobranie sochinenii: Literaturnye proizvedeniia i perepiska*, tom II (1953): 333–364 [see *156*].

First complete publication. See also *249*.

— [repr.] In: P. I. Chaikovskii, *Muzykal´no-kriticheskie stat´i*. Vstup. stat´ia i poiasneniia V. V. Iakovleva. Moskva: Gos. muz. izdat., 1953: 333–364; 2-e izd. (1986) 286–316 [see *133*].

— [French tr.] *Piotr Illiytch Tchaikovski: Voyage à l'étranger*. Tr. et présentation D. Sanadze et S. Hailliot. Paris: Le Castor astral, 1993 (*Les Inattendux*).

AUTOBIOGRAPHY
Article (1889)

[*139*]   **NEITZEL, O. 'Die Russische Musik und ihr berufenster Vertreter'**, *Nord und Süd*, 54 (Jul 1890), 160: 56–71.

Includes Chaikovskii's untitled autobiography: 66–71.

— [rev. repr.] 'P. I. Čajkovskijs Autobiographie aus dem Jahre 1889' (vorgestellt von Alexander Poznansky), *Tschaikowsky-Gesellschaft Mitteilungen*, 7 (2000): 3–11.

— [English tr. (abridged)] 'Recollections of the famous composer Tschaikowsky', *New York Times* (12 Nov 1893).

Reproduced 'as heard from the composer', without reference to its previous publicaton.

— [English tr. (repr.)] 'Tschaikowsky's early life', *Musical Standard* [illus. series], 1 (46) (6 Jan 1894): 10.

— [English tr. (abridged repr.)] In: A. Poznansky, *Tchaikovsky through others' eyes* (1999): 2, 3, 4, 5, 290 [see *380*].

CHAIKOVSKII ON ODESSA
Interview (1893)

[*140*]   **[KUPERNIK, L.] 'Chaikovskii ob Odesse'**, *Odesskii listok* (28 Oct 1893).

A conversation from Jan 1893 with Lev Kupernik, lawyer and member of the Odessa branch of the RMS. First published posthumously

A CONVERSATION WITH P. I. CHAIKOVSKII
Interview (1892)

[*141*]   **B[LOKH], G. 'Beseda s P. I. Chaikovskim'**, *Peterburgskaia zhizn´* (12 Nov 1892).

— [rev. repr.] 'Teatr i muzyka', *Novoe vremia* (13 Nov 1892): 4.

— [repr. (abridged)] 'P. I. Chaikovskii i ego vzgliady', *Nuvellist* (Jan 1893): 4–5.

— [repr. (abridged)] 'Zabytoe interv´iu s P. I. Chaikovskim', *Sovetskaia muzyka* (1949), 7: 59–61.

— [repr.] 'Beseda s Chaikovskim v noiabre 1892 g. v Peterburge'. In: P. I. Chaikovskii, *Polnoe sobranie sochinenii: Literaturnye proizvedeniia i perepiska*, tom II (1953): 367–373 [see *156*].

— [repr.] 'Beseda s Chaikovskim v noiabre 1892 g. v Peterburge'. In: P. I. Chaikovskii, *Muzykal´no-kriticheskie stat´i* (1953): 367–373; 2-e izd. (1986): 317–322 [see *133*].

— [English tr.] In: A. Poznansky, *Tchaikovsky through others' eyes* (1999): 202–208 [see *380*].

— [French tr.] 'Un entretien avec Tchaïkovski en novembre 1892, à Saint-Pétersbourg'. In: *Piotr Tchaïkovski: Écrits critiques, lettres, souvenirs de contemporains* (1985): 107–116 [see *376*].

— [German tr.] In: *Tschaikowsky aus der Nähe* (1994): 220–228 [see *379*].

IN MEMORY OF P. I. CHAIKOVSKII
Interview (1893)

[*142*]   'Pamiati P. I. Chaikovskogo', *Odesskie novosti* (27 Oct 1893).

An interview from Jan 1893 with a reporter from the Odessa newspaper *Odesskie novosti*. First published posthumously.

TSCHAIKOWSKY ON MUSIC IN AMERICA
Interview (1891)

[*143*]   'Tschaikowsky on music in America', *New York Herald* (17 May 1891).

— [repr.] In: E. Yoffe, *Tchaikovsky in America* (1986): 139–142 [see *1864*].

— [repr.] In: A. Poznansky, *Tchaikovsky through others' eyes* (1999): 197–199 [see *380*].

WAGNER AND HIS MUSIC
Article (1891)

[*144*]   CHAIKOVSKII, P. I. 'Wagner and his music', *Morning Journal* (3 May 1891).

— [repr.] In: E. Yoffe, *Tchaikovsky in America* (1986): 71–72 [see *1864*].

— [Russian tr.] '"Vagner i ego muzyka": Neizvestnaia zametka P. I. Chaikovskogo' (perevod G. Baistok), *Sovetskaia muzyka* (1949), 7: 62–63.

— [Russian tr.] In: P. I. Chaikovskii, *Polnoe sobranie sochinenii: Literaturnye proizvedeniia i perepiska.* Tom II (1953): 329–332 [see *156*].

— [Russian tr.] In: P. I. Chaikovskii, *Muzykal´no-kriticheskie stat´i.* Vstup. stat´ia i poiasneniia V. V. Iakovleva (1953): 329–332; 2-e izd. (1986): 284–285 [see *133*].

See also *2106, 2110, 2112*.

WITH P. I. CHAIKOVSKII
Interview (1892)

[*145*]   K[UGULSKII], S. 'U P. I. Chaikovskogo', *Novosti dnia* (13 Apr 1892): 2–3.

— [repr.] In: I. F. Kunin, 'Dva interv´iu' (1965): 30–34 [see *135*].

— [English tr.] In: A. Poznansky, *Tchaikovsky through others' eyes* (1999): 199–202 [see *380*].

— [German tr.] In: *Tschaikowsky aus der Nähe* (1994): 216–220 [see *379*].

WITH P. I. CHAIKOVSKII
Interview (1893)

[*146*]   IAR[ON], M. 'U P .I. Chaikovskogo', *Odesskii listok* (19 Jan 1893).

An interview from Jan 1893 with a reporter from the Odessa newspaper *Odesskii listok*.

WITH THE AUTHOR OF "IOLANTA"
Interview (1892)

[*147*]   'U avtora "Iolanty"', *Peterburgskaia gazeta* (6 Dec 1892): 3.

— [repr.] In: I. F. Kunin, 'Dva interv´iu' (1965): 34–35 [see *135*].

— [English tr.] In: A. Poznansky, *Tchaikovsky through others' eyes* (1999): 208–210 [see *380*].

— [German tr.] In: *Tschaikowsky aus der Nähe* (1994): 229–231 [see *379*].

2.3.3. Translations

HANDBOOK FOR INSTRUMENTATION
Book by F. A. Gevaert, tr. from French to Russian by Chaikovskii (1865)

[*148*]   **GEVAERT, F.-A.** *Rukovodstvo k instrumentovke*. Sochinenie prof. Gevarta. Perevod s frantsuzskogo prof. teorii muzyki pri Moskovskoi konservatorii P. I. Chaikovskogo. Moskva: P. Iurgenson, 1866. 163 p, music.

Review: A. N. Serov, 'O rukovodstve k instrumentovke' (1867) [see *5445*].

— 2-e izd. Perevod P. I. Chaikovskogo. Pod red. Iu. Engelia. Moskva: P. Iurgenson, 1902 [2 vols.].

Review: Iu. K. 'Bibliografiia', *Russkaia muzykal´naia gazeta* (Feb 1902), 7: 223–224 [response by Iu. Engel´, *Russkaia muzykal´naia gazeta* (Mar 1902), 10: 301].

— [repr.] In: P. I. Chaikovskii, *Polnoe sobranie sochinenii: Literaturnye proizvedeniia i perepiska*, tom III-b (1961): 11–359 [see *156*].

MUSICAL CATECHISM
Book by J. C. Lobe, tr. from German to Russian by Chaikovskii (1869)

[*149*]   **LOBE, J. C.** *Muzykal´nyi katekhizis*. Soch. I. Lobe. Perevod s 8-go nemetskogo izdanie P. Chaikovskogo. Moskva: P. Iurgenson, 1870. 132 p.

— 2-e izd. Moskva: P. Iurgenson, 1905. 150 p.

— [repr.] In: P. I. Chaikovskii, *Polnoe sobranie sochinenii: Literaturnye proizvedeniia i perepiska*, tom III-b (1961): 377–482 [see *156*].

NOTES TO THE "STUDIES", Op. 3
Preface by Robert Schumann, tr. from German to Russian by Chaikovskii (1869)

[*150*]   **SCHUMANN, R.** 'Primechaniia k etiudam, op. 3'. In: *Oeuvres complettes pour le piano par R. Schumann*. Edition nouvelle, redigée par N. Rubinstein en six volumes. Tom 1. Moscou: P. I. Jourgenson, 1868.

Chaikovskii's tr. from German to Russian of Schumann's preface to his *Six Studies on Caprices by Paganini*, Op. 3 (1832). Published without the name of the translator.

— [repr.] In: P. I. Chaikovskii, *Polnoe sobranie sochinenii: Literaturnye proizvedeniia i perepiska*, tom III-b (1961): 371–376 [see *156*].

RULEBOOK FOR YOUNG MUSICIANS
Book by Robert Schumann, tr. from German to Russian by Chaikovskii (1868)

[*151*]   **SCHUMANN, R.** *Zhiznennye pravila dlia molodykh muzykantov*. Perevod P. I. Chaikovskogo. Moskva: P. Iurgenson, 1869. 29 p.

Chaikovskii's tr. of Schumann's *Musikalische Haus- und Lebensregeln* (parallel text in Russian and German).

— 7-e izd. *Zhiznennyia pravila i sovety molodym muzykantam*. Moskva: P. Iurgenson, 1914. 29 p.

— [repr.] In: P. I. Chaikovskii, *Polnoe sobranie sochinenii: Literaturnye proizvedeniia i perepiska*, tom III–b (1961): 361–370 [see *156*].

2.4. CORRESPONDENCE

2.4.1. Collections

[152] CHAIKOVSKII, P. I. *Pis´ma k rodnym*. Tom 1: *1850–1879*. Red. i primechaniia V. A. Zhdanova. [Moskva]: Gos. muz. izdat., 1940. 768 p, illus. (*Trudy Doma-muzeia P. I. Chaikovskogo*).

Letters from the composer to Aleksandra Chaikovskaia, Praskov´ia Chaikovskaia, Anatolii Chaikovskii, Il´ia Chaikovskii, Modest Chaikovskii, Lev Davydov and Aleksandra Davydova. See also *451*.

Vol. 2 was not published, but exists in a proof copy at the Klin museum.

[153] OČADLIK, M. *Pražské dopisy P. I. Čajkovského*. Praha: Supraphon, 1949. 25 p. illus.

Facs. of 4 letters from Chaikovskii to Adolf Čech (1888–91), 7 to František Šubert (1887–92) and 2 to Eduard Valečka (1888).

[154] CHAIKOVSKII, P. I. & TANEEV, S. I. *Pis´ma*. Sost. i red. V. A. Zhdanov. Predislovie Iu. Shaporina. [Moskva]: Goskul´turprosvetizdat, 1951. xi, 557 p, illus. (*Gos. literaturnyi muzei*).

Contents: 'Perepiska [P. I. Chaikovskii s S. I. Taneevym] (1874–1893)': 3–202 [see *347*] — 'P. I. Chaikovskii—A. P. Merkling (1871–1893)': 205–256 [see *289*] — 'P. I. Chaikovskii—N. G. Konradi (1876–1893)': 257–287 [see *261*] — 'P. I. Chaikovskii—Iu. P. Shpazhinskoi (1885–1891)': 288–360 [see *329*] — 'P. I. Chaikovskii—N. A. Plesskoi (1879–1893)': 361–370 [see *311*] — 'P. I. Chaikovskii—Dezire Arto (1888–1890)': 371–376 [see *200*].

[155] CHAIKOVSKII, P. I. *Pis´ma k blizkim*. Izbrannoe. Red. i komentarii V. A. Zhdanova. Predislovie Iu. Shaporina. Moskva; Leningrad: Gos. muz. izdat., 1955. xv, 672 p, illus. (*Trudy Gos. Doma-muzeia P. I. Chaikovskogo*).

Selected letters from the composer to Elizaveta Chaikovskaia, Praskov´ia Chaikovskaia, Anatolii Chaikovskii, Il´ia Chaikovskii, Ippolit Chaikovskii, Modest Chaikovskii, Nikolai Chaikovskii, Lev Davydov, Vladimir Davydov and Aleksandra Davydova. Includes: Iu. Shaporin, 'Predislovie': iii–viii [see *908*]. See also *162*.

[156] CHAIKOVSKII, P. I. *Polnoe sobranie sochinenii: Literaturnye proizvedeniia i perepiska*. Moskva, 1953–81 [17 vols.].

Includes almost all Chaikovskii's known letters, and also his books, articles and translations. 248 letters have been censored, in order to remove profanities and abusive vocabulary, references to homosexuality, intimate relationships and illnesses (whether his own or those of his relatives and servants), and passages which were considered ideologically unacceptable [see *192, 195*]. Vols. I and IV not published. See also *182, 259*.

Tom II. [Muzykal´no-kriticheskie stat´i]. Tom podgot. i vstup. stat´ia V. V. Iakovleva. Moskva: Gos. muz. izdat., 1953. xii, 438 p, illus.

Contents: V. V. Iakovlev, 'Chaikovskii—kritik': 1–22 [see *5433*] — 'Muzykal´no-kriticheskie stat´i (1868–1876)': 25–328 — "Vagner i ego muzyka": 329–332 [see *144*] — "Avtobiograficheskoe opisanie puteshestviia za granitsu v 1888 godu": 333–364 [see *138*] — Prilozheniia: "Beseda s Chaikovskim v noiabre 1892 g. v Peterburge": 367–373 [see *141*] — "Pis´mo v redaktsiiu *Golosa*": 374 — 'Primechaniia i poiasneniia': 375–438.

— [rev. repr.] P. I. Chaikovskii, *Muzykal´no-kriticheskie stat´i* (1953) [see *133*].

Tom III–a. [Literaturnye proizvedeniia]. Tom podgot. V. Protopopovym. Moskva: Gos. muz. izdat., 1957. 256 p.

Contents: "Rukovodstvo k prakticheskomu izucheniiu garmonii": 1–162 [see *129*] — "Kratkii uchebnik garmonii": 164–216 [see *130*] — Prilozhenie: 219–253.

Tom III–b. [Perevody]. Tom podgot. V. Protopopovym. Moskva: Gos. muz. izdat., 1961. 524 p.

Contents: 'F. O. Gevart, "Rukovodstvo k instrumentovke"': 11–359 [see *148*] — 'R. Shuman, "Zhiznennye pravila i sovety molodym muzykantam"': 361–370 [see *151*] — 'R. Shuman, "Primechaniia k etiudam op. 3"': 371–376 [see *150*] — 'I. K. Lobe, "Muzykal´nyi katekhizis"': 377–482 [see *149*] — "Betkhoven i ego vremia": 485–520.

Tom V. [Pis´ma (1848–1875)]. Tom podgot. E. D. Gershovskim, K. Iu. Davydovoi i L. Z. Korabel´nikovoi. Moskva: Gos. muz. izdat., 1959. xi, 518 p, illus.

Tom VI. [Pis´ma (1876–1877)]. Tom podgot. N. A. Viktorovoi i B. I. Rabinovichem. Moskva: Gos. muz. izdat., 1961. 396 p, illus.

Tom VII. [Pis´ma (1878)]. Tom podgot. E. D. Gershovskim i I. N. Sokolinskoi. Moskva: Gos. muz. izdat., 1962. 644 p, illus.

Tom VIII. [Pis´ma (1879)]. Tom podgot. K. Iu. Davydovoi, G. I. Labutinoi i N. N. Sin´kovskoi. Moskva: Gos. muz. izdat., 1963. 551 p, illus.

Tom IX. [Pis´ma (1880)]. Tom podgotvlen N. A. Viktorovoi, N. B. Gorlovym i E. A. Pustovit. Moskva: Muzyka, 1965. 407 p, illus.

Tom X. [Pis´ma (1881)]. Tom podgot. N. N. Sin´kovskoi i I. G. Sokolinskoi. Moskva: Muzyka, 1966. 359 p, illus.

Tom XI. [Pis´ma (1882)]. Tom podgot. K. Iu. Davydovoi i G. I. Labutinoi. Moskva: Muzyka, 1966. 359 p, illus.

Tom XII. [Pis´ma (1883–1884)]. Tom podgot. L. V. Muzylevoi i S. S. Muravich. Moskva: Muzyka, 1970. 595 p, illus.

Tom XIII. [Pis´ma (1885–1886)]. Tom podgot. N. A. Viktorovoi i I. S. Poliakovoi. Moskva: Muzyka, 1971. 635 p, illus.

Tom XIV. [Pis´ma (1887–1888)]. Tom podgot. N. N. Sin´kovskoi i I. G. Sokolinskoi. Moskva: Muzyka, 1974. 717 p, illus.

Tom XV–a. [Pis´ma (1889)]. Tom podgot. K. Iu. Davydovoi i G. I. Labutinoi. Moskva: Muzyka, 1976. 296 p, illus.

Tom XV–b. [Pis´ma (1890)]. Tom podgot. K. Iu. Davydovoi i G. I. Labutinoi. Moskva: Muzyka, 1977. 384 p, illus.

Tom XVI–a. [Pis´ma (1891)]. Tom podgot. E. V. Kotominym, S. S. Kotominoi i N. N. Sin´kovskoi. Moskva: Muzyka, 1978. 375 p, illus.

Tom XVI–b. [Pis´ma (1892)]. Tom podgot. E. V. Kotominym, S. S. Kotominoi i N. N. Sin´kovskoi. Moskva: Muzyka, 1979. 278 p, illus.

Tom XVII. [Pis´ma (1893)]. Tom podgot. K. Iu. Davydovoi i G. I. Labutinoi. Moskva: Muzyka, 1981. 358 p, illus.

Reviews: T. Bogdanova, 'Teoreticheskie raboty P. I. Chaikovskogo', *Sovetskaia muzyka* (1958), 10: 143 [vol. III-a] — N. V. Tumanina, 'Pis´ma Chaikovskogo', *Sovetskaia muzyka* (1959), 8: 193–194 [vol. V] — V. A. Kiselev, 'Epistoliarnoe nasledie P. I. Chaikovskogo', *Sovetskaia kul´tura* (13 Oct 1959): 3 [vol. V] — B. Iarustovskii, 'Dlia nastoiashchego i budushchego', *Sovetskaia muzyka* (1964), 9: 125–127 [vols. VII, VIII] — *Revue de musicologie*, 58 (1972), 1: 124–126 [vol. XIII].

[*157*] **ČAJKOVSKIJ, P. I.** *Dopisy*. Usporadal Vladimir Štěpánek. Praha: St. hudební vydavatelstvi, 1965. 289 p (*Hudba v zrcadle doby*; 2).

[*158*] **'Pis´ma k P. I. Chaikovskomu'**, *Sovetskaia muzyka* (1966), 5: 112–118.

Letters to Chaikovskii from various foreign musicians.

[*159*] *Chaikovskii i zarubezhnye muzykanty: Izbrannye pis´ma inostrannykh korrsepondentov.* Sbornik sost. po materialam fondov Doma-muzeia P. I. Chaikovskogo v Klinu. Sost. N. A. Alekseeva. Vstup. stat´ia K. Davydova. Leningrad: Muzyka, 1970. 239 p, music, illus.

Letters to Chaikovskii from Desirée Artôt-Padilla, the Association of Belgian musical artists, Theodore Avé-Lallement, Camille Benois, Francesco Berger, Julius von Bernuth, Enrico Bevignani, Hans von Bülow, Sigmund Bürger, Willy Burmester, Adolf Čech, Marie Červinková-Riegrová, Giovanni Clericci, Paul Collin, Edouard Colonne, Leopold Damrosch, Walter Damrosch, Louis Dershaid, Louis Diémer, Fanny Dürbach, Antonín Dvořák, Henrie Expère, Henry Fink, Wladyslaw Florianskii, Josef Bohuslav Foerster, Berta Foerstrová-Lautererová, Louis Gallet, Frederick Glikson, Edvard Grieg, Lucien Guitry, Karel Haliř, Frits Hartvigson, Michat Hertz, the International Union of Composers, Karl Klindworth, Ivan Knorr, Frederic Lamond, Charles Lamuret, G. Le-Burde, Franz Liszt, Maatschappij tot bevordering der Toonkunst, Félix Mackar, Leon Margulis, Antoine Marmontel, Martin-Pierre Marsik, William Matthews, Sophie Menter, Naples Royal College of Music, New York Philharmonic Club, Adele aus der Ohe, Emil Paladille, Adolf Patera, John Peile, Senfft von Pilsach, Prague National Theatre, Mary Reno, Morris Reno, Hugo Riemann, Franz Rummel, Camille Saint-Saëns, Emil von Sauer, Giovanni Sgambati, Friedrich Sieger, Cecil Silberberg, Charles Villiers Stanford, Sidney Stobn, Sigismund Stojowski, Eduard Strauss, Paul Taffanel, Marie Tayau, Ambroise Thomas, Trompette Chamber Music Society, Umelecká Beseda, André Vainshenck, Pauline Viardot-Garcia, Ružena Vykoukalová-Bradačeva, Hans Wigan, Johannes Wolf, Hermann Wolff and Arma Zenka.

Portions of letters are in German and French.

Review: V. A. Kiselev, 'Korotko o notakh i knigakh', *Sovetskaia muzyka* (1971), 3: 148–149.

[*160*] **'Maloizvestnye pis´ma Chaikovskogo'**, *Inostrannaia literatura* (1970), 10: 273–274.

Regarding the production of *P. I. Tchaikovsky. Letters to his family: An autobiography* (eventually published in 1981) [see *162*].

[*161*] **CHAIKOVSKII, P. I.** *Izbrani pisma*. 1330. Per. ot ruski. Sofiia: Muzika, 1978. 560 p.

[*162*] ***P. I. Tchaikovsky: Letters to his family. An autobiography***. Tr. by Galina von Meck, with additional annotations by Percy M. Young. London: Dobson; New York: Stein & Day, 1981. xxv, 577 p. ISBN: 0-23477-250-6 (UK), 0-8128-2802-X (USA).

Based on *P. I. Chaikovskii: Pis´ma k blizkim* (1955) [see *155*], with some additional material. See also *160*.

— [rev. ed.] New York: Scarborough House, 1982. xxv, 577 p. ISBN: 0-8128-6167-1. (*A Scarborough Book*).

Reviews: G. E. H. Abraham, *Times Literary Suppl.* (1981): 852 — *Stereo Review*, 46 (Nov 1981): 76–77 — *Central Opera Service Bulletin*, 24 (1982), 1: 32 — J. Warrack, *Music & Letters*, 63 (1982), 1/2: 138–141 — D. Brown, *Musical Times*, 123 (Jan 1982): 32 — *High Fidelity*, 32 (Jan 1982): 16 — *School Musician*, 53 (Mar 1982): 16.

2.4.2. Selections

[*163*] **'Mysli P. I. Chaikovskogo (iz ego perepiski)'**, *Solntse Rossii* (1913), 44: 23 [see *583*].

[*164*] **'Peredacha pisem Chaikovskogo Klinskomu muzeiu'**, *Vecherniaia Moskva* (1925), No. 130.

[*165*] **ZHEGIN, N. T.** 'Neopublikovannoe pis´mo P. I. Chaikovskogo', *Muzyka i revoliutsiia* (1928), 11: 27–30.

2 letters from Chaikovskii to Pëtr Iurgenson, 1 to Vasilii Safonov, and 1 to the Moscow Branch of the RMS. with commentary by N. T. Zhegin.

[*166*] **KISELEV, V. A.** 'Neopublikovannoe pis´mo P. I. Chaikovskogo', *Sovetskaia muzyka* (1933), 6: 100–102.

Letters from Chaikovskii to Karl Val´ts and Aleksandr Fedotov. With commentary by V. A. Kiselev, and introductory article by V. V. Iakovlev, 'K publikatsii dvukh neizdannykh pisem Chaikovskogo': 99.

[*167*] **GUSMAN, B. E.** 'Razgovor s Chaikovskim', *Sovetskaia muzyka* (1938), 10/11: 144–153, music, illus.

Selected letters from Chaikovskii to Akhilles Alferaki, Pëtr Iurgenson, Mikhail Ippolitov-Ivanov, Stepan Gedeonov, and to the editor of the Moscow newspaper *Russkie vedomosti*.

[*168*] **'Arkhivy i vystavki'**, *Sovetskaia muzyka* (1938), 7: 77.

[*169*] **'Pis´ma P. I. Chaikovskogo'**, *Sovetskoe iskusstvo* (30 May 1938): 4.

Concerning various autograph letters by Chaikovskii purchased from the collection of S. V. Krivenko.

[*170*] **'Neizvestnye pis´ma P. I. Chaikovskogo'**, *Sovetskaia muzyka* (1939), 8: 55–61, illus.

10 letters from Chaikovskii to Pavel Pereletskii, Vladimir Makovskii, Vasilii Safonov, Pavel Peterssen, Andronik Klimchenko and Aleksandra Iurgenson.

[*171*] **BORTNIKOVA, E. E.** 'Iz perepiski P. I. Chaikovskogo', *Krasnyi arkhiv* (1940), 3: 240–254.

10 letters from Chaikovskii to Sergei Rachinskii, Aleksei Suvorin, Matvei Luzin and Duke Georgii Meklenburg-Strelitskii. Also letters to Chaikovskii from Milii Balakirev and Nikolai Rimskii-Korsakov. With introductory article by E. Bortnikova.

[*172*]   **[Pis´ma P. I. Chaikovskogo]**, *Radians´kaia muzyka* (1940), 2: 44–46, illus.

2 letters from Chaikovskii to Aleksandr Khimichenko (1889, 1892), 1 to N. Nikolaev (1891), 1 to Vasilii Safonov (1891)

[*173*]   **'Pyotr Ilych Tchaikovsky'**. In: *Letters of composers: An anthology, 1603–1945*. Comp. and ed. by Gertrude Norman and Miriam Lubbell Shrifte. New York: Knopf, 1946: 248–267.

Includes letters from Chaikovskii to Vladimir Shilovskii, Nadezhda von Meck, and Grand Duke Konstantin Konstantinovich.

[*174*]   **BELZA, I. 'P. I. Chaikovskii: Pis´ma k cheshskim muzykantam'**, *Sovetskaia muzyka* (1952), 7: 67–72, music, illus.

8 letters from Chaikovskii (1888–93), to Adolf Čech, Josef Bohuslav Foerster and Berta Foerstrová-Lautererová. Russian tr. and commentary by Igor´ Belza.

[*175*]   **LEONT´EVSKII, N. 'Pis´ma Petru Il´ichu Chaikovskomu'**, *Inostrannaia literatura* (1958), 4: 239–246.

Letters to Chaikovskii from Desirée Artôt-Padilla, L'Association des artistes-musiciens Belges, Sigmund Bürger, Walter Damrosch, Frederic Lamond, Franz Liszt, New York Philharmonic Club, John Peile, Prague National Theatre, Charles Villiers Stanford, Camille Saint-Saëns and Emil von Sauer. Russian tr. and commentary by N. Leont´evskii)

[*176*]   **KORABEL´NIKOVA, L. 'Pis´ma Chaikovskogo zarubezhnym muzykantam'**, *Sovetskaia muzyka* (1960), 5: 72–79, music, illus.

4 letters from Chaikovskii to Hans von Bülow (1875): 72–73; to Paul Collin (1892): 74–76; to Sigismund Stojowski (1893): 76–79. Tr. from the French, with commentary by L. Korabel´nikova and K. Iu. Davydova.

[*177*]   **'Peter Ilyitch Tchaikovsky (1840–93)'**. In: *The Musician's world: Great composers in their letters*. London, Thames & Hudson, 1965: 363–373.

Extracts from the composer's letters to Anatolii and Modest Chaikovskii, Nadezhda von Meck, Vladimir Stasov, Sergei Taneev. Mainly concerning Chaikovskii's views on music.

[*178*]   **DAVYDOVA, K. Iu. 'Iz pisem P. I. Chaikovskogo'**, *Sovetskaia muzyka* (1965), 9: 46–51.

9 letters (1888–1893) from Chaikovskii to Osip Paleček, Emil von Sauer, Karl Reinicke, Charles Villiers Stanford and Frederick Maitland.

[*179*]   **KUNIN, I. F. 'Storonnik Moskovskoi konservatorii'**, *Sovetskaia muzyka* (1965), 5: 35–37.

Repr. of a letter to the editor, first published in the journal *Russkie vedomosti* (15 May 1875) under the title "G. Riba v Chekhii" (concerning the administration of the Moscow Conservatory), and signed by 'An advocate of the Moscow Conservatory'. Kunin suggests that the author of the letter was Chaikovskii.

[*180*]   **'Tchaikovsky'**. In: *Letters of composers through six centuries*. Comp. and ed. by Piero Weiss. Foreword by Richard Ellmann. Philadephia: Chilton Book Co., 1967: 361–366, 384.

Includes two letters from Chaikovskii to Nadezhda von Meck and Antonín Dvořák.

[*181*]   **FÉDOROV, V. 'Cajkovskij et la France: Á propos de quelques letteres de Cajkovskij à Félix Mackar'**, *Revue de musicologie*, 54 (1968), 1: 16–95.

Letters from Chaikovskii to Émile Blavet, Edouard Colonne, Henri Delabordé, Willem Kes, Daniel de Lange, Félix Mackar, Camille Saint-Saëns, (Claude) Paul Taffanel and Hermann Wolff.

[*182*]   **DAVYDOVA, K. Iu. 'Problemy epistoliarii'**, *Sovetskaia muzyka* (1986), 6: 87–88.

Overview of Chaikovskii's collected correspondence [see *156*], including information on recently discovered letters, and on Iosif Kotek's revision of the *Valse-Scherzo*.

[*183*]   **'Chaykovski: Spomeni, pisma'**, *Bulgarska muzika*, 41 (1990), 4: 66–82.

[*184*]   **KLIMOVITSKII, A. 'Neizvestnye stranitsy epistoliarii Chaikovskogo'**, *Sovetskaia muzyka* (1990), 6: 99–103 [see *592*].

Letters from Chaikovskii to Vasilii Kandaurov (1885) and Eduard Nápravník (1887).

[185] KORABEL´NIKOVA, L. 'Pis´ma k Chaikovskomu: Dialog s epokhoi', *Sovetskaia muzyka* (1990), 6: 103–114 [see *592*].

Descriptions of letters to Chaikovskii from various correspondents.

— [German tr.] 'Čajkovskij im Dialog mit Zeitgenossen'. In: *Internationales Čajkovskij Symposium, Tübingen 1993: Bericht* (1995): 187–198 [see *596*].

[186] 'Pis´ma, dokumenty', *Sovetskaia muzyka* (1990), 6: 91–98 [see *592*].

Includes letters from Chaikovskii to Ivan Vsevolozhskii, Eduard Nápravník, Francis Jameson, Vera Davydova and Osip Iurgenson; also one letter from Aleksandra Markova to Chaikovskii.

[187] 'Tri dialoga o liubvi: Iz perepiski P. I. Chaikovskogo i vospominanii sovremennikov', *Antrakt* (1990), 7: 9, illus.

Chaikovskii's relationships with Desirée Artôt-Padilla, Antonina Miliukova and Nadezhda von Meck, interpreted through his correspondence.

[188] 'Iz pisem kompozitora', *Sovetskaia kul´tura* (6 Jan 1990), 1: 15.

3 letters from Chaikovskii to Sergei Taneev and Nadzehda von Meck.

[189] KOHLHASE, T. '"Ich bin wahnsinning Müde": Zwei bisher unbekannte Briefe P. I. Cajkovskijs', *Neue Zeitschrift für Musik*, 154 (1993), 5: 45–48.

2 letters to Clotilde Kleeberg (1891) and Aleksandr Ziloti (1893).

[190] *Bisher unbekannte Briefe und musikalische Arbeiten Cajkovskijs*. Übersetzt von Irmgard Wille. Tübingen: Tschaikowsky-Gesellschaft, 1994. 39 p, music. (*Tschaikowsky-Gesellschaft Jahresgabe*).

Contains newly discovered letters from Chaikovskii to an unknown Parisian musician [Jacques Dusautoy] (1887): 4–11; to Clotilde Kleeberg (1891): 12–14; to Aleksandr Ziloti (1893): 15. Also new German trs. of the composer's letters of 20 Aug 1893 to Aleksandra Hubert, Vladimir Davydov, Iulii Konius, Anatolii Chaikovskii, Modest Chaikovskii and Pëtr Iurgenson: 16–24.

— [rev. repr.] 'Drei bisher unbekannte Briefe Čajkovskijs von 1887, 1891 und 1893, sowie sechs weitere Briefe vom 20. August 1893'. In: *Internationales Čajkovskij Symposium, Tübingen 1993: Bericht* (1995): 21–49 [see *596*].

[191] ROZANOVA, Iu. A. 'Russkie poety v perepiske s Chaikovskim (po neopublikovannym pis´mam)'. In: *P. I. Chaikovskii: K 100-letiiu so dnia smerti* (1995): 39–48 [see *597*].

Letters to Chaikovskii from Aleksei Apukhtin and Grand Duke Konstantin Konstantinovich.

[192] SOKOLOV, V. S. 'Pis´ma P. I. Chaikovskogo bez kupiur: Neizvestnye stranitsy epistoliarii'. In: *P. I. Chaikovskii: Zabytoe i novoe* (1995): 118–134 [see *598*].

Publication of previously censored extracts from Chaikovskii's correspondence with his father and his brothers Anatolii and Modest. See also *1950*.

— [German tr.] 'Briefe P. I. Čajkovskijs ohne Kürzungen: Unbekannte Seiten seiner Korrsepondenz (aus dem Russischen von Irmgard Wille)'. In: *Čajkovskijs Homosexualität und sein Tod: Legenden und Wirklichkeit* (1998): 137–162 [see *600*].

[193] LISCHKÉ, A. *Tchaikovski au miroir de ses écrits*. Textes choisis, traduits et présentes par André Lischké. Paris: Fayard, 1996. 434 p, illus.

Reviews: J.-N. von der Weid, 'Le paroxysme au pied de la lettre', *Dissonanz* (Nov 1996), 50: 43–44 — K. Choquer, *L'Avant Scène Opéra*, 175 (Jan/Feb 1997): 126.

[194] KOHLHASE, T. 'Bisher unbekannte Briefe, Notenautographie und andere Čajkovskij-Funde'. In: *Čajkovskijs Homosexualität und sein Tod: Legenden und Wirklichkeit* (1998): 163–298 [see *600*].

Letters from Chaikovskii to Alfred Bruneau, Léonce Détroyat, Louis Gallet, Frits Hartvigson, Édouard Lalo, Julius Laube, Eduard Nápravník, Hermann Wolff, and the Neuen Symphonischen Gesellschaft.

[195] POZNANSKY, A. 'Unknown Tchaikovsky: A reconstruction of previously censored letters to his brothers (1875–1879)'. In: *Tchaikovsky and his world* (1998): 55–96 [see *601*].

Letters from Chaikovskii written in the 1870s to his brothers Anatolii and Modest (their first full publication in English tr.). See also *192*.

[*196*]   KOHLHASE, T. 'Bisher unbekannte Briefe P. I. Čajkovskijs', *Tschaikowsky-Gesellschaft Mitteilungen*, 7
          (2000): 12–46.

          Includes recently-discovered letters from Chaikovskii to Karl Klindworth, Edouard Colonne, German Larosh,
          Velebín Urbánek, Frederic Lamond, John Peile and Alma Aronson.

          See also *99, 102, 105, 373, 376, 963, 1453, 1799, 1945, 2065, 2098, 2948, 3138, 3139.*

                              KARL AL´BREKHT (1836–93)
                         Cellist and director of the Moscow Conservatory

[*197*]   'Perepiska Chaikovskogo: P. I. Chaikovskii i K. K. Al´brekht'. In: *Chaikovskii na moskovskoi stsene*
          (1940): 255–297 [see *2538*].

          16 letters from Chaikovskii to Karl Al´brekht (1876–91), and 5 letters froml Al´brekht to the composer.

                          ANNA ALEKSANDROVA-LEVENSON (1856–1930)
                       Pianist and Chaikovskii's student at the Moscow Conservatory

[*198*]   BULGAKOV, B. 'Pis´ma P. Chaikovskogo k A. Ia. Aleksandrovoi-Levenson', *Sibirskii nabliudatel´*
          (1905), 10: 100–108.

          17 letters from Chaikovskii to Anna Aleksandrova-Levenson (1877–93).

          Review: 'Neizdannye pis´ma P. Chaikovskogo', *Russkaia muzykal´naia gazeta* (16 Apr 1906), 16: 403–404
          [includes repr. of letters from 15 Apr 1881 and 4 Jun 1885].

                               IVAN ARMSGEIMER (1860–1933)
                Ballet composer, conductor and brass player at the Mariinskii Theatre in St. Petersburg

[*199*]   [Pis´mo P. I. Chaikovskogo k I. I. Armsgeimeru], *Biulleten´ Doma-muzeia P. I. Chaikovskogo v Klinu*
          (1951), 1.

          Facs. of 1 letter from Chaikovskii to Ivan Armsgeimer (1891).

          — [repr.] In: *Avtografy P. I. Chaikovskogo v arkhive Doma-muzeia v Klinu*, vyp. 2 (1952) [see *102*].

                            DESIRÉE ARTÔT-PADILLA (1835–1907)
                       Belgian singer and former fiancée of the composer

[*200*]   'P. I. Chaikovskii–Dezire Arto (1888–1890)'. In: *P. I. Chaikovskii—S. I. Taneev: Pis´ma* (1951): 371–376
          [see *154*].

                                LEOPOLD AUER (1845–1930)
                  Violinist, conductor and professor at the St. Petersburg Conservatory

[*201*]   [Pis'ma P. Chaikovskogo k L. Auer']. In: *Voprosy muzykal´no-ispol´nitel´skogo iskusstva*. Vyp. 2. Moscow:
          Muzgiz, 1958: 257–259.

          Russian trs. of 3 letters from Chaikovskii to Auer (1888).

          — [repr.] In: L. Raaben, *L. Auer*. Leningrad: Muzgiz, 1962: 100–103.

                                MILII BALAKIREV (1837–1910)
                            Composer, pianist and conductor

[*202*]   *Perepiska M. A. Balakireva i P. I. Chaikovskogo (1868–1891)*. S predisloviem i primechaniiami S.
          Liapunova. Sankt Peterburg: Iu. G. Tsimmerman [1912]. 100 p, music.

          Includes 43 letters from Chaikovskii to Balakirev (1868–91). See also *203, 204.*

          Review: *Bibliograficheskii listok Russkoi muzykal´noi gazety* (1913), 1: 4–5.

[203]   LIAPUNOV, S. M. 'Iz perepiski M. A. Balakireva s P. I. Chaikovskim', *Vestnik Evropy* (1912), 5: 137–158.

Extracts from *Perepiska M. A. Balakireva i P. I. Chaikovskogo* (1912) [see *202*].

— [repr.] *Russkaia muzykal´naia gazeta* (3/10 Jun 1912), 23/24: 532–534.

— [German tr.] A. Hess, 'Neue Tschaikowski Briefe', *Die Musik* (1911/12), 4: 323–336.

[204]   CALVOCORESSI, M. D. 'The correspondence between Balakirev and Tchaikovsky', *Musical Times*, 53 (Nov 1912): 712–715.

English tr. of extracts from *Perepiska M. A. Balakireva i P. I. Chaikovskogo* (1912) [see *202*].

[205]   ORLOVA, A. A. 'Perepiska s P. I. Chaikovskim'. In: *M. A. Balakirev: Vospominaniia i pis´ma*. Otv. red. E. L. Frid. Vstup. stat´ia S. M. Liapunova i A. S. Liapunovoi. Leningrad: Gos. institut teatra, muzyki i kinematografii, 1962: 115–203, music, illus.

Includes 17 letters from Chaikovskii to Balakirev (1881–91).

[206]   BALAKIREV, M. A. 'Drei Briefe zur "Manfred Sinfonie" an Peter Tschaikowsky'. In: *Tschaikowsky aus der Nähe* (1994): 65–71 [see *379*].

Herr BASKE

German amateur musician

[207]   MÜLLER VON ASOW, E. H. 'Unbekannte Briefe von Peter I. Tschaikowsky', *Österreichische Musikzeitschrift*, 16 (Feb 1961): 68–73, illus.

1 letter from Chaikovskii to Baske (1890).

FRANCESCO BERGER (1834–1919)

English pianist, composer and secretary of the London Philharmonic Society

[208]   'Facsimile letters of musicians' [part 5], *Monthly Musical Record*, 55 (May 1925): 137, illus.

1 letter from Chaikovskii to Francesco Berger (1891).

— [repr.] In: E. Evans, *Tchaikovsky* (1906): 120 [see *1462*].

[209]   SCHANG, F. C. *Visiting Cards of Celebrities*. Paris: Fernand Hazan Editeur, 1971. 271 p.

Includes 1 visiting card with a note from Chaikovskii to Berger (1891).

NIKOLAI BERNARD (1844–1905)

Musical publisher

[210]   [BERNARD, N. M.] *Avtografy muzykal´nykh deiatelei*. Sankt Peterburg: M. I. Bernard, 1889: 34.

Suppl. to the journal *Nuvellist*. Includes 1 letter from Chaikovskii to Nikolai Bernard (1889).

VASILII BESSEL´ (1843–1907)

Violist, music publisher and contemporary at the St. Petersburg Conservatory

[211]   POPOV, S. S. 'Perepiska P. I. Chaikovskogo s Besselem', *K novym beregam* (1923), 1: 42–45; 2: 42–47.

55 letters from Chaikovskii to Bessel´ (1869–73).

[212]   POPOV, S. S. 'Pis´ma P. I. Chaikovskogo k Besseliu', *Muzykal´naia nov´* (1923), 1: 51–55; 3: 43–44.

17 letters from Chaikovskii to Bessel´ (1873).

[213]   ORLOV, G. P. 'Neizdannye pis´ma P. I. Chaikovskogo k V. V. Besseliu', *Sovetskaia muzyka* (1938), 6: 38–57.

26 letters from Chaikovskii to Bessel´ (1874–91). See also *401*.

HUGO BOCK (1848–1932)

Son of the co-founder of the Berlin music-publishing firm Bote & Bock

[214] **BARDI, B. 'Unbekannte Musikerbriefe P. Tschaikowskys: Erstmal veröffentlicht'**, *Berliner Börsen-Courier* (5 Feb 1927).

1 letter from Chaikovskii to Bock (1893).

ADOL´F BRODSKII (1851–1929)

Violinist and concertmaster

[215] **GERSHOVSKII, E. 'Neopublikovannoe pis´mo k A. Brodskomu, 3 iuniia 1882 g.'**, *Sovetskaia muzyka* (1959), 1: 81–83, illus.

[216] **PITFIELD, T. 'Letters from Tchaikovsky to Brodsky'**, *The Listener*, 67 (19 Apr 1962): 683–684, illus.

English trs. of 2 letters from Chaikovskii to Brodskii (1882, 1891).

[217] **'Eshche piatnadtsat´ pisem P. I. Chaikovskogo'**, *Sovetskaia kul´tura* (11 Aug 1962): 4, illus.

The discovery in England of 14 autograph letters from Chaikovskii to Brodskii (of which 3 are published). Also includes the first publication of 1 letter from Chaikovskii to Lev Kupernik.

ALFRED BRUNEAU (1857–1934)

President of the International Composer's Union in Paris

[218] **KOHLHASE, T. 'Čajkovskij und die Union Internationale des Compositeurs: Ein bisher unbekannter Brief Čajkovskijs von 1884'**. In: *Tschaikowsky-Gesellschaft Miteilungen*, 5 (1998): 1–11, illus.

— [repr.] In: *Čajkovskijs Homosexualität und sein Tod: Legenden und Wirklichkeit* (1998): 194–205 [see *600*].

HANS VON BÜLOW (1830–94)

German pianist, conductor, composer and music critc

[219] **ATANOVA, L. 'Pis´ma k P. I. Chaikovskomu'**, *Sovetskaia muzyka* (1966), 5: 112–118.

Eight letters to Chaikovskii from Hans von Bülow (1875–93). With commentary by N. Alekseev and K. Davydova.

[220] **GOLDSTEIN, M. 'Unbekannte Briefe Peter Tschaikowskys an Hans von Bülow'**, *Orchester*, 14 (Jun 1966): 236–238.

1 letter from Chaikovskii to Hans von Bülow (1 Jul 1875).

[221] **'Pis´mo P. I. Chaikovskogo'**, *Muzykal´naia zhizn´* (Dec 1966), 23: 22.

First publication of a letter from Chaikovskii to Hans von Bülow (1 Jul 1875).

WILLY BURMESTER (1869–1933)

German violinst

[222] **BURMESTER, W.** *Fünfzig Jahre Küstlerleben*. Berlin: A. Scherl [1926]: 66–68.

4 letters from Chaikovskii to Burmester (1888–89).

— [English tr.] *Fifty years as a concert violinist*. Tr. from the German by Roberta Franke, in collaboration with Samuel Wolf. Linthicum Heights, Md.: Swand [1975]: 47–49.

[223] **GINZBURG, A. S. 'P. I. Chaikovskii: Pis´ma k V. Burmesteru'**. In: *Muzykal´noe nasledstvo: Sborniki po istorii muzykal'noi kultury SSSR*. Tom 1, Moskva: Gos. Muzykal´noe Izd-vo, 1962: 362–371.

4 letters from Chaikovskii to Burmester (1888–89).

MARIE ČERVINKOVÁ-RIEGROVÁ (1854–95)
Czech writer, translator and librettist

[224] **[Dopis P. Cajkovského]**, *Lidovy noviny* (25 Jan 1937).

1 letter from Chaikovskii to Červinková-Riegrová (1888).

— [Russian tr.] 'Pis´ma P. I. Chaikovskogo', *Muzykal´naia zhizn´* (Apr 1965), 8: 6, facs.

ANTONINA CHAIKOVSKAIA (1849–1917)
Wife of the composer

[225] **'Pis´ma A. I. Chaikovskoi (Miliukovoi) k P. I. Chaikovskomu'.** In: V. Sokolov, *Antonina Chaikovskaia: Istoriia zabytoi zhizni* (1994): 219–251 [see *1887*].

ANATOLII CHAIKOVSKII (1850–1915)
Brother of the composer

[226] **RUBIN, S. 'Neizvestnye pis´ma velikogo kompozitora: Naideny 140 pisem P. I. Chaikovskogo'**, *Sovetskaia kul´tura* (18 Jun 1957): 3.

Concerning 140 autograph letters from Chaikovskii to his brother Anatolii and his wife Praskov´ia from the period 1886–93, found by the author in Leningrad at the home of V. I. Serebriakova, and donated to the Klin house-museum. Includes extracts from the correspondence ('Iz pisem P. I. Chaikovskogo k bratu Anatoliiu'). See also *227–230*.

[227] **RUBIN, S. 'Naideny pis´ma P. I. Chaikovskogo'**, *Vechernii Leningrad* (27 Jul 1957).

[228] **RUBIN, S. 'Neizvestnye pis´ma P. I. Chaikovskogo'**, *Trud* (29 Aug 1957).

[229] **RUBIN, S. 'Iz pisem P. I. Chaikovskogo: Novye materialy'**, *Literaturnaia Gruziia* (1958), 3: 110–113.

[230] **'Pis´ma Chaikovskogo'**, *Moskovskaia pravda* (22 Mar 1958).

ANTON CHEKHOV (1860–1904)
Writer and dramatist

[231] **'P. I. Chaikovskii: Pis´ma Chekhovu'**, *Slovo* (1914), 2: 219–221.

EMILIO COLOMBO (1875–1937)
Italian mucisian

[232] **KASHINA-EVREINOVA, A. 'Naidennoe pis´mo P. I. Chaikovskogo'**, *Novyi zhurnal*, 85 (1966): 271–273.

1 letter from Colombo to Chaikovskii (1891), and Chaikovskii's reply (1892).

EDOUARD COLONNE (1838–1910)
French conductor, violinist and composer

[233] **ZVIGUILSKY, A. 'En marge d'une lettre inedité de Tchaikovsky à Edouard Colonne'**, *Cahiers Ivan Tourgueniev, Pauline Viardot, Maria Malibran*, 14 (1990): 148–154, illus.

EDWARD DANNREUTHER (1844–1905)
English pianist

[234] **'Occasional notes'**, *Musical Times*, 48 (1 Nov 1907): 717.

1 letter from Chaikovskii to Dannreuther (1876).

398   B i b l i o g r a p h y

— [Russian tr.] 'Neizdannoe pis´mo P. Chaikovskogo', *Russkaia muzykal´naia gazeta* (11 Nov 1907), 45: 1033–1034.

KARL DAVYDOV (1838–89)

Cellist, conductor and composer. Teacher and director of the St. Petersburg Conservatory

[*235*] **'Neizdannoe pis´mo Chaikovskogo'**, *Muzykal´noe obrazovanie* (1926), 5/6: 43–45.

1 letter from Chaikovskii to Karl Davydov (1880).

ANTONÍN DVOŘÁK (1840–1906)

Czech composer, conductor, and professor at the Prague Conservatory

[*236*] **ŠOUREK, A.** *Dvořák ve vzpominkách a dopisech*. 9. izd. Praha: Orbis, 1951: 102–105.

3 letters from Chaikovskii to Dvořák (1888–89), in Czech trs.

— [German tr.] In: O. Šourek, *Dvořák im Erinnerungen und Briefe*. Prag: Orbis, 1954.

— [Russian tr.] In: *Dvorzhak v pis´makh i vospominaniiakh*. Moscow: Muzyka, 1964 .

[*237*] **ŠTĔPÁNEK, V.** 'Nové dosud nepublikované rukopisy P. I. Čajkovského', *Hudební rozhledy*, 5 (1952), 17: 22.

Czech tr. of 1 letter from Chaikovskii to Dvořák (1889).

[*238*] **CLAPHAM, J.** 'Dvořák's visit to Russia', *Musical Quarterly*, 51 (Jul 1965), 3: 494.

English tr. and facs. of 1 letter from Chaikovskii to Dvořák (1889).

PAVEL FËDOROV (1809–79)

Author and translator

[*239*] **PETROV, A.** 'Neizdannoe pis´mo P. I. Chaikovskogo ob opere "Undina"', *Gatobovets* (25 Mar 1935).

1 letter from Chaikovskii to Fedorov (1869).

ALEKSANDR FEDOTOV (1841–95)

Actor, director, teacher and dramatist

[*240*] **'Perepiska Chaikovskogo: P. I. Chaikovskii i A. F. Fedotov'**. In: *Chaikovskii na moskovskoi stsene* (1940): 477–481 [see *2538*]

NIKOLAI FIGNER (1857–1918)

Principal tenor with the Imperial Opera in St. Petersburg

[*241*] **'Pis´ma P. I. Chaikovskogo'**, *Novosti i birzhevaia gazeta* (25 Oct 1894).

1 letter from Chaikovskii to Figner (1890).

— [repr.] In: N. N. Figner, *Vospominaniia, pis´ma, materialy*. Leningrad, 1968: 180.

SERGEI FLEROV (1841–1901)

Teacher, journalist and music critic

[*242*] **VASIL´EV, S. [FLEROV, S.V.]** 'Teatral´naia khronika', *Russkoe obozrenie* (Nov 1893): 453.

1 letter from Chaikovskii to Flerov (1881).

[*243*] **'Perepiska Chaikovskogo: P. I. Chaikovskii i S. V. Flerov'**. In: *Chaikovskii na moskovskoi stsene* (1940): 460–466 [see *2538*].

JOSEF BOHUSLAV FOERSTER (1858–1951)
Czech composer and music critic

[244] **BELZA, I. 'Iosef Boguslav Fërster'**, *Sovetskaia muzyka* (1950), 12: 85–90, illus.

Facs. and Russian tr. of 1 letter from Chaikovskii to Foerster (1893).

— [repr. in original French] In: I. F. Belza, *Ocherki razvitiia cheshskoi muzykal'noi klassiki*. Moskva, 1951: 376.

ALEKSANDR GLAZUNOV (1865–1936)
Composer, conductor and professor at the St. Petersburg Conservatory

[245] **KISELEV, V. A. 'Perepiska P. I. Chaikovskogo i A. K. Glazunova'**. In: *Sovetskaia muzyka: 3-i sbornik statei*. Moskva; Leningrad, 1945: 55–66.

Includes 13 letters (1886–92).

IVAN GREKOV (1849–1919)
Actor and manager of the Odessa Opera Theatre

[246] **GREKOV, I. [Pis'mo Chaikovskogo]**, *Odesskii listok* (27 Oct 1893).

1 letter from Chaikovskii to Grekov (21 Oct 1893).

— [repr.] *Novosti dnia* (31 Oct 1893).

— [repr.] *Novosti i birzhevaia gazeta* (1 Nov 1893).

EDVARD GRIEG (1843–1907)
Norwegian composer, pianist and conductor

[247] **ROGAL´-LEVITSKII, D. 'Pis´ma P. I. Chaikovskogo k Edvardu Grigu'**, *Sovetskaia muzyka* (1940), 5/6: 145–148, illus [see *585*].

Russian trs. of 3 letters from Chaikovskii to Grieg (1888).

— [repr.] In: O. Levasheva, *Edvard Grig: Ocherk zhizni i tvorchestva*. Moscow: Muzgiz, 1962: 746–750.

[248] **KISELEV, V. A. 'Pis´ma Edvarda Griga k Chaikovskomu'**, *Sovetskaia muzyka* (1947), 5: 58–60, illus.

Russian tr. of 4 letters from Grieg to Chaikovskii (1888).

[249] **'Druzhba velikikh'**, *Ogonek*, 36 (1957): 25.

Includes 4 letters between Chaikovskii and Grieg (1888), and extracts from Chaikovskii's *Autobiographical account of a tour abroad in the year 1888* [see *138*].

IAKOV GROT (1812–93)
Russian historian and literary academic

[250] **FEDOROV, L. A. 'P. I. Chaikovskii: Sotrudnik slovaria Akademii nauk'**, *Vestnik Akademii nauk SSSR* (1933), 12: 37–40.

2 letters from Chaikovskii to Iakov Grot (1892–93), concerning the composer's editorial work on the *Dictionary of the Russian Language*.

— [repr.] *Russkaia rech´* (1975), 3: 123–126.

MICHAT HERTZ (1844–?)
German conductor, composer and music teacher

[251] **'Perepiska Chaikovskogo: P. I. Chaikovskii i M. Gerts'**. In: *Chaikovskii na moskovskoi stsene* (1940): 482–486 [see *2538*].

ALEKSANDRA HUBERT (1850–1937)

Pianist, wife of Nikolai Hubert, and professor at the Moscow Conservatory

[252]   **'Pis´ma P. I. Chaikovskogo k A. I. i N. A. Gubert'**. Predislovie i primechaniia N. Zhegina i S. Popova. In: *Proshloe russkoi muzyki*, tom 1 (1920): 15–64 [see *584*].

MIKHAIL IPPOLITOV-IVANOV (1859–1935)

Composer, conductor and professor at the Moscow Conservatory

[253]   **POPOV, S. S. 'Perepiska P. I. Chaikovskogo s M. M. Ippolitovym-Ivanovym i ego zhenoi V. M. Zarudnoi-Ivanovoi (1885–1893)'**, *Iskusstvo* (1927), 4: 141–175.

17 letters from Chaikovskii to Ippolitov-Ivanov and his wife Varvara Zarudnaia.

[254]   **'Perepiska M. M. Ippolitova-Ivanova s P. I. Chaikovskim (1885–1893)'**, *Biulleten´ Doma-muzeia P. I. Chaikovskogo v Klinu* (1947), 1: 7–63; 2: 5–61.

Chaikovskii's correspondence with Ippolitov-Ivanov and his wife Varvara Zarudnaia.

— [repr.] In: M. M. Ippolitov-Ivanov, *Pis´ma, stat´i, vospominaniia*. Sost., avtor vstup. stat´i i kommentariev N. N. Sokolov. Moskva: Sovetskii kompozitor, 1986: 39–78, illus.

PËTR IURGENSON (1836–1903)

Chaikovskii's principal publisher

[255]   ***P. I. Chaikovskii: Perepiska s P. I. Iurgensonom*** (1938–52) [2 vols.]. (*Trudy Gos. doma-muzeia P. I. Chaikovskogo*).

Tom 1: 1877–1883. Red. pisem i kommentarii V. A. Zhdanova i N. T. Zhegina. Vstup. stat´ia B. V. Asaf´eva. Moskva: Muzgiz, 1938. 384 p, illus.

Tom 2: 1884–1893. Red. pisem i kommentarii V. A. Zhdanova. Moskva: Gos. muz. izdat., 1952. viii, 344 p, illus.

Reviews: A. Ostretsov, 'Pis´ma P. I. Chaikovskogo k Iurgensonu', *Muzyka* (6 Jul 1937): 4–5 [vol. 1] — B. Iag. 'Novye pis´ma P. I. Chaikovskogo', *Dekada moskovskikh zrelishch* (11 May 1939): 3 [vol. 1].

IAKOV KALISHEVSKII (1856–1923)

Baritone, and choirmaster of the Sofiiskii Cathedral in Kiev

[256]   **[Pis´ma P. I. Chaikovskogo]**, *Muzyka i penie* (1903), 5: 2–3.

6 letters from Chaikovskii to Kalishevskii (1890–91).

VASILII KANDAUROV (1830–88)

Civil servant and librettist

[257]   **[Pis´mo P. I. Chaikovskogo k V. A. Kandaurovu za 1884 g.]**, *Biulleten´ Doma-muzeia P. I. Chaikovskogo v Klinu* (1949), 2: 17–20.

3 letters from Chaikovskii to Kandaurov.

GEORGII KATUAR (1861–1926)

Composer, musicologist and teacher

[258]   **KISELEV, V. A. 'Perepiska P. I. Chaikovskogo i G. L. Katuara'**. In: *Sovetskaia muzyka: 3-i sbornik statei*. Moskva; Leningrad, 1945: 45–54.

3 letters from Chaikovskii and 4 from Katuar (1886).

IVAN KLIMENKO (1841–1914)
Architect and friend of the composer

[*259*] KLIMENKO, T. I. 'Ob odnom adresate Chaikovskogo (pis´ma v redaktsiiu)', *Sovetskaia muzyka* (1977), 2: 103.

Concerning mistakes in the reproduction of Chaikovskii's letters to Ivan Klimenko, in vol. 14 of *Polnoe sobranie sochinenii* [see *156*]. Includes a reply by Kseniia Davydova.

See also *473*.

KARL KLINDWORTH (1830–1916)
Pianist, composer, conductor and professor at the Moscow Consevatory

[*260*] GOLDSTEIN, M. 'Unveröffentlichte Briefe Karl Klindworths an Tschaikowsky', *Musik und Gesellschaft*, 15 (Aug 1965), 8: 547–551, illus.

NIKOLAI KONRADI (1868–1922)
Pupil of the composer's brother Modest

[*261*] 'P. I. Chaikovskii–N. G. Konradi (1876–1893)'. In: *P. I. Chaikovskii–S. I. Taneev: Pis´ma* (1951): 257–287 [see *154*].

GRAND DUKE KONSTANTIN KONSTANTINOVICH (1858–1914)
Poet, amateur composer, nephew of Tsar Aleksandr III

[*262*] 'Iz perepiski P. I. Chaikovskogo', *Nuvellist* (1902), 11: 3–4.

Letters taken from M. I. Chaikovskii, *Zhizn´ Petra Il´icha Chaikovskogo* (1900) [see *1453*].

— [repr.] 'Iz perepiski Chaikovskogo', *Russkie vedomosti* (24 Oct 1902).

[*263*] 'Perepiska "K. R." s A. A. Fetom, Ia. P. Polonskim, P. I. Chaikovskim, A. N. Maikovym', *Novyi zhurnal* (1994), 2/3: 111–144.

[*264*] KUZ´MINA, A. '"Samoe vozvyshennoe iskusstvo—muzyka": Iz perepiski K. R. s P. I. Chaikovskim', *Muzykal´naia zhizn´* (1997), 5: 32–36, illus.

First publication of 3 letters from the Grand Duke to Chaikovskii.

[*265*] 'P. I. Chaikovskii i K. R.'. In: *K. R.: Izbrannaia perepiska.* Sost. L. I. Kuz´mina. Sankt Peterburg: D. Bulanin, 1999: 31–86. (*Rossiiskaia Akademiia nauk. Institut russkoi literatury (Pushkinskii dom)*).

Includes all known correspondence between Chaikovskii and the Grand Duke.

See also *191*.

ARSENII KORESHCHENKO (1870–1921)
Composer, pianist, conductor, teacher and music critic

[*266*] [Pis´ma P. I. Chaikovskogo], *Biulleten´ Doma-muzeia P. I. Chaikovskogo v Klinu* (1951), 1: 36–38.

2 letters from Chaikovskii to Koreshchenko (1892).

[*267*] 'P. I. Chaikovskii: Pis´mo A. I. Koreshchenko', *Sovetskaia muzyka* (1972), 11: 92–93.

1 letter from Chaikovskii to Koreshchenko (1892).

BOGOMIR KORSOV (1843–1920)
Baritone with the Mariinskii and Bol´shoi Theatre companies

[*268*] RUDANOVSKAIA, M. 'Perepiska P. I. Chaikovskogo s B. B. Korsovym', *Sovetskoe iskusstvo* (6 May 1940): 2 [see *853*].

1 letter from Chaikovskii to Korsov, regarding the part of Tomskii in the opera *The Queen of Spades*.

[*269*]   **GERSHOVSKII, E. 'Pis´ma Chaikovskogo k B. Korsovu'**, *Sovetskaia muzyka* (1959), 1: 73–81, illus.
9 letters from Chaikovskii to Korsov (1874–91).

LUDVÍK KUBA (1863–1956)
Czech writer and artist

[*270*]   **DOLEŽAL, J. 'Petr Iljič Čajkovskij a Ludvík Kuba'**, *Hudební rozhledy*, 6 (1953), 16: 760–762.
3 letters from Chaikovskii to Kuba (1888–92).

[*271*]   **'Pis´ma P. I. Chaikovskogo k Liudviku Kube'**. In: *Iz istorii russko-cheshskikh muzykal´nykh sviazei*. Vstup.
stat´ia i kommentarii I. Belzy. Sbornik 2. Moskva: Gos. muz. izdat., 1955: 5–14.
3 letters from Chaikovskii to Kuba (1888–92).
Review: 'Iz istorii russko-cheshskikh sviazei', *Slaviane* (1956), 10: 50.

NIKOLAI KUZNETSOV (1853–1930)
Artist

[*272*]   **'Priobretenie VOKS'**, *Izvestiia* (30 Mar 1946): 3.
The discovery in Yugoslavia of unknown letters from Chaikovskii and I. E. Repin to Nikolai Kuznetsov.

ELIZAVETA LAVROVSKAIA (1845–1919)
Contralto, and professor at the Moscow Conservatory

[*273*]   **SHIKOV, V. 'Etu rol´ia pisal dlia Vas'**, *Kalininskaia pravda* (13 Oct 1970)
2 letters from Chaikovskii to Lavrovskaia (1889), conerning the opera *Evgenii Onegin*.

KARL VON LEDEBUR (1840–1913)
Director of the Schwerin Hoftheater, Germany

[*274*]   **LEDEBUR, K. von. *Aus meinem Tagebuche: Ein Beitrag zur Geschichte des Schweriner Hoftheaters,***
1883–1897. Schwerin, 1897: 175–176.
1 letter from Chaikovskii to Ledebur (1893).

MIKHAIL LENTOVSKII (1843–1906)
Operatic impressario and writer

[*275*]   **'Perepiska Chaikovskogo: P. I. Chaikovskii i M. V. Lentovskii'**. In: *Chaikovskii na moskovskoi stsene*
(1940): 467–470 [see *2538*].

NIKOLAI LENTS (b. 1858)
Lawyer and composer

[*276*]   **[Pis´ma P. I. Chaikovskogo]**, *Den´* (25 Oct 1913).
2 letters from Chaikovskii to Lents (1880–93).

FÉLIX MACKAR (1837–1903)
French music publisher

[277]   FÉDOROV, V. 'Correspondance inédite de P. I. Cajkovskij avec son éditeur français', *Revue de musicologie*, 39 (Jul 1957): 61–70.

[278]   'Pis´ma P. I. Chaikovskogo F. Makkaru', *Sovetskaia muzyka* (1970), 9: 60–77, illus.

Publication of letters from Chaikovskii to Mackar (1885–91). Tr. from French to Russian by G. Shokhman, with notes by Z. Apetian and G. Shokhman.

NADEZHDA VON MECK (1831–94)
Friend and benefactress of the composer

[279]   'Iz perepiski Chaikovskogo', *Russkie vedomosti* (14 Sep 1901).

Compilation of extracts from M. I. Chaikovskii, *Zhizn´ Petra Il´icha Chaikovskogo* (1900–02) [see *1453*].

[280]   *P. I. Chaikovskii: Perepiska s N. F. von-Mekk*. Red. i primechaniia V. A. Zhdanova i N. T. Zhegina. [3 vols.], music, illus. (*Trudy Doma-muzeia P. I. Chaikovskogo*).

Tom 1: 1876–1878. Vstup. stat´ia B. S. Pshibyshevskogo. Moskva; Leningrad: Academia, 1934. xxvii, 643 p.

Tom 2: 1879–1881. Moskva; Leningrad: Academia, 1935. 677 p.

Tom 3: 1882–1890. Moskva; Leningrad: Academia, 1936. 683 p.

Review: S. Ginzburg, 'Kniga o Chaikovskom', *Literaturnyi Leningrad* (20 Jun 1934) [tom 1]. See also *281, 5477*.

[281]   BENNIGSEN, O. 'A bizarre friendship: Tchaikovsky and Mme von Meck', *Musical Quarterly*, 22 (Oct 1936): 420–429, illus.

Includes a review of *P. I. Chaikovskii: Perepiska s N. F. von-Mekk* (1934–36) [see *280*].

[282]   BENNIGSEN, O. 'More Tchaikovsky-von Meck correspondence', *Musical Quarterly*, 24 (Apr 1938): 129–138.

[283]   HOPE, E. 'Tchaikovsky and the Von Meck letters', *Fortnightly Review*, 170 (Dec 1951): 842–847.

[284]   *Teure Freundin: Peter Iljitsch Tschaikowskis in seinen Briefen an Nadeshda von Meck*. Übersetzung des Briefe aus dem Russischen von Ena von Baer; hrsg. von Ena von Baer und Hans Pezold; mit einer Einleitung von Hans Pezold. Leipzig: P. List, 1964. 670 p, illus.

Reviews: *Musik in der Schule*, 16 (1965), 10: 439–440 — *Musik im Unterricht*, 57 (1966): 140 — *Orchester*, 14 (Mar 1966): 126–127 — I. Fellinger, *Die Musikforschung*, 20 (1967), 3: 348–349 — R. Brost, *Musik und Gesellschaft*, 17 (Mar 1967): 202–203 — A. Würz, *Musica*, 21 (1967), 1: 46.

— [new ed.] Hanau: Dausien; Leipizig: Kiepenheuer [1988]. 583 p. ISBN: 3-7684-4899-1 (Hanau), 3-378-00196-8 (Leipzig).

[285]   'The truth will out', *The Times* (18 Oct 1971).

Galina von Meck's tr. of correspondence between Chaikovskii and her grandmother.

[286]   *'To my best friend': Correspondence between Tchaikovsky and Nadezhda von Meck, 1876–1878*. Tr. from the Russian by Galina von Meck. Ed. by Edward Garden and Nigel Gotteri, with an introduction by Edward Garden. Oxford: Clarendon Press; New York: Oxford Univ. Press, 1993. lxxi, 439 p, music, illus. ISBN: 0-19-816158-1.

Reviews: *Musikrevy*, 48 (1993), 4: 39–41 — H. Zajaczkowski, *Musical Times*, 134 (Apr 1993): 211 — P. Griffiths, *Times Literary Suppl.* (4 Jun 1993): 18 — *Classic CD* (Nov 1993), 42: 20–22 [suppl.] — R. Craft, 'Love in a cold climate', *New York Review of Books*, 40 (18 Nov 1993): 37–41 [see *1676*] — M. Meckna, *Choice*, 31 (Dec 1993): 615 — D. Brown, *Music & Letters*, 75 (Feb 1994), 1: 100–102 — A. McMillin, *Slavonic and East European Review* (Apr 1994), 2: 296–297 — M. H. Brown, *Slavic Review*, 54 (win. 1994), 4: 1201–1203.

[287]   MINAEVA, V. 'Duet dlia golosa i miatushcheisia dushi', *Sovetskaia zhenshchina*, 5 (1990): 24–25.

See also *2014, 2086, 2424*.

MIKHAIL MEDVEDEV (1858–1925)

Tenor at the Bol´shoi Theatre in Moscow

[288]   LODGAUZ, L. 'Podlinnye pis´ma Chaikovskogo', *Sovetskoe iskusstvo* (6 May 1939): 1.

ANNA MERKLING (1830–1911)

Daughter of Pëtr Petrovich Chaikovskii (the composer's paternal uncle)

[289]   'P. I. Chaikovskii–A. P. Merkling (1871–1893)'. In: *P. I. Chaikovskii–S. I. Taneev: Pis´ma* (1951): 205–256 [see *154*].

MIKHAIL MIKESHIN (1836–1936)

Artist, sculptor and writer

[290]   NISNEVICH, I. G. 'Belorusskii avtograf Chaikovskogo'. In: I. G. Nisnevich, *Muzykal´no-kriticheskie stat´i*. Leningrad: Sovetskii kompozitor, 1984: 94–95.

         Concerning an autograph note from Chaikovskii (1893), promising to write a march for Mikeshin. See also *500*.

KONSTANTIN MIKHAILOV-STOIAN (1853–1914)

Baritone at the Bol´shoi Theatre in Moscow

[291]   MIKHAILOV-STOIAN, K. I. *Ispoved´ tenora*. Tom 2. Moskva, 1896: 95.

         1 letter from Chaikovskii to Mikhailov-Stoian (1893).

         — [Bulgarian tr.] In: D. Sagaev, 'Pismo na P. I. Chaykovski do K. I. Mikhaylov-Stoyan', *Bulgarska muzika*, 41 (1990), 4: 44–45, illus.

PORFIRII MOLCHANOV (1863–1945)

Composer, professor at the Odessa Conservatory

[292]   ORFEEV, S. 'Avtografy Chaikovskogo i Rimskogo-Korsakova', *Bol´shevistskoe znamia* [Odessa] (5 Jul 1946).

         Includes 1 letter from Chaikovskii to Molchanov (1892).

EDUARD NÁPRAVNÍK (1839–1916)

Czech conductor and composer

[293]   'Perepiska P. I. Chaikovskogo i E. F. Napravnika (1872–1893)'. In: *Chaikovskii: Vospominaniia i pis´ma* (1924): 99–230 [see *373*].

[294]   'Perepiska E. F. Napravnika s P. I. Chaikovskim'. In: *E. F. Napravnik: Avtobiograficheskie, tvorcheskie materialy, dokumenty, pis´ma*. Sost., avtor vstup. stat´i i primechanii L. M. Kutateladze. Pod red. Iu. Keldysh. Leningrad: Gos. Muz. Izdat., 1959: 94–188.

[295]   OROKHOVATSKII, Iu. 'Pered vami: Avtograf Chaikovskogo', *Sovetskaia kul´tura* (15 Nov 1983).

         Publication of an undated letter from Chaikovskii to Eduard Nápravník concerning *The Maid of Orleans*.

[296]   KOZLOV, V. 'Dar fondu kultury: Piat´ pisem Chaikovskogo', *Nashe nasledie* (1990), 4: 24.

         The discovery of five autograph letters from Chaikovskii to Nápravník. See also *297*, *298*.

[297]   MELIKIANTS, G. 'Spustia sto let v dom Chaikovskogo v Klinu vozvratilis´ ego pis´ma', *Izvestiia* (17 Dec 1994): 2.

         The Klin house-museum's acquisition of the five autograph letters from Chaikovskii to Nápravník.

[298]   KOTRELEVA, D. 'Pis´ma vernulis´ k avtoru spustia 100 let', *Trud* (23 Dec 1994).

VLADIMIR NÁPRAVNÍK (1869–1948)
Son of Eduard Nápravník

[*299*] 'Pis´ma P. I. Chaikovskogo k V. E. Napravniku'. In: *E. F. Napravnik: Avtobiograficheskie, tvorcheskie materialy, dokumenty, pis´ma* (1959): 189–203 [see *294*].

VLADIMIR ODOEVSKII(1803-69)
Composer and writer on music

[*300*] KISELEV, V. 'P. I. Chaikovskii i V. F. Odoevskii', *Sovetskaia muzyka* (1940), 5/6: 138–140 [see *585*].
3 letters from Odoevskii to Chaikovskii (1869).

ALEKSANDR OSTROVSKII (1823–86)
Dramatist, writer and librettist

[*301*] IAKOVLEV, V. V. 'A. N. Ostrovskii v perepiske s russkimi kompozitorami'. In: *A. N. Ostrovskii i russkie kompozitory: Pis´ma*. Pod obshchei red. E. M. Kolosovoi i Vl. Filippova Moskva; Leningrad: Iskusstvo, 1937: 5–42.
On Chaikovskii: 25–30. See also *1993*.

WLADYSLAW PACHULSKI (d. 1919)
Violinist, amateur composer and secretary to Nadezhda von Meck

[*302*] 'Pis´ma P. I. Chaikovskogo V. A. Pakhul´skomu', *Sovetskaia muzyka* (1959), 12: 63–78, music, illus.
7 letters from Chaikovskii to Pachulski (1883–91), taken from photocopies of the originals in the USA. Includes introductory article by V. Tsukkerman, 'Ob odnom pedagogicheskom opyte Chaikovskogo': 63–65.

[*303*] MANN, A. 'Tchaikovsky as a teacher'. In: *Music and civilization: Essays in honor of Paul Henry Lang*. Ed. by Edmon Strainchamps, Maria Rika Maniates and Christopher Hatch. New York; London, 1984: 279–296, music, illus. ISBN: 0–3930–1677–3.

[*304*] 'Neizvestnoe pis´mo', *Muzykal´noe obozrenie* (20 Nov 1992): 8.
The discovery of 1 letter from Chaikovskii to Pachulski (1889), in the Paul Sacher Stiftung archive in Switzerland. See also *305*.

[*305*] VAUNTS, V. 'O sud´be pis´ma: Neizvestnyi Stravinskii', *Muzykal´noe obozrenie* (22 Dec 1992): 12.

EMILIIA PAVLOVSKAIA (1853–1935)
Opera artist at the Mariinskii Theatre in St. Petersburg

[*306*] ZHEGIN, N. T. 'P. I. Chaikovskii i E. K. Pavlovskaia', *Sovetskaia muzyka* (1934), 8: 62–64.
5 letters from Chaikovskii to Pavlovskaia (1884–85).

[*307*] 'Perepiska Chaikovskogo: P. I. Chaikovskii i E. K. Pavlovskaia'. In: *Chaikovskii na moskovskoi stsene* (1940): 311–418 [see *2538*].

PAVEL PERELETSKII
Teacher from Rybinsk

[*308*] 'Avtograf P. I. Chaikovskogo', *Russkii vestnik* (1903), 11: 440–444.
1 letter from Chaikovskii to Pereletskii (1885) [facs.: 441–444].

PAVEL PETERSSEN (1831–95)
Pianist and director of the St. Petersburg branch of the Russian Musical Society

[309]   KISELEV, V. 'Neizvestnyte pis´ma Chaikovskogo i Rimskogo-Korsakova', *Sovetskaia muzyka* (1953), 10: 47–49, illus.

3 letters from Chaikovskii to Peterssen (1893).

NATAL´IA PLESKAIA (b. 1837)
Niece of Lev Davydov

[310]   'Pis´ma P. I. Chaikovskogo', *Sovetskoe iskusstvo* (4 Nov 1938): 4.

8 letters from Chaikovskii to Pleskaia (1879–93).

[311]   'P. I. Chaikovskii–N. A. Plesskaia (1879–1893)'. In: *P. I. Chaikovskii–S. I. Taneev: Pis´ma* (1951): 361–370 [see *154*].

KONSTANTIN POBEDONOSTSEV (1827–1906)
Russian statesman and graduate of the Imperial School of Jurisprudence

[312]   *K. P. Pobedonostsev i ego korrespondenty: Pis´ma i zapiski*. Tom 1, polutom 1. Petrograd: Gosizdat, 1923: 235–403.

5 letters from Chaikovskii to Pobedonostsev (1881–86).

IPPOLIT PRIANISHNIKOV (1847–1921)
Singer (baritone) at the Kiev Opera Theatre, music teacher and opera impressario

[313]   'Pis´mo v redaktsiu', *Odesskii listok* (26 Jun 1896).

1 letter from Chaikovskii (1890).

— [repr.] *Russkaia muzykal´naia gazeta* (Aug 1896), 8: 951–952.

DANIEL RAHTER (1828–91)
German music publisher, with offices in Hamburg and St. Petersburg

[314]   VELIMIROVIČ, M. 'Russian autographs at Harvard', *Notes*, 17 (1960), 4: 556–558, illus.

Includes English tr. and partial facs. of 1 letter from Chaikovskii to Rahter (1889).

DANIIL RATGAUZ (1868–1937)
Poet

[315]   'Pis´ma P. I. Chaikovskogo', *Novosti dnia* (5 Oct 1894),

3 letters from Chaikovskii to Ratgauz (1892–93).

[316]   'Novye pis´ma P. I. Chaikovskogo', *Golos Moskvy* (25 Oct 1911).

3 letters from Chaikovskii to Ratgauz (1893).

— [repr.] *Russkaia muzykal´naia gazeta* (3/10 Jun 1912), 23/24: 531.

[317]   'Interesnoe priobretenie', *Sovetskoe iskusstvo* (9 Jul 1940): 2.

2 letters from Chaikovskii to Ratgauz (1893).

[318]   KLIMENKO-RATGAUZ, T. 'Na slova Ratgauza: Vospominaniia ob ottse', *Daugava* (1986), 5: 97–106, illus.

Memoirs of Daniil Ratgauz's daughter, including extracts from Chaikovskii's correspondence with Ratgauz (1892–93).

SERGEI REMEZOV (b. 1854)
Pianist and music teacher

[319] 'Iz arkhiva K. N. Igumnova', *Sovetskaia muzyka* (1946), 1: 84–89.

9 letters from various persons, including 1 letter from Chaikovskii to Remezov (1893).

NIKOLAI RIMSKII-KORSAKOV (1844–1908)
Composer, conductor and professor at the St. Petersburg Conservatory

[320] RIMSKII-KORSAKOV, A. N. 'Perepiska P. I. Chaikovskogo i N. A. Rimskogo-Korsakova'. In: *Sovetskaia muzyka: 3-i sbornik statei*. Moskva; Leningrad, 1945: 121–148.

32 letters from Chaikovskii and Rimskii-Korsakov (1868–91).

[321] 'Perepiska N. A. Rimskogo-Korsakova s P. I. Chaikovskim (1868–1891)'. In: N. A. Rimskii-Korsakov, *Polnoe sobranie sochinenii: Literaturnye proizvedeniia i perepiska*. Tom 7. Moskva: Muzyka, 1970: 12–64.

VASILII SAFONOV (1852–1918)
Pianist, conductor, professor and director of the Moscow Conservatory

[322] RAVICHER, Ia. I. *Vasilii Il´ich Safonov*. Moskva, 1959.

8 letters from Chaikovskii to Safonov (1886–93): 198–213.

ST. PETERSBURG PHILHARMONIC SOCIETY

[323] *100-letnii iubilei Peterburgskogo Filarmonicheskogo obshchestva*. Sankt Peterburg, 1902: 80.

1 letter from Chaikovskii to the St. Petersburg Philharmonic Society (1887).

VASILII SALIN (1843–1907)
Violinist and former student at the St. Petersburg Conservatory.

[324] [Pis´mo P. I. Chaikovskogo], *Sovetskaia Moldaviia* (27 Mar 1941).

1 letter from Chaikovskii to Salin (1893).

PËTR SHCHUROVSKII (1850–1908)
Composer, conductor and music teacher

[325] 'Perepiska Chaikovskogo: P. I. Chaikovskii i P. A. Shchurovskii'. In: *Chaikovskii na moskovskoi stsene* (1940): 456–459 [see *2538*].

KONSTANTIN SHILOVSKII (1849–93)
Artist, poet and musician

[326] 'Perepiska Chaikovskogo: P. I. Chaikovskii i K. S. Shilovskii'. In: *Chaikovskii na moskovskoi stsene* (1940): 298–310 [see *2538*].

VLADIMIR SHILOVSKII (1852–93)
Student of music theory with Chaikovskii in the 1870s

[327] KISELEV, V. 'Pis´ma P. I. Chaikovskogo k V. S. Shilovskomu', *Sovetskaia muzyka* (1940), 5/6: 141–145, illus. [see *585*].

3 letters from Chaikovskii to Vladimir Shilovskii (1873–79).

ANDREI SHISHKOV (d. 1909)
Manager of the Synod Publishing House

[328]   **K. P. S. 'P. I. Chaikovskii i Moskovskii sinodal´nyi khor'**, *Moskovskie vedomosti* (19 Feb 1902).
1 letter from Chaikovskii to to Shishkov (1886).
— [repr. (abridged)] In: V. Metallov, *Sinodal´noe uchilishche tserkovnogo peniia v ego proshlom i nastoiashchem*. Moskva, 1911: 43–44.

IULIIA SHPAZHINSKAIA (d. 1919)
Pianist, wife of Ippolit Shpazhinskii

[329]   **'P. I. Chaikovskii–Iu. P. Shpazhinskaia (1885–1891)'**. In: *P. I. Chaikovskii–S. I. Taneev: Pis´ma* (1951): 288–360 [see *154*].

[330]   **BEZELIANSKII, Iu. 'Odin den´ oktiabria'**, *Nauka i zhizn´*, 10 (1993): 40–44.
Includes 1 letter from Chaikovskii to Shpazhinskaia (1891).

See also *1772, 1999, 4476*.

IPPOLIT SHPAZHINSKII (1848–1917)
Dramatist and librettist

[331]   **'Pis´ma P. I. Chaikovskogo k I. V. Shpazhinskomu'**, *Kul´tura i teatra* (1921), 6: 38–42.
4 letters from Chaikovskii to Shpazhinskii (1888).

[332]   **LAMEY, B. 'Vier unbekannte Briefe Peter Tschaikowsky's'**, *Allgemeine Musik-Zeitung* (1934), 13: 158–160.
1 letter from Chaikovskii to Ivan Shpazhinskii (1887). German tr. and commentary by B. Lamey.

[333]   **'Perepiska Chaikovskogo: P. I. Chaikovskii i I. V. Shpazhinskii'**. In: *Chaikovskii na moskovskoi stsene* (1940): 419–455 [see *2538*].

FRIEDRICH SIEGER
Musical writer, critic, director of the Frankfurt-am-Main Museum-Gesellschaft

[334]   **[Bisher unbekannter Brief Tschaikowskys]**, *Tschaikowsky-Gesellschaft Miteilungen*, 5 (1998): 11–13.
1 letter from Chaikovskii to Sieger (1891), including facs.

JOSEF SITTARD (1846–1903)
German musicologist, organist, teacher and music critic

[335]   **SIEDENTOPF, H. *Musiker der Spätromantik: Unbekannte Briefe aus dem Nachlaß von Josef und Alfred Sittard*.** Tübingen, 1979: 77.
2 letters from Chaikovskii to Sittard (1888–89).

STEPAN SMOLENSKII (1848–1909)
Choirmaster, and Russian church music historian

[336]   **KORABEL´NIKOVA, L. Z., 'S. Smolenskii—entuziast russkoi khorovoi kul´tury'**, *Sovetskaia muzyka* (1959), 12: 83.
2 letters from Chaikovskii to Smolenskii (1893).

NIKOLAI SOLOV´EV (1846–1916)

Composer, music critic, and professor at the St. Petersburg Conservatory

[337] **ANDRONIKOV, I. 'Pis´mo Chaikovskogo'**, *Sovetskaia muzyka* (1956), 4: 117–121, illus.

A letter from Chaikovskii to Solov´ev (1885), regarding the latter's opera *Cordelia*.

— [repr.] 'Ob odnom pis´me P. I. Chaikovskogo'. In: I. Andronikov, *K muzyke*. Moskva: Sovetskii kompozitor, 1975: 154–164.

VLADIMIR STASOV (1824–1906)

Art historian, critic, and director of the arts section of the St. Petersburg Public Library

[338] **KARENIN, V. 'V. V. Stasov i P. I. Chaikovskii: Neizdannye pis´ma'**, *Russkaia mysl´* (1909), 3: 93–149.

20 letters from Chaikovskii to Stasov (1873–93). With introduction and notes by V. Karenin.

Reviews: A. Izmailova, 'Nov´ i star´', *Ezhegodnik Imperatorskikh teatrov* (1909), 4: 183–184 — 'Perepiska V. V. Stasova s P. I. Chaikovskim', *Russkaia muzykal´naia gazeta* (14/21 Jun 1909): 584–587 — M. Ivanov, 'Stranitsa nedavnego proshlogo', *Novoe vremia* (3 Aug 1909).

— [German tr.]. A. Hess, 'Zwanzig Briefe P. J. Tschaikowskys', *Die Musik* (1908/09), 4: 67–94.

[339] **ALEKSEEV, N. M. 'M. Chaikovskii—V. Komarovoi-Stasovoi'**, *Sovetskaia muzyka* (1965), 5: 38–39.

A letter from Modest Chaikovskii (27 Feb 1909) regarding the publication of correspondence between Chaikovskii and Vladimir Stasov.

VÁCLAV SUK (1861–1933)

Czech violinist, conductor and composer

[340] **REMEZOV, I. *Viacheslav Ivanovich Suk: Materialy k biografii*.** Moskva: Muzgiz, 1933: 6–7.

1 letter from Chaikovskii to Suk (1888), with facs.

— [repr.] In: I. Remezov, *Viacheslav Suk*. Moskva, Leningrad: Muzgiz: 1951: 14.

IOSIF SUPRUNENKO (1861–1936)

Music teacher and singer with the Odessa opera company

[341] **SUPRUNENKO, T. 'Neobychnyi avtograf'**, *Neva* (1959), 5: 223–224.

Concerning a letter from Chaikovskii to Iosif Suprunenko (1893), and his autograph on a restaurant menu.

SERGEI TANEEV (1856–1915)

Composer, pianist, conductor, musicologist and professor/director of the Moscow Conservatory

[342] **'Iz perepiski Chaikovskogo'**, *Russkie vedomosti* (31 Oct 1902).

One letter from Chaikovskii to Taneev (14 Jan 1891).

[343] **'Neizdannaia perepiska P. I. Chaikovskogo s S. I. Taneevym (soobshchil M. Chaikovskii)'**, *Belyi kamen´*, 1 (1907): 57–67.

Includes 2 letters from Chaikovskii to Taneev (1880).

[344] **'Iz neopublikovannoi perepiski P. I. Chaikovskogo s S. I. Taneevym'**, *Maski* (1913/14), 2: 1–7.

Includes 2 letters from Chaikovskii to Taneev (1881).

[345] **Pis´ma P. I. Chaikovskogo i S. Taneeva (1874–1893).** Pod red. M. I. Chaikovskogo. Moskva: P. Iurgenson [1916]. iv, 188 p.

— [repr. (extracts)] *Russkaia muzykal´naia gazeta* (20 Mar 1916), 12: 265–268; (27 Mar 1916), 13: 306–309; (24 Apr 1916), 17: 397–399; (1/8 May 1916), 18/19: 425–429.

Review: E. Gunst, 'Iz perepiski Chaikovskogo s Taneevym', *Maski* (1913/14), 2.

[*346*]   **KISELEV, V. 'Neizdannye pis´ma k S. I. Taneevu'**, *Sovetskaia muzyka* (1937), 6: 77.
          1 letter from Chaikovskii to Taneev (1887).

[*347*]   **'Perepiska (1874–1893)'**. In: *P. I. Chaikovskii–S. I. Taneev: Pis´ma* (1951): 3–202 [see *154*].

[*348*]   **RIETHOF, E. 'Meester en leerling: Een brief van Sergej Tanejev aan Tsjaikovski en Tsjaikovski's antwoord'**, *Mens en Melodie*, 35 (Feb 1980): 85–87.

          See also *4615*.

                              PAVEL TRET´IAKOV (1832–98)
          Founder of the Tret´iakov Gallery in Moscow, chief director of the Moscow branch of the RMS

[*349*]   **BOTKINA, A. M. *Pavel Mikhailovich Tret´iakov v zhizni i iskusstve*.** Moskva, 1951: 198–201.
          Includes 5 letters from Chaikovskii to Tret´iakov and his wife Vera (1882–90).

                              KARL VAL´TS (1846–1929)
                         Stage director for the Moscow Theatres

[*350*]   **'Perepiska Chaikovskogo: P. I. Chaikovskii i K. F. Val´ts'.** In: *Chaikovskii na moskovskoi stsene* (1940): 471–476 [see *2538*]

                          PAULINE VIARDOT-GARCIA (1821–1910)
                    Opera singer (soprano), composer and singing tutor

[*351*]   **'Pis´ma Poliny Virado k russkim znakomym'**, *Sovetskaia muzyka* (1960), 8: 89–98, illus.
          Includes 4 letters from Viardot-Garcia to Chaikovskii (1886–89).

                          IVAN VSEVOLOZHSKII (1835–1909)
                         Director of the Imperial Theatres

[*352*]   **ASAF´EV, B. V. 'K istorii izdaniia i postanovki opery P. I. Chaikovskogo "Pikovaia dama"'**, *Orfei*, 1 (1922): 180–185.
          2 letters from Chaikovskii to Vsevolozhskii (1890).

[*353*]   **'Pis´mo P. I. Chaikovskogo k direktoru Imperatorskikh teatrov I. A. Vsevolozhskomu'.** In: *"Pikovaia dama": Opera, muzyka P. I. Chaikovskogo* (1934): 66–68 [see *3546*].
          1 letter (1890) in connection with the opera *The Queen of Spades*.

[*354*]   **SKVIRSKAIA, T. Z. 'K perepiske P. I. Chaikovskogo s I. A. Vsevolozhskim'.** In: *Peterburgskii muzykal´nyi arkhiv: Sbornik statei i materialov*, vyp. 3, Sankt-Peterburg: Sankt-Peterburgskaia konservatoriia, 1999: 181–189.

[*355*]   **GRADSKII, P. 'Rukopisi Chaikovskogo v kipe makulatury'**, *Vechernii Peterburg* (13 Oct 1995): 6.
          The discovery of letters from Chaikovskii to Vsevolozhskii in a rubbish heap in 1921.
          See also *2029*.

                          RUŽENA VYKOUKALOVÁ-BRADAČEVA
                         Czech opera singer (mezzo–soprano)

[*356*]   **ALEKSEEV, N. 'Posle Prazhskoi prem´ery'**, *Muzykal´naia zhizn´* (1968), 23: 22, illus.
          Extracts from Chaikovskii's correspondence with Vykoukalová-Brádačeva (1892–93).

ALEKSANDR ZILOTI (1863–1945)

Pianist, conductor and professor at the Moscow Conservatory

[357]   **[FINDEIZEN] N. F. 'Iz neizdannoi perepiski P. Chaikovskogo'**, *Russkaia muzykal´naia gazeta* (25 Oct 1908), 43: 928–935; (23 Nov 1908), 47: 1041–1049, illus.

11 letters from Chaikovskii to Ziloti (1887–91).

[358]   **ORLOVA, A. A. 'Perepiska A. I. Ziloti s P. I. Chaikovskim'**. In: *Aleksandr Il´ich Ziloti, 1863–1945: Vospominaniia i pis´ma*. Sost., avt. predisl. i primech. L. M. Kutateladze. Pod red. L. N. Raabena. Leningrad, 1963: 79–176.

SERGEI ZILOTI (1862–1914)

Older brother of Aleksandr Ziloti

[359]   **'Dar muzeiu Chaikovskogo'**, *Vechernii Leningrad* (31 Aug 1967): 3.

The presentation to the Klin House-museum archive of a letter from Chaikovskii to Sergei Ziloti (1889).

2.5. DIARIES AND NOTEBOOKS

2.5.1. Critical Editions

[360]   ***Dnevniki P. I. Chaikovskogo (1873–1891)***. Podgot. k pechati Ip. I. Chaikovskim. Predislovie S. Chemodanova. Primechaniia N. T. Zhegina. Moskva; Petrograd: Gosizdat-Muzsektor, 1923. xii, 294 p, music.

Review: *Sovremennaia muzyka* (1924), 1: 28.

— [repr.] Sankt Peterburg: Ego; Severnyi olen´, 1993. xii, 296 p, music. ISBN: 5–8276–0001–6.

Review: A. Kuznetsov, *Novyi mir* (May 1994): 246–247.

— [English tr.] *The diaries of Tchaikovsky*. Tr. from the Russian, with notes, by Wladimir Lakond. New York: W. W. Norton & Co. [1945]. 365 p, music, illus.

Reviews: M. Brunswick, *Kenyon Review*, 8 (1946), 1/4: 686 — A. J. Swan, *Musical Quarterly*, 32 (Apr 1946), 2: 308.

— [English tr. (rev. ed.)]: Westport, Conn.: Greenwood Press [1973]. 385 p, illus. ISBN: 0–8371–5680–7.

With new index (not included in 1945 ed.).

— [German tr.] *P. I. Tschaikowsky: Die Tagebücher*. Hrsg. und mit einem Vorwort versehen von Ernst Kuhn; Übersetzung und Zwischentexte von Hans-Joachim Grimm. Berlin: E. Kuhn, 1992. ix, 386 p, music, illus. ISBN: 3–928864–00–9.

Reviews: H. Grimm, *Beiträge zur Musikwissenschaft*, 34 (1992): 125–126 — *Neue Musikzeitung*, 41 (Jun/Jul 1992): 57 — *Musik in der Schule* (Nov/Dec 1992), 6: 327–328 — *Orchester*, 41 (1993), 4: 449 — W. Stockmeier, *Musik und Kirche*, 63 (Mar/Jun 1993), 3: 170 — M. Bobeth, *Musica*, 48 (May/Jun 1994), 3: 179.

2.5.2. Diary Extracts

[361]   **BASKIN, V. S. 'Iz dnevnika Chaikovskogo: Ocherk´'**, *Niva* (Nov 1895): 567.

[362]   **RIESEMANN, O. von. 'Die Tagebücher Tschaikowsky's'**, *Neue Musik-Zeitung* (1925), 11.

German tr. of extracts from *Dnevniki P. I. Chaikovskogo* (1923) [see *360*].

[363]   **'Pages from a composer's diary'**, *Pester Lloyd* (1 Jan 1925).

English tr. of diary entries 1886–1888 from *Dnevniki P. I. Chaikovskogo* (1923) [see *360*].

— [repr.] *Littell's Living Age*, 324 (7 Mar 1925): 556–561.

[*364*] 'Aus Zeichnungen eines Musikers: Von P. Tschaikowsky aus Tagesbüchern', *Münchener Neuste Nachrichten* (1927), No. 247.

German tr. of extracts from *Dnevniki P. I. Chaikovskogo* (1923) [see *360*].

[*365*] WILSON, E. 'Mice, headache, rehearsal: Tchaikovsky's diaries', *New Yorker*, 21 (19 Jan 1946): 74–77.

[*366*] 'P. I. Chaikovskii: Otryvok iz dnevnika (1886 g.)', *Teatr i zhizn´* (May 1990), 9: 24–25, illus.

[*367*] RAZHEVA, V. 'Neizvestnye dnevniki Chaikovskogo', *Rossiiskaia muzykal´naia gazeta* (1991), 1: 2.

Publication of an entry from Chaikovskii's diary for 1886–88.

See also *138, 368, 631, 1509, 1532, 1857.*

2.5.3. Notebooks

[*368*] 'Zapisnye knizhki i dnevniki'. In: *Avtografy P. I. Chaikovskogo v arkhive Doma-muzeia v Klinu: Spravochnik* [vyp. 1] (1950): 79–92 [see *102*].

A description of Chaikovskii's surviving notebooks and diaries.

[*369*] VAIDMAN, P. E. 'Zamysly 1887–1888 godov', *Sovetskaia muzyka* (1980), 7: 84–90, illus.

Sketches in Chaikovskii's notebooks for 1887 and 1888. Includes facsimiles.

[*370*] VAIDMAN, P. E. 'Kratkoe opisanie zapisnykh knizhek P. I. Chaikovskogo'. In: *Tvorcheskii arkhiv P. I. Chaikovskogo* (1988): 161–164 [see *114*].

2.6. MEMOIRS

2.6.1. Collections

[*371*] *Na pamiat´ o P. I. Chaikovskom*. Stat´i G. A Larosha i N. D. Kashkina. Moskva: Elizaveta Gerbek, 1894. 62 p, illus.

Recollectons of Chaikovskii and analysis of his music. See also *481*.

[*372*] 'P. I. Chaikovskii v vospominaniiakh', *Birzhevye vedomosti* (24 Oct 1913).

Recollections of Chaikovskii by various individuals on the 20th anniversary of his death.

Contents: See *393, 439, 443, 447, 470, 543, 558.*

[*373*] *Chaikovskii: Vospominaniia i pis´ma*. Pod red. Igoria Glebova. Leningrad: Gos. akad. filarmoniia, 1924. 232 p, music, illus.

Contents: A. K. Glazunov, 'Moe znakomstvo s Chaikovskim': 5–12 [see *448*] — V. P. Pogozhev, 'Vospominaniia o P. I. Chaikovskom': 13–98 [see *515*] — 'Perepiska P. I. Chaikovskogo i E. F. Napravnika (1872–1893)': 99–229 [see *293*].

[*374*] *Vospominaniia o P. I. Chaikovskom*. Sost. E. E. Bortnikova, K. Iu. Davydova, G. A. Pribegina. Red. V. V. Protopopov. Moskva: Gos. muz. izdat., 1962. 459 p, illus.

Review: N. Tumanina, 'Sovremenniki o Chaikovskom', *Sovetskaia muzyka* (1963), 4: 136–138.

— Izd. 2-e, pererab. i dop. Moskva: Muzyka, 1973. 559 p, illus.

— Izd. 3-e, ispr. Moskva: Muzyka, 1979. 572 p, illus.

— Izd. 4-e, ispr. Leningrad: Muzyka, 1980. 477 p, illus.

Contents: See *388, 389, 390, 397, 398, 400, 401, 404, 406, 407, 415, 416, 417, 418, 419, 422, 423, 425, 429, 432, 433, 438, 444, 445, 446, 448, 449, 450, 459, 460, 462, 465, 466, 468, 472, 475, 478, 480, 481, 482,*

483, 485, 488, 489, 491, 493, 495, 497, 498, 505, 507, 508, 510, 511, 512, 515, 516, 519, 523, 525, 530, 533, 535, 536, 537, 538, 540, 544, 547, 548, 552, 553, 555, 1701, 1709.

[375] *Piotr Tchaïkovski: Écrits critiques, lettres, souvenirs de contemporains*. Présentation de V. Kharlamov. Choix des textes et notes d'Olga Sakharova; traduit par Dora Sanadze. Moscou: Radouga [1985]. 382 p, illus. ISBN: 5–05–000379–2.

Memoirs of Chaikovskiis contemporaries, and selections from the composer's musical articles, letters and diaries.

Contents: See *407, 415, 416, 419, 438, 456, 466, 482, 483, 485, 491, 498, 508, 510, 512, 516, 519, 1701, 2181.*

[376] LEBRECHT, N. 'Pyotr (Ilyich) Tchaikovsky (1840–1893)'. In: N. Lebrecht, *The book of musical anecdotes*. New York: Free Press, 1985: 217–222.

Includes short extracts from *405, 462, 480,* and Chaikovskii's letters from 1877.

[377] BROWN, D. *Tchaikovsky remembered*. London; Boston: Faber & Faber, 1993. xxxiv, 248 p, illus. ISBN: 0–571–16866–3 (hbk), 0–571–16867–1 (pbk).

Contents: See *388, 389, 390, 394, 397, 398, 399, 404, 405, 406, 416, 417, 419, 421, 423, 429, 432, 433, 444, 445, 446, 448, 449, 450, 452, 453, 454, 456, 457, 459, 460, 462, 464, 465, 472, 475, 478, 480, 481, 482, 483, 484, 485, 491, 493, 495, 497, 505, 507, 508, 510, 511, 512, 515, 516, 519, 523, 530, 531, 533, 535, 539, 540, 546, 547, 1563, 1566, 1701, 2181, 2200.*

Reviews: *The Times* (6 Dec 1993) — *Brio,* 31 (1994), 1: 54–55 — D. Fermon, *Library Journal,* 119 (15 Feb 1994), 3: 161 — J. Shreffler, *Booklist,* 90 (15 Feb 1994): 1051 — H. Zajaczkowski, *Musical Times,* 135 (Apr 1994): 243 — L. Hughes, *Times Literary Suppl.* (15 Apr 1994): 20 — R. J. Wiley, *Music & Letters,* 76 (Feb 1995), 1: 111–113.

— [repr.] Portland, Oregon: Amadeus Press, 1994. xxxiv, 248 p, illus. ISBN: 0–931340–65–9 (hbk); 0–931340–66–7 (pbk).

— [German tr.] *Peter I. Tschaikowsky im Spiegel seiner Zeit.* Aus der Englische von Tobias Döring. Mainz: Atlantis Musikbuch-Verlassen, 1996. 292 p, illus. ISBN: 3–254–00211–3.

Review: *Orchester,* 45 (1997), 4: 63–64.

[378] KORABEL´NIKOVA, L. 'Uchastniki i svideteli zolotogo veka Rossii', *Muzykal´naia akademiia* (1993), 4: 207–210, illus.

Short extracts from various memoirs of Russian emigré artists.

[379] *Tschaikowsky aus der Nähe*. Kritische Würdigungen und Erinnerungen von Zeitgenossen. Unter anderem mit Beiträgen von Mili Balakirew ... sowie einigen Pressinterviews Peter Tschaikowskys. Ausgewählt, übersetzt und hrsg. von Ernst Kuhn. Berlin: E. Kuhn, 1994. xiv, 301 p. (*Musik konkret*; 7). ISBN: 3–928864–09–2.

Collection of memoirs, articles and interviews.

Contents: See *141, 145, 147, 206, 397, 400, 401, 411, 415, 416, 429, 445, 446, 448, 454, 458, 465, 472, 473, 490, 491, 495, 498, 504, 509, 512, 513, 515, 516, 519, 522, 554, 617, 700, 1159, 1678, 1870, 1924, 1948, 2181, 2200, 2265, 3162, 3194, 3704, 3863, 4362, 4364, 4615, 4633, 4655, 4673, 4674, 4808, 4897, 4922, 4955, 5094, 5303, 5326.*

Reviews: *Musikerziehung,* 48 (1994), 1: 42 — *Neue Musikzeitung,* 43 (Aug/Sep 1994): 28 — *Musikerziehung,* 49 (1996), 3: 136–137 — B. Hiltner, *Musik in der Schule,* 2 (Mar/Apr 1996): 109 — K. Kirchberg, *Musik und Bildung,* 28 (Mar/Apr 1996), 2: 62–63 — K. Grönke, *Die Musikforschung,* 49 (Apr/Jun 1996), 2: 219–220 — *Svenska Tidskrift för Musikforskning,* 79 (1997), 2: 173–174.

[380] POZNANSKY, A. *Tchaikovsky through others' eyes*. Compiled, ed. and with an introduction by Alexander Poznansky; trs. from Russian by Ralph C. Burr Jr and Robert Bird. Bloomington, Indiana: Indiana Univ. Press, 1999. 311 p, illus. ISBN 0–253–35545–0.

A compilation of memoirs and interviews with Chaikovskii.

Contents: See *139, 141, 143, 145, 147, 381, 388, 400, 401, 403, 406, 407, 411, 412, 414, 416, 429, 431, 432, 433, 437, 445, 446, 447, 451, 464, 465, 471, 473, 475, 477, 478, 482, 483, 485, 487, 492, 493, 495, 501, 504, 506, 515, 517, 521, 524, 525, 527, 529, 541, 542, 544, 551, 552, 554, 1961, 2181, 2200.*

Review: *Clavier,* 38 (Oct 1999): 2.

See also *183, 618, 1610, 1701, 1709.*

2.6.2. Individual

"V. A."

Former student at the Moscow Conservatory

[*381*] **V. A. 'Iz vospominanii o N. G. Rubinshteine i Moskovskoi konservatorii'**, *Russkii arkhiv*, 3 (1897), 463–470.

Includes the author's recollections of Chaikovskii at the Moscow Conservatory.

— [English tr. (abridged)] In: A. Poznansky, *Tchaikovsky through others' eyes* (1999): 63–64 [see *380*].

SERGEI ANDREEVSKII (1848–1919)

Writer and critic

[*382*] **ANDREEVSKII, S. 'Iz vospominanii: P. I. Chaikovskii'**, *Nash vek* (14 Jun 1918).

ANNA ALEKSANDROVA-LEVENSON (1856–1930)

Pianist and Chaikovskii's student at the Moscow Conservatory

[*383*] **ALEKSANDROVA-LEVENSON, A. Ia. 'Stranichka iz vospominanii o P. I. Chaikovskom'**, *Tomskii Teatral* (Mar 1906), 3/4: 3–5.

ALEKSANDR AMFITEATROV (1862–1938)

Writer and art critic

[*384*] **AMFITEATROV, A. V. 'Vstrecha s P. I. Chaikovskim'**, *Segodnia* (13 Nov 1933).

[*385*] **AMFITEATROV, A. V. 'P. I. Chaikovskii i ego druz´ia'**, *Segodnia* (24 Nov 1933).

[*386*] **AMFITEATROV, A. V. 'Prizraki slavnogo proshlogo: Nik. Rubinshtein i P. Chaikovskii'**, *Segodnia* (25 Jun, 26 Jun, 27 Jun 1937).

See also *1968*.

ALEKSANDRA AMFITEATROVA-LEVITSKAIA (1858–1947)

Soprano and former student at the Moscow Conservatory

[*387*] **AMFITEATROVA-LEVITSKAIA, A. N. 'Pervyi spektakl' "Evgeniia Onegina"'**. In: *Chaikovskii i teatr* (1940): 140–166 [see *2458*].

— [repr.] *Komsomol´skaia pravda* (6 May 1940): 3 [see *862*].

[*388*] **AMFITEATROVA-LEVITSKAIA, A. N. 'Vospominaniia'**. In: *Vospominaniia o P. I. Chaikovskom* (1962): 154–156 [see *374*].

The author's recollections (written in 1940) of her studies in Chaikovskii's classes at the Moscow Conservatory during the 1870s.

— [repr. (abridged)] 'Chaikovskii—uchitel´'. In: *Vospominaniia o P. I. Chaikovskom*, 2-e izd. (1973): 77–80; 3-e izd. (1979): 78–81; 4-e izd. (1980): 66–68 [see *374*].

— [English tr. (abridged)] In: D. Brown, *Tchaikovsky remembered* (1993): 33–34 [see *377*].

— [English tr. (abridged)] In: A. Poznansky, *Tchaikovsky through others' eyes* (1999): 61–62 [see *380*].

[*389*] **AMFITEATROVA-LEVITSKAIA, A. N. 'Vospominaniia o vstrechakh s Chaikovskim v Tiflise'**. In: *Vospominaniia o P. I. Chaikovskom* (1962): 256–259 [see *374*].

The singer's meeting with Chaikovskii in Tiflis in 1890 (written in 1940).

— [repr.] In: *Vospominaniia o P. I. Chaikovskom*, 2-e izd. (1973): 283–286; 3-e izd. (1979): 284–287; 4-e izd. (1980): 241–243 [see *374*].

— [English tr. (abridged)] In: D. Brown, *Tchaikovsky remembered* (1993): 93, 179 [see *377*].

MARIA ANDERSON (1870–1944)
Ballerina at the Imperial Theatres in St. Petersburg

[*390*]   **ANDERSON, M. K. 'Vstrechi s P. I. Chaikovskim'.** In: *Vospominaniia o P. I. Chaikovskom*, 2-e izd. (1973): 237–240 [see *374*].

The author's memoirs (written in 1943) of her encounters with Chaikovskii while performing in his ballets (1889–93).

— [repr.] In: *Vospominaniia o P. I. Chaikovskom*, 3-e izd. (1979): 238–241; 4-e izd. (1980): 202–204 [see *374*].

— [repr. (abridged)] In: O. Ovechkina, 'Khraniatsia v arkhive', *Vechernii Leningrad* (11 Apr 1991): 3, illus.

— [English tr. (abridged)] In: D. Brown, *Tchaikovsky remembered* (1993): 81–82 [see *377*].

IOSIF ANDRONIKASHVILI (1855–1928)
Duke, musician and photographer

[*391*]   **ANDRONIKASHVILI, I. Z. 'Vypiska iz memuarov'.** In: Sh. S. Aslanshvili, *P. I. Chaikovskii v Gruzii* (1940): 27–31 [see *1770*].

WILLIAM APTHORP (1848–1913)
American musician

[*392*]   **APTHORP, W. 'Tchaikovsky in Paris'.** In: W. Apthorp, *By the way: Being a collection of short essays on music and art in general, taken from the program-books of the Boston Symphony Orchestra.* Vol. 2. Boston: Copeland and Day, 1898: 43–47.

The author's recollections of a concert conducted by Chaikovskii in Paris during the season 1890–91.

MIKHAIL ASHKINAZI (1851–1914)
Journalist

[*392a*]   **DELINES, M. [ASHKINAZI, M.] 'Une institutrice française',** *Le Temps* (23 Nov 1896).

Concerning Chaikovskii's childhood governess Fanny Dürbach.

— [Russian tr. (abridged)] 'Guvernantka Chaikovskogo', *Novosti i birzhevaia gazeta* (14 Nov 1896)

LEOPOLD AUER (1845–1930)
Violinist, conductor and professor at the St. Petersburg Conservatory

[*393*]   **AUER, L. 'P. I. Chaikovskii v vospominaniiakh',** *Birzhevye vedomosti* (24 Oct 1913) [see *372*].

[*394*]   **AUER, L. 'Tchaikovsky and the new Russian school'.** In: L. Auer, *My long life in music.* New York: F. A. Stokes, 1923: 139–140, 202–235, illus.

— [repr.] London: Duckworth, 1924: 139–140, 202–235, illus.

— [repr. (abridged)]. In: D. Brown, *Tchaikovsky remembered* (1993): 182–183 [see *377*].

— [Russian tr.] 'Chaikovskii i novaia russkaia shkola'. In: L. Auer, *Sredi muzykantov.* [Leningrad]: Izdat. Sabashnikovykh, 1927: 105–109.

[*395*]   **AUER, L. 'The deaths of Tchaikovsky and Rubinstein'.** In: L. Auer, *My long life in music.* New York: F. A. Stokes, 1923: 284–294, illus.

— [repr.] London: Duckworth, 1924: 202–235, illus.

— [Russian tr.] 'Smert´ Chaikovskogo i Rubinshteina'. In: L. Auer, *Sredi muzykantov.* [Leningrad]: Izdat. Sabashnikovykh, 1927: 138–139.

NIKOLAI AV´ERINO (1872–1948)
Violinist

[*396*]   AV´ERINO, N. K. 'Moi vospominaniia o P. I. Chaikovskom', *Vozrozhdenie* (Jul/Aug 1951), 16: 97–
106.

LÉON BAKST (1866–1924)
Painter, illustrator and theatre designer

[*397*]   **BAKST, L. 'Tschaikowsky aux Ballets russes'**, *Comœdia* (9 Oct 1921).

Bakst's encounter with Chaikovskii during rehersals for *The Sleeping Beauty* in 1890.

—   [English tr. (abridged)] In: D. Brown, *Tchaikovsky remembered* (1993): 82–83 [see *377*].

—   [German tr.] 'Tschaikowskys Ballett "Dornröschen"'. In: *Tschaikowsky aus der Nähe* (1994): 173–174 [see *379*].

—   [Russian tr.] 'Chaikovskii v russkikh baletakh' (tr. K. Davydova), *Sovetskaia muzyka* (1970), 9: 80–82.

—   [Russian tr.] In: *Vospominaniia o P. I. Chaikovskom*, 2-e izd. (1973): 235–236; 3-e izd. (1979): 236–237; 4-e izd. (1980): 200–201 [see *374*].

"BEMOL´"
Correspondent for the newspaper *Novoe vremia*

[*398*]   **BEMOL´. 'Chaikovskii dirizhiruet oratoriei "Vavilonskoe stolpotvorenie"'**, *Novoe vremia* (6 Nov 1893) [suppl.]: 2–3.

Chaikovskii conducting a performance of Anton Rubinstein's cantata *The Tower of Babel* in St. Petersburg in 1889.

—   [repr.] 'Iz vospominanii o P. I. Chaikovskom'. In: *Vospominaniia o P. I. Chaikovskom* (1962): 169–175; 2-e izd. (1973): 265–269; 3-e izd. (1979): 266–270; 4-e izd. (1980): 226–229 [see *374*].

—   [English tr. (abridged)] In: D. Brown, *Tchaikovsky remembered* (1993): 123–126 [see *377*].

FRANCESCO BERGER (1834–1933)
Pianist, composer, and secretary of the London Philharmonic Society

[*399*]   **BERGER, F. 'Some musical celebraties I have known: Tschaikowsky'**. In: F. Berger, *Reminiscences, impressions, anecdotes*. London: Sampson Low, Marson & Co. [1913]: 87–90, illus.

Berger's meetings with Chaikovskii during his visits to England.

—   [repr. (abridged)] In: D. Brown, *Tchaikovsky remembered* (1993): 186–187 [see *377*].

VASILII BERTENSON (1853–1933)
Physician

[*400*]   **BERTENSON, V. B. 'Za tridtsat´ let´: Pëtr i Modest Chaikovskie. Listki iz vospominanii'**, *Istoricheskii vestnik*, 128 (Jun 1912): 806–814.

—   [repr. (excs.)] 'D–r V. Bertenson o Chaikovskom', *Russkaia muzykal´naia gazeta* (17/24 Jun 1912), 25/26: 531–532, 551–559.

—   [repr.] 'Pëtr i Modest Chaikovskie'. In: V. B. Bertenson, *Za 30 let´: Listki iz vospominanii*. Sankt Peterburg: A. S. Suvorin, 1914: 89–99.

—   [repr. (abridged)] 'Listki iz vospominanii'. In: *Vospominaniia o Chaikovskom*, 2-e izd. (1973): 396–402; 3-e izd. (1979): 397–403; 4-e izd. (1980): 338–343 [see *374*].

—   [repr. (extract)] 'Meshok iablok i oblako vaty', *Vechernii Peterburg* (6 May 1994): 3.

—   [English tr. (abridged)] In: S. Bertensson, 'The truth about the mysterious death of Peter Ilyich Tschaikowsky' (1940) [see *2214*].

—   [English tr. (abridged)] In: A. Poznansky, *Tchaikovsky through others' eyes* (1999): 181–186, 256–257 [see *380*].

—   [German tr.] 'Aus meinen Erinnerungen'. In: *Tschaikowsky aus der Nähe* (1994): 257–263 [see *379*].

VASILII BESSEL´ (1843–1907)

Music publisher, violist, and contemporary of Chaikovskii's at the St. Petersburg Conservatory.

[401] **BESSEL´, V. V. 'Moi vospominaniia o Chaikovskom'**, *Ezhegodnik Imperatorskikh teatorv, sezon 1896/1897* (1898), 1 [suppl.]: 19–43.

Recollections of the composer from his studies at the St. Petersburg Conservatory in 1862 up to the premiere of the Symphony No. 6 in 1893. Includes extracts from Chaikovskii's correspondence with Bessel´.

— [offprint] *Iz moikh vospominanii o P. I. Chaikovskom*. Sankt Peterburg: Izdat. Ezhegodnika Imperatorskikh teatrov, 1898. 26 p.

— [repr. (abridged). In: *Vospominaniia o P. I. Chaikovskom* (1962): 406–410 [see *374*].

— [English tr. (abridged)] In: A. Poznansky, *Tchaikovsky through others' eyes* (1999): 32–34 [see *380*].

— [German tr. (abridged)] 'Die Moskauer Verlagsfirma war stärker als wir'. In: *Tschaikowsky aus der Nähe* (1994): 113–120 [see *379*].

See also *3404*.

VASILII BEZEKIRSKII (1835–1919)

Composer, violinist, concert master of the Bol´shoi Theatre Orchestra

[402] **BEZEKIRSKII, V. 'Sovremenniki o P. I. Chaikovskom'**, *Teatr i zhizn´* (25 Oct 1913): 11.

JULIUS BLOCK (1858–1934)

American businessman

[403] **BLOCK, J. H. 'How I came to know Tchaikofsky'.** In: J. H. Block, *Mortals and immortals: Edison, Nikisch, Tchaikofsky, Tolstoy: Episodes under three Tzars*. Bermuda: W. E. Block [distrib. New Haven, Conn.: Yale Univ. Library, 1965]: 26–49.

— [repr.] In: J. H. Block, *Mortals, immortals, life under three Tsars. Music, literature, technology, social, economy, revolutions*. With an introduction by Walter C. Block. Rockville, Md. [Kabel publishers, 1992]: 35–48, illus.

— [repr. (abridged)] In: A. Poznansky, *Tchaikovsky through others' eyes* (1999): 157–161 [see *380*].

— [Russian tr. (abridged)] 'Iu. I. Blok: Vospominaniia o P. I. Chaikovskom' (perevod s angl. O. M. Smirnovoi, publikatsii L. Z. Korabel´nikovoi). In: *P. I. Chaikovskii: Zabytoe i novoe* (1995): 103–116 [see *598*].

ALINA BRIULLOVA (1849–1932)

Mother of Nikolai Konradi (pupil of Modest Chaikovskii)

[404] **BRIULLOVA, A. N. 'Vospominaniia o P. I. Chaikovskom'.** In: *Vospominaniia o P. I. Chaikovskom* (1962): 299–319 [see *374*].

The author's recollections (written in 1929) from her first meetings with Chaikovskii in the 1870s, up to his death in 1893.

— [repr.] In: *Vospominaniia o P. I. Chaikovskom*, 2-e izd. (1973): 123–139; 3-e izd. (1979): 124–140; 4-e izd. (1980): 106–119 [see *374*].

— [English tr. (abridged)] In: D. Brown, *Tchaikovsky remembered* (1993): 15–16, 92, 101–102, 108, 161–162, 165 [see *377*].

ANNA BRODSKAIA (b. 1855)

Wife of Adolf Brodskii

[405] **BRODSKY [BRODSKAIA], A. *Recollections of a Russian home*.** Manchester; London, 1904: 153–167.

Chaikovskii's visits to the Brodskii's home in Lepzig in the late 1880s. Includes accounts of his encounters with Brahms and Grieg.

— [repr. (abridged)] In: D. Brown, *Tchaikovsky remembered* (1993): 138–142, 167 [see *377*].

— [repr. (extract)] In: N. Lebrecht, *The book of musical anecdotes* (1985) [see *376*].

— [Russian tr. (abridged) by V. Nest´ev] In: 'Iz vospominanii', *Sovetskaia muzyka* (1990), 6: 97.

ISAAK BUKINIK (1867–1942)
Violinist and teacher

[*406*]   BUKINIK, I. E. 'Kontserty P. I. Chaikovskogo v Khar´kove (po lichnym vospominaniiam)'. In: *Vospominaniia o P. I. Chaikovskom* (1962): 213–232 [see *374*].

Concerns the rehearsals and feast in honour of the composer during his conducting tour in Khar´kov in Mar 1893.

— [repr.] In: *Vospominaniia o P. I. Chaikovskom*, 2-e izd. (1973): 341–354; 3-e izd. (1979): 342–355; 4-e izd. (1980): 290–301 [see *374*].

— [Dutch tr.] 'Tsjaikovski dirigeert in Charkow: Herinneringen van Isaak J. Boekinik, violist en concertmeester van het Operaorkest von Charkow', *Mens en Melodie*, 34 (Aug 1979): 286–290, illus.

— [English tr. (abridged)] In: D. Brown, *Tchaikovsky remembered* (1993): 130–134, 197 [see *377*].

— [English tr. (abridged)] In: A. Poznansky, *Tchaikovsky through others' eyes* (1999): 222–229 [see *380*].

MIKHAIL BUKINIK (1872–1947)
Cellist and music critic

[*407*]   BUKINIK, M. E. 'Moi vospominaniia o P. I. Chaikovskom', *Novyi zhurnal*, 28 (1952): 238–247.

Recollections of concerts conducted by the composer, and how the news of his death was received in Moscow.

— [repr. (abridged)] '25 oktiabria 1893 goda'. In: *Vospominaniia o P. I. Chaikovskom*, 2-e izd. (1973): 406–411; 3-e izd. (1979): 407–413; 4-e izd. (1980): 346–351 [see *374*].

— [English tr. (abridged)] In: A. Poznansky, *Tchaikovsky through others' eyes* (1999): 217–218 [see *380*].

— [French tr. (abridged)] 'Le 25 octobre 1893'. In: *Piotr Tchaïkovski: Écrits critiques, lettres, souvenirs de contemporains* (1985): 314–319 [see *375*].

WILLY BURMESTER (1869–1933)
German violinst

[*408*]   BURMESTER, W. 'Peter Tschaikowsky und Hans von Bülow'. In: W. Burmester, *Fünfzig Jahre Künstlerleben*. Berlin: A. Scherl [1926]: 62–66.

— [English tr.] 'Peter Tchaikovsky and Hans von Bülow'. In: W. Burmester, *Fifty years as a concert violinist*. Tr. from the German by Roberta Franke, in collaboration with Samuel Wolf. Linthicum Heights, Md.: Swand [1975]: 45–47.

MARIE ČERVINKOVÁ-RIEGROVÁ (1854–95)
Czech writer, translator and librettist

[*409*]   KUNA, M. 'Unknown document on P. I. Tchaikovsky in Prague', *Music News from Prague* (1979), 7: 7.

Extracts from Červinková-Riegrová's notebook.

— [Russian tr. by E. Anikst] 'Chaikovskii v Prage: Novye dokumental´nye materialy', *Muzykal´naia zhizn´* (Dec 1980), 23: 17, illus.

ANTONINA CHAIKOVSKAIA (1849–1917)
Wife of the composer

[*410*]   CHAIKOVSKAIA, A. I. 'U vdovy P. I. Chaikovskogo', *Peterburgskaia gazeta* (5 Dec 1893).

[*411*]   CHAIKOVSKAIA, A. I. 'Iz vospominanii vdovy P. I. Chaikovskogo', *Peterburgskaia gazeta* (3 Apr 1894).

— [repr.] 'Vospominaniia vdovy P. I. Chaikovskogo', *Russkaia muzykal´naia gazeta* (20 Oct 1913), 42: 915–927.

— [repr.] 'Vospominaniia A. I. Chaikovskogo'. In: V. Sokolov, *Antonina Chaikovskaia: Istoriia zabytoi zhizni* (1994): 263–274 [see *1887*].

— [English tr.] In: A. Poznansky, *Tchaikovsky through others' eyes* (1999): 113–121 [see *380*].

— [German tr.] 'Sich selbste nannte er "eine Mischung aus Kind und Greis"'. In: *Tschaikowsky aus der Nähe* (1994): 31–41 [see *379*].

PRASKOV´IA CHAIKOVSKAIA (1864–1956)
Wife of the composer's brother Anatolii

[*412*]   **[CHAIKOVSKAIA, P. V.] 'Mme. Anatol Tchaikovsky: Recollections of Tchaikovsky'**, *Music & Letters*, 21 (Apr 1940), 2: 103–109.

— [repr.] In: O. Zoff, *Great composers through the eyes of their contemporaries* Ed. by Otto Zoff; tr. and assistant ed. Phoebe Rogoff Cave. New York: E. P. Dutton [1951]: 375–383.

— [Russian tr. (abridged)] In: G. Sh[neerson], 'Za rubezhom: Vospominaniia P. V. Chaikovskoi', *Sovetskaia muzyka* (1940), 5/6: 152–153 [see *585*].

ANATOLII CHAIKOVSKII (1850–1915)
Younger brother of the composer

[*413*]   **'U A. I. Chaikovskogo. U V. S. Krivenko. V Ushchilishche Pravovedeniia'**, *Peterburgskaia gazeta* (25 Oct 1903).

Mainly an interview with Anatolii Chaikovskii, with shorter contributions from Modest Chaikovskii, the journalist and theatre-lover V. S. Krivenko, and officials from the School of Jurisprudence in St. Petersburg.

IPPOLIT CHAIKOVSKII (1843–1927)
Younger brother of the composer

[*414*]   **CHAIKOVSKII, I. I. 'Epizody iz moei zhizni'**, *Istoricheskii vestnik*, 131 (1913): 73–74.

Recalling the death of his mother in 1854.

— [English tr. (abridged)] In: A. Poznansky, *Tchaikovsky through others' eyes* (1999): 12–13 [see *380*].

[*415*]   **CHAIKOVSKII, I. I. 'Vospominaniia o prebyvanii P. I. Chaikovskogo v Taganroge i Odesse'**. In: *Vospominaniia o P. I. Chaikovskom* (1962): 206–212 [see *374*].

Ippolit's recollections (written in 1896) of Chaikovskii's visits to Taganrog during the 1880s, and a meeting between them in Odessa in 1893.

— [repr.] In: *Vospominaniia o P. I. Chaikovskom*, 2-e izd. (1973): 355–359; 3-e izd. (1979): 356–360; 4-e izd. (1980): 302–305 [see *374*].

— [repr.] In: B. Ia. Anshakov, *Brat´ia Chaikovskie* (1981): 59–64 [see *1872*].

— [French tr.] 'A Taganrog et Odessa'. In: *Piotr Tchaïkovski: Écrits critiques, lettres, souvenirs de contemporains* (1985): 300–304 [see *375*].

— [German tr.] 'Erinnerungen an die Aufenthalte meines Bruders in Taganrog und Odessa"'. In: *Tschaikowsky aus der Nähe* (1994): 25–30 [see *379*].

MODEST CHAIKOVSKII (1850–1916)
Writer, dramatist and younger brother of the composer

[*416*]   **CHAIKOVSKII, M. I. ['Iz rannikh vospominanii o brate Petre']**. In: *Vospominaniia o P. I. Chaikovskom* (1962): 399–405 [see *374*].

Extracts from Modest's unpublished autobiography (c. 1905), concerning the composer's early life

— [repr. (abridged)] In: *Vospominaniia o P. I. Chaikovskom*, 2-e izd. (1973): 37–40; 3-e izd. (1979): 38–42; 4-e izd. (1980): 33–36 [see *374*].

— [English tr. (abridged)] In: D. Brown, *Tchaikovsky remembered* (1993): 16–18 [see *377*].

— [English tr. (expanded)] In: A. Poznansky, *Tchaikovsky through others' eyes* (1999): 19–26, 82 [see *380*].

— [French tr.] 'Mes premiers souvenirs de mon frère Piotr'. In: *Piotr Tchaïkovski: Écrits critiques, lettres, souvenirs de contemporains* (1985): 186–190 [see *375*].

— [German tr.] 'Frühe Erinnerungen an meinen Bruder Petja'. In: *Tschaikowsky aus der Nähe* (1994): 19–20 [see *379*].

See also *1699, 1700, 1717*.

VIKTOR CHECHOTT (1846–1917)
Russian pianist, composer and music critc

[*417*] **CHECHOTT, V. A. 'Chaikovskii v Kieve'**, *Kievlianin* (6 Sep 1889).
Chaikovskii's attendence at a performance of *Evgenii Onegin* in Kiev in 1889.

— [repr.] In: *Vospominaniia o P. I. Chaikovskom*, 4-e izd. (1980): 412 [see *374*].

— [English tr. (abridged)] In: D. Brown, *Tchaikovsky remembered* (1993): 146 [see *377*].

MARIIA CHEKHOVA (1863–1957)
Sister of Anton Chekhov

[*418*] **CHEKHOVA, M. P. 'A. P. Chekhov i P. I. Chaikovskii'**. In: M. P. Chekhova, *Iz dalekogo proshlogo*. Zapis´ N. A. Sysoeva. Moskva: Gos. izdat. khudozh. literatury, 1966: 57–60, illus.

— [repr.] In: *Vospominaniia o P. I. Chaikovskom*, 2-e izd. (1973): 241–243; 3-e izd. (1979): 242–244; 4-e izd. (1980): 205–207 [see *374*].

DAVID CHERNOMORDIKOV (1869–1947)
Composer, pianist and teacher

[*419*] **CHERNOMORDIKOV, D. A. 'Vystupleniia P. I. Chaikovskogo v Parizhe: Iz zapisok o proshlom'**, *Sovetskaia muzyka* (1940), 5/6: 149–150 [see *585*].
Chaikovskii conducting a performance of his own works in Paris in Feb 1888.

— [repr.] In: *Vospominaniia o P. I. Chaikovskom* (1962): 233–237; 2-e izd. (1973): 287–289; 3-e izd. (1979): 288–290; 4-e izd. (1980): 244–246 [see *374*].

— [English tr. (abridged)] In: D. Brown, *Tchaikovsky remembered* (1993): 120 [see *377*].

— [French tr.] 'P. I. Tchaïkovski à Paris'. In: *Piotr Tchaïkovski: Écrits critiques, lettres, souvenirs de contemporains* (1985): 272–274 [see *375*].

ZAKHARII CHIKHIKVADZE (1862–1930)
Georgian choirmaster

[*420*] **CHIKHIKVADZE, Z. I. 'Chaikovskii: Vospominaniia'**, *Teatri da tskhovreda* (1915), 2: 3; 8: 11–12.
Text in Georgian.

— [Russian tr.] 'Vospominaniia o vstreche' (tr. D. Mshvelidze), *Muzykal´nye kadry* (7 May 1940) [see *873*].

— [Russian tr. (offprint)] Z. I. Chkhikvadze, *P. I. Chaikovskii: Vospominaniia*. Perevod D. Mshvelidze. Lit. obrab. A. Ravikovich. Leningrad: Gos. konservatoriia, 1940. 13 p.

— [Russian tr.] 'Vospominaniia o P. I. Chaikovskom' (perevod i vvodnaia stat´ia I. Bakhtadze, N. Dimitriadi), *Literaturnaia Gruziia* (1990), 6: 201–213.

— [Russian tr. (repr.)] 'Kompozitor P. I. Chaikovskogo: Vospominaniia'. In: *Chaikovskii: Voprosy istorii i teorii* (1991): 31–38 [see *593*].

With introductory article by B. I. Rabinovich: 'Neizvestnaia stranitsa biografii Chaikovskogo': 27–31.

FREDERIC COWEN (1852–1935)
English conductor

[*421*] **COWEN, F. *My art and my friends***. London: Edward Arnold, 1913: 148–149.
On Chaikovskii's visit in London in 1888.

— [repr. (abridged)] In: D. Brown, *Tchaikovsky remembered* (1993): 185 [see *377*].

"D."

Correspondent of the newspaper *Peterburgskii listok*

[422]   D. 'Iz nedavnikh vospominanii', *Peterburgskii listok* (28 Oct 1893).

The composer's visit to Odessa in Jan 1893.

— [repr.] In: *Vospominaniia o P. I. Chaikovskom*, 2-e izd. (1973): 362–363; 3-e izd. (1979): 363–365; 4-e izd. (1980): 308–309 [see *374*].

WALTER DAMROSCH (1862–1930)

American conductor, pianist and composer

[423]   DAMROSCH, W. *My musical life*. New York: C. Scribner's Sons, 1923: 143–146.

Includes Damrosch's accounts of meetings with Chaikovskii during his concert tours of the America in 1891 and Britain in 1893.

— [repr]. In: D. Brown, *Tchaikovsky remembered* (1993): 128, 183, 197–198 [see *377*].

— [Russian tr. (extracts)] G. Shneerson, 'Chaikovskii v Amerike', *Sovetskaia muzyka* (1940), 10: 90–91.

— [Russian tr. (abridged)] 'Vstrechi s Chaikovskim v Amerike i Anglii'. In: *Vospominaniia o P. I. Chaikovskom* (1962): 238–240; 2-e izd. (1973): 316–317; 3-e izd. (1979): 317–318; 4-e izd. (1980): 268–269 [see *374*].

ALEKSANDR DAVYDOV (1872–1944)

Singer

[424]   DAVYDOV, A. M. 'German'. In: *Chaikovskii i teatr* (1940): 211–223 [see *2458*].

The singer's introduction to Chaikovskii in connection with the staging of *The Queen of Spades* in Kiev in 1890.

— [rev. repr.] 'Obraz Germana', *Teatr* (1940), 5: 63–70, illus.

[425]   DAVYDOV, A. M. 'Eto bylo v Kieve...', *Kurortnaia gazeta* (6 May 1940).

Another account of the singer's introduction to Chaikovskii.

— [repr.] 'Nezabyvaemye vstrechi', *Leningradskaia pravda* (6 May 1940): 3.

— [repr.] 'Moia vstrecha s P. I. Chaikovskom'. In: *Vospominaniia o P. I. Chaikovskom* (1962): 184; 2-e izd. (1973): 305–308; 3-e izd. (1979): 306–309; 4-e izd. (1980): 258–260 [see *374*].

IURII DAVYDOV (1876–1965)

Composer's nephew

[426]   DAVYDOV, Iu. L. 'Vospominaniia o Petre Il´iche Chaikovskom', *Ogonek* (1940), 11: 14–15.

Davydov's childhood recollections of his uncle, 1882–93.

[427]   DAVYDOV, Iu. L. 'Vospominaniia o P. I. Chaikovskom', *Udmurtskaia pravda* (10 Jun 1940).

[428]   DAVYDOV, Iu. L. 'Poledenie desiat´ let zhizni P. I. Chaikovskogo v moikh vospominaniiakh'. In: Iu. L. Davydov, *Zapiski o P. I. Chaikovskom* (1962): 59–84 [see *1869*].

[429]   DAVYDOV, Iu. L. 'Poslednie dni zhizni P. I. Chaikovskogo'. In: *Vospominaniia o P. I. Chaikovskom*, 2-e izd. (1973): 382–395 [see *374*]

— [repr.] In: *Vospominaniia o P. I. Chaikovskom*, 3-e izd. (1979): 383–396; 4-e izd. (1980): 326–337 [see *374*].

— [repr.] In: B. Ia. Anshakov, *Brat´ia Chaikovskie* (1981): 64–73 [see *1872*].

— [Dutch tr. (abridged)] *Mens en melodie*, 36 (May 1981): 203–212.

— [English tr. (abridged)] In: D. Brown, *Tchaikovsky remembered* (1993): 209–211 [see *377*].

— [English tr. (abridged)] In: A. Holden, *Tchaikovsky* (1995): 446–449 [see *1554*].

— [English tr. (abridged)] In: A. Poznansky, *Tchaikovsky through others' eyes* (1999): 254–256 [see *380*].

— [German tr.] 'Die letzten Tage im Leben Tschaikowskys nach seiner Ankunft in Petersburg'. In: *Tschaikowsky aus der Nähe* (1994): 242–256 [see *379*].

[*430*]   SENIOR, E. 'The man who knew Tchaikovsky', *Music & Musicians*, 3 (Jan 1955): 18–19, illus.

ANTON DOOR (1833–1919)

Pianist and professor at the Moscow and Vienna Conservatories

[*431*]   DOOR, A. K. 'Tschaikowski erinnerungen', *Neue Freie Presse* ([18]/30 Mar 1901).
— [English tr. (abridged)] In: A. Poznansky, *Tchaikovsky through others' eyes* (1999): 218–219 [see *380*].
— [Russian tr.] 'Vospominaniia o P. I. Chaikovskom', *Moskovskie vedomosti* (28 Mar 1901).
— [Russian tr. (repr.)] 'P. I. Chaikovskii v vospominaniiakh Doora', *Muzyka i penie*, 8 (1901), 10: 4–5.

KONSTANTIN DUMCHEV (1879–1948)

Violinist and teacher

[*432*]   DUMCHEV, K. M. 'Vstrechi', *Znamia kommuny* [Novocherkassk] (6 May 1940).
Dumchev's encounters with Chaikovskii in Odessa in Jan 1893.
— [repr.] In: *Vospominaniia o P. I. Chaikovskom* (1962): 211–213; 4-e izd. (1980): 417 [see *374*].
— [English tr. (abridged)] In: D. Brown, *Tchaikovsky remembered* (1993): 97 [see *377*].
— [English tr.] In: A. Poznansky, *Tchaikovsky through others' eyes* (1999): 221–222 [see *380*].

FANNY DÜRBACH (1822–1901)

Composer's childhood governess

[*433*]   DÜRBACH, F. [Vospominaniia]. In: M. I. Chaikovskii, 'Detstvo i otrochestvo P. I. Chaikovskogo' (1896) [see *1699*].
A compilation of extracts from letters and memoirs written by Fanny Dürbach for Modest Chaikovskii between 1894 and 1896.
— [rev. repr.] In: M. I. Chaikovskii, 'Detskie gody P. I. Chaikovskogo' (1900) [see *1701*].
— [rev. repr.] In: *Vospominaniia o P. I. Chaikovskom* (1962): 389–394 [see *374*].
— [repr.] 'Vospominaniia M-elle Fanny'. In: *P. I. Chaikovskii: Gody detstva* (1983): 91–97 [see *1712*].
— [repr. (abridged)] In: M. Katina, "Eto byl stekliannyi rebënok...": Vospominaniia guvernantki P. I. Chaikovskogo', *Sem´ia i shkola* (1990), 5: 52–53 [see *951*].
— [repr.] 'M-elle Fanny Durbach'. In: *P. I. Chaikovskii: Zabytoe i novoe* (1995): 154–158 [see *598*].
— [English tr. (abridged)] In: O. Zoff, *Great composers through the eyes of their contemporaries*. Ed. by Otto Zoff; tr. and assistant ed., Phoebe Rogoff Cave. New York: E. P. Dutton [1951]: 365–387.
— [English tr. (abridged)] In: D. Brown, *Tchaikovsky remembered* (1993): 4–8 [see *377*].
— [English tr.] In: A. Poznansky, *Tchaikovsky through others' eyes* (1999): 8–12 [see *380*].

SAVELII FEDOROV (1868–1948)

Musician at the Kiev Opera

[*434*]   FEDOROV, S. M. 'Stroki vospominanii: Zapiska I. Samoilenko', *Muzykal´naia zhizn´* (1965), 8: 7.
Fragments from notes made by Fedorov in 1945.

MEDEIA FIGNER (1859–1952)

Soprano at the Mariinskii theatre, wife of Nikolai Figner

[*435*]   'Sovremenniki o P. I. Chaikovskom', *Teatr i zhizn´* (25 Oct 1913): 11.

NIKOLAI FIGNER (1857–1918)

Principal tenor with the Imperial Opera in St. Petersburg

[*436*]   FIGNER, N. N. 'P. I. Chaikovskii: Moi uchitel´´', *Solntse Rossii* (1913), 44: 7–8 [see *583*].

BORIS FITINGOF-SHEL´

Russian Baron, and ballet composer

[437]   **FITINGOF-SHEL´, B. A. 'Al´bom avtografov: Pëtr Il´ich Chaikovskii'**, *Moskovskie vedomosti* (5 Jan 1899).

— [repr.] 'Pëtr Il´ich Chaikovskii'. In: B. A. Fitingof-Shel', *Mirovye znamenitosti: Iz vospominanii barona B. A. Fitingof-Shelia (1848–1898 gg.)*. Sankt Peterburg, 1899: 146–150.

— [English tr.] In: A. Poznansky, *Tchaikovsky through others' eyes* (1999): 173–175 [see *380*].

JOSEF BOHUSLAV FOERSTER (1858–1951)

Czech composer and music critic

[438]   **FOERSTER, J. B. 'Vzpominky na Čajkovskeho'.** In: *Národní divadlo: List dïvadelni práce*. Praha, 1930: 4–5, 20.

The first production of *Evgenii Onegin* at the National Theatre in Prague.

— [French tr.] 'Souvenirs de Tchaïkovski'. In: *Piotr Tchaïkovski: Écrits critiques, lettres, souvenirs de contemporains* (1985): 275–277 [see *375*].

— [Russian tr.] 'Vospominaniia o P. I. Chaikovskom'. In: *Vospominaniia o P. I. Chaikovskom*, 2-e izd. (1973): 295–297; 3-e izd. (1979): 296–298; 4-e izd. (1980): 251–252 [see *374*].

ALEKSANDR FRIBUS

Musical director of the St. Petersburg Conservatory

[439]   **FRIBUS, A. I. 'P. I. Chaikovskii v vospominaniiakh'**, *Birzhevye vedomosti* (24 Oct 1913) [see *372*].

NINA FRIDE (1859–1942)

Mezzo-soprano at the Mariinskii Theatre in St. Petersburg

[440]   **FRIDE, N. A. 'Na repetitsiiakh'**, *Ogonek* (1940), 12: 11.

Brief recollections of productions of *The Enchantress* and *The Queen of Spades*, and meetings with the composer in St. Petersburg and Warsaw.

"I. G—K"

[441]   **G—K, I. 'P. I. Chaikovskii v Odesse: Po lichnym vospominaniiam'**, *Odesskie novosti* (25 Oct 1903).

The composer's visit in Jan 1893.

— [repr.] 'Kur´eznye vospominaniia', *Russkaia muzykal´naia gazeta* (Dec 1903), 50: 1260.

STANISLAV GABEL´ (1849–1924)

Bass singer, and professor at the St. Petersburg Conservatory

[442]   **GABEL´, S. I. 'P. I. Chaikovskii: Drug molodezhi'**, *Solntse Rossii* (1913), 44: 7 [see *583*].

[443]   **GABEL, S. I. 'P. I. Chaikovskii v vospominaniiakh'**, *Birzhevye vedomosti* (24 Oct 1913) [see *372*].

MIKHAIL GAIDAI (1878–1965)

Singer, choirmaster and teacher

[444]   **GAIDAI, M. 'Pis´mo v redaktsiiu'**, *Muzyka i penie* (1903), 9: 21.

On Chaikovskii's visit to Kiev in 1890.

— [repr.] 'Vospominaniia o Chaikovskom', *Russkaia muzykal'naia gazeta* (Nov 1903), 95: 1092–1093.

— [repr.] In: *Vospominaniia o P. I. Chaikovskom*, 4-e izd. (1980): 410 [see *374*].

— [English tr. (abridged)] In: D. Brown, *Tchaikovsky remembered* (1993): 180 [see *377*].

ROSTISLAV GENIKA (1859–1922)
Pianist and former student at the Moscow Conservatory

[*445*]   **GENIKA, R. V. 'Iz konservatorskikh vospominanii (1871–1879 gg.)'**, *Russkaia muzykal'naia gazeta* (4/11 Sep 1916), 36/37: 637–650; (4 Dec 1916), 49, 938–943.

Recollections of Chaikovskii's classes at the Moscow Conservatory.

— [repr.] In: *Vospominaniia o P. I. Chaikovskom* (1962): 147–153; 2-e izd. (1973): 71–76; 3-e izd. (1979): 72–77; 4-e izd. (1980): 61–65 [see *374*].

— [English tr. (abridged)] In: D. Brown, *Tchaikovsky remembered* (1993): 31–32 [see *377*].

— [English tr. (abridged)] In: A. Poznansky, *Tchaikovsky through others' eyes* (1999): 56–59 [see *380*].

— [German tr. (abridged)] 'Meine Studienjahre bei Peter Tschaikowsky'. In: *Tschaikowsky aus der Nähe* (1994): 59–64 [see *379*].

VLADIMIR GERARD (1839–1903)
Lawyer and former student at the Imperial School of Jurisprudence

[*446*]   **GERARD, V. N. 'Chaikovskii v Uchilishche pravovedeniia'.** In: *Vospominaniia o P. I. Chaikovskom*, 2-e izd. (1973): 30–31 [see *374*].

Chaikovskii at the Imperial School of Jurisprudence in the 1850s. See also *1718*.

— [repr.] In: *Vospominaniia o P. I. Chaikovskom*, 3-e izd. (1979): 31–33; 4-e izd. (1980): 27–28 [see *374*].

— [English tr. (abridged)] In: D. Brown, *Tchaikovsky remembered* (1993): 12 [see *377*].

— [English tr.] In: A. Poznansky, *Tchaikovsky through others' eyes* (1999): 16–17 [see *380*]

— [German tr.] 'Peter Tschaikowsky als Schüler der Rechtsschule'. In: *Tschaikowsky aus der Nähe* (1994): 42–43 [see *379*].

ALEKSANDR GLAZUNOV (1865–1936)
Composer, conductor and professor at the St. Petersburg Conservatory

[*447*]   **GLAZUNOV, A. K. 'P. I. Chaikovskii v vospominaniiakh',** *Birzhevye vedomosti* (24 Oct 1913) [see *372*].

— [English tr. (abridged)] In: A. Poznansky, *Tchaikovsky through others' eyes* (1999): 141–142 [see *380*].

[*448*]   **GLAZUNOV, A. K. 'Moe znakomstvo s Chaikovskim'.** In: *Chaikovskii: Vospominaniia i pis'ma* (1924): 5–12 [see *373*].

— [repr.] In: A. K. Glazunov, *Pis'ma, stat'i, vospomonaniia: Izbrannoe.* Sost., vstup. stat'ia i primechaniia M. A. Ganinoi. Moskva: Gos. muz. izdat., 1958: 460–467, illus.

— [repr.] In: *Vospominaniia o P. I. Chaikovskom* (1962): 46–55; 2-e izd. (1973): 244–248; 3-e izd. (1979): 245–249; 4-e izd. (1980): 208–211 [see *374*].

— [English tr. (abridged)] In: D. Brown, *Tchaikovsky remembered* (1993): 71–72, 100, 162–163 [see *377*].

— [German tr.] 'Meine Bekanntschaft mit Peter Tschaikowsky'. In: *Tschaikowsky aus der Nähe* (1994): 101–106 [see *379*].

ALEKSANDR GOL'DENVEIZER (1875–1961)
Pianist, composer and director of the Moscow Conservatory

[*449*]   **GOL'DENVEIZER, A. B. 'Vospominaniia o Chaikovskom'.** In: *Vospominaniia o P. I. Chaikovskom*, 2-e izd. (1973): 368–370 [see *374*].

Chaikovskii as a conductor in the 1890s, including at the premiere of the symphonic ballad *The Voevoda* in Moscow in Nov 1891.

— [repr. (abridged)] In: *A. B. Gol´denveizer o muzykal´nom iskusstve: Sbornik statei*. Sost. obshchaia red., vstup. stat´ia i kommentarii D. D. Blagogo. Moskva: Muzyka, 1975: 164–168.

— [repr.] In: *Vospominaniia o P. I. Chaikovskom*, 3-e izd. (1979): 369–371; 4-e izd. (1980): 314–315 [see *374*].

— [English tr. (abridged)] In: D. Brown, *Tchaikovsky remembered* (1993): 169 [see *377*].

IGOR´ GRABAR´ (1871–1960)
Artist and art historian

[*450*] **GRABAR´, I. E. 'Zavet khudozhnika'.** In: I. E. Grabar´, *Moia zhizn´: Avtobiografiia*. Moskva; Leningrad: Iskusstvo, 1937: 81–84.

Recollections of a dinner with Chaikovskii in St. Petersburg in 1889.

— [repr. (abridged)] *Ogonek* (1940), 12: 14.

— [repr. (abridged)] In: *Vospominaniia o P. I. Chaikovskom* (1962): 66–68; 2-e izd. (1973): 338–340; 3-e izd. (1979): 339–341; 4-e izd. (1980): 288–289 [see *374*].

— [English tr. (abridged)] In: D. Brown, *Tchaikovsky remembered* (1993): 83–85 [see *377*].

MARIIA GUR´E (1853–1938)
Student of Chaikovskii's at the Moscow Conservatory

[*451*] **GUR´E, M. [Vospominaniia o P. I. Chaikovskom].** In: P. I. Chaikovskii, *Pis´ma k rodnym* (1940): 686–687 [see *152*].

— [English tr. (abridged)] In: A. Poznansky, *Tchaikovsky through others' eyes* (1999): 56–61 [see *380*].

GEORGE HENSCHEL (1850–1934)
British baritone

[*452*] **HENSCHEL, G. *Musings & memories of a musician*.** London: Macmillan, 1918. 400 p, illus.

Includes notes on Chaikovskii's visit to England in 1893.

— [repr. (abridged)] In: D. Brown, *Tchaikovsky remembered* (1993): 187–188 [see *377*].

HELEN HENSCHEL (1882–1973)
Singer and pianist, daughter of Sir George Henschel

[*453*] **HENSCHEL, H. *When soft voices die: A musical biography of Sir George Henschel*.** London: John Westhouse, 1944. 216 p, illus.

Includes notes on Chaikovskii's visit to London in 1893.

— 2nd ed. ('About Tchaikovsky'). London: Methuen, 1949. 88–89, illus.

— [repr. (abridged)] In: D. Brown, *Tchaikovsky remembered* (1993): 97–98 [see *377*].

VASILII IASTREBTSEV (1866–1934)
Writer and music critic

[*454*] **IASTREBTSEV, V. V. 'Iz moikh vospominanii o P. I. Chaikovskom',** *Russkaia muzykal´naia gazeta* (6 Mar 1899), 10: 306–310.

Two meetings with the composer in St. Petersburg (1887 & 1893).

— [offprint] *Iz moikh vospominanii o P. I. Chaikovskom*. Novgorod: A. I. Shcherbakov, 1903. 9 p.

— [repr.] In: *Vospominaniia o P. I. Chaikovskom* (1962): 345–350; 3-e izd. (1979): 250–254; 4-e izd. (1980): 212–215 [see *374*].

— [English tr. (abridged)] In: D. Brown, *Tchaikovsky remembered* (1993): 75–77, 233–234 [see *377*].

— [German tr.] 'Aus meinen Erinnerungen an Tschaikowsky'. In: *Tschaikowsky aus der Nähe* (1994): 175–179 [see *379*].

"INIKHOV"

[455]   INIKHOV. 'Vospominaniia o P. I. Chaikovskom', *Pridneprovskii krai* (27 Oct 1903).
        — [repr.] *Novosti i birzhevaia gazeta* (28 Oct 1903).
        — [repr. (abridged)] *Russkaia muzykal´naia gazeta* (1903): 1092–1093.

MIKHAIL IPPOLITOV-IVANOV (1859–1935)

Composer, conductor and professor at the Moscow Conservatory

[456]   IPPOLITOV-IVANOV, M. M. *50-let russkoi muzyki v moikh vozpominaniiakh*. Moskva: Gos. muz.
        izdat., 1934: 48–49, 55–59, 81–83.
        — [repr. (extracts)] In: *Vospominaniia o P. I. Chaikovskom* (1962): 241–255; 2-e izd. (1973): 273–282; 3-e izd.
        (1979): 274–283; 4-e izd. (1980): 233–240 [see *374*].
        — [English tr. (abridged)] In: D. Brown, *Tchaikovsky remembered* (1993): 103, 127, 163–164, 166, 168–169,
        198–199, 203–204 [see *377*].
        — [French tr. (abridged)] In: *Piotr Tchaïkovski: Écrits critiques, lettres, souvenirs de contemporains* (1985): 263–271
        [see *375*].

IURII IUR´EV (1872–1948)

Actor

[457]   IUR´EV, Iu. M. 'Moi vstrechi s P. I. Chaikovskim'. In: Iu. M. Iur´ev, *Zapiski*. Tom 2. Moskva;
        Leningrad, 1945: 72–88.
        Chaikovskii during the 1890s in St. Petersburg, and his death and funeral.
        — [repr. (abridged)] In: Iu. M. Iur´ev, *Zapiski*. Tom 2 [2-e izd.]. Leningrad; Moskva, 1948: 271–283.
        — [repr.] In: *Vospominaniia o P. I. Chaikovskom* (1962): 361–364; 2-e izd. (1973): 327–329; 3-e izd. (1979):
        328–330; 4-e izd. (1980): 278–280 [see *374*].
        — [English tr. (abridged)] In: D. Brown, *Tchaikovsky remembered* (1993): 180 [see *377*].

PËTR IURGENSON (1836–1903)

Chaikovskii's principal publisher

[458]   [IURGENSON, P. I.] 'U Iurgensona', *Peterburgskaia gazeta* (27 Oct 1893) [see *618*].
        — [German tr.] 'Ein Interview aus Anlaß des Ablebens von Peter Tschaikowsky für den Korrespondenten der
        "Peterburgskaja Gazeta"'. In: *Tschaikowsky aus der Nähe* (1994): 273–275 [see *379*].

IVAN IVANOV (1881–1942)

Ballet dancer and producer

[459]   IVANOV, I. ['Vospominaniia']. In: *Vospominaniia o P. I. Chaikovskom*, 4-e izd. (1980): 393–394 [see
        374].
        On the first production of *The Nutcracker* in 1892.
        — [English tr. (abridged)] In: D. Brown, *Tchaikovsky remembered* (1993): 96 [see *377*].

VASILII IVANOV (1865–1912)

Poet and journalist

[459a] IVANOV, V. I. 'P. I. Chaikovskii (iz lichnykh vospominanii)', *Moskovskie vedomosti* (25 Oct 1909).
        About Chaikovskii's visit to Khar´kov in Mar 1893.
        — [repr.] In: *Vospominaniia o P. I. Chaikovskom* (1962): 230–232.

NIKOLAI KASHKIN (1839–1920)

Pianist, music critic and professor at the Moscow Conservatory

[460]   KASHKIN, N. D. 'Pëtr Il´ich Chaikovskii', *Russkie vedomosti* (6 Nov 1893): 2.

— [repr.] In: *Vospominaniia o P. I. Chaikovskom* (1962): 379–388; 3-e izd. (1979): 419–427; abridged in 4-e izd. (1980): 361–362 [see *374*].

— [English tr. (abridged)] In: D. Brown, *Tchaikovsky remembered* (1993): 231–233 [see *377*].

[461]   KASHKIN, N. D. 'Vospominaniia o P. I. Chaikovskom', *Russkoe obozrenie* (Sep 1894): 106–120; (Nov 1894): 276–298; (Jan 1895): 93–110; (Feb 1895): 249–258; (May 1895): 392–407; (Sep 1895): 158–168; (Oct 1895): 679–690; (Nov 1895): 262–281; (Dec 1895): 772–782.

Review: 'Izvestiia otovsiudu', *Nuvellist* (Feb 1896), 2: 7–8.

— [rev. repr.] In: N. D. Kashkin, *Vospominaniia o P. I. Chaikovskom* (1896) [see *462*].

[462]   KASHKIN, N. D. *Vospominaniia o P. I. Chaikovskom*. Moskva: P. Iurgenson, 1896. 163 p.

Reviews: N. F. [Findeizen], *Russkaia muzykal´naia gazeta* (Nov 1896), 11: 1475–1476 — R. H. Newmarch, 'Kashkine's recollections of Tschikowsky', *Musical Times*, 38 (Jun 1897): 449–452.

— 2-e izd. [abridged]. Moskva: Gos. muz. izdat., 1954. Obshchaia red., vstup. stat´ia i primechaniia S. I. Shlifshteina. 227 p. (*Russkaia klassicheskaia muzykal´naia kritika*).

— [repr. (extract)] 'Iz vospominanii o P. I. Chaikovskom'. In: *Vospominaniia o P. I. Chaikovskom* (1962): 165–168 [see *374*].

— [repr. (extracts)] 'V minutu zhizni trudnuiu: Iz vospominanii o Petre Il´iche Chaikovskom', *Muzykal´naia zhizn´* (1997), 11: 37–40, illus.; 12: 27–30.

— [English tr. (abridged)] In: D. Brown, *Tchaikovsky remembered* (1993): 30–31, 39–40, 43–44, 98–99, 109–112, 118, 161, 164, 195–196 [see *377*].

— [English tr. (extract)] In: N. Lebrecht, *The book of musical anecdotes* (1985) [see *376*].

— [German tr.] *Meine Erinnerungen an Peter Tschaikowski*. Von Nikolai Kaschkin. Hrsg. und mit einem Vorwort versehen von Ernst Kuhn; Übersetzung aus dem Russischen von Bärbel Bruder. Berlin: E. Kuhn, 1992. 213 p. (*Musik konkret*; 1). ISBN: 3-928864-01-7.

Also includes German tr. of Kashkin's 'Iz vospominanii o P. I. Chaikovskom' (1896) [see *464*].

Reviews: L. Barkefors, *Svenska Tidskrift för Musikforskning*, 85 (1993), 2: 93–98 — W. Stockmeier, *Musik und Kirche*, 63 (May/Jun 1993), 3: 170 — M. Bobeth, *Musica*, 48 (May/Jun 1994), 3: 179–180 — M. H. Brown, *Slavic Review*, 53 (win. 1994): 1201–1203 — *Orchester*, 43 (1995), 10: 60–61.

[463]   KASHKIN, N. D. 'P. I. Chaikovskii i ego zhizneopisanie', *Moskovskie vedomosti* (11 Jan 1902); (14 May 1902); (11 Jun 1902); (20 Aug 1902); (16 Mar 1903); (27 Jun 1903).

Mainly a review of M. I. Chaikovskii, *Zhizn´ Petra Il´icha Chaikovskogo* (1900–02) [see *1453*], with additoinal recollections by Kashkin.

— [repr. (abridged)] 'Chaikovskii i N. F. von Mekk', *Russkaia muzykal´naia gazeta* (1903), 13: 375–377.

— [repr. (abridged)] In: *P. I. Chaikovskii: Gody detstva* (1983): 107–111 [see *1712*].

[464]   KASHKIN, N. D. 'Iz vospominanii o P. I. Chaikovskom'. In: *Proshloe russkoi muzyki*, tom 1 (1920): 99–132 [see *584*]

Mainly concerning the composer's marriage to Antonina Miliukova (written in 1918).

— [English tr. (abridged)] In: D. Brown, *Tchaikovsky remembered* (1993): 50–63 [see *377*].

— [English tr. (abridged)] In: A. Poznansky, *Tchaikovsky through others' eyes* (1999): 121–133 [see *380*].

— [German tr.] In: *N. D. Kaschkin: Meine Erinnerungen an Peter Tschaikowski* (1992): 179–208 [see *462*].

ABRAM KAUFMAN (1855–1921)

Odessan journalist

[465]   KAUFMAN, A. 'Vstrechi s Chaikovskim (iz lichnykh vospominanii)', *Solntse Rossii* (1913), 44: 15–17 [see *583*].

The composer's tour of Odessa in 1892/93, and the production of *The Queen of Spades*.

— [repr.] *Dlia vas* (1940), No. 19.

— [repr.] *Vospominanii o P. I. Chaikovskom*, 4-e izd. (1980): 419 [see *374*].

— [English tr. (abridged)] In: D. Brown, *Tchaikovsky remembered* (1993): 169–170 [see *377*].

— [English tr. (abridged)] In: A. Poznansky, *Tchaikovsky through others' eyes* (1999): 219–221 [see *380*].

— [German tr.] 'Meine Begegnungen mit Peter Tschaikowsky'. In: *Tschaikowsky aus der Nähe* (1994): 184–188 [see *379*].

ALEKSANDR KHESSIN (1869–1955)
Conductor and music teacher

[*466*]   **KHESSIN, A. B. 'Vstrecha s Chaikovskim'**. In: A. B. Khessin, *Iz moikh vospominanii*. Moskva: Vserossiskoe teatral´noe obshchestvo, 1959: 31–38, illus.

Khessin's recollections (written in 1953) of a meeting with Chaikovskii in St. Petersburg in 1892.

— [repr.] In: *Vospominaniia o P. I. Chaikovskom* (1962): 56–65; 2-e izd. (1973): 330–337; 3-e izd. (1979): 331–338; 4-e izd. (1980): 281–287 [see *374*].

— [French tr.] 'Ma recontre avec Tchaïkovski'. In: *Piotr Tchaïkovski: Écrits critiques, lettres, souvenirs de contemporains* (1985): 292–300 [see *375*].

ALEKSANDR KHIMICHENKO (1856–1947)
Flutist and professor at the Kiev Conservatory

[*467*]   **KHIMICHENKO, A. V. 'Pamiatnye vstrechi'**. In: *P. I. Chaikovskii na Ukraine: Materialy i dokumenty* (1940): 111–113 [see *1782*].

The author's recollections of a meeting with Chaikovskii in Kiev in 1891.

— [repr.] *Sovetskaia Ukraina* (10 Apr 1940).

[*468*]   **KHIMICHENKO, A. V. 'Vospominaniia iz dalekogo proshlogo'**. In: *Vospominaniia o P. I. Chaikovskom* (1962): 159–164.

Based on 'Pamiatnye vstrechi' [see *467*], supplemented by Khimichenko's recollections from 1938 of his days as a student in Chaikovskii's classes at the Moscow Conservatory in the 1870s.

— [repr.] In: *Vospominaniia o P. I. Chaikovskom*, 2-e izd. (1973): 83–86; 3-e izd. (1979): 84–87; 4-e izd. (1980): 71–74 [see *374*].

TSESAR´ KIUI (1835–1918)
Composer and music critic

[*469*]   **KIUI, Ts. A. 'P. I. Chaikovskii: Moskvich'**, *Solntse Rossii* (1913), 44: 7 [see *583*].

[*470*]   **KIUI, Ts. A. 'P. I. Chaikovskii v vospominaniiakh'**, *Birzhevye vedomosti* (24 Oct 1913) [see *372*].

HERMANN KLEIN (1856–1934)
English music critic and teacher

[*471*]   **K[LEIN], H. 'Music and Musicians'**, *Sunday Times* (25 Mar 1888).

Chaikovskii conducting at a concert in London on 22 Mar 1888.

— [repr. (abridged)] In: A. Poznansky, *Tchaikovsky through others' eyes* (1999): 157 [see *380*].

[*472*]   **KLEIN, H. *Thirty years of musical life in London, 1870–1890*.** New York: Century Co., 1903: 343–350.

Klein's meeting with Chaikovskii at Cambridge University in Jun 1893.

— [repr. (abridged)] 'Personal recollections of Tschaikowsky', *Century Magazine*, 65 (Apr 1903): 897–898.

— [repr. (abridged)] In: D. Brown, *Tchaikovsky remembered* (1993): 188–189 [see *377*].

— [Russian tr.] 'Vstrechi s Chaikovskim'. In: *Vospominaniia o P. I. Chaikovskom*, 2-e izd. (1973): 364–366; 3-e izd. (1979): 365–367; 4-e izd. (1980): 310–311 [see *374*].

— [German tr.] 'Eine Begegnung mit Tschaikowsky in England'. In: *Tschaikowsky aus der Nähe* (1994): 180–183 [see *379*].

IVAN KLIMENKO (1841–1914)

Architect and friend of the composer

[473] **KLIMENKO, I. A.** *Moi vospominaniia o Petre Il´iche Chaikovskom*. Riazan´: I. V. Liubomudrov, 1908. 83 p.

Also includes a number of letters from Chaikovskii to Klimenko.

— [repr.] In: *P. I. Chaikovskii: Zabytoe i novoe* (1995): 64–92 [see *598*].

— [excs.] *Rannee utro* (16 May 1908).

— [excs.] 'P. I. Chaikovskii kak iumorist', *Birzhevye vedomosti* (18 May 1908).

— [English tr. (excs.)] In: N. Slonimsky, 'Musical oddities', *Etude*, 70 (Jul 1952): 4; (Sep 1952): 4–5.

— [English tr. (abridged)] In: A. Poznansky, *Tchaikovsky through others' eyes* (1999): 41–42, 64–75, 229–233 [see *380*].

— [German tr. (abridged)] 'Er überließ Laroche das eigene Zimmer und hauste selbst auf dem Korridor'. In: *Tschaikowsky aus der Nähe* (1994): 47–52 [see *379*].

GENNADII KONDRAT´EV (1834–1905)

Director of the Russian Opera

[474] **[KONDRAT´EV, G. P.]** '**Zapiski glavnogo rezhissera russkoi opery G. P. Kondrat´eva**'. In: *Chaikovskii i teatr* (1940): 267–327 [see *2458*].

Kondrat´ev's recollections of the staging of Chaikovskii's operas in St. Petersburg, 1884–99, including those attended by the composer.

NADEZHDA KONDRAT´EVA (1865–??)

Daughter of the composer's friend Nikolai Kondrat´ev

[475] **KONDRAT´EVA, N. N.** '**Vospominaniia o P. I. Chaikovskom**'. In: *Vospominaniia o P. I. Chaikovskom* (1962): 320–339 [see *374*].

The author's recollections of Chaikovskii (from 1940).

— [repr.] In: *Vospominaniia o P. I. Chaikovskom*, 2-e izd. (1973): 102–118; 3-e izd. (1979): 103–119; 4-e izd. (1980): 88–101 [see *374*].

— [English tr. (abridged)] In: D. Brown, *Tchaikovsky remembered* (1993): 41–43 [see *377*].

GRAND DUKE KONSTANTIN KONSTANTINOVICH (1858–1914)

Poet, amateur composer, nephew of Tsar Aleksandr III

[476] **[ROMANOV], K. K. ['Diary']**. In: A. Poznansky, *Tchaikovsky through others' eyes* (1999): 172–173, 265–268 [see *380*].

Extracts from the Grand Duke's previously unpublished diaries concerning Chaikovskii (1880 and 1893).

VASILII KORGANOV (1865–1934)

Army officer, pianist and music teacher

[477] **KORGANOV, V. D.** *Chaikovskii na Kavkaze* (1940): 39–53 [see *1771*].

Korganov's recollections of Chaikovskii's visit to Tiflis in the spring of 1888.

— [repr. (abridged)] In: *P. I. Chaikovskii: Zabytoe i novoe* (1995): 93–102 [see *598*]

— [English tr. (abridged)] In: A. Poznansky, *Tchaikovsky through others' eyes* (1999): 175–181 [see *380*].

RUDOLPH KÜNDINGER (1832–1913)

German pianist and professor at the St. Petersburg Conservatory

[478] **KÜNDINGER, R. V.** '**Zaniatiia s molodym Chaikovskim**'. In: *Vospominaniia o P. I. Chaikovskom* (1962): 397–398 [see *374*].

Chaikovskii's music lessons in the 1850s. See also *1718*.

— [repr.] In: *Vospominaniia o P. I. Chaikovskom*, 2-e izd. (1973): 31–32; 3-e izd. (1979): 36–37; 4-e izd. (1980): 31–32 [see *374*].

— [English tr. (abridged)] In: D. Brown, *Tchaikovsky remembered* (1993): 13 [see *377*].

— [English tr. (abridged)] In: A. Poznansky, *Tchaikovsky through others' eyes* (1999): 17–18 [see *380*].

MARIIA KUZNETSOVA (1880–1966)
Soprano at the Mariinskii Theatre in St. Petersburg

[*479*] **I. M. 'Portret Chaikovskogo (zapisano so slov M. N. Kuznetsovoi-Masne)**, *Vozrozhdenie*, 56 (1956): 14–17.

Chaikovskii in Odessa in 1893, and the portrait painted by the author's father, Nikolai Kuznetsov. See also *561, 565, 569, 575*.

FREDERIC LAMOND (1868–1948)
Scottish pianist, teacher and composer

[*480*] **LAMOND, F. A. 'Tschaikowsky'.** In: F. A. Lamond, *The memoirs of Frederic Lamond*. With a foreword by Ernest Newman. Introduction and postscript by Irene Triesch Lamond. Glasgow: W. MacLellan, 1949: 88–98, illus.

Includes recollections of concerts and correspondence with Chaikovskii in the 1880s and 1890s.

— [repr. (abridged)] In: D. Brown, *Tchaikovsky remembered* (1993): 127, 148–149 [see *377*].

— [repr. (extract)] In: N. Lebrecht, *The book of musical anecdotes* (1985) [see *376*].

— [Dutch tr.] *Volksdageblad* [Amsterdam] (2 May 1940).

— [Russian tr. (abridged)] 'Kontsert b-moll Chaikovskogo'. In: *Vospominaniia o P. I. Chaikovskom*, 2-e izd. (1973): 298–299; 3-e izd. (1979): 299–300; 4-e izd. (1980): 253 [see *374*].

GERMAN LAROSH (1845–1904)
Music critic and professor at the St. Petersburg and Moscow Conservatories

[*481*] **LAROSH, G. A. 'Neskol´ko slov o Petre Il´iche Chaikovskom''**, *Teatral´naia gazeta* (29 Oct 1893): 1–2.

— [repr.] 'Na pamiat´ o P. I. Chaikovskom'. In: *Na pamiat´ o P. I. Chaikovskom* (1894): 55–62 [see *371*].

— [repr.] In: G. A. Larosh, *Sobranie muzykal´no-kriticheskikh statei*, tom 2, chast 1 (1922): 17–21 [see *2311*].

— [repr.] In: *Vospominaniia o P. I. Chaikovskom* (1962): 41–45; 2-e izd. (1973): 412–425; 3-e izd. (1979): 414–418; 4-e izd. (1980): 352–355 [see *374*].

— [repr.] In: G. A. Larosh, *Izbrannye stat´i v piati vypuskakh*, vyp. 2 (1975): 161–165 [see *2376*].

— [English tr. (abridged)] In: D. Brown, *Tchaikovsky remembered* (1993): 240–244 [see *377*].

— [German tr.] 'Einige Worte über Peter Iljitsch Tschaikowsky'. In: G. A. Larosh, *Peter Tschaikowsky: Aufsätze und Erinnerungen* (1993): 169–174 [see *2406*].

[*482*] **LAROSH, G. A, 'Vospominaniia o P. I. Chaikovskom'**, *Novosti i birzhevaia gazeta* (23 Nov 1893): 2.

— [repr.] In: *Na pamiat´ o P. I. Chaikovskom* (1894): 5–24 [see *371*].

— [repr.] In: G. A. Larosh, *Sobranie muzykal´no-kriticheskikh statei*, tom 2, chast 1 (1922): 1–12 [see *2311*].

— [repr.] In: *Vospominaniia o P. I. Chaikovskom* (1962): 11–23; 3-e izd. (1979): 43–54; 4-e izd. (1980): 37–46 [see *374*].

— [repr.] In: G. A. Larosh, *Izbrannye stat´i v piati vypuskakh*, vyp. 2 (1975): 167–175 [see *2376*].

— [English tr. (abridged)] In: D. Brown, *Tchaikovsky remembered* (1993): 18–19, 119 [see *377*].

— [English tr. (abridged)] In: A. Poznansky, *Tchaikovsky through others' eyes* (1999): 34–35 [see *380*].

— [French tr.] 'Souvenirs de Tchaïkovski'. In: *Piotr Tchaïkovski: Écrits critiques, lettres, souvenirs de contemporains* (1985): 191–202 [see *375*].

— [German tr.] 'Erinnerungen an Peter Tschaikowsky'. In: G. A. Larosh, *Peter Tschaikowsky: Aufsätze und Erinnerungen* (1993): 175–188 [see *2406*].

[483] **LAROSH, G. A. 'Iz moikh vospominanii o P. I. Chaikovskom'**, *Severnyi vestnik* (Feb 1894): 175–186.

— [repr.] In: G. A. Larosh, *Sobranie muzykal´no-kriticheskikh statei*, tom 2, chast 1 (1922): 22–35 [see *371*].

— [repr.] In: *Vospominaniia o P. I. Chaikovskom* (1962): 26–41 [see *374*].

— [repr.] In: G. A. Larosh, *Izbrannye stat´i v piati vypuskakh*, vyp. 2 (1975): 176–186 [see *2376*].

— [English tr. (abridged)] In: D. Brown, *Tchaikovsky remembered* (1993): 19–25, 234–238 [see *377*].

— [English tr. (abridged)] In: A. Poznansky, *Tchaikovsky through others' eyes* (1999): 35–41 [see *380*].

— [French tr.] 'En souvenir de P. I. Tchaïkovski'. In: *Piotr Tchaïkovski: Écrits critiques, lettres, souvenirs de contemporains* (1985): 320–324 [see *375*].

— [German tr.] 'Aus meinen Erinnerungen an Peter Tschaikowsky'. In: G. A. Larosh, *Peter Tschaikowsky: Aufsätze und Erinnerungen* (1993): 189–204 [see *2406*].

[484] **LAROSH, G. A. 'Pamiati P. I. Chaikovskogo'**, *Ezhegodnik Imperatorskikh teatrov, sezon 1892/1893* (1894): 496–500.

— [offprint] *Pamiati P. I. Chaikovskogo*. Sankt Peterburg: Izdat. Ezhegodnika Imperatorskikh teatrov, 1894. 7 p.

— [repr. (abridged)] 'Slovo Larosha nad grobom Chaikovskogo', *Solntse Rossii* (1913), 44: 13–15 [see *583*].

— [repr.] In: G. A. Larosh, *Sobranie muzykal´no-kriticheskikh statei*, tom 2, chast 1 (1922): 13–16 [see *2311*].

— [repr.] In: G. A. Larosh, *Izbrannye stat´i v piati vypuskakh*, vyp. 2 (1975): 186–189 [see *2376*].

— [English tr. (abridged)] In: D. Brown, *Tchaikovsky remembered* (1993): 238–239 [see *377*].

[485] **LAROSH, G. A. 'Iz moikh vospominanii: Chaikovskii v konservatorii'**, *Severnyi vestnik* (Sep 1897): 49–60; (Oct 1897): 79–90.

Chaikovskii at the St. Petersburg Conservatory. Prepared for publication by Modest Chaikovskii. See also *1725*.

— [repr.] In: M. I. Chaikovskii, *Zhizn´ Petra Il´icha Chaikovskogo*, tom 1 (1900): 159–188 [see *1453*].

— [repr.] In: G. A. Larosh, *Sobranie muzykal´no-kriticheskikh statei*, tom 2, chast 1 (1922): 36–63 [see *2311*].

— [repr.] In: G. A. Larosh, *Izbrannye stat´i v piati vypuskakh*, vyp. 2 (1975): 277–299 [see *2376*].

— [rev. repr.] 'P. I. Chaikovskii v Peterburgskoi konservatorii'. In: *Vospominaniia o P. I. Chaikovskom*, 2-e izd. (1973): 54–69; 3-e izd. (1979): 55–71; 4-e izd. (1980): 47–60 [see *374*].

— [repr.] In: *Leningradskaia konservatoriia v vospominaniiakh*, kn. 1. Leningrad, 1987:13–19.

— [Dutch tr. (abridged)] 'Uit mijn herinneringen aan Peter Tsjaikovski', *Mens en Melodie*, 35 (Jul 1980): 363–367.

— [English tr. (abridged)] In: O. Zoff, *Great composers through the eyes of their contemporaries*. Ed. by Otto Zoff; tr. and assistant ed., Phoebe Rogoff Cave. New York: E. P. Dutton [1951]: 367–375.

— [English tr. (abridged)] In: D. Brown, *Tchaikovsky remembered* (1993): 19–24 [see *377*].

— [French tr.] 'P. I. Tchaïkovski au Conservatoire de Saint-Pétersbourg'. In: *Piotr Tchaïkovski: Écrits critiques, lettres, souvenirs de contemporains* (1985): 203–218 [see *375*].

[486] **LAROSH, G. A. 'Kniga o Chaikovskom'**, *Rossiia*, (22 Dec 1900): 4

Mainly a review of M. I. Chaikovskii, *Zhizn´ Petra Ilicha Chaikovskogo* (1900–02).

— [repr.] In: G. A. Larosh, *Sobranie muzykal´no kriticheskikh statei*, tom 2, chast 2 (1924): 97–101 [see *2311*].

— [repr.] In: G. A. Larosh, *Izbrannye stat´i v piati vypuskakhh*, vyp. 2 (1975): 334–338 [see *2376*].

KONSTANTIN de LAZARI (1838–1903)
Actor and writer

[487] **LAZARI, K. N. de. 'Vospominaniia o P. I. Chaikovskom'**, *Rossiia* (25 May 1900); (31 May 1900); (12 Jun 1900); (18 Jul 1900).

— [repr. (abridged)] 'Otryvki iz vospominanii'. In: *Pamiatniki kultury: Novye otkrytiia. Ezhegodnik 1996*. Moskva: Nauka, 1998: 186–226.

— [English tr. (abridged)] In: A. Poznansky, *Tchaikovsky through others' eyes* (1999): 82–94, 170–172 [see *380*].

NELSON LE-KIME (1868–?1957)
Belgian music critic

[*488*]   **LE-KIME, N. H. 'P. I. Chaikovskii v Briussele'**. In: *Vospominaniia o P. I. Chaikovskom*, 2-e izd. (1973): 367 [see *374*].

The composer conducting his own music in Brussels in 1893.

— [repr.] In: *Vospominaniia o P. I. Chaikovskom*, 3-e izd. (1979): 368; 4-e izd. (1980): 313 [see *374*].

SEMËN LEVIN
Violinist and teacher

[*489*]   **LEVIN, S. K. 'Moi vospominaniia o velikom kompozitore'**, *Bol´shevistskoe znamia* (22 Mar 1940).

Chaikovskii's rehearsals for concerts in Odessa in Jan 1893.

— [repr.] 'Kontserty Chaikovskogo v Odesse'. In: *Vospominaniia o P. I. Chaikovskom* (1962): 201–205; 2-e izd. (1973): 360–361; 3-e izd. (1979): 361–362; 4-e izd. (1980): 306–307 [see *374*].

ANATOLII LIADOV (1855–1914)
Composer, conductor and professor at the St. Petersburg Conservatory

[*490*]   **LIADOV, A. K. 'P. I. Chaikovskii: Neobychainyi skromnik'**, *Solntse Rossii* (1913), 44: 10 [see *583*].

— [repr.] In: M. Mikhailov, 'Iz neopublikovannykh maloizvestnykh materialov', *Sovetskaia muzyka* (1980), 8: 120.

— [German tr.] 'Peter Tschaikowsky: Ein Mann von ungewöhnlicher Bescheidenheit'. In: *Tschaikowsky aus der Nähe* (1994): 107–108 [see *379*].

IVAN LIPAEV (1865–1942)
Horn player and teacher

[*491*]   **LIPAEV, I. V. 'Pëtr Il´ich Chaikovskii: Iz vospominanii artista-muzykanta'**, *Russkaia starina* (1896), 9: 545–552.

Lipaev's meetings with the composer in the 1890s.

— [repr.] *Russkaia muzykal´naia gazeta* (Nov 1896), 11: 1479–1487.

— [repr.] In: *Vospominaniia o P. I. Chaikovskom* (1962): 186–195; 2-e izd. (1973): 318–326; 3-e izd. (1979): 319–327; 4-e izd. (1980): 270–277 [see *374*].

— [Dutch tr. (abridged)] 'Tsjaikovski en de orkestmusici', *Mens en Melodie*, 34 (Oct 1979): 373–378, illus.

— [English tr. (abridged)] In: D. Brown, *Tchaikovsky remembered* (1993): 149–157 [see *377*].

— [French tr.] 'Souvenirs d'un musicien'. In: *Piotr Tchaïkovski: Écrits critiques, lettres, souvenirs de contemporains* (1985): 283–291 [see *375*].

— [German tr.] 'Tschaikowsky in der Erinnerung eines Orchestermusikers'. In: *Tschaikowsky aus der Nähe* (1994): 137–145 [see *379*].

NAZAR LITROV (d. 1900)
Manservant to Modest Chaikovskii

[*492*]   **LITROV, N. ['Diary']**. In: A. Poznansky, *Tchaikovsky through others' eyes* (1999): 187–191 [see *380*].

Litrov's diary entries relating ot the composition of *The Queen of Spades* in Florence in early 1890.

ALEKSANDR LITVINOV (1861–1933)
Violinist and conductor

[*493*]   **LITVINOV, A. A. 'P. I. Chaikovskii v moei zhizni'**. In: *Vospominaniia o P. I. Chaikovskom* (1962): 157–158 [see *374*].

Chaikovskii at the Moscow Conservatory (written in 1940).

— [repr.] In: *Vospominaniia o P. I. Chaikovskom*, 2-e izd. (1973): 81–82; 3-e izd. (1979): 82–83; 4-e izd. (1980): 69–70 [see *374*].

— [English tr. (abridged)] In: D. Brown, *Tchaikovsky remembered* (1993): 34–35 [see *377*].

— [English tr. (abridged)] In: A. Poznansky, *Tchaikovsky through others' eyes* (1999): 62–63 [see *380*].

NIKOLAI LOSEV

Forester at Votkinsk

[494]   LOSEV, N. 'Vospominaniia o Chaikovskom', *Russkaia muzykal´naia gazeta* (May/Jun 1897), 5/6: 899–900.

The composer's childhood in Votkinsk. Extracted from *Viatskie gubernskie vedomosti* [n. d.].

— [rev. repr.] 'Izvestiia otovsiudu', *Nuvellist* (Apr 1897), 4: 7–8.

FËDOR MASLOV (1840–1915)

Jurist, schoolfriend and colleague of Chaikovskii's at the Ministry of Justice

[495]   MASLOV, F. I. 'P. I. Chaikovskii: Vospominaniia'. In: *Vospominaniia o P. I. Chaikovskom* (1962): 394–396 [see *374*].

Chaikovskii at the Imperial School of Jurisprudence. See also *1718*.

— [repr.] 'Vospominaniia druga'. In: *Vospominaniia o P. I. Chaikovskom*, 2-e izd. (1973): 32–34; 3-e izd. (1979): 33–35; 4-e izd. (1980): 29–30 [see *374*].

— [English tr. (abridged)] In: D. Brown, *Tchaikovsky remembered* (1993): 10–11, 15 [see *377*].

— [English tr.] In: A. Poznansky, *Tchaikovsky through others' eyes* (1999): 13–15 [see *380*].

— [German tr.] 'Erinnerungen an meinen Schulfreund Tschaikowsky'. In: *Tschaikowsky aus der Nähe* (1994): 44–46 [see *379*].

MIKHAIL MATIUSHIN (1861–1934)

Artist

[496]   MATIUSHIN, M. V. 'Vstrechi s P. I. Chaikovskim', *Sovetskaia muzyka* (1940), 5/6: 150–151.

Extracts from Matiushin's unpublished autobiography, concerning Chaikovskii at the Moscow Conservatory, and the first production of *Evgenii Onegin*.

— [repr.] *Leningradskaia pravda* (6 May 1940): 3.

ISAAK MATKOVSKII (1862–1940)

Pianist and teacher

[497]   MATKOVSKII, I. M. 'Nezabyvaemoe', *Ogonek* (1940), 12: 6.

On the composer's resignation from the Moscow Conservatory in 1879, and conducting a concert at Tiflis in 1889.

— [repr.] In: *Vospominaniia o P. I. Chaikovskom*, 4-e izd. (1980): 403 [see *374*].

— [English tr. (abridged)] In: D. Brown, *Tchaikovsky remembered* (1993): 126 [see *377*].

ANNA VON MECK (1864–1942)

Niece of the composer

[498]   MECK, A. L. von 'Iz moikh vospominanii o P. I. Chaikovskom'. In: *Vospominaniia o P. I. Chaikovskom* (1962): 340–344 [see *374*].

The author's recollections of her uncle, and the relationship between Chaikovskii and Nadezhda von Meck (recorded in 1940).

— [repr.] In: *Vospominaniia o P. I. Chaikovskom*, 2-e izd. (1973): 270–272; 3-e izd. (1979): 271–273; 4-e izd. (1980): 230–232 [see *374*].

— [French tr.] 'Pages de mes souvenirs de P. I. Tchaikovski'. In: *Piotr Tchaïkovski: Écrits critiques, lettres, souvenirs de contemporains* (1985): 261–262 [see *375*].

— [German tr.] 'Mein Onkel Peter Tschaikowsky und das Ende seines Briefwechsels mit Nadeshda von Meck'. In: *Tschaikowsky aus der Nähe* (1994): 21–24 [see *379*].

PËTR MEL´NIKOV

Opera director at the Bol´shoi and Mariinskii Theatres, son of the singer Ivan Mel´nikov

[499]   MEL´NIKOV, P. 'Moi vstrechi s P. I. Chaikovskim', *Segodnia* (31 Oct 1939).

MIKHAIL MIKESHIN (1836–1936)

Artist, sculptor and writer

[500]   MIKESHIN, M. O. 'Pamiati P. I. Chaikovskogo', *Peterburgskaia zhizn´* (1893), 52: 498.

Mikeshin's encounter with Chaikovskii in Oct 1893, during which the composer promised to write a march based on Belorussian and Ukrainian folk-tunes. See also *290*.

— [repr.] *Neman* (1969), 11: 131–132.

ALEKSANDR MIKHAILOV (1842–99)

Contemporary of Chaikovskii's at the Imperial School of Jurisprudence

[501]   MIKHAILOV, A. V. 'Iz proshlogo: Vospominaniia pravoveda', *Russkaia shkola*, 1 (1900): 30.

— [English tr. (abridged)] In: A. Poznansky, *Tchaikovsky through others' eyes* (1999): 16 [see *380*].

P. A. MIKHEEV

Postal clerk at Klin

[502]   RIMSKII-KORSAKOV, G. 'Stesnitel´nyi gospodin: Glavy iz vospominanii', *Prostor* (1969), 12: 118–121.

Recollections by P. A. Mikheev and others of Chaikovskii at Frolovskoe, Maidanovo and Klin in the 1880s and 1890s.

— [Polish tr.] 'Czajkowski z bliska', *Ruch Muzyczny*, 5 (1961), 15: 17–18.

NIKOLAI MIKLASHEVSKII

[503]   MIKLASHEVSKII, N. A. 'Moi vospominaniia o P. I. Chaikovskom i A. N. Apukhtine', *Slovo* (1928), No. 1007.

EDUARD NÁPRAVNÍK (1839–1916)

Czech conductor and composer

[504]   NÁPRAVNÍK, E. F. 'P. I. Chaikovskii i "Onegin"', *Solntse Rossii* (1913), 44: 9 [see *583*].

— [English tr.] In: A. Poznansky, *Tchaikovsky through others' eyes* (1999): 142 [see *380*].

— [German tr.] 'Peter Tschaikowsky und seine Oper "Eugen Onegin"'. In: *Tschaikowsky aus der Nähe* (1994): 134 [see *379*].

VLADIMIR NÁPRAVNÍK (1869–1948)

Son of Eduard Nápravník

[505]   NÁPRAVNÍK, V. E. 'Moi vospominaniia o Chaikovskom', *Sovetskaia muzyka* (1949), 7: 63–66, illus.

Chaikovskii in the 1880s and 1890s.

— [repr.] In: *Vospominaniia o P. I. Chaikovskom* (1962): 351–360; 2-e izd. (1973): 254–262; 3-e izd. (1979): 255–263; 4-e izd. (1980): 216–223 [see *374*].

— [English tr. (abridged)] In: D. Brown, *Tchaikovsky remembered* (1993): 93–94, 112–113, 164–165 [see *377*].

[506]   NÁPRAVNÍK, V. E. 'Poslednii priezd P. I. Chaikovskogo v Peterburg: Moi vospominaniia'. In: A. Poznansky, *Tchaikovsky through others' eyes* (1999): 250–254 [see *380*].

Concerning the première of Chaikovskii's *Symphony No. 6*, and news of the composer's death (written c. 1920). See also *1854*.

LEONID NIKOLAEV (1878–1942)

Pianist, composer and professor at the St. Petersburg Conservatory

[507]   **NIKOLAEV, L. V. 'O moikh vstrechakh s P. I. Chaikovskim'**. In: *Vospominaniia o P. I. Chaikovskom* (1962): 196–200 [see *374*].

The author's meetings with Chaikovskii in Kiev in 1890 and 1891.

— [repr.] In: *Vospominaniia o P. I. Chaikovskom*, 2-e izd. (1973): 310–312; 3-e izd. (1979): 311–313 [see *374*].

— [English tr. (abridged)] In: D. Brown, *Tchaikovsky remembered* (1993): 130, 179 [see *377*].

SOF´IA NIUBERG-KASHKINA (1872–1966)

Daughter of Nikolai Kashkin

[508]   **NIUBERG-KASHKINA, S. N. 'O Chaikovskom: Vospominaniia svoi i chuzhie'**. In: *Vospominaniia o P. I. Chaikovskom* (1962): 260–277 [see *374*].

The author's memories of the composer during his last years (written in 1959).

— [repr.] In: *Vospominaniia o P. I. Chaikovskom*, 2-e izd. (1973): 87–101; 3-e izd. (1979): 88–102; 4-e izd. (1980): 75–87 [see *374*].

— [repr. (abridged)] In: 'Iz vospominaniia', *Sovetskaia muzyka* (1990), 6: 98.

— [English tr. (abridged)] In: D. Brown, *Tchaikovsky remembered* (1993): 35–38, 90, 101 [see *377*].

— [French tr.] 'Tchaïkovski'. In: *Piotr Tchaïkovski: Écrits critiques, lettres, souvenirs de contemporains* (1985): 219–233 [see *375*].

OSIP PALEČEK (1842–1915)

Czech singer and music teacher

[509]   **PALECHEK, O. 'P. I. Chaikovskii: Prekrasnyi rezhisser'**, *Solntse Rossii* (1913), 44: 8–9 [see *583*].

— [German tr.] 'Tschaikowsky und die Opernregie'. In: *Tschaikowsky aus der Nähe* (1994): 146–147 [see *379*].

ALEKSANDRA PANAEVA-KARTSOVA (1853–1942)

Singer, and cousin by marriage of Chaikovskii

[510]   **PANAEVA-KARTSOVA, A. V. 'Vospominaniia o P. I. Chaikovskom'**. In: *Vospominaniia o P. I. Chaikovskom* (1962): 278–298 [see *374*].

The author's recollections (written in 1933) of her first meeting with Chaikovskii at the première of *Evgenii Onegin*, Anton Rubinstein's jubilee celebrations in 1889, and Chaikovskii's funeral.

— [repr.] In: *Vospominaniia o P. I. Chaikovskom*, 2-e izd. (1973): 140–161; 3-e izd. (1979): 141–162; 4-e izd. (1980): 120–138 [see *374*].

— [English tr. (abridged)] In: D. Brown, *Tchaikovsky remembered* (1993): 44–45, 67–71 [see *377*].

— [French tr.] 'Souvenirs de Tchaïkovski'. In: *Piotr Tchaïkovski: Écrits critiques, lettres, souvenirs de contemporains* (1985): 234–254 [see *375*].

EMILIIA PAVLOVSKAIA (1853–1935)

Opera artist at the Mariinskii Theatre, St. Petersburg

[511]   **PAVLOVSKAIA, E. K. 'Iz moikh vstrech s P. I. Chaikovskim'**. In: *Vospominaniia o P. I. Chaikovskom* (1962): 139–144 [see *374*].

— [repr.] in *Vospominaniia o P. I. Chaikovskom*, 2-e izd. (1973): 172–175; 3-e izd. (1979): 173–176; 4-e izd. (1980): 148–150 [see *374*].

— [English tr. (abridged)] In: D. Brown, *Tchaikovsky remembered* (1993): 147 [see *377*].

PAVEL PCHEL´NIKOV (1851–1913)

Director of the Moscow Imperial Theatres

[*512*] **PCHEL´NIKOV, P. M. 'Vospominaniia o P. I. Chaikovskom'**, *Moskovskie vedomosti* (27 & 28 Oct 1900).

— [repr.] *Russkaia muzykal´naia gazeta* (5 Nov 1900), 45: 1080–1084.

— [repr.] In: *Vospominaniia o P. I. Chaikovskom*, 2-e izd. (1973): 165–170; 3-e izd. (1979): 166–171; 4-e izd. (1980): 142–146 [see *374*].

— [English tr. (abridged)] In: D. Brown, *Tchaikovsky remembered* (1993): 119, 162 [see *377*].

— [French tr.] 'Souvenirs de P. I. Tchaïkovski'. In: *Piotr Tchaïkovski: Écrits critiques, lettres, souvenirs de contemporains* (1985): 255–260 [see *375*].

— [German tr.] 'Meine Erinnerungen an Tschaikowsky'. In: *Tschaikowsky aus der Nähe* (1994): 153 [see *379*].

MARIUS PETIPA (1822–1910)

Ballet-master and choreographer

[*513*] **PETIPA, M. 'Memuary Mariusa Petipa'.** In: *Marius Petipa: Materialy, vospominannia, stat'i*. Red. A. Nekhenzi, Leningrad: Gos. teatral´nyi muzei, 1971: 54–56.

— [German tr.] 'Aus meiner Zusammenarbeit mit Peter Tschaikowsky und Alexander Glasunow'. In: *Tschaikowsky aus der Nähe* (1994): 159–161 [see *379*].

ISIDOR PHILIPP (1863–1958)

French pianist and teacher

[*514*] **PHILIPP, I. 'Three Russian giants: Glimpses of Tchaikovsky, Rubinstein and Glazunoff'**, *Musical Digest* (Oct/Nov 1948): 18–19.

— [repr.] *Journal of the American Liszt Society*, 8 (Dec 1980): 60–63.

VLADIMIR POGOZHEV (1851–1935)

Manager of the St. Petersburg Imperial Theatres

[*515*] **POGOZHEV, V. P. 'Vospominaniia o P. I. Chaikovskom'**, *Chaikovskii: Vospominaniia i pis´ma* (1924): 13–98 [see *373*].

Includes 10 letters from Chaikovskii to Pogozhev (1887–91). With commentary by I. Glebov [B. V. Asaf´ev], 'Dobavleniia k vospominaniiam V. P. Pogozheva': 89–98.

— [repr.] In: *Vospominaniia o P. I. Chaikovskom* (1962): 69–138; 2-e izd. (1973): 176–234; 3-e izd. (1979): 177–235; 4-e izd. (1980): 151–199 [see *374*].

— [Dutch tr.] 'Persoonlijke onmoetingen met Tsjaikovski', *Mens en melodie*, 34 (Apr 1979): 109–113, illus.

— [English tr. (abridged)] In: D. Brown, *Tchaikovsky remembered* (1993): 72–74, 166–167 [see *377*].

— [English tr. (abridged)] In: A. Poznansky, *Tchaikovsky through others' eyes* (1999): 142–156 [see *380*].

— [German tr. (extract)] 'Eine Episode in meinen Beziehungen zu Tschaikowsky und seinen Verleger Jürgenson'. In: *Tschaikowsky aus der Nähe* (1994): 121–126 [see *379*].

Includes German tr. of Glebov's original commentary ('Notwendige Ergänzung zu Pogoshews Schilderung'): 127–133.

— [German tr. (extract)] 'Tschaikowskys Begräbnis'. In: *Tschaikowsky aus der Nähe* (1994): 280–282 [see *379*].

IULIAN POPLAVSKII (1871–1958)

Cellist and writer

[*516*] **POPLAVSKII, Iu. I. 'Poslednii den´ P. I. Chaikovskogo v Klinu'**, *Artist* (Oct 1894), 42: 116–120.

Description of a short stay at the composer's home in Oct 1893.

— [repr.] in *Vospominaniia o P. I. Chaikovskom* (1962): 365–375; 2-e izd. (1973): 373–381; 3-e izd. (1979): 374–382; 4-e izd. (1980): 318–325 [see *374*].

— [English tr. (abridged)] In: D. Brown, *Tchaikovsky remembered* (1993): 168, 199–203 [see *377*].

— [English tr.] In: A. Poznansky, *Tchaikovsky's last days* (1991): 32–39.

— [French tr.] 'La dernière journée de Tchaïkovski à Kline'. In: *Piotr Tchaïkovski: Écrits critiques, lettres, souvenirs de contemporains* (1985): 305–313 [see *375*].

— [German tr.] 'Tschaikowskys letzter Tag in Klin'. In: *Tschaikowsky aus der Nähe* (1994): 232–241 [see *379*].

[*517*] **POPLAVSKII, Iu. I. 'Pamiati Chaikovskogo'**, *Pravda* (1904), 1: 255–263.

— [repr. (abridged)] 'Pamiati P. I. Chaikovskogo', *Russkaia muzykal'naia gazeta* (Jan 1904): 108–110.

— [English tr. (extract)] In: A. Poznansky, *Tchaikovsky through others' eyes* (1999): 234–238, 268–269 [see *380*].

[*518*] **POPLAVSKII, Iu. I. 'Iz zhizni P. Chaikovskogo: Zapiski sovremennika'**, *Vozrozhdenie* (1965): 5–13.

IPPOLIT PRIANISHNIKOV (1847–1921)
Singer (baritone) at the Kiev Opera Theatre, music teacher and opera impressario

[*519*] **PRIANISHNIKOV, I. P. 'P. I. Chaikovskii kak dirizher: Pis'mo k izdateliu'**, *Russkaia muzykal'naia gazeta* (Sep 1896), 9: 1001–1008.

A letter to the editor (written 9 Aug 1896) recalling Chaikovskii's concerts in Moscow and Kiev in the 1890s.

— [repr.] 'P. I. Chaikovskii kak dirizher'. In: *Vospominaniia o P. I. Chaikovskom* (1962): 178–185; 2-e izd. (1973): 300–304; 3-e izd. (1979): 301–305; 4-e izd. (1980): 254–257 [see *374*].

— [English tr. (abridged)] In: D. Brown, *Tchaikovsky remembered* (1993): 128–129 [see *377*].

— [French tr.] 'P. I. Tchaïkovski chef d'orchestre'. In: *Piotr Tchaïkovski: Écrits critiques, lettres, souvenirs de contemporains* (1985): 278–282 [see *375*].

— [German tr.] 'Peter Tschaikowsky als Dirigent'. In: *Tschaikowsky aus der Nähe* (1994): 148–152 [see *379*].

[*520*] **PRIANISHNIKOV, I. P. 'Sovremenniki o P. I. Chaikovskom'**, *Teatr i zhizn'* (25 Oct 1913): 11.

ARKADII RAICH
Journalist

[*521*] **R[AICH], A. 'K biografii A. N. Apukhtina'**, *Istoricheskii vestnik*, 107 (1907): 580–582.

Includes anecdotes concerning Aleksei Apukhtin and Chaikovskii at the Ministry of Justice.

— [English tr. (abridged)] In: A. Poznansky, *Tchaikovsky through others' eyes* (1999): 18–19 [see *380*].

SERGEI RAKHMANINOV (1873–1943)
Russian composer, pianist and conductor

[*522*] **RAKHMANINOV, S. V. 'Vospominaniia'**. In: *Sergei Rakhmaninov: Literaturnoe nasledie*. Tom 1. Red. Z. Apetian. Moskva: Muzyka, 1978: 53–54.

— [German tr.] 'Tschaikowsky und meine Oper "Aleko"'. In: *Tschaikowsky aus der Nähe* (1994): 111–112 [see *379*].

PËTR RIAZANTSEV (b. 1881)
Trumpet player

[*523*] **RIAZANTSEV, P. ['Vospominaniia']**. In: *Vospominaniia o P. I. Chaikovskom* (1962): 228–230.

Memories of a concert in Khar'kov in Mar 1893 conducted by Chaikovskii.

— [repr.] In: *Vospominaniia o P. I. Chaikovskom*, 4-e izd. (1980): 416 [see *374*].

— [English tr. (abridged)] In: D. Brown, *Tchaikovsky remembered* (1993): 148 [see *377*].

ROMAIN ROLLAND (1866–1944)
French writer and musicologist

[*524*] **ROLLAND, R. 'Le cloitre de la rue d'Ulm'**. In: R. Rolland, *Cahiers Romain Rolland*. Tom 4. Paris, 1952: 190–191.

Concerning concerts conducted by Chaikovskii in Paris in Mar 1888.

— [English tr.] In: A. Poznansky, *Tchaikovsky through others' eyes* (1999): 156–157 [see *380*].

ALEKSANDR RUBETS (1838–1913)
Professor at the St. Petersburg Conservatory

[525]   **RUBETS, A. I. 'Vospominaniia prof. A. I. Rubtsa o pervykh godakh Peterburgskoi konservatorii'**, *Novoe vremia* (27 Aug; 3 Sep 1912).

— [repr. (abridged)] In: *Vospominaniia o P. I. Chaikovskom* (1962): 412; 2-e izd. (1973): 436; 4-e izd. (1980): 371–372 [see *374*].

— [English tr. (abridged)] In: A. Poznansky, *Tchaikovsky through others' eyes* (1999): 45–49 [see *380*].

LEONID SABANEEV (1882–1967)
Composer, conductor and writer

[526]   **SABANEEV, L. S.** *I. Taneev: Mysli o tvorchestve i vospominaniia o zhizni.* Paris: Izd-vo TAIR, 1930: 80–82, 110–112.

Includes Sabaneev's reminiscences of his first meeting with Chaikovskii.

[527]   **SABANEEV, L. 'Moi vstrechi s P. I. Chaikovskim'**, *Russkaia mysl´* (3 Oct 1963).

— [English tr. (abridged)] In: A. Poznansky, *Tchaikovsky through others' eyes* (1999): 214–216 [see *380*].

NADEZHDA SALINA (1864–1956)
Soprano at the Bol´shoi Theatre in Moscow

[528]   **SALINA, N. V. 'Osushchestvlennaia mechta'**, *Ogonek* (1940), 12: 10, illus.

The author's encounters with Chaikovskii while performing in his operas.

VASILII SAPEL´NIKOV (1868–1941)
Russian pianist

[529]   **'U V. L. Sapel´nikova'**, *Odesskie novosti* (14 Nov 1903).

Interview with Sapel´nikov.

— [abridged repr.] *Novosti i birzhevaia gazeta* (18 Nov 1903).

— [abridged repr.] V. L. Sapel´nikov, 'Iz vospominanii o P. I. Chaikovskom', *Teatr*, 539 (1909): 12–13.

— [English tr. (abridged)] In: A. Poznansky, *Tchaikovsky through others' eyes* (1999): 233–234 [see *380*].

KONSTANTIN SARADZHEV (1877–1954)
Violinist and conductor

[530]   **SARADZHEV, K. S. 'O P. I. Chaikovskom'.** In: *K. S. Saradzhev: Stat´i, vospominaniia.* Sost., ref. i avtor biograficheskogo ocherka G. G. Tiranov. Moskva: Sovetskii kompozitor, 1962: 176–180.

The first rehearsal of Chaikovskii's Sixth Symphony at the Moscow Conservatory in 1893.

— [repr.] 'O pervom orkestrovom zvuchanii Shestoi simfonii'. In: *Vospominaniia o P. I. Chaikovskom*, 2-e izd. (1973): 371–372; 3-e izd. (1979): 372–373; 4-e izd. (1980): 316–317 [see *374*].

— [English tr. (abridged)] In: D. Brown, *Tchaikovsky remembered* (1993): 204–205 [see *377*].

EMIL VON SAUER (1862–1942)
Pianist and composer

[531]   **SAUER, E.** *Meine Welt: Bilder aus dem geheimfache meiner Kunst und meines Lebens.* Stuttgart, 1901: 206–207.

The author's meeting with Chaikovskii at a concert in Dresden in 1889.

— [English tr. (abridged)] In: D. Brown, *Tchaikovsky remembered* (1993): 80 [see *377*].

KONSTANTIN SEREBRIAKOV (1852–1919)
Bass at the Mariinskii Theatre

[*532*] SEREBRIAKOV, K. 'Sovremenniki o P. I. Chaikovskom', *Teatr i zhizn'* (25 Oct 1913): 11.

VALENTINA SEROVA (1846–1924)
Composer, and wife of Aleksandr Serov

[*533*] SEROVA, V. 'Trois moments musicales', *Russkaia muzykal'naia gazeta* (Jan 1895), 1: 20–25; (Feb 1895), 2: 131–134.

Meetings with the composer in 1868 and the 1880s, including a performance of the overture-fantasia *Hamlet*.

—— [repr. (abridged)] In: *Vospominaniia o P. I. Chaikovskom*, 2-e izd. (1973): 438–439; 4-e izd. (1980): 373–374 [see *374*].

—— [English tr. (abridged)] In: D. Brown, *Tchaikovsky remembered* (1993): 25 [see *377*].

M. SH—IN

[*534*] SH—IN, M. 'Iz vospominanii o P. I. Chaikovskom', *Russkaia muzykal'naia gazeta* (Jul/Aug 1897), 7/8: 1052–1054.

Chaikovskii's tour of Kiev in 1891.

TAT´IANA SHCHEPKINA-KUPERNIK (1874–1952)
Writer and translator

[*535*] SHCHEPKINA-KUPERNIK, T. L. 'Stranitsy vospominanii', *Komsomol'skaia pravda* (6 May 1940): 3 [see *862*].

The author's meeting with Chaikovskii in Kiev in 1889.

—— [repr.] *Ogonek* (1940), 12: 7, illus.

—— [rev. repr.] 'Chaikovskii'. In: T. L. Shchepkina-Kupernik, *Teatr v moei zhizni*. Moskva; Leningrad, 1948: 48–50.

—— [repr.] In: *Vospominaniia o P. I. Chaikovskom*, 2-e izd. (1973): 313–315; 3-e izd. (1979): 314–316; 4-e izd. (1980): 265–268 [see *374*].

—— [English tr. (abridged)] In: D. Brown, *Tchaikovsky remembered* (1993): 95, 170 [see *377*].

LEV SHTEINBERG (1870–1945)
Conductor, teacher and composer

[*536*] SHTEINBERG, L. P. 'Pamiatnye vstrechi'. *Komsomol'skaia pravda* (6 May 1940): 3 [see *862*].

The author's meetings with Chaikovskii in the early 1890s.

—— [repr.] In: *Vospominaniia o P. I. Chaikovskom* (1962): 176–177; 2-e izd. (1973): 263–264; 3-e izd. (1979): 264–265; 4-e izd. (1980): 224–225 [see *374*].

DMITRII SKALON (1840–1919)
General, President of the Russian Military Historical Society

[*537*] SKALON, D. A. 'Na sluzhbe v leib-ulanakh (1859–1864)', *Russkaia starina*, 10 (1908): 185–186.

—— [repr.] In: *Vospominaniia o P. I. Chaikovskom* (1962): 405–406; 2-e izd. (1973): 432–433; 4-e izd. (1980): 368 [see *374*].

STEPAN SKITALETS (1869–1941)
Writer and poet

[*538*]   **SKITALETS. 'Klochki zhizni (s beregov Nevy): 25 okt. 1893'**, *Rannee utro* (27 Oct 1913): 4.

The reaction in St. Petersburg to the news of the composer's illness and death.

— [repr.] In: *Vospominaniia o P. I. Chaikovskom* (1962): 376–378; 2-e izd. (1973): 403–405; 3-e izd. (1979): 404–406; 4-e izd. (1980): 344–345 [see *374*].

ETHEL SMYTH (1858–1944)

English composer

[*539*]   **SMYTH, E. *Impressions that remained*.** London: Longmans, 1919: 167–168.

— [repr.] In: D. Brown, *Tchaikovsky remembered* (1993): 190–191 [see *377*].

— [Russian tr.] In: 'Iz vospominanii', *Sovetskaia muzyka* (1990), 6: 96.

ALEKSANDRA SNEGIRËVA-IURGENSON (1870–1946)

Daughter of the composer's publisher, Pëtr Iurgenson

[*540*]   **SNEGIRËVA-IURGENSON, A. P. 'P. I. Chaikovskii v sem´e P. I. Iurgensona'.** In: *Vospominaniia o P. I. Chaikovskom*, 2-e izd. (1973): 119–122 [see *374*]

The author's childhood recollections of Chaikovskii in the 1870s and 1880s.

— [repr.] In: *Vospominaniia o P. I. Chaikovskom*, 3-e izd. (1979): 120–123; 4-e izd. (1980): 102–105 [see *374*].

— [English tr. (abridged)] In: D. Brown, *Tchaikovsky remembered* (1993): 91–92 [see *377*].

ALEKSANDRA SOKOLOVA (1836–1914)

Journalist

[*541*]   **SOKOLOVA, A. I. 'Komicheskii sluchai s P. I. Chaikovskim'**, *Istoricheskii vestnik*, 119 (1910): 557–571.

The composer's relationship with the Begichevs and Shilovskiis in the late 1860s.

— [English tr. (abridged)] In: A. Poznansky, *Tchaikovsky through others' eyes* (1999): 97–101 [see *380*].

[*542*]   **SOKOLOVA, A. I. 'Vstrechi i znakomstva'**, *Istoricheskii vestnik*, 127 (1912): 536–538.

Recalling the failure of Chaikovskii's opera *The Voevoda* in 1869.

— [English tr. (abridged)] In: A. Poznansky, *Tchaikovsky through others' eyes* (1999): 94–97 [see *380*].

NIKOLAI SOLOV´EV (1846–1916)

Composer, music critic and professor at the St. Petersburg Conservatory

[*543*]   **SOLOV´EV, N. F. 'P. I. Chaikovskii v vospominaniiakh'**, *Birzhevye vedomosti* (24 Oct 1913) [see *372*].

ADELAIDA SPASSKAIA (b. 1848)

Pianist, music tutor, and fellow student of Chaikovskii's at the St. Petersburg Conservatory

[*544*]   **SPASSKAIA, A. L. 'Tovarishcheskie vospominaniia o P. I. Chaikovskom'**, *Russkaia muzykal´naia gazeta* (31 Oct 1899), 44: 1113–1118.

Chaikovskii at the St. Petersburg Conservatory.

— [repr. (abridged)] In: *Vospominaniia o P. I. Chaikovskom* (1962): 410–412; 2-e izd (1973): 435–436 [see *374*].

— [English tr. (abridged)] In: A. Poznansky, *Tchaikovsky through others' eyes* (1999): 42–45 [see *380*].

ALEKSANDR SPENDIAROV (1871–1928)

Composer, conductor and music teacher

[545]   **SPENDIAROV, A. A. 'Vospominaniia o P. I. Chaikovskom'**, *Literaturnaia Armeniia* (1965), 6: 98–100.
Chaikovskii as conductor. With commentary by K. Grigorian.

—   [repr.] In: *Iz istorii armiano-russkikh muzykal´nykh sviazei: Vospominaniia, pis´ma (1827–1917).* Sost., vstup.
stat´ia i kommentarii K. Grigorian. Erevan: Akademii Nauk Arm. SSR, 1971: 17–22, illus.

CHARLES VILLIERS STANFORD (1852–1924)
Irish composer, conductor, organist and teacher

[546]   **STANFORD, C. V. ['Tchaikovsky'].** In: G. V. Stanford, *Pages from an unwritten diary*. London: Edward
Arnold, 1914: 278–281.
Stanford's memories of Chaikovskii's visit to Cambridge University in 1893.

—   [repr. (abridged)] In: D. Brown, *Tchaikovsky remembered* (1993): 188 [see *377*].

FRANTIŠEK ŠUBERT (1849–1915)
Czech dramatist and director of the National Theatre in Prague

[547]   **ŠUBERT, F. A. 'Skladatel "Eugena Onegina"'.** In: F. A. Šubert, *Moje vzpominky*. Praha: Unie, 1902:
105–116, illus. (*Z uplynulych dob*; 1).
Chaikovskii's visit to Prague in 1888, and the production of *Evgenii Onegin* in the National Teatre.

—   [repr.] In: *Vospominaniia o P. I. Chaikovskom*, 2-e izd. (1973): 290–294; 3-e izd. (1979): 291–295; 4-e izd.
(1980): 247–250 [see *374*].

—   [English tr. (abridged)] In: D. Brown, *Tchaikovsky remembered* (1993): 78, 121–123 [see *377*].

IOAKIM TARTAKOV (1860–1923)
Singer and director at the Mariinskii Theatre in Moscow

[548]   **TARTAKOV, I. V. 'P. I. Chaikovskii: Chudnyi tovarishch'**, *Solntse Rossii* (1913), 44: 6–7 [see *583*].

—   [repr.] In: *Vospominaniia o P. I. Chaikovskom*, 2-e izd. (1973): 309; 3-e izd. (1979): 310; 4-e izd. (1980): 261
[see *374*].

[549]   **TARTAKOV, I. V. 'Sovremenniki o P. I. Chaikovskom'**, *Teatr i zhizn´* (25 Oct 1913): 10.

VLADIMIR TRAVSKII
Producer with the Kononov Private Opera in St. Petersburg

[550]   **'Sovremenniki o P. I. Chaikovskom'**, *Teatr i zhizn´* (25 Oct 1913): 12.

—   [English tr. (abridged)] In: A. Poznansky, *Tchaikovsky's last days: A documentary study* (1997): 70 [see *2270*].

VARVARA TSEKHOVSKAIA (b. 1872)
Journalist for the newspaper *Kievskoe slovo*

[551]   **[TSEKHOVSKAIA, V.] 'Pervaia postanovka "Pikovoi damy"'**, *Solntse Rossii* (1913), 44: 20–22 [see
583].
The premiere of the opera *The Queen of Spades* in Kiev in Dec 1890, which was attended by the composer.

—   [English tr.] In: A. Poznansky, *Tchaikovsky through others' eyes* (1999): 161–163 [see *380*].

IVAN TURCHANINOV (1839–1910)
Contemporary at the Imperial School of Jurisprudence

[552]   **TURCHANINOV, I. N. 'Tovarishcheskie vospominaniia byvshego pravoveda'.** In: *Vospominaniia
o P. I. Chaikovskom* (1962): 406 [see *374*].
See also *1718*.

— [repr.] In: L. V. Konisskaia, *Chaikovskii v Peterburge* (1969): 47–48; 2-e izd. (1974): 51–52 [see *1764*].

— [English tr. (abridged)] In: A. Poznansky, *Tchaikovsky through others' eyes* (1999): 15 [see *380*].

KARL VAL´TS (1846–1929)
Artistic director at the Bol´shoi and Malyi Theatres

[*553*]   **VAL´TS, K. F. 'Iz teatral´nykh memuarov'.** In: K. F. Val´ts, *Shest´desiat piat´ let v teatre*. Leningrad, 1928: 104, 107–108, 117–118, 154–156.

Recalling Chaikovskii's involvement with the productions of this operas and ballets in Moscow.

— [repr.] In: *Vospominaniia o P. I. Chaikovskom*, 2-e izd. (1973): 162–164; 3-e izd. (1979): 163–165; 4-e izd. (1980): 139–141 [see *374*].

KONSTANTIN VARLAMOV (1849–1915)
Actor with the Aleksandrinskii Theatre in St. Petersburg

[*554*]   **VARLAMOV, K. A. 'P. I. Chaikovskii: Chelovek vydaiushcheisia dushevnoi krasoty'**, *Solntse Rossii* (1913), 44: 5 [see *583*].

— [English tr.] In: A. Poznansky, *Tchaikovsky through others' eyes* (1999): 186–187 [see *380*].

— [German tr.] 'Das einzig Merkwürdige an ihm war seine panische Furcht vor Geistern ...'. In: *Tschaikowsky aus der Nähe* (1994): 57–58 [see *379*].

NIKOLAI VIL´DE (d. 1918)
Writer and theatre critic

[*555*]   **VIL´DE, N. N. 'Iz vospominanii ob avtore "Pikovoi damy"'**, *Teatral´naia gazeta* (1915), 50: 14–15.

The author's encounters with Chaikovskii during rehearsals for *Mazepa* and *The Queen of Spades*.

— [repr. (abridged)] In: *Vospominaniia o P. I. Chaikovskom* (1962): 145–146; 2-e izd. (1973): 171; 3-e izd. (1979): 172 ('O Chaikovskom'); 4-e izd. (1980): 147 ('O Chaikovskom') [see *374*].

[*556*]   **VIL´DE, N. N. 'Vozobnovlenie i vospominanie'**, *Russkaia zhizn´* (1917), 17: 4.

Concerns the first production of *Mazepa* in Moscow (1884).

EVGENIIA ZBRUEVA (1868–1936)
Contralto, singer with Bol´shoi and Mariinskii theatres

[*557*]   **ZBRUEVA, E. 'Sovremenniki o P. I. Chaikovskom'**, *Teatr i zhizn´* (25 Oct 1913): 10.

ALEKSANDR ZILOTI (1863–1945)
Pianist, conductor, teacher and professor at the Moscow Conservatory

[*558*]   **ZILOTI, A. I. 'P. I. Chaikovskii v vospominaniiakh'**, *Birzhevye vedomosti* (24 Oct 1913) [see *372*].

VERA ZILOTI (1866–1940)
Wife of Aleksandr Ziloti

[*559*]   **ZILOTI, V. P. 'Znakomstvo s Chaikovskim'.** In: V. P. Ziloti, *V dome Tret´iakova: Memuary V. P. Ziloti*. [New York], 1954: 161–171.

— [repr.] Moskva: Vysshaia shkola, 1992: 161–171. ISBN: 5-0600-2257-9.

2.7. PICTORIAL COLLECTIONS

[560]   'Semeinaia gruppa Chaikovskikh s dagerotipa sniatogo v 1848 godu', *Russkaia muzykal´naia gazeta* (Jan 1897), 1: 79–80.

A photograph of the Chaikovskii family taken in 1848.

[561]   PAVLOVA, I. 'P. I. Chaikovskii: K desiatiletiiu dnia konchiny. Portret raboty N. Kuznetsova v Tret´iakovskoi galleree v Moskve', *Niva* (1903): 857.

Concerning the painting of Chaikovskii made by Nikolai Kuznetsov in 1893. See also *479, 565, 569, 575*.

[562]   'Pictorial biography of P. Tschaikowsky: Tschaikowsky the composer', *Musical Courier* (Jan 1928): 27.

[563]   BUDIAKOVSKII, A. E. *Zhizn´ i tvorchestvo Petra Il´icha Chaikovskogo k stoletiiu so dnia rozhdeniia, 1840–1940.* Foto-al´bom sost. A. E. Budiakovskim. Otv. red. A. V. Ossovskii. [Leningrad]: Gos. nauchno-issledovatel´skii instutut teatra i muzyki, 1940. 75 p. of illus.

Reviews: 'Khudozhestvennye al´bomy o Chaikovskom', *Smena* (29 Jan 1940): 4 — 'Al´bomy, posviashchennye P. I. Chaikovskomu', *Smena* (18 Mar 1940): 4 — 'Moskovskaia khronika: Vsesoiuznyi komitet po oznamenovaniiu stoletiia', *Sovetskoe iskusstvo* (9 Jun 1940): 4 — 'Iubileinyi al´bom', *Sovetskoe iskusstvo* (24 Aug 1940): 4.

[564]   *P. I. Chaikovskii: 1840–1940.* Penza: Penfotokhduzhnik, 1940. 25 p. of illus.

Containing 25 photographs of Chaikovskii, his homes at Votkinsk and Klin, and scenes from productions of his stage works.

[565]   LUK´IANOVA, D. 'Portret', *Ogonek* (1940), 12: 16.

Concerning the donation of Nikolai Kuznetsov's portrait of the composer from the Tret´iakov Gallery in Moscow to the Klin house-museum. See also *479, 561, 569, 575*.

[566]   PETZOLDT, R. *Peter Tschaikowski, 1840–1893: Sein Leben in Bildern*. Leipzig: Bibliographischen Institut, 1953. 44 p, 24 illus.

Review: *Die Musikforschung*, 13 (1960), 1: 93–94.

— 2. Aufl. Leipzig, 1961.

[567]   ORLOVA, A. A. *Pëtr Il´ich Chaikovskii: Zhizn´ i tvorchestvo, 1840–1893*. Foto-vystavka, avtor-sost. A. A. Orlova. Pod red. V. M. Bogdanova-Berezovskogo. Talinn: Estonskoe respublikanskoe otdelenie Muzykal´nogo fonda SSSR, 1955. 40 p, illus. (*Gos. Dom-muzei P. I. Chaikovskogo*).

A folder containing 129 photographs in 11 envelopes relating to the life and work of Chaikovskii, with 11 sheets of captions for use with the photographs when mounted for exhibition, and an explanatory booklet. Text in Russian.

[568]   GITEL´MAKHER, V. 'Redkaia fotografiia', *Muzykal´naia zhizn´* (Jan 1967), 1: 16, illus.

A photograph of the composer with pupils from the Khar´kov Musical Institute, in March 1893.

[569]   IL'IUSHIN, I. 'Portret Chaikovskogo', *Sovetskaia muzyka* (1969), 9: 153.

Concerning the portrait of Chaikovskii by Nikolai Kuznetsov. See also *479, 561, 565, 575*.

[570]   *Pëtr Il´ich Chaikovskii / Pjotr Iljitsch Tschaikowsky*. Sost./Zusammenstellung: P. E. Vaidman, K. Iu. Davydova, I. G. Sokolinskaia. Obshchaia red. / Gesamtred. E. M. Orlova. Moskva: Muzyka; Leipzig: Deutschen Verlag für Musik, 1978. 201 p, illus. (*Trudy Gos. Dom-muzei P. I. Chaikovskogo v Klinu*). ISBN: 0–64201–021–8.

Text in Russian and German. Chiefly illus.

Reviews: *Musik und Gesellschaft*, 30 (Mar 1980): 184 — *Music Forum*, 24 (1980), 5: 31 — N. Alekseenko, *Sovetskaia muzyka* (1981), 5: 118.

[*571*]   ***Pëtr Il´ich Chaikovskii, 1840–1893: Al´bom***. Sost., avtor vstup. stat´i i teksta G. Pribegina. Moskva:
         Muzyka, 1984. 205 p, illus. (*Chelovek, sobytiia, vremia*).
         — [repr.] Moskva: Muzyka, 1985. 205 p, illus. (*Chelovek, sobytiia, vremia*).

[*572*]   ***Chaikovskii 1840–1893: Al´bom***. Sost. G. I. Belonovich, S. S. Kotomina. Otv. red. L. Sidel´nikov.
         Moskva: Muzyka, 1990. 2 vols, illus. ISBN: 5–7140–0137–0 [set], 5–7140–0177–X [vol. 1], 5–7140–
         0130–3 [vol. 2].
         Vol. 1 is a pictorial chronicle of Chaikovskii's life and works. Includes Catalogue of all Chaikovskii's known
         photographs and portraits (pp. 171–223). Vol. 2 deals with the performances of the composer's music in Russia
         and abroad, and with the house-museums at Klin and Votkinsk.

[*573*]   ***Na rodine P. I. Chaikovskogo: Fotokniga***. Avt.-sost. O. F. Prudnikova, T. A. Pozdeeva. Izhevsk: Udmurtiia,
         1990. 159 p.

[*574*]   **BELONOVICH, G.** 'Na pamiat´: 150 let so dnia rozhdeniia P. I. Chaikovskogo', *Nashe nasledie*
         (1990), 2: 24–27, illus.
         On signed photographs of Chaikovskii.

[*575*]   **ELKINA, N. N.** 'Istoriia portreta P. I. Chaikovskogo'. In: *P. I. Chaikovskii i izobrazitel´noe iskusstvo*
         (1991): 20–35 [see *595*].
         See also *479, 561, 565, 569*.

[*576*]   **BELONOVICH, G. I.** 'Chaikovskii i ego okruzhenie na fotografiiakh sovremennikov'. In: *P. I.
         Chaikovskii: Zabytoe i novoe* (1995): 162–199 [see *598*].

         See also *963, 1154, 1229, 1251, 1277, 1301, 1303, 1311, 1945*.

2.8. SOUND RECORDINGS

[*577*]   **KORABEL´NIKOVA, L.** 'Tschaikowskys Stimme auf dem Edisonschen Phonographen?', *Das
         Orchester*, 42 (1994), 10: 20–23.
         The discovery of an Edison-phonograph recording made by Julius Block, which is believed to include
         Chaikovskii's voice. See also *578–582*.

[*578*]   **KORABEL´NIKOVA, L. Z.** 'Predistoriia', *Muzykal´noe obozrenie* (1997), 9: 2.

[*579*]   **VAIDMAN, P. E.** 'Istoriia', *Muzykal´noe obozrenie* (1997), 9: 2.

[*580*]   **ZHURIN, A.** 'Velikii Chaikovskii zagovoril posle 107 let molchaniia. Sensatsionnaia nakhodka
         v Klinu: Vosstanovlena fonogramma s zapis'iu golosa velikogo kompozitora i ego druzei', *Trud* (15
         Nov 1997).

[*581*]   **MARAKHOVSKII, G.** 'Potomkam vozvrashchen golos velikogo kompozitora', *Rossiiskaia gazeta* (18
         Nov 1997): 8.

[*582*]   'Vokrug Chaikovskogo: Sekret Bloka', *Muzykal´naia zhizn´* (1999), 5: 3.

PART 3

APPRECIATION

3.1. COLLECTED ESSAYS

3.2. COMMEMORATION
3.2.1. Russia and the USSR
3.2.2. Europe
3.2.3. America
3.2.4. Asia and Africa

3.3. MUSEUMS AND MONUMENTS
3.3.1. Klin House-Museum
3.3.2. Other Museums
3.3.3. Monuments

3.1. COLLECTED ESSAYS

[583]   'Venok na mogilu P. I. Chaikovskogo', *Solntse Rossii* (1913), 44: 2–23, illus.

Contents: L. A. Saketti, 'P. I. Chaikovskii: Muzykal´nyi kosmopolit': 2 [see *698*] — M. M. Ippolitov-Ivanov, 'P. I. Chaikovskii: Lirik i velichaishii melodist': 2–5 [see *2427*] — K. A. Varlamov, 'P. I. Chaikovskii: Chelovek vydaiushcheisia dushevnoi krasoty': 5 [see *554*] — N. F. Solov´ev, 'P. I. Chaikovskii: Entsiklopedist v muzyke': 6 [see *700*] — I. V. Tartakov, 'P. I. Chaikovskii: Chudnyi tovarishch': 6–7 [see *548*] — M. A. Slavina, 'P. I. Chaikovskii nedootsenen sovremennikami': 7 [see *699*] — Ts. A. Kiui, 'P. I Chaikovskii: Moskvich': 7 [see *469*] — S. I. Gabel´, P. I. Chaikovskii: Drug molodezhi': 7 [see *442*] — M. M. Fokin, 'P. I. Chaikovskii i balet': 7 [see *3808*] — N. N. Figner, 'P. I. Chaikovskii: Moi uchitel´': 7–8 [see *436*] — O. O. Paleček, 'P. I. Chaikovskii: Prekrasnyi rezhisser': 8–9 [see *509*] — E. F. Nápravník, 'P. I. Chaikovskii i "Onegin"': 9 [see *504*] — F. Litvin, 'P. I. Chaikovskii: Genial´nyi lirik': 9 [see *697*] — A. K. Liadov, 'P. I. Chaikovskii: Neobychainyi skromnik': 10 [see *490*] — V. Chechott, '"Evgenii Onegin" na stsene Mariinskogo teatra: K 20-letiiu so dnia smerti Chaikovskogo': 10–12 [see *2866*] — [G. A. Larosh] 'Slovo Larosha nad grobom Chaikovskogo': 13–15 [see *484*] — A. Kaufman, 'Vstrechi s Chaikovskim (iz lichnykh vospominanii)': 15–17 [see *465*] — L. Grigorov, '"Natha-Valse": Tri mgnoveniia': 17–18 [see *5420*] — [V. Tsekhovskaia], 'Pervaia postanovka "Pikovoi damy"': 20-22 [see *551*] — 'Mysli P. I. Chaikovskogo (iz ego perepiski)': 23 [see *163*].

[584]   *Proshloe russkoi muzyki: Materialy i issledovaniia*. Tom 1: *P. I. Chaikovskii*. Pod red. Igoria Glebova i V. Iakovleva. Petrograd: Ogni, 1918 [1920]. 184 p, illus.

Contents: I. Glebov, 'Nash dolg': 7–14 [see *712*] — 'Pis´ma P. I. Chaikovskogo k A. I. i N. A. Gubert': 15–64 [see *251*] — N. T. Zhegin, 'Dom Petra Il´icha Chaikovskogo v Klinu': 65–98 [see *1166*] — N. D. Kashkin, 'Iz vospominanii o P. I. Chaikovskom': 99–132 [see *464*] — V. Ia[kovlev], 'Poezdka v Klin (fevral´ 1919 g.)': 133–139 [see *1162*] — 'Bibliograficheskie i arkhivnye spravki o sochineniiakh P. I. Chaikovskogo i ego muzykal´nyi arkhiv': 140–171 [see *98*] — 'Plan verkhnego etazha doma-muzeia P. I. Chaikovskogo v Klinu': 172 [see *1165*] — 'Katalog portretov (fotografii i graviur), nakhodiashchikhsia v komnatakh Petra Il´icha': 173–175 [see *1163*] — 'Opis´ fotografii, v albomakh i saf´ianovoi korobke, nakodiashchikhsia na stole v gostinoi pered malen´kim divanchikom': 175–182 [see *1164*] — 'Bibliografiia P. I. Chaikovskogo, sobrannaia Modestom Il´ichom i khraniashchiiasia v Klinu v vitrine muzeia': 183–184 [see *15*].

Reviews: In: *Biriuch petrogradskikh akademicheskikh teatrov*. Sbornik statei pod. red. A. Poliakova. Sbornik 2. [Petrograd], 1920: 319–321 — M., *Dela i dni* (1920), 1: 472–473 — E. Braudo, *Vestnik literatury* (1921), 6/7: 13 — Iu. D. Engel´, *Kul´tura i teatr* (1921), 2: 55 — I. Diomidov, *Vestnik prosveshcheniia* (1922), 2: 39 — M. M. Ippolitov-Ivanov, *Vestnik prosveshcheniia* (1922), 2: 39.

[585]   *Sovetskaia muzyka* (1940), 5/6: 1–153, music, illus.

Special Chaikovskii centenary issue.

Contents: B. V. Asaf´ev: 'Chaikovskii': 3–7 [see *794*] — A. Budiakovskii, 'Russkii natsional´nyi genii': 8–17 [see *795*] — Iu. A. Kremlev, 'Printsipy simfonicheskogo razvitiia u Chaikovskogo': 18–34 [see *4405*] — L. V. Danilevich, 'O simfonizme Chaikovskogo': 35–47 [see *4404*] — A. A. Al´shvang, 'Posledniaia simfoniia Chaikovskogo': 48–69 [see *4699*] — B. Iarustovskii, 'Voprosy opernoi dramaturgii Chaikovskogo': 70–87 [see *2572*] — M. Kiselev, 'Balety Chaikovskogo': 88–98 [see *3814*] — K. Kuznetsov, 'Chaikovskii za rubezhom': 99–104 [see *997*] — D. Rogal´-Levitskii, 'Orkestr Chaikovskogo': 105–111 [see *2433*] — K. Igumnov, 'O fortepiannykh sochineniiakh Chaikovskogo': 112–113 [see *5346*] — I. Remezov, 'Obrazy Chaikovskogo na opernoi stsene': 114–123 [see *2573*] — A. Ogolevets, 'Chaikovskii: Avtor uchebnika garmonii': 124–129 [see *5442*] — V. Iakovlev, 'Chaikovskii-dirizher': 130–132 [see *1732*] — 'Dva neopublikovannykh romansa P. I. Chaikovskogo': 133–137 [see *5243*] — V. Kiselev, 'P. I. Chaikovskii i V. F. Odoevskii': 138–140 [see *300*] — V. Kiselev, 'Pis´ma P. I. Chaikovskogo k V. S. Shilovskomu': 141–145 [see *327*] — D. Rogal´-Levitskii, 'Pis´ma P. I. Chaikovskogo k Edvardu Grigu': 145–148 [see *247*] — D. Chernomordikov, 'Vystupleniia P. I. Chaikovskogo v Parizhe': 149–150 [see *419*] — M. V. Matiushin, 'Vstrechi s P. I. Chaikovskim': 150–151 [see *496*] — G. Sh[neerson], 'Za rubezhom: Vospominaniia P. V. Chaikovskoi': 152–153 [see *412*] — 'Stoletie so dnia rozhdeniia P. I. Chaikovskogo': 153 [see *1000*].

[586]   *Tchaikovsky: A symposium*. Ed. by Gerald Abraham. London: L. Drummond, 1945. 252 p, music. (*Music of the Masters*).

Contents: E. Lockspeiser, 'Tchaikovsky the man': 9–23 [see *1644*] — M. Cooper, 'The symphonies': 24–46 [see *4410*] — E. W. Blom, 'Works for solo instrument and orchestra': 47–73 [see *4970*] — R. W. Wood, 'Miscellaneous orchestral works': 74–103 [see *4824*] — C. Mason, 'The chamber music': 104–113 [see *5286*] — A. E. F. Dickinson, 'The piano music': 114–123 [see *5348*] — G. E. H. Abraham, 'Operas and incidental music': 124–183 [see *2580*] — E. Evans, 'The ballets': 184–196 [see *3819*] — A. A. Al´shvang: 'The songs': 197–229 [see *5242*] — G. E. H. Abraham, 'Religious and other choral music': 230–235 [see *5153*] — 'Bibliography': 238–242 — 'List of compositions': 243–252.

— [repr.] London: L. Drummond, 1946. 252 p, music. (*Music of the Masters*).

— [repr.] *The music of Tchaikovsky*. Ed. by Gerald Abraham. New York: W. W. Norton & Co. [1946]. 277 p, music.

— [repr.] Port Washington, N. Y.: Kennikat Press [1969]. 277 p, music.

— [rev. ed.] New York: W. W. Norton [1974]. 280 p; music. (*The Norton Library*; 707). ISBN: 0–3930–0707–3. With updated bibliography.

Review: *Music Educator's Journal*, 61 (Jan 1975): 77.

[587]   ***Russian symphony: Thoughts about Tchaikovsky***. By Dmitri Shostakovich and others. New York: Philosophical Library [1947]. iii, 271 p, illus.

Contents: D. D. Shostakovich, 'Thoughts about Tchaikovsky': 1–5 [see *896*] — B. V. Asaf´ev, 'The great Russian composer': 6–15 [see *2543*] — Iu. Keldysh, 'Tchaikovsky: The man and his outlook': 16–39 [see *1647*] — B. Iarustovskii, 'Operas': 40–85 [see *2480*] — D. V. Zhitomirskii, 'Symphonies': 86–131 [see *4411*] — V. V. Iakovlev, 'The ballets of Tchaikovsky': 132–159 [see *3821*] — A. Alshvang [Al´shvang], 'Chamber music': 160–192 [see *5287*] — K. Iu. Davydova, 'The archives of the Tchaikovsky museum': 198–211 [see *1213*] — 'List of Tchaikovsky's works for the stage': 213–263 [see *9*].

— [repr.] Freeport, N. Y.: Books for Libraries Press [1969]. 271 p, illus. ISBN: 0–8369–1192-X. (*Essay index reprint series*).

[588]   ***P. I. Chaikovskii i russkaia literatura***. Sost. B. Ia. Anshakov, P. E. Vaidman. Nauchnyi red. kandidat iskusstvovedeniia M. E. Rittikh. Izhevsk: Udmurtiia, 1980. 232 p, music, illus. (*Nastoiashchii sbornik podgotovlen po initsiative Gos. Doma-muzeia P. I. Chaikovskogo v g. Votkinske*).

Contents: M. E. Rittikh, 'Predislovie': 3–8 — B. V. Asaf´ev, 'Iunye gody Chaikovskogo i muzyka k "Snegurochke"': 11–18 [see *4358*] — V. V. Iakovlev: 'Chaikovskii i Apukhtin': 19–25 [see *1969*] — M. S. Blok: 'Pomety P. I. Chaikovskogo na proizvedenii L. N. Tolstogo "V chem moia vera"': 26–39 [see *2001*] — E. Z. Balabanovich, 'O nekotorykh chertakh tvorchestva Chekhova i Chaikovskogo': 40–58 [see *1980*] — L. F. Pavlunina, 'P. I. Chaikovskii i V. A. Zhukovskii': 61–74 [see *2146*] — A. E. Shol´p, 'P. I. Chaikovskii i I. S. Turgenev: K probleme sravnitel´no-tipologicheskogo analiza dramaturgii': 75–81 [see *2143*] — N. S. Arshinova: 'K voprosu o psikhologii zhenskogo obraza v pushkinskikh operakh P. I. Chaikovskogo': 82–99 [see *2603*] — T. I. Lavrishcheva, 'Romansy i detskie pesni P. I. Chaikovskogo na stikhi A. N. Pleshcheeva': 100–111 [see *2126*] — I. F. Kunin, 'P. I. Chaikovskii i narodnyi teatr: Neskol´ko soobrazhenii v sviazi s neosushchestvlennymi opernymi zamyslami kompozitora': 112–124 [see *2604*] — B. Ia. Anshakov, 'O nekotorykh chertakh khudozhestvennogo mira P. I. Chaikovskogo i osobennostiakh peresmysleniia pushkinshkikh obrazov v opere "Pikovaia dama"': 125–144 [see *3646*] — G. I. Ivanchenko, 'Traditsii A. S. Pushkina v opere P. I. Chaikovskogo "Pikovaia dama"': 144–154 [see *3649*] — P. E. Vaidman, 'Rabota P. I. Chaikovskogo nad rukopis´iu libretto opery Pikovaia dama': 155–177 [see *3652*] — M. Sh. Bonfel´d, 'Problema dvuiazychiia v opere P. I. Chaikovskogo "Pikovaia dama"': 178–190 [see *3648*] — N. A. Viktorova, 'P. I. Chaikovskii—chitatel´': 191–209 [see *2119*] — I. S. Rozenberg, '"Ia otnoshus´ k stikham, kak muzykant": O vzgliadakh P. I. Chaikovskogo na poeziiu i ego poeticheskom tvorchestve': 210–220 [see *2118*] — 'Prilozhenie': 223–230.

Reviews: V. Ponomareva, *Muzykal´naia zhizn´* (Mar 1981), 6: 24 — P. R. Zaborov, *Russkaia literatura*, 3 (1984): 245–249.

[589]   ***Teatr v zhizni i tvorchestve P. I. Chaikovskogo***. Sost. B. Ia. Anshakov, G. I. Belonovich, M. Sh. Bonfel´d. Nauchnyi red. i avtor predisloviia kandidat iskusstvovedeniia N. N. Sin´kovskaia. Izhevsk: Udmurtiia, 1985. 180 p.

Contents: N. N. Sin´kovskaia, 'Predislovie': 3–5 — L. F. Pavlunina, 'Teatral´nye interesy A. A. i I. P. Chaikovskikh': 6–11 [see *1715*] — V. B. Gorodilina, 'Domashnie predstavleniia v sem´e Chaikovskikh': 12–15 [see *1714*] — G. I. Belonovich, 'P. I. Chaikovskii i frantsuzskii dramicheskii teatr': 16–26 [see *2121*] — N. N. Sin´kovskaia, 'Drama I. V. Shpazhinskogo "Charodeika" i odnoimennaia opera P. I. Chaikovskogo': 27–40 [see *2770*] — M. E. Rittikh, 'Iz istorii vesennei skazki "Snegurochka" A. N. Ostrovskogo—P. I. Chaikovskogo': 40–54 [see *4360*] — A. P. Grigor´eva, 'M. A. Slavina v operakh P. I. Chaikovskogo': 54–63 [see *2611*] — E. A. Pergament, 'P. I. Chaikovskii i Russkoe opernoe Tovarishchestvo I. P. Prianishnikova': 64–75 [see *1957*] — I. I. Savelova, 'Iz istorii formirovaniia zamysla baleta P. I. Chaikovskogo "Shchelkunchik"': 76–88 [see *3993*] — I. A. Nemirovskaia, 'Nekotorye priemy teatral´noi dramaturgii v simfoniiakh P. I. Chaikovskogo': 89–100 [see *4441*] — T. S. Ugriumova, 'Dramaturgiia U. Shekspira v programmnykh simfonicheskikh proizvedenniiakh P. I. Chaikovskogo': 101–109 [see *2140*] — N. S. Arshinova, 'K probleme opernogo psikhologizma v proizvedeniiakh P. I. Chaikovskogo "Oprichnik" i "Charodeika": 110–120 [see *3424*] — G. I. Poberezhnaia,

'Teatral´naia simvolika baleta "Spiashchaia krasavitsa" P. I. Chaikovskogo': 120–129 [see *4115*] — N. S. Zelentsova, 'P. I. Chaikovskii i tipologicheskie osobennosti russkogo realizma kontsa XIX veka': 130–135 [see *2552*] — A. A. Zhuk, '"Pikovaia dama" P. I. Chaikovskogo i problema geroia v russkoi literature poslednei treti XIX v.': 136–145 [see *3668*] — M. Sh. Bonfel´d, '"Pikovaia dama" P. I. Chaikovskogo i nekotorye cherty teatral´noi estetiki XX veka': 145–166 [see *3664*] — G. G. Gusiatnikova, 'A. N. Benua: Postanovshchik Pikovoi damy P. I. Chaikovskogo': 166–172 [see *3666*] — 'Spisok tsitiruemoi literatury': 173–177.

Review: A. Chepalev, 'Izdanie na rodine Chaikovskogo', *Muzykal´naia zhizn´* (1986), 2: 24.

[*590*]   ***P. I. Chaikovskii: Voprosy istorii i stilia.*** K 150-letiiu so dnia rozhdeniia. Sost. i otsvetstvennyi red. M. E. Rittikh. Moskva: Gos. muzykal´no-pedagogicheskii institut im. Gnesinykh, 1989. 176 p, illus. (*Sbornik trudov*; 108).

Contents: Ot sostavitelia': 3–8 —T. Shcherbakova, 'Chaikovskii i muzyka byta': 9–25 [see *2477*] — M. Sh. Bonfel´d, 'Opera P. I. Chaikovskogo "Pikovaia dama": K probleme sviaznosti khudozhestvennogo teksta': 26–46 [see *3678*] — O. Sosnovtseva, 'O soderzhatel´nosti variantnoi formy v muzyke Chaikovskogo': 47–59 [see *2478*] — M. Rittikh, 'Chaikovskii i dramaticheskii teatr: K istorii "Snegurochki"': 60–89 [see *4361*] — A. Iareshko, 'Muzyka kolokol´nykh zvonov v tvorchestve russkikh kompozitorov vtoroi poloviny XIX veka': 90–114 [see *2395*] — I. A. Nemirovskaia, 'Vyrazitel´noe znachenie zhanrovykh splavov i transformatsii v simfoniiakh Chaikovskogo': 115–134 [see *4447*] — A. Baeva, 'Prelomlenie printsipov opernoi dramaturgii Chaikovskogo v sovremennoi sovetskoi opere': 135–149 [see *2616*] — G. Glushchenko, 'P. I. Chaikovskii v russkoi muzykal´noi publitsistike kontsa XIX-nachala XX veka': 150–172 [see *708*].

[*591*]   ***Chaikovskii: K 150-letiiu so dnia rozhdeniia. Voprosy istorii, teorii i ispolnitel´stva.*** Sbornik statei, sost. i red. Iu. Rozanovoi. Obshchaia red. A. I. Kandinskogo. Moskva: Gos. konservatoriia im. P. I. Chaikovskogo, 1990. 137 p.

Contents: Iu. A. Rozanova, 'Sozdavaia novuiu letopis´ zhizni i tvorchestva Chaikovskogo': 4–17 [see *91*] — D. Arutiunov, 'Vzgliady P. I. Chaikovskogo na muzykal´nuiu formu': 17–42 [see *2068*] — E. G. Sorokina, 'Fortepiannye sonaty Chaikovskogo: K probleme stanovleniia klassicheskoi sonaty v russkoi muzyke 2-i poloviny XIX veka': 42–57 [see *5360*] — T. O. Sidorova, 'O nekotorykh spetsificheskikh chertakh tvorcheskogo protsessa Chaikovskogo': 58–76 [see *2480*] — E. Tsarëva, '"Manfred" Bairona u Shumana i Chaikovskogo: K probleme muzyki i slova': 77–94 [see *4490*] — N. P. Savkina, 'Molodoi Prokof´ev i Chaikovskii: Nabliudeniia nad stilem opery "Maddalena"': 94–104 [see *2517*] — T. Gaidamovich, 'Dva varianta odnogo sochineniia, dva varianta ego interpretatsii: "Variatsii na temu rokoko"': 104–119 [see *5140*] — M. G. Mesropova & A. A. Kandinskii-Rybnikov, '"Vremena goda" i "Detskii al´bom" Chaikovskogo: Tsiklichnost´ i problemy ispolneniia': 120–137 [see *5409*].

[*592*]   ***Sovetskaia muzyka*** (1990), 6: 1–142 [special issue], illus.

Special edition to commemorate the 150th anniversary of Chaikovskii's birth.

Contents: 'Pëtr Il´ich o sebe i muzyke': 1, 20, 32, 81, 120, 133 [see *2072*] — M. Pletnev, 'Beskonechnost´ geniia': 2–3 [see *953*] — V. Konyshev, 'Pari nad mirom, russkii genii!': 4, 28, 54, 82, 124, 142 [see *948*] — 'Chaikovskii i my: Kruglyi stol v redaktsii': 5–19 [see *592*] — A. Lunacharskii, 'Vklad P. I. Chaikovskogo v russkuiu kul´turu bestsenen': 21–27 [see *949*] — B. Asaf´ev, 'Chaikovskii rassuzhdaiushchii so svoei sobstvennoi rukopis´iu': 29–31 [see *2479*] — V. Zak, 'Vazhnyi orientir stilia': 33–38 [see *2482*] — Iu. Kholopov, 'O sisteme muzykal´nykh form v simfoniiakh Chaikovskogo': 38–45 [see *4450*] — L. Karagicheva, 'Dva etiuda o "Pikovoi dame"': 46–53 [see *3682*] — L. Z. Korabel´nikova & O. Fel´dman, 'Zavoevyvat´ novye miry v iskusstve': 55–67 [see *3683*] — M. P. Rakhmanova, 'Ogromnoe i eshche edva tronutoe pole deiatel´nosti': 67–74 [see *5158*] — E. Tugarinov, 'Pod znakom ego tvorchestva': 74–80 [see *2506*] — M. Kogan, 'Rodoslovnaia': 81–90 [see *1875*] — 'Pis´ma, dokumenty': 91–98 [see *186*] — A. Klimovitskii, 'Neizvestnye stranitsy epistoliariia Chaikovskogo': 99–103 [see *184*] — L. Korabel´nikova, 'Pis´ma k Chaikovskomu: Dialog s epokhoi': 103–114 [see *185*] — P. Vaidman, '"Zapis´ stanovitsia kosym dozhdem, livnem": Klinskaia tetrad´ B. V. Asaf´eva': 114–117 [see *1304*] — [N. O. Blinov] 'Sobytiia dvukh dnei': 117–123 [see *2240*] — I. Barsova, 'Samye pateticheskie kompozitory evropeiskoi muzyki: Chaikovskii i Maler': 125–132 [see *2512*] — G. Shokhman, 'Vzgliad s drugikh beregov': 134–141 [reviews of *1532, 1534, 1839, 3844*].

[*593*]   ***Chaikovskii: Voprosy istorii i teorii.*** 2-i sbornik, sost. i red. Iu. A. Rozanova; obshchaia red. A. I. Kandinskogo. Moskva: Gos. konservatoriia im. P. I. Chaikovskogo, 1991. 143 p.

Contents: D. Arutiunov, 'P. I. Chaikovskii o krupnykh muzykal´nykh formakh i zhanrakh': 4–20 — N. Sin´kovskaia, 'Brat´ia Chaikovskie v rabote nad libretto "Pikovoi damy"': 20–27 [see *3692*] — D. Chikhikvadze, 'Kompozitor P. I. Chaikovskii: Vospominaniia': 27–38 [see *420*] — I. Skvortsova, '"Shchelkunchik": Problemy pozdnego stilia': 38–54 [see *4002*] — M. Frolova, 'Chaikovskii i Shuman': 54–64 [see *2102*] — A. Albu, 'Chaikovskii i priroda: K izucheniiu khudozhestvennogo naslediia i lichnosti muzykanta': 64–79 [see *2154*] — G. Malinina, 'Nachalo dukhovnogo vozrozhdeniia': 79–94 [see *5216*] — O.

Komarnitskaia, '"Taina" muzykal´noi formy "Pikovoi damy"': 94–112 [see *3691*] — O. Sosnovtseva, 'Spetsifika variantosti v tvorchestve P. I. Chaikovskogo': 112–134 [see *2486*] — G. Mikhailova, 'Tipy stilizatsii v muzyke P. I. Chaikovskogo': 134–143 [see *2485*].

[*594*] **Muzyka P. I. Chaikovskogo: Voprosy interpretatsii**. Sbornik nauchnikh trydov moskovskoi konservatorii. Moskva: Gos. dvazhdy ordena Lenina konservatoriia im. P. I. Chaikovskogo, 1991. 125 p. (*Kafedra istorii i teorii ispolnitel´skogo iskusstva*).

Contents: B. Grigor´ev, 'P. I. Chaikovskii i problemy ispolnitel´skogo iskusstva': 4–17 [see *2402*] — V. Chinaev. 'Vdokhnovennoe, trivial´noe, nostal´gicheskoe: Interpretatsiia Chaikovskogo v svete vremenii': 18–41 [see *2401*] — T. Gaidamovich, 'P. I. Chaikovskii: Trio "Pamiati velikogo khudozhnoka"': 42–59 [see *5312*] — A. Shirinskii, 'Problemy interpretatsii skripichnogo kontserta P. I. Chaikovskogo': 60–71 [see *5112*] — A. Iakovleva, 'Iz istorii sozdaniia i pervykh postanovok opery P. I. Chaikovskogo "Evgenii Onegin"': 72–86 [see *3097*] — V. Berezin, 'Dukhovye instrumenty v rannikh partiturakh Chaikovskogo': 87–101 [see *2484*] — O. Larchenko, 'Tvorchestvo P. I. Chaikovskogo v kritike V. G. Karatygina i sovremennost´': 102–114 [see *2403*] — A. Merkulov, 'Chaikovskii: Avtor fortepiannykh obrabotok i nekotorye kontsertnye obrabotki dlia fortepiannoi muzyki Chaikovskogo', 115–123 [see *5361*].

[*595*] **P. I. Chaikovskii i izobrazitel´noe iskusstvo**. Red-sost. kandidat iskusstvovedeniia M. Sh. Bonfel´d. Izhevsk: Udmurtiia, 1991. 112 p, illus. (*Muzei-usad´ba P. I. Chaikovskogo v Votkinske*). ISBN 5–7659–0390–8.

Contents: T. S. Ugriumova, 'Chaikovskii ob izobrazitel´nom iskusstve': 6–19 [see *2150*] — N. N. Elkina, 'Istoriia portreta P. I. Chaikovskogo': 20–35 [see *575*] — M. Sh. Bonfel´d, 'Vzaimodeistve iskusstv: Organizatsiia dramturgicheskogo prostranstva v opere "Pikovaia dama" i russkoi zhivopisi kontsa XIX–nachala XX vekov': 36–54 [see *3689*] — N. S. Arshinova, 'Psikhologiia vizual´noi obraznosti v operakh P. I. Chaikovskogo': 55–61 [see *2617*] — G. I. Poberzhnaia, 'Izobrazitel´nost´ v baletnoi muzyke P. I. Chaikovskogo': 62–69 [see *3856*] — T. N. Ermolaeva, '"Evgenii Onegin": P. I. Chaikovskogo i liricheskii peizazh XIX veka': 70–78 [see *3095*] — A. P. Grigor´eva, '"Evgenii Onegin" P. I. Chaikovskogo na stsene Opernoi studii Leningradskoi konservatorii v oformlenii T. G. Bruni': 79–86 [see *3096*] — V. S. Belov, 'Balety P. I. Chaikovskogo v tvorchestve S. B. Virsaladze', 87–92 [see *3855*] — G. G. Gusiatnikova, 'Balet P. I. Chaikovskogo "Shchelkunchik" na stsene Leningradskogo Akademicheskogo Malogo teatra opery i baleta': 93–99 [see *4001*] — V. V. Lozhkin, 'Stenografiia opery "Evgenii Onegin" v postanovke Izhevskogo opernogo teatra': 100–107 [see *3098*].

[*596*] **Internationales Čajkovskij Symposium, Tübingen 1993: Bericht**. Hrsg. von Thomas Kohlhase. Mainz [u. a.]: Schott [1995]. 367 p, music. (*Čajkovskij Studien*; 1). ISBN: 3–7957–0295–X.

Proceedings of the symposium held in connection with the Internationales Tschaikowsky-Fest, Tübingen, Oct. 1993. Articles in German or English.

Contents: T. Kohlhase, 'Vorwort': 7–8 — T. Kohlhase, 'Begrussung und Einführung': 9–19 [see *1051*] — 'Drei bisher unbekannte Briefe Čajkovskijs von 1887, 1891 und 1893, sowie sechs weitere Briefe vom 20 August 1893': 21–49 [see *190*] — I. Barsova, 'Mahler: Ein "Schüler" Čajkovskijs?': 51–56 [see *2513*] — G. Belonovich, 'Čajkovskijs letzter Wohnsitz und das Museum in Klin': 57–62 [see *1339*] — M. Bobeth, 'Čajkovskij und das "Mächtige Häuflein"': 63–86 [see *1913*] — S. Dammann, 'Überlegungen zu einer problemgeschichtlichen Untersuchung von Čajkovskijs 4. Sinfonie': 87–102 [see *4617*] — V. Erohin, 'An der Schwelle zum neuen Jahrhundert: Anmerkungen zu Čajkovskijs Harmonik': 103–110 [see *2411*] — T. Frumkis, 'Zu deutschen Vorbildern von Čajkovskijs Harmonielehre': 111–126 [see *2412*] — K. Gronke, 'Zur Rolle des Gremin in Cajkovskijs Oper "Evgenij Onegin"': 127–140 [see *3115*] — A. Holden, 'Čajkovskij's death: Cholera or suicide?': 141–154 [see *2267*] — A. Klimovitskii, 'Čajkovskij und das russische "Silberne Zeitalter"': 155–164 [see *709*] — R.-D. Kluge, 'Čajkovskij und die literarische Kultur Rußlands': 165–176 [see *2123*] — T. Kohlhase, 'Editionsprobleme der Neuen Čajkovskij-Gesamtausgabe am Beispiel der 6. Sinfonie': 177–186 [see *4749*] — L. Korabel´nikova, 'Čajkovskij im Dialog mit Zeitgenossen': 187–198 [see *185*] — L. Lauer, 'Čajkovskijs "Pikovaja Dama" und die Tradition der französischen Opéra-comique-Ballade: 199–206 [see *3710*] — D. Lehmann, 'Čajkovsijs Ansichten über deutsche Komponisten': 207–216 [see *596*] — M. Morita, 'Some observations on Japan's association with Russian music and Čajkovskij': 217–222 [see *1150*] —S. Neef, 'Čajkovskj mit den Augen Stravinskijs gesehen: Zum Verhältnis von ontologischer und psychisch determinierter Zeit in den Opern Čajkovskijs': 223–232 [see *2626*] — A. Poznansky, 'Modest Čajkovskij: In his brother's shadow': 233–246 [see *1903*] — V. Rubtsova, 'Čajkovskij und die russische Kultur seiner Zeit': 247–252 [see *2124*] — V. Smirnov, 'Čajkovskij und Stravinskij': 253–258 [see *2532*] — V. Sokolov, 'Čajkovskijs Tod': 259–280 [see *2253*] — P. E. Vaidman, 'Unbekannter Čajkovskij: Entwürfe zu nicht ausgeführten Komponisten': 281–298 [see *2413*] — P. Weber-Bockholdt, 'Das "Rosen Adagio": Gedanken zur Qualität von Cajkovskijs Balletmusik': 299–306 [see *4135*] — H. Zajaczkowski, 'On Čajkovskij's psychopathology and its relationship with his creativity': 307–328 [see *2173*] — I. Zemtsovskii, 'Čajkovskij and the European melosphere: A case of cantilena-narration': 329–336 [see *2495*].

Reviews: *Muzyka*, 39 (1995), 1: 116–120 — L. Kearney, *Notes*, 53 (Dec 1996), 2: 472–474.

[597]   ***P. I. Chaikovskii: K 100-letiiu so dnia smerti***. Materialy nauchnoi konferentsii. Red.-sost. E. G. Sorokina, Iu. A. Rozanova, A. I. Kandinskii, I. A. Skvortsova. Moskva: Gos. konservatoriia im. P. I. Chaikovskogo, 1995. 116 p. ISBN 5-86419-024-X. (*Nauchnye trudy Moskovskoi gos. konservatorii im. P. I. Chaikovskogo*; 12).

Contents: 'Predislovie': 3–4 — E. M. Tsarëva, 'Chaikovskii v nashi dni: Mezhdu dvumia datami': 5–9 [see *994*] — L. Z. Korabel´nikova, 'Chaikovskii v samosoznanii russkogo zarubezh´ia 20–30-kh godov': 10–18 [see *1005*] — P. E. Vaidman, 'Nekotorye aspekty kompozitorskoi raboty P. I. Chaikovskogo 80–90-kh godov': 19–23 [see *2494*] — Iu. V. Keldysh, 'Uvertiura-fantaziia "Romeo i Dzhul´etta" i ee rol´ v stanovlenii simfonizma Chaikovskogo': 24–30 [see *4917*] — M. G. Aranovskii, 'Nakhodki i oshibki tvorcheskoi intuitsii': 31–39 [see *4493*] — Iu. A. Rozanova, 'Russkie poety v perepiske s Chaikovskim': 39–47 [see *191*] — E. V. Nazaikinskii, 'Ob odnom prieme orkestrovki P. I. Chaikovskogo': 48–54 [see *4789*] — Iu. N. Kholopov, 'Chto zhe delat´ s muzykal´nymi formami Chaikovskogo?': 54–63 [see *2491*] — S. V. Frolov, 'O kontseptsii finala Chetvertoi simfonii Chaikovskogo': 64–72 [see *597*] — T. A. Gaidamovich, 'Trio Chaikovskogo "Pamiati velikogo khudozhnika" i epitafial´naia traditsiia zhanra': 73–83 [see *5314*] — N. N. Sin´kovskaia, 'U istokov stilia': 83–93 [see *2492*] — I. A. Skvortsova, 'Zamysly i ikh sud´ba: Neizvestnye stranitsy tvorcheskogo dialoga: M. I. Petipa i P. I. Chaikovskogo': 94–98 [see *4016*] — G. A. Zhukovskaia, 'Pamiati Pushkina, Glinki i Chaikovskogo': 99–108 [see *2533*] — O. P. Belova, 'Romansovaia melodika Chaikovskogo: Mezhdu printsipom stikha i printsipom prozy': 109–116 [see *5260*].

[598]   ***P. I. Chaikovskii: Zabytoe i novoe***. Vospominaniia sovremennikov, novye materialy i dokumenty: K 100-letiiu Gos. Doma-muzeia P. I. Chaikovskogo v Klinu. Sost. P. E. Vaidman, G. I. Belonovich. Moskva: IIF Mir i kul´tura, 1995. 206 p, music, illus. (*P. I. Chaikovskii—Al´manakh*; 1).

Contents: P. E. Vaidman, 'Otkryvaia novogo Chaikovskogo': 7–15 [see *995*] — 'M. I. Chaikovskii (iz semeinykh vospominanii)': 18–63 [see *1717*] — I. A. Klimenko, 'Moi vospominaniia o Petre Il´iche Chaikovskom': 64–92 [see *473*] — V. D. Korganov, 'Chaikovskii na Kavkaze': 93–102 [see *477*] — 'Iu. I. Blok: Vospominaniia o P. I. Chaikovskom': 103–116 [see *403*] — V. S. Sokolov, 'Pis´ma P. I. Chaikovskogo bez kupiur: Neizvestnye stranitsy epistoliarii': 118–134 [see *192*] — P. E. Vaidman, 'Novye dokumenty P. I. Chaikovskogo: Obzor istochnikov': 135 [see *115*] — K. N. Nikitin, 'Ob odnom khore P. I. Chaikovskogo, schitavshemsia uteriannym': 136–144 [see *5233*] — P. E. Vaidman, 'Rod Chaikovskikh k 1894 g.': 146–147 [see *1879*] — 'Zapiski kadeta Gornogo kadetskogo korpusa I. P. Ch.': 148–150 [see *1895*] — 'Attestat [A. M. Assiera]': 151–153 [see *1874*] — 'M-elle Fanny Dürbach': 154–158 [see *433*] — G. I. Belonovich: 'T. I. Klimenko (vospominaniia ob otse)': 159–160 [see *2003*] — G. I. Belonovich, 'Chaikovskii i ego okruzhenie na fotografiiakh sovremennikov': 162–199 [see *576*].

[599]   ***P. I. Chaikovskii: Issledovaniia i materialy***. Sbornik studencheskikh rabot. Sost. sbornika S. T. Frolov. Sankt Peterburg: Kanon, 1997. 104 p, music, illus.

Contents: S. V. Frolov, 'Ot sostavitelia': 5–11 — E. Efimovskaia, 'O dramaturgicheskom znachenii dueta "Slykhali l´ vy" v opere P. I. Chaikovskogo "Evgenii Onegin"', 12–19 [see *3122*] — N. Tambovskaia, 'Neskol´ko vzgliadov na sud´bu P. I. Chaikovskogo', 20–40 [see *1685*] — N. Remenets, 'Fortepiannaia sonata P. I. Chaikovskogo fa minor': 41–48 [see *5272*] — M. Kirsanova, 'Simfonicheskaia fantaziia "Fatum" P. I. Chaikovskogo', 49–54 [see *4831*] — A. Kalaberda, 'Rannie simfonii Iana Sibeliusa v zerkale pozdnego simfonizma P. I. Chaikovskogo': 55–60 [see *2522*] — S. Tikhomirova, 'Chaikovskii i Larosh: Primer tvorcheskogo sodruzhestva', 61–75 [see *1990*] — L. Dianova, "Avtobiografiia" G. A. Larosha: Materialy k biografii i portretu uchenogo', 76–101 [see *1985*] — 'Prilozhenie': 102.

[600]   ***Čajkovskijs Homosexualität und sein Tod: Legenden und Wirklichkeit***. Mit weiteren Beiträgen zum anderen Themen von Marek Bobéth, Kadja Grönke, Thomas Kohlhase, Lucinde Lauer, Hartmut Schick, Valerij Sokolov und Polina Vajdman. Hrsg. von Thomas Kohlhase. Mainz [u. a.]: Schott [1998]. 602 p. music, illus. (*Čajkovskij-Studien*; 3). ISBN: 3-7957-0341-7.

Contents: A. Poznansky, 'Čajkovskijs Homosexualität und sein Tod: Legenden und Wirklichkeit': 9–136 [see *2250*] — V. S. Sokolov, 'Briefe P. I. Čajkovskijs ohne Kürzungen: Unbekannte Seiten seiner Korrespondenz': 137–162 [see *192*] — T. Kohlhase, '"Paris vant bien une messe!": Bisher unbekannte Briefe, Notenautographe und andere Čajkovskij-Funde': 163–298 [see *194, 218*] — T. Kohlhase, 'Čajkovskijs Wagner-Rezeption: Daten und Texte': 299–326 [see *2112*] — T. Kohlhase, 'Schlagworte, Tendenzen und Texte zur frühen Čajkovskij-Rezeption in Deutschland und Österreich': 327–354 [see *1052*] — M. Bobéth, 'Petr Il´ič Čajkovskij und Hans von Bülow': 355–366 [see *1927*] — K. Grönke, 'Genealogische Tafeln Čajkovskij/Assier, Miljukov, Davydov, fon-Mekk': 367–378 [see *1880*] — K. Grönke, 'Čajkovskijs Tod: Ein kritischer Literaturbericht': 379–404 [see *2266*] — K. Grönke, 'Mädchen singen von Liebe: Anmerkungen zu einem festen Szenen-Typus in Čajkovskijs Puškin-Opern': 405–416 [see *2629*] — T. Kohlhase, 'Musikalishe Kinderszenen bei Čajkovskij': 417–438 [see *2418*] — T. Kohlhase, 'Kritischer Bericht zu Band 69b der Neuen Čajkovskij-Gesamtausgabe': 439–534 [see *5363*] — L. Lauer, 'Čajkovskij und Mozart: Ein Leserbrief Čajkovskijs von 1881': 535–538 [see *2098*] — H.

Schick, 'Dvořak's 8. Sinfonie: Eine Antwort auf Čajkovskijs Fünfte?': 539–556 [see *4656*] — P. Vaidman, '"Hätte mich das Schicksal nicht nach Moskau gestoßen": Beitrag zu einer neuen Čajkovskij-Biographie': 557–569 [see *1689*].

Reviews: *Dissonanz*, 59 (Feb 1999): 54 — *Österreichische Musikzeitschrift*, 54 (May 1999): 71–72.

[*601*]   ***Tchaikovsky and his world***. Ed. by Leslie Kearney. Princeton, N. J.: Princeton Univ. Press, 1998. ISBN 0-691-00429-0 (hbk); 0-691-00430-7 (pbk). (*Bard Music Festival Series*).

Contents: A. Poznansky, 'Tchaikovsky: A life reconsidered': 5–54 [see *1687*] — A. Poznansky, 'Unknown Tchaikovsky: A reconstruction of previously censored letters to his brothers (1875–1879)': 55–96 [see *195*] — L. Botstein, 'Music as the language of psychological realism': 99–144 [see *2151*] — J. E. Kennedy, 'Lines of succession: Three productions of Tchaikovsky's "Sleeping Beauty"': 145–162 [see *4138*] — N. Minibaeva, '"Per Aspera ad Astra": Symphonic tradition in Tchaikovsky's First Suite for orchestra': 163–196 [see *4790*] — S. Dammann, 'An examination of problem history in Tchaikovsky's Fourth Symphony': 197–215 [see *4617*] — C. Emerson, 'Tchaikovsky's Tatiana': 216–219 [see *3125*] — K. Grönke, 'On the role of Gremin: Tchaikovsky's "Eugene Onegin"': 220–233 [see *3115*] — 'Nikolai Kashkin's review of "The Maid of Orleans"': 234–238 [see *3222*] — L. Kearney, 'Tchaikovsky Androgyne: "The Maid of Orleans"': 239–276 [see *3260*] — R. Wortman, 'The Coronation of Alexander III': 277–299 [see *2006*] — R. Bartlett, 'Tchaikovsky, Chekhov and the Russian elegy': 300–318 [see *1984*] — A. Klimovitskii, 'Tchaikovsky and the Russian "Silver Age"': 319–330 [see *709*] — L. K. Neff, 'A documentary glance at Tchaikovsky and Rimsky-Korsakov as music theorists': 333–352 [see *5439*].

Reviews:W. E. Grimm, *Choice*, 36 (Mar 1999), 7: 1277 — *Virginia Quarterly Review*, 75 (Spr. 1999), 2: A56–A57 — M. Frolova-Walker, *Notes*, 56 (Sep 1999), 1: 149–151.

[*602*]   ***Tchaikovsky and his contemporaries: A centennial symposium***. Ed. by Alexandar Mihailovic. Prepared under the auspices of Hofstra Univ. Westport, Conn.: Greenwood Press, 1999. 432 p, music, illus. ISBN 0-313-30825-X. (*Contributions to the Study of Music and Dance*; 49).

Papers read at the conference held at Hofstra Univ., 7–9 Oct 1993.

Contents:A. Mihailovic, 'Tchaikovsky as our contemporary': 1–14 [see *1145*] — R. Taruskin, 'Tchaikovsky: A new view. A centennial essay': 17–60 [see *1686*] — M. H. Brown, 'Tchaikovsky and his music in Anglo-American criticism, 1890s–1950s': 61–74 [see *1143*] — A. Poznansky, 'The Tchaikovsky myths: A critical reassessment': 75–91 [see *1693*] — R. Bartlett, 'Tchaikovsky and Wagner: A reassessment': 95–116 [see *2113*] — J. C. Kraus, 'A comparison of rhythmic structures in the instrumental music of Schumann and Tchaikovsky': 117–128 [see *2497*] — L. Kearney, 'Truth vs. beauty: Comparative text settings by Musorgsky and Tchaikovsky': 129–135 [see *5162*] — S. B. Eggers, 'Culture and nationalism: Tchaikovsky's visions of Russia in "The Oprichink"': 139–146 [see *3431*] — A. Swartz, 'The intrigue of love and illusion in Tchaikovsky's "The Oprichink"': 147–154 [see *3432*] — T. Bullard, 'Tchaikovsky's "Eugene Onegin": Tatiana and Lensky, the third couple': 157–166 [see *3133*] — B. Nelson, '"But was my Eugene happy?": Musical and dramatic tensions in "Eugene Onegin"': 167–176 [see *3134*] — J. Parakilas, 'Musical historicism in "The Queen of Spades"': 177–185 [see *3721*] — O. Dolskaya, 'Tchaikovsky's roots in the Russian choral tradition': 189–196 [see *5161*] — V. Morosan, 'A stranger in a strange land: Tchaikovsky as a composer of church music': 197–226 [see *5163*] — W. H. Parsons, 'Tchaikovsky, the Tsars, and the Tsarist national anthem': 227–233 [see *4833*] — S. Lipman, 'Tchaikovsky: The love that dare not speak its name': 237–244 [see *1144*] — S. Gould, 'The image of the composer in Modest Tchaikovsky's play "The Symphony"': 245–250 [see *1904*] — J. H. Krukones, 'Exploding the romantic myth: Ken Russell's "The Music Lovers"': 251–260 [see *5567*] — 'Biographical issues in Tchaikovsky scholarship': 263–273 [see *1692*] — 'Tchaikovsky in American and Russian musical education': 275–294 [see *1146*] — 'Tchaikovsky's ballets: Interpretation and performance': 295–312 [see *3868*] — 'Musical examples': 315–368 — 'Conference Program': 371–402.

[*603*]   ***P. I. Chaikovskii: Nasledie***. Sbornik nauchnykh statei. Vyp. 1. Sankt-Peterburg: Sankt-Peterburgskaia konservatoriia, 2000. 216 p, music.

Contents: E. M. Orlova, '"Iolanta" Chaikovskogo": Istoriia sozdaniia, filosofskie i esteticheskie osnovy liriki': 5–20 [see *3198*] — Iu. V. Vasil′ev, 'O printsipakh atributsii nekotorykh nabroskov P. I. Chaikovskogo': 21–66 [see *2498*] — N. N. Sin′kovskaia, 'Iz tvorcheskoi istorii "Val′sa-skertso" dlia skripki s orkestrom op. 34 Chaikovskogo': 67–76 [see *5084*] — O. P. Kolovskii, 'O melodii, podgolosochnosti i kontrapunkte v muzyke Chaikovskogo': 77–99 [see *2499*] — P. P. Levando, 'K voprosu o "dukhovnom" i "svetskom" v khorovoi muzyke P. Chaikovskogo': 100–112 [see *5164*] — I. E. Tikhonova, 'Cherta khorovogo pis′ma P. I. Chaikovskogo (na primere svetskikh khorov a cappella)': 113–139 [see *5165*] — N. Iu. Afonina, 'Vzaimodeistvie ritma i faktury v kvartetakh P. I. Chaikovskogo': 140–178 [see *5297*] — A. B. Pavlov-Arbenin, 'Chaikovskii v trudakh Asaf′eva': 179–181 [see *2420*] — B. V. Asaf′ev, 'Muzykal′naia dramaturgiia Chaikovskogo (osnovnye printsipy)': 182–187 [see *2500*] — B. V. Asaf′ev, 'O narodnosti melosa Chaikovskogo': 188–197 [see *2474*].

[*604*]   ***P. I. Chaikovskii: Nasledie***. Sbornik nauchnykh statei. Vyp. 2. Sankt-Peterburg: Sankt-Peterburgskaia konservatoriia, 2000. 198 p, music.

Contents: A. I. Klimovitskii, 'Nekotorye kul´turno-istoricheskie paradoksy bytovaniia tvorcheskogo nasledia Chaikovskogo v Rossii': 6–48 [see *2421*] — E. A. Ruch´evskaia, 'P. I. Chaikovskii i A. K. Tolstoi': 49–80 [see *2003*] — Iu. V. Vasil´ev, 'Etapy tvorcheskoi raboty P. I. Chaikovskogo nad proizvedeniiami 1890-kh godov (na osnove tekstologicheskogo analiza rukopisei)': 81–124 [see *2501*] — E. N. Dulova, '"Spiashchaia krasavitsa" P. I. Chaikovskogo i tipologicheskie osobennosti skazochno baletnogo siuzheta XIX veka': 125–159 [see *4146*] — M. G. Bialik, 'Chaikovskii i Shuman': 160–172 [see *2103*] — A. K. Kenigsberg, 'Chaikovskii i Verdi': 173–185 [see *2104*] — A. P. Grigor´eva, 'Opery P. I. Chaikovskogo na stsene Peterburgskoi— Leningradskoi konservatorii': 186–197 [see *2631*].

3.2. COMMEMORATION

3.2.1. Russia & the USSR

RUSSIA (pre–1917)

[*605*]   **'Khronika'**, *Baian* (Jan 1888), 2: 21.

Tsar Alexander III's award of an annual 3000- rouble pension to Chaikovskii.

[*606*]   **KASHKIN, N. D. '25-letie deiatel´nosti P. I. Chaikovskogo (1865–1890)'**, *Russkoe obozrenie* (Aug 1890), 8: 815–832.

To mark 25 years of Chaikovskii's career as a composer. See also *607, 608*.

[*607*]   **KASHKIN, N. D. 'P. I. Chaikovskii (1865–1890)'**, *Artist* (Sep 1890), 8: 59–60, illus.

[*608*]   **'K iubileiu P. I. Chaikovskogo'**, *Nuvellist* (Sep 1890), 5: 1–2; (Oct 1890), 6: 2–4; (Nov 1890), 7: 1–2; (Dec 1890), 8: 4–5.

[*609*]   **BASKIN, V. S. 'P. I. Chaikovskii'**, *Niva* (1893), 45: 1030–1031.

Obituary notice. See also *610* to *625*.

[*610*]   **'P. I. Chaikovskii'**, *Niva* (1893), 44: 1009.

[*611*]   **'P. I. Chaikovskii: Kompozitor'**, *Vsemirnaia illiustratsiia* (1893), 12: 732; 39: 189.

[*612*]   **KASHKIN, N. D. 'P. I. Chaikovskii'**, *Russkoe slovo* (25 Oct 1893).

[*613*]   **'P. I. Chaikovskii'**, *Novosti i birzhevaia gazeta* (25 Oct 1893).

[*614*]   **'P. I. Chaikovskii'**, *Peterburgskaia gazeta* (25 Oct 1893).

[*615*]   **BASKIN, V. S. 'Pamiati P. I. Chaikovskogo'**, *Peterburgskaia gazeta* (26 Oct 1893).

[*616*]   **'P. I. Chaikovskii'**, *Novoe vremia* (26 Oct 1893): 1–2.

[*617*]   [LAROSH, G. A.] 'P. I. Chaikovskii', *Teatral´naia gazeta* (27 Oct 1893): 1.
          — [repr.] In: G. A. Larosh, *Izbrannye stat´i v piati vypuskakh*, vyp. 2 (1975): 161 [see *2376*].
          — [German tr.] 'Rede am Grabe Tschaikowskys'. In: *Tschaikowsky aus der Nähe* (1994): 276–279 [see *379*].

[*618*]   'Pamiati P. I. Chaikovskogo', *Peterburgskaia gazeta* (27 Oct 1893).
          Includes: 'Iz vospominanii' — 'U P. I. Iurgensona' [see *458*] — 'V Konservatorii' — 'Otpevanie' — 'V muzykal´nou shkole' — 'Panikhidy po P. I. Chaikovskomu' [see *2183*].

[*619*]   'Pamiati P. I. Chaikovskogo', *Peterburgskaia gazeta* (28 Oct 1893).

[*620*]   BASKIN, V. S. 'P. I. Chaikovskii', *Nuvellist* (Nov 1893), 7: 1–3.

[*621*]   [KASHKIN, N. D.] 'Pamiati P. I. Chaikovskogo', *Artist*, 31 (Nov 1893), 11: 174

[*622*]   'Pamiati Petra Il´icha Chaikovskogo', *Artist* (Nov 1893), 31: 174.

[*623*]   IVANOV, M. 'Muzykal´nye nabroski: Pëtr Il´ich Chaikovskii. † 26 okt 1893 goda', *Novoe vremia* (3 Nov 1893); (10 Nov 1893): 2.

[*624*]   'P. I. Chaikovskii', *Sever* (7 Nov 1893): 2317.

[*625*]   'Pamiati Petra Il'icha Chaikovskogo', *Novoe vremia* (9 Nov 1893).

[*626*]   LAROSH, G. A. 'Kontserty i vechera v pamiat´ Chaikovskogo', *Teatral´naia gazeta* (10 Nov 1893): 2.
          Details of concerts orgainsed in memory of the composer.
          — [repr.] In: G. A. Larosh, *Sobranie muzykal´no-kriticheskikh statei*, tom 2, chast 2 (1924): 156–158 [see *2311*].
          — [repr.] In: G. A. Larosh, *Izbrannye stat´i v piati vypuskakh*, vyp. 2 (1975): 165–167 [see *2376*].

[*627*]   KASHKIN, N. D. 'P. I. Chaikovskii: Opyt kharakteristiki ego znacheniia v russkoi muzyke', *Russkoe obozrenie* (Dec 1893), 12: 986–988.
          — [repr.] In: N. D. Kashkin, *Izbrannye stat´i o P. I. Chaikovskom* (1954): 27–43 [see *2349*].

[*628*]   BASKIN, V. S. 'Muzkal´noe obozrenie', *Nuvellist* (Dec 1893), 8: 1–3.
          Concerts in memory of the composer.

[*629*]   'Chestvovanie pamiati P. I. Chaikovskogo', *Novoe vremia* (1894), No. 6432.

[*630*]   [FINDEIZEN, N. F.] 'Muzykal´naia trizna', *Russkaia muzykal´naia gazeta* (Jan 1894), 1: 10–13.
          The musical world's reaction to Chaikovskii's death, and concerts organized to commemorate the composer.
          — [English tr.] In: A. Poznansky, *Tchaikovsky's last days: A documentary study* (1997): 184–189 [see *2270*].

[*631*]   IVANOV, M. 'Muzykal´nye nabroski', *Novoe vremia* (24 Oct 1894): 2.
          A retrospective of the composer on the first anniversary of his death, including extracts from his diaries and accounts of his conducting tours.

[*632*]   'Pamiati P. I. Chaikovskogo', *Novosti dnia* (25 Oct 1894).

[*633*]   'Pamiati P. I. Chaikovskogo', *Peterburgskaia gazeta* (26 Oct 1894).

[*634*]   [Izveshchenie o smerti P. I. Chaikovskogo]. In: *Otchet Moskovskogo otdeleniia IRMO za 1893–94 god*. Moscow, 1895: 7.

[*635*]   'Po povodu dvukh kontsertov v pol´zu fonda Chaikovskogo', *Russkaia muzykal´naia gazeta* (Dec 1896), 12: 1605–1606.

[*636*]   'Raznye izvestiia: 25 Oktiabria, v pamiat´', *Russkaia muzykal´naia gazeta* (Dec 1896). 12: 1619–1620.
          The annual memorial service at the composer's graveside.

[637]   'Odni iz mnogikh: Po povodu piatoi godovshchiny dnia smerti P. I. Chaikovskogo', *Moskovskie vedomosit* (1898), No. 302.

[638]   F[INDEIZEN], N. 'Kontserty v pamiat´ Chaikovskogo, pod upravleniem Art. Nikisha', *Russkaia muzykal´naia gazeta* (Jan 1898), 1: 85–86.

[639]   'Raznye izvestiia', *Russkaia muzykal´naia gazeta* (Oct 1898), 10: 896–897.
        Concerts organised to mark the fifth anniversary of Chaikovskii's death.

[640]   A. K. 'Simfonicheskii kontsert v pamiat´ P. I. Chaikovskogo', *Vestnik teatra i muzyki* (27 Oct 1898), 3: 27–28.
        A memorial concert held on 24 Oct 1898 in St. Petersburg, to mark the fifth anniversary of Chaikovskii's death.

[641]   LIPAEV, I. 'Muzykal´naia zhizn´ Moskvy', *Russkaia muzykal´naia gazeta* (Dec 1898), 12: 1091–1097.
        The fifth anniversary of Chaikovskii's death.

[642]   'Raznye izvestiia', *Russkaia muzykal´naia gazeta* (17 Nov 1900), 46: 1118–1119.
        Events for the seventh anniversary of Chaikovskii's death, including a memorial service by his graveside.

[643]   KOMPANEISKII, N. 'Zaupokoinaia liturgiia v den´ konchiny Chaikovskogo', *Russkaia muzykal´naia gazeta* (3 Nov 1902), 44: 1068–1073.
        A liturgy held at Chaikovskii's graveside to mark the ninth anniversary of his death.

[644]   LIPAEV, I. 'Panikhida po Chaikovskomu: Moskovskie pis´ma', *Russkaia muzykal´naia gazeta* (3 Nov 1902), 44: 1080–1083.
        Events in Moscow to commemorate the ninth anniversary of Chaikovskii's death.

[645]   *Neskol´ko myslei o muzyke i ee predstaviteliakh: Pamiati P. I. Chaikovskogo, 25/X 1893–26/X 1903*. Moskva: 1903 (*Kruzhok liubitelei russkoi muzyki*).

[646]   TURYGINA, L. M. *P. I. Chaikovskii: K desiatiletiiu ego konchiny, 1893–1903*. Pervorazriadnogo zhenskogo uchebnogo zavedeniia L. M. Turyginoi. Sankt-Peterburg: L. M. Turygina, 1903. 20 p.

[647]   IA—SKII, A. 'Muzykal´nyi vecher, posviashchennyi pamiati P. I. Chaikovskogo', *Slovo* (1903), No. 1761.
        Concerts in Kovno (Kaunas), Lithuania, to mark the 10th anniversary of Chaikovskii's death.

[648]   'V pamiat´ P. I. Chaikovskogo', *Nuvellist* (1903), 9: 8.

[649]   NIKOL´SKII, D. 'Pëtr Il´ich Chaikovskii (k desiatiletiiu so dnia smerti)', *Vestnik i biblioteka samoobrazovaniia* (1903), 43.

[650]   'P. I. Chaikovskii', *Niva* (1903), 43: 861–862.
        Includes Aleksandr Kuznetsov's portrait of Chaikovskii: 857.

[651]   'Po povody 10-letiia so dnia smerti P. I. Chaikovskogo: "Pechal´nik" orkestrovykh muzykantov', *Teatr i iskusstvo* (1903), No. 44.

[652]   SHEPLEVSKII, A. M. 'P. I. Chaikovskii: Ego zhizn´ i tvorchestvo', *Pridneprovskii krai* (1903), Nos. 1654, 1658, 1662, 1665.

[653]   FINDEIZEN, N. F. 'Desiat´ let nazad: Pamiati P. I. Chaikovskogo', *Russkaia muzykal´naia gazeta* (19 Oct 1903), 42: 977–982.

[654]   ENGEL´, Iu. D. 'P. I. Chaikovskii', *Russkie vedomosti* (25 Oct 1903; 1 Nov 1903).
        — [rev. repr.] 'Iu. Engel´ o Chaikovskom', *Russkaia muzykal´naia gazeta* (16 Nov 1903), 46: 1125–1126.

[655]   LADOV, V. 'Pamiati P. I. Chaikovskogo', *Peterburgskii listok* (25 Oct 1893).

[656]   'P. I. Chaikovaskii: K 10-letiiu ego konchiny', *Odesskie novosti* (25 Oct 1903).

[657]   'Teatr i muzyka', *Moskovskie vedomosti* (25 Oct 1903).

[658]   VASILEVSKII [NE-BUKVA], I. 'Pamiati P. I. Chaikovskogo', *Sankt-Peterburgskie vedomosti* (25 Oct 1903).

[659]   LEDIN, I. 'U pamiatnika Chaikovskogo', *Novosti i birzhevye gazeta* (26 Oct 1903).
         A requiem mass by Chaikovskii's graveside to commemorate the 10th anniversary of his death.
         — [rev. repr.] 'Zaupokoinaia obednia po P. I. Chaikovskomu', *Russkie vedomosti* (27 Oct 1903).

[660]   'Moskovskie vesti', *Russkie vedomosti* (26 Oct 1903).
         Commemorative events in Kiev.

[661]   A. K. 'Teatr i muzyka: Pervoe simfonicheskoe sobranie', *Sankt-Peterburgskie vedomosti* (27 Oct 1903).

[662]   'P. I. Chaikovskii', *Russkie vedomosti* (27 Oct 1903).
         Special commemorative issue.

[663]   'Den´ Chaikovskogo', *Birzhevye vedomosti* (28 Oct 1903).

[664]   'Kontsert v pamiat´ P. Chaikovskogo', *Sankt-Peterburgskie vedomosti* (28 Oct 1903).

[665]   'P. I. Chaikovskii: Desiat´ let so dnia smerti', *Russkie vedomosti* (28 Oct 1903).

[666]   'Tri kontserta v pamiat´ P. I. Chaikovskogo', *Novosti i birzhevaia gazeta* (28 Oct 1903).

[667]   'Desiatiletie so dnia smerti P. I. Chaikovskogo', *Novosti i birzhevaia gazeta* (29 Oct 1903).

[668]   VAL´TER, V. 'P. I. Chaikovskii: K 10-i godovshchine so dnia ego smerti', *Mir Bozhii* (Nov 1903): 1.

[669]   '10-letie smerti Chaikovskogo', *Russkaia muzykal´naia gazeta* (2 Nov 1903), 44: 1057.

[670]   'Kamernoe sobranie pamiati Chaikovskogo', *Odesskie novosti* (14 Nov 1903).

[671]   LIPAEV, I. 'Moskovskie pis´ma', *Russkaia muzykal´naia gazeta* (16 Nov 1903), 46: 1135–1137.
         Concerts and publications in Moscow marking the 10th anniversary of Chaikovskii's death.

[672]   'K 10-letiiu smerti Chaikovskogo', *Russkaia muzykal´naia gazeta* (16 Nov 1903), 46: 1138–1139.

[673]   'P. I. Chaikovskii: Ego zhizn´ i tvorchestvo (publichnaia lektsiia v zale Angliiskogo kluba, prochitannaia 16 noiabria)', *Pridneprovskii krai* (27 Nov 1903); (29 Nov 1903).

[674]   'Na mogile P. I. Chaikovskogo', *Sankt-Peterburgskie vedomosti* (1904), No. 253.

[675]   'Odinnadtsat´ let so dnia smerti Chaikovskogo', *Sankt Peterburgskie vedomosti* (15 Sep 1904).
         The St. Petersburg Conservatory's commemorations for the 11th anniversary of Chaikovskii's death.

[676]   [Odinnadtsat´ let so dnia smerti Chaikovskogo], *Novosti i birzhevaia gazeta* (1904), No. 295.

[677]   SUVOROVSKII, N. 'Chaikovskii i muzyka budushchego', *Vesy* (1904), 8: 10–20.

[678]   TURCHINOVICH, A. M 'Pamiati Chaikovskogo', *Zapadnyi vestnik* (5 Apr 1904).
         — [offprint] A. M. Turchinovich, *Pamiati P. I. Chaikovskogo: Rech´*. Vil´na, 1904. 21 p.

[679]   ENGEL´, Iu. D. 'Kontserty v pamiat´ Chaikovskogo', *Russkie vedomosti* (19 Apr 1904).

[680]   KOMPANEISKII, N. 'Pis´ma v redaktsiiu', *Russkaia muzykal´naia gazeta* (24 Oct 1904), 43: 984.
         Concerning performances of Chaikovskii's music to mark the 11th anniversary of his death.

[681]   'Panikhidy po P. I. Chaikovskomu', *Rus´* (26 Oct 1904).

[682]   LIPAEV, I. 'Godovshchina Chaikovskogo', *Russkaia muzykal´naia gazeta* (31 Oct 1904), 44: 1031.

[683]   OSSOVSKII, A. V. 'Posle kontserta v pamiat´ P. I. Chaikovskogo', *Slovo* (1906), 2.

[684]   KASHKIN, N. D. 'Pamiati P. I. Chaikovskogo', *Russkoe slovo* (25 Oct 1908).
         — [repr.] In: N. D. Kashkin, *Izbrannye stat´i o P. I. Chaikovskom* (1954): 44–48 [see *2349*].

[685]   KOLOMIITSEV, V. 'Pamiati Chaikovskogo', *Novaia Rus´* (25 Oct 1908).
         A concert conducted by Eduard Nápravník, commemorating the 15th anniversary of Chaikovskii's death,
         — [repr.] In: V. Kolomiitsev, *Stat´i i pis´ma*. Leningrad: Muzyka, 1971: 64–65.

[686]   CHECHOTT, V. A. 'P. I. Chaikovskii: 1840–1893', *Rech´* (1 Dec 1908).

[687]   'Vecher gg. Kalia i Ermakova, posviashchennyi Chaikovskomu', *Birzhevye vedomosti* (28 Oct 1909).
         Report on a lecture on Chaikovskii given in the Hall of the Nobles' Club in St. Petersburg.

[688]   'P. I. Chaikovskii-skomorokh', *Muzyka i zhizn´* (1910), 1: 9–10.
         — [English tr.] In: A. Poznansky, *Tchaikovsky's last days: A documentary study* (1997): 167–168 [see *2270*].

[689]   CHAIKOVSKII, I. P. 'Pis´mo v redaktsiiu: Pochemu ne chestvuetsia pamiat´ P. I. Chaikovskogo',
         Novoe vremia (25 Oct 1911): 5.
         A letter to the editor from the composer's brother Ippolit, concerning the decision of the Aleksandr Nevskii
         cemetery authorities not to allow the traditional memorial service by Chaikovskii's graveside.

[690]   MALKOV, N. 'Po povodu tsikla kontsertov, posviashchennykh proizvedeniiam Chaikovskogo',
         Russkaia muzykal´naia gazeta (30 Sep 1912), 50: 814–817.
         A series of concerts of Chaikovskii's works in St. Petersburg in Sep 1912, conducted by Sergei Kusevitskii. See
         also *691*.

[691]   KOLOMIITSEV, V. 'Tsikl Chaikovskogo', *Den´* (2 Oct 1912).

[692]   MAZARAKII, A. V. *Pamiati P. I. Chaikovskogo: K dvadtsatiletiiu konchiny*. Vinnitsa, 1913. 15 p.

[693]   CHERNOMOR. 'P. I. Chaikovskii', *Za 7 dnei* (1913), 39: 836–837.

[694]   IUR´EV, M. 'Pamiati P. I. Chaikovskogo', *Rampa i zhizn´* (1913), No. 43.

[695]   IVANOV, M. 'P. I. Chaikovskii (po povodu 20-letiia so dnia ego smerti)', *Novoe vremia* (1913), No.
         13511: 5.

[696]   KARATYGIN, V. 'Pamiati P. I. Chaikovskogo', *Teatr i iskusstvo* (1913), 42: 833–836.
         — [repr.] In: *V. G. Karatygin: Izbrannye stat´i*. Moskva; Leningrad: Muzyka, 1965: 92–101.

[697]   LITVIN, F. 'P. I. Chaikovskii: Genial´nyi lirik', *Solntse Rossii* (1913), 44: 9 [see *583*].

[698]   SAKETTI, L. A. 'P. I. Chaikovskii: Muzykal´nyi kosmopolit', *Solntse Rossii* (1913), 44: 2 [see *583*].

[699]   SLAVINA, M. A. 'P. I. Chaikovskii nedootsenen sovremennikami', *Solntse Rossii* (1913), 44: 7 [see
         583].

[700]   SOLOV´EV, N. F. 'P. I. Chaikovskii: Entsiklopedist v muzyke', *Solntse Rossii* (1913), 44: 6 [see *583*].
        — [German tr.] 'Obwhol typisch russisch, wird seine Musik auf der ganzen Welt verstanden'. In: *Tschaikowsky aus der Nähe* (1994): 109–110 [see *379*].

[701]   PROTEI. 'Poet melodii', *Teatr i zhizn´* (25 Oct 1913): 3–4.

[702]   SEREBRIAKOV, K. T. 'P. I. Chaikovskii', *Teatr i zhizn´* (25 Oct 1913): 9–10.

[703]   TIMOFEEV, G. 'Kontsert Arkhangel´skogo Pamiati P. I. Chaikovskogo: 1893–25 oktiabria–1913', *Rech´* (25 Oct 1913): 7.

[704]   SHMULER, A. 'Nash´ Chaikovskii'. In: *Muzykal´nyi al´manakh*. Moskva, 1914: 58–62.

[705]   FINDEIZEN, N. F. 'Pamiati P. I. Chaikovskogo', *Russkaia muzykal´naia gazeta* (20 Oct 1913), 42: 907.

[706]   ENGEL´, Iu. D. 'Pamiati Chaikovskogo', *Russkie vedomosti* (25 Oct 1913).

[707]   'Pamiati P. I. Chaikovskogo', *Teatr i muzyka* (25 Oct 1913): 7.
        Events organised to mark the 20th anniversary of Chaikovskii's death.

[708]   GLUSHCHENKO, G. 'P. I. Chaikovskii v russkoi muzykal´noi publitsistike kontsa XIX-nachala XX veka'. In: *P. I. Chaikovskii: Voprosy istorii i stilia* (1989): 105–172 [see *590*].

[709]   KLIMOVITSKII, A. 'Čajkovskij und das russische "Silberne Zeitalter"'. In: *Internationales Čajkovskij Symposium, Tübingen 1993: Bericht* (1995): 155–164 [see *596*].
        — [English tr.] 'Tchaikovsky and the Russian "Silver Age"'. In: *Tchaikovsky and his world* (1998): 319–330 [see *601*].
        See also *481*.

USSR (1917–91)

[710]   N. K. 'Chaikovskii: Pevets trudovoi intelligentsii', *Muzykal´nyi vestnik* (1919), 2: 1.

[711]   'Pedagogicheskii kontsert i lektsiia', *Zhizn´ iskusstva* (11 Apr 1919): 3.
        A lecture-concert devoted to Chaikovskii's works, introduced by N. Strel´nikov.

[712]   GLEBOV, I. [ASAF´EV, B. V.] 'Nash dolg'. In: *Proshloe russkoi muzyki*, tom 1 (1920): 7–14 [see *584*].

[713]   GLEBOV, I. [ASAF´EV, B. V.] 'P. I. Chaikovskii'. In: *Tsikl akademicheskikh simfonicheskikh kontsertov orkestra i khora Gos. filarmonii*, etc. Petrograd [1921]. 21 p.
        In connection with a series of Philharmonic Society concerts taking place in Jun 1921.

[714]   GLEBOV, I. [ASAF´EV, B. V.] *P. I. Chaikovskii, 1840–1893*. Petrograd: Gos. filarmoniia, 1922. 26 p.
        In connection with a series of Philharmonic Society concerts in Petrograd in 1922.

[715]   GLEBOV, I. [ASAF´EV, B. V.] 'P. I. Chaikovskii'. In: I. Glebov, *Instrumental´noe tvorchestvo Chaikovskogo* (1922): 3–5 [see *2310*].

[716]   BUGOSLAVSKII, S. 'P. Chaikovskii (25 oktiabria 1893 g.–7 noiabria 1923 g.)', *Muzykal´naia nov´* (1923), 3: 22.

[717]   GLEBOV, I. [ASAF´EV, B. V.] 'Muzykal´nye zametki', *Teatr* (1923), 7: 8–9.
        A concert to commemorate the 30th anniversary of Chaikovskii's death.

[718]   IGNATOVICH, V. 'P. I. Chaikovskii (k 30-letiiu so dnia smerti)', *Muzykal´naia nov´* (1923), 3: 20–22.

[719]   MUZALEVSKII, V. I. 'Pod znakom Chaikovskogo', *Vecherniaia krasnaia gazeta* (8 Oct 1923).

[*720*]   MALKOV, N. 'K voprosu o proletarizatsii iskusstva: **Budushchee russkoi muzyki**', *Zhizn´ iskusstva* (1924), 7: 3–4.

[*721*]   'P. I. Chaikovskii', *Rabochii i teatr* (1924), 2: 11.

[*722*]   CHEMODANOV, S. 'P. I. Chaikovskii (k nashim radiokontsertam)', *Novosti radio* (1925), 10: 7.
In connection with a radio broadcast of Chaikovskii's music.

[*723*]   ISLAMEI. 'Vecher Chaikovskogo', *Zhizn´ iskusstva* (1925), 8: 14.

[*724*]   MANSYREV, S. P. 'P. I. Chaikovskii: 25 oktiabria (7 noiabria 1893)', *Nashi poslednie izvestiia* (11 Nov 1926).

[*725*]   BOGDANOV-BEREZOVSKII, V. M. 'Kontsert Akkapelly posviashchennyi pamiati Chaikovskogo', *Muzyka i revoliutsiia* (1928), 10: 36.
A concert of Chaikovskii's choral music to mark the 35th anniversary of this death. See also *729, 730*.

[*726*]   BOGDANOV-BEREZOVSKII, V. M. 'P. I. Chaikovskii', *Rabochii i teatr* (1928), 43: 4–5.
On the 35th anniversary of Chaikovskii's death.

[*727*]   BUGOSLAVSKII, S. 'Pamiati P. I. Chaikovskogo', *Sovremennyi teatr* (1928): 722.

[*728*]   CHUDESNYI. 'Dlia mass ili dlia izbrannykh', *Serp i molot´* (1928), No. 65.

[*729*]   ISLAMEI. 'Opera i kontsert: Otkrytie sezona Akkapelly', *Zhizn´ iskusstva* (1928), 40: 8.
A choral concert to commemorate the 35th anniversary of Chaikovskii's death. See also *724, 730*.

[*730*]   MUZALEVSKII, V. I. 'Pamiati P. I. Chaikovskogo', *Krasnaia panorama* (1928), 45: 14.

[*731*]   OBOLENSKII, L. 'Eshche o Chaikovskom', *Sovremennyi teatr* (1928): 738.

[*732*]   PEKELIS, M. S. 'Chto deistvenno dlia nas o Chaikovskom', *Muzyka i revoliutsiia* (1928), 11: 22.

[*733*]   'Spory o Chaikovskom', *Sovremennyi teatr* (1928), 52: 832.
An assessment of Chaikovskii's music 35 years after his death, with contributions from S. Bismont, N. Pirkovskii, M. Stugin, A. Vinokur and V. Ignatovich.

[*734*]   K. 'Kapella pamiati P. I. Chaikovskogo', *Vecherniaia krasnaia gazeta* (25 Sep 1928).

[*735*]   PROKHOROV, S. A. 'Velikoe v chelovecheskom: Pamiati P. I. Chaikovskogo', *Nov´*, 1 (Oct 1928): 2.

[*736*]   LUNACHARSKII, A. V. 'Chaikovskii i sovremennost', *Vecherniaia krasnaia gazeta* (9 Oct 1928).
— [repr.] In: A. V. Lunacharskii, *V mire muzyki: Stat´i i rechi*. Moskva: Sovetskii kompozitor, 1958: 230–231; 2-e izd. Moskva, 1971: 359–361.

[*737*]   POLIANOVSKII, G. 'Kontserty iz proizvedenii Chaikovskogo', *Pravda* (6 Nov 1928).

[*738*]   CHEMODANOV, S. 'Chaikovskii i my', *Izvestiia* (14 Nov 1928).

[*739*]   POLIANOVSKII, G. 'Chto tsenno dlia nas v Chaikovskom', *Trud* (14 Nov 1928).

[*740*]   'Chaikovskomu ot zemliakov', *Vecherniaia Moskva* (13 Dec 1928).

[*741*]   B[UGOSLAV]SKII, S. 'Chaikovskii v nashi dni', *Sovetskaia filarmoniia* (1928/29), 2: 3.

[*742*]   KOPTIAEV, A. P. 'Chaikovskii na vesakh vremeni: K 30-letiiu so dnia smerti', *Vestnik znaniia* (1929), 19: 963–965.

[*743*]   'Kriticheskoe polozhenie na "kriticheskom fronte"', *Muzyka i revoliutsiia* (1929), 3: 4.
        A critical article, in connection with the 35th anniversary of Chaikovskii's death.

[*744*]   BLOM, V. 'Tak tozhe nel´zia', *Vecherniaia Moskva* (31 Jul 1932).

[*745*]   SOLLERTINSKII, I. 'P. I. Chaikovskii: K 40-letiiu so dnia smerti', *Rabochii i teatr* (1933), 33: 6–7.

[*746*]   'Mesiachnik Chaikovskogo', *Vecherniaia Moskva* (3 Aug 1933).

[*747*]   PSHIBYSHEVSKII, B. 'O Chaikovskom: Kompozitor i epokha', *Sovetskoe iskusstvo* (14 Sep 1933).

[*748*]   GALL´, E. 'Iubilei, priiatnye vo vsekh otnoshenoiakh', *Vecherniaia Moskva* (27 Sep 1933).
        Events marking the 40th anniversary of the composer's death.

[*749*]   KH—I, V. 'Pod znakom Chaikovskogo', *Vecherniaia krasnaia gazeta* (8 Oct 1933).

[*750*]   PASTUKHOV, V. 'Pëtr Il´ich Chaikovskii', *Segodnia* (26 Oct 1933).

[*751*]   'Iskusstvo, teatr i kino', *Leningradskaia pravda* (27 Oct 1933): 4.
        Details of events held in Leningrad to commemorate the 40th anniversary of Chaikovskii's death.

[*752*]   VIN, E. 'Otkrytie kontsertnogo sezona', *Rabochii i teatr* (Oct/Nov 1933). 30/31: 18.
        A vocal-chamber concerts to commemorate the 40th anniversary of Chaikovskii's death.

[*753*]   POLIANOVSKII, G. 'P. I. Chaikovskii: K sorokoletiiu so dnia smerti (1840–1893)', *Za
        kommunisticheskoe prosveshchenie* (12 Nov 1933).

[*754*]   ZAK, I. A. 'O Chaikovskom', *Volzhskaia kommuna* (18 Nov 1933).

[*755*]   K. 'Kamernyi vecher pamiati Chaikovskogo', *Bakinskii rabochii* (26 Nov 1933).

[*756*]   ASAF´EV, B. V. 'O Chaikovskom: K sorokaletiiu so dnia smerti', *Sovetskoe iskusstvo* (8 Dec 1933).

[*757*]   GALL´, E. 'Orkestr bez dirizhera', *Vecherniaia Moskva* (21 Dec 1933).
        Chaikovskii's music performed by 'Persimfans' (a collective orchestra without conductor).

[*758*]   GROMAN-SOLOVTSOV, A. A. 'Neskol´ko myslei o Chaikovskom', *Sovetskaia muzyka* (1934), 2: 24–
        34.

[*759*]   KOSOVANOV, V. 'K kontsertam krasnoiarskogo filarmonicheskogo obshchestva', *Krasnoiarskii
        rabochii* (29 Jan 1934).

[*760*]   DADASHEV, A. 'Pëtr Il´ich Chaikovskii', *Russkii vestnik* (31 Aug 1935).

[*761*]   *Vtoroi kontsert 5-go molodezhnogo abonementa*. Leningrad: [Gos. filarmoniia, 1937]. 12 p.
        A biographical sketch, in connection with a concert of the composer's works.

[*762*]   'Nachalo podgotovki k iubileiu P. I. Chaikovskogo', *Muzyka* (26 Apr 1937), 8: 3.
        Preparations for Chaikovskii's centennial in 1940.

[*763*]   BUDIAKOVSKII, A. 'Chaikovskii i sovetskoe muzykoznanie', *Muzyka* (6 Jul 1937): 4.

[*764*]   GROMAN-SOLOVTSOV, A. & ZHITOMIRSKII, D. V. 'Podlinnyi Chaikovskii', *Muzyka* (6 Jul
        1937): 4–5; (16 Jul 1937): 8.

[*765*]   KHUBOV, G. 'Velikii russkii kompozitor P. I. Chaikovskii', *Pravda* (3 Aug 1937).
        — [repr.] In: G. Khubov, *Muzykal´naia publitsistika raznykh let*. Moskva: Sovetskii kompozitor, 1976: 27–35.

[766]   KOCHAKOV, B. M. *P. I. Chaikovskii: Lektsiia-kontsert 23 apr. 1938 g*. Leningrad: Gos. filarmoniia, 1938. 16 p.

Programme for a lecture and Philharmonic Society concert of Chaikovskii's music in Leningrad on 23 Apr 1938.

[767]   KOCHAKOV, B. M. *P. I. Chaikovskii*. Leningrad: Gos. filarmoniia, 1938. 16 p.

In connection with a series of Philharmonic Society concerts in Kislovodsk in the summer of 1938.

[768]   'Podgotovka k iubileiu P. Chaikovskogo', *Sovetskaia muzyka* (1938), 5: 87.

Preparations for the Chaikovskii centenary in 1940 (see also the following entries).

[769]   'Podgotovka k torzhestvam', *Dekada moskovskikh zrelishch* (1938), 26: 13.

[770]   'Podgotovka k iubileiu P. I. Chaikovskogo', *Sovetskoe iskusstvo* (2 Feb 1938): 4.

[771]   'V Komitete po delam iskusstva', *Sovetskoe iskusstvo* (26 Jun 1938): 4.

On the formation of a committee to organise Chaikovskii's centennial celebrations in 1940.

[772]   '100-letnii iubilei velikikh kompozitorov', *Leningradskaia pravda* (3 Aug 1938): 4.

Considers the birth centenaries of Modest Musorgskii in 1939 and Chaikovskii in 1940.

[773]   SHCHEPKINA-KUPERNIK, T. L. 'Dorogoe imia', *Sovetskoe iskusstvo* (14 Nov 1938).

[774]   *P. I. Chaikovskii, 1840–1893*. [Moskva]: Gos. filarmoniia [1939]. 4 p.

In connection with a symphony concert of Chaikovskii's works on 20 Feb 1939.

[775]   FLEIS, E. P. 'P. I. Chaikovskii', *Molot* (1939), 4/5: 65–76.

[776]   SHTEINPRESS, B. 'Velikie kompozitory zhdut...', *Sovetskoe iskusstvo* (8 Jan 1939): 3.

Preparations for the centennial celebrations of Musorgskii (1939) and Chaikovskii (1940).

[777]   'Festival´ imeni P. I. Chaikovskogo', *Sovetskoe iskusstvo* (11 May 1939): 4.

Preparations for Chaikovskii's jubilee celebrations in May 1940.

[778]   'Podgotovka k iubileiu velikogo russkogo kompozitora', *Dekada moskovskikh zrelishch* (11 May 1939): 9.

[779]   'K stoletiiu so dnia rozhdeniia P. I. Chaikovskogo', *Sovetskoe iskusstvo* (28 Aug 1939): 4.

Events organised to celebrate Chaikovskii's centennial in May 1940.

[780]   'Odni iz blizhadishikh vypuskov "Letopisi" Gosudarstvennogo Literaturnogo Muzeia', *Dekada moskovskikh zrelishch* (21 Sep 1939): 11.

Report on publications to mark the centenary of Chaikovskii's birth, and the 25th anniversary of Sergei Taneev's death.

[781]   'K 100-letiiu so dnia rozhdeniia P. I. Chaikovskogo', *Izvestiia* (30 Sep 1939): 3.

A report from Sverdlovsk on preparations for Chaikovskii's jubilee in the Urals.

[782]   *100-letnii iubilei so dnia rozhdeniia P. I. Chaikovskogo: 25 aprelia (7 maia) 1840 g.—7 Mai 1940 g*. Groznyi [1940]. 32 p, illus. (*Upravlenie po delam iskusstv pri Sovnarkome ChIASSR*).

A biography of Chaikovskii and a programme of jubilee events in Groznyi.

[783]   DRUSKIN, Ia. V. *Pëtr Il´ich Chaikovskii: K 100-letiiu so dnia rozhdeniia*. Rostov na Donu: Rostizdat, 1940. 32 p, illus.

[784]   GLEBOV, I. [ASAF´EV, B. V.] *Pamiati Petra Il´icha Chaikovskogo, 1840–7/V–1940*. Leningrad; Moskva: Gos. muz. izdat., 1940. 32 p., illus.

A short guide to Chaikovskii's life and works.

Review: 'Broshiura Igoria Glebova, posviashchennaia tvorchestvu P. I. Chaikovskogo, vypushena Leningradskim otdeleniem Muzgiza', *Leningradskaia pravda* (26 Aug 1940): 4.

— [repr.] In: B. V. Asaf´ev, *Izbrannye trudy*, tom 2 (1954): 31–47 [see *2348*].

— [repr.] 'Pamiati Petra Il´icha Chaikovskoo'. In: B. V. Asaf´ev, *O muzyke Chaikovskogo: Izbrannoe* (1972): 38–58 [see *2373*].

[785]   **KHINCHIN, L.** *P. I. Chaikovskii: 1840–1940.* Kiev: Mystetstvo, 1940. 160 p, music, illus. (*Kievskaia gos. ordena Lenina konservatoriia. Kafedra istorii muzyki*).

[786]   **KOCHAKOV, B. M.** *Pëtr Il´ich Chaikovskii: K stoletiiu so dnia rozhdeniia, 1840–1940.* Leningrad: Gos. filarmoniia, 1940. 51 p, illus.

[787]   **MELIK-VARTANESIAN, K. E.** *Pëtr Il´ich Chaikovskii: K 100-letiiu so dnia rozhdeniia, 1840–1940.* Erevan: Armgiz, 1940. 70 p, music, illus.

Review: 'Gosizdat Armenii vypustil trud', *Sovetskaia muzyka* (1940), 12: 107

[788]   *P. I. Chaikovskii: K 100-letiiu so dnia rozhdeniia.* Kiev: Gos. filarmoniia, 1940. 40 p, illus.

[789]   *P. I. Chaikovskii: Velikii russkii kompozitor, 1840–1940.* Baku: Azerneshr, 1940. 76 p, illus. (*Upravlenie po delam iskusstv pri SNK AzSSR*).

[790]   *Vystavka posviashchennaia 100-letiiu so dnia rozhdeniia P. I. Chaikovskogo: Katalog.* Vstup. stat´ia V. Filippova. Otv. red. A. B. Gol´denveizer. Moskva: Pravda, 1940. 178 p, music, illus. (*Moskovskaia gos. konservatoriia. Gos. tsentral´nyi muzei im. Iu. A. Bakhrushina. Moskovskaia gos. filarmoniia*).

Catalogue for an exhibition at the Moscow Conservatory to mark the composer's centenary. See also *803*.

[791]   **ROGINSKAIA, G.** *Pëtr Il´ich Chaikovskii: K 100-letiiu so dnia rozhdeniia, 1840–1940.* Sost. G. Roginskaia. Voronezh, 1940. 18 p, illus. (*Voronezhskii Soiuz sovetskikh kompozitorov. Oblastnoi dom narodnogo tvorchestva*).

[792]   **RUBIN, S.** *P. I. Chaikovskii: K 100-letiiu so dnia rozhdeniia.* Sverdlovsk: Sverdlovskaia filarmoniia [1940]. 10 p.

[793]   **VOROB´EVA, M.** *P. I. Chaikovskii: K 100-letiiu so dnia rozhdeniia (7 maia 1840 g.–7 maia 1940 g.).* Perm´, 1940. 12 p. (*Oblastnoi biblioteka im. A. M. Gor´kogo i Oblastnoi teatr opery i baleta*).

[794]   **ASAF´EV, B. V.** 'Chaikovskii', *Sovetskaia muzyka* (1940), 5/6: 3–7 [see *585*].

— [repr.] In: B. V. Asaf´ev, *O muzyke Chaikovskogo: Izbrannoe* (1972): 19–24 [see *2373*].

[795]   **BUDIAKOVSKII, A.** 'Russkii natsional´nyi genii', *Sovetskaia muzyka* (1940), 5/6: 8–17 [see *585*].

[796]   **CHERNYI, O.** 'P. I. Chaikovskii (1840–1893)', *Tridsat´ dnei* (1940), 3/4: 107–113.

[797]   **'Iubilei Chaikovskogo v Talline'**, *Internatsional´naia literatura* (1940), 5/6: 246–247.

[798]   **KARPOVICH, A.** 'Postanovleniem Soveta Narodnykh Komissarov SSSR', *Sovetskaia muzyka* (1940), 1: 97.

Official decrees to mark the Chaikovskii centennial.

[799]   **KHUBOV, G.** 'Velichie i tragizm Chaikovskogo', *Krasnaia nov´* (1940), 9/10: 235–244.

[800]   **'K iubileiu P. I. Chaikovskogo'**, *Sovetskaia muzyka* (1940), 3: 92.

An overview of celebrations planned for Chaikovskii's jubilee, throughout the Soviet Union.

[801]   **'K iubileiu P. I. Chaikovskogo'**, *Sovetskaia muzyka* (1940), 4: 96.

Contains short reports on the Chaikovskii museums at Votkinsk and Kamenka, and preparations for the publication of the composer's complete works and letters. See also *118*.

[802] 'K stoletiiu so dnia rozhdeniia', *Ogonek* (1940), 12: 14.
Reports on films, concerts and exhibitions to mark Chaikovskii's centennial year.

[803] KUNIN, I. F. 'Vystavki k iubileiu P. I. Chaikovskogo', *Sovetskaia muzyka* (1940), 8: 109–110.
An exhibition in Moscow devoted to the composer's life and works. See also *790*.

[804] MARTYNOV, I. 'Velikii russkii kompozitor', *Ogonek* (1940), 12: 2–4, illus.

[805] 'Nauchnaia sessiia, posviashchennaia Chaikovskomu', *Sovetskaia muzyka* (1940), 8: 111.
A special conference at the Moscow Conservatory, dedicated to an analysis of Chaikovskii's music.

[806] OGOLEVETS, A. S. 'P. I. Chaikovskii', *Novyi mir* (1940), 7: 192–209.

[807] 'Otkliki na iubilei Chaikovskogo', *Internatsional´naia literatura* (1940), 5/6: 347.
Report on a Chaikovskii centennial concert in Kaunas, Lithuania.

[808] 'Pëtr Il´ich Chaikovskii', *Sovetskaia muzyka* (1940), 1: 4–7.

[809] R. R. 'Sto let so dnia rozhdeniia P. I. Chaikovskogo', *Literatura i iskusstvo Kazakhstana* (1940), 4/5: 86–90.

[810] SHCHEPKINA-KUPERNIK, T. L. 'Neissiakaemyi istochnik vdokhnoveniia', *Ogonek* (1940), 12.

[811] 'Nakanune iubileiia P. I. Chaikovskogo', *Izvestiia* (6 Jan 1940): 4.

[812] 'Ob oznamenovanii stoletiia so dnia rozhdeniia P. I. Chaikovskogo', *Izvestiia* (9 Jan 1940).
A meeting of the committee set up to organise Chaikovskii's centennial celebrations.

[813] '100-letie so dnia rozhdeniia P. I. Chaikovskogo', *Izvestiia* (14 Jan 1940): 4.
An official bulletin from the Chaikovskii centennial jubilee committee.
— [repr.] *Pravda* (14 Jan 1940).
— [repr.] *Sovetskoe iskusstvo* (14 Jan 1940): 4.

[814] OSSOVSKII, A. V. 'Pered stoletnim iubileem P. I. Chaikovskogo', *Leningradskaia pravda* (18 Jan 1940): 4.
Preparations to mark Chaikovskii's jubilee in Leningrad.

[815] 'K 100-letiiu so dnia rozhdeniia P. I. Chaikovskogo', *Sovetskoe iskusstvo* (21 Jan 1940): 1.
Preparations in Taganrog for Chaikovskii's jubilee celebrations.

[816] 'Pervyi kontsert iz iubileinogo tsikla P. I. Chaikovskogo', *Smena* (27 Jan 1940).

[817] '100 let so dnia rozhdeniia P. I. Chaikovskogo', *Sovetskoe iskusstvo* (29 Jan 1940): 1.

[818] 'Pered iubileem P. I. Chaikovskogo', *Leningradskaia pravda* (30 Jan 1940): 4.

[819] NESTEROV, N. '100 let so dnia rozhdeniia P. I. Chaikovskogo', *Sovetskoe iskusstvo* (4 Feb 1940): 4.
Events to celebrate Chaikovskii's jubilee in Khar´kov.

[820] 'Detiam o Chaikovskom', *Komsomol´skaia pravda* (5 Feb 1940): 4.
Jubilee celebrations organised by the children's branch of the Moscow Philharmonic Society.

[821] 'Podgotovka k iubeleiu Chaikovskogo', *Komsomol´skaia pravda* (5 Feb 1940): 1.
Report on a cycle of concerts by the Leningrad Philharmonic, to mark Chaikovskii's centennial year. See also *822, 823*.

[822] SOLOV´EV, V. 'Pervyi iubileinyi kontsert', *Smena* (6 Feb 1940): 4.

[*823*]   'Muzykal´nyi festival´ iz proizvedenii P. I. Chaikovskogo', *Leningradskaia pravda* (9 Feb 1940).

[*824*]   'Podgotovka k stoletiiu so dnia rozhdeniia Chaikovskogo', *Komsomol´skaia pravda* (9 Feb 1940): 4.

[*825*]   'Akademicheskaia kapella k iubileiu P. I. Chaikovskogo', *Smena* (11 Feb 1940).
          Performances of Chaikovskii's choral works, to mark the 100th anniversary of his birth.

[*826*]   SAFARIAN, L. '100 let so dnia rozhdeniia P. I. Chaikovskogo', *Sovetskoe iskusstvo* (18 Feb 1940): 1.
          Events in Georgia to mark Chaikovskii's centenary year.

[*827*]   'Podgotovka k 100-letiiu so dnia rozhdeniia P. I. Chaikovskogo', *Sovetskoe iskusstvo* (29 Feb 1940):
          1.

[*828*]   GOL´DENVEIZER, A. 'Kontsert iz proizvedenii Chaikovskogo', *Izvestiia* (6 Mar 1940): 4.
          A concert of Chaikovskii's music (overture to *The Storm*, the symphonic ballad *The Voevoda, Suite No. 3*) on 3
          Mar 1940, to celebrate the centenary of his birth.

[*829*]   '100 let so dnia rozhdeniia P. I. Chaikovskogo', *Sovetskoe iskusstvo* (9 Mar 1940): 4.
          Centennial events organised in Moscow, Tblissi, Voronezh, Dnepropetrovsk and Alma-Ata.

[*830*]   GRIGOR´EV, A. 'Na kontsertakh v filarmonii', *Leningradskaia pravda* (9 Mar 1940): 6.
          Continuing the series of Chaikovskii centennial concerts given by the Leningrad Philhamonic Society.

[*831*]   'Iubileinaia dekada posviashchennaia P. I. Chaikovskomu', *Smena* (11 Mar 1940): 4.

[*832*]   'Iubileinaia vystavka P. I. Chaikovskogo', *Pravda* (11 Mar 1940): 6.
          Announcement of an exhibition devoted to Chaikovskii at the Pushkin Museum in Moscow on 29 Apr 1940.
          See also *850*.

[*833*]   SHAVERDIAN, A. 'K 100-letiiu so dnia rozhdeniia P. I. Chaikovskogo', *Pravda* (13 Mar 1940): 6.

[*834*]   'Khar´kov: V sviazi s podgotovkoi k 100-letiiu so dnia rozhdeniia P. I. Chaikovskogo', *Sovetskoe
          iskusstvo* (14 Mar 1940): 4.

[*835*]   'Tsikl lektsii-kontsertov posviashchennykh P. I. Chaikovskomu', *Leningradskaia pravda* (15 Mar
          1940): 4.
          Preview of a series of lecture-concerts by the Leningrad Philharmonic Society (16–28 Mar 1940), to mark
          Chaikovskii's birth centenary.

[*836*]   'Kontserty iz proizvedenii Chaikovskogo v Belostoke', *Komsomol´skaia pravda* (16 Mar 1940): 4.
          A Chaikovskii jubilee concert given by the Belostok Philharmonic Orchestra.

[*837*]   'K 100-letiiu so dnia rozheniia P. I. Chaikovskogo', *Pravda* (18 Mar 1940): 4.
          Preparations for the Chaikovskii centenary in Leningrad and Minsk.

[*838*]   'Vecher, posviashchennyi P. I. Chaikovskomu, sostoialsia v klube Nikol´skoi voinskoi chasti',
          Leningradskaia pravda (28 Mar 1940): 4.
          A jubilee concert given by students of the Leningrad Conservatory.

[*839*]   '100 let so dnia rozhdeniia P. I. Chaikovskogo', *Sovetskoe iskusstvo* (29 Mar 1940): 1.
          Preparations for Chaikovskii's jubilee in Azerbaijan, Georgia, the Ukraine and Sukumi.

[*840*]   'K 100-letiiu so dnia rozhdeniia P. I. Chaikovskogo', *Izvestiia* (16 Apr 1940): 2.

[*841*]   'Pamiati P. I. Chaikovskogo', *Pravda* (17 Apr 1940): 6.
          Celebrations planned at the composer's childhood home at Alapaevsk, to mark the 100th anniversary of his
          birth on 7 May 1940.

[842] '100 let so dnia rozhdeniia P. I. Chaikovskogo', *Sovetskoe iskusstvo* (18 Apr 1940): 4.

Preparations for jubilee celebrations in Khar´kov, Sverdlovsk and Ufa.

[843] 'Iubileinaia sessiia, posviashchennaia P. I. Chaikovskomu', *Smena* (18 Apr 1940): 4.

A conference of musicians in Leningrad on 20 Apr 1940, to celebrate the composer's jubilee. See also *846*.

[844] 'Vystavka, posviashchennaia P. I. Chaikovskomu', *Pravda* (19 Apr 1940): 6.

The opening of an exhibition at the Moscow Conservatory on 19 Apr 1940, with around 2000 exhibits relating to Chaikovskii's life and works. See also *887*.

[845] 'Radiokontserty dlia zagranitsy iz proizvedenii Chaikovskogo', *Komsomol´skaia pravda* (20 Apr 1940): 4.

A series of centennial concerts of Chaikovskii's music, to be broadcast to Latvia, Lithuania and China (20–29 Apr 1940).

[846] 'Plenum, posviashchennyi P. I. Chaikovskomu', *Leningradskaia pravda* (21 Apr 1940): 4.

Report on the Chaikovskii conference in Leningrad. See also *843*.

[847] 'Nakanune stoletiia so dnia rozhdeniia P. I. Chaikovskogo', *Izvestiia* (23 Apr 1940): 1.

Announcement of official celebrations for Chaikovskii's centenary on 7 May, scheduled at Moscow, Klin and Votkinsk.

— [repr.] *Leningradskaia pravda* (23 Apr 1940): 4.

[848] 'Vechera Chaikovskogo v TsDRI', *Sovetskoe iskusstvo* (30 Apr 1940): 4.

A schedule of events and concerts in honour of Chaikovskii's centenary.

[849] PASTUKHOV, V. L. 'Pëtr Il´ich Chaikovskii: K stoletiiu so dnia rozhdeniia', *Den´ russkogo prosveshcheniia* (May/Aug 1940).

[850] 'Otkrytie iubileinoi vystavki k stoletiiu so dnia rozhdeniia P. I. Chaikovskogo', *Leningradskaia pravda* (1 May 1940): 4.

The opening of an exhibition devoted to the composer at the Pushkin museum for the visual arts in Moscow, followed by a chamber concert of Chaikovskii's works.

[851] '100 let so dnia rozhdeniia velikogo kompozitora P. I. Chaikovskogo', *Pravda* (6 May 1940): 4, illus.

Contents: M. Grinberg, 'Vozvyshaiushchii primer' — U. Gadzhibekova, 'Uchitel´' — Iu. Shaporin, 'Genii russkoi muzyki' [see *908*] — 'Prazdnovanii iubileiia v Khar´kove'.

[852] ASAF´EV, B. V. 'Velikii muzykant', *Leningradskaia pravda* (6 May 1940): 3.

— [repr.] In: B. V. Asaf´ev, *Izbrannye trudy*, tom 2 (1954): 48–51 [see *2348*].

— [repr. (abridged)] *Muzykal´naia zhizn´* (1965), 8: 1–2.

— [repr.] In: B. V. Asaf´ev, *O muzyke Chaikovskogo: Izbrannoe* (1972): 24–29 [see *2373*].

[853] 'Chaikovskii', *Sovetskoe iskusstvo* (6 May 1940): 1–3.

Contents: 'Chaikovskii' — 'Torzhestvenoe zasedanie v Bol´shom teatre' — S. Shlifshtein, 'Genii russkoi muzyki' [see *2327*] — A. Shaverdian, 'Melodicheskii stil´ oper Chaikovskogo' [see *2577*] — M. Rudanovskaia, 'Perepiska P. I. Chaikovskogo s B. B. Korsovym': 2 [see *268*] — D. Zhitomirskii, 'Chaikovskii simfonist' [see *4406*] — G. Neigauz, 'Velikoe i prostoe' — E. Grosheva, 'Chaikovskii i russkii muzykal´nyi teatr' [see *2541*].

[854] GARINA, E. 'Velikii russkii kompozitor', *Komsomol´skaia pravda* (6 May 1940).

[855] 'Genii russkogo iskusstva', *Komsomol´skaia pravda* (6 May 1940): 1.

[856] 'Genii russkoi muzyki', *Leningradskaia pravda* (6 May 1940): 1, illus.

[857] GINTSBURG, S. L. 'Chem dorog nam Chaikovskii', *Leningradskaia pravda* (6 May 1940): 3.

Mainly concerning Chaikovskii's musical legacy.

[*858*]   GLIER, R. M. 'Velikii russkii kompzitor', *Literaturnaia gazeta* (6 May 1940): 5.
— [repr.] *Smena* (6 May 1940): 2.

[*859*]   GOL´DENVEIZER, A. 'Chaikovskii v nashi dni', *Izvestiia* (6 May 1940): 3.

[*860*]   IARUSTOVSKII, B. 'Velikii russkii kompozitor', *Trud* (6 May 1940).

[*861*]   'K 100-letiiu so dnia rozhdeniia P. I. Chaikovskogo', *Smena* (6 May 1940).
The opening of an exhibition dedicated to Chaikovskii.

[*862*]   'K 100-letiiu so dnia rozhdeniia P. I. Chaikovskogo', *Komsomol´skaia pravda* (6 May 1940): 3.
Contents: I. Nest´ev, 'Genial´nyi kompozitor' — T. L. Shchepkina-Kupernik, 'Stranitsy vospominanii' [see *535*] — L. P. Shteinberg, 'Pamiatnye vstrechi' [see *536*] — A. N. Amfiteatrova-Levitskaia, 'Pervyi spektakl´' [see *387*] — K. Reznikov, 'Vseobshchee priznanie' — N. Fel´dman, 'On liubil zhizn´' — A. Kalanova, 'Dorogoe millionam imia' — M. Kireevskii, 'Gordost´ naroda'.

[*863*]   'K 100-letiiu so dnia rozhdeniia P. I. Chaikovskogo', *Leningradskaia pravda* (6 May 1940): 3.

[*864*]   'K 100-letiiu so dnia rozhdeniia P. I. Chaikovskogo', *Pravda* (6 May 1940): 1.
Preview of a festival at the Bol´shoi Theatre in Moscow on 7 May 1940, to mark the centenary of Chaikovskii's birth.

[*865*]   LAPONOGOV, I. 'Kompozitor za rabotoi', *Voroshilovogradskaia pravda* (6 May 1940).

[*866*]   'Mastera iskusstv o Chaikovskom', *Komsomol´skaia pravda* (6 May 1940): 2.
ContentsR. Glier, 'Velikii khudozhnik' — D. Arakishvili, 'Betkhoven nashego vremeni' — A. Tigranian, 'Ego tvorchestvo bessmertno' — T. Khrennikov, 'Uchitel´' — A. Maldybaev, 'Ogromnoe nasledstvo' — S. Bogatyrev, 'Vysokie zavety' — 'Radiogramma iz S. Sh. A. ot Leopol´da Stokovskogo'.

[*867*]   'Pamiati velikogo kompozitora', *Izvestiia* (6 May 1940): 1, illus.
Events commemorating the 100th anniversary of Chaikovskii's birth, in Moscow, Leningrad, Georgia and the Ukraine.

[*868*]   'Prazdnik russkoi muzykal´noi kul´tury', *Izvestiia* (6 May 1940): 1.

[*869*]   SHAVERDIAN, A. I. 'Velikii russkii kompozitor: K iubileiu Chaikovskogo', *Izvestiia* (6 May 1940).

[*870*]   'Strana otmechaet 100-letie so dnia rozhdeniia Chaikovskogo', *Komsomol´skaia pravda* (6 May 1940): 4.
Events to mark the centenary of Chaikovskii's birth in Ashkhabad, Omsk, Khar´kov, Nizhnyi Tagil, Klin, Moscow and Kiev.

[*871*]   'Torzhestvennoe zasedanie v Bol´shom teatre', *Sovetskoe iskusstvo* (6 May 1940): 1.
Preparations for a Chaikovskii centennial conference and concert at the Bol´shoi Theatre in Moscow on 7 May 1940. See also *874*.

[*872*]   'Ob oznamenovanii stoletiia so dnia rozhdeniia P. I. Chaikovskogo i uvekovechenii ego pamiati', *Pravda* (7 May 1940): 1.
Announcement of the setting up of a conservatory scholarship fund, to mark the centenary of Chaikovskii's birth.
— [repr.] *Komsomol´skaia pravda* (8 May 1940): 1.
— [repr.] *Sovetskoe iskusstvo* (9 May 1940): 1.

[*873*]   'Sto let so dnia rozhdeniia, genial´nogo russkogo kompozitora P. I. Chaikovskogo', *Muzykal´nye kadry* (7 May 1940) [whole issue], illus.
Contents: 'Velikii russkii kompozitor' — Z. Chikhikvadze, 'Vospominaniia o vstreche': [see *420*] — B. V. Asaf´ev, 'Bol´shaia zhizn´' — A. Budiakovskii, 'Chaikovskii v Konservatorii' [see *1728*] — K. Aleneva, 'Cherty muzykal´noi dramaturgii' — 'Itogi konkursa' — 'Iubileinyi kontsert'.

[874] **'Torzhestvennoe zasedanie v Bol´shom teatre SSSR'**, *Izvestiia* (8 May 1940): 1.

Report on the special conference and concert on 7 May 1940 at the Bol´shoi Theatre in Moscow, to celebrate the 100th anniversary of Chaikovskii's birth. See also *871*.

— [repr.] *Leningradskaia pravda* (8 May 1940): 1.

— [repr.] *Pravda* (8 May 1940): 2.

[875] **'Ukaz Prezidiuma Verkhovnogo Soveta SSSR o prisvoenii imeni P. I. Chaikovskogo Moskovskoi Gosudarstvennoi konservatorii'**, *Izvestiia* (8 May 1940): 1.

Publication of a decree renaming the Moscow Conservatory after Chaikovskii.

— [repr.] *Komsomol´skaia pravda* (8 May 1940): 2.

[876] **NEIGAUZ, G. G. 'Velikoe i prostoe: K stoletiiu so dnia rozhdeniia Chaikovskogo'**, *Sovetskoe iskusstvo* (9 May 1940).

— [repr.] In: G. G. Neigauz, *Razmyshleniia, vospominaniia, dnevniki, izbrannye stat´i, pis´ma k roditeliam*. Moskva: Sovetskii kompozitor, 1975: 179–182.

[877] **'Pamiati genial´nogo kompozitora'**, *Pravda* (9 May 1940): 3.

[878] **'Torzhestvennoe zasedanie v Bol´shom teatre SSSR'**, *Sovetskoe iskusstvo* (9 May 1940): 1.

[879] **'Ukaz Prezidiuma Verkhovnogo Soveta USSR ob uvekovechenii pamiati P. I. Chaikovskogo'**, *Sovetskaia Ukraina* (10 May 1940).

[880] **'Kiev: Upravlenie po delam iskusstv pri SNK USSR ob´iavilo konkurs na nauchnuiu rabotu na temu "P. I. Chaikovskii i ukrainskaia muzykal´naia kul´tura"'**, *Sovetskoe iskusstvo* (14 May 1940): 4.

A competition set for 1 Dec 1940 on the theme 'Chaikovskii and Ukrainian musical culture'.

[881] **'Kontserty i zrelishcha na VSKV'**, *Sovetskoe iskusstvo* (14 May 1940): 1.

News of various events organised during summer 1940 to celebrate Chaikovskii's birth centenary.

[882] **'Transliatsiia kontserta iz Moskvy dlia S. Sh. A.'**, *Pravda* (19 May 1940): 6.

A centennial concert of Chaikovskii's music, broadcast from Moscow to the USA.

[883] **'Iubileinaia sessiia'**, *Muzykal´nye kadry* (20 May 1940).

A conference of musicians in Leningrad, for the Chaikovskii centennial.

[884] **SHNEERSON, G. 'Muzyka v Estonii'**, *Sovetskoe iskusstvo* (4 Jul 1940).

Includes a report on celebrations for Chaikovskii's jubilee in Estonia, and the composition of his piano cycle *Souvenir de Hapsal*.

[885] **'Khar´kov: Gotovias´ k 100-letiiu so dnia rozhdeniia genial´nogo russkogo kompozitora P. I. Chaikovskogo'**, *Izvestiia* (27 Aug 1940): 4.

[886] **LLOYD, A. L. 'Chaikovsky in the Soviet Union'**, *Anglo-Soviet Journal*, 1 (Oct 1940): 321–326.

[887] **'Vystavka, posviashchennaia P. I. Chaikovskomu'**, *Komsomol´skaia pravda* (5 Oct 1940): 4.

The end of the Moscow Conservatory's exhibition devoted to Chaikovskii. See also *844*.

[888] **SHUVALOV, N. A. 'Sto let (1840–1940)'**. In: *P. I. Chaikovskii na stsene teatra opery i baleta im. S. M. Kirova* (1941): 9–16 [see *2542*].

[889] **L´VOV, M. *Pëtr Il´ich Chaikovskii*. Saransk: Mordgiz, 1942. 20 p. (*Velikie predki nashei Rodiny*).

[890] **PAVLOV, K. 'P. I. Tchaikovsky'**, *Voks bull* (1942), 3/4: 71–75, illus.

[891] **IAKOVLEV, V. V. *Pëtr Il´ich Chaikovskii: K 50-letiiu so dnia smerti, 1893–1943*.** Izhevsk: Udmurtgosizdat, 1943. 10 p. (*Gos. Dom-muzei P. I. Chaikovskogo*).

[892]   **P. I. Chaikovskii: K 50-letiiu so dnia smerti**. [Saransk]: Mordovskaia gos. filarmoniia [1943]. 4 p.
        (*Upravlenie po delam iskusstva pri SNK MASSR*).
        For a concert to mark the 50th anniversary of the composer's death. Includes article 'P. I. Chaikovskii' by I. Ia.
        Azhotkin.

[893]   **ASAF'EV, B. V. 'Chaikovskii: K 50-letiiu so dnia smerti'**, *Krasnoflotets*, 17/18 (1943): 52–53.
        — [repr.] In: B. V. Asaf'ev, *Izbrannye trudy*, tom 2 (1954): 26–30 [see *2348*].
        — [repr.] In: B. V. Asaf'ev, *O muzyke Chaikovskogo: Izbrannoe* (1972): 37–38 [see *2373*].

[894]   **ASAF'EV, B. V. 'Pamiati Chaikovskogo: Vydaiushchiisia syny slavianskikh narodov'**, *Slaviane*
        (1943), 2: 40.
        — [repr.] In: B. V. Asaf'ev, *Izbrannye trudy*, tom 2 (1954): 26–30 [see *2348*].
        — [repr.] 'Pamiati Chaikovskogo'. In: B. V. Asaf'ev, *O muzyke Chaikovskogo: Izbrannoe* (1972): 29–34 [see *2373*].

[895]   **ASAF'EV, B. V. 'Chaikovskii—simfonist-dramaturg: K 50-letiiu so dnia smerti P. I.
        Chaikovskogo'**, *Literatura i iskusstvo* (30 Oct 1943).

[896]   **SHOSTAKOVICH, D. D. 'Mysli o Chaikovskom'**, *Literatura i iskusstvo* (7 Nov 1943).
        — [English tr.] 'Thoughts about Tchaikovsky'. In: *Russian Symphony: Thoughts about Tchaikovsky* (1947): 1–5
        [see *587*].

[897]   **ASAF'EV, B. V. 'Chaikovskii: K 50-letiiu so dnia smerti'**, *Pravda* (15 Nov 1943).
        — [repr.] In: B. V. Asaf'ev, *Izbrannye trudy*, tom 2 (1954): 21–23 [see *2348*].
        — [repr.] In: B. V. Asaf'ev, *O muzyke Chaikovskogo: Izbrannoe* (1972): 34–37 [see *2373*].

[898]   **KISELEV, V. A. & KAZANSKII, N. V. P. I. Chaikovskii: Zhizn' i tvorchestvo**. Moskva: Gos. muz.
        izdat., 1947. 49 p, illus. (*Moskovskaia gos. filarmoniia*).
        Guide to an exhibition about the composer in the Chaikovskii Concert Hall of the Moscow State Conservatory.

[899]   **USPENSKAIA, K. 'Velichaishii russkii kompozitor'**, *Ogonek* (1948), 47: 25.
        To mark the 55th anniversary of Chaikovskii's death.

[900]   **LITINA, S. 'Velikii kompozitor, velikogo naroda'**, *Sovetskoe iskusstvo* (9 May 1950): 3.
        For the 110th anniversary of Chaikovskii's birth.

[901]   **LEONOVA, M. 'Vystavka, posviashchennaia zhizni i tvorchestvu P. I. Chaikovskogo'**, *Sovetskaia
        muzyka* (1951), 3: 106, illus.
        An exhibition at the Chaikovskii Hall in Moscow, dedicated to the composer's works.

[902]   **ORLOVA, E. M. P. I. Chaikovskii**. Stenogramma publichnoi lektsii. Leningrad, 1953. 31 p. (*Vsesoiuznoe
        obshchestvo po rasprostraneniiu politicheskikh i nauchnykh znanii*).

[903]   **'P. I. Chaikovskii: Velikii russkii kompozitor'**. In: *Pëtr Il'ich Chaikovskii: Kratkii rekomendatel'nyi
        ukazatel'* (1953): 7–11 [see *23*].

[904]   **POLIANOVSKII, G. 'Čajkovskij a sovětská hudební kultura'**, *Hudební rozhledy*, 6 (1953), 16: 750–
        751.

[905]   **SOKOL'SKII, M. 'Bessmertie geniia'**, *Ogonek* (1953), 44: 9, illus.
        To commemorate the 60th anniversary of the composer's death.

[906]   **MARTYNOV, I. 'Pëtr Il'ch Chaikovskii: K 60-letiiu so dnia smerti'**, *Leningradskaia pravda* (6 Nov
        1953): 4.

[907]   **ASAF'EV, B. V. 'Velikii russkii kompozitor'**. In: B. V. Asaf'ev, *Izbrannye trudy*, tom 2 (1954): 17–20
        [see *2348*].

[908]   SHAPORIN, Iu. 'Predislovie'. In: P. I. Chaikovskii, *Pis´ma k blizkim* (1955): iii–viii [see *155*].

— [repr.] 'Genii russkoi muzyki: P. I. Chaikovskii (Pis´ma k blizkim)'. In: Iu. A. Shaporin, *Stat´i, materialy, vospominaniia*. Moskva, 1989: 115–122.

[909]   **[Pamiati P. I. Chaikovskogo]**, *Muzykal´naia zhizn´* (May 1958), 9: 2, 4.

Celebrations to mark the composer's birthday in Votkinsk and Moscow.

[910]   **'Vchera u pamiatnika P. I. Chaikovskogo'**, *Leningradskaia pravda* (27 Sep 1958): 4.

Report on short ceremony by the composer's grave in Leningrad, attended by prominent musicians.

[911]   IARUSTOVSKII, B. **'Slava i gordost´ russkogo iskusstva: Ocherk o P. I. Chaikovskom'**, *Muzykal´naia zhizn´* (1959), 12: 12–14, illus.

[912]   SHAPORIN, Iu. **'Master of melody'**, *Music Journal*, 18 (Sep 1960): 62, illus.

[913]   KOCH, T. **'The Slavic stamp'**, *Opera News*, 28 (29 Feb 1964): 7.

Concerning a series of postage stamps commemorating Chaikovskii and other composers. See also *938*, *940*.

[914]   KUNIN, I. F. *Pëtr Il´ich Chaikovskii: K 125-letiiu so dnia rozhdeniia*. Moskva: Znanie, 1965. 32 p, illus. (*Novoe v zhizni, nauke i tekhnike*, seriia 6; *Literatura i iskusstvo*; 7).

[915]   **'K 125-letiiu so dnia rozhdeniia P. I. Chaikovskogo'**, *Ogonek* (1965), 17: 8–13, illus.

Contents:A. Sveshnikov, 'Vechno zhivoi': 8 — I. Vershinina, 'Rossii—ego serdtse, miru—ego genii': 9–11 — K. Ivanov, 'Vo vsekh stolitsakh': 11 — E. Popova: 'Slyshna povsiudu': 12–13 [see *1004*].

[916]   SVESHNIKOV, A. **'Muzyka ot vsego serdtsa'**, *Kul´tura i zhizn´* (1965), 5: 39, illus.

An interview with Aleksandr Sveshnikov, conductor and director of the Moscow Conservatory.

[917]   KIRICHENKO, A. **'Rodina volshebnykh melodii: Zavtra ispolniaetsia 125 let so dnia rozhdeniia P. I. Chaikovskogo'**, *Smena* (6 May 1965): 3, illus.

[918]   **'P. I. Chaikovskii, 1840–1965: Akademiia masterstva'**, *Sovetskaia kul´tura* (6 May 1965): 3.

[919]   SOKOL´SKII, M. **'Liubov´ melodiia'**, *Komsomolskaia pravda* (6 May 1965): 3, illus.

[920]   BOGDANOV-BEREZOVSKII, V. **'Nash Chaikovskii: K 125-letiiu so dnia rozhdeniia kompozitora'**, *Leningradskaia pravda* (7 May 1965): 3, illus.

[921]   DMITRIEV, A. **'Slovo o velikom kompozitore: Segodnia 125 let so dnia rozhdeniia P. I. Chaikovskogo'**, *Vechernii Leningrad* (7 May 1965): 2, illus.

[922]   IARUSTOVSKII, B. M. **'Slava i gordost´ zemli russkoi'**, *Sovetskaia kul´tura* (7 May 1965).

[923]   MARTYNOV, I. **'Bessmertie muzyki: K 125-letiiu so dnia rozhdeniia P. I. Chaikovskogo'**, *Izvestiia* (8 May 1965): 6.

[924]   SHOSTAKOVICH, D. D. **'Syn Rossii: K 125-letiiu so dnia rozhdeniia P. I. Chaikovskogo'**, *Pravda* (8 May 1965): 6.

[925]   **'Sto chasov s Chaikovskim'**, *Sovetskaia muzyka* (1966), 6: 149.

A festival dedicated to Chaikovskii's works at Perm´.

[926]   KRUZHIIAMSKAIA, A. **'Priglashenie k znakomstvu'**, *Sovetskaia kul´tura* (12 Jan 1967): 3.

A lecture concert "Chaikovskii" in Moscow, for schoolchildren.

[927]   TSUKKERMAN, V. **'Istoki ekspressii, shirota dykhaniia'**, *Sovetskaia muzyka* (1968), 11: 107–113, music, illus.; 12: 86–94.

For the 75th anniversary of the composer's death.

[*928*]   KORABEL´NIKOVA, L. Z. 'Utverzhdeno V. I. Leninym', *Sovetskaia muzyka* (1971), 9: 100–105.

[*929*]   ANSHAKOV, B. Ia. & VAIDMAN, P. E. 'Torzhestva, posviashchennye Chaikovskomu', *Sovetskaia muzyka* (1974), 9: 159–160.
        Report on the 17th Chaikovskii music festival at Izhevsk.

[*930*]   KHOPROVA, T. A. 'Muzyka Chaikovskogo—bessmertna', *Muzykal´nye kadry* (19 Jun 1980): 4.
        Celebrations at the Leningrad Conservatory to mark the 140th anniversary of Chaikovskii's birth.

[*931*]   NEST´EV, I. 'Sowjetische Musik heute', *Neue Zeitschrift für Musik* (Mar/Apr 1981), 2: 111, illus.

[*932*]   BELYI, P. 'Nepostizhimyi Chaikovskii', *Sovetskaia muzyka* (1982), 6: 75–81.

[*933*]   ROZANOVA, Iu. 'Moi put´ k Chaikovskomu', *Sovetskaia muzyka* (1982), 6: 51–54.
        Interview with Iul´ia Rozanova.

[*934*]   ANSHAKOV, B. Ia. 'Votkinskoe muzykal´no-dramaticheskoe obshchestvo im. P. I. Chaikovskogo'. In: *P. I. Chaikovskii i Ural* (1983): 60–64 [see *1749*].

[*935*]   EMEL´IANOV, A. 'Muzykal´nye merediany: Izhevsk', *Sovetskaia kul´tura* (31 May 1983): 4.
        Report on the annual Chaikovskii music festival in the Urals.

[*936*]   KOROBKOV, V. 'Perm´: Festival´ na beregu Kamy', *Teatr* (1984), 2: 88–90, illus.
        A festival dedicated to Chaikovskii's operas and ballets, in the city of Perm´.

[*937*]   VAIDMAN, P. E. '"Ia vsegda byl pochitatelem velikogo Chaikovskogo"', *Sovetskaia muzyka* (1984), 2: 96–97.
        A. V. Lunacharskii's views on Chaikovskii. See also *949*.

[*938*]   BELIAKOV, V. 'Muzykal´naia filateliia: Chaikovskii na sovetskikh markakh', *Muzykal´naia zhizn´* (1985), 4: 24, illus.
        Chaikovskii as depicted on Soviet postage stamps. See also *913*, *940*.

[*939*]   HARRIS, D. 'Man and superman: How the Soviet Union has covered up for Tchaikovsky', *Connoisseur*, 216 (Jun 1986): 78–83.

[*940*]   BUTOROV, L. 'Chaikovskii: Epokha i obrazy. Iz al´boma kollektsionera', *Muzykal´naia zhizn´* (1987), 3: 19, illus.
        Postage stamps issued in commemoration of Chaikovskii. See also *913*, *938*.

[*941*]   PREISMAN, E. 'Festival v Achinske', *Sovetskaia muzyka* (1987), 10: 180–191.
        Report on the second Achinsk festival dedicated to Chaikovskii's symphonic and chamber music,

[*942*]   ***Muzyka v knizhnom znake: Katalog vystavki k 150-letiiu so dnia rozhdeniia P. I. Chaikovskogo***. Omsk: Uprpoligrafizdat, 1990. 59 p, illus.

[*943*]   'Venok Petru Il´ichu Chaikovskomu: K 150-letiiu so dnia rozhdeniia', *Sovetskaia muzyka* (1990), 5: 2–9, illus.

[*944*]   BUDASHEVSKAIA, L. 'Chaikovskii: Vchera, segodnia, zavtra', *Avrora* (1990), 5: 125–131.
        A conversation with the composer A. Petrov.

[*945*]   'Chaikovskii i my: Kruglyi stol v redaktsii', *Sovetskaia muzyka* (1990), 6: 5–19 [see *592*].
        Discussion of Chaikovskii's music and its relevance to the 20th century, by V. Iuzefovich, V. Gubarenko, N. Karetnikov, I. Zhukov, V. Berlinskii, M. Nest´eva, L. Grabovskii, N. Chernova, S. Korobkov, O. Boshniakovich.

[946]   FEDOSEEV, V. 'Chaikovskii vsegda s nami', *Muzykal´naia zhizn´* (1990), 9: 2–3, illus.

The conductor Vladimir Fedoseev in conversation with V. L´vov.

[947]   'Iubilei russkogo geniia: 150 let P. I. Chaikovskogo', *Muzykal´naia zhizn´* (1990), 1: 1–6.

[948]   KONYSHEV, V. 'Pari nad mirom, russkii genii! (iz vyskazyvanii o kompozitore)', *Sovetskaia muzyka* (1990), 6: 4, 28, 54, 82, 124, 142 [see *592*].

Quotations about Chaikovskii by famous musicians and writers.

[949]   LUNACHARSKII, A. 'Vklad Chaikovskogo v russkuiu kul´turu bestsenen', *Sovetskaia muzyka* (1990), 6: 21–27 [see *592*].

The text of Lunacharskii's speech to mark the 30th anniversary of the composer's death, given on 23 Dec 1923 in the Bol´shoi Theatre, Moscow. Notes and commentary by Polina Vaidman and I. Lunacharskaia. See also *937*.

[950]   MILOVANOVA, N. 'Zvuchit muzyka Chaikovskogo', *Muzykal´naia zhizn´* (1990), 13: 14.

Student performances at the Chaikovskii jubilee festival in Moscow.

[951]   'Muzykal´nyi klub: K 150-letiiu so dnia rozhdeniia P. I. Chaikovskogo', *Sem´ia i shkola* (1990), 5: 50–57.

Contents: V. Gornostaeva, 'Muzyka na vse vremena': 50–52 [see *5408*] — M. Katina, "Eto byl stekliannyi rebënok…": Vospominaniia guvernantki P. I. Chaikovskogo': 52–53 [see *433*] — L. Osipova, 'Pesni Rotshil´da': 53–56 [see *1983*] — M. Zhilinskaia, 'Chaikovskii v krugu rodnykh': 56–57 [see *1876*].

[952]   'Nashe nasledie: Genii russkoi muzyki', *Izvestiia kul´tury Rossii* (1990), 7: 18–25.

News of events celebrating Chaikovskii's jubilee. in Moscow, Votkinsk, Klin and Tambov.

[953]   PLETNEV, M. 'Beskonechnost´ geniia', *Sovetskaia muzyka* (1990), 6: 2–3 [see *592*].

[954]   PLETNEV, M. 'Muzyka na vse vremena: 150 let so dnia rozhdeniia P. I. Chaikovskogo', *Nashe nasledie* (1990), 2: 17–18, illus.

[955]   SMETANNIKOV, L. 'Moi Chaikovskii: K 150-letiiu so dnia rozhdeniia', *Muzykal´naia zhizn´* (1990), 9: 3, illus.

[956]   STRUCHKOVA, R. 'Shkola serdtsa: K 150-letiiu so dnia rozhdeniia P. I. Chaikovskogo', *Sovetskii balet* (1990), 6: 3.

[957]   SVETLANOV, E. 'Velikii syn Rossii: K 150-letiiu so dnia rozhdeniia P. I. Chaikovskogo', *Rossiiskaia muzykal´naia gazeta* (1990), 9: 1, illus.

A Chaikovskii centennial concert at the Bol´shoi Theatre in Moscow on 7 May 1990.

[958]   TIURINA, G. 'Genii chistoi krasoty: K 150-letiiu so dnia rozhdeniia P. I. Chaikovskogo', *Rossiiskaia muzykal´naia gazeta* (1990), 9: 3, illus.

[959]   TULINTSEV, B. 'V pamiat´ o Chaikovskom', *Teatr* (1990), 5: 139–144.

[960]   VASIL´EVA, N. 'God Chaikovskogo: "Ia russkii v polneishem smysle etogo slova"', *Leningradskaia panorama* (1990), 5: 30–31, illus.

Examines the interpretation of his works and the celebrations of his birth centenary.

[961]   ZVEREV, V. 'Mir Chaikovskogo', *Melodiia* (1990), 3: 2–3.

[962]   SVETLANOV, E. 'Velikii syn Rossii', *Sovetskaia kul´tura* (6 Jan 1990), 1: 1, 15.

Outlining the celebrations planned for Chaikovskii's jubilee year.

[963]   'K 150-letiiu so d nia rozhdeniia Petra Il´icha Chaikovskogo: Velikaia zhizn´ v pis´makh i fotografiiakh', *Ekran i stsena* (11 Jan 1990): 8–9, illus.

[*964*]   BANEVICH, S. 'Chto zaveshchal nam Pëtr Il´ich: Zavtra v Leningrade otkryvaetsia Detskii muzykal´nyi festival´, posviashchennyi 150-letiiu so dnia rozhdeniia P. I. Chaikovskogo', *Smena* (23 Mar 1990): 3.

[*965*]   'God P. I. Chaikovskogo', *Sovetskaia kul´tura* (5 May 1990): 9, illus.

Contents: V. Fedoseev, 'Uteshenie i podpora' — R. Muti, 'Za zhizn´ i schast´e' — D. Khvorostovskii, 'On, moia sud´ba' — N. Giaurov, 'Krasota genial´noi muzyki' — N. Shadrina, '"Ioanna d'Ark" na moskovskoi stsene' [see *3251*].

[*966*]   VASIL´EVA, G. 'Zagadochnaia russkaia dusha: Ispolniaetsia 150-let so dnia rozhdeniia P. I. Chaikovskogo', *Komsomol´skaia pravda* (5 May 1990): 4.

An interview with the pianist/conductor Mikhail Pletnev.

[*967*]   BELOUSOV, M. 'Shedevry na vse vremena: K 150-letiiu so dnia rozhdeniia P. I. Chaikovskogo', *Trud* (6 May 1990): 4, illus.

[*968*]   GAKKEL´, L. 'Dumaia o nem, my dumaem o sebe: Zavtra ispolniaetsia 150 let so dnia rozhdeniia Petra Il´icha Chaikovskogo' *Smena* (6 May 1990).

— [repr.] 'Dumaia o Chaikovskom: My dumaem o sebe'. In: L. Gakkel´, *Ia ne boius´—ia muzykant*. Sankt Peterburg, 1993: 29–31.

[*969*]   '"Net bolee menia vliublennogo v matushku Rus´"': K 150-letiiu so dnia rozhdeniia P. I. Chaikovskogo', *Sovetskaia Rossiia* (6 May 1990): 6, illus.

[*970*]   SAZHINA, M. 'O palochke, baletnoi tufel´ke i velikom gorode', *Smena* (6 May 1990).

An exhibition on 'Chaikovskii and musical St. Petersburg' at the Kirov Opera Theatre.

[*971*]   SLONIMSKII, S. 'Vslushaemsia v etu muzyku: K 150-letiiu so dnia rozhdeniia P. I. Chaikovskogo', *Leningradskaia pravda* (6 May 1990): 3, illus.

[*972*]   VAVILINA, A. 'Ot dushi, k dushe: K 150-letiiu so dnia rozhdeniia P. I. Chaikovskogo', *Leningradskaia pravda* (6 May 1990): 3.

On the conductor Evgenii Mravinskii's performances of Chaikovskii's music.

[*973*]   AIZENSHTADT, B. & AIZENSHTADT, M. 'Sledom za Chaikovskim', *Vechernii Leningrad* (7 May 1990): 3.

[*974*]   ZOLOTOV, A. 'V nem, i Rossiia, i ves´ mir: K 50-letiiu so dnia rozhdeniia P. I. Chaikovskogo', *Izvestiia* (7 May 1990): 4, illus.

[*975*]   'Chaikovskii segodnia: Van Klibern i Edison Denisov o muzyke Chaikovskogo', *Literaturnaia gazeta* (9 May 1990): 7, illus.

[*976*]   SHEVCHUK, S. 'Otvetnyi zvuk', *Vechernii Leningrad* (1 Aug 1990).

[*977*]   SHEVCHUK, S. 'Mir slushaet Chaikovskogo', *Vechernii Leningrad* (4 Dec 1990).

[*978*]   NABORSHCHIKOVA, S. 'Balet: Chaikovskii v Tashkente', *Pravda* (8 Dec 1990): 2, illus.

The 'Pas de deux' ballet festival at Tashkent, to celebrate Chaikovskii's jubilee year.

[*979*]   BIALIK, M. 'Posviashchenie: Gala kontsert v Bol´shom zale Leningradskoi filarmonii', *Muzykal´naia zhizn´* (1991), 4: 1, illus.

Report on a gala concert by the Leningrad Philharmonic Orchestra to mark the 150th anniversary of Chaikovskii's birth.

[*980*]   ISTOMINA, A. 'Festivali: Napominanie o garmonii', *Sovetskaia muzyka* (1991), 5: 93–95.

On the 'Chaikovskii's World' music festival at Tol´iatti.

[981]   KORABEL´NIKOVA, L. Z. 'God Chaikovskogo zavershen', *Muzykal´noe obozrenie* (1991), 1: 3, illus.

Conferences and festivals to mark the 150th anniversary of Chaikovskii's birth, and the publication of *Polnoe sobranie sochinenii*, tom 63 (1990) [see *118*].

[982]   'Prazdnika ego radostnye i trevozhnye uroki: K 150-letiiu so dnia rozhdenia P. I. Chaikovskogo', *Sovetskii balet* (1991), 1: 4–9, illus.

A festival devoted to Chaikovskii's ballets.

[983]   ZINKEVICH, E. 'Nauka o Chaikovskom: Vtoroe dykhanie!', *Sovetskaia muzyka* (1991), 2: 99–101.

The conference 'Chaikovskii and world musical culture' held at Votkinsk, 14–18 Oct 1990.

[984]   POZNANSKY, A. 'Tchaikovsky as communist icon'. In: *For SK: In celebration of the life and career of Simon Karlinsky*. Ed. by Michael S. Flier and Robert P. Hughes. Berkeley, Calif.: Berkeley Slavic Specialities, 1994: 233–246, illus. (*Modern Russian literature and culture, studies and texts*; 33).

See also *1399, 2479*.

POST-SOVIET RUSSIA (1991+)

[985]   KORABEL´NIKOVA, L. Z. 'Uchastniki i svideteli zolotogo veka Rossii', *Muzykal´naia akademiia* (1993), 4: 207–210.

[986]   SHENK, P. P. 'Tochno nevidimaia ruka smetala vse sledy', *Smena* (3 Apr 1993).

[987]   MELIKIANTS, G. 'Noiabr´ v Bol´shom teatre budet mesiatsem Chaikovskogo', *Izvestiia* (5 Nov 1993): 2.

A Chaikovskii Festival at the Bol´shoi Theatre in Moscow, marking the centenary of his death. See also *992*.

[988]   BANEVICH, S. 'Sto let odinochestva', *Sankt Peterburgskie vedomosti* (6 Nov 1993).

[989]   GAKKEL´, L. 'My nerazdel´ny s nim', *Sankt Peterburgskie vedomosti* (6 Nov 1993).

[990]   'Delat´ to, k chemu vlechet prizvanie', *Nevskoe vremia* (9 Nov 1993): 5.

The 100th anniversary of Chaikovskii's death.

[991]   LAVROVSKAIA, E. 'Rossiiskaia svirel´ v mirovom orkestre', *Nevskoe vremia* (9 Nov 1993): 5.

[992]   MELIKIANTS, G. 'Festival´ pamiati Chaikovskogo v Bol´shom zavershilsia "Spiashchei krasavitsei"', *Izvestiia* (3 Dec 1993): 8.

[993]   'Posviashchaetsia Chaikovskomu', *Muzykal´naia zhizn´* (1994), 9: 39.

[994]   TSARËVA, E. M. 'Chaikovskii v nashi dni: Mezhdu dvumia datami'. In: *P. I. Chaikovskii: K 100-letiiu so dnia smerti* (1995): 5–9 [see *597*].

[995]   VAIDMAN, P. E. 'Otkryvaia novogo Chaikovskogo'. In: *P. I. Chaikovskii: Zabytoe i novoe* (1995): 7–15 [see *598*].

[996]   KANTOROV, A. 'Chaikovskii opozdal na svoiu prem´eru', *Vechernii Peterburg* (13 Feb 1999): 4.

An interview with Iu. Broido about his 'Unknown Chaikovskii' project.

See also *1146*.

3.2.2. Europe

[997]   KUZNETSOV, K. 'Chaikovskii za rubezhom', *Sovetskaia muzyka* (1940), 5/6: 99–104 [see *585*].

Appreciation of Chaikovskii in Western Europe.

[998]   'Stoletie so dnia rozhdeniia P. I. Chaikovskogo', *Sovetskaia muzyka* (1940), 9: 100.

Events in Bulgaria, Denmark, England, Germany, Italy, The Netherlands, Sweden, Switzerland, and the USA, to commemorate the centenary of Chaikovskii's birth.

[999]   SH[NEERSON], G. 'Khronika zarubezhnoi muzykal´noi zhizni', *Sovetskaia muzyka* (1940), 3: 95.

Centennial concerts of Chaikovskii's works outside Russia. See also *1000*.

[1000]   'Stoletie so dnia rozhdeniia P. I. Chaikovskogo', *Sovetskaia muzyka* (1940), 5/6: 153 [see *585*].

[1001]   'Prazdnovanie iubileia Chaikovskogo za rubezhom', *Izvestiia* (8 Mar 1940).

Events organized in Bulgaria and Germany to celebrate the 100th anniversary of Chaikovskii's birth.
— [repr.] *Leningradskaia pravda* (8 Mar 1940): 4.
— [repr.] *Pravda* (8 Mar 1940).

[1002]   'Prazdnovanie za rubezhom stoletiia so dnia rozhdeniia Chaikovskogo', *Pravda* (7 May 1940): 6.

Reports on celebrations to mark the centenary of Chaikovskii's birth, in England, Estonia, Germany, Latvia, Lithuania and Sweden.
— [repr.] *Leningradskaia pravda* (8 May 1940): 7.

[1003]   'Chestvovanie Chaikovskogo za granitsei', *Pravda* (10 May 1940): 2.

Celebrations in Czechoslovakia, Norway and Bulgaria to mark the 100th anniversary of Chaikovskii's birth.

[1004]   POPOVA, E. 'Slyshna povsiudu', *Ogonek* (1965), 17: 12–13 [see *915*].

Concerts of Chaikovskii's music in Eastern Europe to mark the 125th anniversary of his birth.

[1005]   KORABEL´NIKOVA, L. Z. 'Chaikovskii v samosoznanii russkogo zarubezh´ia 20–30-kh godov'. In: *P. I. Chaikovskii: K 100-letiiu so dnia smerti* (1995): 10–18 [see *597*].

AUSTRIA

[1006]   KORNGOLD, J. 'Peter Tschaikowsky', *Neue Freie Presse* (1 Feb 1912).

See also *1052*.

BULGARIA

[1007]   'Bolgariia: Prazdnovanie stoletiia so dnia rozhdeniia Chaikovskogo', *Internatsional´naia literatura* (1940), 5/6: 345.

Celebrations in Bulgaria to commemorate the 100th anniversary of Chaikovskii's birth. See also *1008*.

[1008]   'Bolgarskaia obshchestvennost´ otmechaet stoletie so dnia rozhdeniia Chaikovskogo', *Pravda* (24 Apr 1940): 6, illus.

[1009]   BORISOV, V. 'Bolgarskaia pechat´ o P. I Chaikovskom', *Sovetskoe iskusstvo* (24 Apr 1940): 3.

Reports on events in Bulgaria to celebrate Chaikovskii's centennial year.

[1010]   'Vystavka pamiati Chaikovskogo v Bolgarii', *Izvestiia* (21 May 1940): 2.

The opening of a Chaikovskii centennial exhibition in Sofia.

[1011]   SJAROV, P. 'Petur Ilich Chaikovski: Po sluchai 60 godini ot smurtta mu', *Bulgarska muzika* (1953), 10: 44–49.

CZECH REPUBLIC

[1012]   LEVICKÝ, A. 'Petr Iljič Čajkovskij: Dne 7. května uplynulo 110 let od narození geniálního ruského skladatele P. J. Čajkovského', *Hudební rozhledy*, 2 (1950): 236–238.

[*1013*] ŠTĚPÁNEK, V. 'Jubileum P. I. Čajkovského', *Hudební rozhledy*, 6 (1953), 16: 748–749.

[*1014*] 'Chas s Chaikovskim', *Sovetskaia kul´tura* (11 Aug 1970): 4.
An exhibition in honour of Chaikovskii in Prague.

[*1015*] SHAPOVALOV, A. 'Charuiushchie zvuki nad Vltavoi: K 150-letiiu P. I. Chaikovskogo', *Smena* (4 May 1990): 3.
Concerts in Prague for the Chaikovskii jubilee.

[*1016*] 'Chaikovskii v Prage', *Kul´tura* (1993), 24: 10.
Commemorations for the 100th anniversary of Chaikovskii's death.

[*1017*] POKORS, M. 'K poctě Cajkovskeho', *Hudební rozhledy*, 46 (1993), 8: 352.

See also *1802*.

FRANCE

[*1018*] 'Muzykal´nye novosti', *Muzykal´nyi mir* (26 Feb 1883): 8.
Chaikovskii's nomination as a correspondent member of the *Academie Française*.

[*1019*] PAROUTY, M. 'Tchaikovski: Star du petit ecran', *Diapason-Harmonie* (Nov 1993), 398: 24.

GERMANY

[*1020*] BÜLOW, H. von. 'Musikalisches aus Italien', *Allgemeine Musik Zeitung* (10/22 Mar 1874).
— [repr.] In: H. von Bülow, Ausgewahlte Schriften (1850–1892). Band 3. Leipzig: Breitkopf & Härtel, 1896: 340–352.

[*1021*] 'Zagrannichnye izvestiia: Germaniia', *Russkaia muzykal´naia gazeta* (Mar 1902), 13: 414; (Apr 1902), 17: 508; (Jul 1902), 26/27: 667.
The Chaikovskii musical festival at Pyrmont, Germany.

[*1022*] IVANOV, M. 'Muzykal´nye nabroski', *Novoe vremia* (25 Mar 1902): 2.
Chaikovskii's reputation in Germany, and preparations for the forthcoming festival in Pyrmont.

[*1023*] POLOVTSOV, A. V. 'Prazdnestvo v pamiat´ P. I. Chaikovskogo v Pirmonte', *Moskovskie vedomosti* (1 Jul 1902).

[*1024*] LESSMANN, O. 'Die Tschaikowsky-Feier in Pyrmont am 28. und 29. Juni 1902', *Allgemeine Musik-Zeitung* (11/18 Jul 1902), 28/29: 512–518.
Includes transcript of a lecture given by Hugo Reimann, 'Peter Iljitsch Tschaikowsky' at the festival in Pyrmont on 28/29 Jun 1902.
— [repr.] In: *Internationales Tschaikowsky-Fest: Tübingen, 23.–27. Oktober 1993. Festschrift* (1993): 144–161 [see *1043*].

[*1025*] KRAUSE, E. 'Tschaikowskys zehnter Todestag', *Musikalisches Wochenblatt* (1903), 43/50.

[*1026*] SPIRO, E. 'Tschaikowskys Stellung im Internationalen Musikleben', *Zeitschrift der Internationalen Musikgesellschaft*, 5 (1903/1904), 8: 307–315.

[*1027*] SIMON, J. 'Zu Tschaikowsky's 30 Todestage', *Blätter der Philharmonie*, 1 (1923), 6.

[*1028*] FABER, R. 'Russkie opery v Germanii', *Zhizn´ iskusstva* (1925), 35: 14.
Concerning the lack of popularity of Chaikovskii's operas in Germany.

[*1029*] 'Iubilei Chaikovskogo v Germanii', *Internatsional´naia literatura* (1940), 5/6: 345.

[*1030*]   SERAUKY, W. 'P. I. Tschaikowski: "Westlich oder östlich orientiert"?', *Musik und Gesellschaft*, 2 (1952), 187–189.

[*1031*]   SIEGMUND-SCHULTZE, W. 'Peter Tschaikowski im Blickpunkt unserer Zeit', *Sowjetwissenschaft: Kunst und Literatur*, 7 (1959): 1115–1125.

[*1032*]   DAVYDOVA, K. Iu. 'Za rubezhom (FRG): Studiia imeni Chaikovskogo', *Sovetskaia muzyka* (1962), 12: 128–130, illus.

On the foundation of the Tschaikowsky-Studio in Hamburg, Germany. See also *1033, 1038. 1039,*

[*1033*]   DIETRICH, R. A. 'Ein deutsches Tschaikowsky-Studio', *Neue Zeitschrift für Musik*, 124 (Apr 1963): 138–139, illus.

[*1034*]   'Komponist im Zwielicht', *Musikhandel*, 16 (1965), 3: 92.

[*1035*]   KERNER, D. 'Nie mit der Gegenwart zufrieden: Zum 125. Geburtstage von Peter Tschaikowski', *Deutsches Ärzteblatt*, 62 (1965), 19: 1080–1087.

[*1036*]   GOLDSTEIN, M. 'Na stsenakh mira: Berlin', *Sovetskaia kul´tura* (6 May 1965): 3.

Celebrations in Germany to mark the 125th anniversary of Chaikovskii's birth.

[*1037*]   KOHLHASE, T. 'Köln: Tschaikowsky-Ausstellung', *Neue Zeitschrift für Musik*, 126 (Dec 1965): 471.

[*1038*]   'Po muzykal´nyim meridianam: Imeni Chaikovskogo', *Muzykal´naia zhizn´* (1969), 21: 20.

The Tschaikowsky-Studio in Hamburg.

[*1039*]   THOMAS, R. 'Tschaikowsky-Studio: Eine Hamburgische Initiative', *Musica*, 23 (1969), 4: 382.

[*1040*]   SCHULZ, F. F. 'Einem großen Künstler zum Gedenken: Zum Verhaltnis Tschaikowsky-Rachmaninow'. In: *Piano-Jahrbuch*. Recklinghausen, 1981: 66–68.

[*1041*]   LEHMANN, H. 'Ein Mensch wie von Puschkin: Zum 150. Geburtstag von Peter Tschaikowski', *Ballet-Journal*, 38 (1990), 3: 44.

[*1042*]   NEEF, S. 'Was ist der Name meiner Gegenwart?: Zum 150. Geburtstag Pjotr Iljitsch Tschaikowskis', *Musik und Gesellschaft*, 40 (Apr 1990): 170–177, illus.

[*1043*]   *Internationales Tschaikowsky-Fest: Tübingen 23.–27 Oktober 1993: Festschrift*. Hrsg. von Thomas Kohlhase. Mainz: B. Schott [1993]. 165 p, illus.

Programme and notes for the international conference devoted to the composer, held in Tübingen, Germany, 23–27 Oct 1993. See also *596, 1048, 1050.*

Contents: 'Das Internationale Tschaikowsky-Fest in Tübingen': 4–5 — 'Grußworte': 6–10 — 'Programmübersicht': 11–19 — 'Die Veranstaltungen im einzelnen': 21–37 — 'Einführungstexte': 39–81 — P. E. Vaidman (tr. I. Wille), 'Ausstellung: Tschaikowsky und die europäische Kultur ... Verzeichnis der Exponate': 83–100 — 'Das Internationale Tschaikowsky-Symposium und die Tschaikowsky-Studien': 101–134 — 'Tschaikowsky-Gesellschaft e.V.': 135–140 — 'Die neue Tschaikowsky-Gesamtausgabe': 141–142 [review of *120*] — 'Die Tschaikowsky-Feier in Bad Pyrmont 1902': 143–161 [see *1024*].

[*1044*]   LASSAHN, B. *Klassik für Einsteiger: Peter Tschaikowsky*. Frankfurt am Main: Eichborn, 1993. 126 p, music, illus. (*Edition Sony Music bei Eichborn*). ISBN: 3-8218-0513-7.

[*1045*]   'Verschiedenes', *Orchester*, 41 (1993), 12: 1359, illus.

[*1046*]   'Vor 100 Jahren Starb Peter Iljitsch Tschaikowski', *Münzen-Revue*, 25 (1993), 12: 1514.

Commemorative coins issued to mark the centenary of Chaikovskii's death.

[*1047*]   KOHLHASE, T. 'Klangmomente ...ich bin wahnsinning müde', *Neue Zeitschrift für Musik*, 154 (Sep 1993): 45–48, music, illus.

[1048] GRÖNKE, K. 'Internationales Cajkovskij-Symposium Tübingen', *Orchester*, 42 (1994): 2: 41–42, illus.

[1049] MORAWSKA, K. 'Internationales Tschaikowsky-Fest, Moguncja 1993' / 'International Tchaikovsky Festival, Munich 1993', *Muzyka*, 39 (1994), 1: 116–117, music.
Text in Polish, with a summary in English.

[1050] GRÖNKE, K. 'International Cajkovskij Symposium, Tübingen, 23.–27. Okt 1993', *Die Musikforschung*, 47 (Jul/Sep 1994), 3: 288.

[1051] KOHLHASE, T. 'Begrüßung und Einführung'. In: *Internationales Čajkovskij Symposium, Tübingen 1993: Bericht* (1995): 9–19 [see 596].

[1052] KOHLHASE, T. 'Schlagworte, Tendenzen und Texte zur frühen Čajkovskijs-Rezeption in Deutschland und Österreich', *Tschaikowsky-Gesellschaft: Mitteilungen*, 3 (1996): 32–59.
— [repr.] In: *Čajkovskijs Homosexualität und sein Tod: Legenden und Wirklichkeit* (1998): 327–354 [see 600].

GREAT BRITAIN

[1053] 'Obituary: M. Tschaikowsky', *The Times* (7 Nov 1893).

[1054] 'Obituary: P. I. Tschaikowsky', *Athenaeum*, 102 (11 Nov 1893): 670.

[1055] SHEDLOCK, J. S. 'Obituary: Peter Iltitsch Tschaikowsky', *Academy*, 44 (11 Nov 1893): 422.

[1056] 'Obituary: P. I. Tchaikovsky', *Harper's Weekly*, 37 (18 Nov 1893): 1112.

[1057] RUNCIMAN, J. F. 'Tschaikowsky in 1916', *Saturday Review*, 121 (15 Jan 1916): 58–59.

[1058] HOL, R. 'The unknown Tschaikowsky', *Musical Mirror* (Nov 1932): 13.

[1059] ABRAHAM, G. E. H. 'Tchaikovsky revalued'. In: G. E. H. Abraham, *Studies in Russian Music: Critical essays on the most important of Rimsky-Korsakov's operas, Borodin's 'Prince Igor', Dargomizhsky's 'Stone Guest', etc.; with chapters on Glinka, Mussorgsky, Balakirev and Tchaikovsky.* London: W. Reeves [1935]: 334–350.
— [repr.] Freeport, N. Y.: Books for Libraries Press [1968]: 334–350. (*Essay Index Reprints*)
— [repr.] London: W. Reeves, 1969: 334–350.

[1060] CALVOCORESSI, M. D. 'Tchaikovsky in the light of recent criticism', *The Listener*, 13 (22 May 1935): 876.

[1061] BLOM, E. W. 'Common prejudices about Tchaikovsky', *The Listener*, 16 (9 Sep 1936): 502.

[1062] ABRAHAM, G. E. H. 'The riddle of Tchaikovsky', *Monthly Musical Record*, 67 (Jul/Aug 1937): 129–131.

[1063] TOYE, F. 'The greatest of Russian composers', *The Listener*, 18 (15 Sep 1937): 582.

[1064] ABRAHAM, G. E. H. 'Pyotr Ilyich Tchaikovsky: Some centennial reflections', *Music & Letters*, 21 (Apr 1940): 110–119.
— [repr.] In: G. E. H. Abraham, *Slavonic and Romantic Music*. Essays and studies. London: Faber & Faber; New York: St. Martin's Press, 1968: 107–115.

[1065] BAYLISS, S. 'Tchaikovsky, 1840–1893', *Choir*, 31 (May 1940): 73–75.

[1066] HOLT, R. 'Peter Tchaikovsky, 1840–1893', *Gramophone*, 17 (May 1940): 409–410, illus.

[1067] SERGUÉFF, N. 'Peter Tchaikovsky, 1840–1893', *Dancing Times*, 356 (May 1940): 468.

[1068] LAMBERT, C. 'Tchaikovsky today', *The Listener*, 23 (2 May 1940): 905.

[*1069*]   HUSSEY, D. 'Tchaikovsky's centenary', *The Spectator*, 164 (17 May 1940): 686.

[*1070*]   TURNER, W. J. 'Tchaikovsky', *New Statesman*, 19 (25 May 1940): 668.

[*1071*]   EVANS, E. 'Chaikovsky today', *Anglo-Soviet Journal*, 1 (Jul 1940): 204–208.

[*1072*]   FISHER, M. 'Peter Iljitch Tchaikovsky', *Nineteenth Century*, 128 (Aug 1940): 180–195.

[*1073*]   WESTBROOK, F. 'Tschaikowsky reconsidered', *Choir*, 32 (Mar 1941): 34–35.

[*1074*]   GODDARD, S. 'The enigma of Tchaikovsky', *Disc*, 1 (win. 1947): 22–28.

[*1075*]   STUART, C. 'Russia and music', *Music* (1950): 36–39.

[*1076*]   WELDON, G. 'In defence of Tschaikowsky', *Music and Musicians*, 1 (Jan 1953): 11, illus.

[*1077*]   LEONARD, R. A. 'Tchaikovsky'. In: R. A. Leonard, *A history of Russian music.* [London]: Jarrolds [1956]: 173–198.

[*1078*]   BERGER, F. 'Music's great sensualist', *Coronet*, 41 (Apr 1957): 16–18, illus.

[*1079*]   'Za rubezhom: Kratkie soobshcheniia', *Sovetskaia muzyka* (1959), 7: 191.
           A report on the 'Tchaikovsky Festival' in London. See also *1080*.

[*1080*]   SENIOR, E. 'Tchaikovsky festival', *Musical Opinion*, 82 (Mar 1959), 369.
           — [Russian tr.] 'Za rubezhom: Festival´ Chaikovskogo v Londone', *Sovetskaia muzyka* (1959), 5: 176–178.

[*1081*]   ANGLES, R. 'Was this his life?: The Tchaikovsky story in Festival Hall', *Music and Musicians*, 11 (1963): 8–9.
           Concerning a lecture-concert of the composer's works in the Royal Festival Hall, London. See also *1082*.

[*1082*]   HENRY, J. D. 'The Tchaikovsky story', *Musical Events*, 18 (Jun 1963): 21.

[*1083*]   GRIFFITHS, P. 'Tchaikovsky works performed at the Edinburgh Festival', *New Yorker*, 68 (28 Sep 1992): 81–83.

[*1084*]   HANCOCK, G. 'The composer Tchaikovsky', *Dancing Times*, 83 (Jan 1993): 411–412.

[*1085*]   HOLLOWAY, R. 'Sugar and spice: The Tchaikovsky centenary', *Musical Times*, 134 (Nov 1993): 620–633, illus.
           Praising Chaikovskii's gift for and audacious use of melody.

[*1086*]   ZAJACZKOWSKI, H. 'Auf der Schwelle zu einer andern Zeit: Tschaikowsky—eine notwendige Neubewertung', *Neuen Züricher Zeitung* (14/15 Aug 1993): 53.
           A centennial reassessment of Chaikovskii.

[*1087*]   STEVENSON, A. B. 'Chaikovski and Mrs. Rosa Newmarch revisted: A contribution to the composer's centennial celebrations', *Inter-American Music Review*, 14 (win/spr 1995), 2: 63–78, music.

[*1088*]   BROUGHTON, S. 'Speaking from the heart', *BBC Music Magazine* (Jan 1998): 18.
           Relating to Simon Broughton's television documentary on the life of the composer. See also *1089*.

[*1089*]   BROUGHTON, S. 'The "Pathétique" tale of a poisoned glass of water', *The Independent* (7 Jan 1998) [*Eye* suppl.].
           See also *1143*.

HUNGARY

[*1090*]   PAPP, M. 'Pjotr Czajkovskij: In memoriam', *Muszika*, 37 (Jan 1994): 3–4, illus.

[*1091*]   HALASZ, P. 'Bacilus vagy mereg? Meg egyszer: Pjotr Czajkovszkij in memorian', *Muzsika*, 37 (Mar 1994): 28–30.

ITALY

[*1092*]   SARKISOV, O. 'Zdes´ zhil Chaikovskii', *Muzykal´naia zhizn´* (1969), 6: 20, illus.

The establishment of a memorial plaque on the house in Florence where the composer stayed in 1878.

[*1093*]   MARTYNOV, I. 'Pamiati Chaikovskogo', *Muzykal´naia zhizn´* (1983), 1: 17.

Concerning the unveiling of a plaque at the Hotel London in Venice (where Chaikovskii stayed on a number of occasions), and the composer's reputation in Italy.

[*1094*]   COMUZIO E. 'Attraverso il fuoco mi son fatto strada: Le vite fiammeggianti idei musicisti sullo schermo e in televisione', *Chigiana*, 42 (1990), 22: 263.

[*1095*]   *Il fanciullo di vetro: Petr Il´ic Cajkovskij a San Pietroburgo*. Cura di Maria Rosaria Boccuni; testi di Mario Bortolotto [et al.]; schede di Elena Valentinovna Anpelogova [et al.]. Bologna: Grafis [1997]. 262 p, illus.

Catalogue of an exhibition in the Museo civico archeologico, Bologna (9 Nov 1997–11 Jan 1998).

THE NETHERLANDS

[*1096*]   RIETHOF, E. 'Tsjaikovski en zijn weldoenster', *Mens en melodie*, 36 (Nov 1981): 544–550.

ROMANIA

[*1097*]   PRICOPE, E. '60 de ani dela moartea lui Ceaicovschi, 1953', *Muzica*, 3 (1953), 4: 54–58.

[*1098*]   VOICANA, M. 'Petr Ilich Tchaikovsky: On the 75th commemoration of his death', *Revue Romaine de l'histoire de l'art*, 6 (1969): 237–241.

SPAIN

[*1099*]   PINTO, J. M. 'Chaikovsky: La musica impudica', *Monsalvat* (May 1990), 182: 15–17, illus.

[*1100*]   'Aniversarios', *Monsalvat* (Feb 1993), 212: 7.

SWEDEN

[*1101*]   'Shvetsiia: Otliki na iubilei Chaikovskogo', *Internatsional´naia literatura* (1940), 5/6: 367.

Events in Sweden commemorating Chaikovskii's birth centenary.

[*1102*]   'Prazdnovanie v Shvetsii 100-letiia so dnia rozhdeniia Chaikovskogo', *Izvestiia* (16 Apr 1940): 2.

— [repr.] *Leningradskaia pravda* (16 Apr 1940): 7.

— [repr.] *Pravda* (16 Apr 1940).

[*1103*]   FORSER, S. 'Ånken, kompositoeren och d 1 100 breven', *Tonfallet*, 6 (1990): 14–15, illus.

SWITZERLAND

[*1104*]   FÉDOROV, V. 'Cajkovskij: Musicien type de XIXe siecle?', *Acta Musicologica*, 42 (1970), 1/2: 59–70.

Discussions at a conference held in Saint-Germain-en-Laye devoted to 19th-century music studies.

YUGOSLAVIA

[*1105*]   PEJOVIČ, R. 'Petar Ilič Čajkovski i njegova dela izvedena u Beogradu', *Zvuk* (1967), 7: 20–26.

3.2.3. America

[*1106*]   BUCHANAN, C. L. 'The unvanquishable Tchaikovsky', *Musical Quarterly*, 5 (Jul 1919): 364–389.

[*1107*]   PRIANI, E. di. 'Secrets of the success of great musicians: Tschaikovsky', *Etude*, 37 (1919): 485–486.

[*1108*]   'Khronika zarubezhnoi muzykal´noi zhizni´: S. Sh. A.', *Sovetskaia muzyka* (1934), 8: 87.
           Report on a five-day music festival in Boston, devoted to Chaikovskii's music.

[*1109*]   ROSENFELD, P. 'The minority and Tschaikowsky', *American Music Lover*, 6 (May 1940): 2–5, illus.

[*1110*]   BEDENKOFF, A. 'The cheerful side of Tchaikovsky', *Musical America*, 60 (25 May 1940): 11.

[*1111*]   'Vecher russkoi muzyki v N´iu-Iorke', *Izvestiia* (1 Jun 1940): 4.
           Report on a concert on 26 May 1940 in New York, to celebrate Chaikovskii's jubilee.

[*1112*]   ZAVADSKY, V. 'Tschaikowsky: The most personal of composers', *Musician*, 50 (Mar 1945): 54–55.

[*1113*]   'Col. Higginson and Tchaikovsky', *Boston Symphony Orchestra Concert Bulletin* (5 Oct 1951), 1: 27–28.
           Colonel Henry Lee Higginson was the founder of the Boston Symphony Orchestra.

[*1114*]   'Composer of the month: Peter Ilyitch Tchaikovsky', *Etude*, 71 (May 1954): 3.

[*1115*]   SMITH, R. 'A fanfare for Piotr Ilyich', *High Fidelity*, 10 (Mar 1960): 48–50, illus.

[*1116*]   JACOBY, S. 'Tchaikovsky's Russia: The lingering passion', *Saturday Review*, 53 (14 Mar 1970): 75–77, illus.

[*1117*]   'Balanchine announces Tchaikovsky festival', *Dance News* (Mar 1981), 1: 16.
           Preview of the festival staged by the New York City Ballet in the summer of 1981. See also *1118* to *1133*, *3839*.

[*1118*]   GRUEN, J. 'The fanfare and the festival: George Balanchine discusses Tchaikovsky', *Dance Magazine*, 55 (Jun 1981): 50–53, illus.

[*1119*]   SEARS, D. 'Joseph Duell: Youngest contributor to New York City Ballet's Tchaikovsky Festival', *Dance News* (Jun 1981): 1–3.

[*1120*]   SUPREE, B. 'Dance: Tchaikovsky Festival — Omlette russe', *Village Voice*, 26 (3 Jun 1981): 75–76.

[*1121*]   ROSENWALD, P. J. 'New York City Ballet's Tchaikovsky Festival', *Wall Street Journal*, 61 (9 Jun 1981): 28.

[*1122*]   'Dance Reviews: New York City Ballet', *Variety*, 303 (10 Jun 1981): 80.

[*1123*]   JOWITT, D. 'Dance: Petr Ilich feted in plastic palace', *Village Voice*, 26 (17 Jun 1981): 71, illus.

[*1124*]   DUFFY, M. 'To Tchaikovsky: A rousing tribute', *Time*, 117 (22 Jun 1981): 74–75, illus.

[*1125*]   SAAL, H. 'Tchaikovsky galore', *Newsweek*, 97 (22 Jun 1981): 63–64, illus.

[*1126*]   JOWITT, D. 'Dance: Who made up this guest list?', *Village Voice*, 26 (24 Jun 1981): 81.

[*1127*]   CROCE, A. 'Dancing', *New Yorker*, 57 (29 Jun 1981): 74–78.
           — [repr.] In: A. Croce, *Going to the dance*. New York: Knopf, 1982: 386–392.

[*1128*]   TOBIAS, T. 'Speech of angels', *New York*, 14 (29 Jun 1981): 40–42, illus.

[*1129*]   KERNER, L. 'Music: But seriously', *Village Voice*, 26 (1 Jul 1981): 72.

[*1130*]   GOODWIN, N. 'Tribute to Tchaikovsky', *Dance and Dancers* (Sep 1981): 21–25, illus.
           Includes comments by Patricia Barnes on the last few performances.

[*1131*]   HAGGIN, B. H. 'In homage to Tchaikovsky', *Ballet News*, 3 (Sep 1981), 3: 20–23, 45, illus.

[*1132*]   MASKEY, J. 'City Ballet choreographers celebrate Tchaikovsky', *Musical America*, 31 (Oct 1981): 8–9, illus.

[*1133*]   TERRY, W. 'A grand high, a new low', *Saturday Review*, 8 (Oct 1981): 52–53, illus.

[*1134*]   LIVINGSTONE, W. 'Classical music briefs', *Stereo Review*, 46 (Nov 1981): 76–77.

[*1135*]   GAINES, C. T. 'Sesquicentennial: Peter Ilyich Tchaikovsky', *Music Clubs Magazine*, 69 (1990), 3: 17–19, illus.

[*1136*]   KLIBERN, V. 'Moi Chaikovskii', *Sovetskaia kul´tura* (13 Jan 1990): 14, illus.
           Interview with the American pianist Van Cliburn.

[*1137*]   WILEY, R. J. 'Reflections on Tchaikovsky', *Dancing Times*, 80 (May 1990): 801–803.

[*1138*]   WILEY, R. J. 'Life sentence on Chaikovsky', *Financial Times* (5 May 1990).

[*1139*]   TARUSKIN, R. 'Tchaikovsky: Fallen from grace', *New York Times* (30 Jun 1991).

[*1140*]   VROON, D. R. 'Overview: Tchaikovsky', *American Record Guide*, 55 (1992), 1: 12, illus.

[*1141*]   BARNES, C. 'Boston, Tchaikovsky and birthdays', *Dance Magazine*, 68 (Jan 1994): 164.

[*1142*]   SCHERER, B. L. 'Tchaikovsky: Guilty pleasure no more', *Wall Street Journal* (28 Aug 1998).
           Review of new biographical and music developments in Chaikovskii studies, on the occasion of Bard music festival dedicated to the composer in Annandale-on-Hudson, New York State.

[*1143*]   BROWN, M. H. 'Tchaikovsky and his music in Anglo-American criticism, 1890s–1950s'. In: *Tchaikovsky and his contemporaries* (1999): 61–74 [see *602*].

[*1144*]   LIPMAN, S. 'Tchaikovsky: The love that dare not speak its name'. In: *Tchaikovsky and his contemporaries* (1999): 237–244 [see *602*].

[*1145*]   MIHAILOVIC, A. 'Tchaikovsky as our contemporary'. In: *Tchaikovsky and his contemporaries* (1999): 1–14 [see *602*].

[*1146*]   'Tchaikovsky in American and Russian musical education'. In: *Tchaikovsky and his contemporaries* (1999): 275–294 [see *602*].
           Round-table discussion, moderated by Joel Sachs

           See also *866, 882, 1000*.

3.2.4. Africa & Asia

JAPAN

[*1147*]   'Korotkie soobshcheniia: Imeni velikogo russkogo kompozitora', *Leningradskaia pravda* (22 May 1960): 3.
           The opening of a ballet school in Tokyo named in honour of Chaikovskii.

[1148] *Chaikofosukii*. Ed. by Minoru Morita. Tokyo, Suntory Museum of Art, 1990, 166 p, illus. ISBN 4–484–90302–4.

Catalogue of an exibition held in the Suntory Museum of Art, Tokyo. Includes articles by Minoru Morita, Liudmila Korabel´nikova, Galina Belonovich, Polina Vaidman and John Warrack.

[1149] DUNAEV, V. 'God Chaikovskogo: Genii chelovechestva', *Sovetskaia kul´tura* (3 Mar 1990): 14.

A conversation with the Japanese conductor Ivaki about Chaikovskii.

[1150] MORITA, M. 'Some observations on Japan's association with Russian music and Čajkovskij'. In: *Internationales Čajkovskij Symposium, Tübingen 1993: Bericht* (1995): 217–222 [see 596].

SOUTH AFRICA

[1151] JACKSON, M. 'Tiger-dance, terukuttu, tango and Tchaikovsky: A politico-cultural view of Indian South-African music before 1948', *World of Music*, 31 (1989), 1: 59–77.

3.3. MUSEUMS AND MONUMENTS

3.3.1. Klin House-Museum

[1152] 'Vid doma v Klinu, gde zhil P. I. Chaikovskii, i ego rabochii kabinet', *Niva* (1893), 48.

[1153] IARTSEV, A. A. 'Tikhii ugolok P. I. Chaikovskogo (k chetvertoi godovshchine smerti kompzoitora)', *Moskovskie vedomosti* (26 Oct 1897); (30 Oct 1897).

[1154] LIPAEV, I. V. 'Iz zapisnoi knizhki: Uiutnyi ugolok P. I. Chaikovskogo', *Russkaia muzykal´naia gazeta* (24 Apr 1899), 17: 489–494.

Includes photographs: 'Kabinet i gostinaia P. I. Chaikovskogo v Klinu': 489–490.

[1155] POLOVTSEV, A. V. *Muzei P. I. Chaikovskogo v Klinu*. Moskva, 1903. 32 p.
— [repr.] *Moskovskie vedomosti* (2 Sep 1903); (3 Sep 1903).

[1156] ROSSIEV, P. 'U P. I. Chaikovskogo', *Birzhevye vedomosti* (25 Oct 1903).

[1157] ROSSIEV, P. 'Gde zhil P. I. Chaikovskii: Putevoi ocherk', *Novyi mir* (1904): 134, illus.

[1158] ZHAK-MELANKHOLIK. 'Pamiati P. I. Chaikovskogo', *Russkoe slovo* (25 Oct 1908).
Chaikovskii at Klin.

[1159] BERTENSON, V. B. 'Dom-muzei P. I. Chaikovskogo v Klinu', *Istoricheskii vestnik*, 129 (1913): 604–615.
— [German tr.] 'Das Tschaikowsky-Museum in Klin'. In: *Tschaikowsky aus der Nähe* (1994): 284–292 [see 379].

[1160] *Ustav Obshchestva druzei Muzeia-doma P. I. Chaikovskogo v Klinu*. Klin, 1920. 8 p.
The founding of the Society of Friends of the Chaikovskii House-Museum at Klin.

[1161] DIOMIDOV, I. 'Muzei P. I. Chaikovskogo', *Izvestiia sovetskikh rabochikh i krest´ianskikh deputatov* (1920), No. 21/22.

[1162] IA[KOVLEV], V. V. 'Poezdka v Klin (fevral´ 1919 g.)'. In: *Proshloe russkoi muzyki*, tom 1 (1920): 133–139 [see 584].

[1163] 'Katalog portretov (fotografii i graviur) nakhodiashchikhsia v komnatakh Petra Il´icha'. In: *Proshloe russkoi muzyki*, tom 1 (1920): 173–175 [see 584].

An inventory of the photographs and paintings preserved in the composer's living room at Klin.

[1164]   'Opis´ fotografii, v albomakh i saf´ianovoi korobke, nakodiashchikhsia na stole v gostinoi pered malen´kim divanchikom'. In: *Proshloe russkoi muzyki*, tom 1 (1920): 175–182 [see *584*].

A list of photographs in the composer's personal collection at Klin.

[1165]   'Plan verkhnego etazha doma-muzeia P. I. Chaikovskogo v Klinu'. In: *Proshloe russkoi muzyki*, tom 1 (1920): 172 [see *584*].

[1166]   ZHEGIN, N. T. 'Dom P. I. Chaikovskogo v Klinu'. In: *Proshloe russkoi muzyki*, tom 1 (1920): 65–98 [see *584*].

[1167]   ZHEGIN, N. T. 'Dom-muzei P. I. Chaikovskogo v Klinu', *Vestnik prosveshcheniia* (1921), 1: 21.

— [repr.] *Kazanskii muzeinyi vestnik* (1922), 1: 169.

[1168]   'Muzei P. I. Chaikovskogo', *Izvestiia* (12 May 1923).

[1169]   ZHEGIN, N. T. 'Obshchestvo druzei Doma-muzeia P. I. Chaikovskogo v Klinu', *Zrelishcha* (1923), 29: 15.

[1170]   V. B. 'Pamiati Chaikovskogo', *Zrelishcha* (1923), 64: 10.

Compiled by the Society of Friends of the Chaikovskii house-museum in Klin, for the 30th anniversary of the composer's death.

[1171]   [IAKOVLEV, V. V.] *Pushkinskaia komnata v Dome-muzee P. I. Chaikovskogo v Klinu*. Iz doklada, prochitannogo na obshchem sobranii obshchestva, sostoiavshchegosia 3 avgusta 1924 g. Moskva: Nauka i prosveshchenie [1924]. 24 p. (*Obshchestvo druzei Doma-muzeia P. I. Chaikovskogo v Klinu*).

[1172]   ZHEGIN, N. T. 'Dom Petra Il´icha Chaikovskogo v Klinu'. In: *Istoriia russkoi muzyki v issledovaniiakh i materialakh*. Pod red. prof. K. A. Kuznetsova. Tom 1. Moskva: Gosizdat-Muzsektor, 1924: 89–92.

[1173]   'Tschaikowsky Museum', *Musical Digest* (19 Feb 1924): 19.

[1174]   DETINOV, S. 'Dom-muzei P. I. Chaikovskogo: K 30-letiiu Doma-muzeia', *Iskusstvo trudiashchimsia* (1925), 16: 11.

The 30th anniversary of the foundation of the house-museum. See also *1175* to *1178*.

[1175]   DETINOV, S. 'Iubileinoe torzhestvo k 30-letiiu Doma-muzeia Chaikovskogo', *Iskusstvo trudiashchimsia* (1925), 21: 17.

[1176]   D[ETINOV], S. 'Muzykal´nyi vecher v Klinu', *Iskusstvo trudiashchimsia* (1925), 27: 12.

[1177]   'Dom-muzei P. I. Chaikovskogo', *Serp i molot´* (1925), No. 4.

[1178]   'Torzhestvennoe zasedanie, posviashchennoe pamiati P. I. Chaikovskogo', *Iskusstvo trudiashchimsia* (1925), 9: 30.

[1179]   'Muzei P. I. Chaikovskogo v Klinu', *Vechernaia krasnaia gazeta* (9 Jan 1925)

[1180]   GLEBOV, I. [ASAF´EV, B. V.] 'Muzykal´no-muzeinoe delo: Moskovskie vpechatleniia', *Krasnaia gazeta* (30 Jan 1926).

[1181]   SIDIAKINA. 'Delegatki: Pobol´she takikh ekskursii', *Serp i molot´* (1927), No. 108.

A tour of the Klin museum.

[1182]   'The Tschaikowsky museum in Klin', *Christian Science Monitor* (16 Jul 1927).

[1183]   'Muzei im. P. I. Chaikovskogo v Klinu', *Rabis* (1928), 42: 4.

[1184]   ZHEGIN, N. T. 'Dom-muzei P. I. Chaikovskogo', *Sovremennyi teatr* (1928), 45: 723.

[1185]   ZHEGIN, N. T. 'Dom-muzei P. I. Chaikovskogo', *Sovetskii muzei* (1931), 4: 98.

[*1186*]   KISELEV, V. 'Dom-muzei P. I. Chaikovskogo v Klinu', *Sovetskaia muzyka* (1933), 6: 104–105.

[*1187*]   S. R. 'V muzee Chaikovskogo', *Vecherniaia Moskva* (4 Jun 1933).

[*1188*]   REMEZOV, I. 'V Klinu', *Muzyka* (6 Jul 1937): 5.
           The history of the house-museum.

[*1189*]   ABOL´NIKOV, S. 'Gorod Chaikovskii', *Sovetskoe iskusstvo* (11 Oct 1937): 4.

[*1190*]   'V dome-muzee P. I. Chaikovskogo', *Sovetskoe iskusstvo* (22 May 1938): 4.
           A concert at the Klin museum on 19 May 1938, to mark the 98th anniversary of Chaikovskii's birth.

[*1191*]   'V dome-muzee P. I. Chaikovsogo', *Sovetskaia muzyka* (1940), 1: 89.

[*1192*]   RUDANOVSKAIA, M. 'Dom-muzei P. I. Chaikovskogo v g. Klin', *Sovetskii muzei* (1940), 1: 48.

[*1193*]   BUDIAKOVSKII, A. 'Novye materialy o P. I. Chaikovskom', *Leningradskaia pravda* (22 Jan 1940): 3.
           Recent research in the Klin archives.

[*1194*]   KHOLODKOVSKII, V. 'Dom v Klinu', *Moskovskii bol´shevik* (27 Apr 1940).

[*1195*]   RUDANOVSKAIA, M. 'V dome-muzee P. I. Chaikovskogo v Klinu', *Sovetskoe iskusstvo* (14 Mar 1940): 4.

[*1196*]   'Pamiati velikogo kompozitora', *Kino* (5 May 1940): 3.
           Review of a short film about the house-museum.

[*1197*]   GABRILOVICH, E. 'Muzei P. I. Chaikovskogo', *Izvestiia* (6 May 1940): 4.

[*1198*]   RODIN, I. 'K stoletiiu so dnia rozhdeniia P. I. Chaikovskogo: V dome-muzee velikogo kompozitora', *Znamia kommuny* [Novocherkassk] (6 May 1940).
           — [rev. repr.] *Krasnaia Bashkiriia* (6 May 1940).

[*1199*]   'Kontsert v dome-muzee Chaikovskogo', *Pravda* (7 May 1940): 6.
           Report on a gala concert held at the house musuem on 6 May 1940, to mark the 100th anniversary of Chaikovskii's birth. See also *1201*.

[*1200*]   GERSONI, V. 'Dom-muzei P. I. Chaikovskogo', *Sovetskaia Sibir´* (8 May 1940).

[*1201*]   'Prazdnovanie v Klinu', *Sovetskoe iskusstvo* (9 May 1940): 4.

[*1202*]   SHVARTS, R. 'Domik v Klinu', *Sovetskoe iskusstvo* (9 May 1940): 4.

[*1203*]   KHOLODKOVSKII, V. *Dom Chaikovskogo v Klinu*. Moskva: Goskinoizdat, 1942. 56 p, illus.
           Up to and after the German occupation in 1941.

[*1204*]   'How the Germans despoiled the Tchaikovsky museum in Klin', *Voks bull* (1942), 3/4: 76–77, illus.

[*1205*]   ZASLAVSKII, D. 'Dom Chaikovskogo v Klinu', *Pravda* (2 Mar 1942).
           On the restoration of the Klin Museum after the German occupation in 1941.
           — [repr.] *Muzykal´naia zhizn´* (Dec 1966), 23: 2, illus.

[*1206*]   'What the Nazi vandals did to Tschaikowsky's home', *Etude*, 61 (May 1943): 300.

[*1207*]   BERTENSON, S. 'The Tchaikovsky museum at Klin', *Musical Quarterly*, 30 (Jul 1944), 3: 329–335, illus.

[1208]   *Kratkii putevoditel' po Domu-muzeiu P. I. Chaikovskogo*. Sost. E. D. Gershovskii, R. A. Iurovskaia. Otv. red. A. I. Mashistov. [Klin] 1945. 40 p, illus. (*Komitet po delam iskusstv pri SNK SSSR. Otdel nauchno-issledovatel'skikh uchrezhdenii*).

[1209]   SUKHOV, V. 'Zdes' zhil Chaikovskii', *Sovetskoe iskusstvo* (10 May 1945): 4, illus.

The re-opening of the house-museum following the German occupation, and celebrations marking the 105th anniversary of Chaikovskii's birth.

[1210]   DAVYDOVA, K. Iu. 'Biuvary Chaikovskogo', *Sovetskoe iskusstvo* (29 Mar 1946): 3, music.

The composer's notes and sketches on his blotting-paper on his desk at Klin.

[1211]   '25-letie Doma-muzeia P. I. Chaikovskogo', *Smena* (22 Nov 1946): 1.

Celebrations marking 25 years since the nationalisation of the house-museum. See also *1212*.

[1212]   '25-letie Doma-muzeia P. I. Chaikovskogo', *Sovetskoe iskusstvo* (22 Nov 1946): 1.

[1213]   DAVYDOVA, K. Iu. 'The archives of the Tchaikovsky museum'. In: *Russian symphony: Thoughts about Tchaikovsky* (1947): 198–211 [see *587*].

[1214]   VOEVODIN, K. 'Dom-muzei P. I. Chaikovskogo', *Smena* (1948), 16: 12.

[1215]   ANAN'EVA, V. 'Domik v Klinu', *Muzykal'nye kadry* (28 Oct 1949): 4.

[1216]   *Dom-muzei P. I. Chaikovskogo v Klinu: Putevoditel'*. Otv. redaktor A. I. Smol'ianov. Avtory V. A. Kiselev, E. M. Orlova, I. Iu. Sokolinskaia. [Moskva]: Iskusstvo, 1950. 64 p, illus. (*Ministerstvo kul'tury SSSR. Glavnoe upravlenie po delam iskusstv. Upravlenie muzykal'nykh uchrezhdenii*).

— [rev. repr.] Moskva: Gos. muz. izdat., 1953. 63 p, illus. (*Ministerstvo kul'tury SSSR. Glavnoe upravlenie po delam iskusstv. Upravlenie muzykal'nykh uchrezhdenii*).

— [rev. repr.] Moskva: Gos. muz. izdat., 1956. 56 p, illus. (*Ministerstvo kul'tury SSSR. Moskovskoe obl. upravlenie kultury*).

— 2-e izd. *Gosudarstvennyi Dom-muzei P. I. Chaikovskogo v Klinu: Putevoditel'*. Sost. K. Iu. Davydova, S. S. Kotomina, I. Iu. Sokolinskaia, M. V. Sutorikhina. Otv. red. G. A. Shamkin. Moskva: Muzyka, 1966. 48 p, illus. Includes 'Kratkii khronograf zhizni i tvorchestva Chaikovskogo': 45–47 — 'Osnovnye trudy, sozdannye na materiale arkhiva Doma-muzeia': 47–48.

— 3-e izd. *Gosudarstvennyi Dom-muzei P. I. Chaikovskogo v Klinu*. Sost. K. Iu. Davydova, S. S. Kotomina, I. Iu. Sokolinskaia, M. V. Sutorikhina. Otv. red. G. A. Shamkin. Moskva: Muzyka, 1974. 90 p, illus.

— 4-e izd. *Gosudarstvennyi Dom-muzei P. I. Chaikovskogo v Klinu*. Sost. K. Iu. Davydova, S. S. Kotomina, I. Iu. Sokolinskaia, M. V. Sutorikhina. Otv. red. G. A. Shamkin. Moskva: Muzyka, 1980. 93 p, illus.

— [English tr.] *The Chaikovsky home-museum in Klin: A short guide*. Comp. by the scientific staff of the Chaikovsky Home-Museum. Tr. from the Russian. Moscow: Foreign Languages Publishing House, 1959. 67 p, illus.

— [English tr. (2nd ed)]. Comp. by the staff of the Chaikovsky Museum. Tr. from the Russian by Vic Schneierson. Moscow: Progress [1967]. 66 p, illus.

— [French tr.] *Musée Tchaikovski à Kline: Petite guide*. Présentation de Léonide Lamm; traduit de russe par Stella Ajsenberg. Moscou: Editions en languages étrangères, 1960. 64 p, illus.

— [French tr. (2nd ed.)] *La Maison-Musée de Tchaikovski à Kline*. Tr. par V. Zhukov. Moscow: Editions du Progrès, 1972.

— [Spanish tr.] Moscow: Foreign Languages Publishing House, 1959. 67 p, illus.

[1217]   'Arkhiv P. I. Chaikovskogo v Dome-muzeia'. In: *Avtografy P. I. Chaikovskogo v arkhive doma-muzeia v Klinu*, vyp. 1 (1950): 3–6 [see *102*].

[1218]   'Domu-muzeiu P. I. Chaikovskogo nado pomoch'', *Sovetskoe iskusstvo* (19 Sep 1950): 3.

An appeal for assistance with repairs to the house-museum.

[1219]   KLIOT, A. 'Dom-muzei P. I. Chaikovskogo', *Sovetskaia muzyka* (1951), 12: 97–99, illus.
         The history of the house-museum.

[1220]   SALISBURY, H. E. 'Tchaikovsky museum', *New York Times* (15 Apr 1951).

[1221]   BELIAVSKII, M. 'Domik v Klinu: K 60 letiiu so dnia smerti P. I. Chaikovskogo', *Sovetskaia kul´tura*
         (3 Nov 1953): 1.

[1222]   KUDRIAVTSEVA, G. 'V dome velikogo kompozitora', *Izvestiia* (12 Nov 1953).
         The Klin House-Musuem's commemoration of the 60th anniversary of Chaikovskii's death.

[1223]   ALEKSEEV, V. 'Dom-muzei P. I. Chaikovskogo v Klinu', *Uchitel´skaia gazeta* (14 Nov 1953).

[1224]   VSEVOLODOV, M. 'Domik v Klinu', *Moskovskaia pravda* (14 Aug 1954).

[1225]   [KORABEL´NIKOVA] L. Z. 'Dom Chaikovskogo v Klinu: Iubilei', *Sovetskaia muzyka* (1955), 2: 158.
         On the 60th anniversary of the house-museum.

[1226]   KORABEL´NIKOVA, L. Z. 'Dom Chaikovskogo v Klinu', *Sovetskaia muzyka* (1955), 2: 113–114.
         On the work of the House-Museum staff.

[1227]   'Im Hause Peter Iljitsch Tschaikowskys', *Neue Zeitschrift für Musik*, 116 (Oct 1955): 38.

[1228]   KRAUSE, E. 'Besuch im Tschaikowski-Haus', *Musica*, 10 (Jul/Aug 1956): 556–557.

[1229]   *Chaikovskii v Klinu: Al´bom fotografii*. Foto L. O. Smirnova. Avtor tekstov G. I. Navtikov. Predislovie
         K. Paustovskogo. Moskva: Gos. muz. izdat., 1958. 72 p, illus.
         — [repr. (extracts) In: K. Paustovskii, 'Pamiat´ o Chaikovskom', *Muzykal´naia zhizn´* (1974), 11: 10–13, illus.

[1230]   GORLOV, N. 'V dome-muzee P. I. Chaikovskogo', *Sovetskaia muzyka* (1958), 1: 157.

[1231]   MARINKOVICH, N. 'V Klinu u Chaikovskogo'. In: N. Marinkovich, *Smysl i liubov*. Moskva, 1958:
         157–161.

[1232]   ARTEMOV, I. 'V dome velikogo kompozitora', *Sovetskaia Latviia* (9 Mar 1958).

[1233]   BRUSIANIN, V. 'V gostiakh u P. I. Chaikovskogo', *Smena* (6 Jul 1958).

[1234]   KHOLODKOVSKII, V. V. *Dom v Klinu*. Moskva: Moskovskii rabochii, 1959. 336 p, illus.
         Reviews: Iu. Teplov, 'Novaia kniga o P. I. Chaikovskom', *Muzykal´naia zhizn´* (1959), 10: 18 — O. Tolmachev,
         'Knizhnoe i notnoe obozrenie', *Sovetskaia muzyka* (1959), 8: 194–195 — G. Navtikov, 'Dom v Klinu', *Leninskoe
         znamia* (10 May 1959) — V. Bortnik 'Naveki veren Rossii', *Moskovskaia pravda* (19 Jun 1959) — 'V gorode, gde
         zhil kompozitor', *Sovetskaia kul´tura* (1 Dec 1959): 2.
         — 2-e izd. Moskva: Moskovskii rabochii, 1960. 342 p, illus.
         — 3-e izd. Moskva: Moskovskii rabochii, 1962. 342 p, illus.
         — 4-e izd. Moskva: Moskovskii rabochii, 1971. 339 p, illus. (*Muzei i vystavki Moskvy i Podmoskov´ia*).
         — 5-e izd. Moskva: Moskovskii rabochii, 1975. 339 p, illus. (*Muzei i vystavki Moskvy i Podmoskov´ia*).
         — 6-e izd. Moskva: Moskovskii rabochii, 1982. 337 p, illus. (*Muzei i vystavki Moskvy i Podmoskov´ia*).

[1235]   'Popolnenie eksponatov v Dome-muzee imeni P. I. Chaikovskogo', *Sovetskaia kul´tura* (12 Mar
         1959).

[1236]   SMOLIAK, Ia. 'Chasy Chaikovskogo', *Sovetskaia kul´tura* (4 Aug 1959).

[1237]   'Podarok Chaikovskomu', *Sovetskaia kul´tura* (6 May 1961): 4, illus.
         The presentation of a miniature violin to the house-museum.

[1238]   KANSKI. 'Dom-muzeum Piotra Czajkowskiego w Kline', *Ruch Muzyczny*, 6 (1962), 21: 18, illus.

[1239] PETROV, E. 'Klin, 16 dekabria'. In: I. Il´f & E. Petrov, *Sobranie sochinenii*. Tom 5. Moskva, 1963: 625–628.

A war correspondent's impression of the damage to the Klin museum, the day after the end of the German occupation in Dec 1941.

[1240] 'Dlia novoi ekspozitsii', *Sovetskaia kul´tura* (3 May 1963): 3.

An appeal by the staff of the house-museum for documents and publications relating to Chaikovskii.

[1241] 'V chest´ dnia rozhdeniia P. I. Chaikovskogo', *Sovetskaia kul´tura* (14 May 1963): 3.

Report on celebrations at Klin and Votkinsk to mark Chaikovskii's birthday.

[1242] AKIVIS, D. *Meetings with Tchaikovsky*. Moscow: Novosti [1965]. [72] p., illus.

— [French tr.] *Rendezvous avec Tschaïkowski*. Moscou, Novosti [1965]. [72] p., illus.

[1243] DAVYDOV, Iu. L. *Klinskie gody tvorchestva Chaikovskogo*. Moskva: Moskovskii rabochii, 1965. 127 p, illus.

Includes: 'Khronologiia poslednikh let zhizni i tvorchestva': 117–126 [see *88*].

Review: 'Korotko o knigakh', *Muzykal´naia zhizn´* (Jan 1966), 2: 17.

[1244] A. B. 'Novosti iz Klina', *Sovetskaia muzyka* (1965), 11: 157, illus.

The musical and educational objectives of the staff of the Klin museum.

[1245] KOVALENKO, N. 'Dokumenty, obviniaiut gitlerovtsev v prestupleniiakh protiv kul´tury: Izuverov ne proshchaiut', *Sovetskaia kul´tura* (9 Mar 1965): 4, illus.

The damage experienced by the house-museum during World War II.

[1246] KIRICHENKO, A. 'Rodina volshebnykh melodii', *Smena* (6 May 1965).

[1247] IOANNISIAN, A. 'Domik v Klinu', *Kommunist* (7 May 1965).

[1248] MAKIEV, M. 'Dom v kotorom zhivet muzyka', *Moskovskaia pravda* (7 May 1965).

[1249] PUZRIN, I. 'Na Klinskoi zemle', *Sovetskaia Rossiia* (7 May 1965).

[1250] SHIROKOV, A. 'Ne zarastet narodnaia tropa: Po zalam muzeia P. I. Chaikovskogo', *Gudok* (7 May 1965).

[1251] 'Inostrannye muzykanty v dome-muzee P. Chaikovskogo v Klinu', *Muzykal´naia zhizn´* (Dec. 1966), 24: 4.

Photographs of foreign musicians at Klin.

[1252] DAVYDOVA, K. Iu. *Dom-muzei P. I. Chaikovskogo v Klinu*. Avtor fotografii V. Tiukkel´ia. Red. A. Obryvalin. Izd. 2-e, pererab. Moskva: Sovetskaia Rossiia, 1967. 16 p, illus.

Text in Russian, English, French and German.

[1253] VERSHININA, G. 'V dome mastera muzyki', *Za bezopasnost´ dvizheniia* (1968), 8: 13.

[1254] KOTOMIN, E. '75-letie Doma Chaikovskogo', *Muzykal´naia zhizn´* (1969), 23: 17–18, illus.

[1255] LEITES, R. 'Puteshestvie k Chaikovskomu'. In. *Zhenskii kalendar´, 1970*. Moskva: Politizdat, 1969: 22.

[1256] 'Čsajkovszkij halalanak 75. evfordulojara', *Muzsika*, 12 (Jan 1969): 4.

[1257] GERBURG, R. 'Klin: Iubilei P. I. Chaikovskogo', *Sovetskaia muzyka* (1970), 8: 65.

[1258] IUR´EV, G. 'Klin: Dom Chaikovskogo', *Sovetskii Soiuz* (1970), 8: 52–53, illus.

[*1259*] KOTOMIN, E. 'Dom-muzei P. I. Chaikovskogo v Klinu', *Kul´tura i zhizn´* (1970), 5: 47–48, illus.

[*1260*] KORABEL´NIKOVA, L. 'Pamiatnye daty sovetskoi muzykal´noi kultury: Utverzhdeno V. I. Leninym', *Sovetskaia muzyka* (1971), 9: 100–105.
The nationalisation of the Klin house-museum in 1921.

[*1261*] KORETSKII, A. 'Dar khudozhnika muzeiu', *Muzykal´naia zhizn´* (1971), 17: 4.
Concerning an account by A. N. Mikhranian on the theme 'A. S. Pushkin and P. I. Chaikovskii', presented to the Klin house-museum.

[*1262*] ROOP, E. W. 'A visit to Tchaikovsky's home', *Clavier*, 10 (1971), 7: 30–33.

[*1263*] JOLLY, C. 'Tchaikovsky at home', *Opera News*, 35 (15 May 1971): 10–15, illus.

[*1264*] NOVIKOV, N & SHAVROV, V. 'Shestaia simfoniia', *Sovetskaia kul´tura* (26 Aug 1971): 2.
The Klin house-museum (where Chaikovskii composed his Symphony No. 6).

[*1265*] MEL´NITSKAIA, M. "S chuvstom velikogo pokloneniia", *Sovetskaia muzyka* (1973), 6: 140–141.
A new exhibition at the Klin museum.

[*1266*] VAIDMAN, P. E. 'Po Sovetskoi strane: Dom-muzei, 7 maia—Klin', *Muzykal´naia zhizn´* (1974), 14: 2.

[*1267*] ZELOV, N. 'Pervyi direktor', *Sovetskaia muzyka* (1974), 4: 138–139.
The centenary of the birth of Nikolai Zhegin, the first director of the house-museum.

[*1268*] MIROVA, A. 'V gostiakh u Chaikovskogo', *Sovetskaia kul´tura* (9 May 1974): 8.
A special concert held at the Klin house-museum, to celebrate the 134th anniversary of Chaikovskii's birth.

[*1269*] GALIMON, N. 'V gosti k Chaikovskomu', *Nedelia* (1975), 47: 17–23.

[*1270*] OVCHINNIKOV, V. 'Pamiati velikogo kompozitora', *Sovetskaia kul´tura* (18 Nov 1975): 8.
A special concert at the house-museum on 16 Nov 1875.

[*1271*] DAVYDOVA, K. Iu. *Chaikovskii v Klinu: Maidanovo, Frolovskoe, Klin*. Moskva: Sovetskaia Rossiia, 1976. 36 p, illus.

[*1272*] GRIGOR´EVA, L. 'Klin, dom Chaikovksogo: Stikhi', *Komsomolskaia pravda* (6 Feb 1977): 2.
A poem about Chaikovskii's home at Klin.

[*1273*] ZVIAGINA, A. 'Klinskie nakhodki', *Ogonek* (May 1977), 20: 20–21.

[*1274*] VAIDMAN, P. E. 'Muzyka, slovo, obraz: Kontserty Iriny Arkhipovoi v Klinu', *Sovetskaia kul´tura* (20 Jan 1978): 4.

[*1275*] RUBCHITS, T. 'Dni pamiati Chaikovskogo', *Sovetskaia muzyka* (1979), 4: 142–143.
A series of concerts at the house-museums in Klin and Votkinsk. See also *1276*.

[*1276*] DANILENKO, G. 'Zvuchit muzyka Chaikovskogo', *Muzykal´naia zhizn´* (Jan 1979), 2: 7.

[*1277*] DAVIDSON, E. 'Tchaikovsky at Klin: Photographs of the composer's home', *Opera News*, 43 (24 Mar 1979): 14–15, illus.

[*1278*] VIKTOROVA, N. 'Biblioteka Petra Il´icha Chaikovskogo', *Muzykal´naia zhizn´* (Jun 1979): 22–23.
The composer's library at Klin.

[*1279*] LETS-ORLETSOVA, L. M. *Tekst ekskursii "P. I. Chaikovskii v Klinu"*. Moskva: Turist, 1980.

[*1280*]   VASIL´EVA, O. "K nemu ne zarastët narodnaia tropa ...", *Sovetskaia muzyka* (1980), 10: 139.

[*1281*]   KALININA, N. 'Pod sen´iu starykh lits', *Sovetskaia kul´tura* (11 Mar 1980): 8, illus.

[*1282*]   VERESHCHAGIN, Iu. 'Osobniak v starom parke', *Gudok* (1 Jul 1980).

[*1283*]   DANILENKO, G. 'Etogo zabyt´ nel´zia: 1941–1981. Sorok let razgroma nemetsko-fashistskikh voisk pod Moskvoi', *Muzykal´naia zhizn´* (1981), 23: 4–5, illus.
            The house-museum since the German occupation in 1941.

[*1284*]   PETROVA, O. 'Panorama novostei: Klin—Novye priobreteniia muzeia', *Muzykal´naia zhizn´* (1983), 15: 5.

[*1285*]   MOSTOVOI, A. 'V chest´ Shestoi "Pateticheskoi": Kakim byt´ muzeiu P. I. Chaikovskogo', *Sovetskaia kul´tura* (7 Jul 1983): 5.

[*1286*]   ARUTIUNIAN, L. 'Rodnye pomety: V Klin, v obitel´ geniia', *Sovetskaia Rossiia* (31 Aug 1983): 4.

[*1287*]   BAILEY, H. 'Klin', *Royal College of Music Magazine*, 80 (1984), 1: 26–29.

[*1288*]   BELONOVICH, G. I. 'Rasskazyvaiut veshchi', *Muzykal´naia zhizn´* (1984), 23: 19, illus.
            The 90th anniversary of foundation of the house-museum.

[*1289*]   PAVLOVA, T. 'O chem povedala staraia tetrad´', *Muzykal´naia zhizn´* (1984), 23: 19–20.
            The visitors' books at the musuem, dating from Dec 1894.

[*1290*]   SIZKO, G. 'Vot i roial´, sletaiut s klavish zvuki', *Muzykal´naia zhizn´* (1984), 23: 18

[*1291*]   VASIL´EV, O. 'Dom, oveiannyi slavoi', *Muzykal´naia zhizn´* (1984), 13: 17–18.
            On the Society of Friends of the house-museum, founded in the 1920s, and former archivists and directors at Klin.

[*1292*]   EPSHTEIN, E. 'Muzyka v moei zhizni: Rabote net kontsa', *Muzykal´naia zhizn´* (1985), 10: 5, illus.
            An interview with Kseniia Davydova, great-niece of Chaikovskii and principal archivist at the Klin museum. See also *1305, 1319*.

[*1293*]   'Chaikovskii-Levitan: Relikvii Doma-muzeia P. I. Chaikovskogo v Klinu. In: *Dekabr´skie vechera VI*. Moskva: Sovetskii khudozhnik, 1986: 17–28.

[*1294*]   VAIDMAN, P. E. 'V dome Chaikovskogo', *Sovetskaia muzyka* (1976), 8: 72–73.
            In connection with a visit by the pianist Vladimir Horowitz to the Klin house-museum.

[*1295*]   FOMINA, I. 'Dom v Klinu', *Sovetskaia kul´tura* (13 May 1986): 1, illus.
            The re-opening of the house-museum after three years of restoration work.

[*1296*]   NADEINSKII, E. 'Dom na okraine Klina', *Krasnaia zvezda* (4 Oct 1986).

[*1297*]   KORABEL´NIKOVA, L. Z. 'Zvuchit Chaikovskii', *Pravda* (26 Apr 1988): 6.
            Concerning a series of historical Chaikovskii concerts by the USSR Radio Symphony Orchestra, at the Chaikovskii house-museum in Klin.

[*1298*]   KOLOSOVA, V. 'Doroga k Chaikovskomu', *Sovetskaia kul´tura* (27 Sep 1988): 4–5.

[*1299*]   MINAEVA, V. 'U Chaikovskogo v Klinu', *Sovetskaia zhenshchina*, 8 (1989), 24: 26.

[*1300*]   *Gosudarstvennyi Dom-muzei P. I. Chaikovskogo v Klinu: Prospekt*. Sost. i avtor teksta G. Belonovich. Moskva: Moskovskii rabochii, 1990. 63 p, illus. ISBN: 5–2390–0161–8.

[*1301*]   BELONOVICH, G. 'Na pamiat´', *Nashe nasledie*, 2 (1990): 24–27.
The collection of Chaikovskii's portraits and photographs in the house-museum.

[*1302*]   UL´IANOVA, M. 'Zdes´ rozhdalas´ ego muzyka', *Televidenie i radioveshchanie*, 7 (1990): 27–29.

[*1303*]   'V Dome-muzee P. I. Chaikovskogo v Klinu', *Sovetskaia muzyka* (1990), 5: 65, illus.
Photographs of the house-museum.

[*1304*]   VAIDMAN, P. E. '"Zapis´ stanovitsia kosym dozhdem, livnem": Klinskaia tetrad´ B. V. Asaf´eva', *Sovetskaia muzyka* (1990), 6: 114–117 [see *592*].
Boris Asaf´ev's work at the Chaikovskii archives.

[*1305*]   SLIUSARENKO, T. 'Vstrecha v Klinu: Takoi, kak vse', *Muzykal´naia zhizn´* (1990), 9: 8–10, illus.
An interview with Chaikovskii's great-niece, Kseniia Davydova, former curator at the Klin house-museum (see also *1292 1319*).

[*1306*]   ZUBACHEV, D. 'Dom v Klinu', *Avrora* (1990), 5: 132–134.

[*1307*]   KOLOSOVA, V. 'Zimnii put´', *Sovetskaia kul´tura* (6 Jan 1990): 15, illus.
A conversation with the director of the house-museum, Galina Belonovich, concerning preparations for the 150th anniversary of Chaikovskii's birth.

[*1308*]   BIRIUKOV, O. 'S imenem Chaikovskogo', *Pravda* (23 Dec 1990): 4.
The formation of the Chaikovskii Society at the Klin house-museum.

[*1309*]   LAURITZEN, P. 'Tchaikovsky at Klin', *Architectural Digest*, 48 (Aug 1991), 8: 124–129, illus.

[*1310*]   *Gosudarstvennyi Dom-muzei P. I. Chaikovskogo v Klinu: Putevoditel´-spravochnik po memorial´noi ekspozitsii*. Sostaviteli G. I. Belonovich, P. E. Vaidman. Moskva: Mir i kultura, 1992. 64 p, illus.
Guide to an exhibition at the Klin museum to commemorate the centenary of Chaikovskii's death.

[*1311*]   KUZNETSOV, A. 'Nash fotoarkhiv', *Muzykal´naia zhizn´* (1992), 21/22: 25, illus.
Photographs showing the damage caused by the German occupation of the house-museum in 1941.

[*1312*]   GONZALEZ, O. J. 'Tchaikovsky at Klin: His own quiet corner', *Classical Music Magazine*, 16 (1993), 5: 25–28, illus.

[*1313*]   BELONOVICH, G. I. *Dom-Muzei P. I. Chaikovskogo v Klinu*. Moskva: Vneshtorgizdat, 1994. 211 p, illus. ISBN 5-8502-5093-X.

[*1314*]   VAIDMAN, P. E. 'Dom-Muzeum Piotra Czajkowskiego w Klinie' / 'Peter Tchaikovsky Museum in Klin', *Muzyka*, 39 (1994), 1: 114–115.
Text in Polish, with a summary in English.

[*1315*]   '100-letie Doma-muzeia Chaikovskogo', *Muzykal´noe obozrenie*, 1 (1995): 7.

[*1316*]   BELONOVICH, G. 'Čajkovskijs letzter Wohnsitz und das Museum in Klin'. In: *Internationales Čajkovskij Symposium, Tübingen 1993: Bericht* (1995): 57–62 [see *596*].

[*1317*]   'Chaikovskii v Klinu', *Muzykal´noe obozrenie* (1996), 1: 5.
The opening of a central square in Klin, in memory of the composer.

[*1318*]   VROON, D. R. 'Point of view: Where Tchaikovsky lived', *American Record Guide*, 60 (1997), 6: 60–61, illus.

[*1319*] SIDOROVA, T. 'Pëtr Chaikovskii: "Ispytal li ia polnotu schast´ia v liubvi? Net, net, net!".
          Nekotorye podrobnosti lichnoi zhizni velikogo russkogo kompozitora', *Komsomol´skaia pravda* (6
          May 1998): 6.

          Kseniia Davydova's last interview, with Tat´iana Sidorova, concerning Chaikovskii and the Klin museum (see
          also *1292, 1305*.

          See also *15, 100, 110, 226, 359, 502, 516, 564, 565, 572, 801, 847, 870, 952, 1897, 2115, 2131, 2767,
          5491*.

3.3.2. Other Museums

[*1320*] NAGIBIN, Iu. 'Chto budem okhraniat´?', *Sovetskaia kul´tura* (26 Aug 1989).

          A proposal to open a Chaikovskii museum at Vosstaniia Square 54/46 in Moscow.

[*1321*] PANIUSHKIN, A. & MEDVEDEVA, I. 'Dom na Kudrinskoi: Budet li on muzeem kompozitora?',
          Rossiiskie vesti (23 Oct 1993).

          Proposal for a museum on Ulitsa Kudrinskaia in Moscow.

ALAPAEVSK HOUSE-MUSEUM

[*1322*] POZDNIAKOV, A. 'Gde zhil Chaikovskii', *Sovetskaia Rossiia* (8 Dec 1956).

[*1323*] ZETEL´, I. 'Entuziasty muzykal´nogo prosveshcheniia: Plody dvadtsatiletnego truda', *Sovetskaia
          muzyka* (1978), 1: 90–93.

[*1324*] 'Tol´ko fakty', *Muzykal´naia zhizn´* (1980), 1: 3.

[*1325*] GORODILINA, V. 'Muzei v Alapaevske', *Teatral´naia zhizn´* (11 Jun 1980), 4, illus.

[*1326*] LETOV, V. '"Anastasiia-val´s": O dome Chaikovskikh v Alapaevsk i pamiati serdtsa', *Izvestiia* (24
          Jul 1984): 3, illus.

          The museum at the site of the former Chaikovskii family home at Alapaevsk, and the composer's governess,
          Anastasiia Petrova.

          See also *1749*.

BRAILOV MUSEUM

[*1327*] SAVINOV, I. 'Zhizn´ vernulas´ vo dvorets', *Rossiiskaia muzykal´naia gazeta* (1990), 9: 3.

          The opening of a museum at the former estate of Nadezhda von Meck at Brailov.

KAMENKA MUSEUM

[*1328*] 'Muzei Chaikovskogo v Kamenke', *Pravda* (25 Apr 1940): 6.

          A short report on the opening of the musuem, at the former home of Chaikovskii's sister Aleksandra Davydova.
          See also *1329*.

[*1329*] 'Kamenka (Kirovogradskaia oblast´): Zdes´ otkryvaetsia muzei P. I. Chaikovskogo', *Izvestiia* (10
          May 1940): 4.

[*1330*] CHERNAIA, E. 'Kamenka', *Sovetskaia muzyka* (1949), 6: 23–31, illus.
          — [rev. repr.] In: E. S. Berliand-Chernaia, *Pushkin i Chaikovskii* (1950): 21–38 [see *2134*].

[*1331*] 'Pis'mo v redaktsiiu: Odnikh obeshchanii malo', *Komsomol´skaia pravda* (22 Jul 1965): 4.

          A letter to the editor from E. Katul´skaia and others, concerning the fate of the Chaikovskii museum at
          Kamenka.

[*1332*]   **FOMIN, B.** 'Otechestvo moe: I pamiat´ Kamenki liubia', *Pravda* (11 Apr 1968): 6.

The Davydov house where Chaikovskii stayed at Kamenka.

[*1333*]   **SHKALIBERDA, M.** *Kamenskii literaturno-memorial´nyi muzei A. S. Pushkina i P. I. Chaikovskogo: Putevoditel´*. Dnepropetrovsk: Promin´, 1972. 75 p, illus.

The re-opening of the building at Kamenka as a joint Chaikovskii—Pushkin museum.

[*1334*]   **KURNOSENKOV, K.** 'Pod nebom Kamenki', *Muzykal´naia zhizn´* (1972), 8: 20–21, illus.

[*1335*]   **KHOKHLOV, N.** 'Pamiat´ Kamenki liubia…', *Izvestiia* (25 May 1980).

[*1336*]   **BABENKO, V. V.** *Kamenskii literaturno-memorial´nyi muzei A. S. Pushkina i P. I. Chaikovskogo: Putevoditel´*. Dnepropetrovsk: Promin´, 1987.

[*1337*]   **IUZEFOVICH, V.** 'Chaikovskii v Muzee imeni Pushkina', *Sovetskaia muzyka* (1987), 5: 77–83, illus.

[*1338*]   **BABENKO, V.** 'Where his magic music was born', *Forum*, 89 (win. 1993): 30–32.

TAGANROG HOUSE-MUSEUM

[*1339*]   **IZIUMSKII, V.** "Taganrog mne ponravilsia…", *Sovetskaia kul´tura* (28 May 1976): 8.

The establishment of a museum at the home of the composer's brother Ippolit in Taganrog.

[*1340*]   **GURVICH, S.** 'Dom-muzei Chaikovskikh', *Sovetskaia muzyka* (1978), 8: 138–139, illus.

VOTKINSK HOUSE-MUSEUM

[*1341*]   'Dom, gde rodilsia P. I. Chaikovskii', *Sovetskoe iskusstvo* (14 Feb 1939): 1.

[*1342*]   **RUKAVISHNIKOV, N.** 'Na rodine velikogo kompozitora', *Ogonek* (1940), 7/8: 18.

[*1343*]   'V Votkinskom dome-muzee P. I. Chaikovskogo', *Sovetskaia muzyka* (1940), 11: 94.

Report on a schoolchildren's tour of the museum, exhibitions, lectures and concerts to mark Chaikovskii's centennial year.

[*1344*]   'Muzei imeni P. I. Chaikovskogo organizovan v Votkinske v dome, gde rodilsia velikii russkii kompozitor', *Pravda* (4 May 1940): 6.

[*1345*]   'Na rodine P. I. Chaikovskogo', *Pravda* (7 May 1940).

Events held at at Votkinsk, to commemorate the 100th anniversary of Chaikovskii's birth.

[*1346*]   'Na rodine P. I. Chaikovskogo', *Pravda* (18 May 1940).

[*1347*]   'Otovsiudu: Dom-muzei P. I. Chaikovskogo otkrylsia', *Pravda* (4 Jan 1950): 2.

The re-opening of the museum after its restoration.

[*1348*]   'Dom-muzei P. I. Chaiovskogo', *Sovetskoe iskusstvo* (7 Jan 1950): 1.

[*1349*]   **LEBEDEV, G.** 'Mechta Chaikovskogo voplotilas´ v zhizn´: Na rodine velikogo kompozitora', *Sovetskaia kul´tura* (17 Nov 1953).

[*1350*]   **MOROV, A.** 'Dom-muzei Chaikovskogo v Votkinske', *Sovetskaia muzyka* (1955), 5: 117–119.

Correspondence relating to the foundation of the birthplace museum at Votkinsk.

[*1351*]   **KRASNOV, A.** 'Dom s mezoninom', *Sovetskaia Rossiia* (28 Sep 1956).

[*1352*]   **CHUVYGIN, N.** 'Na rodine Chaikovskogo', *Sovetskaia Estoniia* (11 Apr 1958).

[*1353*] 'Na rodine Chaikovskogo', *Sovetskaia muzyka* (1960), 3: 158–159, 162, illus.
Celebrations at Votkinsk to mark the 120th anniversary of Chaikovskii's birth. See also *1354*.

[*1354*] 'Na rodine velikogo kompozitora', *Sovetskaia kul´tura* (10 May 1960): 2.

[*1355*] **Dom-muzei P. I. Chaikovskogo v Votkinske: Putevoditel´**. Sost. S. P. Sedusova, E. S. Sheptun. Izhevsk: Udmurtiia, 1962. 57 p, illus.

[*1356*] 'Chaikovskii'. In: *Slovo o zemliakakh*. Izhevsk: Udmurtiia, 1967: 133–140.

[*1357*] MIRONOV, N. 'Tam, gde rodilsia Chaikovskii', *Pravda* (31 Aug 1967): 3.

[*1358*] ANSHAKOV, B. 'Pamiati Chaikovskogo: Votkinsk', *Muzykal´naia zhizn´* (1971), 15: 5.

[*1359*] TIUKALOV, P. 'Na rodine Chaikovskogo', *Sovetskaia muzyka* (1971), 4: 154–155, illus.

[*1360*] KHOMIAKOV, V. 'Kak spasli dom Chaikovskogo', *Sovetskaia kul´tura* (4 Feb 1971): 2.
The restoration of the Votkinsk house-museum.

[*1361*] SAKHAROV, L. S. 'Dom-muzei P. I. Chaikovskogo v gorode Votkinske'. In: *Pamiatniki Otechestva*. Moscow, 1972: 235–238.

[*1362*] ANSHAKOV, B. Ia. 'Chaikovskomu posviashchaetsia', *Sovetskaia muzyka* (1973), 9: 141.
The annual Chaikovskii music festival at Votkinsk.

[*1363*] **Dom-muzei P. I. Chaikovskogo v Votkinske: Putevoditel´**. Tekst podgot. B. Ia. Anshakov. Izhevsk: Udmurtiia, 1974. 79 p, illus.
ReviewsF. Kravtsov, 'Korotko o knigakh', *Muzykal´naia zhizn´* (1974), 18: 24 — E. Permiak, 'Uvlekatel´noe puteshestvie', *Sovetskaia kul´tura* (21 Jan 1975): 4, illus.
— 2-e izd., dop. Izhevsk: Udmurtiia, 1978. 103 p, illus.

[*1364*] TIUKALOV, P. 'Na rodine Chaikovskogo', *Sovetskaia muzyka* (1975), 10: 141.

[*1365*] TIUKALOV, P. 'Dni Glinki, Chaikovskogo, Prokof´eva ... v Votkinske', *Sovetskaia muzyka* (1976), 10: 130.
The annual Chaikovskii music festival.

[*1366*] 'Posviashchaetsa P. I. Chaikovskomu', *Sovetskaia kul´tura* (18 May 1976): 8.

[*1367*] SHUMILOV, E. 'Dom s mezoninom', *Sovetskaia kul´tura* (14 Dec 1976): 8, illus.

[*1368*] 'Pamiat´ o velikom kompozitore', *Vechernii Leningrad* (29 Dec 1976).

[*1369*] TIUKALOV, P. 'Na rodine Chaikovskogo', *Sovetskaia muzyka* (1977), 11: 159.
The annual Chaikovskii musical festival.

[*1370*] ZUBKOV, N. 'Posviashaetsia P. I. Chaikovskomu', *Sovetskaia kul´tura* (24 May 1977): 8.

[*1371*] TIUKALOV, P. 'Na festivaliakh strany: Votkinsk', *Sovetskaia muzyka* (1978), 11: 134.
The annual Chaikovskii music festival.

[*1372*] MAIBUROVA, K. 'Konferentsiia, posviashchennaia 140-i golovshchie P. I. Chaikovskogo v Votkinske', *Sovetskaia muzyka* (1980), 11: 143–144.
Concerning a conference at Votkinsk to mark the 140th anniversary of Chaikovskii's birth, and the 40th anniversary of the opening of the museum.

[*1373*] PONOMAREVA, V. 'Dom v Votkinske', *Muzykal´naia zhizn´* (May 1980), 10: 16–17, illus.

[*1374*] PONOMAREV, I. 'Dom u sinego ozera', *Sel´skaia zhizn´* (5 Apr 1981).

[*1375*]   'Velikomu kompozitoru Rossii', *Pravda* (4 Dec 1984).

[*1376*]   KAKOVKIN, A. 'Bumagi vmesto restavratsii', *Sovetskaia kul´tura* (29 Apr 1986): 2.
           The restoration of the Votkinsk museum.

[*1377*]   SANATIN, V. 'Usad´ba v stile...disko: ochevidnoe—neveroiatnoe', *Komsomol´skaia pravda* (17 Jul
           1986): 2.

[*1378*]   PUZANOVA, N. 'Pust´ kamni muzykoi zvuchat', *Stroitel´naia gazeta* (9 Feb 1989).

[*1379*]   PARAMONOV, K. 'U razbitoi kolybeli', *Sovetskaia kul´tura* (29 Jun 1989).

[*1380*]   GOLUBIN, V. 'Na rodine geniia russkoi muzyki', *Sovetskii balet* (1990), 5: 16–17.
           A festival at Votkinsk to celebrate the 150th anniversary of Chaikovskii's birth.

[*1381*]   'Na rodine Chaikovskogo', *Mir zhenshchiny* (1992), 2 [inside front cover].

           See also *494, 564, 572, 801, 847, 909, 952, 983, 1241, 1275, 1394, 1749, 2116.*

3.3.3. Monuments

[*1382*]   'Pamiatnik Chaikovskomu', *Novoe vremia* (5 Nov 1893): 1–2.
           Editorial on the suggestion of a Chaikovskii memorial.

[*1383*]   'Teatr i muzyka', *Novoe vremia* (31 Jan 1894): 3.
           The setting-up of a Chaikovskii memorial fund. See also *1386*.

[*1384*]   'S vysochaishego soizvoleniia', *Russkaia muzykal´naia gazeta* (Feb 1894), 2: 45–46.

[*1385*]   'Teatr i muzyka', *Novoe vremia* (18 Nov 1896): 3.
           Two symphony concerts in St. Petersburg, in aid of the Chaikovskii memorial fund.

[*1386*]   FINDEIZEN, N. 'Po povodu dvukh kontsertov v pol´zu fonda Chaikovskogo', *Russkaia
           muzykal´naia gazeta* (Dec 1896), 12: 1605–1611.

[*1387*]   'Pamiatnik P. I. Chaikovskomu resheno vozdvignut´ v Sverdlovske', *Izvestiia* (6 May 1940).
           The unveiling of a statue of Chaikovskii next to the Opera and Ballet Theatre.

[*1388*]   NESVITENKO, N. 'Po Sovetskomu Soiuzu: Pamiatnik Chaikovskomu v kolkhoze', *Sovetskoe
           iskusstvo* (14 Jun 1940): 1.
           The laying down of a monument to Chaikovskii at the former Konradi estate at Grankino, near Poltava.

[*1389*]   'Pamiatnik P. I. Chaikovskomu', *Iskusstvo* (1962), 12: 265, illus.
           Photograph of a bronze sculpture of the composer, designed by A. Zavarzin.

[*1390*]   NAUMOV, A. 'Pervaia medal´ pamiati P. I. Chaikovskogo', *Muzykal´naia zhizn´* (1964), 2: 10, illus.
           Notes on a medal commemorating Chaikovskii, issued in Dec 1893.

[*1391*]   KLIMOV, V. 'Velikoe imia: Chaikovskii'. In: *Nash gorod: Chaikovskii*. Perm´, 1967. 172 p.
           The foundation of a new town for young violinists, named in honour of the composer.

[*1392*]   EMEL´IANOVA, N. 'Pamiati Chaikovskogo: Tambov', *Muzykal´naia zhizn´* (1971), 15: 5.
           A memorial statue to Chaikovskii at Usovo.

[*1393*]   NAUMOV, A. 'Bronzovaia siuita', *Muzykal´naia zhizn´* (1974), 1 [cover], illus.
           Statues of Chaikovskii, Gounod and Shaliapin by the sculptor Z. I. Lerner.

[1394]   'God Chaikovskogo: "Muzyka rozhdalas´ v ego dushe"', *Rossiiskaia muzykal´naia gazeta* (1990), 9: 2, illus.

The sculptor O. Komov discusses his ideas for a Chaikovskii memorial at the composer's birthplace at Votkinsk.

[1395]   BOGRAD, G. 'Stranitsy proshlogo listaia: Chaikovskii v Pavlovske', *Leningradskaia pravda* (13 May 1990): 4.

The establishment of a memorial to the composer at Pavlovsk.

See also *1092, 1093*.

ESTONIA

[1396]   'Pamiatnik Chaikovskomu v Khapsalu', *Sovetskaia muzyka* (1940), 11: 94.

The unveiling of a large stone bench in the Estonian town of Haapsalu [Hapsal], where Chaikovskii stayed during the summer of 1867. Carved by the sculptor R. Haavamiagi, and featuring a relief of the composer and music from some of his works. See also *1397, 1398, 1399, 1401*.

[1397]   'Pamiatnik P. I. Chaikovskomu v Khapsalu', *Pravda* (15 Sep 1940): 6.

[1398]   KRESS, M. 'Pamiatnik-skam´ia P. I. Chaikovskomu', *Leninskie iskry* (11 Dec 1946): 4, illus.

[1399]   GARIN, S. 'Skameika na beregu moria', *Muzykal´naia zhizn´* (1960), 9: 14, illus.

[1400]   'P. I. Chaikovskii v Estonii', *Sovetskaia kul´tura* (17 Jan 1975): 3.

The establishment of a memorial to Chaikovskii at the house in Hapsal (Haapsalu) where he stayed during the summer of 1867.

[1401]   KRAUS, O. *Armastusvaarne Haapsalu*. Tallinn: Eesti Raamat, 1992: 26–27.

Photographs of the Chaikovskii monument at Haapsalu.

See also *1777, 1778*.

MOSCOW

[1402]   'Moskva: Raznye izvestiia', *Russkaia muzykal´naia gazeta* (10 Jan 1910): 51.

A collection by the Moscow music circle to raise funds for a Chaikovskii memorial.

[1403]   'Memorial´naia doska P. I. Chaikovskogo', *Vecherniaia Moskva* (22 Dec 1928).

Proposals for a new memorial plaque in the city.

[1404]   LESHCHINSKII, Ia. 'Zabytyi epizod', *Ogonek* (1940), 12: 16.

The story of the sculptor Mikhail Mikeshin's unrealised project to create a memorial to Chaikovskii in Moscow. Includes extracts from Mikeshin's correspondence with Modest Chaikovskii.

[1405]   'Konkurs na proekt pamiatnika P. I. Chaikovskomu', *Pravda* (21 Aug 1940): 6.

The official announcmenent of a competition to design a monument to Chaikovskii to stand in front of the Moscow Conservatory. See also *1406*.
— [repr.] *Izvestiia* (21 Aug 1940)

[1406]   'Moskovskaia khronika: Pered zdaniem Moskovskoi konservatorii im. P. I. Chaikovskogo', *Sovetskoe iskusstvo* (24 Aug 1940): 4.

[1407]   'Vystavka proektov pamiatnika P. I. Chaikovskomu', *Sovetskoe iskusstvo* (23 Feb 1941): 4.

A public exhibition of competing designs for the Chaikovskii monument at the Moscow Conservatory.

[1408]   'Proekt pamiatnika Chaikovskomu', *Sovetskoe iskusstvo* (12 Apr 1946): 2, illus.

Vera Mukhina's chosen design for a memorial to Chaikovskii at the Moscow Conservatory.

[*1409*]   'Proekt pamiatnika P. I. Chaikovskomu', *Ogonek* (2 Mar 1947): 8, illus.

Illustration of the final version of Mukhina's monument to Chaikovskii

[*1410*]   'Otkrytie pamiatnika P. I. Chaikovskomu', *Sovetskaia kul´tura* (16 Nov 1954): 1, illus.

The unveiling of the monument to Chaikovskii by Vera Mukhina, at the Moscow Conservatory. See also *1411*, *1412*, *1413*, *1415*.

[*1411*]   'Otkrytie pamiatnika P. I. Chaikovskomu', *Literaturnaia gazeta* (16 Nov 1954): 2.

[*1412*]   'Otkrytie v Moskve pamiatnika P. I. Chaikovskomu', *Pravda* (16 Nov 1954): 2, illus.

[*1413*]   'Khronika', *Sovetskaia muzyka* (1955), 1: 155.

[*1414*]   EPSHTEIN, E. 'Moskva, sotvori blagodarnuiu pamiat´', *Muzykal´naia zhizn´* (1993), 17/18: 7.

An initiative by the M. I. Glinka Museum of Musical Culture in Moscow to open a cultural centre in memory of Chaikovskii. See also *1416*.

[*1415*]   '"Sam Petr Il´ich goriacho otverg by..." (ob uvekovechenii pamiati P. I. Chaikovskogo)', *Istochnik* (1994), 1: 112–120.

Concerning the Chaikovskii monument at the Moscow Conservatory, designed by Vera Mukhina.

[*1416*]   'Obrashchenie ko vsem pochitateliam tvorchestva Chaikovskogo', *Muzykal´noe obozrenie* (Oct 1994), 10: 2.

The proposed cultural centre in memory of Chaikovskii. See also *1414*.

ST. PETERSBURG / LENINGRAD

[*1417*]   'Teatr i muzyka', *Novoe vremia* (23 Feb 1894): 4.

Proposal for a memorial to Chaikovskii at the St. Petersburg Conservatory.

[*1418*]   'Vysochaishe utverzhdennoi komissiei', *Russkaia muzykal´naia gazeta* (Jul 1896), 7: 750.

The commissioning of a monument for the St. Petersburg Conservatory from the sculptor V. A. Beklemishev.

[*1419*]   'Direktsiei Imperatorskikh teatrov', *Russkaia muzykal´naia gazeta* (Aug 1896), 8: 928–929.

The commissioning of a monument at Chaikovskii's grave in the Aleksandr Nevskii cemetery, from the sculptor Pavel Kamenskii. See *1420* to *1423*.

[*1420*]   'Pamiatnik P. I. Chaikovskogo', *Moskovskie vedomosti* (26 Oct 1897).

[*1421*]   'Raznye izvestiia: V subbotu 25 oktiabria', *Russkaia muzykal´naia gazeta* (Nov 1897), 11: 1619–1620.

The unveiling of Kamenskii's monument at Chaikovskii's grave, to mark the fifth anniversary of the composer's death.

[*1422*]   'Khronika teatra i iskusstva', *Teatr i iskusstvo* (1 Nov 1897): 771.

[*1423*]   'Pamiati P. I. Chaikovskogo', *Muzyka i penie* (15 Nov 1897): 4.

The unveiling of the monument at Chaikovskii's grave in the Aleksandr Nevskii cemetery, and the commissioning of a statue for the St. Petersburg Conservatory.

[*1424*]   'Raznye izvestiia: V nachale aprelia...', *Russkaia muzykal´naia gazeta* (May/Jun 1898), 5/6: 569.

The new memorial statue of Chaikovskii at the St. Petersburg Conservatory, by V. A. Beklemishev. See also *1425*, *1430*.

[*1425*]   IVANOV, M. 'Muzykal´nye nabroski', *Novoe vremia* (26 Oct 1898), 2–3, illus.

[*1426*]   'Raznye izvestiia', *Russkaia muzykal´naia gazeta* (Nov 1898), 11: 984–986.

The ceremonial unveiling of the Chaikovskii monument in the entrance hall of the St. Petersburg Conservatory on 24 Oct 1898. See also *1427*, *1428*, *1429*.

[*1427*]   'Na otkrytii statui Chaikovskogo v foie Konservatorii', *Teatr i iskusstvo* (1 Nov 1898): 777.

[*1428*]   'Otkrytie pamiatnika P. I. Chaikovskomu', *Teatr i iskusstvo* (7 Nov 1898): 782.

[*1429*]   'Statuia P. I. Chaikovskogo raboty skul´ptora prof. Beklemisheva', *Russkaia muzykal´naia gazeta* (Jan 1899), 1: 2.

[*1430*]   'Pamiati P. I. Chaikovskogo', *Peterburgskaia gazeta* (26 Oct 1903).

[*1431*]   'Kapital imeni Chaikovskogo', *Za 7 dnei* (1913), 43: 924.

A proposed new Chaikovskii memorial fund at the St. Petersburg Conservatory. See also *1432*.

[*1432*]   'Teatr i muzyka', *Rech´* (20 Oct 1913): 6.

[*1433*]   'Ko vsem leningradskim muzykal´nym organizatsiiam, teatram i vsei muzykal´noi obshchestvennosti', *Sovetskaia muzyka* (1934), 7: 87.

An open letter from students at the musical colleges in Leningrad and Moscow, campaiging for a monument to Chaikovskii at the Leningrad Conservatory (to coincide with the 45th anniversary of the première of *The Queen of Spades*).

[*1434*]   'Pamiatnik P. I. Chaikovskomu', *Smena* (2 Apr 1940): 4.

Plans for a memorial statue of Chaikovskii in front of the Leningrad Conservatory.

[*1435*]   'V dni vrazheskoi blokady', *Smena* (13 Oct 1945): 4.

Restoration of monuments in the Aleksandr Nevskii cemetery (including Chaikovskii's), which were damaged during World War II.

[*1436*]   KOROSTELEV, K. 'Genii russkoi muzyki', *Smena* (3 Dec 1987): 4.

Plans for a competition to design a memorial statue to Chaikovskii in Leningrad. See also *1437, 1438, 1439*.

[*1437*]   'Pamiatnik Chaikovskomu: Konkurs na luchshii proekt', *Leningradskaia pravda* (15 Dec 1987): 3.

[*1438*]   'Vnimanie, konkurs! Derzai, khudozhnik!', *Smena* (23 Jan 1988): 4.

The announcement of a competition to design the memorial statue to Chaikovskii in Leningrad.
— [repr.] *Vechernii Leningrad* (23 Jan 1988).

[*1439*]   'Velikomu kompozitoru', *Vechernii Leningrad* (18 Apr 1988): 3.

Changes to the rules of the Leningrad memorial competition.

[*1440*]   'God Chaikovskogo: "Peredat´ na sooruzhenie pamiatnika"', *Rossiiskaia muzykal´naia gazeta* (1990), 10: 3.

The winner of the Chaikovskii piano competition is to participate in a charity concert to raise funds for the Chaikovskii memorial.

[*1441*]   KIKTA, V. 'Chaikovskii v skul´pture', *Muzykal´naia zhizn´* (1990), 4: 20–22, illus.

[*1442*]   MAKSOV, A. 'Na pamiatnik Chaikovskomu', *Sovetskii balet* (1990), 4: 15–216, illus.

A musical evening at the Leningrad Conservatory, to raise funds for a memorial statue to Chaikovskii.

[*1443*]   SEBOSHEV, S. 'Gde byt´ pamiatniku P. I. Chaikovskomu?', *Vechernii Leningrad* (11 Jan 1990): 3.

Considers where a new statue of the composer by M. K. Anikushin should stand by the St. Petersburg Conservatory. See also *1445, 1446, 1447, 1448*.

[*1444*]   OROKHOVATSKII, Iu. 'Angely-khraniteli: Upasite ot poruganiia', *Smena* (28 Mar 1990).

Chaikovskii's grave monument and memorial plaque at the house where he died on Malaia Morskaia.

[*1445*]   SEBOSHEV, S. 'Gde byt´ pamiatniku P. I. Chaikovskomu?', *Vechernii Leningrad* (11 Jan 1991).

[*1446*] OROKHOVATSKII, Iu. 'Vechnaia pamiat´, polnaia prorekh', *Smena* (6 Nov 1993).

[*1447*] GRADSKII, P. 'Vstrecha Chaikovskogo s Glinkoi: Sostoitsia li ona?', *Vechernii Peterburg* (17 Mar 1994): 4.

[*1448*] PIRIUTKO, Iu. 'Ishchem mesto dlia pamiatnika', *Sankt Peterburgskie vedomosti* (15 Jun 1994): 5.

[*1449*] STRIZHAK, N. 'Gordit´sia my umeem, ne umeem pomnit´: Pokhozhe net v etom gorode mesta dlia Chaikovskogo', *Smena* (19 Sep 1994).

PART 4

BIOGRAPHY

4.1. GENERAL
4.1.1. Books
4.1.2. Articles

4.2. CHILDHOOD AND YOUTH

4.3. EDUCATION AND EMPLOYMENT
4.3.1. Law Student
4.3.2. Civil Servant
4.3.3. Music Student
4.3.4. Music Teacher
4.3.5. Conductor

4.4. RESIDENCES AND TRAVEL
4.4.1. Russia & Eastern Europe
4.4.2. Western & Central Europe
4.4.3. America

4.5. PERSONAL RELATIONSHIPS
4.5.1. Family
4.5.2. Musicians
4.5.3. Authors
4.5.4. Other
4.5.5. Homosexuality

4.6. VIEWS AND OPINIONS
4.6.1. Music & Musicians
4.6.2. Literature & Writers
4.6.3. Art & Artists
4.6.4. Other

4.7. PSYCHOLOGY AND HEALTH

4.8. DEATH AND BURIAL

4.1. BIOGRAPHY

4.1.1. Books

[*1450*] **CHESHIKHIN, V.** *P. I. Chaikovskii*. Riga; Moscow, 1893. 15 p.

[*1451*] **[MORDVINOV, V. R.]** *Pëtr Il´ich Chaikovskii: Biograficheskie o nem svedeniia i spisok muzykal´nykh sochinenii*. Sankt Peterburg, 1894. 35p.

Contents: 'Pëtr Ili´ch Chaikovskii': 1–16 [see *1572*] — 'Spisok muzykal´nykh sochinenii P. I. Chaikovskogo': 17–35 [see *3*].

[*1452*] **ARENSON, A. K.** *P. I. Chaikovskii*. Riga, 1898. 24 p.

[*1453*] **CHAIKOVSKII, M. I.** *Zhizn´ Petra Il´icha Chaikovskogo*. Po dokumentam, khraniashchimsia v arkhive im. pokoinogo kompozitora v Klinu. V trekh tomakh. S prilozheniem portretov, snimkov i faksimile, ispolnennykh fototsinkograficheskim sposobom. [3 vols] 1900–02. music, illus.

Biography of the composer by his brother Modest. Includes excerpts from selected letters from Chaikovskii to Karl Al´brekht, Anna Aleksandrova-Levenson, Akhilles Al´feraki, Anton Arenskii, Vasilii Bessel´, Adol´f Brodskii, Aleksandra Chaikovskaia, Elizaveta Chaikovskaia, Praskov´ia Chaikovskaia, Anatolii Chaikovskii, Il´ia Chaikovskii, Modest Chaikovskii, Nikolai Chaikovskii, Anton Chekhov, Lev Davydov, Vladimir Davydov, Aleksandra Davydova, Anton Door, Fanny Dürbach, Mariia Ermolova, Adolf Fürstner, Aleksandr Glazunov, Mikhail Ippolitov-Ivanov, Pëtr Iurgenson, Nikolai Kashkin, Ivan Klimenko, Nikolai Konradi, Grand Duke Konstantin Konstantinovich, Nadezhda von Meck, Anna Merkling, Eduard Nápravník, Vladimir Nápravník, Vladimir Obolenskii, Wladyslaw Pachulski, Emiliia Pavlovskaia, Sergei Rachinskii, Daniil Ratgauz, Nikolai Rimskii-Korsakov, Nikolai Rubinshtein, Aleksandr Shidlovskii, Vladimir Shilovskii, Il´ia Slatin, Vladimir Stasov, Sergei Taneev, Leontii Tkachenko, Lev Tolstoi, Eugen Zabel and Varvara Zarudnaia.

See also *262, 446, 485, 1585, 1588, 1589, 1898, 1902, 1961, 1994*.

Tom 1. [1840–1877]. Moskva; Leiptsig: P. Iurgenson, 1900. 573 p, music, illus.

Tom 2. [1878–1885]. Moskva; Leiptsig: P. Iurgenson, 1901. 695 p.

Tom 3. [1885–1893]. Moskva; Leiptsig: P. Iurgenson, 1902. 689, [41] p.

Includes: 'Leiptsigskie retsenzii 1888 goda': 659–667 [see *1827*].

Reviews: G. A. Larosh, 'Kniga o Chaikovskom' (1900) [see *486*] — 'Bibliograficheskie zametki', *Russkie vedomosti* (27 Aug 1901) — N. D. Kashkin, 'P. I. Chaikovskii i ego zhizneopisanie' (1902) [see *463*] — 'Muzykal´no-istoricheskaia literatura', *Teatr i iskusstvo* (1902), 5: 95 — B. D. K., *Russkaia muzykal´naia gazeta* (16 Mar 1903), 11: 332–334.

— 2-e izd., ispr. Moskva; Leiptsig: P. Iurgenson, 1903. (3 vols), music, illus.

Correcting some printing defects in vol. 1.

— [repr. (extract)] 'Zhizn´ Petra Il´icha Chaikovskogo (tom 1, glavy 1–3)'. In: *P. I. Chaikovskii: Gody detstva* (1983): 13–90 [see *1712*].

— [repr.] Moskva: Algoritm, 1997. (3 vols.), music, illus. (*Genii v iskusstve*). ISBN 5-8887-8007-3.

— [English tr.] *The life and letters of Peter Ilich Tchaikovsky (1840–1893)*. By Modeste Tchaikovsky. Ed. from the Russian with an introducton by Rosa Newmarch. London; New York: John Lane, 1906 [1905]. xi, 782 p, music, illus.

Actually abridged tr. from the German ed. of Paul Juon (see also *1087*).

Includes: 'Chronological list of Tchaikovsky's compositions from 1866–1893': 726–749 [see *5*] — 'The plots of Tchaikovsky's chief operas': 750–761 [see *2559*] — 'Extracts from German press notices during Tchaikovsky's tours abroad in 1888 and 1889': 762–777 [see *1827*].

Reviews: 'Tchaikovsky Intime', *Outlook*, 16 (Dec 1905): 824 — *Contemporary Review*, 89 (Feb 1906): 296–301 — *Nation*, 82 (26 Apr 1906): 351.

— [English tr. (repr.)] London: John Lane; New York: Dodd, Mead [1924]. (2 vols.) xi, 782 p, music, illus.

— [English tr. (repr.)] New York: Haskell House Publishers, 1970. (2 vols) xi, 782 p, music, illus. ISBN: 0-8383-0997-6.

— [English tr. (repr.)] New York: Vienna House [1973]. (2 vols) xi, 782 pp, music, illus. ISBN: 0–8443–0034–9.

— [German tr.] *Das Leben Peter Iljitsch Tschaikowsky's*. Von Modest Tschaikowsky. Aus dem Russischen Übersetzt von Paul Juon. In 2 Bänden, mit vielen Portraits, Abbildungen und Facsimile in Zinkographie. (2 vols.), illus., 831 p.

Bd. 1. Moskau; Leipzig: P. Jurgenson [1901]. 539 p.

Bd. 2. Moskau; Leipzig: P. Jurgenson, 1903 [1904]. [292] p.

Reviews: *Nation*, 79 (13 Oct 1904): 298–299 — E. Spiro, 'Das Leben Tschaikowskys', *Signale für die musikalische Welt* (1905), 47: 833–837.

[1454]   KNORR, I. *Peter Jljitsch Tschaikowsky*. Berlin: Harmonie, 1900. 91 p, music, illus. (*Berühmte Musiker. Lebens- und Charakterbilder, nebst Einführung in die Werke der Meister*. Hrsg. von H. Reimann; 9).

Reviews: G. A. Larosh, 'Nemetskaia biografiia P. I. Chaikovskogo', *Rossiia* (2 Dec 1900) (repr. in: G. A.Larosh, *Izbrannye stat´i v piati vypuskakh*, vyp. 2 (1975): 331–334 [see *2376*]) — 'Nemetskaia biografiia P. I. Chaikovskogo', *Literaturnyi vestnik*, 1 (1901), 1: 120.

[1455]   NEWMARCH, R. H. *Tchaikovsky: His life and works*. With extracts from his writings, and the diary of his tour abroad in 1888. London: G. Richards; New York: John Lane, 1900. ix, 232 p, music, illus.
See also *1087*.

Contents: 'Tchaikovsky: His life and works': 1–110 — 'Tchaikovsky as a musical critic': 111–167 [see *5426*] — 'Diary of my tour in 1888' (tr. from the Russian): 168–225 [see *137*].

Reviews: 'Zagranichnaia zhizn´', *Nuvellist* (Jul 1900): 14 — *Academy*, 59 (Jul/Dec 1900): 29 — *Dial*, 29 (1 Jul 1900): 359 — *Athenaeum* (11 Aug 1900), 2: 194 — *The Times* (4 Sep 1900) — *Nation*, 72 (23 May 1901): 418 — [W. H. Hadow], *Times Literary Suppl.* (17 Nov 1905): 397.

— [repr.] London: Greenwood Press [1906]. ix, 232 p, music, illus.

— [2nd ed.] Ed. ... by Edwin Evans. London: W. Reeves; New York: Scribner's, 1908. xvi, 418 p, music, illus.

With new supplements: 'The relation of Tchaikowsky to art-questions of the day': 226–383 [see *2296*] — 'Analyses of selected works': 272–394 — 'Indices for student use: List of Tchaikovsky's works in the arrangement of opus number': 395–401 — 'Classific account of Tchaikovsky's works': 402–409.

See also *1499*.

— [repr. (1st ed.)] New York: Greenwood Press [1969]. ix, 232 p, music, illus.

— [repr. (2nd ed.)] New York: Haskell House Publishers, 1969. xvi, 418 p, music, illus. ISBN: 0–8383–0310–2 (*Studies in music*; 42).

— [repr. (1st ed.)] St. Clair Shores, Mich.: Scholarly Press, 1970. ix, 232 p, music, illus. ISBN: 0–4030–0342–3.

[1456]   G—ICH, E. *P. I. Chaikovskii: Ocherk*. Moskva: A. A. Levenson, 1902. 2 p.

[1457]   HRUBÝ, K. *Peter Tschaikowsky: Eine monographische Studie*. Leipzig: H. Siemann, 1902. 57 p, illus. (*Moderne Musike*).

Review: *Russkaia muzykal´naia gazeta* (21 Sep 1903), 41: 869–870.

[1458]   POOR JORICK. *P. I. Chaikovskii: Biograficheskii ocherk*. Warszawa, 1903. 22 p.

[1459]   LEE, E. M. *Tchaikovski*. London: P. Welby [1904]. xvi, 162 p, music, illus. Ed. by Wakeling Dry (*Music of the Masters*; 2).

— 2nd ed. London: J. Lane, 1906. xv, 164 p.

— 3rd ed. London: J. Lane, 1923. xv, 164 p.

[1460]   MASON, D. G. *Tschaikowsky*. Ed. by Daniel Gregory Mason. Boston, Mass.: Bates & Guild, 1904. 48 p, music, illus. (*Masters in Music*; 4: 23).

[1461]   LIPAEV, I. V. *Pëtr Il´ich Chaikovskii: Biograficheskii ocherk*. Moskva; Leipzig: P. Iurgenson, 1905. 65 p.

[1462] **EVANS, E.** *Tchaikovsky*. London: J. M. Dent; New York: E. P. Dutton & Co, 1906. ix, 207 p, illus. (*The Master Musicians Series*).

Partially based on R. H. Newmarch, *Tchaikovsky: His life and works*, 2nd ed. (1908) [see *1455*].

— [repr.] London: J. M. Dent; New York: E. P. Dutton & Co, 1921. ix, 207 p, illus. (*The Master Musicians Series*).

— [rev. ed.] London: J. M. Dent; New York: E. P. Dutton & Co., 1935. xi, 236 p, illus. (*The Master Musicians New Series*).

Review: *Musical Opinion*, 54 (1936): 504–505.

— [repr.] London: J. M. Dent [1943]. xi, 236 p, illus. (*The Master Musicians New Series*).

Review: W. Dean, *Canon*, 2 (Dec 1948), 5: 216.

— [repr.] New York: Pellegrini & Cudahy, 1949. ix, 236 p, music, illus. (*The Master Musicians New Series*).

— [repr.] London: Dent, 1957. ix, 234 p, music, illus. (*The Master Musicians New Series*).

— [rev. ed.]. New York: Avon Books; London: Dent, 1960. 191 p. (*The Master Musicians Series*).

— [rev. ed.]. Rev. by Gerald Abraham. New York: Collier Books [1963]. 192 p, illus. (*The Master Musicians Series*).

— [rev. ed.] London: J. M. Dent; New York: Farrar, Straus & Giroux, 1966. ix, 226 p, music, illus. (*The Master Musicians Series*).

Reviews: *Musical Opinion*, 90 (Oct 1966): 25 — D. Lloyd-Jones, *Musical Times*, 107 (Jul 1966): 605 — *Opern Welt* (Mar 1967), 3: 6 — A. F. Leighton-Thomas, *Music Review*, 29 (1968), 1: 73–74.

[1463] **LEE, E. M.** *Tchaikovski*. Ed. by George C. Williamson. London: G. Bell & Sons, 1906. viii, 63 p, music, illus. (*Bell's Miniature Series of Musicians*).

[1464] **BRONSKII, P.** *P. I. Chaikovskii: Biograficheskii ocherk*. So spiskom proizvedenii i kratkimi libretto oper. Sankt Peterburg: Gerol´d [1908]. 79 p. (*Vseobshchaia biblioteka*; 31).

[1465] **KLIMENKO, I. A.** *P. I. Chaikovskii: Kratkii biograficheskii ocherk*. Sost. dlia prochteniia v kontserte Muzykal´nogo otdela Riazanskogo literaturno-khudozhestvennogo kruzhka v pamiat´ 15-letiia so dnia konchiny kompozitora. [Moskva]: Iakovlev, 1909. 35 p.

[1466] **BYRON, M. C.** *A day with Peter Ilyich Tchaikovsky*. London: Hukler & Stroughton [1912]. [36] p, illus. (*Days with the Great Composers*).

An anecdotal, semi-fictional portrait of the composer.

— [2nd ed.] *A day with Tchaikovskiy*. London: Hoddler, 1927. 46 p.

[1467] **RONALD, L.** *Tschaikowsky*. London: T. C. & E. C. Jack; New York: F. A. Stokes [c.1912]. 63 p, music, illus. (*Masterpieces of music*).

The latter half of the book is devoted to the composer's piano solos and songs. See also *1471*.

[1468] **KELLER, O.** *Peter Tschaikowsky: Ein Lebensbild*. Leipzig: Breitkopf & Härtel, 1914. 79 p, illus. (*Breitkopf & Härtels Musikbucher: Kleine Musikerbiographien*).

— [2. aufl.]. Leipzig: Breitkopf & Härtel, 1924. 71 p, illus. (*Breitkopf & Härtels Musikbucher: Kleine Musikerbiographien*).

[1469] **KORCHMAREV, K. A.** *P. I. Chaikovskii*. Moskva: Rabis [1921]. 4 p.

[1470] **GLEBOV, I. [ASAF´EV, B. V.]** *P. I. Chaikovskii: Ego zhizn´ i tvorchestvo*. Petrograd: Mysl´, 1922. 184 p. (*Russkie kompozitory*; 1).

Includes: 'Khronograf zhizni P. I. Chaikovskogo i vazhneishikh aktov ego tvorchestva': 153–174 [see *83*].

[1471] **RONALD, L.** *Tschaikowsky*. London: Murdoch, 1922. 28 p, music, illus. (*Mayfair Biographies*; 12).

See also *1467*.

— [repr.] London: Chappell & Co., 1946. 28 p. (*Mayfair Biographies*).

[1472]   IAKOVLEV, V. V. *P. I. Chaikovskii*. Moskva: Nauka i prosveshchenie [1924]. 8 p (*Obshchestvo druzei Doma-muzeia P. I. Chaikovskogo v Klinu*).

— [repr.] Moskva: Nauka i prosveshchenie [1925]. 8 p. (*Obshchestvo druzei Doma-muzeia P. I. Chaikovskogo v Klinu*).

[1473]   STEINITZER, M. *Tschaikowsky*. Leipzig: P. Reclam jun. [1925]. 72 p. (*Reclams Musiker-Biographien*; 38).

[1474]   POPOV, S. M. *Zhizn´ i tvorchestvo P. I. Chaikovskogo: Opyt obshchedostupnogo izlozheniia*. Moskva: Gosizdat-Muzsektor, 1926. 39 p.

— [2-e izd.]. Moskva: Obshchestvo druzei Doma-muzei P. I. Chaikovskogo v Klinu, 1927. 39 p, illus.

Review: M. Ivanov-Boretskii, *Muzykal'noe obrazovanie* (1928), 1: 84.

[1475]   STEIN, R. H. *Tschaikowskij*. Stuttgart; Berlin; Leipzig: Deutsche Verlags-Anstalt, 1927. xix, 508 p, music, illus. (*Klassiker der Musik*).

[1476]   *Tschaikowsky.*London: W. Paxton & Co. [1927]. 17 p, illus. (*Thumb-Nail Sketches of Great Composers*).

[1477]   OSTRETSOV, A. N. *P. I. Chaikovskii: Sotsial´naia i muzykal´naia kharakteristika*. Moskva: Gosizdat-Muzsektor, 1929. 36 p. (*Biblioteka populiarnykh muzykal´nyk znanii*).

[1478]   VLIET, W. van der & THEAKSTON, J. *Peter Iljitch Tschaikowsky: Hans liv og Værker*. København: Haase, 1929. 193 p, illus.

[1479]   DALEN, H. van. *Tschaikowsky*. s'Gravenhaage: J. P. Kruseman [1930]. 112 p, music, illus. (*Beroemde Musici*; 17).

[1480]   BUDIAKOVSKII, A. E. *Chaikovskii: Kratkii ocherk zhizni i tvorchestva*. Leningrad: Triton, 1935. 28 p.

Includes Bibliography ('Iz literatury o Chaikovskom'): [30].

— Izd. 2-e, ispr. i dop. [Leningrad]: Gos. muz. izdat., 1936. 39 p.

With enlarged bibliography ('Rekomendatel´nyi ukazatel´ literatury'): 34–35.

— Izd. 3-e. Leningrad: Iskusstvo, 1938. 44 p.

With updated bibliography ('Rekomendatel´nyi ukazatel´ literatury'): 42–43.

— [Lithuanian tr.]. Perevod Kh. Potashinskas. [Kaunas]: Gos. izdat. khudozh. literatury [1948]. 48 p.

[1481]   ABRAHAM, G. E. H. *Tchaikovsky*. London, Novello & Co. [1938]. 14 p. (*Novello's Biographies of Great Musicians*).

[1482]   FLEIS, E. *Chaikovskii*. Izhevsk: Udmgosizdat, 1939. 44 p, illus.

— [2-e izd.] *P. I. Chaikovskii*. Izhevsk: Udmurtskoe knizhnoe izdat., 1953. 39 p, illus.

[1483]   BERNANDT, G. B. *P. I. Chaikovskii: Kratkii ocherk zhizni i deiatel´nosti*. Moskva; Leningrad: Gos. muz. izdat., 1940. 72 p, illus.

Includes bibliography ('Osnovnaia literatura o P. I. Chaikovskom'): 71–72.

[1484]   ORLOV, N. *P. I. Chaikovskii: Kratkii ocherk zhizni i tvorchestva*. Perevod. T. Mirza. Tashkent: Uzfimgiz, 1940. 40 p, illus.

Text in Uzbek.

[1485]   STOIKO, A. G. *Velikii kompozitor: Iz zhizni P. I. Chaikovskogo*. Chast I: 1877–81. [Gor´kii]: Obl. izdat., 1941. 248 p, illus.

— [new ed.] *Velikii kompozitor: Povest´ o zhizni P. I. Chaikovskogo*. [Leningrad]: Muzyka, 1972. 335 p, illus.

— [Polish tr. by S. Newiadomski]. *Simfonia tesknoty i nadziei, powiesc o Czaikowskim*. Krakow: Polski Wydawnisztwo Muzyczno, 1977. 396 p.

Review: *Ruch Muzyczny*, 23 (1979), 19: 17.

[*1486*]   KHOLODKOVSKII, V. *P. I. Chaikovskii*. Moskva: Goskinoizdat, 1942. 35 p, illus.

[*1487*]   L´VOV, M. *Pëtr Il´ich Chaikovskii*. Saransk: Muz. izd., 1942.

[*1488*]   TIBALDI CHIESA, M. *Ciaikovsky: La vita e l'opera*. [Milano:] Garzanti [1943]. iii, 432 p, music, illus.

— [Spanish tr.] *Tschaikowsky*. Tr. de Alfonso Espronceda. Barcelona: Caralt, 1956. 395 p.

[*1489*]   WEINSTOCK, H. *Tchaikovsky*. New York: Alfred A. Knopf, 1943. xii, 386 p, music, illus.

Includes: 'Catalogue of works': 354–368.

Reviews: A. Berger, *New Republic*, 110 (24 Jan 1944): 124–125 — A. Lourie, *Russian Review*, 4 (fall 1944), 1: 122.

— [repr.] New York: Alfred A. Knopf, 1944. xii, 386 p, music, illus.

— [repr.] London; Toronto: Cassell & Co.; New York: Alfred A. Knopf, 1946. xii, 386 p, illus.

— [repr.] New York: Alfred A. Knopf, 1959. xii, 386 p, illus.

— [repr.] Toronto: Random House, 1966. xii, 386 p, illus.

— [repr.] New York: Alfred A. Knopf, 1973. xii, 386 p, illus.

— [repr.] London; New York: Da Capo Press, 1980. xii, 386 p, illus. (*Da Capo Press Music Reprint Series*). ISBN: 0–306–76040–1 (USA).

— [French tr.] *La vie pathétique de Tchaikovsky*. Traduit de l'anglais. [Paris:] J. B. Janin, 1947. 372 p, illus. (*La flute de pan*).

— [German tr.] *Tschaikovsky*. Aus dem Amerikanischem Übertragen von Reinhold Scharnke. München: Winkler [1948]. 512 p, illus.

— [German tr. (2. Aufl.)]. *Peter Iljitsch Tschaikowsky*. Mit vollständig neu revidiertem Werkverzeichnis. Aus dem Englischen übersetzen von Kurt Michaelis. Adliswil; Lottstetten: E. Kunzelmann, 1993. 393 p, illus.; ISBN: 3–85662–012–0.

— [Spanish tr.]. *Tchaikovski*. Versión española de Jesûs Bal y Gay. México: Nuevo mundo, 1945. 559 p, illus.

[*1490*]   ABRAHAM, G. E. H. *Tchaikovsky: A short biography*. London: Duckworth, 1944. 144 p, illus. (*Great Lives*; 90).

Expanded version of the author's article in *Masters of Russian Music* (1936) [see *1628*].

Review: C. J. Gardner, *Cambridge Review*, 66 (Oct 1944): 342.

— [repr.] London: Duckworth [1949]. 144 p, illus. (*Great Lives*; 90).

Review: S. Markus, 'Opasnyi Chaikovskii', *Sovetskoe iskusstvo* (1 Dec 1949): 4.

— [repr.] Westport, Conn.: Hyperion Press, 1979. 144 p. (*Encore Music Editions*). ISBN: 0–8835–5672–3.

— [repr.] Westport, Conn.: Hyperion Press, 1993. 144 p. (*Encore Music Editions*). ISBN: 0–8835–5672–3.

[*1491*]   CHERNYI, O. & CHERNAIA, E. *Pëtr Il´ich Chaikovskii: Znamenityi kompozitor*. [Moskva]: Molodaia gvardiia, 1944. 64 p. (*Velikie russkie liudi*).

[*1492*]   CÉLIS, H. & RIGHT, W.-P. *Tchaikowsky*. [Bruxelles]: Nouvelle revue Belgique [1945]. 81 p, illus. (*Collection Euterpe*).

[*1493*]   MAYO, W. *Tchaikovsky: His life told in anecdotal form*. Illus. by Andre Dugo. New York: Hyperion Press; Duell Sloan and Pearce, 1945. [40] p, illus.

[*1494*]   AL´SHVANG, A. A. *P. I. Chaikovskii: Popul´iarnyi ocherk*. Moskva; Leningrad: Gos. muz. izdat., 1946. 17 p. (*Komitet po delam iskusstv pri Sovete Ministrov RSFSR*).

[*1495*]   HOFMAN, M. R. *Tchaïkovsky*. Paris: Éditions du Chêne, 1947. 403 p. (*Pour la musique*).

[*1496*]   SERPILIN, L. S. *Chaikovskii*. Kiev: Mistetstvo, 1948. 31 p. (*Klassiki russkoi muzyki*).

Review: T. K., 'Popularnye broshiury o klassikakh', *Sovetskaia muzyka* (1950), 9: 106–108,

— 2-e izd., ispr. i dop. *P. I. Chaikovskii*. Kiev: Muzychna Ukraina, 1985. 29 p.

[*1497*]   **SONOBE, S.** *Chaikofusuki monogatari*. Sonobe Shiro cho. Tokyo: Iwanami Shoten, 1949. vi, 204 p, illus. (*Iwanami shinsho*; 18).

[*1498*]   **BEKE, C.** *De symphonie van het noodlot: Het leven van Peter Iljitsj Tsjakowski (1840–1893)*. Tilburg: Nederland's Boekhuis [1950]. 194 p, music, illus. (*Sonatine-reeks*; 5).

Review: *Mens en Melodie*, 6 (Mar 1951): 91.

— [rev. ed.] *De symphonie van het noodlot: Het leven van Peter Iljitj Tsjaikowski (1840 bis 1893)*. Tilburg: Nederland's Boekhuis, 1958. 212 p, music, illus. (*Sonatine-reeks*; 5).

[*1499*]   **DANILEVICH, L.** *P. I. Chaikovskii*. Moskva; Leningrad: Muzgiz, 1950. 60 p, illus. (*Zamechatel'nye russkie muzykanty*).

[*1500*]   **SCHALLENBERG, E. W.** *Tchaikovsky*. Tr. from the Dutch by M. M. Kessler-Button. London: Sidgwick & Jackson; Stockholm [pr. Amsterdam]: Continental Book Co. [1950]. 60 p, music, illus. (*Symphonia Books*).

Reviews: *Music Parade*, 2 (1951), 5: 22 — *Music & Letters*, 32 (Jan 1951): 75–77.

[*1501*]   **VOS, A. C.** *Het leven van Peter Iljitsj Tsjaikofsky, 1840–1893*. Den Haag: J. P. Krusenam [1950]. 32 p, illus.

[*1502*]   **PECHERSKII, P. L.** *P. I. Chaikovskii: Ocherk zhizni i tvorchestva*. Riga: Latgosizdat, 1951. 224 p, music, illus.

Text in Latvian.

[*1503*]   **SONOBE, S.** *Chaikofusuki no geihutsu*. Tokyo: Iwanami Shoten, 1951. (iv), 213 p, illus.

[*1504*]   **WOLFURT, K. von.** *Peter Iljitsch Tschaikowski: Bildnis des Menschen und Muzikers*. Zürich [pr. Emmendingen]: Atlantis Verlag [1952]. 295 p, music, illus. (*Atlantis-Musik bücherei*).

Review: *Die Musikforschung*, 7 (1954), 2: 238–241.

— 2. Aufl. *Tschaikowski*. Zürich; Freiburg [u. a.]: Atlantis-Verlag, 1978. 296 p, music, illus. ISBN: 3–7611–0290–9.

Reviews: *Bühne* (Feb 1979), 245: 26 — *Neue Musikzeitung*, 28 (1979), 6: 59.

— [Italian tr.] *Ciaikovski*. 2. ed. Trad. di Angela Zamorani. [n.p.]: Accademia, 1963. illus. (*Vite dei musicisti*).

[*1505*]   **ZAGIBA, F.** *Tschaikowsky: Leben und Werk*. Leipzig; Zürich [pr. Wien]: Amalthea-Verlag [1953]. 455 p, illus.

Reviews: *Notes*, 10 (6 Sep 1953): 625–626 — *Die Musikforschung*, 7 (1954), 2: 238–241 — *Neue Zeitschrift für Musik*, 115 (Jan 1954): 34.

[*1506*]   **TÖRNBLOM, F. H.** *Tjajkovskij*. Stockholm: Bonnier, 1955. 229 p, music (*Musikens mästare*).

— [Danish tr.]. *Tjaikovskij*. Oversättung fra svensk af Karen Margrethe og Hans Riis-Vestergaard. København: A. Busck, 1957. 224 p.

Review: *Nordisk Musikkultur*, 6 (Dec 1957): 135.

[*1507*]   **KUNIN, I. F.** *Pëtr Il'ich Chaikovskii*. Moskva: Molodaia Gvardiia, 1958. 368 p, illus. (*Zhizn' zamechatel'nykh liudei*; 17 (265)).

Includes: 'Osnovnye daty zhizni i tvorchestva P. I. Chaikovskogo': 355–359 — 'Literatura o P. I. Chaikovskom': 363–366.

Reviews: A. Narkevich, 'Zhivoi Chaikovskii', *Novyi mir* (1959), 9: 263–265 — 'Velikii kompozitor', *Smena* (26 Mar 1959): 3 — 'V gorode, gde zhil kompozitor', *Sovetskaia kul'tura* (1 Dec 1959): 2 — A. Kulakovskii, 'Populiarnaia kniga o Chaikovskom', *Sovetskaia muzyka* (1960), 3: 194–196.

— [Azerbaijani tr.] Baku: Detiunizdat, 1962. 357 p, illus. (*Zhizn' zamechatel'nykh liudei*).

— [Estonian tr.] Tallin: Estgosizdat, 1963. 319 p, illus. (*Seriia biografii*).

— [Georgian tr.] Tblissi: Sabchota Sakartvelo, 1964. 330 p. (*Stranitsy bol'shoi zhizni*).

— [Japanese tr.] Tr. by Teiichiro Kawagishi. Tokyo: Shin-dokusho-sha, 1970. 254 p.

[*1508*] **MULLER, H. J. M.** *Tsjaikofsky*. Haarlem: J. Gottmer, 1958. 264 p, illus. (*Gottmer-muziekpockets*; 4).

[*1509*] **VIGH, J.** *Ha Csajkovszkij naplót írt volna*. Budapest: Zene munkiadó Vàllalat, 1958. 216 p.
A biography presented in the form of a fictional diary, using extracts from Chaikovskii's diaries and letters.
Review: *Österreichische Musikzeitschrift*, 12 (Dec 1957): 502.
— [French tr.] *Le journal de Tchaikovski, reconstitué à l'aide de documents de l'époque*. Tr. du hongrois par L. Podor. Budapest: Corvina, 1961.
— [German tr.] *Wenn Tschaikowski ein Tagebuch geführt hätte*. [Budapest]: Litteratura [1958]. 234 p.
— [German tr. (2. Aufl.)] Stuttgart; Zürich: Juncker [1967]. 224 p.

[*1510*] **AL´SHVANG, A. A.** *P. I. Chaikovskii*. Moskva: Gos. muz. izdat., 1959. 702 p, music, illus.
Study of the composer's life and principal works. Includes 'Zametki S. I. Taneeva na poliakh klavira "Pikovoi damy"': 687–701 [see *3600*].
Review: *Slovenská Hudba*, 4 (Jun 1960): 332–333.
— 2-e izd. Moskva: Muzyka, 1967. 927 p, music, illus. (*Klassiki mirovoi muzykal´noi kul´tury*).
— 3-e izd. Moskva: Muzyka, 1970. 816 p, music, illus. (*Klassiki mirovoi muzykal´noi kul´tury*).

[*1511*] **GEE, J. & SELBY, E.** *The triumph of Tchaikovsky: A biography*. London: R. Hale [1959]. 206 p, illus.
Reviews: *Musical Times*, 101 (Feb 1960): 89–90 — *Music Magazine*, 164 (May 1962): 53 — *Music & Musicians*, 11 (Nov 1962): 63 — S. Krebs, *Slavic Review*, 22 (Mar 1963), 1: 172.
— [repr.] New York: Vanguard Press [1960]. 206 p, illus.

[*1512*] **HOFMANN, M. R.** *Tschaikovski*. [Paris]: Seuil [1959]. 192 p, music, illus. (*Solféges*; *Microcosme* 11).
Reviews: *Music & Letters*, 43 (Sep 1962): 351— *Tempo*, 63 (win. 1962/63): 48.
— [rev. ed.] *Tchaïkovski*. [Paris:] Seuil [1977]. 184 p, illus. ISBN: 2–0200–0231–0. (*Solféges*; 11).
Includes new 'Discographie' by M. Marnat: 182–184.
— [English tr.] *Tchaikovsky*. Tr. from the French by Angus Herriot. London: J. Calder [pr. the Netherlands, 1962]. 189 p, music, illus. (*Illustrated Calderbook*; *CB 59*).
— [English tr. (rev. ed.)] London: J. Calder; New York: Hillary House, 1966. 192 p, music, illus.
Review: *Sunday Times Magazine* (30 Oct 1977): 39.

[*1513*] **PAHLEN, K. von** *Tschaikowsky: Ein Lebensbild*. Stuttgart: H. E. Günther, 1959. 262 p, music, illus.
Review: *Musikhandel*, 11 (1960), 2: 79.
— [Sonderausgabe] Wiesbaden: Löwit [1977]. 262 p, music, illus.
— [new ed.] München: Goldmann, 1981. 216 p. (*Ein Goldmann-Taschenbuch*; 3927).
— [Dutch tr.] *Tschaikovsky: Een levensbeeld*. Kahnthout-Antwerpen: W. Beckers, 1969. 165 p, illus. (*Interserie*).
— [French tr.] *Tchaikovsky: Le portrait d'une vie*. Kalmthout-Anvers: Beckers, 1971. 306 p.

[*1514*] **STURSHENOV, B.** *P. I. Chaikovski*. Sofia, 1960. 153 p.

[*1515*] **VLADYKINA-BACHINSKAIA, N. M.** *P. I. Chaikovskii*. Moskva: Sovetskiai Rossiia, 1961, 160 p, music, illus. (*Khudozh. samodeiatel´nosti*; 35).
— [Romanian tr.] *Ceaikovski: Monografie*. Tr. din limba rusă de Nicolae Parocescu. Bucureşti: Editura muzicală, 1972. 176 p, illus.
— [Vietnamese tr.] P. I. Trai-cop-xki. Ha Noi, 1978. 198 p, illus.

[*1516*] **GÁL, G. S.** *Pjotr Iljics Csakovskij*. Budapest: Gondolat, 1962. 235 p, illus. (*Kis zenei könyvtár*; 23).

[*1517*] **RUCH´EVSKAIA, E. A.** *Pëtr Il´ich Chaikovskii, 1840–1893: Kratkii ocherk zhizni i tvorchestva*. Popul´iarnaia monografiia E. Ruch´evskaia. Leningrad: Gos. muz. izdat., 1963. 144 p, music, illus. (*Knizhka dlia iunoshestva*).
— 2-e izd., pererab. Leningrad: Muzyka, 1978. 112 p, illus.
— 3-e izd., pererab. Leningrad: Muzyka, 1985. 104 p, illus.
— [4-e izd.]. Moskva: Muzyka, 1998, 133 p, illus. ISBN: 5–7140–0637–2.

[*1518*]   ERISMANN, G. *Piotr Illitch Tchaïkovski: L'homme et son œuvre*. [Paris:] Seghers [1964]. 192 p, illus. (*Musiciens de tous les temps*; 9).

Review: *Musica* (Jul/Aug 1965), 136–137: 41.

— [Japanese tr.] Tr. by Shinji Tanamura. Tokyo: Ongaku-no-tomo, 1971. v, 262 p.

[*1519*]   HANSON, L. & HANSON, E. *Tchaikovsky: A new study of the man and his music*. London: Cassell [1965]. xii, 332 p, music, illus.

Reviews: *Musical Events*, 20 (Jun 1965): 20 — *Musical Times*, 106 (Aug 1965): 599–600 — *Music Teacher*, 44 (Jul 1965): 289.

— [2nd ed.] *Tchaikovsky: The man behind the music*. New York: Dodd, Mead [1966]. xiv, 385 p, music, illus.

Review: B. Schwarz, *Slavic Review*, 27 (Mar 1968), 1: 167.

[*1520*]   ZACCARO, G. *Ciaikowski*. Caltanissetta-Roma: S. Sciascia, 1967. 115 p.

[*1521*]   CH´IEN, I-ju & WU, Hsin-liu. *Ts'ung pei ts'ang tao t'ien o hu*. [Beijing: 1969]. x, 340 p, music.

[*1522*]   JURAMIE, G. *Tchaïkovski*. Paris: Hachette, 1970. 96 p, illus. (*Classiques hachette de la musique*).

Review: *Le Courier Musicale de France* (1971), 33: 35.

— [Italian tr.] *Piotr Iljic Ciakovskii*. Milano: Sugar, 1978. 126 p. (*I classici della musica*; 2).

— [Spanish tr.]. *Tschaikowsky*. Tr. del francés y Feliz Ximenez Sandoval. 2. ed. Madrid: Espassa-Calpe, 1976. 125 p, illus. (*Clásicos de la música*).

— [Spanish tr. (3. ed.)] Madrid: Espassa-Calpe, 1977. 125 p, illus.

— [Spanish tr. (4. ed.)] Madrid: Espassa-Calpe, 1981. 125 p, illus.

— [Spanish tr. (5. ed.)] Madrid: Espassa-Calpe, 1985. 128 p, illus.

[*1523*]   RACHMANOWA, A. *Tschaikowskij: Schicksal und Schaffen*. Aus dem russische Manuskript übersetzt von Arnulf von Hoyer. Wien; Berlin: P. Neff, 1972. 447 p, illus.

Includes bibliography: 429–439.

Review: *Bühne* (Feb 1973), 173: 26.

— [repr.] Berlin; Darmstadt; Wien: Deutsche Buchgemeinschaft; Gütersloh: Bertelsmann; Stuttgart: Europeische Bildungsgemeinschaft; Wien: Buchgemeinschaft Donauland, 1978. 447 p, illus.

[*1524*]   RAEDT, P. de. *Het leven en werk van P. I. Tsjaikofski*. Brüssel: Reinaert Uitg., 1972. 48 p. (*Meesters der toonkunst*; 19).

Text in Dutch.

[*1525*]   BAJER, J. *Petr Iljič Čajkovskij*. Praha: Horizont; České Budějovice: Jihočeské tisk., 1973. 75 p.

[*1526*]   GARDEN, E. *Tchaikovsky*. London: J. M. Dent; New York: Octagon Books, 1973. viii, 194, music, illus. (*The Master Musicians*). ISBN: 0–460–03142–2 (UK pbk), 0–460–03105–8 (UK hbk), 0–460–02187–7 (USA).

Reviews: D. Brown, *Music & Letters*, 54 (1973), 4: 472–473 — *Music in Education*, 37 (1973), 363: 261 — B. Gardiner, 'A new study on Tchaikovsky', *Musical Events*, 28 (Aug 1973): 8–10 — *Times Literary Suppl.* (24 Aug 1973): 974 — R. MacAllister, *Musical Times*, 114 (Sep 1973): 898 — *Music Teacher*, 52 (Nov 1973): 20.

— [repr.] London: J. M. Dent, 1976. viii, 194 p, music, illus. (*The Master Musicians*). ISBN: 0–460–02187–7.

Reviews: *Times Literary Suppl.* (8 Apr 1977): 419 — *Music Review*, 39 (1978), 3–4: 279–280.

— [repr.] London: J. M. Dent, 1984. x, 194 p, music, illus. (*The Dent Master Musicians Series*). ISBN: 0–460–86110–7 (pbk), 0–460–03142–2 (hbk).

Review: *Music Teacher*, 64 (Aug 1985): 20.

— ["4th ed."]. London: J. M. Dent, 1993. x, 178 p, music, illus. (*The Dent Master Musicians*). ISBN: 0–460–86110–7 (pbk.).

Review: A. F. L. Thomas, *Music Review*, 55 (1994), 1: 76–77.

— [German tr.]. *Tschaikowsky: Leben und Werk*. Stuttgart: Deutsche Verlags-Anstalt, 1986. 272 p, music, illus. ISBN: 3–421–06300–1.

Review: S. Schibli, *Neue Zeitschrift für Musik*, 148 (Jul/Aug 1987): 95–96.

— [German tr. (new)] *Tschaikowsky: Eine Biographie*. Ause den Englischen von Konrad Kuster. Frankfurt am Main: Insel Verlag, 1998. 301 p. (Insel Taschenbuch; 2232).

Reviews: T. Kohlhase, *Die Musikforschung* 52 (1999): 383–384 — D. Gojowy, Osterrichische Musik Zeitschrift, 54 (May 1999): 71–72.

[*1527*] **RIETHOF, E.** *Tsjaikovskiej's levenssymfonie: Hat lied van de duizend berken*. 's-Gravenhage: Zuid-Hollandsche U. M.; Forum-boekerij [1973]. 315 p, illus. (*Forum boekerij*). ISBN: 9–0235–8081–8.

[*1528*] **WARRACK, J.** *Tchaikovsky*. London: Hamilton; New York: Scribner's, 1973. xiv, 287 p, music, illus. ISBN: 0–241–02403–X (UK), 0–6841–3558–2 (USA).

Reviews: B. Gardiner, 'Tchaikovsky: The unknown' (1973) [see *2034*] — *Symphony News*, 24 (1973), 5: 31 — S. Sadie, *The Times* (22 Nov 1973) — *Times Literary Suppl.* (30 Nov 1973): 1480 — *Sunday Times* (9 Dec 1973) — A. Bakshian, *National Review*, 26 (18 Jan 1974): 95–96 — P. J. Smith, *Musical America*, 24 (Mar 1974): 30–31 — R. Jacobson, *Opera News*, 38 (23 Mar 1974): 11, illus. — *Music Educator's Journal*, 61 (Feb 1975): 77 — R. Craft, *New York Review of Books*, 26 (1979), 4: 42.

— [rev. ed.] London: Hamilton, 1989. xi, 303 p. ISBN: 0–241–12699–1.

[*1529*] **RUIZ TARAZONA, A.** *Tchaikovsky: Un alma atormentada*. Madrid: Real Musical [1974]. 95 p, illus. (*Colección Músicos*; 1). ISBN: 8–4387–0000–4.

[*1530*] **VOLKOFF, V.** *Tchaikovsky: A self-portrait*. Boston: Crescendo Publishing Co.; London: R. Hale, 1975. 348 p, music, illus. ISBN: 0–7091–4976–X (UK), 0–8759–7088–5 (USA).

— [French tr.] *Tchaïkovski*. [Paris]: Julliard; L'Age d'homme [1983]. 411, [16] p. illus. (*Les vivants*). ISBN: 2–2600–0338–9.

Review: A. Lischké, *L'Avant Scène Opéra*, 55 (1983): 155–156.

[*1531*] **HELM, E. B.** *Peter I. Tschaikowsky: In Selbstzeugnissen und Bilddokumenten*. Reinbek bei Hamburg: Rowohlt, 1976. 149 p, illus. (*Rowohlts Monographien*; 243). ISBN: 3–499–50243–7.

Includes 'Bibliographie': 143–144.

Review: *Musical Opinion*, 100 (Dec 1976): 119.

— [repr.] Reinbek bei Hamburg: Rowohlt, 1977. 149 p, illus. (*Rowohlts Monographien*; 243) ISBN: 3–499–50243–7.

— [repr.] Reinbeck bei Hamburg: Rowohlt, 1979. 149 p, illus. (*Rowohlts Monographien*; 243). ISBN: 3–499–50243–7.

— [repr.] Reinbeck bei Hamburg: Rowohlt, 1980. 149 p, illus. (*Rowohlts Monographien*; 243). ISBN: 3–499–50243–7.

— [repr.] Reinbeck bei Hamburg: Rowohlt, 1983. 149 p, illus. (*Rowohlts Monographien*; 243). ISBN: 3–499–50243–7.

— [repr.] Reinbeck bei Hamburg: Rowohlt, 1985. 149 p, illus. (*Rowohlts Monographien*; 243). ISBN: 3–499–50243–7.

— [repr.] Reinbek bei Hamburg: Rowohlt, 1986. 149 p, illus. (*Rowohlts Monographien*; 243). ISBN: 3–499–50243–7.

— [repr.] Reinbek bei Hamburg: Rowohlt, 1988. 149 p, illus. (*Rowohlts Monographien*; 243). ISBN: 3–499–50243–7.

— 2. Aufl. Reinbek bei Hamburg: Rowohlt, 1990. 157 p, illus. (*Rowohlts Monographien*; 243). ISBN: 3–499–50243–7.

With updated 'Bibliographie': 143–154.

— [repr.] Reinbek bei Hamburg: Rowohlt, 1993. 157 p, illus. (*Rowohlts Mongraphien*; 243). ISBN 3–499–50243–7.

— [repr.] Reinbek bei Hamburg: Rowohlt, 1995. 157 p, illus. (*Rowohlts Mongraphien*; 243). ISBN 3–499–50243–7.

— [Swedish tr.] *Peter Tjajkovskij*. Översättning Torgny Bondestam. Borås: Cete, 1980. 180 p, illus. ISBN: 91–85846–07–4. (*Norma*).

[*1532*]   **P. I. Chaikovskii o muzyke, o zhizni, o sebe**. Literaturnaia kompozitsiia A. A. Orlovoi. Leningrad: Muzyka, 1976. 272 p, illus.

Based on extracts from the composer's letters and diaries.

Review: L. Konisskaia, 'Slovami Chaikovskogo', *Muzykal'naia zhizn'* (Apr 1977), 8: 24.

— [English tr.] *Tchaikovsky: A self-portrait*. Comp. by Alexandra Orlova. Tr. from the Russian by R. M. Davison. With a foreword by David Brown. Oxford; New York: Oxford Univ. Press, 1990. xxiv, 436 p, music, illus. ISBN: 0–19–315319–X.

Expanded to include a new chapter on the composer's death ('26–28 Oct 1893'): 406–414. See also *2242*.

Reviews: G. Shokhman, 'Vzgliad s drugikh beregov', *Sovetskaia muzyka* (1990), 6: 134–141 [see *592*] — J. Warrack, 'Poisonous rumours' (1990) [see *2245*] — F. Welch, 'Why he took arsenic', *Literary Review* (Oct 1990), 148: 43–44 — J. Allison, *Opera*, 42 (May 1991): 516–518 — W. E. Grimm, *Choice*, 28 (Jun 1991): 1650 — H. Zajaczkowski, *Musical Times*, 132 (Jul 1991): 344 — D. Gojowy, *Neue Zeitschrift für Musik*, 152 (Jul/Aug 1991): 94 — E. Garden, *Music & Letters*, 72 (Nov 1991), 4: 618–620 — N. Goodwin, 'Tchaikovsky from far and near' (1992) [see *3859*] — S. Karlinsky, *Slavonic and East European Review*, 70 (Jul 1992): 541–544 — G. R. Seaman, *Notes*, 49 (Mar 1993), 3: 1013–1016.

— [Italian tr.] *Cajkovskij: Un autorittrato*. A cura di Maria Rosaria Boccuni. Torino: EDT, 1993. xxxiii, 447 p. (*Biblioteca di cultura musicale*).

Review: M. Girardi, *Nuovo Rivista Musicale Italiana*, 30 (1995), 1: 301–304.

— [Spanish tr.] *Chaikovski: Un autorretrato*. Versión española de Santiago Martín Bermûdez y Javier Alfaya. Madrid: Alianza [1994]. 457 p, illus. (*Alianza mûsica*; 66).

[*1533*]   SWOLKIEŃ, H. *Piotr Czajkowski*. Wyd. 1. Warszawa: Państwowy Instytut Wydawniczy, 1976. 555 p, illus. (*Ludzie żywi*; 31).

Review: *Ruch Muzyczny*, 21 (1977), 18: 19.

[*1534*]   BROWN, D. *Tchaikovsky: A biographical and critical study*. 1978–91 [4 vols.], music, illus.

Vol. 1: *The early years (1840–1874)*. London: Gollancz; New York: W. W. Norton, 1978. 348 p. ISBN: 0–575–02454–2 (UK), 0–3930–7535–2 (USA).

Vol. 2: *The crisis years (1874–1878)*. London: Gollancz; New York: W. W. Norton, 1982. 312 p. ISBN: 0–575–05426–3 (UK), 0–3830–1707–9 (USA).

See also *1886*.

Vol. 3: *The years of wandering (1878–1885)*. London: Gollancz; New York: W. W. Norton, 1986. 336 p. ISBN: 0–575–03774–1 (UK), 0–3930–2311–7 (USA).

Vol. 4: *The final years (1885–1893)*. London: Gollancz; New York: W. W. Norton, 1991. 526 p. ISBN: 0–575–05094–2 (UK), 0–3930–3099–7 (USA).

Reviews: E. Garden, *Musical Times*, 120 (1979): 402–403 — *The Times* (4 Feb 1979) [suppl.] — R. Craft, *New York Review of Books*, 26 (1979), 4: 42 — J. Warrack, *Opera*, 30 (Mar 1979): 287–288 — *Gramophone*, 56 (May 1979): 1846 — *High Fidelity*, 29 (Jul 1979): 18–19 — *Music & Musicians*, 28 (Oct 1979): 45–46 — *Times Literary Suppl.* (30 Nov 1979): 71 — J. Legrand, *Études classiques*, 48 (1980), 3: 267 — B. Schwarz, *Notes*, 36 (Mar 1980), 3: 649–650 — M. H. Brown, *Journal of the American Musicological Society*, 33 (sum. 1980), 2: 402–407 — R. J. Wiley, *Slavic Review*, 40 (sum. 1981), 2: 330 — H. Zajaczkowski, *Music Review*, 42 (Aug/Nov 1981), 3/4: 290–201 — J. Warrack, *Times Literary Suppl.* (24 Dec 1982): 1412 — *Central Opera Service Bulletin*, 24 (1983), 3: 42 — *South African Music Teacher*, 102 (1983): 13 — *The Economist*, 286 (19 Feb 1983): 109 — *Gramophone*, 60 (Mar 1983): 1091 — R. L. Neighbarger, *Library Journal*, 108 (15 Apr 1983): 826 — *British Books News* (Jun 1983): 379 — E. Garden, *Music & Letters*, 64 (Jul/Oct 1983), 3–4: 248–250 — *Choice*, 21 (Oct 1983): 291 — H. Macdonald, 'Tchaikovsky: Crises and contortions', *Musical Times*, 124 (Oct 1983): 609, 611–612 — *High Fidelity*, 33 (Nov 1983): 18 — G. Martin, *Opera Quarterly*, 1 (win. 1983), 4: 161–164 — *19th Century Music*, 8 (1984): 171–172 — H. Zajaczkowski, *Music Review*, 45 (May 1984), 2: 143–145 — *Gramophone*, 63 (Mar 1986): 1140 — J. Warrack, *Times Literary Suppl.* (21 Mar 1986), 300 — *Literary Review* (May 1986): 51 — *British Books News* (Jun 1986): 350 — K. Gann, *New York Times Book Reviews* (15 Jun 1986): 21 — H. Macdonald, *Musical Times*, 127 (Aug 1986): 441 — E. Garden, *Music & Letters*, 67 (Oct 1986): 392–394 — J. R. Belanger, *Library Journal*, 111 (1 Oct 1986): 98 — H. Zajaczkowski, *Music Review*, 47 (Nov 1986): 301–303 — A. Clements, *New Statesman*, 112 (21 Nov 1986): 27 — G. Shokhman, 'Vzgliad s drugikh beregov', *Sovetskaai muzyka* (1990), 6: 134–141 [see *592*] — H. Canning, 'Love in the time of cholera', *Sunday Times* (8 Dec 1991) — S. Karlinsky, 'Man or myth?' (1992) [see *1671*] — H. Zajaczkowski, *Musical Times*, 133 (Jan 1992): 25 — A. Burgess, 'He kicked Oblomov out of bed', *Observer* (5 Jan 1992) — *Kirkus Reviews* (2 Feb 1992) — T. J. McGee, *Library Journal*, 117 (15 Feb 1992): 168 — N. Goodwin, 'Tchaikovsky from far and near' (May 1992) [see *3859*] — E. Garden, *Music & Letters*, 73 (Nov 1992), 4: 619–621 — *Bloomsbury*

Review, 12 (Dec 1992): 15 — R. Craft, 'Love in a cold climate' (1993) [see *1676*] — R. Taruskin, 'Pathetic symphonist' (1995) [see *1679*].

— [rev. repr. (vols. 1 & 2)] *To the crisis (1840–1878)*. London: Gollancz, 1992. 659 p, music, illus. ISBN: 0–575–05426–3.

— [rev. repr. (vols. 3 & 4)] *The years of fame (1878–1893)*. London: Gollancz, 1992. 849 p, music, illus. ISBN: 0–575–05427–1.

Reviews: *South African Music Teacher* (1992), 121: 18–21 — *Classic CD*, 42 (Nov 1993): 20–22 [suppl.] — J. Allison, 'Coming to terms with Tchaikovsky' (1997) [see *1683*].

[*1535*] **STRUTTE, W.** *Tchaikovsky: His life and times*. Speldhurst: Midas Books, 1979. viii, 158 p, music, illus. ISBN: 0–85936–113–6.

Reviews: C. Nagy, *Clavier*, 19 (1980), 8: 12 — *Music & Musicians*, 28 (Feb 1980): 33–34.

— Expanded ed. Tunbridge Wells: Hippocrene Books; Neptune City, N. J.: Paganiniana Publications [1981]. viii, 156 p, music, illus. ISBN: 0–85936–113–6 (UK). 0–8766–6641–1 (USA).

— [repr.] London: Omnibus Press, 1983. x, 158 p, music, illus. ISBN: 0–7119–0254–2.

— [repr.] Tunbridge Wells: Baton Press, 1984. viii, 158 p, music, illus. ISBN: 0–85936–113–6.

[*1536*] **NÁDOR, T.** *Pjotr Iljics Csajkovszkij életének krónikája*. Budapest: Zeneműkiadó, 1980. 143 p, music. (*Napról napra*; 15). ISBN: 9–6333–0318–4.

[*1537*] **ORLOVA, E. M.** *Pëtr Il´ich Chaikovskii*. Moskva: Muzyka, 1980. 271 p, illus.

Includes: 'Daty zhizni i deiatel´nosti P. I. Chaikovskogo': 243–255 [see *89*].

Review: L. Darinskaia, 'Novyi povorot temy', *Sovetskaia muzyka* (1981), 3: 117–119.

[*1538*] **PARRAMÓN, J. M.** *Tchaikovsky*. Barcelona: Instituto Parramon Ediciones, 1982. 66 p. (*Serie Musica y Musicos*).

Also includes a section on Telemann (with separate pagination).

[*1539*] **SGRIGNOLI, F.** *Cajkovskij*. Milano: Fabbri, 1982. 143 p, illus. (*Grandi della musica*).

[*1540*] **PRIBEGINA, G. A.** *Pëtr Il´ich Chaikovskii: 1840–1893*. Moskva: Muzyka, 1983. 191 p, illus. (*Russkie i sovetskie kompozitory*).

Review: M. Iakovlev, 'O Chaikovskom—s liubov´iu', *Muzykal´naia zhizn´* (1984), 2: 24.

— [repr.] Moskva: Muzyka, 1984. 191 p, illus. (*Russkie i sovetskie kompozitory*).

— 2-e izd, ispr. i dop. Moskva: Muzyka, 1986. 197 p, illus. (*Russkie i sovetskie kompozitory*).

— 3-e izd. Moskva: Muzyka, 1990. 223 p, illus. (*Russkie i sovetskie kompozitory*).

— [German tr.] *Pjotr Iljitsch Tschaikowski*. Aus dem Russische übersetzt und hrsg. von Dieter Lehmann. Berlin: Verlassen Neue Musik, 1988. 270 p, illus. (*Reihe Meister der Russischen und Sowjetischen Musik*). ISBN: 3–7333–0023–8.

[*1541*] **KIRCHHEINER HANSEN, C.** *Tchaikovsky. hans liv, hans musik, hans tid, hans værk, hans samtidige, diskografi, udvalgte værker, bibliografi*. København: Hernov, 1984. 67 p, illus. (*Komponister og deres musik*). ISBN: 8–7721–5162–5.

[*1542*] **MORITA, M.** *Chaikofuskii*. Tokyo: Shincho-sha, 1986. 107 p.

Review: 'Kniga o Chaikovskom v Iaponii', *Muzykal´naia zhizn´* (1988), 17: 25, illus.

[*1543*] *The great composers: Their lives and times*. Vol. 4: *Pyotr Tchaikovsky, 1840–1893*. New York: Marshall Cavendish Corp., 1987. 123 p, illus. ISBN: 0–8630–7776–5 (set).

[*1544*] **KENDALL, A.** *Tchaikovsky: A biography*. London: Bodley Head, 1988. xiii, 257 p, illus. ISBN: 0–3703–1091–8.

[1545] **MOUNTFIELD, D.** *Pyotr Ilyich Tchaikovsky, 1840–1893.* London: Hamlyn; Secaucus, N. J.: Chartwell Books, 1990. 95 p, illus. (*The Great Composers*). ISBN: 0–600–56447–9 (UK), 1–55521–607–2 (USA).

— [French tr.] *Tchaïkovski.* Adapt française de Claude Dovaz. Paris: Librairie Gründ, 1990. 96 p, illus. (*Les grands compositeurs*). ISBN: 2–7000–5503–9.

— [German tr.] *Peter Iljitsch Tschaikowsky, 1840–1893: Leben, Werk und Wirkung.* Aus dem Englischen Übersetzen von Julia Goering. München: Orbis-Verlags, 1992. 95 p, illus. (*Große Komponisten*). ISBN: 3–572–00538–8.

[1546] **NIKITIN, B. S.** *Chaikovskii: Staroe i novoe.* Moskva: Znanie, 1990. 204 p, illus. ISBN: 5–07–000670–3.

[1547] **NICASTRO, A.** *Pëtr Ilîč Čajkovskij.* Pordenone: Studio tesi, 1990. xxiv, 299 p. (*Collezione L'Arte della fuga*; 21). ISBN: 8–8769–2247–4.

Review: G. Moretti, *Nuovo Rivista Musicale Italiana*, 26 (Jul/Dec 1992), 3/4: 599–600.

— [repr.] Pordenone: Studio tesi, 1995. xxiv, 299 p. (*La piacere della musica*)

[1548] **POZNANSKY, A.** *Tchaikovsky: The quest for the inner man.* New York: Schirmer Books; Toronto: Maxwell Macmillan Canada; New York: Maxwell Macmillan International [1991]. xix, 679 p, illus. ISBN: 0–02–871885–2.

Reviews: T. J. McGee, *Library Journal*, 116 (15 Oct 1991): 84 — *Bay Area Reporter*, 21 (27 Nov 1991), 58: 26–28 — *Washington Times* (1 Dec 1991) — *New York Times* (24 Dec 1991) — P. Griffiths, 'The outing of Peter Ilyich', *New York Times Book Reviews* (5 Jan 1992): 24 — S. Karlinsky, 'Man or myth?' (1992) [see *1671*] — *De Gay Krant* (8 Feb 1992), 196: 1–2 — M. Rubin, *Christian Science Monitor* (10 Mar 1992): 15 [Eastern ed.] — P. Gainsley, *Opera News*, 56 (14 Mar 1992): 45 — G. Muns, *Choice*, 29 (Jun 1992): 1556 — H. Zajaczkowski, *Musical Times*, 133 (Nov 1992): 574 — G. R. Seaman, *Notes* (Mar 1993): 1013–1016 — *American Record Guide*, 57 (1994), 3: 232 — M. H. Brown, *Journal of the American Musicological Society*, 47 (sum. 1994), 2: 359–364 — *Lingua Franca* (Jul/Aug 1994): 57–58 — R. Taruskin, 'Pathetic symphonist' (1995) [see *1679*].

— [rev. ed.] London: Lime Tree, 1993. xxii, 679 p, illus. ISBN: 0–4134–5721–4 (hbk), 0–4134–5731–1 (pbk).

Reviews: *Daily Mail* (28 Jan 1993) — *The Times* (30 Jan 1993) — *Sunday Times* (31 Jan 1993) — *The European* (4–7 Feb 1993) — *London Evening Standard* (18 Feb 1993) — *Sunday Telegraph* (14 Mar 1993) — *Classical Music Magazine*, 16 (1993), 5: 31 — *Daily Yomiuri* (27 Jun 1993) — G. Dwyer, 'Zavesa nad tainoi Chaikovskogo pripodnimaetsia', *Art-fonar´*, 7 (1993): 2–3 — *De Volkskrant* (16 Oct 1993).

[1549] **CASINI, C. & DELOGU, M.** *Čajkovskij: La vita, tutte le composizioni.* Milano: Rusconi, 1993. 527 p, illus. (*La Musica*). ISBN: 8–8182–1017–3.

Review: M. Girardi, *Rivista Italiana di Musicologica*, 30 (1995), 1: 301–304.

[1550] **MORITA, M.** *Shin Chaikofuskii kou.* Tokyo: NHK Shuppan, 1993, 368 p, illus. ISBN: 4–1408–0135–2.

Includes chronology ('Chaikofosukii Nendaijun denki'): 305–363 [see *92*].

[1551] **LISCHKÉ, A.** *Piotr Ilyitch Tchaïkovski.* [Paris]: Fayard [1993]. 1132 p, illus. (*Bibliothèque des Grands Musiciens*). ISBN: 2–213–03191–6.

Reviews: *Fanfare*, 17 (1994), 5: 380–383 — *Diapason-Harmonie* (Mar 1994), 402: 28 — M. Weiss, *L'Avant Scène Opéra* (May/Jun 1994): 143–144.

[1552] **POBEREZHNAIA, G.** *Petr Il´ich Chaikovskii.* Kiev, 1994. 356 p, illus. ISBN: 5–8238–0156–4.

[1553] **MORITA, M.** *Senritu no Majutusi, Chaikofusukii.* Tokyo: Ongaku-no-tomo-sha, 1994. 80 p. illus.

[1554] **HOLDEN, A.** *Tchaikovsky.* London: Bantam Press; Toronto: Viking, 1995. xxii, 489 p, illus. ISBN: 0–593–02468–0 (UK), 0–670–84623–6 (Canada).

Includes: 'List of Works and Recommended Recordings': 411–436.

Reviews: C. Milner & N. Farrell, 'Book reopens Tchaikovsky "gay suicide" row', *Sunday Telegraph* (3 Sep 1995) — H. Porter, *Daily Telegraph* (5 Sep 1995) — M. Bragg, 'Gay murder by committee', *The Times* (16 Sep

1995) — M. Shearer, 'A Russian tragedy', *Daily Telegraph* (16 Sep 1995) — H. Canning, *Sunday Times* (1 Oct 1995) — J. Keats, *The Observer* (8 Oct 1995) — *The Economist*, 337 (11 Nov 1995): 3.

— [repr.] *Tchaikovsky: A biography*. New York: Random House [1996]. xxii, 490 p, illus. ISBN: 0–6794–2006–1.

Reviews: A. Hirsch, *Booklist*, 92 (1 Mar 1996): 1116 — T. J. McGee, *Library Journal*, 121 (1 Mar 1996): 79— T. Libbey, 'Unheard melodies', *Washington Post* (31 Mar 1996) — O. Ponomarev, 'Chaikovskogo postigla sud´ba Sokrata?', *Smena* (7 May 1996): 6 — T. Libbey, *Magazine of Music & Sound*, 1 (Jul/Aug 1996), 6: 141 — S. Karlinsky, 'Tchaikovsky and unholy alliance' (fall 1996) [see *1682*] — J. Allison, 'Coming to terms with Tchaikovsky' (1997) [see *1683*].

— [new ed.] *Tchaikovsky*. London: Bantam Press; Toronto: Penguin Books Australia, 1997. xxii, 490 p, illus. ISBN: 0–593–04160–7 (UK), 0–14–017225–4 (Canada).

[*1555*]   **KOOLBERGEN, J.** *Tchaikovsky: 1840–1893*. London: Tiger Books International, 1995. 78 p, illus. ISBN: 1–8550–1787–3.

[*1556*]   **NICE, D.** *Tchaikovsky*. London: Pavilion Books; New York: Simon & Schuster [1995]. 192 p, illus. + 1 CD (*Compact Companions*). ISBN: 1–8579–3670–1 (UK), 0–6848–1357–2 (USA).

        Review: B. J. Dopp, *Library Journal*, 122 (15 Oct 1997): 63.

[*1557*]   **RICH, A.** *Pyotr Ilyich Tchaikovsky: Play by play*. With performances by the Montreal Symphony Orchestra, Charles Dutoit, conductor. San Francisco: HarperCollins, 1995. 155 p, illus. + 1 CD. ISBN: 0–0626–3544–1.

        A short biography, including a CD containing performances of the overture-fantasia *Romeo and Juliet* and the Symphony No. 5.

        Reviews: J. W. Freeman, *Opera News*, 60 (20 Jan 1996): 43 — L. Hanson, *American Record Guide*, 59 (Mar/Apr 1996), 2: 282–283.

[*1558*]   **NICE, D.** *Pyotr Ilyich Tchaikovsky: An essential guide to his life and works*. London: Pavilion Books, 1997. 107 p. (*Classic FM Lifetimes*). ISBN: 1–86205–043–0.

[*1559*]   **HOU, H.-C.** *Yung ch´ang che sheng ming ti ko: Ch´ai-k´o-fu-ssu-chi*. Ti 1 pan. Pei-ching shih: Hsin shih chieh ch´u pan she [1998]. 216 p.

        Text in Chinese, with the cover title in English: *Tchaikovsky*.

[*1560*]   **MUNDY, S.** *Tchaikovsky*. London: Omnibus Press, 1998. 160 p, illus. (*Illustrated Lives of the Great Composers*). ISBN 0–7119–6651–6.

        See also *783, 784, 2322*.

4.1.2. Articles

[*1561*]   'Pëtr Il´ich Chaikovskii'. In: *Nashi deiateli: Gallereia zamechatel´nykh liudei Rossii v portretakh i biografiiakh*. Tom 6. Sankt Peterburg: Bauman, 1879: 75–85.

[*1562*]   **RUBETS, A.** 'P. I. Chaikovskii'. In: A. Rubets, *Biograficheskii leksikon russkikh kompozitorov i muzykal´nykh deiatelei*. Sankt Peterburg: A. Bitner, 1879: 55.

        — 2nd ed. Sankt Peterburg: A. Bitner, 1886: 92–93.

[*1563*]   **POUGIN, A.** 'Tschaikowsky'. In: F.-J. Fétis, *Biographie universelle des musicienes et bibliographie générale de la musique*. Supplément et complément. Publiés sous la direction de M. Artur Pougin. Tom 2-me. Paris, 1880: 588–591.

        — [English tr. (abridged)] In: D. Brown, *Tchaikovsky remembered* (1993): 173 [see *377*].

[*1564*]   **IMBERT, H.** 'P. Tschaikowsky'. In: H. Imbert, *Profils de musiciens: P. Tschaikowsky, J. Brahms, E. Chabrier, Vincent D'Indy, G. Fauré, C. Saint-Saëns*. Avec une preface par Edouard Schure. Paris: Fischbacher, 1888: 3–24.

[1565]   [CHOP, M.] 'P. Tschaikowsky'. In: M. Charles [M. Chop], *Zeitgenössische Tondichter, Neue Folge: Studien und Skizzen*. Leipzig: Rossberg'schen Buchhandlung, 1890: 272–283.

[1566]   DANNREUTHER, E. 'Tschaikowsky'. In: G. A. Grove, *A dictionary of music and musicians (A. D. 1450–1889) by eminent writers, English and foreign*. With illus. and woodcuts. With appendix, ed. by J. A. Fuller Maitland, and index by Mrs. Edmond Wodehouse. Vol. 4. London: Macmillan [1890]: 183, illus.
         — [repr. (abridged)] In: D. Brown, *Tchaikovsky remembered* (1993): 174–175 [see *377*].

[1567]   HENDERSON, H. J. 'Peter Ilitsch Tschaikowsky'. In: *Famous composers and their works*. Ed. by John Knowles Paine, Theodore Thomas and Karl Klauser. Vol. 2. Boston: J. B. Millet, 1891: 803–810.

[1568]   'Pierre-Iljitsch Tschaikowsky', *Monthly Musical Record*, 22 (1892): 241–243.

[1569]   'Tschaikowsky, Peter (Ilyitch)'. In: *Cyclopedia of music and musicians*. Ed. by John Denison Champlin jr. Critical ed. William Foster Apthorp. Vol. 3. New York: C. Scribner's, 1893: 504.

[1570]   SOLOV'EV, N. 'Zhizn´ i deiatel´nost´ P. I. Chaikovskogo', *Novosti i birzhevaia gazeta* (26 Oct 1893) [see *2178*].

[1571]   STEVENSON, E. I. 'Peter Iltitsch Tschaikowsky', *Harper's Weekly*, 37 (18 Nov 1893): 1112; illus.

[1572]   [MORDVINOV, V. R.] 'Chaikovskii, Pëtr Il´ich'. In: *Pamiatnaia knizhka pravoviedov XX vypuska 1859 goda*. Sankt Peterburg, 1894: 177–185.
         — [rev. offprint] 'Pëtr Il´ich Chaikovskii'. In: *Pëtr Il´ich Chaikovskii: Biograficheskie o nem svedeniia i spisok muzykal´nykh sochinenii* (1894): 1–16 [see *1451*].

[1573]   LEGGE, R. 'Peter Tschaikowsky: A sketch', *Musical Opinion*, 17 (Jan 1894): 234.

[1574]   BASKIN, V. 'P. I. Chaikovskii: Segodnia 25 oktiabria', *Peterburgskaia gazeta* (25 Oct 1894).

[1575]   KOPTIAEV, A. P. 'Pëtr Il´ich Chaikovskii: Biograficheskii ocherk', *Russkaia muzykal´naia gazeta* (Jan 1897), 1: 67–86; (Mar 1897), 3: 381–394; (Apr 1897), 4: 604–620.

[1576]   BLACKBURN, V. 'Tschaikowsky'. In: V. Blackburn, *The fringe of an art: Appreciations in music*. London: Unicorn Press, 1898: 151–154, illus.

[1577]   MATHEWS, W. S. B. 'Peter Il´tsch Tschaikowsky'. In: W. S. B. Mathews, *The Masters and their Music: A series of illustrative programs, with biographical, esthetical, and critical annotations, designed as an introduction to music as literature, for the use of clubs, classes, and private study*. Philadelphia: T. Presser, 1898: 206–209.

[1578]   HUNEKER, J. 'A modern music lord'. In: *Mezzotints in Modern Music: Brahms, Tschaikowsky, Chopin, Richard Strauss, Liszt and Wagner*. New York: Scribner's, 1899: 81–140.
         — 2nd ed. New York: Scribner's, 1899: 81–140.
         — 3rd ed. New York: Scribner's, 1905: 81–140.
         — 4th ed. New York: Scribner's, 1912: 81–140.
         — 5th ed. New York: Scribner's, 1913: 81–140.
         — 6th ed. New York: Scribner's, 1920: 81–140.
         — [repr.] London: W. Reeves [n. d.]: 81–140.

[1579]   HERVEY, A. 'Peter Ilitsch Tschaikowsky: A biographical sketch', *Strand Musical Magazine* [new series], 1 (Mar 1899), 3: 35–40, illus.

[1580]   'Tchaikovsky, Peter Iljitch'. In: T. Baker, *A Biographical dictionary of musicians*. Comp. and ed. by Theodore Baker; with portraits from drawings in pen and ink by Alex Gribayedoff. New York: G. Schirmer, 1900: 576–577.
         — 2nd ed. New York: G. Schirmer, 1900: 576–577.

— 3rd ed. 'Tchaikovsky, Piotr [Peter] Ilytch'. In: Baker's biographical dictionary of musicians. Rev. and enlarged by Alfred Remy. New York: G. Schirmer, 1919: 937–939.

— 4th ed. Rev. by Gustave Rese, Gilbert Chase and Robert Geiger; with a suppl. by Nicolas Slonimsky. New York: G. Schirmer, 1940: 1038–1085.

— 5th ed. Completely rev. by Nicolas Slonimsky. New York: G. Schirmer, 1958: 1623–1627.

— [repr.] New York: G. Schirmer, 1971: 1623–1627.

— 6th ed. Completely rev. by Nicolas Slonimsky. New York: Schirmer Books, 1978: 1722–1725.

— 7th ed. Rev. by Nicolas Slonimsky. New York: Schirmer Books, 1978: 2282–2285.

— 8th ed. Rev. by Nicolas Slonimsky. New York: Schirmer Books, 1992: 1858–1860.

See also *1666*.

[*1581*] KEETON, A. E. 'Peter Ilyitch Tschaikovski: Life and work', *Contemporary Review*, 78 (Jul 1900): 74–82.

[*1582*] CHERNOV, E. 'Pëtr Il´ich Chaikovskii: Ocherk ego zhizni i muzykal´noi deiatel´nosti', *Novyi mir* (1901), 58: 186–191.

[*1583*] SCHMIDT, L. 'Peter Tschaikowsky'. In: K. Werckmeister, *Das neunzehnte Jahrhundert in Bildnissen*. Mit Beitragen von Paul Ankel [u. a.]. Hrsg. von Karl Werckmeister. Bd. 5. Berlin: Kunstverlag der Photographischen Gesellschaft, 1901: 857–858.

[*1584*] NEWMAN, E. 'The essential Tchaikovsky', *Contemporary Review*, 79 (Jun 1901): 887–898.

— [repr.] *Littell's Living Age*, 230 (3 Aug 1901): 288–298.

[*1585*] FINDEIZEN, N. F. 'Zhizn´ P. I. Chaikovskogo', *Russkaia muzykal´naia gazeta* (22/29 Jul 1901), 29/30: 717–722.

Partly a review of M. I. Chaikovskii, *Zhizn´ Petra Il´icha Chaikovskogo*, tom 1 (1900) [see *1453*].

[*1586*] STUNT, H. 'Tchaikovsky', *Musical Standard* [illus. series], 16 (20 Jul 1901): 37.

[*1587*] 'Tschaikowsky', *Monthly Musical Record*, 31 (Dec 1901): 269; 32 (Jan 1902): 13–14.

[*1588*] FINDEIZEN, N. F. 'Chaikovskii v 1877–1884 gg: Etiud´´', *Russkaia muzykal´naia gazeta* (30 Jun/6 Jul 1902), 26/27: 641–651; (14/21 Jul 1902), 28/29: 686–688; (28 Jul/4 Aug 1902), 30/31: 720–725; (25 Aug/1 Sep 1902), 34/35: 779–786; (29 Sep 1902), 39: 897–901; (6 Oct 1902), 40:, 935–938.

Consists largely of extracts from M. I. Chaikovskii, *Zhizn´ Petra Il´icha Chaikovskogo*, tom 2 (1901) [see *1453*], with additional material.

[*1589*] FINDEIZEN, N. F. 'Chaikovskii v 1885–1893 gg', *Russkaia muzykal´naia gazeta* (17 Nov 1902): 1121–1125.

Consists largely of extracts from M. I. Chaikovskii, *Zhizn´ Petra Il´icha Chaikovskogo*, tom 3 (1902) [see *1453*].

[*1590*] SOLOV´EV, N. F. 'Chaikovskii, (Pëtr Il´ich)'. In: F. A. Brokgauz. & I. A. Efron, *Entsiklopedicheskii slovar´*. Tom 38. Sankt Peterburg, 1903: 373–375.

[*1591*] 'Chaikovskii'. In: *Biografii kompozitorov s IV–XX vekov*. Inostrannyi i russkii otdel pod red. A. Il´inskogo. Pol´skii otdel pod red. G. Pakhul´skogo. Moskva: K. A. Durnovo, 1904: 544–551.

[*1592*] TURCHINOVICH, A. A. 'Pamiati P. I. Chaikovskogo: Rech´´', *Zapadnyi vestnik*, 91 (1904): 113–114.

— [offprint] *Pamiati P. I. Chaikovskogo: Rech´*. Vil´na, 1904. 21 p.

[*1593*] LAW, F. S. 'Tchaikovsky (1840–1893)', *Musical Standard* [illus. series], 21 (26 Mar 1904): 202–203.

— [repr] *Musician*, 9 (1904), 3: 87–89.

[*1594*]   ZABEL, E. 'P. I. Tschaikowsky', *Deutsche Rundschau*, 124 (1905): 287–288.

[*1595*]   STREATFEILD, R. A. 'Tchaikovsky'. In: R. A. Streatfeild, *Modern music and musicians*. New York; Edinburgh: Macmillan, 1906: 312–325, illus.
— [French tr.] 'Peter Ilitch Tschaïkowski' (tr. de l'anglais par Louis Pennequin), *Revue de temps présent* [année 4], 2 (1910), 3: 43–59.
— [French tr. (offprint)]. Paris, 1910. 15 p.

[*1596*]   VAL´TER, V. G. 'P. I. Chaikovskii (1840–1893 gg)'. In: V. G. Val´ter, *Russkie kompozitory v biograficheskikh ocherkakh*. Vyp 1: *M. I. Glinka, A. G. Rubinshtein i P. I. Chaikovskii*. Moskva: P. Iurgenson, 1907: 85–130.

[*1597*]   'Tschaikowsky, Peter Iljitch (1840–1893)'. In: *Musical biographies*. Comp. by Janet M. Green; W. L. Hubbard, ed. New York: Irving Squire, 1908: 410–412. (*The American History and Encyclopedia of Music*; 2).

[*1598*]   NEWMARCH, R. H. 'Tchaikovsky'. In: *Grove's dictionary of music and musicians*. Ed. by J. A. Fuller Maitland. Vol. 5. London; New York: Macmillan & Co. Ltd. [1910]: 33–49.

[*1599*]   HADDEN, J. C. 'Stars among the planets'. In: J. C. Hadden, *Master musicians: A book for players, singers and listeners*. New York: Holt, 1911: 61–73, illus.
— [repr.] London: T. N. Foulis, 1916: 61–73, illus.

[*1600*]   LAWRENCE, F. 'Peter Ilich Tchaikovsky', *London Quarterly Review*, 116 (Oct 1911): 289–301.

[*1601*]   NARODNY, I. 'Tschaikovsky's stormy inner life', *Musical America*, 16 (1912), 1: 29 illus.

[*1602*]   'Pierre Ilitch Tchaikowsky'. In: *Encyclopædie de la musique et dictionnaire du Conservatoire*. Réd. A. Lavignac et L. de La Laurencie. Vol. 1, part 5. Paris: C. Delagrave [c.1913]: 2560–2565.

[*1603*]   SHARP, R. F. 'Tchaikovsky'. In: R. F. Sharp, *Makers of music: Biographical sketches of great composers, with a chronological summary of their works, portraits, facsimiles of their autograph manuscripts, and a general genealogical table*. 4th ed., rev. and enlarged. New York: Scribner's, 1913: 238–245, illus.

[*1604*]   'Biograficheskie svedeniia o P. I. Chaikovskom', *Teatr i zhizn´* (25 Oct 1913): 4–5.

[*1605*]   MASON, D. G. 'Tchaikovsky's life and work', *New Music Review*, 14 (Jul 1915): 260–264.

[*1606*]   DUNCAN, E. 'Tchaikovsky: A biographical sketch', *Musical Standard* [new series], 8 (16 Sep 1916): 204–205.

[*1607*]   'Tchaikovsky'. In: *The Great Composers: Critical and Biographical Sketches*. Ed. by Louis C. Elson. Part 2. New York: Univ. Society, 1918: 343–346 (*Modern music and musicians for vocalists*; 4).

[*1608*]   'Tschaikowsky', *Musical Herald* (Jan 1919), 850: 7–9.

[*1609*]   KRUG, W. 'Tschaikowsky'. In: *Die neue Musik*. Erlenbach bei Zürich, 1920: 33–35.

[*1610*]   SCHMIDT, L. 'P. Tschaikowsky'. In: *Meister der Tonkunst im neunzehnten Jahrhundert*. Berlin: Hesse [1922]: 223–225.

[*1611*]   SCHOLES, P. A. 'Tchaikovsky (1840–1893)', *School Music Review*, 31 (Dec 1922): 133–135.

[*1612*]   IGNATOVICH, V. 'P. I. Chaikovskii', *Muzykal´naia nov´* (1923), 3: 20.

[*1613*]   'Fragments of biogaphy: 7. Tschaikovsky', *Opera*, 1 (Oct 1923): 10.

[*1614*]   SABANEEV, L. L. 'Chaikovskii', *Izvestiia* (Nov 1923).

[*1615*] KOCHETOV, N. 'P. I. Chaikovskii'. In: N. Kochetov, *Ocherk istorii muzyki*. Moskva: Gosizdat-Muzsektor, 1924: 138.

[*1616*] SABANEEV, L. L. 'Chaikovskii'. In: *Istoriia russkoi muzyki v issledovaniiakh i materialakh*. Pod red. prof. K. A. Kuznetsova. Tom 1. Moskva: Gosizdat-Muzsektor, 1924: 51–63.

[*1617*] SABANEEV, L. L. 'Chaikovskii'. In: L. L. Sabaneev, *Istoriia russkoi muzyki*. Moskva: Rabochii prosveshcheniia, 1924: 51–55.
— [English tr.] 'Tschaikowsky' (tr. by S. W. Pring), *Musical Times*, 70 (Jan 1929): 20–23.
— [English tr. (repr.)] 'Tchaikovsky (born May 7, 1840)', *Musical Times*, 81 (May 1940): 201–202.
— [German tr.] 'Tschaikowsky'. In: *Geschichte der Russischen Musik*. Für deutsche Leser bearbeitet von O. von Reisemann. Leipzig: Breitkopf u. Härtel, 1926: 107–116.
— [German tr.] 'P. Tschaikowsky', *Blätter der Staatsoper* (1929), No. 21.

[*1618*] PEKELIS, M. S. 'P. I. Chaikovskii', *Muzykal´naia nov´* (1924), 11: 35–37.

[*1619*] RIESEMANN, O. von. 'Ein neuer Beitrag zur Biographie Tschaikowsky's', *Die Musik*, 17 (1924), 1: 26.

[*1620*] DOLE, N. H. 'Pyotr Ilyitch Tchaikovsky (1840–1893)'. In: *Famous Composers*. 2nd, rev. ed. New York: Thomas Y. Crowell Co, 1925: 602–626.
— 3rd ed. New York: Thomas Y. Crowell Co., 1929: 602–626
— 4th ed. New York: Thomas Y. Crowell Co., 1929: 602–626

[*1621*] SABANEEV, L. 'Chaikovskii, Pëtr Il´ich'. In: *Entsiklopedicheskii slovar´ bibliograficheskogo obshchestva 'Granat'*. 7-e izd. Tom 45. Moskva: Granat [1926]: 546–553.

[*1622*] SCHMITZ, M. M. 'Little life stories of great masters', *Etude*, 45 (Jan 1927): 10.

[*1623*] LIMBERT, K. E. 'Tchaikovsky (1840–1893)', *Parents' Review*, 40 (Apr 1929): 243–254.
— [repr.] *Parents' Review*, 55 (Apr 1944): 92–100.

[*1624*] DALEN, H. van. 'Tschaikowsky'. In: *Russische muziek en componisten: Belangrijk aangevulde tweeede druk*. s'Gravenhage: Kruseman [1930]: 76–89 (*Beroemde musici*; 13).

[*1625*] MANN, J. 'Tchaikovsky'. In: *The men behind the music*. Ed. by C. H. Warren. London: G. Routledge & Sons, 1931: 117–127.
Offprint of an article from the *Radio Times*.
— [repr.] Port Washington, N. Y.: Kennikat Press, 1970: 117–127.

[*1626*] LUNACHARSKII, A. V. 'Chaikovskii, Pëtr Il´ich'. In: *Malaia sovetskaia entsiklopediia*. Tom 9. Moskva: Sovetskaia entsiklopediia, 1932: 722.

[*1627*] A[SAF´EV], B. V. 'Chaikovskii, Pëtr Il´ich'. In: *Bol´shaia sovetskaia entsiklopediia*. Tom 61. Moskva: Sovetskaia entsiklopediia, 1934: 40–43.

[*1628*] ABRAHAM, G. E. H. 'Tchaikovsky'. In: M. D. Calvocoressi & G. E. H. Abraham, *Masters of Russian Music*. London: Duckworth, 1936: 249–334.
See also *1490*.
— [repr.] In: M. D. Calvocoressi & G. E. H. Abraham, *Masters of Russian Music*. New York: A. A. Knopf, 1946: 249–334
— [repr.] In: M. D. Calvocoressi & G. E. H. Abraham, *Masters of Russian Music*. New York: Johnson Reprint Corp, 1971: 249–334.

[*1629*] EWEN, D. 'Peter Ilitch Tschaikovsky, 1840–1893'. In: D. Ewen, *Composers of yesterday: A biographical and critical guide to the most important composers of the past*. Comp. and ed. by David Ewen. New York: H. W. Wilson Company, 1937: 433–438.

[1630]   SPAETH, S. 'The Troubles of Tschaikowsky'. In: S. Spaeth, *Stories behind the world's great music*. New York; London: Whittlesey House, McGraw-Hill Book Co., 1937: 228–248, illus.

[1631]   'Tchaikovsky: A biographical sketch', *Etude*, 55 (Nov 1937): 750.

[1632]   'Tchaikovsky, Peter'. In: *The Oxford companion to music*. Self-indexed and with a pronouncing glossary by Percy A. Scholes. London; New York: Oxford Univ. Press, 1938: 921–922.
— 2nd ed. London; New York: Oxford Univ. Press, 1940: 921–922.
— 3rd ed. Rev. and with an appendix. London; New York: Oxford Univ. Press, 1941: 921–922.
— 9th ed. Completely rev. and reset with many additions to text and illus. London; New York: Oxford Univ. Press, 1955: 1013–1014.
— 10th ed. Rev. and reset. Ed. by John Owen Ward. London; New York: Oxford Univ. Press, 1970: 1010.

[1633]   'Tschaikovsky, Peter Ilich'. In: *The Macmillan encyclopedia of music and musicians, in 1 volume*. Comp. and ed. by Albert E. Wier. New York: Macmillan Co., 1938: 1890–1892.

[1634]   SLONIMSKY, N. 'Further light on Tchaikovsky', *Musical Quarterly*, 24 (Apr 1938): 139–146; illus.
— [repr.] *Musical Quarterly*, 75 (win. 1991), 4: 70–73.

[1635]   BROCKWAY, W. 'Peter Ilich Tchaikovsky'. In: W. Brockway & H. Weinstock, *Men of music: Their lives, times, and achievements*. New York: Simon & Schuster [1939]: 466–492, illus.
— [rev. repr.] Rev. and enlarged ed. New York: Simon & Schuster [1958]: 502–528, illus.

[1636]   GUSMAN, B. 'Na perelome: Etiud k biografii P. I. Chaikovskogo', *Sovetskaia muzyka* (1939), 1: 60–71.

[1637]   MASON, D. G. 'Peter Ilich Tchaikovsky'. In: *The international cyclopedia of music and musicians*. Ed. by Oscar Thompson. New York: Dodd, Mead & Co, 1939: 1865–1871.
— 2nd ed. New York: Dodd, Mead & Co, 1943: 1865–1871.
— 3rd ed. New York: Dodd, Mead & Co, 1944: 1865–1871.
— 4th ed. New York: Dodd, Mead & Co, 1946: 1865–1871.
— 5th ed. New York: Dodd, Mead & Co, 1949: 1865–1871.
— 6th ed. New York: Dodd, Mead & Co, 1952: 1865–1871.
— 7th ed. Rev. and ed. by Nicolas Slonimsky. New York: Dodd, Mead & Co, 1956: 1865–1871.
— 8th ed. Rev. and ed. by Nicolas Slonimsky. New York: Dodd, Mead & Co, 1958: 1865–1871.
— 9th ed. Ed. by Robert Sabin. New York: Dodd, Mead & Co, 1964: 2188–2194.
— 10th ed. Ed. by Bruce Bohle. New York: Dodd, Mead & Co, 1975: 2245–2251.
— 11th ed. Ed. by Bruce Bohle. New York: Dodd, Mead & Co, 1985: 2245–2251.

[1638]   GROMAN, A. 'Chaikovskii v Moskve 1865–1877: Etiud k biografii P. I. Chaikovskogo', *Sovetskaia muzyka* (May 1939), 5: 48–65, illus.

[1639]   BARNETT, N. 'Neglect of Tschaikowsky's genius', *Musician*, 44 (Dec 1939): 210.

[1640]   'Tchaikovsky'. In: H. Thomas & D. L. Thomas, *Living biographies of great composers*. Garden City, N. Y.: Nelson Doubleday, 1940: 305–325.

[1641]   DOWNES, O. 'Pathetique: The story of a genius', *New York Times* (5 May 1940), illus.

[1642]   'Biografiia Chaikovskogo', *Internatsional'naia literatura* (1941), 5: 249.
Concerning a dramatised account of Chaikovskii's life written by Alfred Lake Literstern, broadcast on BBC radio,

[1643]   BLOM, E. W. 'Tchaikovsky'. In: E. W. Blom, *Some great composers*. London; New York: Oxford Univ. Press, 1945: 107–113.
— [repr.] London: Oxford Univ. Press, 1961: 107–113.

[*1644*] LOCKSPEISER, E. 'Tchaikovsky the man'. In: *Tchaikovsky: A symposium* (1945): 9–23 [see *586*].

[*1645*] BROOK, D. 'Tchaikovsky'. In: D. Brook, *Six Great Russian Composers: Glinka, Borodin, Mussorgsky, Tchaikovsky, Rimsky-Korsakov, Scriabin; their lives and works*. London: Rockliff, 1946: 73–135, music, illus.

[*1646*] OTTELIN, O. 'Tchaikovski'. In: O. Ottelin, *Musiken ett livsvarde*. [Stockholm] Tidningen Studiecameraten [1946]: 6–18.

[*1647*] KELDYSH, Iu. V. 'Tchaikovsky: The man and his outlook'. In: *Russian symphony: Thoughts about Tchaikovsky* (1947): 16–39 [see *587*].

[*1648*] SERAUKY, W. 'P. I. Tschaikowski', *Musik und Gesellshaft* (Jun 1952): 187–189, music, illus.

[*1649*] KHUBOV, G. N. 'Velichie i tragizm Chaikovskogo'. In: G. N. Khubov, *O muzyke i muzykantakh: Ocherki i stat´i*. Moskva, 1959: 147–169 (*Iz russkoi klassiki*).

[*1650*] EWEN, D. 'Tchaikovsky'. In: *The world of great composers*. Ed. by David Ewen. Englewood Cliffs, N. J.: Prentice, 1962: 373–390.

[*1651*] KHOPROVA, T. A. & VASILENKO, S. Ia. 'P. I. Chaikovskii'. In: T. A. Khoprova & S. Ia. Vasilenko, *Ocherki po istorii muzyki XIX veka*. Leningrad, 1964: 248–307.

[*1652*] LLOYD-JONES, D. 'Tschaikowsky'. In: *Die Musik in Geschichte und Gegenwart*. Bd. 13. Hrsg. von F. Blume. Kassel, 1966: 858–868.

[*1653*] POSELL, E. Z. 'Tchaikovsky'. In: *Russian composers*. Boston: Houghton Mifflin Co., 1967: 12–31, illus.

[*1654*] ROSSIKHINA, V. P. 'P. I. Chaikovskii'. In: V. P. Rossikhina, *Rasskazy o russkikh kompozitorakh*. Moskva, 1971: 155–207.

[*1655*] ORLOVA, E. M. 'P. I. Chaikovskii'. In: *Russkaia muzykal´naia literatura*. Obshchaia red. E. L. Frid. Vyp 3. Izd. 4. Leningrad: Muzyka, 1976: 178–325.
— Izd. 6. Leningrad: Muzyka, 1983: 191–341.

[*1656*] BROWN, D. 'Tchaikovsky'. In: *The New Grove dictionary of music and musicians*, Ed. by Stanley Sadie. Vol. 18. London: Macmillan, 1980: 606–636, music, illus.
Includes: 'Works': 629–634 — 'Bibliography': 634–636.
— [rev. repr.] In: *The new grove: Russian masters I. Glinka, Borodin, Balakirev, Mussorgsky, Tchaikovsky*. By David Brown, Gerald Abraham and David Lloyd-Jones. London: Macmillan; New York: W. W. Norton & Co., 1986: 145–252, music, illus. ISBN: 0-3334-0236-7 (UK pbk), 0-3334-0235-9 (UK hbk), 0-3930-2282-X (USA hbk), 0-3933-0102-8 (USA pbk).
Includes revised 'Work-list': 234–243 — 'Bibliography': 244–250.
Reviews: L. Salter, *Musical Times*, 127 (Aug 1986): 441–442 — *Opera News*, 51 (3 Jan 1987): 45.
— [German tr.] 'Tschaikowsky'. In: *Russische Meister des 19. Jahrhunderts. Glinka, Borodin, Balakirev, Mussorgsky, Tschaikowsky*. Von David Brown, Gerald Abraham und David Lloyd-Jones. Stuttgart; Weimar: Metzler, 1995. 300 p, illus.

[*1657*] 'Tchaikovsky, Peter Ilich'. In: *Britannica book of music*. Ed. by Benjamin Hadley; consulting eds. Michael Steinberg, George Gelles. Garden City, N. Y.: Nelson Doubleday; Britannica Books, 1980: 800–803. (*Britannica books*).

[*1658*] BEAUJEAN, A. 'Der Komponist als Selbst porträtist', *Hifi-Stereophonie*, 20 (Jul 1981): 690.

[*1659*] BOBETH, M. 'Tschaikowsky, Piotr (Peter) Iljitch'. In: *Das Grosse Lexikon der Musik in acht Banden*. Hrsg. von Marc Honegger und Gunther Massenkeil. Bd. 8. Freiburg im Breisgau; Basel [u. a.]: Herder, 1982: 186–188.
See also *1681*.

[*1660*]   **KELDYSH, Iu. V. 'Chaikovskii'**. In: *Sovetskaia muzykal´naia entsiklopediia*. Tom 6. Moskva, 1982: 172–189.

Includes: I. S. Poliakova, 'Osnovnye daty zhizni i deiatel´nosti': 183–185 [see *90*] — I. S. Poliakova, 'Bibliografiia': 185–189 [see *43*].

[*1661*]   **ANSHAKOV, B. Ia. & VAIDMAN, P. E. 'Materialy k biografii P. I. Chaikovskogo, 1840–1852 gg.'**. In: *P. I. Chaikovskii: Gody detstva* (1983): 3–12 [see *1712*].

[*1662*]   **BAUMGARTNER, A. 'Pjotr Tschaikowski (1840–93)'**. In: A. Baumgartner, *Musik der Romantik*. Salzburg: Kiesel Verlag, 1983: 599–607. (*Der grosse Musik Fuhrer* ; 4). ISBN 3-7023-4004-1.

[*1663*]   **NORRIS, G. 'Tchaikovsky, Piotr (Ilyich)'**. In: D. Arnold, *The new Oxford companion to music*. Oxford; New York: Oxford Univ. Press, 1983: 1805–1808.

[*1664*]   **BROWN, D. 'Cajkovskij, Petr Il´ic'** In: *Dizionario enciclopedico universale della musica e dei musicisti: Le biografie*. Diretto da Alberto Basso. Tomo 2. Torino: UTET, 1985: 47–67. ISBN 8-8020-3931-3.

[*1665*]   **SMITH, J. S. & CARLSON, B. 'Tchaikovsky'**. In: *The gift of music: Great composers and their influences*. New York: Crossway Books, 1987: 139–144. ISBN: 0-8910-7438-4 (pbk).

[*1666*]   **'Tchaikovsky, Piotr Iyich'**. In: N. Slonimsky, *The concise Baker's biographical dictionary of musicians*. New York: Schirmer Books, 1988: 1246–1249.

Abridged version of the entry in *Bakers Biographical Dictionary*, 7th ed. [see *1580*].

— [new ed.] *The concise edition of Baker's biographical dictionary of musicians*. New York: Schirmer Books, 1994: 1577–1579.

Abridged version of the entry in *Bakers Biographical Dictionary*, 8th ed. [see *1580*].

[*1667*]   **MEYER, H. 'Händel, Schumann, Tschaikowsky: Zum Thema Biographie'**, *Musik und Bildung*, 21 (Jan 1989): 16–22, music, illus.

[*1668*]   **HARRIS, D. 'A Russian musician: Tchaikovsky as a profound nationalist'**, *Opera News*, 53 (18 Mar 1989): 30–32, illus.

[*1669*]   **KELDYSH, Iu. V. 'P. I. Chaikovskii'**. In: *Istoriia russkoi muzyki v desiati tomakh*. Tom 8. Moskva: Muzyka [1990]: 89–245.

[*1670*]   **TSARËVA, E. M. 'Chaikovskii, Pëtr Il´ich'**. In: *Bol´shoi entsiklopedicheskii slovar´ "Muzyka"*. Glavnyi red. G. V. Keldysh. Moskva: Bol´shaia Rossiiskaia entsiklopediia, 1990: 618–619

— [repr.] Moskva, 1998: 618–619.

[*1671*]   **KARLINSKY, S. 'Man or myth?: The retrieval of the true Tchaikovsky'**, *Times Literary Suppl.* (17 Jan 1992): 20–21.

Includes reviews of D. Brown, *Tchaikovsky: A biographical and critical study* (1978–91) [see *1534*] and A. Poznansky, *Tchaikovsky: The quest for the inner man* (1991) [see *1548*].

Reviews: D. Brown, 'Assessing Tchaikovsky', *Times Literary Suppl.* (7 Feb 1992): 13.

[*1672*]   **MYREBERG, A. 'Dramatiskt liv slutade i mystisk död'**, *Populär historia* (1993), 5: 14–19.

[*1673*]   **WIGODER, G. 'Tchaikovsky'**. In: G. Wigoder, *They made history: A biographical dictionary*. New York: Simon & Schuster, 1993: 632–633, illus. ISBN 0-1391-5257-1.

[*1674*]   **ZOLOTOV, A. 'Smert´ i zhizn´ geniia'** (Nov 1993), 43: 13.

[*1675*]   **NAGIBIN, Iu. 'Zagadki Chaikovskogo'**, *Rossiia* (10/16 Nov 1993): 12.

[*1676*]   **CRAFT, R. 'Love in a cold climate'**, *New York Review of Books*, 40 (18 Nov 1993): 37–41.

Includes reviews of *To my best friend* (1993) [see *286*] and D. Brown, *Tchaikovsky: A biogaphical and critical study* (1978–91) [see *1534*].

— [repr.] In: R. Craft, *The moment of existence: Music, literature and the arts, 1990–1995*. Nashville, Tenn.: Vanderbilt Univ. Press, 1996: 196–298. ISBN: 0–8265–1276–3.

[*1677*]   STANLEY, J. 'Tchaikovsky, Peter Ilich, 1840–1893'. In: *Classical music: An introduction to classical music through the great composers and their masterworks*. Foreword by Sir Georg Solti. New York: Reader's Digest Assn., 1994: 156–157, illus. ISBN: 0–8957–7606–5.

[*1678*]   STASOV, V. V. 'Peter ljitsch Tschaikowsky: Ein Fazit'. In: *Tschaikowsky aus der Nähe* (1994): 84–91 [see *379*].

[*1679*]   TARUSKIN, R. **'Pathetic symphonist: Chaikovsky, Russia, sexuality and the study of music'**, *New Republic*, 212 (6 Feb 1995), 6: 26–40, illus.

The perception of Chaikovskii's personality in the West. Includes reviews of D. Brown, *Tchaikovsky: A biographical and critical study* (1978–91) [see *1534*] and A. Poznansky, *Tchaikovsky: The quest for the inner man* (1991) [see *1548*].

[*1680*]   POZNANSKY, A. **'Tchaikovsky: The man behind the myth'**, *Musical Times*, 136 (Apr 1995), 4: 175–182.

— [Japanese tr.] 'Chaikofusukii: Sinwa ni Tutumareta Otoko', *The Ongaku Geijutsu* (Mar 1994): 51–55; (Apr 1994): 72–77.

[*1681*]   BOBETH, M. **'Tschaikowsky, Piotr (Peter) Iljtch'**. In: *Das Neue Lexikon der Musik, in vier Banden*. Neuausg., red. Bearb. Ralf Noltensmeier (Text), Gabriela Rothmund-Gaul (Abbildungen). Bd. 4. Stuttgart: Metzler, [1996]: 560–563. (*Metzler Musik*). ISBN 3–4760–1338–3.

See also *1659*.

[*1682*]   KARLINSKY, S. **'Tchaikovsky and unholy alliance'**, *Harvard Gay & Lesbian Review* (fall 1996): 31–33.

Includes a review of A. Holden, *Tchaikovsky* (1995) [see *1554*].

[*1683*]   ALLISON, J. **'Coming to terms with Tchaikovsky'**, *Opera*, 48 (1997), 4: 417–420.

Includes reviews of D. Brown, *Tchaikovsky: A biographical and critical study* (1978–91) [see *1534*] — A. Holden, *Tchaikovsky* (1995) [see *1554*] — A. Poznansky, *Tchaikovsky's last days: A documentary study* (1997) [see *2270*].

Review: J. Budden, 'Getting it straight', *Opera*, 48 (Jun 1997): 640.

[*1684*]   SCHONBERG, H. C. **'Tchaikovsky, Peter Ilich'**. In: *The lives of the great composers*. 3rd ed. New York: W. W. Norton, 1997. ISBN 0–3930–3857–2.

[*1685*]   TAMBOVSKAIA, N. **'Neskol´ko vzgliadov na sud´bu P. I. Chaikovskogo'**. In: *P. I. Chaikovskii: Issledovaniia i materialy* (1997): 20–40 [see *597*].

[*1686*]   TARUSKIN, R. **'Chaikovskii and the human'**. In: *Defining Russia musically: Historical and hermeneuetical essays*. Princeton: Princeton Univ. Press, 1997: 239–307. ISBN: 0–691–01156–7.

— [repr.] 'Tchaikovsky: A new view. A centennial essay'. In: *Tchaikovsky and his contemporaries* (1999): 17–60 [see *602*].

[*1687*]   POZNANSKY, A. **'Tchaikovsky: A life reconsidered'**. In: *Tchaikovsky and his world* (1998): 3–54 [see *601*].

[*1688*]   'Tchaikovsky, Peter Ilyich'. In: *Encyclopedia of world biography*, vol. 15. Detroit: Gale Research, 1998: 350–352.

[*1689*]   VAIDMAN, P. E. **'"Hätte mich das Schicksal nicht nach Moskau gestoßen": Beitrag zu einer neuen Čajkovskij-Biographie'**. In: *Čajkovskijs Homosexualität und sein Tod: Legenden und Wirklichkeit* (1998): 557–569 [see *600*].

[*1690*]   CRANKSHAW, G. **'TV & video review'**, *Musical Opinion*, 121 (sum. 1998): 296.

In connection with a BBC TV biographical documentary on Chaikovskii in the *Great Composers* series.

[*1691*]   VAIDMAN, P. E. "Chaikovskii-nashe vse", *Kul´tura* (20–26 Aug 1998): 13.

[*1692*]   'Biographical issues in Tchaikovsky scholarship'. In: *Tchaikovsky and his contemporaries* (1999): 263–273 [see *602*].

          Round-table discussion, moderated by John Marcus.

[*1693*]   POZNANSKY, A. 'The Tchaikovsky myths: A critical reasessment'. In: *Tchaikovsky and his contemporaries* (1999): 75–91 [see *602*].

[*1694*]   MORITA, M. 'Sakkyokuka Chaikofusukii no Nayami to sono Jidaisei', *Ritsumeikan Kokusai Kenkyu*, 11 (Mar 1999): 57–72.

[*1695*]   TEACHOUT, T. 'Tchaikovsky's passion', *Commentary*, 107 (Mar 1999), 3: 55–59.

          Includes a brief review section: 'Tchaikovsky on CD: A select discography': 58–59. See *75*.

[*1696*]   VAIDMAN, P. E. 'Biografiia kompozitora kak problema otechestvennoi muzykal´noi istoriografii (na primere biografii Chaikovskogo)'. In: *Keldyshevskii sbornik: Muzykal´no-istoricheskie chteniia pamiati Iu. V. Keldysha, 1997.* Moskva: Rossiiskii institut iskusstvoznania, 1999: 143–155.

[*1697*]   VAIDMAN, P. E. 'Biografiia khudozhnika: Zhizn´ i proizvedeniia (po materialam k biografii P. I. Chaikovskogo)'. In: *Peterburgskii muzykal´nyi arkhiv: Sbornik statei i materialov*, vyp. 3. Sankt-Peterburg: Sankt-Peterburgskaia konservatoriia, 1999: 173–180.

[*1698*]   KOHLHASE, T. 'Čajkovskij, P. I.'. In: *Die Musik in Geschichte und Gegenwart*. 2., neubearbeitete Ausgabe. Personenteil Band 3, Kassel: Bärenreiter & Metzler, 2000: 1596–1655.

          See also *139, 1139*.

4.2. CHILDHOOD AND YOUTH

[*1699*]   CHAIKOVSKII, M. I. 'Detstvo i otrochestvo P. I. Chaikovskogo', *Severnyi vestnik* (1896), 2: 147–166, 3: 176–198.

          Includes recollections by Fanny Dürbach, the Chaikovskii children's governess [see *433*].

          — [repr.] *Russkaia muzykal´naia gazeta* (Mar 1896), 3: 400–408; (Apr 1896), 4: 513–520; (May 1896), 5: 595–607.

[*1700*]   CHAIKOVSKII, M. I. 'Iunost´ i molodost´ P. I. Chaikovskogo', *Severnyi vestnik* (1897), 1: 60–71, 2: 86–96, 3: 117–125, 5: 210–219, 6: 155–166.

          — [repr.] *Russkaia muzykal´naia gazeta* (Mar 1897), 3: 537–544; (Apr 1897), 4: 695–702; (May/Jun 1897), 5/6: 887–898; (Sep 1897), 9: 1261–1262.

[*1701*]   CHAIKOVSKII, M. I. 'Detskie gody P. I. Chaikovskogo'. In: M. I. Chaikovskii, *Zhizn´ Petra Il´icha Chaikovskogo*, tom 1 (1900): 18–80 [see *1453*].

          Includes contributions from family members Lidiia Chaikovskaia and Anna Merkling, and the governess Fanny Dürbach.

          — [repr.] in *Vospominaniia o P. I. Chaikovskom*, 2-e izd. (1973): 11–29; 3-e izd. (1979): 11–30; 4-e izd. (1980): 10–26 [see *374*].

          — [English tr. (abridged)] In: D. Brown, *Tchaikovsky remembered* (1993): 4–10, 14 [see *377*].

          — [French tr.] 'Années d'enfance de Piotr Ilitch Tchaïkovski'. In: *Piotr Tchaïkovski: Écrits critiques, lettres, souvenirs de contemporains* (1985): 167–185 [see *375*].

[*1702*]   'Boyhood of Tchaikovsky', *Musician*, 14 (Jun 1909): 271.

[*1703*]   'K biografii Chaikovskogo', *Russkaia muzykal´naia gazeta* (29 May/5 Jun 1911), 22/23: 504.

          The orchestrina in the Chaikovskii family home. See also *1707*.

[1704]   PARKER, D. C. 'Tschaikovsky's personal side', *Opera Magazine*, 3 (1916), 11: 15, 36.

[1705]   GREW, E. M. 'The childhood of great musicians: 12. Tchaikovsky', *British Musician*, 10 (Sep 1934): 201–203; (Oct 1934): 228–230.

[1706]   COIT, L. E. *The child Tschaikowsky*. Philadelphia: T. Presser Co. [1948]. 20 p, illus.

[1707]   'Orkestrion P. I. Chaikovskogo', *Sovetskoe iskusstvo* (11 Sep 1948): 4.

The orchestrina in the Chaikovskii family home. See also *1703*.

[1708]   MARTINEZ, O. *Tchaikovsky: El sublime atorimentado*. La Habana, 1949. 32 p.

[1709]   'Detskie i iunosheskie gody Chaikovskogo (vyderzhki iz pisem i zapisei)'. In: *Vospominaniia o P. I. Chaikovskom* (1962): 389–413 [see *374*].

Compilation of extracts from letters and memoirs by various writers.

[1710]   IAROVOI, Iu. 'Stekliannyi mal´chik'. In: *Kalendar´-spravochnik Sverdlovskoi oblasti, 1970*. Sverdlovsk: Sverde-Ural´sk. kn. izdat., 1969: 81, illus.

The composer's childhood in Alapaevsk.

[1711]   IAROVOI, Iu. 'Virtovskii roial´´', *Ural* (1972), 6: 124–137.

The piano at the Alapaevsk music school, formerly used by Chaikovskii.

[1712]   *P. I. Chaikovskii: Gody detstva*. Materialy k biografii. Sost. B. Ia. Anshakov, P. E. Vaidman. Izhevsk: Udmurtiia, 1983. 144 p, illus.

Includes: B. Ia. Anshakov & P. E. Vaidman, 'Materialy k biografii P. I. Chaikovskogo, 1840–1852 gg.': 3–12 [see *1661*] — M. I. Chaikovskii, 'Zhizn´ Petra Il´icha Chaikovskogo (tom 1, glavy 1–3)': 13–90 [see *1453*] — 'Vospominaniia M-elle Fanny': 91–97 [see *433*] — 'Zapiski kadeta Gornogo kadetskogo korpusa I. P. Chaikovskogo': 98–101 [see *1895*] — 'Attestat A. M. Assiera': 102–106 [see *1874*] — N. D. Kashkin, 'P. I. Chaikovskii i ego zhizneopisanie': 107–111 [see *463*] — V. V. Iakovlev: 'Modest Il´ich Chaikovskii: Biograf Petra Il´icha Chaikovskogo': 112–130 [see *1902*].

[1713]   SHUMILOV, E. F. 'Plasticheskie iskusstva v Votkinske v I-i polovine 19 veka: K voprosu o khudozhestvennoi srede detstva P. I. Chaikovskogo'. In: *P. I. Chaikovskii i Ural* (1983): 10–15.

[1714]   GORODILINA, V. B. 'Domashnie predstavleniia v sem´e Chaikovskikh'. In: *Teatr v zhizni i tvorchestve P. I. Chaikovskogo* (1985): 12–15 [see *589*].

[1715]   PAVLUNINA, L. F. 'Teatral´nye interesy A. A. i I. P. Chaikovskikh'. In: *Teatr v zhizni i tvorchestve P. I. Chaikovskogo* (1985): 6–11 [see *589*].

[1716]   VAIDMAN, P. E. 'Nachalo: Novye materialy iz arkhiva P. I. Chaikovskogo', *Nashe nasledie* (1990), 2: 19–22.

[1717]   CHAIKOVSKII, M. I. '[Iz semeinykh vospominanii]' (publikatsiia P. E Vaidman). In: *P. I. Chaikovskii: Zabytoe i novoe* (1995): 18–63 [see *598*].

Modest Chaikovskii's account of the composer's childhood and youth (written in 1895).

See also *494, 1326, 1749, 4358, 5455, 5491*.

4.3. EDUCATION AND EMPLOYMENT

4.3.1. Law Student

IMPERIAL SCHOOL OF JURISPRUDENCE (1850–59)

[1718]   CHAIKOVSKII, M. I. [Chaikovskii v Uchilishche pravovedeniia]. In: M. I. Chaikovskii, *Zhizn´ Petra Il´icha Chaikovskogo*, tom 1 (1900): 96–104 [see *1453*].

Includes recollections by Vladimir Gerard [see *446*], Rudolph Kündinger [see *478*], Fëdor Maslov [see *495*] and Ivan Turchaninov [see *552*].

[*1719*]   **ARENIN, E.** 'Iskusstvo bylo ikh kumir: Na beregu Fontanki', *Smena* (13 Oct 1974): 4.

[*1720*]   **POZNANSKY, A.** 'Glavy iz knigi "Genii chuvstva: Zhizn´ i smert´ P. I. Chaikovskogo"'. In: *Portfel´: Literaturnyi sbornik*. Red.-sost. Aleksandr Sumerkin. Dana Point, Calif.: Ardis, 1996: 319–344.

[*1721*]   '**Vokrug Chaikovskogo**', *Muzykal´naia zhizn´* (1999), 5: 3.
            Records from Chaikovskii's studies at the Imperial School of Jurisprudence, and sketches of Chaikovskii's classmate Iakovlev.

            See also *446, 501*.

4.3.2. Civil Servant

MINISTRY OF JUSTICE (1859–63)

[*1722*]   **GERSHOVSKII, E.** 'Chaikovskii v Departamente Iustitsii', *Sovetskaia muzyka* (1959), 1: 83–88, illus.

            See also *521*.

4.3.3. Music Student

ST. PETERSBURG CONSERVATORY (1862–65)

[*1723*]   **STORER, H. J.** 'Tchaikovsky, the student', *Musician*, 22 (Oct 1917): 737.

[*1724*]   **WESTERBY, H.** 'Great masters as students', *Etude*, 48 (May 1930): 319–320, illus.

[*1725*]   **CHAIKOVSKII, M. I.** 'Aufzeichnung der Erinnerungen Laroches an Tschaikowskys Konservatoriumszeit'. In: G. A. Larosh, *Peter Tschaikowsky: Aufsätze und Erinnerungen* (1993): 240–265 [see *2406*].
            In connection with *485*.

            See also *442, 485, 525, 544, 1989*.

4.3.4. Music Teacher

MOSCOW CONSERVATORY (1866–79)

[*1726*]   [**Rech´ P. I. Chaikovskogo na otkrytii Moskovskoi konservatorii**]. In: *Otkrytie Moskovskoi konservatorii 1-go sentiabria 1866 goda*. Moskva, 1866: 9–10.
            A detailled report on Chaikovskii's speech at the opening of the Moscow Conservatory in 1866.

[*1727*]   '**Teatr i muzyka: Bolezn´ g. Chaikovskogo**', *Novosti* (30 Oct 1878).
            Concerning Chaikovskii's resignation from the Moscow Conservatory for health reasons.

[*1728*]   **BUDIAKOVSKII, A.** 'Chaikovskii v Konservatorii', *Muzykal´nye kadry* (7 May 1940) [see *873*].

[*1729*]   **LIVANOVA, T. N.** 'P. I. Chaikovskii i Moskovskaia konservatoriia', *Biulleten´ Doma -muzeia P. I. Chaikovskogo* (1946), 7: 3–7; 8: 4–24.

            See also *179, 381, 388, 445, 493, 496, 497, 1638, 1757*.

4.3.5. Conductor

[*1730*]   '**Muzykal´noe obozrenie**', *Nuvellist* (Apr 1887), 4: 1–2.

Chaikovskii conducting a concert of his own works at a St. Petersburg Philharmonic Society concert on 5 Mar 1887.

[*1731*]   **LAROSH, G. A. 'Muzykal´naia khronika**', *Moskovskie vedomosti* (31 Oct 1889).

Chaikovskii conducting his Violin Concerto and works by other composers at a concert in Moscow on 29 Oct 1889.

— [repr.] 'Chaikovskii-dirizher'. In: G. A. Larosh, *Izbrannye stat´i v piati vypuskakh*, vyp. 2 (1975): 136–137 [see *2376*].

[*1732*]   **IAKOVLEV, V. V. 'Chaikovskii-dirizher**', *Sovetskaia muzyka* (1940), 5/6: 130–132 [see *585*].

— [repr.] In: V. V. Iakovlev, *Izbrannye trudy o muzyke*, tom 1 (1964): 411–416 [see *2362*].

[*1733*]   **VASILENKO, S. 'Moi vospominaniia o dirizherakh**', *Sovetskaia muzyka* (1949), 1: 92–97.

Partly concerning Chaikovskii.

[*1734*]   '**Stranichka shkol´nika: Chaikovskii-dirizher**', *Muzykal´naia zhizn´* (1969), 20: 23.

[*1735*]   **KOPYTOVA, G. 'God Chaikovskogo: Po sledam "Francheski da Rimini"**', *Vechernii Leningrad* (23 Apr 1990): 3.

The story of Chaikovskii's conducting baton. See also *1736*.

[*1736*]   '**Detektivnaia istoriia s dirizherskoi palochkoi Chaikovskogo**', *Antrakt*, 11 (Jun 1990): 3.

[*1737*]   **SIDEL´NIKOV, L. *Chaikovskii-dirizher***. Kiev: Muzychna Ukraina, 1991. 224 p, illus.

Includes: 'Repertuar P. I. Chaikovskogo-dirizhera': 207–214.

[*1738*]   **KOHLHASE, T. 'Čajkovskij als Dirigent**', *Tschaikowsky-Gesellschaft Mitteilungen*, 7 (2000): 62–90.

Includes 'Selbstzeugnisse und Äußerungen von Zeitgenossen': 62–71 — 'Čajkovskij als Dirigent eigener und fremder Werke': 72–90.

See also *398, 407, 419, 421, 449, 488, 489, 497, 519, 523, 545.*

4.4. RESIDENCES AND TRAVEL

4.4.1. Russia & Eastern Europe

(see also 3.3)

[*1739*]   **GURVICH, S. 'P. I. Chaikovskii v Taganroge**', *Don* (1951), 1: 218–219.

The composer's visits to his brother Ippolit in 1886, 1888 and 1890.

[*1740*]   **MARTYNOV, B. 'Chaikovskii v Usovo**', *Literaturnyi Tambov*, 3 (1952): 179–182.

The composer's visits to the Begichev–Shilovskii estate in the 1870s. See also *1743, 1747.*

[*1741*]   **GROMOV, V. & FAINSHTEIN L. 'Zdes' zhil Chaikovskii**', *Smena* (22 Aug 1956).

Chaikovskii's visit to Nadino, near St. Petersburg.

[*1742*]   '**P. I. Chaikovskii vo Frolovskom, gde on zhil v 1888–1891 gg.**', *Muzykal´naia zhizn´* (1959), 12: 12–13, illus.

Chaikovskii's former home at Frolovskoe, near Klin.

[*1743*] EMEL´IANOVA, N. 'P. I. Chaikovskii v Usove'. Tambov, 1973. 14 p.

See also *1740, 1747*.

[*1744*] ILËSHIN, V. 'Russkii v polneishem smysle slova', *Ogonek* (1974), 6: 22–23.

[*1745*] LAGINA, N. 'Liricheskaia ispoved´ dushi: Epizod iz zhizni P. I. Chaikovskogo', *Baikal* (1976), 6: 133–140.

[*1746*] AGAFONOV, A. 'Dom v Pleshcheeve', *Muzykal´naia zhizn´* (3 Feb 1979): 18, illus.

The former country estate of Nadezhda von Meck at Pleshcheevo, where Chaikovskii stayed during the 1880s. See also *1750*.

[*1747*] ILËSHIN, V. 'Chaikovskii v Usove'. In: V. Ilëshin, *I golubye nebesa*. Moskva: Sovetskaia Rossiia, 1981: 39–61.

See also *1740, 1743*.

[*1748*] BOROVKOVA, S. N. 'P. I. Chaikovskii v Glebovo i Podushkino'. In: S. N. Borovkova, *Zapovednaia Zvenigorodskaia zemlia*. 3-e izd. Moskva: Moskovskii rabochii, 1982: 175–190.

[*1749*] *P. I. Chaikovskii i Ural*. Sost. B. Ia. Anshakov, P. E. Vaidman. Izhevsk: Udmurtiia, 1983. 160 p, music, illus. (*Trudy Gos. Dom-muzei P. I. Chaikovskogo v Votkinske*).

Contents: 'Ot sostavitelei': 3–4 — G. I. Oskolkov, 'Sotsial´no-ekonomicheskoe polozhenie gornozavodskogo naseleniia Kamsko-Votkinskogo zavoda v 30–40 gg. 19 veka': 5–10 — E. F. Shumilov, 'Plasticheskie iskusstva v Votkinske v I-i polovine 19 veka: K voprosu o khudozhestvennoi srede detstva P. I. Chaikovskogo': 10–15 [see *1713*] — P. E. Vaidman, 'P. I. Chaikovskii i M. I. Glinka': 15–22 [see *2091*] — N. O. Blinov, 'V. E. Blinov i ego sviazi s sem´ei Chaikovskikh': 23–26 — V. I. Proleeva, 'Doktor S. F. Tugemskii': 26–28 — A. Z. Vorotov, 'Inzhener V. I. Romanov': 29–32 — E. I. Gaevskii, 'I. P. Chaikovskii i master S. Penn': 33–39 [see *1896*] — V. B. Gorodilina, 'Posviashchaetsia Anastasii Petrovoi': 39–44 [see *5370*] — V. I. Adishchev, 'Khorovaia kul´tura Prikam´ia i tvorchestvo P. I. Chaikovskogo': 45–49 [see *5157*] — E. V. Maiburova, 'Iz istorii sozdaniia Sverdlovskogo muzykal´nogo uchilishcha im. P. I. Chaikovskogo': 49–53 — E. N. Voronchikhina, 'Muzyka P. I. Chaikovskogo v dorevoliutsionnoi Viatke': 53–56 — A. V. Shilov, 'Proizvedeniia P. I. Chaikovskogo na Permskoi opernoi stsene': 57-60 [see *2610*] — B. Ia. Anshakov, 'Votkinskoe muzykal´no-dramaticheskoe obshchestvo im. P. I. Chaikovskogo': 60–64 [see *934*] — A. G. Tatarintsev, 'Fol´klor russkogo naseleniia Udmurtii: K voprosu o sostoianii, o svoeobrazii i izuchenii': 65–75 — Z. I. Vlasova, 'O vliianii poeticheskikh traditsii skomorokhov v fol´klore Chaikovskogo raiona, Permskoi oblast': 75–85 — V. A. Al´binskii, 'O traditsiiakh drevnerusskogo skomorosheskogo gudoshnichestva v fol´klore i ob avtorskoi remarke v opere P. I. Chaikovskogo "Charodeika"': 86–91 [see *2769*] — V. V. Blazhes, 'Kollektivnye prozvishcha i etnicheskie epitety v zhanrakh russkogo fol´klora Urala': 91–99 — V. A. Lipatov, 'K probleme rgional´noi spetsifiki fol´klora: O variativnosti zagovorov': 99–108 — L. F. Pavlunina, 'Neskol´ko zametok o istoricheskikh interesakh i sotsial´no-politicheskikh vozzreniiakh P. I. Chaikovskogo': 109–117 [see *2153*] — G. G. Gusiatnikova, 'Iz istorii khudozhestvennogo oformleniia prizhiznennykh postanovok oper i baletov P. I. Chaikovskogo': 118–127 [see *2550*] — T. S. Ugriumova, 'O dramaturgii tsikla v kvartetakh P. I. Chaikovskogo': 127–137 [see *5291*] — I. A. Nemirovskaia, 'Nekotorye osobennosti traktovki pliasovykh i khorovodnykh istokov v muzykal´nom tematizme simfonii P. I. Chaikovskogo': 137–146 [see *4436*] — O. F. Prudnikova, 'Obraz P. I. Chaikovskogo v povestiiakh K. S. Paustovskogo i Iu. M. Nagibina': 146–154 [see *5485*].

[*1750*] LUNEV, M. 'Roial´, na kotorom igral P. I. Chaikovskii', *Muzykal´naia zhizn´* (1986), 14: 5, illus.

Concerning the piano which Chaikovskii used at Nadezhda von Meck's estate at Pleshcheevo. See also *1746*.

[*1751*] MIRONOV, M. 'U lebedinogo ozera', *Stroitel´naia gazeta* (30 Sep 1987).

Anatolii Chaikovskii's former home at Skabeevo, near Moscow, where the composer stayed in 1884. See also *1753*.

[*1752*] *Muzykal´nye prazdniki na rodine P. I. Chaikovskogo: K 150-letiiu so dnia rozhdeniia P. I. Chaikovskogo*. Sost. I. S. Zubkov. Izhevsk: Udmurtiia, 1990. 36 p.

[1753] KARNISHINA, L. 'Znamenityi gost´ Podol´skogo uezda', *Moskovskii zhurnal*, 4 (1995): 44–48.
Chaikovskii's visit to Skabeevo in 1884. See also *1751*.

See also *415, 573, 1271*.

MOSCOW

[1754] GUSMAN, B. 'Chaikovskii v Moskve', *Sovetskaia muzyka* (1939), 5: 48–65.

[1755] GROMAN, A. 'Chaikovskii o Moskve', *Vecherniaia Moskva* (29 Mar 1940).

[1756] ALTAEV, A. & IAMSHCHIKOVA, L. *Chaikovskii v Moskve*. Nauchnaia red. Iu. V. Keldysha. [Moskva]: Moskovskii rabochii, 1951. 307 p, music, illus.
Reviews: A. D´iakonov, 'Iskazhenie obraza velikogo kompozitora', *Sovetskoe iskusstvo* (26 Sep 1951): 3 — T. Livanova, 'Obraz khudozhnika: Romany i povesti o russkikh kompzitorakh', *Sovetskaia muzyka* (1952), 1: 98–102.

[1757] FEDOSIUK, Iu. A. *Chaikovskii v rodnom gorode*. Moskva: Moskovskii rabochii, 1960. 204 p, illus.
Chaikovskii's period of residence in Moscow, and his work for the Moscow Conservatory.

[1758] KARASIKOV, M. 'Gde zhil Chaikovskii?', *Muzykal´naia zhizn´* (Aug 1967), 15: 10, illus.
The house on Ulitsa Frunze (formerly Znamenka), Moscow, where the composer resided from 1869 to 1871.

[1759] IPATOVA, M. 'Kolybel´ Vtoroi simfonii', *Moskva* (1976), 2: 182–183.
The house in Moscow where Chaikovskii worked on his *Symphony No. 2* in 1872 (now Ulitsa Chaikovskogo, 46).

[1760] BLOK, V. 'Komu pomeshal Chaikovskii?', *Trud* (20 Nov 1991).
Should Ulitsa Chaikovskogo in Moscow revert to its old name of Novinskii bulvar?

See also *1320, 1321, 1638*.

SAINT PETERSBURG

[1761] 'Izvestiia otovsiudu', *Nuvellist* (Dec 1886), 8: 8.
A concert and dinner in honour of the composer, held by the St. Petersburg Chamber Music Society on 5 Nov 1886.

[1762] ERMICHEV, A. 'Zdes´ zhil P. I. Chaikovskii', *Vechernii Leningrad* (7 May 1960): 2, illus.
A tour of Chaikovskii's residences in the city.

[1763] KONISSKAIA, L. 'Stranitsa iz zhizni P. I. Chaikovskogo: Dom v Solianom pereulke', *Muzykal´naia zhizn´* (Jun 1966), 11: 8–9, illus.
Extract from the author's forthcoming book *Chaikovskii v Peterburge* [see *1764*], with notes by A. Dolzhanskii.

[1764] KONISSKAIA, L. M. *Chaikovskii v Peterburge*. Leningrad: Lenizdat, 1969. 320 p, illus.
Includes bibliography: 302–307 — List of Chaikovskii's residences in the city ('Ukazatel´ adresov'): 308–318. See also *1763*.
— Izd. 2-e, pererab. i dop. Leningrad: Lenizdat, 1974. 320 p, illus.
Review: O. Snegina, 'Novye izdania: Zdes´ zhil P. I. Chaikovskii', *Muzykal´naia zhizn´* (1974), 19: 24.

[1765] ITKIN, D. 'Na Maloi Morskoi', *Leningradskaia pravda* (29 Apr 1990).
The former apartment of Modest Chaikovskii at Malaia Morskaia 13, where the composer died in 1893. See also *1768*.

[1766] BOGRAD, G. 'Chaikovskii v Pavlovske', *Leningradskaia pravda* (13 May 1990).

[*1767*] 'P. I. Chaikovskii: Entsiklopediia russkoi dushi', *Muzykal´naia zhizn´* (Nov 1993), 21/22: 12–13, illus.

[*1768*] LEUSSKAIA, L. 'Poshla s molotka kvartira, gde zhil Chaikovskii, kakaia sleduiushchaia?', *Sankt-Peterburgskie vedomosti* (13 Jun 1996).

Concerning the sale of the apartment at Malaia Morskaia 13, where Chaikovskii died. See also *1765*.

See also *970, 1095*.

THE CAUCUSES

[*1769*] 'Tiflisskaia zhizn´', *Kavkaz* (20 Apr 1886).

The composer's visit to Tifis in 1886.

— [repr.] 'Chestvovanie P. I. Chaikovskogo'. In: Sh. Aslanshvili, *P. I. Chaikovskii v Gruzii* (1940): 20–21 [see *1770*].

[*1770*] ASLANSHVILI, Sh. S. *P. I. Chaikovskii v Gruzii*. Tbilisi: Sakhelgami, 1940. 32 p, illus.

Includes: 'Chestvovanie P. I. Chaikovskogo': 20–21 [see *1769*] — 'Iz pis´ma M. I. Chaikovskogo k P. G. Bebutovu': 24–26 [see *4700*] — I. Z. Andronikashvili, 'Vypiska iz memuarov': 27–31 [see *391*].

[*1771*] KORGANOV, V. D. *Chaikovskii na Kavkaze*. Po dnevnikam i pis´mam ego, po svedeniiam tifliskikh gazet i po lichnym vospominaniiam. Podgot. k pechati Gos. publichnoi bibliotekoi Armianskoi SSR im. Miasnikiana. Red. teksta A. S. Babaiana. Obshchaia red. i vstup. stat´ia K. S. Saradzheva. Erevan: Armgiz, 1940. xvi, 120 p, illus.

Includes Korganov's personal recollections of Chaikovskii [see *477*], and numerous extracts from the composer's diaries, correspondence and newspaper articles.

Reviews: 'Gosizdat Armenii vypustil trud', *Sovetskaia muzyka* (1940), 12: 107 — Ia. G., *Literaturnoe obozrenie* (1941), 8.

[*1772*] ZHDANOV, V. A. 'Chaikovskii v Tiflise', *Zaria Vostoka* (6 May 1940).

Includes 2 letters from Chaikovskii to Iuliia Shpazhinskaia (1886).

[*1773*] RUBIN, S. 'P. I. Chaikovskii v Tbilisi', *Zaria Vostoka* (13 Nov 1958).

[*1774*] RYBAKOV, I. 'I Chaikovskii pisal o nefti', *Bakinskii rabochii* (7 May 1965).

Chaikovskii's visit to Baku in 1887.

[*1775*] MUSTAFAEV, F. 'Naedine s Baku', *Bakinskii rabochii* (20 Mar 1979).

[*1776*] [Istoriia odnoi fotografii P. I. Chaikovskogo, datirovannoi 22 oktiabria 1890], *Sovetskaia kul´tura* (5 May 1990).

The story of Photograph No. 89, taken during Chaikovskii's visit to Tiflis in 1890.

See also *389, 456, 497*.

ESTONIA

[*1777*] LIUBARSKII, A. 'Chaikovskii v Estonii', *Sovetskaia Estoniia* (25 Mar 1958).

Chaikovskii's visit to Haspsalu (Gapsal) in 1867.

[*1778*] POPOVA, T. 'Pamiati velikogo kompozitora', *Sovetskaia kul´tura* (1 Aug 1978): 5.

Commemorating Chaikovskii's visit to Haapsalu in 1867.

See also *1396* to *1401*.

UKRAINE

[1779]   **'Chaikovskii v Odesse'**, *Odesskii vestnik* (13 Jan 1893).

Chaikovskii's series of concerts in Odessa in Jan 1893.

See also: 'K. prebyvaniiu P. I. Chaikovskogo v Odesse', *Odesskii vestnik* (14 Jan 1893) — '1-e simfonicheskoe sobranie p[od] u[pravleniem] P. I. Chaikovskogo, *Odesskii listok* (17 Jan 1893) — A. Kruglikov, 'Nasha gordost´', *Odesskii listok* (17 Jan 1893) — X, 'Pervoe simfonicheskoe sobranie Odesskogo otdeleniia RMO pod upr. Chaikovskogo', *Odesskii vestnik* (18 Jan 1893) — S. Iar., 'Na simfonicheskom sobranii', *Odesskii listok* (18 Jan 1893) — L. K[uper]nik, 'Pervoe simfonicheskoe sobranie', *Odesskii listok* (18 Jan 1893) — Solo, *Odesskie novosti* (18 Jan 1893) — Verita, *Novorossiiskii telegraf* (18 Jan 1893) — Verita, 'Muzykal´nyi vecher v chest´ Chaikovskogo', *Novorossiiskii telegraf* (22 Jan 1893) — 'Obed v chest´ P. I. Chaikovskogo', *Odesskie novosti* (23 Jan 1893) — V, 'Literaturno-muzykal´nyi vecher v Birzhevom zale', *Odesskii vestnik* (23 Jan 1893) — 'Literaturno-muzykal´nyi vecher', *Novorossiiskii telegraf* (24 Jan 1893) — Verita, *Novorossiiskii telegraf* (25 Jan 1893) — Solo, *Odesskie novosti* (25 Jan 1893) — 'Teatr i muzyka' (25 Jan 1893) — Solo, *Odesskie novosti* (26 Jan 1893) — *Moskovskie vedomosti* (26 Jan 1893).

[1780]   **'Nauka, literatura i iskusstvo'**, *Khar´kovskie gubernskie novosti* (12 Mar 1893).

In connection with Chaikovskii's concert in Khar´kov on 14 Mar 1893.

See also: 'Teatr i muzyka', *Iuzhnyi krai* (12 Mar 1893) — N. Ch., 'Po povodu simfonicheskogo kontserta pod upravleniem P. I. Chaikovskogo', *Iuzhnyi krai* (14 Mar 1893) — *Iuzhnyi krai* (15 Mar 1893)' — *Khar´kovskie vedomosti* (15 Mar 1893) — 'Nauka, literatura i iskusstvo', *Khar´kovskie gubernskie novosti* (15 Mar 1893) — 'Teatr i muzyka', *Iuzhnyi krai* (15 Mar 1893) — 'Nauka, literatura i iskusstvo', *Khar´kovskie gubernskie novosti* (16 Mar 1893) — 'Teatr i muzyka', *Iuzhnyi krai* (16 Mar 1893) — 'Nauka, literatura i iskusstvo', *Khar´kovskie gubernskie novosti* (17 Mar 1893) — 'Teatr i muzyka', *Iuzhnyi krai* (17 Mar 1893) — E. M. B., 'Pis´mo iz Khar´kova', *Moskovskie vedomosti* (19 Mar 1893).

[1781]   **GOL´DSHTEIN, M. M. *P. I. Chaikovskii v Odesse: K 100-letiiu so dnia rozhdeniia velikogo russkogo kompozitora, 1840–1940*.** Odessa: Chernomors´ka kommuna, 1940. 16 p, illus.

[1782]   ***P. I. Chaikovskii na Ukraine: Materialy i dokumenty*.** Red. i predisl. A. V. Ol´khovskogo. Sost. L. D. Fainshtein, O. Ia. Shreer i T. M. Tikhonova. Kiev, 1940. 144 p, music, illus. (*Kievskaia gos. ordena Lenina konservatoriia im. P. I. Chaikovskogo. Kafedra istorii muzyki*).

Text in Ukrainian. See also *467*.

[1783]   **TIUMENEVA, G. A. *Chaikovs´kii i Ukraina*.** Kiev: Mystetstvo, 1955. 54 p, music, illus.

[1784]   **VYSOCHINSKAIA, L. I. *Chaikovskii i Ukraina*.** Stenogramma publichnoi lektsii. Kiev, 1955. 30 p, illus (*Obshchestvo po rasprostraneniiu politicheskikh i nauchnykh znanii Ukrainskoi SSR*; seriia. 4, no. 8).

[1785]   **SVETASHOVA, N. *P. I. Chaikovskii na Cherkasshchine: Pamiatka chitateliu*.** Predislovie M. Shkaliberda. Sost. N. Svetashova. Dnepropetrovsk: Promin´, 1965. 10 p, illus.

[1786]   **MAIBUROVA, E. V. *Chaikovskii na Ukraine*.** Rasshirennaia stenogramma lektsii, prochtannoi studentam muz. zavedenii Ukrainy v ianvare 1965 g. Kiev, 1965. 47 p, music, illus. (*Obshchestvo "Znanie" USSR*; seriia 4, no. 2).

[1787]   **NARODITS´KII, A. *A page from the life of a great composer: P. I. Tchaikovsky in the Sumy region*.** Kiev: Znaniia, 1973. 32 p, illus.

[1788]   **KOGAN, S. 'Česky hudebník v Odese'**, *Hudební rozhledy*, 26 (1973), 11: 516–520.

[1789]   **GOLOTA, V. V. *Teatral´naia Odessa*.** Kiev: Mystetstvo, 1990: 89.

Chaikovskii's visits to Odessa.

[1790]   **HAUSER, Z. 'Czajkowski na Ukrainie'**, *Ruch Muzyczny*, 40 (1996), 17: 38–39, illus.

See also *406, 415, 417, 422, 424, 425, 432, 441, 444, 459a, 465, 479, 489, 507, 523, 534, 535, 551, 568, 880*.

4.4.2. Western & Central Europe

[*1791*]   'Iz oblasti muzykal´noi kritiki', *Baian* (Jan 1888), 3: 29.

Russian tr. of extracts from newspaper reviews of Chaikovskii's concerts in Germany, England and France in 1888.

[*1792*]   'Izvestiia otovsiudu', *Nuvellist* (Mar 1888), 3: 6–7.

Chaikovskii's concert tour of Western Europe in 1888.

[*1793*]   DOMBAEV, G. S. *P. I. Chaikovskii i mirovaia kultura*. Spravochnye materialy, sost. G. Dombaev. Moskva: Sovetskii kompozitor, 1958. 88 p.

Collected extracts from Chaikovskii's letters and diaries relating to foreign culture. Includes a chronicle of the composer's tours of America ('Za granitsei'): 38–88, and lists of foreign performances of Chaikovskii's works, authors of texts, subjects, etc.

[*1794*]   SIDEL´NIKOV, L. 'Ostalis´ pozadi verstovye stolby Rossii: Pervoe zarubezhnoe puteshestvie P. I. Chaikovskogo', *Muzykal´naia zhizn´* (1990), 13: 20–21.

The composer's travels to Germany, Belgium, England and France in 1861.

[*1795*]   STEINEGGER, C. 'Tchaikovski: L'ame russe de l'Europe romantique', *Diapason-Harmonie* (Jan 1993), 389: 39–44, illus.

See also *138, 488*.

AUSTRIA

[*1796*]   G—T, N. 'P. I. Chaikovskii v Avstrii', *Teatral´naia gazeta* (1893), 23: 2.

See also *1052*.

CZECH REPUBLIC

[*1797*]   B[ESSEL´], V. 'P. I. Chaikovskii v Prage', *Muzykal´noe obozrenie* (1888), 9: 65–66.

Extracts from Czech press reviews of Chaikovskii's concert in Prague on 9 Feb 1888.

See also: 'Russkaia muzyka za granitsei', *Baian* (Feb 1888), 6: 58 — 'P. I. Chaikovskii v Prage', *Baian* (Feb 1888), 7: 66.

[*1798*]   VOLKOV, N. 'Serdtse slavianina: K 110-letiiu so dnia rozhdeniia P. I. Chaikovskogo', *Ogonek* (1950), 21: 25, illus.

On the composer's visits to Prague (1887–88).

[*1799*]   ŠTĚPÁNEK, V. *Pražké návštěvy P. I. Čajkovského*. Napsal, materiál vyubral a k tisku připravil V. Štěpánek. Praha: Orbis, 1952. 170 p, illus.

Chaikovskii's visits to Prague, and his relationships with Czech musicians. Includes Czech trs. of letters from Chaikovskii to Adolf Čech, Antonín Dvořák and Berta Foerstrová-Lautererová, Adolf Patera, Josef Sklenář, František Šubert and Eduard Valečka.

Review: I. Belza, 'Chaikovskii v Prage', *Sovetskaia muzyka* (1953), 7: 101, illus.

[*1800*]   ŠTĚPÁNEK, V. 'Přátelství s P. I. Čajkovským', *Zemědělské noviny* (24 Apr 1954).

[*1801*]   ŠÁMAL, J. 'Pëtr Il´ich Chaikovskii i Umeletska beseda'. In: *Puti razvitiia i vzaimosviazi russkogo i chekhoslovatskogo iskusstva*. Otv. red. O. Shvidkovskii. Moskva: Nauka, 1970: 175–182.

On performances of Chaikovskii's works in Prague, and the composer's last visit to the Umělecká beseda.

— [Czech tr.] 'Petr Iljič Čajkovskij a Umělecká beseda'. In: *Cesty rozvoje a vzájemné vztahy ruského a československého umění*. Praha, 1974: 215–240.

[*1802*]   ZVEREV, Iu. A. 'Muzyka Chaikovskogo v Chekhii i ego poseshchenie Pragi'. In: *Voprosy istorii, teorii muzyki i muzykal´nogo vospitania*, sb. 1. Kazan´, 1971: 32–52. (*Uchenye zapiski Kazanskogo gos. pedagog. instituta*).

[*1803*]   'A moment of absolute happiness', *Music News from Prague* (1972), 8: 2–3.

[*1804*]   GINTSBURG, L. 'Češke přátele P. I. Čajkovského'. In: L. Gintsburg. *Svazky–vztahy–pralely* (1973): 11–24.

[*1805*]   'Chaikovskii v Prage', *Televidenie i radioveshchanie*, 3 (Mar 1976): 12.

[*1806*]   KUNA, M. *Pražská epizoda P. I. Čajkovského*. Příspěvek k Česko-ruským vztahům s využitím zápisků a korespondence Marie Červinkové-Riegrové; nejstarší doklad velikonočních slavností v Čechách: Transkripce a analýza rukopisu XIV D. 12 Narodního muzea v Praze Václav Plocek. Praha: Ústav teorie a dějin umění ČSAV, 1978. 153 p, music. (*Uměnovědné studie*; 1)

Text in Czech, with summaries in German and Russian.

[*1807*]   KUNA, M. *Čajkovskij a Praha*. Praha: Supraphon, 1980. 86 p, illus.

Review: *Hudební veda*, 18 (1981), 4: 3656.

[*1808*]   WILEY, R. J. 'Chaikovskii's visit to Prague in 1888', *Slavic Review*, 40 (1981):433–443.

[*1809*]   VOKURKA, Z. 'Minuta absoliutnogo shchast´ia', *Sotsialisticheskaia Chekhoslovakiia* (1988), 7: 20–21.

[*1810*]   SHAPOVALOV, P. 'Charuiushchie zvuki nad Vltavoi', *Smena* (4 May 1990).

[*1811*]   BEZNOSOV, A. 'S monogrammoi "P. Ch.": Neizvestnye stranitsy zhizni velikogo kompozitora', *Pravda* (2 Aug 1990).

See also *409, 438, 547, 1929*.

FRANCE

[*1812*]   'Russkaia muzyka za granitsei', *Muzykal´noe obozrenie* (Oct 1887), 25: 195–200.

Russian tr. of French press reviews of Chaikovskii's concerts in Paris in Feb 1887.

[*1813*]   JOLY, C. 'Tschaikowsky à Paris', *Figaro* (3/15 Mar 1888).

Chaikovskii's concerts in Paris in 1888.

See also: *Art musical* (17/29 Feb 1888) [concert of 16/28 Feb] — *Figaro* (17/29 Feb 1888) — *Gaulois* (18 Feb/1 Mar 1888) — *Temps* (18 Feb/1 Mar 1888) — *Ménestrel* (21 Feb/4 Mar 1888) — *Gaulois* (22 Feb/5 Mar 1888) [concert of 21 Feb/4 Mar] — *Temps* (22 Feb/5 Mar 1888) — H. Leroux, *Temps* (23 Feb/6 Mar 1888) — *Figaro* (24 Feb/9 Mar 1888) — *Ménestrel* (25 Feb/11 Mar 1888) — *Temps* (29 Feb/12 Mar 1888) [concert of 28 Feb/11 Mar] — *Figaro* (2/14 Mar 1888) — A. Landely, 'La musique russe', *Art musical* (3/15 Mar 1888) — *Ménestrel* (6/18 Mar 1888) — *Ménestrel* (13/25 Mar 1888) [concert of 2/14 Mar] — V. V. Bessel´, 'P. I. Chaikovskii v Parizhe', *Muzykal´noe obozrenie* (1888), 9 — V. V. B[essel´], 'Kontserty P. I. Chaikovskogo v Parizhe', *Muzykal´noe obozrenie* (1888), 11: 82–83 — 'Russkaia muzyka za granitsei', *Baian* (Mar 1888), 10: 54.

[*1814*]   [Tschaikowsky à Paris], *Figaro* (22 Mar/3 Apr 1889).

Chaikovskii's concert in Paris on 19/31 Mar 1889.

[*1815*]   PELS, G. 'Tschaikowsky au Châtelet', *Gaulois* (25 Mar/6 Apr 1891).

Chaikovskii's concert in Paris on 24 Mar/5 Apr 1891.

See also *181, 392, 419, 524*.

GERMANY

[*1816*]   **[Tschaikowsky in Leipzig]**, *Neue Zeutschrift für Musik* (30 Dec 1887/11 Jan 1888).

Chaikovskii conducting his own music in Leipzig on 24–25 Dec 1887/5–6 Jan 1888.

See also: *Signale für die musikalische Welt* (30 Dec 1887/11 Jan 1888) — *Musikalisches Wochenblatt* (31 Dec 1887/12 Jan 1888) — 'Russkaia muzyka za granitsei', *Baian* (Jan 1888), 2: 21.

[*1817*]   **[Tschaikowsky in Hamburg]**, *Hamburger Nachtrichten* (9/21 Jan 1888).

Chaikovskii's concert in Hamburg on 8/20 Jan 1888.

See also: V. [Bessel´], 'Russkaia muzyka za granitsei: g. Chaikovskii v Gamburge', *Muzykal´noe obozrenie* (1888), 4: 30–31 — 'Russkaia muzyka za granitsei', *Baian* (Jan 1888), 4: 38 — E. Krause, *Hamburger Fremdenblatt* (9/21 Jan 1888) — J. Sittard, *Hamburger Correspondent* (9/21 Jan 1888) —

[*1818*]   **[Tschaikowsky in Berlin]**, *Berliner Börsen Courier* (28 Jan/9 Feb 1888).

Chaikovskii's concert in Berlin on 27 Jan/8 Feb 1888.

See also: *Vossische Zeitung* (28 Jan/9 Feb 1888) — *National Zeitung* (29 Jan/10 Feb 1888) — 'Russkaia muzyka za granitsei', *Baian* (Feb 1888), 6: 58.

[*1819*]   **'Iz oblasti zagranichnoi muzykal´noi kritiki'**, *Baian* (Feb 1889), 8: 64–65.

Extracts from German newspaper reviews of Chaikovskii's concerts.

See also: 'Zagranichnaia khronika', *Baian* (Apr 1889), 13: 107.

[*1820*]   **[Tschaikowsky in Köln]**, *Rheinische Mercur* (1/13 Feb 1889).

Chaikovskii's concert in Cologne on 31 Jan/12 Feb 1889.

See also: *Kölnischer Volkszeitung* (2/14 Feb 1889) — *Kölnische Zeitung* (2/14 Feb 1889).

[*1821*]   **[Tschaikowsky in Frankfurt]**, *Frankfurter Zeitung* (4/16 Feb 1889).

Chaikovskii's concert in Frankfurt on 4/16 Feb 1889.

See also: *General-Anzeiger* (4/16 Feb 1889) — *Kleine Presse* (4/16 Feb 1889).

[*1822*]   **[Tschaikowsky in Dresden]**, *Dresdner Zeitung* (10/22 Feb 1889).

Chaikovskii's concert in Dresden on 8/20 Feb 1889.

See also: H. Starke, *Dresdner Nachtrichten* (10/22 Feb 1889) — *Dresdner Journal* (10/22 Feb 1889) — F. Gleich, *Dresdner Anzeiger* (10/22 Feb 1889).

[*1823*]   **[Tschaikowsky in Berlin]**, *Fremdenblatt* (14/26 Feb 1889).

Chaikovskii's concert in Berlin on 14/26 Feb 1889.

See also: *Berliner Tageblatt* (15/27 Feb 1889) — *Vossische Zeitung* (15/27 Feb 1889) — *Tägliche Rundschau* (17 Feb/1 Mar 1889) — A. Moszkowsky, 'Berliner Saison (über Tschaikowsky)', *Neue Musik Zeitung* (Mar 1889).

[*1824*]   **[Tschaikowsky in Hamburg]**, *Hamburger Nachtrichten* (4/16 Mar 1889)

Chaikovskii's concert in Hamburg on 3/15 Mar 1889.

See also: 'P. I. Tschaikowsky', *Hamburger Signale* (20 Feb/5 Mar 1889) — *Hamburger Fremdenblatt* (3/15 Mar 1889) — J. Sittard, *Hamburger Correspondent* (4/16 Mar 1889).

[*1825*]   **POLOVTSOV, A. 'P. I. Chaikovskii v Drezdene i Berline'**, *Moskovskie vedomosti* (1898), No. 276.

[*1826*]   **SIMPSON, E. E. 'Tschaikowsky in Leipsic in 1888'**, *Music*, 19 (Dec 1900): 100–109, illus.

Includes extracts from the composer's autobiographical account [see *137*].

[*1827*]   **'Leiptsigskie retsenzii 1888 goda'**. In: M. I. Chaikovskii, *Zhizn´ Petra Il´icha Chaikovskogo*, tom 3 (1902): 659–667 [see *1453*].

Russian tr. of German newspaper reviews of the composer's concerts in 1888.

— [English tr.] 'Extracts from German press notices during Tchaikovsky's tours abroad in 1888 and 1889'. In: M. I. Chaikovskii, *The life and letters of Peter Ilich Tchaikovsky* (1906): 762–777 [see *1453*].

Includes additonal references compiled by Rosa Newmarch.

[*1828*]   ENGEL´, R. 'Za rubezhom: Chaikovskii v Germanii', *Muzyka* (1922), 4: 87.

Accounts of Chaikovskii's travels to Germany, 1888–92.

[*1829*]   GOLDSTEIN, M. 'Der erste Besuch Tschaikowskis in Berlin', *Musik und Gesellschaft*, 13 (Jun 1963): 372–373, illus.

[*1830*]   BOLLERT, W. 'Tschaikowsky in Berlin', *Philharmonische Blätter* (1977/78), 8: 20–21.

See also *1052*.

GREAT BRITAIN

[*1831*]   'St. James's Hall concert', *The Times* (11/23 Mar 1888).

Chaikovskii's concert in London on 10/22 Mar 1888.

See also: *Daily Chronicle* (11/23 Mar 1888) — *Daily Telegraph* (11/23 Mar 1888) — *Musical Times* (20 Mar/1 Apr 1888) — *The Times* (1/13 Apr 1888) — A. P. 'P. I. Chaikovskii v Londone', *Muzykal´noe obozrenie* (1888), 13: 99–100 — 'Russkaia muzyka za granitsei', *Baian* (Mar 1888), 12: 111.

[*1832*]   'St. James's Hall concert', *The Times* (1/13 Apr 1889).

Chaikovskii's concert in London on 30 Mar/11 Apr 1889.

See also: *Daily Telegraph* (1/13 Apr 1889) — *London Musical Courier* (1/13 Apr 1889) — *Musical Times* (30 Mar/11 Apr 1889).

[*1833*]   'Philharmonic Society concert', *Daily Telegraph* (21 May/2 Jun 1893).

Chaikovskii's concert in London on 20 May/1 Jun 1893.

See also: *Daily Chronicle* (21 May/2 Jun 1893) — *The Times* (22 May/3 Jun 1893).

[*1834*]   'Teatr i muzyka', *Novoe vremia* (17 Jun 1893): 3.

Concerning Chaikovskii's honorary doctorate from Cambridge University.

[*1835*]   NEWMARCH, R. H. 'Tchaikovsky's last visit to England', *Musical Times*, 45 (Feb 1904): 95–97.

Chaikovskii's visit to Cambridge University in 1893.

[*1836*]   "LA MAIN GAUCHE". 'Tchaikovsky in England', *Musical Opinion*, 63 (Jun 1940): 396.

[*1837*]   DAVYDOVA, K. Iu. 'Chaikovskii v Kembridzhe', *Muzykal´naia zhizn´* (Jun 1966), 11: 10, illus.

Russian tr. of English press reports from 1893.

[*1838*]   VLASTO, J. 'A Cambridge occasion', *Musical Times*, 109 (Jul 1968): 616–618.

[*1839*]   NORRIS, G. *Stanford, the Cambridge Jubilee, and Tchaikovsky*. Newton Abbot, Devon; North Pomfret, Vt.: David & Charles [1980]. 584 p. ISBN: 0–7153–7856–2.

Reviews: *Times Ediucational Suppl.* (25 Mar 1980): 22 — *Times Literary Suppl.* (25 Jul 1980): 830 — *Music & Musicians*, 28 (Aug 1980): 39 — S. Banfield, *Music & Letters*, 61 (1980), 3/4: 433–435 — W. S. Newman, *Journal of the American Liszt Society*, 10 (1981): 96–100 — G. Shokhman, 'Vzgliad s drugikh beregov', *Sovetskaia muzyka* (1990), 6: 134–141 [see *592*].

[*1840*]   'V Kembridzhe pozdravliali na latyni', *Sankt Peterburgskie vedomosti* (6 Nov 1993).

See also *399, 421, 423, 452, 453, 471, 472, 546.*

ITALY

[*1841*]   POZHIDAEV, G. A.. 'Kaprichchio: Malen´kaia povest´', *Muzykal´naia zhizn´* (Apr 1968), 7: 15–17, illus.

Extract from Pozhidaev's forthcoming book *Chaikovskii v Rime* [see *1842*].

Review D. Kabalevskii, 'K malen´koi povesti G. Pozhideva "Kaprichchio". In: *Panorama*. Vyp. 6. Moskva: Molodaia gvardiia, 1973: 158–188.

[*1842*]   **POZHIDAEV, G. A.** *Chaikovskii v Rime: "Ital´ianskoe kaprichchio"*. Moskva: Muzyka, 1976. 40 p, illus. (*Rasskazy o muzyke dlia shkol´nikov*).

See also *1841*.

See also *492, 1092, 1093*.

POLAND

[*1843*]   **'Czajkowskij v Warszawe'**, *Warszawskij dnevnik* (2 Jan 1892).

Chaikovskii's concert in Warsaw on 2 Jan 1892.

See also: *Warszawskij dnevnik* (9 Jan 1892) — N. N., 'Pis'mo iz Varshavy', *Moskovskie vedomosti* (13 Jan 1892).

SWITZERLAND

[*1844*]   **[Tschaikowsky à Géneve]**, *Art musical* (3/15 Mar 1889).

Chaikovskii's concert in Geneva on 25 Feb/9 Mar 1889.

See also: *Art musical* (19/31 Mar 1889).

[*1845*]   **MEYLEN, P.** 'Tschaikowsky à Clarens', *Feuilles musicales*, 7 (1954): 34–36.

4.4.3. America

[*1846*]   **'Tschaikowsky is here'**, *New York Herald* (15/27 Apr 1891).

Chaikovskii's appearances at the opening of the Carnegie Music Hall in New York.

See also: 'Russian great composer P. Tschaikowsky spends his first day in New York', *New York World* (16/28 Apr 1891) — 'The festival at the New Music Hall next week', *Mail & Express* (20 Apr/2 May 1891) — *Evening Post* (20 Apr/2 May 1891) — 'Tschaikowsky's March', *American Art Journal* (23 Apr/5 May 1891) — 'Carnegie Music Hall opened', *The Press* (24 Apr/6 May 1891) — 'The first concert in the new music hall', *New York Times* (24 Apr/6 May 1891) — 'The first night of the music festival', *The Sun* (24 Apr/6 May 1891) — 'Music crowned in its new home', *New York Herald* (24 Apr/6 May 1891) — 'The Music Hall opened', *New York Tribune* (24 Apr/6 May 1891) — 'Music's new home', *Morning Journal* (24 Apr/6 May 1891) — 'The new Music Hall', *Evening Post* (24 Apr/6 May 1891) — 'Mr. Damrosch's third concert', *The Press* (26 Apr/8 May 1891) — 'The Music Festival', *Brooklyn Daily Eagle* (26 Apr/8 May 1891) — 'The Music Festival', *Evening Post* (26 Apr/8 May 1891) — 'Music warm and strong', *Morning Journal* (26 Apr/8 May 1891) — 'Tchaikovsky's ovation at the Music Festival', *New York World* (26 Apr/8 May 1891) — *Evening Telegram* (26 Apr/8 May 1891) — 'Chorus singing without orchestra at the Festival', *Morning Journal* (27 Apr/9 May 1891) [see *5188*] — 'The Music Festival', *Evening Post* (27 Apr/9 May 1891) — 'The Music Hall concerts', *New York Times* (27 Apr/9 May 1891) — 'Close of the Music Festival', *The Press* (28 Apr/10 May 1891) — 'The end of the Festival: M. Tschaikowsky has another ovation at the Music Hall', *New York World* (28 Apr/10 May 1891) — 'Last of Festival concerts', *New York Daily Tribune* (28 Apr/10 May 1891) — 'The Music Hall concerts', *New York Times* (28 Apr/10 May 1891) — 'End of the Music Festival', *Evening Post* (29 Apr/11 May 1891).

Extracts from many of the above are repr. in: E. Yoffe, *Tchaikovsky in America* (1986) [see *1864*].

[*1847*]   **BLUMENBURG, M. A.** 'The music at the Festival', *Musical Courier* (1/13 May 1891).

[*1848*]   **'Great composer and director'**, *Harper's Weekly*, 35 (4/16 May 1891): 372, illus.

[*1849*]   **'Tchaikovsky has no superiors as a leader of musicians'**, *Baltimore American* (4/16 May 1891).

Chaikovskii's concert in Baltimore on 3/15 May 1891.

See also: 'Great Tchaikovsky', *The Sun* [Baltimore] (4/16 May 1891) — 'The eminent Russian composer Tchaikovsky directs the performance of two of his works at the Academy of Music', *North American* (19 May 1891).

[*1850*]   'Tchaikovsky and other celebrities in a notable Musical Festival', *Philadelphia Press* (7/19 May 1891).

Chaikovskii's concert in Philadelphia on 6/18 May 1891.

See also: 'Tchaikovsky's concert', *Daily Evening Telegraph* (7/19 May 1891).

[*1851*]   BLUMENBURG, M. A. 'The raconteur', *Musical Courier* (8/20 May 1891).

[*1852*]   'The world of music', *New York World* (8/20 May 1891).

[*1853*]   'The reception for Tchaikovsky: A pleasant farewell to the popular composer', *New York Daily Tribune* (9/21 May 1891).

[*1854*]   'Tschaikowsky in America', *New York Herald* (12/24 May 1891).

[*1855*]   'When Tchaikovsky visited Gustav-Schirmer', *Musician*, 34 (Oct 1929): 10, illus.

[*1856*]   MULLEN, J. M. 'Tchaikowsky's visit to Baltimore', *Maryland Historical Magazine*, 34 (Mar 1939): 41–45.

[*1857*]   BEDENKOFF, A. 'Tchaikovsky in America: As told in his diary', *Musical America*, 60 (Jul 1940): 5, illus.

[*1858*]   MAREK, G. 'Tchaikovsky on Broadway', *Good Housekeeping*, 112 (Apr 1941): 12, illus.

[*1859*]   FICKES, M. P. 'Master of melody: The opening night concert of Carnegie hall — a high spot in the life of Tchaikovsky', *Etude*, 70 (Mar 1952): 10–11, illus.

[*1860*]   'A bit of nostalgia', *Musical Courier*, 149 (1 Mar 1954): 9, illus.

Chaikovskii at the opening of Carnegie Hall in 1891.

[*1861*]   KOLODIN, I. 'Tchaikovsky in America', *Opera News*, 22 (2 Dec 1957): 12–13.

[*1862*]   SCHICKEL, R. 'Amazing people, these Americans'. In: R. Schickel, *The world of Carnegie Hall*. New York: Julian Messner, Inc, 1960: 37–55.

[*1863*]   'Carnegie Hall reaches 80', *Music & Artists*, 4 (1971), 4: 8.

[*1864*]   YOFFE, E. *Tchaikovsky in America: The composer's visit in 1891.* Comp. by Elkhonon Yoffe. Trs. from the Russian by Lidya Yoffe. New York; Oxford: Oxford Univ. Press, 1986. x, 216 p, illus. ISBN: 0-19-504117-8.

Reviews: R. W. Richart, *Library Journal*, 111 (15 Sep 1986): 89 — *Music Magazine*, 10 (1987), 2: 25 — *Opera Journal*, 20 (1987), 2: 32–33 — *Ovation*, 8 (Apr 1987): 39 — J. E. Johnson, *Choice*, 24 (May 1987): 1409 — E. Garden, *Music & Letters*, 68 (Oct 1987), 4: 381–383 — S. Johnson, *Musical Times*, 129 (Jan 1988): 21–22.

[*1865*]   BROWN, D. 'Tchaikovsky: The spirited mind', *Arête*, 2 (Jan/Feb 1990), 4: 54–57.

[*1866*]   SHAL´NEV, A. 'Bez trinadtsatogo etazha', *Sovetskaia kul´tura* (26 May 1990).

[*1867*]   SIDEL´NIKOV, L. & PRIBEGINA, G. A. *25 dnei v Amerike: K 100-letiiu gastrol´noi poezdki P. I. Chaikovskogo / 25 days in America: For the centenary of Peter Tchaikovsky's concert tour.* Moskva: Muzyka, 1991. 125 + 109 p, illus. ISBN: 5-7140-0371-3.

Text in Russian and English.

[*1868*]   KUZNETSOV, S. 'Mir iskusstva: Den´ rozhdeniia v N´iu-Iorke', *Sovetskaia kul´tura* (5 May 1991): 9.

An exhibition 'Chaikovskii at Carnegie Hall', to commemorate the centenary of the composer's visit to the opening of the hall in 1891. See also *423, 1793, 3092, 5472*.

4.5. PERSONAL RELATIONSHIPS

4.5.1. Family

[1869]   **DAVYDOV, Iu. L. *Zapiski o P. I. Chaikovskom*.** Obshchaia red. i primechaniia G. I. Navtikova. Moskva: Gos. muz. izdat., 1962. 114 p, music, illus.

Contents: 'Chaikovskii i sem´ia Davydovykh': 3–43 — 'Peterburgskie i moskovskie rodnye i blizkie P. I. Chaikovskogo': 44–58 [see *1870*] — 'Posledenie desiat´ let zhizni P. I. Chaikovskogo v moikh vospominaniiakh': 59–84 [see *428*].

Reviews: A. Shirokov, 'Vnuk dekabrista, plemiannik Chaikovskogo', *Vechernii Leningrad* (4 Jun 1963): 3 — *Musik und Gesellschaft*, 15 (Nov 1965): 777.

[1870]   **DAVYDOV, Iu. L. 'Peterburgskie i moskovskie rodnye i blizkie P. I. Chaikovskogo'.** In: *Zapiski o P. I. Chaikovskom* (1962): 44–58 [see *1869*].

— [German tr.] 'Verwandte und Bekannte Peter Tschaikowskys in Moskau und St. Petersburg'. In: *Tschaikowsky aus der Nähe* (1994): 1–18 [see *379*].

[1871]   **PROLEEVA, V. I. 'K istorii rodoslovnoi Chaikovskikh'.** In: B. Ia. Anshakov, *Il´ia Petrovich Chaikovskii* (1976): 8–14 [see *1893*].

[1872]   **ANSHAKOV, B. Ia. *Brat´ia Chaikovskie: Ocherk*.** Izhevsk: Udmurtiia, 1981. 84 p, illus.

Includes: I. I. Chaikovskii, 'Vospominaniia o prebyvanii P. I. Chaikovskogo v Taganroge i Odesse': 59–64 [see *415*] — Iu. L. Davydov, 'Poslednie dni zhizni P. I. Chaikovskogo': 64–73 [see *429*].

[1873]   **PROLEEVA, V. I. 'K rodoslovnoi P. I. Chaikovskogo',** *Sovetskie arkhivy* (1981), 1: 65–66.

[1874]   **'Attestat A. M. Assiera'.** In: *P. I. Chaikovskii: Gody detstva* (1983): 102–106 [see *1712*].

The attestation certificate of Chaikovskii's grandfather Andrei Assier, issued to him upon his retirement in 1831.

— [repr.] In: *P. I. Chaikovskii: Zabytoe i novoe* (1995): 151–153 [see *598*].

[1875]   **KOGAN, M. 'Rodoslovnaia',** *Sovetskaia muzyka* (1990), 6: 81–90 [see *592*].

Genealogies of the Chaikovskii and Assier families.

[1876]   **ZHILINSKAIA, M. 'Chaikovskii v krugu rodnykh',** *Sem´ia i shkola* (1990), 5: 50–52 [see *951*].

[1877]   **DAVYDOV, G. 'Relikvii iz Afriki',** *Sovetskaia kul´tura* (26 Jan 1991).

Relatives on the Davydov side of Chaikovskii's family.

[1878]   **TKACHUK, T. 'Novoe v rodoslovnoi Chaikovskogo',** *Muzykal´naia zhizn´* (Dec 1991), 23/24: 9.

[1879]   **VAIDMAN, P. E. 'Rod Chaikovskikh k 1894 godu'.** In: *P. I. Chaikovskii: Zabytoe i novoe* (1995): 146–147 [see *598*].

[1880]   **GRÖNKE, K. 'Genealogische Tafeln Čajkovskij/Assier, Miljukov, Davydov, fon-Mekk'.** In: *Čajkovskijs Homosexualität und sein Tod: Legenden und Wirklichkeit* (1998): 367–378 [see *600*].

A series of genealogical tables for the Chaikovskii, Assier, Miliukov, Davydov and Von Meck families.

See also *560, 1712*.

ANTONINA CHAIKOVSKAIA (1849–1917)

Wife

[1881]   **K[UREPIN, A. D.] 'Moskovskii fel´eton: Bolezn´ Chaikovskogo',** *Novoe vremia* (22 Oct 1877).

Report on Chaikovskii's departure from Russia on health grounds (following the failure of his marriage).

[1882] **'Zhenit´ba P. I. Chaikovskogo'**, *Nuvellist* (1902), 7: 5–6.

Chaikovskii's marriage, based on Nikolai Kashkin's memoirs [see *463*].

[1883] **HADDEN, J. C. 'Tchaikowsky's peculiar marriage'**, *Musical Opinion*, 33 (Feb 1910): 328–329; illus.

— [rev. repr.] *New Music Review*, 11 (Nov 1912): 498–501.

[1884] **'Tchaikowski's strange marriage'**, *Etude*, 42 (Jul 1924): 450.

[1885] **ABRAHAM, G. E. H. '"Eugene Onegin" and Tchaikovsky's marriage'**, *Monthly Musical Record*, 64 (Dec 1934): 222–223, music.

— [rev. repr.] In: G. E. H. Abraham, *On Russian Music: Critical and historical studies of Glinka's operas, Balakirev's works, etc., with chapters dealing with compositions by Borodin, Rimsky-Korsakov, Tchaikovsky, Mussorgsky, Glazunov, and various other aspects of Russian music*. London: W. Reeves [1939]: 225–233.

— [repr.] New York: Johnson Reprint Corp. [1970]: 225–233.

— [repr.] Freeport, N. Y.: Books for Libraries Press, 1980: 225–233. (*Essay Index Reprint Series*). ISBN 0-8369-1900-9.

[1886] **BROWN, D. 'Tchaikovsky's marriage'**, *Musical Times*, 123 (Nov 1982): 754–756, illus.

Extracted from D. Brown, *Tchaikovsky: A biographical and critical study*, vol. 2 (1982) [see *1534*].

[1887] **SOKOLOV, V. *Antonina Chaikovskaia: Istoriia zabytoi zhizni*.** Moskva: Muzyka, 1994. 293 p, illus. ISBN: 5-7140-0565-1.

Includes supplements: 'Pis´ma A. I. Chaikovskoi (Miliukovoi) k P. I. Chaikovskomu': 219–251 [see *225*] —'Interview A. I. Chaikovskoi "Peterburgskoi gazete". Pis´ma A. I. Chaikovskoi k raznym litsam': 251–262 — 'Vospominaniia A. I. Chaikovskoi': 263–274 [see *411*].

Reviews: T. Veligura, 'Strannaia zhenshchina', *Kul´tura* (29 Jan 1994) — O. Krylova, 'Zhenshchiny, tak i ne stavshie sud´boi Chaikovskogo', *Smena* (28 Dec 1995): 4.

[1888] **SOKOLOV, V. S. 'Semeinaia drama Petra Il´icha'**, *Vechernii klub* (25 Feb 1995).

[1889] **SOKOLOV, V. S. 'Pis´mo v redaktsiiu'**, *Vechernii klub* (25 Apr 1995).

[1890] **NESMELOVA, S. 'Zhena kompozitora'**, *Kur'er* (26 Mar 1996).

See also *187, 410, 411, 464, 3120*.

IL´IA CHAIKOVSKII (1795–1880)
Father

[1891] **'Nekrolog: I. P. Chaikovskii'**, *Golos* (11 Jan 1880): 2.

Obituary of Chaikovskii's father.

[1892] **IAROVOI, Iu. 'Otets velikogo kompozitora'**. In: *Kalendar´-spravochnik Sverdlovskoi oblasti, 1970*. Sverdlovsk: Sverde-Ural´skie kniga izdat., 1969: 120, illus.

Concerning a forthcoming biography of Il´ia Petrovich Chaikovskii by Boris Anshakov [see *1893*].

[1893] **ANSHAKOV, B. Ia. *Il´ia Petrovich Chaikovskii: Ocherki zhizni i deiatel´nosti*.** Sost. B. Ia. Anshakov. Izhevsk: Udmurtiia, 1976. 90 p.

Contents: A. P. Loshkarev, 'Sluga Otechestva': 5–7 — V. I. Proleeva, 'K istorii rodoslovnoi Chaikovskikh': 8–14 [see *1871*] — M. A. Dement´eva & K. I. Dement´ev, 'Znachenie geologicheskikh issledovanii I. P. Chaikovskogo na territorii glavnogo devonskogo polia (v predelakh Novgorodskoi oblasti)': 15–20 — G. I. Oskolkov, 'I. P. Chaikovskii na Kamsko-Votkinskom zavode (1837–1848)': 21–34 — A. Z.- Vorotov, 'I. P. Chaikovskii-osnovatel´ sudostroeniia na Kamsko-Votkinskom zavode': 35–40 — N. S. Sharin, 'I. P. Chaikovskii v Alapaevske': 41–46 — S. I. Kudoiarova, 'I. P. Chaikovskii—Direktor Sankt-Peterburgskogo prakticheskogo tekhnologicheskogo instituta (1858–1863)': 47–58 — B. Ia. Anshakov, 'Il´ia Petrovich i Petr Il´ich Chaikovskie': 59–78 — 'Iz pisem Il´ia Petrovicha Chaikovskogo k Aleksandre Andreevne Chaikovskoi' : 80–85 — 'Pis´mo glavnogo nachal´nika upravleni zavodov general-leitenanta V. A Glinki, ministru finansov

F. P. Vronchenko': 86–87 — 'Kratkii khonograf zhizni I. P. Chaikovskogo' : 88–89 — 'Osnovnaia literatura v kotoroi osviashchaetsia zhizn´ i deiatel´nost´ I. P. Chaikovskogo': 90.

See also *1892*.

— 2-izd, ispr. i dop. Izhevsk: Udmurtiia, 1979. 106 p, illus.

[*1894*]   **ANSHAKOV, B. Ia. 'Otets kompozitora'**, *Muzykal´naia zhizn´* (Jul 1977), 13: 19–20, illus.

[*1895*]   **[CHAIKOVSKII, I. P.] 'Zapiski kadeta Gornogo kadetskogo korpusa I. P. Chaikovskogo'**. In: *P. I. Chaikovskii: Gody detstva* (1983): 98–101 [see *1712*].
The unfinished memoirs of Chaikovskii's father.
— [repr.] In: *P. I. Chaikovskii: Zabytoe i novoe* (1995): 148–150 [see *598*].

[*1896*]   **GAEVSKII, E. I. 'I. P. Chaikovskii i master S. Penn'**. In: *P. I. Chaikovskii i Ural* (1983): 33–39 [see *1749*].

See also *1715*.

MODEST CHAIKOVSKII (1850–1915)
Younger brother

[*1897*]   **VLAD, A. 'V dome P. I. Chaikovskogo'**, *Sem´ia* (1897): 2–5.
Interview with Modest Chaikovskii, partly concerning the Klin house-museum.

[*1898*]   **'Biografiia P. I. Chaikovskogo'**, *Moskovskie vedomosti* (29 Oct 1897).
Concerning Modest Chaikovskii's work on his biography of the composer [see *1453*].

[*1899*]   **KASHKIN, N. D. 'Nekrolog: M. I. Chaikovskii'**, *Khronika zhurnala Muzykal´nyi sovremennik* (1916), 14: 33–34.
Modest Chaikovskii's obituary.

[*1900*]   **'Zaveshchanie M. I. Chaikovskogo'**, *Muzykal´nyi sovremennik* (1916), 20: 28.
A transcript of Modest Chaikovskii's will.

[*1901*]   **KUZNETSOVA, G. V. 'Modest Il´ich Chaikovskii kak surdopedagog'**. In: *Voprosy defektologii*. Moskva: Moskovskii pedagogicheskii institut im V. I. Lenina, 1964: 198–209.

[*1902*]   **IAKOVLEV, V. V. 'Modest Il´ich Chaikovskii: Biograf Petra Il´icha Chaikovskogo'**. In: *P. I. Chaikovskii: Gody detstva* (1983): 112–130 [see *1712*].
Concerning M. I. Chaikovskii, *Zhizn´ Petra Il´cha Chaikovskogo* (1900–02) [see *1453*].

[*1903*]   **POZNANSKY, A. 'Modest Čajkovskij: In his brother's shadow'**. In: *Internationales Čajkovskij Symposium, Tübingen 1993: Bericht* (1995): 233–246 [see *596*].

[*1904*]   **GOULD, S. 'The image of the composer in Modest Tchaikovsky's play "The Symphony"'**. In: *Tchaikovsky and his contemporaries* (1999): 245–250 [see *602*].

See also *1872, 3652, 3692*.

PËTR FEDOROVICH CHAIKOVSKII (1745–1818)
Grandfather

[*1905*]   **PROLEEVA, V. 'Pëtr Chaikovskii: Ded kompozitora'**, *Muzykal´naia zhizn´* (May 1980), 10: 16–17, illus.

[*1906*]   **KULIK, I. 'Rodoslovnaia velikogo kompozitora'**, *Druzhba narodov* (1984), 7: 265.

[*1907*]   PROLEEVA, V. I. *K rodoslovnoi P. I. Chaikovskogo: Zhizn' i deiatel'nost' P. F. Chaikovskogo.* Izhevsk: Udmurtiia, 1990. 31 p, illus. ISBN 5-7659-9265-0.

4.5.2. Musicians

[*1908*]   K. P. S. 'P. I. Chaikovskii i Moskovskii sinodal'nyi khor', *Moskovskie vedomosti* (19 Feb 1902).

[*1909*]   KOLODIN, I. 'Tchaikovsky on "The Five"'. In: I. Kolodin, *The critical composer* (1940): 198–201 [see *2055*].

Chaikovskii's views on Milii Balakirev, Aleksandr Borodin, Tsesar Kiui, Nikolai Rimskii-Korsakov, and Modest Musorgskii.

[*1910*]   NAVTIKOV, G. 'Zarubezhnye vstrechi Chaikovskogo', *Kul'tura i zhizn'* (1960), 5: 46–48, illus.

On the composer's meetings with prominent musicians, 1875–93 (Feruccio Busoni, Artur Nikisch, Antonín Dvořák, Johannes Brahms, Camille Saint-Saëns and Edvard Grieg).

[*1911*]   SIN'KOVSKAIA, N. 'Nachalo odnoi tvorcheskoi druzhby', *Sovetskaia muzyka* (1978), 5: 97–100.

Chaikovskii's relationships with the composers Ivan Armsgeimer, Sergei Rakhmaninov and Aleksandr Ziloti.

[*1912*]   RIDENOUR, R. C. *Nationalism, modernism and personal rivalry in nineteenth-century Russian Music.* Ann Arbor: UMI Research Press [1981]. 258 p.

[*1913*]   BOBETH, M. 'Čajkovskij und das Mächtige Häuflein'. In: *Internationales Čajkovskij Symposium, Tübingen 1993: Bericht* (1995): 63–86 [see *596*].

Chaikovskii's relationships with Milii Balakirev, Aleksandr Borodin, Tsesar Kiui, Nikolai Rimskii-Korsakov, Modest Musorgskii and Vladimir Stasov.

See also *159*.

DESIRÉE ARTÔT-PADILLA (1835–1907)
Belgian singer and former fiancée of the composer

[*1914*]   KEETON, A. E. 'One of Tchaikovski's love episodes', *Monthly Musical Record*, 34 (Mar 1904): 43–45.

[*1915*]   SLONIMSKY, N. 'The most amazing romance in musical history', *Etude*, 53 (Oct 1935): 575–576; (Nov 1935): 645–646, illus.

[*1916*]   RUKAVISHNIKOV, N. K. 'Vstrechi Chaikovskogo s Desire Arto', *Sovetskaia muzyka*, (1937), 9: 43–54.

[*1917*]   DUPE, G. 'Le curieux amour de Tchaikovsky', *Musica* (Aug 1960), 77: 40–44, illus.

See also *187, 2004*.

MILII BALAKIREV (1837–1910)
Composer, pianist, conductor, and founder of the Free Music School in St. Petersburg

[*1918*]   SAVVIN, N. A. 'Iz perepiski M. A. Balakireva', *Russkaia muzykal'naia gazeta* (1910), 41: 874–882.

Extracts from Balakirev's correspondence, including his views on Chaikovskii and other composers.

[*1919*]   IVANOV, M. 'Iz nedavnego proshlogo russkogo iskusstva', *Novoe vremia* (1912), No. 13194: 4.

The relationship between Chaikovskii and Balakirev.

[*1920*]   V—A, O. 'Chaikovskii i programmnaia muzyka', *Russkaia muzykal´naia gazeta* (20 Oct 1913), 42: 927–933.
The influence of Balakirev on Chaikovskii's early programmatic works.

[*1921*]   BROWN, D. 'Balakirev, Tchaikovsky and Nationalism', *Music & Letters*, 42 (Jul 1961), 3: 227–241.

[*1922*]   GARDEN, E. 'The influence of Balakirev on Tchaikovsky', *Proceedings of the Royal Musical Association*, 107 (1981): 86–100, music.

See also *4475, 4916*.

ALEKSANDR BORODIN (1833–87)
Composer and Professor of Chemistry

[*1923*]   IAKOVLEV, V. 'Borodin i Chaikovskii', *Sovetskaia muzyka* (1954), 1: 66–74.

[*1924*]   BORODIN, A. 'Aus einem Brief an seine Fray Jekaterina Borodina'. In: *Tschaikowsky aus der Nähe* (1994): 72 [see *379*].

JOHANNES BRAHMS (1833–97)
German composer and pianist

[*1925*]   BRENT SMITH, A. 'Imperfect sympathies', *The Chesterian*, 11 (1929), 77: 161.

[*1926*]   KOLODIN, I. 'Tchaikovsky on Brahms'. In: I. Kolodin, *The critical composer* (1940): 202–205 [see *2055*].

See also *405*.

HANS VON BÜLOW (1830–94)
German pianist, conductor and music critc

[*1927*]   BOBÉTH, M. 'Pëtr Il´ič Čajkovskij und Hans von Bülow', *Tschaikowsky-Gesellschaft: Mitteilungen*, 2 (1995): 15–29.
— [rev. repr.] In: *Čajkovskijs Homosexualität und sein Tod: Legenden und Wirklichkeit* (1998): 355–366 [see *600*].

See also *1020*.

ANTONÍN DVOŘÁK (1840–1906)
Czech composer, conductor, and professor at the Prague Conservatory

[*1928*]   [Vzpominka na Dvořáka], *Dalibor*, 18 (1896): 3.

[*1929*]   BELZA, I. *Antonín Dvorzhak*. Moskva; Leningrad: Muzgiz, 1949: 82–84.
Includes details of Chaikovskii's visits to Prague in Jan and Nov 1888, where he met Dvořák.

[*1930*]   KISELEV, V. 'Antonin Dvorzhak v Rossii', *Sovetskaia muzyka* (1951), 11: 78–82, illus.

[*1931*]   VRBA, P. 'Zamechatel´naia druzhba', *Muzykal´naia zhizn´* (1961), 17: 11–12, illus.
On Dvořák's meetings with Chaikovskii (1888–90).

[*1932*]   MIKUSA, K. 'Přátelství Antoíina Dvořáka a Petra Iljice Čajkovského', *Dvořákuv Karlovarski podzím* (1963), 5: 32.

[*1933*]   CLAPHAM, J. 'Dvořák's visit to Russia', *Musical Quarterly*, 51 (1965), 3: 493–506, illus.

[*1934*]   'Dvořák—Čajkovskij posedme', *Hudební rozhledy*, 37 (1984), 2: 69.

[*1935*] **LANDOVSKA, V. 'Chaikovskii i Dvorzhak'**. In: V. Landovska, *O muzyke*. Moskva, 1991: 331.

[*1936*] **'Dvořák a Čajkovskij: Poznámky k Dvořákové osme symfonii'**, *Hudební veda*, 28 (1991), 3: 244–256, music.

Text in Czech, with a summary in German.

ALEKSANDR GLAZUNOV (1865–1936)
Composer, conductor and professor at the St. Petersburg Conservatory

[*1937*] **GOZENPUD, A. A. 'A. K. Glazunov i P. I. Chaikovskii'**. In: *A. K. Glazunov: Issledovaniia, materialy, publikatsii, pis´ma*. Tom 1. Leningrad: Gos. muz. izdat, 1959: 353–375.

CHARLES GOUNOD (1818–93)
French composer, conductor and organist

[*1938*] **ALEKSEEVSKII, A. 'Guno i ego russkie tseniteli'**, *Muzykal´naia zhizn´* (Oct 1993), 19/20: 21–22.

EDVARD GRIEG (1843–1907)
Norwegian composer, pianist and conductor

[*1939*] **BJØRKVOLD, J.-R. 'Peter Čajkovskij og Edvard Grieg: En kontakt mellom to åndsfrender'**, *Studia Musicologica Norvegica*, 2 (1976): 37–50, music.

Includes bibliography and summary in English.

[*1940*] **MOKHOV, N. 'Grieg and Russia'**, *Studia Musicologica Norvegica*, 19 (1993): 123–124.

[*1941*] **SHATOV, N. 'Sovremenniki i druz´ia'**, *Muzykal´naia zhizn´* (1993), 21/22: 19–20, illus.

[*1942*] **MARTINOTTI, S. 'Rivisitazione di Grieg'**, *Nuovo Rivista Musicale Italiana*, 29 (1995), 4: 655–656.

See also *405*.

ARSENII KORESHCHENKO (1870–1921)
Composer, pianist, conductor, teacher and music critic

[*1944*] **KORESHCHENKO, A. N. 'Neutomimyi truzhenik i entuziast: Dva dokumenta k biografii'**, *Sovetskaia muzyka* (1972), 11: 92–94.

IOSIF KOTEK (1855–85)
Violinist and former student of Chaikovskii's

[*1945*] **'Redkaia fotografiia P. I. Chaikovskogo'**, *Muzykal´naia zhizn´* (1959), 15: 20, illus.

Concerning three newly-discovered letters from Chaikovskii to Iosif Kotek's sisters (Iuliia Chistiakova-Mikhalevskaia and Evgeniia Zhukovskaia), written in 1885 shortly after Kotek's death. Also a photograph of Chaikovskii with Kotek.

SOPHIE MENTER (1846–1918)
Pianist, composer and professor at the St. Petersburg Conservatory

[*1946*] **NAVRATIL, C. 'The 'immortal beloved' who guided Tchaikovsky's music'**, *Musical America* (1932), 4: 22.

Concerning Chaikovskii's relationship with Sophie Menter. See also *4992* to *4997*.

MODEST MUSORGSKII (1839–81)
Russian composer

[*1947*]   **VILOKOVIR, E. 'M. P. Musorgskii: K 45-letiiu so dnia smerti'**, *Muzyka i revoliutsiia* (1926), 5: 8–9.
Includes Musorgskii's views on Chaikovskii and other Russian composers.

[*1948*]   **MUSORGSKII, M. M. 'Tschaikowsky: Ein Anhänger der Religion bedingungsloser Schönheit'.**
In: *Tschaikowsky aus der Nähe* (1994): 76–79 [see *379*].
Extract from a letter from Musorgskii to Vladimir Stasov concerning Chaikovskii.

See also *2618, 5162*.

EDUARD NÁPRAVNÍK (1839–1916)
Czech conductor and composer

[*1949*]   **POSTLER, M. 'Přátelské vzrahy Čajkovského k Nápravníkoví'**, *Hudební rozhledy*, 11 (1958): 782–784.

[*1950*]   **KHENTOVA, S. 'Druzhba, rozhdennaia muzykoi'**, *Vechernii Leningrad* (6 Jun 1970): 2–3.
The relationship between Chaikovskii and Nápravník.

[*1951*]   **KHENTOVA, S. 'Chaikovskii i Napravnik'**, *Muzykal´naia zhizn´* (1971), 11: 15–16, illus.

[*1952*]   **MIKHEEVA, L. V. 'Napravnik i Chaikovskii'.** In: L. V. Mikheeva, *Eduard Frantsevich Napravnik*.
Moskva: Muzyka. 1985: 75–84.

[*1953*]   **NÁPRAVNÍK, V. E.** *Eduard Frantsevich Napravnik i ego sovremenniki*. Leningrad: Muzyka, 1991:
222–323, illus. ISBN 5-07140-0412-4.
Chaikovskii's relationship with Eduard Nápravník and his son Vladimir.

MARIIA PAL´CHIKOVA-LOGINOVA
Chaikovskii's first music teacher

[*1954*]   **PRESNETSOV, R. '"Ot starogo uchenika...": Istoriia odnoi fotografii'**, *Muzykal´naia zhizn´* (Mar
1978), 5: 20–21, illus.

EMILIIA PAVLOVSKAIA (1853–1935)
Opera artist at the Mariinskii Theatre in St. Petersburg

[*1955*]   **ZHEGIN, N. T. 'P. I. Chaikovskii i E. K. Pavlovskaia'**, *Sovetskaia muzyka* (1934), 8: 62–64.

IPPOLIT PRIANISHNIKOV (1847–1921)
Singer (baritone) at the Kiev Opera Theatre, music teacher and opera impressario

[*1956*]   **PERGAMENT, E. A. 'Neotsenimaia pomoshch´: K izucheniiu tvorcheskoi biografii P. I.
Chaikovskogo'**, *Sovetskaia muzyka* (1980), 7: 94–99.

[*1957*]   **PERGAMENT, E. A. 'P. I. Chaikovskii i Russkoe opernoe tovarishchestvo I. P. Prianishnikova'.**
In: *Teatr v zhizni i tvorchestve P. I. Chaikovskogo* (1985): 64–75 [see *589*].

NIKOLAI RIMSKII-KORSAKOV (1844–1908)
Composer, conductor and professor at the St. Petersburg Conservatory

[*1958*]   **FINDEIZEN, N. F. 'Chaikovskii i Rimskii-Korsakov: Opyt sravneniia kompozitor-
sovremennikov'**, *Niva* (1910), 1: 91 [suppl.].

[*1959*]   DIVANOVA, T. N. 'Rimskii-Korsakov i Chaikovskii'. In: T. N. Divanova, *Stat´i, vospominaniia.* Moskva: Muzyka, 1989: 103–113.

ANTON RUBINSHTEIN (1829–94)
Russian composer and pianist, older brother of Nikolai Rubinshtein

[*1960*]   ZABEL, E. *Anton Rubinstein: Ein Künstlerleben.* [Leipzig?], 1892: 271–276.

Includes 1 letter from Chaikovskii to Zabel (1892), concerning Anton Rubinshtein.

— [Russian tr. (abridged)] *Teatral´nyi mirok* (10 Jan 1893).

— [Russian tr.] 'P. Chaikovskii ob A. G. Rubinshtein', *Nuvellist* (Feb 1893), 2: 3–4.

[*1961*]   CHAIKOVSKII, M. I. [Chaikovskii i A. G. Rubinshtein]. In: M. I. Chaikovskii, *Zhizn´ Petra Il´icha Chaikovskogo*, tom 1 (1900): 331–332, 591–592 [see *1453*].

— [English tr.] In: A. Poznansky, *Tchaikovsky through others' eyes* (1999): 31 [see *380*].

[*1962*]   IVANOV, M. 'Desiatiletie so smerti P. I. Chaikovskogo: Po povodu A. Rubinshteina', *Novoe vremia* (1903), No. 9924.

[*1963*]   IVANOV, M. 'A. G. Rubinshtein', *Russkii vestnik* (1905), 1: 313, 321.

[*1964*]   CHERVINSKII, P. 'Vostorg i bol´ Chaikovskogo: Po sledam zabytogo pis´ma', *Muzykal´naia zhizn´* (1992), 17/18: 24.

A letter written by Chaikovskii concerning Anton Rubinshtein's 50th year as a musician.

See also *1966*.

NIKOLAI RUBINSHTEIN (1835–81)
Pianist, conductor, music teacher and founder of the Moscow Conservatory

[*1965*]   IAKOVLEV, V. V. 'P. I. Chaikovskii i N. G. Rubinshtein (1866–1881 gg.)'. In: *Istoriia russkoi muzyki v issledovaniiakh i materialakh.* Pod red. prof. K. A. Kuznetsova. Tom 1. Moskva: Gosizdat-Muzsektor, 1924: 153–182.

— [repr.] In: V. V. Iakovlev, *Izbrannye trudy o muzyke.* Tom 3. Moskva: Sovetskii kompozitor, 1983: 175–178.

[*1966*]   'Brat´ia Rubinsheteiny i Chaikovskii (ikh skhodstva i kontrasty)', *Segodnia* (25 Oct 1937).

4.5.3. Authors

ALEKSEI APUKHTIN (1841–93)
Writer, poet and school-friend of the composer

[*1967*]   POPOV, P. S. 'Poslanie A. N. Apukhtina P. I. Chaikovskomu', *Golos minuvshego* (1919), 1–4: 100.

[*1968*]   AMFITEATROV, A. V. 'Chaikovskii i Apukhtin: Druzhba', *Segodnia* (8 Sep 1933).

[*1969*]   IAKOVLEV, V. V. 'Chaikovskii i Apukhtin'. In: V. V. Iakovlev, *Izbrannye trudy o muzyke*, tom 1 (1964): 373–378 [see *2362*].

— [repr.] In: *P. I. Chaikovskii i russkaia literatura* (1980): 19–25 [see *588*].

[*1970*]   "V svoi my verili talanty...", *Muzykal´naia zhizn´* (1991), 9/10: 3.

[*1971*]   MARKOV, V. M. 'Chaikovskii i Apukhtin: K 100-letiiu so dnia smerti', *Vestnik Udmurtskogo universiteta*, 4 (1993):129–133.

Commemorating the centenary of Apukhtin's death. See also *191, 521*.

ANTON CHEKHOV (1860–1904)
Writer and dramatist

[*1972*]   SUVOROVSKII, N. 'Chaikovskii i Chekhov: Kak poety toski', *Kur´er* (25 Oct 1893).

[*1973*]   KUZMIN, M. 'Chekhov i Chaikovskii', *Zhizn´ iskusstva* (20 Oct 1918), 1: 11–13.

     — [repr.] In: M. Kuzmin, *Uslovnosti: Stat´i ob iskusstve*. Petrograd: Poliarnaia zvezda (1927): 144–147.

[*1974*]   LUNACHARSKII, A. V. 'Chem mozhet byt´: Chekhov dlia nas', *Pechat´ i revoliutsiia* (1924), 4: 19.

     On Chekhov's relationship with Chaikovskii.

     — [repr.] in A. V. Lunacharskii, *Literaturnye siluety*. Moskva: Gosizdat, 1925: 114–133.

[*1975*]   N. M. 'Chekhovskie nastroeniia v muzyke', *Zhizn´ izkusstva* (1924), 29: 10.

     Chekhov's views on Russian composers, including Chaikovskii.

[*1976*]   PUTINTSEV, N. 'Chekhov i Chaikovskii', *Kurortnaia gazeta* (8 May 1940).

[*1977*]   BALABANOVICH, E. Z. 'Chekhov i Chaikovskii: K 100-letiiu so dnia rozhdeniia velikogo russkogo pisatelia', *Muzykal´naia zhizn´* (1960), 2: 4–5, illus.

[*1978*]   RIGOTTI, D. 'Chechov librettista mancato', *La Scala* (Aug/Sep 1960): 26–27.

[*1979*]   BALABANOVICH, E. Z. *Chekov i Chaikovskii*. [Moskva]: Moskovskii rabochii, 1970. 184 p, illus.

     Reviews: V. Kiselev, 'Novye izdaniia', *Muzykal´naia zhizn´* (1971), 2: 24 — A. Kuznetsov, 'Obzory i retsenzii: Pisatel´ i iskusstvo', *Voprosy literatury* (1971), 4: 189–191 — E. Sholok, 'Velikie sovremenniki', *Teatr* (1972), 7: 84–85.

     — 2-e izd. Moskva: Moskovskii rabochii, 1973. 182 p, illus.

     Review: E. Sholok, 'Velikoe rodstvo', *Moskva* (1974), 11: 222–223.

     — 3-e izd., dop. Moskva: Moskovskii rabochii, 1978. 184 p, illus.

     See also *1980*.

     Review: P. R. Zaborov, *Russkaia literatura*, 3 (1984): 245–249.

     — [Japanese tr.] Tr. Nobuyuki Nakamoto. Tokyo: Shin-jidai-sha, 1970. 352 p.

[*1980*]   BALABANOVICH, E. Z. 'O nekotorykh chertakh tvorchestva Chekhova i Chaikovskogo'. In: *P. I. Chaikovskii i russkaia literatura* (1980): 40–58 [see *588*].

     Extracted from E. Z. Balabanovich, *Chekhov i Chaikovskii* (1978): 148–183 [see *1979*].

[*1981*]   BROWN, D. 'Tchaikovsky and Chekhov'. In: *Slavonic and Western music: Essays for Gerald Abraham*. Ed. by Malcolm H. Brown and Roland John Wiley. Oxford: Clarendon Press; Ann Arbor: UMI Research [1985]: 197–205, illus. (*U. M. I. Russian Music Studies*; 12). ISBN 0–8357–1594–9 (USA).

[*1982*]   MAKAROV, V. A. & MAKAROVA, L. A. 'A. P. Chekhov i P. I. Chaikovskii'. In: V. A. Makarova & I. A. Makarova, *Chekhovskie chteniia*. Oblastnaia nauchnia konferentsiia posviashchennaia izucheniiu zhizni i tvorchestva A. P. Chekhova i ego sviazei s Sumschinoi. Sumy, 1989: 37–38.

[*1983*]   OSIPOVA, L. 'Pesni Rotshil´da', *Sem´ia i shkola* (1990), 5: 53–56 [see *951*].

[*1984*]   BARTLETT, R. 'Tchaikovsky, Chekhov and the Russian elegy'. In: *Tchaikovsky and his world* (1998): 300–318 [see *601*].

     See also *418, 2000, 2004*.

GERMAN LAROSH (1845–1904)
Music and literary critic, and colleague at the St. Petersburg and Moscow Conservatories

[*1985*]   IAKOVLEV, V. V. 'Larosh o Chaikovskom'. In: G. A. Larosh, *Sobranie muzykal´no-kriticheskikh statei*, tom 2, chast 2 (1924): iii–xx [see *2311*].

[*1986*] SHUPER, D. S. 'Larosh i Chaikovskii'. In: D. S. Shuper, 'G. A. Larosh'. Dissertatsiia, predstavlennaia na soiskanie uchenoi stepenii kandidata. Leningrad: Gos. Konservatoriia, 1946: 107–144.

[*1987*] SABININA, M. 'Larosh i Chaikovskii (k 50-letiiu so dnia smerti G. Larosha)', *Sovetskaia muzyka* (1954), 10: 67–76, illus.

[*1988*] BERNANDT, G. B. 'Larosh i Chaikovskii'. In: G. A. Larosh, *Izbrannye stat´i v piati tomakh*, vyp. 2 (1975): 5–22 [see *2376*].

[*1989*] DIANOVA, L. '"Avtobiografiia" G. A. Larosha: Materialy k biografii i portretu uchenogo'. In: *P. I. Chaikovskii: Issledovaniia i materialy* (1997): 76–101 [see *599*].

[*1990*] TIKHOMIROVA, S. 'Chaikovskii i Larosh: Primer tvorcheskogo sodruzhestva'. In: *P. I. Chaikovskii: Issledovaniia i materialy* (1997): 61–75 [see *599*].

ALEKSANDR OSTROVSKII (1823–86)
Dramatist, translator and librettist

[*1991*] IAKOVLEV, V. V. 'A. N. Ostrovskii i muzykal´naia stikhiia'. In: *Ostrovskii: K 100-letiiu so dnia rozhdeniia, 1823–1923*. Iubileinyi sbornik, pod red. A. A. Bakhrushina, N. L. Brodskogo, N. A. Popova. Moskva: Izdat. Russkogo teatral´nogo obschestva, 1923: 60–63.

[*1992*] DURYLIN, S. 'Istoriia odnoi druzhby', *Sovetskii teatr* (1936), 6: 15–16.

Chaikovskii's collaboration with Ostrovskii on *The Voevoda* and *The Snow Maiden*.

[*1993*] POPOV, S. 'A. N. Ostrovskii i P. I. Chaikovskii'. In: *A. N. Ostrovskii i russkie kompozitory: Pis´ma*. Pod obshchei red. E. M. Kolosovoi i Vl. Filippova Moskva; Leningrad: Iskusstvo, 1937: 141–171.

See also *301*.

See also *3806, 4358, 4360*.

LEV TOLSTOI (1828–1910)
Novellist and playwright

[*1994*] 'Znakomstvo P. I. Chaikovskogo s grafom L. N. Tolstym', *Russkie vedomosti* (27 Aug 1901).

Compilation of extracts from M. I. Chaikovskii, *Zhizn´ Petra Il´icha Chaikovskogo* (1900–02) [see *1453*].

— [rev. repr.] 'P. I. Chaikovskii i L. N. Tolstoi', *Nuvellist* (1901), 10: 10.

[*1995*] NEWMARCH, R. H. 'Tchaikovsky and Tolstoi', *Contemporary Review*, 83 (Jan 1903): 112–118.

— [repr.] *Littell's Living Age*, series 7 (4 Apr 1903), 237: 58–63.

— [German tr.] 'Tschaikowsky und Tolstoj' (Deutsche Übersetzung von H. J. Conrat), *Die Musik*, 2 (15 Jul 1903), 20: 116–122.

— [German tr. (repr.)] *Allgemeine Musik-Zeitung* (1908), 39.

[*1996*] TOLSTOI, S. L. 'Lev Tolstoi i Chaikovskii: Ikh znakomstvo i vzaimootnosheniia'. In: *Istoriia russkoi muzyki v issledovaniiakh i materialakh*. Pod red. prof. K. A. Kuznetsova. Tom 1. Moskva: Gosizdat-Muzsektor, 1924: 114–124.

[*1997*] FELBEY, R. 'Tchaikovsky and Tolstoy', *The Chesterian* (Dec 1930), 91: 65–69.

[*1998*] BRAUDO, E. 'Tolstoi o Chaikovskom', *Literaturnaia gazeta* (20 Nov 1935): 4.

[*1999*]   ZAIDENSHNUR, E. 'Chaikovskii i Tolstoi', *Sovetskoe iskusstvo* (10 Sep 1938).

Extract from a letter from Chaikovskii to Shpazhinskaia (1887).

— [Ukrainian tr.] *Proletarskaia pravda* (9 Sep 1938).

[*2000*]   'L. Tolstoi o Chaikovskom', *Ogonek* (1940), 12: 4.

Extracts from letters by Tolstoi, Turgenev and Chekhov, concerning their views on Chaikovskii.

[*2001*]   BLOK, M. S. 'Neizdannye pomety P. I. Chaikovskogo na publitsisticheskikh proizvedeniiakh
L. N. Tolstogo'. In: *Iasnopolianskii sbornik: Literaturno-kriticheskie stat´i i materialy o zhizni i tvorchestve L. N.
Tolstogo*. Tula, 1955: 214–225.

— [rev. repr.] 'Pomety P. I. Chaikovskogo na proizvedenii L. N. Tolstogo "V chem moia vera"', In: *P. I.
Chaikovskii i russkaia literatura* (1980): 26–39 [see *588*].

[*2002*]   GARDEN, E. 'Tchaikovsky and Tolstoy', *Music & Letters*, 55 (Jul 1974), 3: 307–316.

[*2003*]   RUCH´EVSKAIA, E. A. 'P. I. Chaikovskii i A. K. Tolstoi'. In: *P. I. Chaikovskii: Nasledie*, vyp. 2
(2000): 49–80 [see *604*].

4.5.4. Others

[*2004*]   BROWN, D. 'Shedding a mask: Tchaikovsky's personal relationships', *The Listener*, 123 (1 Feb
1990): 44.

In connection with a series of three broadcasts by the author on BBC Radio 3, entitled *A sympathetic person*
(examining the composer's relationships with Leontii Tkachenko, Désirée Artôt and Anton Chekhov).

See also *385*.

ALEXANDER III (1845–94)

Tsar of Russia

[*2005*]   PLATEK, Ia. 'V dome Romanovykh', *Muzykal´naia zhizn´* (1994), 1: 32–35.

[*2006*]   WORTMAN, R. 'The Coronation of Alexander III'. In: *Tchaikovsky and his world* (1998): 277–299
[see *601*].

See also *605, 4833*.

PËTR IURGENSON (1836–1903)

Chaikovskii's principal publisher

[*2007*]   'P. I. Iurgenson: Biograficheskii nabrosok', *Russkaia muzykal´naia gazeta* (11 Apr 1904), 15: 385–391.

[*2008*]   NADEINSKII, E. 'Dinastiia iz doma na Neglinnoi', *Muzykal´naia zhizn´* (1990), 9: 14.

See also *530*.

IVAN KLIMENKO (1841–1914)

Architect and friend of the composer

[*2009*]   KLIMENKO, I. V. 'Pis´mo v redaktsiiu', *Russkaia muzykal´naia gazeta* (22/29 Jun 1903), 25/26: 605–
606.

[*2010*]   BELONOVICH, G. I. 'T. I. Klimenko (vospominaniia ob otse)'. In: *P. I. Chaikovskii: Zabytoe i novoe*
(1995): 159–160 [see *598*].

Tat´iana Klimenko's recollections (from 1992) of her father's relationship with Chaikovskii. See also *473*.

NADEZHDA VON MECK (1831–94)
Correspondent and benefactress of the composer

[2011]   TIDEBÖHL, E. von. 'P. I. Tschaikowsky and Mme. von Meck', *Monthly Musical Record*, 35 (Apr 1905): 65–67; (May 1905): 87–88.

[2012]   BIENEFELD, E. 'Tschaikowsky und Frau f. Meck', *Deutsche Musiker-Zeitung*, 58 (1927), 49.

[2013]   BOWEN, C. D. & MECK, B. von. *"Beloved friend": The story of Tchaikowsky and Nadejda von Meck*. London: Hutchinson & Co., 1937. 528 p, illus.

Includes extracts from correspondence between the composer and Nadezhda von Meck.

Reviews: G. A[braham], *Music & Letters*, 18 (1937): 408–410 — M. Bach-Wayskaja, *Die Musik*, 29 (1937): 832–837 — W. J. Henderson, 'I write music for you', *Saturday Review*, 15 (30 Jan 1937): 5 — 'Queer musician', *Time*, 29 (1 Feb 1937): 63 — *Music Journal*, 20 (Jan 1962): 104.

— [rev. ed.] New York: Random House, 1937. viii, 484 p, music, illus.

— [repr.] New York: Garden City, 1940. viii, 484 p, music, illus.

— [repr.] New York: Dover, 1946. viii, 484 p, music, illus.

— [repr.] Boston: Brown [1961]. viii, 484 p, music, illus.

— [repr.] Westport, Conn: Greenwood Press, 1976. 484 p, music, illus. ISBN: 0–8371–6861–9.

— 2nd ed. (abridged). *"The Music Lovers": The story of Tchaikowsky and Nadejda von Meck*. London: Hodder Paperbacks, 1971. 317 p, illus. ISBN: 0–340–15154–4.

— [Danish tr.] *Tschaikovsky og fru von Meck*. København: Jespersen og Pios Forl, 1940. 320 p.

— [French tr.] *L'ami bien-aimé*. Traduit par M. Rémon. Paris: Gallimard, 1940.

— [German tr.] *"Geliebte Freundin": Tschaikowskys Leben und sein Briefwechsel mit Nadeshsa von Meck*. Aus der Englische unter Benutzung der russische Original-Briefe von Wolfgang E. Groeger. Leipzig: P. List [1938]. 476 p, music, illus.

ReviewsR. Petzoldt, '"Geliebte Freundin": Peter Tschaikowsky und Nadeschda von Meck', *Allgemeine Musik Zeitung*, 65 (1938): 297–298 — M. Bach-Wayskaja & H. Gerigk, *Musik und Kultur*, 30 (1938): 840–842.

— [German tr. (2nd ed.)] *P. I. Tschaikowsky: Briefwechsel mit N. F. von Meck*. Deutsch von W. E. Groeger, nach der Ausgabe von W. A. Shdanow und N. T. Schegin; englisch von C. Drinker-Bowen. Leipzig: Paul List Verlag, 1949. 460 p.

— [German tr. (repr.)] Leipzig: P. List [1951]. 460 p.

Review: *Musikhandel*, 19 (1968), 8: 416.

[2014]   BORTKIEWICZ, S. *Die seltsame Liebe Peter Tschaikowskys und der Nadjeschda von Meck*. Nach dem Originalbriefwechsel Peter Tschaikowskys mit Frau Nadjeschda von Meck aus dem Russische übersetzt von Sergei Bortkiewicz. Leipzig: Kochler & Amelang [1938]. 319 p.

Reviews: M. Bach-Wayskaja, *Die Musik*, 30 (1938): 842–843 — B. Disertori, *Rivista musicale italiana*, 42 (1938): 671–673 — R. Petzoldt, *Allgemeine Musik Zeitung*, 65 (1938): 741 — G. Struck, *Lübeck Blätter*, 80 (1938): 710–711.

[2015]   HARRISON, S. 'Tchaikovsky never spoke to his chief benefactor'. In: S. Harrison, *Musical box*. New York, 1941: 107–110.

[2016]   MAREK, G. 'Woman beside the genius', *Good Housekeeping*, 118 (Jan 1944): 151–152.

[2017]   WILLIAMS, R. 'Who were the women composers have loved?', *House Buyer*, 87 (Jun 1945): 88–89.

[2018]   SLONIMSKY, N. 'Musical oddities', *Etude*, 70 (Nov 1952): 4–5.

[2019]   RIMSKI-KORSAKOW, G. 'Rozmowa z wnuczka Nadiezdy von Meck', *Ruch Muzyczny*, 5 (1961), 15: 18.

[2020]   MECK, G. von. *As I remember them*. London: Dobson, 1973. 448, [33] p, illus. ISBN 0–234–77454–1.

Memoirs of Nadezhda von Meck's granddaugter and Chaikovskii's grand-nece, Galina von Meck.

Reviews: *Musical Events*, 28 (Jun 1973): 6 — J. Warrack, *Musical Times*, 114 (Jul 1973): 699–700.

— [Russian tr.] G. Fon Mekk, *Kak ia ikh pomniu*. Perevod. s angl. Borisa Nikitina. Moskva: Fond im. I. D. Sytina, 1999. ISBN 5–8686–3107–2.

[*2021*] REULING, K. F. 'Part of the past', *Opera News*, 42 (18 Feb 1978): 14–17, illus.
Interview with Galina von Meck.

[*2022*] BANNOUR, W. *L'étrange baronne von Mekk: La dame de pique de Tchaïkovsky*. Paris: Librarie académique Perrin [1988]. 252 p, illus. (*Collection Terre des femmes*). ISBN: 2–2620–0509–5
Reviews: *Revue musicale de Suisse Romande*, 41 (1988), 2: 89–90 — E. Pérez Adrián, *Revista de Occidente*, 4 (Mar 1988), 82: 153.

[*2023*] MALYGINA, S. 'Milyi, dorogoi, bestsennyi drug', *Sovetskii patriot* (11 Oct 1988).

[*2024*] ATTERFORS, G. 'Nadezhda von Meck: Unik brevsamling', *Musikrevy*, 48 (1993), 4: 39–431.

[*2025*] BUROV, F. 'Ot Fanni do Nadezhdy: Bez nadezhdy na liubov', *Daidzhest/24 chasa* (1993), 50: 10–11.

[*2026*] BEVAN, V. 'Nadezhda von Meck: An unseen angel', *Classic CD* (Nov 1993), 42: 11–12 [suppl.].

[*2027*] TOMMASINI, A. 'The patroness who made Tchaikovsky Tchaikovsky', *New York Times* (2 Sep 1998).

[*2028*] HÄUSLER, J. 'Čajkovskij und die russischen "Eisenbahnkönige"', *Tschaikowsky-Gesellschaft Mitteilungen*, 7 (2000): 91–98.

See also *187, 281, 463, 498, 1746, 1750, 2085, 3120, 5492, 5493*.

MARIUS PETIPA (1818–1910)

Balletmaster and choreographer

[*2029*] SLONIMSKII, Iu. 'Chaikovskii o Petipa', *Neva* (1974), 1: 220.
Extract from a letter from Chaikovskii to Ivan Vsevolozhskii, regarding Petipa.

KONSTANTIN SHILOVSKII (1849–93)

Artist, poet and musician

[*2030*] ENDII. 'Iz zhizni P. I. Chaikovskogo', *Peterburgskii listok* (24 Oct 1895).
Concerning the composer's visits to Shilovskii's Glebovo estate.

VLADIMIR STASOV (1824–1906)

Art historian, critic, and director of the arts section of the St. Petersburg Public Library.

[*2031*] KARENIN, V. 'Stasov i Chaikovskii'. In: *Vladimir Stasov: Ocherk ego zhizni i deiatel´nosti*. Tom 2. Leningrad: Mysl´, 1927: 438–451.
Includes: 'V. V. Stasov o VI simfonii Chaikovskogo': 440–441 [see *4688*].

[*2032*] 'Pis´ma V. V. Stasova k A. N. Molas', *Sovetskaia muzyka* (1949), 1: 86–91.
A letter written by Stasov in 1870, giving his views on Chaikovskii and 'The Five'.

4.5.5. Homosexuality

[*2033*] SMITH, A. E. 'Peter Ilyich Tchaikovsky: His life and loves re-examined', *ONE Instutute Quarterly Homophile Studies*, 4 (Dec 1961): 20–36.

[2034]   GARDINER B. 'Tchaikovsky: The unknown', *Musical Opinion*, 97 (Apr 1974): 283.
Includes a review of J. Warrack, *Tchaikovsky* (1973) [see *1528*].

[2035]   LONG, R. 'The unmade bed', *Fugue*, 4 (Feb 1980): 32.
Unmarried composers.

[2036]   ORLOVA, A. A. 'Taina zhizni Chaikovskogo', *Novyi Amerikanets* (5–11 Nov 1980), 39: 20–21.
— [rev. repr.] 'Taina zhizni i smerti Chaikovskogo' (1987) [see *2233*].

[2037]   WALLACE, I. *The intimate sex lives of famous people*. New York: Del, 1981: 256–257.

[2038]   MAYER, H. 'Lüdvig von Bavaria und Peter Ilitsch Tschaikowsky'. In: H. Mayer, *Aussenseiter*. Frankfurt am Main: Suhrkamp, 1975: 247–259.
— [English tr.] 'Ludwig of Bavaria and Peter Ilitch Tchaikovsky'. In: H. Mayer, 'Outsiders: A study in life and letters'. Tr. by Denis M. Sweet. Cambridge, Mass.: MIT Press, 1982: 210–221.

[2039]   OSMOND-SMITH, D. 'Tchaikovsky: The relationship between music and homosexuality', *European Gay Review* (1986): 25–31.
Interview with Professor David Brown.

[2040]   KARLINSKY, S. 'Should we retire Tchaikovsky?', *Christopher Street*, 11 (May 1988), 3: 16–21.
— [German tr. (abridged)] 'Tschaikowskis Selbstmord: Mytos und Realität' (übers. von M. Beitner), *Capri*, 2 (Dec 1988), 3: 29–36.

[2041]   JOHANSSON, W. 'Tchaikovsky, Peter Il´ich (1840–1893)'. In: *Encyclopedia of homosexuality*, vol. 2. Wayne R. Dynes, ed. New York: Garland, 1990: 1279–1280.

[2042]   POZNANSKY, A. 'Tchaikovsky's candour', *New York Times Book Reviews* (2 Feb 1992).

[2043]   SMITH, N. 'Perceptions of homosexuality in Tchaikovsky criticism', *Context* (sum. 1992–93), 4: 3–9.

[2044]   RUSSELL, P. 'Tchaikovsky'. In: *The gay 100: A ranking of the most influential gay men and lesbians, past and present*. New York: Carol, 1994: 117–120, illus.

[2045]   HENRY, S. 'Tchaikovsky, Peter Ilich'. In: *Gay and lesbian biography*. Detroit: St. James Press, 1997: 427–429.

See also *2250, 4460*.

4.6. VIEWS AND OPINIONS

4.6.1. Music & Musicians

[2046]   VEIMARN, P. 'Khudozhestvennye vozzreniia P. I. Chaikovskogo na muzykal´noe iskusstvo', *Syn Otechestva* (1898), Nos. 176, 179.

[2047]   SIMPSON, E. E. 'Tschaikowsky as a music critic', *Music*, 19 (Mar 1901): 460–469.
English tr. of extracts from *Muzykal´nye fel´etony i zametki Petra Il´icha Chaikovskogo* (1898) [see *131*].

[2048]   NERUDA, E. 'Tschaikowsky als Kritiker', *Neue Zeitschrift für Musik*, 99 (1903), 10: 148–149.

[2049]   VAL´TER, V. 'Chto pisal ob opere Pëtr Il´ich Chaikovskii', *Russkaia muzykal´naia gazeta* (19 Oct 1903), 42: 983–990.
Extracts from Chaikovskii's writings on the subject of opera.

[2050]   ALTMANN, W. 'Tschaikowsky als Beurteiler anderer Komponisten', *Zeitschrift der Internationalen Musikgesellschaft*, 5 (1903/04), 2: 58–62.

[2051]   DANILOVICH, A. 'Tschaikowsky als Kritiker', *Le Courier musicale*, 12 (1907).

[2052]   KNORR, I. 'Tschaikowsky als Kritiker und Musikschriftsteller', *Blätter der Staatsoper* (1929), 21.

[2053]   'Tschaikowsky über Komponisten und über Komponieren: Aus unveröffentlichten Briefen', *Die Musik*, 30 (1938): 239–244.

[2054]   'Tschaikowsky über Programm-musik', *Die Musik*, 31 (1938): 32–33.

[2055]   KOLODIN, I. *The critical composer: The musical writings of Berlioz, Wagner, Schumann, Tchaikovsky and others*. Ed. by Irving Kolodin. New York: Howell, Soskin & Co. [1940]. vi, 275 p, music.

Chaikovskii's views and opinions on various composers derived from his diaries and letters. Includes 'Tchaikovsky on Beethoven': 83–85 [see *2078*] — 'Tchaikovsky on Wagner': 191–197 [see *2109*] — 'Tchaikovsky on "The Five"': 198–201 [see *1909*] — 'Tchaikovsky on Brahms': 202–205 [see *1926*].

— [repr.] Port Washington, N. Y.: Kennikat Press; Freeport, N. Y.: Books for Libraries press [1969]. vi, 275 p, music. (*Essay and General literature index reprint series*). ISBN: 0–8046–0566–1.

[2056]   GOLOVINSKII, G. 'Chaikovskii: Muzykal´nyi kritik', *Sovetskaia muzyka* (1950), 8: 81–87.

[2057]   'Nachalo kriticheskoi deiatel´nosti P. I. Chaikovskogo', *Sovetskaia muzyka* (1951), 11: 112.

[2058]   *P. I. Chaikovskii o kompozitorskom masterstve: Izbrannye otryvki iz pisem i statei*. Sost., red. i kommentarii I. F. Kunina. Moskva: Gos. muz. izdat., 1952. 156 p, music, illus. (*Russkaia klassicheskaia muz. kritika*).

Includes bibliography: 145–148.

— 2-e izd., pererab. i dop. *P. I. Chaikovskii o kompozitorskom tvorchestve i masterstve: Izbrannye otryvki iz pisem i statei*. Sost., red. i kommentarii I. F. Kunina. Moskva: Muzyka, 1964. 271 p, music, illus. (*Russkaia klassicheskaia muz. kritika*).

Includes bibliography: 258–261.

Review: *Muzykal´naia zhizn´* (1965), 15: 24.

[2059]   *P. I. Chaikovskii o narodnom i natsional´nom elemente v muzyke: Izbrannye otryvki iz pisem i statei*. Sost., red. i kommentarii I. F. Kunina. Moskva: Gos. muz. izdat., 1952. 108 p. (*Russkaia klassicheskaia muz. kritika*).

Includes bibliography: 97–100.

Review: Ia. El´sberg, 'Mysli Chaikovskogo', *Literaturnaia gazeta* (28 Oct 1952): 4,

— 2-e izd, pererab. *P. I. Chaikovskii o Rossii i russkoi kul´ture: Izbrannye otryvki iz pisem i statei*. Sost., predislovie, red. i komentarii I. F. Kunina. Moskva: Gos. muz. izdat., 1961. 196 p. (*Russkaia klassicheskaia muzykal´naia kritika*).

[2060]   *P. I. Chaikovskii ob opere: Izbrannye otryvki iz pisem i statei*. Sost., red. i kommentarii I. F. Kunina. Moskva; Leningrad: Gos. muz. izdat., 1952. 196 p. (*Russkaia klassicheskaia muzykal´naia kritika*).

Includes bibliography: 186–189.

Review: N. Shumskaia, 'Mysli Chaikovskogo ob opere i programmnoi muzyke', *Sovetskaia muzyka* (1952), 10: 93–94, music.

— 2-e izd., dop. *P. I. Chaikovskii ob opere i balete: Izbrannye otryvki iz pisem i statei*. Sost., red., predislovie i kommentarii I. F. Kunina. Moskva: Gos. muz. izdat., 1960. 292 p. (*Russkaia klassicheskaia muz. kritika*).

Includes bibliography: 275–279.

[2061]   *P. I. Chaikovskii o programmnoi muzyke: Izbrannye otryvki iz pisem i statei*. Sost., red. i kommentarii I. F. Kunina. Moskva; Leningrad: Gos. muz. izdat., 1952. 112 p, music. (*Russkaia klassicheskaia muzykal´naia kritika*).

Includes bibliography: 105–108.

Review:N. Shumskaia, 'Mysli Chaikovskogo ob opere i programmnoi muzyke', *Sovetskaia muzyka* (1952), 10: 93–94.

— 2-e izd., pererab. i dop. *P. I. Chaikovskii o simfonicheskoi muzyke: Izbrannye otryvki iz pisem i statei*. Sost., red., vstup. stat´ia i kommentarii I. F. Kunina. Moskva: Gos. muz. izdat., 1963. 311 p, music. (*Russkaia klassicheskaia muz. kritika*).

Includes bibliography: 293–298.

[2062]   'Iz vyskazyvanii P. I. Chaikovskogo'. In: *Pëtr Il´ich Chaikovskii: Kratkii rekomendatel´nyi ukazatel´* (1953): 12–17 [see *23*].

[2063]   'P. I. Chaikovskii i narodno-pesennoe tvorchestvo', *Muzykal´nye kadry* (5 Nov 1953): 4.

Extracts from Chaikovskii's articles and correspondence concerning Russian folk-songs.

[2064]   OGOLEVETS, A. S. *Materialy i dokumenty po istorii russkoi realisticheskoi muzykal´noi estetiki*. Klassiki russkoi muzyki i muzykal´noi kritiki ob iskusstve. Dopushcheno v kachestve ucheb. posobiia dlia vysshikh muzykal´nykh ucheb. zavedenii. Tom 2: *V. V. Stasov, M. P. Musorgskii, A. P. Borodin, P. I. Chaikovskii, N. A. Rimskii-Korsakov*. Moskva: Gos. muz. izdat. [c.1955], music, illus.

Textbook for music students.

[2065]   'Peter Ilyitch Tchaikovsky, 1840–1893'. In: *Composers on music: An anthology of composer's writings from Palestrina to Copland*. Ed. by Sam Morgenstern. New York: Pantheon Books, 1956: 249–257.

Extracts from Chaikovskii's correspondence with Nadezhda von Meck.

— 2nd ed. *Composers on music: Eight centuries of writings*. Ed. by Josiah Fisk. Boston: Northeastern University Press, 1997:152-160.

With additional extracts from Chaikovskii's letters to his brother Anatolii, and Vladimir Davydov.

[2066]   *P. I. Chaikovskii i narodnaia pesnia: Izbrannye otryvki iz pisem i statei*. Sost., red. predislovie i kommentarii B. I. Rabinovicha. Moskva: Gos. muz. izdat., 1963. 159 p, music. (*Russkaia klassicheskaia muzykal´naia kritika*).

Includes 'Ukazatel´ proizvedenii Chaikovskogo, v kotorykh ispol´zuiutsia narodnye pesni': 120–137 [see *2361*] — 'Notnoe prilozhenie': 138–141 — 'Kommentarii k notnomu prilozheniiu': 142–144 — 'Bibliografiia': 145–149.

[2067]   RAPZE, E. 'Mysli kompozitora', *Neva* (1965), 5: 197–198.

Extracts from Chaikovskii's letters and critical articles.

[2068]   ARUTIUNOV, D. A. 'Iz vyskazyvanii P. I. Chaikovskogo o muzykal´noi forme'. In: D. A. Arutiunov, *Sochineniia P. I. Chaikovskogo v kurse analiza muzykal´nykh proizvedenii* (1989): 96–109 [see *2393*].

— [rev. repr.] 'Vzgliady P. I. Chaikovskogo na muzykal´nuiu formu (po materialam vyskazyvanii)'. In: *Chaikovskii: K 150-letiiu so dnia rozhdeniia. Voprosy istorii, teorii i ispolnitel´stva* (1990): 17–42 [see *591*].

[2069]   GERDT, O. "Ia pretenduiu na shedevr etogo zhanra", *Sovetskii balet* (1990), 6: 4–6.

References to ballet in Chaikovskii's correspondence.

[2070]   'O vremeni, o muzyke, o sebe: Iz pisem, dnevnikov, statei P. I. Chaikovskogo', *Muzykal´naia gazeta* (1990), 9: 4.

[2071]   ORLOVA, A. A. 'P. I. Chaikovskii o muzyke: K 150-letiiu so dnia rozhdeniia kompozitora', *Grani* (1990): 283-305.

[2072]   'Pëtr Il´ich o sebe i muzyke', *Sovetskaia muzyka* (1990), 6: 1, 20, 32, 81, 120, 133 [see *592*].

[2073]   'Chaikovskii: Mysli o muzyke', *Muzyka v SSSR* (Jan/Mar 1990): 12–15, illus.

[2074]   ARUTIUNOV, D. 'P. I. Chaikovskii o krupnykh muzykal´nykh formakh i zhanrakh'. In: *Chaikovskii: Voprosy istorii i teorii* (1991): 4–20 [see *593*].

[2075]   **CAMPBELL, S.** *Russians on Russian music, 1830–1880: An anthology*. Ed. and tr. by Stuart Campbell. Cambridge; New York: Cambridge Univ. Press, 1994. xxi, 295 p, illus.
Review: *Music & Letters*, 76 (1995), 4: 627–629.

See also *177, 1532, 2599*.

DANIEL AUBER (1781–1871)
French composer

[2076]   'Tchaikovsky on Auber (1781–1871)', *Musical Opinion*, 94 (Sep 1971): 625.
Tr. of extracts from Chaikovskii's musical articles.

LUDWIG VAN BEETHOVEN (1770–1827)
German composer and pianist

[2077]   **MIASKOVSKII, N. Ia.** 'Chaikovskii i Betkhoven', *Muzyka* (16 May 1912): 431–440, illus.
The influence of Beethoven on Chaikovskii's music.
Review: I. Raiskii: 'Artisticheskii vostorg i issledovatel´skaia glubina' (1980) [see *2384*].
— [offprint] *Chaikovskii i Betkhoven*. Moskva, 1912. 14 p.
— [repr.] In: N. Ia. Miaskovskii, *Avtobiografiia, stat´i, zametki, otzyvy, iz perepiski*. Pod red. S. Shlifshtein. Tom 2. Moskva: Sovetskii kompozitor, 1960: 56–63.
— [repr.] In: N. Ia. Miaskovskii, *Literaturnoe nasledie, pis´ma: Sobranie materialov*, Red., sost. i primechaniia S. Shlifshteina. Tom 2. 2-e izd. Moskva: Muzyka, 1964: 62–71.
— [repr.] In: *Iz istorii sovetskoi Betkhoveniany*. Moskva: Sovetskii kompozitor, 1972: 35–39.

[2078]   **KOLODIN, I.** 'Tchaikovsky on Beethoven'. In: I. Kolodin, *The critical composer* (1940): 83–85 [see *2055*].

[2079]   **HARLING-COMYNS, F.** 'Tschaikowsky on the "Eroica" and "Fidelio"', *Musical Opinion*, 90 (Jan 1967): 201.
Tr. from Chaikovskii's articles for the *Moskovskie vedomosti*, 1871–75.

[2080]   'Peter Ilich Tschaikowsky'. In: *The Beethoven companion*. Ed. by Thomas K. Scherman and Louis Biancolli. Garden City, N. Y.: Doubleday, 1972: 1158–1160.

[2081]   **KHOKHLOV, Iu. N.** 'Betkhoven ili Chaikovskii?'. In: *Russko-nemetskie muzykal´nye sviazi*. Red.-sost. I. I. Nikolaevskaia, Iu. N. Khokhlov. Moskva: Muzyka, 1996: 136–178.

DMITRI BORTNIANSKII (1751–1825)
Russian composer

[2082]   **KUZMA, M.** 'Bortniansky à la Bortniansky: An examination of the sources of Dmitry Bortniansky's Choral Concertos', *Journal of Musicology*, 14 (1996), 2: 183–212, music, illus.
Concerning Chaikovskii's editorial work on the complete edition of Bortnianskii's church music.

FRANÇOIS COUPERIN (1668–1733)
French composer and organist

[2083]   **LANDOVSKA, V.** 'Chaikovskii i Kuperen'. In: V. Landovska, *O muzyke*. Moskva, 1991: 330.

ALEKSANDR DARGOMYZHSKII (1813–69)
Russian composer and pianist

[2084]   'Chaikovskii o Glinke i Dargomyzhskom', *Nuvellist* (1903), 2: 67.

Chaikovskii's views on Glinka and Dargomyzhskii.

CLAUDE DEBUSSY (1862–1918)
French pianist, composer and critic

[2085]   LOCKSPEISER, E. 'Debussy, Tchaïkovsky et Mme von Meck', *La revue musicale*, 16 (Nov 1935): 245.
— [English tr.] 'Debussy, Tchaikovsky and Madame von Meck', *Musical Quarterly*, 22 (Jan 1936): 38–44.

[2086]   LOCKSPEISER, E. 'Claude Debussy in the correspondence of Tchaikovsky and Madame von Meck', *Musical Opinion*, 60 (May 1937): 691–692.

[2087]   SLONIMSKY, N. 'Musical oddities', *Etude*, 70 (Nov 1952): 4–5.

See also *2013, 2509, 2510*.

MIKHAIL GLINKA (1804–57)
Russian composer

[2088]   KONSKII, P. 'Cherez Glinku k sovremennosti?', *Rabochii i teatr* (1925), 40: 7.
The influence of Glinka on Chaikovskii and other composers.

[2089]   MARTYNOV, I. I. 'Chaikovskii i Glinka', *Sovetskaia muzyka* (1940), 1: 28–37, illus.

[2090]   VAIDMAN, P. E. 'Az prinadlezhu i esm´ porozhdenie Glinki', *Sovetskaia muzyka* (1979), 7: 84–88.

[2091]   VAIDMAN, P. E. 'P. I. Chaikovskii i M. I. Glinka'. In: *P. I. Chaikovskii i Ural* (1992): 15–22 [see *1749*].

See also *2084*.

WOLFGANG AMADEUS MOZART (1756–91)
Austrian composer, conductor and pianist

[2092]   'Chaikovskii i Motsart', *Zhizn´ iskusstva* (1924), 2: 30.

[2093]   WALSALL, A. 'Tschaikowsky's adoration of Mozart', *Etude*, 43 (Sep 1925): 661.

[2094]   SAKVA, K. 'Chaikovskii o Mozarte'. In: *Bericht über den internationalen musikwissenschaftlichen Kongreß Wien, Mozartjahr 1956*. Wien, 1956: 537–543.

[2095]   'Tchaikovsky on Mozart', *Musical Times*, 97 (Jan 1956): 42.

[2096]   LENZON, V. 'Russkaia Motsartiana', *Muzykal´naia zhizn´* (1985), 21: 18.
Concerning the collection of Mozart's scores in Chaikovskii's library at Klin, and the Suite No. 4, *Mozartiana*.

[2097]   SCHAUER, J. 'Mozart and the romantics', *San Francisco Opera Magazine*, 69 (1991), 4: 50–54, illus.

[2098]   LAUER, L. 'Čajkovskij und Mozart: Ein Leserbrief von 1881'. In *Tschaikowsky-Gesellschaft: Mitteilungen*, 2 (1995): 55–58.
Chaikovskii's letter to the editor of the journal *Signale für die musikalische Welt*, concerning an arrangement of Mozart's opera *Don Giovanni*.
— [repr.] In: *Čajkovskijs Homosexualität und sein Tod: Legenden und Wirklichkeit* (1998): 535–538 [see *600*].

[2099]   SYSOEVA, E. V. 'Chaikovskii i Motsart'. In: *Pamiati N. S. Nikolaevoi*. Moskva: Gos. konservatoriia im. P. I. Chaikovskogo, 1996: 114–120. (*Nauchnye trudy MGK im P. I. Chaikovskogo*; 14).

          — [repr.] In: *Motsart: Prostranstvo stseny*. Red.-sost. R. G. Kosacheva, M. E. Tarakanov. Moskva: Gitis, 1998: 84–99. ISBN 5-7196-02328-0.

[2100]   KLIMOVITSKII, A. I. 'Motsart Chaikovskogo: Fragmenty siuzheta'. In: *K 75-letiiu E. R. Ruch´evskoi: Sbornik statei*. Sankt Peterburg: Gos. konservatoriia im. N. A. Rimskogo-Korsakova, 1998: 45–104.

          See also *4820, 4830*.

ROBERT SCHUMANN (1810–56)
German composer, conductor, pianist and critic

[2101]   BLANK, G. 'Über die Beziehungen P. I. Tschaikowsky zum Schaffen Robert Schumanns', *Wissenschaftliche Zeitschrift der Padagogischen Hochschule Zwickau*, 9 (1973), 2: 108–127.

[2102]   FROLOVA, M. 'Chaikovskii i Shuman'. In: *Chaikovskii: Voprosy istorii i teorii* (1991): 54–64 [see *593*].

[2103]   BIALIK, M. G. 'Chaikovskii i Shuman'. In: *P. I. Chaikovskii: Nasledie*, vyp. 2 (2000): 160–172 [see *604*].

          See also *117, 2497*.

GIUSEPPE VERDI (1813–1901)
Italian composer

[2104]   KENIGSBERG, A. K. 'Chaikovskii i Verdi'. In: *P. I. Chaikovskii: Nasledie*, vyp. 2 (2000): 173–185 [see *604*].

RICHARD WAGNER (1813–83)
German composer, conductor and writer

[2105]   KIUI, Ts. A. 'Muzykal´nye zametki: Pis´mo g. Chaikovskogo', *Sankt Peterburgskie vedomosti* (20 Mar 1873).

          Repr. of Chaikovskii's letter in the journal *Golos* (6 Mar 1873): 2, regarding Wagner's overtures to *Tannhauser* and *Die Valküre*.

[2106]   SEIDL, A. 'A defence of Wagner', *Morning Journal* (10 May 1891).

          A response to Chaikovskii's article 'Wagner and his music' [see *145*]. See also *2110*.

          — [repr.] In: E. Yoffe, *Tchaikovsky in America* (1986): 125–127 [see *1864*].

[2107]   LAROSH, G. A. 'O "Val´kirii", R. Vagnere i vagnerisme', *Ezhegodnik Imperatorskikh teatrov, 1899/1900* (1900), prilozh. 1: 60–81.

          Includes references to Chaikovskii's relationship with Wagner.

[2108]   [BACH-WAYSKAJA, M.] 'Tschaikowsky über Wagner', *Allgemeine Musik Zeitung*, 65 (1938): 87.

[2109]   KOLODIN, I. 'Tchaikovsky on Wagner'. In: I. Kolodin, *The critical composer* (1940): 191–197 [see *2055*].

[2110]   PEYSER, H. F. 'Recalling a once-celebrated controversy', *Musical America*, 63 (10 Jan 1943): 7–9, illus.

          Seidl's rebuttal to Chaikovskii's article 'Wagner and his music' [see *2106*]. See also *2106*.

[2111]   'Tchaikovsky and Wagner', *About the House*, 4 (1975), 10: 26–31, illus.

[*2112*] KOHLHASE, T. 'Čakovskijs Wagner-Rezeption: Daten und Texte', *Tschaikowsky-Gesellschaft: Mitteilungen*, 4 (1997): 70–96.

Chaikovskii's critical writings on Wagner.

— [repr.] In: *Čajkovskijs Homosexualität und sein Tod: Legenden und Wirklichkeit* (1998): 299–326 [see *600*].

[*2113*] BARTLETT, R. 'Tchaikovsky and Wagner: A reassessment'. In: *Tchaikovsky and his contemporaries* (1999): 95–116 [see *602*].

See also *145*, *4658*.

CARL MARIA VON WEBER (1786–1826)
German composer, conductor and pianist

[*2114*] SKORBIASHCHENSKAIA, O. 'Chaikovskii i Veber', *Sovetskaia muzyka* (1990), 12: 101–105, music.

4.6.2. Literature & Writers

[*2115*] ORLOVA, A. A. 'Biblioteka kompozitora', *Ogonek* (1940), 12: 15.

Chaikovskii's opinions on various writers, and a description of his library at the Klin house-museum.

[*2116*] P. V. 'Konferentsii, seminary, vstrechi', *Sovetskaia muzyka* (1979), 5: 143.

A conference on the theme 'P. I. Chaikovskii and Russian Literature', held at the Votkinsk house-museum.

[*2117*] ANCHUGOVA, T. 'Vysshaia potrebnost´', *V mire knig* (1980), 7: 74–76.

Chaikovskii's literary interests.

[*2118*] ROZENBERG, I. S. '"Ia otnoshus´ k stikham kak muzykant": O vzgliadakh P. I. Chaikovskogo na poeziiu i ego poeticheskom tvorchestve'. In: *P. I. Chaikovskii i russkaia literatura* (1980): 210–221 [see *588*].

[*2119*] VIKTOROVA, N. A. 'P. I. Chaikovskii—chitatel´'. In: *P. I. Chaikovskii i russkaia literatura* (1980): 191–209 [see *588*].

[*2120*] PLATEK, Ia. 'Pod sen´iu druzhnykh muz: Po stranitsam pisem Petra Il´icha Chaikovskogo', *Muzykal´naia zhizn´* (1984), 1: 18–19, 3: 20–21, 6: 15–17, 9: 18–19, 11: 18–20, illus.

Chaikovskii's literary interests as revealed in his correspondence.

— [rev. repr.] 'Pis´ma P. I. Chaikovskogo'. In: Ia. Platek, *Pod sen´iu druzhnykh muz*. Moskva: Sovetskii kompozitor, 1987: 113–178.

[*2121*] BELONOVICH, G. I. 'P. I. Chaikovskii i frantsuzskii dramaticheskii teatr'. In: *Teatr v zhizni i tvorchestve P. I. Chaikovskogo* (1985): 16–26 [see *589*].

[*2122*] ZAKHAROVA, O. 'Chaikovskii chitaet Bibliiu', *Nashe nasledie*, 2 (1990): 22–24, illus.

[*2123*] KLUGE, R.-D. 'Cajkovskij und die literarische Kultur Rußlands'. In: *Internationales Čajkovskij Symposium, Tübingen 1993: Bericht* (1995): 165–176 [see *596*].

[*2124*] RUBTSOVA, V. 'Čajkovskij und die russische Kultur seiner Zeit'. In: *Internationales Čajkovskij Symposium, Tübingen 1993: Bericht* (1995): 247–252 [see *596*].

Mainly concerning Chaikovskii's literary interests.

[*2125*] MAMONTOVA, L. I. *Obrazy v muzyke: Literaturno-poeticheskaia kompozitsiia k proizvedeniiam P. I. Chaikovskogo i R. Shumana*. Sankt Peterburg: Znanie Rossii, 1995. 30 p, music, illus. ISBN: 5-7320-0382-7.

See also *588*, *1278*.

ALEKSEI PLESHCHEEV (1825–93)

Russian poet and translator

[2126]   LAVRISHCHEVA, T. I. 'Romansy i detskie pesni P. I. Chaikovskogo na stikhi A. N. Pleshcheeva'. In: *P. I. Chaikovskii i russkaia literatura* (1980): 100–111 [see *588*].

ALEKSANDR PUSHKIN (1799–1837)

Russian poet and novellist

[2127]   IANOVSKII, B. 'Pushkin i Chaikovskii', *Rul´* (30 Jan 1912).

[2128]   BLIUM, V. I. 'Chaikovskii i Pushkin', *Radioslushatel´* (1930), 9: 5.

[2129]   MEIERKHOL´D, V. E. 'Pushkin i Chaikovskii'. In: *Pikovaia dama* (1935): 5–11 [see *3545*].

[2130]   GRACHEV, P. 'Pushkin i russkaia opera', *Zvezda* (1937), 1: 33–40.

—   [repr.] In: *Pushkin v iskusstve*. Otv. red. N. Shuvalov. Leningrad; Moskva: Iskusstvo, 1937: 28–57.

[2131]   RUKAVISHNIKOV, N. K. 'Pushkin v biblioteke P. Chaikovskogo', *Sovetskaia muzyka* (1937), 1: 60–81.

[2132]   IAKOVLEV, V. V. 'Chaikovskii i Pushkin'. In: *Chaikovskii i teatr* (1940): 1–36 [see *2537*].

—   [repr.] 'Pushkin i Chaikovskii'. In: V. V. Iakovlev, *Pushkin i muzyka*. Moskva; Leningrad: Muzgiz, 1949: 174–180; 2nd ed. Moskva: Muzgiz, 1957: 118–179.

—   [repr.] 'Pushkin i Chaikovskii'. In: V. V. Iakovlev, *Izbrannye trudy o muzyke*, tom 1 (1964): 332–372 [see *2362*].

[2133]   NEISHTADT, V. 'Chaikovskii i Pushkin', *Literaturnaia gazeta* (6 May 1940): 5.

[2134]   BERLIAND-CHERNAIA, E. S. *Pushkin i Chaikovskii*. [Moskva]: Gos. muz. izdat., 1950. 144 p, illus.

Includes 'Do "Onegina"': 3–21 — 'Kamenka': 21–38 [see *1330*] — "Evgenii Onegin": 38–76 [see *2962*] — "Mazepa": 77–99 [see *3317*] — "Pikovaia dama": 100–142 [see *3587*].

[2135]   HUCK, W. 'The music in Pushkin', *San Francisco Opera Magazine* (fall 1987), 10: 54–59.

[2136]   PLATEK, Ia. "Edinyi lavr ikh druzhno obvivaet...", *Muzykal´naia zhizn´* (1990), 9: 22–24; 10: 21–23; 11: 20–22, illus.

[2137]   MOISEEV, Ia. 'Izbiratel´noe srodstvo: Chaikovskii o Pushkine', *Muzykal´naia zhizn´* (1999), 6: 3–5, illus.

See also *1171, 2564, 2595, 2603, 2625, 2628, 2630, 2841, 2854, 3060, 5493*.

WILLIAM SHAKESPEARE (1564–1616)

English playwright and poet

[2138]   SOLLERTINSKII, I. 'Ot Berlioza do Shostakovicha: Shekspir v muzyke', *Sovetskoe iskusstvo* (8 Dec 1933).

[2139]   KREMLEV, Iu. A. 'Shekspir v muzyke Chaikovskogo'. In: *Shekspir v muzyke*. Otv. red. L. N. Raaben. Leningrad: Muzyka, 1964: 212–275, illus.

[2140]   UGRIUMOVA, T. S. 'Dramaturgiia U. Shekspira v programmnykh simfonicheskikh proizvedeniiakh P. I. Chaikovskogo'. In: *Teatr v zhizni i tvorchestve P. I. Chaikovskogo* (1985): 101–109 [see *589*].

IVAN TURGENEV (1818–83)
Russian poet and translator

[2141]   'Turgenev o muzyke', *Nuvellist* (Feb 1889), 2: 4–6.

Turgenev's opinons of Russian composers, including Chaikovskii.

[2142]   ZIL´BERSHTEIN, I. S. 'Triumf russkoi muzyki: Turgenev o Musorgskom i Chaikovskom',
Ogonek (1973), 3: 22–23, illus.

Extracts from Turgenev's correspondence.

[2143]   SHOL´P, A. E. 'P. I. Chaikovskii i I. S. Turgenev: K probeme sravnitel´no-tipologicheskogo
analiza dramturgii'. In: *P. I. Chaikovskii i russkaia literatura* (1980): 75–81 [see *588*].

[2144]   PLATEK, Ia. 'Turgenev i Chaikovskii: Vstrechi i nevstrechi', *Muzykal´naia zhizn´* (1993) 5: 20–21.

[2145]   PLATEK, Ia. '"No i liubov´ melodii...": Ivan Turgenev v muzykal´nom zerkale ego pisem',
Muzykal´naia zhizn´ (1998), 12: 30–34.

See also *2833, 3036*.

VASILII ZHUKOVSKII (1783–1852)
Russian poet, dramatist and librettist

[2146]   PAVLUNINA, L. F. 'P. I. Chaikovskii i V. A. Zhukovskii'. In: *P. I. Chaikovskii i russkaia literatura*
(1980): 61–74 [see *588*].

4.6.3. Art & Artists

[2147]   RUCH´EVSKAIA, E. 'Ob esteticheskikh vzgliadakh Chaikovskogo: K 60-letiiu so dnia smerti
P. I. Chaikovskogo', *Muzykal´nye kadry* (5 Nov 1953): 4.

[2148]   KARANDAEVA, T. S. 'P. I. Chaikovskii ob esteticheskoi tsennosti proizvedeniia iskusstva i
khudozhestvennoi kritiki'. In: *Esteticheskoe sozdanie i khudozhestvennaia kul´tura obshchestva*. Moskva:
Gos. univ. im. Lomovosova, 1981: 41–48.

Adapted from dissertation: 'Esteticheskie vzgliady P. I. Chaikovskogo' (summary published Moskva: MGU
im. M. V. Lomonosova, 1983. 24 p).

[2149]   *P. I. Chaikovskii ob iskusstve: Izbrannye fragmenty pisem, zametok, statei*. Pod red. M. S. Bonfel´da.
Izhevsk: Udmurtiia, 1989. 369 p, illus.

[2150]   UGRIUMOVA, T. S. 'Chaikovskii ob izobrazitel´nom iskusstve (po pis´mam i
vospominaniiam)'. In: *P. I. Chaikovskii i izobrazitel´noe iskusstvo* (1991): 6–19 [see *595*].

[2151]   BOTSTEIN, L. 'Music as the language of psychological realism: Tchaikovsky and Russian art'.
In: *Tchaikovsky and his world* (1998): 99–144 [see *601*].

4.6.4. Other

[2152]   KAIGORODOV, D. N. *P. I. Chaikovskii i priroda: Biograficheskii ocherk*. Sankt Peterburg: Suvorin,
1907. 46 p.

Reviews·N. Bernshtein, 'Zhizn´ P. I. Chaikovskogo', *Tovar* (Dec 1907) — V. G., *Russkaia muzykal´naia gazeta*
(Dec 1907): 1125 — 'Raznye izvestiia', *Russkaia muzykal´naia gazeta* (Mar 1911), 11: 321–322.

[2153]   PAVLUNINA, L. F. 'Neskol´ko zametok o istoricheskikh interesakh i sotsial´no-politicheskikh vozzreniiakh P. I. Chaikovskogo'. In: *P. I. Chaikovskii i Ural* (1983): 109–117 [see *1749*].

[2154]   ALBU, A. 'Chaikovskii i priroda: K izucheniiu khudozhestvennogo naslediia i lichnosti muzykanta'. In: *Chaikovskii: Voprosy istorii i teorii* (1991): 64–79 [see *593*].

4.7. PSYCHOLOGY AND HEALTH

[2155]   GILMAN, L. 'Tchaikovsky and Richard Strauss and the idea of death', *Musical World*, 8 (1903): 12–14.

[2156]   GOULD, G. M. 'Tchaikovsky', *Boston Medical and Surgical Journal*, 154 (1906), 513–517, 552–557.
— [repr] In: *Biographic clinics: Essays concerning the influence of visual function, pathologic and phsiologic, upon the health of patients*. Vol. 4. Philadelphia: P. Blakiston's, 1906: 119–151.

[2157]   'Tchaikovsky's melancholy self-portrayal', *Current Literature*, 40 (Mar 1906): 316–318.

[2158]   SEGALIN, G. V. 'Patogenez i biogenez zamechatel´nykh liudei: Chaikovskii'. In: *Klinichecheskii arkhiv genial´nostu i odarennosti (evropatologii), posviashchennyi voprosam patologii genial´no-odarennoi lichnosti, a takzhe voprosam tvorchestva*. Pod red. G. V. Segalina, vyp. 1 (1925): 69–70.

[2159]   HEINTZ, J. 'Tschaikovsky's black beast', *Open court*, 44 (Nov 1930): 643–646, illus.
Concerning Chaikovskii's 'dread of an endless death'.

[2160]   RABENECK, N. 'To be or not to be: A portrait of Tchaikovsky in mid-career', *Opera News*, 22 (2 Dec 1957): 10–12, illus.

[2161]   BRUSSEL, J. A. 'The Tchaikowsky troika', *Psychiatric Quarterly Supplement*, 36 (1962), 2: 304–322.
— [offprint] *The Tchaikowsky troika*. Utica, N. Y.: State Hospitals Press [1962]. 18 p.

[2162]   MÜHLENDAHL, K. E. von. *Die Psychose Tschaikowskis und der Einfluss seiner Musik auf gleichartige Psychotiker*. München: A. Schubert, 1964. 35 p.
Dissertation.

[2163]   KERNER, D. 'Nie mit der Gegenwart zufrieden: Zum Geburtstag von Peter Tschaikowski', *Deutsches Ärzteblatt*, 19 (1965): 1080–1087.

[2164]   KERNER, D. 'Peter Tschaikowsky (1840–1893)'. In: *Krankheiten Grosser Musiker*. Bd. 2. Stuttgart; New York: F. K. Schattauer Verlag, 1977: 103–115.

[2165]   BØHME, G. *Medizinische Porträts berhümter Komponisten*. Wolfgang Amadeus Mozart, Ludwig van Beethoven, Carl Maria von Weber, Frédéric Chopin, Peter Iljitsch Tschaikowski, Béla Bartók. Stuttgart: Fischer, 1979. 191 p, illus. ISBN 3-437-10555-8.
Reviews: *Schweizerische Musikzeitung*, 120 (1980), 2: 113–114 — *Orchester*, 27 (Oct 1979): 774.

[2166]   ZAJACZKOWSKI, H. 'Tchaikovsky: The missing piece of the jigsaw puzzle', *Musical Times*, 131 (May 1990): 238–242, music, illus.
Concerning a dream by Chaikovskii and *The Maid of Orleans*. See also *2167*, *2168*.

[2167]   ZAJACZKOWSKI, H. 'Letters to the editor: Tchaikovsky's vices?', *Musical Times*, 131 (Jun 1990): 298.
In connection with *2166*.

[2168]   KLINE, P. 'Letters to the editor: Zajaczkowski on Tchaikovsky', *Musical Times*, 131 (Aug 1990): 406.
Response to *2166*, *2167*. Includes reply by H. Zajaczkowski.

[2169]   NEUMAYR, A. 'Peter Ilyitsch Tschaikowsky (1840–1893)'. In: *Musik und Medizin*. Bd. 3: *Chopin, Smetana, Tschaikowsky, Mahler*. Wien: Edition Wien [1991]: 201–226, illus. ISBN: 3–85058–074–1.

— [English tr.] 'Peter Ilyich Tchaikovsky (1840–1893)'. In: *Music and medicine*. Vol. 3: *Chopin, Smetana, Tchaikovsky, Mahler: Notes on their lives, works and medical histories*. Tr. by David J. Parent. Bloomington: Medi-Ed. Press, 1994: 207–310, illus. ISBN 0–936741–08–2.

— [Russian tr.] 'Pëtr Il´ich Chaikovskii'. In: Muzykanty v zerkale meditsiny, Perevod. E. S. Samoilovicha. Rostov-na-Donu; Moskva: Zevs, 1997: 217–338. (*Sled v istorii*).

[2170]   ZAJACZKOWSKI, H. 'Tchaikovsky's feelings: The psychology behind the music', *Musical Times*, 133 (Jun 1992): 276.

[2171]   SAFFLE, M. & SAFFLE, J. R. 'Medical histories of prominent composers: Recent research and discoveries', *Acta Musicologica*, 65 (1993), 2: 98.

[2172]   TANNER, M. 'Tchaikovsky: Inside his mind', *Classic CD* (Nov 1993), 42: 4–5 [suppl.], illus.

[2173]   ZAJACZKOWSKI, H. 'On Čajkovskij's psychopathology and its relationship with his creativity'. In: *Internationales Čajkovskij Symposium, Tübingen 1993: Bericht* (1995): 307–328, music [see *596*].

[2174]   VOGELAAR, P. W. 'The agony of Peter Ilyich Tchaikovsky', *Medical Problems of Performing Artists*, 11 (Sep 1996), 3: 75–82, illus.

[2175]   'P. I. Chaikovskii (1840–1983)'. In: *Poroki i bolezni velikikh liudei*. Sost. E. E. Laptsenok. Minsk: Literatura, 1998: 389–394 (*Entsiklopediia tain i sensatsii*).

See also *1727, 1881, 2488, 4619, 5328*.

4.8. DEATH AND BURIAL

[2176]   'Khronika: P. I. Chaikovskii', *Novoe vremia* (25 Oct 1893).

[2177]   'Bolezn´ i konchina P. I. Chaikovskogo', *Peterburgskaia gazeta* (26 Oct 1893).

Contents: 'V kvartire pokoinogo' — 'U prakha pokoinogo' — 'Nachalo rokovoi bolezni' — 'Mnenie d-ra Bertensona' — 'Ne sbyvshiesia nadezhdy' — 'Rokovaia razviazka' — 'Posledniia minuty' — 'Chaikovskii kak chelovek' — 'Slova N. N. Fignera' — 'Pervaia panikhida' — 'Vecherniaia panikhida' — 'Polozhenie v grob' — 'Vynostela' — 'Pokhorony' — 'Panikhida v Uchilishche Pravovedeniia'.

— [English tr. (extract)] 'Interview with Dr. Bertenson'. In: A. Holden, *Tchaikovsky* (1995): 437–438 [see *1554*].

[2178]   'P. I. Chaikovskii', *Novosti i birzhevaia gazeta* (26 Oct 1893).

Contents: I. Lialechkin, 'Na smert´ P. I. Chaikovskogo' [see *5509*] — 'Traur iskusstva i nauki' — G. Gradovskii, 'Velikaia utrata' — N. F. Solov´ev, 'Zhizn´ i deiatel´nost' P. I. Chaikovskogo' [see *1570*] — [E. Napravnik & K. Davydov], 'Pis´ma o P. I. Chaikovskom' — 'Bolezn´ i posledniia minuty P. I. Chaikovskogo: U doktora N. N. Mamonova' — 'U N.N. Fignera' — 'Panikhidy po P. I. Chaikovskom'.

— [English tr. (extract)] 'Interview with Dr Nikolai Mamonov'. In: A. Poznansky, *Tchaikovsky through others' eyes* (1999): 259–260 [see *380*].

[2179]   'P. I. Chaikovskii', *Novoe vremia* (26 Oct 1893).

[2180]   'A famous composer dead', *New York Times* (26 Oct/7 Nov 1893).

[2181]   BERTENSON, L. B. 'Bolezn´ P. I. Chaikovskogo', *Novoe vremia* (27 Oct 1893).

— [English tr.] In: A. A. Orlova, 'Tchaikovsky: The last chapter' (1981): 138–139 [see *2222*].

— [English tr.] In: D. Brown, *Tchaikovsky remembered* (1993): 213–215 [see *377*].

— [English tr.] In: A. Holden, *Tchaikovsky* (1995): 440–442 [see *1554*].

— [English tr. (with additional material)] In: A. Poznansky, *Tchaikovsky through others' eyes* (1999): 257–259 [see *380*].

— [French tr.] In: *Piotr Tchaïkovski: Écrits critiques, lettres, souvenirs de contemporains* (1985): 369–370 [see *375*].

— [German tr.] In: *Tschaikowsky aus der Nähe* (1994): 232–241 [see *379*].

[*2182*]   **'P. I. Chaikovskii'**, *Novosti i birzhevaia gazeta* (27 Oct 1893).

Contents:'Telegrammy' — 'Otkliki inostrannoi pechati' — 'U groba P. I. Chaikovskogo' — 'V pamiat´ P. I. Chaikovskogo'.

[*2183*]   **'Panikhidy po P. I. Chaikovskomu'**, *Peterburgskaia gazeta* (27 Oct 1893) [see *618*].

[*2184*]   **'Sredi gazet i zhurnalov'**, *Novoe vremia* (27 Oct 1893).

[*2185*]   **'U groba P. I. Chaikovskogo'**, *Novoe vremia* (27 Oct 1893).

[*2186*]   **'Khronika: U groba P. I. Chaikovskogo'**, *Novoe vremia* (28 Oct 1893).

[*2187*]   **'P. I. Chaikovskii'**, *Novosti i birzhevaia gazeta* (28 Oct 1893).

Includes: O. Chumina, 'Pamiati P. I. Chaikovskogo' [see *5510*] — 'Telegrammy' — 'U groba P. I. Chaikovskogo' — 'V sobranii literatorov' — 'V direktsii Imperatorskikh teatrov'.

[*2188*]   **'Pokhorony P. I. Chaikovskogo'**, *Novoe vremia* (29 Oct 1893).

[*2189*]   **'Pokhorony P. I. Chaikovskogo'**, *Novosti i birzhevaia gazeta* (29 Oct 1893).

Contents: 'Nachalo protsessii' — 'U Mariinskogo teatra' — 'V Kazanskom sobore' — 'Posle otpevaniia' — 'V Aleksandro-Nevskoi Lavre'.

[*2190*]   **'Pokhorony P. I. Chaikovskogo'**, *Peterburgskaia gazeta* (29 Oct 1893).

[*2191*]   **['Funeral of M. Tschaikowsky']**, *The Times* (29 Oct/10 Nov 1893).

[*2192*]   **'Moskovskiia pis´ma'**, *Novosti i birzhevaia gazeta* (30 Oct 1893).

[*2193*]   **'P. I. Chaikovskii'**, *Novosti i birzhevaia gazeta* (30 Oct 1893).

[*2194*]   **'Sredi gazet i zhurnalov'**, *Novoe vremia* (30 Oct 1893).

[*2195*]   **'Zloby dnia'**, *Peterburgskaia gazeta* (30 Oct 1893).

[*2196*]   **'Moskva u groba P. I. Chaikovskogo'**, *Novosti i birzhevaia gazeta* (31 Oct 1893).

[*2197*]   **'Na ocheredi: Istoricheskoe znachenie pokhron P. I. Chaikovskogo'**, *Novosti i birzhevaia gazeta* (31 Oct 1893).

[*2198*]   K—V, K. **'Smert´ i pokhrony P. I. Chaikovskogo'**, *Russkoe obozrenie* (Nov 1893), 11: 508–512.

[*2199*]   **'Nad mogiloi Chaikovskogo'**, *Teatral´naia gazeta* (Nov 1893), 22: 7.

Chaikovskii's burial service.

[*2200*]   **CHAIKOVSKII, M. I. 'Pis´mo v redaktsiiu: Poslednie dni zhizni P. I. Chaikovskogo'**, *Novosti i birzhevaia gazeta* (1 Nov 1893).

— [repr.] 'Pis´mo v redaktsiiu: Bolezn´ P. I. Chaikovskogo', *Novoe vremia* (1 Nov 1893).

— [repr.] In: M. I. Chaikovskii, *Zhizn´ Petra Il´icha Chaikovskogo*, tom 3 (1902): 648–654 [see *1453*].

— [English tr.] In: A. Orlova, 'Tchaikovsky: The last chapter' (1981): 140–144 [see *2222*].

— [English tr.] In: D. Brown, *Tchaikovsky remembered* (1993): 210–212, 215–219 [see *377*].

— [English tr.] In: A. Holden, *Tchaikovsky* (1995): 442–445 [see *1554*].

— [English tr. (with additional material)] In: A. Poznansky, *Tchaikovsky through others' eyes* (1999): 247–250, 260–265 [see *380*].

— [German tr.] 'Der Erkrankung Peter Tschaikowskys'. In: *Tschaikowsky aus der Nähe* (1994): 266–272 [see *379*].

[*2201*] **'Moskva ili Peterburg?'**, *Novosti i birzhevaia gazeta* (2 Nov 1893).
The question of where Chaikovskii should be buried.

[*2202*] **SUVORIN, A.** 'Malen´kie pis´ma', *Novoe vremia* (3 Nov 1893).
— [German tr. (abridged)] In: *Internationales Čajkovskij-Symposium, Tübingen 1993: Bericht* (1995): 272–274 [see *596, 2253*].

[*2203*] **'Zloby dnia'**, *Peterburgskaia gazeta* (4 Nov 1893).

[*2204*] **'Kto dolzhen byl lechit´ P. I. Chaikovskogo?'**, *Peterburgskaia gazeta* (5 Nov 1893).

[*2205*] **PETERBURZHETS.** 'Malen´kaia khronika', *Novoe vremia* (5 Nov 1893).

[*2206*] **CHAIKOVSKII, M. I.** 'Pis´mo v redaktsiiu', *Novoe vremia* (7 Nov 1893).
— [German tr. (abridged)] In: *Internationales Čajkovskij-Symposium, Tübingen 1993: Bericht* (1995): 274 [see *596, 21400*].

[*2207*] **'O chem govoriat'**, *Novosti i birzhevaia gazeta* (7 Nov 1893).
— [German tr. (abridged)] In: *Internationales Čajkovskij-Symposium, Tübingen 1993: Bericht* (1995): 274 [see *596, 2253*].

[*2208*] **'Pokhorony P. I. Chaikovskogo'**, *Sever* (7 Nov 1893).

[*2209*] **[DOROSHEVICH, V.]** 'Eshche odno pis´mo g. M. Chaikovskogo', *Peterburgskaia gazeta* (8 Nov 1893).
— [German tr. (abridged)] In: *Internationales Čajkovskij-Symposium, Tübingen 1993: Bericht* (1995): 275 [see *596, 2253*].

[*2210*] **PETERBURZHETS.** 'Malen´kaia khronika', *Novoe vremia* (8 Nov 1893).

[*2211*] **LEL´.** 'Pokhorony P. I. Chaikovskogo: Chestvovanie ego pamiati', *Artist* (Dec 1893), 32: 169–171.

[*2212*] **KENYON, C. F.** 'Correspondence: Tchaikovsky', *Academy*, 59 (Jul/Dec 1900): 58.
A letter to the editor, concerning the composer's 'morbid' personality, and rumours of his suicide.

[*2213*] **'O polednikh dniakh zhizni Chaikovskogo'**, *Volzhskii vestnik* (1903), No. 231.

[*2214*] **BERTENSON, S.** 'The truth about the mysterious death of Peter Ilyich Tschaikowsky: Short pages from family memoirs—Study of Tschaikowsky's interesting personality', *Etude*, 58 (Jun 1940): 369, 420, illus.
Includes abridged English tr. of V. B. Bertenson, 'Pëtr i Modest Chaikovskie' [see *400*].

[*2215*] **OBER, W. B.** 'De mortibus musicorum: Some cases drawn from a pathologist's notebook', *Stereo Review*, 25 (Nov 1970): 84.

[*2216*] **DONALSON, N. & DONALSON, B.** *How did they die?*. New York: St. Martin Press, 1980: 355–356.

[*2217*] **ORLOVA, A. A.** 'Taina smerti Chaikovskogo', *Novyi Amerikanets* (12–18 Nov 1980), 40: 22–23.
Claims that Chaikovskii was forced to commit suicide. See also *2218, 2219*.
— [rev. repr.] 'Taina zhizni i smerti Chaikovskogo' (1987) [see *2233*].

[*2218*] **ARENSKII, K.** 'Taina smerti P. I. Chaikovskogo', *Novoe russkoe slovo* (19 Dec 1980).
Critical response to *2217*. See also *2219*.

[*2219*]   ORLOVA, A. A. 'Eshche raz o smerti Chaikovskogo', *Novoe russkoe slovo* (13 Jan 1981).
Reply to *2218*. See also *2221*.

[*2220*]   SPIEGELMAN, J. 'The trial, condemnation and death of Tchaikovsky', *High Fidelity*, 31 (Feb 1981): 49–51, illus.
— [Russian tr.] In: 'Smert´ Chaikovskogo: Tochki zreniia' (1993) [see *2252*].

[*2221*]   ARENSKII, K. 'Snova o smerti P. I. Chaikovskogo', *Novoe russkoe slovo* (5 Feb 1981).
Response to *2219*.

[*2222*]   ORLOVA, A. A. 'Tchaikovsky: The last chapter' (tr. from the Russian by David Brown), *Music & Letters*, 62 (Apr 1981), 2: 125–145.

[*2223*]   ORLOVA, A. A. 'Kholera ili samoubistvo?', *Novyi Amerikanets* (19–25 Jul 1981), 75: 38–42.

[*2224*]   HENAHAN, D. 'Did Tchaikovsky really commit suicide?', *New York Times* (26 Jul 1981).
See also *2226*.
— [repr.] *International Herald Tribune* (28 Jul 1981).

[*2225*]   BERBEROVA, N. N., BROWN, M. H. & KARLINSKY, S. 'Tchaikovsky's 'suicide' reconsidered: A rebuttal', *High Fidelity*, 31 (Aug 1981), 8: 49, 85.
— [Russian tr. (abridged)] *Novyi Amerkianets* (19–25 Jul 1981), 75: 39.
— [Russian tr.] In: 'Smert´ Chaikovskogo: Tochki zreniia' (1993) [see *2252*].

[*2226*]   BERBEROVA, N. N., BROWN, M. H. & KARLINSKY, S. 'Doubts about Tchaikovsky', *New York Times* (9 Aug 1981).
Response to *2224*. Includes D. Henahan's reply.

[*2227*]   KRIEGSMAN, A. 'The great suicide debate', *Washington Post* (28 Mar 1982).

[*2228*]   LISCHKÉ, A. 'Tchaikovski s'est il suicidé?', *Diapason* (Jun 1983), 284: 27–29.

[*2229*]   ORLOVA, A. A. 'Posledni dni Chaikovskogo', *Sem´ dnei*, 7 (16 Dec 1983): 44–49.

[*2230*]   ACOCELLA, J. R. 'Tchaikovsky's death: A summary of the controversy', *Dance Magazine*, 59 (Dec 1985): 90–91, illus.

[*2231*]   CHAIKOVSKAIA, O. G. 'Pikovye damy', *Novyi mir* (1986), 10: 235–250.
The first reaction to Orlova's story of the composer's death to appear in the Soviet Union. See also *2232*.
— [repr.] In: O. G. Chaikovskaia, *Soperniki vremeni: Opyty poeticheskogo vospriiatiia proshlogo*. Moskva: Sovetskii pisatel´, 1990: 83–119.

[*2232*]   ORLOVA, A. A. 'O glasnosti i emigrantskikh perepalkakh: Po povodu odnoi repliki', *Vremia i my*, 98 (1987): 226–230.
Partly concerning Ol´ga Chaikovskaia's article [see *2231*].

[*2233*]   ORLOVA, A. A. 'Taina zhizni i smerti Chaikovskogo', *Kontinent*, 53 (1987): 311–336.
Rev. repr. of *2036*, *2217*.
— [repr.] *Niva* (9–10 Oct 1991), 19: 2; (17–23 Oct 1991), 20: 2; (30–31 Oct 1991), 21: 8.

[*2234*]   ORLOVA, A. A. 'Tragediia Chaikovskogo i gorbachevskaia glasnost´', *Novoe russkoe slovo* (25 Jan 1987).

[*2235*]   REITHOF van HEULEN, E. 'De raadsels rond de dood van Tsjaikovskie blijven: Zijn de onthullingen van Orlova wel voldønde onderzocht?', *Mens en Melodie*, 42 (Jul/Aug 1987): 307–317.

[2236]   POZNANSKY, A. 'Tchaikovsky's suicide: Myth and reality' (tr. by Ralph C. Burr jr.), *19th Century Music*, 11 (spr. 1988), 3: 199–220.

Refutation of the claim that Chaikovskii committed suicide. See also *2238, 2239*.

[2237]   HENAHAN, D. 'Tchaikovsky's death: The riddle endures', *New York Times* (20 Nov 1988).

[2238]   BROWN, D. 'Comment and chronicle', *19th Century Music*, 13 (1989), 1: 73–84.

Response to *2236*. Includes reply by A. Poznansky. See also *2239*.

[2239]   KARLINSKY, S. 'Comment and chronicle', *19th Century Music*, 13 (aut. 1989), 2: 179–180.

Follow-up to *2236, 2238*.

[2240]   [BLINOV, N. O.] 'Sobytiia dvukh dnei: Khronika po soobshcheniiam peterburgskikh gazet i svidetel´stvam sovremennikov', *Sovetskaia muzyka* (1990), 6: 117–123 [see *592*].

A chronology of 25–26 Oct 1893.

[2241]   NAGIBIN, Iu. 'Chaikovskiy: Final tragedii', *Megapolis ekspress*, 16 (1990): 13.

— [repr.] *Daidzhest: 24 chasa* (1990), 42: 8–9.

— [rev. repr.] 'Chaikovskii: Final tragedii' & 'Zagadki Chaikovskogo'. In: Iu. Nagibin, *Vechnaia muzyka*. Moskva: Podkova, 1998: 435–452. ISBN: 5-8951-7012-9.

[2242]   ORLOVA, A. A. '26–28 Oct 1893'. In: *Tchaikovsky: A self-portrait* (1990): 406–414 [see *1532*].

[2243]   WOODSIDE, M. S. 'Comment and chronicle: Tchaikovsky's suicide', *19th Century Music*, 13 (1990), 3: 273–274.

Includes response by A. Poznansky.

[2244]   ACOCELLA, J. R. 'Tchaikovsky's death: The autopsy continues', *Dance Magazine*, 64 (Nov 1990): 54–57, illus.

[2245]   WARRACK, J. 'Poisonous rumours', *Times Literary Suppl.* (9–15 Nov 1990).

An overview of the controversy, and a review of A. Orlova's book *Tchaikovsky: A self-portrait* (1990) [see *1532*].

[2246]   SELLORS, A. 'Out into the open', *Classic CD*, 11 (Mar 1991): 32–33.

[2247]   GÖRLICH, J. G. 'Mysteriöser Tod', *Neue Musikzeitung*, 40 (Apr/May 1991): 50.

[2248]   BROEDER, M. 'O pijn! De boosaardige fabel van Tsjaikovski's zelfmoord', *De Groene Amsterdammer* (9 Sep 1992).

[2249]   ORLOVA, A. 'Vosstanavlivaia gor´kuiu pravdu', *Novoe russkoe slovo* (6 Nov 1992) and (7/8 Nov 1992).

[2250]   POZNANSKY, A. *Samoubiistvo Chaikovskogo: Mif i real´nost´*. K 100-letiiu so dnia smerti Petra Il´icha Chaikovskogo. Moskva: Glagol, 1993. 190 p. (*Glagol*; 17). ISBN: 5-87532-019-2.

Reviews: K. Gorelik, 'Grekhi ego byli strashny?', *Stolitsa* (1994), 20: 47 — V. Zhuravlev, 'Kak izbezhat´ samoubiistva', *Nezavisimaia gazeta* (2 Apr 1994) — P. Gradskii, 'Zagadki smerti Chaikovskogo: Iad ili kholera', *Vechernii Peterburg* (12 Aug 1994).

— [repr. (chapter 1)] A. Poznansky, '"Molva" (iz knigi "Samoubiistvo Chaikovskogo")' , *Nezavisimaia gazeta* (3 Nov 1993).

— [repr. (chapter 3)] A. Poznansky, 'Prestuplenie bez nakazaniia', *Art-fonar´* (1994), 1: 13–16.

— [German tr.] *Tschaikowskys Tod: Geschichte und Revision einer Legende*. [Aus dem Russischen von Irmgard Wille]. Mainz: Atlantis Musikbuch-Verlag, 1998. 218 p, illus. (*Serie Musik, Atlantis-Schott*; Bd 8373). ISBN 3-254-08373-3.

Reviews: V. Tarnow, 'In Rosafarbenen Schatten des Zarenhof', *Die Welt* (29 May 1998) — K. Grönke, 'Der Tod in den Zeiten der Cholera', *Frankfurter Allgemaine Zeitung* (13 Aug 1998) — B. Feuchtner, 'Wieder eine verschworung weniger', *Opernwelt* (Sep/Oct 1998): 32–33 — D. Gojowy, *Österreichische Musik Zeitschrift*, 54 (1999), 5: 71–72.

— [German tr.] 'Čajkovskijs Homosexualität und sein Tod: Legenden und Wirklichkeit'. In: *Čajkovskijs Homosexualität und sein Tod: Legenden und Wirklichkeit* (1998): 9–136 [see *600*].

[*2251*]   LAVRIN, A. 'Chaikovskii, Pëtr Il´ich'. In: A. Lavrin, *Khroniki Kharona: Entsiklopediia smerti*. Moskva: Moskovskii rabochii, 1993: 505–506.

[*2252*]   'Smert´ Chaikovskogo: Tochki zreniia', *Gay slaviane* (1993), 1: 2–28.
Includes Russian tr. of J. Spiegelman, 'The trial, condemnation and death of Tchaikovsky' (1981) [see *2220*] and N. N. Berberova, M. H. Brown & S. Karlinsky, 'Tchaikovsky's 'suicide' reconsidered: A rebuttal' (1981) [see *2225*].

[*2253*]   SOKOLOV, V. S. 'Do i posle tragedii: Smert´ P. I. Chaikovskogo v dokumentakh', *Znamia*, 11 (1993): 143–169.
— [repr.] In: N. O. Blinov, *Posledniaia bolezn´ i smert´ P. I. Chaikovskogo* (1994): 147–203 [see *2265*].
— [German tr. (rev.)] 'Čajkovskijs Tod', In: *Internationales Čajkovskij Symposium, Tübingen 1993: Bericht* (1995): 259–280 [see *596*]. See also *2202, 2206, 2207, 2209*.

[*2254*]   SCHER, V. 'One thing is certain: Tchaikovsky is dead', *Union Tribune* (29 Aug 1993).

[*2255*]   'Tchaikovsky suicide theory triggers overtures of dissent', *The Sunday Times* (29 Aug 1993).

[*2256*]   POZNANSKY, A. 'Experts clash over Tchaikovsky', *The Sunday Times* (12 Sep 1993).

[*2257*]   BROWN, D. 'Culture forum: Tchaikovsky', *The Sunday Times* (10 Oct 1993).

[*2258*]   HOLDEN, A. 'Who killed Tchaikovsky?', *The Sunday Express* (24 Oct 1993).
In connection with a BBC TV documentary by the author. See also *2264*.

[*2259*]   BROWN, D. 'Secrets of the abyss', *BBC Music Magazine*, 11 (Nov 1993): 26–29.

[*2260*]   MILLS, R. 'Who killed Tchaikovsky?', *Classic CD* (Nov 1993), 42: 28–29 [suppl.], illus.

[*2261*]   STUTTFORD, T. 'How did the great composer die?', *The Times* (4 Nov 1993)

[*2262*]   KETTLE, M. A. 'A whiff of scandal', *The Guardian* (5 Nov 1993), illus.

[*2263*]   SKORBIASHCHENSKAIA, O. 'Taina smerti: Mif i real´nost´', *Vechernii Peterburg* (12 Nov 1993): 6.

[*2264*]   FAWKES, R. 'Anatomy of death', *Classical Music Magazine* (4 Dec 1993): 33.
Relating to Anthony Holden's television documentary. See also *2258*.

[*2265*]   BLINOV, N. O. *Posledniaia bolezn´ i smert´ P. I. Chaikovskogo*. Podgot. k publikatsii i komentarii V. S. Sokolova. Moskva: Muzyka, 1994. 207 p, illus. ISBN: 5–7140–0564–3.
Includes newspaper reports, diary entries and memoirs of Chaikovskii's contemporaries concerning his last illness. With a suppl. by V. S. Sokolov, 'Do i posle tragedii': 147–203 [see *2253*].
Review: G. Liatiev, 'Ponevole il´ po vole?' *Nezavisimaia gazeta* (23 Dec 1995).

[*2266*]   GRÖNKE, K. 'Čajkovskijs Tod: Ein kritischer Literaturbericht', *Tschaikowsky-Gesellschaft: Mitteilungen*, 3 (1995): 31–54.
— [rev. repr.] In: *Čajkovskijs Homosexualität und sein Tod: Legenden und Wirklichkeit* (1998): 379–404 [see *600*].

[*2267*]   HOLDEN, A. 'Čajkovskij's death: Cholera or suicide?'. In: *Internationales Čajkovskij Symposium, Tübingen 1993: Bericht* (1995): 141–154 [see *596*].

[*2268*]   HOLDEN, A. 'Coda of silence', *The Guardian* (29 Aug 1995).

[2269] PFUHL, W. 'Das merkwurdige Marchen vom gemüchelten Meister: Zum Selbstmord gezungen oder Opfer für Cholera. Ein deutsch-russisches Forscher-Team untserucht das Gesamtwerk and das Leben Tschaikowskys', *Die Welt* (2 Dec 1995).

[2270] POZNANSKY, A. *Tchaikovsky's last days: A documentary study*. Oxford: Clarendon Press; New York: Oxford Univ. Press, 1996. xvii, 236 p, illus. ISBN: 0–19–816596–X.

Reviews: T. J. McGee, *Library Journal*, 121 (1 Oct 1996): 80 — D. Fallowell, *The Times* (21 Nov 1996) — R. P. Sasscer, *Choice*, 34 (1997): 1348 — M. Scott, *The Spectator* (7 Dec 1996) — J. Allison, 'Coming to terms with Tchaikovsky' (1997) [see *1683*] — D. J. R. Bruckner, *New York Times Book Review* (2 Feb 1997) — *Contemporary Review*, 271 (Aug 1997): 111 — A. McMillin, *Slavonic and East European Review*, 75 (Oct 1997), 4: 712–713 — D. Brown, 'How did Tchaikovsky come to die?' (Nov 1997) [see *2271*] — D. Wyeth, *Chamber Music*, 14 (Dec 1997), 6: 29–30 — M. H. Brown, *Notes*, 54 (Mar 1998), 3: 701–703.

[2271] BROWN, D. 'How did Tchaikovsky come to die—and does it really matter?', *Music & Letters*, 78 (Nov 1997), 4: 581–588.

See also *2272*.

[2272] POZNANSKY, A. 'Letters to the editor: Why it matters how Tchaikovsky came to die', *Music & Letters*, 79 (Aug 1998), 3: 463–469.

Response to *2271*. Also includes a letter from R. Taruskin, and replies from D. Brown.

See also *395, 407, 506, 510, 538, 1765, 1768, 5504*.

PART 5

WORKS

5.1. MUSIC
5.1.1. General

5.1.2. Style

5.1.3. Influence

5.2. STAGE WORKS
5.2.1. General

5.2.2. Operas

5.2.3. Ballets

5.2.4. Incidental Music

5.3. ORCHESTRAL WORKS
5.3.1. General

5.3.2. Symphonies

5.3.3. Suites

5.3.4. Overtures

5.4. CONCERTOS
5.4.1. General

5.4.2. Piano and Orchestra

5.4.3. Violin and Orchestra

5.4.4. Cello and Orchestra

5.5. VOCAL WORKS
5.5.1. Choral

5.5.2. Songs and Duets

5.6. CHAMBER-INSTRUMENTAL WORKS
5.6.1. Chamber Works

5.6.2. Piano Works

5.7. WRITINGS

5.1. MUSIC

5.1.1. General

[2273]   [RAZMADZE, A. S.] 'Korrespondentsiia: Moskva', *Muzykal´nyi listok* (29 Apr 1873; 6 May 1873).

[2274]   MOSKVICH. 'Moskovskie zametki', *Grazhdanin* (28 May 1873).
Partly concerning Chaikovskii.

[2275]   TUISA, N. 'Vchera, segodnia, zavtra: Kak provodit vremia odin "znamenityi russkii kompozitor"', *Sovremennye izvestiia* (4 Jan 1876).

[2276]   'Pëtr Il´ich Chaikovskii', *Krugozor* (15 May 1876).

[2277]   LAROSH, G. A. 'Muzykal´nye ocherki: Russkaia muzykal´naia literatura 1874–1875 godov', *Golos* (10 Jun 1876).
— [repr.] 'P. Chaikovskii i obychnoe otnositel´no nego nedorazumenie'. In: G. A. Larosh, *Sobranie muzykal´no-kriticheskikh statei*, tom 2, chast´ 2 (1924): 38–43 [see *2311*].
— [repr.] 'P. Chaikovskii i obychnoe otnositel´no nego nedorazumenie'. In: G. A. Larosh, *Izbrannye stat´i v piati vypuskakh*, vyp. 2 (1975): 82–86 [see *2376*].
— [German tr.] 'Peter Tschaikowsky und die üblichen über ihn verbreiteten Irrtümer'. In: G. A. Larosh, *Peter Tschaikowsky: Aufsätze und Erinnerungen* (1993): 96–101 [see *2406*].

[2278]   BÜLOW, H. von 'Autokritisches von einer Reise in den Nebeln', *Signale für die Musikalische Welt*, 36 (1878), 69: 1089–1091.
— [repr.] In: H. von Bülow, Ausgewahlte Schriften (1850–1892). Band 3. Leipzig: Breitkopf & Härtel, 1896: 379–392.
— [Russian tr. (excs.)] 'Moskovskie zametki: Biulov o russkom muzykal´nom genie. Predstavitel´ ego g. Chaikovskii', *Golos* (13 Mar 1879).

[2279]   'Pëtr Il´ich Chaikovskii', *Niva* (1880), 51.

[2280]   AMICUS [MONTEVERDE, P. A.] 'Beseda', *Sankt Peterburgskie vedomosti* (27 Mar 1880).
Report on a concert devoted to Chaikovskii's works in St. Petersburg on 25 Mar 1880.

[2281]   [KIUI, Ts. A.] 'La musique en Russie: Tchaikowsky', *Revue et gazette musicale de Paris* (29 Aug 1880).

[2282]   STASOV, V. V. 'Nasha muzyka za poslednie 25 let', *Vestnik Evropy* (1883), 10: 616–619.

[2283]   'Pëtr Il´ich Chaikovskii', *Akkord* (1885), 5: 125–126.

[2284]   BASKIN, V. S. 'P. I. Chaikovskii: Ocherk muzykal´noi deiatel´nosti', *Russkaia mysl´*, 7 (1886), 2: 237.

[2285]   BASKIN, V. S. 'P. I. Chaikovskii: Obzor ego muzykal´noi deiatel´nosti', *Trud´*, (1890), 5: 277, 485; 6: 55, 270, 613; 7: 46, 170, 298.
See also *2286*.

[2286]   BASKIN, V. S. *P. I. Chaikovskii: Ocherk ego deiatel´nosti*. Sankt Peterburg: A. F. Marks, 1895. 202 p, illus. (*Russkie kompozitory*; 4).
Expanded version of *2285*.
Review:A. V. Ossovskii, 'Muzykal´nyi kritik osobogo roda', *Russkaia muzykal´naia gazeta* (Jan 1895), 1: 64–71.

[2287] **LAROSH, G. A. 'Predislovie perevodchika'.** In: E. Hanslick, *O muzykal´no-prekrasnom.* Moskva: P. Iurgenson, 1895.

Includes Larosh's comments on Hanslick's relationship with Chaikovskii. See also *2290.*

— [repr.] In: G. A. Larosh, *Sobranie muzykal´no-kriticheskikh statei.* Tom 1. Moskva, 1913: 337–361.

[2288] **S[CHÖNAICH], G. 'Peter Iljitsch Tschaikowsky'**, *Neue Musikalische Presse,* 4 (1895), 10: 1–2.

[2289] **BEREZOVSKII, V. V. 'Chaikovskii'.** In: V. V. Berezovskii, *Russkaia muzyka: Kritiko-istoricheskii ocherk natsional´noi muzykal´noi shkoly v eia predstaviteliakh.* Sankt Peterburg: Iu. I. Erlikh, 1898: 279–360.

[2290] **P—SKII, E. 'Ganslick o Chaikovskom'**, *Russkaia muzykal´naia gazeta* (21 Nov 1899), 47: 1189–1197; (5 Dec 1899), 49: 1259–1263; (12 Dec 1899), 50: 1296–1297; (19 Dec 1899), 51: 1329–1335.

Russian tr. of extracts from Edward Hanslick's reviews of Chaikovskii's music.

[2291] **CARTER, V. 'The happier Tschaikovsky'**, *Musical Standard* [illus. series], 14 (20 Oct 1900): 242].

[2292] **MASON, D. G.** *From Grieg to Brahms.* Studies of some modern composers (Grieg, Dvořák, Saint-Saëns, Franck, Tschaïkowsky, Brahms) and their art. New York: Outlook Co., 1902: 151–171.

— [repr.] New York: Macmillan, 1927: 151–171, illus.

— [repr.] New York: Macmillan, 1936: 151–171, illus.

— [repr.] New York: AMS Press, 1971: 151–171, illus.

[2293] **MASON, D. G. 'Tchaikovsky and his music'**, *Outlook,* 72 (1 Nov 1902): 548–554, illus.

[2294] **LIEBLING, F. 'The compositions of Tschaikowsky considered in their practical relation to music teaching'**, *Musician,* 7 (1903), 12: 426.

[2295] **BESSEL´, V. V. 'Pëtr Il´ich Chaikovskii'.** In: V. V. Bessel´, *Kratkii ocherk muzyki v Rossii.* Sankt Peterburg: V. Bessel´ & Ko., 1905: 30–33.

[2296] **EVANS, E. 'The relation of Tchaikovsky to art-questions of to-day'**, *Musical Standard* [illus. series], 27 (30 Mar 1907): 198–199; (18 May 1907): 309–310; (1 Jun 1907): 345–346; (15 Jun 1907): 374–375; (29 Jun 1907): 410–412; (29 Jun 1907): 28; (13 Jul 1907): 25–26.

In six parts: 1. 'On Tchaikovsky's musical opinions' [on orchestration] — 2. 'Tchaikovsky and form' — 3. 'Tchaikovsky and idealism' — 4. 'Tchaikovsky and nationalism' — 5. 'Tchaikovsky and individuality' — 6. 'Tchaikovsky and criticism'.

— [rev repr.] In: R. H. Newmarch, *Tchaikovsky: His life and works,* 2nd ed. (1908): 226–393 [see *1455*].

[2297] **KOPTIAEV, A. P.** *Pëtr Il´ich Chaikovskii.* Sankt Peterburg: Udelov, 1909. ii, 71 p (*Istoriia novoi russkoi muzyki v kharakteristikakh;* 1).

Reviews:A. Kal´, *Ezhegodnik Imperatorskikh teatrov* (1909), 4: 197 — *Russkaia muzykal´naia gazeta* (12/19 Jul 1909), 28/29: 651–652 — M M. Ivanov, 'Novosti muzykal´noi kritiicheskoi literatury', *Novoe vremia* (22 Mar 1910): 4.

— 2-e izd. Sankt Peterburg, 1913. ii, 71 p.

[2298] **WILLIAMS, C. F. A.** *The rhythm of modern music.* London: Macmillan & Co., 1909. xvii, 321 p.

Includes analysis of various works by Chaikovskii.

[2299] **TRACY, J. M. 'Tchaikovsky: Talented composer'**, *Musician,* 14 (Aug 1909): 351.

[2300] **OSSOVSKII, A. V. 'P. I. Chaikovskii'**, *Muzyka* (23 Jun 1911): 636–639.

Mainly concerned with the nationalistic aspects of Chaikovskii's music.

[2301] **LAWRENCE, F. 'Peter Ilich Tchaikovsky'**, *London Quarterly Review,* 116 (Oct 1911): 289–301.

— [repr.] In: F. Lawrence, *Musicians of sorrow and romance.* London: C. H. Kelly, 1913: 93–105.

[2302]   RONALD, L. *Tschaikowsky and his music*. Ed. by E. Hatzfield. London; Edinburgh; New York: F. A. Stokes [1912].

[2303]   'Teatr i muzyka', *Novoe vremia* (13 Mar 1913): 6; (16 Mar 1913): 6; (1 Apr 1913): 6.

Reports on a series of three lectures concerning Chaikovskii's music, given by Aleksandr Koptiaev in St. Petersburg on 11 Mar, 15 Mar, 31 Mar 1913.

[2304]   'Tvorchestvo P. I. Chaikovskogo', *Teatr i zhizn´*, (25 Oct 1913): 5–10.

Includes contributions from Aleksandr Glazunov, Liverii Saketti, Tsezar Kiui, Nikolai Solov´ev, Pëtr Shenk, Anatolii Liadov, Osip Paleček, N. N. Bogoliubov, F. Litvin, Ioakim Tartakov, Evgeniia Zbrueva, G. A. Bosse.

[2305]   MONTAGU-NATHAN, M. 'Tchaikovsky, Rubinstein and the eclectics'. In: M. Montagu-Nathan, *A history of Russian music: Being an account of the rise and progress of the Russian school of composers*. With a survey of their lives and a description of their works. London: W. Reeves, 1914: 260–273.

— 2nd ed., rev. and corrected. London: W. Reeves, 1918: 260–273, illus.

— [repr.] New York: Biblo and Tannen, 1969: 260–273, illus.

[2306]   VIATKIN, G. 'O Chaikovskom', *Novyi zhurnal dlia vsekh* (1915), 4: 55–57.

[2307]   MONTAGU-NATHAN, M. 'The Story of Russian music: II. Tchaikovsky', *Music Student*, 9 (Jul 1917): 169–171, illus.

[2308]   KARATYGIN, V. G. 'Chaikovskii', *Nash vek* (1918), No. 107.

— [repr.] In: V. G. Karatygin, *Zhizn´, deiatel´nost´, stat´i i materialy*. Leningrad: Academia, 1927: 220–221.

[2309]   FORSYTH, C. 'A note on Tschaikowsky', *Monthly Musical Record*, 51 (Jan 1921): 57–58; (Mar 1921): 130.

[2310]   GLEBOV, I. [ASAF´EV, B. V.] *Instrumental´noe tvorchestvo Chaikovskogo*. Petrograd [Gos. filarmoniia], 1922. 69 p.

Contents: 'P. I. Chaikovskii': 3–5 [see *715*] — 'O simfonizme': 5–13 — 'Simfonizm Chaikovskogo': 13–32 [see *4396*] — 'Simfonicheskie poemy Chaikovskogo': 32–42 [see *4822*] — 'Siuity': 43–57 [see *4757*] — 'Kontsertnyi stil´ Chaikovskogo': 57–63 [see *4969*] — 'Kamernyi stil´ Chaikovskogo': 63–69 [see *5283*].

— [repr.] In: B. V. Asaf´ev, *O muzyke Chaikovskogo: Izbrannoe* (1972): 234–290 [see *2373*].

— [repr.] 'Chaikovskii'. In B. V. Asaf´ev, *O simfonicheskoi i kamernoi muzyke*. Moskva: Muzyka, 1981: 94–138.

[2311]   LAROSH, G. A. *Sobranie muzykal´no-kriticheskikh statei*. So vstup. stat´ei M. I. Chaikovskogo i vospominaniiami N. D. Kashkina. Pod red. V. Iakovleva. Tom 2: *P. I. Chaikovskii*.

Reprint of selected articles by German Larosh (see also *2376, 2406*).

Chast´ 1. Moskva: Gosizdat-Muzsektor, 1922. viii, 183 p.

Contents: See *481, 482, 483, 484, 486, 2638, 2728, 2783, 2786, 3359, 3364, 3376, 3763, 3779, 3789, 4037, 4164, 5425*.

Chast´ 2. Moskva; Petrograd: Gosizdat-Muzsektor, 1924. xx, 158 p.

Contents: See *626, 1985, 2277, 2422, 2535, 3731, 4537, 4568, 4581, 4797, 4827, 4829, 4840, 5001, 5182, 5318*.

[2312]   CARSE, A. 'The period of Brahms–Tchaikovsky'. In: A. Carse, *The history of orchestration*. London: Kegan Paul, Trench, Trubner & Co. Ltd.; New York: E. P. Dutton & Co., 1925: 290–311, music, illus.

— [repr] New York: Dover [1964]: 290–311.

— [Russian tr. (rev.)] 'Period Bramsa i Chaikovskogo'. In: A. Kars, *Istoriia orkestrovka*. Perevod s angliiskogo E. Lenartova i V. Fermana. Pod red. M. Ivanova-Boretskogo. Moskva: Gosizdat, 1932: 224–248.

[2313]   SPALDING, W. 'Les écoles nationales: Tschaikovsky'. In: W. Spalding, *Manuel d´analyse musicale*. Paris: Payot, 1927: 354–356.

[2314]   MOSOLOV, A. 'Motsart–Glazunov–Chaikovskii', *Persimfans* (1928), 2: 11.

[*2315*]   BRAUDO, E. M. 'P. I. Chaikovskii'. In: E. M. Braudo, *Szhatyi ocherk istorii muzyki*. Moskva: Gosizdat-Muzsektor, 1929: 240–241.

[*2316*]   CHEMODANOV, S. 'P. I. Chaikovskii'. In: *Chto nuzhno znat´ kazhdomu o muzyke*. Moskva: Moskovskii rabochii, 1930: 101–102.

[*2317*]   'Tchaikovsky'. In: G. Upton & F. Borowski, *The standard concert guide*. Chicago, A. C. McClurg, 1930: 489–503.

[*2318*]   BOUQUET, R. 'Les maîtres de la musique russe: Tchaikovsky', *Musique et Concours* (Mar 1932).

[*2319*]   ASAF´EV, B. V. 'Tvorchestvo P. I. Chaikovskogo'. In: *Pikovaia dama: Opera, muzyka P. I. Chaikovskogo* (1935): 10–23 [see *3546*].

   — [repr. (abridged)] 'Tvorchestvo P. I. Chaikovskogo (1840–1893)'. In: B. V. Asaf´ev, *Izbrannye trudy*, tom 2 (1954): 52–56 [see *2348*].

   — [repr. (abridged)] In: B. V. Asaf´ev, *O muzyke Chaikovskogo: Izbrannoe* (1972): 209–214 [see *2373*].

[*2320*]   HALE, P. 'Peter Ilitch Tchaikovsky'. In: P. Hale, *Great Concert Music: Philip Hale's Boston Symphony programme notes: Historical, critical, and descriptive comment on music and composers*. Ed. by John N. Burk; with an introduction by Lawrence Gilman. New York: Garden City Publishing Co, 1935: 343–362.

   — 2nd ed. New York: Garden City Pub. Co, 1939: 343–362.

[*2321*]   FASOLIS, A. 'Qualche osservazioni su Tschaikowsky', *Schewiz-Instrumentalmusik*, 25 (1936): 257–258.

[*2322*]   PALS, N. van der. *Peter Tschaikowsky*. Potsdam, 1939.

   Review: 'Germaniia: Kniga o Chaikovskom', *Internatsional´naia literatura* (1940), 7/8: 321.

[*2323*]   IARUSTOVSKII, B. M. *P. I. Chaikovskii: Zhizn´ i tvorchestvo*. Pod red. M. S. Pekelisa. Moskva, 1940. 40 p, music. (*Besedy po istorii muzyki*).

   Review: I. F. Kunin, 'Beseda po istorii muziki', *Sovetskaia muzyka* (1941), 3: 93–95.

   — 2-e izd. *Chaikovskii*. Moskva: Gos. muz. izdat., 1961. 47 p, illus. (*Bibliotechka liubitelia muzyki*).

[*2324*]   *Spisok izbrannykh vokal´nykh i instrumental´nykh proizvedenii P. I. Chaikovskogo dlia khudozhestvennoi samodeiatel´nosti*. Moskva: Tsentral´nyi dom Krasnoi Armii im. M. V. Frunze i vsesoiuznyi dom narodnogo tvorchestva im. N. K. Krupskoi, 1940. 9 p.

   — [repr.] Krasnodar: Krasnodarskii kraevoi dom narodnogo tvorchestva, 1940. 8 p.

[*2325*]   KHUBOV, G. N. 'Velichie i tragizm Chaikovskogo', *Krasnaia nov´* (1940), 9/10.

   — [repr.] In: G. N. Khubov, *O muzyke i muzykantakh: Ocherki i stat´i*. Moskva: Sovetskii kompozitor, 1959: 146–169.

[*2326*]   ZHITOMIRSKII, D. V. 'P. I. Chaikovskii'. In: *Istoriia russkoi muzyki*. Pod red. prof. M. S. Pekelisa. Tom 2. Moskva: Gos. konservatoriia, 1940: 334–429.

[*2327*]   SHLIFSHTEIN, S. 'Genii russkoi muzyki', *Sovetskoe iskusstvo* (6 May 1940): 2 [see *853*].

[*2328*]   SPAETH, S. G. 'Classical czar of Tin Pan Alley', *Etude*, 60 (1942): 665, illus.

[*2329*]   ASAF´EV, B. V. 'Chaikovskii simfonist-dramaturg: K 50-letiu so dnia smerti P. I. Chaikovskogo', *Literatura i iskusstvo* (30 Oct 1943).

[*2330*]   BUGOSLAVSKII, S. A. *Pëtr Il´ich Chaikovskii*. Stenogramma publichnoi lektsii prochitannoi 10 dek. 1944 g. v Kolonnom zale Doma Soiuzov v Moskve. Moskva, 1945. 25 p. (*Lektsionnoe biuro po delam vysshei shkoly pri SNK SSSR*).

[*2231*]   MAREK, G. 'Man with the emotional music', *Good Housekeeping*, 123 (Nov 1946): 4–5.

[2332] LANG, P. H. 'Melody: Is it dated?', *Saturday Review*, 30 (11 Jan 1947): 28–29.

[2333] CHERBULIEZ, A.-E. *Tschaikowsky und die russische Musik*. Mit 4 Kunstdrucktafeln und 21
Notenbeispielen. Rüschlikon-Zürich: A. Müller [1948]. 208 p, music, illus. (*Meister der Musik im 19. und
20. Jahrhundert*).
Review: *Die Musikforschung*, 7 (1954), 2: 238–241.

[2334] DANILEVICH, L. V. *P. I. Chaikovskii*. Moskva; Leningrad: Gos. muz. izdat., 1950. 60 p, illus.
(*Zamechatel´nye russkie muzykanty*).
Review: I. F. Kunin, 'Novye knigi o Chaikovskom', *Sovetskaia kniga* (1951), 2: 114–120.
— [Uzbek tr.] Tashkent: Sredniaia i vysshaia shkola, 1963. 62 p, illus.

[2335] ALPATOV, M. V. 'Pyotr Chaikovsky'. In: M. V. Alpatov, *Russian impact on art*. Ed. and with a preface
by Martin L. Wolf; tr. from the Russian by Ivy Litvinov. New York, Philosophical Library [1950]: 270–
272.

[2336] ROSENWALD, H. 'The unknown Tchaikovsky', *Music News*, 42 (May 1950): 18–19.

[2337] MURDOCH, W. J. 'Treasure that lay deep', *Etude*, 68 (Sep 1950): 54, illus.

[2338] AL´SHVANG, A. A. *Opyt analiza tvorchestva P. I. Chaikovskogo (1864–1878)*. Moskva; Leningrad:
Gos. muz. izdat., 1951. 256 p, music, illus.
Review: I. F. Kunin, *Sovetskaia muzyka* (1952), 4: 111–114.

[2339] IARUSTOVSKII, B. M. *P. I. Chaikovskii: Lektsiia*. Moskva; Leningrad: Gos. muz. izdat., 1951, 35
p. (*V pomoshch´ slushateliu muzyki*).
Review: T. Karysheva, 'Populiarnye broshiury-lektsii', *Sovetskaia muzyka* (1952), 8: 108–110.
— [2-e izd.] Moskva: Gos. muz. izdat., 1953, 35 p. (*V pomoshch´ slushateliu muzyki*).
— [3-e izd.] Moskva: Gos. muz. izdat., 1957. 41 p. (*V pomoshch´ slushateliu muzyki*).

[2340] SERAUKY, W. 'P. I. Tschaikowski in seinem Verhältnis zu Romantik und Realismus'. In:
Wissenschaftlich Zeitschrift der Universität Leipzig Gesellschafts-Sprachwissenschaftlich Reiche (1951/52), 5: 1–7.

[2341] PERMIAKOV, S. M. 'Esteticheskie vzgliady P. I. Chaikovskogo'. Moskva, 1952.
Dissertation (Moscow Univ.).
Reviews:*Voprosy filosofii* (1953), 1: 233 — N. Goriunov, 'Stepen´ nevezhestva, ili nevezhestvo so stepen´iu',
Sovetskaia muzyka (1954), 2: 149–151.

[2342] 'Peter Ilitch Tschaikowsky'. In: G. von Westerman & K. Schuman, *Knaurs Konzertführer*. Mit einem
Geleitwort von Wilhelm Furtwängler. München: Drömer Knaur [1952]: 287–297 (Knaur-
Taschenbucher; 240).
— [English tr.] *The concert guide: A handbook for concert-goers and music-lovers*. Preface by John Russell. Foreword
by Wilhelm Furtwängler. Tr. and ed. by Cornelius Cardew. New York: Arco [1963]: 287–297.

[2343] SERAUKY, W. 'Tschaikowsky: Westlich oder östlich orientiert?', *Musik und Gesellschaft* (1952),
2: 187–189.

[2344] POLIANOVSKII, G. A. *Material k lektsii na temu "P. I. Chaikovskii: Genii russkoi muzyki"*. Moskva,
1953. 36 p. (*Vsesoiuznoe obshchestvo po rasprostraneniiu politicheskikh i nauchnykh znanii*).
Notes in connection with a lecture-concert (analysis of Chaikovskii's works).

[2345] 'Vazhneishie muzykal´nye proizvedeniia P. I. Chaikovskogo'. In: *Pëtr Il´ich Chaikovskii: Kratkii
rekomendatel´nyi ukazatel´* (1953): 5–6 [see 23].

[2346] '"Tin Pan Alley" tunes by Peter Ilyitch Tschaikowsky', *Music Journal*, 11 (Aug 1953): 6.

[2347]   SOKOL´SKII, M. 'Vdokhnovenie, rozhdennoe trudom: Kak rabotal P. I. Chaikovskii', *Sovetskaia kul´tura* (14 Nov 1953): 3.

Examines selected works dating from 1868, 1878 and 1890.

[2348]   ASAF´EV, B. V. 'P. I. Chaikovskii'. In: B. V. Asaf´ev, *Izbrannye trudy*. Pod red. E. M. Orlovoi. Tom 2. Moskva: Akademiia Nauk SSSR, 1954: 5–190.

Selected articles by Boris Asaf´ev (see *784, 852, 893, 894, 897, 907, 2319, 2437, 2439, 2543, 2565, 2750, 2952, 4043, 5239*). Includes introductory article: V. V. Protopopov, 'Raboty B. V. Asaf´eva o Chaikovskom', 5–16.

[2349]   KASHKIN, N. D. *Izbrannye stat´i o P. I. Chaikovskom*. Obshchaia red., vstup. stat´ia i primechaniia S. I. Shlifshteina. Moskva: Gos. muz. izdat., 1954. 239 p. (*Russkaia klassicheskaia muzykal´naia kritika*).

Repr. of selected reviews by Nikolai Kashkin (see *627, 684, 2640, 2717, 2730, 2840, 2858, 3158, 3159, 3222, 3384, 3438, 3444, 3450, 3787, 4040, 4153, 4555, 4632, 4670, 4836*). Includes introductory article: S. I. Shlifshtein, 'Kashkin o Chaikovskom', 3–26.

[2350]   POLIANOVSKII, G. *Pëtr Il´ich Chaikovskii*. Moskva: Goskul´turprosvetizdat, 1954. 62 p. (*V pomoshch´ lektoru*; 6).

[2351]   BLOK, M. 'Problemy muzykal´nogo ispolnitel´stva v estetike P. I. Chaikovskogo'. In: *O muzykal´nom ispolnitel´stve*. Moskva, 1954: 78–172.

[2352]   LEONARD, R. A. 'Tchaikovsky'. In: R. A. Leonard, *A history of Russian music*. [London]: Jarrolds [1956]: 173–198; illus.

[2353]   *Muzykal´noe nasledie Chaikovskogo: Iz istorii ego proizvedenii*. Red. kollegiia: K. Iu. Davydova, V. V. Protopopov, N. V. Tumanina. Moskva: Izdat. Akademii Nauk SSSR, 1958. 541 p, music, illus.

A detailed history of each of Chaikovskii's musical works, with copious bibliographical references, indexes, bibliography and appendices.

Review: A. A. Orlova, 'Kniga o Chaikovskom', *Sovetskaia muzyka* (1960), 1: 187–190.

[2354]   KELDYSH, Iu. 'Puti sovremennogo novatorstva: Stat´ia vtoraia', *Sovetskaia muzyka* (1958), 12: 25–39.

Includes a section on Chaikovskii's works: 26–28.

[2355]   MAZEL´, L. A. 'Dve zametki o vzaimovliianii opernykh i simfonicheskikh printsipov u Chaikovskogo', *Sovetskaia muzyka* (1958), 9: 72–80, music, illus.

Contents: 'K voprosu o dramaturgii Shestoi simfonii': 72–75 [see *4714*] — 'K voprosu o simfonizme "Pikovoi damy"': 75–80 [see 3599].

[2356]   IARUSTOVSKII, B. 'Klassiki russkoi muzyki: Slava i gordost´ russkogo iskusstva', *Muzykal´naia zhizn´* (1959), 12: 12–14, illus.

[2357]   'Ob odnom pedagogicheskom opyte Chaikovskogo', *Sovetskaia muzyka* (1959), 12: 63–78, music, illus.

[2358]   TUMANINA, N. V. *Chaikovskii: Put´ k masterstvu, 1840–1877*. Moskva: Izdat. Akademii Nauk SSSR, 1962. 559 p, music, illus.

Review: A. Kandinskii, *Sovetskaia muzyka* (1971), 3: 138–143.

[2359]   GRICKAT-RADULOVIČ, I. 'Associacije iz muzike uz delo Ive Andrica', *Zvuk* (1962), 55: 513–518.

[2360]   STUPEL´, A. 'Muzyka dlia detei i o detiakh', *Doshkol´noe vospitanie* (1962), 10: 76–80.

[2361]   'Ukazatel´ proizvedenii Chaikovskogo, v kotorykh ispol´zuiutsia narodnye pesni'. In: *P. I. Chaikovskii i narodnaia pesnia* (1963): 120–137 [see *2066*].

[2362] **IAKOVLEV, V. V.** *Izbrannye trudy o muzyke*. Tom 1: *P. I. Chaikovskii (1840–1893)*. Red.-sost. i avtory primechanii D. Zhitomirskii i T. Sokolova. Moskva: Muzyka, 1964. 506 p, illus.

Mostly repr. of selected articles by Vasilii Iakovlev (see *1732, 1969, 2132, 2363, 2539, 2565, 2590*).

Reviews: I. F. Kunin, 'Chaikovskii v trudakh V. V. Iakovleva', *Muzykal'naia zhizn'* (1965), 8: 24 — N. Sin'kovskaia, 'Neutomimyi izyskatel', *Sovetskaia muzyka* (1965), 9: 137–139.

[2363] **IAKOVLEV, V. V.** 'Opyt tvorcheskoi biografii'. In: V. V. Iakovlev, *Izbrannye trudy o muzyke*, tom 1 (1964) : 37–126 [see *2362*].

[2364] **DAVIDSON, P.** 'Tchaikovsky'. In: P. Davidson, *Ge´onim be-mamlekhet ha-musikah*. [n.p., 1964(?)]: 81–96, music, illus.

Text in Hebrew.

[2365] **EWEN, D.** 'Peter Ilitch Tchaikovsky'. In: D. Ewen, *The complete book of classical music*. Englewood Cliffs (N. J.): Prentice-Hall [1965]: 737–765.

[2366] **KUNIN, I. F.** 'Stranichka shkol´nika: Serebrianyi rozhok', *Muzykal'naia zhizn'* (Sep 1966), 18: 22.

[2367] **TUMANINA, N. V.** *Chaikovskii: Tvorcheskii put´ velikogo mastera (1840–1893)*. Moskva: Institut istorii iskusstv, 1967. 47 p.

Dissertation summary (Institute of History of Arts, Moscow).

[2368] **TUMANINA, N. V.** *Chaikovskii: Velikii master, 1878–1893*. Moskva: Nauka, 1968. 487 p, music, illus. (*Akademii Nauk SSSR. Institut istorii iskusstva*).

Review: A. Kandinskii, *Sovetskaia muzyka* (1971), 3: 138–143.

[2369] **WHITWELL, D.** '19th century Russian composers: Their music for winds', *The Instrumentalist*, 22 (Feb 1968): 52–54.

[2370] **LAVRISHCHEVA, T. I.** 'O nekotorykh osobennostiakh vneshnikh uslovii tvorchestva P. I. Chaikovskogo'. In: *Voprosy muzykal´nogo obrazovaniia: Sbornik statei*. Saratov, 1969: 119–127, music. (*Ministerstvo prosveshcheniia RSFSR. Saratovskii gos. pedagogicheskii institut*).

[2371] **TSUKKERMAN, V. A.** 'Quellen des Ausdrucks und Write des Atems bei Tschaikowski', *Sowetwissenschaft*, 17 (1969), 6: 631–632, music.

[2372] **LAVRISHCHEVA, T. I.** 'P. I. Chaikovskii o portrebnosti k tvorcheskoi deiatel´nosti'. In: *Voprosy muzykal´nogo obrazovaniia*. Vyp. 2. Saratov, 1970: 58–67. (*Ministerstvo prosveshcheniia RSFSR. Saratovskii gos. pedagogicheskii institut*).

[2373] **ASAF´EV, B. V.** *O muzyke Chaikovskogo: Izbrannoe*. Vstup. stat´ia E. Orlovoi. Leningrad: Muzyka, 1972. 376 p.

Repr. of selected articles by Boris Asaf´ev (see *784, 794, 852, 893, 894, 897, 2310, 2319, 2429, 2437, 2543, 2565, 2750, 2952, 3509, 4043, 4358, 4409, 4602, 4647, 5402*).

[2374] **TIULIN, Iu. N.** *Proizvedeniia Chaikovskogo: Strukturnyi analiz*. Moskva: Muzyka, 1973. 274 p, music.

[2375] **SOLLERTINSKII, I. I.** 'Tezisy, plany, zametki: O Malere i Chaikovskom. O Mozartianstve Chaikovskogo. O soderzhanii 4-i simfonii Chaikovskogo'. In: *Pamiati I. I. Sollertinskogo: Vospominaniia, materialy, issledovaniia*. Sost. L. V. Mikheeva. Leningrad; Moskva, 1974: 217–218.

— 2-e izd, dop. Leningrad: Sovetskii kompozitor, 1978: 217–218, illus.

[2376] **LAROSH, G. A.** *Izbrannye stat´i v piati tomakh*. Otv. red. A. A. Gozenpud. Vyp. 2: *P. I. Chaikovskii*. Leningrad: Muzyka, 1975. 368 p. illus. (*Russkaia klassicheskaia muzykal'naia kritika*).

Repr. of selected reviews and articles by German Larosh (see *481, 482, 483, 484, 485, 486, 617, 626, 1454, 1731, 1988, 2311, 2422, 2535, 2638, 2728, 2783, 2786, 3280, 3359, 3364, 3376, 3390, 3402, 3478, 3479, 3731, 3763, 3779, 3789, 4037, 4164, 4469, 4471, 4537, 4548, 4545, 4568, 4581, 4635, 4666, 4797, 4824, 4827, 4840, 4876, 4931, 5001, 5182, 5196, 5269, 5275, 5304, 5318, 5416, 5425*).

[2377]   TAYLOR, P. 'Correspondence: Tchaikovsky borrowings', *Gramophone*, 52 (Jan 1975): 1320.

[2378]   KAMIEN, R. 'Peter Ilych Tchaikovsky'. In: R. Kamien, *Music: An appreciation*. New York: McGraw-Hill, 1976: 301–308.
— 2nd ed. New York: McGraw-Hill, 1980: 316–322
— 3rd ed. New York: McGraw-Hill, 1984: 337–343.
— 4th ed. New York: McGraw-Hill, 1988: 337–343.

[2379]   TRET´IAKOVA, L. S. 'Pëtr Il´ich Chaikovskii'. In: *Russkaia muzyka XIX veka*. Moskva: Prosveshchenie, 1976: 163–197.

[2380]   STREET, D. 'The modes of limited transposition', *Musical Times*, 117 (Oct 1976): 819–821, illus.

[2381]   STUDWELL, W. E. *Chaikovskii, Delibes, Stravinskii: Four essays on three masters*. Chicago: Prophet Press, 1977. 59 p.

[2382]   HEERENOVÁ, P. *Skladatelé boje s osudem: Petr Iljič Čajkovskij, Sergej Prokofjev*. Metodický text pro účastníky soutěže. O zemi, kde zítra již znamená včera zpracovala Petra Heerenová. Brno: SVK, 1980. 38 p, illus.

[2383]   AUERBAKH, L. 'Val´s u Chaikovskogo'. In: L. Auerbakh, *Rasskazy o val´se*. Moskva: Sovetskii kompozitor, 1980: 116–125.

[2384]   RAISKII, I. 'Artisticheskii vostorg i issledovatel´skaia glubina: N. Miaskovskii o P. I. Chaikovskom-simfoniste'. In: *Kritika i muzykoznanie: Sbornik statei*. Vyp. 2. Moskva: Muzyka, 1980: 207–216.
Concerning Miaskovskii's critical articles on Chaikovskii, in particular 'Chaikovskii i Betkhoven' (1912) [see 2077].

[2385]   TANIS, J. 'Was Tschaikovsky the grandfather of rock?', *Songwriter*, 6 (Oct 1980): 34–36.

[2386]   ROZANOVA, Iu. 'P. I. Chaikovskii'. In: *Istoriia russkoi muzyki*. Obshchaia red. A. I. Kandinskogo. Tom 2: *Vtoraia polovina XIX veka*. Kniga 3: *P. I. Chaikovskii*. Moskva: Muzyka [1981]. 308 p, illus.
— Izd. 2-e, ispr. i dop. Moskva: Muzyka, 1986.

[2387]   GUREWITSCH, M. A. 'New steps to Tchaikovsky', *New Leader*, 64 (7 Sep 1981): 20–21.

[2388]   MITCHELL, D. 'Catching on to the technique in "Pagoda-Land"', *Tempo* (Sep 1983), 146: 18–20, illus.

[2389]   MAGNITSKAIA, T. 'Zhivoe dykhanie melodii', *Sovetskaia muzyka* (1984), 4: 98–100, illus.

[2390]   PICCARDI, C. 'Realta e virtualita del decadentismo', *Studia Musicologica*, 14 (1985), 2: 269–271.

[2391]   BELYI, P. 'Nepostizhimyi Chaikovskii: Zametki kompozitora', *Sovetskaia muzyka* (1986), 6: 75–80.
Chaikovskii's works viewed as part of an overall cyclical scheme.

[2392]   BROWN, D. 'Tchaikovsky's ciphers', *Times Literary Suppl.* (4 Apr 1986): 359.

[2393]   ARUTIUNOV, D. *Sochineniia P. I. Chaikovskogo v kurse analiza muzykal´nykh proizvedenii*. Moskva: Muzyka, 1989. 111 p, music.
Includes: 'Iz vyskazyvanii P. I. Chaikovskogo o muzykal´noi forme': 96–109 [see 2068].

[2394]   GRIFFITHS, P. 'Peter Ilych Tchaikovsky'. In: *Heritage of music*. Ed. by Michael Raeburn and Alan Kendall. Oxford; New York: Oxford University Press, 1989: 43–61.

[2395] IARESHKO, A. 'Muzyka kolokol´nykh zvonov v tvorchestve russkikh kompozitorov vtoroi polovny XIX veka (P. Chaikovskii, M. Musorgskii, N. Rimksii-Korsakov)'. In: *P. I. Chaikovskii: Voprosy istorii i stilia* (1989): 90–114 [see *590*].

[2396] WILEY, R. J. 'Pattern and meaning in Tchaikovsky', *San Francisco Performing Arts Library and Museum Journal* (spr. 1989), 1: 39–49 [see *4310*].

[2397] BELLINGARDI, L. *Invito all'ascolto di Petr Il´ič Čajkovskij*. Milano: Mursia [1990]. 232 p.

Review: U. Padroni, *Nuova Rivista Musicale Italiana*, 25 (Jul/Dec 1991), 3/4: 522–523.

[2398] *Tvorcheskoe nasledie P. I. Chaikovskogo, 1840–1893: Materialy k obsuzhdeniiu na pedagogicheskom seminare*. Leningrad, 1990. 29 p.

[2399] 'Chaikovskii, Pëtr Il´ch'. In: *Slovo o muzyke: Kniga dlia uchashchiksia studencheskikh klassov*. Sost. V. Grigorovich, Z. Andreeva. 2 izd., ispr. Moskva: Prosveshchenie, 1990: 271–317.

[2400] SMIRNOV, M. 'Chaikovskii: Vechnost´ mgnoveniia'. In: M. Smirnov, *Emotsional´nyi mir muzyki: Issledovanie*. Moskva: Muzyka, 1990: 264–268.

[2401] CHINAEV, V. 'Vdokhnovennoe, trivial´noe, nostal´gicheskoe: Interpretatsiia Chaikovskogo v svete vremenii'. In: *Muzyka P. I. Chaikovskogo: Voprosy interpretatsii* (1991): 18–41 [see *594*].

[2402] GRIGOR´EV, B. 'P. I. Chaikovskii i problemy ispolnitel´skogo iskusstva'. In: *Muzyka P. I. Chaikovskogo: Voprosy interpretatsii* (1991): 4–17 [see *594*].

[2403] LARCHENKO, O. 'Tvorchestvo P. I. Chaikovskogo v kritike V. G. Karatygina i sovremennost´'. In: *Muzyka P. I. Chaikovskogo: Voprosy interpretatsii* (1991): 102–114 [see *594*].

[2404] SIDEL´NIKOV, L. *P. I. Chaikovskii*. Moskva: Iskusstvo, 1992. 351, (24) p, illus. (*Zhizn´ v iskusstve*). ISBN: 5–210–02306–0.

Review: M. H. Brown, *Slavic Review*, 53 (win. 1994): 1201–1203.

[2405] KOHLHASE, T. 'Čajkovskij, Petr Il´ič'. In: *Metzler Komponisten Lexikon*. Hrsg. von Horst Weber. Weimar: J. B. Metzler, 1992: 130–133.

[2406] LAROSH, G. A. *Peter Tschaikowsky: Aufsätze und Erinnerungen*. Ausegwählt, übersetzt und hrsg. von Ernst Kuhn. Mit Texten zur Person Hermann Laroches aus der Feder von Modest Tschaikowsky und Nikolai Kaschkin sowie einem Orignalal-Beitrag von Thomas Kohlhase. Berlin: E. Kuhn, 1993. 314 p. (*Musik konkret*; 5). ISBN: 3–928864–07–6.

Contents: T. Kohlhase, 'Hermann Laroche: Ein russischer Hanslick': 12–40 — M. Chaikovskii, 'In memorian Hermann Laroche': 41–59 — N. Kashkin, 'Meine Erinnerungen an Hermann Laroche': 266–280 — 'Tschaikowskys Biographie in Stichworten': 306–307.

See also *13, 47, 481, 482, 483, 1725, 2277, 2728, 2783, 3359, 3478, 3789, 4037, 4164, 4469, 4537, 4568, 4581, 4666, 4797, 4827, 4829, 5001, 5196, 5425*.

Reviews: L. Barkefors, *Svenska Tidskrift för Musikforskning*, 85 (1993), 2: 93–98 — *Orchester*, 42 (1994), 10: 63–64 — M. Betz, *Die Musikforschung*, 48 (Jan/Mar 1995), 1: 90–91.

[2407] POPOV, V. S. *Tschaikowsky: Orchester Studien—Fagott*. Hrsg. V. S. Popov. Frankfurt: Zimmermann, 1993.

Review: *Orchester*, 42 (1994), 1: 69–70.

[2408] CAMPBELL, S. *Russians on Russian music: An anthology*. Ed. and tr. by Stuart Campbell. Cambridge; New York: Cambridge Univ. Press [1994]: 134–145, 240–272. xxi, 295 p, illus. ISBN: 0–521–40267–0.

English trs. of selected reviews by Chaikovskii, and of Chaikovskii's music. Includes: P. Tchaikovsky, 'The revival of "Ruslan and Lyudmila": 134–140 — P. Tchaikovsky, '"Dargomyzhsky's "Rusalka", The Italian Opera': 141–145 — H. Laroche, '"Oprichnik": An opera in four acts': 240–245 [see *3359*] — H. Laroche, 'Tchaikovsky's "Eugene Onegin", in the Conservatoire's production': 245–248 [see *2783*] — C. Cui, 'Notes on music: "Eugene Onegin"': 248–254 [see *2829*] — H. Laroche, 'A new Russian symphony': 255–260 [see *4537*] — H. Laroche, 'Russian musical composition in our day': 260–272 [see *2422*].

[2409]   MÜHLBACH, M. 'Der Klassiker Tschaikowsky'. In: *Russische Musikgeschichte im Überblick: Ein Handbuch*. Berlin: E. Kuhn, 1994: 209–257.

[2410]   SIN´KOVSKAIA, N. 'P. I. Chaikovskii: K izucheniiu tvorcheskogo protsessa'. In: *Protsessy muzykal´nogo tvorchestva: Sbornik trudov*, vyp. 134. Moskva: Ministerstvo kul´tury Rossiiskoi Federatsii, 1994: 78–89.

[2411]   EROHIN, V. 'An der Schwelle zum neuen Jahrhundert: Anmerkungen zu Cajkovskijs Harmonik'. In: *Internationales Čajkovskij Symposium, Tübingen 1993: Bericht* (1995): 103–110 [see 596].

[2412]   FRUMKIS, T. 'Zu deutschen Vorbildern von Čajkovskijs Harmonielehre'. In: *Internationales Čajkovskij Symposium, Tübingen 1993: Bericht* (1995): 111–126 [see 596].

[2413]   VAIDMAN, P. E. 'Unbekannter Čajkovskij: Entwürfe zu nicht ausgeführten Komponisten'. In: *Internationales Čajkovskij Symposium, Tübingen 1993: Bericht* (1995): 281–298 [see 596].

[2414]   HERRUER, P. 'De Weense wals van Schoenberg, Berg en Webern, een duidelijk een-twee-drie?', *Mens en Melodie*, 50 (Jul/Aug 1995): 419–425

[2415]   KOHLHASE, T. *Einführungen in ausgewählte Werke Petr Il´ič Čajkovskijs*. Mainz: Schott, 1996. (*Čajkovskij Studien*; 2). ISBN: 3-7957-0324-7.

[2416]   BUHLER, J. 'Informal music analysis: A critique of formalism, semiology, and narratology as discourses on music'. Philadelphia: Univ. of Pennsylvania, 1996. 270 p.

          Dissertation (Ph. D.). Considers contemporary musical analysis of Mahler and Chaikovskii.

[2417]   JACKSON, T. L. 'The tragic reversed recapitulation in the German classical tradition', *Journal of Music Theory*, 40 (spr. 1996): 61–111.

[2418]   KOHLHASE, T. 'Musikalische Kinderszenen bei Čajkovskij', *Tschaikowsky-Gesellschaft Mitteilungen*, 4 (1997): 31–52.

          — [repr.] In: *Čajkovskijs Homosexualität und sein Tod: Legenden und Wirklichkeit* (1998): 417–438 [see 600].

[2419]   AFONINA, N. 'Evolution of meter in Russian music of the nineteenth century and the beginning of the twentieth century', *Tijdschrift voor Muziektheorie*, 3 (May 1998): 110–112.

[2420]   PAVLOV-ARBENIN, A. B. 'Chaikovskii v trudakh Asaf´eva'. In: *P. I. Chaikovskii: Nasledie*, vyp. 1 (2000): 179–182 [see 603].

          The writings of Boris Asaf´ev (Igor Glebov) concerning Chaikovskii's music.

[2421]   KLIMOVITSKII, A. N. 'Nekotorye kul´turno-istoricheskie paradoksy bytovaniia tvorcheskogo nasledia Chaikovskogo v Rossii'. In: *P. I. Chaikovskii: Nasledie*, vyp. 2 (2000): 6–48 [see 604].

          See also *594, 805, 1243*.

5.1.2. Style

[2422]   LAROSH, G. A. 'Russkaia muzykal´naia kompozitsiia nashikh dnei: Obshchaia kharakteristika tvorchestva P. Chaikovskogo', *Golos* (28 Nov 1873): 1–3.

          — [repr.] In: G. A. Larosh, *Sobranie muzykal´no-kriticheskikh statei*, tom 2, chast´ 2 (1924): 17–32 [see 2311].

          — [repr.] In: G. A. Larosh, *Izbrannye stat´i v piati vypuskakh*, vyp. 2 (1975): 38–51 [see 2376].

          — [English tr.] 'Russian musical composition in our day'. In: S. Campbell, *Russians on Russian music* (1994): 260–272 [see 2408].

[2423]   TIMOFEEV, G. N. 'Natsional´naia muzyka i ee predstaviteli v Rossii', *Russkii vestnik* (1900), 45: 255–258.

[2424]   'Protsess muzykal´nogo tvorchestva: Iz perepiski Chaikovskogo', *Russkie vedomosti* (23 Sep 1901).
Extracts from 2 letters from Chaikovskii to Nadezhda von Meck, concerning the process of composition.

[2425]   BORMAN, E. 'Dies und Jenes über Tschaikowsky', *Neue Zeitschrift für Musik*, 46 (1912): 645–647.

[2426]   MASON, D. G. '"Yankee Doodle" as it might have been treated by Tschaikowsky', *Outlook*, 100 (27 Jan 1912): 219–224, illus.

[2427]   IPPOLITOV-IVANOV, M. M. 'P. I. Chaikovskii: Lirik i velichaishii melodist', *Solntse Rossii* (1913), 44: 2–5 [see *583*]

[2428]   GUNST, E. O. 'O kompozitorskoi rabote P. I. Chaikovskogo', *Maski* (1913/14), 2: 8–20.

[2429]   GLEBOV, I. [ASAF´EV, B. V.] *Chaikovskii: Opyt kharakteristiki*. Petrograd: Svetozar, 1922. 62 p, illus.
— [2-e izd.] Petrograd; Berlin [pr. Leipzig]: Svetozar, 1923. 48 p, illus.
— [repr.] In: B. V. Asaf´ev, *O muzyke Chaikovskogo: Izbrannoe* (1972): 214–234 [see *2373*].

[2430]   LOGE. 'Chaikovskii i narodnaia pesnia', *Zhizn´ iskusstva* (1931), 811: 6.

[2431]   IARUSTOVSKII, B. M. 'Oblik Chaikovskogo', *Sovetskaia muzyka* (1938), 6: 32–37.
Chaikovskii's basic working methods.

[2432]   KREMLEV, Iu. A. 'Nekotorye istoki melodicheskikh intonatsii Chaikovskogo', *Sovetskaia muzyka* (1940), 3: 30–38, illus.

[2433]   ROGAL´-LEVITSKII, D. 'Orkestr Chaikovskogo', *Sovetskaia muzyka* (1940), 5/6: 105–111, illus [see *585*].

[2434]   SHASTIN, N. 'Narodnyi genii', *Ogonek* (1940), 12: 5–6, music, illus.
The influence of folk-music on Chaikovskii's works.

[2435]   TSUKKERMAN, V. 'Vyrazitel'nye sredstva liriki Chaikovskogo', *Sovetskaia muzyka* (1940), 9: 49–67.
See also *2458*.

[2436]   GRINBERG, M. 'Chaikovskii: 1840–1940', *Teatr* (May 1940), 5: 11–16.

[2437]   ASAF´EV, B. V. 'O napravlennosti formy u Chaikovskogo'. In: *Sovetskaia muzyka: 3-i sbornik statei*. Moskva; Leningrad, 1945: 5–9.
— [repr.] In: B. V. Asaf´ev, *Izbrannye trudy*, tom 2 (1954): 64–70 [see *2348*].
— [repr.] In: B. V. Asaf´ev, *O muzyke Chaikovskogo: Izbrannoe* (1972): 67–73 [see *2373*].

[2438]   ZHITOMIRSKII, D. V. 'Zametki ob instrumentovke Chaikovskogo'. In: *Sovetskaia muzyka: 3-i sbornik statei*. Moskva; Leningrad, 1945: 10–22.

[2439]   ASAF´EV, B. V. 'Poteria melodii', *Voprosy filosofii* (1948), 1: 146–147.
Partly concerning Chaikovskii.
— [repr. (abridged)] 'O melodizme muzyki Chaikovskogo'. In: B. V. Asaf´ev, *Izbrannye trudy*, tom 2 (1954): 71–72 [see *2348*].

[2440]   SLONIMSKY, N. 'Musical miscellany: Tchaikovsky's method of work', *Etude*, 68 (Dec 1950): 7.

[2441]   KOSTAREV, V. 'Preobrazovanie melodiko-tematicheskikh elementov v proizvedenniiakh P. I. Chaikovskogo'. In: *Nauchno-metodicheskie zapiski*. Tom 2. Sverdlovsk: Ural´skaia gos. konservatoriia, 1953: 183–217, music.

[2442]   SOKOL´SKII, M. 'Vdokhnovenie, rozhdennoe trudom: Kak rabotal P. I. Chaikovskii', *Sovetskaia kul´tura* (14 Nov 1953).

[2443]   DANILEVICH, L. 'Ob orkestrovom masterstve', *Sovetskaia muzyka* (1954), 5: 18–24.
          Includes a section on Chaikovskii's orchestration: 19–20.

[2444]   AL´SHVANG, A. A. 'Pesennye istoki simfonizma Chaikovskogo', *Sovetskaia muzyka* (1955), 12: 52–60, music, illus.
          The influence of Russian folk-song on Chaikovskii's orchestral works.
          — [repr.] In: A. A. Al´shvang, *Izbrannye stat´i*. Moskva, 1959: 172–183.
          — [repr.] In: A. A. Al´shvang, *Izbrannye sochineniia*. Tom 1. Moskva, 1964: 104–117.

[2445]   BUIANOVSKII, V. M. 'Rol´ voltorny v simfonicheskom i opernom orkestre P. I. Chaikovskogo'. Leningrad: Gos. Konservatoriia im N. A. Rimskogo-Korsakova, 1955. 21 p.
          Summary of dissertation (Leningrad Conservatory).

[2445a]   GORDEICHUK, N. M. 'Chaikovskii i ukrainskie narodnye pesni'. In: *Russko-ukrainskie sviazi v oblasti iskusstva*. Kiev, 1955: 65–73.

[2446]   VEPRIK, A. 'Orkestrovaia faktura proizvedenii Chaikovskogo'. In: A. Veprik, *Ocherki po voprosam orkestrovykh stilei*. Moskva: Sovetskii kompozitor, 1961: 19–68?, music.
          — 2-e izd, ispr. Moskva: Sovetskii kompozitor, 1978: 22–74, music.

[2447]   PROTOPOPOV, V. V. 'Polifoniia P. Chaikovskogo'. In: V. V. Protopopov, *Istoriia polifonii v eë vazhneishikh iavleniiakh*. Moskva: Muzyka, 1962: 102–132. (*Russkaia klassicheskaia i sovetskaia muzyka*).

[2448]   GUSAROVA, O. V. 'Dialogichnist´ u polifonii P. I. Chaikovskogo'. In: *Naukovo-metodichni zepiski*. Kiev, 1963: 71–83.
          Text in Ukrainian.

[2449]   JODAL, G. 'Arta orchestraţiei la P. I. Ceaikovski', *Lucrări de Muzicologie*, 1 (1965): 45–57, illus.
          Text in Romanian, with summaries in Russian, French, German and Italian.

[2450]   KONSTANTIN, A. 'Chaikovskii—natsional´nyi kompozitor', *Pravoslavnyi put´* (1965): 165–192.
          The religious aspects of the composer's music.

[2451]   GUSAROVA, O. V. 'Nekotorye osobennosti polifonii P. I. Chaikovskogo'. Kiev: Gos. konservatoriia im. P. I. Chaikovskogo, 1966. 16 p.
          Summary of dissertation (Kiev Conservatory).
          — [rev. repr.] 'Nekotorye voprosy polifonii P. I. Chaikovskogo'. In: *Ukrainskoe muzykovedenie: Nauchno-metodicheskii mezhvedomstvennyi ezhegodnik*. Kiev, Mystetstvo, 1966: 32–73, illus.

[2452]   ROITERSHTEIN, M. 'O edinstve sonato-tsiklicheskoi formy u Chaikovskogo'. In: M. Roitershtein, *Voprosy muzykal´noi formy: Sbornik statei*. Vyp. 1. Pod red. V. Protopopova. Moskva: Muzyka, 1966: 121–150, music.

[2453]   TIUMENEVA, G. 'Chaikovskii i ukrainskaia narodnaia pesnia'. In: *Iz istorii russko-ukrainskikh muzykal´nykh sviazei*. Moskva, 1966: 182–203.

[2454]   TSUKKERMAN, V. 'Istoki ekspressii, shirota dykhaniia: K 75-letiiu so dnia smerti P. I. Chaikovskogo', *Sovetskaia muzyka* (1968), 11: 107–113, illus.; 12: 86–94.

[2455]   LAVRISHCHEVA, T. I. 'P. I. Chaikovskii o rezhime kompozitorskogo truda'. In: *Voprosy muzykal´nogo obrazovaniia: Sbornik statei*. Saratov, 1969: 109–118, music. (*Ministerstvo prosveshcheniia RSFSR. Saratovskii gos. pedagogicheskii institut*).

[2456] SAVINIKH, V. F. 'Russkaia garmonika v tvorchestve P. I. Chaikovskogo'. In: *Voprosy iskusstvoznaniia*. Vyp. 1. Khar´kov, 1969: 246–255. (*Nauchno- metodologicheskie raboty Khar´kovskogo instituta iskusstv*).

[2457] KOSTAREV, V. P. 'Stroenie sonatnykh razrabotok v proizvedeniiakh P. I. Chaikovskogo'. In: *Nauchno-metodicheskoe zapiski Ural´skoi gos. konservatorii im. M. P. Musorgskogo*. Vyp. 6. Sverdlovsk: Sredne-Ural´skoe knizhnoe izdat., 1970: 63–114, music.

Dissertation.

— [partial repr.] *Stroenie i tematicheskoe razvitie v sonatnykh razrabotkakh proizvedenii P. I. Chaikovskogo*. Sverdlovsk, 1972. 22 p.

— [partial repr.] *Stroenie i tematicheskoe razvitie v sonatnykh razrabotkakh proizvedenii P. I. Chaikovskogo*. Leningrad: Gos. konservatorii im. N. A. Rimskogo-Korsakova, 1973. 21 p.

[2458] TSUKKERMAN, V. *Vyrazitel´nye sredstva liriki Chaikovskogo*. Moskva: Muzyka, 1971. 245 p, music.

See also *2435*.

Review: D. V. Zhitomirskii, 'Kniga o Chaikovskom', *Sovetskaia muzyka* (1973), 6: 113–117.

[2459] KNEPLER, G. 'Cajkovskij: Musicien type de XIXe siecle?', *Acta Musicologica*, 43 (1971), 3/4: 205–235.

[2460] MIASOEDOV, A. *Traditsii Chaikovskogo v prepodavanii garmonii*. Moskva, 1973. 61 p.

[2461] LAVRISHCHEVA, T. I. 'Psikhologicheskie osobennosti tvorcheskogo protsessa P. I. Chaikovskogo'. Erevan: Konservatoriia, 1973. 23 p.

Summary of dissertation (Erevan Conservatory).

[2462] NORRIS, G. 'Tchaikovsky and the 18th Century', *Musical Times*, 118 (Sep 1977): 715–716, illus.

[2463] VITACHEK, F. E. *Ocherki po iskusstvu orkestrovki XIX veka: Istoricheskii-stilisticheskii analiz partitur Berlioza, Glinki, Vagnera, Chaikovskogo i Rimskogo-Korsakova*. Moskva: Muzyka, 1978. 149 p, music.

[2464] IVANCHENKO, G. I. *Ritm kak faktor formoobrazovaniia i dramaturgii v simfonicheskom tvorchestve P. I. Chaikovskogo*. Leningrad, 1982. 24 p, music.

Dissertation summary (Leningrad Conservatory).

[2465] STOLZ, R. F. G. 'Temporal incongruence in selected compositions of Peter Ilich Tchaikovsky'. Columbus: Ohio State Univ., 1982. xii, 160 p, music, illus.

Dissertation (Ph. D.). Includes bibliography: 143–148.

[2466] ZAJACZKOWSKI, H. 'The function of obsessive elements in Tchaikovsky's style', *Music Review*, 43 (Feb 1982), 1: 24–30, music.

[2467] SIN´KOVSKAIA, N. N. *O garmonii P. I. Chaikovskogo*. Moskva: Muzyka, 1983. 79 p, music. (*Voprosy istorii, teorii, metodiki*).

Review: N. Makarova, *Sovetskaia muzyka* (1984), 11: 107.

[2468] TARASOV, A. 'O tembrovom var´irovanii na neizvestnuiu temu (Rimskii-Korsakov i Chaikovskii)'. In: *Muzykal´naia klassika i sovremennost´: Voprosy istorii i estetiki. Sbornik trudov*. Leningrad, 1983: 34–45.

[2469] WILEY, R. J. 'Tchaikovsky's harmony'. In: R. J. Wiley, *Tchaikovsky's ballets* (1985): 345–353 [see *3844*].

[2470] ZAJACZKOWSKI, H. 'Tchaikovsky's musical style'. Sheffield, 1985.

Thesis (Ph. D), Sheffield Univ.

— [rev. repr.] *Tchaikovsky's musical style*. Ann Arbor; London: UMI Research Press [1987]. x, 245 p, music, illus. (*Russian Music Studies*; 19). ISBN: 0-8357-1806-9.

Reviews: *Central Opera Service Bulletin*, 28 (1988), 4: 169 — *Ovation*, 10 (Sep 1989): 69 — R. W. Oldani, *Slavic Review*, 48 (aut. 1989), 3: 530 — D. Brown, *Music & Letters*, 70 (Nov 1989), 4: 566–568 (with response by H. Zajackowski, *Music & Letters*, 71 (Aug 1990), 3: 474–476).

[2471]   PROTOPOPOV, V. 'Polifoniia P. I. Chaikovskogo'. In: *Istoriia polifonii*. Vyp. 5: *Polifoniia v russkoi muzyke XVII-nachale XX v.* Moskva: Muzyka, 1987: 164–189.

[2472]   VASIL´EV, Iu. V. 'Formirovanie orkestrovoi tkani v proizvedeniakh P. I. Chaikovskogo 1890-kh godov: Na materiale avtorskikh rukopisei'. In: *Orkestrovye stili v russkoi muzyke*. Leningrad: Muzyka, 1987: 21–39.

[2473]   VASIL´EV, Iu. V. 'Stanovlenie khudozhestvennogo teksta v tvorchestve P. I. Chaikovskogo: Na materiale rukopisei proizvedeniia 90-kh godov'. Leningrad: Gos. konservatoriia im. N. A. Rimskogo-Korsakova, 1987. 25 p.

         Dissertation (Leningrad Conservatory).

[2474]   ASAF´EV, B. V. 'O narodnosti melosa Chaikovskogo' (publikuetsia vpervye, podgot. k pechati A. Pavlova-Arenina), *Muzykal´nye kadry* (18 Apr 1988): 4.

         — [repr.] In: *P. I. Chaikovskii: Nasledie*, vyp. 1 (2000): 188–197 [see *603*].

[2475]   ARUTIUNOV, D. A. *Sochineniia P. I. Chaikovskogo v kurse analiza muzykal´nykh proizvedenii*. Moskva: Muzyka, 1989. 112 p.

[2476]   ISTOMIN, I. 'Garmoniia Chaikovskogo'. In: *Ocherki po istorii garmonii v russkoi i sovetskoi muzyke*. Vyp. 3. Moskva: Muzyka, 1989: 5–35, music.

[2477]   SHCHERBAKOVA, T. 'Chaikovskii i muzyka byta'. In: *P. I. Chaikovskii: Voprosy istorii i stilia* (1989): 9–25 [see *590*].

[2478]   SOSNOVTSEVA, O. 'O soderzhatel´nosti variantnoi formy v muzyke Chaikovskogo'. In: *P. I. Chaikovskii: Voprosy istorii i stilia* (1989): 47–59 [see *590*].

[2479]   ASAF´EV, B. V. 'Chaikovskii, rassuzhdaiushchii so svoei sobstvennoi rukopis´iu: Monolog ili dialog?', *Sovetskaia muzyka* (1990), 6: 29–31 [see *592*].

         Boris Asaf´ev's ficitionalised account of Chaikovskii's compositional methods.

[2480]   SIDOROVA, T. O. 'O nekotorykh spetsificheskikh chertakh tvorcheskogo protsessa Chaikovskogo'. In: *Chaikovskii: K 150-letiiu so dnia rozhdeniia. Voprosy istorii, teorii i ispolnitel´stva* (1990): 58–76 [see *591*].

[2481]   TSUKKERMAN, V. A. 'Chaikovskii'. In: V. A. Tsukkerman, *Analiz muzykal´nykh proizvedenii: Rondo v ego istoricheskom razvitii. Uchebnik dlia muzykovedcheskikh otdelenii konservatorii*. Chast´ 2. Moskva: Muzyka, 1990: 112 –124, music.

[2482]   ZAK, V. 'Vazhnyi orientir stilia', *Sovetskaia muzyka* (1990), 6: 33–38, music [see *592*].

[2483]   WERNER, E. 'Dass er ein Schöpfer der Melodie war', *Acta Mozartiana*, 37 (Aug 1990), 3: 53–57.

[2484]   BEREZIN, V. 'Dukhovye instrumenty v rannikh partiturakh Chaikovskogo'. In: *Muzyka P. I. Chaikovskogo: Voprosy interpretatsii* (1991): 87–101 [see *594*].

[2485]   MIKHAILOVA, G. 'Tipy stilizatsii v muzyke P. I. Chaikovskogo'. In: *Chaikovskii: Voprosy istorii i teorii* (1991): 134–143 [see *593*].

[2486]   SOSNOVTSEVA, O. 'Spetsifika variantosti v tvorchestve P. I. Chaikovskogo'. In: *Chaikovskii: Voprosy istorii i teorii* (1991): 112–134 [see *593*].

[2487] KHOLOPOVA, V. '"Forma emocjonalna" u Czajkowskiego: Próba postawienia problemu' / 'An attempt at exploring the problem of "emotional form" in Tchaikovsky's music', *Muzyka*, 39 (1994), 1: 3–17, music.

Text in Polish, with a summary in English.

[2488] POBEREŹNA, H. 'Osobowość Czajkowskiego jako jeden z wyznaczników stylu jego twórczości' / 'The personality of Tchaikovsky as a determinant of his style', *Muzyka*, 39 (1994), 1: 73–88, music.

Text in Polish, with a summary in English.

[2489] BRIANTSEVA, V. N. 'O pretvorenii val´sovosti v tvorchestve P. I. Chaikovskogo i S. V. Rakhmaninova'. In: *S. V. Rakhmaninov: K 120-letiiu so dnia rozhdeniia (1873–1993)*. Materialy nauchnoi konferentsii. Red, sost. i vstupit. stat´ia A. I. Kandinskogo. Moskva: Gos. konservatoriia im. P. I. Chaikovskogo, 1995: 120–128.

[2490] CHEKAN, Iu. I. 'Ob intonatsionnoi kontseptsii tvorchestva Chaikovskogo 90-kh godov'. In: *Ocherki po istorii russkoi muzyki: Tematicheskii sbornik nauchnykh trudov*. Kiev: Slavianskii universitet, 1995: 110–121 (*Natsional´naia Muzykal´naia Akademiia im. P. I. Chaikovskogo*).

[2491] KHOLOPOV, Iu. N. 'Chto zhe delat´ s muzykal´nymi formami Chaikovskogo?'. In: *P. I. Chaikovskii: K 100-letiiu so dnia smerti* (1995): 54–64 [see *597*].

[2492] SIN´KOVSKAIA, N. N. 'U istokov stilia'. In: *P. I. Chaikovskii: K 100-letiiu so dnia smerti* (1995): 83–93 [see *597*].

Mainly concerned with Chaikovskii's early works.

[2493] TARUSKIN, R. 'Busnoys and Chaikovsky', *International Journal of Musicology*, 4 (1995): 111–139.

[2494] VAIDMAN, P. E. 'Nekotorye aspekty kompozitorskoi raboty P. I. Chaikovskogo 80–90-kh godov (po materialam arkhiva kompozitora)'. In: *P. I. Chaikovskii: K 100-letiiu so dnia smerti* (1995): 19–23 [see *597*].

[2495] ZEMTSOVSKII, I. 'Čajkovskij and the European melosphere: A case of cantilena-narration'. In: *Internationales Čajkovskij Symposium, Tübingen 1993: Bericht* (1995): 329–336 [see *596*].

[2496] SOSNOVTSEVA, O. B. 'Variantnoe razvitie i variantnaia forma v tvorchestve P. I. Chaikovskogo'. Moskva, Rossiiskaia akademiia muzyki im. Gnesinykh, 1997. 25 p.

Summary of dissertation (Russian Academy of Music).

[2497] KRAUS, J. C. 'A comparison of rhythmic structures in the instrumental music of Schumann and Tchaikovsky'. In: *Tchaikovsky and his contemporaries* (1999): 117–128 [see *602*].

[2498] VASIL´EV, Iu. V. 'O printsipakh atributsii nekotorykh nabroskov P. I. Chaikovskogo'. In: *P. I. Chaikovskii: Nasledie*, vyp. 1 (2000): 21–66 [see *603*].

[2499] KOLOVSKII, O. P. 'O melodii, podgolosochnosti i kontrapunkte v muzyke Chaikovskogo'. In: *P. I. Chaikovskii: Nasledie*, vyp. 1 (2000): 77–99 [see *603*].

[2500] ASAF´EV, B. V. 'Muzykal´naia dramaturgiia Chaikovskogo (osnovnye printsipy)'. In: *P. I. Chaikovskii: Nasledie*, vyp. 1 (2000): 182–187 [see *603*].

[2501] VASIL´EV, Iu. V. 'Etapy tvorcheskoi raboty P. I. Chaikovskogo nad proizvedeniiami 1890-kh godov (na osnove tekstologicheskogo analiza rukopisei)'. In: *P. I. Chaikovskii: Nasledie*, vyp. 2 (2000): 81–124 [see *604*].

See also *114, 4450*.

5.1.3. Influence

[2502] SUVOROVSKII, N. 'Chaikovskii i muzyka budushego', *Vesy* (1904), 8: 10–20.

[2503] RUDER, W. 'Tschaikowsky und die weltliche Musik', *Neue Musik-Zeitung* (1926), 3: 49.

[2504] DIMITRIADI, N. 'P. I. Chaikovskii i gruzinskaia muzykal´naia kul´tura', *Literaturnaia Gruziia* (1988), 6: 203–221.

[2505] 'Peter Tchaikovsky (1840–1893)'. In: J. L. Holmes, *Composers on composers*. New York: Greenwood Press, 1990: 147–148.
The views of Sergei Taneev, Igor Stravinskii, Sergei Prokof´ev and Gustav Mahler on Chaikovskii's music.

[2506] TUGARINOV, E. 'Pod znakom ego tvorchestva', *Sovetskaia muzyka* (1990), 6: 74–80 [see *592*].
The influence of Chaikovskii's music on the choirmaster Vasilii Orlov, and other contemporary Soviet musicians.

[2507] TULINTSEV, B. 'Iz istorii kul´tury: V pamiat´ o Chaikovskom', *Teatr* (1990), 5: 139–144.
The influence of Chaikovskii's music on the works of Skriabin, Stravinskii and Shostakovich.

[2508] LEHMANN, D. 'Čajkovsijs Ansichten über deutsche Komponisten'. In: *Internationales Čajkovskij Symposium, Tübingen 1993: Bericht* (1995): 207–216 [see *596*].

CLAUDE DEBUSSY (1862–1918)
French pianist, composer and critic

[2509] PALMER, C. 'Tchaikovsky and Debussy', *Musical Opinion*, 95 (Nov 1971): 69–70.

[2510] KUPETS, L. A. 'Frantsuzskie obrazy russkoi muzyki'. In: *Russkaia kul´tura i mir: Tezisy dokladov uchastnikov II mezhdunarodnoi nauchnoi konferentsii*. Chast´ 2. Nizhnii Novgorod: NGLU im. N. A. Dobroliubova, 1994: 154–155.

See also *2085, 2086, 2087*.

REINHOLD GLIER (1875–1956)
Russian composer and conductor

[2511] GLIER, R. M. 'Pamiati velikogo kompozitora: K 100-letiiu so dnia rozhdeniia P. I. Chaikovskogo', *Oktiabr´* (1940), 4/5: 296–299.
Chaikovskii's influence on Glier.
— [repr.] 'Velikii russkii kompozitor'. In: *Reingold Moritsevich Glier: Stat´i, vospominaniia, materialy*. Pod red. V. M. Bogdanova-Berezovskogo. Tom 1. Moskva; Leningrad: Muzyka, 1965: 65–67, illus.
— [repr.] In: R. M. Glier, *Stat´i i vospominaniia*. Sost.-red.V. A. Kiselev. Moskva: Muzyka, 1975: 37–44, illus.

See also *858, 866*.

GUSTAV MAHLER (1860–1911)
Austrian composer, conductor and pianist

[2512] BORISOVA, I. '"Samye pateticheskie kompozitory evropeiskoi muzyki": Chaikovskii i Maler', *Sovetskaia muzyka* (1990), 6: 125–132 [see *592*].
Comparing Chaikovskii and Mahler as symphonists.

[2513]   BARSOVA, I. 'Mahler—ein 'Schüler' Cajkovskijs?'. In: *Internationales Čajkovskij Symposium, Tübingen 1993: Bericht* (1995): 51–56 [see *596*].

[2514]   BARSOVA, L. 'Mahler und Russland', *Muzik & Wetenschap*, 5 (1995–96), 3: 290–293, music.

NIKOLAI METNER [MEDTNER] (1880–1951)
Russian composer and pianist

[2515]   DROZDOV, A. 'N. K. Metner: K ego priezdu v SSSR', *Muzyka i revoliutsiia* (1927), 4: 20.

[2516]   VAINKOP, Iu, 'Nikolai Metner', *Rabochii i teatr* (1927), 14: 13.

SERGEI PROKOF´EV (1891–1953)
Russian composer and pianist

[2517]   SAVKINA, N. P. 'Molodoi Prokof´ev i Chaikovskii: Nabliudeniia nad stilem opery "Maddalena"'. In: *Chaikovskii: K 150-letiiu so dnia rozhdeniia. Voprosy istorii, teorii i ispolnitel´stva* (1990): 94–104 [see *591*].

SERGEI RAKHMANINOV (1873–1943)
Russian composer, pianist and conductor

[2518]   KARATYGIN, V. G. 'Chaikovskii i Rakhmaninov', *Zhizn´ iskusstva*, 1 (1923), 40: 10; 41: 10.

[2519]   SABANEEV, L. 'Pismo iz Parizha: Chetvertyi kontsert Rakhmaninova', *Muzyka i revoliutsiia* (1927), 5/6: 51–52.

The influence of Chaikovskii on Rakhmaninov.

See also *522, 1911*.

RODION SHCHEDRIN (1932–)
Russian composer

[2520]   ROZANOVA, Iu. '"Anna Karenina" R. K. Shchedrina i traditsii P. I. Chaikovskogo'. In: *Muzyka i khoreografiia sovremennogo baleta*, vyp. 4. Leningrad, 1982. 194–201.

DMITRII SHOSTAKOVICH (1906–975)
Russian composer and pianist

[2521]   WOLTER, G. 'Universal messages: Reflections in conversation', *Tempo*, 200 (Apr 1997): 14–19.

Includes an interview with Solomon Volkov concerning the influence of Chaikovskii on Shostakovich.

See also *896, 924, 2507*.

JEAN SIBELIUS (1865–1957)
Finnish composer

[2522]   KALBERDA, A. 'Rannie simfonii Iana Sibeliusa v zerkale pozdnego simfonizma P. I. Chaikovskogo'. In: *P. I. Chaikovskii: Issledovaniia i materialy* (1997): 55–60 [see *599*].

ALEKSANDR SKRIABIN (1872–1915)
Russian composer and pianist

[2523]   MARTYNOV, I. 'Skriabin i Chaikovskii'. In: *Sovetskaia muzyka: 3-i sbornik statei*. Moskva; Leningrad, 1945: 23–31.

Chaikovskii's influence on Skriabin, and a comparison of their compositional techniques.

See also *2507*.

IGOR STRAVINSKII (1882–1971)
Russian composer, conductor, pianist and writer

[2524]   SABANEEV, L. 'Beseda so Stravinskim: Ot nashego Parizhskogo korrespondenta', *Zhizn´ iskusstva* (1927), 24: 6–7.

An interview with Stravinskii, touching on his relationship with Chaikovskii.

[2525]   KABI, P. 'Muzykal´naia zhizn´ Parizha', *Muzyka i revoliutsiia* (1929), 4.

Chaikovskii's influence on Stravinskii, and the latter's ballet *The Fairy's Kiss*. See also *2586*.

[2526]   MORTON, L. 'Stravinsky and Tchaikovsky: Le baiser de la fée', *Musical Quarterly*, 48 (Jul 1962), 3: 313–326, music, illus.

Stravinsky's one-act ballet *La baiser de la fée* (*The Fairy's Kiss*) was an arrangement of piano pieces and songs by Chaikovskii, with interpolated material of Stravinsky's own (orchestrated 1928, revised 1950). See also *2525, 2531*.

—   [repr.] In: P. H. Lang, *Stravinsky: A new appraisal of his work*. New York: Norton, 1963: 47–60, music.

[2527]   SCHNEIDER, H. 'Die Parodieverfahren Igor Strawinskys', *Acta Musicologica*, 54 (1982), 1/2: 280–281.

[2528]   BJØRKVOLD, J. R. 'En drøfting av russiske trekk i Igor Stravinskijs musikk', *Studia Musicologica Norvegica*, 9 (1983): 164, illus.

Text in Norwegian with summary in English.

[2529]   ROZHDESTVENSKII, G. 'Stravinskii i Chaikovskii'. In: *I. F. Stravinskii: Stat´i, vospominaniia*. Moskva: Sovetskii kompozitor, 1985: 248–261.

[2530]   SAVENKO, S. "Schitaiu sebia iz plemeni, porozhdennogo Chaikovskim", *Sovetskaia muzyka* (1990), 9: 112–115, music.

[2531]   ZHUKOVSKAIA, G. '"Potselui fei": Osobennosti orkestrovogo stilia (K probleme "Stravinskii i Chaikovskii")'. In: *Moskovsii muzykoved: Ezhegodnik*. Vyp. 2. Moskva, 1991: 258–269.

Stravinskii's treatment of Chaikovskii's music in *The Fairy's Kiss*.

[2532]   SMIRNOV, V. 'Čajkovskij und Stravinskij'. In: *Internationales Čajkovskij Symposium, Tübingen 1993: Bericht* (1995): 253–258 [see *596*].

[2533]   ZHUKOVSKAIA, G. V. 'Pamiati Pushkina, Glinki i Chaikovskogo (o posviashchenii opery "Mavra" I. Stravinskogo)'. In: *P. I. Chaikovskii: K 100-letiiu so dnia smerti* (1995): 99–108 [see *597*].

[2534]   ZHUKOVSKAIA, G. V. 'Stravinskii i Chaikovskii'. Moskva: Gos. Konservatoriia im. P. I. Chaikovskogo, 1995. 24 p.

Summary of dissertation (Moscow Conservatory).

See also *2507, 2626*.

5.2. STAGE WORKS

5.2.1. General

[2535] **LAROSH, G. A. 'P. I. Chaikovskii kak dramaticheskii kompozitor'**, *Ezhegodnik Imperatorskikh teatrov, sezon 1893/94* (1894), 1 (suppl.): 81–182, illus.

— [offprint] *P. I. Chaikovskii kak dramaticheskii kompozitor*. Sankt Peterburg: Izdat. Ezhegodnika Imperatorskikh teatrov, 1895. 102 p, illus.

— [repr.] In: G. A. Larosh, *Sobranie muzykal´no-kriticheskikh statei*, tom 2, chast´ 2 (1924): 49–149 [see *2311*].

— [repr.] In: G. A. Larosh, *Izbrannye stat´i v piati vypuskakh*, vyp. 2 (1975): 195–277 [see *2376*].

[2536] **BOGDANOV-BEREZOVSKII, V. M.** *Opernoe i baletnoe tvorchestvo Chaikovskogo: Ocherki.* Leningrad; Moskva: Iskusstvo, 1940. 117 p, illus.

[2537] *Chaikovskii i teatr: Stat´i i materialy k 100-letiiu so dnia rozhdeniia.* Pod red. A. I. Shaverdiana. Moskva; Leningrad: Iskusstvo, 1940. lxxii, 359 p, illus. (*Vserossiiskoe teatral´noe obshchestvo*).

Contents:'Ot redaktora': v-viii — A. Shaverdian, 'Chaikovskii i russkii opernyi teatr': ix-lxxii [see *2574*] — V. V. Iakovlev, 'Chaikovskii i Pushkin': 1–36 [see *2132*] — I. Nest´ev & B. Iarustovskii, 'Stsenicheskaia istoriia "Evgeniia Onegina"': 37–79 [see *2946*] — Iu. Bakhrushin, 'Balety Chaikovskogo i ikh stsenicheskaia istoriia': 80–139 [see *3812*] — A. N. Amfiteatrova-Levitskaia, 'Pervyi spektakl´ "Evgeniia Onegina"': 140–166 [see *387*] — M. L. Mel´ttser, 'Rabota K. S. Stanislavskogo nad "Evgeniem Oneginym"': 167–175 [see *2944*] — M I. Brian, 'Tat´iana': 176–182 [see *2942*] — G. V. Zhukovskaia, 'Rodnoi obraz': 183–187 [see *2947*] — S. Ia. Lemeshev, 'Bessmertnyi obraz': 188–194 [see *2943*] — S. I. Migai, 'Eletskii i Onegin': 195–202 [see *2945*] — K. G. Derzhinskaia, 'Chaikovskii v moei zhizni': 203–210 [see *3572*] — A. M. Davydov, 'German': 211–223 [see *424*] — N. K. Pechkovskii, 'V poiskakh, pravdivogo obraza': 224–231 [see *3573*] — K. E. Antarova, 'Moia rabota nad rol´iu grafini v "Pikovoi dame"': 232–239 [see *3571*] — G. S. Ulanova, 'Lebed´': 240–244 [see *4213*] — 'Programmy M. Petipa "Spiashchaia krasavitsa"': 245–256 [see *4058*] — "Shchelkunchik": 257–266 [see *3930*] — 'Zapiski glavnogo rezhissera russkoi opery G. P. Kondrat´eva: 267–327 [see *474*] — Primechaniia: 328–355.

Reviews: 'Korotko o knigakh', *Literaturnoe obozrenie* (1940), 17: 38 — 'Dva sbornika o Chaikovskom', *Literaturnaia gazeta* (6 May 1940): 6 — P. Vasil´ev, 'Bibliografiia: Chaikovskii i teatr', *Sovetskoe iskusstvo* (19 Jan 1941): 4.

[2538] *Chaikovskii na Moskovskoi stsene: Pervye postanovki v gody ego zhizni.* Pod red. V. V. Iakovleva. Moskva; Leningrad: Iskusstvo, 1940. 502 p, music, illus. (*Gos. Tsentral´nyi teatral´nyi muzei im. A. A. Bakhrushina*).

Contents: V. V. Iakovlev, 'Chaikovskii v Moskovskikh teatrakh': 5–244 [see *2539*] — 'Perepiska P. I. Chaikovskogo': 255–486 [see *197, 240, 243, 252, 275, 307, 325, 326, 333, 350*] — 'Podlinnaia partitura P. I. Chaikovskogo "Stseish domovogo" (melodrama) iz p´esy A. N. Ostrovskogo "Voevoda" (1886 g.)': 487–500 [see *122*].

Reviews.*Literaturnaia gazeta* (20 Mar 1940): 6 — 'Dva sbornika o Chaikovskom', *Literaturnaia gazeta* (6 May 1940): 6 — P. Vasil´ev, 'Chaikovskii i teatr', *Sovetskoe iskusstvo* (19 Jan 1941): 4.

[2539] **IAKOVLEV, V. V. 'Chaikovskii v moskovskikh teatrakh: Pervye postanovki v Moskve ego muzykal´no-stsenicheskikh proizvedenyi'.** In: *Chaikovskii na Moskovskoi stsene* (1940): 5–244 [see *2538*].

— [repr.] In: V. V. Iakovlev, *Izbrannye trudy o muzyke*, tom 1 (1964): 127–331 [see *2362*].

[2540] **BOGDANOV-BEREZOVSKII, V. 'Reformator muzykal´nogo teatra'**, *Iskusstvo i zhizn´* (May 1940), 5: 19–23, illus.

[2541] **GROSHEVA, E. 'Chaikovskii i russkii muzykal´nyi teatr'**, *Sovetskoe iskusstvo* (6 May 1940): 3 [see *853*].

[2542]   **P. I. Chaikovskii na stsene teatra opery i baleta im. S. M. Kirova (b. Mariinskii): Sbornik statei.** Otv. red. N. A. Shuvalov. [Leningrad]: Leningradskii Gos. ordena V. I. Lenina Akademicheskii teatr opery i baleta im. S. M Kirova, 1941. 448 p, music, illus.

Contents: 'Sto let (1840–1940)': 9–16 [see *888*] — E. Stark, 'Stsenicheskaia istoriia oper P. I. Chaikovskogo v byvsh. Mariinskom teatre': 17–154 [see *2578*] — S. A. Tsvetaev, 'Problema ispolnitel´stva v operakh P. I. Chaikovskogo': 155–238 [see *2579*] — V. M. Bogdanov-Berezovskii, 'Muzykal´naia dramaturgiia baletov P. I. Chaikovskogo': 239–286 [see *3816*] — N. N. Nosilov, 'Balety P. I. Chaikovskogo na stsene teatra opery i baleta im. S. M. Kirova': 287–404 [see *3817*] — N. V. Mamuna, 'Notnye avtografy i neizdannye pis´ma P. I. Chaikovskogo': 405–422 [see *99*] — A. M. Brianskii, 'Materialy k russkoi literature o P. I. Chaikovskom': 423–449 [see *20*].

[2543]   ASAF´EV, B. V. 'Kompozitor-dramaturg Pëtr Il´ich Chaikovskii'. In: *Teatr*. Moskva, 1944: 218–222.

— [repr.] In: B. V. Asaf´ev, *Izbrannye trudy*, tom 2 (1954): 57–63 [see *2348*].

— [repr.] In: B. V. Asaf´ev, *O muzyke Chaikovskogo: Izbrannoe* (1972): 60–67 [see *2373*].

— [English tr.] 'The great Russian composer'. In: *Russian symphony: Thoughts about Tchaikovsky* (1947): 6–15 [see *587*].

[2544]   BEYER, W. 'State of the theater: Music in my heart', *School & Society*, 66 (27 Dec 1947): 508–509.

[2545]   SEAMAN, G. 'Tchaikovsky in the theatre', *The Listener*, 60 (6 Nov 1958): 752.

[2546]   INOZEMTSEVA, G. 'Dramaturgiia Chaikovskogo: K 120-letiiu so dnia rozhdeniia P. I. Chaikovskogo', *Teatral´naia zhizn´* (1960), 9: 22.

[2547]   TUMANINA, N. V. *Chaikovskii i muzykal´nyi teatr: Kniga dlia liubitelei muzyki*. Moskva: Gos. muz. izdat., 1961. 254 p, music, illus.

[2548]   OSTER, O. 'Peter Iljitsch Tschaikowsky', *Musik und Szene*, 6 (1962), 11: 121–124.

[2549]   NIEMÜLLER, K. W. 'Tschaikowsky und Puschkin', *Das Opernjournal* (1969/70), 5: 7–10.

[2550]   GUSIATNIKOVA, G. G. 'Iz istorii khudozhestvennogo oformleniia prizhiznennykh postanovok oper i baletov P. I. Chaikovskogo'. In: *P. I. Chaikovskii i Ural* (1983): 118–127 [see *1749*].

[2551]   BUIANOVA, G. 'Znatoki otvechaiut: "Postavleny vpervye"', *Leningradskaia pravda* (28 Jul 1984): 4.

The first performances of Chaikovskii's operas and ballets in St. Petersburg.

[2552]   ZELENTSOVA, N. S. 'P. I. Chaikovskii i tipologicheskie osobennosti russkogo realizma kontsa XIX veka'. In: *Teatr v zhizni i tvorchestve P. I. Chaikovskogo* (1985): 130–135 [see *589*].

[2553]   IL´ICHEV, V. 'Chaikovskii i Bol´shoi teatr: Iz istorii postanovki oper baletov kompozitora na stsene Bol´shogo teatra', *Sovetskii artist* (13 Apr 1990).

5.2.2. Operas

[2554]   CHESHIKHIN, V. E. 'Istoriia russkoi opery: Pëtr Il´ich Chaikovskii', *Russkaia muzykal´naia gazeta* (18 Nov 1901), 46: 1155–1158; (25 Nov 1901), 47: 1187–1190; (2 Dec 1901), 48: 1213–1219; (9 Dec 1901), 49: 1244–1249.

— [rev. repr.] 'Petr Il´ich Chaikovskii'. In: V. E. Cheshikhin, Istoriia russkoi opery: s 1674 po 1903 g. Sankt Peterburg, 1902. (*Istoriia russkoi muzyki*; 1).

— [rev. repr.] 'Petr Il´ich Chaikovskii'. In: V. E. Cheshikhin, Istoriia russkoi opery: s 1674 po 1903 g. 2., ispr. i znachitel´no dop. izd. Moskva: P. Iurgenson, 1905: 276–357. (*Istoriia russkoi muzyki*; 1).

[2555]   NEWMARCH, R. H. 'National opera in Russia: Tchaikovsky', *Proceedings of the Musical Association*, 30 (1903): 57–73.

[2556]   F[INDEIZEN], N. F. 'Zhenskie tipy v operakh Chaikovskogo: Etiud', *Russkaia muzykal´naia gazeta* (19 Oct 1903), 42: 998–1005.

[2557]   KEETON, A. E. 'Tshaikovski's operas', *Contemporary Review*, 85 (Apr 1904): 487–495.

[2558]   NEWMARCH, R. H. 'Tchaikovsky's early lyrical operas', *Monthly Journal of the International Musical Society*, 6 (Oct 1904), 10: 29–34.
   — [repr.] *Zeitschrift der Internationalen Musikgesellschaft*, 6 (1904/1905), 1: 29–34.

[2559]   NEWMARCH, R. H. 'The plots of Tchaikovsky's chief operas'. In: M. I. Chaikovskii, *The life and letters of Peter Ilich Tchaikovsky* (1906): 750–761 [see *1453*].

[2560]   GILMAN, L. 'Music and the opera: Tschaikowsky as opera-maker', *Harper's Weekly*, 52 (15 Feb 1908), 6: 28, illus.

[2561]   IVANOV, M. M. 'Opernye kompozitory prodolzhateli zapadnykh veianii'. In: M. M. Ivanov, *Istoriia muzykal´nogo razvitiia Rossii*. Tom 2. Sankt Peterburg: A. S. Suvorin, 1912: 53–68.
   Mainly concerned with Chaikovskiii's operatic style.

[2562]   NEWMARCH, R. H. 'Tchaikovsky'. In: R. H. Newmarch, *The Russian opera*. London: H. Jenkins; New York: E. P. Dutton [1914]: 334–361, illus.
   — [repr.] Westport, Conn.: Greenwood Press [1972]. xv, 403 p, illus.

[2563]   BAKLANOFF, G. 'About the operas of Tschaikowsky', *Musical Courier*, 77 (1918), 21: 8–9.

[2564]   GLEBOV, I. [ASAF´EV, B. V.] 'Pushkin v pretvorenii Glinki i Chaikovskogo'. In: *Pamiati Pushkina*. Petrograd: Gos. Akad. teatry, 1922: 7–15 p.

[2565]   GLEBOV, I. [ASAF´EV, B. V.] 'Opery Chaikovskogo'. In: I. Glebov, *Simfonicheskie etiudy*. Petrograd: Gos. filarmoniia, 1922: 160–200.
   — [repr. (extracts)] In: B. V. Asaf´ev, *Izbrannye trudy*, tom 2 (1954): 169–174 [see *2348*].
   — [repr.] In: B. V. Asaf´ev, *Simfonicheskie etiudy*. Obshchaia red. i vstup. stat´ia E. M. Orlovoi. Leningrad: Muzyka, 1970: 127–158.
   — [repr.] In: B. V. Asaf´ev, *O muzyke Chaikovskogo: Izbrannoe* (1972): 297–327 [see *2373*].

[2566]   BAZYLIEV, A. 'Opery Chaikovskogo', *Muzykal´naia nov´* (1924), 9: 27.

[2567]   ASAF´EV, B. V. 'Opery Chaikovskogo i Rimskogo-Korsakova'. In: B. V. Asaf´ev, *Russkaia muzyka ot nachala XIX stoletiia*. Moskva; Leningrad: Academia, 1930: 25–29.

[2568]   IAKOVLEV, V. V. 'Chaikovskii v poiskakh opernogo libretto'. In: *Muzykal´noe nasledstvo: Sbornik materialov po istorii muzykal´noi kul´tury v Rossii*. Pod red. prof. M. V. Ivanova-Boretskogo. Vyp. 1. Moskva: Ogiz, 1935: 50–75.
   — [repr.] In: V. V. Iakovlev, *Izbrannye trudy o muzyke*, tom 1 (1964): 379–410 [see *2362*].

[2569]   HOZENPUD, A. *Operna dramaturhia Chaikovs´kogo: Narysi*. [Kharkhiv]: Mystetstvo, 1940. 145 p, illus.
   Text in Ukrainian.
   Review: 'Opernaia dramaturgiia Chaikovskogo', *Sovetskoe iskusstvo* (20 Apr 1941): 4.

[2570]   GRINBERG, M. 'Chaikovskii: 1840–1940', *Teatr* (1940), 5: 11–16, illus.
   An overview of Chaikovskii's works, with particular emphasis on his operas.

[*2571*]   IARUSTOVSKII, B. M. 'Voprosy opernoi dramaturgii P. I. Chaikovskogo: 1. O rabote Chaikovskogo nad opernym libretto', *Sovetskaia muzyka* (1940), 1: 38–48.

See also *2572*.

[*2572*]   IARUSTOVSKII, B. M. 'Voprosy opernoi dramaturgii Chaikovskogo: 2. Problema "skvoznogo deistviia" v opere', *Sovetskaia muzyka* (1940), 2: 40–45.

— [repr.] *Sovetskaia muzyka* (1940), 5/6: 70–87 [see *585*].

[*2573*]   REMEZOV, I. 'Obrazy Chaikovskogo na opernoi stsene', *Sovetskaia muzyka* (1940), 5/6: 114–123, illus. [see *585*]

[*2574*]   SHAVERDIAN, A. I. 'Chaikovskii i russkii opernyi teatr'. In: *Chaikovskii i teatr* (1940): ix-lxxii [see *2537*].

— [repr.] In: A. I. Shaverdian, *Sbornik statei*. Sost. R. A. Shaverdian. Moskva: Sovetskii kompozitor, 1958: 289–364.

[*2575*]   SHAVERDIAN, A. I. 'Zametki ob opernom stile Chaikovskogo', *Teatr* (1940), 5: 17–33, illus.

[*2576*]   SHAVERDIAN, A. I. 'Chaikovskii i pevtsy', *Sovetskoe iskusstvo* (18 Apr 1940).

[*2577*]   SHAVERDIAN, A. I. 'Melodicheskii stil´ oper Chaikovskogo', *Sovetskoe iskusstvo* (6 May 1940): 2 [see *853*].

[*2578*]   STARK, E. 'Stsenicheskaia istoriia oper P. I. Chaikovskogo v byvsh. Mariinskom teatre'. In: *P. I. Chaikovskii na stsene teatra opery i baleta im. S. M. Kirova* (1941): 17–154 [see *2542*].

[*2579*]   TSVETAEV, A. 'Problema ispolnitel´stva v operakh P. I. Chaikovskogo'. In: *P. I. Chaikovskii na stsene teatra opery i baleta im. S. M. Kirova* (1941): 155–238 [see *2542*].

[*2580*]   ABRAHAM, G. E. H. 'Operas and incidental music'. In: *Tchaikovsky: A symposium* (1945): 124–183 [see *586*].

— [rev. repr.] 'Tchaikovsky's operas'. In: G. E. H. Abraham, *Slavonic and Romantic Music*. Essays and studies. London: Faber & Faber; New York: St. Martin's Press, 1968: 116–177.

[*2581*]   IARUSTOVSKII, B. M. *Opernaia dramaturgiia Chaikovskogo*. Moskva; Leningrad: Gos. muz. izdat., 1947. 244 p, music.

Reviews: E. Gordeeva, 'Novaia rabota o Chaikovskom', *Sovetskoe iskusstvo* (11 Sep 1948): 4.

[*2582*]   IARUSTOVSKII, B. M. 'Operas'. In: *Russian symphony: Thoughts about Tchaikovsky* (1947): 40–85 [see *587*].

[*2583*]   SHAWE-TAYLOR, D. 'The neglect of Tchaikovsky', *Opera*, 1 (Apr 1950), 2: 15–21, illus.

[*2584*]   IARUSTOVSKII, B. 'Rabota klassikov nad opernym stsenariem', *Sovetskaia muzyka* (1952), 7: 10–18.

[*2585*]   BIANCOLLI, L. 'Peter Iljitsch Tschaikowsky'. In: *The opera reader: A complete guide to the best loved operas*. Comp. and ed. by Louis Biancolli. New York: McGraw-Hill [1953]: 505–521.

Includes: "Eugene Onegin": 508–515 [see *2970*] — "Pique Dame": 516–521 [see *3599*].

[*2586*]   KHOKHLOVKINA, A. 'Voprosy spetsifiki opernogo obraza'. In: *Sovetskaia muzyka: Teoreticheskie i kriticheskie stat´i*, Moskva: Muzgiz, 1954: 278–326.

[*2587*]   WEINSTOCK, H. 'Russian opera on microgroove', *High Fidelity*, 6 (Nov 1956): 115–118.

Includes a guide to recordings of Chaikovskii's operas.

[*2588*]   PROTOPOPOV, V. V. & TUMANINA, N. V. *Opernoe tvorcherstvo Chaikovskogo*. Moskva: Izdat. Akademii Nauk SSSR, 1957. 370 p, music, illus.

[2589] SEAMAN, G. 'Tchaikovsky as opera composer', *The Listener*, 69 (4 Apr 1963): 613.

[2590] IAKOVLEV, V. V. 'Modest Il´ich Chaikovskii: Avtor opernykh tekstov'. In: V. V. Iakovlev, *Izbrannye trudy o muzyke*, tom 1 (1964): 417–481 [see *2362*].

[2591] OSBORNE, C. 'The richness of Russian opera', *High Fidelity*, 16 (Jan 1966): 74–76, illus.

[2592] *Opery P. I. Chaikovskogo: Putevoditel´*. Moskva: Muzyka, 1970. 384 p, music, illus.
Contents: See *2593, 2692, 2765, 3012, 3184, 3325, 3625*.

[2593] ROZANOVA, Iu. 'Opernoe tvorchestvo Chaikovskogo'. In: *Opery P. I. Chaikovskogo: Putevoditel´* (1970): 3–16 [see *2592*].

[2594] DEL´MAN, V. 'V poedinke so vremenem', *Sovetskaia muzyka* (1971), 2: 61–67.
In connection with performances of *The Enchantress, Cherevichki* and *The Maid of Orleans* in Perm´.

[2595] COOPER, M. 'Pushkin and the opera in Russia', *Opera*, 22 (Feb 1971): 96–100.

[2596] BLAGOOBRAZOVA, V. 'Narodnaia pesnia v khorovom tvorchestve P. I. Chaikovskogo'. In: *Voprosy russkoi i sovetskoi khorovoi kul´tury*. Vyp. 23. Moskva, 1975: 85–105.
Mainly concerning Chaikovskii's use of folk-songs in his operatic choruses.

[2597] KOLODIN, I. 'An American debut: The big Bolshoi brand of grand opera', *Saturday Review*, 2 (28 Jun 1975): 29–32, illus.

[2598] KRAUSE, E. 'Tschaikowski'. In: E. Krause, *Oper von A-Z: Ein Opernführer*. Leipzig: Deutscher Verlag für Musik, 1976: 512–521.
Includes: "Eugen Onegin": 513–517 [see *3038*] — "Pique Dame": 517–521 [see *3635*].
— 2. Aufl. Leipzig: Deutscher Verlag für Musik, 1977: 512–521.
— [repr.] Leipzig: Deutscher Verlag für Musik, 1979: 512–521.
— 3. Aufl. Leipzig: Deutscher Verlag für Musik, 1980: 512–521.
— 4. Aufl. Leipzig: Deutscher Verlag für Musik, 1981: 512–521.

[2599] 'Pjotr I. Tschaikowsky'. In: L. F. Schiedermair, *Die Oper: Premieren im Spiegel ihrer Zeit*. Erweitete und neu durchgesehene Ausg. München: Langen Muller, 1979: 273–280.
Includes extracts from Chaikovskii's letters concerning his own operas, and opera in general.

[2600] FORBES, E. 'The operas of Pyotr Ilich Tchaikovsky, 1840–1893', *About the House*, 5 (1979), 8: 69.
A list including names of librettists and date of first performances.

[2601] GURAL´NIK, U. A. 'Idei i obrazy literatury na iazyke drugikh iskusstv'. In: *Russkaia literatura v istoriko-funktsional´nom osveshchenii*. Moskva: Nauka, 1979: 41–97.

[2602] MATSOKINA, E. M. 'Polifoniia v operakh P. I. Chaikovskogo'. Leningrad: Gos. konservatoriia im. N. A. Rimskogo-Korsakova, 1979. 25 p.
Dissertation summary (Leningrad Conservatory).

[2603] ARSHINOVA, N. S. 'K voprosu o psikhologii zhenskogo obraza v pushkinskikh operakh P. I. Chaikovskogo'. In: *P. I. Chaikovskii i russkaia literatura* (1980): 82–99 [see *588*].

[2604] KUNIN, I. F. 'P. I. Chaikovskii i narodnyi teatr: Neskol´ko soobrazhenii v sviazi s neosushchestvlennymi opernymi zamyslami kompozitora'. In: *P. I. Chaikovskii i russkaia literatura* (1980): 112–124 [see *588*].

[2605] LOVELAND, K. 'Tchaikovsky at the opera', *Opera*, 31 (Jan 1980): 91–92.

[2606]   RICHARDS, D. 'Records: Tchaikovsky's operas', *Music & Musicians*, 28 (Jun 1980): 28–30.
          A guide to recordings.

[2607]   'Tschaikowski'. In: D. Zochling, *Die Oper: Westermanns farbiger Führer durch Oper, Operette, Musical*. Mit
          einem Vorwort von Placido Domingo. Braunschweig: Westermann, 1981: 553–561.

[2608]   BORTOLOTTO, M. 'Fiori cuori picche ansiose bocche'. In: M. Bortolotto, *Consacrazione della casa*.
          Milano: Adelphi, 1982: 93–130. (*Saggi*; 22)

[2609]   BELENKOVA, I. Ia. 'K probleme dialoga v opere: Na materiale liriko-psikhologicheskoi opery
          P. I. Chaikovskogo'. Leningrad: Gos. institut teatra, muzyka i kinematografii, 1983. 206 p.
          Dissertation (Leningrad Institute of Theatre, Music and Cinematography).
          — [rev. repr. (summary)] Leningrad: Gos. institut teatra, muzyka i kinematografii, 1983. 18 p.

[2610]   SHILOV, A. V. 'Proizvedeniia P. I. Chaikovskogo na Permskoi opernoi stsene'. In: *P. I. Chaikovskii
          i Ural* (1983): 57-60 [see *1749*].

[2611]   GRIGOR´EVA, A. P. 'M. A. Slavina v operakh P. I. Chaikovskogo'. In: *Teatr v zhizni i tvorchestve
          P. I. Chaikovskogo* (1985): 54–63 [see *589*].

[2612]   'Pjotr Iljitsch Tschaikowski'. In: S. Neef, *Handbuch der russischen und sowjetischen Oper*. Berlin:
          Henschelverlag Kunst und Gesellschaft, 1985: 658–702.

[2613]   KRASINSKAIA, L. *Opernaia melodika P. I. Chaikovskogo: K voprosu o vzaimodeistvii melodii i
          rechevoi intonatsii*. Leningrad: Muzyka, 1986. 247 p, music.

[2614]   BANNOUR, W. 'Vierges et sorcières: Les heroines d'opéra de Tchaikovsky'. In: *Littérature et opéra*.
          Grenoble: 1987: 129–141.

[2615]   STEINBERG, M. 'Tchaikovskiana', *San Francisco Opera Magazine* (aut. 1987), 10: 26–27, music, illus.

[2616]   BAEVA, A. 'Prelomlenie printsipov opernoi dramaturgii Chaikovskogo v sovremennoi sovetskoi
          opere (na primere "Marii Stiuart" S. Slonimskogo)'. In: *P. I. Chaikovskii: Voprosy istorii i stilia* (1989):
          135–149 [see *590*].

[2617]   ARSHINOVA, N. S. 'Psikhologiia vizual´noi obraznosti v operakh P. I. Chaikovskogo:
          Dialektika "sveta" i "mraka"'. In: *P. I. Chaikovskii i izobrazitel´noe iskusstvo* (1991): 55–61 [see *595*].

[2618]   MUROV, A. 'Chto zhe stavit´ segodnia?: Lichnye nabliudeniia kompozitora nad paradoksami
          otechestvennoi opery'. In: *Muzyka Rossii: Muzykal´noe tvorchestvo i muzykal´naia zhizn´ respublik Rossiiskoi
          Federatsii*. Vyp. 9. Sost. A. Grigor´eva. Moskva, 1991: 80–89.
          Comparison of operas by Chaikovskii and Musorgskii.

[2619]   TARUSKIN, R. 'Tchaikovsky, Pyotr Il´ych'. In: *The new Grove dictionary of opera*. Ed. by Stanley
          Sadie. Vol. 4. London: Macmillan; New York: Grove's Dictionaries of Music, 1992: 663–672.

[2620]   'Tchaikovsky, Pyotr'. In: J. Warrack & E. West, *The Oxford dictionary of opera*. London: Oxford Univ.
          Press, 1992: 700–702.

[2621]   LIPPMANN, F. 'Melancholy in music: Two examples (Beethoven and Tchaikovsky)', *Nuova
          rivista musicale italiana*, 26 (Apr/Jun 1992), 2: 213.

[2622]   PETERSÉN, G. 'Operatonsättaren Pjotr Tjajkovskij', *Operan* (1992/93), 3: 12–14.

[2623]   SALMON, G. 'Tchaikovsky, Petr'. In: *International dictionary of opera*. Ed. C. Steven LaRue. Vol. 2.
          Detroit : St. James Press, 1993: 1322–1326.

[2624]   TANNER, M. 'Drama and drudgery: The operas', *Classic CD* (Nov 1993), 42: 14–15 [suppl.], illus.

[2625] KLIMOVITSKII, A. I. 'Otzvuki russkogo sentimentalizma v Pushkinskikh operakh Chaikovskogo', *Muzykal´naia akademiia* (1995), 1: 167–168.

[2626] NEEF, S. 'Čajkovskj mit den Augen Stravinskijs gesehen: Zum Verhältnis von ontologischer und psychisch determinierter Zeit in den Opern Čajkovskijs'. In: *Internationales Čajkovskij Symposium, Tübingen 1993: Bericht* (1995): 223–232 [see *596*].

[2627] BOYDEN, M. 'Tchaikovsky, Peter Ilich'. In: *Opera: The rough guide*. With contributions from Joe Staines (et al). Ed. by Jonathan Buckley. London: Rough Guides, 1997: 306–307, illus. ISBN 1-8582-8138-5.

[2628] GOULD, S. L. 'Romantic literary narrative into opera: Towards a poetics of transposition'. Madison: Univ. of Wisconsin, 1997. 305 p.

Dissertation (Ph. D.). Includes references to Chaikovskii's adaptation of Pushkin's novels.

[2629] GRÖNKE, K. 'Mädchen singen von Liebe: Anmerkungen zu einem festen Szenen-Typus in Čajkovskijs Puškin-Opern'. In: *Čajkovskijs Homosexualität und sein Tod: Legenden und Wirklichkeit* (1998): 405–416 [see *600*].

[2630] BRIGGS, A. D. 'Tchaikovsky and Pushkin: Men of Russian Letters', *Opera*, 49 (May 1998), 5: 516–522, illus.

The composer's adaptations of Pushkin's text, in his operas *Evgenii Onegin*, *Mazepa* and *The Queen of Spades*.

[2631] GRIGOR´EVA, A. P. 'Opery P. I. Chaikovskogo na stsene Peterburgskoi—Leningradskoi konservatorii'. In: *P. I. Chaikovskii: Nasledie*, vyp. 2 (2000): 186–197 [see *604*].

See also *64, 70, 77, 79, 80, 81, 474, 1028, 2049, 2130, 2132*.

CHEREVICHKI
Opera in 4 acts (1885)
[see also *Vakula the Smith*]

[2632] *"Cherevichki": Muzyka P. I. Chaikovskogo*. Libretto iz povesti Gogolia "Noch´ pered rozhdestvom" sost. Ia. P. Polonskim. Moskva: P. Iurgenson, 1886. 63 p.

Original libretto.

— 2-e izd. Moskva: P. Iurgenson, 1898. 63 p.

— 3-e izd. Moskva: P. Iurgenson, 1906. 63 p.

[2633] 'Teatr i muzyka', *Russkie vedomosti* (20 Jan 1887).

The first production of the opera on 19 Jan 1887 in Moscow (see also *2634* to *2637*).

[2634] ["Cherevichki"], *Moskovskie vedomosti* (21 Jan 1887).

[2635] KRUGLIKOV, S. N. '"Cherevichki": Opera P. I. Chaikovskogo', *Sovremennye izvestiia* (24 Jan 1887).

[2636] ["Cherevichki"], *Moskovskie vedomosti* (30 Jan 1887).

[2637] KRUGLIKOV, S. N. '"Cherevichki": Opera P. I. Chaikovskogo', *Sovremennye izvestiia* (31 Jan 1887).

[2638] LAROSH, G. A. 'Opernye novinki sezona: "Cherevichki" P. Chaikovskogo', *Russkii vestnik* (31 Oct 1887).

— [repr.] In: G. A. Larosh, *Sobranie muzykal´no-kriticheskikh statei*, tom 2, chast´ 1 (1924): 146–152 [see *2311*].

— [repr.] In: G. A. Larosh, *Izbrannye stat´i v piati vypuskakh*, vyp. 2 (1975): 124–129 [see *2376*].

[*2639*]   CHECHOTT, V. 'Korrespondentsii: Moskva, 8 marta', *Muzykal´noe obozrenie* (1888), 11: 85–86.
Analysis of the opera.

[*2640*]   KASHKIN, N. D. 'Ia. P. Polonskii i P. I. Chaikovskii, kak avtory odnogo obshchego
proizvedeniia (lektsiia, chitannaia v auditorii Istoricheskogo muzeia, 22 noiabria)', *Moskovskie
vedomosti* (23 Nov 1898).
Transcript of a lecture given by Nikolai Kashkin on 22 Nov 1898, mainly concerning the opera *Vakula the
Smith*/*Cherevichki*.
— [repr.] In: N. D. Kashkin, *Izbrannye stat´i o P. I. Chaikovskom* (1954): 58–67 [see *2349*].

[*2641*]   *"Cherevichki": Komiko-fantasticheskaia opera*. Libretto Ia. P. Polonskogo. Muzyka P. I. Chaikovskogo.
Kazan´, 1903. 61 p.
Synopsis of the opera, including short article 'P. I. Chaikovskogo i ego opera "Cherevichki"'.

[*2642*]   K[UZNETSO]V, N. *"Cherevichki"*. Moskva, 1903. 4 p. (*Teatr Ermitazh. Tovarishchestvo Moskovskoi
Chastnoi opery*).

[*2643*]   *"Cherevichki": Opera. Muzyka P. I. Chaikovskogo*. Kratkoe soderzhanie s sokhranieniem glavnykh
numerov peniia. Kiev: Z. M. Sakhin, 1904. 27 p.

[*2644*]   '"Cherevichki" Chaikovskogo', *Russkaia muzykal´naia gazeta* (11 Sep 1905), 35: 852–854.

[*2645*]   *"Cherevichki"*. Odessa: Izdat. Odesskogo Gorodskogo teatra, 1906.

[*2646*]   OSSOVSKII, A. V. '"Cherevichki" Chaikovskogo v Mariinskom teatre', *Slovo* (31 Dec 1906): 5.

[*2647*]   'Teatr i muzyka', *Novoe vremia* (31 Dec 1906): 5.

[*2648*]   T[IMOFEEV], G. 'Teatr i muzyka: Mariinskii teatr', *Rech´* (31 Dec 1906): 4.

[*2649*]   OSSOVSKII, A. V. '"Cherevichki": Komiko-fantasticheskaia opera P. I. Chaikovskogo', *Slovo*
(1907), 41.
— [repr.] In: A. V. Ossovskii, *Muzykal´nyo-kriticheskie stat´i, 1894–1912*. Leningrad: Muzyka, 1971: 190–196.

[*2650*]   'Mariinskii teatr: "Cherevichki"', *Russkaia muzykal´naia gazeta* (1 Jan 1907), 1: 29–30.

[*2651*]   *P. I. Chaikovskii: "Cherevichki" ("Vakula kuznets")*. Opera. Libretto s biografiei kompozitora.
Khar´kov, 1913. 12 p.
— 2-e izd. Khar´kov, 1914. [12] p.

[*2652*]   '"Cherevichki" P. Chaikovskogo na Mariinskoi stsene', *Khronika zhurnala "Muzykal´nyi Sovremennik"*
(1915), 10: 9–10.

[*2653*]   TIMOFEEV, G. 'Mariinskii teatr, "Cherevichki" Chaikovskogo', *Rech´* (3 Dec 1915): 5.

[*2654*]   *"Cherevichki"*. In: G. Angert, *100 oper*. Libretto oper pod red. L. Sabaneeva. Moskva: Russkoe
teatral´naia obshchestvo, 1927: 260–261.

[*2655*]   *"Cherevichki": Komicheskaia opera v 3 deistviiakh po Gogoliu*. Muzyka P. I. Chaikovskogo. Vstup.
stat´ia I. Malkova o postanovke opery. Moskva: Teakinopechat´, 1930. 16 p, illus. (*Putevoditel´ po
opernym spektakliam*).
— Izd. 2-e [Moskva]: Gos. izdat. khudozh. literatury, 1931. 16 p, illus. (*V pomoshch´ zriteliu*).

[*2656*]   SONNEMAN, K. "Die goldenen Schuhe", *Allgemeine Musik Zeitung* (1932), 49.
The first production in Germany. See also *2657* to *2660*.

[*2657*]   EIMERT. "Der Pantoffelnheld", *Signale für die Musikalische Welt* (1933), 1.

[2658] HUNEK, R. "Die goldenen Schuhe", *Signale fur die Musikalische Welt* (1933), 1.

[2659] LAUX, K. 'P. Tschaikowsky "Die goldenen Schuhe"', *Die Musik* (1933), 4: 284.

[2660] 'Die Oper "Tscherewitschki" von Tschaikowskij', *Die Musik* (1933), 4: 315.

[2661] BRUN, M. '"Cherevichki": Opera Chaikovskogo', *Saratovskii rabochii* (10 Jan 1934).

[2662] *"Cherevichki": Komiko-fantasticheskaia opera*. Muzyka P. I. Chaikovskogo. Tekst Ia. Polonskogo, po povesti Gogolia "Noch´ pered Rozhdestvom". Tiflis: Vsegryzrabis, 1936. 16 p.

[2663] *"Cherevichki"*. Sverdlovsk: Gos. teatr opery i baleta im. Lunacharskogo, 1938. 12 p.

[2664] *Cherevichki: Opera v 4 deistviiakh*. Muzyka P. I. Chaikovskogo. Libretto Ia. P. Polonskogo po povesti N. V. Gogolia "Noch´ pered rozhdestvom". Gor´kii: Gor´kovskii Obl. teatr opery i baleta imeni A. S. Pushkina, 1938. 51 p.

[2665] *"Cherevichki"*. Sbornik k postanovke opery v Leningradskom Gos. ordena V. I. Lenina Akad. Malom opernyi teatr. Leningrad: Gos. Akad. Malyi opernye teatr, 1940. 64 p, illus.

Contents:A. E. Budiakovskii, 'P. I. Chaikovskii i ego opera "Cherevichki"': 3–21 — 'Libretto opery (Polnyi tekst)': 22–61 — 'Programma spektaklia': 61–64.

[2666] VINER, A. B. 'Liubimaia opera Chaikovskogo', *Sovetskoe iskusstvo* (9 May 1940): 3.

[2667] KHUBOV, G. '"Cherevichki" v Leningradskom Malom opernom teatre', *Pravda* (13 May 1940).
A new production of the opera at the Malyi Theatre in Leningrad, to celebrate the 100th anniversary of Chaikovskii's birth. See also *2669* to *2673*.
— [repr.] In: G. Khubov, *Muzykal´naia publitsistika raznykh let*. Moskva: Sovetskii kompozitor, 1976: 178–183.

[2668] '"Cherevichki" Chaikovskogo', *Izvestiia* (14 May 1940).

[2669] '"Cherevichki": Spektakl´ Malogo opernogo teatra', *Komsomol´skaia pravda* (14 May 1940): 3.

[2670] GROSHEVA, E. "Cherevichki", *Sovetskoe iskusstvo* (14 May 1940): 2.

[2671] RABINOVICH, D. A. '"Cherevichki": Prem´era Leningradskogo Malogo opernogo teatra v Moskve', *Leningradskaia pravda* (14 May 1940): 8.

[2672] SHAVERDIAN, A. '"Cherevichki": Postanovka Leningradskogo gosudarstvennogo ordena Lenina Akademicheskogo Malogo opernogo teatra', *Izvestiia* (14 May 1940): 4.

[2673] BOGDANOV-BEREZOVSKII, V. M. '"Cherevichki" v Malom opernom teatre', *Iskusstvo i zhizn´* (Jun 1940), 6: 23–25.

[2674] *"Cherevichki"*. Leningrad: Tsentral´naia teatral´naia kassa upravleniia po delam iskusstv Lengorispolkoma, 1941. 64 p, illus.

Contents: A. Budiakovskii: 'Opera Chaikovskogo "Cherevichki"': 3–24 — K. N. Derzhavin: '"Noch´ pered rozhdestvom" i ukrainskie povesti Gogola': 25–55 — 'Kratkoe soderzhanie opery "Cherevichki"': 56–64.

[2675] '"Cherevichki" v filiale Bol´shogo teatra SSSR', *Izvestiia* (15 Jan 1941).
In connection with a new production at the Bol´shoi Theatre in Moscow. See also *2676, 2677, 2678, 2679*.

[2676] GORODINSKII, V. '"Cherevichki", *Pravda* (15 Jan 1941): 4.
— [repr.] In: V. Gorodinskii, *Izbrannye stat´i*. Moskva: Sovetskii kompozitor, 1963: 237–238.

[2677] GRINBERG, M. '"Cherevichki" (novaia postanovka filiala Gosudarstvennogo Akademicheskogo Bol´shogo teatra SSSR)', *Komsomol´skaia pravda* (15 Jan 1941): 4.

[2678]   KELDYSH, Iu. "Cherevichki", *Sovetskoe iskusstvo* (19 Jan 1941): 3.

[2679]   RUZ, G. 'Iskusstvo: "Cherevichki" v Bol´shom teatre', *Ogonek* (7 Feb 1941): 18.

[2680]   GOL´DENBLIUM, A. *"Cherevichki"*. [Moskva]: Sovetskoe iskusstvo, 1944. 6 p. (*Programma Moskovskie zrelishcha Gos. ordena Lenina Akademicheskogo Bol´shoi Teatr SSSR*).

[2681]   SHOSTAKOVICH, D. D. '"Cherevichki": Opera Chaikovskogo na ekrane', *Sovetskoe iskusstvo* (18 May 1945): 3, illus.

[2682]   *Cherevichki*. [Sverdlovsk]: Sverdlovskii Gos. teatr opery i baleta im. A. V. Lunacharskogo, 1947. 12 p.

[2683]   IARUSTOVSKII, B. '"Kuznets Vakula"—"Cherevichki": O nekotorykh printsipakh opernoi dramaturgii Chaikovskogo', *Teatral´nyi al´manakh*, 7 (1948): 209–227, illus.

[2684]   *"Cherevichki": Komiko-fantasticheskaia opera v 4-kh deistviiakh i 8-mi kartinakh*. Muzyka P. I. Chaikovskogo. Libretto Ia. P. Polonskogo po povesti N. V. Gogolia. Moskva: Gos. Akad. Bol´shoi teatr SSSR, 1949. 8 p.

[2685]   VANSLOV, V. V. *"Cherevichki" P. Chaikovskogo*. Moskva; Leningrad: Gos. muz. izdat., 1949. 44 p, music, illus. (*Putevoditeli po russkoi muzyke*).
          Review: I. F. Kunin, 'Novye knigi o Chaikovskom', *Sovetskaia kniga* (1951), 2: 114–120.

[2686]   FERMAN, V. E. '"Cherevichki" ("Kuznets Vakula") Chaikovskogo i "Noch´ pered Rozhdestvom" Rimskogo-Korsakova: Opyt sravneniia opernoi dramaturgii i muzykal´nogo stilia'. In: *Voprosy muzykoznaniia*. Vyp. 1. Moskva, 1954: 205–238.

[2687]   *"The Golden Slippers": Opera by P. I. Tschaikovsky*. Book by J. Polonsky, based on Gogol's story "Christmas Eve"; English version by Ruth and Thomas Martin. New York: G. Schirmer [1955]. 31 p. (*G. Schirmer's collection of opera librettos*).
          English tr. of libretto.

[2688]   EYER, R. 'Rare Tchaikovsky opera staged', *Musical America*, 75 (1 Nov 1955): 15, illus.

[2689]   SABIN, R. "Cherevichki", *American Record Guide*, 31 (Jun 1965): 1006–1007.
          A new recording of the opera.

[2690]   '"The Empress's Shoes": BBC Third Programme', *Opera*, 18 (May 1967): 432–433.
          In connection with a radio broadcast of the opera.

[2691]   DEL´MAN, V. 'Ispytanie na sovremennost´', *Sovetskaia muzyka* (1969), 1: 45–52, illus.
          In connection with performances of *The Enchantress* and *Cherevichki* in Perm´.

[2692]   FINKEL´SHTEIN, Z. "Cherevichki". In: *Opery P. I. Chaikovskogo: Putevoditel´* (1970): 17–57 [see 2592].

[2693]   STRÄTER, L. 'Tschaikowskij und die Volksmusik: Russische Aufnahme der "Pantöffelchen"', *Opern Welt*, 21 (1980), 5: 56.

[2694]   STENGER, M. 'Tschaikowskys "Pantöffelchen"', *Musica*, 36 (1982), 1: 59–60, illus.

[2695]   TAYLOR, P. *Gogolian Interludes: Gogol's story "Christmas Eve" as the subject of the operas by Tchaikovsky and Rimsky-Korsakov*. London: Collets, 1984. iv, 264 p, music, illus. ISBN: 0–5690–8806–2.
          Includes the librettos in Russian (transliteration) and English tr.
          Review: J. Warrack, *Music & Letters*, 67 (Apr 1986), 2: 199–200.

[2696]   POSPISIL, V. 'Cajkovskeho "Strevicky" v Liberci', *Hudenbí rozhledy*, 37 (1984), 4: 162–163.

[2697]   JOHNSON, S. "Cherevichki", *Musical Times*, 124 (Jul 1984): 400.

[2698]   DOWNES, E. 'Tchaikovsky's "Beloved child"', *Opera*, 40 (Dec 1989), 12: 1426–1431.

[2699]   *"The Little Shoes"*. In: *Opera plot index: A guide to locating plots and descriptions of operas, operettas, and other works of the musical theater, and associated material.* Comp. by William E. Studwell, David A. Hamilton. New York: Garland, 1990: 219. (*Garland Reference Library of the Humanities*; 1099).

[2700]   BORISOVA, M. "Tscherewitscki". In: *Pipers Enzyklopadie des Musiktheaters: Oper, Operette, Musical, Ballet.* Hrsg. von Carl Dahlhaus und dem Forschungsinstitut fur Musiktheater der Universität Bayreuth unter Leitung von Sieghart Dohring. Band 6. München: Piper, 1997: 330–333.

THE ENCHANTRESS
Opera in 4 acts (1885–87)

[2701]   'Izvestiia otovsiudu', *Nuvellist* (Sep 1885), 5: 7.
Concerning Chaikovskii's decision to reject a libretto based on Pushkin's *The Captain's Daughter*, in favour of Shpazhinskii's *The Enchantress*.

[2702]   *"Charodeika" ("Nizhegorodskoe predanie"): Opera v chetyrekh deistviiakh.* Libretto I. V. Shpazhinskogo. Muzyka P. I. Chaikovskogo. Moskva: P. Iurgenson, 1887. 106 p.
Original libretto.
— 2-e izd. Moskva: P. Iurgenson, 1901. 42 p.

[2703]   GALLER, K. P. 'Muzykal´naia zametka', *Sankt Peterburgskie vedomosti* (7 Mar 1887).
Reviewing extracts performed in St. Petersburg on 5 Mar 1887.

[2704]   SOLOV´EV, N. F. 'Teatr i muzyka', *Novosti i birzhevaia gazeta* (7 Mar 1887).
Reviewing extracts performed in Moscow on 22 Feb 1887. See also *2705, 2706*.

[2705]   Z[INOV´EV], P. 'Kontsert filarmonicheskogo obshchestva', *Peterburgskaia gazeta* (7 Mar 1887).

[2706]   'Kontsert filarmonicheskogo obshchestva', *Novoe vremia* (8 Mar 1887).

[2707]   M[AKARO]V, P. S. 'Teatr i muzyka', *Birzhevye vedomosti* (21 Oct 1887).
The first production of the opera on 20 Oct 1887 in St. Petersburg. See also *2708* to *2723*.

[2708]   ZINOV´EV, P. 'Russkaia opera', *Peterburgskaia gazeta* (21 Oct 1887).

[2709]   'Novaia russkaia opera', *Muzykal´noe obozrenie* (22 Oct 1887): 35–36.

[2710]   '"Charodeika": Opera v 4-kh deistviiakh', *Peterburgskii listok* (22 Oct 1887).

[2711]   SOLOV´EV, N. F. '"Charodeika": Opera v 4-kh deistviiakh g. Chaikovskogo', *Novosti i birzhevaia gazeta* (22 Oct 1887).

[2712]   ZINOV´EV, P. 'Teatral´noe ekho', *Peterburgskaia gazeta* (22 Oct 1887).

[2713]   '"Charodeika": Opera v 4-kh deistviiakh', *Peterburgskii listok* (23 Oct 1887).

[2714]   SOLOV´EV, N. F. 'Eshche ob opere g. Chaikovskogo', *Novosti i birzhevaia gazeta* (23 Oct 1887).

[2715]   IVANOV, M. M. '"Charodeika": Opera v 4-kh deistviiakh', *Novoe vremia* (26 Oct 1887).

[2716]   GALLER, K. P. '"Charodeika": Opera P. I. Chaikovskogo', *Sankt Peterburgskie vedomosti* (28 Oct 1887).

598   B i b l i o g r a p h y

[*2717*]   K[ASHKIN], N. D. '"Charodeika": Opera v 4-kh deistviiakh P. I. Chaikovskogo', *Russkie vedomosti* (28 Oct 1887).

       — [repr.] In: N. D. Kashkin, *Izbrannye stat´i o P. I. Chaikovskom* (1954): 85–94 [see *2349*].

[*2718*]   [KIUI, Ts. A.] 'Muzykal´nye zametki: "Charodeika", opera g. Chaikovskogo', *Grazhdanin* (28 Oct 1887).

[*2719*]   MAKAROV, P. S. 'Muzykal´naia beseda', *Birzhevye vedomosti* (28 Oct 1887).

[*2720*]   [KIUI, Ts. A.] '"Charodeika": Opera v 4-kh deistviiakh', *Muzykal´noe obozrenie* (29 Oct 1887): 43–44; (5 Nov 1887): 294–297.

[*2721*]   LAROSH, G. A. '"Cherevichki" P. I. Chaikovskogo', *Russkii vestnik* (31 Oct 1887).

[*2722*]   'Muzykal´noe obozrenie', *Nuvellist* (Nov 1887): 1–3.

[*2723*]   [KIUI, Ts. A.] '"La charmeuse": Opéra de P. Tschaikowsky', *Supplément littéraire de l'Indépendance Belge* (18/30 Nov 1887).

       — [rev. repr.] 'Correspondance de Saint Pétersbourg: "La Charmeuse", opéra en quatre actes', *Le Ménestrel* (20 Nov/11 Dec 1887).

[*2724*]   BASKIN, V. '"Charodeika" P. I. Chaikovskogo], *Zhivopisnoe obozrenie* (31 Dec 1887).
The first production in Tiflis on 14 Dec 1887.

[*2725*]   KASHKIN, N. D. '"Charodeika": Opera v 4-kh deistviiakh P. I. Chaikovskogo, libretto I. V. Shpazhinskogo', *Artist* (Feb 1890), 6: 106–108.
The first production in Moscow on 2 Feb 1890. See also *2726, 2727, 2728*.

[*2726*]   K[ASHKI]N, N. D. 'Teatr i muzyka', *Russkie vedomosti* (4 Feb 1890).

[*2727*]   KONIUS, G. '"Charodeika" na stsene Bol´shogo teatra', *Moskovskie vedomosti* (4 Feb 1890).

[*2728*]   LAROSH, G. A. 'P. Chaikovskii i muzykal´naia drama', *Moskovskie vedomosti* (8 Feb 1890): 3–4.

       — [repr.] In: G. A. Larosh, *Sobranie muzykal´no-kriticheskikh statei*, tom 2, chast´ 1 (1924): 153–165 [see *2311*].

       — [repr.] In: G. A. Larosh, *Izbrannye stat´i v piati vypuskakh*, vyp. 2 (1975): 145–155 [see *2376*].

       — [German tr.] 'Peter Tschaikowsky und die Musikdrama'. In: G. A. Larosh, *Peter Tschaikowsky: Aufsätze und Erinnerungen* (1993): 146–160 [see *2406*].

[*2729*]   ENGEL´, Iu. D. '"Charodeika" Chaikovskogo', *Kur´er* (28 Nov 1900).

       — [repr.] In: Iu. D. Engel´, *Glazami sovremennika*. Moskva, 1971: 74–75.

[*2730*]   KASHKIN, N. D. ["Charodeika"], *Moskovskie vedomosti* (28 Nov 1900; 5 Dec 1900).

       — [repr.] In: N. D. Kashkin, *Izbrannye stat´i o P. I. Chaikovskom* (1954): 95–113 [see *2349*].

[*2731*]   LIPAEV, I. 'Iz Moskvy', *Russkaia muzykal´naia gazeta* (Dec 1900): 1208–1211.

[*2732*]   *"Charodeika": Ocherk*. Muzyka P. I. Chaikovskogo. Izlozhenie soderzhaniia s sokhraneniem glavnykh numerov peniia. Kiev: Z. M. Sakhina, 1902. 28 p.

[*2733*]   'Teatr i muzyka', *Novaia muzyka* (12 Jun 1902): 7.

[*2734*]   *"Charodeika": Opera*. Libretto I. Shpazhinskogo. Muzyka P. I. Chaikovskogo. Soderzhanie opery s sokhraneniem teksta glavnykh arii. Kiev: S. M. Boguslavskii, 1909. 16 p.

[*2735*]   *"Charodeika": Opera*. Izlozhenie soderzhaniia s sokhraneniem glavnykh numerov peniia. Irkutsk, 1912. 28 p.

[2736]   IUR'EV, M. 'Zametki o teatre: "Charodeika"', *Rampa i zhizn'* (1913), No. 48.

[2737]   "Charodeika". In: G. Angert, *100 oper*. Libretto oper pod red. L. Sabaneeva. Moskva: Russkoe teatral'noe obshchestvo, 1927: 239–240.

[2738]   *"Charodeika": Opera v 4 deistviiakh P. I. Chaikovskogo*. [Moskva]: Gos. Akad. Bol'shoi teatr [1937]. 39 p.

[2739]   *"Die Zauberin": Oper in 4 akten (6 bildern)*. Unter Benutzung des Textes von Schpashchinsky für die deutsche Bühne bearbeitet von Julius Kapp. Wien [1940]. 282 p. (*Universal Edition* Nr. 11242).

[2740]   '"Charodeika" Chaikovskogo na germanskoi stsene', *Internatsional'naia literatura* (1940), 7/8: 321. Report on the first production of the opera in Berlin.

[2741]   [FEDOROVSKII, F.] "Charodeika", *Iskusstvo i zhizn'* (Jun 1940), 6: 28/29, illus. Concerning Fedorovskii's scenic designs for Act II of the opera.

[2742]   GRINBERG, M. "Charodeika", *Sovetskoe iskusstvo* (24 Aug 1940): 3.

[2743]   *"Charodeika": Muzyka P. I. Chaikovskogo*. [Leningrad]: Gos. ordena Lenina Akad. teatr opery i baleta im. S. M. Kirova [1941]. 64 p, illus.
Contents: 'Ot teatra': 3–16 — N. V. Mamuna, 'Istoriia sozdaniia i pervoi postanovki "Charodeiki"': 17–52 — 'Libretto opery "Charodeika"': 53–64.

[2744]   'Opera Chaikovskogo "Charodeika" na stsene Berlinskogo opernogo teatra', *Pravda* (3 Feb 1941): 5.

[2745]   SHAVERDIAN, A. '"Charodeika": Novaia postanovka Teatra opery i baleta im. S. M. Kirova', *Izvestiia* (25 Mar 1941): 4.

[2746]   SOLLERTINSKII, I. '"Charodeika": Novaia postanovka Leningradskogo teatra opery i baleta im. Kirova', *Pravda* (25 Mar 1941): 6.

[2747]   ENTELIS, L. '"Charodeika": Prem'era v teatre im S. M. Kirova', *Smena* (28 Mar 1941): 3.

[2748]   RABINOVICH, D. 'Vtoroe rozhdenie "Charodeiki"', *Sovetskoe iskusstvo* (6 Apr 1941): 3.

[2749]   *"Charodeiki"*. Leningrad: Gos. ordena Lenina Akad. teatr opery i baleta im. S. M. Kirova, 1946. 40 p.

[2750]   ASAF'EV, B. V. *"Charodeika", opera P. I. Chaikovskogo: Opyt raskrytiia intonatsionnogo soderzhaniia*. Moskva; Leningrad: Gos. muz. izdat., 1947. 40 p, music.
— [repr.] In: B. V. Asaf'ev, *Izbrannye trudy*, tom 2 (1954): 142–168 [see 2348].
— [repr.] In: B. V. Asaf'ev, *O muzyke Chaikovskogo: Izbrannoe* (1972): 162–197 [see 2373].

[2751]   "Charodeika", *Sovetskaia muzyka* (1951), 8: 112.
The 65th anniversary of the opera's composition.

[2752]   ECKSTEIN, P. 'První setkánís Čajkovského "Čarodějkou": K československé premiéře opery v Státním divadle v Ostravě', *Hudební rozhledy*, 6 (1953), 16: 752–754.

[2753]   'Tschaikowskys "Zauberin" in Bielefeld', *Musikleben*, 6 (Jan 1953): 21.

[2754]   D'IAKONOV, A. 'Iz kontsertnykh zalov: "Charodeika" v kontsertnom ispolnenii', *Sovetskaia muzyka* (1954), 4: 114–115.

[2755]   LEVASHOV, V. & ORLOV, V. 'Zapiski o Novosibirskoi opere', *Sovetskaia muzyka* (1954), 5: 99–102.

[2756]   SOKOL´SKII, M. '"Charodeika" Chaikovskogo v kontsertnom ispolnenii', *Literaturnaia gazeta* (13 Feb 1954): 3.

[2757]   STRUCK, G. "Die Zauberin", *Musica*, 10 (Jun 1956): 406.

[2758]   RABINOVICH, D. '"Charodeika" v Bol´shom teatre', *Sovetskaia muzyka* (1958), 7: 79–83, illus. In connection with a new production of the opera in Moscow. See also *2759*.

[2759]   IARUSTOVSKII, B. 'Novaia postanovka "Charodeika"', *Muzykal´naia zhizn´* (Apr 1958), 7: 5–6, 8, illus.

[2760]   SEAMAN, G. 'Tchaikovsky in the theatre', *The Listener*, 60 (6 Nov 1958): 752.

[2761]   SIN´KOVSKAIA, N. *Opera P. I. Chaikovskogo "Charodeika"*. Moskva: Gos. muz. izdat., 1959. 62 p, music, illus. (*Putevoditeli po operam*).

[2762]   SIN´KOVSKAIA, N. 'Varianty dramaturgicheskoi kontseptsii "Charodeiki" Chaikovskogo po chernovym rukopisiam'. In: *Moskovskaia Gosudarstvennaia konservatoriia im. P. I. Chaikovskogo: Trudy kafedry teorii muzyki*. Vyp. 1. Moskva, 1960: 37–112, music, illus.

[2763]   GÜLKE, P. 'Die originale "Zauberin": Dokumente und Überlegungen zur Neubearbeitung einer Tschaikowski-Oper', *Musik und Gesellschaft*, 14 (Feb 1964): 86–93, illus.

[2764]   SIN´KOVSKAIA, N. *"Charodeika", opera P. I. Chaikovskogo: K probleme opernogo simfonizma*. Moskva: Gos. konservatoriia im. P. I. Chaikovskogo, 1965. 12 p. Dissertation (Moscow Conservatory).

[2765]   SIN´KOVSKAIA, N. "Charodeika". In: *Opery P. I. Chaikovskogo: Putevoditel´* (1970): 171–216 [see *2592*].

[2766]   ECKSTEIN, P. '"Čarodejka" portreti cesky', *Hudební rozhledy*, 24 (1971), 4: 158–160.

[2767]   ZARANKIN, Iu. 'V dome kompozitora', *Teatral´naia zhizn´* (1976), 20: 30, illus. A special performance of the opera *The Enchantress*, in the concert hall of the house-museum at Klin.

[2768]   NORRIS, G. 'Tchaikovsky's "Enchantress"', *Musical Times*, 121 (1980): 109.

[2769]   AL´BINSKII, V. A. 'O traditsiiakh drevnerusskogo skomorosheskogo gudoshnichestva v fol´klore i ob avtorskoi remarke v opere P. I. Chaikovskogo "Charodeika"'. In: *P. I. Chaikovskii i Ural* (1983): 86–91 [see *1749*].

[2770]   SIN´KOVSKAIA, N. N. 'Drama I. V. Shpazhinskogo "Charodeika" i odnoimennaia opera P. I. Chaikovskogo'. In: *Teatr v zhizni i tvorchestve P. I. Chaikovskogo* (1985): 27–40 [see *589*].

[2771]   *"The Sorceress"*. In: *Opera plot index: A guide to locating plots and descriptions of operas, operettas, and other works of the musical theater, and associated material*. Comp. by William E. Studwell, David A. Hamilton. New York: Garland, 1990: 366. (*Garland Reference Library of the Humanities*; 1099).

[2772]   ALLISON, J. 'Tchaikovsky and his "Enchantress"', *Opera*, 47 (May 1996), 5: 519–524, illus.

[2773]   BRUCE, D. 'Source and sorcery', *Musical Times*, 137 (Aug 1996): 11–15.

[2774]   LAUER, L. "Tscharodeika". In: *Pipers Enzyklopadie des Musiktheaters: Oper, Operette, Musical, Ballet. Hrsg. von Carl Dahlhaus und dem Forschungsinstitut fur Musiktheater der Universität Bayreuth unter Leitung von Sieghart Dohring*. Band 6. München: Piper, 1997: 344–346.

See also *2691, 3424*.

EVGENII ONEGIN
Lyrical scenes in 3 acts, Op. 24 (1877-78)

[2775]   'Muzykal'naia novost'', *Novosti* (3 Sep 1878).

Concerning Chaikovskii's work on the opera. See also *2776* to *2780*.

[2776]   'Muzykal'naia novost'', *Novosti* (11 Sep 1878).

[2777]   'Raznye izvestiia', *Saratovskii spravochnyi listok* (16 Sep 1878).

[2778]   'Chronique', *Journal d'Odessa* (16/28 Sep 1878).

[2779]   'Teatral'nye novosti', *Sankt Peterburgskie vedomosti* (1 Oct 1878).

[2780]   L[EVENSON], O. '"Evgenii Onegin" v muzyke Chaikovskogo', *Moskovskie vedomosti* (22 Oct 1878).

[2781]   T. '"Evgenii Onegin" novaia opera P. Chaikovskogo', *Russkaia pravda* (14 Dec 1878).

Rehearsals of the first four scenes of the opera on 16 Dec 1878 by students of the Moscow Conservatory. See also *2782, 2783*.

[2782]   K[UREPIN], A. D. 'Eshche o "Evgenii Onegine" Chaikovskogo', *Novoe vremia* (16 Dec 1878).

[2783]   LAROSH, G. A. 'Nedelia v Moskve. "Evgenii Onegin" v konservatorii', *Golos* (31 Dec 1878).

— [repr.] In: G. A. Larosh, *Sobranie muzykal'no- kriticheskikh statei*, tom 2, chast' 1 (1924): 136–141 [see *2311*].

— [repr.] In: G. A. Larosh, *Izbrannye stat'i v piati vypuskakh*, vyp. 2 (1975): 102–106 [see *2376*].

— [English tr.] 'Tchaikovsky's "Eugene Onegin", in the Conservatoire's production'. In: S. Campbell, *Russians on Russian music* (1994): 245–248 [see *2408*].

— [German tr.] 'Tschaikowskys "Eugen Onegin" als Aufführung des Moskauer Konservatoriums'. In: G. A. Larosh, *Peter Tschaikowsky: Aufsätze und Erinnerungen* (1993): 110–114 [see *2406*].

[2784]   *"Evgenii Onegin": Liricheskie stseny v 3 deistviiakh*. Tekst po Pushkinu. Muzyka P. I. Chaikovskogo. Moskva: P. Iurgenson, 1879. 71 p.

Original libretto. See also *2863*.

— [2-e izd.] Moskva: P. Iurgenson, 1880. 72 p.

— [3-e izd.] *"Evgenii Onegin": Liricheskiia stseny v 3-kh deistviiakh*. Siuzhet zaimstvovan iz poemy A. S. Pushkina (s sokhraneniem ego stikhov). Muzyka P. Chaikovskogo. Moskva: Tipografiia Imperatorskikh Moskovskikh teatrov, 1881. 64 p.

— 4-e izd. Moskva: P. Iurgenson, 1884 [1883]. 67 p.

— 5-e izd. Moskva: P. Iurgenson, 1885. 67 p.

— 6-e izd. Moskva: P. Iurgenson, 1886. 67 p.

— 7-e izd. Moskva: P. Iurgenson, 1890. 64 p.

— 8-e izd. Moskva: P. Iurgenson, 1896. 64 p.

— 9-e izd. Moskva: P. Iurgenson, 1898. 46 p.

Parallel text in Russian and Italian.

[2785]   INCOGNITO 'Teatr i muzyka', *Sovremennye izvestiia* (20 Mar 1879).

The first production of the opera on 17 Mar 1879 at the Moscow Conservatory. See also *2786* to *2791, 2948, 2950*.

[2786]   [LAROSH, G. A.] '"Evgenii Onegin" Chaikovskogo v spektakle konservatorii', *Moskovskie vedomosti* (22 Mar 1879): 3.

— [repr.] In: G. A. Larosh, *Sobranie muzykal'no- kriticheskikh statei*, tom 2, chast' 1 (1924): 141–145 [see *2311*].

— [repr.] In: G. A. Larosh, *Izbrannye stat'i v piati vypuskakh*, vyp. 2 (1975): 106–109 [see *2376*].

[2787]   BOTK—, N. 'Konservatorskii spektakl´ 17 Marta. "Evgenii Onegin": Liricheskie stseny P. I.
          Chaikovskogo', *Sovremennye izvestiia* (24 Mar 1879).

[2788]   KICHEEV, N. P. & NEMTSROVICH, V. I. 'Uchenicheskii spektakl´ v konservatorii', *Budil´nik*
          (26 Mar 1879).

[2789]   L[EVENSON], O. Ia. 'Chaikovskii: "Evgenii Onegin"', *Russkie vedomosti* (28 Mar 1879).
          — [repr.] In: O. Ia. Levenson, *V kontsertnoi zale*. Moskva, 1880: 369–380.

[2790]   V. A. 'Russkaia opera vo vtoroi polovine posta: "Evgenii Onegin", novaia opera Chaikovskogo,
          ispolnennaia uchenikami konservatorii', *Saratovskii spravochnyi listok* (30 Mar 1879).

[2791]   ZN—EN. 'Pis´ma k redaktoru: "Evgenii Onegin", opera g. Chaikovskogo', *Sankt-Peterburgskie
          vedomosti* (6 Apr 1879).

[2792]   'Evgenii Onegin", opera v 3-kh d., P. I. Chaikovskogo', *Budil´nik* (25 Jun 1879).

[2793]   '"Evgenii Onegin": Liricheskie stseny P. Chaikovskogo', *Voskresenyi listok muzyki i obiavlenii* (Oct
          1879), 45: 1–2.

[2794]   A. B. '"Evgenii Onegin": Liricheskie stseny P. Chaikovskogo' (7 Oct 1879).

[2795]   IVANOV, M. M., '"Evgenii Onegin", liricheskie stseny g. Chaikovskogo', *Novoe vremia* (11 Feb
          1880).

[2796]   'Opera "Evgenii Onegin": Abonement na russkuiu operu', *Russkaia gazeta* (14 Jul 1880).

[2797]   'Izvestiia otovsiudu', *Nuvellist* (Oct 1880), 6: 9–12.
          Report on preparations to stage the opera at the Bol´shoi Theatre in Moscow.

[2798]   K[UREPIN], A. D. *Peterburgskaia gazeta* (16 Jan 1881).
          The first performance at the Bol´shoi Theatre in Moscow on 11 Jan 1881. See also *2799* to *2804*.

[2799]   K. 'Moskovskii fel´eton ob "Evgenii Onegine" v Bol´shom teatre', *Novoe vremia* (17 Jan 1881).

[2800]   IGNOTUS [FLEROV, S. V.] '"Evgenii Onegin", opera g. Chaikovskogo', *Moskovskie vedomosti* (20
          Jan 1881).

[2801]   'Teatr i muzyka. Russkaia opera: Ispolnenie opery "Evgenii Onegin" Chaikovskogo', *Sovremennye
          izvestiia* (23 Jan 1881).

[2802]   'Moskovskie zametki', *Golos* (27 Jan 1881).

[2803]   'Izvestiia otovsiudu', *Nuvellist* (Feb 1881): 9.

[2804]   BOBORYKIN, P. 'Moskovskie teatry', *Russkie vedomosti* (8 Feb 1881).

[2805]   'Teatr i muzyka', *Novoe vremia* (8 Mar 1883).
          A new production of the opera at the Kononov Theatre in St. Petersburg. See also *2806* to *2815*.

[2806]   'Teatral´noe ekho', *Peterburgskaia gazeta* (13 Mar 1883).

[2807]   'Muzykal´nye novosti', *Muzykal´nyi mir* (2 Apr 1883): 8.

[2808]   M. R. 'Ezhenedel´noe obozrenie: "Evgenii Onegin" Chaikovskogo', *Muzykal´nyi i teatral´nyi vestnik*
          (24 Apr 1883): 5.

[2809]   NEMO. 'Nouveles à la main', *Sufler* (24 Apr 1883).

[*2810*] 'Teatr i muzyka', *Novoe vremia* (25 Apr 1883).

[*2811*] SOLOV´EV, N. F. 'Teatr i muzyka', *Sankt Peterburgskie vedomosti* (27 Apr 1883).

[*2812*] V. 'Teatral´nyi kur´er', *Peterburgskii listok* (29 Apr 1883).

[*2813*] M. R. 'Ezhenedel´noe obozrenie: "Evgenii Onegin", opera Chaikovskogo', *Muzykal´nyi i teatral´nyi vestnik* (1 May 1883): 5–6.

[*2814*] MEYER, E. ["Eugen Onegin"], *St. Petersburger Zeitung* (3 May 1883).

[*2815*] ["Evgenii Onegin"], *Vsemirnaia illiustratsiia* (7 May 1883).

[*2816*] V. V. 'Korrespondentsiia: Moskva', *Muzykal´nyi i teatral´nyi vestnik* (9 Oct 1883): 8–9.

[*2817*] 'Vesti otovsiudu: Khar´kov', *Muzykal´nyi i teatral´nyi vestnik* (4 Dec 1883): 6.
The first performance of the opera in Khar´kov on 31 Oct 1883.

[*2818*] 'Moskva', *Muzykal´nyi i teatral´nyi vestnik* (20 Dec 1883): 6.

[*2819*] IVANOV, M. M. 'Muzykal´nye nabroski', *Novoe vremia* (15 Oct 1884): 2.
A new production of the opera at the Bol´shoi Theatre in St. Petersburg. See also *2820* to *2830*.

[*2820*] 'Teatr i muzyka', *Novoe vremia* (21 Oct 1884): 4.

[*2821*] 'Teatr i muzyka', *Novosti i birzhevaia gazeta* (21 Oct 1884).

[*2822*] 'Teatral´nyi kur´er: Russkaia opera', *Peterburgskii listok* (21 Oct 1884).

[*2823*] GALLER, K. P. 'Teatr i muzyka', *Sankt Peterburgskie vedomosti* (21 Oct 1884).

[*2824*] GALLER, K. P. 'Muzykal´noe obozrenie', *Sankt Peterburgskie vedomosti* (22 Oct 1884).

[*2825*] IVANOV, M. M. '"Evgenii Onegin", liricheskie stseny g. Chaikovskogo', *Novoe vremia* (22 Oct 1884): 2.

[*2826*] SOLOV´EV, N. F. 'Muzykal´noe obozrenie: "Evgenii Onegin", opera g. Chaikovskogo', *Novosti i birzhevaia gazeta* (23 Oct 1884).

[*2827*] MAKAROV, P. S. 'Muzykal´naia beseda', *Birzhevye vedomosti* (24 Oct 1884).

[*2828*] IVANOV, M. M. 'Muzykal´noe obozrenie', *Nuvellist* (Nov 1884), 7: 1–4.

[*2829*] [KIUI, Ts. A.] 'Muzykal´nye zametki: "Evgenii Onegin", liricheskie stseny g. Chaikovskogo', *Nedelia* (4 Nov 1884): 1539–1544.
— [English tr.] 'Notes on music: "Eugene Onegin"'. In: S. Campbell, *Russians on Russian music* (1994): 248–254 [see *2408*].

[*2830*] SUVORIN, A. S. 'Malen´kaia khronika', *Novoe vremia* (8 Nov 1884).

[*2831*] 'Vchera i segodnia: Malen´kie novosti', *Novosti i birzhevaia gazeta* (11 Nov 1884).

[*2832*] GALLER, K. '"Evgenii Onegin", liricheskie stseny v 3-kh deistviiakh', *Vsemirnaia illiustratsiia*, 32 (1884), No. 827: 392, 395.

[*2833*] M. 'Turgenev o muzyke', *Nuvellist* (Jan 1885), 1: 7–8.
Turgenev's opinons of the music and libretto of *Evgenii Onegin*.

[*2834*]   NABLIUDATEL´, 'Razgovor na muzykal´no-literaturnuiu temu'. *Sankt Peterburgskie vedomosti* (4 Nov 1887).

[*2835*]   'Russkaia muzyka za granitsei', *Baian* (Dec 1888): 350.
The first performance of the opera in Prague on 24 Nov/6 Dec 1888.

[*2836*]   *"Eugen Onegin": Lyrische Scenen in drei Aufzügen*. Text nach Puschkin, deutsch von A. Bernhard. Musik von P. Tschaikowsky. Leipzig: D. Rahter [?1889]. 52 p.
German tr. of the libretto.

[*2837*]   'Izvestiia otovsiudu', *Nuvellist* (Jan 1889): 6–7.
News of the first production in Prague.

[*2838*]   KRUGLIKOV, S. '"Evgenii Onegin": Opera P. I. Chaikovskogo', *Artist* (Oct 1889), 2: 75–83.

[*2839*]   *"Evgenii Onegin"*. Sankt Peterburg: Ia. Volkov, 1890. 32 p (*Sokrashchennye libretto oper*; 65).

[*2840*]   KASHKIN, N. D. 'Muzykal´noe obozrenie', *Sovremennoe obozrenie* (1890), 2: 435–436.
— [repr.] 'Figner v role Lenskogo'. In: N. D. Kashkin, *Izbrannye stat´i o P. I. Chaikovskom* (1954): 68–70 [see 2349].

[*2841*]   MIRSCH, P. '"Eugen Onegin": Text nach Puschkin, musik von Tschaikowsky', *Hamburger Nachtrichten* (8/20 Jan 1892).
The first production in Hamburg on 7/19 Jan 1892. See also *2842*, *2843*.

[*2842*]   ARMBRUST, C. ["Eugen Onegin"], *Hamburger Fremdenblatt* (8/20 Jan 1892).

[*2843*]   LISSARD, I. ["Eugen Onegin"], *Hamburger Correspondent* (8/20 Jan 1892).

[*2844*]   'Tschaikowsky's opera "Eugeny Onegin"', *Musical Times*, 33 (Oct 1892): 585–586, music.

[*2845*]   *"Evgenii Onegin" Chaikovskogo*. Odessa: I. T. Loginov, 1894. 4 p.
Synopsis, and short biography of the composer.

[*2846*]   'Tschaikowsky and his "Eugene Onegin"', *American Monthly Review of Reviews*, 9 (Jan 1894): 88–89, music, illus.

[*2847*]   'Russkaia muzyka zagranitsei', *Russkaia muzykal´naia gazeta* (Jul 1894), 7: 155.
Report of extracts from the opera performed in Oxford, England.

[*2848*]   *"Evgenii Onegin"*. Odesssa: Izdat. Odesskogo gorodskogo teatra, 1895. 16 p.
— [2-e izd.] Odessa: Izdat. Odesskogo gorodskogo teatra, 1897. 16 p.
— [3-e izd.] Odessa: Izdat. Odesskogo Gorodskogo teatra, 1900. 16 p.
— [4-e izd.] Odessa: Izdat. Odesskogo Gorodskogo teatra, 1901. 16 p.

[*2849*]   *"Evgenii Onegin": Opera, muzyka P. I. Chaikovskogo*. Sankt Peterburg: I. Katz, 1898. 24 p.

[*2850*]   *Kratkoe libretto opery "Evgenii Onegin" Chaikovskogo*. Irkutsk, 1898. 4 p.

[*2851*]   BUKINIK, M. E. '"Evgenii Onegin" Chaikovskogo v Berline', *Russkaia muzykal´naia gazeta* (Oct 1898), 10: 905–907.

[*2852*]   *Evgenii Onegin: Opera v 3 deistviiakh*. Muzyka P. I. Chaikovskogo. Odessa: I. T. Loginov, 1899. 4 p.

[*2853*]   *Podrobnoe libretto opery "Evgenii Onegin"*. Odessa: S. V. Mozharovskii, 1899. 13 p.

[2854] IVANOV, M. M. 'Muzykal´nye nabroski: Pushkin v muzyke', *Novoe vremia* (22 Mar; 26 Apr; 3 May 1899).

Includes analysis of Chaikovskii's *Evgenii Onegin*.

[2855] **Libretto: Opera "Evgenii Onegin"**. Rasskaz soderzhaniia s sokhraneniem glavnykh numerov peniia. Kiev: Z. M. Sakhnin, 1901. 20 p.

— [new ed.] *P. I. Chaikovskii: "Evgenii Onegin"*. Libretto po A. S. Pushkinu. Soderzhanie opery s sokhraneniem teksta glavnykh arii. Kiev: S. M. Boguslavskii, 1910. 16 p.

— [2-e izd.] *P. I. Chaikovskii: "Evgenii Onegin"*. Tekst po Pushkinu. Podrobnoe izlozhenie soderzhaniia opery s sokhraneniem teksta vsekh glavnykh arii i numerov peniia. Kiev: Z. M. Sakhin, 1915. 16 p.

[2856] **K—OV, N. "Evgenii Onegin": Liricheskie stseny, muzyka P. I. Chaikovskogo**. Moskva, 1902. 7 p.

— [2-e izd.] Moskva, 1903. 6 p. (*Teatr Ermitazh. Tovarishchestvo Moskvoskoi chastnoi opery*).

[2857] **Libretto "Evgenii Onegin"**. Odessa: Izdat. Odesskogo gorodskogo teatra, 1903.

[2858] KASHKIN, N. D. 'Novaia postanovka "Evgeniia Onegina"', *Russkoe slovo* (29 Oct 1908).

— [repr.] In: N. D. Kashkin, *Izbrannye stat´i o P. I. Chaikovskom* (1954): 71–79 [see 2349].

[2859] ENGEL´, Iu. D. "Evgenii Onegin", *Russkie vedomosti* (2 Nov 1908).

— [repr.] In: Iu. D. Engel´, *Glazami sovremennika*. Moskva, 1971: 223–225.

[2860] '25-letie "Evgeniia Onegina"', *Russkaia muzykal´naia gazeta* (25 Oct 1909), 43: 957–959.

[2861] **"Evgenii Onegin"**. Libretto. Tiflis, 1910. 4 p.

[2862] SINGLETON, E. '"Eugene Onegin": Synopsis'. In: E. Singleton, *Guide to modern opera*. New York: Dodd, 1911: 49–53.

[2863] **"Evgenii Onegin"**. Tekst po Pushkinu. Moskva: P. Iurgenson, 1912. 147 p.

[2864] ENGEL´, Iu. D. "Evgenii Onegin", *Russkie vedomosti* (8 Nov 1912).

— [repr.] In: Iu. D. Engel´, *Glazami sovremennika*. Moskva, 1971: 353–360.

[2865] BOGOLIUBOV, N. N. 'Stranichka vospominanii: "Evgenii Onegin" v Drezdene, 1909'. *Russkaia zhizn´* (1913), 42: 7–8.

On the staging of the opera in the Dresden Imperial Theatre in 1909.

[2866] CHECHOTT, V. '"Evgenii Onegin" na stsene Mariinskogo teatra: K 20-letiiu so dnia smerti Chaikovskogo', *Solntse Rossii* (1913), 44: 10–12 [see 583].

[2867] 'Kak byl sozdan "Evgenii Onegin"', *Teatr i zhizn´* (25 Oct 1913): 13–14.

[2868] "Evgenii Onegin", *Teatr i zhizn´* (25 Oct 1913): 14–15.

[2869] MONTAGU-NATHAN, M. '"Evgenie Oniegin": Abstract of a Lecture, June 23', *Musical Standard*, 5 (1915): 8.

[2870] TOMASHEVSKII, B. 'Zametki o Pushkine'. In: *Pushkin i ego sovremenniki: Materialy i issledovaniia*, tom 38. Sankt-Peterburg, 1917: 67–70.

Concerning Triquet's couplets. See also 2978.

[2871] [ASAF´EV, B. V.] 'Mariinskii teatr', *Russkaia volia* (30 Sep 1917).

[2872] [ASAF´EV, B. V.] 'Mariinskii teatr (po povodu vystupleniia artisticheskoi molodezhi)', *Russkaia volia* (1 Oct 1917).

[2873] *"Evgenii Onegin"*. Kratkoe libretto s sokhraneniem teksta glavnykh arii. Petrograd: Izdat. Znamenskoi skoropechatni, 1918. 11 p.
— 2-e izd. Petrograd, 1918. 11 p.

[2874] PEYSER, H. F. '"Eugene Onegin" is final novelty at the Metropolitan', *Musical America*, 31 (1920), 23: 1, 3–4.
The first American staging of the opera on 24 Mar 1920 at the Metropolitan Opera in New York. See also *2875*.

[2875] MASON, D. G. 'Byronism in opera: "Eugene Onegin" at the Metropolitan', *Arts and Decoration*, 12 (Apr 1920): 424, illus.

[2876] DAVIDSON, G. 'Tchaikovsky: "Eugene Onegin"'. In: G. Davidson, *Stories from the Russian opera*. London: T. Laurie; Philadelphia, J. B. Lippincott [1922]: 193–205, illus.

[2877] MARKOV, P. 'O novom teatre: Posle "Onegina"', *Teatr i muzyka* (1922), 9: 108.

[2878] IAKOVLEV, V. *"Evgenii Onegin": Liricheskie stseny P. I. Chaikovskogo*. Moskva: Khudozhestvennaia pechat´, 1924. 39 p, music. (*Putevoditel´ dlia slushatelei i ispolnitelei opery. Muzykal´naia biblioteka*; 8).

[2879] SHUVALOV, E. K. *"Evgenii Onegin"*. Libretto, s portretom i kratkoi biografiei kompozitora. Kazan´: Glavpolitprosvet, 1924. 23 p.

[2880] KAMKAROVICH, A. 'P. I. Chaikovskii: "Evgenii Onegin"'. In: A. Kamkarovich, *Putevoditel´ po operam*. Leningrad, 1926: 16–19.

[2881] *"Evgenii Onegin": Liricheskie stseny v 3-kh deistviiakh*. Muzyka P. I. Chaikovskogo. Tekst po romanu A. S. Pushkina. Libretto opery, vvedenie i primechaniia S. Bugoslavskogo. Moskva: Gosizdat-Muzsektor, 1927. 54 p. (*Radioperedacha*).

[2882] ALAMAZOV. *"Evgenii Onegin"*. Podrobnoe libretto, kharakteristika i kriticheskie zamechaniia. Pod red. i predisloviem V. Bliuma. [Moskva, 1927]. 28 p. (*Sputnik v opere*).

[2883] CHEMODANOV, S. *"Evgenii Onegin"*. [Moskva]: Teakinopechat´ [1927]. 15 p.

[2884] CHEMODANOV, S. "Evgenii Onegin", *Novosti radio* (1927), 2: 5.
In connection with a radio broadcast of the opera.

[2885] "Evgenii Onegin". In: G. Angert, *100 oper*. Libretto oper pod red. L. Sabaneeva. Moskva: Russkoe teatral´naia obshchestvo, 1927: 256–257.

[2886] BELIAEV, V. '"Evgenii Onegin" v postanovke studii im. Stanislavskogo'. In: *Gosudarstvennaia opernaia studiia-teatr im. narodnogo artista respubliki K. S. Stanislavskogo*. Tekst V. Beliaeva. Moskva: Izdat. Obshchestva druzei opernoi studii-teatra im K. S. Stanislavskogo, 1928: 29–32, illus.

[2887] MAZING, B. '"Evgenii Onegin" v opernoi studii Stanislavskogo', *Rabochii i teatr* (1928), 20: 7.

[2888] *Evgenii Onegin*. [Moskva]: Teakinopechat´, 1929. 16 p, illus. (*Putevoditel´ po opernym spektakliam*).
— 2-e izd. [Moskva]: Teakinopechat´, 1930. 16 p, illus. (*Putevoditel´ po opernym spektakliam*).
— 3-e izd. [Petrograd; Moskva]: Teakinopechat´, 1930. 16 p, illus. (*Putevoditel´ po opernym spektakliam*).

[2889] *"Evgenii Onegin": Opera, muzyka P. I. Chaikovskogo*. Red. K. K. Obolenskogo. Moskva: Teakinopechat´, 1929. 95 p.
Complete libretto. Includes introductory article: 'Korotko o kompozitore i ego opere'.

[2890] GILEV, S. 'Pervyi "Onegin"', *Rabis* (1929), 15: 5.
The 50th anniversary of the first production of the opera. See also *2891, 2892, 2893*.

[2891] LEVITSKAIA-AMFITEATROVA, A. N. 'Pervye repetitsii "Onegina"', *Rabis* (1929), 15: 4.

[2892] ZBRUEVA, E. 'Sluchainaia fraza', *Rabis* (1929), 15: 4.

[2893] ZHEGIN, N. T. 'K 50-letiiu postanovki "Onegina"', *Serp i molot* (5–12 Apr 1929).

[2894] NEWMARCH, R. H. 'Tchaikovsky: Valse from "Eugene Onegin"'. In: R. H. Newmarch, *The concert-goer's library of descriptive notes. Part III: Suites and ballet suites for orchestra, rhapsodies and fantasias, miscellaneous dances*. London: Oxford Univ. Press; H. Milford, 1930: 144.

[2895] ANNESLEY, C. "Eugen Onegin". In: C. Annesley, *The standard operaglass. Detailed plots of the celebrated operas, with critical and biographical remarks and dates by Charles Annesley. With a prelude by James Huneker. Rev. ed. New York, Brentano's, 1931: 808–810.
— [rev. repr.] In: C. Annesley, *Home book of the opera*. New York: Dial Press, 1937: 198–199.

[2896] *"Evgenii Onegin"*. Baku: Gos. opernyi teatr im. M. F. Akhundova, 1931. 7 p.

[2897] *"Evgenii Onegin"*. Moskva: Gos. izdat. khudozh. literatury, 1931. 16 p (*V pomoshch´ zriteliu*).
Synopsis of the opera.

[2898] RIADNOVA, N. *"Evgenii Onegin": Opera P. Chaikovskogo*. Kratkoe soderzhanie i muzykal´noe obzorenie. Tiflis: Gos. opernyi teatr, 1931. 16 p.

[2899] '"Onegin" iubilar: Istoricheskaia spravka', *Sovetskoe iskusstvo* (1931), 8: 4.

[2900] *"Evgenii Onegin"*. Sverdlovsk: Gos. teatr opery i baleta im. A.V. Lunacharskogo, 1932. 8 p.
Synopsis of the opera.
— [2-e izd.] Sverdlovsk: Gos. teatr opery i baleta im. A. V. Lunacharskogo, 1933. 6 p.

[2901] IANKOVSKII, M. 'Pushkin ili Turgenev', *Rabochii i teatr* (1932), 14/15: 16.

[2902] BOGDANOV-BEREZOVSKII, V. M. *Chto nado znat´ ob opere "Evgenii Onegin"*. Leningrad: Biuro obsluzivaniia rabochego zritelia pri upravlenii Leningradskikh Gos. teatrov, 1933. 23 p. (*V pomoshch´ zriteliu*).

[2903] *Desiat´ let opernoi studii 1922/23 - 1932/33 i iiubileinyi spektakl´: Novaia postanovka "Evgeniia Onegina"*. Leningrad: Gos. konservatoriia [1933]. 15 p. (*Opernaia studiia*).

[2904] *"Evgenii Onegin"*. Moskva: Gos. Akad. Bol´shoi teatr SSSR, 1933. 19 p, illus. (*Muzei-vystavka Gos. Bol´shogo teatra SSSR*).

[2905] *"Evgenii Onegin"*. Saratov: Nizhne-Volzskii kraevedcheskii teatr opery i baleta im. N. G. Chernyshevskogo [1933]. 16 p. (*Muzyka v massy*).

[2906] MUZALEVSKII, V. I. '70 let Leningradskoi konservatorii', *Rabochii i teatr* (1933), No. 8/9: 13.
Includes details of a performance of the opera at the Leningrad Conservatory.

[2907] TARANUSHCHENKO, V. '"Evgenii Onegin" na stsene GABTa', *Sovetskaia muzyka* (1933), 4: 165–166.

[2908] ZHITOMIRSKII, D. V. '"Evgenii Onegin" i "Pikovaia dama"', *Muzykal´naia samodeiatel´nost´* (1933), 12: 5–13.

[2909] GLEBOV, I. [ASAF´EV, B. V.] 'Dva "Onegina": K vozobnovlenniiu opery Chaikovskogo', *Sovetskoe iskusstvo* (26 Apr 1933): 3
In connection with a revival of the opera in the Bol´shoi Theatre, Moscow.
— [repr.] In: B. V. Asaf´ev, *Ob opere*. Leningrad: Muzyka, 1976: 206–210.

[*2910*]   POLIANOVSKII, G. 'Kompozitor, poet i khudozhnik: "Evgenii Onegin" na stsene Bol´shogo
            teatra SSSR', *Sovetskoe iskusstvo* (26 Apr 1933), No. 27.

[*2911*]   KANN, E. 'I zamysel ne nov: "Evgenii Onegin" v Bol´shom teatre', *Vecherniaia Moskva* (27 Apr
            1933).

[*2912*]   KANN, E. 'Pis´ma ob "Onegine": Neopublikovannaia perepiska P. I. Chaikovskogo', *Vecherniaia
            Moskva* (24 Sep 1933).
            Extracts from Chaikovskii's letters from 1877/78, concerning the opera.

[*2913*]   *"Evgenii Onegin": Liricheskie stseny P. I. Chaikovskogo*. Khar´kov: Izdat. Oblastnogo Gos. Teatral´nogo
            Tresta, 1934. 12 p.

[*2914*]   REMEZOV, I. *"Evgenii Onegin": Liricheskie stseny v 3-kh deistviiakh*. Tekst po Pushkinu. Muzyka
            Chaikovskogo. [Moskva]: Upravlennyi treatrami NKP RSFSR, 1934. 68 p, illus.
            Includes complete libretto.

[*2915*]   '"Evgenii Onegin" v tatarskoi opere', *Vecherniaia Moskva* (1934), No. 205.

[*2916*]   K. S. '"Evgenii Onegin" v ispolnenii opernogo klassa muzykal´nogo tekhnikuma im.
            Gnesinykh', *Sovetskaia muzyka* (1934), 7: 69–70.

[*2917*]   VOR, V. '"Evgenii Onegin": Obsuzhdenie radiomontazha opery Chaikovskogo', *Radiogazeta*
            (1934), 2: 2.

[*2918*]   *"Evgenii Onegin"*. [Kolomna]: 1935. 14 p. (*Opernaia studiia*).
            Comparing the characters in the opera with those in Pushkin's novel.

[*2919*]   *"Evgenii Onegin": Liricheskie stseny v 3-kh deistvaiiakh i 7-mi kartinakh*. Leningrad: Gos. Akad. teatr
            opery i baleta, 1935. 8 p.
            In connection with a production of the opera on 3 June 1935 in Leningrad.

[*2920*]   *"Evgenii Onegin": Opera P. I. Chaikovskogo*. Saratov: Saratovskii kraevoi teatr opery i baleta im. N. G.
            Chernyshevskogo, 1935. 24 p. (*Muzyka v massy*).
            — [rev. repr.] Voronezh: Saratovskii kraevoi teatr opery i baleta im. N. G. Chernyshevskogo, 1936. 26 p.
            (*Muzyka v massy*).

[*2921*]   GÖTZE, W. ´Tschaikowskys "Eugen Onegin"'. In: W. Götze, *Studien zum Formbildung der Oper*.
            Frankfurt am Main, 1935: 31–38.

[*2922*]   *"Evgenii Onegin"*. Gor´kii: Gor´kovskii kraevoi teatr opery i baleta, 1936. 30 p, illus.

[*2923*]   *"Evgenii Onegin"*. Kuibyshev: Kuibyshevskii teatr opery i baleta, 1937. 8 p.

[*2924*]   *"Evgenii Onegin": Liricheskie stseny P. I. Chaikovskogo*. Baku: Gos. Bol´shoi teatr opery i baleta im.
            M. F. Akhundova, 1936. 8 p.

[*2925*]   *"Evgenii Onegin": Opera*. Cheliabinsk: Cheliabinskii oblastnoi opernyi teatr, 1937. 5 p.

[*2926*]   *"Evgenii Onegin": Liricheskie stseny P. I. Chaikovskogo*. Leningrad: Gos. Akad. teatr opery i baleta,
            1937. 32 p, illus.
            Contents: A. F. 'Kratkoe soderzhanie opery': 3–5 — V. M. Bogdanov-Berezovskii, 'Muzykal´no stsenicheskoe
            razvitie opery': 6–15 — V. M. Bogdanov-Berezovskii, 'Obshchestvennoe i muzykal´no-khudozhestvennoe
            znachenie opery':16–21 — A. Finagin, 'K istorii postanovok opery "Evgenii Onegin"': 22–30.

[*2927*]   *"Evgenii Onegin": Liricheskie stseny v 3-kh deistviiakh, 7 kartinakh*. Muzyka P. I. Chaikovskogo.
            [Leningrad]: Leningradskii Gos. Malyi opernyi teatr, 1937. 56 p, illus.
            Contents:'Ot teatra': : 3–4 — V. M. Bogdanov-Berezovskii, '"Evgenii Onegin" P. I. Chaikovskogo': 5–19 —
            B. Khaikin, 'Moi rabota nad "Oneginym"': 20–22 — N. Smolich, 'O rezhisserskoi zadache': 23–26 — L.

Pumpianskii, '"Evgenii Onegin" A. S. Pushkina': 27–46 — 'K istorii postanovok opery "Evgenii Onegin"': 47–50 — 'Programma spektaklia': 51–54.

[2928] **Evgenii Onegin: Opera P. I. Chaikovskogo.** Leningrad; Moskva: Iskusstvo, 1937. 64 p, illus.

Contents: B. Tomashevskii, "Evgenii Onegin" Pushkina': 5–21 — A. Budiakovskii, '"Evgenii Onegin" Chaikovskogo': 22–54 — '"Evgenii Onegin": Stsenicheskoe razvitie deistviia' [libretto]: 55–63.

[2929] **"Evgenii Onegin": Opera P. I. Chaikovskogo.** Moskva: Gos. muz. izdat., 1937. 80 p, illus.

Complete libretto. Includes introductory article by A. Ostretsov, '"Evgenii Onegin", opera P. I. Chaikovskogo': 3–14.

— [2-e izd.] *"Evgenii Onegin".* Liricheskie stseny po A. S. Pushkinu. Muzyka P. I. Chaikovskogo. Moskva: Gos. muz. izdat., 1937. 80 p.

[2930] **Opera P. I. Chaikovskogo "Evgenii Onegin" po romanu A. S. Pushkina: Poiasneniia.** K predstoiashchei transliatsii po radio 7 fevralia 1937 goda. Leningrad: Leningradskii komitet po radioveshchaniiu i radiofikatsii, 1937, 16 p.

In connection with a radio broadcast of the opera on 7 Feb 1937.

[2931] **P. N. P. 'Opernoe libretto "Evgeniia Onegina"',** *Gor´kovskii rabochii* (7 Jan 1937).

[2932] **"Evgenii Onegin".** Kazan´: Permskii Gos. teatr opery i baleta, 1938. 12 p.

[2933] **"Evgenii Onegin".** Moskva: Gos. ordena Lenina Akad. Bol´shoi teatr Soiuza SSR, 1938. 4 p.

[2934] **"Evgenii Onegin": Libretto opery i programma.** Saratov: Saratovskii kraevoi teatr opery i baleta im. N. G. Chernyshevskogo, 1938. 15 p.

[2935] **"Evgenii Onegin": Liricheskie stseny, muzyka P. I. Chaikovskogo.** Alma-Ata: Ob´edinennyi teatr kazakhshoi i russkoi opery i baleta, 1938. 10 p.

[2936] **Chaikovskii: "Evgenii Onegin".** Saratov: Saratovskii kraevoi teatr opery i baleta im. N. G. Chernyshevskogo, 1939. 16 p.

[2937] **"Evgenii Onegin": Foto-reproduktsii.** Moskva: Gos. ordena Lenina Akad. Bol´shoi teatr Soiuza SSR, 1939. 13 p.

[2938] **'Teatral´nyi muzei im. Bakhrushina otkryvaetsia vo vtoroi polovine marta',** *Sovetskoe iskusstvo* (6 Mar 1939): 4.

The opening of an exhibition at the Bakhrushin Theatrical Museum in Moscow, to mark the 60th anniversary of the first performance of *Evgenii Onegin*. See also *2939, 2940*.

[2939] **'Teatral´nye vystavki Chaikovskogo i Musorgskogo',** *Sovetskoe iskusstvo* (10 Mar 1939): 4.

[2940] **'Po vystavkam',** *Dekada moskovskikh zrelishch* (11 Apr 1939): 13.

[2941] **"Evgenii Onegin": Liricheskie stseny v 3-kh deistviiakh.** Kiev: Gos. konservatoriia im. P. I. Chaikovskogo, 1940, 18 p.

[2942] **BRIAN, M. I. 'Tat´iana'.** In: *Chaikovskii i teatr* (1940): 176–182 [see *2537*].

[2943] **LEMESHEV, S. Ia. 'Bessmertnyi obraz'.** In: *Chaikovskii i teatr* (1940): 188–194 [see *2537*].

[2944] **MEL´TTSER, M. L. 'Rabota K. S. Stanislavskogo nad "Evgeniem Oneginym"'.** In: *Chaikovskii i teatr* (1940): 167–175 [see *2537*].

— [repr.] In: *Muzykal´no-tvorcheskoe vospitanie artistov opernoi stseny.* Moskva, 1981: 45–70. (*Sbornik trudov GMPI im. Gnesnykh*; 57).

[*2945*]   **MIGAI, S. I. 'Eletskii i Onegin'.** In: *Chaikovskii i teatr* (1940): 195–202 [see *2537*].

[*2946*]   **NEST´EV, I. & IARUSTOVSKII, B. 'Stsenicheskaia istoriia "Evgeniia Onegina"'.** In: *Chaikovskii i teatr* (1940): 37–79 [see *2537*].

[*2947*]   **ZHUKOVSKAIA, G. V. 'Rodnoi obraz'.** In: *Chaikovskii i teatr* (1940): 183–187 [see *2537*].

[*2948*]   **IVASHCHENKO, A. 'P. I. Chaikovskii: Otryvki iz pisem',** *Literaturnaia gazeta* (6 May 1940): 5.
Extracts from Chaikovskii's letters to Nikolai Rubinshtein and Karl Al´brekht, concerning the production of *Evgenii Onegin* by students of the Moscow Conservatory in 1879.

[*2949*]   **VINOGRADOV, V. 'Kompozitor i poet',** *Sovetskaia Ukraina* (6 May 1940).

[*2950*]   **SHISHOV, I. 'Pervaia Tat´iana',** *Znamia kommuny* [Novocherkassk] (16 May 1940).
Concerning Aleksandra Panaeva-Kartsova, who first performed the role of Tat´iana in the opera.

[*2951*]   **WESTRUP, J. A. 'Tchaikovsky's best opera',** *The Listener*, 26 (16 Oct 1941): 545.

[*2952*]   **ASAF´EV, B. V. *"Evgenii Onegin", liricheskie stseny P. I. Chaikovskogo:. Opyt intonatsionnogo analiza stilia i muzykal´noi dramaturgii.*** Moskva; Leningrad: Gos. muz. izdat., 1944. 89 p.
— [repr.] In: B. V. Asaf´ev, *Izbrannye trudy*, tom 2 (1954): 73–141 [see *2348*]
— [repr.] In: B. V. Asaf´ev, *O muzyke Chaikovskogo: Izbrannoe* (1972): 73–162 [see *2373*].
— [German tr.] *Tschaikowskys "Eugen Onegin".* Von B. W. Assafjew-Glebow. Versuch einer Analyse des Stils und der musikalischen Dramaturgie. Übersetzung: Guido Waldmann. Potsdam: Athenaion [1949]. 150 p.
Reviews: *Das Musikleben*, 4 (May 1951): 153 — *Musica*, 6 (Oct 1952): 441.

[*2953*]   **'Molodye sily',** *Sovetskoe iskusstvo* (5 Apr 1945).
In connection with a production at the Opera Studio of the Moscow Conservatory.

[*2954*]   **DRUSKIN, M. S. *"Evgenii Onegin" P. I. Chaikovskogo: Ocherk.*** Leningrad: Gos. ordena Lenina Akad. teatr opery i baleta im. S. M. Kirova, 1946. 32 p, illus.

[*2955*]   ***"Eugene Onegin": An opera in three acts.*** Words adapted from the poem of Alexander Pushkin by P. Tchaikovsky and C. S. Shilovsky. English version by Edward J. Dent. London: Oxford Univ. Press, 1946. 67 p.

[*2956*]   **"Eugen Onegin",** *Theatre Arts*, 31 (Mar 1947): 25.

[*2957*]   **NECHAEV, I. 'Opera v dni blokady'.** In: I. Nechaev, *Leningradskie teatry v gody Velikoi Otechestvennoi voiny.* Leningrad; Moskva: Iskusstvo, 1948: 517–531.

[*2958*]   **COOPER, M. 'Tchaikovsky's "Eugene Onegin",** *The Listener*, 39 (29 Apr 1948): 716.

[*2959*]   ***"Evgenii Onegin": Liricheskie stseny v 3-kh deistviiakh, 7-mi kartinakh, P. I. Chaikovskogo.*** Tekst po Pushkinu. Moskva: Gos. Akad. Bol´shoi teatr SSSR, 1949.

[*2960*]   **SHEKHONINA, I. *"Evgenii Onegin" P. Chaikovskogo.*** Moskva; Leningrad, 1949. 74 p, music, illus. (*Putevoditel´ po pushkinskim operam*).
Review: I. F. Kunin, 'Novye knigi o Chaikovskom', *Sovetskaia kniga* (1951), 2: 114–120.

[*2961*]   **IAGOLIM, B. 'Liubimaia russkaia opera',** *Ogonek* (1949), 17: 28.
For the 70th anniversary of the first performance of the opera.

[*2962*]   **BERLIAND-CHERNAIA, E. "Evgenii Onegin".** In: E. Berliand-Chernaia, *Pushkin i Chaikovskii* (1950): 38–76 [see *2134*].

[*2963*]   ***Evgenii Onegin.*** Moskva: Iskusstvo, 1951. 24 p, illus.
The history of the opera at the Bol´shoi Theatre in Moscow.

[2964]   RYZHKIN, I. Ia. 'Asaf'evskii analiz "Pikovoi damy" i "Evgeniia Onegina" Chaikovskogo'. In: *Pamiati akademika Borisa Vladimirovicha Asaf'eva: Sbornik statei o nauchno-kriticheskom nasledii*. Moskva: Akademii Nauk SSSR, 1951: 55–67.

[2965]   DOBRYNINA, E. 'V opernoi studii Moskovskii konservatorii', *Sovetskaia muzyka* (1952), 7: 76–78.

[2966]   'Zamysel "Evgeniia Onegina"', *Sovetskaia muzyka* (1952), 5: 12–13.
         The 75th anniversary of Chaikovskii's earliest work on the opera.

[2967]   BUSH, A. "Eugen Onegin", *Opera*, 3 (May 1952): 269–272, illus.

[2968]   MONTAGU, G. 'Tchaikowsky's "Eugen Onegin"', *London Musical Events*, 7 (May 1952): 24–25, illus.

[2969]   SEMEONOFF, B. '"Eugene Onegin": A synopsis and discography', *Record Collector*, 7 (Jun/Jul 1952): 141–149.

[2970]   BIANCOLLI, L. "Eugene Onegin". In: L. Biancolli, *The opera reader: A complete guide to the best loved operas* (1953) [see *2585*].

[2971]   GOLOVANOV, N. 'The most popular opera in Soviet Russia', *Music and Musicians*, 2 (Nov 1953): 13, illus.

[2972]   '75-letie opery "Evgenii Onegin"', *Teatr* (1954), 4: 190–191.

[2973]   IKONNIKOV, 'Opernaia klassika na belorusskoi stsene', *Sovetskaia muzyka* (1955), 5: 88–91.

[2974]   KLOPPENBURG, W. C. 'Tsjaikowsky's "Eugen Onegin": Bij de opvoering tijdens het Holland-Festival 1955', *Mens en melodie*, 10 (May 1955): 141–144, music.

[2975]   *"Eugene Onegin"*. Original libretto in Russian, with an English transliteration and line-by-line translation. London: Decca Record Co., 1956. 70 p.

[2976]   TUMASHEV, L. 'Opera "Evgenii Onegin" v Pekine', *Sovetskaia muzyka* (1956), 10: 142.
         A production of the opera in China.

[2977]   'The story of Tchaikovsky's "Eugene Onegin"', *Opera News*, 20 (5 Mar 1956): 22–24, illus.

[2978]   IAKOVLEV, V. V. 'O kupletakh Trike'. In: V. V. Iakovlev, *Pushkin i muzyka*. Moskva: Muzgiz, 1957: 253–263.
         Discussion with B. Tomashevskii. See also *2870*.

[2979]   BROOK, P. 'A realistic approach to "Eugene Onegin"', *New York Times* (27 Oct 1957).

[2980]   "Eugene Onegin", *New Yorker*, 33 (9 Nov 1957): 121.

[2981]   "Eugene Onegin", *New Republic*, 137 (25 Nov 1957): 22.

[2982]   "Eugene Onegin", *Opera News*, 22 (2 Dec 1957), illus. [whole issue].
         Includes: M. E. Peltz: 'Seen through a letter: Notes on "Eugene Onegin"'.

[2983]   *"Evgenii Onegin" P. I. Chaikovskogo: Liricheskie stseny v 3-kh deistviiakh, 7-mi kartinakh*. Libretto kompozitora pri uchastii K. Shilovskogo po A. S. Pushkinu. Moskva: Gos. muz. izdat., 1958. 75 p. (*Opernye libretto*).
         — 2-e izd. Moskva: Gos. muz. izdat., 1963. 72 p (*Opernye libretto*).
         — 3-e izd. Moskva: Muzyka, 1976. 60 p. (*Opernye libretto*).

[2984]   "Eugene Onegin", *Saturday Review*, 41 (27 Dec 1958): 22.

[2985]   IVANOV, B. E. *Dal´ svobodnogo romana*. Moskva: Sovetskii pisatel´, 1959. 715 p, illus.

[2986]   APOSTOLOV, P. 'Fil´m-opera "Evgenii Onegin"', *Sovetskaia muzyka* (1959), 6: 124–127.

[2987]   CHERNAIA, E. 'Besedy o muzyke: "Evgenii Onegin"', *Muzykal´naia zhizn´* (1959), 20: 11–12.
         The 80th anniversary of the first production.

[2988]   'Otvechaem na pis´ma chitatelei', *Muzykal´naia zhizn´* (1959), 8: 17.

[2989]   POLIAKOVA, L. '"Evgenii Onegin" na ekrane', *Sovetskaia muzyka* (1959), 6: 119–123, illus.

[2990]   TUGGLE, R. A. "Eugene Onegin", *Opera News*, 24 (12 Dec 1959): 26.

[2991]   CHERNAIA, E. *"Evgenii Onegin" P. I. Chaikovskogo*. Moskva: Gos. muz. izdat., 1960. 99 p, music.
         (*Putivodeitel´ po operam*).
         Includes short bibliography ('Chto chitat´ ob operakh P. I. Chaikovskogo'): 99.

[2992]   SHOL´P, A. E. 'I. S. Turgenev i "Evgenii Onegin" Chaikovskogo'. In: *I. S. Turgenev (1818–1883–
         1958): Stat´i i materialy*. Pod red. M. P. Alekseeva. [Orel]: Orlovskoe knizhnoe izdat., 1960: 159–183,
         illus. (*Gos. muzei I. S. Turgeneva*).

[2993]   BADRIDZE, E. '"Evgenii Onegin" v Khanoe', *Sovetskaia muzyka* (1961), 11: 127–133.
         A production of the opera in Hanoi, South Vietnam.

[2994]   BLAUKOPF, K. 'Zur musikalischen Physiognomie', *Musik und Szene*, 6 (1962), 11: 124–127.

[2995]   MELIK-PASHAEV, A. '"Pikovaia dama" v Kovent-Gardene', *Sovetskaia muzyka* (1962), 4: 85–89.

[2996]   JOACHIM, H. 'Balanchine's "Eugene Onegin"', *Opera*, 13 (May 1962): 314–315, illus.

[2997]   SHOL´P, A. E. 'Do pitanniia prodramaturgie operi "Evgenii Onegin" P. I. Chaikovskogo'. In:
         Naukovo-metodichni zapiski. Kiev, 1963: 71–83.
         Text in Ukrainian.

[2998]   SHOL´P, A. E. 'Chaikovskii v bor'be za realisticheskii stil´ v russkoi opere: Rezhisserskii analiz
         dramaturgii "Evgenii Onegin"'. Kiev: Gos. konservatoriia im. P. I. Chaikovskogo, 1964, 18 p.
         Dissertation, Kiev Univ.

[2999]   KUZNETSOVA, I. '"Onegin": Georg Ots', *Sovetskaia muzyka* (1964), 5: 41–45.

[3000]   'On records: "Eugene Onegin"', *Opera News*, 28 (29 Feb 1964): 34.

[3001]   STEDMAN, J. W. 'A smiling sigh', *Opera News*, 28 (29 Feb 1964): 24–25, music.

[3002]   HELM, E. B. 'Eine eintönlge Saison', *Neue Zeitschrift für Musik*, 125 (May 1964), 209–210, illus.

[3003]   RUBINSHTEIN, L. 'Belaia ten´', *Muzykal´naia zhizn´* (1965), 8: 8–9.
         The origins of the opera.

[3004]   DOLGOPOLOV, M. "Ia liubliu vas!", *Izvestiia* (14 Nov 1965): 3, illus.
         An analysis of the role of Lenskii by the opera artist S. Lemeshev.

[3005]   SHOL´P, A. 'Problema siuzhetnogo varianta v epiloge "Evgeniia Onegina" Chaikovskogo'. In:
         Ukrainskoe muzykovedenie: Nauchno-metodicheskii mezhvedomstvennyi ezhegodnik. Kiev: Mistetstvo, 1966: 82–
         93, illus.

[3006]   *"Eugene Onegin": Opera in three acts by P. I. Tchaikovsky*. Libretto from the poem by Alexander
         Pushkin; English version by Donald Miller. [n.p.] D. Miller, 1968. 32 p.

[*3007*] KANSKI, J. '"Dama" i "Eugeniusz"', *Ruch Muzyczny*, 12 (1968), 4: 10–11, illus.

[*3008*] OSIPOVA, V. 'Rozhdenie prekrasnogo', *Sovetskaia muzyka* (1968), 8: 63–67.

[*3009*] *"Eugene Onegin": Lyrical scenes in three acts*. Text (after Pushkin) and music by Peter Tchaikovsky; English version by Boris Goldovsky. New York: G Schirmer [1969]. vii, 20 p. (*G. Schirmer's collection of opera librettos*; 2791).

[*3010*] RUMIANTSEV, P. I. "Evgenii Onegin". In: P. I. Rumiantsev, *Stanislavskii i opera*. Moskva: Iskusstvo, 1969: 77–202.

[*3011*] *"Eugene Onegin": Lyrical scenes in three acts and seven scenes*. Libretto by Konstantin Shilovsky and Pyotr Tchaikovsky, based on Alexander Pushkin's novel in verse of the same name; English version by David Lloyd-Jones. London: Friends of Covent Garden, 1970. 40 p.

[*3012*] CHERNAIA, E. "Evgenii Onegin". In: *Opery P. I. Chaikovskogo: Putevoditel´* (1970): 58–131 [see *2592*].

[*3013*] COLDING-JØRGENSEN, I. '"Eugen Onegin" i radioen', *Dansk Musiktidsskrift*, 46 (1970), 7–8: 212–213.

[*3014*] PORTER, A. 'Tchaikovsky's finest opera', *About the House*, 3 (1970), 7: 32–37, illus.

[*3015*] RUSSELL, J. '"Onegin" - an anti opera?', *About the House*, 3 (1970), 7: 28–31, illus.

[*3016*] DAVIS, P. G. 'Tchaikovsky's musical novel', *High Fidelity*, 20 (Oct 1970): 87–88.

[*3017*] BARKER, F. G. 'Muted passion', *Music & Musicians*, 19 (Apr 1971): 56–57.

[*3018*] WOCKER, K. H., 'Weltschmerz als Kammermusik', *Opern Welt* (Apr 1971), 4: 14–22, illus.

[*3019*] SCHREIBER, U. 'Anatomie von Zuständen', *Opern Welt* (May 1971), 5: 16–18, illus.

[*3020*] *"Evgenii Onegin": Liricheskie stseny v 3-kh deistviiakh, 7-mi kartinakh*. Libretto (po romanu v stikakh A. Pushkina) P. Chaikovskogo i K. Shilovskogo. Moskva: Gos. ordena Lenina Akad. Bol´shogo teatra SSSR [1972]. 14 p, illus.

[*3021*] SCHMIDGALL, G. 'What ever happened to "Eugen Onegin"?', *Opera Canada*, 13 (1972), 3: 39–40.

[*3022*] SCHNEIDERS, H. L. 'Wo jede Liebe noch ein Liebestod ist', *Neue Musikzeitung*, 21 (Jun/Jul 1972): 17.

[*3023*] SCHNEIDERS, H. L. 'Tschaikowskij ist nicht Pushkin', *Opern Welt* (Jul 1972), 7: 8.

[*3024*] WENDLAND, J. 'Das Übliche: Nur etwas schlimmer', *Opern Welt* (Jul 1972), 7: 8–9.

[*3025*] BOGDANOVA, A. 'Stseny iz opery Chaikovskogo', *Sovetskaia muzyka* (1973), 7: 58–60, illus.

[*3026*] KOCH, H. W. '"Onegin" zwischen zwei Weltern', *Opern Welt* (Mar 1973), 3: 48.

[*3027*] BRIUKHACHEVA, E. 'Aranzhirovka trudnoispolnimykh mest klavira opery "Evgenii Onegin"'. In: *O rabote kontsertmeistera*. Moskva: Muzyka, 1974: 135–159.

[*3028*] DROZDOVA, M. F. 'Opery Chaikovskogo na Pushkinskie siuzhety: "Evgenii Onegin"'. In: *V pomoshch uchiteliu russkogo iazyka i literatury*, vyp. 7. Cheliabinsk, 1974: 3–15.

[*3029*] EISENDOORN, J. 'Tsjaikowski over zijn opera "Jevgeny Onjegin"', *Opera Journaal* (1974), 6: 2, illus.

[*3030*] MAHLKE, S. 'Romantische Opern-Tschaikowskijs "Eugen Onegin" in Berlin', *Opern Welt* (Jun 1974), 6: 32, illus.

[3031]   'Een parallel tussen Tsjaikowski en de titelroi in "Onjegin"?', *Opera Journaal* (1974/75), 6: 3, illus.

[3032]   "Jevgeny Onjegin", *Opera Journaal* (1974/75), 7: 4–5.

[3033]   KARKHOFF, H. 'De muziek van Tsjaikowski', *Opera Journaal* (1974/75), 6: 3.

[3034]   'Poesjkien's "Jevgeny Onjegin" prentenboek', *Opera Journaal* (1974/75), 6: 2.

[3035]   SHOL´P, A. E. 'Turgenev o Lenskom Chaikovskogo', *Nauchnye trudy Kurskogo pedagogicheskogo instituta*, 50 (1975): 163–169.

[3036]   EAST, L. "Yevgeniy Onyegin", *Music & Musicians*, 23 (Aug 1975): 41–42.

[3037]   "Eugene Onegin". In: G. Kobbe, *Kobbe's complete opera book*. Ed. and rev. by the Earl of Harewood. London: Putnam, 1976: 908–917.
          — [rev. ed.] G. Kobbe, *The definitive Kobbe's opera book*. Ed., rev. and updated by the Earl of Harewood. New York: Putnam, 1987: 730–737.

[3038]   KRAUSE, E. "Eugen Onegin". In: E. Krause, *Oper von A-Z: Ein Opernführer* (1976): 513–517 [see 2598].

[3039]   "Onegin", *About the House*, 5 (1976), 1: 50–51, illus.

[3040]   SCHWARZ, B. 'Two Tchaikovsky masterpieces', *Saturday Review* (Mar 1976), 3: 38–39.

[3041]   SCHMIDGALL, G. 'Tchaikovsky's "Eugene Onegin"'. In: G. Schmidgall, *Literature as Opera*. New York: Oxford Univ. Press, 1977: 217–246. ISBN: 0–19–502213–0.

[3042]   STANISLAVSKII, K. S. '"Evgenii Onegin" P. Chaikovskogo'. In: *Stanislavskii: Reformator opernogo iskusstva*. Moskva: Muzyka, 1977: 79–111.
          — 4-e izd. Moskva: Muzyka, 1988: 80–107.

[3043]   PAPP, M. 'Az "Anyegin" Szegeden', *Muzsika*, 20 (Feb 1977): 11–12, illus.

[3044]   "Eugene Onegin", *New Republic*, 177 (26 Nov 1977): 22–23.

[3045]   VAKHROMEEV, V. 'Besedy o muzyke: "Evgenii Onegin" P. I. Chaikovskogo (K 100-letiiu sozdaniia opery)', *Muzykal´naia zhizn´* (24 Dec 1977): 15–17, music, illus.

[3046]   SHAW, G. B. 'Tchaikovsky: "Evgene Onegin", 26 October 1892'. In: G. B. Shaw, *The great composers: Reviews and bombardments*. Ed. with an introduction by Louis Crompton. Berkeley: Univ. of California Press [1978]: 299–301.

[3047]   ASHBROOK, W. 'Intimate revelations', *Opera News*, 42 (18 Feb 1978): 20, illus.

[3048]   LANIER, T. P. '"Eugene Onegin": Tchaikovsky troika', *Opera News*, 42 (18 Feb 1978): 31.

[3049]   SCHMIDGALL, G. 'An ironic twist', *Opera News*, 42 (18 Feb 1978): 10–13, illus.
          On Chaikovskii's adaptation of Pushkin's story.

[3050]   KERENYI, M. 'Uj szereplok az Anyeginben', *Muzsika*, 21 (Apr 1978): 21–23, illus.

[3051]   ANDREEVA, E. 'U teatra khoroshie perspektivy', *Sovetskaia muzyka* (1979), 1: 68–72.
          In connection with a production of the opera in Kazakhstan.

[3052]   BLYTH, A. "Eugene Onegin". In: *Opera on record*. Ed. by Alan Blyth; discographies comp. by Malcolm Walker. London: Hutchinson, 1979: 520–631.

[3053]   SADIE, S. 'Tchaikovsky: "Eugene Onegin"', *Musical Times*, 120 (1979): 239.

[3054] BLYTH, A. 'Opera on the gramophone: "Eugene Onegin"', *Opera*, 30 (Feb 1979): 121–128; (Mar 1979): 219–224.

[3055] "Eugene Onegin", *Music & Musicians*, 28 (Nov 1979): 41.

[3055a] KESTNER, J. 'From cynicism to compassion: In adapting Pushkin's verse novel, Tchaikovsky opted for humanism', *Opera News*, 44 (8 Dec 1979): 8–17, illus.

[3056] SHEVIAKOVA, V. 'Spustia sto let', *Sovetskaia kul´tura* (18 Dec 1979): 5.
The 100th anniversary of the first performance.

[3057] DEMIDOV, A. 'Liubov´ artista: K 100-letiiu pervoi postanovki opery P. I. Chaikovskogo "Evgenii Onegin"', *Teatr* (1980), 2: 56–57.

[3058] KUNIN, I. F. 'Vek nyneshnii i vek minuvshii', *Sovetskaia muzyka* (1980), 4: 138–139, illus.

[3059] FAWKES, R. 'The great "Onegin" boom', *Music & Musicians*, 28 (Feb 1980): 20–23.

[3060] BERLIN, I. 'Tchaikovsky, Pushkin and Onegin', *Musical Times*, 121 (Mar 1980): 163–168, illus.

[3061] TIKHOVOV, K. K. 'Vokal´nye ansambli v operakh Chaikovskogo "Evgenii Onegin" i "Pikovaia dama"'. In: *Muzykal´no-tvorcheskoe vospitanie artistov opernoi stseny*. Moskva, 1981: 75–107. (*Sbornik trudov GMPI im. Gnesnykh*; 57).

[3062] LEVINOVSKII, V. 'Zabytaia stranitsa russkogo opernogo iskusstva', *Muzykal´naia zhizn´* (Jan 1981), 2: 15–17, illus.
Concerning a 1906 production of the opera in Moscow by L. Superzhitskii.

[3063] TORADZE, G. 'Snova na Tbilisskoi stsene: "Evgenii Onegin", ot 1883 do 1981 goda', *Muzykal´naia zhizn´* (May 1981), 10: 7.
The history of the opera at the Paliashvili Theatre in Tblissi.

[3064] SHOL´P, A. E. *"Evgenii Onegin" P. I. Chaikovskogo: Ocherki*. Leningrad: Muzyka, 1982. 168 p, music.
Reviews: M. Tur´ian, '"Evgenii Onegin": Pushkin i Chaikovskii', *Voprosy literatury* (1984), 3: 241–247 — P. R. Zaborov, *Russkaia literatura*, 3 (1984): 245–249.

[3065] *Tchaïkovski: "Eugène Onéguine"*. Regards sur Szymanowski. Paris: L'Avant-Scene, 1982. 181 p, music, illus. (*L'Avant Scène Opéra*; 43).
Includes the libretto of the opera in French tr. and Russian (transliterated).

[3066] KAZENIN, I. 'Skvoz´ gody', *Teatral´naia zhizn´* (1982), 19: 17, illus.
The 60th anniversary of Stanislavskii's production of the opera.

[3067] IAKOVLEV, V. V. '"Evgenii Onegin" P. I. Chaikovskogo i reforma K. S. Stanislavskogo: Neskol´ko nabliudenii'. In: V. V. Iakovlev, *Izbrannye trudy o muzyke*. Tom 3. Moskva: Sovetskii kompozitor, 1983: 405–419.

[3068] KANSKI, J. 'Oniegin inaczej', *Ruch Muzyczny*, 27 (1983), 18: 6–7.

[3069] SCHLÄDER, J. 'Operndramaturgie und musikalische Konzeption: Zu Tschaikowskijs Opern "Eugen Onegin" und "Pique Dame" und ihren literarischen Vorlagen' / 'Opera dramturgy and musical conception: Tchaikovsky's operas "Eugen Onegin" and "Pique Dame" and their literary sources', *Deutsche Vierteljahrsschrift für Literaturwissenschaft und Geistesgeschichte*, 57 (1983), 4: 525–568,.Summary in German and English.

[3070] SCHUMANN, O. "Eugen Onegin". In: O. Schumann, *Der grosse Opern- und Operettenführer*. Herrsching: M. Pawlak [1983]: 243–244.

[3071]   GLEIDE, E. '"Eugen Onegin": Metamorphosen eines Stoffes. Puschkins Versroman—
         Tschaikowskys Oper—Crankos Ballett', *Musik und Bildung*, 15 (Sep 1983), 9: 18–24, illus.

[3072]   "Eugene Onegin". In: J. W. Freeman, *The Metropolitan Opera stories of the great operas*. Vol. 1. New York:
         Metropolitan Opera Guild; W. W. Norton [1984]: 427–431.

[3073]   GROSHEVA, E. 'Na riadovom spektakle', *Sovetskaia muzyka* (1984), 1: 32–34.

[3074]   TUR´IAN, M. '"Evgenii Onegin" i Chaikovskii', *Voprosy literatury* (1984), 3: 241–247.

[3075]   *Peter Tschaikowsky: "Eugen Onegin". Texte, Materialien, Kommentare*. Hrsg. von Atilla Csampai und
         Dietmar Holland. Reinbeck bei Hamburg: Rowohlt, 1985. 232 p, music, illus. (*Rororo Opernbücher*;
         7896). ISBN: 3–499–17896–6.

[3076]   '"Eugene Onegin": Broadcast of February 23', *Opera News*, 49 (16 Feb 1985): 26–28, illus.
         Includes a history, synopsis and discography of the opera.

[3077]   THOMAS, C. J. 'Mussorgsky: "Boris Godunov" and Tchaikovsky "Eugene Onegin"', *Opera
         Quarterly* (sum. 1985): 139.

[3078]   MARCHESI, G. "Evgenij Onegin". In: G. Marchesi, *L'opera lirica: Guida storico-critica dalle origini al
         Novecento*. [Milano]: Ricordi; [Firenze]: Giunti [1986]: 149–154. (*Guide alla musica*).

[3079]   ROTONDELLA, G. 'Alla Sacla: Da Ciaikovskij a Debussy', *Rassegna Musicale Curci*, 39 (1986), 3:
         11–14.

[3080]   SADIE, S. "Eugene Onegin", *Musical Times*, 127 (Aug 1986): 448.

[3081]   JACOBS, A. 'Tchaikovsky: "The Queen of Spades" and "Eugene Onegin"', *Times Literary Suppl.*
         (5 Sep 1986): 976.

[3082]   "Eugene Onegin", *San Francisco Opera Magazine*, 8 (aut. 1986), illus. [whole issue].

[3083]   HILLER, C. H. 'Durchaus nicht verstaubt: Musiktheatereindrücke aus Moskau und Leningrad',
         Opern Welt, 28 (1987), 11: 58–59, illus.

[3084]   LAZARUS, J. "Eugene Onegin". In: J. Lazarus, *The opera handbook*. Boston (Mass.): G. K. Hall, 1987:
         199–200. (*G. K. Hall performing arts handbooks*).

[3085]   ZEKULIN, N. G. '"Evgenii Onegin": Pushkin and Tchaikovsky—the art of adaptation (novel to
         opera)', *Canadian Slavonic Papers*, 29 (Jun/Sep 1987), 2/3: 279–291.

[3086]   "Eugene Onegin". Music by Pyotr Tchaikovsky. Libretto tr. from the Russian by David-Lloyd Jones. Ed.
         by N. John. London: J. Calder; New York: Riverrun Press, 1988. 96 p, music, illus. (*Opera Guides*; 38).
         ISBN: 0–71454–146–X (US pbk).
         Review: D. Brown, *Musical Times*, 129 (Sep 1988): 464–465.

[3087]   WILEY, R. J. 'The dances in "Eugene Onegin"', *Dance Research*, 6 (aut. 1988), 2: 48–60.

[3088]   '"Eugene Onegin": Broadcast of March 25', *Opera News*, 53 (18 Mar 1989): 26–29, illus.
         Includes a brief history of the opera, synopsis of the plot, discography and interviews with the cast and
         conductor.

[3089]   WARRACK, J. 'Tchaikovsky's "Eugene Onegin"', *Times Literary Suppl.* (21 Apr 1989): 425.

[3090]   AIZENSHTADT, M. & AIZENSHTADT, B. 'Zabytyi muzykal´nyi salon', *Vechernii Leningrad*
         (1990), No. 211: 3.
         Recalling a private performance of the opera at the home of Iuliia Abaza in St. Petersburg on 6 Mar 1868.

[3091] VOLKONSKII, S. M. 'Bessmertno to, chto my liubim', *Muzykal´naia zhizn´* (1990), 9: 25.

[3092] SHAL´NEV, A. 'Poiski, nakhodki: Avtograf iz Karnegi-kholl', *Izvestiia* (3 Mar 1990): 5, illus.
An autograph fragment from the opera, signed by the composer and dated 11/23 Apr 1893. Now preserved in Carnegie Hall, New York.

[3093] PAPP, M. 'Orosz klasszika, szovjet modern: Csajkovszkij es Sosztakovics a Dresdai Unnepi Jatekokom', *Muzsika*, 33 (Sep 1990): 27–33, illus.

[3094] *"Eugenij Onegin": Scene liriche in tre atti e sette quadri*. Libretto di P. I. Cajkovskij e K. S. Silovskij dall'omonimo romanzo in versi di A. S. Puskin. Musica di Piotr Il´ic Cajkovskij. À curo di Claudio Del Monte e Vincenzo Raffaele Segreto. Parma: Grafiche Step, 1991. [45], 55 p.

[3095] ERMOLAEVA, T. N. '"Evgenii Onegin": P. I. Chaikovskogo i liricheskii peizazh XIX veka'. In: *P. I. Chaikovskii i izobrazitel´noe iskusstvo* (1991): 70–78 [see 595].

[3096] GRIGOR´EVA, A. P. '"Evgenii Onegin" P. I. Chaikovskogo na stsene Opernoi studii Leningradskoi konservatorii v oformlenii T. G. Bruni'. In: *P. I. Chaikovskii i izobrazitel´noe iskusstvo* (1991): 79–86 [see 595].

[3097] IAKOVLEVA, A. 'Iz istorii sozdaniia i pervykh postanovok opery P. I. Chaikovskogo "Evgenii Onegin". In: *Muzyka P. I. Chaikovskogo: Voprosy interpretatsii* (1991): 72–86 [see 594].

[3098] LOZHKIN, V. V. 'Stenografiia opery "Evgenii Onegin" v postanovke Izhevskogo opernogo teatra'. In: *P. I. Chaikovskii i izobrazitel´noe iskusstvo* (1991): 100–107 [see 595].

[3099] SÅLLSTRØM, G. 'Tva versioner av "Eugen Onegin"', *Musikrevy*, 46 (1991), 5: 266–268, illus.

[3100] DOLFUS, P. 'Tchaikovsky dans "Eugene Oneguine" et "La dame de pique"'. Maitrise: Univ. de Strasbourg (Sciences Humaines), 1992. illus.
Dissertation.

[3101] LIPPERMANN, F. 'La melanconia nella musica: Due esempi (Beethoven e Cajkovskij)', *Nuovo Rivista Musicale Italiana*, 26 (1992), 2: 17–20, illus.

[3102] 'Tchaikovsky: "Eugene Onegin"', *Gramophone* (Feb 1992): 89.

[3103] "Eugene Onegin", *Opera News*, 57 (Dec 1992): 28–31, illus.
Includes bibliography and discography.

[3104] SWANSTON, H. F. G. 'Missed connections: In "Eugene Onegin", Pushkin and Tchaikovsky show how social conventions prevent the expression of feelings', *Opera News*, 57 (19 Dec 1992): 12–14, illus.

[3105] PESTALOZZA, L. 'Possiamo dire che "Oneghin" si colloca fra Dostoevskij e Cechov?', *Musica/Realtà*, 14 (1993), 41: 69–77.

[3106] BLETSHACHER, R. 'Vom Gluck und seiner Unerrechbarkeit: Tschaikowskijs "Eugen Onegin"'. In: R. Bletschacher, *Apollons Vermachtnis: Vier Jahrhunderte Oper*. Wien: Überreuter [1994]: 350–353. ISBN 3-8000-3498-0.

[3107] DANOVA, I. V. 'Emotsional´naia vyrazitel´nost´ v russkoi vokal´noi shkole po sravneniiu s ital´ianskoi (na primere ispolneniia arii Lenskogo L. Sobinovym i E. Karuso'. In: *Khudozhestvennyi tip cheloveka: Kompleksnye issledovaniia*. Moskva: Gos. konservatoriia im. P. I. Chaikovskogo, 1994: 170–184. (*Eksperimental´no-teoreticheskie issledovaniia*).

[3108] "Eugenio Oneguin". In: F. E. Valenti, *La opera: Pasion y encuentro*. Buenos Aires: Ediciones de Arte Gaglianone, 1994: 377–380. ISBN 9-5072-0017-7.

[*3109*]   FORMAN, D. "Eugene Onegin". In: D. Forman, *The good opera guide*. London: Weidenfeld & Nicolson, 1994: 201–208.

— [American ed.] *A night at the opera: An irreverent guide to the plots, the singers, the composers, the recordings*. New York: Random House, 1994: 201–208.

[*3110*]   KHRIPIN, A. 'Tania liubit Zheniu', *Argumenty i fakty* (1994), 1: 8.

Analysis of *Evgenii Onegin*.

[*3111*]   PLOTKIN, F. '"Eugene Onegin": Romantic opera'. In: F. Plotkin, *Opera 101: A complete guide to learning and loving opera*. New York: Hyperion, 1994: 296–311.

[*3112*]   SADIE, S. 'Tchaikovsky's "Yevgeny Onegin"', *Times Literary Suppl.* (24 Jun 1994): 19.

[*3113*]   PARIN, A. "Uzhel´ ta samaia Tat´iana?", *Segodnia* (23 Sep 1994): 1.

[*3114*]   CLARK, A. 'Originalfassung in der Scheune', *Opern Welt* (Nov 1994), 11: 48.

[*3115*]   GRÖNKE, K. 'Zur Rolle des Gremin in Cajkovskijs Oper "Evgenij Onegin"'. In: *Internationales Čajkovskij Symposium, Tübingen 1993: Bericht* (1995): 127–140 [see *596*].

— [English tr.] 'On the role of Gremin: Tchaikovsky's "Eugene Onegin"' (tr. by A. D. Humel). In: *Tchaikovsky and his world* (1998): 220–233 [see *601*].

[*3116*]   MÖSCH, S. 'Tschaikowsky: "Eugen Onegin", irgendwo und nirgendwo', *Opern Welt* (Feb 1995): 43–44.

[*3117*]   SCHWINGER, E. 'Tschaikowsky: "Eugen Onegin", trost aus der Flasche', *Opern Welt* (Feb 1995): 36.

[*3118*]   BARINOVA, L. N. 'Rabota K. S. Stanislavskogo nad operoi "Evgenii Onegin": Opernaia studiia Bol´shogo teatra, 1922 god'. Moskva: Gos. institut iskusstvoznaniia, 1996. 271 p.

Dissertation.

[*3119*]   BÖKSLE, E. 'Peter Tschaikowskij: "Eugen Onegin"', *Nye Musikken*, 5 (1996), 3: 45.

[*3120*]   BRENER, M. 'A most unusual triangle'. In: M. Brener, *Opera offstage: Passion and politics behind the great operas*. New York: Walker and Co., 1996: 141–152. ISBN 0–8027–1313–0.

The composition of *Evgenii Onregin* and Chaikovskii's relationships with Antonina Miliukova and Nadezhda von Meck.

[*3121*]   BERSHADSKAIA, T. S. 'Garmoniia kak sredstvo kharakteristiki deistvuiushchikh lits v opere P. Chaikovskogo "Evgenii Onegin"'. In: T. S. Bershadskaia, *Garmoniia kak element muzykal´noi sistemy*. Sankt Peterburg: Gos. konservatorii im. N. A. Rimskogo-Korsakova, 1997: 159–177.

[*3122*]   EFIMOVSKAIA, E. 'O dramaturgicheskom znachenii dueta "Slykhali l´ vy" v opere P. I. Chaikovskogo "Evgenii Onegin"'. In: *P. I. Chaikovskii: Issledovaniia i materialy* (1997): 12–19 [see *599*].

[*3123*]   LAUER, L. "Jewgeni Onegin". In: *Pipers Enzyklopadie des Musiktheaters: Oper, Operette, Musical, Ballet. Hrsg. von Carl Dahlhaus und dem Forschungsinstitut fur Musiktheater der Universität Bayreuth unter Leitung von Sieghart Dohring*. Band 6. München: Piper, 1997: 333–339.

[*3124*]   TARUSKIN, R. 'P. I. Chaikovskii and the ghetto'. In: *Defining Russia musically: Historical and hermeneuetical essays*. Princeton: Princeton Univ. Press, 1997: 48–60. ISBN: 0–691–01156–7.

Review: *Notes*, 55 (Sep 1998): 71–74.

[*3125*]   EMERSON, C. 'Tchaikovsky's Tatiana', *Metropolitan Opera Stagebill* (Mar 1997): 3.

— [repr.] In: *Tchaikovsky and his world* (1998): 216–219 [see *601*].

[*3126*] POZNANSKY, A. 'Notes on "Eugene Onegin"', *Metropolitan Opera Stagebill* (Mar 1997), 3: 21–22, 47–48.

[*3127*] TEACHOUT, T. 'A quiet place: Tchaikovsky's "Eugene Onegin" succeeds despite its absence of action', *Opera News*, 61 (19 Apr 1997): 20–23, illus.

[*3128*] FINK, M. 'Ballszenen in Opern', *International Review of the Aesthetics and Sociology of Music*, 28 (Dec 1997): 181–183.

Text in German, with summaries in Croatian and English.

[*3129*] TARUSKIN, R. 'Tchaikovsky and the literary folk: A study in misplaced derision', *San Francisco Opera Magazine* (1997/98), 10: 10–15.

A comparision of Chaikovskii's opera with Pushkin's novel.

[*3130*] NEST´EVA, M. '"Evgenii Onegin": Stsenicheskie interpretatsii', *Muzykal´naia akademiia* (1998), 2: 70–74.

[*3131*] SKVIRSKAIA, T. Z. '"Dragotsennost´ P. A. Vakara": Ob odnom avtografe P. I. Chaikovskogo'. In: *Peterburgskii muzykal´nyi arkhiv: Sbornik statei i materialov*. Vyp. 2. Sankt Peterburg: Kanon, 1998: 144–149.

Concerning a four-bar autograph from the Letter Scene in *Onegin*, written by Chaikovskii for Platom Vakar in 1884.

[*3132*] TALLIAN, T. 'Nevelodesi regenyek: Csajkovszkij: "Anyegin"', *Muzsika*, 41 (Apr 1998): 37–39.

[*3133*] BULLARD, T. 'Tchaikovsky's "Eugene Onegin": Tatiana and Lensky, the third couple'. In: *Tchaikovsky and his contemporaries* (1999): 157–166 [see *602*].

[*3134*] NELSON, B, '"But was my Eugene happy?": Musical and dramatic tensions in "Eugene Onegin"'. In: *Tchaikovsky and his contemporaries* (1999): 167–176 [see *602*].

[*3135*] PARIN, A. V. 'Berezki na fone kolonn'. In: A. V. Parin, *Khozhdenie v Nevidimyi grad: Paradigmy russkoi klassicheskoi opery*. Moskva: AGRAF, 1999: 361–382.

[*3136*] PARIN, A. V. 'Elegiia na zasnezhennykh postorakh vselennoi'. In: A. V. Parin, *Khozhdenie v Nevidimyi grad: Paradigmy russkoi klassicheskoi opery*. Moskva: AGRAF, 1999: 143–176.

[*3137*] TAMBOVSKAIA, N. A. '"Evgenii Onegin" i "Orleanskaia deva" kak tragicheskii "sverkhtsikl" v tvorchestve Chaikovskogo'. In: *Keldyshevskii sbornik: Muzykal´no-istoricheskie chteniia pamiati Iu. V. Keldysha, 1997*. Moskva: Rossiiskii institut iskusstvoznaniia, 1999: 155–164.

See also *196, 273, 387, 417, 438, 496, 504, 510, 547, 1885, 3680, 3782, 5552, 5553, 5628*.

HYPERBOLA

Projected opera (1854)

[*3138*] DVINSKII, M. M. 'Opera ne napisannaia Chaikovskim', *Vecherniaia krasnaia gazeta* (29 May 1933).

Includes two letters from the composer to Viktor Olkhovskii concerning the projected opera *Hyperbola*.

[*3139*] 'Opera "Giperbola": Dva pis´ma P. I. Chaikovskogo', *Vecherniaia Moskva* (22 Aug 1936).

IOLANTA

Opera in 1 act, Op. 69 (1891)

[*3140*] *"Iolanta": Opera v odnom deistvii*. Muzyka P. I. Chaikovskogo. Siuzhet zaimstvovan iz dramaticheskoi poemy datskogo poeta Geinrikha Gertsa. Tekst M. I. Chaikovskogo. Sankt Peterburg: P. Iurgenson, 1892. 46 p.

Original libretto.

— [2-e izd.] Moskva: P. Iurgenson, 1892. 46 p.

[*3141*]   V. F. 'Novaia opera P. Chaikovskogo', *Peterburgskii listok* (6 Dec 1892).
Outlining the story of the opera.

[*3142*]   BASKIN, V. 'Teatral´noe ekho: "Iolanta"', *Peterburgskaia gazeta* (7 Dec 1892).
The first production of the opera on 6 Dec 1892, in St. Petersburg. See also *3143* to *3157*.

[*3143*]   I—CH, G. 'Mariinskii teatr: "Iolanta", opera P. I. Chaikovskogo', *Birzhevye vedomosti* (7 Dec 1892).

[*3144*]   IVANOV, M. M. 'Teatr i muzyka', *Novoe vremia* (7 Dec 1892): 3.

[*3145*]   V. F. 'Opera "Iolanta"', *Peterburgskii listok* (7 Dec 1892).

[*3146*]   BASKIN, V. 'Teatral´noe ekho: "Iolanta"', *Peterburgskaia gazeta* (8 Dec 1892).

[*3147*]   Ia. D. '"Iolanta": Opera v odnom akte P. I. Chaikovskogo', *Sankt Peterburgskie vedomosti* (8 Dec 1892).

[*3148*]   'Teatr i muzyka: "Iolanta" g. Chaikovskogo', *Den´* (8 Dec 1892).

[*3149*]   IPPOLITOV. 'Opera "Iolanta" i balet "Shchelkunchik" Chaikovskogo', *Grazhdanin* (8 Dec 1892).

[*3150*]   V. F. 'Opera "Iolanta"', *Peterburgskii listok* (8 Dec 1892).

[*3151*]   VEIMARN, P. 'Opera "Iolanta" i balet "Shchelkunchik" P. I. Chaikovskogo', *Syn Otechestva* (8 Dec 1892).

[*3152*]   IPPOLITOV. 'Opera "Iolanta" i balet "Shchelkunchik"'. *Grazhdanin* (9 Dec 1892).

[*3153*]   IUGORSKII, S. 'Pis´mo iz Peterburga', *Moskovskie vedomosti* (9 Dec 1892).

[*3154*]   'Teatral´noe ekho', *Peterburgskaia gazeta* (10 Dec 1892).

[*3155*]   DOMINO. 'Nasha obshchestvennaia zhizn´', *Birzhevye vedomosti* (13 Dec 1892).

[*3156*]   IVANOV, M. M. 'Muzykal´nye nabroski', *Novoe vremia* (14 Dec 1892): 2.

[*3157*]   LEL´. '"Iolanta" i "Shchelkunchik" P. I. Chaikovskogo', *Artist* (Jan 1893), 26: 175–177.

[*3158*]   KASHKIN, N. D. '"Iolanta": Opera v 1-m deistvii. Tekst M. I. Chaikovskogo. Muzyka P. I. Chaikovskogo', *Artist* (Dec 1893): 110–114.
The first performance in Moscow, on 11 Nov 1893.
— [repr.] In: N. D. Kashkin, *Izbrannye stat´i o P. I. Chaikovskom* (1954): 164–177 [see *2349*].

[*3159*]   KASHKIN, N. D. 'Ispolnenie "Iolanty" Chaikovskogo', *Artist* (Dec 1893): 142–143.
— [repr.] in N. D. Kashkin, *Izbrannye stat´i o P. I. Chaikovskom* (1954): 178–181 [see *2349*].

[*3160*]   CHESHIKHIN, V. 'Chaikovskii: "Iolanta"'. In: V. Cheshikhin, *Otgoloski opery i kontserta*. Sankt Peterburg, 1896: 134–145.

[*3161*]   *"Iolanta"*. Odessa: I. T. Loginov, 1898. 4 p.
Includes a short biography of the composer.

[*3162*]   HANSLICK, E. 'Die Oper "Jolanthe"'. In: E. Hanslick, *Aus neuer und neuester Zeit*. Musikalische Kritiken und Schilderungen von Eduard Hanslick. Berlin, 1900: 30–33.
— [repr.] 'Die Tschaikowsky-Rezensionen'. In: *Tschaikowsky aus der Nähe* (1994): 210–213 [see *379*].

[3163] '"Iolanta" P. I. Chaikovskogo', *Russkaia muzykal'naia gazeta* (16/23 Jul 1900), 29/30: 689–695.

[3164] *"Iolanta": Liricheskaia opera.* Muzyka P. I. Chaikovskogo. Moskva, 1902. 2 p.

[3165] **K—OV, N.** *Libretto opera "Iolanta".* Moskva: N. Ketkhudov, 1903. 4 p.

[3166] *"Iolanta": Opera.* Libretto s sokhraneniem teksta glavnykh arii. Kiev: S. M. Boguslavskii, 1908. 15 p.

[3167] *"Iolanthe": Lyrische Oper in einem Aufzüge.* Text (russisch) nach Heinrik Hertz' 'König Renés Tochter' von Modest Tschaikovsky. Deutsche Umdichtung von Hans Schmidt. Musik von P. Tschaikovsky, Op. 69. Hamburg: D. Rahter [190–?]. 40 p.

[3168] *"Iolanta": Opera v 1 deistvii P. I. Chaikovskogo.* Kratkoe soderzhanie s sokhraneniem glavnykh numerov peniia. Kiev: Z. M. Sakhina, 1913. 24 p.

[3169] **DAVIDSON, G.** 'Tchaikovsky: "Iolanta"'. In: G. Davidson, *Stories from the Russian opera.* London: T. Laurie; Philadelphia, J. B. Lippincott [1922]: 206–224, illus.

[3170] "Iolanta", *Ezhenedel'nik Petrogradskikh Gosudarstvennykh akademcheskikh teatrov* (1923), 29/30: 7.

[3171] "Iolanta". In: G. Angert, *100 oper.* Libretto oper pod red. L. Sabaneeva. Moskva: Russkoe teatral'naia obshchestvo, 1927: 202–203.

[3172] **KANKAROVICH, A.** 'P. I. Chaikovskii: "Iolanta"'. In: A. Kankarovich, *Putevoditel' po operam.* Tom 2. Leningrad, 1927: 34–42.

[3173] **BRAUDO, E. M.** '"Iolanta" v kontsertnom ispolnenii', *Sovetskoe iskusstvo* (12 Feb 1939): 3.
A concert performance of the opera in Moscow on 6 Feb 1939.

[3174] *"Iolanta": Opera v 2-kh kartinakh.* Leningrad: Gos. ordena Lenina Akad. Malyi opernyi teatr, 1946. 24 p.

[3175] **KOREV, Iu.** *Opera "Iolanta" P. I. Chaikovskogo: Poiasnenie.* Moskva: Gos. muz. izdat., 1957. 31 p, music. (*V pomoshch' slushateliu muzyki*).

[3176] *"Iolanta" P. I. Chaikovskogo: Liricheskaia opera v 1-m deistviia.* Libretto M. I. Chaikovskogo po drame G. Gertsa 'Doch' korolia Rene'. Polnyi tekst. Predislovie E. Eremeevoi. Moskva: Gos. muz. izdat., 1960. 76 p. (*Opernye libretto*).
— 2-e izd. Moskva: Muzyka, 1977. 55 p. (*Opernye libretto*).

[3177] **AGAIANTS, S.** '"Iolanta", "Melodii Dunaevskogo"', *Sovetskaia muzyka* (1963), 9: 158–159.
Concerning a film version of the opera.

[3178] **MILLER, P. L.** 'The first recording of Tchaikovsky's "Iolantha"', *American Record Guide*, 30 (Jun 1964): 972.

[3179] **SEROFF, V.** 'Posthumous Tchaikovsky', *Saturday Review*, 47 (25 Jul 1964): 48.

[3180] **POPOV, I. K.**, "Yolanta", *Bulgarska muzika*, 18 (1967), 6: 40–42, illus.

[3181] **LLOYD-JONES, D.** 'A Background to "Iolanta"', *Musical Times*, 109 (Mar 1968): 225–226.

[3182] **PAYNE, A.** 'Russian Rarities', *Music and Musicians*, 16 (Mar 1968): 34–35.
On Rimskii-Korsakov's *Mozart and Salieri* and Chaikovskii's *Iolanta.*

[3183] **WOCKER, K. H.** 'Opern—von und mit Mozart', *Opern Welt* (May 1968), 5: 32–33.

[3184] **PRIBEGINA, G. A.** "Iolanta". In: *Opery P. I. Chaikovskogo: Putevoditel'* (1970): 326–382 [see *2592*].

[*3185*]   SHPILLER, N. 'Teatr smelogo eksperimenta', *Sovetskaia muzyka* (1975), 2: 60–67.
In connection with a new production of the opera in Leningrad.

[*3186*]   GROUM-GRJIMAILO, T. 'Moscou: Pyotr Ilyitch Tchaikovski "Yolande"', *Schweizerische Musikzeitung*, 115 (1975), 6: 320–321.

[*3187*]   "Iolanta". In: G. Kobbe, *Kobbe's complete opera book*. Ed. and rev. by the Earl of Harewood. London: Putnam, 1976: 932–934.
— [rev. ed.] G. Kobbe, *The definitive Kobbe's opera book*. Ed., rev. and updated by the Earl of Harewood. New York: Putnam, 1987: 749–751.

[*3188*]   STRÄTER, L. 'Eine Opern-Rarität: Tschaikowskijs "Jolanthe", *Opern Welt*, 19 (1978), 9: 54.

[*3189*]   BOLLERT, W. 'Tchaikovsky: "Iolanthe"', *Musica*, 33 (1979), 2: 192–194.

[*3190*]   ROBINSON, H. 'Moscow', *Opera News*, 43 (Mar 1979): 36.

[*3191*]   *"Iolanta"*. Music by Piotr Ilyich Tchaikovsky. Libretto by Modeste Tchaikovsky. [Washington, D. C.: National Symphony Orchestra, 1982]. [43] p.

[*3192*]   *"Iolanta"*. In: *Opera plot index: A guide to locating plots and descriptions of operas, operettas, and other works of the musical theater, and associated material*. Comp. by William E. Studwell, David A. Hamilton. New York: Garland, 1990: 179. (*Garland Reference Library of the Humanities*; 1099).

[*3193*]   SCHWINGER, E. 'Nur die Schlusspointe ist hintersinnig', *Opern Welt*, 34 (Aug 1993): 44, illus.

[*3194*]   RIMSKII-KORSAKOV, N. A. 'Wo Streicher am Platze wären, verwendet er Bläser... '. In: *Tschaikowsky aus der Nähe* (1994): 80–83 [see *379*].
The author's reaction to Chaikovskii's *Iolanta*, extracted from the German tr. of Rimskii-Korsakov's memoirs *Letopis' moei muzykal'nyi zhizn'* (1909).

[*3195*]   "Iolanta". In: J. W. Freeman, *The Metropolitan Opera stories of the great operas*. Vol. 2. New York: Metropolitan Opera Guild; W. W. Norton [1997]: 387–389.

[*3196*]   PARIN, A. V. "Iolanta". In: *Pipers Enzyklopadie des Musiktheaters: Oper, Operette, Musical, Ballet. Hrsg. von Carl Dahlhaus und dem Forschungsinstitut fur Musiktheater der Universität Bayreuth unter Leitung von Sieghart Dohring*. Band 6. München: Piper, 1997: 350–352.

[*3197*]   PARIN, A. V. 'Ogon´ voda i svet bez plameni'. In: A. V. Parin, *Khozhdenie v Nevidimyi grad: Paradigmy russkoi klassicheskoi opery*. Moskva: AGRAF, 1999: 229–312
Concerning *Iolanta* and *The Maid of Orleans*.

[*3198*]   ORLOVA, E. M. '"Iolanta" Chaikovskogo": Istoriia sozdaniia, filosofskie i esteticheskie osnovy liriki'. In: *P. I. Chaikovskii: Nasledie*, vyp. 1 (2000): 5–20 [see *603*].

THE MAID OF ORLEANS

Opera in 4 acts (1878–79)

[*3199*]   'Teatral´noe ekho', *Peterburgskaia gazeta* (16 Sep 1879).
Reporting Chaikovskii's work on the opera. See also *3200, 3201*.

[*3200*]   'Letopis´ iskusstv. Teatra i muzyki', *Vsemirnaia illiustratsiia* (22 Sep 1879).

[*3201*]   NIKS & KIKS [KICHEEV, N. P. & NEMTSROVICH, V. I.] 'Novaia opera P. I. Chaikovskogo', *Budil´nik* (1880), 40.

[3202]   *"Orleanskaia deva": Opera v chetyrekh deistviiakh.* Libretto (mnogie stseny zaimstvovany u
          Zhukovskogo). Muzyka P. I. Chaikovskogo. Moskva: P. Iurgenson, 1881. 68 p.

          Original libretto.

          — [repr.] *Russkii muzykal´nyi vestnik* (1881), 9: 3, 10: 3–4, 11: 3.

          — 2-e izd. Moskva: P. Iurgenson, 1881. 68 p.

          — 3-e izd. Moskva: P. Iurgenson, 1886. 68 p.

          — [4-e izd.] Moskva: P. Iurgenson, 1904. 64 p.

[3203]   'Sredi muzykal´nykh retsenzii', *Russkaia muzykal´naia gazeta* (1881), 8: 3–4.

          The first production on 13 Feb 1881 in St. Petersburg. See also *3204* to *3214*.

[3204]   'Muzyka i teatr', *Novoe vremia* (14 Feb 1881).

[3205]   SOLOV´EV, N. F. 'Pervoe predstavlenie opery "Orleanskaia deva" g. Chaikovskogo", *Sankt
          Peterburgskie vedomosti* (14 Feb 1881).

[3206]   GALLER, K. P. "Orleanskaia deva", *Novosti i birzhevaia gazeta* (15 Feb 1881).

[3207]   'Ot nemuzykal´nogo retsenzenta', *Molva* (15 Feb 1881).

[3208]   'Teatral´nyi kur´er', *Peterburgskii listok* (15 Feb 1881).

[3209]   IVANOV, M. M. "Orleanskaia deva", *Novoe vremia* (16 Feb 1881).

[3210]   MAKAROV, P. S. "Orleanskaia deva", *Birzhevye vedomosti* (17 Feb 1881).

[3211]   [KIUI, Ts. A.] '"Orleanskaia deva", opera g. Chaikovskogo', *Golos* (19 Feb 1881): 2.

[3212]   Z[INOV´EV], P. 'Teatral´noe ekho', *Peterburgskaia gazeta* (19 Feb 1881).

[3213]   LEVENSON, O. ["Orleanskaia deva"], *Russkie vedomosti* (21 Feb 1881).

[3214]   'Muzykal´noe obozrenie', *Nuvellist* (Mar 1881): 1–4.

[3215]   CHVALA, E. ["Orleanskaja deva"], *Politik* (18/30 Jul 1882).

          The first production in Prague on 16/28 Jul 1882. See also *3216, 3217, 3237*.

[3216]   NOVOTNY, J. ["Orleanskaja deva"], *Pokrok* (18/30 Jul 1882).

[3217]   ["Orleanskaja deva"], *Narodny listy* (18/30 Jul 1882).

[3218]   'Prem´era opery P. Chaikovskogo "Orleanskaia deva", *Muzykal´nyi mir* (8 Dec 1882): 5.

[3219]   M. 'Muzykal´noe obozrenie', *Muzykal´nyi mir* (8 Jan 1883): 4.

[3220]   GALLER, K. P. ["Orleanskaia deva"], *Vsemirnaia illiustratsiia* (15 Jan 1883).

[3221]   LIPAEV, I. 'Iz Moskvy: "Orleanskaia deva" Chaikovskogo', *Russkaia muzykal´naia gazeta* (Feb
          1899), 9: 286–290.

          The first production in Moscow, on 3 Feb 1899. See also *3222* to *3225*.

[3222]   DMITRIEV, N. [KASHKIN, N. D.] '"Orleanskaia deva" Chaikovskogo', *Moskovskie vedomosti* (5
          Feb 1899).

          — [repr.] In: N. D. Kashkin, *Izbrannye stat´i o P. I. Chaikovskogo* (1954): 80–84 [see *2349*].

          — [English tr.] 'Nikolai Kashkin's review of "The Maid of Orleans"'. In: *Tchaikovsky and his world* (1998):
          234–238 [see *601*].

[3223]   ENGEL´, Iu. D. "Orleanskaia deva", *Kur´er* (6 Feb 1899).

[3224]   'Opera i kontserty', *Russkaia muzykal´naia gazeta* (Mar 1899): 353.

[3225]   **'Teatr i muzyka'**, *Novoe vremia* (11 Mar 1899): 4.

[3226]   *"Orleanskaia deva": Opera*. Tekst po Shilleru i Zhukovskomu. Muzyka P. I. Chaikovskogo. Podrobnoe soderzhanie opery s sokhraneniem glavnykh nomerov peniia. Podrobnoe libretto. Kiev: Z. M. Sakhnin, 1903. 30 p.

   — 8-e izd., peresmotrennoe i dop. Kiev: Z. M. Sakhnin, 1909. 30 p.

   — [new ed.] vnov´ peresmotrennoe i dop. Kiev: Z. M. Sakhnin, 1911. 16 p.

   — [repr.] Kiev: Z. M. Sakhnin, 1915. 16 p.

[3227]   **A. K. 'Moskovskaia khronika'**, *Zolotoe runo* (1906), 3: 125–128.

   The 25th anniversary production at the Winter Theatre in Moscow.

[3228]   **KOL´TSOV, K. M.** *"Orleanskaia deva": Opera P. I. Chaikovskogo*. Istoricheskaia zametka. Moskva, 1907. 32 p, illus.

[3229]   **ENGEL´, Iu. D.** 'Novoe slovo v opernom dele: "Orleanskaia deva" Chaikovskogo na stsene Novogo teatra', *Russkie vedomosti* (23 Sep 1907; 26 Sep 1907).

[3230]   **ENGEL´, Iu. D.** 'Pis´ma o moskovskoi opere', *Russkaia muzykal´naia gazeta* (30 Sep 1907), 39: 849–884.

[3231]   *"Orleanskaia deva": Opera P. I. Chaikovskogo*. Libretto po Shilleru i Zhukovskomu. Soderzhanie opery s sokhraneniem teksta glavnykh arii. Kiev: S. M. Boguslavskii, 1909. 16 p.

   — 2-e izd. *"Orleanskaia deva": Muzyka P. I. Chaikovskogo*. Soderzhanie opery s sokhraneniem glavnykh arii. Kiev: S. M. Boguslavskii, 1915. 16 p.

[3232]   *"Orleanskaia deva"*. In: G. Angert, *100 oper*. Libretto oper pod red. L. Sabaneeva. Moskva: Russkoe teatral´naia obshchestvo, 1927: 265–267.

[3233]   **BOGDANOV-BEREZOVSKII, V. M.** *"Orleanskaia deva" P. I. Chaikovskogo*. Leningrad: Gos. ordena Lenina Akad. teatr opery i baleta im. S. M. Kirova, 1945. 20 p, illus.

[3234]   **KALGANOV, Iu.** '"Orleanskaia deva": Prem´era v teatre opery i baleta im. S. M. Kirova', *Smena* (20 Dec 1945): 3.

   The revival of the opera in Leningrad, including a short history and analysis of the music.

   — [repr.] *Leningradskaia pravda* (25 Dec 1945): 3.

[3235]   **BOGDANOV-BEREZOVSKII, V. M.** 'Vozrozhdennaia opera Chaikovskogo: "Orleanskaia deva" v Leningradskom ordena Lenina teatre opery i baleta im. S. M. Kirova', *Sovetskaia muzyka* (1946), 8/9: 87–90.

[3236]   **GRINBERG, M.** '"Orleanskaia deva": Prem´era v Leningradskom teatre opery i baleta im. Kirova', *Sovetskoe iskusstvo* (25 Jan 1946): 3.

[3237]   'Pervaia postanovka "Orleanskoi devy" v Prage', *Sovetskaia muzyka* (1952), 7: 120.

   Recalling the first performance of the opera in Prague in 1882.

[3238]   **JOLLY, C.** 'Saint Joan in Love', *Opera News*, 21 (10 Dec 1956): 32.

[3239]   **'Sagra Umbra Musicale in Perugia'**, *Neue Zeitschrift für Musik*, 118 (Feb 1957): 106.

[3240]   **RABINOVICH, D.** '"Orleanskaia deva" v Sverdlovskom teatre', *Sovetskaia muzyka* (1958), 3: 87–89.

[3241]   **SOKOL´SKII, M.** '"Orleanskaia deva": Prem´era v Leningradskom Gosudarstvennom teatre opery i baleta im. Kirova'. In: M. Sokol´skii, *Slushaia vremia*. Moskva: Muzyka, 1964: 189–197.

[3242]   KRAUSE, E. 'Ernstes nach Schiller, Heiteres nach Sheridan', *Opern Welt* (May 1970), 5: 26–27, illus.

[3243]   DEL'MAN, V. 'V poedinke so vremenem', *Sovetskaia muzyka*, 35 (Feb 1971): 61–67.
          In connection with the staging of the opea in the Perm´ Opera Theatre.

[3244]   DAVIS, P. G. 'Tchaikovsky's "Joan of Arc"', *High Fidelity*, 21 (Aug 1971): 96.

[3245]   REGITZ, H. 'Tschaikowskys "Jungfrau von Orleans"', *Musica*, 29 (1975), 3: 239–240, illus.

[3246]   "The Maid of Orleans". In: G. Kobbe, *Kobbe's complete opera book*. Ed. and rev. by the Earl of Harewood. London: Putnam, 1976: 917–920.
          — [rev. ed.] G. Kobbe, The definitive Kobbe's opera book. Ed., rev. and updated by the Earl of Harewood. New York: Putnam, 1987: 737–739.

[3247]   *"Joan of Arc" / "The Maid of Orleans": An opera in four acts by Petr Ilyich Tchaikovsky*. Tr. by Richard Balthazar. [Montreal]: R. Balthazar [1978]. 27 p.
          English tr. of the libretto.

[3248]   'Tchaikovsky's St. Joan', *Music & Musicians*, 26 (Feb 1978): 12–15.

[3250]   *"The Maid of Orleans"*. In: *Opera plot index: A guide to locating plots and descriptions of operas, operettas, and other works of the musical theater, and associated material*. Comp. by William E. Studwell, David A. Hamilton. New York: Garland, 1990: 231. (*Garland Reference Library of the Humanities*; 1099).

[3251]   SHADRINA, N. '"Ioanna d'Ark" na moskovskoi stsene', *Sovetskaia kul´tura* (5 May 1990): 9, illus. [see *965*].

[3252]   SOROKINA, I. 'Istoriia odnoi zhizni: Iz opernogo naslediia Chaikovskogo', *Muzykal´naia zhizn´* (1990), 9: 19–20, illus.
          The history of the composition and production of the opera.

[3253]   MAYER, M. "The Maid of Orleans", *Opera*, 41 (Jul 1990): 814.

[3254]   MOROZOV, D. 'Bol´shoi teatr v god Chaikovskogo', *Muzykal´naia zhizn´* (1991), 5: 8–9, illus.
          A production of the opera at the Bol´shoi Theatre in Moscow to mark Chaikovskii's birth centennial.

[3255]   ZAJACZKOWSKI, H. 'Tchaikovsky: His dream, the "Maid of Orleans" and his creative impulse', *Musical Times*, 132 (Feb 1991): 62–63.

[3256]   GOODWIN, N. "The Maid of Orleans", *Opera News*, 55 (2 Feb 1991): 39.

[3257]   CHERKASINA, M. 'Tchaikovsky—"The Maid of Orleans": The problem of the genre and the specific treatment of the subject', *International Journal of Musicology*, 3 (1994): 175–186.

[3258]   JACOBS, A. "The Maid of Orleans", *Opera*, 46 (Sep 1995): 1124–1125.

[3259]   PARIN, A. V. "Orleanskaja deva". In: *Pipers Enzyklopadie des Musiktheaters: Oper, Operette, Musical, Ballet. Hrsg. von Carl Dahlhaus und dem Forschungsinstitut fur Musiktheater der Universität Bayreuth unter Leitung von Sieghart Dohring*. Band 6. München: Piper, 1997: 339–342.

[3260]   KEARNEY, L. 'Tchaikovsky androgyne: "The Maid of Orleans"'. In: *Tchaikovsky and his world* (1998): 239–276 [see *601*].

          See also *2166, 3197, 3420, 4900*.

MAZEPA
Opera in 3 acts (1881–83)

[*3261*]   'Muzykal´nye novosti', *Muzykal´nyi mir* (8 Dec 1882): 5.
Report on Chaikovskii's work on the opera.

[*3262*]   *"Mazepa": Opera*. Siuzhet zaimstvovan iz poemy Pushkina. Muzyka P. Chaikovskogo. Moskva: P. Iurgenson, 1883. 66 p.
Original libretto.
— 2-e izd. Moskva: P. Iurgenson, 1884. 64 p.
— 3-e izd. Moskva: P. Iurgenson, 1885. 63 p.
— 4-e izd. Moskva: P. Iurgenson, 1890. 63 p.
— 5-e izd. Moskva: P. Iurgenson, 1903. 49 p.

[*3263*]   *"Mazepa": Opera, muzyka P. I. Chaikovskogo*. Sankt Peterburg [1883]. 6 p. (*Sokrashchennye libretto i programmy oper i baletov*; 53).

[*3264*]   '"Mazepa": Opera P. I. Chaikovskogo', *Akkord* (1884), 3: 61–62.
The first production of the opera on 3 Feb 1884 in Moscow. See also *3265, 3271, 3272*.

[*3265*]   IGNOTUS [FLEROV, S. V.] '"Mazepa": Novaia opera P. I. Chaikovskogo", *Moskovskie vedomosti* (7 Feb 1884).

[*3266*]   'Teatr i muzyka: "Mazepa", opera Chaikovskogo v Moskve', *Sankt Peterburgskie vedomosti* (7 Feb 1884).
The first production in St. Petersburg on 6 Feb 1884. See also *3267 to 3270, 3273 to 3279*.

[*3267*]   M. P. 'Teatral´noe ekho: Pervoe predstavlenie opery "Mazepa"', *Peterburgskaia gazeta* (7 Feb 1884).

[*3268*]   IVANOV, M. M. '1-oe predstavlenie "Mazepy"', *Novoe vremia* (8 Feb 1884): 3.

[*3269*]   SOLOV´EV, N. F. 'Teatr i muzyka: Pervoe predstavlenie opery "Mazepa" Chaikovskogo', *Sankt Peterburgskie vedomosti* (8 Feb 1884).

[*3270*]   V. 'Teatral´nyi kur´er: Bol´shoi teatr', *Peterburgskii listok* (8 Feb 1884).

[*3271*]   IGNOTUS [FLEROV, S. V.] '"Mazepa": Novaia opera P. I. Chaikovskogo", *Moskovskie vedomosti* (9 Feb 1884).

[*3272*]   L[EVENSO]N, O. '"Mazepa": Opera v 3-kh deistviiakh i 6 kartinakh P. I. Chaikovskogo', *Russkie vedomosti* (9 Feb 1884).

[*3273*]   MAKAROV, P. S. "Mazepa", *Birzhevye vedomosti* (10 Feb 1884).

[*3274*]   GALLER, K. '"Mazepa", opera P. I. Chaikovskogo', *Novosti i birzhevaia gazeta* (11 Feb 1884).

[*3275*]   [KIUI, Ts. A.] '"Mazepa", opera g. Chaikovskogo'. *Nedelia* (12 Feb 1884): 234–239.

[*3276*]   IVANOV, M. M. 'Muzykal´nye nabroski', *Novoe vremia* (13 Feb 1884): 2.

[*3277*]   MOLODOI MUZYKANT [KRUGLIKOV, S. N.]. "Muzykal´naia khronika: "Mazepa" Chaikovskogo', *Sovremennye izvestiia* (14 Feb 1884).

[*3278*]   SOLOV´EV, N. F. 'Muzykal´noe obozrenie: "Mazepa", opera g. Chaikovskogo', *Sankt Peterburgskie vedomosti* (14 Feb 1884).

[*3279*]   IVANOV, M. M. 'Muzykal´noe i kontsertnoe obozrenie', *Nuvellist* (Apr 1884): 1–3.

[*3280*] LAROSH, G. A. '"Mazepa" P. I. Chaikovskogo', *Moskovskie vedomosti* (2 Jan 1889): 3–4.
— [repr.] In: G. A. Larosh, *Izbrannye stat´i v piati vypuskakh*, vyp. 2 (1975): 129–135 [see *2376*].

[*3281*] *"Mazepa": Opera Chaikovskogo*. Libretto. Kazan´, 1890. 23 p.

[*3282*] *"Mazepa": Opera, muzyka P. I. Chaikovskogo*. Kazan´: Izdat. Tovarishchestva opernykh i dramaticheskikh artistov, predstavitel´ A. M. Gorin-Gorianov, 1891. 4 p.

[*3283*] ENGEL´, Iu. D. "Mazepa", *Kur´er* (3 Sep 1899).

[*3284*] *Kratkoe libretto opery "Mazepa"*. S nebol´shoi biografiei kompozitora. Irkutsk, 1898. 4 p.

[*3285*] *"Mazepa": Opera P. I. Chaikovskogo*. Odessa: Odesskoi gorodskoi teatr, 1900.

[*3286*] ENGEL´, Iu. D. 'Chastnaia opera. "Mazepa", opera Chaikovskogo', *Kur´er* (8 Feb 1900).

[*3287*] *Libretto opery "Mazepa"*. Kiev: Z. M. Sakhnin, 1902. 23 p.

[*3288*] *Kratkoe libretto opery "Mazepa"*. Kiev: S. M. Boguslavskii, 1908. 15 p.
— 2-e izd. Kiev: S. M. Boguslavskii, 1909. 16 p.

[*3289*] *"Mazepa": Opera, muzyka P. I. Chaikovskogo*. Moskva [1911]. 4 p.

[*3290*] *"Mazepa": Opera P. I. Chaikovskogo*. Libretto i biografiia Chaikovskogo. Khar´kov [1914]. 12 p.

[*3291*] LEL´. '"Mazepa" v Muzykal´noi drame', *Russkaia muzykal´naia gazeta* (5 Jan 1914), 1: 24.

[*3292*] TIDEBÖHL, E. von. 'Tchaikovsky's opera "Mazeppa"', *Monthly Musical Record*, 48 (Aug 1918): 174–176.

[*3293*] ASAF´EV, B. V. '"Mazepa": Opera v Tavricheskom sadu', *Zhizn´ iskusstva* (28 Jul 1920).
— [repr.] In: B. V. Asaf´ev, *Ob opere*. Leningrad: Muzyka, 1976: 211–212.

[*3294*] "Mazepa". In: G. Angert, *100 oper*. Libretto oper pod red. L. Sabaneeva. Moskva: Russkoe teatral´naia obshchestvo, 1927: 263–265.

[*3295*] NEWMARCH, R. H. 'Tchaikovsky: "Danse cosaque" from "Mazeppa"'. In: R. H. Newmarch, *The concert-goer's library of descriptive notes. Part III: Suites and ballet suites for orchestra, rhapsodies and fantasias, miscellaneous dances*. London: Oxford Univ. Press; H. Milford, 1930: 144.

[*3296*] N. Iu. '"Mazepa", opera P. Chaikovskogo: Soderzhanie opery', *Radioslushatel´* (1930), 18: 14.

[*3297*] UNGERER, J. "Mazeppa", *Allgemeine Musik Zeitung* (1931), 23.
The first production in Germany. See also *3298*, *3299*.

[*3298*] DORN. "Mazeppa", *Signale für die Musikalische Welt* (1931), 25/26.

[*3299*] HÖCHSTER, E. "Mazeppa", *Die Musik* (1931), 10: 759.

[*3300*] MANUILOV, V. & DRANISHNIKOV, V. A. *"Mazepa": Muzyka P. I. Chaikovskogo*. [Leningrad]: Leningradskii Gos. Akad. teatr opery i baleta, 1934. 67 p, illus.
Contents: V. A. Manuilov, '"Poltava" Pushkina': 3–31 — 'Muzykal´no-stsenicheskoe razvitie opery': 32–45 — V. Dranishnikov, 'Opera "Mazepa" (k istorii ee sochineniia): 45–64.
— 2-e izd. [Leningrad]: Leningradskoe Gos. Akad. teatr opery i baleta im. S. M. Kirova, 1936. 66 p, illus.

[*3301*] *"Mazepa": Opera, muzyka P. I. Chaikovskogo*. Sbornik. Moskva: Gos. Akad. Bol´shoi teatr SSSR, 1934. 47 p, illus. (*Muzei vystavka*).

Contents: A. P. Svetov, 'Istoricheskaia spravka': 3–8 — L. Grossman, '"Poltava" Pushkina': 9–19 — A. A. Groman-Solovtsov, '"Mazepa" i opernoe nasledie Chaikovskogo': 20–27 — L. P. Shteinberg, 'O "Mazepe"': 28–34 — L. V. Baratov, 'K postanovke "Mazepy"': 35–45.

[*3302*]   REMEZOV, I. *"Mazepa": Kriticheskii ocherk o "Poltave" Pushkina, "Mazepe" Chaikovskogo i libretto V. P. Burenina.* [Moskva]: Upravlenie teatrami NKP RSFSR, 1934. 99 p, illus.

— Izd. 2-e, dop. Moskva: Upravlenie teatrami NKP RSFSR, 1935. 103 p., illus.

[*3303*]   BLIUM, V. 'V zashchity starogo tipa', *Radiogazeta* (1934), 25: 2.

Concerning a radio broadcast of *Mazepa*.

[*3304*]   SIMSKII, M. 'Novye opernye transliatsii', *Radiogazeta* (1934), 24: 3.

Relating to a broadcast of *Mazepa* from the Bol´shoi Theatre, Moscow.

[*3305*]   KANN, E. '"Mazepa" v filiale Bol´shogo', *Vecherniaia Moskva* (16 May 1934).

[*3306*]   *"Mazepa": Opera P. I. Chaikovskogo.* Sverdlovsk: Gos. teatr opery i baleta im. A. V. Lunacharskogo, 1935. 10 p.

[*3307*]   RIADNOVA, N. *"Mazepa".* Tbilisi: Tbilisskii Gos. opernyi teatr. [c.1935]. 23 p.

[*3308*]   *"Mazepa": Opera, muzyka P. I. Chaikovskogo.* Gor´kii: Gor´kovskii obl. teatr opery i baleta im. A. S. Pushkina, 1937. 63 p.

Includes Pushkin's poem 'Poltava', and a synopsis of the opera.

[*3309*]   *"Mazepa": Opera, muzyka P. I. Chaikovskogo po poeme A. S. Pushkina 'Poltava'.* Saratov: Saratovskii teatr opery i baleta im. N. G. Chernyshevskogo, 1937. 17 p, illus.

A new production of the opera to mark the centenary of Pushkin's death.

— [2nd izd.] Saratov: Direktsiia oblastnogo teatra opery i baleta [1937]. 19 p, illus.

[*3310*]   *"Mazepa".* Libretto opery P. I. Chaikovskogo. Moskva: Gos. ordena Lenina Akad. Bol´shoi teatr SSSR, 1938. 4 p.

[*3311*]   *"Mazepa".* Polnyi tekst libretto. Moskva: Iskusstvo, 1938. 84 p.

Complete libretto, with introduction by B. Iarustovskii, '"Mazepa" P. I. Chaikovskogo'.

[*3312*]   *"Mazepa": Opera P. I. Chaikovskogo.* Programma i libretto. Perm´: Permskii teatr opery i baleta, 1938. 10 p.

[*3313*]   *"Mazepa": Opera P. I. Chaikovskogo.* Tekst V. P. Burenina. Kuibyshev: Kuibyshevskii teatr opery i baleta, 1938. 4 p.

[*3314*]   'Kalendar´ iskusstv: 20 fevralia 1884', *Dekada moskovskikh zrelishch* (Feb 1939), 6: 14.

The 55th anniversary of the first production of the opera in St. Petersburg.

[*3315*]   *"Mazepa": Opera v 6-ti kartinakh.* Muzyka P. I. Chaikovskogo. Libretto M. I. Chaikovskogo po povesti A. S. Pushkina. Moskva: Gos. Akad. Bol´shoi teatr SSSR, 1949. 8 p.

[*3316*]   NEST´EV, I. *"Mazepa" P. Chaikovskogo.* Moskva; Leningrad: Gos. muz. izdat., 1949. 56 p, music, illus. (*Putevoditeli po pushkinskim operam*).

Review: I. F. Kunin, 'Novye knigi o Chaikovskom', *Sovetskaia kniga* (1951), 2: 114–120.

— 2-e izd. Moskva: Gos. muz. izdat., 1959. 55 p, music, illus. (*Putevoditeli po russkoi muzyke*).

[*3317*]   BERLIAND-CHERNAIA, E. *"Mazepa".* In: E. Berliand-Chernaia, *Pushkin i Chaikovskii* (1950): 77–99 [see *2134*].

[*3318*] *"Mazepa"*. Moskva: Iskusstvo, 1951. 23 p, illus.

[*3319*] 'Group puts on Tchaikovsky's "Mazeppa"', *Musical America*, 71 (1 Dec 1951): 19.

[*3320*] *"Mazepa": Opera v 3-kh deistviiakh*. Siuzhet´ zaimstvovan iz poemy Pushkina. Muzyka P. Chaikovskogo. Moskva: Gos. muz. izdat., 1953. 79 p. (*Opernye libretto*).
Complete libretto.
— 2-e izd. *"Mazepa": Opera v 3 deistviiakh i 6 kartinakh*. Libretto V. P. Burenin. Polnyi tekst. V pererabotke P. I. Chaikovskogo. Vstup. stat´ia E. Eremeevoi. Moskva: Muzyka, 1964. 87 p. (*Opernye libretto*).

[*3321*] SEROFF, V. "Tchaikovsky's "Mazeppa"', *Saturday Review*, 37 (27 Nov 1954): 52.
A survey of recordings of the opera.

[*3322*] SLONIMSKY, N. "Mazeppa", *Musical Quarterly*, 42 (Jan 1956): 128–129.

[*3323*] 'Listok iz zapisnoi knizhki Chaikovskogo', *Sovetskaia kul´tura* (12 Nov 1959).
The discovery of a page of sketches for *Mazepa*.

[*3324*] PAULS, J. P. 'Musical works based on the legend of Mazeppa', *Ukrainian Review*, 11 (win. 1964): 61–64.

[*3325*] NEST´EV, I. "Mazepa". In: N. Nikolaeva, *Opery P. I. Chaikovskogo: Putevoditel´* (1970): 132–170 [see 2592].

[*3326*] PROTOPOPOV, V. 'Muzyka petrovskogo vremeni o pobede pod Poltavoi', *Sovetskaia muzyka* (1971), 12: 97–105, illus.

[*3327*] "Mazepa". In: G. Kobbe, *Kobbe's complete opera book*. Ed. and rev. by the Earl of Harewood. London: Putnam, 1976: 920–926.
— [rev. ed.] G. Kobbe, The definitive Kobbe's opera book. Ed., rev. and updated by the Earl of Harewood. New York: Putnam, 1987: 739–744.

[*3328*] NORRIS, G. "Mazeppa", *Musical Times*, 121 (May 1980): 332.

[*3329*] FEIN, M. T. 'From poem to libretto: A comparison of Pushkin's "Poltava" and Cajkovskij's "Mazepa"'. Chapel Hill: Univ. of North Carolina, 1984. 72 p.
Dissertation.

[*3330*] BROWN, D. 'Tchaikovsky's "Mazeppa"', *Musical Times*, 125 (Dec 1984): 696–698, music.

[*3331*] WARRACK, J. 'Tchaikovsky's "Mazeppa"', *Opera*, 35 (Dec 1984), 12: 1309–1315, illus.

[*3332*] SADIE, S. 'Tchaikovsky's "Mazeppa"', *Musical Times*, 126 (1985): 106.

[*3333*] GUEST, G. 'More on "Mazeppa"', *Opera*, 36 (Jul 1985): 765.

[*3334*] SEIBERT, D. C. 'The dramaturgy of Tchaikovsky's "Mazeppa"': An interview with Mark Elder', *Music Review*, 49 (Nov 1988), 4: 272–288, music.

[*3335*] *"Mazeppa"*. In: *Opera plot index: A guide to locating plots and descriptions of operas, operettas, and other works of the musical theater, and associated material*. Comp. by William E. Studwell, David A. Hamilton. New York: Garland, 1990: 245. (*Garland Reference Library of the Humanities*; 1099).

[*3336*] PARIN, A. V. 'Liebe und Macht in Tschaikowskys Oper "Mazeppa". In: *Peter Tschaikowsky: "Mazeppa". Programmheft der Bregenzer Festspiele*. Bregenz: 1991: 16–19.

[*3337*] WAKELING, D. W. 'Tchaikovsky: "Mazeppa"', *Opera Quarterly* (sum. 1991): 186–188.

[3338]   *"Mazeppa": Opera in three acts by Pyotr Ilyich Tchaikovsky.* Libretto by the composer and Viktor
          Burenin after the lyric poem "Poltava" by Alexander Pushkin. [New York]: Opera Orchestra of New
          York [1993]. 56 p, music, illus.
          Text in English and Russian. Includes commentary by Benton Hess.

[3339]   **RUDICHENKO, T.** "Mazeppa", *Opera*, 46 (Jul 1995): 839–840.

[3340]   **PARIN, A. V.** 'Mazepa: Istoricheskoe litso, literaturnyi geroi, politecheskii simvol', *Mariinskii
          teatr* (1996), 3/4: 2–3.
          Examining the historical basis for Chaikovskii's opera.

[3341]   **KANSKI, J.** "Mazeppa", *Opera*, 47 (Nov 1996): 1341–1342.

[3342]   **NEEF, S.** "Masepa". In: *Pipers Enzyklopadie des Musiktheaters: Oper, Operette, Musical, Ballet. Hrsg. von
          Carl Dahlhaus und dem Forschungsinstitut fur Musiktheater der Universität Bayreuth unter Leitung von Sieghart
          Dohring.* Band 6. München: Piper, 1997: 342–344.

[3343]   **BELLINGARDI, L.** "Mazeppa", *Opera*, 48 (Feb 1997): 211.

[3344]   **EDGECOMBE, R. S.** 'Wagnerian elements in Tchaikovsky's "Mazeppa"', *Opera Journal*, 30 (Dec
          1997), 4: 21–30.

[3345]   **LOOMIS, G. W.** 'Shadow and Light', *Opera News*, 62 (11 Apr 1998), 15: 28–31.

[3346]   **TARUSKIN, R.** '"Mazeppa": Tchaikovsky's opera of dark cravings', *New York Times* (3 May 1998):
          16.
          In connection with the Kirov Opera's production at the Metropolitan Opera. See also *3347*.

[3347]   **TOMMASSINI, A.** 'Historical accuracy aside, true psychological battles', *New York Times* (4 May
          1998)m illus.

          See also *555, 556*.

THE OPRICHNIK
(1870–72)

[3348]   'Novosti', *Muzykal´nyi listok* (1872/73), 4: 59–62.
          Report of Chaikovskii's work on the opera.

[3349]   *"Oprichnik": Opera P. Chaikovskogo.* Siuzhet zaimstvovan iz dramy Lazhechnikova. Sankt Peterburg:
          V. Bessel, 1874. 44 p.
          Original libretto.
          — [2-e izd.] *"Oprichnik": Opera v 4 deistviiakh P. Chaikovskogo.* Siuzhet zaimstvovan iz dramy Lazhechnikova.
          Sankt Peterburg: V. Bessel´, 1878. 39 p.
          — [repr.] Sankt Peterburg: V. Bessel´, 1896, 1900, 1903, 1905, 1906.
          — [3-e izd.] *"Oprichnik": Opera v 4 deistviiakh.* Siuzhet zaimstvovan iz dramy Lazhechnikova. Muzyka P. I.
          Chaikovskogo. Petrograd; Moskva, 1917. 48 p.

[3350]   'Muzykal´nye novosti', *Muzykal´nyi svet* (Jan 1874), 1: 7.
          Preparations for the first production. See also *3351, 3352*.

[3351]   'Peterburgskaia letopis´', *Syn Otechestva* (28 Mar 1874).

[3352]   'Teatr i muzyka', *Sankt Peterburgskie vedomosti* (28 Mar 1874).

[3353]   **S.** 'Muzykal´noe obozrenie', *Birzhevye vedomosti* (13 Apr 1874).
          The first production of the opera on 12 Apr 1874 in St. Petersburg. See also *3354 to 3371*.

[3354] 'Teatr i muzyka', *Sankt Peterburgskie vedomosti* (14 Apr 1874).

[3355] 'Teatral'nyi kur'er', *Peterburgskii listok* (14 Apr 1874).

[3356] T. '"Oprichnik": Opera P. I. Chaikovskogo', *Russkie vedomosti* (16 Apr 1874).

[3357] 'Teatr i muzyka', *Sankt Peterburgskie vedomosti* (16 Apr 1874).

[3358] [BASKIN, V. S.] '"Oprichnik", opera Chaikovskogo', *Peterburgskii listok* (17 Apr 1874).

[3359] LAROSH, G. A. '"Oprichnik", opera v 4-kh deistviiakh', *Golos* (17 Apr 1874): 1.
— [repr.] In: G. A. Larosh, *Sobranie muzykal'no- kriticheskikh statei*, tom 2, chast' 1 (1924): 116–123 [see *2311*].
— [repr.] In: G. A. Larosh, *Izbrannye stat'i v piati vypuskakh*, vyp. 2 (1975): 55–61 [see *2376*].
— [English tr.] '"Oprichnik": An opera in four acts'. In: S. Campbell, *Russians on Russian music* (1994): 240–245 [see *2408*].
— [German tr.] '"Der Opritschnik": Eine Oper in vier Akten von Peter Tschaikowsky'. In: G. A. Larosh, *Peter Tschaikowsky: Aufsätze und Erinnerungen* (1993): 80–88 [see *2406*].

[3360] R[OSTISLAV], M. *Russkii mir* (17 Apr 1874).

[3361] GOST. 'Stolichnye tolki: Novaia opera "Oprichnik"...Tolki ob muzyke Chaikovskogo', *Vsemirnaia illiustratsiia* (20 Apr 1874).

[3362] [LENZ, V.] 'Opéra russe: "L'Opritchnik" (Le garde du corps), opéra et 5 tableaux', *Journal de St. Pétersbourg* (20 Apr/2 May 1874).

[3363] S. 'Muzykal'noe obozrenie', *Birzhevye vedomosti* (20 Apr 1874).

[3364] LAROSH, G. A. '"Oprichnik": Opera P. Chaikovskogo', *Muzykal'nyi listok* (21 Apr 1874): 321–325; (28 Apr 1874): 337–344.
— [repr.] In: G. A. Larosh, *Muzykal'no-kriticheskie stat'i*, Sankt Peterburg: V. Bessel', 1894: 45–55.
— [repr.] In: G. A. Larosh, *Sobranie muzykal'no-kriticheskikh statei*, tom 2, chast' 1 (1924): 106–115 [see *2311*].
— [repr.] In: G. A. Larosh, *Izbrannye stat'i v piati vypuskakh*, vyp. 2 (1975): 61–69 [see *2376*].

[3365] B. V. '"Oprichnik": Opera g. Chaikovskogo', *Peterburgskaia gazeta* (23 Apr 1874).

[3366] 'Fel'eton: "Oprichnik" opera Chaikovskogo', *Modnyi svet* (23 Apr 1874).

[3367] [KIUI, Ts. A.] 'Muzykal'nye zametki: "Oprichnik", opera g. Chaikovskogo', *Sankt Peterburgskie vedomosti* (23 Apr 1874): 1–2.

[3368] B. V. '"Oprichnik": Opera g. Chaikovskogo', *Peterburgskaia gazeta* (25 Apr 1874).

[3369] MAKAROV, P. '"Oprichnik": Opera, soch. P. I. Chaikovskogo', *Muzykal'nyi svet* (11 May 1874): 33–37.

[3370] ORFEI. 'Tolki ob "Oprichnike"', *Muzykal'nyi svet* (11 May 1874).

[3371] M[AGUR], D. A. '"Oprichnik" (opera P. I. Chaikovskogo)', *Vsemirnaia illiustratsiia* (1 Jun 1874): 366.

[3372] A. S. 'Un nouvelle opéra russe: "L'Opritchnik" de m. Tchaikofsky', *Journal d'Odessa* (13/25 Jul 1874).
Concerning the first production of the opera in Odessa on 16 Jul 1874. See also *3373, 3374, 3375*.

[3373] [Predstavlenie opery "Oprichnik"], *Odesskii vestnik* (30 Jul 1874).

[*3374*]   A. S. '"L'Opritchnik" de m. Tchaikofsky sur la scène d'Ermitage', *Journal d'Odessa* (3/15 Aug 1874).

[*3375*]   M. 'Muzykal´nye zametki: "Oprichnik", opera P. I. Chaikovskogo', *Odesskii vestnik* (4 Aug 1874).

[*3376*]   [LAROSH, G. A.]. 'Vnutrennie novosti: Peterburgskaia khronika', *Golos* (6 Oct 1874): 3.
        — [repr.] In: G. A. Larosh, *Sobranie muzykal´no-kriticheskikh statei*, tom 2, chast´ 1 (1924): 124 [see *2311*].
        — [repr.] 'Vozobnovlenie "Oprichnika"'. In: G. A. Larosh, *Izbrannye stat´i v piati vypuskakh*, vyp. 2 (1975): 72–73 [see *2376*].

[*3377*]   'Muzykal´nye zametki', *Peterburgskaia gazeta* (8 Oct 1874).
        The revival of the opera in St. Petersburg. See also *3378*.

[*3378*]   'Fel´eton´', *Vsemirnaia illiustratsiia* (16 Nov 1874).

[*3379*]   "Oprichnik", *Kievskii listok ob´iavlennii* (18 Dec 1874).
        The first production in Kiev on 9 Dec 1874. See also *3380*.

[*3380*]   N. 'Russkaia opera v Kieve: "Oprichnik"', *Kievlianin* (21 Dec 1874).

[*3381*]   *"Oprichnik": Opera P. Chaikovskogo*. Podrobnoe izlozhenie soderzhaniia opery. Kiev, 1875. 14 p.

[*3382*]   'Moskovskie zametki: Neozhidannaia sopernitsa g. Chaikovskogo', *Golos* (6 May 1875).
        The first production in Moscow on 4 May 1875. See also *3383* to *3386*.

[*3383*]   [HUBERT, N. A.] '"Oprichnik", opera v 4-kh deistviiakh P. I. Chaikovskogo', *Moskovskie vedomosti* (11 May 1875).

[*3384*]   KASHKIN, N. D. '"Oprichnik" na moskovskoi stsene', *Russkie vedomosti* (11 May 1875).
        — [repr.] In: N. D. Kashkin, *Izbrannye stat´i o P. I. Chaikovskom* (1954): 53–57 [see *2349*].

[*3385*]   'Teatr i muzyka', *Novoe vremia* (20 May 1875).

[*3386*]   B. 'Russkaia opera', *Odesskii vestnik* (1 Jul 1875).

[*3387*]   SAM PO SEBE. 'Russkie dramaticheskie spektakli', *Kievlianin* (15 Jul 1875).

[*3388*]   'Teatr i muzyka', *Novoe vremia* (21 Sep 1875).

[*3389*]   G[ALLER], K. P. 'Mariinskii teatr: "Oprichnik", opera P. I. Chaikovskogo. Debiut g-zhi Kadminoi', *Birzhevye vedomosti* (24 Oct 1875).

[*3390*]   [LAROSH, G. A. "Oprichnik"], *Golos* (24 Oct 1875).
        — [repr.] In: G. A. Larosh, *Izbrannye stat´i v piati vypuskakh*, vyp. 2 (1975): 77–78 [see *2376*].

[*3391*]   N. 'Russkaia opera v Kieve', *Kievlianin* (8 Nov 1877).

[*3392*]   VBR. '"Oprichnik": Bol´shaia opera v chetyrekh deistviiakh P. I. Chaikovskogo', *Saratovskii spravochnyi listok* (28 May 1878).

[*3393*]   LA. 'Opera "Oprichnik"', *Saratovskii spravochnyi listok* (15 Jun 1878).

[*3394*]   NEMO [IUSKEVICH-KRASKOVSKII, A. I.] 'Russkaia opera v Kieve, "Oprichnik" Chaikovskogo', *Kievskii listok* (11 Nov 1878).

[*3395*]   AMICUS [MONTEVERDE, P. A.] 'Beseda: Strannoe prikliuchenie s "Oprichnikom"', *Sankt Peterburgskie vedomosti* (30 Jan 1880).
        Concerning rumours that the opera was to be withdrawn from the repertoire on the instructions of the state censor. See also *3396*.

[3396] LUKIN, A. 'Tainstvennye prichiny, pomeshavshie opere g. Chaikovskogo "Oprichnik" byt´ postavlennoi na stsene: Uchastie v etom dele g. Shchurovskogo', *Molva* (9 Feb 1880).

[3397] ADE. '"Oprichnik", opera Chaikovskogo', *Sovremennye izvestiia* (18 Feb 1880).

[3398] 'Russkaia opera: Opera "Oprichnik" Chaikovskogo i predstavlenie ee na stsene zdeshnego Bol´shogo teatra', *Sovremennye izvestiia* (25 Feb 1880).
Revival of the opera at the Bol´shoi Theatre in Moscow.

[3399] 'Izvestiia otovsiudu', *Nuvellist* (Mar 1880): 8–11.

[3400] 'Nashi muzykal´nye i teatral´nye kritiki', *Russkaia gazeta* (2 Mar 1880).

[3401] RAZMADZE, A. S. 'Teatr i muzyka', *Russkii kur´er* (30 Nov 1880).

[3402] R. [LAROSH, G. A.] 'Pis´mo iz Peterburga', *Moskovskie vedomosti* (2 Feb 1890): 6.
A production of the opera by students of the St. Petersburg Conservatory on 18 Dec 1889.
— [repr.] In: G. A. Larosh, *Izbrannye stat´i v piati vypuskakh*, vyp. 2 (1975): 144–145 [see *2376*].

[3403] 'Teatr i muzyka', *Novoe vremia* (14 Nov 1893): 4.
Chaikovskii's work on *The Oprichnik*.

[3404] BESSEL´, V. V. 'Iz vospominanii o P. I. Chaikovskom: "Oprichnik"', *Novoe vremia* (7 Oct 1896).

[3405] 'Teatr i muzyka', *Novoe vremia* (21 Oct 1896): 3.
On the first publication of the full score.

[3406] *"Oprichnik": Opera P. Chaikovskogo*. Odessa: I. T. Loginov, 1897. 4 p.

[3407] 'Raznye izvestiia: Firma V. Bessel´ i komp.', *Russkaia muzykal´naia gazeta* (Jan 1897), 1: 156.
Negotiations between the publishing firm Bessel´ and the Imperial Theatres concerning a revival of the opera.

[3408] 'Muzykal´noe obozrenie', *Nuvellist* (Oct 1897), 6: 1–2.

[3409] BESSEL´, V. V. 'Neskol´ko slov po povodu vozobnovleniia "Oprichnika" P. Chaikovskogo na stsene Mariinskogo teatra', *Russkaia muzykal´naia gazeta* (Dec 1897), 12: 1717–1720.

[3410] *Libretto opery "Oprichnik"*. Kiev: Z. M. Sakhnin, 1901. 23 p.

[3411] *"Oprichnik": Opera v 4 deistviiakh P. Chaikovskogo*. Sankt Peterburg [V. Travskii], 1903. 15 p.

[3412] KOMPANEISKII, N. 'Po povodu protsessa iz-za "Oprichnika" (pis´ma v redaktsiiu)', *Russkaia muzykal´naia gazeta* (19/26 Dec 1904), 51/52: 1274–1275.
Regarding the publication of the score by Bessel´.

[3413] *Libretto opery "Oprichnik"*. Muzyka P. I. Chaikovskogo. Soderzhanie opery s sokhraneniem teksta glavnykh arii. Kiev, S. M. Boguslavskii, 1909. 15 p.
— 2-e izd. *P. I. Chaikovskii: "Oprichnik"*. Libretto po drame I. I. Lazechnikova. Soderzhanie opery s sokhraneniem teksta glavnykh arii. Kiev: S. M. Boguslavskii, 1909 [1910]. 15 p.

[3414] IUR´EV, M. "Oprichnik", *Rampa i zhizn´* (1911), No. 38.

[3415] *"Oprichnik": Opera, muzyka P. I. Chaikovskogo*. Riga, 1914. 7 p.

[3416] *"Oprichnik": Opera v 4 deistviiakh*. Libretto i biografiei P. I. Chaikovskogo. Khar´kov, 1914. 12 p.

[*3417*]   STEPANOVICH, A. I. *Mysli ob opere P. I. Chaikovskogo "Oprichnik"*. Nezhin, 1915. 15 p.

[*3418*]   '"Oprichnik" v sverdlovskoi opere', *Sovetskoe iskusstvo* (24 May 1940): 1.
           A special production of the opera in Sverdlovsk, to mark the centenary of Chaikovskii's birth.

[*3419*]   VOLGII, Iu. '"Oprichnik": Novyi spektakl´ Kirgiz. Gos. teatra opery i baleta', *Sovetskaia Kirgiziia*
           (12 Jun 1957).

[*3420*]   'On records: Tchaikovsky's "Oprichnik", "Maid of Orleans"', *Opera News*, 30 (Jun 1966): 30.

[*3421*]   LESS, A. 'Neizvestnyi avtograf Chaikovskogo', *Muzykal´naia zhizn´* (1972), 7: 16, illus.
           Concerning a one bar phrase from Natal´ia's arioso ('Akh vy vetry buinye') written by Chaikovskii in an
           album belonging to the singer Aleksandra Men´shikova, on 5 Nov 1889.

[*3422*]   LEHEL, F. 'Au coeur de l'opera russe', *Harmonie-Antenne* (Oct 1979): 10–11.

[*3423*]   *"The Oprichnik": An opera in 4 acts*. Libretto and music by Pyotr Ilich Tchaikovsky. Tr. and notes by
           Philip Taylor. London: Collet's, 1980. 85 p, music, illus. ISBN: 0-5690-8605-1.
           Libretto in English and Russian (Cyrillic). Includes synopsis in English and notes by German Larosh.
           Review: J. Warrack, *Opera*, 31 (Oct 1980): 1022–1023.

[*3424*]   ARSHINOVA, N. S. 'K probleme opernogo psikhologizma v proizvedeniiakh P. I. Chaikovskogo
           "Oprichnik" i "Charodeika"'. In: *Teatr v zhizni i tvorchestve P. I. Chaikovskogo* (1985): 110–120 [see
           589].

[*3425*]   SIN´KOVSKAIA, N. 'Neizvestnaia stranitsa', *Sovetskaia muzyka* (1986), 6: 81–86, music, illus.
           The discovery in the Klin House-Museum archives of an additional aria for Viazminskii, written by
           Chaikovskii in 1878 for the singer Bogomir Korsov. Includes the complete score. See also *3426*.

[*3426*]   SIN´KOVSKAIA, N. 'Zabytaia partitura: Naidena novaia stranitsa opery "Oprichnik"', *Sovetskaia
           Rossiia* (25 Apr 1986): 6.

[*3427*]   *"Oprichnik"*. In: *Opera plot index: A guide to locating plots and descriptions of operas, operettas, and other works
           of the musical theater, and associated material*. Comp. by William E. Studwell, David A. Hamilton. New
           York: Garland, 1990: 281. (*Garland Reference Library of the Humanities*; 1099).

[*3428*]   ZAJACZKOWSKI, H. 'Tchaikovsky's "Oprichnik": A great work', *Musical Times*, 133 (Oct 1992):
           537.

[*3429*]   MUGINSTEIN, M. "Opritschnik". In: *Pipers Enzyklopadie des Musiktheaters: Oper, Operette, Musical,
           Ballet. Hrsg. von Carl Dahlhaus und dem Forschungsinstitut fur Musiktheater der Universität Bayreuth unter
           Leitung von Sieghart Dohring*. Band 6. München: Piper, 1997: 329–330.

[*3430*]   CUNNINGHAM, T. T. 'Terrible visions: The sublime image of Ivan the Terrible in Russian
           opera'. Princeton: Princeton University, 1999. 164 p.
           Dissertation (Ph. D.).

[*3431*]   EGGERS, S. B. 'Culture and nationalism: Tchaikovsky's visions of Russia in "The Oprichink".
           In: *Tchaikovsky and his contemporaries* (1999): 139–146 [see *602*]

[*3432*]   SWARTZ, A. 'The intrigue of love and illusion in Tchaikovsky's "The Oprichink"'. In: *Tchaikovsky
           and his contemporaries* (1999): 147–154 [see *602*].

[*3433*]   GRUM-GRZHIMAILO, T. '"Oprichnik"—on zhe kromeshnik', *Literaturnaia gazeta* (17 Feb 1999):
           11, illus.
           A new production of the opera at the Bol´shoi Theatre in Moscow.

OTHELLO
Projected opera in 4 acts (1876–77)

[*3434*] 'Muzykal´nye i teatral´nye novosti', *Muzykal´nyi svet* (16 Jan 1877): 35.

A report that Chaikovskii is considering a libretto on Shakespeare's *Othello*.

THE QUEEN OF SPADES
Opera in 3 acts, Op. 68 (1890)

[*3435*] ***"Pikovaia dama": Opera v 3-kh deistviiakh i 7 kartinakh***. Muzyka P. Chaikovskogo. Tekst Modesta Chaikovskogo (na siuzhet A. S. Pushkina). Moskva: P. Iurgenson, 1890. 67 p.

Original libretto.

— 2-e izd. Moskva: P. Iurgenson, 1900. 67 p.

[*3436*] ***"Pikovaia dama": Opera v trekh deistviiakh i semi kartinakh***. Muzyka P. I. Chaikovskogo. Sankt Peterburg: Izdat. tip. Imperatorskikh teatrov, 1890. 15 p.

[*3437*] ***"Pique-Dame": Oper in 3 Akten und 7 Bildern***. Text von M. Tschaikowsky nach einer Puschkin'schen Novelle. Für die deutsche Bühne bearbeitet von Max Kalbeck. Musik von P. Tschaikovsky, Op. 68. Hamburg, Leipzig: D. Rahter [1890?]. 68 p.

[*3438*] KASHKIN, N. D. '"Pikovaia dama": Opera v 3-kh deistviiakh i 7-mi kartinakh', *Russkoe obozrenie* (Dec 1890), 6: 780–793.

The first production on 7 Dec 1890 in St. Petersburg. See also *3439* to *3445, 3447, 3448, 3449*.

— [repr.] In: N. D. Kashkin, *Izbrannye stat´i o P. I. Chaikovskom* (1954): 129–147 [see *2349*].

[*3439*] "Pikovaia dama", *Novosti i birzhevaia gazeta* (8 Dec 1890).

[*3440*] BASKIN, V. "Pikovaia dama", *Peterburgskaia gazeta* (9 Dec 1890).

[*3441*] SOLOV´EV, N. F. '"Pikovaia dama": Opera P. Chaikovskogo', *Novosti i birzhevaia gazeta* (9 Dec 1890).

[*3442*] IVANOV, M. M. "Pikovaia dama", *Novoe vremia* (10 Dec 1890).

[*3443*] DELIER, Ia. '"Pikovaia dama": P. I. Chaikovskogo', *Sankt Peterburgskie vedomosti* (12 Dec 1890).

[*3444*] KASHKIN, N. D. "Pikovaia dama", *Russkie vedomosti* (14 Dec 1890).

— [repr.] In: N. D. Kashkin, *Izbrannye stat´i o P. I. Chaikovskom* (1954): 114–128 [see *2349*].

[*3445*] '"Pikovaia dama": Opera v 3-kh deistviiakh i 7 kartinakh', *Peterburgskii listok* (20 Dec 1890).

[*3446*] CHECHOTT, V. A. 'Opernyi teatr', *Kievlianin* (21 Dec 1890).

The first production in Kiev on 19 Dec 1890.

[*3447*] FINDEIZEN, N. F. '"Pikovaia dama": Opera P. I. Chaikovskogo'. In: N. F. Findeizen, *Muzykal´nye ocherki i eskizy*. Sankt Peterburg, 1891: 28–45.

[*3448*] KASHKIN, N. D. '"Pikovaia dama": Opera v 3-kh deistviiakh i 7-mi kartinakh', *Artist* (Jan 1891), 12: 171–178.

[*3449*] N. 'Pis´mo iz Peterburga', *Moskovskie vedomosti* (1 Jan 1891).

[*3450*] KASHKIN, N. D. "Pikovaia dama", *Russkie vedomosti* (5 Nov 1891).

The first production in Moscow on 4 Nov 1891. See also *3451* to *3457*.

— [repr.] In: N. D. Kashkin, *Izbrannye stat´i o P. I. Chaikovskom* (1954): 159–163 [see *2349*].

[*3451*]   'Teatr i muzyka', *Russkii listok* (5 Nov 1891).

[*3452*]   'Teatral´nye i muzykal´nye izvestiia', *Moskovskie vedomosti* (6 Nov 1891).

[*3453*]   K[ASHK]IN, N. D. '"Pikovaia dama" v Bol´shom teatre', *Moskovskii listok* (7 Nov 1891).

[*3454*]   'Teatral´nye i muzykal´nye izvestiia', *Moskovskie vedomosti* (7 Nov 1891).

[*3455*]   KASHKIN, N. D. "Pikovaia dama", *Russkie vedomosti* (10 Nov 1891).

[*3456*]   'Teatral´nye i muzykal´nye izvestiia', *Moskovskie vedomosti* (11 Nov 1891).

[*3457*]   'Teatral´nye i muzykal´nye izvestiia', *Moskovskie vedomosti* (21 Dec 1891).

[*3458*]   *Kratkoe soderzhanie opery v 3 deistviiakh i 7 kartinakh "Pikovaia dama" (na siuzhet A. S. Pushkina).*
             Muzyka P. I. Chaikovskogo. Moskva: A. A. Levenson, 1892. 16 p.
             — [repr.] Moskva: Tipografiia Imperatorskikh teatrov, 1893. 16 p.

[*3459*]   'Zagranichnaia khronika', *Artist* (Oct 1892): 198.
             The first production in Prague on 30 Sep/12 Oct 1892. See also *3460* to *3465*.

[*3460*]   CHVALA, E. "Piková dáma", *Narodni Politika* (1/13 Oct 1892).

[*3461*]   HEYDA, F. "Piková dáma", *Dalibor* (1/13 Oct 1892).

[*3462*]   NOVOTNY, J. ["Piková dáma"], *Hlas Naroda* (1/13 Oct 1892).

[*3463*]   '"Pikovaia dama" v Prage', *Moskovskie vedomosti* (5 Oct 1892).

[*3464*]   'Teatr i muzyka', *Novoe vremia* (7 Oct 1892): 3.

[*3465*]   'Izvestiia otovsiudu', *Nuvellist* (Nov 1892), 7: 6–8.

[*3466*]   W. '"Pikovaia dama" P. I. Chaikovsogo' *Saratovskii dnevnik* (2 Dec 1892).
             The first production in Saratov on 23 Nov 1892.

[*3467*]   N. N. '"Pikovaia dama" P. I. Chaikovskogo', *Odesskie novosti* (19 Jan 1893).
             The first production in Odessa on 19 Jan 1893. See also *3468* to *3476*.

[*3468*]   REBIKOV, V. '"Pikovaia dama": Opera P. I. Chaikovskogo', *Odesskii listok* (19 Jan 1893).

[*3469*]   LAPIS 'Gorodskoi teatr', *Odesskie novosti* (20 Jan 1893).

[*3470*]   O[BOLENSKII], L. 'Muzyka Chaikovskogo voobshche i "Pikovoi damy" v osobennosti', *Odesskie novosti* (20 Jan 1893).

[*3471*]   'Teatr i muzyka', *Odesskii listok* (20 Jan 1893).

[*3472*]   HOMO-NOVUS. 'Gorodskoi teatr: "Pikovaia dama"', *Odesskii listok* (21 Jan 1893).

[*3473*]   MAESTRO. 'Iskusstvo i literatura: Gorodskoi teatr', *Odesskii vestnik* (21 Jan 1893).

[*3474*]   OBOLENSKII, L. E. 'Muzyka Chaikovskogo voobshche i "Pikovoi damy" v osobennosti', *Odesskie novosti* (21 Jan 1893).

[*3475*]   SOLO "Pikovaia dama", *Odesskie novosti* (21 Jan 1893).

[*3476*]   VERITA. "Russkaia opera", *Novorossiiskii telegraf* (21 Jan 1893).

[3477] *"Pikovaia dama": Opera P. I. Chaikovskogo*. Sokrashchennoe libretto. Kiev: Kievskii gorodskoi teatr, 1895. 15 p.

[3478] LAROSH, G. A. 'Mariinskii teatr: Vozobnovlenie "Pikovoi damy" 14 aprelia', *Novosti i birzhevaia gazeta* (16 Apr 1895): 3.
— [repr.] In: G. A. Larosh, *Izbrannye stat´i v piati vypuskakh*, vyp. 2 (1975): 189–193 [see *2376*].
— [German tr.] 'Tschaikowskys Oper "Pique Dame"'. In: G. A. Larosh, *Peter Tschaikowsky: Aufsätze und Erinnerungen* (1993): 164–168 [see *2406*].

[3479] LAROSH, G. A. '"Pikovaia dama" v Mariinskom teatre 27 aprelia', *Novosti i birzhevaia gazeta* (29 Apr 1895): 3.
— [repr.] In: G. A. Larosh, *Izbrannye stat´i v piati vypuskakh*, vyp. 2 (1975): 193–195 [see *2376*].

[3480] *Soderzhanie opery "Pikovaia dama"*. Muzyka P. I. Chaikovskogo. Odessa: I. T. Loginov, 1898. 5 p.

[3481] *"Pikovaia dama"*. Odessa: Odesskii gorodskoi teatr, 1899.
— [repr.] Odessa: Odesskii gorodskoi teatr, 1900.

[3482] BORMAN, M. 'Muzykal´nye zametki', *Severnyi kur´er* (26 Mar 1900).

[3483] E. P. 'Mariinskii teatr', *Russkaia muzykal´naia gazeta* (7/14 May 1900), 19/20: 540–542.

[3484] *Libretto opery "Pikovaia dama"*. Kiev: Z. M. Sakhnin, 1901. 23 p.

[3485] ENGEL´, Iu. D. "Pikovaia dama", *Russkie vedomosti* (26 Oct 1901).

[3486] N. K. *"Pikovaia dama": Opera P. I. Chaikovskogo*. Moskva: A. A. Levenson, 1902. 7 p.
— [rev. repr.] Moskva, 1903. 6 p. (*Teatr Ermitazh. Tovarishchestvo Moskovskoi Chastnoi opery*).

[3487] *Soderzhanie opery "Pikovaia dama"*. Muzyka P. I. Chaikovskogo. Odessa: I. T. Loginov, 1902.

[3488] KARPATH, L. '"Pique Dame": Zur Erstaufführung in der Hofoper in Wien am 9. Dezember 1902', *Signale für die Musikalische Welt* (1902), 64/65.
The first production in Vienna.

[3489] VANCSA, M. "Pique-Dame", *Neue Musikalische Presse*, 11 (1902), 50 :657–659.

[3490] *Kratkoe libretto opery "Pikovaia dama"P. I. Chaikovskogo*. Sankt Peterburg: Ia. I. Baskin [1904]. 20 p.

[3491] *Libretto opery "Pikovaia dama"*. Muzyka P. I. Chaikovskogo. Odessa: Odesskii gorodskoi teatr, 1904.

[3492] *"La dama di picche"*. Dramma lirico in tre atti e sette quadri, tratto dalla novella omonima di Pushkin. Musica di Pietro Tcaikowski. Milano: G. Ricordi, 1906. 39 p.
Italian tr. of the libretto.

[3493] SCHWERS, P. 'Peter Tschaikowskys Oper "Pique Dame"L Besprechung der Erstaufführung an der Berliner Königlichen Oper, 20. März 1906', *Allgemeine Musik-Zeitung* (1906), 13.
The first production in Berlin.

[3494] VERZHBITSKII, I. K. *Opera "Pikovaia dama": Muzyka P. I. Chaikovskogo*. Sankt Peterburg, 1909. 26 p.

[3495] AL´ZUTSKII, I. Ia. *Kritika muzyki i libretto opery "Pikovaia dama" P. I. Chaikovskogo i M. I. Chaikovskogo*. Sankt Peterburg: Pechatnoe iskusstvo, 1910. 133 p, illus.

[3496] *"Pikovaia dama"*. Soderzhanie opery s sokhraneniem teksta glavnykh arii. Izd. 3-e. Kiev: S. M. Boguslavskii, 1910. 16 p.
— [repr.] Kiev: S. M. Boguslavskii, 1918. 16 p.

[*3497*]   *"Pikovaia dama": Opera na siuzhet A. S. Pushkina*. Muzyka P. I. Chaikovskogo. Moskva, 1910. 6 p.

[*3498*]   GILMAN, L. 'Tchaikovsky's opera "The Queen of Spades"', *Harper's Weekly*, 54 (19 Mar 1910), 7: 25.

[*3499*]   ENGEL´, Iu. D. '"Pikovaia dama" Chaikovskogo: Opera Zimina', *Russkie vedomosti* (3 Dec 1910).

[*3500*]   *"La Dame de Pique": Roman lyrique en trois actes et sept tableaux, d'aprés A. Pouchkine et M. Tschaïkowsky*. Paroles françaises de Michel Delines. Musique de P. Tschaikowsky, op. 68. Paris: A. Noël, 1911. 76 p.
— [repr.] Paris: A. Noël, 1932. 76 p.

[*3501*]   *"The Queen of Spades" / "Pique Dame": An opera in three acts and seven scenes*. Libretto by Modeste Tchaikovsky, founded on the tale by A. S. Pushkin; music by P. Tchaikovsky; English version by Rosa Newmarch. London & Brighton: J. & W. Chester [1915]. 47 p.

[*3502*]   *"Pikovaia dama": Opera P. I. Chaikovskogo*. Podrobnoe izlozhenie soderzhaniia opery s sokhraneniem teksta vsekh arii i numerov peniia. Kiev: Z. M. Sakhnin, 1915. 16 p.

[*3503*]   'Dva iubileia russkoi opery: "Pikovaia dama"', *Russkaia muzykal´naia gazeta* (8 Nov 1915), 45: 705–711.
The 25th anniversary of the first production of *The Queen of Spades* at the Mariinskii Theatre in St. Petersburg.

[*3504*]   NEWMAN, E. 'Tchaikovsky's "Pique Dame"', *Nation*, 17 (5 Jun 1915): 319–320.

[*3505*]   ARFWADSON, C. A. 'Tshaikovsky and "Pikovaia dama"', *20th Century Music*, 1 (Sep 1915): 52–54.

[*3506*]   *"Pikovaia dama": Opera P. I. Chaikovskogo*. Kratkoe libretto s sokhraneniem teksta glavnykh arii. Petrograd: Znamenskoi skoropechatni, 1918. 12 p.
— 2-e izd. Petrograd: Znamenskoi skorpoechatni, 1918. 12 p.

[*3507*]   *"Pique Dame" ("The Queen of Spades"): Opera in three acts*. Words by M. I. Tschaikovsky, founded on Pushkin's story of the same title. Music by P. I. Tschaikowsky. New York: F. Rullman [191–?]. 55 p.

[*3508*]   GLEBOV, I. [ASAF´EV, B. V.] 'Muzykal´naia restavratsiia opery Chaikovskogo v b. Mariinskom teatre'. In: *Biriuch petrogradskikh akadamecheskikh teatrov*. Sbornik statei pod. red. A. Poliakova. Sbornik. [Petrograd], 1920: 182–185.

[*3509*]   GLEBOV, I. [ASAF´EV, B. V.] *"Pikovaia dama": Opera v 3-kh deistviiakh i 7-mi kartinakh (na siuzhet A. S. Pushkina)*. Muzyka P. I. Chaikovskogo. Dekoratsiia po eskizam khudozhnika Aleksandra Benua. Petrograd: [Gos. Akad. teatr opery i baleta, 1921]. 39 p, illus.
— [repr.] In: B. V. Asaf´ev, *Kriticheskie stat´i, ocherki i retsenzii*. Moskva; Leningrad: Muzyka, 1967: 130–158.
— [repr.] In: B. V. Asaf´ev, *Simfonicheskie etiudy*. Leningrad: Muzyka, 1970: 158–194.
— [repr.] In: B. V. Asaf´ev, *O muzyke Chaikovskogo: Izbrannoe* (1972): 327–362 [see *2373*].

[*3510*]   GLEBOV, I. [ASAF´EV, B. V] *"Pikovaia dama": Opera P. I. Chaikovskogo (1840–1893)*. Petrograd [1921]. 11 p.

[*3511*]   '"Pikovaia dama" P. I. Chaikovskogo', *Kul´tura i teatr* (1921), 1: 27.

[*3512*]   DAVIDSON, G. 'Tchaikovsky: "The Queen of Spades"'. In: G. Davidson, *Stories from the Russian opera*. London: T. Laurie; Philadelphia, J. B. Lippincott [1922]: 225–238, illus.

[*3513*]   GLEBOV, I. [ASAF´EV, B. V] '"Pikovaia dama"'. In: I. Glebov, *Simfonicheskie etiudy*. Petrograd: Gos. filarmoniia, 1922: 201–247.
— [repr.] In: B. V. Asaf´ev, *Simfonicheskie etiudy*. Obshchaia red. i vstup. stat´ia E. M. Orlovoi. Leningrad: Muzyka, 1970: 141–158.

[*3514*] GLEBOV, I. [ASAF´EV, B. V.] 'K istorii izdaniia i postanovki opery P. I. Chaikovskogo "Pikovaia dama"', *Orfei* (1922), 1: 179–186.

[*3515*] NIKOL´SKAIA, G. '"Pikovaia dama": K 35-letiiu so dnia pervoi postanovki', *Rabochii i teatr* (Dec 1925), 50: 14.

The 35th anniversary of the first production.

[*3516*] GINTSBURG, S. 'Iubilei "Pikovoi damy"', *Krasnaia gazeta* (17 Jan 1926).

[*3517*] KANKAROVICH, A. 'P. I. Chaikovskii: "Pikovaia dama"'. In: A. Kankarovich, *Putevoditel´ po operam*. Leningrad, 1926: 20–24.

[*3518*] *"Pikovaia dama"*. Soderzhanie opery. Moskva: Teakinopechat´ [1927]. 7 p.

[*3519*] "Pikovaia dama". In: G. Angert, *100 oper*. Libretto oper pod red. L. Sabaneeva. Moskva: Russkoe teatral´noe obshchestvo, 1927: 257–260.

[*3520*] CH[EMODANOV], S. "Pikovaia dama", *Novosti radio* (1927), 6: 5.

In connection with a live radio broadcast from the Bol´shoi Theatre in Moscow.

[*3521*] *"Pikovaia dama" P. I. Chaikovskogo: Libretto opery*. Text M. Chaikovskogo. Vvedenie i podstrochnye primechaniia S. Chemodanova. Moskva: Gosizdat-Muzsektor, 1928, 63 p. (*Radioperedacha*).

[*3522*] BRAUDO, E. 'Muzykal´naia chast´ "Pikovoi damy"', *Sovremennyi teatr* (1928), 2: 28.

[*3523*] FEVRAL´SKII, A. '"Pikovaia dama": Problemy muzykal´noi dramy', *Sovremennyi teatr* (1928), 2: 26.

[*3524*] LIUTSH, V. "Pikovaia dama", *Muzyka i revolutsiia* (1928), 2: 33.

[*3525*] SHKLIAR, I. '"Pikovaia dama", muzyka Chaikovskogo', *Turkmenskaia iskra* (2 Jul 1928).

[*3526*] E. K. '"Pikovaia dama": Muzyka Chaikovskogo', *Polesskaia pravda* (4 Jul 1928).

[*3527*] *"Pikovaia dama": Opera P. I. Chaikovskogo*. Tekst izdaniia pod red. A. Obolenskogo. Moskva: Teakinopechat´, 1929. 103 p, illus.

— [2-e izd.] Moskva: Teakinopechat´, 1930. 95 p, illus.

[*3528*] *"Pikovaia dama": Opera v 3-kh deistviiakh, 7-mi kartinakh*. Muzyka P. I. Chaikovskogo. Tekst M. I. Chaikovskogo, na siuzhet A. S. Pushkina. [Moskva]: Teakinopechat´ i Boro, 1929. 16 p, illus. (*Putevoditel´ po opernym spektakliam*).

— 2-e izd. [Moskva]: Teakinopechat´, 1929. 16 p. (*Putevoditel´ po opernym spektakliam*).

— 3-e izd., ispr. [Moskva]: Teakinopechat´, 1930. 16 p, music, illus. (*Putevoditel´ po opernym spektaliam*).

— 4-e izd. [Moskva]: OGIZ; Gos. izdat. khudozh. literatury, 1931. 16 p. (*V pomoshch´ zriteliu*).

[*3529*] SHAVERDIAN, A. 'Opera v 44 dnia', *Radioslushatel´* (1929), 8: 10.

[*3530*] GINTSBURG, S. 'Eshche odna "Pikovaia dama"', *Vecherniaia Moskva* (4 Mar 1930).

In connection with a Stanislavskii Theatre production.

[*3531*] CHEMODANOV, S. "Pikovaia dama: Teatr im. Stanislavskogo", *Izvestiia* (24 Mar 1930).

[*3532*] ANNESLEY, C. "Pique Dame". In: C. Annesley, *The standard operaglass*. Detailed plots of the celebrated operas, with critical and biographical remarks and dates by Charles Annesley. With a prelude by James Huneker. Rev. ed. New York, Brentano's, 1931: 841–843.

— [rev. repr.] In: C. Annesley, *Home book of the opera*. New York: Dial Press, 1937: 533–534.

[*3533*]   **CHEPENSKAIA, K.** 'Nasledstvo proshlogo', *Zaochnoe muzykal´noe obuchenie* (1931), 6: 1–4.

A comparison of the roles of Liza in *The Queen of Spades* and Parasia in Musorgskii's *Sorochinskii Fair*.

[*3534*]   **RIADNOVA, N.** *"Pikovaia dama": Opera v 3-kh deistviiakh i v 7-mi kartinakh*. Kratkoe soderzhanie i muzykal´naia obzor. Tiflis: Tiflisskii Gos. opernyi teatr [1931]. 28 p.

[*3535*]   **"Pikovaia dama"**, *Sovetskoe iskusstvo* (23 May 1931).

Interview with N. Smolich.

[*3536*]   *"Pikovaia dama"*. Saratov: Saratovskii Obl. teatr opery i baleta im. N. G. Chernyshevskogo, 1933. 6 p.

[*3537*]   *"Pikovaia dama"*. Libretto pod red. S. A. Tsvetaeva. [Leningrad]: Biuro obsluzhivaniia rabochego zritelia pri upravlenii Leningradskikh Gos. opernykh teatrov, 1933. 62 p. (*V pomoshch´ zriteliu*).

Includes: S. Tsvetaev, 'P. I. Chaikovskii: Kratkii obzor ego tvorcheskogo puti i kratkii razbor muzykal´nyi dramaturgii opery "Pikovoi damy"': 39–62.

—   [2-e izd.] [Leningrad]: Leningradskii Gos. Akad. teatr opery i baleta, 1934. 48 p, illus.

[*3538*]   *"Pikovaia dama"*. Khar´kov: Gos. opernyi teatr im. K. S. Stanislavskogo, 1934. 10 p.

[*3539*]   *"Pikovaia dama"*. Saratov: Nizhne-Volzhskii kraevoi teatr opery i baleta im. Chernyshevskogo [1934]. 12 p. (*Muzyka v massy*).

[*3540*]   **REMEZOV, I.** *"Pikovaia dama": Opera v 3-kh deistviiakh*. Muzyka P. I. Chaikovskogo. Tekst M. I. Chaikovskogo. Risunki zasluzhennykh deiatelei iskusstv D. N. Kardovskogo i O. L. Della-Vos-Kardovskoi. [Moskva]: Upravlenie teatrami NKP RSFSR, 1934. 68 p, illus.

—   Izd. 2-e, dop. [Moskva]: Upravlenie teatrami NKPS RSFSR, 1935. 103 p, illus.

[*3541*]   **KUT, A.** 'Meierkhol´d o "Pikovoi dame"', *Sovetskoe iskusstvo* (1934), 54: 4.

Concerning Vsevolod Meierkhol´d's new production of the opera in Leningrad. See also *3542, 3543, 3545, 3547, 3548, 3549, 3551, 3552, 3556, 3604, 3636, 3683, 3703*.

[*3542*]   **ORLOVA, L.** 'Iz muzykal´noi zhizni Leningrada', *Sovetskaia muzyka* (1934), 11: 66–67.

[*3543*]   '"Pikovaia dama" v Gos. Malom opernom teatre', *Rabochii i teatr* (1934),2: 17.

[*3544*]   **GROMAN-SOLOVTSOV, A. A.** *Beseda ob opere "Pikovaia dama"*. Moskva: Upravlenie mestnogo veshchaniia VRK, 1935. 12 p.

[*3545*]   *"Pikovaia dama"*. Sbornik statei i materialov k postanovke opery 'Pikovaia dama' narodnym artistom respubliki V. E. Meierkhol´dom v Gos. Akad. Malom opernom teatre. Leningrad: Gos. Akad. Malyi opernyi teatre, 1935. 52 p, illus.

Contents: 'Ot teatra': 1–4 — V. E. Meierkhol´d, 'Pushkin i Chaikovskii': 5–11 [see *2129*] — A. Piotrovskii, '"Pikovaia dama" v Malom opernom teatre': 12–19   — B. V. Asaf´ev, 'O lirike "Pikovoi damy" Chaikovskogo': 20–24 — S. A. Samosud, 'Neskol´ko slov ot dirizhera': 25–26 — M. Kalaushin, 'Rabota Pushkina nad "Pikovoi damoi"': 27–37 — I. Sollertinskii, 'Meierkhol´d i muzykal´nyi teatr': 38–41 — A. M. 'Stsenicheskaia istoriia "Pikovoi damy"': 42–45   — 'Iz literaturnogo arkhiva': 46–50.

[*3546*]   *"Pikovaia dama": Opera, muzyka P. I. Chaikovskogo*. K 45-letiiu so dnia pervoi postanovki na stsene byvsh. Mariinskogo teatra, 1890–1935. Sbornik statei, pod red. Aleksandra Brodskogo. [Leningrad]: Leningradskii Gos. Akad. teatra opery i baleta im. S. M. Kirova, 1935. 119 p, music, illus.

Contents: 'Ot teatra': 6–9 — B. V. Asaf´ev, 'Tvorchestvo P. I. Chaikovskogo': 10–23 [see *2319*] — V. A. Dranishnikov, 'Muzykal´naia dramaturgiia "Pikovoi damy"': 24–56 — I. I. Sollertinskii, 'P. I. Chaikovskii i russkii simfonizm': 57–65 [see *4369*] — 'Pis´mo P. I. Chaikovskogo k I. A. Vsevolozhskomu': 66–68 [see *353*] — N. V. Smolich, 'O postanovke "Pikovoi damy"': 68–75 — E. A. Stark, 'Otzyvy pechati o pervoi postanovke "Pikovoi damy"': 76–88 — V. A. Manuilov, '"Pikovaia dama" Pushkina': 89–117 — A. M. B[rianskii], 'Primechaniia k iliustratsiiam': 118–119.

[*3547*]   **G. T.** 'Diskussia o "Pikovoi dame" v postanovke V. E. Meierkhol´da, 30/I 1935 g.', *Sovetskaia muzyka* (1935), 4: 95–96.

[3548] GRES, S. '"Pikovaia dama": Kriticheskii ocherk v dialogakh', *Zvezda* (1935), 5: 200–210.

[3549] SOLLERTINSKII, I. 'Chaikovskii i Meierkhol´d', *Rabochii i teatr* (1935), 3: 3–5.

[3550] ASAF´EV, B. V. 'Lirika "Pikovoi damy"', *Sovetskoe iskusstvo* (11 Jan 1935).
— [repr. (extract)] In: B. V. Asaf´ev, *Ob opere*. Leningrad: Muzyka, 1976: 212–216.

[3551] GINTSBURG, S. '"Pikovaia dama" v postanovke Meierkhol´da', *Krasnaia gazeta* (29 Jan 1935).

[3552] SMOLIICH, M. 'Postanovshchik o spektakle: K postanovke "Pikovoi damy" v Kirovskom teatre', *Leningradskaia pravda* (30 Jan 1935): 4.

[3553] BOGDANOV-BEREZOVSKII, V. M. "Pikovaia dama", *Literaturnyi Leningrad* (1 Feb 1935).

[3554] *"Pikovaia dama"*. Saratov: Saratovskii kraevoi teatr opery i baleta im. Chernyshevskogo, 1936. 40 p.

[3555] *"Pikovaia dama"*. Voronezh: Saratovskii kraevoi teatr opery i baleta im. Chernyshevskogo, 1936. 24 p.

[3556] CHEMODANOV, S. 'Leningradskii Malyi opernyi teatr', *Novyi mir* (1936), 4: 274–280.
Includes a section on Meierkhol´d's new production of *The Queen of Spades*. See also *3557*.

[3557] SHAVERDIAN, A. 'Put´ sovetskogo opernogo teatra', *Sovetskaia muzyka* (1936), 3: 61–69.

[3558] BUDIAKOVSKII, A. E. *"Pikovaia dama": Opera, muzyka P. I. Chaikovskogo*. Leningrad: Gos. Akad. teatr opery i baleta im. S. M. Kirova, 1937. 22 p, illus.
A comparison of the opera and Pushkin's novel.

[3559] BUDIAKOVSKII, A. E. *"Pikovaia dama": Opera v 7-mi kartinakh*. Muzyka P. I. Chaikovskogo. Tekst M. I. Chaikovskogo. Saratov: Obl. teatr opery i baleta, 1937. 10 p. (*Upravlenie po delam iskusstv pri Saratovskom oblispolkome*).

[3560] *"Pikovaia dama"*. Gor´kii: Gor´kovskii teatr opery i baleta im. A. S. Pushkina, 1937. 15 p, illus.

[3561] *"Pikovaia dama"*. Perm´: Permskii teatr opery i baleta, 1937. 16 p.

[3562] *"Pikovaia dama"*. Tekst M. I. Chaikovskogo. Moskva: Gos. muz. izdat., 1937. 96 p, illus.
Complete libretto. With introductory article by A. Ostretsov, '"Pikovaia dama" Chaikovskogo': 3–14.

[3563] 'Znamenatel´nye daty: 19 dekabria 1890 g. v Peterburgskom Mariinskom teatre byla vpervye postavlena "Pikovaia dama" Chaikovskogo', *Muzyka* (16 Dec 1937): 8.

[3564] OSTRETSOV, A. N. *"Pikovaia dama"*. Moskva: Gos. muz. izdat. 1938. 192 p, illus. (*Putevoditel´ po opere*).
History of the opera, musical analysis and libretto.

[3565] *"Pikovaia dama"*. Kuibyshev: Kuibyshevskii teatr opery i baleta, 1938. 4 p.

[3566] *"Pikovaia dama"*. Leningrad; Moskva: Iskusstvo, 1938. 104 p, illus.
Contents:M. Kalaushin, 'Rabota Pushkina nad "Pikovoi damoi": 3–52 — A. F. Stsenicheskaia istoriia opery "Pikovaia dama"': 52–71 — V. Bogdanov-Berezovskii: 'Opera P. Chaikovskogo "Pikovaia dama"': 71–93 — 'Stsenicheskoe izlozhenie deistviia': 94–101.

[3567] *"Pikovaia dama"*. Perm´: Permskii teatr opery i baleta, 1938. 8 p.

[3568] *"Pikovaia dama"*. Soderzhanie opery i programma. Rostov na Donu: Khar´kovskii Akad. teatr opery i baleta, 1938. 8 p.

[3569] *"Pikovaia dama": Foto*. Moskva: Soiuz foto-khudozhnik, 1938. 10 p.
Photographic record of the 1938 production at the Kirov Theatre, Leningrad.

[*3570*]   GRINBERG, M. 'Filosofokie motivy opery "Pikovaia dama": Zametki o muzykal´noi dramaturgii Chaikovskogo', *Teatr* (1938), 8: 86–107, 9: 88–106, illus.

[*3571*]   ANTAROVA, K. E. 'Moia rabota nad rol´iu grafini v "Pikovoi dame"'. In: *Chaikovskii i teatr* (1940): 232–239 [see *2537*].

[*3572*]   DERZHINSKAIA, K. G. 'Chaikovskii v moei zhizni'. In: *Chaikovskii i teatr* (1940): 203–210 [see *2537*].

[*3573*]   PECHKOVSKII, N. K. 'V poiskakh pravdivogo obraza'. In: *Chaikovskii i teatr* (1940): 224–231 [see *2537*].

[*3574*]   RUKAVISHNIKOV, N. K. 'Kak sozdavalas "Pastoral" iz "Pikovoi damy"', *Sovetskaia muzyka* (1940), 3: 45–46.

        Includes extracts from Chaikovskii's correspondence with his brother Modest.

[*3575*]   'Teatral´nyi kalendar´: 19 dekabria 1890 g.—Pervoe predstavlenie "Pikovoi damy" P. I. Chaikovskogo v Peterburge', *Teatr* (1940), 12: 144.

        The 50th anniversary of the first production.

[*3576*]   '"Pikovaia dama" na samodeiatel´noi stsene', *Pravda* (7 Feb 1940): 6.

        Concerning a special production of the opera in Leningrad to mark the centenary of Chaikovskii's birth. See also *3577*.

[*3577*]   KHUBOV, G. '"Pikovaia dama": Spektakl´ Leningradskogo teatra opery i baleta im S. M. Kirova', *Pravda* (19 May 1940).

        — [repr.] In: G. Khubov, *Muzykal´naia publitsistika raznykh let*. Moskva: Sovetskii kompozitor, 1976: 183–187.

[*3578*]   'Opere "Pikovaia dama": 50-let', *Leningradskaia pravda* (8 Dec 1940): 3.

[*3579*]   'V stolitse Uzbekistana: "Pikovaia dama" na uzbekskom iazyke', *Sovetskoe iskusstvo* (25 May 1945): 4.

        An Uzbek-language production of the opera in Tashkent (tr. by Khamid Guliam).

[*3580*]   '"Pikovaia dama" na ekrane', *Sovetskoe iskusstvo* (5 Oct 1945): 2.

        Plans for a film of the opera.

[*3581*]   BOGDANOV-BEREZOVSKII, V. M. *"Pikovaia dama" P. I. Chaikovskogo*. Leningrad: Gos. ordena Lenina Akad. teatr opery baleta im. S. M. Kirova, 1946. 25 p, illus.

[*3582*]   *"Pikovaia dama"*. Khar´kov: Khar´kovskii Gos. Akad. teatr opery i baleta im. M. V. Lysenko, 1947. 24 p.

        Text in Ukrainian and Russian

[*3583*]   *"Pikovaia dama"*. Kratkie poiasneniia k opere P. I. Chaikovskogo. Siuzhet zaimstvovan iz odnoimennoi povesti A. S. Pushkina. Kazan´ [Tatgosizdat], 1947. 15 p, illus.

[*3584*]   *"Pikovaia dama"*. Opera v 3-kh deistviiakh i 7-mi kartinakh. Muzyka P. I. Chaikovskogo. Libretto M. I. Chaikovskogo po povesti A. S. Pushkina. Moskva: Gos. Akad. Bol´shoi teatr SSSR, 1949. 12 p.

[*3585*]   SOLOVTSOV, A. A. *"Pikovaia dama" P. I. Chaikovskogo*. Moskva; Leningrad: Gos. muz. izdat,.1949. 103 p, music, illus. (*Putevoditeli po pushkinskim operam*).

        Review: I. F. Kunin, 'Novye knigi o Chaikovskom', *Sovetskaia kniga* (1951), 2: 114–120.

        — 2-e izd., pererab. Moskva: Gos. muz. izdat., 1954. 140 p, music, illus.

        Review: M. Teroganian, 'Opernye putevoditeli', *Sovetskaia muzyka* (1955), 2: 145–148.

        — 3-e izd. Moskva: Gos. muz. izdat., 1959. 151 p, music, illus.

[3586] IARUSTOVSKII, B. 'Literaturnye obrazy Pushkina v opernykh libretto ("Boris Godunov" i "Pikovaia dama")', *Sovetskaia muzyka* (1949), 5: 43–52.

[3587] BERLIAND-CHERNAIA, E. "Pikovaia Dama". In: E. Berliand-Chernaia, *Pushkin i Chaikovskii* (1950): 100–142 [see *2134*].

[3588] COOPER, M. 'Tchaikovsky's "Queen of Spades"', *The Listener*, 43 (5 Jan 1950): 40.

[3589] MONTAGU, G. 'Tchaikovsky's "The Queen of Spades"', *London Musical Events*, 5 (Dec 1950): 26–28, illus.

[3590] *"Pikovaia dama"*. Moskva: Iskusstvo, 1951. 23 p, illus.

[3591] IAGOLIM, B. 'Iz istorii "Pikovoi damy" (vystavka v Klinu)', *Sovetskaia muzyka* (1951), 1: 109–111, illus.

        In connection with an exhibition at the Klin museum.

[3592] RYZHKIN, I. Ia. 'Asaf'evskii analiz "Pikovoi damy" i "Evgeniia Onegina" Chaikovskogo'. In: *Pamiati akademika Borisa Vladimirovicha Asaf'eva. Sbornik statei o nauchno-kriticheskom nasledii.* Moskva, Izd-vo Akademii Nauk SSSR, 1951: 55–67.

[3593] TREVES, P. 'A Londra la Dama di picche', *La Scala* (Apr 1951): 38–39, illus.

[3594] MITCHELL, D. C. 'A note on Tchaikovsky's "Queen of Spades"', *The Chesterian*, 25 (Apr 1951): 86–89.

[3595] BIANCOLLI, L. "Pique Dame"'. In: L. Biancolli, *The opera reader: A complete guide to the best loved operas* (1953): 516–521 [see *2585*].

[3596] 'Pervoe predstavlenie "Pikovoi damy"', *Teatr* (Dec 1955): 186–188, illus.

        A short history of the composition and staging of the opera.

[3597] *"Pikovaia dama" P. I. Chaikovskogo*. Opera v 3-kh deistviiakh (7-mi kartinakh). Libretto M. I. Chaikovskogo. Siuzhet zaimstvovan iz povesti A. S. Pushkin. Libretto M. I. Chaikovskogo. Polnyi tekst. Vstup. stat'ia O. Melikian. Moskva: Gos. muz. izdat., 1956. 93 p. (*Opernye libretto*).

        — [rev. ed.] Predislovie E. Eremeevoi. Moskva: Gos. muz. izd., 1958. 94 p. (*Opernye libretto*).

        — 2-e izd. Moskva: Gos. muz. izdat., 1963. 93 p. (*Opernye libretto*).

[3598] KLOPPENBURG, W. C. 'Tsjaikowsky's opera "Pique dame"', *Mens en melodie*, 11 (Nov 1956): 330–334, music, illus.

[3599] MAZEL', L. A. 'K voprosu o simfonizme "Pikovoi damy"', *Sovetskaia muzyka* (1958), 9: 75–80 [see *2355*].

[3600] [TANEEV, S. I.] 'Zametki S. I. Taneeva na poliakh klavira "Pikovoi damy"'. In: A. A. Al'shvang, *P. I. Chaikovskii* (1959): 687–701 [see *1510*].

[3601] *Pietro Ciaicovskii: "La dama di picche"*. Opera in tre atti e sette quadri di Modesto Ciaicovski, tratta dalla novella di Puskin. Versione italiana de B[runo] B[runi]. Trieste: Tip. triestina, 1960. 68 p.

[3602] DOLZHANSKII, A. N. 'Eshche o "Pikovoi dame" i Shestoi simfonii Chaikovskogo', *Sovetskaia muzyka* (1960), 7: 88–100, music.

        Review: B. Iarustovskii, 'Eshche raz o "Pikovoi dame" (v sviazi so stat'ei A. Dolzhanskogo)', *Sovetskaia muzyka* (1961), 1: 64–67.

        — [repr.] 'Eshche o "Pikovoi dame" i Shestoi simfonii Chaikovskogo'. In: A. Dolzhanskii, *Izbrannye stat'i*. Leningrad: Muzyka, 1973: 162–178.

[3603]   *"The Queen of Spades": Opera in three acts.* Words by Modest Tchaikovsky, based on a tale by Alexander Pushkin. New English version by Arthur Jacobs. Music by Piotr Ilyich Tchaikovsky Oxford: Oxford Univ. Press, 1961. xii, 60 p.

[3604]   KAPLAN, E. 'Meierkhol´d stavit "Pikovuiu damu"', *Sovetskaia muzyka* (1961), 8: 59–65, illus.
          Recalling the first production of the opera by Vsevolod Meierkhol´d in the 1930s.

[3605]   DIETHER, J. '"Queen of Spades" filmed', *Musical America*, 81 (Nov 1961): 40.

[3606]   MNATSAKANOVA, E. 'Besedy o muzyke: "Pikovaia dama"', *Muzykal´naia zhizn´* (1962), 1: 13–14, 2: 11–12, illus.

[3607]   BOR, V. '"Pikova dama" a upravy', *Hudební rozhledy*, 16 (1963), 21: 902.

[3608]   VANSLOV, V. 'Vopreki muzyke', *Sovetskaia muzyka* (1964), 9: 18–22.
          Partly concerning a production of the opera in Novosibirsk.

[3609]   ANUFRIEV, V. 'Khandev v "Pikovoi dame"', *Teatr* (1965), 5: 93–97, illus.
          The role of Hermann in the opera.

[3610]   MERKLING, F. 'Trump and no-trump', *Opera News*, 29 (20 Mar 1965): 33.

[3611]   KANSKI, J. 'Z krakowskiego Teatru Muzycznego', *Ruch Muzyczny*, 10 (1966), 12: 8–9, illus.

[3612]   GOLDOVSKY, B. 'The third man', *Opera News*, 30 (15 Jan 1966): 26–27, music.
          On the role of Prince Eletskii.

[3613]   "Queen of Spades", *Opera News*, 30 (15 Jan 1966): 19–22, illus.

[3614]   ABRAHAM, G. E. H. "The Queen of Spades", *The Listener*, 76 (29 Sep 1966): 478, illus.

[3615]   JEFFERSON, A. 'Tchaikovsky's card-sharp countess', *Music and Musicians*, 15 (Oct 1966): 16–17, music.

[3616]   JEFFERSON, A. 'Misdeal for Tchaikovsky', *Music and Musicians*, 15 (Nov 1966): 28–29, illus.

[3617]   SOKOL´SKII, M. 'Iz stat´i "Filosofskie motivy opery "Pikovaia dama"'. In: M. Sokol´skii, *Slushaia vremia*. Moskva: Muzyka, 1967: 37–86.

[3618]   FRIDECZKY, F. '"Pique Dame": Bemutato a Szegedi Nemzeti Szinhazban', *Muzsika*, 10 (Apr 1967): 13–14.

[3619]   OPPENS, K. 'Chagall begegnet Mozart', *Opern Welt* (May 1967), 5: 10–12.

[3620]   TARKHOV, L. F. 'Moia rabota nad partiei Germana v opere Chaikovskogo "Pikovaia dama"'. In: *Muzykal´noe nasledstvo*. Vyp. 2, chast´ 2. Moskva: Muzyka, 1968: 198–213.

[3621]   CRANKSHAW, G. 'Lifelike St. Petersburg', *Music & Musicians*, 16 (May 1968): 38, illus.

[3622]   MATSOKINA, E. M. 'O vyrazitel´nom znachenii polifonicheskikh priemov v opere "Pikovaia dama" P. I. Chaikovskogo'. In: *Sbornik statei po muzykoznaniiu*. Otv. red. A. N. Kotliarevskii. Vyp. 3. Novosibirsk: Zap.-Sib. kn. izdat., 1969: 103–129.

[3623]   ZANETTI, E. "La dama di picche". Venezia: Teatro La Fenice, 1969. 20 p.

[3624]   MATSOKINA, E. M. 'O ravnotemnoi polifonii v opere Chaikovskogo "Pikovaia dama"'. In: *Nauchno-metodicheskie zapiski: Sbornik statei*. Vyp. 5. Novosibirsk: Zapadno-Sibirskoe izdat., 1970: 177–194.

[3625]   SOLOVTSOV, A. "Pikovaia dama". In: *Opery P. I. Chaikovskogo: Putevoditel´* (1970): 217–325 [see 2592].

[3626]   DEL´MAN, V. 'V bor´be protivorechii', *Sovetskaia muzyka* (1971), 11: 70–76.

[3627]   KOLODIN, I. 'Music to my ears', *Saturday Review*, 54 (Mar 1971): 6–7.

[3628]   SMITH, P. J. 'N. E. T.: "The Queen of Spades"', *Musical America*, 21 (May 1971): 23.

[3629]   NES´TEVA, M. 'Teatr zasluzhivaet podderzhki i nuzhdaetsia v nei', *Sovetskaia muzyka* (1972), 3: 28–35, illus.

[3630]   JIRKO, I. 'Obnoveny Čajkovskij v Narodnim divadle', *Hudební rozhledy*, 26 (1973), 5: 202–203, illus.

[3631]   POSPIŠIL, V. 'Velka operni udalost', *Hudební rozhledy*, 26 (1973), 7: 293–297, illus.

[3632]   KOLODIN, I. 'A new deal for "The Queen of Spades"', *Saturday Review* (20 Jan 1973), 1: 73.

[3633]   SOLODKINA, D. "Pikovaia dama", *Sovetskaia muzyka* (1975), 3: 55–57.

[3634]   VENETSKII, A. "Pikovaia dama", *Sovetskaia muzyka* (1975), 3: 61–62.
         In connection with a production of the opera in Donetsk.

[3635]   KRAUSE, E. "Pique Dame". In: E. Krause, *Oper von A-Z: Ein Opernführer* (1976): 517–521 [see 2598].

[3636]   POTAPOVA, L. 'O nekotorykh osobennostiakh spektaklia "Pikovaia dama" v postanovke V. E. Meierkhol´da'. In: *Trudy Leningradskogo Gos. instituta teatra, muzyki i kinematografii*, 6 (1976): 142–162.

[3637]   "The Queen of Spades". In: G. Kobbe, *Kobbe's complete opera book*. Ed. and rev. by the Earl of Harewood. London: Putnam, 1976: 926–931.
         — [rev. ed.] G. Kobbe, The definitive Kobbe's opera book. Ed., rev. and updated by the Earl of Harewood. New York: Putnam, 1987: 744–749.

[3638]   SCHWARZ, B. 'Two Tchaikovsky masterpieces', *Saturday Review*, 3 (6 Mar 1976): 38–39.

[3639]   IARUSTOVSKII, B. 'I vnov´ "Pikovaia dama"', *Sovetskaia muzyka* (1977), 9: 131–135.
         In connection with the premiere of the Stanislavskii/Nemirovich-Danchenko production of the opera in Moscow.

[3640]   STANISLAVSKII, K. S. '"Pikovaia dama" Chaikovskogo'. In: *Stanislavskii: Reformator opernogo iskusstva*. Moskva: Muzyka, 1977: 172–184.
         — 4-e izd. Moskva: Muzyka, 1988: 165–180.

[3641]   FORBES, E. 'Tchaikovsky: "Pique Dame"', *Opera News*, 43 (1978), 1: 36.

[3642]   FREEMAN, J. 'Tchaikovsky: "Pique Dame"', *Opera News*, 43 (1978), 3: 80.

[3643]   'Tchaikovsky: "Queen of Spades"', *High Fidelity*, 28 (Jul 1978): 100–101.

[3644]   'Pod titlom "Iskrennost´ pastushki"', *Muzykal´naia zhizn´* (Nov 1978), 21: 3, music.
         Concerning the *Interlude* from Act II of the opera.

[3645]   ROBERTS, C. 'Pushkin's "Pikovaja dama" and the Opera Libretto', *Canadian Review of Comparative Literature* 6 (1979): 9–26.

[3646]   ANSHAKOV, B. Ia. 'O nekotorykh chertakh khudozhestvennogo mira P. I. Chaikovsogo i osobennostiakh pereosmyslenia pushkinskikh obrazov v opere "Pikovaia dama"'. In: *P. I. Chaikovskii i russkaia literatura* (1980): 125–144 [see 588].

[*3647*]   **BENUA [BENOIS], A.** "Pikovaia dama". In: A. Benua, *Moi vospominaniia.* Izd. podgot. N. I. Aleksandrova [et al.]. Predisl. D. S. Likhacheva. Tom 1. Moskva: Nauka, 1980: 651–658. (*Literaturnye pamiatniki*)

— 2-e izd., dop. *Moi vospominaniia: V piati knigakh.* Izd. podgot. N. I. Aleksandrova [et al]. Otv. red. D. S. Likhachev. Tom 1. Moskva: Nauka, 1990: 649–656. (*Literaturnye pamiatniki*).

[*3648*]   **BONFEL´D, M. Sh.** 'Problema dvuiazychiia v opere P. I. Chaikovskogo "Pikovaia dama"'. In: *P. I. Chaikovskii i russkaia literatura* (1980): 178–190 [see *588*].

[*3649*]   **IVANCHENKO, G. I.** 'Traditsii A. S. Pushkina v opere P. I. Chaikovskogo "Pikovaia dama"'. In: *P. I. Chaikovskii i russkaia literatura* (1980): 144–154 [see *588*].

[*3650*]   **KANSKI, J.** '"Dama Pikowa": Opera czy symfonia?', *Ruch Muzyczny,* 24 (1980), 10: 11, illus.

[*3651*]   **MUGINSHTEIN, E.** 'Dramaturgicheskii "rezonans" v opere', *Sovetskaia muzyka* (1980), 12: 73–75.

[*3652*]   **VAIDMAN, P. E.** 'Rabota P. I. Chaikovskogo nad rukopis´iu libretto opery "Pikovaia dama"'. In: *P. I. Chaikovskii i russkaia literatura* (1980): 155–177 [see *588*].

[*3653*]   **VASIL´EV, Iu.** 'K rukopisiam "Pikovoi damy": K izucheniu tvorcheskoi biografii P. I. Chaikovskogo', *Sovetskaia muzyka* (1980), 7: 99–103, illus.

Analysis of Chaikovskii's sketches for the first two scenes of the opera.

[*3654*]   **"The Queen of Spades",** *San Francisco Opera Magazine* (1982), 7 [whole issue], illus.

[*3655*]   **HARBISON, J.** 'Thoughts on Tchaikovsky and his "Queen of Spades"', *San Francisco Opera Magazine* (fall 1982), 7: 58–60, illus.

[*3656*]   **BLETSCHACHER, R.** 'Liebe, Spiel und Wahnsinn', *Bühne* (Nov 1982), 290: 23, illus.

[*3657*]   **BIALIK, M.** 'Das Romanische in Tschaikowskis "Pique Dame"'. In: *Romantikkonferenz (2) 1982.* Hrsg. Gunther Stephan und Hans John. Dresden, 1983: 104–107.

[*3658*]   **MIOLI, P.** 'Tchaikovsky: "Queen of Spades"', *Opera,* 34 (1983), 8: 854–855.

[*3659*]   **SCHUMANN, O.** "Pique Dame". In: O. Schumann, *Der grosse Opern- und Operettenführer.* Herrsching: M. Pawlak [1983]: 245–246.

[*3660*]   **STEANE, J.** "The Queen of Spades". In: *Opera on record 2.* Ed. by Alan Blyth; discographies comp. by Malcolm Walker. London: Hutchinson, 1983: 268–281.

[*3661*]   **KATS, B.** 'Vslushivaias´ v "Pikovuiu damu": Analiticheskie primechaniia k nabliudeniiam B. V. Asaf´eva', *Sovetskaia muzyka* (1984), 7: 52–58, music.

[*3662*]   **MILKA, A. L.** 'Novoe o rukopisi introduktsii k "Pikovoi dame" P. I. Chaikovskogo'. In *Pamiatniki kul´tury: Novye otkrytiia. Ezhegodnik 1982.* Leningrad: Nauka, 1984: 197–207.

[*3663*]   **FREEMAN, J. W.** "Queen of Spades". In: J. W. Freeman, *The Metropolitan Opera stories of the great operas.* Vol. 1. New York: Metropolitan Opera Guild; W. W. Norton [1984]: 431–434.

[*3664*]   **BONFEL´D, M. Sh.** '"Pikovaia dama" P. I. Chaikovskogo i nekotorye cherty teatral´noi estetiki XX veka.'. In: *Teatr v zhizni i tvorchestve P. I. Chaikovskogo* (1985): 145–166 [see *589*].

[*3665*]   **EWELL, B. C.** '"The Queen of Spades" and the processes of artistic transformation', *Opera Journal,* 18 (1985), 1: 19–26.

[*3666*]   **GUSIATNIKOVA, G. G.** 'A. N. Benua: Postanovshchik "Pikovoi damy" P. I. Chaikovskogo'. In: *Teatr v zhizni i tvorchestve P. I. Chaikovskogo* (1985): 166–172 [see *589*].

[3667] KOCH, H. W. 'Beruhigung durch den beunruhiger?', *Opern Welt*, 26 (1985), 9: 49.

[3668] ZHUK, A. A. '"Pikovaia dama" P. I. Chaikovskogo i problema geroia v russkoi literature poslednei treti XIX v. (k tipologicheskim sootvetstviiam v iskusstve)'. In: *Teatr v zhizni i tvorchestve P. I. Chaikovskogo* (1985): 136–145 [see 589].

[3369] MARCHESI, G. "La dama di picche". In: G. Marchesi, *L'opera lirica: Guida storico-critica dalle origini al Novecento*. [Milano]: Ricordi; [Firenze]: Giunti [1986]: 154–160. (*Guide alla musica*).

[3670] LAZARUS, J. "Queen of Spades". In: J. Lazarus, *The opera handbook*. Boston (Mass.): G. K. Hall, 1987: 200. (*G. K. Hall performing arts handbooks*).

[3671] TANNER, M. "Queen of Spades", *Times Literary Suppl.* (21 Aug 1987): 901.

[3672] "The Queen of Spades", *San Francisco Opera Magazine* (aut. 1987), 10 [whole issue], illus.

[3673] ARNOSI, E. 'Tchaikovsky and "The Queen of Spades"', *Opera*, 38 (Nov 1987): 1308–1309.

[3674] LISCHKÉ, A. 'From Weber's "Die Freischütz" to Tchaikovsky's "Pique Dame": Magic infallibility and its consequences', *L'Avant Scène Opéra*, 105/106 (Jan/Feb 1988): 152–153.

[3675] FORBES, E. "The Queen of Spades", *Opera News*, 54 (Sep 1988): 48–49.

[3676] GREEN, L. 'Tchaikovsky: "The Queen of Spades"', *Opera Quarterly*, 6 (win. 1988), 2: 111–112.

[3677] *Tchaikovski: "La dame de pique"*. Livret russe intégral (translittéré) Modeste Tchaïkovski, d'aprés la nouvelle d'Alexandre Pouchkine traduction en français de Lily Denis. Commentaire musical et littéraire d'André Lischke. Paris: L'Avant Scène, 1989. (*L'Avant Scène Opéra*; 119/120).

Contents: A. Duault, 'Présentation': 3 — V. Hofmann, 'Une genése difficile': 4–11 — M.-F. Vieuille, 'Quelques sources européennes': 12–17 — J. M. Brèque, 'De Pouchkine à Tchaïkovski': 18–25 — A. Duault, 'Miroir d'une ville, miroir d'une âme': 26–29 — W. Bannour, 'Le double assassinat à l'Opéra': 30–33 — A. Duault, 'Argument': 34–35 — "La Dame de Pique": 37–105 [complete original libretto transliterated from the Russian, with a a French tr. by Lily Denis, and commentary by André Lischke] — A. Lischke, 'Le Comte de Saint-Hermann': 106–108 — M.-F. Vieuille, 'La Comtesse sortit à minuit': 109–118 — A. Schnittke, 'Pour un traitement rénové de la partition': 119–121 — V. Meyerhold, 'Une mise en scène qui éclaire Pouchkine'': 122–129 — A. Tubeuf, 'Les bonnes maniéres des suicidaires': 130–133 — P. Kaminski, 'Discographie': 134–141 — G. Voisin, 'Les airs séparés': 142–145 — M. Pazdro, 'L'ouevre à l'affiche': 148–155 — E. Giuliani, 'Bibliographie': 157 — A. Butaux, 'Cette année-là: 1890': 158–159 — 'La Dame de l'Opéra de Varsovie': 160–167.

[3678] BONFEL'D, M. Sh. 'Opera P. I. Chaikovskogo "Pikovaia dama": K probleme sviaznosti khudozhestvennogo teksta'. In: *P. I. Chaikovskii: Voprosy istorii i stilia* (1989): 26–46 [see 590].

[3679] PISARENKO, O. 'Sprawa "Damy pikowej"', *Ruch Muzyczny*, 33 (1989), 16–17: 15–16.

[3680] SHAROEV, I. G. 'Chaikovskii-rezhisser: O "Pikovoi dame" i "Evgenii Onegine"'. In: I. G. Sharoev, *Muzyka, kotoruiu my vidim*. Moskva: Sovetskii kompozitor, 1989: 33–40.

[3681] ARKAD'EV, M. 'O neskhodstve skhodnogo: "Pikovaia dama" i mif o tsare Edipe (opyt sopostavleniia nesopostavimogo)', *Rossiskaia muzykal'naia gazeta* (1990), 2: 4–5.
Analysis of the libretto and Pushkin's text.

[3682] KARAGICHEVA, L. 'Dva etiuda o "Pikovoi dame": Modest Chaikovskii ili Pushkin? Pochemu arietta iz opery Gretri?', *Sovetskaia muzyka* (1990), 6: 46–53, music [see 592].

[3683] KORABEL'NIKOVA, L. Z. & FEL'DMAN, O. 'Zavoevyvat´ novye miry v iskusstve: D. Shostakovich, I. Sollertinskii, Vs. Meierkhol'd', *Sovetskaia muzyka* (1990), 6: 55–67 [see 592].
A discussion of Vsevolod Meierkhol'd's controversial production of the opera on 25 Jan 1935.

[*3684*]   **MIKHAILOV, M. K. 'Ob istokakh odnoi temy Chaikovskogo'**. In: M. K. Mikhailov, *Etiudy o stile v muzyke: Stat´i i fragmenty*. Leningrad: Muzyka, 1990: 268–269, music.

Concerning the theme of the duet from the *Intermezzo* in Act II.

[*3685*]   *"The Queen of Spades"*. In: *Opera plot index: A guide to locating plots and descriptions of operas, operettas, and other works of the musical theater, and associated material*. Comp. by William E. Studwell, David A. Hamilton. New York: Garland, 1990: 317. (*Garland Reference Library of the Humanities*; 1099).

[*3687*]   **CANNING, H. "Queen of Spades"**, *Opera*, 41 (Mar 1990): 340–341.

[*3688*]   **GALVERT, M. de. "Queen of Spades"**, *Opera*, 41 (May 1990): 555.

[*3689*]   **BONFEL´D, M. Sh. 'Vzaimodeistvie iskusstv: Organizatsiia dramaturgicheskogo prostranstva v opere "Pikovaia dama" i russkoi zhivopisi kontsa XIX–nachala XX vekov'**. In: *P. I. Chaikovskii i izobrazitel´noe iskusstvo* (1991): 36–54 [see *595*].

[*3690*]   **KOMARNITSKAIA, O. V. 'Kompozitsiia opery v sviazi s zhanrovoi i stilevoi spetsifikoi v russkoi klassicheskoi muzyke XIX veka'**. Kiev: Gos. ordena Lenina konservatorii im. P. I. Chaikovskogo, 1991. 28 p.

Dissertation (Kiev Conservatory), mainly concerned with the dramaturgy of *The Queen of Spades*.

[*3691*]   **KOMARNITSKAIA, O. V. '"Taina" muzykal´noi formy "Pikovoi damy"'**. In: *Chaikovskii: Voprosy istorii i teorii* (1991): 94–112 [see *593*].

[*3692*]   **SIN´KOVSKAIA, N. 'Brat´ia Chaikovskie v rabote nad libretto "Pikovoi damy"'**. In: *Chaikovskii: Voprosy istorii i teorii* (1991): 20–27 [see *593*].

[*3693*]   **'Interv´iu postanovshchikov i ispolnitelei opery P. I. Chaikovskogo "Pikovaia dama"'**, *Sovetskaia kul´tura* (21 Jul 1991): 14.

[*3694*]   **TELLEZ, J. L. '"Pikovaya dama": El verismo y algo mas'**, *Monsalvat* (Jan 1992), 200: 31–32, illus.

[*3695*]   **WARRACK, J. 'Tchaikovsky's "Queen of Spades"'**, *Times Literary Suppl.* (26 Jun 1992): 18.

[*3696*]   **GORODECKI, M. 'Tchaikovsky's mastery'**, *Musical Times*, 133 (Aug 1992): 419.

[*3697*]   **BONFEL´D, M. Sh. 'K probleme mnogourovnevosti khudozhestvennogo teksta: Otmechaia 100-letiie so dnia smerti P. I. Chaikovskogo'**, *Muzykal´naia akademiia* (1993), 4: 197–203.

[*3698*]   **HAGMAN, B. '"Nøtnkåpparen"; "Spader Dam"'**, *Musikrevy*, 48 (1993), 4: 36–38, illus.

[*3700*]   **"The Queen of Spades"**, *San Francisco Opera Magazine*, 71 (1993), 12: 25–26, illus.

[*3701*]   **RAKU, M. 'Ne ver´te v iskrennost´ pastushki: Otmechaia 100-letie so dnia smerti P. I. Chaikovskogo'**, *Muzykal´naia akademiia* (1993), 4: 203–206, music.

[*3702*]   **TARUSKIN, R. 'A masterpiece of musical surrealism ("The Queen of Spades")'**, *San Francisco Opera Magazine*, 71 (1993), 12: 16–20, illus.

[*3703*]   **MEIERKHOL´D, V. E. *"Pikovaia dama": Zamysel, voploshshenie, sud'ba*. Dokumenty i materialy. Sost., vstup. stat´ia i kommentarii G. V. Kopytovoi. Sankt Peterburg: Kompozitor, 1994. 404 p, illus. ISBN: 5–8528–5327–5.

Russian text, with summary and table of contents in English.

[*3704*]   **BENOIS, A. 'Meine Eindrücke von der Premiere der Oper "Pique Dame"'**. In: *Tschaikowsky aus der Nähe* (1994): 163–172 [see *379*].

[3705] BLETSCHACHER, R. '"Was ist das Leben? Ein Spiel!": Tschaikowskijs schwarze oper "Pique Dame"'. In: R. Bletschacher, *Apollons Vermachtnis: Vier Jahrhunderte Oper*. Wien: Überreuter [1994]: 354–355. ISBN 3-8000-3498-0.

[3706] **"La Dama de Pique"**. In: F. E. Valenti, *La opera: Pasion y encuentro*. Buenos Aires: Ediciones de Arte Gaglianone, 1994: 420–423. ISBN 9-5072-0017-7.

[3707] KLIMOVITSKII, A. I. '"Pikovaia dama" Chaikovskogo: Kul´turnaia pamiat´ i kul´turnye predchuvstviia'. In: *Rossiia—Evropa: Kontakty muzykal´nykh kul´tur*. Sbornik nauchnykh trudov, sost. i otv. red. E. S. Khodorkovskaia. Sankt Peterburg, 1994: 221–274.

[3708] VON BUCHAU, S. **"The Queen of Spades"**, *Opera News*, 58 (19 Feb 1994): 34.

[3709] KOROBKOV, S. '"Pikovaia dama" oznachaet tainuiu nedobrozhelatel´nost', *Muzykal´naia akademiia* (1995), 4/5: 104–110, illus.

[3710] LAUER, L. 'Čajkovskijs "Pikovaja Dama" und die Tradition der französischen Opéra-comique-Ballade'. In: *Internationales Čajkovskij Symposium, Tübingen 1993: Bericht* (1995): 199–206 [see *596*].

[3711] POZNANSKY, A. 'Fate and game: Tchaikovsky in "The Queen of Spades"', *Metropolitan Opera Stagebill* (Nov 1995): 8–14.

[3712] ROBINSON, H. 'The Russian bard: Alexander Pushkin and "The Queen of Spades"', *Opera News*, 60 (23 Dec 1995): 20–23, illus.

[3713] TARUSKIN, R. 'Another world: Why "The Queen of Spades" is the great Symbolist opera', *Opera News*, 60 (23 Dec 1995): 8–10, music, illus.

[3714] MERLIN, C. **"Pique Dame"**, *L'Avant Scène Opéra*, 171 (May/Jun 1996): 119.

[3715] LOBANOVA, M. **"Reflections on Tchaikovsky's opera "The Queen of Spades"'**, *Die Musikforschung*, 49 (Jul/Sep 1996), 3: 275–286.

[3716] LOBANOVA, M. 'Drei, Sieben, As: Zu der Opera "Pique Dame" von Pjotr Iljitsch Cajkovskij', *Die Musikforschüng*, 49 (Sep/Dec 1996), 3: 275–287, music.

[3717] MORRISON, S. A. 'Russian opera and symbolist poetics'. Princeton: Princeton Univ., 1997. 277 p. Dissertation (Ph. D.). Includes a section on *The Queen of Spades*.

[3718] PARIN, A. V. **"Pikowaja dama"**. In: *Pipers Enzyklopadie des Musiktheaters: Oper, Operette, Musical, Ballet*. Hrsg. von Carl Dahlhaus und dem Forschungsinstitut fur Musiktheater der Universität Bayreuth unter Leitung von Sieghart Dohring. Band 6. München: Piper, 1997: 346–350.

[3719] TCHEKAN, U. '"Le Demon" de Rubinstein et le Guerman de Tchaikovski'. In: *Proceedings of the International Musicological Convention in Vorzel (Ukraine), May 4th-6th, 1996*. Yelena S. Zinkevich (ed.). Heilbronn: Music Edition Lucie Galland, 1997: 11–17.

[3720] STARODUB, T. F. 'Nekotorye osobennosti mifa lichnosti v "Pikovoi dame" P. Chaikovskogo'. In: *Muzykal´nyi mir romantizma: Ot proshlogo k budushchemu*. Materialy nauchnoi konferentsii. Rostov-na-Donu: Gos. konservatorii im. S. V. Rakhmaninova, 1998: 76–79.

[3721] PARAKILAS, J. 'Musical historicism in "The Queen of Spades"'. In: *Tchaikovsky and his contemporaries* (1999): 177–185 [see *602*].

[3722] FREEMAN, J. W. 'It's in the cards: Life's a gamble', *Opera News*, 63 (Apr 1999), 10: 30–33.

[3723] MELICK, J. 'Phantom lady: The figure of the Old Countess gives "The Queen of Spades" its mysterious edge', *Opera News*, 63 (Apr 1999): 34–37.

[3724] KOEGLER, H. 'Tchaikovsky "The Queen of Spades"', *Opera News*, 63 (May 1999): 79–80.

[3725]   **PARIN, A. V.** 'Strashnaia starukha, tsvetushchaia krasavitsa, rokovaia karta'. In: A. V. Parin, *Khozhdenie v Nevidimyi grad: Paradigmy russkoi klassicheskoi opery*. Moskva: AGRAF, 1999: 313–358.

[3726]   **KHOMUTOV, A.** *"Pikovaia dama" A. S. Pushkina: Opera P. I. Chaikovskogo i ee libretto*. Sankt-Peterburg: Muzyka, 1999. 38 p. ISBN: 5-85772-007-9.

[3727]   **RAKU, M.** '"Pikovaia dama" brat´ev Chaikovskikh: Opyt intertekstual´nogo analiza', *Muzykal´naia akademiia*, 2 (1999): 9–21.

          See also *268, 352, 424, 425, 465, 492, 551, 555, 1433, 2911, 2945, 3007, 3061, 3069, 3081, 3100, 3137, 5618, 5619, 5683, 5684, 5686.*

ROMEO AND JULIET
Projected opera (1878–81)

[3728]   **ENGEL, Iu.** 'Muzyka v Moskve', *Khronika zhurnala "Muzykal´nyi Sovremennik"* (1916), 11/12: 21–25. Review of a performance of the duet scena, completed by Sergei Taneev.

          See also *5068.*

UNDINA
Opera in 3 acts (1869)

[3729]   **R—NKO, V.** 'Moskovskaia zhizn´: Novaia opera g. Chaikovskogo', *Sovremennaia letopis´* (14 Sep 1869).
          Report of Chaikovskii's work on the opera.

[3730]   **P.** 'Muzykal´naia khronika', *Moskovskie vedomosti* (15 Mar 1870).
          Report that excerpts from *Undina* are to be performed in Moscow on 16 Mar 1870.

[3731]   **LAROSH, G. A.** 'Muzykal´naia khronika', *Moskovskie vedomosti* (3 Apr 1870): 4.
          Review of extracts from the opera performed on 16 Mar 1870 in Moscow. Also includes a review of the Six Romances, Op. 6.
          — [repr.] In: G. A. Larosh, *Sobranie muzykal´no-kriticheskikh statei*, tom 2, chast´ 2 (1924): 14–15 [see *2311*].
          — [repr.] 'O romansakh i otryvkakh iz opery "Undina"'. In: G. A. Larosh, *Izbrannye stat´i v piati vypuskakh*, vyp. 2 (1975): 31–32 [see *2376*].

[3732]   **[KIUI, Ts. A.]** 'Muzykal´nye zametki', *Sankt-Peterburgskie vedomosti* (9 May 1870).

[3733]   **DAMPF, A.** '"Undina": Ne Undina, no nechto undinnoe v nei est´', *Muzykal´noe obozrenie* (1994), 7/8: 10.
          A performance of surviving scenes from the opera on 11 May 1994 in Moscow.

          See also *239.*

VAKULA THE SMITH
Comic opera in 3 acts, Op. 14 (1874)
[See also *Cherevichki* (1885)]

[3734]   'Teatr', *Novosti* (7 Nov 1874).
          On Chaikovskii's submission of the opera to the competition committee. See also *3735*.

[*3735*]   'Khronika', *Golos* (26 Oct 1875).

[*3736*]   KONSTANTIN [GRAND DUKE KONSTANTIN NIKOLAEVICH]. 'Zametki i izvestiia: Reskript na imia g. Chaikovskogo', *Sovremennye izvestiia* (8 Nov 1875).

The award of first prize in the opera competition to Chaikovskii's *Vakula the Smith*. See also *3737* to *3740*, *3742* to *3744*.

[*3737*]   'Teatr i muzyka', *Novoe vremia* (10 Nov 1875).

Publication of a letter from the Grand Duke Konstantin Nikolaevich to Chaikovskii, concerning the awarding of the prize for *Vakula the Smith*.

[*3738*]   'Iz drugikh gubernii', *Varshavskii dnevnik* (13/25 Nov 1875).

[*3739*]   'Vnutrennie izvestiia', *Kavkaz* (19 Nov 1875).

[*3740*]   'Izvestiia iz Rossii', *Muzykal´nyi listok* (1875/76), 6: 88, 9: 26–29.

[*3741*]   *"Vakula kuznets"*. Libretto dlia opery Ia. P. Polonskogo. Muzyka P. I. Chaikovskogo. Sankt Peterburg: E. Goppe, 1876. 81 p.

Original libretto.

— 2-e izd. *Kuznets Vakula*. Muzyka P. I. Chaikovskogo. Slova Ia. P. Polonskogo. Libretto dlia opery. Sankt Peterburg: E. Goppe, 1878. 61 p.

[*3742*]   'Iz drugikh gubernii', *Varshavskii dnevnik* (18 Feb/1 Mar 1876).

[*3743*]   'Smes´´', *Astrakhanskii spravochnyi listok* (26 Feb 1876).

[*3744*]   G[ALLER], K. '"Kuznets Vakula", opera P. I. Chaikovskogo', *Muzykal´nyi svet* (16 May 1876): 152; (23 May 1876): 157–158; (30 May 1876): 167–168; (6 Jun 1876): 174–176.

[*3745*]   'Teatr i muzyka', *Novoe vremia* (16 Aug 1876).

Preparations for the first production. See also *3746* to *3748*.

[*3746*]   'Sankt Peterburg: Muzykal´nye i teatral´nye novosti', *Muzykal´nyi svet* (Nov 1876): 394.

[*3747*]   'Teatral´nyi kur´er', *Peterburgskii listok* (17 Nov 1876).

[*3748*]   'Teatral´nye novosti', *Teatral´naia gazeta* (23 Nov 1876).

[*3749*]   KARTSOV, N. 'Teatral´nyi kur´er'. *Peterburgskii listok* (25 Nov 1876).

The first production of the opera on 24 Nov 1876 in St. Petersburg. See also *3750* to *3774*, *3776*.

[*3750*]   [KIUI, Ts. A.] 'Teatr i muzyka', *Sankt Peterburgskie vedomosti* (26 Nov 1876).

[*3751*]   'Teatr i muzyka', *Novoe vremia* (26 Nov 1876).

[*3752*]   'Peterburg, 24 Noiabria', *Teatral´naia gazeta* (26 Nov 1876).

[*3753*]   ROSTISLAV ["Vakoula le forgeron"], *Journal de St. Petersbourg* (27 Nov 1876).

[*3754*]   KARTSOV, N. 'Mariinskii teatr: Russkaia opera. "Kuznets Vakula", opera P. I. Chaikovskogo', *Muzykal´nyi svet* (28 Nov 1876).

[*3755*]   'Pervoe predstavlenie opery "Kuznets Vakula" P. I. Chaikovskogo', *Peterburgskaia gazeta* (28 Nov 1876).

[*3756*]   [GALLER, K. P.] 'Novaia opera na Mariinskoi stsene: "Kuznets Vakula", opera P. I. Chaikovskogo', *Birzhevye vedomosti* (29 Nov 1876).

[*3757*]   IVANOV, M. M. '"Kuznets Vakula": Komicheskaia opera', *Novoe vremia* (29 Nov 1876).

[*3758*]   'Peterburgskie gazety po povodu predstavleniia opery P. Chaikovskogo "Vakula-kuznets"', *Teatral´naia gazeta* (29 Nov 1876).

[*3759*]   [KIUI, Ts. A.] '"Kuznets Vakula", opera g. Chaikovskogo', *Sankt Peterburgskie vedomosti* (30 Nov 1876): 2–3.

[*3760*]   G. 'P. I. Chaikovskii i ego opera "Kuznets Vakula"', *Syn Otechestva* (1 Dec 1876).

[*3761*]   DOLD, G. A. 'Russische Oper "Wakula der Schmeid": Komische Oper in 3 Akten. Musik von P. Tschaikowski', *St. Petersburger Herold* (2/14 Dec; 5/17 Dec 1876).

[*3762*]   FAMINTSYN, A. 'Russische Oper: "Wakula der Schmeid", komischphantastische Oper in drei Akten. Musik von Peter Tschaikowski', *St. Petersburger Zeitung* (2/14 Dec 1876).

[*3763*]   LAROSH, G. A. 'Opera "Vakula-Kuznets" na Mariinskoi stsene', *Golos* (2 Dec 1876): 1–2.
       — [repr.] In: G. A. Larosh, *Sobranie muzykal´no-kriticheskikh statei*, tom 2, chast´ 1 (1924): 125–134 [see *2311*].
       — [repr.] In: G. A. Larosh, *Izbrannye stat´i v piati vypuskakh*, vyp. 2 (1975): 86–93 [see *2376*].

[*3764*]   '"Vakula-kuznets": Opera Chaikovskogo', *Teatral´naia gazeta* (3 Dec 1876).

[*3765*]   P. [KARTSOV, N.] 'Muzykal´nye nabroski: "Kuznets Vakula", opera P. I. Chaikovskogo', *Peterburgskii listok* (4 Dec; 5 Dec; 9 Dec; 15 Dec 1876).

[*3766*]   BUKVA [VASILEVSKII, I. F.] '"Golos iz publiki" o novoi opere g. Chaikovskogo', *Birzhevye vedomosti* (5 Dec 1876).

[*3767*]   IVANOV, M. M. '"Kuznets Vakula", komicheskaia opera P. Chaikovskogo', *Pchela* (5 Dec 1876).

[*3768*]   ROSTISLAV [TOLSTOI, F. M.] 'Peterburgskie pis´ma: O muzyke i teatrakh', *Moskovskie vedomosti* (5 Dec 1876).

[*3769*]   SHUROVSKII, P. 'Pervoe predstavlenie opery "Vakula-kuznets" soch. P. I. Chaikovskogo, 24 Noiabria v Peterburge', *Moskovskoe obozrenie* (5 Dec 1876).

[*3770*]   'Po povodu libretto opery "Vakula-kuznets"', *Teatral´naia gazeta* (7 Dec 1876).

[*3771*]   'Teatr i muzyka', *Modnyi svet* (8 Dec 1876).

[*3772*]   'Teatral´noe ekho', *Peterburgskaia gazeta* (9 Dec 1876).

[*3773*]   KASHKIN, N. D. '"Kuznets Vakula" (opera P. I. Chaikovskogo na stsene Mariinskogo teatra v Peterburge)', *Russkie vedomosti* (16 Dec 1876).

[*3774*]   DILETANT. 'Muzykal´naia zametka', *Sovremennye izvestiia* (21 Dec 1876).

[*3775*]   IVANOV, M. M. 'Peterburgskaia khronika', *Muzykal´nyi listok* (1876/77), 6: 86–90.
       A concert performance of the dances from the opera on 20 Nov 1876 in St. Petersburg.

[*3776*]   GALLER, K. P. 'Razbor sochinenii: Konkursy Imperatorskogo Russkogo Muzykal´nogo Obshchestva', *Muzykal´nyi svet* (2 Jan 1877): 4–6.

[*3777*]   S[ARIOTTI], M. I. 'Imperatorskaia russkaia opera: "Kuznets Vakula", opera v 4 deistviiakh g. Chaikovskogo', *Vsemirnaia illiustratsiia* (29 Jan 1877).

[*3778*]   '"Kuznets Vakula" g. Chaikovskogo v Peterburge', *Teatral´naia gazeta* (12 Oct 1877).
       The revival of the opera in St. Petersburg. See also *3779*.

[*3779*]   LAROSH, G. A. 'Dva slova o "Vakule-Kuznetse"', *Golos* (13 Oct 1877).

— [repr.] In: G. A. Larosh, *Sobranie muzykal´no-kriticheskikh statei*, tom 2, chast´ 1 (1924): 135 [see *2311*].

— [repr.] In: G. A. Larosh, *Izbrannye stat´i v piati vypuskakh*, vyp. 2 (1975): 93–94 [see *2376*].

[*3780*]   'Teatr i muzyka', *Novoe vremia* (9 Feb 1902): 4.

The 25th anniversary of the first performance.

[*3781*]   JACOBS, A. '"Vakula the Smith": BBC Radio 3', *Opera*, 41 (Feb 1990): 243–245.

In connection with a radio broadcast of the opera.

[*3782*]   'Die werkgeschichtlichen Einführungen der alten Čajkovskijs-Gesamtausgabe', *Tschaikowsky-Gesellschaft Mitteilungen*, 7 (2000): 99–123.

Concerning the scores of *Vakula the Smith* and *Evgenii Onegin* in vols. 35 and 36 of *PSSM* [see *118*].

THE VOEVODA

Opera in 3 acts, Op. 3 (1867–68)

[*3783*]   'Letopis´ moskovskikh kontsertov', *Antrakt* (25 Feb 1868).

The first performance of the *Entr'acte and Dances of the Chambermaids* from the opera on 19 Feb 1868 in Moscow.

[*3784*]   *"Voevoda": Opera v 3-kh deistviiakh*. Siuzhet zaimstvovan iz dramy A. N. Ostrovskogo 'Son na Volge'. Muzyka P. I. Chaikovskogo. Moskva: P. Iurgenson, 1869. 39 p.

Original libretto.

[*3785*]   'Stolichnaia zhizn´': Moskva. "Voevoda" soch. Chaikovskogo', *Vsemirnyi trud*, 2 (1869), 4: 184.

The first production of the opera on 30 Jan 1869 in Moscow. See also *3786* to *3796*.

[*3786*]   'Muzykal´noe izvestie', *Russkie vedomosti* (30 Jan 1869).

[*3787*]   [KASHKIN, N. D.] '"Voevoda": Opera g. Chaikovskogo', *Russkie vedomosti* (5 Feb 1869).

— [repr.] In: N. D. Kashkin, *Izbrannye stat´i o P. I. Chaikovskom* (1954): 49–52 [see *2349*].

[*3788*]   'Teatr i muzyka', *Novoe vremia* (7 Feb 1869).

[*3789*]   LAROSH [G. A.] 'Novaia russkaia opera: "Voevoda" g. Chaikovskogo. Benefis g-zhi Men´shikovoi 30 ianvaria', *Sovremennaia letopis´* (9 Feb 1869): 10–11.

— [repr.] In: G. A. Larosh, *Sobranie muzykal´no-kriticheskikh statei*, tom 2, chast´ 1 (1924): 102–105 [see *2311*].

— [repr.] In: G. A. Larosh, *Izbrannye stat´i v piati vypuskakh*, vyp. 2 (1975): 23–25 [see *2376*].

— [German tr.] '"Der Wojewode" von Herrn Tschaikowsky: Eine neue russische Oper'. In: G. A. Larosh, *Peter Tschaikowsky: Aufsätze und Erinnerungen* (1993): 61–66 [see *2406*].

[*3790*]   P. 'Moskovskii listok', *Severnaia pchela* (9 Feb 1869).

[*3791*]   K. 'Korrespondentsiia: Moskva, 9 fevralia', *Vest´* (14 Feb 1869).

[*3792*]   I. U. 'Obzor vnutrennei zhizni Rossii: Novaia opera g. Chaikovskogo', *Voronezhskii telegraf* (18 Feb 1869).

[*3793*]   S. P. 'Moskovskaia zhizn´', *Golos* (4 Mar 1869).

[*3794*]   'Obzor muzykal´nogo sveta: Sankt Peterburg, aprel´ 1869', *Muzykal´nyi svet* (Apr 1869), 4: 13.

[*3795*]   'Telegraf', *Nuvellist* (Apr 1869): 31.

[*3796*]   N. G. 'Stsena iz opery "Voevoda" g. Chaikovskogo', *Vsemirnaia illiustratsiia* (24 May 1869).

[*3797*]   POPOV, S. 'Pervaia opera Chaikovskogo', *Kul´tura i teatra* (1921), 5/6: 27.

[*3798*]   'Wiederauffindung des Manuskriptes der verschollenen Oper "Der Wojewode" von Peter Tschaikowsky', *Allgemeine Musik Zeitung*, 63 (1936): 127.

[*3799*]   'Kalendar´ iskusstva: 11 fevralia 1869 g. v moskovskom Bol´shom teatre', *Sovetskoe iskusstvo* (12 Feb 1939): 4.
           The 60th anniversary of the first production.

[*3800*]   BOGDANOV-BEREZOVSKII, V. 'Pervaia opera Chaikovskogo: Postanovka "Voevoda" v Malom opernom teatre', *Vechernii Leningrad* (8 Oct 1949): 3.
           The new production of the opera at the Malyi Theatre in Leningrad in 1949. See also *3801* to *3804*.

[*3801*]   EVDAKHOV, O. '"Voevoda" (opera P. I. Chaikovskogo v Malom teatre', *Leningradskaia pravda* (3 Nov 1949): 3.

[*3802*]   IARUSTOVSKII, B. 'Vtoroe rozhdenie opery', *Sovetskaia muzyka* (1950), 5: 58–64, music, illus.

[*3803*]   SAVINOV, N. 'Vozrozhdenie opery', *Ogonek* (1950), 34: 25.
           Comparing the first production of *The Voevoda* in Moscow in 1869, with the reconstructed version at the Malyi Theatre, Leningrad, in 1949.

[*3804*]   SOKOL´SKII, M. 'Vozrozhdennaia klassika: "Voevoda" P. I. Chaikovskogo v Leningradskom Malom opernom teatre', *Sovetskoe iskusstvo* (28 Jul 1950): 2.

[*3805*]   ABRAHAM, G. E. H. 'Tchaikovsky's first opera'. In: *Festschrift Karl Gustav Fellerer zum sechzigsten Geburtstag am 7. Juli 1962.* Hrsg. von Heinrich Hüschen, Regensburg: G. Bosse, 1962: 12–19, music, illus.

[*3806*]   GOZENPUD, A. 'Ostrovskii na opernoi stsene: "Voevoda" Chaikovskogo i "Vrazh´ia sila" Serova'. In: A. Gozenpud, *Russkii opernyi teatr XIX veka, 1857–1872.* Leningrad: Muzyka, 1971: 240–275.

           See also *111, 542, 1992, 1993, 4338, 5416.*

5.2.3. Ballets

[*3807*]   KEETON, A. E. 'Tchaikovski as a ballet composer', *Contemporary Review*, 86 (Oct 1904): 566–575.

[*3808*]   FOKIN, M. M. 'P. I. Chaikovskii i balet', *Solntse Rossii* (1913), 44: 7 [see *583*].

[*3809*]   LEVINSON. 'Chaikovskii v balete', *Zhizn´ iskusstva* (29 Oct 1918).

[*3810*]   LESHKOV, D. 'Chaikovskii's ballets'. In: *Marius Petipa (1822–1910): K stoletiiu ego rozhdeniia.* Petrograd: Petrogradskikh Akad. teatrov, 1922: 38–47. (*Teatral´naia biblioteka*; 1).

[*3811*]   KRIUGER, A. N. *Baletnye siuity Chaikovskogo.* Leningrad: Leningradskaia filarmoniia, 1940. 32 p, music. (*Putevoditel´ po kontsertam*).
           Concerning the published suites compiled from each of Chaikovskii's ballets.

[*3812*]   BAKHRUSHIN, Iu. 'Balety Chaikovskogo i ikh stsenicheskaia istoriia'. In: *Chaikovskii i teatr* (1940): 80–139 [see *2537*].

[*3813*]   BAKHRUSHIN, Iu. 'Balety Chaikovskogo na stsene', *Teatr* (1940), 5: 35–50, illus.
           The stage history of Chaikovskii's ballets in Moscow and Leningrad.

[*3814*] KISELEV, M. 'Balety Chaikovskogo', *Sovetskaia muzyka* (1940), 5/6: 88–98 [see *585*].

[*3815*] EVANS, E. 'A great master of ballet music: The Tchaikovsky centenary', *Dancing Times*, 356 (May 1940): 468–469.

[*3816*] BOGDANOV-BEREZOVSKII, V. M. 'Muzykal´naia dramaturgiia baletov P. I. Chaikovskogo'. In: *P. I. Chaikovskii na stsene teatra opery i baleta im. S. M. Kirova* (1941): 239–286 [see *2542*].

[*3817*] NOSILOV, N. N. 'Balety P. I. Chaikovskogo na stsene teatra opery i baleta im. S. M. Kirova'. In: *P. I. Chaikovskii na stsene teatra opery i baleta im. S. M. Kirova* (1941): 287–404 [see *2542*].

[*3818*] LAWSON, J. 'Tchaikovsky and the ballet: Some hitherto unknown facts', *Dancing Times*, 375 (Dec 1941): 124–127, illus.

[*3819*] EVANS. E, 'The ballets'. In: *Tchaikovsky: A symposium* (1945): 184–196 [see *586*].

[*3820*] BOGDANOV-BEREZOVSKII, V. M. 'Stsenicheskaia problema baletov Chaikovskogo', *Teatral´nyi al´manakh*, 3 (1946), 5: 153–169, illus.

[*3821*] IAKOVLEV, V. V. 'The ballets of Tchaikovsky'. In: *Russian symphony: Thoughts about Tchaikovsky* (1947): 132–159 [see *587*].

[*3822*] ZHITOMIRSKII, D. V. *Balety P. Chaikovskogo: "Lebedinoe ozero", "Spiashchaia krasavitsa", "Shchelkunchik"*. Moskva; Leningrad: Gos. muz. izdat., 1950. 155 p, illus. (*Putevoditeli po russkoi muzyke*).
Review: I. F. Kunin, 'Novye knigi o Chaikovskom', *Sovetskaia kniga* (1951), 2: 114–120.
— [rev. ed.] *Balety Chaikovskogo: Nauchno-populyarnyi ocherk*. Moskva: Gos. muz. izdat., 1957. 120 p, music, illus.

[*3823*] 'Tchaikovsky's ballets', *Notes*, 8 (Sep 1951): 744–745.
On piano arrangements of *Swan Lake* (by E. Langer), *The Sleeping Beauty* (A. Ziloti) and *The Nutcracker* (S. Taneev) published 1949–50 by the Tschaikowsky Foundaton of New York. The score of *Swan Lake* is a new compilation by P. March, consisting of Langer's arrangement published in 1896, together with other material from the original version.

[*3824*] BOURGEOIS, J. & JACQUES, H. 'La musique de ballet de Tchaikowsky', *Disques*, 4 (Nov 1951): 4, illus.
Mainly a review of recordings.

[*3825*] SOKOL´SKII, M. 'Zametki o balete: Vechno zhivoi Chaikovskii', *Sovetskoe iskusstvo* (2 Jul 1952): 3.

[*3826*] SLONIMSKII, Iu. I. *P. I. Chaikovskii i baletnyi teatr ego vremeni*. Pod red. D. V. Zhitomirskogo. Moskva: Gos. muz. izdat., 1956. 335 p, illus. (*Gos. nauchno-issledovatel´skii institut teatra i muzyki*).
Review: L. Serebrovskaia, 'Knizhnoe obozrenie: Balety Chaikovskogo', *Sovetskaia muzyka* (1957), 1: 145–147.

[*3827*] LINDLAR, H. 'Tchaikovsky als ballettkomponist', *Musik und Szene*, 3 (1958/59), 9: 100–103.

[*3828*] SLONIMSKII, Iu. 'Writings on Lev Ivanov', *Dance Perspectives* (1959), 2 [whole issue].
Includes references to Ivanov's work on *Swan Lake* and *The Nutcracker*.

[*3829*] IVANOVA, S. 'Mariia Semenova v baletakh Chaikovskogo: K 125-letiiu so dnia rozhdeniia P. I. Chaikovskogo', *Teatr* (1965), 5: 98–104, illus.
The role of the designer Mariia Semenova in Chaikovskii's ballets.

[*3830*] DEMIDOV, A. 'Lirika, teatral´nost´, geroika baletov Chaikovskogo v postanovke Grigorovicha', *Teatr* (1970), 7: 41–49, illus.

[*3831*] KNIGHT, J. 'Music for dance', *Composer* (win. 1970/71), 38: 11.

[*3832*]   ASAF'EV, B. V. *O balete: Stati´i, retsenzii, vospominaniia*. Leningrad: Muzyka, 1974. 296 p.

Includes: "Lebedinoe ozero": 26–27 — "Spiashchaia krasavitsa": 76–85 [see *4043*] — 'Tridtsatiletie "Shchelkunchika"': 102–107 [see *3903*] — 'K postanovke baleta P. I. Chaikovskogo "Lebedinoe ozero"': 177–193 [see *4202*] — "Shchelkunchik" [I]: 193–194 —"Shchelkunchik" [II]: 194–197 — 'Iz Klinskikh novell: Prosnetsia li "Spiashchaia krasavitsa"?': 199–205 — '"Spiashchaia krasavitsa" ili "Spiashchaia tsarevna"?': 205–212.

[*3833*]   STUDWELL, W. E., *Delibes and Chaikovskii: The origins of modern ballet music*. [DeKalb, Illinois]: W. E. Studwell, 1974. 57 p.

[*3834*]   MASKEY, J. 'The dance', *Musical America*, 25 (May 1975): 14–15.

[*3835*]   TERRY, W. 'Ballet's multiple styles', *Saturday Review* (20 Sep 1975), 2: 46–47.

[*3836*]   ROZANOVA, Iu. A. *Simfonicheskie printsipy baletov Chaikovskogo*. Moskva: Muzyka, 1976. 160 p, music, illus.

Review: R. J. Wiley, *Cord*, 10 (fall/win. 1977), 1: 23–24.

[*3837*]   WARRACK, J. *Tchaikovsky's ballet music*. London: British Broadcasting Corporation; Seattle: Univ. of Washington Press, 1979. 72 p, music. (*BBC Music Guides*; 41). ISBN: 0–563–12860–7 (UK), 0–2959–5697–6 (USA).

Reviews: E. Garden, *Musical Times*, 120 (Oct 1979): 831 — *The Times* (14 Oct 1979) [suppl.]— *Music & Musicians*, 28 (Feb 1980): 33–34 — *Music Teacher*, 60 (Jan 1981): 29 — *American Music Teacher*, 31 (1982), 4: 62 — H. Zajaczkowski, *Music Review*, 45 (Feb 1984), 1: 61–62.

— [Chinese tr.] London: BBC, 1995. ISBN: 957–8996–66–7.

— [Italian tr.] *Ciajkovskij: I balletti*. Trad. di Luca Ripanti. Milano: Rugginenti, 1994. 102 p. (*Guide musicali Rugginenti-BBC*).

[*3838*]   TURSKA, I. *Balety Piotra Czajkowskiego*, wyd 1. Kraków: Polskie Wydn. 1. Muzyczne, 1981. 146 p, music, illus. (*Mała biblioteka baletowa*; 4) ISBN: 8–3224–0170–1.

[*3839*]   ACOCELLA, J. R. 'The mystery, magic and mastery of Tchaikovsky and the ballet', *Dance Magazine*, 55 (Jun 1981), 6: 53–56, illus.

Partly in connection with the Chaikovskii ballet festival in New York.

[*3840*]   KOEGLER, H. 'Tchaikovsky', *Ballet News*, 2 (Dec 1981): 35.

[*3841*]   MILNES, R. 'Tchaikovsky and dance: An introduction', *Dance Gazette* (Oct 1982), 181: 7–9, illus.

[*3842*]   LISCHKÉ, A. 'Tchaikovski et l'évolution du ballet russe', *Opéra de Paris*, 6 (Jan 1983): 22–24, illus.

[*3843*]   VOLKOV, S. *Balanchine's Tchaikovsky: Interviews with George Balanchine*. Tr. from the Russian by Antonia W. Bouis. New York: Simon & Schuster [1985]. xxvii, 252 p, illus. ISBN: 0–6714–9875–4.

Reviews: J. Anderson, *New York Times Book Review* (26 May 1985): 17 — J. Stahl, *Library Journal*, 110 (1 Jun 1985): 140 — B. Genne, *Dancing Times* (Sep 1985): 1047–1048 — H. Koegler, *Ballett-International*, 8 (Oct 1985), 10: 52–53 — *Musical America*, 35 (Nov 1985): 18–19 — J. R. Acocella, *Dance Magazine*, 59 (Dec 1985): 87–92 — G. E. Dorris, 'Tchaikovsky and the ballet', *Dance Chronicle*, 9 (1986), 2: 262–263 — H. Muschamp, *Artforum*, 24 (Jan 1986), 5: 13 — *Neue Zeitschrift für Musik* (Apr 1986), 4: 78 — S. J. Cohen, *Dance Research Journal*, 18 (win. 1986): 64–65.

— [2nd ed.] *Balanchine's Tchaikovsky: Conversations with Balanchine on his life, ballet and music*. New York: Anchor Books, 1992. xxvii, 202 p, illus. ISBN: 0–385–42387–X.

Reviews: *American Record Guide*, 56 (1993), 2: 215 — *Fanfare*, 16 (1993), 4: 434 — A. Poznansky, *Slavic Review*, 52 (win. 1993), 4: 864–865 — B. Jennings, *Attitude*, 9 (win. 1993), 1: 60 — *Dancing Times*, 84 (Jan 1994): 379.

— [repr.] London: Faber & Faber, 1993. xxi, 202 p, illus. ISBN: 0–571–17056–0 (pbk).

— [French tr.] *Conversations avec George Balanchine: Variations sur Tchaïkovski*. Texte français de Carole Dany. Préface de Maurice Béjart. Paris: L'Arche [1988]. 222 p, illus. ISBN: 2–85181–210–3.

— [German tr.] *Schlaflose Nächte mit Tschaikowsky: Das Leben Balanchines*. In Gesprächen mit Solomon Volkov, aus dem Amerikanische von Heide Sommer und Olivin Ziemer. Vorwort von Maurice Bëjart. Übersetzt des russische Orig.-Ms. ins Amerikan von Antonina W. Bouis. Weinheim [u. a.]: Beltz; Quadriga-Verlags, 1994. 220 p, illus. ISBN: 3–88679–220–X.

Reviews: H. Koegler, *Ballett International* (Jun 1994): 50 — *Orchester*, 43 (1995), 1: 59–60 — K. Kirchberg, *Neue Zeitschrift für Musik* (May/Jun 1995), 3: 77.

[3844]   **WILEY, R. J. *Tchaikovsky's ballets: "Swan Lake", "Sleeping Beauty", "Nutcracker"***. Oxford: Clarendon Press; New York: Oxford Univ. Press [1985]. xv, 429 p, music, illus. ISBN: 0–19–315314–9. (*Oxford monographs on music*).

Includes: 'Tchaikovsky's harmony': 345–353 [see *2469*].

Reviews: N. Goodwin, *Dance & Dancers* (1985): 33–34 — J. Warrack, *Music & Letters*, 66 (1985): 375–376 — A. Macaulay, 'Wiley's Tchaikovsky', *Dancing Times*, 75 (Mar 1985): 502–504, illus. — G. E. H. Abraham, *Times Literary Suppl.* (29 Mar 1985): 339 — E. Garden, *Musical Times*, 126 (Jul 1985): 409, 411 — R. G. Whaley, *Choice*, 23 (Oct 1985): 304 — J. R. Acocella, *Dance Magazine*, 59 (Dec 1985): 92–93 —G. E. Dorris, 'Tchaikovsky and the ballet', *Dance Chronicle*, 9 (1986), 2: 256–263 — R. Craft, *New York Review of Books*, 33 (13 Feb 1986): 29–30 — A. Croce, 'Dancing: The dreamer of the dream' (24 Feb 1986) [see *3846*] — G. Eberle, *Neue Zeitschrift für Musik* (Oct 1986), 10: 72 — E. Willinger, 'Wiley's Tchaikovsky', *Ballet Review*, 15 (spr. 1987), 1: 13–18 — T. Kohlhase, *Die Musikforschung*, 40 (Oct/Dec 1987), 4: 377–378 — *Slavic and East European Journal*, 31 (win. 1987), 4: 639–640 — H. Zajaczkowski, *Music Review*, 49 (May 1988), 2: 150–154 — M. Mazo, *Journal of the American Musicological Society*, 42 (spr. 1989), 1: 194–203 — E. D. Carpenter, *Slavic Review*, 48 (win. 1989), 4: 698–699 — G. Shokhman, 'Vzgliad s drugikh beregov', *Sovetskaia muzyka* (1990), 6: 134–141 [see *592*].

— [repr.] London: Oxford Univ. Press, 1986. ISBN: 0–19–315314–9.

— [repr.] London: Oxford Univ. Press, 1991. ISBN: 0–19–816249–9 (pbk).

— [repr.] London: Oxford Univ. Press, 1997. ISBN: 0–19–816249–9 (pbk).

[3845]   **WILEY, R. J. 'Dramatic time and music in Tchaikovsky's ballets'**. In: *Slavonic and Western music: Essays for Gerald Abraham*. Ed. by Malcolm H. Brown and Roland John Wiley. Oxford: Clarendon Press; Ann Arbor: UMI Research [1985]: 187–195, illus. music. (*U. M. I. Russian Music Studies*; 12). ISBN 0–8357–1594–9 (US).

[3846]   **CROCE, A. 'Dancing: The dreamer of the dream'**, *New Yorker*, 62 (24 Feb 1986): 76–79.

Includes a review of R. J. Wiley, *Tchaikovsky's ballets* (1985) [see *3844*].

[3847]   **DULOVA, E. *Balety P. I. Chaikovskogo i zhanrovaia stilistika baletnoi muzyki XIX veka***. Leningrad: Gos. konservatoriia im. N. A. Rimskogo-Korsakova, 1989. 58 p.

[3848]   **LLORENS, P. 'Chaikovsky: El ballet en el siglo'**, *Monsalvat* (May 1990), 182: 26–27, illus.

[3849]   **WILEY, R. J. 'Reflections on Tchaikovsky'**, *Dancing Times*, 80 (May 1990): 801–803, illus.

[3850]   **MACAULAY, A. 'Ermler's Tchaikovsky'**, *Dancing Times*, 80 (Sep 1990): 1179–1181, illus.

Interview with the conductor of the Bol´shoi Theatre Orchestra, Mark Ermler.

[3851]   **'Festival´ "Balety P. I. Chaikovskogo"'**, *Izvestiia* (20 Sep 1990): 6.

Concerning a festival in Moscow devoted to Chaikovskii's ballets. See also *3852, 3853, 3854*.

[3582]   **'Teatry Rossii na stsene Bol´shogo: Festival´ baleta'**, *Sovetskaia kul´tura* (29 Sep 1990): 9.

[3853]   **PERKINA, L. 'Balet i Chaikovskii'**, *Pravda* (1 Oct 1990): 6.

[3854]   **ONCHUROVA, N. 'Iz muzeinykh arkhivov: Iurii Bakhrushin o baletakh Chaikovskogo'**. *Sovetskii balet*, 6 (Nov/Dec 1990): 9.

[3855]   **BELOV, V. S. 'Balety P. I. Chaikovskogo v tvorchestve S. B. Virsaladze'**. In: *P. I. Chaikovskii i izobrazitel´noe iskusstvo* (1991): 87–92 [see *595*].

[*3856*]   POBERZHNAIA, G. I. 'Izobrazitel´nost´ v baletnoi muzyke P. I. Chaikovskogo'. In: *P. I. Chaikovskii i izobrazitel´noe iskusstvo* (1991): 62–69 [see *595*].

[*3857*]   JOHNSON, R. 'Tchaikovsky's Balanchine', *New Dance Review*, 3 (Jan/Mar 1991), 3: 16–17.

[*3858*]   VALIS-HILL, C. 'Tchaikovsky jubilee at New York City Ballet', *Attitude*, 7 (win./spr.1991), 2: 36, illus.

[*3859*]   GOODWIN, N. 'Tchaikovsky from far and near', *Dance and Dancers* (May 1992): 16–17, illus.

Discussion of Chaikovskii's ballet music as presented in A. Orlova, *Tchaikovsky: A self-portrait* (1990) [see *1532*], and D. Brown, *Tchaikovsky: A biographical and critical study*, vol. 4 (1991) [see *1534*].

[*3860*]   CONSTANTI, S. 'Fresh dances for the late Tchaikovsky', *Dancing Times*, 83 (Aug 1993): 1080; 84 (Jan 1994): 331.

[*3861*]   SWANSTON, R. 'Success and failure at the ballet', *Classic CD* (Nov 1993), 42: 8–9 [suppl.], illus.

[*3862*]   PERCIVAL, J. 'All in the music: Tchaikovsky and Balanchine', *Dance and Dancers* (Nov/Dec 1993): 9–11.

[*3863*]   FOKINE, M. 'Tschaikowsky und das Ballett'. In: *Tschaikowsky aus der Nähe* (1994): 162 [see *379*].

[*3864*]   KRZEMIEŃ-KOLPANOWICZ, B. 'Modele opracowania muzycznego w baletach Czajkowskiego' / 'Models of musical treatment in Tchaikovsky's ballets', *Muzyka*, 39 (1994), 1: 33–59, music.

Text in Polish, with a summary in English.

[*3865*]   WILEY, R. J. 'The Life and Works of Lev Ivanov: Choreographer of "The Nutcracker" and "Swan Lake"'. Oxford: Oxford Univ. Press, 1997. 306 p. ISBN 0–1981–6567–6.

[*3866*]   GOODWIN, N. 'Tchaikovsky, Petr Il´'ich'. In: *International encyclopedia of dance: A project of Dance Perspectives Foundation, Inc.* Founding ed. Selma Jeanne Cohen. Vol. 6. New York: Oxford Univ. Press, 1998: 1114–1117.

[*3867*]   JACOBS, L. 'Tchaikovsky at the millennium', *New Criterion*, 18 (Sep 1999), 1: 21–28.

Concerning recent productions of *Swan Lake* by Matthew Bourne, and *The Sleeping Beauty* by the Kirov Ballet.

[*3868*]   'Tchaikovsky's ballets: Interpretation and performance'. In: *Tchaikovsky and his contemporaries* (1999): 295–312 [see *602*].

A round-table discussion, moderated by Jeanne Fuchs.

See also *76, 78, 82*.

THE NUTCRACKER
Fairy-ballet in 2 acts, Op. 71 (1891–92)
[see also the *Suite* from the ballet]

[*3869*]   *"Shchelkunchik": Balet-feeriia*. Muzyka P. I. Chaikovskogo. Sankt Peterburg: Tipografiia Imperatorskikh teatrov, 1892. 20 p.

Original libretto.

— [English tr.] in R. J. Wiley, *Tchaikovsky's ballets* (1982): 333–341 [see *3844*].

[*3870*]   'Teatr i muzyka', *Birzhevye vedomosti* (29 Sep 1892): 3.

Rehearsals for the first production of the ballet in St. Petersburg.

[*3871*]   'Teatral´noe ekho', *Peterburgskaia gazeta* (5 Dec 1892).

[3872] 'Novyi balet-feeriia', *Peterburgskii listok* (6 Dec 1892).

The first production of the ballet on 6 Dec 1892 in St. Petersburg. See also *3149, 3154, 3155, 3157, 3783 to 3891.*

[3873] BASKIN, V. 'Teatral´noe ekho: "Shchelkunchik"', *Peterburgskaia gazeta* (7 Dec 1892).

[3874] IPPOLITOV [RAPGOF, I. P.]. 'Muzykal´naia zhizn´', *Grazhdanin* (7 Dec 1892).

[3875] R. 'Pervoe predstavlenie "Shchelkunchika"', *Peterburgskii listok* (7 Dec 1892).

[3876] S. 'Teatr i muzyka', *Novoe vremia* (7 Dec 1892): 3.

[3877] A. 'Teatr i muzyka', *Novoe vremia* (8 Dec 1892): 3.

[3878] B. "Shchelkunchik", *Peterburgskaia gazeta* (8 Dec 1892).

[3879] DOMINO. 'Mariinskii teatr: "Shchelkunchik", balet-feeriia, muzyka P. I. Chaikovskogo', *Birzhevye vedomosti* (8 Dec 1892): 2.

[3880] [SKAL´KOVSKII, K. A.] 'Balet', *Novosti i birzhevaia gazeta* (8 Dec 1892): 3–4.

[3881] 'Teatr i muzyka: "Shchelkunchik"', *Den´* (8 Dec 1892).

[3882] BASKIN, V. S. 'Teatral´noe ekho', *Peterburgskaia gazeta* (9 Dec 1892): 4.

[3883] IPPOLITOV [RAPGOF, I. P.] 'Balet "Shchelkunchik"', *Grazhdanin* (9 Dec 1892).

[3884] IUGORSKII, S. 'Pis´mo iz Peterburga', *Moskovskie vedomosti* (9 Dec 1892).

[3885] 'Teatral´nyi kur´er', *Peterburgskii listok* (9 Dec 1892).

[3886] STARYI BALETOMAN. 'Teatral´noe ekho', *Peterburgskaia gazeta* (10 Dec 1892).

[3887] BUKVA [VASIL´EVSKII, I. F.] 'Peterburgskie nabroski', *Russkie vedomosti* (13 Dec 1892).

[3888] DOMINO. "Shchelkunchik", *Birzhevye vedomosti* (13 Dec 1892).

[3889] IVANOV, M. 'Muzykal´nye zametki', *Novoe vremia* (14 Dec 1892).

[3890] BASKIN, V. S. 'Peterburgskaia muzykal´naia zhizn´', *Nabliudatel´* (1893), 6: 232–234.

[3891] 'Muzykal´noe obozrenie', *Nuvellist* (Jan 1893): 2.

[3892] KORESHCHENKO, A. 'Peterburgskie teatry', *Moskovskie vedomosti* (31 Oct 1895).

[3893] 'Teatr i muzyka', *Novoe vremia* (24 Apr 1900).

[3894] B. 'Balet', *Peterburgskaia gazeta* (9 Oct 1900).

[3895] ARAKCHIEV, [ARAKISHVILI] D. I. 'Pis´mo v redaktsiiu: Po nedorazumenniu', *Russkaia muzykal´naia gazeta* (18 Mar 1901), 11: 335–338.

Letter to the editor concerning the Georgian origins of the Arabian Dance in *The Nutcracker.*

[3896] 'Balet', *Birzhevye vedomosti* (1 Feb 1905).

[3897] KUDRIN, K. 'Benefis kordebaleta', *Teatr i iskusstvo* (1909), 51: 22–25.

[3898] NE-BALETOMAN. 'Benefis kordabaleta', *Peterburgskaia gazeta* (14 Dec 1909).

[3899] KOZLIANINOV, L. "Shchelkunchik", *Novoe vremia* (15 Dec 1909).

[*3900*]   E. B. 'Feia kukol-Shchelkunchik', *Birzhevye vedomosti* (28 Dec 1909).

[*3901*]   SVETLOV, V. 'Balet', *Peterburgskaia gazeta* (24 Oct 1911).

[*3902*]   VOLYNSKII, A. "Shchelkunchik", *Birzhevye vedomosti* (1 Nov 1912).

[*3903*]   L[EVENSO]N, A. "Feia kukol´: "Shchelkunchik", *Rech* (30 Oct 1912).

[*3904*]   '"Shchelkunchik" v postanovke A. A. Gorskogo', *Vestnik teatra* (1919), 30: 4–5.

[*3905*]   EL. "Shchelkunchik", *Izvestiia* (18 Sep 1919).

[*3906*]   GERONSKII. '"Shchelkunchik" v Novom teatre', *Ekran* (1922), 24/25: 9–10.

[*3907*]   GLEBOV, I. [ASAF´EV, B. V.] 'Tridsatiletie "Shchelkunchika". Gofman-Chaikovskii i Petipa-Vsevolozhskii. Russkoe buntarstvo i russkii empire. O finale "Shchelkunchika", o russkikh finalakh voobshche i o finalakh Chaikovskogo v osobennosti', *K novym beregam* (1923), 1: 37–41.
           — [repr.] 'Tridsatiletie "Shchelkunchika"'. In: B. V. Asaf´ev, *O balete: Stati´i, retsenzii, vospominaniia* (1974): 102–107 [see *3832*].

[*3908*]   STARK, E. 'V balete', *Krasnaia gazeta* (5 Feb 1923).

[*3909*]   VOLYNSKII, A. 'Maliar negodnyi', *Zhizn´ iskusstva* (20 Feb 1923), 7: 4–5.
           — [English tr. (excs.)] in R. J. Wiley, *Tchaikovsky's ballets* (1982): 388 [see *3844*].

[*3910*]   'Iubilei P. I. Chaikovskogo', *Vecherniaia krasnaia gazeta* (15 Aug 1928).
           Concerning a production of 'The Nutcracker', for the 35th anniversary of Chaikovskii's death.

[*3911*]   'K iubileiu P. I. Chaikovskogo', *Vecherniaia krasnaia gazeta* (8 Sep 1928).

[*3912*]   'Prem´era "Shchelkunchika"', *Pechat´ i revoliutsiia* (1929), 11: 116–117.

[*3913*]   "Shchelkunchik", *Zhizn´ iskusstva* (1929), 42: 11–12.

[*3914*]   VSEVOLODSKII, V. 'Pravda o balete', *Zhizn´ iskusstva* (1929), 16: 7–8.

[*3915*]   "Shchelkunchik", *Rabochii i teatr* (Nov 1929), 45 [whole issue], illus.
           In connection with a new production of the ballet in Leningrad. Includes: N. Zapadinskii, 'Na granitse zdravogo smysla': 7–8 — V. M. Bogdanov-Berezovskii, 'Luchshee v spektakle: Muzyka': 9–10.

[*3916*]   SOLLERTINSKII, I. "Shchelkunchik", *Krasnaia gazeta* (1 Nov 1929).

[*3917*]   GVOZDEV, A. 'Novyi "Shchelkunchik"', *Krasnaia gazeta* (28 Nov 1929).

[*3918*]   ***"Shchelkunchik": Balet v 3-kh aktakh i 22-kh epizodakh, s prologom i epilogom***. Libretto, postanovka i tekst F. L. Lopukhova. Sistema peredvizhnykh sten. butaforiia, kostiumy, grim po proektu i eskizam V. V. Dmitrieva. Muzyka P. I. Chaikovskogo. [Moskva]: Teakinopechat´, 1930. 16 p. (*V pomoshch´ zriteliu*).

[*3919*]   ***"Shchelkunchik": Balet P. I. Chaikovskogo***. Moskva: Gos. izdat. khudozh. literatury, 1932. 31 p, illus. (*Gos. Akad. Bol´shoi teatr SSSR*).

[*3920*]   GABOVICH, M. 'O kadrakh i "Shchelkunchike"', *Sovetskoe iskusstvo* (21 Apr 1932).

[*3921*]   SLONIMSKII, Iu. A. *"Shchelkunchik"*. Muzyka P. I. Chaikovskogo. [Leningrad]: Gos. Akad. teatr opery i baleta, 1934. 40 p, illus.
           — 2-e izd. Leningrad: Gos. Akad. teatr opery i baleta, 1934. 23 p, illus.
           — 3-e izd. Leningrad: Gos. Akad. teatr opery i baleta im. S. M. Kirova, 1936. 21 p, illus.

[3922]   GRAVE, A. &. SIMONOV, A. '"Shelkunchik": Teatr opery i baleta', *Leningradskaia pravda* (28 Feb 1934).

[3923]   IANKOVSKII, M. '"Shelkunchik": Prem'era v GATOBE', *Krasnaia gazeta* (2 Mar 1934).

[3924]   VALER'IANOV, B. 'Nevozrozhdennyi "Shchelkunchik": Prem'era v Lengosteatre opery i baleta', *Sovetskoe iskusstvo* (11 Mar 1934): 3.

[3925]   *"Shchelkunchik"*. Khoreograficheskaia studiia. [Tiflis], 1936. 18 p, illus.

[3926]   VAINONEN, V. '"Shchelkunchik": Balet P. I. Chaikvoskogo v Bol'shom teatre', *Pravda* (6 Feb 1939): 6.
         The author's new production of the ballet in Moscow. See also *3927*.

[3927]   VAINONEN, V. '"Shchelkunchik": Balet P. I. Chaikovskogo', *Dekada moskovskikh zrelishch* (11 Mar 1939), 8: 13.

[3928]   ERLIKH, A. '"Shchelkunchik": Novaia postanovka baleta Chaikovskogo v Bol'shom teatre', *Pravda* (10 May 1939): 5.

[3929]   POTAPOV, V. I. 'Vo sne i naiavu', *Sovetskoe iskusstvo* (11 May 1939).

[3930]   'Programmy M. Petipa: "Shchelkunchik"'. In: *Chaikovskii i teatr* (1940): 257–266 [see *2537*].

[3931]   GORODINSKII, V. '"Shchelkunchik": Tretii baletnyi spektakl' molodezhi v Bol'shom teatre', *Komsomol'skaia pravda* (26 Mar 1940): 4.
         — [repr.] In: V. Gorodinskii, *Izbrannye stat'i*. Moskva: Sovetskii kompozitor, 1963: 222–227.

[3932]   *"Shchelkunchik": Balet P. I. Chaikovskogo*. Sost. V. M. Bogdanov-Berezovskii. Leningrad: Leningradskii Akad. teatr opery i baleta, 1941. 40 p.

[3933]   IVING, V. '"Shchelkunchik" v filiale Bol'shogo Akad. teatra', *Izvestiia* (3 Aug 1943).

[3934]   BAKHRUSHIN, Iu. *"Shchelkunchik"*. [Moskva]: Sovetskoe iskusstvo, 1944. 6 p. (*Programmy moskovskikh zrelishch. Gos. Akad. Bol'shoi teatr SSSR*).

[3935]   KRASOVSKAIA, V. '"Shchelkunchik", vozobnovlenie baleta', *Vechernii Leningrad* (20 Apr 1947).

[3936]   KROKOVER, R. 'New York City Ballet will give whole "Nutcracker"', *Musical Courier*, 149 (1 Jan 1954): 16.

[3937]   AUDEN, W. H. 'Ballet's present Eden: Example of "The Nutcracker"', *Center*, 1 (Feb 1954): 2–4, illus.

[3938]   WEINSTOCK, H. 'Chronology of "The Nutcracker"', *Center*, 1 (Feb 1954): 5–6.

[3939]   KOLODIN, I. 'The compleat "Nutcracker"', *Saturday Review*, 37 (29 May 1954): 40, illus.

[3940]   CARP, L. 'Small fry and "The Nutcracker"', *Dance magazine*, 31 (1957), 12: 38–40, 92.

[3941]   CHAPPELL, W. *"The Nutcracker"*. Adapted and illus. by Warren Chappell; based on the Alexandre Dumas père's version of the story by E. T. A. Hoffmann; with themes from the music by Peter Ilyich Tschaikovsky. New York: A. A. Knopf [1958]. [40] p, music, illus.
         — [repr.] New York: Schocken Books, 1980. [40] p, music, illus.

[3942]   CROWLE, P. *"The Nutcracker" ballet: A Christmas fantasy and its history*. Photographs by Mike Davis; with a foreword by Alexandre Benois, and a preface by David Lichine. London: Faber & Faber [1958]. 52 p, illus.

[*3943*]   BARBES, C. '"The Nutcracker": Music', *Dance and Dancers*, 9 (Feb 1958): 15.

[*3944*]   WALDEN, D. *"The Nutcracker"*. Pictures by Harold Berson. Philadelphia: Lippincott, 1959. 45 p.

[*3945*]   APPLEBY, W. & FOWLER, F. *"Nutcracker" and "Swan Lake"*. Illus. by Audrey Walker. London: Oxford Univ. Press [1960]. 57 p, illus. (*The Young Reader's Guides to Music*; 3).
        — [repr.] New York: H. Z. Walck, 1968. 57 p, illus. (*The Young Reader's Guides to Music*; 3).

[*3946*]   SWINSON, C. *"The Nutcracker" ("Casse-noisette"): The story of the ballet*. London: A & C Black [1960]. 96 p, illus.

[*3947*]   HALL, G. *"The Nutcracker": The story of the ballet*. London: Ballet Books [1961]. [24] p, illus.

[*3948*]   SKUDINA, G. 'Stranichka shkol´nika: "Shchelkunchik"', *Muzykal´naia zhizn´* (1962), 24: 14–15.
        The 70th anniversary of the first performance.

[*3949*]   BOOKSPAN, M. 'Tchaikovsky's "Nutcracker"', *Stereo Review* (Dec 1962): 35.

[*3950*]   CHISTIAKOVA, V. 'Zagadka "Shchelkunchika"', *Teatr* (1966), 6: 21–31.

[*3951*]   GUSEV, P. 'Novyi "Shchelkunchik"', *Sovetskaia muzyka* (1966), 7: 68–78, illus.

[*3952*]   KRIGER, V. 'Vozrozhdennyi "Shchelkunchik"', *Izvestiia* (19 Mar 1966).

[*3953*]   CHERNOVA, N. 'Logika rezhissera', *Moskovskii komsomolets* (8 Apr 1966).

[*3954*]   GUEST, I. "Casse noisette", *About the House*, 2 (1967), 8: 4–11, illus.

[*3955*]   TERRY, W. 'World of dance', *Saturday review*, 50 (2 Dec 1967): 51–52, illus.
        The history of the ballet in the United States.

[*3956*]   SOLTÉSZ, G. *"Diótôro", Pjortr Hjies Csajkovszkij*. Budapest: Zenenukiadó, 1968. 27 p, illus.
        The story of the ballet (with two 7-inch records).

[*3957*]   'Nicholas Georgiadis talks about his designs for "The Nutcracker" and "Aida"', *About the House*, 2 (1968), 9: 46–47, illus.

[*3958*]   GOODWIN, N. '"The Nutcracker": What Tchaikovsky thought', *Dance and Dancers*, 19 (Apr 1968): 28–29.

[*3959*]   SURIN, E. 'Novye dissertatsii: Pervyi moskovskii "Shchelkunchik": K 50-letiiu postanovki A. Gorskogo', *Teatr* (1969), 5: 86–94, illus.
        The 50th anniversary of the first production in Moscow.

[*3960*]   PLEKHANOVA, N. 'Poisk napolovinu: "Shchelkunchik"', *Trud* (23 Nov 1969).

[*3961*]   DEMIDOV, A. 'Kukol´nyi dom', *Teatr* (1970), 3: 30–35.

[*3962*]   ALEKSANDROV, A. "Shchelkunchik", *Vechernii Leningrad* (24 Feb 1970).

[*3963*]   KUSHIDA, M. *Kurumiwarningyo*. [Tokyo]: Gakken [1971]. 2 vols, music, illus. [+1 LP record].
        — [English tr.] *P. I. Tchaikovsky's "The Nutcracker"*. Based on Tchaikovsky's ballet after the story by E. T. A. Hoffmann. Illus. by Fumiko Hori, adapted by Magoichi Kushida, tr. by Ann King Herring. [Tokyo]: Gakken [1971]. [28] p, illus. (*Fantasia pictorial*; 8).
        — [English tr. (repr.)] London: F. Warne, 1974. [30] p, illus. (*Fantasia pictorial*; 8). ISBN: 0–7232–1760–2.

[*3964*]   MAYNARD, O. "The Nutcracker", *Dance Magazine*, 47 (Dec 1973): 51–74.

[3965] HORI, F. *P. I. Tchaikovsky's "The Nutcracker"*. Based on Tchaikovsky's ballet. London: F. Warne, 1974. ISBN: 0–7232–1760–2.

[3966] VASIL´KOVA, N. 'Dlia bol´shikh i malen´kikh', *Sovetskaia kul´tura* (1 Jan 1974): 5, illus.

[3967] BARYSHNIKOV, M. *"Nutcracker": Ballet in 2 acts*. Choreographer: Mikhail Baryshnikov. Composer: Peter Ilich Tchaikovsky. [n.p.] American Ballet Theatre, 1976. 219 p.
Mainly choreographic notation, but includes a review and brief synopsis of the ballet.

[3968] *"Lo Schiaccianoci" di Petr I. Ciaikovskij*. Milano: Teatro alla Scala, 1977. (*Teatro alla Scala: Stagione d'opera e balletto 1976/77*). 43 p, illus.

[3969] BALANCHINE, G. & MASON, F. "The Nutcracker". In: *Balanchine's complete stories of the great ballets*. Rev. and enlarged ed. Garden (N. Y.): Doubleday, 1977: 387–395.

[3970] TERRY, W. 'A ballet for all seasons', *Saturday Review*, 4 (5 Mar 1977): 49–50, illus.

[3971] WILES, E. 'Tchaikovsky's "Casse-noisette"', *Music Teacher*, 56 (Jun 1977): 15–17.

[3972] WILLIAMS, M. D. 'The greatest hits of U. S. symphony orchestras', *Music Journal*, 36 (Sep 1978): 6.

[3973] ANDERSON, J. *The "Nutcracker" ballet*. London: Bison; New York: Mayflower Books [1979]. ix, 297 p, illus. ISBN: 0–8317–6486–4 (USA).

[3974] 'Records: "The Nutcracker"', *Ballet News*, 1 (May 1979): 50.

[3975] MICHELMAN, F. '"The Nutcracker": Tchaikovsky's ballet of good and evil endures as a classic', *Horizon*, 22 (Dec 1979): 51–55, illus.

[3976] JACOBSON, R. 'Viewpoint', *Ballet News*, 2 (Dec 1980): 4.

[3977] MURPHY, A. 'Visions of sugarplums', *Ballet News*, 2 (Dec 1980): 10–12, illus.

[3978] TERRY, W. '"Nuts" around the world', *Saturday Review* (Dec 1980), 7: 90, illus.

[3979] ROSENWALD, P. J. 'Dancing into the Kingdom of Sweets and reveries', *Wall Street Journal*, 61 (26 Dec 1980): 5.

[3980] LIVIO, A. *"Lo Schiaccianoci"*. Trad. di Patrizia Luppi. Roma: Di Giacomo [1982]. 135 p, illus. (*La danza e il balletto*).

[3981] LUTTER, F. 'Zwei Unterrichtssendungen des Bildungsfernsehens für den Musikunterricht des Klasse 3', *Musik in der Schule*, 33 (1982), 7–8: 243–244.

[3982] KLEIN, N. *Baryshnikov's "Nutcracker"*. With photographs by Ken Regan; additional photographs by Christopher Little and Martha Swope. New York: Putnam [1983]. [64] p, illus. ISBN: 0–3991–2887–5.

[3983] KLEIMENOVA, M. & URAL´SKAIA, V. 'Mir dobra i radosti: Balet P. Chaikovskogo "Shchelkunchik" v Bol´shom Teatre opery i baleta Belorusskoi SSR', *Sovetskii balet* (1983), 2: 8–10, illus.

[3984] MILNES, R. 'Tchaikovsky's ballet scores: "Nutcracker"', *Dance Gazette* (Oct 1983), 184: 18–20, illus.

[3985] CRISP, C. "The Nutcracker", *About the House*, 6 (1984), 12: 44–47, illus.
Notes on some historic performances.

[3986] WILEY, R. J. 'On meaning in "Nutcracker"', *Dance Research*, 3 (aut. 1984), 1: 3–28.

[3987]   WILEY, R. J. 'The symphonic element in "Nutcracker"', *Musical Times*, 125 (Dec 1984): 693–695.

[3988]   WILEY, R. J. 'Cracking "The Nutcracker"', *The Guardian* (14 Dec 1984).

[3989]   NEWMAN, B. *Stories of the ballets: "The Nutcracker"*. London [pr. Belgium]: Auran Press; New York: Barron's, 1985. 48 p.
         Includes a short biography of the composer.

[3990]   SWITZER, E. E. *"The Nutcracker": Story and a ballet*. Photographs by Steven Caras & Costas. New York: Atheneum, 1985. 101 p, illus.
         Review: A. Silvey, *Horn Book*, 61 (Nov/Dec 1985): 721.

[3991]   DEMIDOV, A. 'Stremlenie k mechte: Iz stsenicheskoi istorii baleta "Shchelkunchik"', *Muzykal´naia zhizn´* (1985), 20: 20–21, illus.

[3992]   "Der Nußknacker (Casse Noisette)". In: *Reclams Ballettführer*. Von Hartmut Regitz, Otto Friedrich Regner, Heinz-Ludwig Schneiders. Stuttgart: Reclam, 1985: 425–429. (*Universal-Bibliothek*; 8042).

[3993]   SAVELOVA, I. I. 'Iz istorii formirovaniia zamysla baleta P. I. Chaikovskogo "Shchelkunchik"'. In: *Teatr v zhizni i tvorchestve P. I. Chaikovskogo* (1985): 76–88 [see 589].

[3994]   SCHULLER, G. & STEIERT, T. "Schtschelkunchik". In: *Pipers Enzyklopädie des Musiktheaters: Oper, Operette, Musical, Ballet. Hrsg. von Carl Dahlhaus und dem Forschungsinstitut für Musiktheater der Universität Bayreuth unter Leitung von Sieghart Dohring*. Band 3. München: Piper, 1989: 157–161.

[3995]   SKVORTSOVA, I. 'Balet P. Chaikovskogo "Shchelkunchik": O novizne traktovki zhanra'. In: *Muzykal´nyi zhanry i sovremennost´: Tezisy dokladov molodykh muzykovedov*. Gor´kii: Gork´ovskaia konservatoriia, 1989: 110–113.

[3996]   SKVORTSOVA, I. 'K voprosu o variantakh muzykal´no-stsenicheskoi interpretatsii: "Shchelkunchik" Chaikovskogo—Novyi tip baletnogo spektaklia'. In: *Muzykal´no-ispolnitel´skoe iskusstvo: Problemy stilia i interpretatsii*. Sbornik nauchnykh trudov. Moskva: Gos. konservatoriia, 1989: 69–83.

[3997]   ASAF´EV, B. V. 'O tainakh baleta "Shchelkunchik", *Sovetskii balet* (1990), 5: 44–46, illus.

[3998]   GIPPO, J. '"The Nutcracker" and the piccolo', *Flute Talk*, 9 (Feb 1990): 32, music.

[3999]   KENNICOTT, P. 'Notes on "The Nutcracker"', *Dance Magazine*, 64 (Dec 1990): 76–77, illus.

[4000]   STUART, O. 'Tchaikovsky's enduring "Nutcracker"', *Classical*, 2 (Dec 1990): 40–46, illus.

[4001]   GUSIATNIKOVA, G. G. 'Balet P. I. Chaikovskogo "Shchelkunchik" na stsene Leningradskogo Akademicheskogo Malogo teatra opery i baleta (postanovka I. Bel´skogo, stsenografiia E. Stenberga)'. In: *P. I. Chaikovskii i izobrazitel´noe iskusstvo* (1991): 93–99 [see 595].

[4002]   SKVORTSOVA, I. A. '"Shchelkunchik": Problemy pozdnego stilia'. In: *Chaikovskii: Voprosy istorii i teorii* (1991): 38–54 [see 593].

[4003]   *"Der Nußknacker": Nach dem Ballet von Peter Iljitsch Tschaikowsky*. Bilder von Diane Goode. Deutsche übersetzen von Regina Zwerger. Wien: Überreuter, 1992. illus. ISBN: 3-8000-2041-6.
         Photographs and illustrations from a stage production of the ballet.

[4004]   SHERIKHOVA, G. 'Besedy o muzyke: Snovideniia po Gofmanu', *Muzykal´naia zhizn´* (1992), 23/24: 19–20.
         The 100th anniversary of the first performance of *The Nutcracker*.

[4005]   SKVORTSOVA, I. A. 'Muzykal'naia poetika baleta P. I. Chaikovskogo "Shchelkunchik"'.
         Moskva: Gos. konservatoriia im. P. I. Chaikovskogo, 1992. 25 p.
         Summary of dissertation (Moscow Conservatory).

[4006]   GIPPO, J. 'Let's talk picc: "The Nutcracker's" faux pas', *Flute Talk*, 12 (Sep 1992): 36–37, music.

[4007]   MEYEROWITZ, J. *George Balanchine's "The Nutcracker"*. Photographed and told by Joel Meyerowitz
         of the ballet by New York City Ballet. Boston, etc. [pr. Italy]: Elektra Entertainment; Little, Brown &
         Co., 1993. [78] p. (*A Floyd Yearout Book*).

[4008]   COPPERTHWAITE, D. B. 'The immortal "Nutcracker"', *Classical Music Magazine*, 16 (1993), 5:
         16–20, illus.

[4009]   GAMALEY, Iu. 'Balet "Shchelkunchik": Ego zhizn' s 1934 po 1954 god', *Balet* (1993), 5/6: 41–44,
         illus.

[4010]   BROWN, D. 'Tchaikovsky's ballets', *Dance Now*, 2 (aut. 1993), 3: 28–39, illus.

[4011]   INOZEMTSEVA, G. '"Shchelkunchik": Tri moskovskikh spektaklia', *Balet* (1994), 6: 9–11, illus.
         Comparing three different productions of the ballet in Moscow.

[4012]   *"Lo Schiaccianoci" di Petr Il'ic Cajkovskij*. Milano: Teatro alla Scala, 1994. 76 p, illus. (*Teatro alla
         Scala: Stagione d'opera e balletto 1994/95*).

[4013]   ROSE, C. 'Tchaikovsky "Casse-noisette": "La valse des fleurs"', *L'education musicale*, 50 (1994),
         411: 9–11.

[4014]   SKWORCOWA, I. [SKVORTSOVA, I. A.] '"Dziadek do orzechów" Piotr Czaikowskiego:
         Problemy koncepcji i stylu' / '"The Nutcracker": The problems of the conception and style',
         Muzyka, 39 (1994), 1: 61–72, music.
         Text in Polish, with a summary in English.

[4015]   SWANSTON, R. 'Tchaikovsky's "The Nutcracker"', *Classic CD* (Jan 1994), 44: 36–41, illus.

[4016]   SKVORTSOVA, I. A. 'Zamysly i ikh sud'ba: Neizvestnye stranitsy tvorcheskogo dialoga: M. I.
         Petipa i P. I. Chaikovskogo'. In: *P. I. Chaikovskii: K 100-letiiu so dnia smerti* (1995): 94–98 [see *597*].

[4017]   DOBROVOL'SKAIA, G. N. *"Shchelkunchik"*. Sankt Peterburg: MOL, 1996. 200 p, illus (*Shchedevry
         baleta*). ISBN 5-86345-028-0.

[4018]   KOEGLER, H. 'Ein Amerikanischer mythos: Zum "Nußknacker-kult in Nordamerika', *Ballett-
         International* (1996), 3: 46–50.

[4019]   SIEGEL, M. B. 'Kingdom of the Sweet', *Hudson Review*, 50 (sum. 1997): 255–267.
         The ballet's production history and social aspects.

[4020]   BLAIN, T. 'Tchaikovsky: "The Nutcracker"', *Classic CD* (Dec 1997): 46–49, illus.

[4021]   FISHER, J. J. 'The annual "Nutcracker": A participant-oriented, contextualized study of "The
         Nutcracker" ballet as it has evolved into a Christmas ritual in the United States and Canada'.
         Riverside: Univ. of California, 1998. 481 p.
         Dissertation (Ph. D.).

[4022]   'Rasshifrovannye tainy "Shelkunchika"', *Kul'tura* (1–7 Oct 1998): 5.
         Sergei Vikharev's revival of the original choreography in Novosibirsk.

         See also *459, 3865, 5459, 5598, 5599, 5647*.

THE SLEEPING BEAUTY
Ballet in a prologue and 3 acts, Op. 66 (1888–89)

[4023]   *"Spiashchaia krasavitsa": Balet-feeriia v 3 deistviiakh s prologom*. Muzyka P. I. Chaikovskogo. Postanovka i tantsy M. I. Petipa. Sankt Peterburg: Izdat. Imperatorskikh Sankt Peterburgskikh teatrov, 1889. 21 p.

Original libretto.

— [2-e izd.] Moskva: P. Iurgenson, 1890. 22 p.

— 3-e izd. Moskva: P. Iurgenson, 1899. 18 p.

— [English tr.] in R. J. Wiley, *Tchaikovsky's ballets* (1982): 327–333 [see *3844*].

— [English tr.] in *A Century of Russian ballet: Documents and accounts, 1810-1910*. Selected and tr. by Roland John Wiley. Oxford: Clarendon Press; New York : Oxford Univ. Press, 1990: 360–372.

[4024]   'Khronika: Peterburg', *Artist* (1889), 4: 182.

Rehearsals for the ballet in St. Petersburg.

[4025]   'Teatral´noe ekho: "Spiashchaia krasavitsa" (novyi balet)', *Peterburgskaia gazeta* (4 Jan 1890): 3.

The first production of the ballet on 3 Jan 1890 in St. Petersburg. See also *4026* to *4039*.

[4026]   'Eshche o novom balete', *Peterburgskaia gazeta* (4 Jan 1890): 3.

[4027]   'Balet "Spiashchaia krasavitsa"', *Syn Otechestva* (4 Jan 1890): 3.

[4028]   'Eshche o novom balete', *Peterburgskii listok* (5 Jan 1890): 3.

[4029]   N. 'Novyi balet', *Novosti i birzhevaia gazeta* (5 Jan 1890): 3.

[4030]   SKAL´KOVSKII, K. A. 'Teatr i muzyka', *Novoe vremia* (5 Jan 1890): 2.

— [English tr.] In: *A Century of Russian ballet: Documents and accounts, 1810-1910*. Selected and tr. by Roland John Wiley. Oxford: Clarendon Press; New York : Oxford Univ. Press, 1990: 373–376.

[4031]   'Teatral´noe ekho', *Peterburgskaia gazeta* (6 Jan 1890): 3.

[4032]   'Teatral´noe ekho',, *Peterburgskaia gazeta* (8 Jan 1890): 3.

[4033]   'Teatr i muzyka', *Novoe vremia* (9 Jan 1890): 4.

[4034]   BUKVA. 'Peterburgskie nabroski', *Russkie vedomosti* (14 Jan 1890): 2.

[4035]   IVANOV, M. M. 'Muzykal´nye zametki', *Novoe vremia* (16 Jan 1890).

[4036]   L. 'Teatral´noe ekho', *Peterburgskaia gazeta* (16 Jan 1890).

[4037]   LAROSH, G. A. 'Muzykal´noe pis´mo iz Peterburga', *Moskovskie vedomosti* (17 Jan 1890): 3–4.

— [repr.] In: G. A. Larosh, *Sobranie muzykal´no-kriticheskikh statei*, tom 2, chast´ 1 (1924): 171–179 [see *2311*].

— [repr.] In: G. A. Larosh, *Izbrannye stat´i v piati vypuskakh*, vyp. 2 (1975): 137–144 [see *2376*].

— [English tr.] In: *A Century of Russian ballet: Documents and accounts, 1810-1910*. Selected and tr. by Roland John Wiley. Oxford: Clarendon Press; New York : Oxford Univ. Press, 1990: 377–384.

— [German tr.] 'Tschaikowskys Ballett "Dornröschen"'. In: G. A. Larosh, *Peter Tschaikowsky: Aufsätze und Erinnerungen* (1993): 136–145 [see *2406*].

[4038]   IVANOV, M. M. '"Spiashchaia krasavitsa" P. I. Chaikovskogo', *Novoe vremia* (22 Jan 1890).

[4039]   '"Spiashchaia krasavitsa": Balet-feeriia v 3-kh deistviiakh s prologom M. Petipa. Muzyka P. I. Chaikovskogo', *Nuvellist* (Feb 1890): 3–5.

[4040] KASHKIN, N. D. '"Spiashchaia krasavitsa" Chaikovskogo', *Moskovskie vedomosti* (19 Jan 1899).

— [repr.] In: N. D. Kashkin, *Izbrannye stat´i o P. I. Chaikovskom* (1954): 187–192 [see 2349].

[4041] BEAUMONT, C. W. *"The Sleeping Princess": Music by Peter Tchaikovsky*. Written by C. W. Beaumont, decorated by Randolph Schwabe. London: C. W. Beaumont [1921]. 2 vols, illus. (*Impressions of the Russian Ballet, 1921*; 1).

[4042] BAKST, L. *L'oeuvre de Léon Bakst pour "La belle au bois dormant"*. Ballet en cinq actes d'après le conte de Perrault. Musique de Tchaikovsky. Préface d'André Levinson. Paris: M. de Brunoff, 1922. 21 p, illus.

Mainly illustrations of designs for the ballet.

— [English tr.] *The designs of Léon Bakst for "The Sleeping Princess", a ballet in five acts after Perrault*. Music by Tchaikovsky. Preface by André Levinson. New York: Scribner's; London: Benn Bros., 1923. 18 p, illus.

— [English tr. (repr.)] New York: B. Blom, 1971. 18 p, illus.

[4043] GLEBOV, I. [ASAF´EV, B. V.] 'Pis´ma o russkoi opere i balete: III. "Spiashchaia krasavitsa"', *Ezhenedel´nik Petrogradskikh Gosudarstvennykh akademcheskikh teatrov* (1922), 5: 28–36.

— [repr.] "Spiashchaia krasavitsa". In: B. V. Asaf´ev, *Izbrannye trudy*, tom 2 (1954): 175–181 [see *2348*].

— [repr.] "Spiashchaia krasavitsa". In: B. V. Asaf´ev, *Kriticheskie stat´i, ocherki i retsenzii*. Moskva; Leningrad, 1967: 158–167.

— [repr.] "Spiashchaia krasavitsa". In: B. V. Asaf´ev, *O muzyke Chaikovskogo: Izbrannoe* (1972): 362–370 [see *2373*].

— [repr.] "Spiashchaia krasavitsa". In: B. V. Asaf´ev, *O balete: Stati´i, retsenzii, vospominaniia* (1974): 76–85 [see *3832*].

[4044] "Spiashchaia krasavitsa", *Zhizn´ iskusstva* (1923), 45: 3.

[4045] VOLYNSKII, A. L. "Spiashchaia krasavitsa", *Zhizn´ iskusstva* (1923), 48: 7.

[4046] *"Spiashchaia krasavitsa"*. Moskva: Teakinopechat´, 1928. 8 p.

[4047] BRODERSEN, Iu. & MALKOV, N. *"Spiashchaia krasavitsa"*. Siuzhet zaimstvovan iz skazok Sh. Perro. Stsenicheskaia razrabotka M. I. Petipa. Muzyka P. I. Chaikovskogo. [Moskva]: Teakinopechat´, 1930. 15 p. (*V pomoshch´ zriteliu*).

[4048] *"Spiashchaia krasavitsa": Balet, muzyka P. I. Chaikovskogo*. Moskva: Teakinopechat´, 1930. 61 p. (*Kratkoe libretto*).

[4049] NEWMARCH, R. H. 'Tchaikovsky: Valse from "The Sleeping Beauty"'. In: R. H. Newmarch, *The concert-goer's library of descriptive notes. Part III: Suites and ballet suites for orchestra, rhapsodies and fantasias, miscellaneous dances*. London: Oxford Univ. Press; H. Milford, 1930: 143–144.

[4050] BOGDANOV-BEREZOVSKII, V. M. *Chto nado znat´ o balete "Spiashchaia krasavitsa"*. Leningrad: Biuro obsluzhivaniia rabochego zritelia pri upravlennii Leningradskikh Gos. teatrov, 1933. 31 p. (*V pomoshch´ zriteliu*).

[4051] SHAGINIAN, M. "Spiashchaia krasavitsa", *Izvestiia* (4 Dec 1933).

[4052] BOGDANOV-BEREZOVSKII, V. M. *"Spiashchaia krasavitsa": Balet v 3 deistviiakh s prologom*. Muzyka P. I. Chaikovskogo. [Leningrad]: Gos. Akad. teatr opery i baleta, 1934. 27 p, illus.

Includes libretto.

— Izd. 2-e. Leningrad: Gos. Akad. teatr opery i baleta, 1935. 27 p, illus.

— Izd. 3-e. Leningrad: Gos. Akad. teatr opery i baleta im. S. M. Kirova, 1937. 25 p, illus.

— [Izd. 4-e.] Leningrad: Gos. Akad. teatr opery i balet im S. M. Kirova, 1940. 25 p, illus.

[4053] *"Spiashchaia krasavitsa": Balet v 3-kh aktakh*. Muzyka P. I. Chaikovskogo. Moskva: Gos. Akad. Bol´shoi teatr Soiuza SSR, 1936. 44 p.

Includes: V. M. Bogdanov-Berezovskii, '"Spiashchaia krasavitsa" v istorii russkogo baleta': 5–12 — N. Rukavishnikov, '"Spiashchaia krasavitsa": Balet P. I. Chaikovskogo (istoricheskaia spravka)': 13–21.

[*4054*]   GORODINSKII, V. "Spiashchaia krasavitsa", *Komsomol´skaia pravda* (30 Dec 1936).

— [repr.] In: V. Gorodinskii, *Izbrannye stat´i*. Moskva: Sovetskii kompozitor, 1963: 194–198.

[*4055*]   CARTER, E. "The Sleeping Beauty", *Modern Music*, 14 (1937): 175–176.

[*4056*]   MARTIN, J. J. 'A premiere: Philadelphia Ballet to give first American performance of Tchaikovsky work', *New York Times* (7 Feb 1937).

[*4057*]   SHAGINIAN, M. "Spiashchaia krasavitsa", *Izvestiia* (4 Dec 1938).

[*4058*]   'Programmy M. Petipa: "Spiashchaia krasavitsa"'. In: *Chaikovskii i teatr* (1940): 245–256 [see *2537*].
Petipa's original ballet-master's plan.

— [repr.] In: P. I. Chaikovskii, *Polnoe sobranie sochinenii*, tom 12G (1952): 368–375 [see *118*].

— [rev. repr.] In: Iu. I. Slonimskii, *P. I. Chaikovskii i baletnyi teatr ego vremeni* (1956): 312–22 [see *3826*].

— [English tr. by J. Lawson], *Dancing Times* (Dec 1942): 112–114; (Jan 1943): 168–170; (Feb 1943): 218–220; (Mar 1943): 270–271.

— [English tr. (abridged)] In: S. J. Cohen, *Dance as a theatre art*. Source readings in dance history from 1581 to the present. Ed. with a commentary by Selma Jeanne Cohen. New York: Harper & Row [1974]: 95–102; 2nd ed. Princeton, N. J.: Princeton Book Co. [1992]: 95–102. (*Dance horizons*).

— [English tr.] 'The balletmaster's plan for "Sleeping Beauty". In: R. J. Wiley, *Tchaikovsky's Ballets* (1985): 359–370 [see *3844*].

— [German tr.] 'Musikalisch-szenischer Plan zu "Dornröschen"', *Musik und Bildung*, 15 (Sep 1983): 49–50.

[*4059*]   ANTHONY, G. *"The Sleeping Princess": Camera studies by Gordon Anthony*. With text by Nadia Benois, Arnold Haskell and Constant Lambert. London: G. Routledge & Sons Ltd, 1940 [1942]. xi, 49 p, illus.
Published in connection with a revival of *The Sleeping Beauty* at Sadler's Wells, 2 Feb 1939.
Includes: C. Lambert, 'Tchaikovsky and the Ballet' — N. Benois: 'Decor and costumes' — A. L. Haskell: 'Aurora truly wedded'.

[*4060*]   BAKHRUSHIN, Iu. *"Spiashchaia krasavitsa"*. [Moskva]: Sovetskoe iskusstvo, 1944. 6 p. (*Programmy moskovskikh zrelishch Gos. ordena Lenina Akad. Bol´shoi teatr SSSR*).

[*4061*]   POSNER, S. *"The Sleeping Princess": The story of the ballet*. With decorations by Joyce Millen. London: Newman Wolsey, 1945. 96 p, illus.
The history of the ballet.

[*4062*]   BEAUMONT, C. W. *"The Sleeping Beauty" as presented by The Sadler's Wells Ballet, 1946*. A photographic record by Edward Mandinian the story of the ballet by Cyril W. Beaumont. London, C. W. Beaumont [1946]. viii, 15 p, illus.

[*4063*]   BEAUMONT, C. W. *"The Sleeping Beauty" as presented by The Sadler's Wells Ballet, 1946*. A photographic record by Russell Sedgwick; the story of the ballet by Cyril W. Beaumont. London, C. W. Beaumont [1946]. 8 p, illus.

[*4064*]   *"Spiashchaia krasavitsa"*. Leningrad: Gos. ordena Lenina Akad. teatr opery i baleta im. S. M. Kirova, 1946. 24 p.

[*4065*]   HUSSEY, D. 'The composer of "The Sleeping Beauty"', *Dancing Times*, 427 (Apr 1946): 333–335, illus.

[*4066*]   HUSSEY, D. 'Tchaikovsky and the fairies', *Dancing Times* (Jul 1946): 504–506.

[*4067*]   HASKELL, A. *"The Sleeping Beauty"*. London: Bodley Head, 1949. 56 p, music, illus.

[*4068*]   RITTIKH, M. '"Spiashchaia krasavitsa" na stsene Bol´shogo teatra', *Sovetskaia muzyka* (1952), 7: 73–75.

[4069]   KRASOVSKAIA, V. 'Vozvrashchenie "Spiashchei krasavitsy"', *Sovetskoe iskusstvo* (19 Apr 1952).

[4070]   'Das verwandelte "Dornröschen"', *Musica*, 8 (Sep 1954): 408–409.

[4071]   CLOUGH, F. F. 'Tchaikovsky: "The Sleeping Beauty" ballet, op. 66', *Gramophone*, 33 (May 1955): 486–487.

          Lists which numbers from the ballet are included in seven recordings.

[4072]   KROKOVER, R. 'A total "Sleeping Beauty", more graceful than rapturous', *High Fidelity*, 5 (Sep 1955): 64.

          First complete recording of the ballet. See also *4073*.

[4073]   '"The Sleeping Beauty" unabridged', *American Record Guide*, 22 (Nov 1955): 38–39.

[4074]   DEAS, S. 'The music of "Coppellia" and "The sleeping beauty"', *Ballet annual*, 14 (1960): 73–76.

[4075]   NUSSAC, S. de. "La belle au bois dormant", *Musica* (Dec 1960), 81: 40–43, illus.

[4076]   CHAPPELL, W. *"The Sleeping Beauty"*. From the tales of Charles Perrault. Music by Peter Ilyich Tchaikovsky. Adapted and illus. by Warren Chappell. London, 1961. 38 p, music, illus.

        — [repr.] London: Kaye & Ward, 1973. 38 p, music, illus.

        — [repr.] New York: Knopf, 1982. 38 p, music, illus. ISBN: 0–8052–0683–3 (pbk.).

[4077]   HALL, G. *"Sleeping Beauty": The story of the ballet*. London: Ballet Books [1961]. [24] p, illus.

[4078]   *"Spiashchaia krasavitsa": Balet v 3-kh deistviiakh P. Chaikovskogo*. Libretto I. Vsevolozhskogo i M. Petipa po motivam skazok Sharlia Perro. Moskva: Akademiia Nauk, 1963. 17 p, illus.

[4079]   KANSKI, J. '"Spiaca Krolewna" na wschodzie i na zachodzie', *Ruch muzyczny*, 7 (1963), 1: 12–13.

[4080]   SHOSTAKOVICH, D. D. 'Balet na ekrane', *Izvestiia* (14 May 1964).

[4081]   APPLEBY, W. & FOWLER, F. *"The Sleeping Beauty" and "The Firebird": Stories from the ballet*. Illustrated by Alan Clark. New York: H. Z. Walck, 1965. 58 p, illus.; music. (*The Young Reader's Guides to Music*).

[4082]   D'AMICO, F. *Cajkovskii e la rivincita di Pepita*. Roma: Teatro del' Opera, 1965. 15 p.

[4083]   ROZANOVA, Iu. A. *O simfonizme v balete Chaikovskogo "Spiashchaia krasavitsa"*. Moskva: Muzyka, 1965. 64 p, music. (*V pomoshch´ pedagogu-muzykantu*).

[4084]   SLONIMSKII, Iu. 'Gordost´ russkoi kul´tury', *Vechernii Leningrad* (15 Jan 1965): 3.

          The 75th anniversary of the first performance.

[4085]   CRISP, C. 'Vsevolozhsky and "The Sleeping Beauty"', *About the House*, 2 (Nov 1968), 12: 26–34, illus.

[4086]   "The Sleeping Beauty", *About the House*, 3 (1969), 1: 42–45, illus.

[4087]   GOODWIN, N. & PERCIVAL, J. 'Tchaikovsky: "The Sleeping Beauty", op. 66', *Dance and Dancers*, 20 (Mar 1969): 18–20.

          A comparison of four different productions.

[4088]   LOPUKHOV, F. V. "Spiashchaia krasavitsa". In: F. V. Lopukhov, *Khoreograficheskie otkrovennosti*. Moskva: Iskusstvo, 1972: 79–102.

[4089]   KRASOVSKAIA, V. *Marius Petipa and "The Sleeping Beauty"* (tr. from the Russian by Cynthia Read), *Dance Perspectives* (spr. 1972), 49: 1–56, illus.

[*4090*]   VANSLOV, V. '"Spiashchaia krasavitsa" Chaikovskogo i novyi spektakl´ Bol´shogo teatr',
Sovetskaia muzyka (1973), 10: 38–45, illus.

In connection with a new production of the ballet in Moscow by Iurii Grigorovich.

[*4091*]   CRISP, C. "The Sleeping Beauty", *Financial Times* (16 Mar 1973).

— [repr.] *About the House*, 4 (1973), 3: 18–21.

[*4092*]   BRODSKAIA, G. 'Ot Petipa do Grigorovicha', *Teatr* (1974), 4: 41–53, illus.

The history of *The Sleeping Beauty* at the Bol´shoi Theatre in Moscow.

[*4093*]   HARRIS, D. 'Tchaikovsky's bible for balletomanes', *High Fidelity*, 25 (Mar 1975): 71–72.

Comparison of recordings.

[*4094*]   GOLDNER, N. 'American Ballet's supreme test: First U. S. version of full-length "Sleeping
Beauty" is still like dress rehearsal', *Christian Science Monitor*, 68 (21 Jun 1976): 22.

[*4095*]   CROCE, A. 'Dancing: "Beauty" in distress', *New Yorker*, 52 (5 Jul 1976): 78–80.

Comparing the 1976 American Ballet Theatre and 1946 Covent Garden productions of the ballet.

[*4096*]   BALANCHINE, G. & MASON, F. "The Sleeping Beauty". In: *Balanchine's complete stories of the great
ballets*. Rev. and enlarged ed. Garden (N. Y.): Doubleday, 1977: 540–559.

[*4097*]   BENUA [BENOIS], A. 'Iz vospominanii: "Spiashchaia krasavitsa"'. In: *Muzyka i khoreografiia
sovremennogo baleta*. Vyp. 2. Leningrad: Muzyka, 1977: 216–234.

— [repr.] In: A. Benua, Moi vospominaniia. Izd. podgot. N. I. Aleksandrova [et al]. Predisl. D. S.
Likhacheva. Tom 1. Moskva: Nauka, 1980: 601–607. (*Literaturnye pamiatniki*).

— 2-e izd. Tom 1. Moskva: Nauka, 1990: 600-606. (*Literaturnye pamiatniki*).

— [English tr.] in *A Century of Russian ballet: Documents and accounts, 1810-1910*. Selected and tr. by Roland
John Wiley. Oxford: Clarendon Press; New York : Oxford Univ. Press, 1990: 385–391.

[*4098*]   SPILSTED, G. 'Ballet reform and the Diaghilev Ballets Russes to 1913', *Studies in Music*, 2 (1977):
127–128.

[*4099*]   MASKEY, J. 'The dance', *Musical America*, 27 (Nov 1977): 12–13, illus.

[*4100*]   *"La bella addormentata nel bosco" di Piotr I. Ciaikovskij*. Milano: Teatro alla Scala, 1978. 43 p, illus.
(*Teatro alla Scala: Stagione del Bicentenario 1778/1978*).

[*4101*]   REGITZ, H. 'Ein "Dornröschen": Traum', *Bühne* (Sep 1978), 240: 20, illus.

[*4102*]   'Records: "The Sleeping Beauty"', *Ballet News*, 1 (May 1979): 50.

[*4103*]   "The Sleeping Beauty", *Ballet News*, 1 (May 1979): 27–30, illus.

[*4104*]   VILL, S. 'Prima la musica—poi la danza?': Zum Verhältnis Musik (Choreographie im
Tanztheater)', *Musik und Bildung*, 12 (Sep 1980): 530–534.

[*4105*]   HAHNL, H. H. '"Dornröschen" in der Staatsoper', *Österreichische Musikzeitschrift*, 35 (Dec 1980):
666–667.

[*4106*]   '"Spiashchaia krasavitsa": Prem´era 31 maia 1973 g.'. In: *Bol´shoi teatr SSSR, 1972/1973-
1973/1974*. Moskva: Sovetskii kompozitor, 1981: 54–68, illus.

Includes: 'Ekspozitsiia spektaklia' — 'Baletmeister Iu. Grirgorovich' — E. Shumilova, 'Poema o mechte' —
V. Krasovskaia, 'Vozvrashchenie "Spiashchei krasavitsy"'.

[*4107*]   '"The Sleeping Beauty": A chronology', *Dance magazine*, 55 (Jun 1981), 6: 57–58, illus.

Identifies dates and personalia for the first and other important productions of the ballet.

[4108] BRUBACH, H. 'Classic Beauty', *Atlantic Monthly*, 248 (Dec 1981): 81–86.

[4109] DEMIDOV, A. 'Okhota printsa Dezire, ili istoriia "Spiashchei krasavitsy"', *Muzykal´naia zhizn´* (1983), 11: 15–16, illus.
Concerning the first production by Marius Petipa in 1890.

[4110] DEMIDOV, A. 'Polowanie ksiecia Desire czuli historia "Spacej krolewny"', *Ruch Muzyczny*, 27 (1983), 21: 25–27.

[4111] MILNES, R. 'Tchaikovsky's ballet scores: "Sleeping Beauty"', *Dance Gazette* (Jul 1983), 183: 17–18, illus.

[4112] JENNINGS, L. *"The Sleeping Beauty": The story of the ballet*. Illus. by Francesca Crespi; text by Linda Jennings. London: Hodder & Stoughton, 1984. [32] p, illus. ISBN: 0-3403-3518-1.

[4113] *P. Chaikovskii: "Spiashchaia krasavitsa"*. Balet v 3-kh deistviiakh. Libretto I. Vsevolozhskogo i M. Petipa po skazhke Sharlia Perro. Moskva, 1984. 22 p, illus.

[4114] **"Dornröschen (La belle au bois dormant)"**. In: *Reclams Ballettführer*. Von Hartmut Regitz, Otto Friedrich Regner, Heinz-Ludwig Schneiders. Stuttgart: Reclam, 1985: 168–178. (*Universal-Bibliothek*; 8042).

[4115] POBEREZHNAIA, G. I. 'Teatral´naia simvolika baleta "Spiashchaia krasavitsa" P. I. Chaikovskogo'. In: *Teatr v zhizni i tvorchestve P. I. Chaikovskogo* (1985): 120–129 [see *589*].

[4116] WOLFF, H. C., 'Katzenmusik', *Musica*, 39 (1985), 2: 161–163, music.

[4117] WOLFF, H. C. 'Tchaikovsky's "Dornröschen" and Stravinsky: Stylistic change around 1922', *Beiträge zur Musikwissenschaft*, 28 (1986): 267–276.

[4118] DULOVA, E. N. 'Balet "Spiashchaia krasavitsa" P. I. Chaikovskogo v kontekste avtorskogo stiliia'. Leningrad: Gos. konservatoriia im. N. A. Rimskogo-Korsakova, 1989. 22 p.
Summary of dissertation (Leningrad Conservatory).
— [rev. repr.] '"Spiashchaia krasavitsa" v kontekste pozdnego stiliia Chaikovskogo'. In: *Formy i stil´: Sbornik nauchnykh trudov*. Chast´ 1. Leningrad: Gos. konservatoriia im. N. A. Rimskogo-Korsakova, 1990: 115–149.

[4119] DULOVA, E. N. 'Utverzhdaia "glavenstvo soderzhaniia": 100 let baletu P. I. Chaikovskogo "Spiashchaia krasavitsa"', *Sovetskii balet* (1989), 1: 30–32, illus.

[4120] KONSTANTINOVA, M. E. *"Spiashchaia krasavitsa"*. Moskva: Iskusstvo, 1990. 239 p, illus. (*Shedevry baleta*). ISBN: 5-210-00344-2.

[4121] IL´ICHEVA, M. 'Na grani bessmertiia i "psevdo-zhizni"', *Sovetskii balet* (1990), 6: 12–14, illus.
The stage history of *The Sleeping Beauty*.

[4122] REGITZ, H. '100 Jahre "Dornröschen"-Ballet', *Ballett-Journal*, 38 (1990), 2: 52.

[4123] PERCIVAL, J. 'A beauty past compare: Petipa's scenario for "The Sleeping Beauty"', *Dance & Dancers* (Mar 1990): 14–15.

[4124] GOODWIN, N. 'A tale of two entr'actes: Aspects of Tchaikovsky and the "Sleeping Beauty"', *Dance & Dancers* (May 1990): 14–15.

[4125] MACAULAY, A. 'The big sleep: The "Sleeping Beauty" at its centenary: Tchaikovsky-Petipa collaboration', *Dancing Times*, 80 (May 1990): 805–808.

[4126] WILEY, R. J. 'Musical form in "The Sleeping Beauty"', *Dance* (Oct 1990): 31–34.

[*4127*] KOEGLER, H. "Spjashtschaja krassaviza". In: *Pipers Enzyklopadie des Musiktheaters: Oper, Operette, Musical, Ballet. Hrsg. von Carl Dahlhaus und dem Forschungsinstitut fur Musiktheater der Universität Bayreuth unter Leitung von Sieghart Dohring*. Band 4. München: Piper, 1991: 724–729.

[*4128*] ROTHENAICHER, P. 'Märchen—Symbolik—Musik: "Dornröschen—Verbindungen zwischen der Märchensymbolik und der Symbolik der Musik am Beispiel der Grimmschen Märchens "Dornröschen" und Tschaikowskis Ballet "The Sleeping Beauty"', *Musiktherapeutische Umschau*, 12 (1991), 3: 270.

[*4129*] POLETTI, S. 'A different "Beauty"', *Dance & Dancers* (Jan 1991): 33–34.

[*4130*] SCHOLL, T. 'Anticipating a new "Sleeping Beauty"', *Ballet Review*, 19 (spr. 1991): 43–45.

[*4131*] HAGMAN, B. "Tørnrosa', *Musikrevy*, 48 (1993), 4: 28–29, illus.

[*4132*] BROWN, D. 'Tchaikovsky's ballets', *Dance Now*, 2 (sum. 1993), 2: 34–41, music, illus.

[*4133*] PRITCHARD, J. [et al.], 'The awakened beauty', *Dancing Times*, 84 (Dec 1993): 225.

[*4134*] KOEGLER, H. 'Zeitlos und unkritisch, opulent und beliebig: Zu den "Dornröschen" inszenierungen der letzten Spielzeit', *Ballett International* (1995), 6: 40.

[*4135*] WEBER-BOCKHOLDT, P. 'Das "Rosen Adagio": Gedanken zur Qualität von Cajkovskijs Balletmusik'. In: *Internationales Čajkovskij Symposium, Tübingen 1993: Bericht* (1995): 299–306 [see *596*].

[*4136*] LLOYD-JONES, D. 'Tchaikovsky: Suite from "The Sleeping Beauty", op. 66a'. In: *The musician's guide to symphonic music: Essays from the Eulenberg scores*. Corey Field, ed. Mainz; New York: Schott, 1997: 646–647.

[*4137*] GUBSKAIA, I. T. 'Evoliutsiia baletnogo spektaklia (ot "Spiashchei krasavitsy" M. Petipa k "Mal´ro, ili Metamorfozy bogov" M. Bezhara)', *Vestnik Akademii russkogo baleta im. A. Ia. Vaganovoi* (1998), 6: 128–142.

[*4138*] KENNEDY, J. E. 'Lines of succession: Three productions of Tchaikovsky's "Sleeping Beauty"'. In: *Tchaikovsky and his world* (1998): 145–162 [see *601*].
          Examines the St. Petersburg première in 1892, and the London productions of 1921 and 1946.

[*4139*] WILEY, R. J. 'Tchaikovsky and "The Sleeping Beauty"', *Dancing Times*, 89 (Dec 1998): 239–242; (Jan 1999): 335–338, illus.

[*4140*] BROIDO, Iu. 'Probuzhdenie Avrory', *Vechernii Peterburg* (29 Apr 1999): 1, illus.
          Sergei Bikharev's new revival of the original production of the ballet, at the Mariinskii Theatre in St. Petersburg. See also *4141* to *4145*.

[*4141*] STOLIAROVA, G. 'Skromnoe obainie antikvariata', *Nevskoe vremia* (8 May 1999): 2.

[*4142*] ABYZOVA, L. 'Prem´era: Imperatorskii balet "vstal na mesto"', *Smena* (11 May 1999): 3, illus.

[*4143*] IAKOVLEVA, Iu. 'Mechta o "Spiashchei krasavitse": Nuzhen li teatru spektakl´ stoletnei davnosti?', *Sankt Peterburgskie vedomosti* (11 May 1999): 3, illus.

[*4144*] GOSUDAREV, A. 'Desiat´ let spustia, ili vremia feerii', *Chas pik* (12 May 1999): 15, illus.

[*4145*] DRUZHININA, E. 'Prem´era: Prosnulas´ "Spiashchaia krasavitsa"', *Trud* (29 May 1999): 5.

[*4146*] DULOVA, E. N. '"Spiashchaia krasavitsa" P. I. Chaikovskogo i tipologicheskie osobennosti skazochnogo baletnogo siuzheta XIX veka'. In: *P. I. Chaikovskii: Nasledie*, vyp. 2 (2000): 125–159 [see *604*].

See also *397*, *5598*, *5599*, *5714*.

SWAN LAKE
Ballet in 4 acts, Op. 20 (1875–76)

[*4147*]   '"Lebedinoe ozero": **Balet v chetyrekh deistviiakh. Muzyka P. I. Chaikovskogo**', *Teatral´naia gazeta* (19 Oct 1876): 390–391.

Original libretto. See also *4148*.

— [English tr. (rev.)] In: R. J. Wiley, *Tchaikovsky's ballets* (1985): 321–327 [see *3844*].

[*4148*]   *"Lebedinoe ozero": Balet v 4 deistviiakh*. Muzyka P. I. Chaikovskogo. Moskva: P. Iurgenson, 1877. 22 p

[*4149*]   [SOKOLOV], A. 'Moskovskie pis´ma: Pis´mo No. 2', *Peterburgskii listok* (10 Feb 1877).

Rehearsals for the first production of the ballet.

[*4150*]   '"Lebedinoe ozero"', *Teatral´naia gazeta* (21 Feb 1877): 174.

The first production of the ballet on 20 Feb 1877 in Moscow. See also *4151* to *4160*.

[*4151*]   A. D. '"Lebedinoe ozero", balet g. Reizingera. Muzyka g. Chaikovskogo', *Teatral´naia gazeta* (22 Feb 1877): 178.

[*4152*]   N. '"Lebedinoe ozero", balet g. Reizingera, muzyka P. I. Chaikovskogo: Korrespondentsiia iz Moskvy', *Sankt Peterburgskie vedomosti* (23 Feb 1877): 3.

[*4153*]   KASHKIN, N. D. '"Lebedinoe ozero": balet, muzyka soch. g. Chaikovskogo', *Russkie vedomosti* (25 Feb 1877).

— [repr.] In: V. V. Iakovlev, *N. D. Kashkin*. Moskva; Leningrad, 1950: 31.

— [repr.] In: N. D. Kashkin, *Izbrannye stat´i o P. I. Chaikovskom* (1954): 182–186 [see *2349*].

[*4154*]   A. L. 'Moskovskie pis´ma: Novyi balet "Lebedinoe ozero"', *Birzhevye vedomosti* (26 Feb 1877).

[*4155*]   KUREPIN, A. D. 'Moskovskii fel´eton: "Lebedinoe ozero" Chaikovskogo', *Novoe vremia* (26 Feb 1877): 2.

[*4156*]   SKROMNYI NABLIUDATEL´. 'Nablideniia i zametki', *Russkie vedomosti* (26 Feb 1877): 2.

[*4157*]   ZUB [SHCHUROVSKII, P. A.] 'Benefis Karpakovoi: "Lebedinoe ozero", balet Reizingera, muzyka Chaikovskogo', *Sovremennye izvestiia* (26 Feb 1877): 1.

[*4158*]   KASHKIN, N. D. 'Muzykal´naia khronika: Ispolnenie baleta "Lebedinoe ozero"', *Russkie vedomosti* (3 Mar 1877).

[*4159*]   'Chto pishut v gazetakh', *Teatral´naia gazeta* (4 Mar 1877).

[*4160*]   ZHELIABUZHSKII, E. D. '"Lebedinoe ozero", balet v 4-kh deistviiakh, soch. Reizingera, muzyka P. I. Chaikovskogo', *Vsemirnaia illustratsiia* (23 Apr 1877): 334.

[*4161*]   SKROMNYI NABLIUDATEL´. 'Nabliudeniia i zametki', *Russkie vedomosti* (8 May 1877).

[*4162*]   'Moskovskie zametki', *Golos* (24 Aug 1877).

[*4163*]   'Zrelishcha i uveseleniia', *Russkie vedomosti* (1 Sep 1877).

[*4164*]   LAROSH, G. A. 'Muzykal´nye nabliudeniia i vpechatleniia (iz Moskvy)', *Golos* (14 Sep 1878).

— [repr.] In: G. A. Larosh, *Sobranie muzykal´no-kriticheskikh statei*, tom 2, chast´ 1 (1924): 166–170 [see *2311*].

— [repr.] "Lebedinoe ozero". In: G. A. Larosh, *Izbrannye stat´i v piati vypuskakh*, vyp. 2 (1975): 97–101 [see *2376*].

— [German tr.] 'Tschaikowskys Ballett "Schwanensee"'. In: G. A. Larosh, *Peter Tschaikowsky: Aufsätze und Erinnerungen* (1993): 102–106 [see *2406*].

[4165]   'Moskovskie teatry: Bol´shoi teatr', *Sufler* (27 Jan 1880).

[4166]   K[ASHKIN], N. 'Muzykal´naia khronika', *Russkie vedomosti* (25 Feb 1884).

[4167]   *"Lebedinoe ozero": Muzyka P. I. Chaikovskogo*. Sankt Peterburg: Izdat. Imperatorskikh Sankt Peterburgskikh teatrov, 1895. 22 p.

[4168]   A. B. 'Teatr i muzyka', *Novoe vremia* (17 Jan 1895): 3.
The first production in St. Petersburg on 15 Jan 1895. See also *4169* to *4174*.

[4169]   P[ETROVSKII, E. M.]. '"Lebedinoe ozero" Chaikovskogo', *Russkaia muzykal´naia gazeta* (Feb 1895), 2: 154–156.

[4170]   B. 'Teatral´noe ekho: Benefis P´eriny Len´iani', *Peterburgskaia gazeta* (16 Jan 1895): 3.

[4171]   B. V. "Lebedinoe ozero", *Teatral´nyi kur´er* (17 Jan 1895).

[4172]   VRERAN. 'Balet "Lebedinoe ozero"', *Novosti i birzhevaia gazeta* (17 Jan 1895): 3.

[4173]   'Mariinskii teatr', *Peterburgskii listok* (17 Jan 1895): 4.

[4174]   'Benefis Mlle Legnani', *Sankt Peterburgskie vedomosti* (17 Jan 1895): 3.

[4175]   F[INDEIZEN], N. F. 'Balet: Khronika teatra i iskusstva', *Teatr i iskusstvo* (29 Nov 1898): 871.

[4176]   'Teatr i muzyka', *Novoe vremia* (16 Jan 1901).

[4177]   MUKHIN, D. "Lebedinoe ozero", *Moskovskie vedomosti* (19 Jan 1901).

[4178]   K. D. "Lebedinoe ozero", *Russkoe slovo* (25 Jan 1901).

[4179]   'Teatr i muzyka', *Moskovskie vedomosti* (25 Jan 1901).

[4180]   ENGEL´, Iu. D. 'Teatr i muzyka', *Russkie vedomosti* (28 Jan 1901).

[4181]   MATOV [MAMONTOV], S. 'Teatr i muzyka', *Rossiia* (9 Feb 1901).

[4182]   T[IMOFEEV], G. 'Teatr i muzyka: Mariinskii teatr', *Rech´* (3 Oct 1906): 4.
In connection with the revival of *Swan Lake* in St. Petersburg.

[4183]   SVETLOV, V. 'Balet "Lebedinoe ozero"', *Slovo* (28 Nov 1906): 3.

[4184]   KOZLIANINOV, L. 'Debiuty v moskovskom balete: Novoe "Lebedinoe ozero"', *Novoe vremia* (3 May 1910).

[4185]   ZIGFRID [STARK, E.] 'Otkrytie baletnogo sezona', *Obozrenie teatrov* (6 Sep 1911).

[4186]   MAMONTOV, S. 'Benefis kordebaleta', *Russkoe slovo* (11 Dec 1912).

[4187]   K-O, 'Tsaritsa "Lebedinogo ozera"', *Karsavina* (11 Mar 1913).

[4188]   CHEREPNIN, A. A. "Lebedinoe ozero", *Teatral´naia gazeta* (29 Nov 1916).

[4189]   '"Lebedinoe ozero" P. I. Chaikovskogo', *Kul´tura i teatra* (1921), 2: 27.

[4190]   L[ESHKOV], D. *"Lebedinoe ozero"*. Fantasticheskii balet, muzyka P. I. Chaikovskogo. Petrograd: Gos. Akad. teatr opery i baleta, 1922. 9 p.

[4191]   VOLYNSKII, A. '"Lebedinoe ozero": Lebed´ v muzyke', *Zhizn´ iskusstva* (1923), 47: 4–5.

[4192]   *"Lebedinoe ozero": Balet P. I. Chaikovskogo*. Kiev, 1927. 7 p.

[4193]   SOKOLOVA, N. 'Neskol´ko slov o "Lebedinom ozere"', *Sovremennyi teatr* (1 Jul 1928).

[4194]   K. R. "Lebedinoe ozero", *Tikhookeanskaia zvezda* (23 Aug 1928).

[4195]   "Lebedinoe ozero", *Krasnoe znamia* (31 Aug 1928).

[4196]   *"Lebedinoe ozero": Balet P. I. Chaikovskogo*. Tekst izd. pod red. L. Obolenskogo. Moskva: Teakinopechat´, 1929. 40 p, illus.

[4197]   IVING, V. *"Lebedinoe ozero"*. Pod red. L. Obolenskogo. Moskva: Teakinopechat´, 1930. 32 p, illus.

[4198]   GVOZDEV, A. *"Lebedinoe ozero"*. Moskva: Gos. izdat. khudozh. literatury, 1931. 16 p, illus.

[4199]   *"Lebedinoe ozero"*. Baku: Bol´shoi Gos. opernyi teatr im. M. F. Akhundova, 1931. 7 p.

[4200]   RIADNOVA, N. *"Lebedinoe ozero": Balet, muzyka P. I. Chaikovskogo*. Tiflis: Tilfiskii Gos. opernyi teatr, 1931. 8 p.

[4201]   SOLLERTINSKII, I. *"Lebedinoe ozero"*. [Moskva]: Gos. izdat. khudozh. literatury, 1931. 15 p, illus. (*V pomoshch´ zriteliu*).
         Libretto of the 1895 production. With introductory article by I. Sollertinskii, 'O balete i ego avtore'.

[4202]   GLEBOV, I. [ASAF´EV, B. V.] *Lebedinoe ozero*. [Leningrad]: Leningradskii Gos. Akad. teatr opery i baleta, 1933. 40 p, illus.
         Contents: "Lebedinoe ozero": Vozobnovlenie i postanovka A. Ia. Vaganovoi': 3–5 — 'Kratkoe soderzhanie': 6–9 — 'K postanovke baleta P. I. Chaikovskogo "Lebedinoe ozero"': 10–40.
         — 2-e izd. Leningrad: Gos. Akad. teatr opery i baleta, 1934. 34 p, illus.
         — 3-e izd. [Leningrad: Gos. Akad. teatr opery i baleta im. S. M. Kirova, 1935. 34 p, illus.
         — 4-e izd. Leningrad: Gos. Akad. teatr opery i baleta im. S. M. Kirova, 1937. 31 p, illus.
         — 6-e izd. *Lebedinoe ozero*. Leningrad: Gos. Alad. teatr opery i baleta im S. M. Kirova, 1938. 35 p, illus.
         — [repr.] 'K postanovke baleta P. I. Chaikovskogo "Lebedinoe ozero"'. In: B. V. Asaf´ev, *O balete: Stati´i, retsenzii, vospominaniia* (1974): 177–193 [see *3832*].
         — [Ukrainian tr.] "5-e izd." *Lebedyne ozero*. Kyiv: Derzh. Akad. teatru opery i baletu URSR, 1937. 30 p, illus.

[4203]   SOLLERTINSKII, I. "Lebedinoe ozero", *Rabochii i teatr*, 12 (1933): 14–16.

[4204]   *"Lebedinoe ozero"*. Erevan: SSR Armianskii teatr opery i baleta, 1934. 8 p.

[4205]   *"Lebedinoe ozero"*. Saratov: Nizhne-Volzhskii kraiev. teatr opery i baleta [1934]. 12 p.

[4206]   *"Lebedinoe ozero": Libretto*. Tbilisi: Teatr opery i baleta im. Z. Paliashvili, 1937. 12 p.
         Text in Russian and Georgian.

[4207]   BOGDANOV-BEREZOVSKII, V. M. *"Lebedinoe ozero": Balet v 4-kh deistviiakh*. Libretto i kratkii ocherk. Moskva: Gos. Akad. Bol´shoi teatr SSSR, 1938, 22 p.

[4208]   *"Lebedinoe ozero"*. Alma-Ata: Ob´edinennyi teatr Kazakhskoi i Russkoi opery i baleta, 1938. 6 p.

[4209]   *"Lebedinoe ozero"*. Rostov na Donu: Khar´kovskii Akad. Gos. teatr opery i baleta, 1938. 8 p.

[4210]   M. Z. "Lebedinoe ozero", *Dekada moskovskikh zrelishch* (11 Dec 1938): 3.

[4211]   ROZENFEL´D, S. 'Teatral´nyi dnevnik: "Lebedinoe ozero" v teatre opery i baleta', *Iskusstvo i zhizn´* (1938), 11/12: 58–60.
         The history of the ballet at the Mariinskii/Kirov Theatre in St. Petersburg/Leningrad.

[*4212*]   TAL´NIKOV, A. 'Kompozitor i dve baleriny', *Teatr* (1940), 5: 51–62, illus.
The roles of Odette and Odile in *Swan Lake*.

[*4213*]   ULANOVA, G. S. 'Lebed'. In: *Chaikovskii i teatr* (1940): 240–244 [see *2537*]

[*4214*]   BERN, L. '"Lebedinoe ozero": Na smotre molodezhi Bol´shogo teatra', *Vechernaia Moskva* (29 Mar 1940).

[*4215*]   '"Lebedinoe ozero" v estonskom teatre', *Izvestiia* (12 Apr 1940): 9.
Report on a production of the ballet at the Estonia Theatre in Tallinn.

[*4216*]   GRINBERG, M. "Lebedinoe ozero", *Pravda* (26 May 1940): 6.
In connection with a new production on the Moscow stage by the Kirov Ballet Company. See also *4217*, *4218*.

[*4217*]   VOLKOV, N. "Lebedinoe ozero", *Izvestiia* (26 May 1940): 4.

[*4218*]   GRINBERG, M. "Lebedinoe ozero", *Pravda* (26 May 1940): 6.

[*4219*]   CHURCHILL, D. W. '"Le lac des Cygnes": The ballet, the music and the records', *Gramophone*, 20 (Jun 1942): 10–11.
Includes discography.

[*4220*]   SLONIMSKII, Iu. *"Lebedinoe ozero"*. Moskva: Sovetskoe iskusstvo, 1944. 6 p. (*Programmy moskovskikh zrelishch. Gos. ordena Lenina Akad. Bol´shoi teatr SSSR*).

[*4221*]   GRIGOR´EV, A. "Lebedinoe ozero", *Leningrad* (1945), 19/20: 26–28, illus.
The stage history of the ballet, and review of a new production at the Kirov Theatre in Leningrad. See also *4222*.

[*4222*]   GUROVSKII, M. '"Lebedinoe ozero": Prem´era v teatre opery i baleta imeni S. M. Kirova', *Leningradskaia pravda* (4 Jul 1945): 3.

[*4223*]   *"Lebedinoe ozero"*. Leningrad: Gos. ordena Lenina Akad. teatr opery i baleta im. S. M. Kirova, 1946. 32 p.

[*4224*]   *"Lebedinoe ozero"*. Odessa: Gos. Akad. teatr opery i baleta, 1946. 23 p, illus

[*4225*]   LYNHAM, D. *Tales from the ballet: "Swan Lake", "Petrouchka"*. Retold by Deryck Lynham. Lithographs by Sylvia Green. London: Sylvan Press, 1946. 23 p, illus.

[*4226*]   BEAUMONT, C. W. *"The Swan Lake" as presented by the Sadler's Wells Ballet*. A photographic record by Russell Sedgwick of Tunbridge & Sedgwick; the story of the ballet by Cyril W. Beaumont. London, C. W. Beaumont [1947]. 8 p, illus.

[*4227*]   *"Lebedinoe ozero"*. Novosibirsk: Novosibirskii Gos. teatr opery i baleta, 1947. 8 p. (*Komitet po delam iskusstv pri Sovete Ministrov RSFSR*).
Includes libretto.

[*4228*]   ROBERTSON, M. *The story of the ballet "Swan Lake" ("Le lac des cygnes")*. With decorations by Joyce Millen. London: Newman Wolsey, 1947. 96 p., illus.
A detailed synopsis of the ballet.

[*4229*]   SENIOR, E. 'Tchaikovsky: Music that dances', *Dance and Dancers*, 1 (Mar 1950): 10, 18, music, illus.

[*4230*]   *"Lebedinoe ozero"*. Moskva: Iskusstvo, 1951. 23 p, illus. (*Gos. Akad. Bol´shoi teatr*).

[4231] BEAUMONT, C. W. *The ballet called "Swan Lake"*. London: C. W. Beaumont, 1952. 176 p, illus.
Historical, critical and technical study.
— New York: Dance Horizons, 1982. 176 p, illus. ISBN: 0-8712-7128-1 (pbk).

[4232] KOLODIN, I. 'Total "Swan Lake"', *Saturday Review*, 35 (28 Jun 1952): 45.

[4233] MOISEEV, I. 'Tvorcheskoe otnoshenie k baletnoi klassike', *Sovetskaia muzyka* (1953), 8: 49–52.
A new production of the ballet at the Stanislavskii Theatre in Moscow for the 75th anniversary of its first performance, using Chaikovskii's original score. See also *4234* to *4238*.

[4234] SMOL´IANOV, A. & DAVYDOVA, K. Iu. 'Vosstanovlenie partitury Chaikovskogo', *Sovetskaia muzyka* (1953), 8: 53–61.

[4235] SURITS, E. 'Po Chaikovskomu (o novoi postanovke "Lebedinogo ozera")', *Teatr* (1953), 8: 22–28.

[4236] ULANOVA, G. 'Plodotvornost´ iskanii', *Sovetskoe iskusstvo* (9 May 1953): 2–3.

[4237] SEMENOVA, M. '"Lebedinoe ozero": Novaia postanovka baleta P. I. Chaikovskogo', *Izvestiia* (17 May 1953): 3.

[4238] LEPESHINSKAIA, O. 'Traditsii i novatorstvo: Novaia postanovka baleta "Lebedinoe ozero"', *Pravda* (21 May 1953): 3.

[4239] IKONNIKOV, A. '"Lebedinoe ozero" v Cheliabinskom teatre', *Sovetskaia muzyka* (1958), 2: 72.

[4240] 'A Tchaikovsky original', *American Record Guide*, 21 (May 1955): 288–289.
New recording of the original version of the ballet.

[4241] CLOUGH, F. F. 'Tchaikovsky: "Swan Lake" ballet, op. 20', *Gramophone*, 33 (Aug 1955): 106.
A concordance table, showing which numbers from the ballet are included in 11 recordings.

[4242] 'Vozobnovlenie "Lebedinogo ozera" v postanovke Petipa i Ivanova', *Sovetskaia kul´tura* (26 Jul 1958): 1.
A revival of the 1895 St. Petersburg production at the Malyi Theatre in Leningrad. See also *4243*.

[4243] EVDAKHOV, O. '"Lebedinoe ozero": Novaia postanovka v Malom opernom teatre', *Leningradskaia pravda* (28 Nov 1958): 4.

[4244] KUNIN, I. F. 'Besedy o muzyke: "Lebedinoe ozero" Chaikovskogo', *Muzykal´naia zhizn´* (1959), 24: 13–14, music, illus.

[4245] 'Tchaikowski: "Le lac des cygnes"', *Disques* (1960), 117: 252–253.

[4246] GOLOVASHCHENKO, Iu. 'Cherty sovetskogo baleta', *Sovetskaia muzyka* (1960), 8: 51–52.

[4247] SABIN, R. 'Russians film complete "Swan Lake"', *Musical America*, 80 (Feb 1960): 251.

[4248] HALL, G. *"Swan Lake": The story of the ballet*. London: Ballet Books [1961]. [24] p, illus.

[4249] GOLEA, A. 'Altes—neu in der Grossen Oper', *Neue Zeitschrift für Musik*, 122 (Feb 1961): 69–70.

[4250] NUSSAC, S. de. "Le lac des Cygnes", *Musica* (Feb 1961), 83: 25–29.

[4251] SLONIMSKII, Iu. I. *"Lebedinoe ozero" P. Chaikovskogo*. Leningrad: Gos. muz. izdat., 1962. 79 p, illus. (*Sokrovishcha sovetskogo baletnogo teatra*).

[4252] GUEST, I. "Swan Lake", *About the House*, 1 (1963), 5: 24–28.

[4253] LANCHBERY, J. 'Tchaikovsky's "Swan Lake"', *Dancing Times*, 54 (Dec 1963): 129, music, illus.

[4254] *"Lebedinoe ozero": Balet v 4-kh deistviiakh P. Chaikovskogo*. Libretto V. Begicheva i V. Gel´tsera Moskva: Nauka, 1964. 13 p, illus.

[4255] COTON, A. V. 'Another look at "Swan Lake", *About the House*, 1 (1964), 6: 38–39.

[4256] BRINSON, P. 'The new old "Swan Lake"', *About the House*, 1 (1965), 11: 2–5, illus.

[4257] KUTSCHERA, A. C. 'Tschaikowskys "Schwanensee" in der Staatsoper', *Oesterrichische Musikzeitschrift*, 19 (1965): 546–547.

[4258] '1000-i raz', *Sovetskaia muzyka* (1966), 1: 147, illus.
The 1000th performance of the ballet at the Bol´shoi Theatre in Moscow, on 20 Oct 1965.

[4259] GOODWIN, N. 'Back to the Lake: Music', *Dance and Dancers*, 17 (May 1966): 33–35.
Compares the numbers in the original score with various staged versions.

[4260] '"Lebedinoe ozero" v 500-i raz!', *Sovetskaia kul´tura* (19 Aug 1967): 1.
The 500th production of the ballet in Leningrad.

[4261] OGURA, S. *Hakucho no mizuumi no bigaku*. Tokyo [1968]. 345 p, illus.

[4262] SLONIMSKII, Iu. 'Den´ rozhdeniia shedevra', *Vechernii Leningrad* (1 Mar 1969): 3.
The 75th anniversary of the first production of Act II of the ballet in St. Petersburg (17 Feb 1894).

[4263] DIENES, G. 'A Hattyuk tava-filmen', *Muzsika*, 12 (Dec 1969): 17–18.
Concerning a new filmed version of the ballet.

[4264] KISHIDA, E. *P. I. Tchaikovsky's "Swan lake"*. Illus. by Shigeru Hatsuyama; adapted by Eriko Kishida; tr. by Ann King Herring. [Tokyo:] Gakken [1970]. [27] p, illus. (*Fantasia pictorial*).
— [repr.] London: F. Warne [1974?]. [27] p, illus. (*Fantasia pictorial*). ISBN: 0–7232–1759–9.

[4265] DUTSKAIA, E. 'Tribuna kritika: V protivorechii s partituroi', *Teatral´naia zhizn´* (1970), 15: 15.
A new production of the ballet in Moscow by Iu. Grigorovich, using on Chaikovskii's original score. See also *4266, 4267, 4268, 4271*.

[4266] ROSLAVLEVA, N. 'Vernoe i spornoe: Novaia postanovka "Lebedinogo ozera" v Bol´shom teatre SSSR', *Muzykal´naia zhizn´* (1970), 12: 7–9.

[4267] VANSLOV, V. '"Lebedinoe ozero" v Bol´shom teatre', *Sovetskaia muzyka* (1970), 3: 44–50.

[4268] LOPUKHOV, F. 'Teatr: Traditsionno i novo', *Izvestiia* (3 Jan 1970): 4.

[4269] ENTELIS, L. 'Vysokaia poeziia tantsa: K 75-letiiu spektaklia "Lebedinoe ozero" v postanovke M. Petipa', *Leningradskaia pravda* (27 Jan 1970): 4.
The 75th anniversary of the first production in St. Petersburg. See also *4270*.

[4270] 'Neuviadaemaia krasota', *Vechernii Leningrad* (27 Jan 1970): 3, illus.

[4271] DEMIDOV, A. 'Vozvrashchenie: "Lebedinoe ozero" v postanovke Iu. Grigorovicha', *Komsomol´skaia pravda* (19 Feb 1970): 4.

[4272] DARRELL, R. D. 'Recharting the muddled waters of "Swan Lake"', *High Fidelity*, 20 (Apr 1970): 79–81, illus.
Survey of recordings.

[4273] KRESH, P. 'A new champion in the "Swan Lake" regatta', *Stereo Review*, 24 (Apr 1970): 79–80.

[4274] ROZANOVA, Iu. '"Lebedinoe ozero" P. Chaikovskogo: Pervyi russkii klassicheskii balet'. In: *Iz istorii russkoi i sovetskoi muzyki*. Moskva: Muzyka, 1971: 257–275.

[4275] LOPUKHOV, F. V. '"Lebedinoe ozero" kak russkii balet'. In: F. V. Lopukhov, *Khoreograficheskie otkrovennosti*. Moskva: Iskusstvo, 1972: 103–111.

[4276] SCHNEIDERS, H. L. 'Den "Schwanensee" gründlich verunreinigt: Tschaikowskys Ballett in Bremen "umfunktioniert"', *Neue Musikzeitung*, 21 (1972), 1: 17.

[4277] "Lebedinoe ozero". In: *Bol´shoi teatr SSSR, 1969/1970*. Moskva: Sovetskii kompozitor, 1973: 42–57, illus.

Includes: 'Prem´era 25 dek. 1969 g.' — B. L´vov-Anokhin, 'O pervom variante spektaklia' — F. Lopukhov, 'Traditsionno i novo' — P. Gusev, 'Razmyshleniia o baletnom klassicheskom nasledii'.

[4278] KHOKHLOV, B. 'Iubilei spektakliia', *Sovetskaia kul´tura* (10 Jul 1973): 8.

The 700th performance of W. Burmeister's production of the ballet. See also *4304*.

[4279] HATSUYAMA, S. *P. I. Tchaikovsky's "Swan Lake"*. Adapted and illus. by Shigeru Hatsuyama. London: F. Warne, 1974. ISBN: 0–7232–1759–9.

[4280] SURITS, E. Ia. '"Lebedinoe ozero": Postanovka A. Gorskogo i Vl. Nemirovicha-Danchenko, 1920'. In: *Muzyka i khoreografiia sovremennogo baleta: Sbornik statei*. Moskva: Muzyka, 1974: 243–263.

[4281] WILEY, R. J. 'Tchaikovsky's "Swan Lake": The first productions in Moscow and St. Petersburg'. Cambridge, Mass: Harvard Univ., 1974. xiv, 430 p, illus.

Thesis.

[4282] BALANCHINE, G. & MASON, F. "Swan Lake". In: *Balanchine's complete stories of the great ballets*. Rev. and enlarged ed. Garden City (N. Y.): Doubleday, 1977: 585–603.

[4283] GODANTSEVA, I. 'Polet v buduschee: K 100-letiiu pervoi postanovki baleta P. I. Chaikovskogo "Lebedinoe ozero"', *Teatral´naia zhizn´* (Feb 1977), 4: 27, illus.

[4284] ZHITOMIRSKII, D. V. '"Lebedinoe ozero" Chaikovskogo: K 100-letiiu so dnia prem´ery', *Muzykal´naia zhizn´* (Feb 1977), 4: 15–16, illus.

[4285] DORRIS, G. 'Once more to lake (Tchaikovsky's "Swan Lake")', *Ballet Review*, 6 (1978), 4: 99–105.

[4286] SCHÄFER, H. '"Schwanensee": Original und neu', *Musik und Gesellschaft*, 28 (May 1978): 288–290, illus.

[4287] LEVIEUX, F. & MASSON, C. *"Le Lac des cygnes"*. Paris: Albin Michel, 1979.

Photographic study.

[4288] CROCE, A. 'Dancing: "Swan Lake" and its alternatives', *New Yorker*, 55 (11 Jun 1979): 142–144.

[4289] DIAMOND, D. *"Swan Lake"*. Adapted and illus. by Donna Diamond. Introduction by Clive Barnes. New York: Holiday House [1980]. [32] p, illus. ISBN: 0–8234–0356–4.

[4290] NOVICK, J. 'Who's afraid of the virgin swan?', *Village Voice*, 25 (19 May 1980): 83, illus.

[4291] IGNAT´EVA, M. & INOZEMTSEVA, G. 'Vsekh linii taian´e i pen´e', *Sovetskaia kul´tura* (27 Jun 1980): 4, illus.

Swan Lake at the Bol´shoi Theatre in Moscow.

[4292] LUTEN, C. J. 'The new "Swan Lake": It's the one to have', *American Record Guide*, 43 (Jul/Aug 1980): 43–45.

[*4293*]   '"Swan Lake": A chronology', *Dance magazine*, 55 (Jun 1981), 6: 57–58, illus.

Identifies dates and personalia for the first and other important productions of the ballet.

[*4294*]   GRILLO, E. *"Il lago dei cigni"*. Roma: Di Giacomo [1982]. 189 p, illus. (*La danza e il baletto*; 6).

[*4295*]   MILNES, R. 'Tchaikovsky's ballet scores: "Swan Lake"', *Dance Gazette* (Mar 1983), 182: 8–9, illus.

[*4296*]   BROWN, D. 'Tchaikovsky and "Swan Lake"', *Ballet Review*, 11 (spr. 1983), 1: 68–83.

[*4297*]   *"Le Lac des Cygnes": Ballet en quatre actes de P. Tchaïkovski*. Paris: L'Avant Scène, 1984. 95 p, illus. (*Ballet/danse*; 12). ISBN: 2–900130–03–4.

Contents:G. Mannoni, 'Présentation', 1–3 — M. Schneider, 'D'un conte à l'autre: Naissance d'une légende': 4–9 — A. Duault, 'Tchaïkovski: L'éternel orphelin: 10–13 — J.-C. Diens, 'Lev Ivanov: Le choréographe mal-aimé": 14–17 — G. Erismann, 'La musique: Instrument du destin': 18–23 — N. Kachkine [N. Kashkin]: 'Souvenirs': 24–25 — D. Dabbadie & N. Dabbadie, 'Naissance d'une choréographie': 26–29 — A. Livio, 'Le mystère de l'eau et du lac des cugnes': 30–37 — I. Lidova, 'Les ballerines à l'âme slave": 38–43 — A.-P. Hersin & O. Mauraisin, 'L'école française à l'épreuve du Lac des cygnes", 1960–1984': 44–545 — A. Livio, 'Quelques cugnes en exil': 56–59 — D. Dabbadie & R. Sirvin, 'Aux sources du ballet: Les arguments de 1877 et 1895': 60–69 — R. Sirvin, 'Une choréographie en perpétuelle mouvance': 70–81 — R. Sirvin, 'Cinq partitons du Lac des cygnes': 82–87 — M. Babsky, 'Le Lac des cygnes sur lesscènes du monde': 88–90 — E. Giuliani, 'Bibliographie': 93–94.

[*4298*]   DEMIDOV, A. P. *"Lebedinoe ozero"*. Moskva: Iskusstvo, 1985. 366 p, illus. (*Shchedevry baleta*).

Reviews:A. Sokolov-Kaminskii, 'Talantlivyi zachin', *Sovetskii balet* (1988), 3: 59–60 — M. Rittikh, 'Ostaviv v storone partituru', *Sovetskii balet* (1988), 3: 60–61.

[*4299*]   NEWMAN, B. *Stories of the ballets: "Swan Lake"*. London [pr. Belgium]: Auran Press; New York: Barron's, 1985. 48 p.

[*4300*]   "Schwanensee (Le Lac des Cygnes)". In: *Reclams Ballettführer*. Von Hartmut Regitz, Otto Friedrich Regner, Heinz-Ludwig Schneiders. Stuttgart: Reclam, 1985: 542–559. (*Universal-Bibliothek*; 8042).

[*4301*]   WILEY, R. J. 'On "Swan Lake" and tradition", *About the House*, 7 (1985), 3: 18–25.

[*4302*]   GRIGOROVICH, Iu. & DEMIDOV, A. *The official Bolshoi Ballet book of "Swan Lake"*. Photography by Vladimir Pcholkin. Tr. from the Russian by Yuri S. Shirokov. Neptune, N. J.: T. F. H. Publications [1986]. 139 p, illus. ISBN: 0–8662–2328–2.

— 2nd ed. Neptune, N. J.: T. F. H. Publications [1988]. 139 p, illus. ISBN: 0–8662–2644–3.

[*4303*]   DEMIDOV, A. 'Iz istorii baleta: Kakim bylo "Lebedinoe ozero"', *Muzykal´naia zhizn´* (1986), 4: 17–18, illus.

[*4304*]   KAZENIN, I. 'Iubilei: Dolgaia i schastlivaia zhizn´', *Teatr* (1986), 11: 154–155, illus.

The 1000th production of W. Burmeister's production of the ballet in Moscow. See also *4278*.

[*4305*]   WILEY, R. J. 'The revival of "Swan Lake": A guest editorial', *Dancing Times*, 77 (Mar 1987): 492.

[*4306*]   WILEY, R. J. 'New life for an old swan', *Financial Times* (7 Mar 1987).

[*4307*]   WILEY, R. J. 'A rose revived', *About the House*, 7 (sum. 1987), 9: 15–17, illus.

[*4308*]   CHELOMBIT´KO, G. '160 let so dnia rozhdeniia baletmeistera, pervogo postanovshchika baleta "Lebedinoe ozero" Vatslava Reizingera', *Sovetskii balet* (1988), 1: 59–61, illus.

[*4309*]   VINOGRADOVA, S. 'Problemy tekushchego repertuara: Cherez tri s polovinoi desiatiletiia', *Sovetskii balet* (1988), 5: 43–44.

The 35th year of W. Burmeister's production of the ballet in Moscow.

[4310] 'Why a Swan?: Essays, interviews, and conversations on "Swan Lake"', *San Francisco Performing Arts Library and Museum Journal* (spr. 1989), 1 [whole issue].

Includes: R. J. Wiley, 'Pattern and meaning in Tchaikovsky': 39–49 [see *2396*].

[4311] BUCK, D. C. 'The journey of the swan maiden: A verse narrative retelling of an ancient myth'. Boston (Mass.): Boston Univ., 1990. 104 p.

Dissertation (Ph. D.). Concerning the story on which the ballet is based.

[4312] LADYGIN, D. 'Mnogostradal´naia istoriia muzyki baleta prodolzhaetsia'. In: *Moskovskii muzykoved: Ezhegodnik*. Vyp. 1. Moskva: Muzyka, 1990: 65–80.

The stage history of the ballet.

[4313] LADYGIN, D. 'Partitura "Lebedinogo ozera": Trevozhnye fakty ee biografii', *Sovetskii balet* (1990), 4: 17–21.

[4314] NEEF, H. '"Schwanensee": Die Tragödie der gehorsamen Kinder', *Musik und Gesellschaft*, 40 (Apr 1990): 178–181, illus.

[4315] PUDELEK, J. '"Swan Lake" in Warsaw, 1900', *Dance Chronicle*, 13 (1990/91), 3: 359–367, illus.

[4316] JASINSKI, R. 'A communication: Some recollections of "Swan Lake" in Warsaw', *Dance Chronicle*, 14 (1991), 1: 102–107, illus.

[4317] HAGMAN, B. 'Svansjøn', *Musikrevy*, 48 (1993), 4: 34–35, illus.

[4318] BROWN, D. 'Tchaikovsky's ballets', *Dance Now*, 2 (spr. 1993), 1: 26–34, illus.

[4319] WOHLFAHRT, H. T. 'Auf Schwanenflugeln: zum 100. Todestag von Pjotr Iljitsch Tschaikowsky', *Ballett-Journal/Das Tanzarchiv*, 41 (Dec 1993), 5: 60–63, illus.

In a fictional letter to the Chaikovskii, the author describes how *Swan Lake* has become an international cultural property.

[4320] KOEGLER, H. "Lebedinoe ozero". In: *Pipers Enzyklopadie des Musiktheaters: Oper, Operette, Musical, Ballet*. Hrsg. von Carl Dahlhaus und dem Forschungsinstitut fur Musiktheater der Universität Bayreuth unter Leitung von Sieghart Dohring. Band 5. München: Piper, 1994: 212–218.

[4321] REGITZ, H. 'Ein Stück vollkommenheit: Vor 100 Jahren gaben Marius Petipa und Lew Iwanow dem "Schwanensee"-Ballett seine endgütlige Gestalt', *Ballet-Journal*, 43 (1995), 2: 50–51.

[4322] ROZANOVA, O. 'Koldovskaia vlast´ "Lebedinogo ozera"', *Mariinskii teatr* (1995), 2: 2.

The 100th anniversary of the first production in St. Petersburg.

[4323] CLARKE, M. 'The choreographer and composer of "Swan Lake": Petipa and Tchaikovsky', *Dancing Times*, 85 (Feb 1995): 523; (Mar 1995): 627.

[4324] 'Simvol mirovogo baleta', *Nevskoe vremia* (15 Feb 1995): 2.

The 100th anniversary of the first production.

[4325] KUZOVLEVA, T. 'Po muzyke—luchshii, po tantsam—bednyi', *Chas pik* (22 Feb 1995): 15.

[4326] CURTIS, J. M. '"Swan Lake" at 100', *Dance Magazine*, 69 (Jun 1995): 38–41, illus.

[4327] KNEISS, U. "Schwanenkönigen", *Bühne* (1996), 11: 24.

[4328] MELIKIANTS, G. '"Lebedinoe ozero" bez chernogo lebedia i bez belogo tozhe', *Izvestiia* (24 Dec 1996): 4.

In connection with a new production of the ballet at the Bol´shoi Theatre in Moscow.

[*4329*]   **LLOYD-JONES, D.** 'Tchaikovsky: "Swan Lake" suite, Op. 20'. In: *The musician's guide to symphonic music: Essays from the Eulenberg scores*. Corey Field, ed. Mainz; New York: Schott, 1997: 653.

[*4330*]   **'Teatr baleta Gosudarstvennogo Kremlevskogo dvortsa'**, *Muzykal´noe obozrenie* (1997), 3: 8A.
A special production of the ballet to commemorate the 120th anniversary of the first performance.

[*4331*]   **WILEY, R. J.** '"Ars longa": An imperial "Swan Lake" is heard again', *Dancing Times* (Sep 1997), 9: 1074–1075.

[*4332*]   **TOPAZ, M.** 'Adventures in choreography', *Dance magazine*, 72 (Oct 1998), 10: 52–53.

[*4333*]   **STEYN, M.** "Swan Lake", *New Criterion*, 17 (Nov 1998), 3: 43–47.

[*4334*]   **MORITA, M.** 'Eien no "Hakucho no Mizuumi"'. Tokyo: Shinshokan, 1999. 354 p. ISBN 4–4032–3064–4.

[*4335*]   **KOTYKHOV, V.** 'Ozero smerti i liubvi', *Moskovskii komsomolets* (3 Dec 1999).

See also *3865, 3945, 5725, 5727.*

5.2.4. Incidental Music

[*4336*]   **GLUMOV, A.** *Muzyka v russkom dramaticheskom teatre: Istoricheskie ocherki.* Moskva: Gos. muz. izdat., 1955. 435 p.
Includes analysis of Chaikovskii's incidental music: "Dmitrii Samozvanets": 264–267 — "Snegurochka": 267–293 — "Monolog domovogo": 297–308 — "Gamlet": 309–326. With an appendix including the scores for "Kuplety grafa Al´mavivy": 412–413 — "Introduktsiia k 1-mu deistviiu Dmitriia Samozvantsa": 414–428 — "Monolog Domovogo": 429–433.

See also *2580.*

THE BARBER OF SEVILLE
Music for Count Almaviva's couplets (1872)

[*4337*]   **L.** 'Kuplety grafa Al´mavivy iz "Sevil´skogo tsirul´nika" P. Chaikovskogo', *Russkaia muzykal´naia gazeta* (26 Feb 1906), 9: 231.
The publication of the score by Iurgenson.

DMITRII THE PRETENDER AND VASILII SHUISKII
Music for A. N. Ostrovskii's play (1866–67)

[*4338*]   **VAIDMAN, P. E.** 'Listy iz al'boma', *Muzykal´naia zhizn´* (1986), 20: 9, 14, illus
The first publication of Chaikovskii's piano arrangement of the *Mazurka* for Ostrovskii's play. Also includes a fragment from the opera *The Voevoda*.

HAMLET
Music to Shakespeare's tragedy, Op. 67a (1891)

[*4339*]   **'Teatra i muzyka'**, *Novoe vremia* (10 Feb 1891).
The first production in St. Petersburg.

[*4340*]   **'Frantsuzskii teatr'**, *Novosti i birzhevaia gazeta* (11 Feb 1891).

[*4341*]   **'Mikhailovskii teatr: "Gamlet"'**, *Peterburgskii listok* (11 Feb 1891).

[*4342*]   IUGORSKII, S. 'Pis´mo iz Peterburga', *Moskovskie vedomosti* (19 Feb 1891).

[*4343*]   VASIL´EV, S. 'Teatral´naia khronika', *Moskovskie vedomosti* (21 Oct 1891).

[*4344*]   P—SKII, E. '"Gamlet" Chaikovskogo', *Russkaia muzykal´naia gazeta* (1895), 8: 495–501.
           Review of the score published by Iurgenson.

THE SNOW MAIDEN

Music for A. N. Ostrovskii's spring fairy-tale, Op. 12 (1873)

[*4345*]   X. 'Iz Moskvy', *Sankt Peterburgskie vedomosti* (23 May 1873).
           The first performance on 11 May 1873 in Moscow. See *4346, 4347*.

[*4346*]   AKILOV, P. 'Bol´shoi teatr: Novoe proizvedenie A. N. Ostrovskogo s noveisheiu muzykoiu P. I.
           Chaikovskogo', *Razvlechenie* (25 May 1873).

[*4347*]   'Moskovskie zametki: "Snegurochka"', *Golos* (26 May 1873).

[*4348*]   [KIUI, Ts. A.] 'Muzykal´nye zametki: Piat´ nomerov iz "Snegurochki" gg. Ostrovskogo i
           Chaikovskogo', *Sankt Peterburgskie vedomosti* (7 Nov 1873): 2.
           Publication of extracts from the vocal score. See also *4349*.

[*4349*]   [KIUI, Ts. A.] 'P. Chaikovskii, "Snegurochka": Muzyka k vesennei skazke A. Ostrovskogo', *Sankt
           Peterburgskie vedomosti* (21 Aug 1874): 1.

[*4350*]   'Letnii teatr', *Don* (25 May 1878).

[*4351*]   'Teatr i muzyka', *Novoe vremia* (16 Dec 1894): 3.
           The first performance in St. Petersburg, on 14 Dec 1894. See also *4352*.

[*4352*]   'Muzykal´noe obozrenie', *Nuvellist* (Jan 1895): 2.

[*4353*]   '"Snegurochka" s muzykoi Chaikovskogo', *Russkaia muzykal´naia gazeta* (14 Jan 1901), 2: 52.

[*4354*]   'Kalendar´ iskusstv: 65 let tomu nazad', *Dekada moskovskikh zrelishch* (1938), 15: 13.
           Recalling the first production in 1873.

[*4355*]   SHUMSKAIA, N. 'Iskusstvo strany "Kalevaly"', *Sovetskaia muzyka* (1959), 11: 101–105.
           A new production of *The Snow Maiden* in Petrozavodsk.

[*4356*]   NOVIKOVA, E. 'K 75-letiiu so dnia smerti A. N. Ostrovskogo: Skazka o "Snegurochke"',
           Muzykal´naia zhizn´ (1961), 11: 16–17.
           On Chaikovskii's music for *The Snow Maiden*, and Rimskii-Korsakov's opera on the same subject.

[*4357*]   SEROFF, V. '"Snow Maiden" by Tchaikovsky', *Saturday Review*, 45 (27 Jan 1962): 56.

[*4358*]   ASAF´EV, B. V. 'Iunye gody Chaikovskogo i muzyka k "Snegurochke"'. In: B. V. Asaf´ev, *O
           muzyke Chaikovskogo: Izbrannoe* (1972): 198–202 [see *2373*].
           — [repr.] In: *P. I. Chaikovskii i russkaia literatura* (1980): 11–18 [see *588*].

[*4359*]   KARASIKOV, M. 'Muzyka Chaikovskogo k "Snegurochke": K 100-letiiu so dnia pervoi
           postanovki', *Muzykal´naia zhizn´* (1973), 8: 17–18.

[*4360*]   RITTIKH, M. E. 'Iz istorii vesennei skazki "Snegurochka" A. N. Ostrovskogo—P. I.
           Chaikovskogo'. In: *Teatr v zhizni i tvorchestve P. I. Chaikovskogo* (1985): 40–54 [see *589*].

[4361]   RITTIKH, M. E. 'Chaikovskii i dramaticheskii teatr: K istorii "Snegurochki"'. In: *P. I. Chaikovskii: Voprosy istorii i stilia* (1989): 60–89 [see *590*].

See also *1992, 1993, 5715* to *5719*.

5.3. ORCHESTRAL WORKS

5.3.1. General

[4362]   SITTARD, J. 'Peter Tschaikowsky als Orchesterkomponist', *Hamburger Correspondent* (21 Jan 1888).

— [repr.] In: J. Sittard, *Studien und Charakteristiken*. Bd. 2: *Künstler-Charakteristiken: Aus dem Konzertsaal*. Hamburg; Leipzig; Berlin, 1889: 138–145.

— [repr.] In: *Tschaikowsky aus der Nähe* (1994): 190–195 [see *379*].

[4363]   BEYER, C. *Peter Tschaikowsky's Orchesterwerke*. Erläutert mit Notenbeispeilen von C. Beyer. Berlin: Schlesinger [1911]. 137 p, music. (*Schlesinger'sche Musikbibliothek*).

[4364]   RIEMANN, H. *P. Tschaikowsky's Orchesterwerke*. Berlin; Wien [1911]. (*Meisterführer*; 14).

— [repr. (abridged)] 'Die Tschaikowsky-Rezensionen'. In: *Tschaikowsky aus der Nähe* (1994): 46–48 [see *379*].

[4365]   LUCAS, C. 'Tschaikowsky's orchestral and chamber works', *Musical Courier*, 77 (1918), 21: 7–8.

[4366]   BLOM, E. W. *Tchaikovsky: Orchestral works*. Oxford: Oxford Univ. Press; London: H. Milford, 1927. 51 p, music, illus. (*Musical Pilgrim*; 25).

Analysis of 4 selected works. For contents see *4593, 4772, 4903, 5018*.

— [repr.] London: Oxford Univ. Press [1948]. 51 p, music. (*Musical Pilgrim*).

— [repr.] Westport (Conn.): Greenwood Press [1971]. 51 p, music. (*Musical Pilgrim*). ISBN: 0–8371–4202–4.

[4367]   BOTSTEIBER, H. *Symphonie und Suite, von Berlioz bis zur Gegenwart*. Leipzig, 1932: 30–45.

[4368]   BUDIAKOVSKII, A. E. *P. I. Chaikovskii: Simfonicheskaia muzyka*. Leningrad: Leningradskaia filarmoniia, 1935. 273 p, music, illus. (*Knigi o simfonicheskoi muzyke*).

Includes: 'Spisok sochinenii Chaikovskogo': 260–264 — 'Literatura o Chaikovskom': 264–273.

[4369]   SOLLERTINSKII, I. I. 'P. I. Chaikovskii i ruskii simfonizm'. In: *Pikovaia dama: Opera, muzyka P. I. Chaikovskogo* (1935): 57–65 [see *3546*].

[4370]   ZHITOMIRSKII, D. V. *Simfonicheskoe tvorchestvo Chaikovskogo: Putevoditel´*. Moskva: Gos. filarmoniia, 1936. ii, 62 p, music, illus.

Analysis of selected orchestral works.

[4371]   SPAETH, S. G. 'Peter Ilitch Tschaikowsky'. In: S. G. Spaeth, *A guide to great orchestral music*. New York: The Modern Library [1943]: 206–225. (*The modern library of the world's best books*).

[4372]   BIANCOLLI, L. *Tschaikowsky and his orchestral music*. [New York: Philharmonic-Symphonic Society of New York, 1944]. 48 p, illus.

Includes: 'Complete list of recordings by the Philarmonic-Symphony Society of New York': 46–48 [see *52*].

— [rev. ed.] New York: Grosset & Dunlap [1950]. 56 p. illus.

Includes: 'Complete list of recordings by the Philarmonic-Symphony Society of New York': 53–56 [see *52*].

Review: *Etude*, 69 (Apr 1951): 7.

[4373]   WOLFURT, K. von. *Die sinfonischen Werke von Peter Tschaikowski*. Einführungen. Berlin: Bote & Bock [1947]. 64 p, music.

[4374]   'Tchaikovsky works discovered', *Music News*, 41 (Nov 1949): 17.

[4375]   FERGUSON, D. N. 'Tchaikovsky'. In: D. N. Ferguson, *Masterworks of the orchestral repertoire: A guide for listeners*. Minneapolis: Univ. of Minnesota Press [1954]: 586–603.

[4376]   DOLZHANSKII, A. N. *Muzyka Chaikovskogo: Simfonicheskie proizvedeniia*. Nauchno-populiarnye ocherki. Leningrad: Gos. muz. izdat., 1960. 269 p, music, illus.

  See also *4378*.

[4377]   RENNER, H. 'Peter Iljitsch Tschaikowsky'. In: H. Renner, *Reclams Konzertführer: Orchestermusik*. 6. Aufl. Stuttgart: Reclam, 1963: 404–428. (*Universal-Bibliothek*; 7720/31).

  — 9. Aufl., mit ein Erganzung des Hauptteils von Klaus Schweizer. Stuttgart: Reclam, 1972: 404–428. (*Universal-Bibliothek*; 7720/31).

[4378]   DOLZHANSKII, A. N. *Simfonicheskaia muzyka Chaikovskogo: Izbrannye proizvedeniia*. Moskva; Leningrad: Muzyka, 1965. 240 p, music.

  See alsoo *4376*.

  — 2-e izd. Leningrad: Muzyka, 1981. 208 p, music.

[4379]   KLEIN, R. 'Pjotr Iljitsch Tschaikowsky'. In: R. Klein, *Das Symphoniekonzert: Ein Stilführer durch das Konzertrepertoire*. Hrsg. in Zsarb. mit des Osterreichischer Geschichte für Musik. Wien; München: Jugend & Volk [1971]: 180–186. (*J & V Musik*).

[4380]   'Pjotr Iljitsch Tschaikowski'. In: *Konzertbuch: Orchestermusik*. Hrsg. von Hansjurgen Schaefer; begrundet von Karl Schonewolf. 3., unveranderte Aufl. Band 3. Leipzig: Deutscher Verlag für Musik, 1975: 495–538.

[4381]   RICH, A. 'Peter Ilyitch Tchaikovsky'. In: A. Rich, *Classical music: Orchestral*. With the assistance of Daniel Schillaci. New York: Simon & Schuster, 1980: 89–91. (*Simon & Schuster listener's guides to music*).

[4382]   SCHUMANN, O. 'Peter Tschaikowsky'. In: O. Schumann, *Der grosse Konzertführer*. Herrsching: M. Pawlak, 1983: 373–391.

[4383]   'Peter Iljitsch Tschaikowsky'. In: *Lexikon Orchestermusik Romantik*. Hrsg. Wulf Konold; mit Beitragen von Alfred Beaujean [et al]. Originalausg. Band 2: *S–Z*. Mainz: Schott; München: Piper, 1989: 954–1019 (*Serie Musik Piper-Schott*).

[4384]   ENGSTRØM, B. O. 'Tjajkovskij: Orkestermusiken', *Musikrevy*, 48 (1993), 4: 18–25, illus.

[4385]   MOLINARI, G. 'Ciaikowsky e la musica sinfonica della scuola russa', *Rassegna Musicale Curci*, 46 (1993), 2: 26–32.

[4386]   BRIANTSEVA, V. 'O pretvorenii val´sovosti v tvorchestve P. I Chaikovskogo i S.V. Rakhmaninova'. In: *S. V. Rakhmaninov. K 120-letiiu so dnia rozhdeniia (1873–1993)*. Materialy nauchnoi konferentsii, red.-sost. A. I. Kandinskii. Moskva: [Moskovskaia konservatoriia], 1995: 120–128. ISBN: 5-8641-9016-0.

[4387]   RZEHULKA, B. 'Pjotr Iljitsch Tschaikowsky'. In: *Der Konzertführer: Orchestermusik von 1700 bis zur Gegenwart*. Hrsg. von Attila Csampai und Dietmar Holland; in Zusammenarbeit mit Irmelin Burgers. Uberarbeitete und erw. Neuausg. [Tubingen]: Wunderlich [1996]: 536–567.

5.3.2. Symphonies

[4388]   MATHEWS, W. S. B. 'The symphonies of Tschaikowsky', *Music*, 17 (Apr 1900): 612–614.

[*4389*]   NEWMAN, E. 'Tschaikowsky and the symphony', *Monthly Musical Record*, 32 (Aug 1902): 122–124;
(Sep 1902): 145–147; (Oct 1902): 163–164.

[*4390*]   CH[ERNOV], K. N. 'Simfonii Chaikovskogo s ikh tematicheskim ukazatelem', *Russkaia
muzykal´naia gazeta* (7 Mar 1904), 10: 257–265; (14 Mar 1904), 11: 289–301; (21 Mar 1904), 12: 321–
335; (28 Mar/4 Apr 1904), 13/14: 354–357.
         — [offprint] K. N. Chernov, *Simfonii Chaikovskogo s ikh kratkim tematicheskim ukazatelem*. Sankt Peterburg:
1904. 62 p.

[*4391*]   ENGEL´, Iu. D. 'Simfonii Chaikovskogo: K kontsertam A. Nikisha', *Russkie vedomosti* (14 Apr
1904).
         In connection with a cycle of the symphonies conducted by Artur Nikisch.

[*4392*]   'Lektsiia Iu. Engelia o Chaikovskom, kak simfoniste', *Russkaia muzykal´naia gazeta* (21 Apr/2 May
1904), 17/18: 471–473.

[*4393*]   STILLMAN-KELLEY, E. 'Tschaikowsky as symphonist', *Musical Courier*, 53 (1906), 24: 5, 25: 5–8.

[*4393*]   GOEPP, P. H. 'Tschaikowsky'. In: P. H. Goepp, *Symphonies and their meaning*. 7th ed. [3 vols. in one].
Philadelphia: J. B. Lippincott, 1908. 2: 422–433; 3: 114–142.

[*4395*]   ENGEL´, Iu. D. 'Tsikl Chaikovskogo', *Russkie vedomosti* (19 Sep 1912; 21 Sep 1912; 23 Sep 1912;
25 Sep 1912).
         In connection with a concert cycle of the symphonies.

[*4396*]   GLEBOV, I. [ASAF´EV, B. V.] 'Simfonizm Chaikovskogo'. In: I. Glebov, *Instrumental´noe tvorchestvo
Chaikovskogo* (1922): 13–32 [see *2310*].

[*4397*]   BLOM, E. W. 'The early Tchaikovsky symphonies'. In: E. W. Blom, *Stepchildren of music*. London:
G. T. Foulis [1925]: 153–160.
         Symphonies Nos. 1, 2 and 3.
         — [repr.] Freeport, N. Y.: Books for Libraries Press [1967]. (*Essay index reprint series*).

[*4398*]   ABRAHAM, G. E. H. 'The great unplayed: Tchaikovsky's earlier symphonies', *Musical Standard*
[new series], 26 (11 Jul 1925): 12.
         Symphonies Nos. 1, 2 and 3.

[*4399*]   ZHITOMIRSKII, D. V. 'O simfonizme Chaikovskogo', *Sovetskaia muzyka* (1933), 6: 60–65.

[*4400*]   O'CONNELL, C. 'Peter I. Tschaikowsky'. In: C. O'Connell, *The Victor book of the symphony*. New York:
Simon & Schuster, 1934: 443–478.
         — Rev. ed. New York: Simon & Schuster, 1941: 552–589.

[*4401*]   DOWNES, O. 'Peter Ilyitch Tchaikovsky'. In: O. Downes, *Symphonic masterpieces*. New York: Dial
Press, 1935: 184–201.

[*4402*]   SPAETH, S. G. 'Tschaikowsky'. In: S. G. Spaeth, *Great symphonies: How to recognize and remember them*.
Garden City, N. Y.:Garden City Publishing Co. [1936]: 224–248.

[*4403*]   BUDIAKOVSKII, A. 'Chaikovskii simfonist', *Iskusstvo i zhizn´* (1940): 22–23.

[*4404*]   DANILEVICH, L. V. 'O simfonizme Chaikovskogo', *Sovetskaia muzyka* (1940), 1: 8–15; 5/6: 35–47,
music, illus. [see *585*].
         Concerning the first four symphonies.

[*4405*]   KREMLEV, Iu. A. 'Printsipy simfonicheskogo razvitiia u Chaikovskogo', *Sovetskaia muzyka* (1940),
5/6: 18–34 [see *585*].
         — [repr.] In: Iu. A. Kremlev, *Izbrannye stat´i*. Leningrad: Muzyka, 1976: 106–125.

[4406] ZHITOMIRSKII, D. V. 'Chaikovskii simfonist', *Sovetskoe iskusstvo* (6 May 1940): 3 [see *853*].

[4407] WESTRUP, J. A. 'Tchaikovsky and the Symphony', *Musical Times*, 81 (Jun 1940): 249–252, music.

[4408] BLOM, E. W. 'Tchaikovsky as symphonist', *The Listener*, 26 (25 Sep 1941): 449.

[4409] ASAF´EV, B. V. *Velikii russkii simfonist*. [Moskva]: Gos. filarmoniia [1943]. 2 p.
Programme suppl. for a series of Philharmonic Society concerts in Moscow. on 16, 18, 21, 24 Nov 1943.
— [repr.] In: B. V. Asaf´ev, *O muzyke Chaikovskogo: Izbrannoe* (1972): 58–60 [see *2373*].

[4410] COOPER, M. 'The symphonies'. In: *Tchaikovsky: A symposium* (1945): 24–46 [see *586*].

[4411] ZHITOMIRSKII, D. V. 'Symphonies'. In: *Russian symphony: Thoughts about Tchaikovsky* (1947): 86–131 [see *587*].

[4412] COOPER, M. 'Peter Ilich Tchaikovsky'. In: *The symphony*. Ed. by Ralph Hill. Harmondsworth: Penguin Books, 1949: 261–275. (*Pelican books*).
— [repr.] St. Clair Shores, Mich.: Scholarly Press, 1978: 261–275.

[4413] ELLIOT, J. H. 'Tchaikovsky as symphonist', *Hallé* (Sep 1949): 9–11, illus.

[4414] KREMLEV, Iu. A. *Simfonii P. I. Chaikovskogo*. Moskva: Gos. muz. izdat., 1955. 304 p, music, illus.
Review: L. Danilevich, 'Kniga o simfoniiakh Chaikovskogo', *Sovetskaia muzyka* (1956), 9: 146–149.

[4415] WILLIAMS, R. 'How to enjoy a symphony', *House Buyer*, 98 (Jul 1956): 49–50.

[4416] SHLIFSHTEIN, S. *Simfonii P. I. Chaikovskogo*. Moskva: Gos. filarmoniia, 1957. 50 p. (*V pomoshch´ slushateliam kontsertov*).

[4417] NIKOLAEVA, N. S. *Simfonii P. I. Chaikovskogo: Ot "Zimnikh grez" k "Pateticheskoi"*. Moskva: Gos. muz. izdat., 1958. 298 p, music, illus.
Review: O. Leont´ev, 'Kniga o simfoniiakh Chaikovskogo', *Sovetskaia muzyka* (1959), 1: 187–188.

[4418] NIKOLAEVA, N. S. 'O dramaturgicheskom konflikte v simfoniiakh Chaikovskogo', *Sovetskaia muzyka* (1958), 1: 57–68, music, illus.

[4419] KELLER, H. 'The new in review', *Music Review*, 20 (May 1959): 160–161.

[4420] IARUSTOVSKII, B. *Simfonii Chaikovskogo*. 2-e izd. Moskva: Muzgiz, 1961. 45 p, music. (*Biblioteka slushatelia kontsertov*).

[4421] HAMBURGER, P. *Tjajkofskij som symfoniker*. København [Rhodos, 1962]. 89 p, music, illus. (*Folkeuniversitets bibliotek: Musik*; 1).
Review: *Dansk Musiktidsskrift*, 38 (1963), 1: 31.

[4422] KLOIBER, R. 'Pjotr (Peter) Iljitsch Tschaikowsky'. In: R. Kloiber, *Handbuch der klassischen und romantischen Symphonie*. Wiesbaden: Breitkopf & Hartel, 1964: 241–265.
— 2., erw. Aufl. Wiesbaden: Breitkopf & Härtel, 1976: 297–318.

[4423] KIRCHBERG, K. 'Tschaikowsky "ohne Weltanschauung"?', *Phonoprisma* (Nov/Dec 1966), 6: 172–175.
Relating to new recordings of the symphonies by Lorin Maazel and the Vienna Philharmonic Orchestra.

[4424] WARRACK, J. *Tchaikovsky symphonies and concertos*. London: British Broadcasting Corporation, 1969. vii, 56 p, music. (*BBC Music Guides*; 16). ISBN: 0-563-09203-3.
Reviews: *Royal College of Music Magazine*, 66 (1970), 1: 22–23 — *Music Teacher*, 49 (Mar 1970): 35 — *Musical Times*, 111 (Jul 1970): 712 — *Music Review*, 32 (1971), 4: 362–363 — *Music in Education*, 39 (1975), 372: 71.

— [repr.] Seattle: Univ. of Washington Press [1971]. vii, 56 p, music. (*BBC Music Guides*; 16). ISBN 0-2959-5109-5.

— Rev. ed. London: British Broadcasting Corporation, 1974. viii, 64 p, music. (*BBC Music Guides*). ISBN: 0-563-12773-2.

With revisions to the text, and a new section on "Manfred".

— [repr.] London: British Broadcasting Corporation, 1980. viii, 64 p, music. (*BBC Music Guides*). ISBN 0-563-12773-2.

[*4425*]   **BOGATYREV, S. S. 'Nekotorye osobennosti izlozheniia v poslednikh simfoniiakh Chaikovskogo'.** In: S. S. Bogatyrev: *Issledovaniia, stat'i, vospominaniia*. Red.-sost. G. A. Tiumeneva i Iu. N. Kholopov. Moskva: Sovetskii kompozitor, 1972: 53–68.

[*4426*]   **KELLER, H. 'Peter Ilyich Tchaikovsky'.** In: *The symphony*. Ed. by Robert Simpson. Vol. 1.Newton Abbot: David & Charles, 1972: 342–353.

[*4427*]   **CUYLER, L. E. 'The symphonies of Tchaikovsky'.** In: L. E. Cuyler, *The symphony*. New York: Harcourt Brace Jovanovich, [1973]: 154–158. (*Harbrace history of musical forms*).

— 2nd ed. Warren, Mich.: Harmonie Park Press, 1995: 154–158. (Detroit monographs in musicology/Studies in music; 16).

[*4428*]   **HART, P. 'Tchaikovsky overdone, underdone and done in',** *High Fidelity*, 25 (Jul 1975): 63–66.
Survey of recordings.

[*4429*]   **SCHUMANN, K. 'Symphonien aus dem Nichts: Anmerkungen zu Tschaikowskys frühen Orchesterwerken',** *Philharmonische Blätter* (1976/77), 8: 8–9, 11.

[*4430*]   **KONDRASHIN, K. P.** *O dirizherskom prochtenii simfonii P. I. Chaikovskogo*. Moskva: Muzyka, 1977. 240 p, music.

[*4431*]   **MARCH, I. 'The symphonies of Tchaikovsky',** *Gramophone*, 55 (Dec 1977): 1037–1038, illus.

[*4432*]   **SCHUMANN, K. 'Die grundidee gab Beethoven: Die Schicksalthematik in dem Symphonien Tschaikowskys',** *Philharmonische Blätter* (1977/78), 2: 2–5.

[*4433*]   **SEGALINI, S. 'Discographie comparée: Les symphonies des Tchaikovski',** *Harmonie* (Apr 1978), 136: 94–101.

[*4434*]   **STEDMAN, P. 'Peter Ilyich Tchaikovsky'.** In: P. Stedman, *The symphony*. Englewood Cliffs, N. J.: Prentice-Hall, 1979: 159–170.

— 2nd ed. Englewood Cliffs, N. J.: Prentice Hall, 1992: 166–178.

[*4435*]   **SKREBKOV, S. S. 'Simfonicheskaia polifoniia Chaikovskogo'.** In: S. S. Skrebkov, *Izbrannye stat´i*. Red.-sost. D. A. Arutiunov, Moskva: Muzyka, 1980.

[*4436*]   **NEMIROVSKAIA, I. A. 'Nekotorye osobennosti traktovki pliasovykh i khorovodnykh istokov v muzykal´nom tematizme simfonii P. I. Chaikovskogo'.** In: *P. I. Chaikovskii i Ural* (1982): 137–146 [see *1749*].

[*4437*]   **NEMIROVSKAIA, I. A. 'O printsipe simfonicheskogo kontrdeistviia',** *Sovetskaia muzyka* (1983), 8: 105–107.

[*4438*]   **RICHARD, J. V. 'A survey of symphonic works composed contemporaneously to Brahms' four symphonies, 1869–1876',** *L'Avant Scène Opéra*, 53 (1983): 22–23.

[*4439*]   **NEMIROVSKAIA, I. A. 'Znachenie bytovykh zhanrov i muzykal´noi dramaturgii simfonii Chaikovskogo i Bramsa'.** Moskva: Moskovskaia Gos. Konservatoriia im P. I. Chaikovskogo, 1984. 24 p.
Summary of dissertation (Moscow State Conservatory).

[*4440*] NEISHTADT, I. N. 'Zhanrovaia struktura simfonii P. I. Chaikovskogo'. Vil´nius: Gos. Konservatoriia Litovskoi SSR, 1985. 22 p.

Summary of dissertation (Lithuanian State Conservatory).

[*4441*] NEMIROVSKAIA, I. A. 'Nekotorye priemy teatral´noi dramaturgii v simfoniiakh P. I. Chaikovskogo'. In: *Teatr v zhizni i tvorchestve P. I. Chaikovskogo* (1985): 89–100 [see *589*].

[*4442*] HOPKINS, A. 'Tchaikovsky'. In: A. Hopkins, *The Dent concetgoers companion*. Vol. 2: *Holst to Webern*. London: J. M. Dent, 1986: 311–328.

Includes: 'Symphony No. 4 in F minor': 314–318 [see *4610*] — 'Symphony No. 5 in E minor': 319–323 [see *4651*] — 'Symphony No. 6 in B minor': 323–328 [see *4736*].

— [2nd ed. (vols. 1 & 2 combined)]. *The Dent concertgoers companion*. London, J. M. Dent, 1993: 601–618.

[*4443*] LISCHKÉ, A. 'Piotr Ilyitch Tchaikovski'. In: *Guide de la musique symphonique*. Sous la direction de Francois-Rene Tranchefort; avec la collaboration de Andre Lischké, Michel Parouty, Marc Vignal. [Paris]: Fayard, [1986]: 788–805. (*Collection les indispensables de la musique*).

[*4444*] POCIEJ, B. 'Symfonia', *Ruch Muzyczny*, 31 (1987), 6: 14–15, illus.

[*4445*] 'Tchaikovsky, Dvořák and Sibelius'. In: *The great symphonies, the great orchestras, the great conductors*. Ed. by Clive Unger Hamilton and Peter Van der Spek. London: Sidgwick & Jackson, 1988: 106–114.

[*4446*] 'Cajkovskij, Petr Il'ich'. In: *Repertorio di musica sinfonica: Gli autori, le composizioni dal Seicento a oggi*. A cura di Piero Santi. Ricordi : Giunti [1989]: 171–181. (*Guide alla musica*).

[*4447*] NEMIROVSKAIA, I. A. 'Vyrazitel´noe znachenie zhanrovykh splavov i transformatsii v simfoniiakh Chaikovskogo'. In: *P. I. Chaikovskii: Voprosy istorii i stilia* (1989): 115–134 [see *590*].

[*4448*] ITKINA, Zh. M. 'Nekotorye osobennosti ispolnitel´skikh traktovok Natana Rakhlina v ego kazanskikh programmakh'. In: *Natan Rakhlin: Stat´i, interv´iu, vospominaniia*. Obshchaia red., sost. i predislovie G. Ia. Iudina. Moskva, 1990: 61–68.

Concerning Chaikovskii's symphonies.

[*4449*] KELDYSH, Iu. V. 'Simfonizm Chaikovskogo i evoliutsiia simfonicheskogo myshleniia v XIX veke', *Sovetskaia muzyka* (1990), 12: 92–101.

[*4450*] KHOLOPOV, Iu. 'O sisteme muzykal´nykh form v simfoniiakh Chaikovskogo: K probleme klasssifikatsii muzykal´nykh form', *Sovetskaia muzyka* (1990), 6: 38–45 [see *592*].

[*4451*] ANGERER, M. 'Ästhetik der Symphonie und russishce Symphonik', *Österreichische Musikzeitschrift*, 45 (May 1990): 237–244, music, illus.

[*4452*] SZERSNOVICZ, P. 'Tchaikovsky symphoniste—Le sentimental caché—Un maître de la form', *Le Monde de la Musique* (Nov 1992), 160: 15–17.

[*4453*] BROWN, D. 'Russia before the Revolution'. In: *A Companion to the symphony*. Ed. by Robert Layton. London; New York: Simon & Schuster, 1993: 262–291.

— [repr.] *A guide to the symphony*. Ed. by Robert Layton. Oxford; New York: Oxford Univ. Press, 1995: 262–291.

[*4454*] KOZLOVSKII, A. 'O nekotorykh izustnykh traditsiiakh i korrektivakh ispolneniia: Na osnove vstrech i besed s muzykantami ushedshego pokoleniia', *Muzykal´naia akademiia* (1993), 2: 99–100.

Concerning observations on the performance of Chaikovskii's symphonies.

[*4455*] LAYTON. R. 'Just how great are the symphonies?', *Classic CD* (Nov 1993), 42 [suppl.]: 6–7, illus.

[*4456*] CHION, M. 'Les ambassadeurs: Borodine, Tchaikovski, Dvořák'. In: M. Chion, *La symphonie a l'époque romantique: De Beethoven à Mahler*. Paris: Fayard [1994]:179–200. (*Collection les chemins de la musique*).

[4457]　**TREZISE, S.** 'Tchaikovsky symphonies', *Classic CD* (Apr 1994), 47: 68.

[4458]　**STEINBERG, M.** *The symphony: A listener's guide*. New York: Oxford Univ. Press, 1995. xvii, 678 p, music. ISBN: 0–19–506177–2.

　　　　Includes analyses of Chaikovskii's symphonies nos. 4–6: 624–643.

[4459]　**IVANOVA, L. P.** 'O edinstve tsikla v pervykh trekh simfoniiakh Chaikovskogo'. In: *Trudy kafedry teorii muzyki*. Vyp. 1. Sankt Peterburg, 1995: 51–71. (*Ministerstvo kul´tury Rossiiskoi Federatsii. Sankt Peterburgskaia gos. konservatoriia im. N. A. Rimskogo-Korsakova*).

[4460]　**JACKSON, T. L.** 'Aspects of sexuality and structure in the later symphonies of Tchaikovsky', *Music Analysis*, 14 (Mar 1995), 1: 3–25, music.

[4461]　**DAMMANN, S.** 'Gattung und Einzelwerk im symphonischen Frühwerk Cajkovskijs'. Stuttgart: M & P Verlag für Musikwissenschaft und Forschung, 1996. 479 p, music. ISBN: 3–476–45155–0. Dissertation (Kiel Univ.).

[4462]　**MOLINARI, G.** 'Anton Bruckner e la Sinfonia del secondo Ottocento', *Rassegna Musicale Curci*, 49 (1996), 2: 21–22.

[4463]　**KRAUS, J. C.** 'Tchaikovsky'. In: *The nineteenth century symphony*. Ed. D. Kern Holoman. New York: Schirmer, 1997: 299–326.

[4464]　'Pjotr Iljitsch Tschaikowskij'. In: *Reclams Konzertführer: Orchestermusik*. Von Klaus Schweizer und Arnold Werner-Jensen. Stuttgart: Reclam, 1998: 482–504.

　　　　See also *2512, 2522*.

MANFRED
Symphony in 4 scenes after Byron, Op. 58 (1885)

[4465]　'Teatr i muzyka', *Russkie vedomosti* (13 Mar 1886).

　　　　The first performance of the symphony on 11 Mar 1886 in Moscow. See also *4466, 4467*.

[4466]　'Posledniaia pochta', *Moskovskie vedomosti* (13 Mar 1886).

[4467]　'"Manfred": Simfoniia Chaikovskogo', *Teatr i zhizn´* (16 Mar 1886).

[4468]　'Teatr i muzyka', *Novoe vremia* (18 May 1886).

　　　　The first performances in Pavlovsk on 2 and 16 May 1886.

[4469]　**LAROSH, G. A.** 'Muzykal´noe obozrenie', *Russkii vestnik* (Oct 1886).

　　　　— [repr.] 'Kvartet No. 2 (F-dur), op. 22. Simfoniia "Manfred" (h-moll), op. 58'. In: G. A. Larosh, *Izbrannye stat´i v piati vypuskakh*, vyp. 2 (1975): 122–124 [see *2376*].

　　　　— [German tr.] 'Tschaikowskys Sinfonie "Manfred", op. 58'. In: G. A. Larosh, *Peter Tschaikowsky: Aufsätze und Erinnerungen* (1993): 133–135 [see *2406*].

[4470]　[KIUI, Ts. A.] '"Manfred": Simfoniia P. Chaikovskogo', *Muzykal´noe obozrenie* (31 Dec 1886).

　　　　The first performance in St. Petersburg on 27 Dec 1886.

[4471]　**LAROSH, G. A.** 'Kontsert 11 avgusta v Pavlovske: "Manfred" i "Gamlet" Chaikovskogo', *Teatral´naia gazeta* (15 Aug 1893): 6.

　　　　— [repr.] In: G. A. Larosh, *Izbrannye stat´i v piati vypuskakh*, vyp. 2 (1975): 155–159 [see *2376*].

[4472]　**RIEMANN, H.** *Peter Iljitsch Tschaikowsky: Symphonie "Manfred" (H-moll), Op. 58*. Erlautert von Hugo Riemann. Frankfurt am Main: H. Bechhold [c.1895]. 23 p, music. (*Musikführer*; 141).

— [Russian tr.] *"Manfred" P. I. Chaikovskogo*. Simfoniia v 4 kartinakh (H-moll, Op. 58) na siuzhet dramaticheskoi poemy Bairona. Tematicheskoe raziasnenie soderzhaniia, sost. G. Riman; perevod B. Iu[rgenson]. Moskva: P. Iuurgenson, 1903. 25 p, music.

[4473] ENGEL´, Iu. D. '"Manfred" Chaikovskogo i "Pesn´ o veshchem Olege" Rimskogo-Korsakova: K kontsertu Russkogo Muzykal´nogo obshchestva 1 dekiabria', *Russkie vedomosti* (1 Dec 1901; 3 Dec 1901).

— [repr.] '"Manfred" pod upravleniem Safonova', In: Iu. D. Engel´, *Glazami sovremennika*. Moskva, 1971: 89–95.

[4474] "Manfred", *Russkaia muzykal´naia gazeta* (1 Jan 1906), 1: 16–17.

[4475] 'Chaikovskii v svoem tvorchestve', *Muzyka* (16 May 1912): 455.
Extracts from Chaikovskii's correspondence with Balakirev concerning *Manfred*.

[4476] MEDVEDEVA, N. 'Neopublikovannoe pis´mo o "Manfrede"', *Sovetskoe iskusstvo* (6 Jul 1937).
A letter from Chaikovskii to Iuliia Shpazhinskaia (1886) concerning the symphony.

[4477] NIKOLAEVA, N. *Simfoniia Chaikovskogo "Manfred": Poiasnenie*. Moskva: Gos. muz. izdat., 1952. 27 p, music. (*V pomoshch´ slushateliu muzyki*).

— [2-e izd.] Moskva: Gos. muz. izdat., 1959. 24 p, music. (*Biblioteka slushatelia kontsertov*).

[4478] ZHITOMIRSKII, D. V. *Chaikovskii: "Manfred". Simfoniia v 4-kh kartinakh (po Baironu)*. [Moskva: Gos. filarmoniia, 1954]. 7 p. (*V pomoshch´ slushateliam kontsertov*).

[4479] DIETHER, J. 'From Everest: Yet another abridged "Manfred" symphony', *American Record Guide*, 26 (Apr 1960): 636–637.
Survey of recordings.

[4480] ORLOVA, A. A. 'Iz istorii programmy simfonii Chaikovskogo "Manfred"', *Sovetskaia muzyka* (1961), 2: 69–73.
Comparing Balakirev's, Stasov's and Chaikovskii's programmes for the symphony.

[4481] HARRISON, J. S. 'The New York music scene', *Musical America*, 83 (Nov 1963): 29.

[4482] KEMPSTER, R. A. 'Tchaikovsky rewritten', *Music & Musicians*, 15 (May 1967): 18.
A letter to the editor concerning the *Manfred* symphony.

[4483] DUBRAVSKAIA, T. 'Simfoniia "Manfred" Chaikovskogo', *Muzykal´naia zhizn´* (1974), 11: 14–15, music.

[4484] YUNGKANS, J. "Manfred", *Fugue*, 3 (May 1979): 32–34, illus.

[4485] MANNONI, G. '"Manfred" selon Noureev', *Harmonie* (Nov 1979), 152: 63–64.

[4486] VELAZCO, J. 'Cronica de "Manfredo"', *Heterofonia*, 17 (1984), 85: 44–47/

[4487] DUCK, L. 'The Manchester scene', *Musical Opinion*, 110 (Apr 1987): 120–121.

[4488] SCHOUTEN, R. 'Lord Byron of de muzikale weerklank van een charismatisch dichter', *Mens en melodie*, 43 (Mar 1988): 178–180.

[4489] KOLMAKOVA, M. 'Vse simfonii Chaikovskogo: Zagadka Mastera', *Muzykal´naia zhizn´* (1990), 22: 19–21, illus.

[4490] TSARËVA, E. '"Manfred" Bairona u Shumana i Chaikovskogo: K probleme muzyki i slova'. In: *Chaikovskii: K 150-letiiu so dnia rozhdeniia. Voprosy istorii, teorii i ispolnitel´stva* (1990): 77–94 [see *591*].

[4491]   ARANOVSKII, A. 'Dva etiuda o tvorcheskom protsesse. 2. Konstruktsiia i obraz (simfoniia
P. Chaikovskogo "Manfred"). In: *Prostessy muzykal'nogo tvorchestva: Sbornik trudov.* Moskva, 1994: 69–
77. (*Ministerstvo kul'tury Rossiiskoi Federatsii. Rossiiskaia Akademiia muzyki im. Gnesnykh*).

[4492]   ERMOLAEVA, T. N. 'O "Manfrede" P. I. Chaikovskogo: Stanovlenie obraza glavnogo geroia (po
materialam chernovykh eskizov)'. In: *Russkaia kul'tura i mir: Tezisy dokladov uchastnikov II
mezhdunarodnoi nauchnoi konferentsii.* Tom 2. Nizhnii Novgorod: NGLU im N. A. Dobroliubova, 1994:
167–168.

[4493]   ARANOVSKII, M. G. 'Nakhodki i oshibki tvorcheskoi intuitsii (iz rukopisnogo arkhiva P. I.
Chaikovskogo)'. In: *P. I. Chaikovskii: K 100-letiiu so dnia smerti* (1995): 31–38 [see *597*].
Concerning Chaikovskii's sketches for *Manfred* and the Symphony No. 5.

[4494]   ABRAHAM, G. E. H. 'Tchaikovsky: "Manfred" symphony, op. 58'. In: *The musician's guide to
symphonic music: Essays from the Eulenberg scores.* Corey Field, ed. Mainz; New York: Schott, 1997: 633–
638.

See also *110, 206, 1920, 2512, 5657, 5659.*

SYMPHONY in E flat major
[unfinshed; completed by Semën Bogatyrev] (1892)

[4495]   RABINOVICH, D. A. 'Vozrozhdennaia simfoniia', *Sovetskaia muzyka* (1957), 5: 128–133, music,
illus.
Includes a review of the first performance of Bogatyrev's reconstruction of symphony on 7 Feb 1957 in
Moscow.

[4496]   BOGATYREV, S. S. 'Ot redaktora' / 'Editor's note'. In: *P. I. Chaikovskii: Simfoniia Es-dur.*
Vosstanovlenie, instrumentovka i red. S. Bogatyreva. Partitura. Moskva: Gos. muz. izdat., 1961: 5–18,
music.
Bogatyrev's foreword to the score of his reconstruction. Text in Russian and English.

[4497]   SCHONBERG, H. 'Tchaikovsky's Seventh', *New York Times* (12 Nov 1961).
A new recording of the reconstructed symphony, by the Philadelphia Orchestra conducted by Eugene
Ormandy.

[4498]   SARGEANT, W. 'Musical events', *New Yorker*, 38 (10 Mar 1962): 127–129.
The first performance of the symphony in New York on 27 Feb 1962. See also *4499, 4500, 4501, 4502,
4504.*

[4499]   'Music to my ears', *Saturday Review*, 45 (17 Mar 1962): 43.

[4500]   GELLATT, R. 'Music makers', *High Fidelity*, 12 (Apr 1962): 59.

[4501]   GOODFRIEND, J. 'Philadelphia Orchestra', *Musical America*, 82 (Apr 1962): 54.

[4502]   SCHAUENSEE, M. de, 'Operatic merger', *Musical America*, 82 (Apr 1962): 24.

[4503]   SINGER, S. L. 'Philadelphia', *Music Magazine*, 164 (Apr 1962): 62–63.

[4504]   COHN, A. 'New York', *Music Magazine*, 164 (May 1962): 55.

[4505]   HOLDE, A. 'Eine VII. Symphonie von Tschaikowsky', *Neue Zeitschrift für Musik*, 123 (May 1962):
240.

[4506]   HOLDE, A. 'USA: Eine VII. Symphonie von Tschaikowsky', *Orchester*, 10 (Jul/Aug 1962): 245–246.

[*4507*]   LUTEN, C. J. 'That's right—the Tchaikovsky Seventh Symphony', *American Record Guide*, 28 (Aug 1962): 947.

[*4508*]   SCOTT-MADDOCKS, D. 'Tchaikovsky's Seventh', *Music and Musicians*, 11 (Sep 1962): 30, illus.

[*4509*]   ANGLES, R. 'Tchaikovsky's ghost', *Music and Musicians*, 11 (Nov 1962): 54.

[*4510*]   CHAPMAN, E. 'Tchaikovsky's "7th" Symphony', *Musical Events*, 17 (Nov 1962): 20.

[*4511*]   COOPER, M. 'Great Britain', *Musical America*, 82 (Nov 1962): 26.
            On the first performance of the symphony in London.

[*4512*]   MYERS, R. H. 'London music', *Canon*, 16 (Nov 1962): 78.

[*4513*]   'New Tchaikovsky symphony', *Strad*, 73 (Nov 1962): 267.

[*4514*]   K. P. 'Otvechaem chitateliam: Vozrozhdennaia simfoniia', *Muzykal´naia zhizn´* (1963), 22: 15.
            Letter to the editor.

[*4515*]   'Eine wiederhergestellte Sinfonie Tschaikowskis', *Musik und Gesellschaft*, 15 (Mar 1965): 198–199.

[*4516*]   THOMAS, R. 'Tschaikowskys Es-Dur Sinfonie und Idee einer Sinfonie "Das Leben"', *Neue Zeitschrift für Musik*, 128 (Apr 1967): 160–162, illus.

[*4517*]   BLOK, V. M. 'Vosstanovlenie simfonii Es-dur Chaikovskogo'. In: S. S. Bogatyrev, *Issledovaniia, stat´i, vospominaniia*. Red.-sost. G. A. Tiumeneva i Iu. N. Kholopov. Moskva: Sovetskii kompozitor, 1972: 214–237, illus.

[*4518*]   BLOK, V. M. 'Vozrozhdennaia simfoniia Chaikovskogo', *Muzykal´naia zhizn´* (20 Oct 1976): 8–9.

[*4519*]   'Tchaikovsky's lost symphony: Chandos releases a reconstruction of Tchaikovsky's last symphony—not the "Pathetique", but the "Seventh"', *Classic CD* (Feb 1993), 33: 8, illus.

            See also *111*.

SYMPHONY NO. 1
"Winter Daydreams", Op. 13 (1866, rev. 1874)

[*4520*]   A. D. 'Simfoniia P. I. Chaikovskogo', *Peterburgskaia gazeta* (19 Feb 1867).
            The first complete performance of the symphony on 3 Feb 1868 in Moscow.

[*4521*]   'Muzykal´noe obozrenie', *Nuvellist* (Nov 1886), 7: 3–4.
            The first performance of the revised version in St. Petersburg on 22 Oct 1886.

[*4522*]   PROKOF´EV, G. 'Moskovskie kontserty: 1-aia simfoniia', *Russkaia muzykal´naia gazeta* (11 Oct 1909), 41: 1001–1002.

[*4523*]   CARSE, A. 'First Symphonies: Studies in Orchestration. 4. Brahms—Tchaikovsky', *Musical Opinion*, 44 (Sep 1920): 957–958.
            Includes analysis of Chaikovskii's *Symphony No. 1*.

[*4524*]   MALKOV, N. P. *Pervaia simfoniia Chaikovskogo*. [Leningrad]: Leningradskaia filarmoniia, 1940. 32 p. (*Putevoditel´ po kontsertam*).

[*4525*]   ZHITOMIRSKII, D. V. 'Ranniaia redaktsiia "Zimnikh grëz"', *Sovetskaia muzyka* (1950), 5: 65–66, music.
            The discovery of the score of the original version of the symphony, in the library of the Moscow Conservatory.

[4526]   CHERNAIA, E. 'Besedy o muzyke: "Zimnie grëzy"—Pervaia simfoniia Chaikovskogo', *Muzykal´naia zhizn´* (1964), 1: 11–13, music, illus.

[4527]   'Verschiedenes', *Musik und Gesellschaft*, 18 (Oct 1968): 720.

[4528]   BOWEN, M. 'Interestingly off-beat', *Music & Musicians*, 18 (Dec 1969): 53.

[4529]   SIMMONS, D. 'London music', *Musical Opinion*, 93 (Dec 1969): 123.

[4530]   KANNY, M. '"Winter Dreams": The newest and best', *American Record Guide*, 38 (May 1971): 592–593.
          Survey of recordings.

[4531]   LENZON, V. 'Besedy o muzyke: "Zimnie grëzy"', *Muzykal´naia zhizn´* (1986), 3: 15–16.

[4532]   SHERIKHOVA, G. 'Vse simfonii Chaikovskogo: Zimnii put´', *Muzykal´naia zhizn´* (1990), 9: 10–11, illus.

[4533]   ABEL, J. M. 'Peter Tschaikowski und seine 1. Sinfonie g-Moll'. In: J. M. Abel, *Die Entstehung der sinfonischen Musik in Russland*. Berlin: E. Kuhn, 1996: 306–322. (*Studia Slavica musicologica*; 7).

[4534]   KLIMOVITSKII, A. I. 'Etiudy k probleme: Traditsiia, tvorchestvo, muzykal´nyi tekst'. In: *Muzyka: Analiz i estetika*. Sbornik statei k 90-letiiu L. A. Mazelia. Sankt Peterburg, 1997: 63–88.
          Concerning the first movements of Chaikovskii's *Symphony No. 1*, and symphonies by Beethoven, Schumann, Brahms and Mozart.

[4535]   LLOYD-JONES, D. 'Tchaikovsky: Symphony No. 1 in G minor, Op. 13 ("Winter reveries")'. In: *The musician's guide to symphonic music: Essays from the Eulenberg scores*. Corey Field, ed. Mainz; New York: Schott, 1997: 654–655.

          See also *5590, 5591, 5592, 5724, 5744*.

SYMPHONY NO. 2
"Little Russian", Op. 17 (1872, rev. 1879–80)

[4536]   'Novosti', *Muzykal´nyi listok* (1872/73), 9: 140–142.
          Report on Chaikovskii's work on the symphony.

[4537]   LAROSH, G. A. 'Novaia russkaia simfoniia', *Moskovskie vedomosti* (7 Feb 1873): 3.
          The first performance of the symphony on 26 Jan 1873 in Moscow. See also *4538, 4539*.
          — [repr.] In: G. A. Larosh, *Sobranie muzykal´no-kriticheskikh statei*, tom 2, chast´ 2 (1924): 9–14 [see *2311*].
          — [repr.] In: G. A. Larosh, *Izbrannye stat´i v piati vypuskakh*, vyp. 2 (1975): 34–38 [see *2376*].
          — [English tr.] 'A new Russian symphony'. In: S. Campbell, *Russians on Russian music* (1994): 255–260 [see *2408*].
          — [German tr.] 'Eine neue russische Sinfonie'. In: G. A. Larosh, *Peter Tschaikowsky: Aufsätze und Erinnerungen* (1993): 74–79 [see *2406*].

[4538]   LAROSH, G. A. 'Novaia simfoniia g. Chaikovskogo', *Golos* (7 Feb 1873): 1.
          — [repr.] In: G. A. Larosh, *Izbrannye stat´i v piati vypuskakh*, vyp. 2 (1975): 38 [see *2376*].

[4539]   MOSKVICH. 'Moskovskie zametki', *Grazhdanin* (19 Feb 1873).

[4540]   RAZMADZE, A. 'Korrespondentsiia: Moskva', *Muzykal´nyi listok* (1872/73), 26: 414–416, 27: 431–432.
          The third performance of the symphony in one concert season. See also *4541*.

[4541] 'Novosti', *Muzykal'nyi listok* (1872/73), 27: 439–441, 28: 458–460.

[4542] 'Telegraf: Moskva', *Nuvellist* (Dec 1873), 12: 113.
The Russian Musical Society's presentation to Chaikovskii.

[4543] [KIUI, Ts. A.] 'Novaia simfoniia g. Chaikovskogo', *Sankt Peterburgskie vedomosti* (1 Mar 1874): 2.
Publication of Chaikovskii's piano duet arrangement of the symphony. See also *4544, 4545, 4546.*

[4544] FAMINTSYN, A. 'Peterburgskaia khronika', *Muzykal'nyi listok* (2 Mar 1874): 278–280.

[4545] LAROSH, G. A. 'Sochineniia P. Chaikovskogo: Vtoraia simfoniia', *Muzykal'nyi listok* (2 Mar 1874): 273–277, music.
— [repr.] In: G. A. Larosh, *Izbrannye stat'i v piati vypuskakh*, vyp. 2 (1975): 52–55 [see *2376*].

[4546] [KIUI, Ts. A.] 'Vtoraia simfonia g. Chaikovskogo (chetyrekhruchnoe perelozhenie avtora)', *Sankt Peterburgskie vedomosti* (21 Jul 1874): 2.

[4547] 'Izvestiia iz Rossii', *Muzykal'nyi listok* (1876/77), 21: 331–332.
News of a successful performance of the symphony in Hannover, Germany.

[4548] 'Desiatoe sobranie Muzykal'nogo obshchestva', *Golos* (2 Feb 1881).
The first performance of the revised version on 31 Jan 1881 in St. Petersburg. See also *4549, 4550, 4551.*

[4549] 'Teatr i muzyka', *Birzhevye vedomosti* (4 Feb 1881).

[4550] GALLER, K. 'Desiatoe simfonicheskoe sobranie', *Novosti i birzhevaia gazeta* (4 Feb 1881).

[4551] [KIUI, Ts. A.], 'Poslednii kontsert Russkogo muzykal'nogo obschestva', *Golos* (11 Feb 1881): 1.

[4552] IVANOV, M. M. 'Muzykal'nyi nabrosok', *Novoe vremia* (23 Feb 1881).
Publication of the revised version.

[4553] IGNOTUS [FLEROV, S. V.] 'Vtoraia simfoniia P. I. Chaikovskogo', *Moskovskie vedomosti* (24 Nov 1881).
First performance of the revised version in Moscow on 21 Nov 1881. See also *4554.*

[4554] 'Teatr i muzyka', *Sovremennye izvestiia* (25 Nov 1881).

[4555] KASHKIN, N. D. 'Vtoraia sinfoniia P. I. Chaikovskogo', *Russkie vedomosti* (6 Jan 1896).
— [repr.] In: N. D. Kashkin, *Izbrannye stat'i o P. I. Chaikovskom* (1954): 193–194 [see *2349*]

[4556] 'Final iz 2-oi simfonii', *Russkaia muzykal'naia gazeta* (1907): 793–794.

[4557] MALKOV, N. P. *Vtoraia simfoniia P. I. Chaikovskogo*. [Leningrad]: Leningradskaia filarmoniia, 1939. 30 p, music. (*Putevoditel' po kontsertam*).

[4558] BARNETT, S. 'Tschaikowsky's Second Symphony: A neglected masterpiece', *Musician*, 45 (May 1940): 94.

[4559] 'Pervaia redaktsiia 2-i simfonii Chaikovskogo', *Sovetskoe iskusstvo* (17 Sep 1949): 2.
The reconstruction of the symphony's original version from orchestral parts preserved in the Moscow Conservatory.

[4560] IARUSTOVSKII, B. M. *Vtoraia simfoniia Chaikovskogo: Poiasnenie*. Moskva; Leningrad, 1950. 10 p, music. (*V pomoshch' slushateliu muzyki*).

[4561] MONTAGU-NATHAN, M. 'Tchaikovsky's Second Symphony', *Hallé* (Oct 1951): 3–6.

[4562]   BOOKSPAN, M. 'The basic repertoire: Tchaikovsky's "Little Russian"', *Stereo Review* (Jun 1969): 55.

[4563]   BOGATYREV, S. S. 'O pervonachal´noi redaktsii Vtoroi simfonii P. I. Chaikovskogo'. In: S. S. Bogatyrev: *Issledovaniia, stat'i, vospominaniia.* Red.-sost. G. A. Tiumeneva i Iu. N. Kholopov. Moskva: Sovetskii kompozitor, 1972: 144–158.

[4564]   BELYI, P. 'Besedy o muzyke: Vtoraia i Tret´ia simfonii Chaikovskogo', *Muzykal´naia zhizn´* (Nov 1975), 22: 15–16.

[4565]   SLIUSARENKO, T. 'Vse simfonii Chaikovskogo: Bez lozhnoi skromnosti skazhu…', *Muzykal´naia zhizn´* (1990), 12: 19–21.

[4566]   ABRAHAM, G. E. H. 'Tchaikovsky: Symphony No. 2 in C minor, Op. 17'. In: *The musician's guide to symphonic music: Essays from the Eulenberg scores.* Corey Field, ed. Mainz; New York: Schott, 1997: 656–659.

See also *1759.*

SYMPHONY NO. 3
Op. 29 (1875)

[4567]   GUBERT, N. A. 'Pervoe simfonicheskoe sobranie RMO', *Moskovskie vedomosti* (28 Nov 1875).
The first performances of the Symphony No. 3 and the Piano Concerto No. 1 on 7 Nov 1875 in Moscow.

[4568]   LAROSH, G. A. '5-i kontsert Russkogo muzykal´nogo obshchestva 24 ianvaria', *Golos* (28 Jan 1876): 1.
The first performance in St. Petersburg on 24 Jan 1876. Also includes a review of the String Quartet No. 2.
— [repr.] In: G. A. Larosh, *Sobranie muzykal´no-kriticheskikh statei,* tom 2, chast´ 2 (1924): 35–38 [see *2311*].
— [repr.] In: G. A. Larosh, *Izbrannye stat´i v piati vypuskakh,* vyp. 2 (1975): 79–82 [see *2376*].
— [German tr.] 'Zwei neue Werke von Tschaikowsky'. In: G. A. Larosh, *Peter Tschaikowsky: Aufsätze und Erinnerungen* (1993): 91–95 [see *2406*].

[4569]   'Tret´ia simfoniia', *Russkaia muzykal´naia gazeta* (22 Feb 1904), 8: 212–213.

[4570]   KRIUGER, A. N. *Tret´ia simfoniia Chaikovskogo.* Leningrad: Leningradskaia filarmoniia, 1938. 32 p, music. (*Putevoditel´ po kontsertam*).

[4571]   ALEXANDER, D. R. 'Tchaikovsky's Third Symphony: An analysis of its form, harmony and style'. Phoenix: Univ. of Arizona, 1989. 298 p.
Dissertation (M.M.).

[4572]   RIMSKII, L. 'Vse simfonii Chaikovskogo: Glubokoe i utonchennoe iskusstvo', *Muzykal´naia zhizn´* (1990), 14: 19.

[4573]   ABRAHAM, G. E. H. 'Tchaikovsky: Symphony No. 3 in D, Op. 29'. In: *The musician's guide to symphonic music: Essays from the Eulenberg scores.* Corey Field, ed. Mainz; New York: Schott, 1997: 660–661.

See also *4564, 5590, 5591, 5592, 5651, 5653.*

SYMPHONY NO. 4
Op. 36 (1877–78)

[4574]   'Raznye izvestiia', *Muzykal´nyi svet* (5 Feb 1878): 62.
Preview of the first performance of the symphony.

[*4575*] **F[LEROV], S. V.** *Moskovskie vedomosti* (17 Feb 1878).

The first performance of the symphony on 10 Feb 1878 in Moscow. See also *4576*.

[*4576*] **'Raznye izvestiia'**, *Muzykal´nyi svet* (19 Feb 1878): 84.

[*4577*] **'Muzykal´naia khronika'**, *Voskresnyi listok muzyki i ob´iavlenii* (Nov 1878), 2: 5.

The first performance in St. Petersburg on 10 Nov 1878. See also *4578* to *4582*.

[*4578*] **'Chetvertaia simfoniia g. Chaikovskogo'**, *Peterburgskaia gazeta* (29 Nov 1878).

[*4579*] **GALLER, K. P.** 'Chetvertaia simfoniia P. Chaikovskogo', *Birzhevye vedomosti* (3 Dec 1878).

[*4580*] **IVANOV, M. M.** 'Chetvertaia simfoniia Chaikovskogo', *Novoe vremia* (4 Dec 1878).

[*4581*] **LAROSH, G. A.** 'Muzykal´nye ocherki: 4, 5, 6-i kontserty Muzykal´nogo obshchestva', *Golos* (7 Dec 1878).

— [repr.] In: G. A. Larosh, *Sobranie muzykal´no-kriticheskikh statei*, tom 2, chast´ 2 (1924): 150–151 [see *2311*].

— [repr.] 'Chetvertaia simfoniia (f-moll), op. 36'. In: G. A. Larosh, *Izbrannye stat´i v piati vypuskakh*, vyp. 2 (1975): 101–102 [see *2376*].

— [German tr.] 'Tschaikowskys Vierte Sinfonie f-Moll, Op. 36'. In: G. A. Larosh, *Peter Tschaikowsky: Aufsätze und Erinnerungen* (1993): 107–109 [see *2406*].

[*4582*] **SOLOV´EV, N. F.** 'Chetvertaia simfoniia g. Chaikovskogo', *Sankt Peterburgskie vedomosti* (9 Dec 1878).

[*4583*] **GALLER, K. P.** 'Simfoniia No. 4 dlia orkestra, soch. 30-e P. I. Chaikovskogo, perelozhennoe dlia fortepiano v 4 ruki S. Taneevym', *Novosti* (11 Oct 1879).

[*4584*] **IVANOV, M. M.** 'Kontsertnoe i teatral´noe obozrenie', *Nuvellist* (Jan 1879).

[*4585*] **'Concert de M. Colonne'**, *La Gazette Musicale* (21 Jan/1 Feb 1880).

The first performance in Paris on 13/25 Jan 1880.

[*4586*] **TEIBLER, H.** *Peter Tschaikowsky: Vierte Symphonie, F-moll, für grosses orchester, Op. 36*. Erlautert von Hermann Teibler. Berlin; Leipzig: Hermann Seeman nachfolger [c.1895]. 24 p, music. (*Musikführer*; 255).

[*4587*] **CHESHIKHIN, V.** 'Chetvertaia i shestaia simfonii Chaikovskogo'. In: V. Cheshikhin, *Otgoloski opery i kontserta*. Sankt Peterburg, 1896: 176–181.

[*4588*] **BLEIKHMAN, Iu.** 'Muzykal´nye zametki', *Teatr i iskusstvo* (8 Nov 1898): 802.

[*4589*] **'Teatr i iskusstvo'**, *Novoe vremia* (20 Nov 1904): 4.

[*4590*] **'"Gamlet" i 4-aia simfoniia'**, *Russkaia muzykal´naia gazeta* (2 Nov 1908), 44: 977–978.

[*4591*] **GANGELIN, A.** *Chetvertaia simfoniia Chaikovskogo v stikhakh*. Sankt Peterburg: Chevalier, 1911. 128 p.

The author's impressions of the Fourth Symphony expressed in verse.

[*4592*] **'Tschaikowsky's Fourth Symphony'**, *Etude*, 44 (Jul 1926): 502.

[*4593*] **BLOM, E. W.** 'Symphony No. 4 in F minor (op. 36)'. In: E. W. Blom, *Tchaikovsky: Orchestral works* (1927): 23–42 [see *4366*].

[4594]   NEWMARCH, R. H. 'Tchaikovsky: Symphony No. 4 in F minor (op. 36)'. In: R. H. Newmarch, *The concert-goer's library of descriptive notes*. Part IV: *Symphonies, overtures, concertos*. London: Oxford Univ. Press; H. Milford, 1931: 52–56.

[4595]   DOWNES, O. 'Tchaikovsky: Symphony No. 4'. In: O. Downes, *Symphonic broadcasts*. New York: L. MacVeagh: Dial Press, 1932: 8–14.

[4596]   MUZALEVSKII, V. I. *Chetvertaia simfoniia Chaikovskogo*. [Leningrad]: Leningradskaia filarmoniia, 1935. 32 p, illus. (*Putevoditel´ po kontsertam*).

[4597]   GREW, S. 'Tschaikowsky's "Fate" symphony: The composer's exposition', *American Music Lover*, 6 (Aug 1940): 112–115.
         The composer's programme for the Fourth Symphony, as described in a letter to Nadezhda von Meck.

[4598]   IARUSTOVSKII, B. *Chetvertaia simfoniia Chaikovskogo: Poiasnenie*. Moskva; Leningrad: Gos. muz. izdat., 1950. 12 p, music. (*V pomoshch´ slushateliu muzyki*).

[4599]   KAINE, A. 'Three ways to conduct the Tchaikovsky Fourth', *American Record Guide*, 25 (May 1959): 635–639.
         A comparison of recordings.

[4600]   'Tchaikovsky's Symphony No. 4', *Stereo Review* (Sep 1959): 18.

[4601]   LANG, P. H. 'Tchaikovsky: Symphony No. 4 in F minor'. In: *The Symphony, 1800–1900*. Ed. by Paul Henry Lang. New York: W. J. Norton [1969]: 445–539, music. (*Norton Music Anthologies*).

[4602]   ASAF´EV, B. V. 'Dva annotatsii: [4-i simfoniia]'. In: B. V. Asaf´ev, *O muzyke Chaikovskogo: Izbrannoe* (1972): 290–294 [see *2373*].
         First published in the programme of a symphony concert in Petrograd on 20 Sep 1919.

[4603]   DUBRAVSKAIA, T. 'Besedy o muzyke: Chetvertaia simfoniia Chaikovskogo', *Muzykal´naia zhizn´* (1972), 22: 15–16, 24, illus.

[4604]   WAGNER, C. 'Experimentelle Untersuchungen über das Tempo', *Österreichischer Musikzeitschrift*, 29 (1974): 589–604.

[4605]   WILLIAMS, M. D. 'The greatest hits of U. S. symphony orchestras', *Music Journal*, 36 (Sep 1978): 8.

[4606]   DEMIN, V. 'Muzyka i slovo', *Pravda* (23 Mar 1980): 3.
         Partly concerning a television documentary ("Iskrennee dvizhenie dushi") about the symphony.

[4607]   SZESKUS, R. 'Nationale Züge im Schaffen russischer und sowjetischer Komponisten', *Musik in der Schule*, 33 (1982), 11: 358–359, illus.

[4608]   STEPHENS, H. 'Set works for 'O'-level Tchaikovsky: Symphony No. 4 in F minor, third movement (Scherzo: Pizzacato ostinato)', *Music Teacher*, 62 (Mar 1983): 22.

[4609]   ZAJACZKOWSKI, H. 'Tchaikovsky's Fourth Symphony', *Music Review*, 45 (Aug/Nov 1984), 3/4: 265–276, music.

[4610]   HOPKINS, A. 'Tchaikovsky: Symphony No. 4 in F minor'. In: A. Hopkins, *The concetgoers companion*, vol. 2 (1986): 314–318 [see *4442*].
         — [2nd ed. (vols. 1 & 2 combined)]. *The Dent concertgoers companion* (1993): 604–608 [see *4442*].

[4611]   AKHMATOVA, G. 'Chelovek i sud´ba', *Muzykal´naia zhizn´* (1990), 16: 19.

[4612]   ROBINSON, H. 'Tchaikovsky: Symphony #4', *International Society of Bassists* (spr. 1990): 56–53.

[4613] DIETEL, G. 'Tschaikowsky, der Progressive?: Bemerkungen zu seiner Vierten Sinfonie, für die Gebildeten unter seinen Verächtern', *Das Orchester*, 39 (1991), 3: 264–269, music, illus.

[4614] KHOKHLOV, Iu. 'Piataia Betkhovena i Chetvertaia Chaikovskogo: Opyt sravnitel´noi kharakteristiki', *Muzykal´naia akademiia* (1993), 4: 211–212.

[4615] TANEEV, S. I. 'Ich zähle offen alles auf, was mir an Ihrer Vierten Sinfonie nicht gefällt'. In: *Tschaikowsky aus der Nähe* (1994): 92–100 [see *379*].

       German tr. of a letter from Taneev to Chaikovskii (1878) regarding the symphony, and Chaikovskii's response.

[4616] SOKOLOFF, L. 'Let's talk picc: Tchaikovsky's 4th', *Flute Talk*, 14 (Oct 1994): 36–37, music.

       Concerning the piccolo part in the Scherzo. Includes fingering charts.

[4617] DAMMANN, S. 'Überlegungen zu einer problemgeschichtlichen Untersuchung von Čajkovskijs 4. Sinfonie'. In: *Internationales Čajkovskij Symposium, Tübingen 1993: Bericht* (1995): 87–102 [see *596*].

       — [English tr.] 'An examination of problem history in Tchaikovsky's Fourth Symphony' (tr. A. D. Humel). In: *Tchaikovsky and his world* (1998): 197–215 [see *601*].

[4618] FROLOV, S. V. 'O kontseptsii finala Chetvertoi simfonii Chaikovskogo'. In: *P. I. Chaikovskii: K 100-letiiu so dnia smerti* (1995): 64–72 [see *597*].

[4619] HOFFMANN, F. '"Die Qualen und die Seligkeit der Liebe": Tschaikowsky als homosexueller Komponist und seine 4. Sinfonie', *Musik im Unterricht*, 6 (1995), 32: 41–48.

[4620] LLOYD-JONES, D. 'Tchaikovsky: Symphony No. 4 in F minor, op. 36'. In: *The musician's guide to symphonic music: Essays from the Eulenberg scores*. Corey Field, ed. Mainz; New York: Schott, 1997: 662–665.

[4621] SJÖBERG, L. 'När demonerna är som häftigast: Tjajkovskij och hans fjärde symfoni', *Musik* [Stockholm] (1998), 2: 12–16.

SYMPHONY NO. 5
Op. 64 (1888)

[4622] 'Kontsert Filarmonicheskogo obshchestva', *Peterburgskii listok* (6 Nov 1888).

       The first performances in St. Petersburg of the *Symphony No. 5* and *Piano Concerto No. 2* on 5 Nov 1888, conducted by Chaikovskii. See also *4623* to *4627*.

[4623] 'Teatr i muzyka', *Novoe vremia* (7 Nov 1888).

[4624] L. 'Kontsert Filarmonicheskogo obshchestva', *Peterburgskaia gazeta* (7 Nov 1888).

[4625] SOLOV´EV, N. F. 'Kontsert Filarmonicheskogo obshchestva', *Novosti i birzhevaia gazeta* (7 Nov 1888).

       Reviews of the *Symphony No. 5* and *Piano Concerto No. 2*.

[4626] Ia. D. 'Kontsert g. Chaikovskogo', *Sankt Peterburgskie vedomosti* (8 Nov 1888).

[4627] IVANOV, M. M. 'Kontsert Filarmonicheskogo obshchestva', *Novoe vremia* (9 Nov 1888).

[4628] [KIUI, Ts. A.] 'Kontsert Filarmonicheskogo obshchestva iz proizvedenii g. Chaikovskogo', *Muzykal´noe obozrenie* (17 Nov 1888): 195–196.

       The second performance of the symphony, on 12 Nov 1888 in St. Petersburg. See also *4629*.

[4629] BERENDEI. 'Novye proizvedeniia russkikh avtorov: Sochineniia P. I. Chaikovskogo', *Baian* (Nov 1888): 315–316, 323–324.

       Concerning the *Symphony No. 5* and the overture-fantasia *Hamlet*.

[*4630*]   'Muzykal´noe obozrenie', *Nuvellist* (Dec 1888), 8: 3.

[*4631*]   'Obshchedostupnyi kontsert RMO iz proizvedenii Chaikovskogo', *Moskovskie vedomosti* (12 Dec 1888).
           The first performance in Moscow on 10 Dec 1888, conducted by Chaikovskii. See also *4632*.

[*4632*]   KASHKIN, N. D. 'Novaia simfoniia P. I. Chaikovskogo', *Russkaia mysl´* (Jan 1889).
           — [repr.] In: N. D. Kashkin, *Izbrannye stat´i o P. I. Chaikovskom* (1954): 199–202 [see *2349*].

[*4633*]   HANSLICK, E. 'Tschaikowskys Funfte Symphonie e-moll'. In: E. Hanslick, *Am Ende des Jahrhunderts (1895–1899). Musikalische Kritiken und Schilderungen von Eduard Hanslick*. Berlin, 1899: 194–196.
           — [repr.] 'Die Tschaikowsky-Rezensionen'. In: *Tschaikowsky aus der Nähe* (1994): 206–207 [see *379*].

[*4634*]   BEYER, C. *Peter Tschaikowsky: Symphonie in E-moll (nr. 5), Op. 64*. Berlin: Schlesinger [c.1900]. 16 p, music. (*Musikführer*; 146).

[*4635*]   L[AROSH, G. A.] 'Teatr i muzyka', *Rossiia* (15 Nov 1900): 3.
           Reviews of the *Symphony No. 5* and the overture-fantasia *Hamlet*.
           — [repr.] In: G. A. Larosh, *Izbrannye stat´i v piati vypuskakh*, vyp. 2 (1975): 325–326 [see *2376*].

[*4636*]   EVANS, E. 'Tchaikovsky analyses: 4. Symphony no. 5 in E minor, op. 64', *Musical Standard* [illus. series], 28 (12 Oct 1907): 229–232; (26 Oct 1907): 261–264, music.

[*4637*]   ENGEL´, Iu. D. 'Piataia simfoniia Chaikovskogo pod upravleniem Kusevitskogo', *Russkie vedomosti* (6 Nov 1909).

[*4638*]   WHITE, R. T. 'Tchaikovsky's Fifth Symphony', *Music Teacher*, 4 (Oct 1925): 614, music.

[*4639*]   NEWMARCH, R. H. 'Tchaikovsky: Symphony No. 5 in E minor and major, op. 64'. In: R. H. Newmarch, *The concert-goer's library of descriptive notes*. Part I: *Symphonies, overtures, concertos*. London: Oxford Univ. Press; H. Milford, 1928: 48–52.

[*4640*]   KOCHAKOV, B. M. *Piataia simfoniia Chaikovskogo*. [Leningrad]: Leningradskaia filarmoniia, 1937. 31 p, music.
           — 2nd ed., ispr. Leningrad: Leningradskii Gos. filarmoniia, 1946. 23 p

[*4641*]   TOVEY, D. F. 'Tchaikovsky: Symphony in E minor, no. 5, op. 64'. In: D. F. Tovey, *Essays in musical analysis*. Vol. 6. London: Oxford Univ. Press, Humphrey Milford, 1939: 58–65.
           — [repr.] London: Oxford Univ. Press, Humphrey Milford, 1939: 58–65
           — [new ed.] Vol. 1: *Symphonies and other orchestral works*. London; New York: Oxford Univ. Press, 1981: 512–519.

[*4642*]   LEONIDOV, M. 'Moskovskie gastroli Mravinskogo', *Sovetskaia muzyka* (1949), 6: 82–84.
           Largely concerning the conductor Evgenii Mravinskii's interpretation of Chaikovskii's Fifth Symphony.

[*4643*]   IARUSTOVSKII, B. *Piataia simfoniia Chaikovskogo: Poiasnenie*. Moskva; Leningrad: Gos. muz. izdat., 1950. 10 p, music. (*V pomoshch´ slushateliu muzyki*).

[*4644*]   BOOKSPAN, M. 'Tchaikovsky's Fifth Symphony', *Stereo Review*, 5 (Dec 1960): 16, illus.
           Survey of recordings.

[*4645*]   ADORNO, T. W. 'Musikalische Warenanalysen: Tschaikowsky e-moll Symphonie, lamgsamer Satz'. In: T. W. Adorno, *Quasi una fantasia: Musikalische Schriften II*. Frankfurt am Main, 1963: 64–66.

[*4646*]   DOLZHANSKII, A. 'Piatia simfoniia', *Muzykal´naia zhizn´* (1965), 8: 3–5, music.

[4647] ASAF´EV, B. V. 'Dve annotatsii: [5-i simfoniia]'. In: B. V. Asaf´ev, *O muzyke Chaikovskogo: Izbrannoe* (1972): 294–297 [see *2373*].

First published in the programme of a Philharmonic Society concert in Leningrad on 11 Dec 1926.

[4648] FITZSIMMONS, W. E. 'A historical and interpretive study of four works for orchestra'. Kansas City: Univ. of Missouri, 1972. 196 p.

Dissertation.

[4649] BOOKSPAN, M. 'The basic repertoire', *Stereo Review*, 36 (Feb 1976): 50.

Survey of recordings.

[4650] WILLIAMS, M. D. 'The greatest hits of U. S. symphony orchestras', *Music Journal*, 36 (Sep 1978): 6.

[4651] HOPKINS, A. 'Tchaikovsky: Symphony No. 5 in E minor'. In: A. Hopkins, *The concetgoers companion*, vol. 2 (1986): 319–323 [see *4442*].

— [2nd ed. (vols. 1 & 2 combined)]. *The Dent concertgoers companion* (1993): 609–613 [see *4442*].

[4652] SLIUSARENKO, T. 'Mezhdu zhizn´iu i smert´iu', *Muzykal´naia zhizn´* (1990), 18:19—20.

[4653] SEIBERT, D. C. 'The Tchaikovsky Fifth: A symphony without a programme', *Music Review*, 51 (Feb 1990), 1: 36–45, music.

[4654] KRAUS, J. C. 'Tonal plan and narrative plot in Tchaikovsky's Symphony No. 5 in E minor', *Music Theory Spectrum*, 13 (spr. 1991), 1: 21–47, music.

[4655] DANIELSON, D. 'Die Rettung der Fünften Sinfonie Tschaikowskys durch Arthur Nikisch'. In: *Tschaikowsky aus der Nähe* (1994): 136 [see *379*].

[4656] SCHICK, H. 'Dvořák's Eighth Symphony: A response to Tchaikovsky?'. In: *Rethinking Dvořák: Views from five countries*. Ed. David Beveridge. Oxford: Oxford Univ. Press, 1996: 155–168.

— [German tr.] 'Dvořák's 8. Sinfonie: Eine Antwort auf Čajkovskijs Fünfte?'. In: *Čajkovskijs Homosexualität und sein Tod: Legenden und Wirklichkeit* (1998): 539–555 [see *600*].

[4657] LLOYD-JONES, D. 'Tchaikovsky: Symphony No. 5 in E minor, op. 64'. In: *The musician's guide to symphonic music: Essays from the Eulenberg scores*. Corey Field, ed. Mainz; New York: Schott, 1997: 666–668.

[4658] KLIMOVITSKII, A. I. '"Leitmotiv sud´by" Vagnera i Piatoi simfonii Chaikovskogo i nekotorye problemy intertekstual´nosti', *Muzykal´naia akademiia*, 2 (1998), 3/4: 280–285.

See also *1557, 4493, 5234, 5490, 5692, 5693*.

SYMPHONY NO. 6
"Pathetique", Op. 74 (1893)

[4659] P. V. 'Pervoe simfonicheskoe sobranie RMO', *Syn Otechestva* (17 Oct 1893).

The first performance of the symphony on 16 Oct 1893 in St. Petersburg, conducted by Chaikovskii. See also *4660* to *4666*.

[4660] E. K. 'Pervoe simfonicheskoe sobranie', *Sankt Peterburgskie vedomosti* (18 Oct 1893).

[4661] 'Pervoe simfonicheskoe sobranie', *Birzhevye vedomosti* (18 Oct 1893).

[4662] 'Teatr i muzyka', *Novoe vremia* (18 Oct 1893).

[*4663*]   'Pervoe simfonicheskoe sobranie', *Novosti i birzhevaia gazeta* (18 Oct 1893).

[*4664*]   'Pervoe simfonicheskoe sobranie', *Peterburgskaia gazeta* (18 Oct 1893).

[*4665*]   RAPGOF, I. P. 'Pervoe simfonicheskoe sobranie', *Grazhdanin* (19 Oct 1893).

[*4666*]   LAROSH, G. A. 'Pervyi simfonicheskii kontsert muzykal´nogo obshchestva 16 oktiabria',
            Teatral´naia gazeta (22 Oct 1893).
            — [repr.] In: G. A. Larosh, *Izbrannye stat´i v piati vypuskakh*, vyp. 2 (1975): 159–161 [see *2376*].
            — [German tr.] 'Tschaikowskys Sechste Sinfonie h-Moll, Op. 74'. In: G. A. Larosh, *Peter Tschaikowsky:
            Aufsätze und Erinnerungen* (1993): 161–163 [see *2406*].

[*4667*]   'Teatr i muzyka', *Novoe vremia* (7 Nov 1893): 4.
            The performance of the symphony at a Chaikovskii memorial concert in St. Petersburg on 6 Nov 1893. See
            also *4668*.

[*4668*]   'Teatr i muzyka', *Novoe vremia* (8 Nov 1893): 3.

[*4669*]   BASKIN, V. 'Muzykal´noe obozrenie', *Nuvellist* (Dec 1893), 8: 1–3.
            The first performance in Moscow on 4 Dec 1893. See also *4670*.

[*4670*]   KASHKIN, N. D. [Shestaia simfoniia Chaikovskogo], *Russkie vedomosti* (6 Dec 1893).
            — [repr.] In: N. D. Kashkin, *Izbrannye stat´i o P. I. Chaikovskom* (1954): 203–204 [see *2349*].

[*4671*]   'Imperatorskoe Russkoe Muzykal´noe Obshchestvo: Simfonicheskie sobraniia', *Russkaia
            muzykal´naia gazeta* (Jan 1894), 1: 17–18.

[*4672*]   'Tschaikowsky's new symphony', *The Critic*, 24 [new series 21] (12/24 Mar 1894): 208.
            The first performance in New York on 4/16 Mar 1894. See also *New York Post* (7/19 Mar 1894), *New York
            Times* (7/19 Mar 1894).

[*4673*]   HANSLICK, E. 'Tschaikowskys Symphonie pathetique'. In: E. Hanslick, *Fünf Jahre Musik (1891–
            95). Kritiken von Eduard Hanslick*. Berlin, 1896: 300–303.
            — [repr.] 'Die Tschaikowsky-Rezensionen'. In: *Tschaikowsky aus der Nähe* (1994): 199–206 [see *379*].

[*4674*]   RIEMANN, H. *Peter Iljitsch Tschaikowsky: Sechste symphonie (H-moll, Pathétique), Op. 74*. Erlautert
            von Hugo Riemann. Berlin: Schlesinger [c.1895]. 16 p, music. (*Musikführer*; 130).
            — [2. Aufl.] *P. Tschaikoffsky: VI. Symphonie (h-moll) - (Symphonie pathétique, Op. 74)*. Erläutert von Hugo
            Riemann. Leipzig, H. Seemann; Berlin: Schlesinger [1898]. (*Der Musikführer*; 130). 17 p, music.
            — [rev. repr.] 'Einleitung zu einer Einführung in Tschaikowskys VI. Symphonie h-Moll'. In: *Tschaikowsky aus
            der Nähe* (1994): 196–213 [see *379*].
            — [Russian tr.] *P. I. Chaikovskii: VI Simfoniia, op. 74*. Tematicheskoe raz´iasnenie soderzhaniia. Sost. G.
            Riman. Perevod B. Iu[rgenson]. Moskva: P. Iurgenson, 1898. 16 p, music.

[*4675*]   WEINGARTNER, F. 'Tschaikowskys "Symphonie Pathétique"', *Allgemeine Musik-Zeitung* (1896), 1.

[*4676*]   RUNCIMAN, J. F. 'Tschaikowsky and his "Pathetic" symphony', *Dome* (1897), 2: 108–118.
            — [repr.] In: J. F. Runciman, *Old scores and new readings: discussions on music & certain musicians*. London
            [Unicorn Press], 1899: 270–278.
            — 2nd ed., rev. and enlarged. London [Unicorn Press], 1901: 270–278.
            — [repr.] 'Tchaikovsky and his "Pathetic" symphony', *Music* (1950): 122–130.

[*4677*]   MALHERBE, C. T. *Notice sur la symphonie pathétique (op. 74) de P. Tschaïkowsky*. Paris: A. Noël
            [1900]. 42 p, illus.

[*4678*]   [EVANS, E.] 'The "Pathetic" Symphony: A new reading', *Musical Standard* [illus. series], 18 (1 Nov
            1902): 271.

[*4679*]   HOLT, R. 'A symphony for everyone: Tschaikowsky's "Pathetic"', *Musician*, 9 (1904), 1: 14–16.

[*4680*]   'Russkaia muzyka za granitsei', *Russkaia muzykal´naia gazeta* (18 Apr 1904), 16: 447.

            Report on a lecture 'P. Chaikovskii and his *Pathétique* symphony' in Dortmund, Germany.

[*4681*]   'Conception and working out of the "Pathetic" symphony', *Current Literature*, 37 (Oct 1904): 336–338.

[*4682*]   EVANS, E. 'Tchaikovsky analyses: 3. Symphony no. 6 in B minor, op. 74 (The "Pathetic")',
            Musical Standard [illus. series] (17 Aug 1907), 28: 105–107; (31 Aug 1907), 29: 137–140; (14 Sep
            1907): 29: 165–167; (28 Sep 1907), 29: 197–200.

[*4683*]   MASON, D. G. 'Short studies of great masterpieces. VIII. Symphony No. VI, "Pathétique"' by
            P. Tschaikowsky, op. 76 [sic]. First performance, October 28, 1893', *New Music Review*, 16 (1917):
            574–578.

            — [repr.] '"Symphonie pathétique": Tschaikowsky'. In: D. G. Mason, *The appreciation of music*. Vol. 3: *Short
            studies of great masterpieces*. New York: H. W. Gray, 1918: 101–106.

[*4684*]   DONALD, P. 'Great orchestral works by modern composers: 22. Symphony No. 6, in B minor,
            "Pathetic", op. 74. by Peter Tschaikowsky', *Metronome*, 34 (1918), 7: 45; 8: 43, 60.

[*4685*]   BOURHUÈS, L & DENÉRÉAZ, A. 'Tschaikovsky'. In: *La musique et la vie intérieure*. Paris: Alcan;
            Lausanne: Bridel [1921]: 524–526.

            On the psychology of the Sixth Symphony.

[*4686*]   GILMAN, L. 'Two masterworks reconsidered: Strauss's "Ein heldenleben" and Tchaikovsky's
            "Pathétique" symphony', *North American Review*, 213 (Feb 1921): 266–272.

[*4687*]   BIART, V. 'Great orchestral masterpieces: "Pathétique" symphony', *Etude*, 43 (Dec 1925): 851–852, illus.

[*4688*]   [STASOV, V. V.] 'V. V. Stasov o VI simfonii Chaikovskogo'. In: V. Karenin, 'Stasov i Chaikovskii'
            (1927): 440–441 [see *2031*].

[*4689*]   STEIN, R. 'Tschaikowsky's Abschied vom Leben', *Die Musik*, 19 (1926), 3: 153–161.

[*4690*]   'Tschaikowsky at rehearsals', *Etude*, 46 (Aug 1928): 586.

[*4691*]   ANDERSON, M. 'Adagio from Tschaikowsky's "Pathetic" symphony as a piano study piece',
            Musician, 37 (Mar 1932): 13–15, illus.

[*4692*]   BUDIAKOVSKII, A. E. *Shestaia simfoniia Chaikovskogo*. [Leningrad]: Leningradskaia filarmoniia,
            1935. 30 p, music. (*Putevoditel´ po kontsertam*).

            — [2-e izd.] Leningrad: [Leningradskaia Gos. filarmoniia], 1940. 39 p, music, illus. (*Programmy kontsertov*).

[*4693*]   SHLIFSHTEIN, S. 'Shestaia simfoniia Chaikovskogo', *Muzykal´naia samodeiatel´nost´* (Jul 1935),
            7: 16–25, music.

            See also *4694*.

[*4694*]   SHLIFSHTEIN, S. 'Pis´mo v redaktsiiu', *Muzykal´naia samodeitel´nost´* (Aug 1935), 8: 43.

            The author's corrections to the above article.

[*4695*]   TOVEY, D. F. 'Tchaikovsky: Pathetic Symphony, No. 6, op. 74'. In: D. F. Tovey, *Essays in musical
            analysis*. Vol. 2. London: Oxford Univ. Press, Humphrey Milford, 1935: 84–89, music.

            — [repr.] London: Oxford Univ. Press, 1972: 84–89.

            — [new ed.] Vol. 1: *Symphonies and other orchestral works*. London; New York: Oxford Univ. Press, 1981: 519–
            524, music. ISBN: 0-19-315147-2 (pbk); 0-19-315146-4 (hbk).

[*4696*]   B[UDIAKOVSKII], A. 'Programma VI simfonii', *Muzyka* (6 Jul 1937): 5.

Chaikovskii's programme for the symphony.

[*4697*]   ABRAHAM, G. E. H. 'The Programme of the "Pathétique" Symphony'. In: G. E. H. Abraham, *On Russian music: Critical and historical studies of Glinka's operas, Balakirev's works, etc., with chapters dealing with compositions by Borodin, Rimsky-Korsakov, Tchaikovsky, Mussorgsky, Glazunov, and various other aspects of Russian music.* London: W. Reeves [1939]: 143–146.

— [repr.] New York: Johnson Reprint Corp. [1970]: 143–146.

— [repr.] Freeport, N. Y.: Books for Libraries Press, 1980: 143–146. (*Essay Index Reprint Series*). ISBN 0-8369-1900-9.

[*4698*]   STRAKHOVA, E. *Razgadka (VI) shestoi simfonii Chaikovskogo*. Moskva [1939]. 24 p.

[*4699*]   AL´SHVANG, A. A. 'Posledniaia simfoniia Chaikovskogo', *Sovetskaia muzyka* (1940), 5/6: 48–69, music, illus. [see *585*]

[*4700*]   'Vyderzhka iz pis´ma M. I. Chaikovskogo k P. G. Bebutovu ot 18 oktiiabria 1893 g.'. In: Sh. S. Ashlanshvili, *P. I. Chaikovskii v Gruzii* (1940): 20–21 [see *1770*].

Concerning the programme of the *Symphony No. 6* as set out in four verses by Modest Chaikovskii (the dating of the letter to Oct 1893 is doubtful).

[*4701*]   KODZHAK, I. B. *Pateticheskaia simfoniia: K 50-letiiu 6-i simfonii P. I. Chaikovskogo*. [Kharbin]: M. V. Zaitesva [1943]. 46 p.

[*4702*]   RYZHKIN, I. Ia. 'Shestaia simfoniia Chaikovskogo', *Sovetskaia muzyka* (1946), 1: 70–83; 2/3: 96–107.

A detailled musical analysis of the symphony, and its programmatic content.

[*4703*]   DUKAS, P. 'La "Symphonie pathétique" de Tchaikowsky'. In: *Les écrits de Paul Dukas sur la musique.* Paris: Société d'editions françaises et internationales, 1948: 407–409. (*Musique et musiciens*).

[*4704*]   IARUSTOVSKII, B. *Shestaia simfoniia Chaikovskogo: Poiasnenie*. Moskva; Leningrad: Gos. muz. izdat., 1950. 10 p, music. (*V pomoshch´ slushateliu muzyki*).

[*4705*]   'Lethal "Pathétique"', *Musical America*, 70 (Feb 1950): 133.

[*4706*]   'Waxing eloquent: Tchaikovsky: Symphony No. 6 in B minor, op. 74', *Canon*, 4 (Sep 1950), 2: 65.

Comparison of recordings.

[*4707*]   STOMENGER, K. '"Symfonia patetyczna" Czajkowskiego', *Poradnik muzyczny*, 5 (1951), 9: 4–5.

[*4708*]   SUCKLING, N. 'The tragic symphony', *Monthly Musical Record*, 81 (Jul/Aug 1951): 143–149.

[*4709*]   MEYER, A. *Den store koncert*. Aalborg: H. Müller, 1953. 21 p, illus.

[*4710*]   ZAGIBA, F. 'Die "Symphonie pathétique": Eine Lebensschilderung des Meisters (zum 60. Todestag P. I. Tschaikowskijs)', *Die Musikerziehung*, 7 (Jun 1954), 4: 208–210.

[*4711*]   OTTAWAY, H. 'Some reflections on Tchaikovsky's Sixth Symphony', *Musical Opinion*, 80 (Oct 1956): 15–17.

[*4712*]   HOLLANDER, H. 'Das Finale-Problem in Tschaikowskys Sechster Symphonie', *Neue Zeitschrift für Musik*, 118 (Jan 1957): 13–15.

[*4713*]   MACHLIS, J. 'Tchaikovsky: "Pathetique" symphony'. In: J. Machlis, *The enjoyment of music: An introduction to perceptive listening*. New York: W. W. Norton, 1957: 142–144.

— 2nd ed. New York: W. W. Norton, 1963: 142–144.

— 3rd ed. New York: W. W. Norton, 1970: 156–159.

[*4714*] MAZEL´, L. 'K voprosu o dramaturgii Shestoi simfonii', *Sovetskaia muzyka* (1958), 9: 72–75 [see *2355*].

[*4715*] MNATSAKANOVA, E. 'Shestaia simfoniia Chaikovskogo', *Muzykal´naia zhizn´* (1958), 18: 12–13.
Includes facs. from autograph score.

[*4716*] PIGGOTT, J. 'Tchaikovsky's last great symphony', *Music and Musicians*, 7 (Nov 1958): 15, illus.

[*4717*] GUIDE, R. de. 'La symphonie no. 6 de Tchaikovsky devient...la "Pathétique"', *Musica* (Oct 1959), 67: 5–7.

[*4718*] [BOOKSPAN, M.] 'Martin Bookspan rates the basic repertoire', *Stereo Review*, 10 (May 1960): 18–19.
Survey of recordings.

[*4719*] POZHIDAEV, I. 'Puteshestvie v stranu Simfoniiu', *Iunost´* (1962), 3: 56–60.
Includes supplementary article by D. Kabalevskii, 'Primeta vremeni'.

[*4720*] WIENKE, G. 'Tschaikowsky Symphonie Nr. 6: Eine vergleichende Discographie', *Phonograph*, 9 (1962), 2: 32–35.

[*4721*] IARUSTOVSKII, B. 'Velikaia simfoniia', *Komsomol´skaia pravda* (29 Apr 1962): 4.

[*4722*] DREIDEN, C. D. "Pateticheskaia simfoniia", *Sovetskaia muzyka* (1965), 4: 5–15.

[*4723*] RINGGER, R. U. 'Peter Tschaikowskijs "Pathetique" und das Spätburgerliche', *Schweizer Monatshefte*, 45 (1965/66): 77–80.

[*4724*] BERNSTEIN, L. 'Tchaikovsky: Symphony No 6 in B minor, Opus 74, "Pathetique"'. In: L. Bernstein, *The infinite variety of music*. New York, Simon & Schuster, 1966: 171–193.

[*4725*] GOLLAND, T. 'Faksimile "Pateticheskoi": Izdatel´stvo "Muzyka" o sebe', *Sovetskaia kul´tura* (11 Jan 1966): 2.
Plans for a facsimile edition of Chaikovskii's manuscript score for the symphony [see *124*].

[*4726*] LEVASHEV, Iu. 'Lebedinaia pesn´: K 75-letiiu so dnia ispolneniia Shestoi simfonii P. I. Chaikovskogo', *Muzykal´nye kadry* (13 Dec 1968): 4.

[*4727*] BLOK, V. M. 'Na puti k "Pateticheskoi"', *Sovetskaia muzyka* (1970), 9: 78–80, music.

[*4728*] MIKHAILOV, A. 'My smotrim Shestuiu', *Sovetskaia kul´tura* (1 Apr 1972): 3.
Review of a television documentary film 'P. I. Chaikovskii: Shestaia simfoniia', with the conductor Iurii Temirkanov.

[*4729*] PRIBEGINA, G. A. 'O rabote P. I. Chaikovskogo nad Shestoi simfoniei: Po materialam rukopisei'. In: *Iz istorii russkoi i sovetskoi muzyki*. Sost. A. Kandinskii. Vyp. 2. Moskva: Muzyka, 1976: 115–145. (*Moskovskaia Gos. konservatoriia im. P. I. Chaikovskogo. Kafedra istorii muzyki narodov SSSR*).
An analysis of the text of the symphony from the manuscript full score and sketches.

[*4730*] HOLDRIDGE, L. B. *Symphony in B minor, "Pathétique": A confession for narrator and orchestra in four movements*. The passion of Peter Ilitch Tchaikovsky, according to Larry Holdridge. Illus. by Ferebe Street. Owings Mills, Md: Stemmer House Publishers, 1978. 57 p, illus. ISBN: 0-9161-4426-7 (hbk), 0-9161-44275 (pbk). (*A Barbara Holdridge Book*).
Mainly poems.

[*4731*] MAZEL´, L. A. 'O pervoi chasti Shestoi simfonii Chaikovskogo: K voprosu o vliianii opery na simfoniiu'. In: L. A. Mazel´, *Voprosy analiza muzyki*. Moskva: Sovetskii kompozitor, 1978: 311–319.
— 2-e izd., dop. Moskva, 1991: 302–308.

[*4732*]   SHAW, G. B. 'Tchaikovsky: Sixth Symphony, 7 March 1894'. In: G. B. Shaw, *The great composers: Reviews and bombardments*. Ed. with an introduction by Louis Crompton. Berkeley: Univ. of California Press [1978]: 153–154.

[*4733*]   PATLAENKO, Z. N. 'Ob odnoi osobennosti pervoi chasti Shestoi simfonii P. I. Chaikovskogo'. In: *Nauchno-metodologicheskaia konferentsiia, posviashchennaia 60-letiiu Sovetskoi Karelii (15–16 sent. 1980)*. Tezisy dokladov. Petrazavodsk: PF LOLGK im N. A. Rimskogo-Korsakova SK KaSSR, 1980: 34–36.

[*4734*]   DUBRAVSKAIA, T. 'Besedy o muzyke: Shestaia simfoniia Chaikovskogo', *Muzykal´naia zhizn´* (Oct 1980), 20: 15–16, music.

[*4735*]   KEENER, A. 'Tchaikovsky's "Pathetique"', *Strad*, 91 (1981): 697.

[*4736*]   HOPKINS, A. 'Tchaikovsky: Symphony No. 6 in B minor'. In: A. Hopkins, *The concetgoers companion*, vol. 2 (1986): 323–328 [see *4442*].
          — [2nd ed. (vols. 1 & 2 combined)]. *The Dent concertgoers companion* (1993): 613–618 [see *4442*].

[*4737*]   KERNER, L. 'Music: Muscle and blood', *Village Voice*, 31 (14 Oct 1986): 88.

[*4738*]   KLIMOVITSKII, A. I. 'Zametki o Shestoi simfonii: K probleme Chaikovskogo na poroge XX veka'. In: *Problemy muzykal´nogo romantizma*. Sbornik nauchnykh trudov. Leningrad, 1987: 108–127, music.

[*4739*]   ESKINA, M. 'Vse simfonii Chaikovskogo: Geometriia sud´by', *Muzykal´naia zhizn´* (1990), 20: 19–21.

[*4740*]   FEDIANINA, L. D. 'Poetika "tikhogo sveta" v kontseptsii Shestoi simfonii Chaikovskogo'. In: *Otechestvennaia kul´tura XX veka i dukhovnaia muzyka*. Rostov-na-Donu, 1990: 29–31.

[*4741*]   BRODIN, G. 'Tjajkovskij Symfoni nr 6, "Pathéthique"', *Hör här!* (1990/91), 4: 19 .

[*4742*]   JANSSON, A. 'Pjotr Tjajkovskij: Sista verket', *Konsertnytt*, 26 (1990/91), 8: 13–14.

[*4743*]   BUSKE, P. 'Aufwühlende Seelenbeichte', *Orchester*, 39 (1991), 6: 720.

[*4744*]   KHRUSHCHEV, V. "Pateticheskaia simfoniia", *Muzykal´naia zhizn´*, (1993) 7/8: 19, illus.

[*4745*]   ZAJACZKOWSKI, H. 'Not to be born were best', *Musical Times*, 134 (Oct 1993): 561–566.

[*4746*]   SWAIN, J. 'Tchaikovsky's Sixth Symphony, "Pathetique"', *Gramophone*, 71 (Nov 1993): 28–32.

[*4747*]   MURPHY, E. W. 'The dominant complex/climax in selected works of the late nineteenth century', *Music Review*, 55 (1994), 2: 104–118, music, illus.
          Includes analysis of Chaikovskii's *Symphony No. 6*.

[*4748*]   POBEREZHNA, H. 'O programmie VI Symfonii Piotra Czajkowskiego' / 'On the program of Tchaikovsky's Sixth Symphony', *Muzyka*, 39 (1994), 1: 19–32, music.
          Text in Polish, with a summary in English.

[*4749*]   KOHLHASE, T. 'Editionsprobleme der Neuen Čajkovskij-Gesamtausgabe am Beispiel der 6. Sinfonie'. In: *Internationales Čajkovskij Symposium, Tübingen 1993: Bericht* (1995): 177–186 [see *596*].
          Concerning the New Complete Edition of Chaikovskii's works [see *120*].

[*4750*]   'Tchaikovsky: Symphony No. 6 in B minor, op. 74'. In: A. J. Rudel, *Classical music top 40*. New York: Simon & Schuster, 1995: 340–345.

[*4751*]   BOWEN, J. A. 'Tempo, duration and flexibility: Techniques in the analysis of performance', *Journal of Musicological Research*, 16 (Dec 1996), 2: 111–156, music.

[4752] **LLOYD-JONES, D. 'Tchaikovsky: Symphony No. 6 in B minor, op. 74, "Pathétique"'**. In: *The musician's guide to symphonic music: Essays from the Eulenberg scores*. Corey Field, ed. Mainz; New York: Schott, 1997: 669–671.

[4753] **OTT, L. 'Tchaikovsky: Symphony No. 6'**. In: L. Ott, *Orchestration and orchestral style of major symphonic works: Analytical perspectives*. Lewiston, N. Y.: E. Mellen Press, 1997: 97–117. (*Studies in the history and interpretation of music*; 55).

[4754] **PFANN, W. '"Hat er es denn beschlossen...": Anmerkungen zu einem neuen Verständnis von Cajkovskijs "Symphonie Pathetique"'**, *Die Musikforschung*, 51 (Apr/Jun 1998), 2: 191–209.

[4755] **MARCOTTE, G. 'Ecoute à la "Symphonie pathétique" de Tchaikovski'**, *Liberté*, 40 (Jun 1998), 3: 95–102.

[4756] **JACKSON, T. L. *Tchaikovsky: Symphony No. 6 ("Pathetique")***. Cambridge: Cambridge Univ. Press, 1999, 154 p, music. (*Cambridge Music Handbooks*). ISBN: 0–52164–111–X (hbk); 0–52164–676–6 (pbk.).
Review: R. Drakeford, *Musical Times* (win. 1999): 62–63.

See also *119, 123, 124, 506, 530, 1264, 3602, 4587, 5482, 5484, 5581, 5587, 5588, 5589, 5649, 5666, 5667, 5678, 5679.*

5.3.3. Suites

[4757] **GLEBOV, I. [ASAF´EV, B. V.] 'Suiity'**. In: I. Glebov, *Instrumental´noe tvorchestvo Chaikovskogo* (1922): 43–57 [see *2310*].

[4758] **KHOKHLOV, Iu. N. *Orkestrovye siuity Chaikovskogo***. Moskva: Gos. Muz. Izd, 1961. 92 p, music. (*Biblioteka slushatelia kontsertov*).

[4759] **LUTEN, C. J. 'Four Tchaikovsky suites'**, *American Record Guide*, 33 (Mar 1967): 555, illus.

[4760] **BELYI, P. 'Besedy o muzyke: Siuity Chaikovskogo'**, *Muzykal´naia zhizn´* (Jul 1978), 14: 15–16; (Aug 1978), 15: 17–19.
Analysis of the four orchestral suites and the *Serenade for String Orchestra*.

[4761] **'Classical reviews'**, *High Fidelity*, 39 (Jun 1989): 70–71.

See *1285*.

THE NUTCRACKER
Suite from the ballet, Op. 71a (1892)

[4762] **BASKIN, V. 'Teatral´noe ekho: Deviatoe simfonicheskoe sobranie'**, *Peterburgskaia gazeta* (9 Mar 1892).
The first performance of the suite on 7 Mar 1892 in St. Petersburg, conducted by Chaikovskii. See also *4763* to *4768*.

[4763] **'Deviatoe simfonicheskoe sobranie'**, *Peterburgskii listok* (9 Mar 1892).

[4764] **P. G. 'Simfonicheskoe sobranie'**, *Birzhevye vedomosti* (9 Mar 1892).

[4765] **SOLOV´EV, N. F. 'Deviatoe simfonicheskoe sobranie'**, *Novosti i birzhevaia gazeta* (9 Mar 1892).

[4766] **'Teatr i muzyka'**, *Novoe vremia* (9 Mar 1892): 3.

[4767]   VEIMARN, P. 'Deviatoe simfonicheskoe sobranie Russkogo muzykal´nogo obshchestva', *Syn Otechestva* (9 Mar 1892).

[4768]   D. N. 'Deviatoe simfonicheskoe sobranie', *Grazhdanin* (12 Mar 1892).

[4769]   'Pervyi simfonicheskii kontsert V. I. Glavacha', *Moskovskie vedomosti* (6 Jul 1892).
          The first performance in Moscow, on 4 Jul 1892.

[4770]   RIEMENSCHNEIDER, G. *Peter Tschaikowsky: "Der Nussknacker", suite für grosses orchester, Op. 71a.* Erlautert von Georg Riemenschneider. Leipzig: H. Seemann [c. 1895]. 23 p, music. (*Musikführer*; 232).

[4771]   DONALD, P. 'Great orchestral works by modern composers: 1. "Nutcracker" ("Casse-Noisette"), suite by by Peter I. Tschaikowsky', *Metronome*, 32 (1916), 4: 22, 45–47.

[4772]   BLOM, E. W. 'Suite from the ballet "Casse-Noisette" (op. 71a)'. In: E. W. Blom, *Tchaikovsky: Orchestral Works* (1927): 42–51 [see *4366*].

[4773]   BIART, V. 'Master lesson upon the dainty "Nutcracker" suite', *Etude*, 46 (Sep 1928): 672; (Oct 1928): 748, illus.

[4774]   NEWMARCH, R. H. 'Tchaikovsky: Suite from the ballet "Casse-Noisette" (op. 71a)'. In: R. H. Newmarch, *The concert-goer's library of descriptive notes*. Part III: *Suites and ballet suites for orchestra, rhapsodies and fantasias, miscellaneous dances*. London: Oxford Univ. Press; H. Milford, 1930: 86–88.

[4775]   MONAGHAN, K. 'Christmas concert: The story behind the music of Tschaikowsky's "Nutcracker Suite" (radio play)', *Scholastic Review*, 38 (16 Dec 1940): 17–18.

[4776]   BURKE, D. & DUDLEY, J., 'Interpretations of the "Nutcracker Suite"', *Scholastic Arts*, 43 (Mar 1944): 250, illus.

[4777]   ARNOLD, K. & DUDLEY, J. '"Nutcracker Suite" inspirations', *Scholastic Arts*, 45 (Mar 1946): 249.

[4778]   MAREK, G. 'Practically everybody's favorite: "Nutcracker Suite"', *Good Housekeeping*, 131 (Aug 1950): 4, illus.

[4779]   HUNGAR, E. & HEIDINGER, T. 'Christmas and the "Nutcracker Suite"', *Scholastic Arts*, 55 (Dec 1955): 27, illus.

[4780]   KUNIN, I. F. '"Ideal´neishaia forma"', *Sovetskaia muzyka* (1968), 11: 113–116.

[4781]   VIERTEL, K. H. '"Nussknacker-Suite": Eine Rätsel-Sendereihe mit Stefan Lux', *Musik und Gesellschaft*, 25 (Oct 1975): 626–627.

[4782]   '"The Nutcracker' suite, op. 71a", *Clavier*, 36 (Nov 1997): 36.

          See also *110, 3811, 5554, 5641*.

SUITE NO. 1
Op. 43 (1878–79)

[4783]   L[EVENSON], O. 'Shestoi kontsert Muzykal´nogo obshchestva', *Russkie vedomosti* (8 Dec; 15 Dec 1879).
          The first performance of the suite on 6 Dec 1879 in Moscow. See also *4784*.
          — [repr.] 'Chaikovskii: Siuita dlia orkestra', In: O. Ia. Levenson, *V kontsertnoi zale*. Moskva, 1880: 222.

[4784]   'Shestoi kontsert Muzykal´nogo obshchestva', *Sovremennye izvestiia* (17 Dec 1879).

[*4785*]   'Muzykal´nye novosti', *Muzykal´nyi mir* (21 Nov 1882): 5.

News of a performance of the suite in Berlin.

[*4786*]   ENGEL´, Iu. D. 'Pervaia siuita Chaikovskogo', *Kur´er* (5 Mar 1900).

— [repr.] In: Iu. D. Engel´, *Glazami sovremennika.* Moskva, 1971: 59–60.

[*4787*]   TEIBLER, H. *Peter Tschaikowsky: Erste Suite, D moll, für grosses Orchester, Op. 43.* Erlautert von Hermann Teibler. Leipzig: H. Seeman Nachf. [1902]. 19 p, music. (*Musik Führer*; 264)

[*4788*]   NEWMARCH, R. H. 'Tchaikovsky: Suite no. 1, in D minor (op. 43)'. In: R. H. Newmarch, *The concert-goer's library of descriptive notes.* Part III: *Suites and ballet suites for orchestra, rhapsodies and fantasias, miscellaneous dances.* London: Oxford Univ. Press; H. Milford, 1930: 57–61.

[*4789*]   NAZAIKINSKII, E. V. 'Ob odnom prieme orkestrovki P. I. Chaikovskogo'. In: *P. I. Chaikovskii: K 100-letiiu so dnia smerti* (1995): 48–54 [see *597*].

Concerning the fugue in the first movement of the Suite No. 1.

[*4790*]   MINIBAEVA, N. '"Per aspera ad astra": Symphonic tradition in Tchaikovsky's First Suite for orchestra'. In: *Tchaikovsky and his world* (1998): 163–196 [see *601*].

See also *5669, 5697*.

SUITE NO. 2
Op. 53 (1883)

[*4791*]   L[EVENSO]N, O. 'Muzykal´naia khronika: Ekstrennoe sobranie Muzykal´nogo obshchestva', *Russkie vedomosti* (11 Feb 1884).

The first performance of the suite on 4 Feb 1884 in Moscow. See also *4792*.

[*4792*]   [KRUGLIKOV, S. N.] 'Ekstrennoe sobranie Muzykal´nogo obshchestva', *Sovremennye izvestiia* (18 Feb 1884).

[*4793*]   SOLOV´EV, N. F. 'Kontsert Filarmonicheskogo obshchestva', *Novosti i birzhevaia gazeta* (5 Mar 1886).

The first performance in St. Petersburg, 5 Mar 1887. See also *4794, 4795, 4796*.

[*4794*]   Z[INOV´EV], P. 'Kontsert Filarmonicheskogo obshchestva', *Peterburgskaia gazeta* (7 Mar 1887).

[*4795*]   'Kontsert Filarmonicheskogo obshchestva', *Novoe vremia* (8 Mar 1887).

[*4796*]   [KIUI, Ts. A.] 'Kontsert SPb Filarmonicheskogo obshchestva', *Muzykal´noe obozrenie* (12 Mar 1887).

[*4797*]   SUIKERMAN, J. 'Een onbekende suite van P. I. Tschaikowsky', *Vereenigde tijdschriften Cæcilie en Het muziekcollege* (May 1929): 202–204.

See also *5728*.

SUITE NO. 3
Op. 55 (1884)

[*4798*]   Z[INOV´EV], P. 'Piatoe simfonicheskoe sobranie RMO', *Peterburgskaia gazeta* (14 Jan 1885).

The first performance of the suite on 12 Jan 1885 in St. Petersburg. See also *4799, 4800, 4801*.

[*4799*]   SOLOV´EV, N. F. 'Piatoe simfonicheskoe sobranie RMO', *Novosti i birzhevaia gazeta* (14 Jan 1885).

[*4800*]   '5-e simfonicheskoe sobranie RMO', *Peterburgskii listok* (15 Jan 1885).

[*4801*]   **GALLER, K. P.** 'Piatoe simfonicheskoe sobranie RMO', *Sankt Peterburgskie vedomosti* (18 Jan 1885).

[*4802*]   **LAROSH, G. A.** 'Muzykal´noe obozrenie: P. Chaikovskii i ego novaia siuita', *Russkii vestnik* (Jan 1885).

The first performance in Moscow, on 19 Jan 1885. See also *4803, 4804.*

— [repr.] In: G. A. Larosh, *Sobranie muzykal´no-kriticheskikh statei*, tom 2, chast´ 2 (1924): 151–156 [see *2311*].

— [repr.] 'Obshchaia kharakteristika tvorchestva P. Chaikovskogo', In: G. A. Larosh, *Izbrannye stat´i v piati vypuskakh*, vyp. 2 (1975): 118–122 [see *2376*].

— [German tr.] 'Tschaikowskys Dritte Orchestersuite, Op. 55'. In: G. A. Larosh, *Peter Tschaikowsky: Aufsätze und Erinnerungen* (1993): 127–132 [see *2406*].

[*4803*]   'Simfonicheskoe sobranie Muzykal´nogo obshchestva', *Moskovskie vedomosti* (21 Jan 1885).

[*4804*]   'Simfonicheskoe sobranie RMO', *Russkie vedomosti* (24 Jan 1885).

[*4805*]   [**KIUI, Ts. A.**] 'Tret´e simfonicheskoe sobranie Russkogo muzykal´nogo obshchestva', *Muzykal´noe obozrenie* (4 Jan 1886): 105–106.

[*4806*]   'Tchaikovsky's ovation at the music festival', *New York World* (26 Apr/8 May 1891).

A performance of the suite at Carnegie Hall, New York on 25 Apr/7 May 1891, conducted by Chaikovskii. See also *1846, 4807.*

[*4807*]   'Tschaikowsky's Suite', *American Art Journal* (2/14 May 1891).

[*4808*]   **HANSLICK, E.** 'Tschaikowskys Dritte Orchester-Suite, Op. 55'. In: E. Hanslick, *Am Ende des Jahrhunderts (1895–1899). Musikalische Kritiken und Schilderungen von Eduard Hanslick.* Berlin, 1899: 285–286.

— [repr.] 'Die Tschaikowsky-Rezensionen'. In: *Tschaikowsky aus der Nähe* (1994): 209 [see *379*].

[*4809*]   **KNORR, I.** *Peter Tschaikowsky: Suite no. 3 (G-dur) für orchester, Op. 55.* Erlautert von Jwan Knorr. Frankfurt am Main: H. Bechhold [c.1900]. 21 p, music. (*Musikführer*; 5).

[*4810*]   **NEWMARCH, R. H.** 'Tchaikovsky: Suite No. 3, in G major (op. 55)'. In: R. H. Newmarch, *The concert-goer's library of descriptive notes.* Part III: *Suites and ballet suites for orchestra, rhapsodies and fantasias, miscellaneous dances.* London: Oxford Univ. Press; H. Milford, 1930: 61–64.

[*4811*]   **JOHANSEN, B.** 'Tema och variationer', *Operan* (1994/95), 6: 5–7.

[*4812*]   **ABRAHAM, G. E. H.** 'Tchaikovsky: Suite No. 3 in G, op. 55'. In: *The musician's guide to symphonic music: Essays from the Eulenberg scores.* Corey Field, ed. Mainz; New York: Schott, 1997: 648–650.

See also *5687, 5732, 5734.*

SUITE NO. 4
"Mozartiana", Op. 61 (1887)

[*4813*]   **KASHKIN, N. D.** 'Vtoroe simfonicheskoe sobranie RMO', *Russkie vedomosti* (15 Nov 1887).

The first performance of the Suite on 14 Nov 1887 in Moscow, conducted by Chaikovskii. See also *4814, 4815, 4816.*

[*4814*]   'Vtoroe simfonicheskoe sobranie RMO', *Novosti i birzhevaia gazeta* (15 Nov 1887).

[*4815*]   'Vtoroe simfonicheskoe sobranie RMO', *Moskovskie vedomosti* (17 Nov 1887).

[4816] K[ASHKIN], N. D. 'P. I. Chaikovskii i kontserty Muzykal´nogo obshchestva 14 i 15 noiabria', *Russkie vedomosti* (21 Nov 1887).

[4817] [KIUI, Ts. A.] 'Tret´e simfonicheskoe sobranie Russkogo muzykal´nogo obshchestva', *Muzykal´noe obozrenie* (17 Dec 1887): 341–342.

The first performance in St. Petersburg, 12 Dec 1887.

— [rev. repr.] 'Tretii kontsert Russkogo muzykal´nogo obshchestva', *Grazhdanin* (23 Dec 1887).

[4818] NIEMANN, W. *Peter Tschaikowsky: Mozartiana-suite, Op. 61*. Erlautert von Walter Niemann. Leipzig: H. Seemann [n. d.]. 18 p, music. (*Musikführer*; 233).

[4819] NEWMARCH, R. H. 'Tchaikovsky: Suite no. 4, "Mozartiana"'. In: R. H. Newmarch, *The concertgoer's library of descriptive notes*. Part III: *Suites and ballet suites for orchestra, rhapsodies and fantasias, miscellaneous dances*. London: Oxford Univ. Press; H. Milford, 1930: 64–65.

[4820] GÖBEL, A. '"Unvergleichliche Schönheiten": Mozarts Variation über "Unser dummer Pöbel meint" und ihre Bearbeitung bei Tschaikowsky', *Musik und Bildung*, 27 (Nov/Dec 1995): 47–51, music, illus.

— [repr.] *Deutsche Tonkünstler Zeitung*, 27 (1995), 6: 47–52.

[4821] UNGER, M. 'Tchaikovsky: "Mozartiana", Suite No. 4, op. 61'. In: *The musician's guide to symphonic music: Essays from the Eulenberg scores*. Corey Field, ed. Mainz; New York: Schott, 1997: 651–652.

See also *2096, 5671* to *5676*.

5.3.4. Overtures

[4822] GLEBOV, I. [ASAF´EV, B. V.] 'Simfonicheskie poemy Chaikovskogo'. In: I. Glebov, *Instrumental´noe tvorchestvo Chaikovskogo* (1922): 32–42 [see *2310*].

[4823] BUDIAKOVSKII, A. E. *Simfonicheskie poemy Chaikovskogo*. [Leningrad]: Leningradskaia filarmoniia, 1935. iii, 32 p, illus. (*Putevoditel´ po kontsertam*).

[4824] WOOD, R. W. 'Miscellaneous orchestral works'. In: *Tchaikovsky: A symposium* (1945): 74–103 [see *586*].

[4825] BUDDEN, R. *Tchaikovsky: Miscellaneous orchestral works*. London: Cassell, 1952. 32 p, illus. (*Decca Music Guides*; 11).

See also *1920, 2140*.

CHARACTERISTIC DANCES
(1864–65)

[4826] KUNIN, I. F. 'Chaikovskii i Iogann Shtraus', *Sovetskaia muzyka* (1965), 8: 158, illus.

The 100th anniversary of Strauss conducting the first performance of the dances in Pavlovsk on 30 Aug 1865.

FATUM
Symphonic fantasia, Op. 77 (1869)

[4827] LAROSH, G. A. 'Kontserty Russkogo muzykal´nogo obshchestva 7-i, 8-i i 9-i', *Sovremennaia letopis´* (9 Mar 1869).

The first performance of the fantasia on 15 Feb 1869 in Moscow.

— [repr.] In: G. A. Larosh, *Sobranie muzykal´no-kriticheskikh statei*, tom 2, chast´ 2 (1924): 1–5 [see *2311*].

— [repr.] 'Simfonicheskaia fantaziia "Fatum"'. In: G. A. Larosh, *Izbrannye stat'i v piati vypuskakh*, vyp. 2 (1975): 26–29 [see *2376*].

— [German tr.] 'Die Sinfonische Fantaisie "Fatum" von Herrn Tschaikowsky', In: G. A. Larosh, *Peter Tschaikowsky: Aufsätze und Erinnerungen* (1993): 66–70 [see *2406*].

[4828]   **[KIUI, Ts. A.] 'Deviatyi kontsert Russkogo muzykal'nogo obshchestva'**, *Sankt Peterburgiskie vedomosti* (1 Apr 1869).

The first performance in St. Petersburg on 17 Mar 1869.

— [repr.] In: Ts. A. Kiui, *Izbrannye stat'i*. Leningrad, 1952: 151–154.

[4829]   **LAROSH, G. A. 'Eshche o "Fatume" g. Chaikovskogo'**, *Sovremennaia letopis'* (16 Apr 1869): 12.
Concerning the fantasia's epigraph. Includes part of a letter from S. A. Rachinskii.

— [repr.] In: G. A. Larosh, *Sobranie muzykal'no-kriticheskikh statei*, tom 2, chast' 2 (1924): 5–7 [see *2311*].

— [repr.] In: G. A. Larosh, *Izbrannye stat'i v piati vypuskakh*, vyp. 2 (1975): 29–31 [see *2376*].

— [German tr.] 'Noch einmal zu Herrn Tschaikowskys Sinfonischer Fantasie "Fatum"', In: G. A. Larosh, *Peter Tschaikowsky: Aufsätze und Erinnerungen* (1993): 71–73 [see *2406*].

[4830]   **CHERNOV, K. N. '"Fatum" P. I. Chaikovskogo i Motsarta** (1909). Sankt Peterburg: Izdat. zhurnala "Svetlyi luch", 1909. 25 p.

Review: B. T., *Russkaia muzykal'naia gazeta* (18 Apr 1910), 16: 402.

[4831]   **KIRSANOVA, M. 'Simfonicheskaia fantaziia "Fatum" P. I. Chaikovskogo'**. In: *P. I. Chaikovskii: Issledovaniia i materialy* (1997): 49–54 [see *599*].

See also *1920*.

FESTIVAL OVERTURE ON THE DANISH NATIONAL ANTHEM
Op. 15 (1866)

[4832]   **ROSTISLAV [TOLSTOI, F. M.], 'Kratkii obzor minuvshego kontsertnogo sezona'**, *Golos* (12 Apr 1867): 1.

The first performance of the overture on 29 Jan 1867 in Moscow.

[4833]   **PARSONS, W. H. 'Tchaikovsky, the Tsars, and the Tsarist national anthem'**. In: *Tchaikovsky and his contemporaries* (1999): 227–233 [see *602*].

FRANCESCA DA RIMINI
Fantasia after Dante, Op. 32 (1876)

[4834]   **'Izvestiia iz Rossii'**, *Muzykal'nyi listok* (1876/77), 8: 127–128.
Report of Chaikovskii's work on the fantasia.

[4835]   **'Korrespondentsiia: Moskva'**, *Muzykal'nyi listok* (1876/77), 16: 247–251.
The first performance on 25 Feb 1877 in Moscow. See also *4836, 4837*.

[4836]   **KASHKIN, N. D. 'Desiatoe sobranie muzykal'nogo obshchestva i novaia fantaziia g. Chaikovskogo'**, *Russkie vedomosti* (3 Mar 1877).

— [repr.] In: N. D. Kashkin, *Izbrannye stat'i o P. I. Chaikovskom* (1954): 195–198 [see *2349*].

[4837]   **ZUB [SHCHUROVSKII, P. A.] 'Muzykal'naia zametka'**, *Sovremennye izvestiia* (16 Mar 1877).

[4838]   **GALLER, K. P. '"Francheska da Rimini" g. Chaikovskogo'**, *Birzhevye vedomosti* (14 Mar 1878).
The first performance in St. Petersburg on 11 Mar 1878. See also *4839*.

[4839]   **IVANOV, M. 'Muzykal'nye nabroski'**, *Novoe vremia* (20 Mar 1878).

[4840] LAROSH, G. A. 'Muzykal´nye ocherki', *Golos* (3 Apr 1878).

Performances of *Francesca da Rimini* and the Piano Concerto No. 1 in St. Petersburg.

— [repr.] In: G. A. Larosh, *Sobranie muzykal´no-kriticheskikh statei*, tom 2, chast´ 2 (1924): 43–48 [see *2311*].

— [repr.] '"Francesca da Rimini". Fortepiannyi kontsert op. 23'. In: G. A. Larosh, *Izbrannye stat´i v piati vypuskakh*, vyp. 2 (1975): 94–97 [see *2376*].

[4841] TAUBERT, E. E.[Tschaikowskys "Francesca da Rimini"], *Die Post* (5/17 Sep 1878).

The first performance in Berlin on 2/14 Sep 1878. See also *4842* to *4846*.

[4842] URBAN, H. [Tschaikowskys "Francesca da Rimini"], *Vossische Zeitung* (5/17 Sep 1878).

[4843] WUERST, R. [Tschaikowskys "Francesca da Rimini"], *Berliner fremdenblatt* (5/17 Sep 1878).

[4844] ZUMPRECHT, O. [Tschaikowskys "Francesca da Rimini"], *National Zeitung* (5/17 Sep 1878).

[4845] EHRLICH, H. [Tschaikowskys "Francesca da Rimini"], *Berliner Tageblatt* (6/18 Sep 1878).

[4846] [Tschaikowskys "Francesca da Rimini"], *Neue Prüssische Zeitung* (6/18 Sep 1878).

[4847] [KIUI, Ts. A.] 'Poslednii kontsert Muzykal´nogo obshchestva', *Nedelia* (14 Apr 1885).

[4848] NIEMANN, W. *Peter Tschaikowsky: "Francesca da Rimini", Op. 32*. Erlautert von Walter Niemann. Leipzig: H. Seemann [c.1895]. 19 p, music; 17 cm. (*Musikführer*; 239).

[4849] DONALD, P. 'Great orchestral works by modern composers: 2. "Franceska da Rimini", fantazia, after Dante, by Peter I. Tschaikowsky', *Metronome*, 32 (1916), 5: 44–46.

[4850] GLEBOV, I. [ASAF´EV, B. V.] 'Dante i russkie kompozitory'. In: *Dante, 1321–1921*. Petrograd: Gos. filarmoniia, 1921: 42–50.

[4851] NEWMARCH, R. H. 'Tchaikovsky: Symphonic fantasia "Francesca da Rimini" (op. 32)'. In: R. H. Newmarch, *The concert-goer's library of descriptive notes. Part II: Wagnerian excerpts, symphonic poems and fantasias, marches*. London: Oxford Univ. Press; H. Milford, 1929: 88–90.

[4852] 'Simfoniia "Francheska da Rimini"', *Sovetskaia muzyka* (1941), 7: 96.

[4853] KENIGSBERG, A. 'Na spektakliakh rizhskogo teatra', *Sovteskaia muzyka* (1962), 6: 59–67.

[4854] SKUDINA, G. 'Besedy o muzyke: "Francheska da Rimini" P. I. Chaikovskogo', *Muzykal´naia zhizn'* (1962), 17: 13–14, music.

[4855] SOKOLOVA, T. *"Francheska da Rimini": Simfonicheskaia fantaziia Chaikovskogo*. Moskva: Muzyka, 1964. 54 pp, music, illus. (*Biblioteka slushatelia kontsertov. V pomoshch´ slushateliam universitov kul´tury*).

[4856] BOOKSPAN, M. 'The basic repertoire: Tchaikovsky's "Francesca da Rimini"', *Stereo Review*, 28 (Mar 1972): 49.

Survey of recordings.

[4857] GILNES, D. 'Further prose tone-poems', *Music News*, 6 (1976), 1: 22.

[4858] TIRDATOVA, E. 'Obrazy Dante u Lista i Chaikovskogo'. In: *Iz istorii zarubezhnoi muzyki*. Sost. M. Pekelis, I. Givental´. Vyp. 3. Moskva: Muzyka, 1979: 5–28, music. (*Gos. muzykal´no-pedagogicheskii institut im. Gnesinykh. Kafedra istorii zarubezhnoi muzyki*).

Analysis of Liszt's *Dante* symphony, and Chaikovskii's *Francesca da Rimini*.

[4859] BARRICELLI, J. P. 'Liszt's journey through Dante's hereafter', *Journal of the American Liszt Society*, 14 (1983): 3–15, illus.

Comparing Liszt's and Chaikovskii's settings of Dante's poem.

[4860]　LLOYD-JONES, D. 'Tchaikovsky: "Francesca da Rimini", op. 32'. In: *The musician's guide to symphonic music: Essays from the Eulenberg scores*. Corey Field, ed. Mainz; New York: Schott, 1997: 628–630.

[4861]　COPPOLA, C. 'The elusive fantasy: Genre, form and program in Tchaikovsky's "Francesca da Rimini"', *Nineteenth-Century Music*, 22 (fall 1998), 2: 169–189.

See also *1735, 5633* to *5640*.

HAMLET
Overture-fantasia, Op. 67 (1888)

[4862]　Ia. D. 'Tret´e simfonicheskoe sobranie', *Sankt Peterburgskie vedomosti* (14 Nov 1888).
The first performance on 12 Nov 1888 in St. Petersburg, conducted by Chaikovskii. See also *4863* to *4869*.

[4863]　L. 'Tret´e simfonicheskoe sobranie RMO', *Peterburgskaia gazeta* (14 Nov 1888).

[4864]　SOLOV´EV, N. F. 'Tret´e simfonicheskoe sobranie RMO', *Novosti i birzhevaia gazeta* (14 Nov 1888).

[4865]　'Tret´e simfonicheskoe sobranie RMO', *Peterburgskii listok* (14 Nov 1888).

[4866]　'Tret´e simfonicheskoe sobranie RMO', *Novoe vremia* (15 Nov 1888).

[4867]　G. G. 'Tret´e simfonicheskoe sobranie Russkogo muzykal´nogo obshchestva', *Birzhevye vedomosti* (16 Nov 1888).

[4868]　[KIUI, Ts. A.] 'Tretii kontsert Russkogo muzykal´nogo obshchestva', *Muzykal´noe obozrenie* (17 Nov 1888).

[4869]　'Chaikovskii v Filarmonicheskom obshchestve', *Den´* (27 Nov 1888).

[4870]　FINK, H. T. 'Brooklyn Philharmonic', *Evening Post* (16 Feb 1891).
The first performance in Brooklyn, New York, on 2/14 Feb 1891.
— [repr.] In: E. Yoffe, *Tchaikovsky in America* (1986): 22–23 [see *1864*].

[4871]　FINK, H. T. [Tchaikovsky's "Hamlet"], *Evening Post* (13 Apr 1891).
Includes extracts from Fink's correspondence with Chaikovskii concerning *Hamlet*.
— [repr.] In: E. Yoffe, *Tchaikovsky in America* (1986): 23 [see *1864*].

[4872]　K[ASHKIN], N. 'Teatr i muzyka', *Russkie vedomosti* (14 Feb 1893).
The first performance in Moscow on 14 Feb 1893. See also *4873*.

[4873]　'Simfonicheskii kontsert RMO', *Moskovskie vedomosti* (14 Feb 1893).

[4874]　TEIBLER, H. *Peter Tschaikowsky: "Hamlet"*. Erlautert von Hermann Teibler. Leipzig: Hermann Seemann nachfolger [c.1895]. 14 p, music. (*Musikführer*; 214).

[4875]　P—SKI, E. '"Gamlet" Chaikovskogo', *Russkaia muzykal´naia gazeta* (Aug 1895), 8: 495–501.

[4876]　LAROSH, G. A. 'Dva slova o Chaikovskom', *Rossiia* (17 Nov 1900): 2.
— [repr.] 'Dva slova o Chaikovskom (po povodu "Gamleta"). In: G. A. Larosh, *Izbrannye stat´i v piati vypuskakh*, vyp. 2 (1975): 326–328 [see *2376*].

[4877]　KESSLER, G. 'Kleine Enträuschungen', *Opern Welt* (May 1967), 5: 13.

[4878]   ABRAHAM, G. E. H. 'Tchaikovsky: "Hamlet", fantasy-overture, op. 67'. In: *The musician's guide to symphonic music: Essays from the Eulenberg scores*. Corey Field, ed. Mainz; New York: Schott, 1997: 631–632.

See also *533, 4471, 4567, 4590, 4269, 4635, 5642, 5643, 5644, 5646, 5665.*

ITALIAN CAPRICCIO
Op. 45 (1880)

[4879]   L[EVENSO]N, O. 'Muzykal´naia khronika'. *Russkie vedomosti* (6 Dec 1880).

The first performance on 6 Dec 1880 in Moscow. See also *4880, 4881, 4882.*

[4880]   IGNOTUS [FLEROV, S. V.] 'Sed´moe simfonicheskoe sobranie', *Moskovskie vedomosti* (10 Dec 1880).

[4881]   L[EVENSO]N, O. 'Muzykal´naia khronika', *Russkie vedomosti* (15 Dec 1880).

[4882]   KRUGLIKOV, S. N. ["Ital´ianskoe kaprichchio" Chaikovskogo]. *Sovremennye izvestiia* (19 Dec 1880).

[4883]   [KIUI, Ts. A.] 'Kontsert artistov orkestra russkoi opery', *Golos* (31 Dec 1880).

The first performance of the *Italian Capriccio* in St. Petersburg, and an 'Arioso' from *The Maid of Orleans* on 26 Dec 1880. See also *4884, 4885.*

[4884]   MAKAROV, P. S. ["Ital´ianskoe kaprichchio" Chaikovskogo], *Birzhevye vedomosti* (6 Jan 1881).

[4885]   'Teatr i muzyka', *Novoe vremia* (7 Jan 1881).

[4886]   TEIBLER, H. *Peter Tschaikowsky: "Capriccio italien" für grosses orchester*. Erlautert von Hermann Teibler. Leipzig: Hermann Seeman nachfolger [c.1900]. 13 p, music. (*Musikführer*; 250).

[4887]   DONALD, P. 'Great orchestral works by modern composers: 4. "Italian Caprice" for orchestra, op. 45 by Peter I. Tschaikowsky', *Metronome*, 32 (1916), 7: 42–43.

[4888]   POZHIDAEV, G. 'O chem rasskazala muzyka', *Sovetskaia muzyka* (1964), 7: 88–92.

With introduction by D. Kabalevskii, 'Neskol´ko slov ob avtore': 88–89.

[4889]   BAS, L. A. 'Ital´ianskoe kaprichchio'. In: L. A. Bas, *Rasskazy o kompozitorakh*. Kiev: Muzyka Ukraina, 1967: 33–38, illus.

[4890]   BOOKSPAN, M. 'The basic repertoire', *Stereo Review*, 29 (Oct 1972): 59.

Survey of recordings.

See also *1841, 1842, 5488, 5607.*

OVERTURE in C minor
(1865–66)

[4891]   ABRAMOV, A. 'Novinki Chaikovskogo', *Izvestiia* (2 Aug 1934).

The first performance of the overture in Moscow on 30 Jul 1934.

See also *109.*

ROMEO AND JULIET
Overture-fantasia after Shakespeare
(1869, rev. 1870, 1880)

[4892]   RAZMADZE, A. 'Korrespondentsii: Moskva', *Muzykal´nyi sezon* (19 Mar 1870): 3–4.
          The first performance of the overture on 4 Mar 1870 in Moscow. See also *4688*.

[4893]   A. R. 'Muzykal´nyi fel´eton', *Muzykal´nyi vestnik* (Apr 1870), 4: 3–4.

[4894]   [KIUI, Ts. A.] 'Prodolzhenie muzykal´noi bibliografii', *Sankt Peterburgskie vedomosti* (1 Oct 1871).

[4895]   [KIUI, Ts. A.] 'Chetvertyi kontsert Russkogo muzykal´nogo obshchestva', *Sankt Peterburgskie vedomosti* (9 Feb 1872).
          The first performance of the 2nd version on 5 Feb 1872 in St. Petersburg.

[4896]   [KIUI, Ts. A.] 'Muzykal´nye zametki: Uvertiura g. Chaikovskogo "Romeo"', *Sankt Peterburgskie vedomosti* (25 Oct 1872).
          Publication of the piano duet arrangement (2nd version).
          — [repr.] In: Ts. A. Kiui, *Izbrannye stat´i*. Leningrad, 1952: 213–215.

[4897]   HANSLICK, E. 'Tschaikowskys Ouvertüre zu Shakespeares "Romeo und Julia"', *Neue Freie Presse* (30 Nov 1876).
          On the first performance in Vienna, on 14/26 Nov 1876.
          — [repr.] In: E. Hanslick, *Concerte, Componisten und Virtuosen der letzten fünfzehn Jahre, 1870–1885*. Kritiken von Eduard Hanslick. Berlin: Allgemeiner Verein für Deutsche Literatur, 1886: 174–176
          — [repr.] 'Die Tschaikowsky-Rezensionen'. In: *Tschaikowsky aus der Nähe* (1994): 196–197 [see *379*].

[4898]   'Zagranichnye izvestiia', *Muzykal´nyi listok* (1876/77), 2: 26–27, 3: 41–42, 4: 107–108.
          The first performances in Boston, Vienna and Paris.

[4899]   [KIUI, Ts. A.] 'Pervyi simfonicheskii kontsert Russkogo muzykal´nogo obshchestva', *Muzykal´noe obozrenie* (19 Nov 1887).
          — [rev. repr.] 'Pervoe simfonicheskoe sobranie Russkogo muzykal´nogo obshchestva', *Grazhdanin* (23 Nov 1887): 3.

[4900]   TEIBLER, H. *Peter Tschaikowsky: "Romeo und Julia", ouverture-fantasie nach Shakespeare*. Erlautert von Hermann Tiebler. Leipzig: Hermann Seemann nachfolger [c. 1895]. 14 p, music. (*Musikführer*; 219).

[4901]   DONALD, P. 'Great orchestral works by modern composers: 3. "Romeo and Juliet", overture-fantasia after Shakespeare, by Peter I. Tschaikowsky', *Metronome*, 32 (1916), 6: 48–51.

[4902]   RUTTERS, H. 'Tsjaikofskiana', *Cæcilia*, 76 (1918), 1: 4–6, 2: 20–26, 3: 34–37.

[4903]   BLOM, E W. '"Romeo and Juliet", fantasy-overture'. In: E. W. Blom, *Tchaikovsky: Orchestral works* (1927): 5–12 [see *4366*].

[4904]   NEWMARCH, R. H. 'Tchaikovsky: Overture-fantasia "Romeo and Juliet"'. In: R. H. Newmarch, *The concert-goer's library of descriptive notes*. Part I: *Symphonies, overtures, concertos*. London: Oxford Univ. Press; H. Milford, 1928: 79–80.

[4905]   SOLOVTSOV, A. A. *"Romeo i Dzhul´etta": Uvertiura-fantaziia P. I. Chaikovskogo*. Poiasnenie A. Solovtsova. Moskva: Gos. muz. izdat., 1953. 36 p, music. (*V pomoshch´ slushateliu muzyki*).
          — [2-e izd.] Moskva: Gos. muz. izdat., 1960. 28 p, music (*Biblioteka slushatelia kontsertov*).

[4906]   AL´SHVANG, A. A. 'Pesennye istoki simfonizma Chaikovskogo', *Sovetskaia muzyka* (1955), 6: 52–60, music, illus.
          The possible origins of the overture's love theme in the Russian folk-song 'Iskhodila mladen´ka'.

[4907]   FREINDLIKH, G. 'Uvertiura-fantaziia P. I. Chaikovskogo "Romeo i Dzhul´etta"'. In: *Ocherki po teoreticheskomu muzykoznaniiu*. Leningrad, 1959: 88–119.

[4908]   SUTTON, W. 'Tchaikovsky's "Romeo and Juliet"', *Music in Education*, 26 (15 Nov 1962): 171, mus.

[4909]   MEYER, E. R. 'Measure for measure: Shakespeare and music', *Music Educator's Journal*, 54 (Mar 1968): 38–39.

[4910]   BOOKSPAN, M. 'The basic repertoire: Tchaikovsky's "Romeo and Juliet"', *Stereo Review* (Jan 1969): 57.

[4911]   KUNIN, I. F. 'Besedy o muzyke: Uvertiura-fantaziia "Romeo i Dzhul´etta"', *Muzykal´naia zhizn´* (1970), 1: 15–16.

[4912]   RICHARDS, D. '"Peer Gynt" and "Romeo and Juliet"', *Music & Musicians*, 27 (Dec 1978): 42.

[4913]   RICHARDSON, B. *Tchaikovsky fantasy-overture: "Romeo and Juliet"*. Leeds: Mayflower Enterprises, 1985. (*Mayflower Study Guides*; 8). ISBN: 0–9468–9614–3.

[4914]   GILINSKY, J. E. 'Unity and opposition in the orchestration of Tchaikovsky's "Romeo and Juliet" overture'. New York: Manhattan School of Music, 1990. 166 p.
          Dissertation (M. M.).

[4915]   DVILIANSKII, A. Ia. 'P. Chaikovskii: Uvertiura-fantaziia "Romeo i Dzhul´etta" (vstuplenie, taktov 1–10)'. In: A. I. Dvilianskii, *Kompleksnyi garmonicheskii analiz*. Bishkek, 1993: 96–98, music.

[4916]   SLIUSARENKO, T. 'Linii sud´by', *Muzykal´naia zhizn´* (1993), 19/20: 19–20.
          Milii Balakirev's influence on *Romeo and Juliet*.

[4917]   KELDYSH, Iu. V. 'Uvertiura-fantaziia "Romeo i Dzhul´etta" i ee rol´ v stanovlenii simfonizma Chaikovskogo'. In: *P. I. Chaikovskii: K 100-letiiu so dnia smerti* (1995): 24–30 [see *597*].

          See also *1557, 1920, 5700* to *5707*.

SERENADE FOR STRING ORCHESTRA
Op. 48 (1880)

[4918]   LEVENSON, O. Ia. 'Sed´moe simfonicheskoe sobranie RMO', *Russkie vedomosti* (17 Jan 1882).
          The first performance in Moscow on 16 Jan 1882. See also *4918*.

[4919]   IGNOTUS [FLEROV, S. V.] 'Simfonicheskoe sobranie RMO', *Moskovskie vedomosti* (22 Jan 1882).

[4920]   'Muzykal´naia khronika', *Sovremennye izvestiia* (5 Jul 1882).

[4921]   KNORR, J. *Peter Tschaikowsky: Serenade für streichorchester, Op. 48*. Erlautert von Jwan Knorr. Frankfurt am Main: H. Bechhold [c.1895]. 16 p, music. (*Musikführer*; 17).

[4922]   HANSLICK, E. 'Tschaikowskys "Serenade" für Streichorchester, Op. 48'. In: E. Hanslick, *Fünf Jahre Musik (1891–95)*. Kritiken von Eduard Hanslick. Berlin, 1896: 181–182.
          — [repr.] 'Die Tschaikowsky-Rezensionen'. In: *Tschaikowsky aus der Nähe* (1994): 199 [see *379*].

[4923]   RAWLINSON, H. 'Some famous works for string orchestra: "Serenade for string orchestra", op. 48, Peter Ilyich Tchaikovsky', *Strad* (Nov 1947): 154–158, music, illus.

[4924]   BOOKSPAN, M. 'The basic repertoire: Tchaikovsky's "Serenade for Strings"', *Stereo Review*, 14 (Mar 1965): 41–42.

[4925]   UNGER, M. 'Tchaikovsky: Serenade for string orchestra, op. 48'. In: *The musician's guide to symphonic music: Essays from the Eulenberg scores*. Corey Field, ed. Mainz; New York: Schott, 1997: 645.

          See also *4760, 5625* to *5627, 5710* to *5713*.

SLAVONIC MARCH
Op. 31 (1876)

[4926]   'Izvestiia iz Rossii', *Muzykal´nyi listok* (1876/77), 9: 138.

          The first performance of the march on 5 Nov 1876 in Moscow.

[4927]   NEWMARCH, R. H. 'Tchaikovsky: Marche Slave (op. 31)'. In: R. H. Newmarch, *The concert-goer's library of descriptive notes*. Part II: *Wagnerian excerpts, symphonic poems and fantasias, marches*. London: Oxford Univ. Press; H. Milford, 1929: 106.

THE STORM
Overture to Ostrovskii's drama, Op. 76 (1864)

[4928]   F[INDEIZEN], N. F. 'II-i i III-i russkie simfonicheskie kontserty (17 i 24 fevr.)', *Russkaia muzykal´naia gazeta* (Mar 1896), 3: 350.

          The first public performance of the overture on 24 Feb 1896 in St. Petersburg.

THE TEMPEST
Fantasia after Shakespeare's drama, Op. 18 (1873)

[4929]   RAZMADZE, A. S. '"Buria" g. Chaikovskogo', *Muzykal´nyi listok* (20 Jan 1874): 139–141.

          The first performance of the fantasia on 7 Dec 1873 in Moscow.

[4930]   [KIUI, Ts. A.] 'Russkoe muzykal´noe obshchestvo', *Sankt Peterburgskie vedomosti* (19 Nov 1874): 1.

          The first performance in St. Petersburg on 16 Nov 1874. See also *4931*.

[4931]   LAROSH, G. A. 'Vtoroi simfonicheskii kontsert Russkogo muzykal´nogo obshchestva', *Golos* (22 Nov 1874): 1–2.

          — [repr.] In: G. A. Larosh, *Izbrannye stat´i v piati vypuskakh*, vyp. 2 (1975): 73–74 [see *2376*].

[4932]   C'EST MOI. 'Nashi zagorodnye uveseleniia: Muzykal´naia i inaia parallel´', *Muzykal´nyi svet* (21 Aug 1877): 389–390.

[4933]   [2-me concert russe], *Le Figaro* (4/16 Sep 1878).

          The first performance in Paris on 2/14 Sep 1878. See also *4933* to *4938*.

[4934]   ["La tempête"], *La Gazette Musicale* (10/22 Sep 1878).

[4935]   ["La tempête"], *Le Ménestrel* (10/22 Sep 1878).

[4936]   LEFEVRE, G. ["La tempête"], *Paris Journal* (27 Feb/11 Mar 1879).

[4937]   ELI ["La tempête"], *Art Musical* (8/20 Mar 1879).

[4938]   ["La tempête"], *Le Ménestrel* (8/20 Mar 1879).

[4939]   'Muzykal´noe obozrenie', *Nuvellist* (Dec 1881): 4.

          The first performance of the fantasia in St. Petersburg. See also *4940*.

[4940]   IGNOTUS [FLEROV, S. V.] 'Muzykal´naia khronika', *Moskovskie vedomosti* (3 Dec 1881).

[4941]   KRUGLIKOV, S. N. '"Buria" Chaikovskogo', *Sovremennye izvestiia* (14 Aug 1882).

[4942]   [KIUI, Ts. A.] 'Obshchedostupnyi russkii simfonicheskii kontsert', *Muzykal´noe obrozrenie* (5 Dec 1885): 81–84.

          — [repr.] In: Ts. A. Kiui, *Izbrannye stat´i*. Leningrad, 1952: 335–340.

[4943]   NEWMARCH, R. H. 'Tchaikovsky: Symphonic fantasia (op. 18), "The Tempest"'. In: R. H. Newmarch, *The concert-goer's library of descriptive notes*. Part II: *Wagnerian excerpts, symphonic poems and fantasias, marches*. London: Oxford Univ. Press; H. Milford, 1929: 87–88.

[4944]   ILESHIN, B. 'Russkii v polneishem smysle slova', *Ogonek* (Feb 1974), 6: 22–23, illus.
The origins of *The Tempest*.

[4945]   ERMOLAEVA, T. N. 'Vzgliad na "Buriu" A. K. Glazunova i P. I. Chaikovskogo'. In: *Glazunov, Nil´sen, Sibelius: Zhizn´, tvorchestvo, epokha (K 130-letiiu so dnia rozhdeniia)*. Petrozavodsk, 1996: 19–20.

See also *5096*.

THE VOEVODA

Symphonic ballad, Op. 78 (1890–91)

[4946]   K[ASHKIN], N. 'Teatr i muzyka', *Russkie vedomosti* (8 Nov 1891).
The first performance on 6 Nov 1891 in Moscow, conducted by Chaikovskii. See also *4947, 4948*.

[4947]   [Kontsert g. Ziloti], *Russkii listok* (8 Nov 1891).

[4948]   'Teatral´nye i muzykal´nye izvestiia', *Moskovskie vedomosti* (9 Nov 1891).

[4949]   'Inostrannaia muzykal´naia pechat´ soobshchaet', *Russkaia muzykal´naia gazeta* (Oct 1896), 10: 1288.
Publication of the reconstructed score by Beliaeff.

[4950]   'Teatr i muzyka', *Novoe vremia* (24 Mar 1897): 3.
The first performance of the ballad in St. Petersburg in Mar 1897.

[4951]   AINSLEY, R. 'Rubbish!', *Classic CD* (Dec 1993), 43: 38–40, illus.

See also *449*.

THE YEAR 1812

Op. 49 (1880)

[4952]   IGNOTUS [FLEROV, S. V.] 'Kontsert g. Chaikovskogo', *Moskovskie vedomosti* (13 Aug 1882).
The first performance of the overture on 8 Aug 1882 in Moscow. See also *4953*.

[4953]   KRUGLIKOV, S. N. 'Kontsert g. Chaikovskogo', *Sovremennye izvestiia* (14 Aug 1882).

[4954]   SOLOV´EV, N. F. 'Torzhestvennaia uvertiura "1812 god" soch. Chaikovskogo', *Muzykal´nyi i teatral´nyi vestnik* (16 Jan 1883): 7.
Publication of the score by Iurgenson.

[4955]   HANSLICK, E. 'Die Ouvertüre "1812"'. In: E. Hanslick, *Aus neuer und neuester Zeit*. Musikalische Kritiken und Schilderungen von Eduard Hanslick. Berlin, 1900: 79–80.
— [repr.] 'Die Tschaikowsky-Rezensionen'. In: *Tschaikowsky aus der Nähe* (1994): 210 [see *379*].

[4956]   TEIBLER, H. *Peter Tschaikowsky. "1812" Overture für grosses Orchester, Op 49*. Erlautert von Hermann Teibler. Leipzig, H. Seeman Nachf. [1902]. 16 p, music. (*Musikführer*; 254)

[4957]   'Tschaikovsky's "1812"', *The Christian Science Monitor* (23 Jan 1929).

[4958]   'V Filarmonii: Patrioticheskaia uvertiura Chaikovskogo "1812 god"', *Smena* (9 Dec 1941): 4.
A special performance of the overture in Leningrad on 7 Dec 1941, in support of Russia's involvement into the Second World War.

[*4959*] 'Shotgun symphony: 1812 overture', *Time*, 40 (30 Nov 1942): 74, illus.

[*4960*] KUSHNAREVA, L. *"1812 god": Torzhestvennaia uvertiura Chaikovskogo*. Poiasnenie. Moskva: Gos. muz. izdat., 1954. 19 p, music (*V pomoshch´ slushateliu muzyki*).

[*4961*] CONLY, J. M. 'The brass includes a cannon', *High Fidelity*, 6 (May 1956): 74.
Review of new recordings.

[*4962*] DARRELL, R. D. 'A brand-new 1812: Served to the taste of the commissars', *High Fidelity*, 9 (Aug 1959): 60.
A new Soviet recording of the overture, omitting the quotation from "God Save the Tsar".

[*4963*] 'Prazdnik voennykh orkestrov', *Muzykal´naia zhizn´* (1960): 2.
The representation of the Napoleonic War in Chaikovskii's overture.

[*4964*] KIRBY, F. '"War of 1812" rages again', *Billboard* (13 Feb 1971): 1.

[*4965*] BOOKSPAN, M. 'The basic repertoire: Tchaikovsky's "1812" overture', *Stereo Review*, 26 (May 1971): 53.
Survey of recordings.

[*4966*] RZHAKSINSKII, F. 'Vozvrashchenie uvertiury', *Vechernii Leningrad* (7 May 1980): 3.
The return of the overture to Soviet concert halls.

[*4967*] MONTERO GARCIA, J. 'Comentario didactico con musicograma de la obertura "1812", op. 49 de Tchaikovsky: Ejemplo practico para alumnos de educacion primaria y secundaria', *Música y educación*, 7 (20 Dec 1994): 59–66.

[*4968*] 'Tchaikovsky: "1812 Overture", op. 49'. In: A. J. Rudel, *Classical music top 40*. New York: Simon & Schuster, 1995: 334–339.

See also *5096*.

5.4. CONCERTOS

5.4.1. General

[*4969*] GLEBOV, I. [ASAF´EV, B. V.] 'Kontsertnyi stil´ Chaikovskogo'. In: I. Glebov, *Instrumental´noe tvorchestvo Chaikovskogo* (1922): 57–63 [see *2310*].

[*4970*] BLOM, E. W. 'Works for solo instrument and orchestra'. In: *Tchaikovsky: A symposium* (1945): 47–73 [see *586*].

[*4971*] GERMAIN, J. & GOLEA, A. 'Les concerti de Tchaikowsky', *Disques*, 3 (15 Sep 1950): 623–624.

[*4972*] SARADZHEV, K. S. 'Protiv iskazheniia avtorskogo teksta', *Sovetskaia muzyka* (1951), 1: 64.
A letter to the editor, in which the author argues against restoring the 'authentic' texts of Chaikovskii's concertos in the complete editon of his works [see *118*]. See also *4973, 4974, 4975*.

[*4973*] MOSTRAS, K. & OISTRAKH, D. 'Tribuna: K voprosu o redaktsii muzykal´nykh tekstov', *Sovetskaia muzyka* (1951), 5: 84–85.
Response to *4972*.

[*4974*] GOL´DENVEIZER, A. 'V zashchitu avtorskogo teksta', *Sovetskaia muzyka* (1951), 5: 85.

[*4975*] GAUK, A. 'Vosstanovit´ avtorskii tekst', *Sovetskaia muzyka* (1951), 5: 86.

[4976] HERBAGE, J. 'Peter Ilich Tchaikovsky'. In: R. Hill, *The concerto*. Ed. by Ralph Hill. London: Penguin Books, 1952: 219–233.

— [repr.] Westport, Conn.: Greenwood Press, 1978: 219–233.

[4977] KLOIBER, R. 'Tschaikowsky'. In: R. Kloiber, *Handbuch des Instrumentalkonzerts*. Band 2. Wiesbaden: Breitkopf & Härtel, 1973: 153–171.

[4978] BROWN, D. 'The concerto in pre-revolutionary Russia'. In: *A companion to the concerto*. Ed. by Robert Layton. London: Christopher Helm, 1988: 177–202.

— [repr.] In: *A guide to the concerto*. Ed. by Robert Layton. Oxford; New York: Oxford Univ. Press, 1996: 177–202.

[4979] BEADLE, J. J. 'The strange story of the concertos', *Classic CD* (1993), 42: 16–17 [Nov suppl.], illus.

[4980] ROEDER, M. T. 'Piotr Ilich Tchaikovsky'. In: M. T. Roeder, *A history of the concerto*. Portland, Or.: Amadeus Press [1994]: 293–298.

[4981] STEINBERG, M. 'Piotr Ilych Tchaikovsky'. In: M. Steinberg, *The concerto: A listener's guide*. New York: Oxford Univ. Press, 1998: 471–491.

See also *4424*.

5.4.2. Piano & Orchestra

[4982] DRUSKIN, M. S. *Fortepiannye kontserty Chaikovskogo*. Leningrad: Leningradskaia filarmoniia, 1938. 36 p, illus. (*Putevoditel´ po kontsertam*).

[4983] FISKE, R. E. 'Tchaikovsky's later piano concertos', *Musical Opinion*, 62 (Oct 1938): 17–18; (Nov 1938): 114–115; (Dec 1938): 209–210; music.

Concertos Nos. 2 and 3, the Concert Fantasia, and the Andante and Finale.

[4984] VOLLMER, E. 'Tschaikowsky's Klavierkonzerte: Unter besonderer Berücksichtigung seines Klaviersatzes'. [n. p., 1956]. iv, 88 p.

Dissertation.

[4985] NIEBUHR, U. 'Der Einfluß Anton Rubensteins auf die Klavierkonzerte Peter Tschaikowskys', *Die Musikforschung*, 27 (1974), 4: 412–434, illus.

[4986] HALL, D. 'Tchaikovsky's piano concertos', *Stereo Review*, 32 (Jan 1974): 112.

Comparison of recordings.

[4987] NORRIS, J. 'The Piano Concertos of Peter Tchaikovsky'. In: *The Russian piano concerto*. Vol. 1: *The nineteenth century*. Bloomington, Ind.: Indiana Univ. Press [1994]: 114–185, illus.

Reviews: J. Belanger, *Choice*, 32 (Nov 1994): 466 — *Music & Letters*, 76 (1995), 3: 455–457.

[4988] 'Tchaikovsky reconsidered: Andrei Hoteev talks to Martin Anderson', *Fanfare*, 22 (Mar/Apr 1999): 74.

In connection with Andrei Hoteev's complete recordings of Chaikovskii's works for piano with orchestra.

See also *5347*.

CONCERT FANTASIA
For piano with orchestra, Op. 56 (1884)

[4989] 'Desiatoe simfonicheskoe sobranie RMO', *Moskovskie vedomosti* (25 Feb 1885).

The first performance of the Fantasia on 22 Feb 1885 in Moscow. See also *4990*.

[*4990*]   **T. 'Teatr i muzyka'**, *Russkie vedomosti* (27 Feb 1885).

[*4991*]   **[KIUI, Ts. A.] 'Simfonicheskie sobraniia Russkogo muzykal´nogo obshchestva'**, *Muzykal´noe obozrenie* (10 Apr 1886): 201–203.

The first performance in St. Petersburg on 4 Apr 1886.

See also *5614*.

FANTASIA ON GYPSY MELODIES
Composed by S. Menter/F. Liszt. Arranged by Chaikovskii for piano with orchestra (1892)

[*4992*]   **'Iskusstvo i literatura'**, *Odesskii vestnik* (25 Jan 1893).

The first performance on 23 Jan 1893 in Odessa, by Sophie Menter, cond. Chaikovskii.

[*4993*]   **KISELEV, V. A. 'Posledniaia instrumentovka'**, *Sovetskaia muzyka* (1968), 11: 116–117.

[*4994*]   **HARDEN, I. 'Liszt oder Menter'**, *Hifi Stereophonie*, 21 (Feb 1982): 183.

[*4995*]   **HOLLAND, B. 'Is it really Liszt?'**, *New York Times* (1 Apr 1982).
— [repr.] *Journal of the American Liszt Society*, 11 (1982): 106.

[*4996*]   **HINSON, M. 'Long lost Liszt Concerto?'**, *Journal of the Amercian Liszt Society*, 13 (1983): 53–58, illus.

[*4997*]   **ECKHARDT, M. 'Uj Liszt-zongoraverseny?'**, *Muzsika*, 26 (Mar 1983): 6–7, music, illus.

PIANO CONCERTO NO. 1
Op. 23 (1875, rev. 1879, 1889)

[*4997a*]   **'The von Bülow concert'**, *Boston Globe* (26 Oct. 1875).

The first performance in Boston on 13/25 Oct 1875, given by Hans von Bülow. See also 'Concerts', *Dwight's Journal of Music*, 35 (13 Nov 1875): 125–126 — *New York Tribune* (23 Nov 1875) — *New York Times* (23 Nov 1875).

[*4998*]   **M[AKARO]V, P. 'Pervyi kontsert Russkogo muzykal´nogo obshchestva'**, *Muzykal´nyi svet* (Nov 1875), 19: 7–8.

The first performance in St. Petersburg on 1 Nov 1875. See also *4999* to *5002*.

[*4999*]   **'Teatr i muzyka: Pervoe simfoncheskoe sobranie'**, *Birzhevye vedomosti* (5 Nov 1875).

[*5000*]   **SOLOV´EV, N. F. 'Muzykal´noe obozrenie'**, *Novoe vremia* (5 Nov 1875).

[*5001*]   **LAROSH, G. A. '4, 5, 6-i kontserty Muzykal´nogo obshchestva'**, *Golos* (5 Nov 1875).
— [repr.] In: G. A. Larosh, *Sobranie muzykal´no-kriticheskikh statei*, tom 2, chast´ 2 (1924): 33–34 [see *2311*].
— [repr.] 'O fortepiannom kontserte (b-moll), Op. 23'. In: G. A. Larosh, *Izbrannye stat´i v piati vypuskakh*, vyp. 2 (1975): 78–79 [see *2376*].
— [German tr.] 'Über Tschaikowskys Klavierkonzert b-Moll, Op. 23'. In: G. A. Larosh, *Peter Tschaikowsky: Aufsätze und Erinnerungen* (1993): 89–90 [see *2406*].

[*5002*]   **[KIUI, Ts. A.] 'Pervyi kvartet i pervyi kontsert Russkogo muzykal´nogo obshchestva'**, *Sankt Peterburgskie vedomosti* (6 Nov 1875).

[*5003*]   **'Teatr i muzyka'**, *Sankt Peterburgskie vedomosti* (19 Nov 1875).

Reports of the first performance of the concerto on 13/25 Oct 1875 in Boston, USA. See also *5006*.

[*5004*]   **FAMINTSYN, A. 'Peterburgskaia khronika'** *Muzykal´nyi listok* (1875/76), 7: 105–109, 11: 169–173.

The first performance in Moscow on 21 Nov 1875. See also *5005*.

[5005]   'Izvestiia iz Rossii', *Muzykal´nyi listok* (1875/76), 5: 76–77.

[5006]   'Zagranichnye izvestiia', *Muzykal´nyi listok* (1875/76), 6: 92–94.

[5007]   **[Fortepiannyi kontsert Chaikovskogo]**, *Muzykal´nyi svet* (14 Mar 1876).
         The first performance in London, on 28 Feb/11 Mar 1876.

[5008]   **[La première concert russe]**, *Art musical* (31 Aug/12 Sep 1878).
         The first performance in Paris, on 28 Aug/9 Sep 1878. See also *5009* to *5013*.

[5009]   **[La première concert russe]**, *La Gazette Musicale* (3/15 Sep 1878).

[5010]   **[La première concert russe]**, *Le Ménestrel* (3/15 Sep 1878).

[5011]   **[La première concert russe]**, *La Gazette Musicale* (7/19 Sep 1878).

[5012]   **[La première concert russe]**, *Le Moniteur Universal* (22 Sep/3 Oct 1878).

[5013]   **[La première concert russe]**, *La Gazette Musicale* (25 Sep/6 Oct 1878).

[5014]   **LEVENSON, O. Ia.** 'Chaikovskii: B-moll´nyi f-p kontsert'. In: O. Ia. Levenson, *V kontsertnoi zale*.
         Moskva, 1880: 14–16.

[5015]   **[KIUI, Ts. A.]** 'Simfonicheskie sobraniia Russkogo muzykal´nogo obshchestva', *Muzykal´noe
         obozrenie* (20 Mar 1886): 177–178.

[5016]   **'The end of the Festival: M. Tschaikowsky has another ovation at the Music Hall'**, *New York
         World* (28 Apr/10 May 1891).
         The first performace in New York, on 27 Apr/9 May 1891, conducted by Chaikovskii. See also *1846*.

[5017]   **EVANS, E.** 'Tchaikovsky analyses: 2. Piano concerto in B flat minor, op. 23', *Musical Standard*
         [illus. series], 28 (3 Aug 1907): 73–76, music.

[5018]   **BLOM, E. W.** 'Piano Concerto No. 1, in B flat minor (op. 23)'. In: E. W. Blom, *Tchaikovsky:
         Orchestral works* (1927): 13–23 [see *4366*].

[5019]   **NEWMARCH, R. H.** 'Tchaikovsky: Concerto no. 1, in B flat minor, op. 23, for pianoforte and
         orchestra'. In: R. H. Newmarch, *The concert-goer's library of descriptive notes*. Part I: *Symphonies, overtures,
         concertos*. London: Oxford Univ. Press; H. Milford, 1928: 102–105.

[5020]   **MAREK, G.** 'It will never be so good: Piano Concerto in B flat minor', *Good Housekeeping*, 113 (Oct
         1941): 12–13.

[5021]   **BLOM, E. W.** 'A sin of omission', *Monthly Musical Record*, 73 (Mar/Apr 1943): 60–62.

[5022]   **MAREK, G.** 'Most popular piano concerto: Tchaikovsky's First Concerto', *Good Housekeeping*, 126
         (Apr 1948): 4–5, illus.

[5023]   **'Tchaikovsky's First Piano Concerto: World premiere took place in Boston on October 25,
         1875'**, *Etude*, 67 (Jul 1949): 405.

[5024]   **'When Boston first heard Tchaikovsky'**, *Boston Symphony Orchestra Concert Bulletin* (15 Dec 1950),
         8: 367–368.

[5025]   **'Tchaikovsky note'**, *Music Journal*, 10 (Feb 1952): 51.

[5026]   **SVETOZAROV, D. A.** 'Opyt ispolnitel´skogo analiza pervogo fortepiannogo kontserta
         Chaikovskogo'. Leningrad: Gos. konservatorii im. N. A. Rimskogo-Korsakova, 1954. 16 p.
         Summary of dissertation (Leningrad Conservatory).

[5027]   GRAVES, N. R. 'Christmas concerto: The story of the famous B-flat minor piano concerto',
         Etude, 72 (Dec 1954): 11, illus.

[5028]   CHASINS, A. 'Tchaikovsky's pianistic warhorse', *Saturday Review*, 38 (31 Dec 1955): 38–39.

[5029]   OBORIN, L. 'Klassicheskie instrumental´nye kontserty: Pervyi fortep´iannyi kontsert P. I.
         Chaikovskogo', *Muzykal´naia zhizn´* (1958), 5: 3–4, illus.

[5030]   SOKOL´SKII, M. 'Velikii kontsert', *Komsomol´skaia pravda* (6 Aug 1959): 4.

[5031]   DAN´KO, L. 'Gimn zhizni i radosti: K 120-letiiu so dnia rozhdeniia P. I. Chaikovskogo',
         Muzykal´naia zhizn´ (1960), 9: 12–13, music, illus.

[5032]   NIKOLAEV, A. *Pervyi fortepiannyi kontsert Chaikovskogo*. Moskva: Gos. muz. izdat., 1960. 40 p, illus.
         (*K mezhdunarodomu konkursu im. P. I. Chaikovskogo*).

[5033]   AKSEL´ROD, G. 'Ob ispolnenii Pervogo kontserta dlia fortepiano P. I. Chaikovskogo'. In:
         Voprosy fortepiannogo ispolnitel´stva. Vyp. 2. Moskva: Muzyka, 1968: 113–125.

[5034]   GOL´DENVEIZER A., NEIGAUZ, G. & FEINBERG, S. 'Nekotorye zamechaniia po povodu
         ispolneniia kontserta Chaikovskogo'. In: *Voprosy fortepiannogo ispolitel´stva*. Vyp. 2. Moskva: Muzyka,
         1968: 126–152.

[5035]   FRISKIN, J. 'The text of Tchaikovsky's B flat minor concerto', *Music & Letters*, 50 (Apr 1969), 2:
         246–251, music, illus.
         After the author's death the unfinished article was completed by Mrs Friskin and Malcolm Frager.

[5036]   KHENTOVA, S. 'Kontsert Chaikovskogo', *Verchernii Leningrad* (15 Feb 1969): 2–3.

[5037]   ENTELIS, L. 'Pervyi kontsert Chaikovskogo', *Smena* (12 Nov 1971): 4.

[5038]   EIL´BERKVIT, M. 'Biografiia shedevra', *Sovetskaia kul´tura* (17 May 1974): 4.

[5039]   LIMMERT, E. 'Tschaikowskij-Aufnahme mit Lazar Berman', *Opern Welt* (Jul 1976), 7: 51.

[5040]   FAUCHEREAU, S. 'Tchaikovsky Concerto Nr. 1', *Quinzaine littéraire*, 291 (1978): 24.

[5041]   BLOK, V. M. 'Fortepiannye kontserty Chaikovskogo', *Muzykal´naia zhizn´* (May 1978), 9: 15–17.

[5042]   VERMEULEN, E. 'Een verouderde kritiek?: J. C. Hol over Tsjaikowski's Eerste Pianoconcert',
         Mens en melodie, 33 (Jul 1978): 227–230.

[5043]   GARDEN, E. 'Three Russian piano concertos', *Music & Letters*, 60 (1979), 2: 174–179, illus.

[5044]   NIKOLAEVA, A. 'Vozvrashchenie k originalu', *Sovetskaia muzyka* (1980), 10: 91–92.
         Comparing the three versions of the concerto.

[5045]   GARDEN, E. 'A Note on Tchaikovsky's First Piano Concerto', *Musical Times*, 122 (Apr 1981): 238–
         239.

[5046]   MACDONALD, H. 'Tchaikovsky's First Piano Concerto', *Musical Times*, 122 (1981): 366.

[5047]   BROWN, D. 'Tchaikovsky's First Piano Concerto', *Musical Times*, 122 (1981): 524.

[5048]   ZAJACZKOWSKI, H. 'Letters to the editor: Tchaikovsky's First Piano Concerto', *Musical Times*,
         123 (Feb 1982): 89–90.

[5049]   FEOFANOV, D. 'Tchaikovsky's First Piano Concerto', *American Music Teacher*, 34 (1984/85), 4: 34–
         35, music, illus.
         Comparison of the printed editions with the original score.

[5050] NORRIS, J. 'The piano concertos of Anton Rubinstein', *Music Review*, 46 (1985), 4: 266–269, music.

[5051] ZEMTSOVSKII, I. *Po sledam vesnianki iz fortepiannogo kontserta P. Chaikovskogo: Istoricheskaia morfologiia narodnoi pesni*. Leningrad: Muzyka, 1987. 128 p, music.
Review: *Ethnomusicology*, 34 (1990), 1: 163–165.

[5052] BAKHIDOV, A. A. 'P. Chaikovskii "Kontsert dlia fortepiano s orkestrom No. 1: Final. Analiz'.
In: A. A. Bakhidov, *Fortepiannoe iskusstvo i fol'klor*. Tiflis, 1988: 31–39.

[5053] SLIUSARENKO, T. 'Besedy o muzyke: Rubezh', *Muzykal'naia zhizn'* (1988), 6: 19–21, illus.

[5054] SLEZAK, P. 'Tschaikowskys Klavierkonzert Nr 1 fehlerhaft?', *Orchester*, 36 (May 1988), 5: 493–494, music, illus.

[5055] GREENFIELD, E. 'Building a library: Tchaikovsky's Piano Concerto No. 1', *BBC Music Magazine*, 4 (1996), 5: 49–51.

[5056] ABRAHAM, G. E. H. 'Tchaikovsky: Piano Concerto, op. 23, in B flat minor'. In: *The musician's guide to symphonic music: Essays from the Eulenberg scores*. Corey Field, ed. Mainz; New York: Schott, 1997: 639–641.

See also *480, 4567, 4840, 5593, 5616.*

PIANO CONCERTO NO. 2
Op. 44 (1879–80)

[5056a] 'Philharmonic Society Concert', *New York Times* (13 Nov 1881).
The world premiere of the Concerto, given by Madeleine Schiller in New York on 31 Oct/12 Nov 1881.

[5057] [Pervyi simfonicheskii kontsert], *Moskovskie vedomosti* (19 May 1882).
Preview of the first performance in Moscow, on 21 May 1882.

[5058] KARATYGIN, V. '2-i kontsert A. Ziloti', *Rech'* (27 Oct 1915).
A detrimental review of the concerto. See also *5059*.

[5059] ZAGORSKII, E. V. 'Pis'mo v redaktsiiu', *Russkaia muzykal'naia gazeta* (8 Nov 1915), 45: 711–712.
Response to *5058*.

[5060] KRAVCHENKO, T. P. 'Vtoroi i tretii kontserty dlia fortepiano s orkestrom P. I. Chaikovskogo'.
Leningrad, 1954. 10 p. (*Leningradskaia ordena Lenina Gos. konservatoriia im. N. A. Rimskogo-Korsakova. Kafedra spetsial'nogo fortepiano*).
Summary of dissertation (Leningrad Conservatory).

[5061] KRAVCHENKO, T. 'O redaktsiiakh vtorogo kontserta dlia fortepiano s orkestrom P. I. Chaikovskogo'. In: *Voprosy muzykal'no-ispolnitel'skogo iskusstva*. Vyp. 2. Moskva: Muzgiz, 1958: 341–373.

[5062] 'Notes from our correspondents', *High Fidelity*, 15 (May 1965): 16.

[5063] SHAW, G. B. 'Tchaikovsky: Concerto No. 2, 2 May 1890'. In: G. B. Shaw, *The great composers: Reviews and bombardments*. Ed. with an introduction by Louis Crompton. Berkeley: Univ. of California Press [1978]: 152.

[5064] BRUBACH, H. 'Balanchine's Tchaikovsky', *Atlantic Monthly*, 247 (Jun 1981), 6: 90–94, illus.
George Balanchine's choreography of Chaikovskii's *Piano Concerto No. 2*. See also *5065, 5066, 5602 to 5605*.

[*5065*]   MORK, E. 'Tchaikovsky's Piano Concerto No. 2', *Dance Magazine*, 56 (Sep 1993): 90.

[*5066*]   WHITAKER, R. 'Tchaikovsky's Piano Concerto No. 2', *Ballet Review*, 23 (fall 1995), 3: 49–50.

[*5067*]   LLOYD-JONES, D. 'Tchaikovsky: Piano Concerto No. 2 in G, op. 44'. In: *The musician's guide to symphonic music: Essays from the Eulenberg scores*. Corey Field, ed. Mainz; New York: Schott, 1997: 642–644.

See also *4622* to *4627*.

PIANO CONCERTO NO. 3
Op. 75 (1893)

[*5068*]   KORESHCHENKO, A. N. 'P. I. Chaikovskii: Dva posmertnykh sochineniia', *Moskovskie vedomosti* (27 Sep 1894): 3.

Concerning Chaikovskii's unfinished sketches for the Piano Concerto No. 3 and the duet scena for an opera on *Romeo and Juliet* (both later completed by Sergei Taneev).

— [repr.] In: *Kritika i muzykoznanie: Sbornik statei*. Vyp. 2. Leningrad: Muzyka, 1980: 249–252.

[*5069*]   'Teatr i muzyka', *Novoe vremia* (9 Jan 1895): 3.

The first performance of the concerto on 7 Jan 1895 in St. Petersburg. See also *5070*.

[*5070*]   'Muzykal´noe obozrenie', *Nuvellist* (Feb 1895), 2: 1–2.

[*5071*]   'Tchaikovsky: Piano Concerto No. 3 in E flat major, op. 75', *Musical Courier*, 142 (15 Nov 1950): 31.

[*5072*]   LIMMERT, E. 'Unbekannter Tchaikowsky', *Das Orchester*, 6 (1958): 45.

— [repr.] *Neue Zeitschrift für Musik*, 119 (Feb 1958): 85.

[*5073*]   'Notes from our correspondents', *High Fidelity*, 15 (May 1965): 16.

[*5074*]   SENIOR, E. 'Mixed music', *Music and Musicians*, 17 (Dec 1968): 57.

[*5075*]   'Speaking of records: A 'new' Tchaikovsky piano concerto' (1972), *High Fidelity*, 22 (Mar 1972): 14.

First recording of the Concerto with Taneev's completion of the Andante and Finale (Michael Ponti, Radio Luxembourg Orch).

See also *5060, 5584, 5585, 5586*.

5.4.3. Violin & Orchestra

[*5076*]   RAABEN, L. N. *Skripichnye i violonchel´nye proizvedeniia P. I. Chaikovskogo*. Moskva: Gos. muz. izdat., 1958. 119 p, music, illus.

Mainly dealing with the works for violin or cello with orchestra.

[*5077*]   KRAULKIS, G. V. *Skripichnye proizvedeniia P. I. Chaikovskogo*. Moskva: Gos. muz. izdat., 1961. 50 p. (*K mezhdunarodnomu konkursu im P. I. Chaikovskogo*).

[*5078*]   TUROK, P. 'Tchaikovsky: Violin Concerto, "Serenade Melancholique", "Valse-Scherzo"', *Music Journal*, 36 (1978), 9: 28.

[*5079*]   TURNER, B. C. 'Tchaikovsky'. In: *The living violin*. New York: Knopf, 1996 + 1 CD. ISBN: 0–6798–8177–8.

Intended for younger readers.

SÉRÉNADE MÉLANCOLIQUE
For violin with orchestra, Op. 26 (1875)

[5080] IVANOV, M. M. 'Peterburgskaia khronika', *Muzykal'nyi listok* (1876/77), 5: 70–73.

The first performance of the *Sérénade* in St. Petersburg on 6 Nov 1876.

See also *5081, 5082, 5083*.

VALSE-SCHERZO
For violin with orchestra, Op. 34 (1877)

[5081] [3-me concert russe], *Le Voltaire* (13/25 Sep 1878).

The first performance of the *Valse-scherzo* and the *Sérénade mélancolique* in Paris on 8/20 Sep 1878. See also *5082, 5083*.

[5082] [3-me concert russe], *La Gazette Musicale* (17/29 Sep 1878).

[5083] [3-me concert russe], *Le Ménestrel* (17/29 Sep 1878).

[5084] SIN'KOVSKAIA, N. N. 'Iz tvorcheskoi istorii "Val'sa-skertso" dlia skripki s orkestrom op. 34 Chaikovskogo'. In: *P. I. Chaikovskii: Nasledie*, vyp. 1 (2000): 67–76 [see *603*].

See also *182, 5746*.

VIOLIN CONCERTO
Op. 35 (1878)

[5085] BERGRUEN, O. [Tschaikowskys Violinkonzert], *Morgen Post* (23 Nov/5 Dec 1881).

The first performance on 22 Nov/4 Dec 1881 in Vienna. See also *5086* to *5095*.

[5086] GOERING, F. [Tschaikowskys Violinkonzert], *Deutsche Zeitung* (24 Nov/6 Dec 1881).

[5087] SPIEDLER, L. [Tschaikowskys Violinkonzert], *Fremdenblatt* (24 Nov/6 Dec 1881).

[5088] FREI, W. [Tschaikowskys Violinkonzert], *Neues Wiener Tageblatt* (25 Nov/7 Dec 1881).

[5089] WÖRTZ, D. [Tschaikowskys Violinkonzert], *Wiener Sonn- und Montagszeitung* (26 Nov/8 Dec 1881).

[5090] FF [Tschaikowskys Violinkonzert], *Wiener Abendpost* (27 Nov/9 Dec 1881).

[5091] HELM, T. [Tschaikowskys Violinkonzert], *Wiener Signale* (28 Nov/10 Dec 1881).

[5092] BEER, M. [Tschaikowskys Violinkonzert], *Deutsche Kunst- und Musikzeitung* (1/13 Dec 1881).

[5093] KALBECK, M. [Tschaikowskys Violinkonzert], *Wiener Allgemeine Zeitung* (8/20 Dec 1881).

[5094] HANSLICK, E. 'Tschaikowskys Violin-Konzert, Op. 35 (Herr Brodsky)', *Neue Freie Presse* (12/24 Dec 1881).

— [repr.] In: E. Hanslick, *Concerte, Componisten und Virtuosen der letzten fünfzehn Jahre, 1870–1885*. Kritiken von Eduard Hanslick. Berlin: Allgemeiner Verein für Deutsche Literatur, 1886: 295–296.

— [repr.] Berlin: Allgemeiner Verein für Deutsche Literatur, 1896: 295–296.

— [repr.] Farnborough: Gregg International, 1971: 295–296.

— [repr.] 'Die Tschaikowsky-Rezensionen'. In: *Tschaikowsky aus der Nähe* (1994): 197–198 [see *379*].

[5095] IGNOTUS [FLEROV, S. V.], 'Muzykal'naia khronika', *Moskovskie vedomosti* (20 Dec 1881).

[*5096*]   "MOLODOI MUZYKANT" [KRUGLIKOV, S. N.]. 'Muzykal´naia khronika', *Sovremennye izvestiia*
(14 Aug 1882).

The first performance of the *Violin Concerto* and *The Year 1812* and *The Tempest*, in Moscow on 8 Aug 1882.
See also *5097*.

[*5097*]   L[EVENSON], O. 'Muzykal´naia khronika', *Russkie vedomosti* (15 Aug 1882).

[*5098*]   'Teatralnoe ekho: Poslednii simfonicheskii kontsert v Pavlovske', *Peterburgskaia gazeta* (28 Aug
1894).

[*5099*]   NEWMARCH, R. H. 'Tchaikovsky: Concerto in D (op. 35), for violin and orchestra'. In: R. H.
Newmarch, *The concert-goer's library of descriptive notes*. Part IV: *Symphonies, overtures, concertos*. London:
Oxford Univ. Press; H. Milford, 1931: 121–123.

[*5100*]   RICH, T. 'Master lesson upon "Canzonetta" from Concerto, op. 35 in D major', *Etude*, 58 (Jun
1940): 388–400, music.

[*5101*]   MAKAROV, V. A. *Konsert dlia skripki P. I. Chaikovskogo: Poiasnenie*. Moskva: Gos. muz. izdat.,
1954. 32 p, music. (*V pomoshch´ slushateliu muzyki*).

[*5102*]   RAABEN, L. 'Ob ispolnenii skripichnogo kontserta Chaikovskogo'. In: *O muzykal´nom
ispolnitel´stve*. Moskva, 1954: 256–278.

[*5103*]   IAMPOL´SKII, I. 'Kontsert dlia skripki s orkestrom P. I. Chaikovskogo', *Muzykal´naia zhizn´*
(1958), 5: 3–4.

[*5104*]   BOOKSPAN, M. 'Tchaikovsky's Violin Concerto in D major', *Stereo Review*, 4 (Jan 1960): 18–19.

[*5105*]   KRUMMACHER, F. 'Virtuosität und Komponisten im Violinkonzert: Probleme der Gattung
zwischen Beethoven und Brahms', *Neue Zeitschrift für Musik*, 135 (1974), 10: 604–613.

[*5106*]   FAUCHEREAU, S. 'Tchaikovsky Concerto pour violon', *Quinzaine littéraire*, 291 (1978): 24.

[*5107*]   BLOK, V. M. 'Skripichnyi kontsert P. Chaikovskogo', *Muzykal´naia zhizn´* (Mar 1979), 5: 15–17,
music.

[*5108*]   CHANG, M. S. 'The Tchaikovsky Violin Concerto, op. 35 in D major: An interpretive study of
the first movement'. Philadelphia: Temple Univ., 1988. 100 p.

Dissertation (D. M. A.).

[*5109*]   'Classical reviews', *High Fidelity*, 39 (Jun 1989): 71.

[*5110*]   BROWN, D. 'In the beginning', *Strad* (Jul 1989), 100: 551–552.

[*5111*]   FORREST, J. 'Spoilt for choice: The Tchaikovsky Violin Concerto on CD—and before', *Strad*,
100 (Jul 1989): 553–554.

Survey of recordings.

[*5112*]   SHIRINSKII, A. 'Problemy interpretatsii skripichnogo kontserta P. I. Chaikovskogo'. In: *Muzyka
P. I. Chaikovskogo: Voprosy interpretatsii* (1991): 60–71 [see *594*].

[*5113*]   SOLNTSEV, V. 'Skripichnye kontserty P. I. Chaikovskogo i I. Bramsa (k probleme
natsional´nykh osobennostei kompozitorskogo myshleniia)'. In: *Russkaia muzyka IX–XX vekov v
kontekste traditsii kul´tury Vostok-Zapad: Tezisy Vsesoiuznoi konferentsii, 5–7 maia 1991 g*. Novosibirsk: Gos.
konservatoriia im. M. I. Glinki, 1991: 98–100 (*Zapadno-russkie muzykal´nye sviazi*).

[*5114*]   DENTON, D. 'Tchaikovsky's Violin Concerto', *Strad*, 103 (Apr 1992): 368–369, illus.

A survey of 40 available recordings.

[5115]   JAMESON, M. 'Tchaikovsky: Violin Concerto', *Classic CD* (Aug 1995), 64: 36–39, illus.

[5116]   SHPINITSKAIA, Iu. N. 'O natsional´nykh traditsiiakh v skripichnykh kontsertakh Chaikovskogo i Glazunova'. In: *Glazunov, Nil´sen, Sibelius: Zhizn´, tvorchestvo, epokha (K 130-letiiu so dnia rozhdeniia).* Petrozavodsk, 1996: 14–15.

[5117]   LLOYD-JONES, D. 'Tchaikovsky's Violin Concerto'. In: *The musician's guide to symphonic music: Essays from the Eulenberg scores.* Corey Field, ed. Mainz; New York: Schott, 1997: 672–674.

[5118]   DENTON, D. 'Tchaikovsky's Violin Concerto in D major', *Strad*, 108 (Nov 1997): 1265.

See also *1731, 5612, 5617.*

5.4.4. Cello & Orchestra

[5119]   STOGORSKII, A. 'Po povodu akademicheskogo izdaniia Chaikovskogo', *Sovetskaia muzyka* (1959), 1: 100–103, music.

Concerning the critical edition of the works for cello with orchestra, published in vols. 30B and 55B of P. I. Chaikovskii, *Polnoe sobranie sochinenii* (1956), prepared by Viktor Kubatskii [see *118*].

[5120]   GAIDAMOVICH, T. A. *Violonchel´nye p´esy Chaikovskogo—Violonchel´nyi kontsert Gliera.* Moskva: Gos. muz. izdat., 1963. 35 p. (*Biblioteka slushatelia kontsertov*).

A study of Chaikovskii's cello works and Gliére's Cello Concerto, Op. 87.

See also *5076.*

NOCTURNE
Arranged for cello with orchestra by Chaikovskii (1888)

[5121]   NEWMAN, M. 'Tchaikovsky: "Nocturne" in D minor, op. 19, no. 4', *Strad*, 100 (May 1989): 405.

PEZZO CAPRICCIOSO
For cello with orchestra, Op. 62 (1887)

[5122]   KONIUS, G. 'Ekstrennoe sobranie Russkogo muzykal´nogo obshchestva (25 noiabria)', *Moskovskie vedomosti* (27 Nov 1889).

The first performance in Moscow on 25 Nov 1889. See also *5123.*

[5123]   KASHKIN, N. D. 'Teatr i muzyka', *Russkie vedomosti* (28 Nov 1889).

VARIATIONS ON A ROCOCO THEME
For cello with orchestra, Op. 33 (1876)

[5124]   KUBATSKII, V. 'Vosstanovlennyi Chaikovskii', *Izvestiia* (7 Dec 1940): 4.

The reconstruction of Chaikovskii's original score of the *Variations on a Rococo Theme.*

[5125]   IAMPOL´SKII, I. M. 'Neopublikovannye rukopisi "Variatsii na temu rokoko" Chaikovskogo'. In: *Sovetskaia muzyka: 3-i sbornik statei.* Moskva; Leningrad, 1945: 32–44.

— [repr.] In: I. M. Iampol´skii: *Izbrannye issledovaniia i stat´i.* Moskva: Sovetskii kompozitor, 1985: 110–119.

[5126]   MONTAGU-NATHAN, M. 'Displaced variations', *Strad*, 57 (Aug 1946): 108–114.

[5127]   STANFIELD, M. B. 'Some 'cellistic landmarks', *Violins and Violinists*, 11 (Mar/Apr 1950): 127–128.

[*5128*] DOBROKHOTOV, B. 'Notograficheskie zametki: "Variatsii na temu rokoko"', *Sovetskaia muzyka* (1955), 2: 148–149.
First publication of the original score of the Variations, edited by Aleksandr Stogorskii. See also *5129, 5130*.

[*5129*] [KNUSHEVITSKII, S.] 'Zamechaniia o redaktsii "Variatsii na temu rokoko" Chaikovskogo', *Sovetskaia muzyka* (1956), 7: 150–152, music, illus.

[*5130*] STOGORSKII, A. 'Pis´ma v redaktsiiu: Eshche o "Variatsiiakh na temu rokoko"', *Sovetskaia muzyka* (1956), 11: 151–154.
Response to *5129*.

[*5131*] FYODOROVA, Z. 'They found what Tchaikovsky really wrote', *Music and Musicians*, 5 (Jul 1957): 11, illus.
Deals with Fitzenhagen's alterations to the text of the Variations.

[*5132*] KOTLER, Iu. 'Vtoroe rozhdenie "Variatsii"', *Komsomol´skaia pravda* (18 Aug 1957).
The reconstruction of the original text of the Variations by Viktor Kubatskii.

[*5133*] 'Von Manuskripten und ihren seltsamen Shicksalen', *Musica*, 11 (Nov 1957): 667.

[*5134*] CHERVOV, B. 'Ob ispolnenii "Variatsii na temu rokoko" P. I. Chaikovskogo'. In: *Ukrainskoe muzykovedenie: Nauchnyi mezvedomstvennyi ezhegodnik*. Gl. 2, red. Z. A. Dashak. Kiev: Muzyka Ukraina, 1967: 25–41, music.

[*5135*] 'Pablo Kazal´o o "Variatsiiakh" Chaikovskogo', *Muzykal´naia zhizn´* (1974), 11: 19.
Publication of a letter of 6 Nov 1954 from Pablo Casals to A. Stogorskii concerning the original edition of the cello-piano arrangement of Chaikovskii's Rococo Variations.

[*5136*] STOGORSKII, A. 'Pis´mo v redaktsiiu: "Variatsii na temu rokoko" (sud´ba bessmertnogo shedevra)', *Muzykal´naia zhizn´* (1983), 21: 16.

[*5137*] KEENER, A. 'Original "Rococo"', *Strad*, 94 (Aug 1983): 241–242.
First recording of the original version (Raphael Wallfisch and the English Chamber Orchestra.)

[*5138*] PACEY, M. 'Concert notes: London', *Strad*, 96 (Oct 1985): 391.

[*5139*] BLOK, V. M. 'K istorii znamenitykh "Variatsii"', *Muzykal´naia zhizn´* (1990), 23: 19.

[*5140*] GAIDAMOVICH, T. 'Dva varianta odnogo sochineniia, dva varianta ego interpretatsii: "Variatsii na temu rokoko"'. In: *Chaikovskii: K 150-letiiu so dnia rozhdeniia. Voprosy istorii, teorii i ispolnitel´stva* (1990): 104–119 [see *591*].

[*5141*] TOBIAS, P. '"Rococo" at variance', *Strad*, 104 (Sep 1993): 814–819.

[*5142*] DENTON, D. 'A "Rococo" round-up', *Strad*, 104 (Sep 1993): 876–878.
Survey of 15 recordings.

[*5143*] MATTERN, J. 'The Tchaikovsky Rococo Variations: Its versions and editions'. Bloomington: Indiana Univ., 1994. ix, 196 p.
Thesis (D. Mus.).

[*5144*] TOMMASINI, A. 'A cellist unearths a rarity', *New York Times* (31 May 1997).
The original score of the variations, performed by Carter Bray.

[*5145*] BRUEGGE, J. '"Mozartismen" in Peter I. Tschaikowskys "Rokoko-Variationen, op. 33": Ein Beitrag zur Mozartrezeption im 19. Jahrhundert', *Acta Mozartiana*, 45 (Jul 1998): 1–9.

See also *111, 5696*.

5.5. VOCAL WORKS

5.5.1. Choral

[5146] LISITSYN, M. A. 'P. I. Chaikovskii kak dukhovnyi kompozitor', *Russkaia muzykal´naia gazeta* (Sep 1897), 9: 1199–1214.

[5147] PREOBRAZHENSKII, A. 'Iz "Slovaria russkogo tserkovnogo peniia"', *Russkaia muzykal´naia gazeta* (1897): 628–630.
A short evaluation of Chaikovskii as a composer of church music.

[5148] KONINSKII, K. M. 'Chaikovskii o russkoi tserkovnoi muzyke', *Russkaia muzykal´naia gazeta* (9 Jan 1899), 2: 50–52.

[5149] TITKOV, V. 'Pis´mo v redaktsiiu', *Russkaia muzykal´naia gazeta* (30 Sep 1900). 40: 924.
Concerning Chaikovskii's choral harmonisation of the folk-song 'Tis Not the Wind That Bends the Branch'.

[5150] KOMPANEISKII, N. 'Sankt-Peterburg: Khronika', *Russkaia muzykal´naia gazeta* (30 Mar 1903), 13: 380–388.
Includes a section on Chaikovskii as a composer of church music.

[5151] NIKOL´SKII, A. V. 'P. I. Chaikovskii kak dukhovnyi kompozitor', *Muzyka i zhizn´* (1908), 9: 4–8; 10: 6–9; 11: 4–8.
— [repr. (abridged)] *Muzykal´naia zhizn´* (1990), 9: 12–13.

[5152] MARTSENKO, N. F. *P. I. Chaikovskii v nashei tserkovnoi muzyke: Muzykal´no-kriticheskii ocherk.* Odessa: Odesskikh regentskikh kursov, 1913. 30 p.
Review: *Bibliograficheskii listok Russkoi muzykal´noi gazety*, 8 (1913): 73.

[5153] ABRAHAM, G. E. H. 'Religious and other choral music'. In: *Tchaikovsky: A symposium* (1945): 230–235 [see *586*].

[5154] VANSON, F. 'Tchaikovsky: Church composer', *Choir*, 53 (Oct 1962): 177.

[5155] PONOMAR´KOV, I. P. 'Khorovoe tvorchestvo P. I. Chaikovskogo'. In: *Russkaia khorovaia literatura: Ocherki.* Vyp. 2. Pod red. S. V. Popova. Moskva: Muzyka, 1969: 108–148, music.

[5156] KRYLOV, A. 'O khorakh a kapella Chaikovskogo'. In: *Khorovoe iskusstvo.* Vyp. 3. Leningrad: Muzyka, 1977: 114–128.

[5157] ADISHCHEV, V. I. 'Khorovaia kul´tura Prikam´ia i tvorchestvo P. I. Chaikovskogo'. In: *P. I. Chaikovskii i Ural* (1983): 45–49 [see *1749*].

[5158] RAKHMANOVA, M. P. 'Ogromnoe i eshche edva tronutoe pole deiatel´nosti', *Sovetskaia muzyka* (1990), 6: 67–74, music [see *592*].
Chaikovskii's sacred choral works, published in P. I. Chaikovskii, *Polnoe sobranie sochinenii*, tom 63 (1990) [see *118*].

[5159] RAKHMANOVA, M. P. 'Uwagi o muzyce cerkiewnej Piotra Czajkowskiego' / 'On Tchaikovsky's Orthodox Church music', *Muzyka*, 39 (1994), 1: 89–108, music.
Text in Polish, with a summary in English.

[5160] MOROSAN, V. 'The sacred choral works of Peter Tchaikovsky'. In: *Peter Tchaikovsky: The complete sacred choral works* (1996): xli–cxix [see *121*].

[*5161*]   DOLSKAYA, O. 'Tchaikovsky's roots in the Russian choral tradition'. In: *Tchaikovsky and his contemporaries* (1999): 189–196 [see *602*].

[*5162*]   KEARNEY, L. 'Truth vs. beauty: Comparative text settings by Musorgsky and Tchaikovsky'. In: *Tchaikovsky and his contemporaries* (1999): 129–135.

[*5163*]   MOROSAN, V. 'A stranger in a strange land: Tchaikovsky as a composer of church music'. In: *Tchaikovsky and his contemporaries* (1999): 197–226 [see *602*].

[*5164*]   LEVANDO, P. P. 'K voprosu o "dukhovnom" i "svetskom" v khorovoi muzyke P. Chaikovskogo'. In: *P. I. Chaikovskii: Nasledie*, vyp. 1 (2000): 100–112 [see *603*].

[*5165*]   TIKHONOVA, I. E. 'Cherta khorovogo pis´ma P. I. Chaikovskogo (na primere svetskikh khorov a cappella)'. In: *P. I. Chaikovskii: Nasledie*, vyp. 1 (2000): 113–139 [see *603*].

See also *2596*.

ALL-NIGHT VIGIL

For unaccompanied voices, Op. 52 (1881–82)

[*5166*]   KOHLHASE, T. 'Tschaikowsky als Kirchenmusiker: Die Vsenoščnaja und ihre liturgischen Vorlagen'. In: *Festschrift Georg von Dadelsen zum 60. Geburtstag*. Neuhausen-Stuttgart, 1978: 189–229, music.

[*5167*]   MAL´SHEVA, T. F. 'Kanonicheskie osnovy "Vsenoshchnogo bdeniia" i ikh traktovke P. I. Chaikovskim'. In: *Otechestvennaia kul´tura XX veka i dukhovnaia muzyka*. Rostov-na-Donu, 1990: 130–132.

[*5168*]   KOHLHASE, T. 'Petr I. Cajkovskij: Ein Erneurer der mehrstimmigen Russishcen Kirchenmusik. II. "Die Vsenoščnaja", Op. 52, und einzelne Chöre', *Hermeneia*, 6 (1990), 1: 6.

[*5169*]   KOHLHASE, T. '"Russische Samen säen...": Peter I. Cajkovskijs ursprüngliches Vorwort zur "Ganznächtlichen Vigil" wiederntdeckt', *Neue Zeitschrift für Musik*, 151 (May 1990): 16–21, music, illus.

[*5170*]   CHERNUSHENKO, V. 'Kak molitva vsevyshnemu', *Peterburgskaia panorama* (1993), 6: 4–5.

[*5171*]   PROTOPOPOV, V. 'Muzyka prednachinatel´nogo psalma vo "Vsenoshchnom bdenii"', *Muzykal´naia akademiia* (1999), 1: 1–7.

Settings of the Vigil by Chaikovskii, Sergei Rakhmaninov and Aleksei L´vov.

CANTATA FOR THE OPENING OF THE POLYTECHNIC EXPOSITION

For chorus, orchestra and tenor solo (1872)

[*5172*]   'Otkrytie Politekhnicheskoi vystavki', *Moskovskie vedomosti* (1 Jun 1872).

The first performance of the cantata on 31 May 1872 at the opening of the Moscow Polytechnic Exposition. See also *5173*, *5174*.

[*5173*]   'Moskovskaia Politekhnicheskaia vystavka', *Azovskii vestnik* (4 Jun 1872).

[*5174*]   'Muzykal´nyi otdel na Politekhnicheskoi vystavke v Moskve', *Nuvellist* (Jul 1872), 7: 54–55.

[*5175*]   'Kantata dlia otkrytiia Politekhnicheskoi vystavki', *Russkaia muzykal´naia gazeta* (16/23 Jan 1905), 3/4: 89.

[5176] 'Neopublikovannaia kantata Chaikovskogo', *Sovetskoe iskusstvo* (8 Jan 1949): 3.

Report of a lecture by Semën Bogatyrev concerning the cantata. See also *5179*.

[5177] 'An unpublished cantata discovered', *Musical Courier* (1 Mar 1949), 139: 15.

[5178] 'Unpublished Tchaikovsky cantata found in former home', *Musical America*, 69 (Jul 1949): 34.

[5179] BOGATYREV, S. S. 'O kantate P. I. Chaikovskogo "Na otkrytie Politekhnicheskoi vystavki v 1872 godu"'. In: *S. S. Bogatyrev: Issledovaniia, stat´i, vospominaniia*. Red.-sost. G. A. Tiumeneva i Iu. N. Kholopov. Moskva: Sovetskii kompozitor, 1972: 130–143.

[5180] BOGUSLAVSKII, G. 'Pamiatnoe sobytie: K izucheniiu tvorcheskoi biografii P. I. Chaikovskogo', *Sovetskaia muzyka* (1980), 7: 90–93.

CANTATA FOR THE JUBILEE OF O. A. PETROV
For soloist, chorus and orchestra (1875)

[5181] 'Izvestiia iz Rossii', *Muzykal´nyi listok* (1875/76): 233.

The first performance of the cantata, on 24 Apr 1876 in St. Petersburg.

CHORUS OF FLOWERS AND INSECTS
For mixed and children's voices with orchestra (1869–70)

[5182] LAROSH, G. A. 'Muzykal´naia khronika', *Sovremennaia letopis´* (25 Jan 1871): 13.

The first performance of the chorus, on 18 Dec 1870 in Moscow.

— [repr.] In: G. A. Larosh, *Sobranie muzykal´no-kriticheskikh statei*, tom 2, chast´ 2 (1924): 16 [see *2311*].

— [repr.] 'Khor el´fov (tsvetov i nasekomykh) iz opery "Mandragora"'. In: G. A. Larosh, *Izbrannye stat´i v piati vypuskakh*, vyp. 2 (1975): 32 [see *2376*].

[5183] [KIUI, Ts. A.] 'Muzykal´nye zametki: Vtoroi kontsert Besplatnoi shkoly', *Sankt Peterburgskie vedomosti* (11 Jan 1872).

The first performance in St. Petersburg on 18 Dec 1871.

—[repr.] In: Ts. A. Kiui, *Izbrannye stat´i*. Leningrad, 1952: 191–194.

[5184] GR[ODZ]KII, B. V. 'P. Chaikovskii: Khor tsvetov i nasekomykh iz opery "Mandragora"', *Nuvellist* (Sep 1904), 9: 5.

Publication of the full score by Iurgenson, in an orchestration by Aleksandr Glazunov. See also *5185*.

[5185] L. 'P. Chaikovskii (Posmertnoe izd.). Khor tsvetov i nasekomykh iz opery "Mandragora". Izd. P. Iurgensona', *Russkaia muzykal´naia gazeta* (19 Nov 1904), 46: 1102.

THE GOLDEN CLOUD DID SLEEP
Chorus (1887)

[5186] 'The manuscript of Chaikovskii's song', *Musical Times*, 108 (Jul 1967): 595.

GREETING TO A. G. RUBINSHTEIN
Chorus (1889)

[5187] 'Neizvestnyi avtograf P. I. Chaikovskogo'. In: *Iz fondov kabineta rukopisei: Publikatsii i obzory*. Sost. i otvetstvennyi red. G. V. Kopytova, Sankt Peterburg: Rossiiskii Institut istorii iskusstv, 1998: 15–22.

A four-bar fragment of the chorus, written by Chaikovskii on the back of a poem by Iakov Polonskii in 1889. Includes facsimile.

LEGEND

Children's song, arr. for mixed voices (1889)

[*5188*]   **'Chorus singing without orchestra at the Festival'**, *Morning Journal* (27 Apr/9 May 1891).

The first performance in New York on 26 Apr/8 May 1891, conducted by Chaikovskii.

LITURGY OF ST. JOHN CHRYSOSTOM

For unaccompanied voices, Op. 41 (1878)

[*5189*]   **'Peterburgskaia khronika'**, *Sovremennost´* (3 May 1879).

[*5190*]   **["Liturgiia" Chaikovskogo v universitetskoi tserkvi]**, *Kievlianin* (17 May 1879).

Previewing the first performance of the Liturgy in Kiev.

[*5191*]   **VASIL´EV, S. '"Liturgiia sv. Ioanna Zlatoustogo' v muzykal´nom perelozhenii g. Chaikovskogo'**, *Moskovskie vedomosti* (22 Jun 1879).

The first performance of the Liturgy in Jun 1879 in Kiev.

[*5192*]   **'Peterburgskaia khronika'**, *Sovremennost´* (26 Jun 1879).

On the legal proceedings surrounding the confiscation of Iurgenson's editions. See also *5193, 5194, 5195*.

[*5193*]   **'Vnutrennie novosti'**, *Golos* (28 Jun 1879).

[*5194*]   **'Peterburgskaia letopis´'**, *Syn Otechestva* (29 Jun 1879).

[*5195*]   **'Strannyi sluchai s sochineniem g. Chaikovskogo'**, *Novosti* (29 Jul 1879).

[*5196*]   **LAROSH, G. A. 'Muzykal´nye ocherki: "Liturgiia sv. Ioanna Zlatoustogo" dlia 4-golosnogo smeshannogo khora'**, *Russkii vestnik* (Jan 1880), 1: 416–427.

Publication of the score by Iurgenson, after delays caused by the legal proceedings. See also *5197*.

— [repr.] In: G. A. Larosh, *Izbrannye stat´i v piati vypuskakh*, vyp. 2 (1975): 109–118 [see *2376*].

— [German tr.] 'Die "Liturgie des heiligen Johannes Chysostomus" für vierstimmigen gemischten Chor, Op. 41 von Peter Tschaikowsky'. In: G. A. Larosh, *Peter Tschaikowsky: Aufsätze und Erinnerungen* (1993): 115–126 [see *2406*].

[*5197*]   **REGENT. '"Liturgiia sv. Ioanna Zlatousta" dlia chetyrekhgolosnogo smeshannogo khora: Sochinenie P. Chaikovskogo'**, *Russkii muzykal´nyi vestnik* (22 Apr 1880): 2; (1 May 1880): 2; (15 May 1880): 1–2; (22 May 1880): 2–3; (1 Jun 1880): 1–3.

— [repr.] *Russkii muzykal´nyi listok* (1880), Nos. 1, 2, 3, 5, 6.

[*5198*]   **L[EVENSON], O. 'Muzykal´naia khronika'**, *Russkie vedomosti* (15 Dec 1880).

[*5199*]   **'Posledniaia pochta'**, *Moskovskie vedomosti* (19 Dec 1880).

The first public performance in Moscow, on 18 Dec 1880.

[*5200*]   **AMVROSIIA [KLIUCHAREV, A. I.] 'Dukhovnyi kontsert v zale Rossiiskogo Blagorodnogo sobraniia'**, *Rus´* (3 Jan 1881), 8: 13–14.

A letter to the editor, criticising Chaikovskii for 'daring' to write the *Liturgy*.

[*5201*]   **IGNOTUS [FLEROV, S. V.] 'Muzykal´naia khronika'**, *Moskovskie vedomosti* (3 Jan 1881).

[*5202*]   **LEVENSON, O. ["Liturgiia" P. I. Chaikovskogo]**, *Russkie vedomosti* (8 Jan 1881).

[*5203*]   **RE, SI, SOL. '"Liturgiia" Chaikovskogo'**, *Sovremennye izvestiia* (22 Jan 1881).

[*5204*]   **[KIUI, Ts. A.] 'Chetvertaia kontsertnaia nedeliia'**, *Golos* (17 Mar 1882): 2.

[5205]   'Kontsertnoe obozrenie', *Nuvellist* (Apr 1882), 4: 3–4.

[5206]   SMOLENSKII, S. V. 'O "Liturgii", op. 41, soch. Chaikovskogo: Iz istoriko-iuridicheskikh vospominanii', *Russkaia muzykal´naia gazeta* (19 Oct 1903), 42: 991–998; (26 Oct 1903), 43: 1009–1023.

   — [offprint] *'O "Liturgii", op. 41, soch. Chaikovskogo: Iz literaturno-iuridicheskikh vospominanii'.* Sankt Peterburg: Izdat. Russkaia muzykal´naia gazeta, 1903. 33 p.

[5207]   STROM, F. 'The Tchaikovsky choral settings of the "Liturgy of St. John Chrysostom"', New York: Univ. of Rochester, 1948.

   Thesis (M. M.), Eastman School of Music.

[5208]   RABENECK, N. 'Liturgy by Tchaikovsky performed at Russian church service', *Musical Courier*, 157 (Feb 1958): 16.

[5209]   BECKWITH, R. S. 'Choral music in the liturgy: How to write a Russian mass', *American Choral Review*, 10 (sum. 1968): 4: 178–185.

   Includes a table outlining the order of worship for the liturgy.

[5210]   GOLEA, A. 'Au festival de Dubrovnik: Un Tchaikowsky inconnu', *Journal Musical Français* (Nov 1969), 186: 29.

[5211]   FREEMAN, J. W. 'Tchaikovsky: "Liturgy of St. John Chysostom"', *Opera News*, 44 (8 Dec 1979): 28.

[5212]   RAKHMANOVA, M. P. 'Muzykal´naia restavratsiia: Kontsertnoe obozrenie', *Sovetskaia muzyka* (1981), 6: 98–99.

[5213]   CHERNUSHENKO, V. '"Veruiu": O "Liturgii" Chaikovskogo', *Muzykal´naia zhizn´* (1988), 21: 19–20, illus.

[5214]   KOHLHASE, T. 'Petr I. Cajkovskij: Ein Erneurer der mehrstimmigen Russishcen Kirchenmusik. I. Die "Liturgie", Op. 41', *Hermeneia*, 5 (1989), 1: 6.

[5215]   VARVARINA, M. 'Voskreshënnaia "Liturgiia"', *Novoe vremia* (1990), No. 39: 47.

   The revival of Chaikovskiii's Liturgy.

[5216]   MALININA, G. 'Nachalo dukhovnogo vozrozhdeniia'. In: *Chaikovskii: Voprosy istorii i teorii* (1991): 79–94 [see *593*].

MOSCOW
Coronation cantata (1883)

[5217]   IVANOV, M. M. 'Muzykal´noe obozrenie', *Nuvellist* (Feb 1884), 2: 5.

   The first performance of the cantata in St. Petersburg, on 8 Jan 1884.

[5218]   *Kantata napisannaia ko dniu sviashchennogo koronovanniia ikh Imperatorskikh velichestv Gosudaria Imperatora i Gosudaryni Imperatritsy.* Stikhi A. Maikova. Muzyka P. Chaikovskogo (13 fevral´ia 1894 g., Moskva). Sankt Peterburg, 1894. 14 p.

   The words of the cantata, as used at the Coronation of Tsar Nikolai II in 1894.

[5219]   KHUBOV, G. '"Moskva": Kantata Chaikovskogo', *Literatura i iskusstvo* (8 Feb 1942).

   — [repr.] In: G. Khubov, *Muzykal´naia publitsistika raznykh let.* Moskva: Sovetskii kompozitor, 1976: 226–228.

[5220]   SHEKHONINA, I. & POPOV, I. 'Temy Moskvy v muzyke', *Sovetskoe iskusstvo* (5 Sep 1947): 3.

   Includes a section on the cantata *Moscow*.

[*5221*] BELLINGARDI, L. 'Rachmaninoff's "Vesna" and Tchaikovsky's "Moskva"', *Opera*, 43 (Feb 1992): 216.

[*5222*] KIREEV, D. 'Rossii doch´ liubima', *Muzykal´naia zhizn´* (1997), 9: 27–28.
The history of the cantata.

[*5223*] FRUMKIS, T. 'Kantata P. I. Chaikovskogo "Moskva": (ne)sluchainyi tekst v (ne)sluchainom kontekste'. In: *Moskva i moskovskii tekst russkoi kul´tury: Sbornik statei.* Otv. red. G. S. Knabe. Moskva: Rossiiskii Gos. gumanitarnyi institut, 1998: 119–136, illus.
— [German tr.] 'P. I. Čajkovskijs Kantate "Moskva"', *Tschaikowsky-Gesellschaft Mitteilungen*, 7 (2000): 47–61.

NINE CHURCH PIECES
For unaccompanied voices (1884–85)

[*5224*] KOMPANEISKII, N. 'Kontsert pridvornoi pevcheskoi kapelly', *Russkaia muzykal´naia gazeta* (Feb 1902): 143–144.
Includes a review of 'Blessed are they whom thou hast chosen' (No. 7).

[*5225*] KOMPANEISKII, N. '"Zadostoinik" Turchaninova i "Dostoino" Chaikovskogo', *Russkaia muzykal´naia gazeta* (May 1902), 18/19: 514–519.
Concerning 'It is truly fitting' (No. 5).

[*5226*] KOMPANEISKII, N. 'Tserkovno-pevcheskoe delo: "Kheruvimskaia pesn´ No. 3" (C-dur) P. I. Chaikovskogo'. In: *Russkaia muzykal´naia gazeta* (31 Oct 1904), 44: 1019–1023.

[*5227*] 'Reviewed in brief: "Tebe poyem" ("We hymn thee"), Peter Tchaikovsky, P. Chesnokov (arr.)', *Choral Journal*, 37 (Dec 1996), 5: 70.

ODE TO JOY
Music to Schiller's hymn (1865)

[*5228*] [KIUI, Ts. A.] 'Muzykal´nye zametki: Konservatorskie solisty i kompozitor', *Sankt Peterburgskie vedomosti* (24 Mar 1866).
The first performance of the cantata, on 29 Dec 1865 in St. Petersburg.

[*5229*] 'Auffindung einer unbekannten Vertonung von Schillers "Lied an die Freude" durch Peter Tschaikowsky im Archiv des Leningrader Konservatoriums', *Allgemeine Musik Zeitung*, 63 (1936), 402.
The discovery of the MS of the cantata in the library of the St. Petersburg Conservatory. See also *5229*.
— [repr.] *Die Musik-Woche*, 4 (1936), 22: 21.

[*5230*] 'Dnevnik iskusstv', *Izvestiia* (15 May 1936): 4.

[*5231*] GROMOV, M. 'Vtoroe rozhdenie', *Ogonek* (1949), 36: 28.
Comparing the first performance of the cantata in 1865, and a radio broadcast performance in 1949.

[*5232*] 'Rare Tchaikovsky and Elgar', *Music & Musicians*, 27 (Nov 1978): 30–31.

SPRING
Chorus (1871)

[*5233*] NIKITIN, K. N. 'Ob odnom khore P. I. Chaikovskogo, schitavshemsia uteriannym'. In: *P. I. Chaikovskii: Zabytoe i novoe* (1995): 136–144 [see *598*].
Concerning the choruses *Spring* and *Evening*.

THREE CHORUSES
For unaccompanied voices (1891)

[5234] VAIDMAN, P. E. 'Tri nabroska P. I. Chaikovskogo', *Sovetskaia muzyka* (1979), 2: 98–101.

The composer's sketches for the chorus *Without Time, Without Season*, formerly believed to be for the *Symphony No. 5*.

5.5.2. Songs & Duets

[5235] TIMOFEEV, G. N. 'Ocherk razvitiia russkogo romansa: Lektsiia, chitannaia 23 fevr. 1895 g.', *Russkaia muzykal´naia gazeta* (1895): 362–368.

Includes: 'Romansovoe tvorchestvo Chaikovskogo': 362–365.

[5236] KIUI, Ts. A. 'Russkii romans: Chaikovskii', *Nedelia* (18 Jun 1895); (25 Jun 1895).

See also *5261*.

— [repr.] 'P. I. Chaikovskii (1840–1893)'. In: Ts. A. Kiui, *Russkii romans: Ocherk ego razvitiia*. Sankt Peterburg: N. F. Findeizen, 1896: 108–135.

— [English tr.] 'The Russian Romance: Peter Il´ich Chaikovsky'. Tr. by James Walker. In: *Classical Essays on the development of the Russian art song*. [Northfield, Minn.]: J. Walker, 1993: 61-75.

[5237] NEWMAN, E. 'Tschaikowsky as a song-writer', *Monthly Musical Record*, 31 (Aug 1901): 173–175.

— [repr.] *Musical Standard* [illus. series], 16 (10 Aug 1901): 87–88.

[5238] FINDEIZEN, N. F. 'Chaikovskii'. In: N. F. Findeizen, *Russkaia khudozhestvennaia pesnia (romans): Istoricheskii orcherk ee razvitiia*. Moskva; Leipzig: P. Iurgenson, 1905: 66–71, music.

— [English tr.] 'Peter Il´ich Chaikovskii'. Tr. by James Walker. In: *Classical Essays on the development of the Russian art song*. [Northfield, Minn.]: J. Walker, 1993: 83–90.

[5239] ASAF´EV, B. V. 'Russkii romans XIX veka'. In: B. V. Asaf´ev, *Russkaia muzyka ot nachala XIX stoletiia*. Moskva; Leningrad: Academia, 1930: 80–84.

— [repr.] In: B. V. Asaf´ev, *Izbrannye trudy*, tom 2 (1954): 182–183 [see *2348*].

— [repr.] In: B. V. Asaf´ev, *Russkaia muzyka: XIX v nachalo XX veka*. Leningrad, 1968: 36–40; 2-e izd. Leningrad, 1979: 37–41.

[5240] [ABRAHAM, G. E. H.]. 'Tchaikovsky as a song-writer', *The Listener*, 16 (21 Oct 1936): 788.

[5241] AL´SHVANG, A. A. *Romansy i pesni Chaikovskogo*. [Moskva]: Moskovskaia Gos. filarmoniia, 1938. 13 p.

[5242] AL´SHVANG, A. A. 'Romansy P. I. Chaikovskogo', *Sovetskaia muzyka* (1939), 9/10: 100–122; (1940), 1: 14–27.

— [English tr. (abridged)] 'The Songs'. In: *Tchaikovsky: A symposium* (1945): 197–229 [see *586*].

[5243] 'Dva neopublikovannykh romansa P. I. Chaikovskogo', *Sovetskaia muzyka* (1940), 5/6: 133–137 [see *585*].

Includes: "Moi genii, moi angel, moi drug": 133–134 — "Pesnia Zemfiry": 135–137.

[5244] SHUL´MAN, M. 'Romansy Chaikovskogo', *Dekada moskovskikh zrelishch* (1940), 2: 20.

[5245] TSUKKERMAN, V. 'Vyrazitel´nye sredstva liriki Chaikovskogo', *Sovetskaia muzyka* (1940), 9: 49–67, music.

[5246] EVANS, E. 'Tchaikovsky's songs', *The Listener*, 23 (25 Apr 1940): 856.

[*5247*]   'Neizvestnye romansy P. I. Chaikovskogo', *Sovetskoe iskusstvo* (28 Nov 1944): 1.

A realisation by Boris Asaf´ev of Chaikovskii's sketches for two projected songs: 'Oh no, do not love me just for beauty alone' and 'I saw you in a dream'.

[*5248*]   ORLOVA, E. M. *Romansy Chaikovskogo*. Moskva; Leningrad: Gos. muz. izdat., 1948. 164 p, music.

Includes: 'Perechen´ i kratkaia kharakteristika notnykh eskizov, chernovykh i chistovykh rukopisei romansov, khraniashchikhsia v arkhive P. I. Chaikovskogo v Dome-muzee v Klinu': 139–142 [see *100*].

[*5249*]   VASINA-GROSSMAN, V. A. 'Romansy P. I. Chaikovskogo'. In: V. A. Vasina-Grossman, *Russkii klassicheskii romans XIX veka*. Otv. red. I. F. Belza. Moskva: Izdat. Akademii Nauk SSSR, 1956: 265–298, illus.

[*5250*]   ABRAHAM, G. E. H. 'Russia'. In: D. A. Stevens, *A history of song*. Ed. by D. Stevens. London: Hutchinson [1960]: 338–381, music.

— [repr.] New York: W. W. Norton [1961]. 491 p, illus.

— [repr.] London: Hutchinson, 1971. 491 p, illus. SBN 09–104680–7. (*A Radius Book*)

— [repr.] Westport, Conn: Greenwood Press, 1982. 491 p, music.

— [rev. repr.] 'Russian song'. In: G. E. H. Abraham, *Essays on Russian and East European Music*. Oxford: Clarendon Press; New York: Oxford Univ. Press, 1985: 1–39, music.

[*5251*]   OGOLEVETS, A. 'Vyrazitel´nye sredstva vysshego poriadka v romansakh Chaikovskogo'. In: *Voprosy muzykoznaniia: Sbornik statei*. Moskva, 1960: 165–193.

[*5252*]   RABINOVICH, B. I. 'Neizvestnyi romans P. I. Chaikovskogo', *Muzykal´naia zhizn´*, (1965), 8: 10, music, illus.

Sketches for a romance "Liubi, poka liubit´ ty mozhesh´" ('Love me as much as you can') to words by A. N. Pleshcheev. Includes a facsimile of the autograph and publication of the text. [Later research has concluded that Chaikovskii was not the author of the sketches].

[*5253*]   MAIBUROVA, K. 'Romansy Chaikovskogo i Rakhmaninova na slova Shevchenko'. In: *Shevchenko i muzyka*. Sbornik statei. Kiev: Mistetstvo, 1966: 42–54, music.

[*5254*]   DUNAEVSKII, B. 'Romansy P. I. Chaikovskogo', *Molodezhnaia estrada* (1970), 1: 154–158.

[*5255*]   VLADIMIROV, L. 'Romansy Chaikovskogo: Ekzamen artista', *Sovetskaia muzyka* (1970), 9: 52–53.

A discussion with the Russian tenor Vladimir Atlantov.

[*5256*]   PAVLOVA, G. 'V mire filofonii: Romansy P. I. Chaikovskogo', *Muzykal´naia zhizn´* (1972), 3: 16.

A complete set of Chaikovskii's songs issued on Melodiya gramophone records.

[*5257*]   'P. I. Tchaikovski: Songs', *Recorded Sound* (Apr/Jul 1978), 70–71: 781–788.

A list of Chaikovskii's songs, with opus numbers, and titles in Russian (Cyrillic) and English.

[*5258*]   PEREVERZEV, N. 'Uvelichennye kvarty i umen´shennye kvinty v romansakh P. I. Chaikovskogo: Umen´shennye kvarty v vokal´nom tvorchestve Chaikovskogo'. In: N. Pereverzev, *Ispolnitel´skaia intonatsiia*. Moskva: Muzyka, 1989: 114–137, music.

[*5259*]   LERNER, O. 'Vokal´naia lirika Chaikovskogo v kontsertmeisterskom klasse'. In: *Sbornik metodicheskikh razrabotok po voprosam muzykal´noi pedagogiki i ispolitel´stva*. Sost. V. Sradzhev. Tashkent, 1991: 68–76.

[*5260*]   BELOVA, O. P. 'Romansovaia melodika Chaikovskogo: Mezhdu printsipom stikha i printsipom prozy'. In: *P. I. Chaikovskii: K 100-letiiu so dnia smerti* (1993): 109–116 [see *597*].

[*5261*]   BELOVA, O. P. 'Dialog cherez leta: K voprosu o kritike Kiui romansov Chaikovskogo'. In: *100 let russkoi muzyki (1890–1990): Voprosy teorii, istorii, traditsii i novatorstva*. Red. I. B. Baranova, A. A. Zonderger. Petrozadovsk, 1995: 43–45.

[*5262*]   SKOBTSOVA, Zh. G. 'Prelomlenie bytovykh zhanrov v kamerno-vokal´nom tvorchestve P. I. Chaikovskogo'. In: *Voprosy muzykal´nogo iskusstva: Sbornik statei.* Vyp. 1. Donetsk: Gos. konservatoriia im. S. S. Prokof´eva, 1996: 74–77. (*Iz rabot muzykantov-ispolnitelei*).

[*5263*]   TANNER, M. 'When the lily needs gilding', *Classic CD* (Feb 1996), 70: 50.

[*5264*]   KEARNEY, L. 'Truth vs. beauty: Comparative text settings by Musorgsky and Tchaikovsky'. In: *Tchaikovsky and his contemporaries* (1999): 129–135 [see *602*].

See also *1467, 2126, 5287, 5735*.

CHILDREN'S SONGS ON RUSSIAN AND UKRAINIAN TUNES
Compiled by Mariia Mamontova
Harmonized by Chaikovskii (1872–77)

[*5265*]   [KIUI, Ts. A.] 'Muzykal´naia bibliografiia', *Sankt Peterburgskie vedomosti* (6 Sep 1872).
Concerning the publication of the score by Iurgenson.
— [repr.] In: Ts. A. Kiui, *Izbrannye stat´i.* Leningrad, 1952: 209–213.

[*5266*]   SHCHUROVSKII, P. A. 'Detskie pesni Mamontovoi', *Moskovskie vedomosti* (15 Oct 1872).

See also *5387*.

SEVEN ROMANCES
Op. 47 (1880)

[*5267*]   [KIUI, Ts. A.] 'Chetvertoe simfonicheskoe sobranie Russkogo muzykal´nogo obshchestva', *Grazhdanin* (9 Jan 1888).
A performance of the orchestral version of 'Was I not a little blade of grass in the field?' (No. 7) on 26 Dec 1887 in St. Petersburg.

SIX DUETS
Op. 46 (1880)

[*5268*]   BERRY, C. 'The secular dialogue duet: 1600–1900', *Music Review*, 40 (1979), 4: 280.
On the 'Scottish Ballad (Edward)' (No. 2).

SIX FRENCH SONGS
Op. 65 (1888)

[*5269*]   LAROSH, G. A. 'Sechs Lieder für eine Singstime mit Begleitung des Pianoforte, von P. Tschaikowsky', *Moskovskie vedomosti* (3 Aug 1889): 5, music.
Publication of the score by Rahter.
— [repr.] In: G. A. Larosh, *Izbrannye stat´i v piati vypuskakh*, vyp. 2 (1975): 135–136 [see *2376*].

SIX ROMANCES
Op. 6 (1869)

[*5270*]   [KIUI, Ts. A.] '6 romansov, muzyka P. I. Chaikovskogo, op. 6. Moskva, u P. I. Iurgensona', *Sankt Peterburgskie vedomosti* (25 Apr 1870).

[*5271*]   [KIUI, Ts. A.] 'Muzykal´nyi vecher v pol´zu nedostatochnykh uchenikov konservatorii', *Sankt Peterburgskie vedomosti* (28 Dec 1873).
Concerning 'None But the Lonely Heart' (Op. 6, No. 6) and 'O Sing That Song' (Op. 16, No. 4).

[*5272*]   **[KIUI, Ts. A.]** '**Muzykal´nye zametki**', *Golos* (12 Nov 1876).
            Concerning 'Not a word, o my friend' (No. 2).

[*5273*]   **[KIUI, Ts. A.]** '**Chetvertyi kontsert Russkogo muzykal´nogo obshchestva**', *Golos* (12 Nov 1880):
            1.
            Concerning 'None but the lonely heart' (No. 6).

            See also *3731*.

                                    SIX ROMANCES
                                   Op. 16 (1872–73)

[*5274*]   **[KIUI, Ts. A.]** '**Muzykal´naia bibliografiia**', *Sankt Peterburgskie vedomosti* (20 Apr 1873): 2.
            Publication of the score by Bessel´.

            See also *5271*.

                                    SIX ROMANCES
                                    Op. 25 (1875)

[*5275*]   **LAROSH, G. A.** '**Bibliografiia: Sochineniia P. Chaikovskogo—6 romansov, op. 25**', *Muzykal´nyi*
            listok (19 Oct 1875): 17–20.
            — [repr.] In: G. A. Larosh, *Muzykal´no-kriticheskikh statei*. Sankt Peterburg: V. Bessel´, 1894: 139–143.
            — [repr.] In: G. A. Larosh, *Izbrannye stat´i v piati vypuskakh*, vyp. 2 (1975): 74–77 [see *2376*].

[*5276*]   **[KIUI, Ts. A.]** '**Muzykal´nye zametki: Muzykal´naia bibliografiia**', *Sankt Peterburgskie vedomosti* (9
            Jan 1876): 1.
            Publication of the Six Romances, Op. 25 by Bessel´ and the sets of Six Romances, Op. 27 and Op. 28 by
            Iurgenson.
            — [repr.] In: Ts. A. Kiui, *Izbrannye stat´i*. Leningrad, 1952: 264–267.

                                    SIX ROMANCES
                                    Op. 38 (1878)

[*5277*]   '**Interesno znat´: Posle bala**', *Muzykal´naia zhizn´* (1999), 4: 49.
            Aleksei Tolstoi's poem 'Amid the din of the ball', and its setting by Chaikovskii (No. 3).

                                    SIX ROMANCES
                                    Op. 73 (1893)

[*5278*]   **IV—, W.** '**Chaikovskii i Ratgauz**', *Istorik i sovremennik* (1922), 4: 284–285.

            See also *5556*.

                              SIXTEEN SONGS FOR CHILDREN
                                   Op. 54 (1881–83)

[*5279*]   **IGNOTUS [FLEROV, S. V.]**, '**Muzykal´naia bibliografiia**', *Moskovskie vedomosti* (24 Mar 1884).

[*5280*]   **ROZINER, F.** '**Gde zhivet Lizochek?**', *Muzykal´naia zhizn´* (1970): 22–23.

65 RUSSIAN FOLK-SONGS

Collected by Vladimir Prokunin. Edited by Chaikovskii (1872–73)

[5281]   **[KIUI, Ts. A.] 'Muzykal´naia bibliografiia'**, *Sankt Peterburgskie vedomosti* (1 Mar 1873).
Publication of the score by Iurgenson.

5.6. CHAMBER-INSTRUMENTAL WORKS

5.6.1. Chamber Works

[5282]   **VAL´TER, V. G. 'Kamernaia muzyka P. I. Chaikovskogo'**, *Russkaia muzykal´naia gazeta* (20 Oct 1913), 42: 908–914.

[5283]   **GLEBOV, I. [ASAF´EV, B. V.] 'Kamernyi stil´ Chaikovskogo'**. In: I. Glebov, *Instrumental´noe tvorchestvo Chaikovskogo* (1922): 63–69 [see *2310*].

[5284]   **FINDEIZEN, N. F.** *Kamernaia muzyka Chaikovskogo*. Moskva: Gosizdat-Muzsektor, 1930. 38 p, music.
— [English tr.] 'Tchaikovsky'. In: *Cobbett's cyclopedic survey of chamber music*. Comp. and ed. by Walter Wilson Cobbett. Vol. 2. London: Oxford Univ. Press, 1930: 490–500, music.
— [English tr. (2nd ed.)] In: *Cobbett's cyclopedic survey of chamber music*. Comp. and ed. by Walter Wilson Cobbett. With supplementary material ed. by Colin Mason. London: Oxford Univ. Press, 1963: 490–500, music.

[5285]   **ABRAHAM, G. E. H. 'The story of Russian chamber music'**, *Strad*, 47 (Feb 1937): 445–446.
Mainly concerning Chaikovskii.

[5286]   **MASON, C. 'The chamber music'**. In: *Tchaikovsky: A symposium* (1945): 104–113 [see *586*].

[5827]   **AL´SHVANG, A. A. 'Chamber music'**. In: *Russian symphony: Thoughts about Tchaikovsky* (1947): 160–192 [see *587*].
Includes sections on the songs and solo piano works.

[5288]   **SOKHOR, A.** *Kamernoe tvorchestvo P. I. Chaikovskogo*. Leningrad: Ispolkom Lengorsoveta [1949]. 11 p.

[5289]   **MIASOEDOV, A.** *Instrumental´nyi ansambl´ Chaikovskogo*. Moskva: Gos. filarmoniia, 1958. 16 p. (*V pomoshch´ slushateliam kontsertov*).

[5290]   **RAABEN, L.** *Instrumentalnyi ansambl v russkoi muzyke*. Moskva: Gos. muz. izdat., 1961.

[5291]   **UGRIUMOVA, T. S. 'O dramaturgii tsikla v kvartetakh P. I. Chaikovskogo'**. In: *P. I. Chaikovskii i Ural* (1983): 127–137 [see *1749*].

[5292]   **BERGER, M. 'Tchaikovsky, Peter Ilich'**. In: *Guide to chamber music*. New York: Dodd, Mead, 1985: 437–438. ISBN: 0–3960–8385–4.

[5293]   **SJØQVIST, G. 'Tjajkovskijs kammarmusik'**, *Musikrevy*, 48 (1993), 4: 26–27.

[5294]   **TREZISE, S. 'The unknown chamber music'**, *Classic CD* (1993), 42: 18–19 [Nov suppl.], illus.

[5295]   **KHRAMOVA, I. M. 'Chaikovskii i Shuman: O nekotorykh paralleliakh v traktovke strunnogo kvarteta'**. In: *Russkaia kul´tura i mir: Tezisy dokladov uchastnikov II mezhdunarodnoi nauchnoi konferentsii*. Tom 2. Nizhnii Novgorod: NGLU im. N. A. Dobroliubova, 1994: 167–168.

[5296]   TREZISE, S. 'Tchaikovsky in miniature', *Classic CD* (Mar 1994), 46: 47.

[5297]   AFONINA, N. Iu. 'Vzaimodeistvie ritma i faktury v kvartetakh P. I. Chaikovskogo'. In: *P. I. Chaikovskii: Nasledie*, vyp. 1 (2000): 140–178 [see *603*].

See also *4365, 5662, 5664, 5708.*

PIANO TRIO
Op. 50 (1881–82)

[5298]   L[EVENSO]N, O. 'Muzykal´naia khronika', *Russkie vedomosti* (16 Oct 1882).
The publication of the score by Iurgenson.

[5299]   IGNOTUS [FLEROV, S. V.] 'Muzykal´naia khronika', *Moskovskie vedomosti* (22 Oct 1882).
The first public performance on 18 Oct 1882 in Moscow. See also *5300, 5301*.

[5300]   MOLODOI MUZYKANT [KRUGLIKOV, S. N.] 'Muzykal´naia khronika', *Sovremennye izvestiia* (23 Oct 1882).

[5301]   L[EVENSO]N, O. 'Muzykal´naia khronika', *Russkie vedomosti* (23 Oct 1882).

[5302]   'Muzykal´noe obozrenie', *Muzykal´nyi mir* (8 Dec 1888): 4.

[5303]   HANSLICK, E. 'Tschaikowskys Klaviertrio a-moll, op. 50'. In: E. Hanslick, *Am Ende des Jahrhunderts (1895–1899). Musikalische Kritiken und Schilderungen von Eduard Hanslick*. Berlin, 1899: 228–230.
— [repr.] 'Die Tschaikowsky-Rezensionen'. In: *Tschaikowsky aus der Nähe* (1994): 207–208 [see *379*].

[5304]   R. R. [LAROSH, G. A.] 'Teatr i muzyka', *Rossiia* (23 Nov 1900).
Includes a review of Chaikovskii's Trio.
— [repr. (extract)] In: G. A. Larosh, *Izbrannye stat´i v piati vypuskakh*, vyp. 2 (1975): 331 [see *2376*].

[5305]   EVANS, E. 'Tchaikovsky analyses: 1. The Trio in A minor, op. 50', *Musical Standard* [illus. series], 28 (20 Jul 1907): 41–44, music.

[5306]   'Neopublikovannoe pis´mo S. I. Taneeva', *Sovetskaia muzyka* (1936), 6: 55–62.
Publication of a letter of 5 Feb 1913 from Taneev to A. V. Nikolaev, concerning the the fugue from Chaikovskii's *Piano Trio*.

[5307]   AUERBAKH, L. D. *Trio Chaikovskogo "Pamiati velikogo khudozhnika": Putevoditel´*. Moskva: Muzyka, 1977. 60 p, music. (*Putevoditel´ po operam i baletam*).

[5308]   CRADDOCK, P. 'Piano Trio in A minor, op. 50', *Strad*, 90 (1979): 450.

[5309]   'The Tchaikovsky "Trio": A centennial discography', *Fanfare*, 5 (1981), 2: 261–262.

[5310]   GAIDAMOVICH, T. 'Besedy o muzyke: Trio "Pamiati velikogo khudozhnika', *Muzykal´naia zhizn´* (1982), 5: 15–16.

[5311]   ARUTIUNOV, D. A. 'Trio Chaikovskogo "Pamiati velikogo khudozhnika": Ob evoliutsii avtorskogo otnosheniia k zhanru'. In: *Muzykal´no-ispolitel´skoe iskusstvo: Problemy stilia i interpretatsii*. Sbornik nauchnykh trudov. Moskva: Gos. konservatoriia, 1989: 97–104

[5312]   GAIDAMOVICH, T. 'P. I. Chaikovskii: Trio "Pamiati velikogo khudozhnoka" (k istorii sozdaniia i interpretatsii)'. In: *Muzyka P. I. Chaikovskogo: Voprosy interpretatsii* (1991): 42–59 [see *594*].

[5313]   ALT, Y. C. 'Famous opus 50s', *Classic CD* (Jul 1994), 50: 36–37, illus.

[*5314*] GAIDAMOVICH, T. A. 'Trio Chaikovskogo "Pamiati velikogo khudozhnika" i epitafial´naia traditsiia zhanra'. In: *P. I. Chaikovskii: K 100-letiiu so dnia smerti* (1995): 73–83 [see *597*].

See also *5582, 5583, 5588, 5589*.

SOUVENIR DE FLORENCE
String sextet, Op. 70 (1890, rev. 1891–92)

[*5315*] LEL´. 'Piatoe kvartetnoe sobranie RMO', *Artist* (Jan 1893), 26: 178.

The first performance of the revised sextet in Moscow on 3 Dec 1892.

See also *5670, 5720*.

STRING QUARTET in B-flat major
[in 1 movement] (1865)

[*5316*] BORISOVSKII, V. 'B-dur´nyi kvartet P. I. Chaikovskogo', *Sovetskaia muzyka* (1941), 3: 101.

STRING QUARTET NO. 1
Op. 11 (1871)

[*5317*] 'Raznye izvestiia', *Muzykal´nyi vestnik* (Apr 1871), 4: 8.

The first performance of the quartet on 16 Mar 1871, at a concert of Chaikovskii's works in Moscow. See also *5318*.

[*5318*] LAROSH, G. A. 'Kontsert g. Chaikovskogo, 16 marta', *Sovremennaia letopis´* (12 Apr 1871).
— [repr.] In: G. A. Larosh, *Sobranie muzykal´no-kriticheskikh statei*, tom 2, chast´ 2 (1924): 8–9 [see *2311*].
— [repr.] In: G. A. Larosh, *Izbrannye stat´i v piati vypuskakh*, vyp. 2 (1975): 32–34 [see *2376*].

[*5319*] 'Kontserty Russkogo muzykal´nogo obshchestva i kvartetnye sobraniia', *Muzykal´nyi svet* (Dec 1872), 12: 92–94.

The first performance in St. Petersburg on 24 Oct 1872. See also *5320, 5321*.

[*5320*] 'Khronika', *Muzykal´nyi listok* (1872/73), 7: 118–121.

[*5321*] 'Telegraf: Moskva', *Nuvellist* (Feb 1873), 2: 16.

[*5322*] L[EVENSON], O. 'Pervyi kvartet Chaikovskogo', *Russkie vedomosti* (22 Nov 1880).

[*5323*] [KIUI, Ts. A.] 'Vtoroe sobranie "Russkogo kvarteta"', *Golos* (24 Dec 1880): 2.

[*5324*] [KIUI, Ts. A.] 'Kvartetnye sobraniia' *Golos* (29 Sep 1882): 1.

[*5325*] [KIUI, Ts. A.] 'Pervoe kvartetnoe sobranie Russkogo muzykal´nogo obshchestva (Vtoraia seriia)'. *Muzykal´noe obozrenie* (7 Nov 1885): 49–51.

[*5326*] HANSLICK, E. 'Tschaikowskys Erstes Streichquartett, Op. 11'. In: E. Hanslick, *Concerte, Componisten und Virtuosen der letzten fünfzehn Jahre, 1870–1885*. Kritiken von Eduard Hanslick. Berlin: Allgemeiner Verein für Deutsche Literatur, 1886: 305–306.
— [repr.] Berlin: Allgemeiner Verein für Deutsche Literatur, 1896: 305–306.
— [repr.] Farnborough: Gregg International, 1971: 305–306.
— [repr.] 'Die Tschaikowsky-Rezensionen'. In: *Tschaikowsky aus der Nähe* (1994): 198 [see *379*].

[*5327*] 'Tschaikovsky's Quartet in D major', *The Violinist*, 15 (1913), 1: 23–24.

[5328]   KLEVEZAL´, E. 'Patologicheskie cherty tvorchestva Chaikovskogo', *Ural´skii meditsinskii zhurnal* (1929), 5: 51.

          Analysis of the psychological aspects of the Andante cantabile from the First Quartet.

[5329]   SZESKUS, R. 'Nationale Züge im Schaffen russischer und sowjetischer Komponisten', *Musik in der Schule*, 33 (1982), 11: 360, illus.

[5330]   DAVIDIAN, R. 'Pervyi kvartet Chaikovskogo D-dur, op. 11'. In: R. Davidian, *Kvartetnoe iskusstvo: Problemy ispolnitel´stva teoreticheskie osnovy, prakticheskii opyt*. Moskva, 1994: 281–283.

[5331]   MORTON, M. 'The latest score: "Andante cantabile", op. 11 by Peter Ilyich Tchaikovsky: Transcribed for double bass and piano by Yuri Golubev', *International Society of Bassists*, 20 (win. 1996), 3: 51.

                                    STRING QUARTET NO. 2
                                        Op. 22 (1874)

[5332]   'Vtoroe kvartetnoe sobranie RMO', *Muzykal´nyi listok* (Mar 1874).

          The first public performance of the quartet on 10 Mar 1874 in Moscow.

[5333]   [KIUI, Ts. A.] 'Kvartet No. 2 g. Chaikovskogo'', *Sankt Peterburgskie vedomosti* (6 Nov 1874).

          The first performance in St. Petersburg on 24 Oct 1874. See also *5333*.

[5334]   FAMINTSYN, A. 'Peterburgskaia khronika', *Muzykal´nyi listok* (1874/75), 3: 38–44.

[5335]   'Izvestiia iz Rossii', *Muzykal´nyi listok* (1875/76), 45: 233.

[5336]   'Muzykal´nye novosti', *Muzykal´nyi mir* (29 Jan 1883): 6.

          Performances of String Quartets Nos. 2 and 3 in Cologne, Germany.

[5337]   [ABRAHAM, G. E. H.] 'Tchaikovsky's Quartet in F, op. 22', *The Listener*, 16 (15 Jul 1936): 141–142.

          See also *4568*.

                                    STRING QUARTET NO. 3
                                        Op. 30 (1876)

[5338]   RAZMADZE, A. 'Muzykal´naia khronika', *Russkie vedomosti* (1 Apr 1876).

          The first public performance of the quartet on 18 Mar 1876 in Moscow.

[5339]   [KIUI, Ts. A.] 'Tret´e kvartetnoe sobranie Russkogo muzykal´nogo obshchestva', *Sankt Peterburgskie vedomosti* (26 Oct 1876): 2.

          The first performance in St. Petersburg on 19 Oct 1876. See also *5340*.

[5340]   IVANOV, M. M. 'Peterburgskaia khronika', *Muzykal´nyi listok* (1876/77), 2: 22–24.

[5341]   'Muzykal´naia khronika', *Russkii muzykal´nyi vestnik* (1880), 26: 3.

[5342]   [KIUI, Ts. A.] 'Chetvertoe kvartetnoe i tret´e simfonicheskoe sobranie Russkogo muzykal´nogo obshchestva'. *Golos* (5 Nov 1880): 1.

          See also *5336*.

5.6.2. Piano Works

[5343]   GENIKA, R. V. 'Fortepiannoe tvorchestvo P. I. Chaikovskogo', *Russkaia muzykal´naia gazeta* (1 Jan 1908): 1: 9–12; (13 Jan 1908), 2: 33–40; (3 Feb 1908), 5: 120–125; (17 Feb 1908), 7: 187–192; (16 Mar 1908), 11: 257–260; (23 Mar 1908), 12: 289–294; (28 Apr 1908), 13: 329–332; (25 Oct 1908), 43: 935–944; (2 Nov 1908), 44: 961–967; (9 Nov 1908), 45: 995–996; (23 Nov 1908), 47: 1049–1055; (14 Dec 1908), 50: 1137–1145; (21/28 Dec 1908), 51/52: 1174–1177.

— [offprint] *Fortepiannoe tvorchestvo P. I. Chaikovskogo*. Sankt Peterburg [c.1909]. 131 p.

[5344]   ARONSON, M. 'Tschaikowsky's piano compositions', *Musical Courier*, 66 (1918), 21: 6–7.

[5345]   DRUSKIN, M. 'Fortepiannoe tvorchestvo Chaikovskogo', *Iskusstvo i zhizn´* (1940), 5: 24–25, illus.

[5346]   IGUMNOV, K. 'O fortepiannykh sochineniiakh Chaikovskogo', *Sovetskaia muzyka* (1940), 5/6: 112–113 [see *585*].

[5347]   JOHNSON, T. A. 'The piano works of Tchaikovsky', *Musical Opinion*, 63 (Jul 1940): 438–439.
Includes the piano concertos.

[5348]   DICKINSON, A. E. F. 'The piano music'. In: *Tchaikovsky: A symposium* (1945): 114–123 [see *586*].

[5349]   MIAG, P. 'Tschaikowskys Klaviermusik', *Schweizerische Musikzeitung* (1 Oct 1948): 377–382, music.

[5350]   NIKOLAEV, A. A. *Fortepiannoe nasledie Chaikovskogo*. Moskva; Leningrad: Gos. muz. izdat, 1949. 208 p, music, illus. (*Moskovskaia Gos. ordena Lenina konservatoriia im. P. I. Chaikovskogo; Trudy kafedry istorii pianizma i metodiki obucheniia igre na fortepiano*).
Includes: 'Perechen´ rukopisei fortepiannykh socinenenii P. I. Chaikovskogo khraniashchikhsia v Gos. tsentral´nom muzee muzykal´noi kul´tury im. M. I. Glinki': 204–205 [see *101*] — Kratkaia bibliografiia: 206–207.
Review: T. Livanova, 'Novaia kniga o Chaikovskom', *Sovetskaia muzyka* (1950), 6: 99–102.

— 2-e izd, pererab. Moskva: Gos. muz. izdat., 1958. 285 p, music, illus.
Includes: 'Perechen´ rukopisei fortepiannykh sochinenenii P. I. Chaikovskogo khraniashchikhsia v Gos. tsentral´nom muzee muzykal´noi kul´tury im. M. I. Glinki': 275–277 [see *101*] — 'Kratkaia bibliografiia': 280–282.

[5351]   FROLOVA, S. *Fortepiannye sonaty P. I. Chaikovskogo: Poiasnenie*. Moskva: Gos. muz. izdat., 1955. 40 p, music. (*V pomoshch´ slushateliu muzyki*).

[5352]   NIKOLAEV, A. A. *Fortepiannye proizvedeniia P. I. Chaikovskogo*. Moskva: Gos. muz. izdat., 1957. 72 p, illus.

[5353]   ALEKSEEV, A. D. 'Fortepiannoe tvorchestvo Chaikovskogo: Cherty stilia, p´esy razlichnykh zhanrov, proizvedeniia krupnoi formy'. In: A. D. Alekseev, *Russkaia fortepiannaia muzyka: Konets XIX–nachalo XX veka*. Moskva, 1969: 11–62.

[5354]   ROITERSHTEIN, M. I. 'O edinstve sonatnogo tsikla P. I. Chaikovskogo'. Leningrad: Gos. konservatoriia im. N. A. Rimskogo-Korsakova, 1970. 20 p.
Summary of dissertation (Leningrad Conservatory).

[5355]   KOSTAREV, V. P. 'Stroenie i tematicheskoe razvitie v sonatnykh razrabotkakh proizvedenii P. I. Chaikovskogo'. Leningrad: Gos. Konservatoriia im N. A. Rimskogo-Korsakova, 1973. 21 p.
Summary of dissertation (Leningrad Conservatory).

[5356]   IGUMNOV, K. 'O fortepiannykh sochineniiakh P. I. Chaikovskogo: Stat´i o kompozitorakh'. In: *Pianisty rasskazyvaiut*. Vyp. 1. Sost. M. Sokolov. Moskva: Sovetskii kompozitor, 1979: 201–203.

— 2-e izd. Moskva, 1990: 150–152.

[*5357*] 'Peter (Pjotr) Iljitscha Tschaikowski'. In: *Klaviermusik A–Z*. Hrsg. von Christof Ruger. 1. Aufl. Leipzig: Deutscher Verlag für Musik, 1979: 739–752. (*Konzertbuch*).

— 2., unveranderte Aufl. Leipzig: Deutscher Verlag für Musik, 1982: 739–752. (*Konzertbuch*).

[*5358*] SMIRNOV, M. A. 'Ob odnoi osobennosti ispolneniia fortepiannykh p´es Chaikovskogo'. In: *Voprosy muzykal´noi pedagogiki*. Vyp. 1. Moskva: Muzyka, 1979: 107–114.

[*5359*] OVCHINNIKOV, M. A. 'Problemy pianizma v osmyslenii vedushchikh muzykal´nykh kritikov vtoroi poloviny XIX veka: P. I. Chaikovskii'. In: M. A. Ovchinnikov, *Fortepiannoe ispolnitel´stvo i russkaia muzykal´naia kritika XIX veka*. Moskva: Muzyka, 1987: 162–168.

[*5360*] SOROKINA, E. G. 'Fortepiannye sonaty Chaikovskogo: K probleme stanovleniia klassicheskoi sonaty v russkoi muzyke 2-i poloviny XIX veka'. In: *Chaikovskii: K 150-letiiu so dnia rozhdeniia. Voprosy istorii, teorii i ispolnitel´stva* (1990): 42–57 [see *591*].

[*5361*] MERKULOV, A. 'Chaikovskii: Avtor fortepiannykh obrabotok i nekotorye kontsertnye obrabotki dlia fortepiannoi muzyki Chaikovskogo'. In: *Muzyka P. I. Chaikovskogo: Voprosy interpretatsii* (1991): 115–123 [see *594*].

[*5362*] GALLOTTA, B. 'La musica pianistica di Ciakovskji', *Rassegna Musicale Curci*, 47 (1994), 3: 4–10.

[*5363*] KOHLHASE, T. 'Kritischer Bericht zu Band 69 b der Neuen Čajkovskij-Gesamtausgabe (NČE)'. In: *Čajkovskijs Homosexualität und sein Tod: Legenden und Wirklichkeit* (1998): 439–533 [see *600*].

Includes: 'Kritischer Bericht zur "Grande Sonate" Op. 37': 442–492 — 'Kritischer Bericht zum "Kinderalbum" Op. 39': 493–533.

See also *1467, 5287*.

ALLEGRO in F minor
[unfinished] (1863–64)

[*5364*] VLASOV, V. & KOBLIAKOV, A. 'Novaia stranichka tvorchestva velikogo kompozitora', *Muzykal´naia zhizn´* (19 Oct 1978): 17, music.

Concerning Konstantin Kalinenko's completion of the score.

[*5365*] MATTHEW-WALKER, R. 'A new Tchaikovsky completion', *Musical Times*, 132 (Oct 1991): 498.

Leslie Howard's completion of the score.

[*5366*] REMENETS, N. 'Fortepiannaia sonata P. I. Chaikovskogo fa minor'. In: *P. I. Chaikovskii: Issledovaniia i materialy* (1997): 41–48 [see *599*].

ANASTASIE-VALSE
(1854)

[*5367*] ZAITSEV, P. 'Iunosheskoe proizvedenie P. I. Chaikovskogo', *Den´* (21 Oct 1913) [suppl. *Literatura. Isskustvo. Nauka*].

A description and facsimile of the newly-discovered autograph of the *Anastasie-Valse*, the composer's earliest surviving work.

[*5368*] 'Pervoe muzykal´noe proizvedenie P. I. Chaikovskogo', *Teatr i zhizn´* (25 Oct 1913): 15.

[*5369*] ZAGORNYI, N. N. 'Pervoe sochinenie P. I. Chaikovskogo'. In: *Muzykal´noe nasledstvo*. Sborniki po istorii muzykal´noi kultury SSSR, Moskva: Gos. Muzykal´noe Izd-vo, 1962: 463–464.

Includes the score of the *Valse*: 587–591.

[5370] GORODILINA, V. B. 'Posviashchaetsia Anastasii Petrovoi'. In: *P. I. Chaikovskii i Ural* (1983): 39–44 [see *1749*].

See also *1326*.

CHILDREN'S ALBUM
24 simple pieces, Op. 39 (1878)

[5371] LOVELOCK, W. 'Some practical aids to the better playing of "Mazurka" in D minor by Tschaikowsky', *Piano Student* [new series], 2 (Jun 1936): 198–199, music;
No. 11 from the set.

[5372] LOVELOCK, W. 'Master lessons in miniature: "Sweet dreams" by Tschaikowsky', *Music Teacher*, 16 (Dec 1937): 677–678, music.
Reverie (No. 21).

[5373] TULUPOVA, B. '"Detskii al´bom" P. I. Chaikovskogo'. In: *Nauchnye raboty studentov. Vyp. 3: Gumanitarnye nauki*. Pod obshchei red. G. G. Moshkovich. Krasnodar: Krasnodarskii Gos. pedagogicheskii institut im. 15-letiia VLKSM, 1963: 117–123. (*Nauchnoe studencheskoe obshchestvo*).

[5374] GORSKAIA, E. 'Stranichka shkol´nika: "Detskii al´bom"', *Muzykal´naia zhizn´* (Nov 1965), 22: 22–23, illus.

[5375] KOROLEVA, E. 'O "Detskom al´bome" P. I. Chaikovskogo', *Nachal´naia shkola* (1966), 2: 93–94.

[5376] BLOK, V. M. '"Detskii al´bom" P. I. Chaikovskogo', *Muzykal´naia zhizn´* (May 1977), 10: 14–24, music.

[5377] GORSKAIA, E. '"Detskii al´bom" P. I. Chaikovskogo'. In: *Muzyka i ty: Al´manakh dlia shkol´nikov*. Vyp. 7. Moskva: Sovetskii kompozitorov, 1988: 25–38, illus.

[5378] SCHMITT, R. 'Puppenspiele zu Tschaikowskys Musik: Eine Anregung zu fachübergreifendem Musikunterricht in der Grundschule', *Musik und Bildung*, 20 (Jul/Aug 1988): 597–600, music, illus.

[5379] MOLIN, D. 'Listaia "Iunym o muzyke: Detskii al'bom"', *Muzykal´naia zhizn´* (1990), 1: 19, illus.

[5380] DVILIANSKII, A. Ia. 'P. Chaikovskii: "Utrennee razmyshlenie", soch. 39, no. 1'. In: A. I. Dvilianskii, *Kompleksnyi garmonicheskii analiz: Uchebnik posobie dlia muzykal´nykh uchilishch*. Bishkek: Ilim, 1993: 22–24, music.

[5381] MESROPOVA, M. G. & KANDINSKII-RYBNIKOV, A. A. 'O neopublikovannoi P. I. Chaikovskim pervoi redaktsii "Detskogo al´boma" Chaikovskogo'. In: *Voprosy muzykal´noi pedagogiki*. Vyp. 11. Moskva: Gos. konservatoriia im. P. I. Chaikovskim', 1997: 138–150.

See also *126, 127, 5409*.

DUMKA
Op. 59 (1886)

[5382] LEE, E. M. 'The amateur's repertoire: Tchaikovsky's "Dumka", op. 56' [sic], *Musical Opinion*, 53 (Nov 1929), 136–137, music.

[5383] VAKHIDOV, A. A. 'P. Chaikovskii "Dumka": Analiz'. In: A. A. Vakhidov, *Fortepiannoe iskusstvo i fol´klor*. Tiflis, 1988: 22–31.

FIFTY RUSSIAN FOLK SONGS
Arranged for piano duet by Chaikovskii (1868–69)

[5384] DEM´IANOVA, O. A. '50 russkikh narodnykh pesen v obrabotke Chaikovskogo', *Soobshcheniia Instituta istorii iskusstv*, 15 (1959): 88–117, music.

[5385] DEM´IANOVA, O. A. 'Neizvestnyi avtograf P. Chaikovskogo', *Sovetskaia muzyka* (1960), 5: 80–81, music, illus.

The discovery of Chaikovskii's sketches for the folksongs, in P. Villebois' collection *100 russkikh pesen*.

[5386] LEHMANN, 'Tschaikowsky als Bearbeiter russischer Volkslieder', *Revue Belge de Musicologie*, 19 (1965), 1: 28–52.

[5387] EVSEEV, S. V. *Narodnye pesni v obrabotke P. I. Chaikovskogo*. Red., predislovie i kommentarii B. I. Rabinovicha. Moskva: Muzyka, 1973. 139 p, music.

Includes: 'Ukazatel´´ istochnikov pesen, obrabotannykh Chaikovskim v sbornike "50 pesen". Posleduiushchie obrabotki tekh zhe pesen': 134–136 — 'Ukazate´ istochnikov dlia obrabotok v "Detskikh pesniakh" M. Mamontovoi': 137–138.

GRAND SONATA
Op. 37 (1878)

[5388] L[EVENSON], O. Ia. 'Fortepiannaia sonata Chaikovskogo', *Russkie vedomosti* (20 Oct 1879).

— [repr.] 'Chaikovskii: Fortepiannoe sonata', In: O. Ia. Levenson, *V kontsertnoi zale*. Moskva, 1880: 127–131.

[5389] A. P. 'Kontsert N. G. Rubinshteina', *Moskovskie vedomosti* (16 Mar 1880).

NATHALIE-VALSE
(1878)

[5390] KISELEV, V. A. 'Neizvestnaia rukopis´ Chaikovskogo', *Sovetskoe iskusstvo* (16 Sep 1938): 3.

The discovery of Chaikovskii's autograph score of the waltz.

See also *5420*.

PIANO SONATA in C-sharp minor
Op. 80 (1865)

[5391] 'P. Tschaikowsky: Sonate (Oevure posthume) composée en 1865', *Russkaia muzykal´naia gazeta* (1903), 23/24: 590–591.

Publication of the score by Iurgenson.

ROMANCE
Op. 5 (1868)

[5392] GROELING, C. R. 'New music reviews: Ensemble, "Romance" by Peter I. Tchaikovsky, arr. by Myron Zakopets', *Instrumentalist*, 51 (Feb 1997), 7: 67.

SCHERZO À LA RUSSE
Op. 1, No. 1 (1867)

[5393] 'Tchaikovsky's "Scherzo à la russe"', *Musical Courier*, 140 (Sep 1949): 31.

THE SEASONS
Op. 37-bis (1875–76)

[5394]   G. 'Chaikovskii, prikazhite!', *Peterburgskii listok* (19 May 1876).

Report on the composer's contribution of the pieces to the journal *Nuvellist*.

[5395]   HAMBOURG, M. 'A master lesson on Tchaikovsky's "April"', *Etude*, 68 (Apr 1950): 26, 32–33, music.

[5396]   POLIAKOVA, L. V. *"Vremena goda" P. I. Chaikovskogo: Poiasnenie*. Moskva; Leningrad, 1951. 31 p, music. (*V pomoshch´ slushateliu muzyki*).

Reviews: N. Shakhnazarova, 'Populiarnye broshiury o muzyke', *Sovetskaia muzyka* (1952), 5: 101–103 — A. G. Shnitke, 'O neudachnykh poiasneniiakh L. Poliakovoi', *Vestnik Leningradskoi ordena Lenina Konservatorii*, 1 (1952): 328–334.

— 2-e izd. Moskva: Gos. muz. izdat., 1960. 27 p, music. (*Biblioteka slushatelia kontsertov*).

[5397]   BRECKENRIDGE, W. K, *Anecdotes of great musicians: With a discussion of some works of Schumann and Tchaikovsky*. New York: Pageant Press [1955].

Includes analysis of Chaikovskiii's *The Seasons*.

[5398]   POLIAKOVA, L. "Vremena goda", *Muzykal´naia zhizn´* (1958), 23/24: 17–18.

[5399]   EPSHTEIN, V. M. *"Vremena goda" Chaikovskogo v interpretatsii K. N. Igumnova*. V pomoshch´ studentu-zaochniku. Minsk: Vysheishaia shkola, 1966. 96 p, music. (*Belorossiskaia Gos. konservatoriia*).

[5400]   KHENTOVA, S. "Vremena goda", *Vechernii Leningrad* (18 Jan 1969): 2–3.

[5401]   KURTSMAN, A. 'Stranichka shkol´nika: God nachinaet novyi krug', *Muzykal´naia zhizn´* (1971), 1: 20–21.

[5402]   ASAF´EV, B. V. "Vremena goda". In: B. V. Asaf´ev, *O muzyke Chaikovskogo: Izbrannoe*. Leningrad: Muzyka, 1972: 203–206 [see *2373*].

[5403]   BLAGOI, D. 'Besedy o muzyke: "Vremena goda" Chaikovskogo (k 100-letiiu so vremeni sozdaniia)', *Muzykal´naia zhizn´* (Aug 1976), 16: 8–10, music.

[5404]   ELDER, D. 'Tchaikovsky: "The Seasons"', *Clavier*, 17 (1978), 9: 11.

[5405]   KRESH, P. 'Chef Tchaikovsky's best musical pancakes, with syrup and without', *Stereo Review*, 42 (May 1979): 96.

Comparison of recordings.

[5406]   GORNOSTAEVA, V. "Vremena goda", *Sovetskaia kul´tura* (24 Oct 1980): 6.

[5407]   ALEKSEEVA, A. 'Klub "Muzyka s toboi": "Vremena goda"', *Smena* (1984), 5: 16–19, illus.

[5408]   GORNOSTAEVA, V. 'Muzyka na vse vremena', *Sem´ia i shkola* (1990), 5: 50–52 [see *951*].

[5409]   MESROPOVA, M. G. & KANDINSKII-RYBNIKOV, A. A. '"Vremena goda" i "Detskii al´bom" Chaikovskogo: Tsiklichnost´ i problemy ispolneniia' (1990) [see above]. In: *Chaikovskii: K 150-letiiu so dnia rozhdeniia. Voprosy istorii, teorii i ispolnitel´stva* (1990): 120–137 [see *591*].

[5410]   DVILIANSKII, A. Ia. 'P. Chaikovskii: "Mart" ("Pesn´ zhavoronka"), soch. 37 bis, No. 3'. In: A. I. Dvilianskii, *Kompleksnyi garmonicheskii analiz: Uchebnoe posobie dlia muzykal´nykh uchilishch*. Bishkek: Ilim, 1993: 90–91.

[5411]   DVILIANSKII, A. Ia. 'P. Chaikovskii: "Oktiabr´" ("Osenniaia pesn´"), soch. 37 bis, No. 10'. In: A. I. Dvilianskii, *Kompleksnyi garmonicheskii analiz: Uchebnoe posobie dlia muzykal´nykh uchilishch*. Bishkek: Ilim, 1993: 37–38.

[*5412*]   LANDRUM, M. M. 'Tchaikovsky's "The Seasons": Analytical and pedagogical perspectives'.
          Philadelphia: Temple Univ., 1997. ii, 138 p; music
          Dissertation (D. M. A.).

[*5413*]   BOYES, K. 'The months of the year portrayed in piano works by Fanny Hensel, Charles-
          Valentin Alkan, Peter Tchaikovsky and Judith Lang Zaimont'. Cincinatti: Univ. of Cincinatti,
          1998. 465 p.
          Dissertation.

[*5414*]   PICCIRILLI, D. "June: Barcarolle", *Clavier*, 37 (May/Jun 1998), 5: 34.

[*5415*]   'Die "Jahreszeiten"', *Clavier*, 37 (Oct 1998), 8: 32.

          See also *125, 5600, 5601, 5631, 5632, 5656, 5699*.

SIX PIECES
Op. 19 (1873)

[*5416*]   LAROSH, G. A. 'P. Chaikovskii: 6 fortepiannykh p´es, op. 19 i op. 21', *Golos* (1 May 1874).
          Publication of the scores of the piano pieces Op. 19 and Op. 21, and also extracts from *The Snow Maiden* and
          The Voevoda.
          — [repr.] In: G. A. Larosh, *Izbrannye stat´i v piati vypuskakh*, vyp. 2 (1975): 69–72 [see *2376*].

[*5417*]   M[AKAROV], P. [Kontsert N. G. Rubinshteina], *Muzykal´nyi svet* (14 Mar 1876).
          Concerning a performance of the *Thème original et variations* (No. 6) in Moscow.

[*5418*]   ZICH, J. 'Komoroni pianista', *Hudební rozhledy*, 46 (1993), 3: 141–143, music.
          On the *Nocturne* (No. 4).

          See also *5121*.

SIX PIECES
Op. 21 (1873)

[*5419*]   [KIUI, Ts. A.] 'Muzykal´naia bibliografiia', *Sankt Peterburgskie vedomosti* (29 Jan 1876): 3.

          See also *5416*.

SIX PIECES
Op. 51 (1882)

[*5420*]   GRIGOROV, L. '"Natha-Valse": Tri mgnoveniia', *Solntse Rossii* (1913), 44: 17–18 [see *583*].

          See also *5390*.

TWELVE PIECES
Op. 40 (1878)

[*5421*]   MAGRATH, J. 'New music reviews: Peter Ilyich Tchaikovsky, "Twelve Pieces for Piano, op.
          40"', *Clavier*, 35 (May/Jun 1996), 5: 35–36.

[*5422*]   SULLIVAN, M. '"Twelve Pieces for piano, Opus 40" by P. I. Tchaikovsky', *American Music Teacher*,
          46 (1997), 5: 101–102.

          See also *128*.

SIX PIECES
Op. 51 (1882)

[5423]   'Muzykal´nye novosti', *Muzykal´nyi mir* (24 Oct 1882): 6.
Publication of the score by Iurgenson.

5.7. WRITINGS

[5424]   [KIUI, Ts. A.] 'Kur´ezy, sluchaiushchiesia s muzykal´nymi retsenzentami', *Sankt Peterburgskie vedomosti* (1 Mar 1873).
Criticism of Chaikovskii's review articles in the *Russkie vedomosti*. Chaikovskii responded by writing to the editor of the journal *Golos* (see letter 291).

[5425]   LAROSH, G. A. 'Predislovie'. In: G. A. Larosh, *Muzykal´nye fel´etony i zametki Petra Il´icha Chaikovskogo (1868–1876)* (1898): i–xxxii [see *131*].
— [repr.] in G. A. Larosh, *Sobranie muzykal´no-kriticheskikh statei*, tom 2, chast´ 1 (1922): 64–96 [see *2311*].
— [repr.] in G. A. Larosh, *Izbrannye stat´i v piati vypuskakh*, vyp. 2 (1975): 299–325 [see *2376*].
— [German tr.] 'Vorwort zur russischen Erstausgabe der "Musikalsichen Feuilletons" Tschaikowskys'. In: G. A. Larosh, *Peter Tschaikowsky: Aufsätze und Erinnerungen* (1993): 205–239 [see *2406*].

[5426]   NEWMARCH, R. H. 'Tchaikovsky as a music critic', *Musical Standard* [illus. series], 11 (14 Jan 1898): 22–23; (21 Jan 1898): 36–38; (28 Jan 1898): 50–51; (4 Feb 1898): 66–68.
English tr. of extracts from *Muzykal´nye fel´etony i zametki Petra Il´icha Chaikovskogo* (1898) [see *131*].
— [rev. repr.] 'Tchaikovsky as a musical critic'. In: R. H. Newmarch, *Tchaikovsky: His life and works* (1900): 111–167 [see *1455*].

[5427]   TIMOFEEV, G. N. 'P. I. Chaikovskii v roli muzykal´nogo kritika', *Russkaia muzykal´naia gazeta* (17/24 Jul 1899), 29/30: 707–714; (31 Jul/7 Aug 1899), 31/32: 742–748; (14/21 Aug 1899), 33/34: 769–774.
— [offprint] *P. I. Chaikovskii v roli muzykal´nogo kritika*. Sankt Peterburg: Izdat. Russkaia muzykal´naia gazeta, 1899. 46 p.

[5428]   POLOVTSOV, A. V. 'P. I. Chaikovskii kak pisatel´', *Moskovskie vedomosti* (25 Oct 1903).
—[rev. repr.] *P. I. Chaikovskii kak pisatel´*. Moskva, 1903. 51 p.

[5429]   BERNANDT, G. B. 'Chaikovskii-publitsist', *Sovetskaia muzyka* (1940), 3: 39–44.

[5430]   MALININ, F. N. 'Zametki o poeticheskom nasledii P. I. Chaikovskogo', *Novyi mir* (1940), 7: 210–217, illus.

[5431]   ZHDANOV, V. A. 'Chaikovskii i muzykal´naia kritika', *Sovetskoe iskusstvo* (29 Mar 1940): 4.

[5432]   SOKOL´SKII, M. 'Perechityvaia stat´i Chaikovskogo', *Sovetskaia muzyka* (1953), 11: 72–75.

[5433]   IAKOVLEV, V. V. 'Chaikovskii-kritik'. In: P. I. Chaikovskii, *Polnoe sobranie sochinenii: Literaturnye proizvedeniia i perepiska*, tom II (1953): 1–22 [see *133*].
— [German tr.] 'Tschaikowski als Kritiker'. In: *P. I. Tschaikowsky: Erinnerungen und Musikkritiken* (1961) [see *134*].

[5434]   'Literaturnye proizvedeniia P. I. Chaikovskogo'. In: *Pëtr Il´ich Chaikovskii: Kratkii rekomendatel´nyi ukazatel´* (1953): 17 [see *23*].

[5435]   SLONIMSKY, N. 'Musical oddities', *Etude*, 73 (Jan 1955): 4.

[*5436*]   PARSHINA, T. 'Literaturnyi talant Chaikovskogo', *Literaturnaia ucheba* (1981), 3: 214–223.

[*5437*]   PLATEK, Ia. 'Vmeste s muzykoi: Chaikovskii—literator', *Muzykal´naia zhizn´* (1984), 23: 16–17.

[*5438*]   OVCHINNIKOV, M. 'Chaikovskii-kritik'. In: P. I. Chaikovskii, *Muzykal´no-kriticheskie stat´i*, 2-e izd. (1986): 1–24 [see *133*].

[*5439*]   NEFF, L. K. 'A documentary glance at Tchaikovsky and Rimsky-Korsakov as music theorists'. In: *Tchaikovsky and his world* (1998): 333–354 [see *601*].

Includes an English tr. of the Chaikovskii's Preface to his *Guide to the Practical Study of Harmony*, and letters to Wladyslaw Pachulski (1883) and Nikolai Rimskii-Korsakov (1885).

See also *250, 2118, 2635*.

GUIDE TO THE PRACTICAL STUDY OF HARMONY
Book (1872)

[*5440*]   LAROSH, G. A. 'Istoricheskii metod prepodavaniia teorii muzyki', *Muzykal´nyi listok* (1872/73): 2–5.
— [repr.] In: G. A. Larosh, *Muzykal´no-kriticheskie stat´i*. Moscow: V. Bessel´, 1894.
— [repr.] In: G. A. Larosh, *Sobranie muzykal´no-kriticheskikh statei*. Tom 1. Moskva, 1913: 275.

[*5441*]   JUON, P. *Prilozhenie k uchebniku garmonii P. Chaikovskogo*. Moskva: P. Iurgenson, 1900. [2 vols.]

[*5442*]   OGOLEVETS, A. 'Chaikovskii: Avtor uchebnika garmonii', *Sovetskaia muzyka* (1940), 5/6: 124–129, illus. [see *585*].

[*5443*]   'Uchebnik garmonii P. I. Chaikovskogo', *Sovetskaia muzyka* (1951), 8: 110.

[*5444*]   STEPANOV, A. A. 'Voprosy garmonicheskoi struktury i funktsional´nosti v "Rukovodstve po prakticheskomu izucheniiu garmonii" P. I. Chaikovskogo'. In: *Voprosy muzykovedeniia: Sbornik statei*. Red.-sost. Iu. N. Rags. Chast´ 2. Moskva, 1972: 152–177, music. (*Trudy Gos. muzykal´no-pedagogicheskogo instituta im. Gnesinykh*; 2).

See also *129, 5439*.

HANDBOOK FOR INSTRUMENTATION
Book by F. A. Gevaert. Tr. from French to Russian by Chaikovskii (1865)

[*5445*]   SEROV, A. N. 'O rukovodstve k instrumentovke', *Muzyka i teatr* (1867): 16.
— [repr.] In: A. N. Serov, *Kriticheskie stat´i 1864–1867*. Tom 4. Moskva, 1868: 1794–1800].

See also *148*.

THE MUSICAL SOCIETY. REPLY TO AN ANONYMOUS CORRESPONDENT. TWO EXAMPLES OF MOSCOW MUSICAL CRITICISM
Article for the journal *Russkie vedomosti* (1875)

[*5446*]   'Moskovskie zametki: G. Chaikovskomu', *Golos* (2 Dec 1875).
Concerning Chaikovskii's criticism of the singer Dmitrii Slavianskii. See also *5447*.

[*5447*]   BEZPECHAL´NYI, I. [NEFEDOV, F. D.] 'Iz Moskvy v Peterburg (ocherki i zametki): Pevets Slavianskii i muzykal´nyi kritik g. Chaikovskii', *Sankt Peterburgskie vedomosti* (9 Dec 1875).

A VOICE FROM MOSCOW'S MUSICAL WORLD
Article for the journal *Sovremennaia letopis´* (1869)

[*5448*]　**S[TASOV], V. 'Khronika'**, *Sankt Peterburgskie vedomosti* (14 May 1869).
Response to Chaikovskii's article on Milii Balakirev. See also *5449*.

[*5449*]　**'Vermischtes: St. Petersburg'**, *Rigasche Zeitung* (20 May/1 Jun 1869).

PART 6

MISCELLANEA

6.1. JUVENILE LITERATURE

6.2. NOVELS

6.3. SHORT STORIES AND PLAYS

6.4. POETRY

6.5. MOTION PICTURES

6.6. OPERAS & MUSICALS

6.7. BALLETS

6.1. JUVENILE LITERATURE

[5450] **GOLOVSKAIA, K. V. & DYSHEVSKAIA, V. N. *P. I. Chaikovskii: Metodicheskaia razrabotka dlia uchitelei muzyki i rukovoditelei kruzhkov srednei shkoly*.** Moskva: NNKP RSFSR. Tsentral′nyi dom khudozhestvennogo vospitaniia detei, 1940. 43 p, music.

Guidelines for analysis of Chaikovskii's music for secondary school children. Includes: 'Spisok proizvedenyi, rekomenduemykh dlia ispolneniia det′mi': 38–43.

— [new ed.] Moskva: Uchpedgiz, 1990. 44 p, music.

[5451] **VLADYKINA, N. & RATSKAIA, Ts. *P. I. Chaikovskii: Dlia shkol′nikov starshego vozrasta*.** Moskva: Gos. muz. izdat., 1940. 213 p, illus. (*Zhizn′ zamechatel′nykh muzykantov*).

[5452] **PURDY, C. L. *Stormy victory: The story of Tchaikovsky*.** With decorations by Vera Bock; music drawings by Rudolf W. Kohl. New York: J. Messner [1942]. xiv, 248 p, music, illus.

[5453] **GRONOWICZ, A. *Tchaïkovsky*.** Montréal, L. Parizeau, 1945. 202 p.

— [English tr.] *Tchaikovsky*. Tr. from the Polish by Joseph Vetter; drawings by George Avison. New York; Edinburgh, T. Nelson & Sons [1946]. 192 p, illus.

[5454] **RATSKAIA, Ts. *P. I. Chaikovskii (1840–1893)*.** Moskva: Institut khudozhestvennogo vospitaniia Akademii pedagogicheskikh nauk RSFSR, 1948. 55 p, illus.

[5455] **WHEELER, O. *The story of Peter Tschaikowsky*.** Illus. by Christine Price. New York: E. P. Dutton & Co., 1953. [119 p.], music, illus.

Mainly concerning the composer's childhood. Includes some simple piano pieces.

Reviews: *Music Teacher*, 33 (Nov 1954): 555 — *Canon*, 14 (Aug 1960): 22.

— [repr.] London: Faber & Faber, 1954. [119 p], music, illus.

[5456] **ALTAEV, A. *Chaikovskii*.** Predislovie V. Iakovleva. Posleslovie i primechanie I. Kunina. Illus. I. Astapova. Moskva: Gos. izdat. detskoi literatury, 1954. 528 p, illus. (*Shkol′naia biblioteka*).

Biographical novel, for older children.

Review: L. Rozenbaum, 'Zhivoi Chaikovskii', *Kurskaia pravda* (6 Mar 1955).

— 2-e izd. Moskva: Gos. izdat. detskoi literatury, 1956. 543 p, illus. (*Shkol′naia biblioteka*).

[5457] **ORLOVA, A. A. *Pëtr Il′ich Chaikovskii: Kratkii ocherk zhizni i tvorchestva*.** Knizhka dlia detei srednego vozrasta. Leningrad: Gos. muz. izdat, 1955. 101 p, music, illus.

Review: M. Terogzniak, 'Detiam o klassikakh', *Sovetskaia muzyka* (1958), 2: 150.

[5458] **VLADYKINA-BACHINSKAIA, N. M. *P. I. Chaikovskii*.** Moskva: Gos. muz. izdat., 1957. 232 p, music, illus. (*Shkol′naia biblioteka*).

Review: S. Borisova, 'Populiarnaia kniga o Chaikovskom', *Sovetskaia muzyka* (1958), 8: 154.

— 2-e izd., dop. Moskva: Muzyka, 1964. 196 p, music, illus. (*Shkol′naia biblioteka*).

— 3-e izd. Moskva: Muzyka, 1971. 229 p, music, illus. (*Shkol′naia biblioteka*).

— 4-e izd. Moskva: Muzyka, 1975. 205 p, illus. (*Shkol′naia biblioteka*).

[5459] **WHEELER, O. *Peter Tschaikowsky and the "Nutcracker" ballet*.** Illus. by Christine Price. New York: E. P. Dutton & Co. [1959]. 95 p, illus.

A fictionalised biography of the composer for young children, including some short piano pieces and only a small section on *The Nutcracker*.

— [repr.] London: Faber & Faber, 1960. 95 p, illus.

[5460] **CARDONA-PEÑA, A. *Tchaikovsky*.** Ed. Alfredo Cardona-Peña. Naucalpan de Juarez: Organizacion Editorial Novaro, 1965. 21 p. (*Vidas ilustres*).

In comic book format.

[*5461*] **YOUNG, P. M.** *Tchaikovsky*. Illus. by Richard Shirley Smith. London: Benn; New York: D. White, 1968. 76 p, music, illus. (*Masters of Music*). ISBN: 0–5101–3734–2 (UK), 0–8725–0434–4 (USA).

Reviews: *Music in Education*, 33 (1969), 336: 89 — *Music Teacher*, 48 (Feb 1969): 37 — *Musical Times*, 110 (May 1969): 493 — *Musical Opinion*, 93 (Feb 1970): 253.

— 2nd ed. New York: Princeton Book Co., 1976. 76 p, music, illus. ISBN: 0–8725–0236–7.

[*5462*] **CLARK, M. W. F.** *Tchaikovsky: The lonely way*: The story of a creative life. Richmond, Virginia: Dietz Press, 1983. vii, 199 p, illus.

[*5463*] **CLARK, E.** *Tchaikovsky*. Illus. by Tony Morris. Hove: Wayland; New York: Bookwright Press, 1988. 32 p, illus. (*Great Lives*). ISBN: 1–8521–0178–4 (UK), 0–5311–8245–2 (USA).

[*5464*] **KALININA, N. A.** *P. I. Chaikovskii: Povest´*. Moskva: Detskaia literatura, 1988. 143 p, illus.

[*5465*] **TAMES, R.** *Tchaikovsky*. London; New York; Sydney: F. Watts, 1991. 32 p, illus. (*Life Times*). ISBN: 0–7496–0462–X (UK & Australia), 0–5311–4108–X (USA).

[*5466*] **POLLARD, M.** *Peter Ilyich Tchaikovsky*. Watford: Exley Publications [1992]. 64 p, illus. (*The World's Greatest Composers*). ISBN: 1–8501–5303–5.

— [Swedish tr.] *Peter Iljitj Tjajkovskij*. Översättning Kerstin Gårsjo. Örebro: Libris [1995]. 63 p, illus. (*Musikens mästare*). ISBN: 91–7195–032–X (hbk.); 91–7195–070–2 (pbk.)

[*5467*] **KRULL, K.** 'Tchaikovsky'. In: *Lives of the musicians: Good times, bad times (and what the neighbors thought)*. Illus. by Kathryn Hewitt. New York: Harcourt Brace Jovanovich, 1993: 54–57, illus. ISBN 0–1524–8010–2.

[*5468*] **RACHLIN, A.** *Tchaikovsky*. Illus. by Susan Hellard. London: Gollancz; Hauppage, N. Y.: Barron's, 1993. [22] p, illus. (*Famous Children*). ISBN: 0–575–05550–2 (UK hbk), 0–575–05554–5 (UK pbk), 0–8120–1545–2 (US).

[*5469*] **THOMPSON, W.** *Pyotr Ilyich Tchaikovsky*. London: Faber & Faber; New York: Viking [1993]. 48 p, music, illus. (*Composer's World*). ISBN: 0–5715–1270–4 (UK), 0–6708–4476–4.

Review: *International Journal of Music Education* (1994), 24: 90.

[*5470*] **HOOBLER, D. & HOOBLER, T.** *Russian Portraits*. Illus. by John Edens. New York: Raintree Stack-Vaughn Pubs, 1994: 53–58, illus.

[*5471*] **VENEZIA, M.** *Peter Tchaikovsky*. Written and illus. by Mike Venezia. Consultants: Donald Freund, Amelia S. Kaplan. Chicago: Childrens Press [1994]. 32 p. (*Getting to Know the World's Greatest Composers*). ISBN: 0–516–04537–7.

— 2nd ed. Chicago: Childrens Press, 1995. 32 p. (*Getting to Know the World's Greatest Composers*). ISBN: 0–516–44537–5.

[*5472*] **KALMAN, E.** *Tchaikovsky discovers America*. Illus. by Laura Fernandez and Rick Jacobson New York: Orchard Books, 1995. [40] p, illus. ISBN: 0–5310–6894–3.

A fictional account of meetings between the composer and a young girl in New York.

Reviews:S. Hammond, *Performing Arts in Canada*, 28 (Fall 1993), 3: 30 [preview] — S. Ellis, *Quill & Quire*, 61 (Feb 1995): 38 — S. Zvirin, *Booklist*, 91 (15 Mar 1995): 1331 — E. S. Watson, *Horn Book*, 71 (Mar/Apr 1995): 190 — B. P. Abrahams, *School Library Journal*, 41 (Apr 1995): 132.

See also *926, 951*.

6.2. NOVELS

[*5473*] **PLATEK, Ia.** 'Besposhchadnaia pravda', *Muzykal´naia zhizn´* (1993), 11/12: 28–29, illus.

The music of Chaikovskii and Shostakovich in the novels of Aleksandr Solzhenitsyn.

Alexander von Andreevsky
TSCHAIKOWSKY: ROMAN SEINES LEBENS
Novel (1957)

[*5474*]   ANDREEVSKY, A. von. *Tschaikowsky: Roman seines Lebens*. Berlin: Bote & Bock [1957]. 319 p, illus.
Review: *Österreichische Musikzeitschrift*, 12 (Dec 1957): 502.

Nina Berberova
CHAIKOVSKII: ISTORIIA ODINOKOI ZHIZNI
Novel (1936)

[*5475*]   BERBEROVA, N. N. *Chaikovskii: Istoriia odinokoi zhizni*. Berlin: Petropolis, 1936. 300 p, illus.
— [new ed.] Red. B. Averin, S. Iaskenskii; posleslovie N. Bochkarevoi. Sankt Peterburg: Petro-RIF, 1993. 237 p, illus. ISBN: 5-85388-003-9. (*Lichnost´ i istoriia*).
    Reviews: A. Kuznetsov, *Novyi mir* (Jan 1998): 229-231.
— [repr.] Moskva: Roman-Gazeta, 1994. 63 p. (*Roman-Gazeta*; 1238).
— [rev. ed.] Sankt Peterburg: Limbus Press, 1997. 256 p, illus.
— [rev. ed.] Moskva: Izdatel´stvo imeni Sabashnikovykh, 1997. 574 p. ISBN: 5-8242-0061-0.
— [Dutch tr.] *Tsjaikovski: De geschiedenis van een eenzaam leven*. Naar het Russisch bewerkt en met aantekeningen voorzien door J. A. Loerink. Amsterdam: A. J. G. Strengholt [1948]. 256 p. (*Maesters der muziek*).
— [Dutch tr. (rev. ed.)] *Tsjaikovski: Biografie*. Vertaald door Frans de Haan. Amsterdam: Uitgeverij De Arbeiderspers [1988]. 240 p. (*Open Domein*; 17). ISBN: 9-0295-0232-0.
— [Finnish tr.] *Tsaikovski*. Yksin aisen ihmisen tarina Kajsa Rootz enin ruotsinkielisest a laitoksesta suomentanut Anna-Maija Oksanen. Helsinki: Oy Fazerin Musiikkikauppa, 1958. 244 p. illus.
— [French tr.] *Tchaïkovsky: Histoire d'une vie solitaire*. Traduit du russe par l'auteur et M. Journot. Paris: Egloff [1948]. 252 p, illus.
— [French tr. (rev. ed.)] *Tchaïkovski: Biographie*. Arles: Actes Sud, 1987. 218 p.
Review: A. Lischké, *L'Avant Scène Opéra*, 99 (Jun 1987): 152.
— [French tr. (rev. ed.)] Arles: Actes Sud, 1990. 249 p (*Presses pocket*; 5).
— [German tr.] *Tschaikowsky: Geschichte ein einsamen Lebens*. Aus dem Russische Übertragen und bearbeitet von Leo Borchard. Berlin: G. Kiepenheuer, 1938. 391 p, illus.
— [German tr. (repr.)] Berlin: G. Kiepenheuer, 1941. 391 p.
— [German tr. (rev ed.)] *Tschaikowsky: Biographie*. Deutsche Übersetzt aus dem Französischen von Anna Kamp. Düsseldorf: Claassen, 1989. 279 p. ISBN: 3-546-41297-4.
— [German tr.] 2. Auflage. Reinbek bei Hamburg: Rowohlt, 1994. 279 p. (*Rororo*; 13044). ISBN: 3-499-13044-0.
— [Italian tr.] *Il ragazzo di vetro: Cajkovskij*. Traduzione di Riccardo Mainardi. Parma: Guanda, 1993. 233 p. (*Biblioteca della Fenice*).
— [Latvian tr.] *Cajkovskijs: Vientuļas dzives gājums*. Romans. No kirevu valodas tulkojis H. Dorbe. Rigā: Grāmatu draugs [1937]. 219 p, illus. (*Ievērojamu personu dzives romāni*).
— [Latvian tr (extracts)] In: N. N. Berberova, 'Čajkovska pedejie gadi', *Musikas Apskats*, 4 (1937), 236-245.
— [Spanish tr.] *Chaikovski*. Traducci on y ap endice bibliografico y fonographico para la edici on española de Santiago Mart in Bermudez. [Madrid]: Aguilar [1990]. 326 p, illus. ISBN: 8-4036-0080-1.
— [Swedish tr.] *Tjajkovskij: En ensam människas historia*. Stockholm: Medén, 1936. 274 p.

[*5476*]   BERBEROVA, N. N. 'Looking back at Tchaikovsky' (tr. Vincent Giroud), *Yale Review*, 80 (Jul 1992): 60-73.

[*5477*]   BERBEROVA, N. 'Predislovie ili posleslovie k knige "P. I. Chaikovskii: Istoriia odnikoi zhizni', *Muzykal´naia zhizn´* (1994), 5: 35-39, illus.

[*5478*]   DEOTTO, P. 'Nina Berberova's biography of Tchaikovsky: The problem of the genre', *Russian literature*, 45 (15 May 1999), 4: 391-400.

Jacques Brenner
LA NUIT D'OCTOBRE
Novel (1993)

[*5479*] **BRENNER, J.** *Tchaïkowsky, ou, La nuit d'octobre: 1840–1893*. Monaco: Editions du Rocher [1993]. 259 p. (*Rocher Littérature*). ISBN: 2-2680-1473-8.

Dominique Fernandez
TRIBUNAL D'HONNEUR
Novel (1996)

[*5480*] **FERNANDEZ, D.** *Tribunal d'honneur*. Roman par Dominique Fernandez. Paris: Grasset [1996]. 505 p.

Review: A. Orlova, 'Oshibki, netochnosti i pravda o smerti Chaikovskogo', *Novoe russkoe slovo* (1 Aug 1997).

Ivan Izakovič
CHVILE ŠITASTIA, ROKY MÚK
Novel (1983)

[*5481*] **IZAKOVIČ, I.** *Chvile šitastia, roky múk: O Čajkovskom*. Vyd. 1. Bratislava: Tatran, 1983. 433 p, illus. (*Osudy slávnych*; 19)

Klaus Mann
SYMPHONIE PATHÉTIQUE
Novel (1935)

[*5482*] **MANN, K.** *Symphonie Pathétique: Ein Tschaikowsky-Roman*. Amsterdam: Querido, 1935. 398 p.
— [repr.] Berlin: Blanvalet, 1952. 398 p.
— [Sonderausg.] Hrsg. und mit einem Nachwort von Martin Gregor-Dellin. [München:] Nymphenburger Verlagshandlung [1970]. 407 p. (*Bucher der Neunzehn*; 189).
Review: *Neue Musikzeitung*, 20 (1971), 1: 13.
— [repr.] München: Spangenberg [1979]. 407 p. ISBN: 3-7707-2527-1.
— 3. Aufl. Mit einem Nachwort von Martin Gregor-Dellin. Reinbek bei Hamburg: Rowohlt, 1981. 281 p. (*Rororo*; 4844). ISBN: 3-499-14844-7.
— [repr.] Reinbek bei Hamburg: Rowohlt, 1985. 281 p. (*Rororo*; 4844). ISBN: 3-499-14844-7.
— [repr.] Reinbek bei Hamburg: Rowohlt, 1989. 281 p. (*Rororo*; 1844). ISBN: 3-499-14844-7.
— [repr.] Reinbek bei Hamburg: Rowohlt, 1991. 281 p. (*Rororo*; 4844). ISBN: 3-499-14844-7.
— [repr.] Reinbek bei Hamburg: Rowohlt, 1993). 281 p. (*Rororo*; 4844). ISBN: 3-499-14844-7.
— [English tr.] *Pathetic Symphony: A Tchaikovsky novel*. English version by Hermon Ould. London: Gollancz, 1938. 445 p.
— [English tr. (2nd. ed.)] New York: Allen, Towne & Heath [1948]. 346 p.
A new version by the author; the chapters are divided into sections named after the movts. of the Sixth Symphony.
— [English tr. (repr.)] New York: Marcus Wiener, 1985. 346 p. ISBN: 0-9101-2924-X.
Review: *Ovation*, 7 (Mar 1986): 30.
— [English tr. (repr.)] New York: M. Wiener, 1994. 346 p. ISBN: 0-910-12924-X.
— [French tr.] *Symphonie Pathétique: Le roman de Tchaikovski*. Traduit par F. Daber et G. Merchez. Paris: Jean Cyrille Godefroy, 1984.
— [Serbo-Croat tr.] *Patetična simfonija*. Belgrade: Rad, 1958. 290 p.
Review: 'Za rubezhom: Iugoslaviia', *Muzykal'naia zhizn'* (Jan 1958), 2: 18

[5483]   SHEVCHENKO, E. 'Versiia Klausa Manna', *Muzykal´naia zhizn´* (1993), 21/22: 21–22.

[5484]   SHEVCHENKO, E. 'Paticheskaia simfoniia P. I. Chaikovskogo v odnoimennom romane **Klausa Manna'**. In: *Russkaia kul´tura i mir: Tezisy dokladov uchastnikov II mezhdunarodnoi konferentsii*. Tom 2. Nizhnii Novgorod: NGU im N. A. Dobroliubova, 1994: 168–171.

Josef Mühlberger
IM SCHATTEN DES SHICKSALS
Novel (1950)

[5485]   MÜHLBERGER, J. *Im Schatten des Schicksals: Der Lebensroman Peter Tschaikowskijs*. Esslingen: Bechtle [1950]. 202 p, illus.

Konstantin Paustovskii
POVEST´ O LESAKH
Novel (1940)

[5486]   PRUDNIKOVA, O. F. 'Obraz P. I. Chaikovskogo v povestiakh K. S. Paustovskogo i Iu. M. **Nagibina'**. In: *P. I. Chaikovskii i Ural* (1983): 146–154 [see *1749*].

[5487]   PAUSTOVSKII, K. 'Preodolenie vremenii: Povest´ o lesakh', *Ogonek* (1948), Nos. 27–36.

Serialisation of the first part of a novel dedicated to Chaikovskii.

— [repr.] In: K. Paustovskii, Sobranie sochinenii v shesti tomakh, tom 2. Moskva: Gos. izdat. khudozhestvennoi literatury, 1957: 305–325 .

6.3. SHORT STORIES & PLAYS

Claude Borell
CAPRICCIO ITALIEN
Story (1981)

[5488]   BORELL, C. "Capriccio Italien". In: C. Borell, Doch die Holle siegt. München: Wilhelm Goldmann, 1981: 312–342.

Aleksandr Gidoni
VIDENIE CHASHI
Story (1989)

[5489]   GIDONI, A. 'Videnie chashi'. In: A. Gidoni, *Khomo Eros: Novellotskil*. N´iu Iork; Toronto, 1989: 161–200.

Warren Kenfield
ELEGY ON THE DEATH OF A BROTHER IN BATTLE
Story (1970)

[5490]   KENFIELD, W. G. *The programme for Tchaikovsky's Fifth Symphony: "Elegy on the death of a brother in battle"*. A manuscript by Warren Geoffrey Kenfield, Paris, early 1888; ed., with a history of the manuscript, by Frank Edwin Egler. [Norfolk, Ct.: F. E. Egler, 1970]. 31 p.

A fictional account of the 'programme', supposedly related to the author during a brief encounter with Chaikovskii.

V. Maistrakh

VOSPOMINANIIA ORKESTRINY CHAIKOVSKOGO

Short story (1914)

[*5491*]   **MAISTRAKH, V.** *Vospominaniia orkestriny Chaikovskogo*. Moskva, 1914. 24 p.
A fictionalised account of the orchestrina in the Chaikovskii home at Votkinsk.

Iurii Nagibin

KAK BYL KUPLEN LES

Short story (1975)

[*5492*]   **NAGIBIN, Iu.** "**Kak byl kuplen les**". In: *Tsarskosel´skoe utro: Povesti, rasskazy*. Moskva: Sovetskii
pisatel´, 1983: 120–163.
A fictional short story concerning Chaikovskii and Nadezhda von Meck.

Iurii Nagibin

KOGDA POGAS FEIERVERK

Short story (1975)

[*5493*]   **NAGIBIN, Iu.** "**Kogda pogas feierverk**". In: *Tsarskosel´skoe utro: Povesti, rasskazy*. Moskva: Sovetskii
pisatel´, 1983: 164–196.
A fictional short story concerning Chaikovskii and Nadezhda von Meck.

6.4. POETRY

Margarita Aliger

DANCE OF THE LITTLE SWANS

Poem (1959)

[*5494*]   **ALIGER, M.** '**Tanets malen´kikh lebedei**'. In: *Stikhi o muzyke*. Moskva: Sovetskii kompozitor, 1982:
104.

Aleksei Apukthin

THE POET'S GENIUS

Poem

[*5495*]   **APUKHTIN, A. N.** '**Genii poeta**'. In: A. N. Apukhtin, *Polnoe sobranie stikhotvorenii*. Leningrad: Sovetskii
pisatel´, 1991: 267.

Aleksei Apukthin

TO P. I. CHAIKOVSKII

Poem ("K ot´ezdu muzykanta druga...")

[*5496*]   **APUKHTIN, A. N.** '**P. I. Chaikovskomu**'. In: A. N. Apukhtin, *Polnoe sobranie stikhotvorenii*. Leningrad:
Sovetskii pisatel´, 1991: 302.

Aleksei Apukthin

TO P. I. CHAIKOVSKII

Poem ("Net, nad pis´mom tvoim ...")

[5497]   **APUKHTIN, A. N. 'P. I. Chaikovskomu'**. In: A. N. Apukhtin, *Polnoe sobranie stikhotvorenii*. Leningrad: Sovetskii pisatel´, 1991: 270–271.

Aleksei Apukthin
TO P. I. CHAIKOVSKII
Poem ("Ty pomnish´, kak zabivshis´ ...")

[5498]   **APUKHTIN, A. N. 'P. I. Chaikovskomu'**. In: A. N. Apukhtin, *Polnoe sobranie stikhotvorenii*. Leningrad: Sovetskii pisatel´, 1991: 206.

A. Butkovskii
AT THE GRAVE OF P. I. CHAIKOVSKII
Epitaph (1893)

[5499]   **BUTKOVSKII, A.** *Na mogilu P. I. Chaikovskogo*. Kiev: Kievskoe slovo, 1893. 1 p.

O. Chumina
IN MEMORY OF P. I. CHAIKOVSKII
Epitaph (1893)

[5500]   **CHUMINA, O. 'Pamiati P. I. Chaikovskogo'**, *Novosti i birzhevaia gazeta* (28 Oct 1893) [see *2187*].

H. G. Dwight
TSCHAIKOVSKY
Poem (1912)

[5501]   **DWIGHT, H. G. 'Tschaikovsky: A poem'**, *Century Magazine*, 83 (Mar 1912): 765.

Afanasii Fet
TO PËTR IL´ICH CHAIKOVSKII
Poem (1891)

[5502]   **FET, A. A. 'Petru Il'ichu Chaikovskomu (Tomu ne lestny nashi ody)'**. In: *Liricheskie stikhotvoreniia A. Feta v 2-kh chastiakh*. Tom 2. Sankt-Peterburg: Br. Panteleevykh, 1894: 319.
   — [repr.] 'P. I. Chaikovskomu'. In: *Zhizn´ Petra Il´icha Chaikovskogo*, tom 3 (1902): 502 [see *1453*].
   — [repr.] 'P. I. Chaikovskomu: "Tomu ne lestnyi nash ody"'. In: A. A. Fet, *Polnoe sobranie stikhotvorenii*. Tom 1. Sankt Peterburg: A. Marks, 1912: 434.

Vasilii Ivanov
IN MEMORY OF CHAIKOVSKII
Poem (1908)

[5503]   **IVANOV, V. 'Pamiati Chaikovskogo: 25 oktiabria 1893 g.–1908 g.'**, *Moskovskie vedomosti* (1908): 248.

Kosta Khetagurov
IN MEMORY OF P. I. CHAIKOVSKII
Epitaph (1893)

[5504]   **KHETAGUROV, K. 'Pamiati P. I. Chaikovskogo'**, *Severnyi Kavkaz* (23 Dec 1893).
   — [repr.] 'Kosta Khetagurov o Chaikovskom', *Sovetskaia muzyka* (1940), 1: 50–51.
   — [repr.] In: K. Khetagurov, *Poeziia*. Moskva: Sovetskaia Rossiia, 1986: 130.

Lev Kondyrev
CHAIKOVSKII
Poem (1993)

[*5505*]   **KONDYREV, L. 'Chaikovskii'**. In: L. Kondyrev, *Dnevnik Pushkina*. Moskva: RMTK "Moskva", 1993:
159–160.

I. Lialechkin
ON THE DEATH OF P. I. CHAIKOVSKII
Epitaph (1893)

[*5506*]   **LIALECHKIN, I. 'Na smert´ P. I. Chaikovskogo'**, *Novosti i birzhevaia gazeta* (25 Oct 1893) [see
2178].

Desanka Maksimovich
CHAIKOVSKII'S VIOLIN
Poem (1975)

[*5507*]   **MAKSIMOVICH, D. 'Skripki Chaikovskogo'**. In: *Stikhi o muzyke*. Moskva: Sovetskii kompozitor,
1982: 217–218.

B. Niditch
TCHAIKOVSKY BATHING
Poem (1983)

[*5508*]   **NIDITCH, B. Z. 'Tchaikovsky bathing'**, *Antigonish Review*, 53 (1983): 97.

Grand Duke Konstantin Konstantinovich
O, HOW OFTEN YOU ALL HURT ME SO SHARPLY
Poem (1889)

[*5509*]   **R[OMANOV], K. 'O, liudi, vy chasto menia iazvili tak bol´no'**. In: K. R., *Tretii sbornik stikhotvorenii,
1889–1899*. Sankt-Peterburg: Akademiia Nauk, 1900: 50.

Daniil Ratgauz
CRY ALL OF US
Poem (1893)

[*5510*]   **RATGAUZ, D. 'Plach´te, vse, v ch´em serdtse zhivy'**, *Kievlianin* (27 Oct 1893).

Vsevolod Rozhdestvenskii
CHAIKOVSKII
Poem (1974)

[*5511*]   **ROZHDESTVENSKII, V. 'Chaikovskii'**. In: *Stikhi o muzyke*. Moskva: Sovetskii kompozitor, 1982:
52.

A. M. Scruggs
TSCHAÏKOWSKY
Poem (1945)

[*5512*]   **SCRUGGS, A. M. 'Tschaikowsky'**, *Hygeia*, 23 (Nov 1945): 846.

Igor´ Severianin
IN MEMORY OF P. I. CHAIKOVSKII
Poem (1908)

[5513]   **SEVERIANIN, I. 'Pamiati P.I. Chaikovskogo'.** In: I. Severianin, *Victoria Regia: Chetvertaia kniga poez.*
Moskva: Nashi dni, 1915: 116.

— [repr.] In: I. Severianin, *Tost bezotvetnyi: Stikhotvoreniia, poemy, proza.* Moskva: Respublika, 1999: 139
(*Proshloe i nastoiashchee*).

Igor´ Severianin
CHAIKOVSKII
Poem (1926)

[5514]   **SEVERIANIN, I. 'Chaikovskii' ("Proslyshan´e potustoronnikh zvukov...")'**, *Segodnia* (2 Mar
1926).

— [repr.] In: I. Severianin, *Medal´ony: Sonety i variatsii o poetakh, pisateliakh i kompozitorakh.* Belgrad, 1934: 97.

— [repr.] In: I. Severianin, *Tost bezotvetnyi: Stikhotvoreniia, poemy, proza.* Moskva: Respublika, 1999: 392
(*Proshloe i nastoiashchee*).

See also *1272.*

6.5. MOTION PICTURES

[5515]   **'Amerikanskii fil´m o kompozitore Chaikovskom'**, *Leningradskaia pravda* (29 Aug 1937): 4.

[5516]   **IURENEV, R. 'Tri fil´ma o P. I. Chaikovskom'**, *Iskusstvo kino* (1940), 6: 44–46, illus.
Reviews of 3 documentary films about Chaikovskii: 'Chaikovskii' — 'Domik v Klinu' — 'Spetsial´nyi nomer
kinozhurnala *Sovetskoe iskusstvo*'.

[5517]   **'Pamiati velikogo kompozitora'**, *Kino* (5 May 1940).
Concerning a planned film about Chaikovskii.

[5518]   **BELIAVSKII, M. 'Kinoocherk o Chaikovskom'**, *Muzykal´naia zhizn´* (1959), 7: 8, illus.
A film directed by Ia. Mirimov. Scenario by A. Belokurov & Boris Iarustovskii.

[5519]   **BAULIN, V. 'Fil´m o Petipa i Chaikovskom'**, *Sovetskaia muzyka* (1964), 12: 154.
An idea for a film about Chaikovskii's relationship with Marius Petipa.

[5520]   **BUSYGIN, S. 'Posviashchaetsia Chaikovskomu'**, *Sovetskaia kul´tura* (7 Dec 1976): 6.
On a documentary film: *Simfoniia: Zhizn´* (about Chaikovskii's music).

[5521]   **ARBATOV, Iu. 'Aprokrif'**, *Kinostsenarii*, 3 (1997): 28–63.
Script for a projected film about Chaikovskii and Antonina Miliukova.

CHAIKOVSKII
Directed by Igor´ Talankin. Music arranged and conducted by Dmitrii Tiomkin (1969).

[5522]   **GOODWIN, N. 'Epic Tchaikovsky'**, *Music and Musicians*, 14 (Apr 1966): 31.
On the making of the film about the life of the composer, in Moscow.

[5523]   **'"Chaikovskii": Fil´m o velikom russkom kompozitore'**, *Sovetskoe iskusstvo* (29 Jun 1967): 3.

[5524]   'Soviet starts composer biopic', *Variety* (Jun 1968), 251: 33.

[5525]   KEIMAKH, T. 'Mir informatsii', *Sovetskaia kul´tura* (2 Jul 1968): 1, illus.

[5526]   GERASICHEVA, G. 'Zhizn´ otdannaia iskusstvu: Snimaetsia fil´m o Chaikovskom', *Leningradskaia pravda* (27 Mar 1969): 4, illus.

[5527]   PITMAN, J. 'If it's all-Russian, can "Tschaikowsky" be much of a WB co-production?', *Variety* (5 Nov 1969), 256: 19.

[5528]   ALEKSANDROV, M. 'Eto nadolgo zapomnitsia', *Ogonek* (1970), 39: 31, illus.

[5529]   CHERTOK, S. '"Chaikovskii": Novaia lenta "Mosfil´ma"', *Sovetskii Soiuz* (1970), 9: 28–29.

[5530]   IVANOVA, T. 'Kinoprem´era: "Tvorchestvo trebuet zhizni"', *Sovetskii ekran* (1970), 14: 10–12.

[5531]   MEDVEDEV, A. 'Novye fil´my: Svidanie s Chaikovskim', *Muzykal´naia zhizn´* (1970): 19–21, illus.

[5532]   'Tschaikovsky film grows', *Music Journal*, 28 (Jan 1970): 73.

[5533]   'Zhizn´ prozhitaia v tvorchestve: Rezhisser Igor´ Talankin rasskazyvaet o svoem novom fil´me "Chaikovskii"', *Smena* (25 Mar 1970): 4.

[5534]   METAL´NIKOV, B. 'Tsena tvorchestva', *Sovetskaia kul´tura* (20 Jun 1970): 3, illus.

[5535]   KUZNETSOV, M. 'Talantlivye proby', *Komsomol´skaia pravda* (10 Sep 1970): 4.

[5536]   TESS, T. 'Kino: "Chaikovskii"', *Izvestiia* (11 Sep 1970): 3.
          — [rev. repr.] *Kul´tura i zhizn´* (1971), 1: 2–6, illus.

[5537]   MURAV´EV, A. 'Chaikovskii dalekii i blizkii', *Sovetskaia kul´tura* (19 Sep 1970): 3, illus.

[5538]   LYNDINA, E. 'Kino: "Muzyka—dusha moia"', *Sovetskaia Rossiia* (20 Sep 1970): 3.

[5539]   BELZA, I. 'Zhizn´ v muzyke', *Literaturnaia gazeta* (23 Sep 1970): 8.

[5540]   STISHOV, E. 'Skazanie o Chaikovskom', *Literaturnaia Rossiia* (2 Oct 1970): 21, illus.

[5541]   PASI, M. 'Un film su Ciakowski', *Rassegna Musicale Curci*, 24 (1971), 2: 17–20, illus.

[5542]   SOKOL´SKII, M. '"Chaikovskii" i Chaikovskii', *Sovetskaia muzyka* (1971), 3: 63–67, illus.
          — [German tr.] 'Der Film "Tschaikowski" und der wahre Tschaikowski', *Kunst und Literatur*, 20 (Mar 1972): 319–326.

[5543]   '"Tchaikovsky": A movie', *Clavier*, 10 (1971), 2: 18.

[5544]   GARDINER, B. 'The Tchaikovsky film', *Musical Events*, 26 (May 1971): 13–14.

[5545]   PALMER, C. 'Tiomkin's "Tchaikovsky"', *Musical Opinon*, 95 (Dec 1971): 122–124.

[5546]   TAYLOR, J. R. "Tchaikovsky", *The Times* (2 Feb 1973).

[5547]   "Tchaikovsky", *Sunday Times* (4 Feb 1973).

[5548]   GARDINER, B. 'Soviet Tchaikovsky: New Moscow film', *Musical Events*, 28 (Mar 1973): 10–11.

[5549]   PALMER, C. 'St. Petersburg to Hollywood', *Music & Musicians*, 21 (Apr 1973): 18–20.
          Comparing Talankin's and Russell's films.

ES WAR EINE RAUSCHENDE BALLNACHT
Directed by Carl Froelich (1939)

[5550] **"Es war eine rauschende Ballnacht"**. In: P. Cadars & F. Courtade, *Le cinema nazi*. [Paris]: E. Losfeld [1972]: 246–247 (*Collection cinématheque de Toulouse*).

[5551] **"Es was eine rauschende Ballnacht"**. In: B. Drewniak, *Der deutsche Film 1938–1945: Eine Gesamtuberblick*. Düsseldorf: Droste, 1987: 444, 804–805.

EVGENII ONEGIN
Silent film based on Chaikovskii's opera. Directed by Aleksandr Khanzhonkov (1911)

[5552] **A. [O fil´me Khanzhonkova]**, *Vestnik kinematografii* (1911), 4: 12, 5: 25–26.

[5553] **KHANZHONKOV, A. 'Dorevolitsionnye kinoinstsenirovki proizvedenii A. S. Pushkina'**, *Iskusstvo kino* (1940), 6: 44–46.

FANTASIA
Cartoon film by Walt Disney (1940)
[partly set to Chaikovskii's *Nutcracker* suite]

[5554] **TAYLOR, D. "Nutcracker Suite"**. In: D. Taylor, *Walt Disney's Fantasia*. With a foreword by Leopold Stokowski. New York: Simon & Schuster, 1940: 22–45.

[5555] **PAULUS, I. 'Klasicna glazba u crtanom filmu "Fantazija" Walta Disneya'**, *Arti Musices*, 28 (1997), 1/2: 115.

LAST SPRING
Television film (1982)

[5556] **ARNAUTOVA, O. "Posledneiu vesnoiu …"**, *Sovetskaia muzyka* (1982), 6: 48.
Concerning the Soviet television film of the same name, based on Chaikovskii's *Six Romances*, Op. 73.

THE MUSIC LOVERS
Directed by Ken Russell (1971)

[5557] **WOCKER, K. H. 'Ken Russells Tschaikowsky-Film'**, *Musica*, 25 (1971), 3: 259–262, illus.

[5558] **HAYMAN, R. 'Ken Russell's Tchaikovsky'**, *The Times* (6 Jan 1971).

[5559] **EGOROV, E. 'Kinopaskvilianty za rabotoi'**, *Sovetskaia kul´tura* (26 Jan 1971): 4.

[5560] **KANFER, S. 'False notes'**, *Time*, 87 (8 Feb 1971): 82–83.

[5561] **FARBER, S. 'A dream blasted by sexual reality'**, *New York Times* (21 Feb 1971).
— [repr.] In: *The New York Times Film Reviews (1971–1972)*. New York: New York Times & Arno Press, 1973: 22.

[5562] **TAYLOR, J. R. 'Russell's pathetic fallacy'**, *The Times* (24 Feb 1971).

[5563] **COUGHLAN, J. 'Flicks: "The Music Lovers"'**, *Jazz & Pop*, 10 (Mar 1971): 28.

[5564] **SUTCLIFFE, T. 'Gentlemen in love'**, *Music & Musicians*, 19 (Apr 1972): 20–21, illus.

[5565] **ZACHARY, R. 'Films'**, *Opera News*, 37 (23/30 Dec 1972): 41.

[*5566*] PALMER, C. 'Film, play', *Musical Times*, 114 (Apr 1973): 412.

[*5567*] KRUKONES, J. H. 'Exploding the romantic myth: Ken Russell's "The Music Lovers"'. In: *Tchaikovsky and his contemporaries* (1999): 251–260 [see *602*].

See also *5549*.

THE SLEEPING BEAUTY
Animated film by the Walt Disney Corporation. Directed by Clyde Geronim (1958)

[*5568*] WEILER, A. H. "Sleeping Beauty", *New York Times* (18 Feb 1959): 36.

SONG OF MY HEART
Directed by Benjamin Glazer (1947)

[*5569*] CROWTHER, B. 'The screen: "Song of my heart"', *New York Times* (5 Mar 1948), 17.
— [repr] In: *The New York Times Film Reviews, 1913-1968*. Vol. 3. New York, 1970: 2240.

6.6. OPERAS & MUSICALS

CHAIKOVSKII
Literary-musical spectacle. Words by L. Boleslavskii

[*5570*] IL´IN, V. 'Geniiu muzyki', *Sovetskaia kul´tura* (25 Jan 1980): 8.

The performance in Moscow of the musical 'Chaikovskii', based on a poem by L. Boleslavskii. For the 140th anniversary of the composer's birth.

MUSIC IN MY HEART
Musical by F. Steininger

[*5571*] '"Muzyka v moei dushe": Romanticheskaia muzykal´naia p´esa s melodiiami iz Chaikovskogo'. In: Iu. Zhukov, *Iz boia v boi, 1946/1970*. Moskva: Mysl´, 1970: 149–150.

Steininger's musical on the life of Chaikovskii, performed on Broadway, New York.

SHAMEFUL VICE
Opera by Michael Finnissy (1995)

[*5572*] DRIVER, P. 'Vice admirable', *Sunday Times* (2 Apr 1995).

[*5573*] 'Shameful Vice'. In: *Uncommon ground: The music of Michael Finnissy*. Ed. by Henrietta Bougham, Christopher Fox and Ian Pace. Aldershot: Ashgate, 1997: 340–344, 393.

SYMPOSION
Opera by Peter Schat (1982)

[*5574*] SCHAT, P. "Symposion". In: P. Schat, *Toonklok*. Amsterdam: Meulenhoff, 1984.
— [English tr.] In: P. Schat, *The Tone Clock*. Tr. from the Dutch and intr. by Jenny McLeod. Langhorne; Pennsylvania; Chur: Harwood Academic Publishers, 1993: 118-193, music. ISBN: 3–7186–5369–9 (hbk), 3–7186–5370–2 (pbk). (*Contemporary Music Studies*; 7).

Score and libretto of the opera, which is based on the story of Chaikovskii's supposed 'suicide'.

[*5575*] 'Comments and events', *Key Notes*, 28 (1994), 3: 24.

[5576] DOUW, A. '"Symposion", opera van Peter Schat en Komrij: Gifmenger van het eerste uur', *Mens en melodie*, 49 (Apr 1994): 210–217, music.

[5577] DAVIDSON, M. 'Netherlands: Interminable "Symposion"', *Opera*, 45 (Sep 1994): 1097–1098.

[5578] KASOW, J. 'Amsterdam', *Opera News*, 59 (Oct 1994): 60.

[5579] "Symposion", *Key Notes*, 28 (Dec 1994), 4: 15–17, illus.

6.7. BALLETS

[5580] 'Other Tchaikovsky ballets', *Dance magazine*, 55 (Jun 1981), 6: 58, illus.
A short list of ballets by others set to Chaikovskii's music.

ADAGIO LAMENTOSO
Ballet by George Balanchine (1981)
[based on movt. IV from the *Symphony No. 6*]

[5581] 'Symphonie No. 6, "Pathétique": Fourth movement, Adagio Lamentoso'. In: *Choreography by George Balanchine: A catalogue of works*. New York: Eakins Press Foundation, 1983: 284.

ALEKO
Ballet by Leonide Massine (1942)
[based on the *Trio* in A minor]

[5582] "Aleko". In: *The dance encyclopedia*. Comp. and ed. by Anatole Chujoy and P. W. Manchester. Rev. and enlarged ed. New York: Simon & Schuster [1967]: 10.

[5583] "Aleko". In: W. Terry, *Ballet guide: Background, listings, credits, and descriptions of more than five hundred of the world's major ballets*. New York: Dodd & Mead, 1976: 34.

ALLEGRO BRILLANTE
Ballet by George Balanchine (1956)
[based on movt. I from the *Piano Concerto No. 3*]

[5584] "Allegro brilliante". In: *The dance encyclopedia*. Comp. and ed. by Anatole Chujoy and P. W. Manchester. Rev. and enlarged ed. New York: Simon & Schuster [1967]: 14.

[5585] "Allegro brillante". In: G. Balanchine, *Balanchine's new complete stories of the great ballets*. Ed. by Francis Mason. Drawings by Marta Becket. Garden City (N. Y.): Doubleday [1968]: 13.

[5586] "Allegro brillante". In: W. Terry, *Ballet guide: Background, listings, credits, and descriptions of more than five hundred of the world's major ballets*. New York: Dodd & Mead, 1976: 34–35.

ALLEGRO CON GRAZIA
Ballet by Jerome Robbins (1981)
[based on movt. II from the *Symphony No. 6*]

[5587] 'Symphonie No. 6, "Pathétique": Second movement, Allegro con grazia'. In: *Choreography by George Balanchine: A catalogue of works*. New York: Eakins Press Foundation, 1983: 284.

[5588] "Allegro con grazia". In: *International dictionary of ballet*. Ed. Martha Bremser. Vol. 2. Detroit: St. James Press, 1993: 1201.

L'AMOUR ET SON DESTIN
Ballet by Serge Lifar (1957)

[based on the *Symphony No. 6*]

[*5589*] **"L'amour et son Destin"**. In: J. Laurent, & J. Sazonova. *Serge Lifar: Rènovateur du ballet Française.* [Paris]: Buchet; Chastel [1960]: 218–219.

ANASTASIA
Ballet by Kenneth MacMillan (1967, rev. 1972)

[based on *Symphony No. 1* & *Symphony No. 3*]

[*5590*] **"Anastasia"**. In: G. B. L. Wilson, *A dictionary of ballet.* New York: Theatre Arts Books, 1974: 15.

[*5591*] **"Anastasia"**. In: W. Terry, *Ballet guide: Background, listings, credits, and descriptions of more than five hundred of the world's major ballets.* New York: Dodd & Mead, 1976: 35–36.

[*5592*] **"Anastasia"**. In: *International dictionary of ballet.* Ed. Martha Bremser. Vol. 1. Detroit: St. James Press, 1993: 22–24.

ANCIENT RUSSIA
Ballet by Bronislava Nijinska (1943)

[based on the Piano Concerto No. 1]

[*5593*] **"Ancient Russia"**. In: *The dance encyclopedia.* Comp. and ed. by Anatole Chujoy and P. W. Manchester. Rev. and enlarged ed. New York: Simon & Schuster [1967]: 51.

ANDANTINO
Ballet by Michel Fokine (1916)

[*5594*] **"Melodiia"**. In: M. Fokin, *Protiv techeniia: Vospominaniia baletmeistera; stsenarii i zamysly baletov, stat´i, interv´iu i pis´ma.* Leningrad: Iskusstvo, 1981: 467.

[*5595*] **"Andantino"**. In: *International dictionary of ballet.* Ed. Martha Bremser. Vol. 1. Detroit: St. James Press, 1993: 503.

ANDANTINO
Ballet by Jerome Robbins (1981)

[*5596*] **"Andantino"**. In: *International dictionary of ballet.* Ed. Martha Bremser. Vol. 2. Detroit: St. James Press, 1993: 1201.

AT A BALL
Ballet by Boris Romanov (1927)

[*5597*] **"At a Ball"**. In: *International dictionary of ballet.* Ed. Martha Bremser. Vol. 2. Detroit: St. James Press, 1993: 1205.

AURORA'S WEDDING (LE MARIAGE D'AURORE)
Ballet after Marius Petipa, mounted by Nicholas Sergeyev with additional dances by Bronislava Nijinska (1981)

[based on *The Sleeping Beauty* & *The Nutcracker*]

[*5598*] **"Le mariage d'Aurore"**. In: *The book of ballets, classic and modern.* Ed. by Gerald Goode. New York: Crown [1939]: 149–152.

[*5599*] **"Aurora's Wedding"**. In: W. Terry, *Ballet guide: Background, listings, credits, and descriptions of more than five hundred of the world's major ballets.* New York: Dodd & Mead, 1976: 43–44.

AUTUMN SONG

Ballet by Bronislava Nijinska (1915)

[based on *The Seasons*]

[*5600*]   "Autumn song". In: *International dictionary of ballet*. Ed. Martha Bremser. Vol. 2. Detroit: St. James Press, 1993: 1017.

AUTUMN SONG

Ballet by Michel Fokine (1917)

[based on *The Seasons*]

[*5601*]   "Osenniaia pesnia". In: M. Fokin, *Protiv techeniia: Vospominaniia baletmeistera; stsenarii i zamysly baletov, stat´i, interv´iu i pis´ma*. Leningrad: Iskusstvo, 1981: 467.

BALLET IMPERIAL

Ballet by George Balanchine (1941)

[based on the *Piano Concerto No. 2*]

[*5602*]   "Ballet Imperial". In: *The dance encyclopedia*. Comp. and ed. by Anatole Chujoy and P. W. Manchester. Rev. and enlarged ed. New York: Simon & Schuster [1967]: 90.

[*5603*]   "Ballet Imperial". In: G. Balanchine, *Balanchine's new complete stories of the great ballets*. Ed. by Francis Mason. Drawings by Marta Becket. Garden City (N. Y.): Doubleday [1968]: 35–36.

[*5604*]   "Ballet Imperial". In: W. Terry, *Ballet guide: Background, listings, credits, and descriptions of more than five hundred of the world's major ballets*. New York: Dodd & Mead, 1976: 48–49.

[*5605*]   "Ballet Imperial". In: G. Balanchine & F. Mason, *Balanchine's complete stories of the great ballets*. Rev. and enlarged ed. Garden City (N. Y.): Doubleday, 1977: 48–51.

See also *5064, 5065, 5066.*

BEAUTY AND THE BEAST

Ballet by Lew Christensen (1958)

[*5606*]   "Beauty and the beast". In: *International dictionary of ballet*. Ed. Martha Bremser. Vol. 1. Detroit: St. James Press, 1993: 276.

CAPRICCIO ITALIEN

Ballet by Peter Martins (1981)

[based on the *Italian Capriccio*]

[*5607*]   "Capriccio italien". In: *International dictionary of ballet*. Ed. Martha Bremser. Vol. 2. Detroit: St. James Press, 1993: 916.

CHAIKOVSKII

Ballet by Boris Eifman (1993)

[based on the *Symphony No. 5*; *Liturgy of St. John Chrysostom* (no. 6); *Serenade for String Orchestra* (movts. II & III); *Italian Capriccio*; *Symphony No. 6* (movt. IV)]

[*5608*]   MAINIETSE, V. 'Moskovskie gastroli: Po zavetam Dostoevskogo', *Muzykal´naia zhizn´* (1994), 5: 8–9, illus.

[*5609*]   SVESHNIKOVA, A. 'Chto khochet uvidet´ zritel´?: Chaikovskii v Sankt-Peterburgskom teatre baleta Borisa Eifmana'. In: *Vestnik: Belorusskii baletnyi zhurnal* (1994), 3: 114–116.

[*5610*]   WELZIEN, L. 'Mein Tschaikowsky ist keine cola: Ein gespräch mit Boris Eifman', *Tanzdrama* (1995), 29: 4–8.
An interview with Boris Eifman.

[*5611*]   KISSELGOFF, A. 'A tortured composer embracing his desires', *New York Times* (13 Apr 1998).

[*5612*]   ACOCELLA, J. '"Pathetique": Russian ballet in torment', *New Yorker* (8 Feb 1999): 82–84.

LE CHAT BOTTÉ
Ballet by Roland Petit (1985)

[*5613*]   "Le Chat botté". In: *International dictionary of ballet*. Ed. Martha Bremser. Vol. 2. Detroit: St. James Press, 1993: 1115.

CONCERT FANTASY
Ballet by Jacque D'Amboise (1981)
[based on the *Concert Fantasia*]

[*5614*]   "Concert Fantasy". In: *International dictionary of ballet*. Ed. Martha Bremser. Vol. 1. Detroit: St. James Press, 1993: 327.

CONCERTO
Ballet by Herbert Ross (1958)
[based on the *Violin Concerto*]

[*5615*]   'Ross, Herbert'. In: *The dance encyclopedia*. Comp. and ed. by Anatole Chujoy and P. W. Manchester. Rev. and enlarged ed. New York: Simon & Schuster [1967]: 780.

CONCERTO COREOGRAFICO
Ballet by Tamara Grigorieva (1951)
[based on the *Piano Concerto No. 1*]

[*5616*]   "Concerto coreografico". In: *The dance encyclopedia*. Comp. and ed. by Anatole Chujoy and P. W. Manchester. Rev. and enlarged ed. New York: Simon & Schuster [1967]: 220.

CONCERTO IN WHITE
Ballet by Nikita Dolgushin (1969)
[based on the *Violin Concerto*]

[*5617*]   "Kontsert v belom". In: A. Degen & I. Stupnikov, *Leningradskii balet, 1917–1987. Slovar´-spravochnik: Solistki, solisty, baletmeistery, pedagogi, dirizhery*. Leningrad: Sovetskii kompozitor, 1988: 248.

LA DAME DE PIQUE
Ballet by Serge Lifar (1960)
[based on *The Queen of Spades*]

[*5618*]   "La Dame de Pique". In: *International dictionary of ballet*. Ed. Martha Bremser. Vol. 2. Detroit: St. James Press, 1993: 864.

LA DAME DE PIQUE
Ballet by Roland Petit (1978)
[based on *The Queen of Spades*]

[*5619*] **"La Dame de Pique"**. In: H. Koegler, *The concise Oxford dictionary of ballet*. London; New York: Oxford Univ. Press, 1982: 112.

THE DANCE DREAM
Ballet by Alexander Gorskii
[partially based on various works by Tchaikovsky]

[*5620*] **"The Dance Dream"**. In: C. W. Beaumont, *Complete book of ballets: A guide to the principal ballets of the nineteenth and twentieth centuries*. New York: Grosset & Dunlap, 1938: 623–625.

DESIGNS WITH STRINGS
Ballet by John Taras (1948)
[based on movt. II from the *Trio in A minor*]

[*5621*] **"Designs with strings"**. In: G. Balanchine, *Balanchine's new complete stories of the great ballets*. Ed. by Francis Mason. Drawings by Marta Becket. Garden City (N. Y.): Doubleday [1968]: 115–116.

[*5622*] **"Designs with strings"**. In: W. Terry, *Ballet guide: Background, listings, credits, and descriptions of more than five hundred of the world's major ballets*. New York: Dodd & Mead [1976]: 109.

ELEGIE
Ballet by John Neumeier (1978)

[*5623*] **"Elegie"**. In: *International dictionary of ballet*. Ed. Martha Bremser. Vol. 2. Detroit: St. James Press, 1993: 1011.

EPISODES
Ballet by Frank Staff (1968)

[*5624*] **"Episodes"**. In: *International dictionary of ballet*. Ed. Martha Bremser. Vol. 2. Detroit: St. James Press, 1993: 1345.

EROS
Ballet by Michel Fokine (1915)
[based on the *Serenade for Strings*]

[*5625*] **'New productions in Russia'**. In: C. W. Beaumont, *Michel Fokine and his ballets*. London: C. W. Beaumont, 1935: 115–117.

[*5626*] **'Balet "Eros"'**, *Smena* (26 Mar 1940): 4.
A production of the ballet at the Kirov Theatre in Leningrad.

[*5627*] **'M. I. Chaikovskomu'**. In: M. Fokin, *Protiv techeniia: Vospominaniia baletmeistera; stsenarii i zamysly baletov, stat´i, interv´iu i pis´ma*. Leningrad: Iskusstvo, 1981: 376–377, 466.

EUGENE ONEGIN
Ballet by Victor Gsovsky (1954)
[based on *Evgenii Onegin*]

[*5628*] **"Eugene Onegin"**. In: *International dictionary of ballet*. Ed. Martha Bremser. Vol. 1. Detroit: St. James Press, 1993: 620.

FAMILY PORTRAITS
Ballet by Birgit Cullberg (1985)

[5629] **"Family portraits"**. In: *International dictionary of ballet*. Ed. Martha Bremser. Vol. 1. Detroit: St. James Press, 1993: 318.

FANTASIA ON CHAIKOVSKII'S MELODY
Ballet by Michel Fokine (1907)

[5630] **"Fantaziia na melodiiu P. Chaikovskogo"**. In: M. Fokin, *Protiv techeniia: Vospominaniia baletmeistera; stsenarii i zamysly baletov, stat´i, interv´iu i pis´ma*. Leningrad: Iskusstvo, 1981: 463.

THE FOUR SEASONS
Ballet by Michel Fokine (1908)
[based on *The Seasons*]

[5631] **"Vremena goda"**. In: M. Fokin, *Protiv techeniia: Vospominaniia baletmeistera; stsenarii i zamysly baletov, stat´i, interv´iu i pis´ma*. Leningrad: Iskusstvo, 1981: 464.

[5632] **"The Four Seasons"**. In: *International dictionary of ballet*. Ed. Martha Bremser. Vol. 1. Detroit: St. James Press, 1993: 501.

FRANCESCA DA RIMINI
Ballet by Michel Fokine (1915)
[based on *Francesca da Rimini*]

[5633] **'New productions in Russia'**. In: C. W. Beaumont, *Michel Fokine and his ballets*. London: C. W. Beaumont, 1935: 115–117.

[5634] **"Francesca da Rimini"**. In: C. W. Beaumont, *Complete book of ballets: A guide to the principal ballets of the nineteenth and twentieth centuries*. New York: Grosset & Dunlap, 1938: 832–835.

[5635] **"M. I. Chaikovskomu"** & **"Eros"**. In: M. Fokin, *Protiv techeniia: Vospominaniia baletmeistera; stsenarii i zamysly baletov, stat´i, interv´iu i pis´ma*. Leningrad: Iskusstvo, 1981 376-377; 466

FRANCESCA DA RIMINI
Ballet by David Lichine (1937)
[based on *Francesca da Rimini*]

[5636] **"Francesca da Rimini"**. In: *The book of ballets, classic and modern*. Ed. by Gerald Goode. New York: Crown [1939]: 108–110.

FRANCESCA DA RIMINI
Ballet by Serge Lifar (1958)
[based on *Francesca da Rimini*]

[5637] **"Franceska da Rimini"**. In: J. Laurent, & J. Sazonova. *Serge Lifar: Renovateur du ballet Francais*. [Paris]: Buchet; Chastel [1960]: 228.

FRANCESCA DA RIMINI
Ballet by Konstantin Boiarskii (1959)
[based on *Francesca da Rimini*]

[5638] **ENTELIS, L. 'Balety na muzyku Chaikovskogo'**, *Leningradskaia pravda* (7 May 1959).

[5639] **"Francheska da Rimini"**. In: A. Degen & I. Stupnikov, *Leningradskii balet, 1917–1987. Slovar´-spravochnik: Solistki, solisty, baletmeistery, pedagogi, dirizhery*. Leningrad: Sovetskii kompozitor, 1988: 256.

FRANCESCA DA RIMINI
Ballet by John Taras (1986)

[based on *Francesca da Rimini*]

[*5640*]   **"Francesca da Rimini"**. In: *International dictionary of ballet*. Ed. Martha Bremser. Vol. 2. Detroit: St. James Press, 1993: 1388.

FROLICKING GODS
Ballet by Michel Fokine (1923)

[based on *The Nutcracker* suite]

[*5641*]   **"Veseliashchiesia bogi"**. In: M. Fokin, *Protiv techeniia: Vospominaniia baletmeistera; stsenarii i zamysly baletov, stat´i, interv´iu i pis´ma*. Leningrad: Iskusstvo, 1981: 468.

HAMLET
Ballet by Robert Helpmann (1942)

[based on the overture-fantasia *Hamlet*]

[*5642*]   **BONAVIA, F. 'Dancing "Hamlet" to Tchaikovsky'**, *New York Times* (21 Jun 1942).

[*5643*]   **"Hamlet"**. In: G. Balanchine, *Balanchine's new complete stories of the great ballets*. Ed. by Francis Mason. Drawings by Marta Becket. Garden City (N. Y.): Doubleday [1968]: 195–197.

[*5644*]   **"Hamlet"**. In: W. Terry, *Ballet guide: Background, listings, credits, and descriptions of more than five hundred of the world's major ballets*. New York: Dodd & Mead [1976]: 172–173.

[*5645*]   **"Hamlet"**. In: G. Balanchine & F. Mason, *Balanchine's complete stories of the great ballets*. Rev. and enlarged ed. Garden City (N. Y.): Doubleday, 1977: 286–288.

[*5646*]   **'"Hamlet": Photo essay'**, *About the House*, 6 (1981), 3: 36–37.

THE HARD NUT
Ballet by Mark Morris (1991)

[based on *The Nutcracker*]

[*5647*]   **"Hard Nut"**. In: *International dictionary of ballet*. Ed. Martha Bremser. Vol. 2. Detroit: St. James Press, 1993: 989.

THE IDIOT (1980)
Ballet by Boris Eifman

[based on the *Symphony No. 6*]

[*5648*]   **EVTUSHENKO, E. 'Dostoevskii: A famous novel translated into ballet'**, *Soviet Life* (1981), 11: 50–53.

An ballet adaptation of Dostoevskii's *The Idiot*, using music from Chaikovskii's Sixth Symphony, in a Royal Ballet production.

[*5649*]   **"Idiot"**. In: A. Degen & I. Stupnikov, *Leningradskii balet, 1917–1987. Slovar´-spravochnik: Solistki, solisty, baletmeistery, pedagogi, dirizhery*. Leningrad: Sovetskii kompozitor, 1988: 246.

IMPROMPTU (THE NYMPH AND THE TWO)
Choreographic miniature by Leonid Iakobson (1938)

[*5650*]   **"Nymph and the Two"**. In: *International dictionary of ballet*. Ed. Martha Bremser. Vol. 2. Detroit: St. James Press, 1993: 1552.

JEWELS
Ballet by George Balanchine (1967)

["Diamonds" section based on the *Symphony No. 3*]

[*5651*]   "**Jewels**". In: G. Balanchine, *Balanchine's new complete stories of the great ballets*. Ed. by Francis Mason. Drawings by Marta Becket. Garden City (N. Y.): Doubleday [1968]: 222–223.

[*5652*]   "**Jewels**". In: G. Balanchine & F. Mason, *Balanchine's complete stories of the great ballets*. Rev. and enlarged ed. Garden City (N. Y.): Doubleday, 1977: 324–325.

[*5653*]   "**Jewels**". In: *Choreography by George Balanchine: A catalogue of works*. New York: Eakins Press Foundation, 1983: 250.

JOKE
Choreographic miniature by Leonid Iakobson (1949)

[*5654*]   "**Joke**". In: *International dictionary of ballet*. Ed. Martha Bremser. Vol. 2. Detroit: St. James Press, 1993: 1552.

KITTENS
Choreographic miniature by Leonid Iakobson (1936)

[*5655*]   "**Kittens**". In: *International dictionary of ballet*. Ed. Martha Bremser. Vol. 2. Detroit: St. James Press, 1993: 1552.

LOVE BALLAD
Ballet by Fëdor Lopukhov (1959)

[based on *The Seasons*]

[*5656*]   "**Ballada o liubvi**". In: A. Degen & I. Stupnikov, *Leningradskii balet, 1917–1987. Slovar´-spravochnik: Solistki, solisty, baletmeistery, pedagogi, dirizhery*. Leningrad: Sovetskii kompozitor, 1988: 133–136, 242.

MANFRED
Ballet by Rudolf Nureev (1979)

[based on the symphony *Manfred*]

[*5657*]   "**Manfred**". In: *Phaidon book of the ballet*. Preface by Rudolf Nureyev. Oxford: Phaidon, 1981: 317.

[*5658*]   "**Manfred**". In: *Reclams Ballettführer*. Von Hartmut Regitz, Otto Friedrich Regner, Heinz-Ludwig Schneiders. Stuttgart: Reclam, 1985: 365–370. (*Universal-Bibliothek*; 8042).

[*5659*]   "**Manfred**". In: *International dictionary of ballet*. Ed. Martha Bremser. Vol. 2. Detroit: St. James Press, 1993: 1035.

MARCHE SLAVE
Ballet by Isadora Duncan (1917)

[based on the *Slavonic March*]

[*5660*]   "**Marche slave**". In: D. McDonagh, *The complete guide to modern dance*. Garden City (N. Y.): Doubleday, 1976: 17.

MEDITATIONS
Choreographic miniature by Leonid Iakobson (1938)

[*5661*]   "**Meditations**". In: *International dictionary of ballet*. Ed. Martha Bremser. Vol. 2. Detroit: St. James Press, 1993: 1552.

MEDITATIONS
Ballet by George Balanchine (1963)
[based on *Méditation*, op. 42, no. 1]

[5662] **"Meditations"**. In: G. Balanchine, *Balanchine's new complete stories of the great ballets*. Ed. by Francis Mason. Drawings by Marta Becket. Garden City (N. Y.): Doubleday [1968]: 246–247.

[5663] **"Mediations"**. In: G. Balanchine & F. Mason, *Balanchine's complete stories of the great ballets*. Rev. and enlarged ed. Garden City (N. Y.): Doubleday, 1977: 357.

[5664] **"Meditations"**. In: *Choreography by George Balanchine: A catalogue of works*. New York: Eakins Press Foundation, 1983: 242–243.

MEDITATIONS
Ballet by Nikita Dolgushin (1969)
[based on the overture-fantasiia *Hamlet*]

[5665] **"Razmyshleniia"**. In: A. Degen & I. Stupnikov, *Leningradskii balet, 1917–1987. Slovar´-spravochnik: Solistki, solisty, baletmeistery, pedagogi, dirizhery*. Leningrad: Sovetskii kompozitor, 1988: 252.

MEDUSA
Ballet by Michel Fokine (1924)
[based on the *Symphony No. 6*]

[5666] **"Medusa"**. In: C. W. Beaumont, *Michel Fokine and his ballets*. London: C. W. Beaumont, 1935:127.

[5667] **"Medusa"**. In: M. Fokin, *Protiv techeniia: Vospominaniia baletmeistera; stsenarii i zamysly baletov, stat´i, interv´iu i pis´ma*. Leningrad: Iskusstvo, 1981: 468.

THE MIRROR WALKERS
Ballet by Peter Wright (1962)
[based on the *Suite No. 1*]

[5668] **"The Mirror Walkers"**. In: *Reclams Ballettführer*. Von Otto Friedrich Regner, Heinz-Ludwig Schneiders. Stuttgart: Reclam,1972: 294–297.

[5669] **"Mirror Walkers"**. In: *International dictionary of ballet*. Ed. Martha Bremser. Vol. 2. Detroit: St. James Press, 1993: 1548.

MOMENTUM
Ballet by Dennis Nahat (1968)
[based on *Souvenir de Florence*]

[5670] **"Momentum"**. In: G. Balanchine & F. Mason, *Balanchine's Complete stories of the great ballets*. Rev. and enlarged ed. Garden City (N. Y.): Doubleday, 1977: 362.

MOZARTIANA
Ballet by George Balanchine (1933, rev. 1981)
[based on the *Suite No. 4*]

[5671] **"Mozartiana"**. In: *Choreography by George Balanchine: A catalogue of works*. New York: Eakins Press Foundation, 1983: 112–113, 282–283.

[*5672*]   **MAIORANO, R. & BROOKS**, V. *Balanchine's "Mozartiana": The making of a masterpiece*. New York: Freundlich Books [distrib. Scribner's], 1985. xix, 188 p, illus.
Review: L. Shapiro, *Newsweek*, 105 (18 Mar 1985): 79.

[*5673*]   **"Mozartiana"**. In: *International dictionary of ballet*. Ed. Martha Bremser. Vol. 2. Detroit: St. James Press, 1993: 990–992.

MOZARTIANA
Ballet by Nikita Dolgushin (1970)
[based on the *Suite No. 4*]

[*5674*]   **"Mozartiana"**. In: A. Degen & I. Stupnikov, *Leningradskii balet, 1917–1987. Slovar´-spravochnik: Solistki, solisty, baletmeistery, pedagogi, dirizhery*. Leningrad: Sovetskii kompozitor, 1988: 249.

MOZARTIANA
Ballet by Willam Christensen (1972)
[based on the *Suite No. 4*]

[*5675*]   **"Mozartiana"**. In: *International dictionary of ballet*. Ed. Martha Bremser. Vol. 1. Detroit: St. James Press, 1993: 278.

MOZARTIANA
Ballet by Ronald Hynd (1973)
[based on the *Suite No. 4*]

[*5676*]   **"Mozartiana"**. In: H. Koegler, *The concise Oxford dictionary of ballet*. London; New York : Oxford Univ. Press, 1982: 292.

NI FLEURS NI COURONNES
Ballet by Maurice Bejart (1968)

[*5677*]   **"Ni Fleures ni Couronnes"**. In: M. Bejart, *Le ballet des mots*. [Paris]: Les Belles Lettres; Archimbaud, 1994: 484.

NIJINSKY: CLOWN OF GOD
Ballet by Maurice Bejart (1971)
[based on the *Symphony No. 6*]

[*5678*]   **"Nijinsky, clown de Dieu"**. In: M. Bejart, *Le ballet des mots*. [Paris]: Les Belles Lettres; Archimbaud, 1994: 433–436.

[*5679*]   **"Nijinsky, clown of God"**. In: W. Terry, *Ballet guide: Background, listings, credits, and descriptions of more than five hundred of the world's major ballets*. New York: Dodd & Mead [1976]: 226.

[*5680*]   **"Njinsky, clown de Dieu"**. In: *International dictionary of ballet*. Ed. Martha Bremser. Vol. 2. Detroit: St. James Press, 1993: 1020–1021.

LES OISEAUX D'OR
Ballet by David Lichine (1954)

[*5681*]   **"L'oiseaux d'or"**. In: *International dictionary of ballet*. Ed. Martha Bremser. Vol. 2. Detroit: St. James Press, 1993: 853.

ONEGIN
Ballet by John Cranko (1965)
[based on various compositions by Chaikovskii]

[5682]   **"Onegin"**. In: *Reclams Ballettführer*. Von Otto Friedrich Regner, Heinz-Ludwig Schneiders. Stuttgart: Reclam, 1972: 335–338.

[5683]   **"Onegin"**. In: G. B. L. Wilson, *A dictionary of ballet*. New York: Theatre Arts Books, 1974: 367.

[5684]   **"Eugene Onegin"**. In: W. Terry, *Ballet guide: Background, listings, credits, and descriptions of more than five hundred of the world's major ballets*. New York: Dodd & Mead [1976]: 128–129.

[5685]   **"Eugene Onegin"**. In: G. Balanchine & F. Mason, *Balanchine's complete stories of the great ballets*. Rev. and enlarged ed. Garden City (N. Y.): Doubleday, 1977: 208–210.

[5686]   **"Onegin"**. In: *Phaidon book of the ballet*. Preface by Rudolf Nureyev. Oxford: Phaidon, 1981: 272.

PARURES
Ballet by Anthony Burke (1948)
[based on the *Suite No. 3*]

[5687]   **"Tchaikovsky"**. In: *The dance encyclopedia*. Comp. and ed. by Anatole Chujoy and P. W. Manchester. Rev. and enlarged ed. New York: Simon & Schuster [1967]: 895,

PAS DE DEUX
Ballet by Jerome Robbins (1981)

[5688]   **"Pas de deux"**. In: *International dictionary of ballet*. Ed. Martha Bremser. Vol. 2. Detroit: St. James Press, 1993: 1201.

PIANO PIECES
Ballet by Jerome Robbins (1981)

[5689]   **"Piano Pieces"**. In: *International dictionary of ballet*. Ed. Martha Bremser. Vol. 2. Detroit: St. James Press, 1993: 1201.

PIOTR ILLITCH TCHAIKOWSKY: L'ENFANT DE PORCELAINE
Ballet by Jorge Lefebre (1981)
[based on various works by Chaikovskii]

[5690]   **HERSIN, A. P. 'Tchaïkovsky: "L'enfant de porcelaine", á Charlevoi'**, *Les Saisons de la Danse* (Nov 1981), 138: 16, illus.
In connection with a production at at the Palais des Beaux Arts, Charlevoi, 2–4 Oct 1981.

LES PRÈSAGES (THE FATES)
Ballet by Leonide Massine
[based on the *Symphony No. 5*]

[5691]   **"Les Prèsages"**. In: C. W. Beaumont, *Complete book of ballets: A guide to the principal ballets of the nineteenth and twentieth centuries*. New York: Grosset & Dunlap, 1938: 746–748.

[5692]   **"Le Prèsage"**. In: *The book of ballets, classic and modern*. Ed. by Gerald Goode. New York: Crown [1939]: 179–181.

[5693]   **"Les Prèsages"**. In: W. Terry, *Ballet guide: Background, listings, credits, and descriptions of more than five hundred of the world's major ballets*. New York: Dodd & Mead [1976]: 260–261.

THE REAPER'S DREAM
Ballet by Lydia Kyasht (1913)

[5694]   **"The Reaper's Dream"**. In: *International dictionary of ballet*. Ed. Martha Bremser. Vol. 1. Detroit: St. James Press, 1993: 794.

REFLECTIONS
Ballet by Gerald Arpino (1971)
[based on *Variations on a Roccoco Theme*]

[5695]   **"Reflections"**. In: G. Balanchine & F. Mason, *Balanchine's complete stories of the great ballets*. Rev. and enlarged ed. Garden City (N. Y.): Doubleday, 1977: 472.

[5696]   **"Reflections"**. In: *International dictionary of ballet*. Ed. Martha Bremser. Vol. 1. Detroit: St. James Press, 1993: 46.

REVERIES (later SUITE No. 1)
Ballet by John Clifford (1969)
[based on the *Suite No 1*]

[5697]   **"Reveries"**. In: W. Terry, *Ballet guide: Background, listings, credits, and descriptions of more than five hundred of the world's major ballets*. New York: Dodd & Mead [1976]: 272.

[5698]   **"Reveries"**. In: G. Balanchine & F. Mason, *Balanchine's complete stories of the great ballets*. Rev. and enlarged ed. Garden City (N. Y.): Doubleday, 1977: 480–482.

ROMANCE (1915)
Ballet by Michele Fokine

[5699]   **"Romans"**. In: M. Fokin, *Protiv techeniia: Vospominaniia baletmeistera; stsenarii i zamysly baletov, stat´i, interv´iu i pis´ma*. Leningrad: Iskusstvo, 1981: 466.

ROMEO AND JULIET
Ballet by Birger Bartholin (1937, rev. 1950)
[based on the overture-fantasia *Romeo and Juliet*]

[5700]   **"Romeo and Juliet"**. In: *The dance encyclopedia*. Comp. and ed. by Anatole Chujoy and P. W. Manchester. Rev. and enlarged ed. New York: Simon & Schuster [1967]: 776.

ROMEO AND JULIET
Ballet by Willam Christensen (1938)
[based on the overture-fantasia *Romeo and Juliet*]

[5701]   **"Romeo and Juliet"**. In: *International dictionary of ballet*. Ed. Martha Bremser. Vol. 1. Detroit: St. James Press, 1993: 278 .

ROMEO AND JULIET
Ballet by Gyula Harangozo (1939)
[based on the overture-fantasia *Romeo and Juliet*]

[5702]   **"Romeo and Juliet"**. In: *International dictionary of ballet*. Ed. Martha Bremser. Vol. 1. Detroit: St. James Press, 1993: 635.

ROMEO AND JULIET
Ballet by Serge Lifar (1942)
[based on the overture-fantasia *Romeo and Juliet*]

[5703] **"Romeo et Juliette"**. In: J. Laurent, & J. Sazonova. *Serge Lifar: Rènovateur du ballet Française*. [Paris]: Buchet; Chastel [1960]: 160.

ROMEO AND JULIET
Ballet by Leonid Iakobson (1944)
[based on the overture-fantasia *Romeo and Juliet*]

[5704] **"Romeo i Dzhul´etta"**. In: A. Degen & I. Stupnikov, *Leningradskii balet, 1917–1987. Slovar´-spravochnik: Solistki, solisty, baletmeistery, pedagogi, dirizhery*. Leningrad: Sovetskii kompozitor, 1988: 225.

ROMEO AND JULIET: A TRAGEDY IN VERONA
Ballet by George Skibine (1950)
[based on the overture-fantasia *Romeo and Juliet*]

[5705] **"Romeo and Juliet"**. In: *The dance encyclopedia*. Comp. and ed. by Anatole Chujoy and P. W. Manchester. Rev. and enlarged ed. New York: Simon & Schuster [1967]: 776.

ROMEO AND JULIET
Ballet by Nikita Dolgushin (1971)
[based on the overture-fantasia *Romeo and Juliet*]

[5706] **"Romeo i Dzhul´etta"**. In: A. Degen & I. Stupnikov, *Leningradskii balet, 1917–1987. Slovar´-spravochnik: Solistki, solisty, baletmeistery, pedagogi, dirizhery*. Leningrad: Sovetskii kompozitor, 1988: 252.

ROMEO AND JULIET
Ballet by Sergei Vikulov (1982)
[based on the overture-fantasia *Romeo and Juliet*]

[5707] **"Romeo i Dzhul´etta"**. In: A. Degen & I. Stupnikov, *Leningradskii balet, 1917–1987. Slovar´-spravochnik: Solistki, solisty, baletmeistery, pedagogi, dirizhery*. Leningrad: Sovetskii kompozitor, 1988: 252.

SCHERZO, OPUS 42
Ballet by Jacque D'Amboise (1981)
[based on no. 2 from the *Souvenir d'un lieu cher*]

[5708] **"Scherzo, Opus 42"**. In: *International dictionary of ballet*. Ed. Martha Bremser. Vol. 1. Detroit: St. James Press, 1993: 327.

THE SEASONS
Ballet by Leonid Lavrovsky (1928)
[based on *The Seasons*]

[5709] **"The Seasons"**. In: *International dictionary of ballet*. Ed. Martha Bremser. Vol. 1. Detroit: St. James Press, 1993: 829.

SERENADE (1935)
Ballet by George Balanchine (1935)
[based on the *Serenade for String Orchestra*]

[5710]   KUZNETSOV, I. 'Na spektakliakh gostei', *Sovetskaia muzyka* (1963), 1: 42–51.

[5711]   "Serenade". In: G. Balanchine, *Balanchine's new complete stories of the great ballets*. Ed. by Francis Mason. Drawings by Marta Becket. Garden City (N. Y.): Doubleday [1968]: 363–364.

[5712]   "Serenade". In: G. Balanchine & F. Mason, *Balanchine's complete stories of the great ballets*. Rev. and enlarged ed. Garden City (N. Y.): Doubleday, 1977: 530–533.

[5713]   "Serenade". In: *Choreography by George Balanchine: A catalogue of works*. New York: Eakins Press Foundation, 1983: 117–119.

SLEEPING BEAUTY: THE LAST TSAR'S DAUGHTER
Ballet by Youri Vamos (1993)
[based on *The Sleeping Beauty*]

[5714]   "Dornröschen". In: *Pipers Enzyklopadie des Musiktheaters: Oper, Operette, Musical, Ballet*. Hrsg. von Carl Dahlhaus und dem Forschungsinstitut für Musiktheater der Universität Bayreuth unter Leitung von Sieghart Dohring. Bd. 6. München: Piper [1995]: 377–378.

THE SNOW MAIDEN
Ballet by Vladimir Burmeister (1961)
[based on *The Snow Maiden* and movts. I and II from the *Symphony No. 1*]

[5715]   GOODWIN, N. '"The Snow Maiden": Music', *Dance and Dancers*, 12 (Sep 1961): 12–13.
          The premiere of the ballet at the Festival Hall in London.

[5716]   'Nashe iskusstvo za rubezhom: Russkaia "Snegurochka" lomaet led", *Sovetskaia kul´tura* (6 Jan 1962): 1.

[5717]   KRIGER, V. '"Snegurochka" prishla v balet', *Pravda* (28 Nov 1963): 4.
          The premiere of the ballet in Moscow.

[5718]   EL´IASH, N. 'Tantsuet "Snegurochka"', *Sovetskaia kul´tura* (30 Nov 1963): 3, illus.

[5719]   "Snow Maiden". In: *International dictionary of ballet*. Ed. Martha Bremser. Vol. 1. Detroit: St. James Press, 1993: 215.

SOUVENIR DE FLORENCE
Ballet by John Taras (1981)
[based on *Souvenir de Florence*]

[5720]   "Souvenir de Florence". In: *International dictionary of ballet*. Ed. Martha Bremser. Vol. 2. Detroit: St. James Press, 1993: 1388.

SOUVENIR DE LENINGRAD
Ballet by Maurice Bejart (1987)

[5721]   "Souvenir de Leningrad". In: M. Bejart, *Le ballet des mots* [Paris]: Les Belles Lettres; Archimbaud, 1994: 493.

SPRING FAIRY TALE
Ballet by Fëdor Lopukhov (1947)
[based on various pieces by Chaikovskii, compiled by Boris Asaf´ev]

[5722]   "Vesenniaia skazka". In: A. Degen & I. Stupnikov, *Leningradskii balet, 1917–1987. Slovar´-spravochnik: Solistki, solisty, baletmeistery, pedagogi, dirizhery*. Leningrad: Sovetskii kompozitor, 1988: 243.

THE STORM
Ballet by Oleg Aver´ianov & Vladimir Fedianin (1982)

[5723]   **"Groza"**. In: A. Degen & I. Stupnikov, *Leningradskii balet, 1917–1987. Slovar´-spravochnik: Solistki, solisty, baletmeistery, pedagogi, dirizhery*. Leningrad: Sovetskii kompozitor, 1988: 244.

SYMPHONY NO. 1
Ballet by Peter Martins (1981)
[based on the *Symphony No. 1*]

[5724]   **"Symphony No 1"**. In: *International dictionary of ballet*. Ed. Martha Bremser. Vol. 2. Detroit: St. James Press, 1993: 916.

TCHAIKOVSKY PAS DE DEUX
Ballet by George Balanchine (1960)
[based on excerpts from *Swan Lake*]

[5725]   **"Tchaikovsky Pas de deux"**. In: G. Balanchine, *Balanchine's new complete stories of the great ballets*. Ed. by Francis Mason. Drawings by Marta Becket. Garden City (N. Y.): Doubleday [1968]: 432.

[5726]   **"Tchaikovsky Pas de deux"**. In: G. Balanchine & F. Mason, *Balanchine's complete stories of the great ballets*. Rev. and enlarged ed. Garden City (N. Y.): Doubleday, 1977: 632–633.

[5727]   **"Pas de deux"**. In: *Choreography by George Balanchine: A catalogue of works*. New York: Eakins Press Foundation, 1983: 232.

TCHAIKOVSKY SUITE NO. 2
Ballet by Jacques d'Amboise (1969)
[based on the *Suite No. 2*]

[5728]   **"Tchaikovsky Suite No. 2"**. In: W. Terry, *Ballet guide: Background, listings, credits, and descriptions of more than five hundred of the world's major ballets*. New York: Dodd & Mead [1976]: 339.

[5729]   **"Tchaikovsky Suite No 2"**. In: G. Balanchine & F. Mason, *Balanchine's complete stories of the great ballets*. Rev. and enlarged ed. Garden City (N. Y.): Doubleday, 1977: 633.

TCHAIKOVSKY SUITE NO. 3
[original title: *Theme and Variations*]
Ballet by George Balanchine (1947, rev. 1970)
[based on movt. IV from the *Suite No. 3*]

[5730]   **"Theme and variations"**. In: G. Balanchine, *Balanchine's new complete stories of the great ballets*. Ed. by Francis Mason. Drawings by Marta Becket. Garden City (N. Y.): Doubleday [1968]: 433–434.

[5731]   **"Tchaikovsky Suite No 3"**. In: G. Balanchine & F. Mason, *Balanchine's complete stories of the great ballets*. Rev. and enlarged ed. Garden City (N. Y.): Doubleday, 1977: 633–634.

[5732]   **"Theme and variations"**. In: *Choreography by George Balanchine: A catalogue of works*. New York: Eakins Press Foundation, 1983: 242.

TCHAIKOVSKY WALTZ
Ballet by John Taras (1946)

[5733]   **"Tchaikovsky Waltz"**. In: *International dictionary of ballet*. Ed. Martha Bremser. Vol. 2. Detroit: St. James Press, 1993: 1386.

THE TEMPEST

Ballet by Rudolf Nureev (1982)

[based on the *Suite No. 3* (movt. IV finale), *Suite No. 1* (movt. II) and *The Tempest*]

[5734]   **"The Tempest"**, *About the House*, 6 (1983), 8: 27–29, illus.
Photographic study of Nureev's ballet.

TIME PASSED SUMMER

Ballet by Benjamin Harkarvy (1974)

[based on 11 songs by Chaikovskii]

[5735]   'Time Passed Summer'. In: W. Terry, *Ballet guide: Background, listings, credits, and descriptions of more than five hundred of the world's major ballets*. New York: Dodd & Mead [1976]: 345–346.

[5736]   **"Time Past Summer"**. In: G. Balanchine & F. Mason, *Balanchine's complete stories of the great ballets*. Rev. and enlarged ed. Garden City (N. Y.): Doubleday, 1977: 645.

TRIO

Ballet by John Taras (1991)

[5737]   **"Trio"**. In: *International dictionary of ballet*. Ed. Martha Bremser. Vol. 2. Detroit: St. James Press, 1993: 1388.

TSCHAIKOWSKY

Ballet by Horst Müller (1979)

[5738]   **"Tschaikowsky"**. In: H. Koegler, *The concise Oxford dictionary of ballet*. London; New York: Oxford Univ. Press, 1982: 412.

TSCHAIKOWSKY

Ballet by Youri Vamos (1980)

[based on Chaikovskii's chamber music]

[5739]   **"Tschaikowsky"**. In: H. Koegler, *The concise Oxford dictionary of ballet*. London, New York: Oxford Univ. Press, 1982: 412.

VALSE-SCHERZO

Part of the ballet *Tempo di Valse* by Jacques D'Amboise (1981)

[5740]   **"Valse-scherzo"**. In: *International dictionary of ballet*. Ed. Martha Bremser. Vol. 1. Detroit: St. James Press, 1993: 327.

WALTZ

Choreographic miniature by Leonid Iakobson (1948)

[5741]   **"Waltz"**. In: *International dictionary of ballet*. Ed. Martha Bremser. Vol. 2. Detroit: St. James Press, 1993: 1552.

WALTZ-SCHERZO

Ballet by George Balanchine (1958)

[based on the *Valse-Scherzo*, op. 34]

[5742]   **"Waltz-scherzo"**. In: *Choreography by George Balanchine: A catalogue of works*. New York: Eakins Press Foundation, 1983: 226.

WAR AND PEACE

Ballet by Valery Panov (1980)

[5743]   **"War and Peace"**. In: *International dictionary of ballet*. Ed. Martha Bremser. Vol. 2. Detroit: St. James Press, 1993: 1070.

WINTER DREAMS

Ballet by Kenneth MacMillan (1991)

[based on the *Symphony No. 1*]

[5744]   **"Winter dreams"**. In: *International dictionary of ballet*. Ed. Martha Bremser. Vol. 2. Detroit: St. James Press, 1993: 891.

YOUTH

Choreographic miniature by Leonid Iakobson (1949)

[5745]   **"Youth"**. In: *International dictionary of ballet*. Ed. Martha Bremser. Vol. 2. Detroit: St. James Press, 1993: 1552.

YOUTH SUITE

Choreographic miniature by Leonid Iakobson (1950)

[5746]   **"Youth Suite"**. In: *International dictionary of ballet*. Ed. Martha Bremser. Vol. 2. Detroit: St. James Press, 1993: 1553.

BIBLIOGRAPHY INDEX

2257, 2259, 2270, 2392, 2470, 3086, 3330, 3859, 4010, 4132, 4296, 4318, 4453, 4978, 5047, 5110

Brown, Malcolm H. 286, 462, 602, 1143, 1534, 1548, 1981, 2225, 2226, 2252, 2270, 2404, 3845

Brubach, H. 4108, 5064

Bruckner, D. J. R. 2270

Bruce, D. 2773

Bruder, Bärbel 462

Bruegge, J. 5145

Brun, M. 2661

Bruneau, Alfred 194, 218

Bruni, T. G. 595

Brunswick, M. 360

Brusianin, V. 1233

Brussel, James A. 2161

"B. T." 4830

Buchanan, Charles L. 1106

Buck, Dorothy C. 4311

Buckley, Jonathan 2627

Budashevskaia, L. 944

Budden, Julian 1683

Budden, Roy 4825

Budiakovskii, Andrei E. 563, 585, 763, 795, 873, 1193, 1480, 1728, 2665, 2674, 2928, 3558, 3559, 4368, 4403, 4692, 4696, 4823

Budil´nik 2788, 2792, 3201

Bugoslavskii, Sergei 716, 727, 741, 2330, 2881

Buhler, James 2416

Bühne [Vienna, Austria] 1504, 1523, 3656, 4101, 4327

Buianova, G. 2551

Buianovskii, V. M. 2445

Bukinik, Isaak E. 406

Bukinik, Mikhail E. 407, 2851

"Bukva" — *see* Vasilevskii, I. F.

Bulai, L. G. 34

Bulgakov, B. 198

Bulgarska muzika [Sofia, Bulgaria] 183, 291, 1011, 3180

Bullard, Truman 602, 3133

Bülow, Hans G. von 132, 159, 176, 219–221, 1020, 1927, 2278, 4997a

Bunimovich, Vladimir I, ("Muzalevskii, Vladimir") 719, 730, 2553, 2906, 4596

Burenin, Viktor 3302, 3313, 3320, 3338

Bürger, Sigmund 159, 175

Burgess, Anthony 1534

Burk, John N. 2320

Burke, Anthony 5687

Burke, D. 4776

Burmeister, Vladimir 4278, 4304, 4309, 5715–5719

Burmester, Willy 159, 222, 223, 408

Burov, F. 2025

Burr, Ralph C. 380, 2236

Bush, Alan 2967

Buske, P. 4743

Busoni, Feruccio 1910

Busygin, S. 5520

Butaux, A. 3677

Butkovskii, A. 5499

Butorov, L. 940

"B. V." 3365, 3368, 4171

Byron, George G. 4472, 4478, 4488, 4490

Byron, May C. 1466

Cadars, P. 5550

Cæcilia [Strasbourg, France] 4902

Calvocoressi, Michel D. 204, 1060

Cambridge Review [Cambridge, England] 1490

Campbell, Stuart 141, 143, 2075, 2408

Canadian Review of Comparative Literature [Ottawa, Canadal] 3645

Canadian Slavonic Papers [Ottawa, Canada] 3085

Canning, Hugh 1534, 1554, 3687

Canon [Sydney, Australia] 1462, 4706, 5455

Cantata for the Jubilee of O. A. Petrov **(68)** 5181

Cantata for the Opening of the Polytechnic Exposition **(24)** 5172–5180

Caras, Steven 3990

Cardew, Cornelius 2342

Cardona-Peña, Alfredo 5460

Carlson, B. 1665

Carp, L. 3940

Carpenter, E. D. 3844

Carse, Adam 2312, 4523

Carter, Elliot 4055

Carter, Vivian 2291

Caruso, Enrico 3107

Casals, Pablo 5135

Casini, Claudio 1549

Catoire, Georges — *see* Katuar, Georgii

Cave, Phoebe Rogoff 412, 433, 485

Čech, Adolf 153, 159, 174, 1799

Célis, Henri 1492

Center 3937, 3938

Central Opera Service Bulletin [New York, USA] 162, 1534, 2470

Century Magazine [New York, USA] 472, 5501

Červinková-Riegrová, Marie 159, 224, 409, 1806

"C'est Moi" 4932

Chaikovskaia, Aleksandra A. [mother] 152, 589, 1453, 1715, 1893

Chaikovskaia, Antonina I. [wife] — *see* Miliukova, Antonina

Chaikovskaia, Elizaveta M. [stepmother] 155, 1453

Chaikovskaia, Lidiia 1701

Chaikovskaia, Ol´ga S. [sister-in-law] 2231, 2232

Chaikovskaia, Praskov´ia V. [sister-in-law] 152, 155, 226, 412, 1453

Chaikovskii, Anatolii I. [brother] 152, 155, 177, 190, 192, 195, 226–230, 413, 1453, 1751, 2065

Chaikovskii, Il´ia P. [father] 152, 155, 589, 1453, 1712, 1715, 1891–1896

Chaikovskii, Ippolit I. [brother] 155, 360, 414, 415, 689, 1339, 1872

Chaikovskii, Modest I. [brother] 15, 97, 98, 99, 137, 152, 155, 177, 190, 192, 195, 279, 339,

Constanti, S. 3860
Contemporary Review [London, England] 1453, 1581, 1584, 1995, 2270, 2557, 3807
Context 2043
Conus — *see* Konius
Cooper, Martin 586, 2595, 2958, 3588, 4410, 4412, 4511
Courtade, F. 5550
Copperthwaite, D. B. 4008
Coppola, C. 4861
Cord 3836
Coronet 1078
Costas 3990
Coton, A. V. 4255
Coughlan, J. 5563
Couperin, François 2083
(Le) Courier Musicale [Paris, France] 2051
(Le) Courier Musicale de France [Paris, France] 1522
Cowen, Frederic 421
Craddock, P. 5308
Craft, Robert 286, 1528, 1534, 1676, 3844
Cranko, John 5682–5686
Crankshaw, G. 1690, 3621
Crespi, Francesca 4112
Crisp, Clement 3985, 4085, 4091
(The) Critic 4672
Croce, Arlene 1127, 3844, 3846, 4095, 4288
Croissant, C. R. 77
Crompton, Louis 3046, 4732, 5063
Crowle, Pigeon (Eileen Georgina Beatrice) 3942
Crowther, B. 5569
Csampai, Attila 3075, 4387
Cui — *see* Kiui
Cuming, G. J. 55
Current Literature [New York, USA] 2157, 4681
Curtis, J. M. 4326
Cuyler, L. E. 4427

Dabbadie, D. 4297
Dabbadie, N. 4297
Daberet, F. 5482
Dadashev, A. 760
Dahlhaus, Carl 2700, 2774, 3123, 3196, 3259, 3342, 3429, 3718, 3994, 4127, 4320, 5714
Daidzhest/24 chasa 2025, 2241
Daily Chronicle [London, England] 1831, 1833
Daily Evening Telegraph 1850
Daily Mail [London, England] 1548
Daily Telegraph [London, England] 1554, 1831–1833
Daily Yomiuri [Tokyo, Japan] 1548
Dalen, Hugo van 1479, 1624
Dalibor [Prague, Czech Republic] 1928, 3461
D´Amboise, Jacques 82, 5614, 5708, 5728, 5729, 5740
D´Amico, F. 4082
Dammann, Susanne 596, 601, 4461, 4617
Dampf, A. 3733
Damrosch, Leopold 159
Damrosch, Walter 175, 423

Dance [New York, USA] 4126
Dance Chronicle [New York, USA] 3843, 3844, 4315, 4316
Dance & Dancers [London, England] 1130, 3844, 3859, 3862, 3943, 3958, 4087, 4123, 4124, 4129, 4229, 4259, 5715
Dance Gazette 3841, 3984, 4111, 4295
Dance Magazine [New York, USA] 1118, 1141, 2230, 2244, 3839, 3843, 3844, 3940, 3964, 3999, 4107, 4293, 4326, 4332, 5065, 5580
Dance News [New York, USA] 1117, 1119
Dance Now 4010, 4132, 4318
Dance Perspectives [New York, USA] 3828, 4089
Dance Research Journal [Brockport (N. Y.), USA] 3087, 3843, 3986
Dancing Times [London, England] 1067, 1084, 1137, 3815, 3818, 3843, 3844, 3849, 3850, 3860, 4058, 4065, 4066, 4125, 4133, 4139, 4253, 4305, 4323, 4331
Danielson, D. 4655
Danilenko, G. 1276, 1283
Danilevich, Lev V. 585, 1499, 2334, 2443, 4404, 4414
Danilovich, A. 2051
Dan´ko, Larisa 5031
Dan´ko, Kseniia (Danko, Xenia) 124, 125
Dannreuther, Edward 234
Danova, I. V. 3107
Dansk Musiktidsskrift [Copenhagen, Denmark] 3013, 4421
Dante Alighieri 4849, 4850, 4858, 4859
Dany, Carole 3843
Dargomyzhskii, Aleksandr S. 118, 141, 1059, 2084
Darinskaia, L. 1537
Darrell, R. D. 50, 4272, 4962
Dashak, Z. A. 5134
Daugava 318
Davidian, R. 5330
Davidson, E. 1277
Davidson, Gladys 2876, 3169, 3512
Davidson, M. 5577
Davidson, Philip 2364
Davis, Mike 3942
Davis, P. G. 3016, 3244
Davison, R. M. 1532
Davydov, Aleksandr 424, 425, 2537
Davydov, G. 1877
Davydov, Iurii L. [nephew] 88, 426–430, 1243, 1869, 1870, 1872
Davydov, Karl Iu. 235, 2178
Davydov, Lev V. [brother-in-law] 152, 155, 1453
Davydov, Vladimir L. [nephew] 155, 190, 1453, 2065
Davydova, Aleksandra I. [sister] 152, 155, 1328
Davydova, Anna L. [niece] — *see* Meck, Anna L. von
Davydova, Kseniia Iu. [great-niece] 102, 156, 159, 176, 178, 182, 219, 259, 374, 397, 570, 587, 1032, 1210, 1213, 1216, 1252, 1271, 1292, 1305, 1319, 1837, 2353, 4234

5633–5640
Franke, Roberta 222, 408
Frankfurter Allgemeine Zeitung [Frankfurt, Germany] 2250
Frankfurter Zeitung [Frankfurt, Germany] 1821
Freed, R. 71
Freeman, J. W. 1557, 3072, 3195, 3363, 3642, 3722, 5211
Frei, W. 5088
Freindlikh, G. 4907
Freindling, G. R. 102
Fremdenblatt 1823, 5087
(6) French Songs **(108)** 5269
Freund, Donald 5471
Fribus, Aleksandr 439
Frid, E. L. 205, 1655
Fride, Nina 440
Frideczky, F. 3618
Friskin, James 5035
Friskin, Mrs James 5035
Froelich, Carl 5550–5553
Frolov, Sergei T. 597, 599, 4618
Frolova (Frolova-Walker), M. 593, 601, 2102
Frolova, S. 5351
Frumkis, Tat´iana 596, 2412, 5223
Fuchs, Jeanne 3868
Fugue [Toronto, Canada] 2035, 4484
Fuller Maitland, J. A. 1566, 1598
Fürstner, Adolf 1453
Furtwängler, Wilhelm 2342
Fyodorova, Zoya 5131

Gabel´, Stanislav 442, 443, 583
Gabovich, M. 3920
Gabrilovich, E. 1197
Gadzhibekova, U. 851
Gaevskii, E. I. 1749, 1896
Gaidai, Mikhail 444
Gaidamovich, Tat´iana A. 591, 594, 597, 5120, 5140, 5310, 5312, 5314
Gaines, C. T. 1135
Gainsley, P. 1548
Gakkel´, Leonid 968, 989
Gál, György S. 1516
Galimon, N. 1269
Gall´, E. 748, 757
Galler, Konstantin P. 129, 2703, 2716, 2823, 2824, 2832, 3206, 3220, 3274, 3389, 3744, 3756, 3776, 4550, 4579, 4583, 4801, 4838
Gallet, Louis 159, 194
Gallotta, B. 5362
Galvert, M. de. 3688
Gamaley, Iu. 4009
Gann, K. 1534
Gangelin, A. 4591
Garden, Edward J. C. 286, 1526, 1532, 1534, 1864, 1922, 2022, 3837, 3844, 5043, 5045
Gardiner, B. 1526, 1528, 2034, 5544, 5548
Gardner, C. J. 1490

Garin, S. 1399
Garina, E. 854
Gårsjo, Kerstin 5466
Gatobovets 239
Gauk, Aleksandr 4975
Gaulois [Paris, France] 1813, 1815
Gay slaviane [St. Petersburg, Russia] 2252
(Le) Gazette Musicale [Paris, France] 4585, 4934, 5009, 5011, 5013, 5082
Gedeonov, Stepan A. 167
Gee, John 1511
Geiger, Robert 1580
Gellatt, R. 4500
Gelles, G. 1657
Gel´tser, Vasilii 4254
General-Anzeiger [Elberfield, Germany] 1821
Genika, Rostislav V. 445, 5343
Genne, Beth 3843
Georgiadis, N. 3957
Gerard, Vladimir N. 446, 1718
Gerasicheva, G. 5526
Gerburg, R. 1257
Gerdt, O. 2069
Gerigk, H. 2013
Gerlach, Hannelore 134
Germain, J. 4971
"Geronskii" 3906
Gershovskii, Evgenii 156, 215, 269, 1208, 1722
Gersoni, V. 1200
Gevaert, François-Auguste 148, 156
"G. G." 4867
Giaurov, Nikolai 965
Gidoni, Aleksandr 5489
G—ich, E. 1456
Gilev, Sergei 2890
Gilinsky, Joshua Earl 4914
Gilman, Lawrence 50, 2155, 2320, 2560, 3498, 4686
Gilnes, D. 4857
Gintsburg, Lev 1804
Gintsburg, S. 857, 3516, 3530, 3551
Ginzburg, A. S. 223
Gippo, J. 3998, 4006
Girardi, M. 1532, 1549
Giroud, Vincent 5476
Gitel´makher, V. 568
Giuliani, E. 3677, 4297
Glavach, V. I. 4769
Glazer, Benjamin 5569
Glazunov, Aleksandr K. 245, 373, 447, 448, 513, 514, 1453, 1937, 2304, 4697, 4945, 5116, 5184
Glebov, Igor´ — *see* Asaf´ev, B. V.
Gleich, F. 1822
Gleide, E. 3071
Glier, Reingold (Gliere, Reinhold) 858, 866, 2511, 5120
Glikson, Frederick 159
Glinka, Mikhail I. 597, 1059, 1365, 1447, 1645, 1656, 1749, 2084, 2088–2091, 2463, 2533,

3516, 3551, 3908, 3916, 3917, 3923
Krasnaia nov´ [Moscow, Russia] 799, 2325
Krasnaia panorama [Moscow, Russia] 730
Krasnaia zvezda [Moscow, Russia] 1296
Krasnoe znamia [Taganrog, Russia] 4195
Krasnoflotets [Moscow, Russia] 893
Krasnoiarskii rabochii [Krasnoiarsk, Russia] 759
Krasnov, A. 1351
Krasnyi arkhiv [Moscow, Russia] 171
Krasovskaia, Vera 3935, 4069, 4089, 4106
Krauklis, Georgii V. 5077
Kraus, Joseph 602, 2497, 4463, 4654
Kraus, Oscar 1401
Krause, Ernst 1025, 1228, 1817, 2598, 3038, 3242,
     3635
Kravchenko, Tat'iana P. 5060, 5061
Kravtsov, F. 1363
Krebs, S. 1511
Kremlev, Iulii A. 585, 2139, 2432, 4405, 4414
Kresh, P. 4273, 5405
Kress, M. 1398
Kriegsman, Alan 2227
Kriger, Viktorina 3952, 5717
Kriuger, A. N. 3811, 4570
Krivenko, S. V. 169
Krivenko, V. S. 413
Krokover, R. 3936, 4072
Krug, W. 1609
Kruglikov, Semën N. 1779, 2635, 2637, 2838, 3277,
     4792, 4882, 4941, 4953, 5096, 5300
Krugozor [Moscow, Russia] 2276
Krukones, James 602, 5567
Krull, K. 5467
Krummacher, F. 5105
Kruzhiiamskaia, A. 926
Krylov, A. 5156
Krylova, O. 1887
Krzemien-Kolpanowicz, B. 3864
"K. S." 2916
Kuba, Ludvik 270, 271
Kubatskii, Viktor 118, 5119, 5124, 5132
Kudoiarova, S. I. 1893
Kudriavtseva, G. 1222
Kudrin, K. 3897
Kugul´skii, Semën 145
Kuhn, Ernst 360, 379, 462, 2406
Kulakovskaia, T. 113
Kulakovskii, A. 1507
Kulik, I. 1906
Kul´tura [Moscow, Russia] 1016, 1691, 1887, 4022
Kul´tura i teatr [Moscow, Russia] 331, 584, 3511,
     3797, 4189
Kul´tura i zhizn´ [Moscow, Russia] 916, 1259, 1910,
     5536
Kuna, Milan 409, 1806, 1807
Kündinger, Rudolf 478, 1718
Kunin, Iosif F. 23, 135, 145, 147, 179, 588, 803,
     914, 1507, 2058–2061, 2323, 2334, 2338, 2362,
     2366, 2604, 2685, 2960, 3058, 3316, 3585,

3822, 4244, 4780, 4826, 4911, 5456
Kunst und Literatur [Berlin, Germany] 1031, 2371,
     5542
Kupernik, Lev A. 140, 217, 1779
Kupets, L. A. 2510
Kurepin, Aleksandr 1881, 2782, 2798, 4155
Kur´er 1890, 1972, 2729, 3223, 3283, 3286, 4786
Kurnosenkov, K. 1334
Kurortnaia gazeta 425, 1976
Kurskaia pravda [Kursk, Russia] 5456
Kurtsman, Alisa 5401
Kusevitskii, Sergei 690, 4637
Kushida, Magoichi 3963
Kushnareva, L. 4960
Kuster, Konrad 1526
Kut, A. 3541
Kutateladze, Larisa 294, 358
Kutschera, A. C. 4257
Kuzma, M. 2082
Kuzmin, Mikhail 1973
Kuz´mina, A. 264
Kuz´mina, Liudmila 265
Kuznetsov, Aleksandr 360, 650, 1311, 1979, 5475
Kuznetsov, I. 5710
Kuznetsov, Konstantin A. 585, 997, 1172, 1616,
     1965, 1996
Kuznetsov, M. 5535
Kuznetsov, N. 2642
Kuznetsov, Nikolai 272, 479, 561, 569
Kuznetsov, S. 1868
Kuznetsova, G. V. 1901
Kuznetsova, I. 2999
Kuznetsova, Mariia 479
Kuzovleva, T. 4325
K—v, K. 2198
Kyasht, Lydia 5694

"L." 4036, 4337, 4624, 4863, 5185
"La" 3393
Labutina, Galina 156
Ladov, V. 655
Ladygin, D. 4312, 4313
Lagina, N. 1745
Lakond, Wladimir (Lake, Walter) 360
La Laurencie, L. de 1602
Lalo, Édouard 194
"La Main Gauche" 1836
Lambert, Constant 1068, 4059
Lamey, B. 332
Lamm, Léonide 1216
Lamm, Pavel G. 118
Lamond, Frederic 159, 175, 196, 480
Lamond, Irene Triesch 480
Lamuret, Charles 159
Lanchbery, John 4253
Landely, A. 1813
Landovska, Wanda 1935, 2083
Landrum, Michael McRee 5412
Lang, Paul Henry 303, 2332, 4601

4678, 4682, 5017, 5237, 5305, 5426

Musical Times [London, England] 129, 162, 204, 234, 286, 377, 462, 1085, 1462, 1511, 1519, 1526, 1532, 1534, 1548, 1617, 1656, 1680, 1831, 1832, 1835, 1838, 1864, 1886, 2020, 2095, 2166–2168, 2170, 2380, 2462, 2697, 2768, 2773, 2844, 3053, 3060, 3080, 3086, 3181, 3255, 3328, 3330, 3332, 3428, 3696, 3837, 3844, 3987, 4407, 4424, 4745, 4756, 5045–5048, 5186, 5365, 5461, 5566

Musical World [Boston, USA] 2155

Music Analysis [Oxford, England] 4460

Music & Artists [New York, USA] 1863

Música y educación [Madird, Spain] 4967

Music Clubs Magazine [Indianapolis, USA] 1135

Music Educator´s Journal [Reston (Virgina), USA] 586, 1528, 4909

Music Forum 570

Musician [Philadelphia, USA] 1112, 1593, 1639, 1702, 1723, 1855, 2294, 2299, 4558, 4679, 4691

Music in Education [London, England] 1526, 4424, 4908, 5461

Music Journal [New York, USA] 912, 2013, 2346, 3972, 4605, 4650, 5025, 5078, 5532

Music & Letters [Oxford, England] 162, 286, 377, 412, 1064, 1500, 1512, 1526, 1532, 1534, 1839, 1864, 1921, 2002, 2013, 2075, 2222, 2271, 2272, 2470, 2695, 3844, 4987, 5035, 5043

Music Magazine [Toronto, Canada] 1511, 1864, 4503, 4504

Music & Musicians [London, England] 430, 1076, 1081, 1511, 1534, 1535, 1839, 2606, 2971, 3017, 3036, 3055, 3059, 3182, 3248, 3615, 3616, 3621, 3837, 4482, 4508, 4509, 4528, 4716, 4912, 5074, 5131, 5232, 5522, 5549, 5564

Music News [Chicago, USA] 2336, 4374, 4857

Music News from Prague [Prague, Czech Republic] 409, 1803

Music Parade [London, England] 1500

Music Review [Cambridge, England] 1462, 1526, 1534, 2466, 3334, 3837, 3844, 4419, 4609, 4653, 4747, 5050, 5268

Music Student [Leeds, England] 2307

Music Teacher [London, England] 1519, 1526, 3837, 3971, 4424, 4608, 4638, 5372, 5455, 5461

Music Theory Spectrum [Bloomington, USA] 4654

(Die) Musik [Berlin; Lepizig; Stuttgart, Germany] 203, 338, 1619, 1995, 2013, 2014, 2053, 2054, 2659, 2660, 3299, 4621, 4689

Musikalisches Wochenblatt [Berlin, Germany] 1025, 1816

Musikas Apskats 5475

(Die) Musikerziehung [Vienna, Austria] 63, 379, 4710

(Die) Musikforschung [Kassel, Germany; Basel, Switzerland] 11, 284, 379, 566, 1050, 1504, 1505, 1526, 2333, 2406, 3715, 3716, 3844, 4754, 4985

Musikhandel [Bonn, Germany] 11,1034, 1513, 2013

Musik im Unterricht [Mainz, Germany] 284, 4619

Musik in der Schule [Berlin, Germany] 134, 284, 360, 379, 3981, 4607, 5329

(Das) Musikleben [Mainz, Germany] 2753, 2952

Musikrevy [Stockholm, Sweden] 286, 2024, 3099, 3698, 4131, 4317, 4384, 5293

Musiktherapeutische Umschau [Stuttgart, Germany] 4128

Musik und Bildung [Mainz, Germany] 11, 379, 1667, 3071, 4058, 4104, 4820, 5378

Musik und Gesellschaft [Berlin, Germany] 11, 134, 260, 284, 570, 1030, 1042, 1648, 1829, 1869, 2343, 2763, 4286, 4314, 4515, 4527, 4781

Musik und Kirche [Kassel, Germany; Basel, Switzerland] 360, 462

Musik und Kultur [Regensburg, Germany] 2013

Musik und Szene [Düsseldorf, Germany] 2548, 2994, 3827

(Die) Musik-Woche [Berlin, Germany] 5229

Musique et Concours [Paris, France] 2318

Musorgskii, Modest P. 602, 772, 776, 1059, 1645, 1656, 1909, 1913, 1947, 1948, 2142, 2395, 2618, 2939, 3077, 3533, 4697, 5264

Mustafaev, F. 1775

Muti, Ricardo 965

Muzalevskii, Vladimir. — *see* Bunimovich, Vladimir I.

Muzica [Bucharest, Romania] 1097

Muzik & Wetenschap 2514

Muzsika [Budapest, Hungary] 1090, 1091, 1256, 3043, 3050, 3093, 3132, 3618, 4263, 4997

Muzyka [Moscow, Russia] 255, 762–764, 1188, 1828, 2077, 2300, 3563, 4475, 4696

Muzyka [Warsaw, Poland] 48, 95, 596, 1049, 1314, 2487, 2488, 3864, 4014, 4748, 5159

Muzyka i penie [St. Petersburg, Russia] 256, 431, 444, 1423

Muzyka i revoliutsiia [Moscow, Russia] 16, 165, 725, 732, 743, 1947, 2515, 2519, 2525, 3524

Muzyka i teatr 5445

Muzyka i zhizn´ [Leningrad, Russia] 688, 5151

Muzykal´naia akademiia [Moscow, Russia] 94, 378, 985, 2625, 3130, 3697, 3699, 3701, 3709, 3727, 4454, 4614, 4658, 5171

Muzykal´naia nov´ [Moscow; Petrograd, Russia] 212, 716, 718, 1612, 1618, 2566

Muzykal´naia samodeiatel´nost´ [Moscow, Russia] 2908, 4693, 4694

Muzykal´naia zhizn´ [Moscow, Russia] 112, 221, 224, 264, 356, 409, 434, 462, 568, 582, 588, 589, 852, 909, 911, 938, 940, 946, 947, 950, 955, 979, 993, 1038, 1092, 1093, 1205, 1229, 1234, 1243, 1251, 1254, 1261, 1266, 1276, 1278, 1283, 1284, 1288, 1289, 1290, 1291, 1292, 1305, 1311, 1324, 1334, 1358, 1363, 1373, 1390, 1392, 1393, 1399, 1414, 1441, 1532, 1540, 1542, 1721, 1734, 1742, 1746, 1750, 1758, 1763, 1764, 1767, 1794, 1837, 1841, 1878, 1894, 1905, 1931, 1938, 1941, 1945, 1951, 1954, 1964, 1970, 1977, 1979,

Popov, Serafim 5155
Popov, V. S. 2407
Popova, E. 915, 1004
Popova, Tat´iana 1778
Populär historia 1672
Poradnik muzyczny [Lodz, Poland] 4707
Porter, Andrew 3014
Porter, H. 1554
Posell, Elsa Z. 1653
Posner, Sandy 4061
Pospisil, Vilem 2696, 3631
Postler, Miroslav 1949
Potapov, V. I. 3929
Potapova, L. 3636
Potashkinas, Kh. 1480
Pougin, Artur 1563
Pozdeeva, T. A. 573
Pozdniakov, A. 1322
Pozhidaev, Gennadi A. 1841, 1842, 4888
Pozhidaev, I. 4719
Poznansky, Alexander 139, 141, 143, 145, 147, 195,
    380, 381, 388, 400, 401, 403, 406, 407, 411,
    414, 416, 429, 431–433, 437, 445–447, 451, 464,
    465, 471, 473, 476–478, 482, 483, 487, 492, 493,
    495, 501, 506, 515–517, 521, 524, 525, 527, 529,
    541, 542, 544, 550–552, 596, 600–602, 630, 688,
    984, 1548, 1671, 1679, 1680, 1683, 1687, 1693,
    1720, 1903, 1961, 2042, 2178, 2236, 2238,
    2243, 2250, 2256, 2270, 2272, 3126, 3711, 3843
Prague National Theatre [Prague, Czech Republic]
    175
Pravda [Moscow, Russia] 517, 737, 765, 813, 832,
    833, 837, 841, 844, 851, 864, 872, 874, 877,
    882, 897, 924, 978, 1001–1003, 1008, 1102,
    1199, 1205, 1297, 1308, 1328, 1332, 1344–1347,
    1357, 1397, 1405, 1412, 1811, 2667, 2676,
    2744, 2746, 3576, 3577, 3853, 3926, 3928,
    4216, 4218, 4238, 4606, 5717
Pravoslavnyi put´ [Jordanville (N. Y.), USA] 2450
Preisman, E. 941
Preobrazhenskii, Antonii 5147
Presnetsov, R. 1954
Press 1846
Priani, E. di. 1107
Prianishnikov, Ippolit P. 313, 519, 520, 589, 1956,
    1957
Pribegina, Galina A. 124, 374, 571, 1540, 1867,
    3184, 4729
Price, Christine 5455, 5459
Pricope, E. 1097
Pridneprovskii krai 455, 652, 673
Pring, S. W. 1617
Pritchard, J. 4133
Proceedings of the Musical Association [London,
    England] 2555
Proceedings of the Royal Musical Association [London,
    England] 1922
Prokhorov, S. A. 735
Prokof´ev, Georgii 4522

Prokof´ev, Sergei 1365, 2505, 2517
Prokunin, Vasilii P. 118
Proleeva, Vera I. 1749, 1871, 1873, 1893, 1905,
    1907
Proletarskaia pravda [Riga, Latvia] 1999
Prostor 502
"Protei" 701
Protopopov, Vladimir V. 102, 118, 135, 156, 374,
    2348, 2353, 2447, 2452, 2471, 2588, 3326,
    5171
Prudnikova, O. F. 573, 1749, 5486
Pshibyshevskii, Boleslav 280, 747
P—skii, E. 2290, 4344, 4875
Psychiatric Quarterly Supplement [New York, USA]
    2161
Pudelek, Janina 4315
Pumpianskii, Lev 2927
Purdy, Claire Lee 5452
Pushkin, Aleksandr S. 588, 597, 1261, 2127–2137,
    2533, 2595, 2625, 2628, 2629, 2630, 2701,
    2784, 2836, 2841, 2855, 2863, 2881, 2914,
    2918, 2927, 2928, 2929, 2930, 2955, 2959,
    2983, 3006, 3009, 3011, 3020, 3023, 3034,
    3064, 3071, 3094, 3104, 3129, 3249, 3262,
    3301, 3302, 3308, 3309, 3315, 3317, 3320,
    3329, 3338, 3435, 3458, 3492, 3497, 3500,
    3501, 3507, 3509, 3528, 3545, 3558, 3566,
    3583, 3584, 3586, 3587, 3597, 3601, 3603,
    3645, 3646, 3649, 3677, 3681, 3682, 3712,
    3726, 5553
Pustovit, E. 156
Putintsev, N. 1976
Puzanova, N. 1378
Puzrin, I. 1249
"P. V." 4659

(The) Queen of Spades **(10)** 118, 268, 353, 424, 440,
    465, 492, 551, 555, 1433, 3435–3727, 5618,
    5619
Quill & Quire [Toronto, Canada] 5472
Quinzaine littéraire [Paris, France] 5040, 5106

"R." — *see* Larosh, German A.
Raaben, Lev N. 201, 358, 2139, 5076, 5102, 5290
Rabeneck, Nicolai 2160, 5208
Rabinovich, Boleslav I. 156, 420, 2066, 5252, 5387
Rabinovich, David A. 2671, 2748, 2758, 3240, 4495
Rabis [Moscow, Russia] 1183, 2890, 2891, 2892
Rabochii i teatr [Leningrad, Russia] 721, 726, 745,
    752, 2088, 2516, 2887, 2901, 2906, 3515, 3543,
    3549, 3915, 4203
Rachinskii, Sergei A. 171, 1453, 4829
Rachlin, Ann 5468
Rachmanowa, Alja 1523
Radians´kaia muzyka [Kiev, Ukraine] 172
Radiogazeta [Moscow, Russia] 2917, 3303, 3304
Radioslushatel´ [Moscow, Russia] 2128, 3296, 3529
Raeburn, Michael 2394
Raedt, Paul de 1524

Tikhonova, I. E. 603, 5165
Tikhonova, T. M. 1782
Tikhookeanskaia zvezda [Khabarovsk, Russia] 4194
Time [Chicago, USA] 1124, 2013, 4959, 5560
(The) Times [London, England] 285, 377, 1053,
 1455, 1528, 1534, 1548, 1554, 1831–1833, 2191,
 2261, 2270, 3837, 5546, 5558, 5562
Times Educational Supplement [London, England]
 1839
Times Literary Supplement [London, England] 162,
 286, 377, 1455, 1526, 1534, 1671, 1839, 2245,
 2392, 3081, 3089, 3112, 3671, 3695, 3844
Timofeev, Grigorii A. 703, 2423, 2648, 2653, 4182,
 5235, 5427
Tiomkin, Dmitrii 5522–5549
Tiranov, G. G. 530
Tirdatova, Evgeniia 4858
Titkov, V. 108, 5149
Tiukalov, P. 1359, 1364, 1365, 1369, 1371
Tiukkel´, V. 1252
Tiulin, Iurii N. 2374
Tiumeneva, Galina A. 1783, 2453, 4425, 4517,
 4563, 5179
Tiurina, G. 958
"T. K." 1496
Tkachenko, Leontii G. 1453, 2004
Tkachuk, T. 1878
Tobias, P. 5141
Tobias, T. 1128
Tolmachev, O. 1234
Tolstoi, Aleksei 604, 5277
Tolstoi, Feofil 3753, 3768, 4832
Tolstoi, Lev N. 403, 588, 1453, 1994–2003
Tolstoi, Sergei 1996
Tomashevskii, Boris 2870, 2928, 2978
Tommasini, Anthony 2027, 3347, 5144
Tomskii Teatral [Tomsk, Russia] 383
Tonfallet [Stockholm, Sweden] 1103
Topaz, M. 4332
Toradze, Gulbat 3063
Törnblom, Folke H. 1506
Tovar 2152
Tovey, Donald F. 4641, 4695
Towers, Deirdre 78
Toye, Francis 1063
Tracy, J. M. 2299
Travskii, Vladimir 550
Tret´iakov, Pavel M. 349
Tret´iakova, L. S. 2379
Tret´iakova, Vera N. 349
Treves, P. 3593
Trezise, S. 4457, 5294, 5296
Tridtsat´ dnei [Moscow, Russia] 796
Trompette Chamber Music Society 159
Trud [Moscow, Russia] 228, 298, 580, 739, 860,
 967, 1760, 2285, 3960, 4145
Tsareva, Ekaterina 591, 597, 994, 1670, 4490
Tschaikowsky-Gesellschaft Mitteilungen [Tübingen,
 Germany] 118, 139, 218, 334, 1738, 1928,

 2112, 2266, 2418, 3782, 5223
Tserkovnyi vestnik [Warsaw, Poland] 130
Tsekhovskaia, Varvara 551, 583
Tsukkerman, Viktor A. 302, 927, 2371, 2435,
 2454, 2458, 2481, 5245
Tsvetaev, Serafim 2542, 2579, 3537
Tubeuf, A. 3677
Tugarinov, E. 592, 2506
Tugemskii, S. F. 1749
Tuggle, R. A. 2990
Tuisa, N. 2275
Tulintsev, Boris 959, 2507
Tulupova, B. 5373
Tumanina, Nadezhda V. 156, 374, 2353, 2358,
 2367, 2368, 2547, 2588
Tumashev, L. 2976
Turchaninov, Ivan 552, 1718
Turchaninov, Pëtr 5225
Turchinovich, A. M. 678, 1592
Turgenev, Ivan S. 233, 588, 2000, 2141–2145,
 2833
Tur´ian, M. 3064, 3074
Turkmenskaia iskra [Potrudnik, Turkmenistan] 352?
Turner, B. C. 5079
Turner, J. Rigbie 105
Turner, W. J. 1070
Turok, P. 5078
Turska, Irena 3838
Turygina, Lidiia M. 646
Tyler, T. H. 50

Uchitel´skaia gazeta [Moscow, Russia] 1223
Udmurtskaia pravda [Izhevsk, Russia] 427
Ugriumova, T. S. 589, 595, 1749, 2140, 2150,
 5291
Ukrainian Review [Kiev, Ukraine] 3324
Ulanova, Galina 2537, 4213, 4236
Ul´ianova, M. 1302
Umelecká Beseda [Prague, Czech Republic] 159
Undina (2) [opera] 118, 239, 3729–3733
Unger, M. 4821, 4925
Ungerer, J. 3297
Union Tribune 2254
Upton, G. 2317
Ural 1711
Ural´skaia, V. 3983
Ural´skii meditsinskii zhurnal [Sverdlovsk, Russia]
 5328
Urban, H. 4842
Urbánek, Velebín 196
Uspenskaia, K. 899
Uspenskaia, Sof´ia 24–26, 30, 31, 33

"V." 1779, 2812, 3270
"V. A." 381, 2790
Vaganova, Antonina 4137, 4202
Vaidman, Polina E. 114, 115, 117, 120, 128, 369,
 370, 570, 579, 588, 592, 596–598, 600, 929,
 937, 949, 995, 1043, 1148, 1266, 1274, 1294,